[THE JYZE MILLENNIUM]

Annals of The Jyze Age
____

Jyzeburst

Jyzemelt

Jyze and Jyze Alone

Jyze in Love

Deep Jyze

The Jyze Millennium

Jyze of the Heavenly Year

Scat Jyze

Also by G.P. Sandefjord
____

Have Mercy (a novel)

The Jyze Millennium

G.P. Sandefjord

Annal Six of The Jyze Age

Cover art by GPS
Published by House of Jyze
ISBN 978-0-9964173-7-2
Library of Congress CIP Pending
www.HouseOfJyze.com

For the fabulous Zoelie B.

To me, jyze is somebody standing up,
so to speak, and saying, with as little
concealment as possible, what it is for
him or her to be on earth at this moment.

                -- Galway Kinnell
                [but he said "poetry"
                for "jyze"]

PART I

Jyze of the Far Out

BOOK A

[Got to Jyze It Up]

‑‑‑‑‑

1

‑‑‑‑‑

Opening day of jyze season. And here I stand at
the upper end of the high bridge taking in the panoramic
view to the west. J-town cityscape, deep blue bay and
the waters beyond (a freighter and a ferry and numerous
small craft plying), the islands and promontories, the
snowcapped peaks on the far side horizontally streaked
with dark gray clouds. And arrayed roughly a hundred
feet below me here, the complex intersection of two
major freeways and a number of lesser roads, vehicles
rolling along on numerous levels in every which
direction and at widely varying speeds, though mostly
not so fast.

It's where I wanted to be for this occasion. Good
weather too -- scattered puffy white clouds on this side
of the water, light breeze, no need for the jacket I
brought along just in case. But I've left myself little
time. Cutting back my usual "morning" ritual by half
wasn't nearly enough. In about two hours I'm due to
meet Zoelie and Kat down at the hideaway. And the walk
in from here should take roughly a third of that.

(Literally standing I am. J-book spread atop a
pitted and mossy concrete podium of sorts at just above
waist level. Bridge traffic growling by at my back.
What do they think? A jyzer at work -- Cawk dude in
tattered chucks, worn jeans, ragged black hoodie with
the hood down, scruffy ponytail. Must've crawled up
from "the jungle" or "the rez" -- the homeless
encampments in the greenbelt flanking the freeways on
the hillsides below, some featuring incongruously bright
and shapely camping tents visible from here. A few feet

7

to my left a dirt path leads down that way. Just beyond
the path, a supermarket cart sprawls on its back in the
grass, three of its four wheels missing.)

It's Earth Day. As good a day as any, I figured,
to start up a millennial jyze annal. If all goes more
or less according to plan -- and that's always a
possibility although way, way, way short of a certainty
-- these pages will witness the official rollover of the
thousand-year Christian epoch at about their two-thirds
mark, to be followed some three months later by the
true, at least as I see it, millennium, and this will
still leave slightly more than a month for denouement
and whatever else might come along.

But will the planet still exist at that point? Or
how about fifty years from then? A century on? Another
thousand years on? -- Or even if the planet itself
manages to survive in one piece, what about the human
species? The chances there -- and of course for a great
many other species -- are definitely not looking good.

Regardless, but also for that very reason, it's TJM
time. TJM: The Jyze Millennium. For 367 days the jyzer
will follow the jyzegeist -- see where it leads. Over
this period churn out a thousand pages of jyze as a
fitting tribute: an M for the TJM. That's my pledge
here. (367 days, not 365, because next year is a leap
year and Earth Day will be the last day of this annal as
well as the first.)

-- And just in case all the millennial doings
aren't enough to keep things hopping, Z and I will also
be getting hitched this year. Yes. I shouldn't fail to
mention this here at the top, or as close as I can get
to it now without scratching out some or all of the
above. Barring some disaster of the personal kind --
which itself would keep things hopping, I suspect -- the
ceremony will take place on September 25th, just a
little over five months from now.

And throughout it all the jyze rules observed for
the first five annals in this series will continue to
apply in this one. And the usual quirky jyze lingo will
surely be cropping up here and there as well.

So, anyway...the start-up. Cornflakes and coffee
at noon, altering an artsy postcard to leave on Z's
pillow (it's become a tradition), a quick flip through
the paper and then out I came -- well, not exactly
pinwheeling. But then as I was hurrying along the two
blocks across the hilltop and the long curving steeply
downhill block to the bridge, a flock of butterflies did
take to swarming -- in my gut. The yips, yes. Or the
yips, yup. Yipe! I mean I've been thinking about this
TJM launch for a long time.

And then out with the J-stick, a shake or two to
get the ink flowing after the long layoff, and soon
everything was okay again.

-- And...now what? Just a quick look around. Lift
my gaze up a bit and right there, ten blocks or so
straight west from this perch, rise two huge stadiums,
one a concrete dome dating from a quarter century back
and the other, to the left of the dome, a brand-new
brick-and-steel major-league ballpark with a movable
roof. The new stadium will have its grand opening later
this summer; the concrete dome is scheduled to be blown
up sometime before closing day of this TJM project. Or
blown in, I should say -- "imploded." No one knows
exactly when the big boom will take place; but if jyze
is lucky, it will be sometime next March or April,
helping to make for a gangbusters TJM climax.

Stretched out for several miles to the left of the
new stadium, the industrial/port district with its giant
harbor cranes and coffee-company headquarters building.
Half a mile to the right of the dome, the downtown
highrise cluster jaggedly mounting its steep hillside to
the east.

And at the western base of that hill, just to the
north of the dome, lies the old historic quarter, and in
the middle of that stands my usual first destination of
the day, the hideaway, that is, my Jyzer Ink office and
writing cubbyhole. From here I can see just a small
chunk of the building it's in. And a diagonal block
northeast of that, also partly visible, rises the dozen-
story city utility building with Z's office on the fifth

floor; that's probably where she and Kat are right now. And some eight blocks north and two east of that, all uphill, but completely obscured from here by the main downtown skyline, stands the twenty-five-story building which is still the site of my same old nightscoper "day job." And that's my ultimate destination tonight, just as it has been most other nights for the past decade and a half or so.

My usual workaday turf. Other than the hilltop hood Z and I are homeys of here, and the Asian quarter that sprawls between here and the stadiums as well as the historic quarter and the downtown, all of which I walk through on most days on my way in to work, what I've just noted is pretty much it.

And then looming behind me and a couple of hundred feet up at the northern prow of our ridge-shaped hill (which runs five or six miles north and south), halfway between here and the apartment, is the massive orange-brick art-deco edifice of what was once the marine hospital. This castle-like structure, some sixteen stories tall and almost as wide at the base, has now, after standing mostly empty for several years, been leased out for the next decade to one of the more obnoxious dot-coms around (and by the way, the stock market set new highs on five straight days last week, with high-tech companies like this one -- the core of the so-called "new economy" -- leading the charge as usual). The refurbishing of the hospital and its grounds is already underway. Bulldozers are rumbling. The dot-commers will start moving in next month, their numbers eventually expected to reach about two thousand. The fallout in our hood could be...jyzeworthy, yeah.

As for news out there in the non-local world, I should mention we're currently engaged in yet another undeclared war, USAn planes bombing not just Iraq (as they've been doing for years) but now also the Kosovo region of Yugoslavia. To me this looks like the latest phase of our brazen effort to extend our "new world order" hegemony right up to the borders of Russia. And then the truly riveting news is a murderous rampage --

thirteen dead -- by two black-trenchcoated students at a
suburban high school not far from my former abode about
a thousand miles southeast of here. The media are agog
over it.

     (Now a couple of burly men emerge from the bushes,
at least as startled by my presence here as I am by
theirs. Black hair and hawklike noses, thus quite
possibly tribal dudes, perhaps associated somehow with
the Natusan center at the far end of the bridge. Yet
both are so neatly dressed -- and wearing such
expensive-looking watches -- they could well be
plainclothes cops. -- So I asked one of them for the
time. "Hey, it's ten to two, bro." Didn't sound very
street to me and not very Native either. In any case
I'd better be packing it in here real soon.)

     But first a few quick nature notes. Cherry trees
are still blooming along the far side of the Natusan
center; I can see several from here. And one county to
the north some eighty square miles of tulips are doing
likewise, coming in just a little late this year owing
to the nasty La Nina winter. And snowfall up in the
mountains another county farther north is already
ninety-one feet for the season with four months still to
go, supposedly within two feet of the "world record" (as
if anyone could know what that actually is).

     And that's it -- can't be late for Zoelie and Kat.
Gonna hafta sprint a little maybe. But I'm in shape for
it, I insist. A marryin' kind of man certainly should
be, I think, yes I do. And so here I go.

                        [+2]

     Two days on, the next installment.
     First something more about the previous one. When
Z got home that same evening she found I'd left a stove
burner turned on, half a pot of coffee still simmering.
The first time I've ever done anything like that, I
swear. I who am forever hounding her about not leaving
flammable food wrappers on the burners. (She also said

I'd been "obviously distracted" the previous couple of days and hadn't been my "usual affectionate self" that morning when I came to bed. -- And of course, as I immediately owned up, it's all jyze's fault. And she said that's exactly what she was assuming and therefore she would let me off the hook this time. But I'd better be very, very careful over the TJM year ahead because it's certain to cough up plenty more distractions.

So now the hideaway. It's a warm and sunny Saturday afternoon out there, a rarity for this time of year, and here I am cooped up indoors in a nearly empty building.

These days I usually arrive down here between three and four o'clock -- and in fact it's three-forty now. But it's unusual for me to be here on a Saturday afternoon. This is the one day of the week Z and I both have off from our jobs and, as has been the case ever since we met, we almost always spend much or all of it together. Today, however, I asked for a pass for jyze reasons -- just for the afternoon -- and she obliged me. Then I blew a big chunk of the allotted time browsing at the only real bookstore, also known as (still) (by us) the ORB.

So this office. Not too many changes here over the three months (almost four really) during which jyze has been on R&R. The paintings on the walls are the same, the lamps, the armchair, the green rug, the bookshelves, Mother's old spinning cylindrical wooden bookcase topped with its canted dictionary stand, the shades and blinds on all three full-size windows (door window included), the abundant bric-a-brac and memorabilia, the inspirational slogans tacked here and there, the hat rack hung with drying workout gear -- all pretty much the same. (Earlier this afternoon I noticed for the very first time -- after renting this office for more than three years now -- that if I stand in the center of the room I can reach within a foot of everything in here at shoulder level. But I'd need a good-size stepladder to touch the ceiling; it's just under eight feet above the top of my head when I'm standing.)

And...the sorry truth is I've again failed to leave
myself enough time. It's almost four now and I need to
be home by five-thirty to shower and dress for tonight's
extravaganza, a formal church wedding to be followed by
a gala reception at the downtown art museum. Ramona,
one of Z's coworkers and a longtime friend of hers, is
marrying the twenty-years-older Joseph (or as she calls
him, Pepe) (I've never spent more than a minute or two
with either of them). He's an obscenely rich Eurusan
man (she's Mexusan) who leans far to the right
politically, from what I'm told, and tends to be a bit
uptight about it in this famously liberal city. But
we're still invited and we're still planning to go.

It's a big year for weddings among people we know.
Two have occurred already, another will go down next
week. Wei and Alison's will take place in early summer,
Jess and Gwen's (actually a same-sex commitment
ceremony) in midsummer, and then a few days past the end
of summer the baddest of them all: ours.

It's solely because of the one tonight -- hyped to
be far fancier than any of the others we've attended or
will attend, this year or probably any year, certainly
including our own -- that over the past week I've gone
out and bought, piece by piece, the outfit I'll wear not
just tonight but also for, yes, our own. Months in
advance! At great expense! (True, I'm borrowing the
money, but because I'm paying interest on the loan -- to
Z -- this only makes the eventual cost even higher.)
And yet I'm enjoying it too, playing it for all it's
worth, both the glad-rag and the po-boy aspects.
Letting myself be trussed up and domesticated but
bucking and kicking every step of the way. For laughs.
Fact is if I could find a way to avoid such ritual
formality, or perhaps better to call it semiformality,
I'd do so. But it's not gonna happen.

*

And now a change. What I'd rather do is return
tomorrrow night for a special session. In general I'm
thinking I'll hit the J-book every other day; but only
J-day itself, the start of a new chapter (every eighth

day for most of this annal as it's currently sketched
out), will be set in stone, pretty much. During the
rest of the J-week I'll try to be more flexible.

I hadn't wanted to start bending the rules right at
the beginning, but -- it's happening.

And again one last note. A touching moment with
Kat on Thursday. The three of us were sitting right
here -- in these very tight quarters -- waiting for her
mother to arrive, and Kat was playing with a handful of
electric tapers she'd made off with from the opening
celebration of the city's Millennium Project which she
and Z had earlier attended together. Now she suddenly
stuck one up under my shirt, saying, "Let's see how it
looks!" -- inserting it in such a way that it formed a
long, narrow cone with light shining through the shirt
fabric at the tip. She quickly followed this with
another and then another and another, some six or seven
in all, until I was bristling like an electrified
hedgehog. "Wow, you're all lit up, Glen! Too bad you
can't see!" (But I could see -- see myself ablaze with
the Millennium Project, both mine (uncapped) and the
city's (capped), absolutely. Pretty damn hokey, true,
but still. And Z loved it -- the taper tepees, each
with its sexy little areolar glow as on the breasts of
the kitschy hula girls on the lamps at a certain coffee
shop she and I sometimes visit.) (Yes, she's still the
same splendidly bawdy Z. -- And still has the same
fabulous sexual talent to go with her many other gifts:
I'll just note that right here. And also say I'm pretty
much keeping up with her in the sexual realm, thank the
gods, after the prolonged feeble start two years ago.)

[+1]

A fine walk in. From the high bridge I could see a
dozen isolated shafts of sunlight streaming down and
silvering the entire bay in "palomino patches." Quiet
Sunday streets. No line at the upper AQ (Asian quarter)
grocery where I buy bananas. No train engine spewing

smoke from under the street-level bridge next to the
station. No baseball crowds in the HQ (historic
quarter) -- the team's on the road. A slow day for
panhandlers, pushers, street-stall peddlers.

I did notice that the sun had moved one sawtooth
notch farther north in the mountains since the last time
I saw it setting. Another eight weeks or so and it will
reverse directions and start ratcheting down millennium-
ward peak by peak (though at the very end, on the winter
solstice, it will have to hang one last U-ie and then
bounce back a few degrees before the rollover proper).

It's quiet up here now. The cleanup team just
passed through and for some reason this has become the
last floor they do. They start on the first, then go up
to the sixth (top) and work their way back down to our
floor, the second. Lately they've begun tossing down
tied trash bags and flattened cardboard boxes from the
interior balconies of the atrium (our floor is where the
atrium starts and thus we're nobody's balcony). You're
taking your life in your hands out there if you don't
follow just the right wall-hugging path to the restrooms
while this bombardment's underway. (Which could be why
our floor gets cleaned last, it just dawned on me.
Efficiency. The buck doesn't stop here but the trash
does.)

-- And so last night's wedding. It was even posher
than Z had warned me to expect. The reception at the
art museum had the run of the bottom two floors as well
as the grand staircase between. It featured two bands,
one mariachi and the other a jazzy fifteen-piece
ballroom-dance outfit. The spread was so sumptuous I
went back for seconds and thirds and probably packed in
enough top-grade meat and fish to fill my protein needs
for a month. The wedding cake was a bizarre modernistic
affair of boxlike layers of different types of cake
stacked seemingly haphazardly atop each other like huge
flattened children's blocks in a structure about six
feet high. After Pepe and Ramona carved out the first
two pieces, a uniformed crew of four servers handled the
cutting for everyone else, using a stepladder to access

the upper layers, their flashing knives making them look
like moonlighting sword dancers.

Tuxes and low-cut gowns were the order of the day.
Among the roughly three hundred attendees I was the only
male who showed up without a tie -- with collar open --
and one of only two without a suitcoat, and the other
guy had a good excuse: his right arm was massively
casted and riding in a sling (though I suspected it was
all a phony and wished I'd thought up such a good ruse
-- but then what would be my excuse for being tieless,
as he was not?).

The wedding itself went down atop east hill in the
huge cathedral overlooking the entire downtown. Even
with a crowd of hundreds present the sanctuary was no
more than a quarter or a fifth full -- or who knows, a
tenth? The portly Eurusan priest in charge, after
saying he'd overheard someone referring to the
proceedings as "the wedding of the century," rather
smugly allowed as how it was probably just that.
Mercifully the ceremony itself was much less elaborate
than expected, at least temporally: it lasted only about
forty-five minutes. Even so I found myself inwardly
gagging over some of the religious content of the ritual
script. Nor was I the only one who reacted this way.
Later at the reception I was pleased to hear Gerry J.,
who'd been sitting just two seats away from me, voicing
some of the same gripes I'd been keeping to myself.

Most of the bride's friends from the utility
gravitated to the same area in the cathedral. How odd
it seemed that I knew nearly everyone within several
rows. Gerry and Leola and Jess and a gay man she
recruited to escort her for the evening (Gwen's out of
town for work-related training) were to the left;
Serafina and family (her two daughters served as the
flower girls) were behind me, as were June and D'Arcy
and several others; and to my right, between me and Z,
was Aida. She performed all the ritual required of true
believers; Z performed none of it (and told me later she
thought the senior D's, seated behind us and to our left
-- they're the parents of Aida and Sera, I should

16

probably note -- she thought they observed this and most likely took some offense at it). And in front of us were -- ach, never mind! The point is I'm practically one of the gang now. An adjunct member, however, no doubt still on some sort of probation with a number of the old-timers.

Ramona is a member of one of Z's "girls' night out" groups (she has several). They've known each other for almost a decade. Ramona and Pepe met about the same time Z and I did and the two romances were often the subject of group scuttlebutt as they moved along more or less parallel tracks. In a few ways Pepe and Ramona's story is similar to ours, Z tells me -- like me, Pepe pulled out all the courtship stops -- but in most it's the polar opposite. Pepe is a hospital administrator with, as mentioned before, lots of bucks and deeply conservative views (he refers to Z as Ramona's "pinko friend"). All night long people were asking us, usually but not always with a wink, if our wedding would be like Pepe and Ramona's, and all night long we were saying ours would be the utter antithesis: "the antiwedding of the century." After a while Z got into the spirit of this too (pleasing me no end) though I don't really expect her to stick with it all the way to the altar.

Among the attractions at the reception was a wandering caricaturist. Z and I had ours done and it drew lots of oohs. Z's only objection to it is she thinks it makes her look older than me (which of course she is, though only by eighteen months). But she still likes it enough that she's talking about using it on the cover of our wedding invitation. It shows us holding hands and striding along in traditional wedding garb -- the very tux I wasn't wearing last night and won't be for our ceremony either. (Z's theory about the caricaturist: "He's gay and he liked you and that's why he made me into such a crone.")

-- And speaking of our wedding, here's the skinny on that.

For starters, I like to say we're already married. It happened back on January 27th when we were talking about setting a date, the kind of ceremony we'd have, the size of the wedding party, so on and so forth. I said I'd go along with whatever she wanted, but in return I'd like her to agree that in the eyes of my own personal deities (totally fictional though they of course were then and still are) -- in the eyes of those deities we were marrying right at that exact moment on the 27th. I was sitting in the black armchair in the living room at the time and she was in her rattan armchair a few feet away. She stood up, took two steps toward me, knelt between my legs, clasped my cheeks in her hands, brought her face within inches of mine and said intensely, with a good strong dose of the high drama she's such a master of, "I do. I do, Glen. I'm married to you right now!" And then after a delicious melting-eyes pause: "Well, what about it, Mr. G? Aren't you going to kiss the bride?" And kiss her I did, and she kissed back -- full tilt, as is also her usual wont (and want) -- and the official marital consummation followed shortly thereafter on the living-room couch.

I memorialized the occasion with a framed card and a hand-painted "loving cup," and ever since I've felt much better about all the other wedding rigmarole we've been going through. That is, the authentically "official stuff." And as she says: "This wedding thing is all for my community of friends who are expecting it and will be very hurt if I let them down. And don't forget, they're your friends now too."

A few months earlier, as reported in last year's jyze, she had agreed to something else: if she could pick the year, I could pick the date. She went for this year, even though one of her Chiusan friends -- June probably -- told her it's unlucky by certain traditional Chinese calendrical notions (but not by others); I chose September 25th, the day of the Chinese Autumn Moon Festival (among other reasons, to appease any lunar astrologers -- June included to be sure -- who might be disturbed by the choice of year).

The next step was to find a lawyer who could affirm I'm officially marriageable. (Lady S had said several

times she would obtain a divorce, but if she had
actually done so, I'd never heard about it. Then again
I hadn't heard anything at all from her in four or five
years. And knowing Lady S I doubted she would've taken
the step.)
    We -- mostly I -- let this matter of obtaining
legal help drag on for months, rejecting several
possible candidates (one because of high fees, another
because of scant knowledge about Asia, a third because
we learned belatedly that he was the one who botched
Aida's divorce). Finally in late March we came up with
a woman whose office is just a block from mine, Evelyn
H. (Evie). Of part-Chinese ancestry herself, an avid
reader of so-called "literary fiction" (she actually
calls it that!), politically pretty much in sync with
us, and not too expensive. By then we were calling what
we sought a "fail-safe divorce," and the early part of
the process, at least, turned out to be a good deal less
complicated than expected. Notification of Lady S could
be handled by certified letter sent to the most recent
address I had for her, and because she's moved out of
the country since living there and didn't leave a
forwarding address (or so Mother told me back then), the
divorce would almost certainly not be contested, Evie
said, and the court would automatically approve it after
a required waiting period of ninety days. And so in all
likelihood it would become official in mid to late
August. This would give us breathing space of a month
or so before the wedding.
    We agreed we should, just in case, continue to call
the September 25 date tentative. But we decided to go
ahead with the planning as if it were certain, and
that's what we -- but mostly she, Z -- have been doing
ever since. Should some obstacle arise, we'll simply
postpone the wedding until the obstacle goes away. This
is her preferred solution. (And I just pray no obstacle
does arise. After what she went through with the
infamous Arvin during her one other close encounter with
the altar -- canceling the wedding just a week
beforehand, after some of the out-of-town guests had

already begun to arrive -- she might not survive a
second such disaster.)

There's much more to be said about this ongoing
process. All kinds of trauma to describe regarding the
decision of how to marry and where and before whom and
saying what and wearing what and doing what at the
reception afterwards, where, arranged by whom, with whom
assisting, whom decorating, whom entertaining, whom
toasting, whom cleaning up, on and on and on. But later
for that. This is more than enough connubial jyzing for
one day.

I do want to note, though, Z looked terrific in her
low-cut, short-skirted black dress last night. And she
danced funkily as always even though the new black pumps
she bought in haste yesterday afternoon didn't quite fit
right, raising a couple of blisters that gave her fits
afterwards. My own entirely new outfit -- new socks,
shirt, slacks, belt, T-shirt, and even new hemp briefs,
my first ever, chosen by her but then it turned out I
liked them too -- the outfit as a whole, I say, seemed
to fill the bill adequately. And then in the fifteen
hours between our return home last night and my
departure for downtown this afternoon we got it on no
fewer than three times, including once on that same
living-room couch. To which I say -- and she too --
hallelujah! Let's go to a fancy-pants wedding and
devour lots of red meat every week! Every day if
possible! (The "Hallelujah Chorus," incidentally, is
what the pipe organ burst into after the priest told
Pepe he could kiss the bride.)

[+1]

It's not the usual Monday night. Here's the
conference-room table at the scope office. Straight
ahead out the windows, up-close skyscraper midriffs,
scores and scores of brightly lit rooms without a single
human or any other kind of living being in sight.
Street sounds straggling up from far below. Half a

block to the right, long shiny cars slowly circling the
fountain at street level in front of the four-star (or
is it five now?) hotel -- but I can see them only if I
stand up and lean toward the windows.

All this is the usual, true, despite what I just
said; it's my being here on Monday night that isn't.
Fortunately for me, I had a rush job to take on --
meaning next week I won't be quite so monetarily hard up
as I'd been thinking -- and now I've left myself about
seventy-five minutes in which to do a semi-rush job on
the jyze itself.

Earlier, on the way in, I stopped by the usual
downtown chain burger joint to pick up a vanilla yogurt
cone. There I noticed that loud classical music is no
longer playing outside to drive away the so-called gang-
banger types, a few of whom were loitering tentatively
about. Maybe the franchise owners are afraid these kids
(most are "of color" -- not pink though -- and appear to
be high-school age) will build up immunity to the music
if they hear too much of it. Could even be they'll
start to like it. First thing you know the "gang-
bangers" will be chowing down at the symphony-hall
restaurant and the symphonygoers will be switching over
to the chain burger joints and the entire established
order will be turned on its head forever. Or not. Or
just call this another jyze fantasy.

Before the cone, it was, again, pretty much the
usual Monday, except that everything had to be moved up
an hour because Z volunteered to meet Wei and Alison at
the airport tonight. They're back from a three-week
trip to Ecuador and the Galapagos. I would've met them
with her if I'd known how long this rush job would take,
but I had no way to figure that out in advance.

A quick story to tell. Last night I stuffed my
soiled workout clothes into my old blue cloth "Remember"
bag (from Japan days) to take home for washing, topping
them off with that bunch of bananas from the AQ grocery.
At the bus stop a block and a half up from the hideaway
I set the bag down on a shelter bench while scribbling
some notes and suddenly the bus roared up, and in the

confusion I forgot to remember the "Remember" bag on the bench. I didn't realize this until I was walking home from the bus stop atop south hill -- and then I jumped in Z's car and raced back downtown in hopes the bag would still be there.

As I pulled up to the bus stop, a small Cawk druggie mutterer I've noticed around the area before was walking away from the shelter and carrying a pair of what I immediately recognized as my gym shorts. He was also -- and I loved this -- chomping on a banana. I called out to him -- "Hey!" -- and he took off running, turning the corner and disappearing down the hill. Meanwhile I saw the blue "Remember" bag itself lying on the sidewalk next to the shelter and the bunch of bananas -- smaller now -- neatly arranged almost like the subject of a still life atop the covered trash receptacle, which was brightly lit up as always by, aptly enough, the bus-stop crime lights. No one else was around. And when I went to pick up the "Remember" bag I found my three moldy T-shirts and one pair of moldy shorts strewn on the sidewalk nearby -- rejected by the mutterer dude.

The shame of this.

Replacing the shorts will cost me about thirty bucks. Right now I can't afford to do it. But I do have three other pairs of shorts, though they're all raggedy cheapos. Still: I'm not so badly off. What if it had been my backpack I'd left down there? (Z's worried about me: first I forgot to turn the stove off, now this. But in a way I'm pleased to be so distracted. I take it to mean my subconscious has found this TJM project to be something truly worthy of grinding away at. -- And on the way home I chomped on one of the bananas myself. I mean, the peel may have been contaminated but the meat inside was still good, yes? Seemed so to me. Or to put it another way, all this chasing around was making me late for dinner.)

(Other stories I'd get into if I had the time might include some locker-room talk with Willis E. at the WOC about the "wedding of the century" -- he too was an

attendee, and almost certainly the only former Black
Panther present -- and the orgy of media analysis about
the high-school massacre. Gene, also at the WOC and a
former Air Force pilot (Cawk) with strong law-and-order
tendencies although he's also quite friendly, used to
live half a mile from that same high school, and so he
and I got into it a bit today, but not too badly. I'd
also try to say something about the grim spectacle of
NATO, which is to say our USAn posse in Europe,
celebrating its fiftieth anniversary by ramping up the
air attacks on Serbia.)

   Onward. A few words about a matter touched on
earlier. In brief, I'm just barely scraping by
financially. without all the expenses associated with
the wedding I'd probably be all right, but as of the end
of the month -- Saturday, five days from now -- my bank
account will be down to under twenty bucks. The bump
from the rush job will help, but in recent months rush
jobs have been few and far between and I can't count on
being rescued by them too often, especially during the
slow summer months. Eventually I'll almost certainly
have to do some more borrowing from Z. And this is
acceptable to her on the understanding that early next
year, when there's no penalty to do it, I'll take money
out of my deep reserves to pay her back. As of this
moment those reserves, despite the continuing boisterous
bull market, are worth less than they were at the start
three and a half years ago. My hopes of being able to
hang on to most of them for a rainy day or (should I
last so long) my retirement years are going up in smoke.

   Not that there's anything really surprising about
any of this.

   Meanwhile I do have other work concerns. One, what
happens if Naomi's carpal tunnel worsens or she injures
herself in some other way or falls sick or quits
reporting for some reason -- for example, Larry, her
husband (still), is promoted, as rumor often says he
will be, to Justice Department headquarters back east?
I'll be in big trouble for sure. But suppress that one
too. And then there's the celebrated "Y2K problem."

All along I've believed the extent of this gargantuan
planet-wide high-tech snafu predicted to occur at the
exact moment of the millennial rollover has been vastly
overblown. It's a serious matter, yes, but apocalyptic
hysteria associated with the grand occasion is of course
what's causing most of the uproar. And yet there's
still a chance it could affect either one or both of my
Jyzer Ink computers. These are the ones I use to do my
job. They're both old. Neither's been checked out for
Y2K-bug symptoms -- it would cost too much. I just have
to hope they'll be able to ride out the storm, assuming
there really is one. And they might, since the kind of
work I do isn't particularly time-dependent: basically
it's all just a more elaborate version of word-
processing with a steno-translation wrinkle to it. I'm
thinking the odds are about three to one in my favor.
     (J-town is tearing up its streets right now as it
wires itself for the next stage of the digital
revolution. With the world's largest software company
just a few miles up the road and lots of other big cyber
companies nearby, this city has become an epicenter of
the revolution. Like it or not, it's affecting just
about everything here, myself absolutely included,
except with respect to financial prosperity.) ---

[+2]

     "Tis-Z wants to keep G mitey happy!" So says
tonight's note awaiting me under the red heart-shaped "I
lub you" rock in my armchair (where I now sit, changed
into the flimsy ripped-side black backup shorts and
loose long-sleeve khaki henley). The note's written
with color-over markers, the words surrounding a pair of
hand-drawn kiss-ready lips, and placed at the center of
the lips is a tin of "Hot Love" breath mints.
     I like it, I like it! (The "Tis-Z" plays off a
remark someone made at work that she's always in a tizzy
these days because of wedding preparations, which of
course at this point have scarcely even begun; the

"mitey" refers to her newly revived war against dust
mites in this apartment, about which I've been giving
her a hard time, though in a gently goofing way, I'd
like to think.)

And for her I have a freshly altered art postcard
(also referring to tizzies and mites) and a copy of the
new issue of a neocounterculturish magazine featuring a
whole section on "Alternative Weddings," and I'll leave
both for her to find on her armchair when she gets up in
the morning.

How much longer I can keep the altered-postcard
campaign going I don't know. In the bedroom there's a
stack of maybe three hundred of these cards which I've
made for her over the past two years. It's reached the
point where if I check the stands at bookstores and
elsewhere for art postcards, I've usually seen them all
before. The catch is that I've let it slip to her --
several times -- I'll be doing a thousand of them on a
kind of installment plan as one of my wedding presents
for her. But then again we haven't really discussed how
long the remaining seven hundred installments might
take. And my other main wedding present, I should
mention, is this TJM project going down right here, and
years or even decades may pass before it's in any kind
of shape for presentation.

Two days on. Three-twenty a.m. The newly
normalized living room. Yesterday I took down all the
banners, crepe paper, and balloons, stripped the
remaining birthday items from the coffee table -- lots
of small stuff, mostly magnets and altered political
buttons, since this year's shtick was to give Z presents
in a number matching her age (her big day was more than
six weeks ago already!) -- and also finally removed the
art supplies from the back half of the dining table
which they'd been occupying since a couple of weeks
before Christmas. The impetus behind all this
normalizing is the meeting of Z's book group which will
take place here Friday evening. She's planning to stay
home from work tomorrow to tackle the final phase of the
preparatory cleanup.

(Pause to nibble at a whole-wheat fig bar. -- And did I just hear the paper arrive? Maybe not, so I'll check later. No need to rush down there at this hour: even if it has come, no one's likely to rip it off before six at the earliest. But I'll mention that a second far-coast-megalopolis paper is now being delivered daily (except Sunday) to someone in our building and it's the right-wing business paper. Ironically, this is probably another early effect of the dot-com move-in at the hospital. It's still several weeks away but already we're seeing plenty of move-outs and move-ins and upscaling around here, including in our building. -- And as I like to remind Z, in a sense she and I are part of the upscaling ourselves, although more like precursors to it. When we arrived on the scene some sixteen months ago no papers at all were being delivered to this building, and certainly not the snooty far-coast "All the fits that fit" paper that we get.)

-- On a related matter, the plan to purchase the building for conversion to condos which we considered enlisting in back around Christmas, that's literally gone south on us. Doug and Thuy in 303 directly above us, the ringleaders of that scheme, bailed out and bought a house a mile or two farther south on the hill. And in truth we were never strongly interested anyway. Now with the dot-com's arrival just a little over a block down the street it's likely the price on our building will zoom out of sight. From overheard bus talk I know the waiting lists for rooms and apartments at other nearby hilltop buildings are lengthy. Our own building is fully occupied again but this has usually been the case while we've lived here, presumably because even though it's one of the newer buildings in the hood, the rent's not too steep -- yet.

No big news has erupted out there in the world in these past couple of days. Funerals in the high-school massacre, misguided (intentionally?) USAn missiles in Serbia. This means I have room to mention an item which in the inconceivably distant future might mean more than anything else that's happened in the entire millennium now about to stagger to its close. Just last week astronomers announced the first sighting of another solar system. It's forty light years away, something like that. And if two solar systems can be found in such a relatively microscopic speck of the universe, a great many almost certainly must exist in more distant realms. This has long been suspected, of course, especially by sci-fi freaks, but until now hard evidence has been lacking. (So does the universe suddenly seem a friendlier place? Is that why the news is being so widely welcomed? Could it be we're unconsciously hoping some of these aliens will save us from ourselves?)

-- But it's getting late. What should I cross off the list of things I wanted to mention? Maybe everything. Okay, everything, let's go for it. Except this:

How do Z and I fit in with our compatriots? I noticed a figure in the paper today: $34,000 is the average annual salary for the bottom ninety percent of USAns. (Including the upper ten percent would skew the figures into absurdity.) Interestingly, Z makes almost exactly as much above that amount as I make below it, meaning as a unit we're just about average for the non-ruling class, which is to say we're the exact middle of the middle class. As boojie as they get, that's right. Who knew? Not us! (By another measure, per-capita income in our state -- growing fast in these boom times, despite widening inequality -- is $27,000. That's for every man, woman, and child in the state. And I earn well under half that amount. Which to be sure for much of the world would still be an unimaginable fortune.)

And one last note. I finally learned why all the plants on our balcony died this winter: there was an unbroken weeklong spell of subfreezing weather. Somehow I didn't even notice it at the time (though I still knew it was pretty damn cold out there for a while).

That's it. Night's over for me. At four a.m. the news comes on and keeps going for five hours; all-night jazz is done and late-night jyze with it.

2

    Stopping on the way in, western edge of the AQ.
And outdoors. Even though rain is threatening. -- On a
wooden bench in the back section of the above-ground
portion of the underground bus station.
    Lots of brick and wrought iron on display. Low-
lying Victorian-mod structures, a color scheme of
purple, green, and pink. Thirty or forty feet straight
down an open shaft to my left the tops of double-length
buses glide by on their way -- along with the rest of
the bus, right -- into or out of the downtown tunnel.
    Construction everywhere around here. Crossing
almost directly overhead at the moment, the arm of a
huge yellow crane swinging a load of what I'd guess is
rebar into the bare frame of a new office building about
ten stories up. At my back the entire train depot (the
more eastward of the two) is swathed in gray plastic as
it undergoes restoration, looking like a building-wrap
art project. (The ceremonial veiling was pictured in
this morning's J-town paper.) At least half a dozen
other good-size buildings, most of which will be twelve
stories or more, are starting to take shape nearby. A
little farther to the southwest the movable roof of the
new ballpark carves out a big chunk of skyline, as do,
just north of it, the upper reaches of the great gray
concrete dome (which will be replaced by yet another
stadium built on the same spot after the domesday
demolition, so that two stadiums will soon stand, by a
kind of halitosis -- or no, make that mitosis -- where
before there was only one). And local software/dot-com
money is behind most of this construction spree if not

all of it.

That's true as well, of course, of the conversion of our south-hill marine hospital. "The castle." That official landmark structure could also be seen from here except for a seven-story dirty-cream-colored apartment building blocking the view across the street. (In a sense our hood up there is just a sort of upper-deck extension of the one down here.)

Came walking straight down through the heart of the AQ. My favorite route in but not the fastest -- the sidewalks are crowded and the narrow streets jammed with traffic (much of it double-parked) and I can't take advantage of my usual time-saving diagonal short-cuts through parking lots farther up, near or under the freeway overpass.

The cherry blossoms are already gone, I noticed, except for a few on the trees outside the Japanese Buddhist "Church," as it's called on the sign, I guess in a concession to Western ways -- quite possibly inspired by the internment crackdown almost sixty years ago, yes indeed. That same crackdown, I should note, stripped many of the Japusan residents of our hilltop hood of their homes and property, including the family that lived where our apartment building now stands.

Today's trek has been uneventful so far except for an incident right at the start. A scruffy gray-bearded hobo dude was sprawled on the sidewalk near our driveway and as I approached he rose unsteadily, turned, and unleashed a mighty stream of bright-yellow urine on the neighbor's riprap. Just as he did this a bus rolled by and gave an appreciative toot -- or a disapproving toot, who knows. "Fuckers," the dude grumbled as I slid stealthily by, at the same time doing a little jig to avoid the torrent surging across the sidewalk. -- This being the kind of south-hill street life (along with the sporadic open prostitution and drug-dealing and car-prowling at night) which in our era has so far kept the rents low and the residents' senses healthily alert.

Yesterday's hike in, on the other hand, offered several hints of the hood's new trend. First an

expensive red convertible sports car bearing four young
Cawk men, two wearing ball caps turned backwards, roared
up and the driver, pointing up at the biggest structure
around, asked, "Do you know, would this be the old
mariner hospital?" When I said it was -- but marine,
not mariner -- they pulled into the inner-campus drive
and took a slow but noisy spin around the landscaped
circle at the center. From their banter it was obvious
they were dot-commers -- maybe millionaires already --
dropping by to scope out their new digs.

Not long after that, as I reached the bridge, a
young Cawk woman with short hair dyed incandescent red,
a black miniskirt, platform shoes, tattoos and piercings
-- the whole schmear -- came clomping by, presumably
headed home after work; and just seconds later a young
and svelte and almost suburban-looking Cawk woman jogged
past me going north. First time I can recall seeing
either type on or anywhere near the hill.

(All these Cawks -- it shouldn't be surprising in a
city where the percentage of Eurusans almost exactly
matches that for the country as a whole, or about
seventy-two percent. But nonetheless it is surprising,
because until very recently a number of outrageous land-
use practices forced most folks of non-pink complexion
to live in this end of town. For the same reason most
of the public and private agencies serving the poor and
the homeless and the jail/prison releasees were also
located in this area and remain here now, and those in
need of such services are more or less herded in this
direction -- which is why many people living here refer
to it as a "sacrifice zone." If you live here, you
sacrifice so that the mostly Cawk north, west, and east
parts of town may be relatively untroubled. -- But now
at least some things about the zone are changing, yes.
Not that I'm saying this is all or even mostly for the
better. It's a lot more complicated than that.)

(And going by right now, here's another example of
that change: a dynamic tough-guy Asiusan/Eurusan pair of
cops on foot patrol. And we're all glad they're on the
job, because large numbers of variously complected but

still more or less equally nasty drunks and drug dealers
hang out around here. The notorious east-depot saloon
stands right across the street. Late at night this bus
stop where I'm sitting is one of the most perilous in
town; my own bus is often delayed here by deployments of
cop cars, transit vans, aid vehicles, fire equipment, or
just a backup of coaches as a trolley stalled at the
front of the line, perhaps because of an onboard fight
or some other kind of incident, awaits assistance.)

     -- And speaking of dynamic Asiusan/Eurusan duos,
the Z-woman (who, being biracial, is of course one of
those duos all by herself) is staying home from work
again today, finishing up what she calls her
"blitzklean" in preparation for tonight's book-group
meeting. But yesterday was another hot one for us. A
very fine shag in the morning, surely one of our most
multiply-orgasmed (for her, I probably don't need to
say) and longest-lasting of the "plan A" type ever. And
it ended -- "Better come soon!" -- only because she was
getting too raw to go on. ("Plan A" is a recent term of
ours for sexual engagement with intercourse permitted,
as opposed to "plan B" in which it's banned because a
herpes outbreak is occurring or seems imminent.)

     -- On goes my jacket. The wind's turning chilly.
(A knot of construction workers clatters out of the site
to the south, lunch buckets and hard hats and tool belts
aswing -- homeward bound.) "Forest green" canvas work
jacket. Z's never liked it a whole lot but it's perfect
for the streets with its attached hood, rain repellancy,
warmth, size (large enough to accommodate three layers
underneath including a heavy sweatshirt). (And here's
my same old beat-up brown backpack -- "college size,"
it's called, expandable for books, and I've never even
tried it in its slimmer mode. At this point shiny black
duct tape, itself fraying in places, is all that keeps
it in one piece. Not to play down the rest of the way I
dress -- "street camo" -- but this backpack is probably
the main reason I'm sometimes taken as a hobo dude
myself. Along with the hair, of course.)

     And then finally a few calendrical notes. First,

it's the last day of the month and I have bills to pay.
It's also Arbor Day and to do my bit I'll now put in a
good word for trees. You grow, trees! Z and I had
intended to help kick off the city's massive tree-
planting campaign today -- another part of the official
Millennium Project -- but her stay-home decision
scotched that. (As still another part of the same
project, the city's begun work, it appears, on the
display lighting for the high bridge. Two crews were
going at it with a backhoe in appropriate spots down
below as I walked across maybe ninety minutes ago.)

     And then in a few hours we'll be into Walpurgis
Night, always good for some wild times up in the Scandi
quarter -- but this partial Scandi right here will be
locking himself in the scope office for the evening and
then going straight home. -- And tomorrow's a doozy,
with opening day of the boating season happening to fall
on May Day this year, meaning spiffy yacht captains will
be mixing it up with black-masked anarchists. Are the
riot police ready for this? Everyone's saying it'll be
a kind of tune-up for the big protests planned for the
WTO "ministerial" which will be held here in Jyze City
in November. And I for one am hoping that's true --
there really will be big protests -- but fearing it's
not. And wondering, in light of the eco-apocalypse
looming ahead, whether it could possibly matter.

[+2]

     -- Door cracked open six inches, fan pushing out
mustiness and fustiness. No other signs of life around
here. Two days on and I'm sprawled in my hideaway
armchair, feet propped against the hassock to bolster my
left thigh for use as a J-book stand.
     Just back from a downtown stroll. Browsed at the
public-market bookstore, dropped off our rent check at
the post office, indulged in my weekly vanilla yogurt
cone at the usual chain burger joint. It was the
typical Sunday-night scene out there: sidewalks and

streets relatively quiet but at the same time far from
lacking in interest not to mention conflict. Among
tonight's notables of the human kind: at the post-office
bus stop, a couple of super-heavyweight crazies
bellowing walruslike at each other as bystanders
scrambled for safety; near the HQ entertainment zone, a
group of three very tall young men filing silently by
carrying instrument cases and wearing black trench coats
as if in emulation of the perpetrators of the high-
school massacre; and in the alley right behind the
hideaway building, a camel's-hair-coated business type
(I'd say) examining a computer monitor in the trash
piled next to an overloaded dumpster as a pair of
grizzled drifters eyed the fancy brown leather briefcase
he'd perhaps unthinkingly set down on the pavement by
his feet and was himself slowly drifting away from.
(Note: all the folks just mentioned were male and Cawk.)
    At the burger joint I read a few pages in my book
before a saggy-garbed punk, also male and Cawk and of
clearly dubious intentions, plopped down at my two-seat
table even though several empty tables stood nearby;
this convinced me it was time to move on. And then just
outside the door a box of frozen burger patties nearly
bonked me when it came flying off an oddly canted
conveyor belt emerging from an illegally parked trailer
truck. (But I want to note classical music is back on
the burger joint's PA. My guess is the country-and-
western they were experimenting with over the past few
days drew in more undesirables than it drove away.)
    Earlier this afternoon Z and I saw a movie called
"Hideous Kinky" that turned out to be very bad. Set in
the high hippie era, it was about a young Eurusan mother
bumming around Morocco ostensibly in search of Sufi
enlightenment, her two daughters in tow. At least one
review made it sound good, and with Z's longstanding
interest in Sufism -- she even has an official Sufi
name, Daena, which means something like "bright dawn" (a
tribute to her well-deserved rep as a "lark": an early
riser) -- we agreed we couldn't pass it up. Especially
not when our own wedding is set to feature a quasi-Sufi

ceremony, as chosen by Z and agreed to by me. But it
was quickly obvious the movie was a dud. About ten
minutes in Z muttered "I hate this" and repeated it
several times over the next few minutes before abruptly
decamping for the lobby. I was about to pack up to join
her there when she slipped back in, and we hung on for
another ten or fifteen minutes before leaving together
and for good.

-- But weddings continue to be big for us these
days even when we're not focusing on our own. Last
night we attended another reception, this time for a
former housemate of Z's from more than a decade back,
Max Y. (who's now a mover and shaker at the local
chapter of the ACLU). He and his bride, Leah -- both
Jewish Eurusans who attended the same far-coast-
megalopolis high school at the same time -- never even
met until a year or two ago and that was out here, and
it's the first marriage for both. A lot like our story!
-- Except that Z and I didn't go to the same high
school back then when we lived a few miles apart in, or
in my case near, Centropolis, and we didn't know each
other; and of course I fall seriously short on the
"first marriage" clause (but she doesn't).

The reception was held at a state park I'd never
heard of before near a remote burb neither of us had
ever visited before. It was blessedly low-key, with a
three-piece Jewish band playing and lots of urban Jewish
Eurusan folks in attendance. For the occasion I wore my
engineer boots (only the third or fourth time I've
broken them out in the past decade) along with some
freshly washed (and dried) jeans, a khaki dress shirt,
and my brown five-dollar thrift-shop sports jacket: a
look Z had never seen me in before. "Passable," she
said grimly. (At one point during the speechifying a
chorus of oohs and aahs arose from the audience when a
bald eagle landed on a tree outside the big picture
window directly behind the podium. Such an amusingly
gratified and yet perplexed look the speaker radiated
until he realized people weren't necessarily reacting to
his rambling toast to the bride and groom.)

Z used to engage in "punfest contests" with "the M&M boys," her housemates Max (the groom at the wedding) and Manny (later Kat's adoptive father). Max was a little uncomfortable with both of them back then, she told me, because he wasn't much of a socializer and she and Manny had parades of paramours tramping in and out "at all hours of the day and night." Another former housemate of theirs was present for the reception, Phoebe M., a platinum-blond Eurusan (probable Scandi roots) now living in the southern megalopolis of the megastate to our south, and Z said of her, "I could tell right away she still hates me, and the funny thing is I still don't know why." (One possible reason, though, which she did mention later in passing: Phoebe used to play her stereo at very high volume in the room directly below Z's, and Z several times confronted her about it. Z doubts this would've done the trick all by itself, but I think she's wrong about that. Few can confront more memorably than Z when she's really upset, and other people's loud music can definitely do it.)

I didn't know a single person at this wedding. A couple of faces seemed vaguely familiar, possibly from ACLU meetings I long ago attended on a few occasions with Lady U. But I couldn't definitely ID anyone.

(Z again looked especially good, I thought, in white leggings -- no underwear, though I'm pretty sure I'm the only one besides Z herself who knew about that -- and her black dress with the red coastal-indigene markings. Weddings do seem to suit her well. And the salmon was excellent. And I was relieved to see she was comfortable with this type of reception, casual and unshowy. -- But now, after hearing Max regale the crowd with a long tale of the ordeal he and Leah underwent to find a "hall" for their reception, we're both worried about coming up with something even half as good -- and preferably much closer in -- for ours.)

-- Earlier in the day the exceptionally labile Z-woman had briefly burst into tears when I said -- thinking I was just talking lightly -- if I had my druthers I'd do marriage the same way brother Rob did,

in a court chamber with only the judge and a single
outside witness present as required by law. The stress
is getting to her, she admitted. (And today one of her,
and therefore in a sense my, stress symptoms is back:
the herpes "prodomo" tingles.)

    Also on the wedding front, Aida is again stirring
up trouble. She's back with Z's former lover Kirk M.
and on the phone yesterday she said she'd like to bring
him to our reception. Almost five months early she's
saying this! She wouldn't haul him along to the wedding
itself -- she's to be Z's "first witness" (equivalent to
a maid of honor) -- but to the reception, yes. Z's
puzzling overtime on this. "I think maybe it's a kind
of unconscious provocation." I see it as that and more
-- as a continuation of what Aida's been engaged in all
along with both of us, which might be described as a
medium-intensity guerrilla campaign to alienate Z from
me and/or me from Z. But I don't want to be going into
that right now, or maybe anytime. Best just to think of
it as an unavoidable part of the price, and certainly
well worth paying, of nupping up with Zoelie B.

    (But...okay, I'll say one more thing about Aida.
In that same call she told Z that Kirk had told her that
when he leans in close he can see himself reflected in
her, Aida's, eyes, which are very dark. And then she
said to Z, "You can't do that with white people's eyes
and so they've always seemed empty to me. Is that how
you feel when you look in Glen's eyes?" -- And Z, I'm
happy to report, told her this: "Oh no, I love his eyes.
He has swarms of big horny Norwegians in there.")

    We got home at eleven last night and Z hit the sack
right away. As usual on Saturday nights I lay in bed
reading next to her until my current normal bedtime,
four-thirty a.m., meanwhile nibbling on cookies and
fruit left over from her book-group meeting (attendance
was less than expected: only seven). My favorite time
of the week, these leisurely late Saturday nights in bed
with the extraordinary Z-woman...in fact, because of our
maximally conflicting work/sleep schedules, it's the
only time we spend more than an hour or two there

together all week long, with rare exceptions. And this
has been so pretty much since the day we met. (At one
point Z thought our shortage of shared bed hours was a
major cause of my shameful sexual foozles of that first
year. Now she's done a one-eighty and declared it's a
main reason we're so hot for each other. -- Could be
she's correct on both scores, I'd say.)

[+2]

     This turns out just right. Forty-six hours later,
give or take a few minutes, and sun's blazing down on
the gray marble stage at the downtown central plaza.
I'm settled in at stage right front, and a marble
column's got my back with respect to a cluster of Cawk
skateboarders, half a dozen or more, perched vulturelike
in dark gray and black hoodies along the low rear wall.
Clatter of a few active boards hitting brick or concrete
here and there (the skaters have to be at least a little
wary because it's illegal in the plaza). Four lanes of
rush-hour traffic groaning northward. Through the Wall
of Water fountain, whose water is shut off today for
some reason, I can peer at the agonizingly compressed
faces of passengers riding jam-packed buses (okay, a
slight exaggeration there in "agonizingly"; in most
cases "blankly" would be more accurate). -- And on the
far side of the street, shoppers traipsing in and out of
the arcade and a row of corporate chain stores.
     Lift my head, a view of many more shoppers crowding
the sidewalks of the great white way -- also called "the
glitz strip" -- this being the city's main shopping
district, which runs east and west, perpendicular to the
street here. Turn my gaze to the right and two blocks
to the south I see the white marble of my very own scope
building, the upper twenty or so stories. Stars and
Stripes rippling fitfully way up there eight or nine
stories above where I'll be working tonight just as I do
most nights, five or sometimes six per week. But before
then Z and I will be meeting at the hideaway and then

hitting a nearby blues club for dinner.

     -- Oops, suddenly everything darkens, a chill
shudders my shoulders, a raindrop splashes on my
forehead. Yike, where'd this big black cloud come from?
                              *

     Back at the same spot a few minutes later. Sun's
out again already! But probably not for long. More
puffy dark gray clouds appear to be rolling this way
across the bay. Something like the aftermath of cannon
fire, I'd say, from a massive naval battle farther out,
maybe over by the naval base at the transit port I came
to know so well during my commuting years. A mock
battle, I suppose, sort of like the war games with live
ammo that USAn forces engage in off the Korean coast and
a good many other places around the world. Because --
you never know when we might need to gin up another war
or two or three. And you gotta be ready. This is how
it is when you're de facto ruler of the planet.

     I took shelter by the side of one of the supports
for the Wall of Water. Didn't realize the pools under
the fountain overhang remain full even when the
fountain's shut off. I literally stepped on the water
in one of them but pulled my foot back before it broke
the surface. Not even a ripple so far as I could see.
Yet I could swear I felt the surface sort of push back
like an invisible plastic sheet. (Could it be the old
walking-on-water delusion? Surely not!)

     Nowhere else in the blocklong triangular space of
the plaza is there a sheltered seat or bench. This is
by design, of course. Though jyzers probably weren't
intended to be the main target.

     -- Now darkening again, new chill, new occasional
raindrop splashes. A few of the drops are interacting
with my black ink in intriguing Rorschachian ways.
Blurry splatter patterns. Or authenticating jyze
watermarks, could say.

     -- Can go for one more paragraph, I think, if I
hunch over just so. Tale of the walk straight up this
street right here, the "very high road." The best and
also the most difficult part comes at the small

municipal plaza where I must pick my way through long
lines of urban nomads awaiting the nightly charity hot
meals served there. A block farther down, as a kind of
preparation for that, an overture of screams from the
city jail courses over all passersby, especially on warm
days, but also even on days like today, though not as
loud or as long. But at all times those screams can be
heart-rending. And also once in a while, it must be
said, quite funny. "Hey you down there, throw me up
some deodorant, will you? I stink!!!" (That was one I
heard a few weeks ago and it's still echoing.)

    -- Sun again. Well. Another brief respite, it
appears. The clouds seem to have switched over to a
slightly more northerly track.

    So I'll mention a bizarre sight. Two blocks south
of here, at one of the busiest downtown intersections
(right across from the scope building), a burly cop in
shades was hunched over on a motorcycle standing on the
sidewalk. This was almost flush against the show window
of a corner storefront set back about fifteen feet from
the street. He looked just like one of those cardboard
cutouts of a motorcycle cop propped up in front of a
highway billboard to scare motorists. Or could it be he
was seriously waiting for a speeder to pass by? He did
seem to be intently eyeing the street traffic. The
strangest part of it was that people (pedestrians) kept
stopping to stare at him and he never reacted at all --
didn't move a muscle -- sort of like those bronze-
painted live mime "statues" at the public market.

    -- And now a new cloud appears, much more ominous,
the fierce fighting mother bear of all clouds with a
couple of feisty adolescent cubs nearby. I'm packing it
in, pulling out my folding umbrella, moving on. And
it's almost time anyway.

*   *

    -- Now up in the very scope office I was gazing at
from the plaza some six hours ago. Holding forth at the
reception desk. This at the far end of the hall from
the conference room where jyze was going down during its
last session here.

What do we have in this zone? A brief inventory
reveals a couple of desktop computers and monitors, a
fancy-looking phone with buttons for twelve extensions
and two dozen reporters, an old-timey adding machine,
reference books, a high counter as in a dentist's
office, a sign with a big red arrow and the legend
"Complaint Dept. 6,342 miles" (it's pointing due west,
so be prepared for the onslaught, Beijingers). At my
back stands another desk on which perches an ancient
electric typewriter, used to fill out unfamiliar court
forms that pop up from time to time. And next to this
desk squats the big (five feet high) gray floor safe in
which all the grand-jury materials and laptops are kept,
including mine. I could probably dial in the
combination for that safe with my eyes closed. And
behind the safe, a window looking out on the usual
downtown night scene, mid-canyon-wall level.

Also on that other desk is displayed a greeting
card for National Secretary's Day, which took place last
week. "To Nell." I have no idea who Nell is. I still
know a few of the staff people here but it's been at
least six months since I've visited the office during
daylight hours. And yet I'm a kind of staff person
myself -- just an independently contracted one. Also it
could be said I'm a kind of secretary or perhaps a
digital-age scrivener, a possibility jyze has expanded
on in previous annals. "Legal worker" is how the
authorities now classify me for tax purposes, replacing
the "information systems worker" of last year's tax
return. "Nightscoper" is still my preferred term.

Z and I did meet right on time at the hideaway and
had a fine evening. A bit of canoodling in the armchair
there before we strolled over to our favorite blues
joint, where I crammed down a super-jumbo burger and
thus won a chance at the grand drawing to win a free
pass for two to the live-music event of my choice over
the next year at that same joint. Then to the ORB (only
real bookstore) for an hour of parallel browsing and
then dessert at the cafe downstairs, site of our very
first scheduled date (broken by her). Then up to the

notoriously nasty bus stop at the AQ terminal where we
practiced synchronized back-to-back "davening" ("you
watch mine, I'll watch yours") for ten minutes or so
until an ancient fume-belching hilltop-bound diesel
coach came poking along and I bade the lady farewell.

At one point I was describing to her various things
I'd been jyzing about earlier -- the "living statue"
cop, the walruslike bellowers, the vulturelike skater-
boys. Observed Z: "My babe really loves the urban
scene." Now that really stopped me in my tracks. How I
appreciated her saying that!

Tomorrow, I should mention, is Midspring Day, also
known as Cinco de Mayo, which just happens to be our "FF
Anniversary." Last night I stealthily retrieved our FF
celebratory candle sculpture from its high shelf in the
bedroom as Z slept and then I added a whole new layer of
foofaraw to it; tonight I'll set it up on her chair to
greet her when she arises in the morning (ideally just
after completing an anniversary F -- except that she
still hasn't taken herself off prodomo quarantine, so
probably not) (but "plan B" stuff of course is not ruled
out; in fact, it's for occasions like this that we
appropriated the term in the first place). (At the ORB
cafe tonight she confessed she sometimes fears our era
of high romantic excitement ("limerence") will soon be
passing simply because everyone says that's what happens
after a couple's been together two years. I insist that
it just can't turn out that way for us. And goddamnit,
I believe this!)

I've got another thirty minutes or so to burn here.
Time to haul out my handy list of miscellaneous items.

(1) Last night June dropped by at two a.m. It was
my turn to help edit one of her law-school papers. She
conked out on the living-room couch as I read the draft,
unable to prevent myself from stealing a glance or two
at her to admire her female attractiveness and even more
to marvel at her strong resemblance to Lady S. She
wound up sleeping over on the fold-out bed in Z's room.

(2) It appears Z and I will indeed be having the
same trouble Max and Leah did in finding a "hall" for

our reception. Interestingly, Z's now talking about
renting a large tent and using Jess and Gwen's yard for
the festivities. Earlier it was Aida's yard that topped
the list, but Z admitted tonight she's once again
seriously down on Aida. "It's terrible to say, but if
she doesn't care about hurting my feelings maybe I
shouldn't care so much about hurting hers." (Yesterday
Aida failed to show up for a lunch appointment with Z,
and then she failed to call to apologize afterwards.
This on top of the business about bringing Kirk to the
reception was just too much.)

   (3) Z's decided to forgo buying an air conditioner
in this year of high wedding-related expenses, thereby
"saving" more than a thousand dollars; instead we'll
order a forty-dollar clip-on cooler like the one she
bought last year for her mother, who raves about it.

   (4) Yesterday I noticed a laminated sign tacked on
the tree by our driveway. It advertised (in pencil,
with many touchingly misspelled words) dressmaking and
mending services available in unit 102 of our building.
That's where the enigmatic Filusan Ciro lives with an
older woman who apparently speaks only Tagalog and we
assume is his mother. Tonight Z told me she's putting
together a bag of items to be mended by her and jokingly
suggested I could come up with an additional bag or two
all by myself just from the stuff I regularly wear.

   (5) One evening last week when I set up my GJ
laptop on the conference table here I saw a lovely sight
out the window. In the gap between two of the tallest
highrises to the southeast the full moon shone,
appearing to be floating like a big pale cherry on top
of a fogbank that rose two-thirds of the way up the gap.
It looked something like a giant schematic highball out
there. And because of the way the fog was streaming,
the cherry seemed to be bobbing slightly, as if it were
riding an upwelling of champagne bubbles. (Not that I
think champagne is a normal highball ingredient.)

   -- And now, at five to one, I'd better be about my
business of locking the GJ laptop and various documents
back in the safe (tonight's job, by the way, took under

forty minutes) and unhooking the Jyzer Ink desktop computer from the battery of printers and rolling it back down the hall on its rickety cart to its usual parking spot for the current era in the northwest corner of the conference room.

[+2]

Tonight it's not looking so good. Z melted down over wedding plans this afternoon -- got upset enough to charge me with "ruining everything" for her. It's the first time we've had to invoke our emergency quarrel guidelines -- the "Moskstraumen Measures" -- in many months. Maybe half a year or more.

It took about an hour to patch things up. I suppose I should just be grateful the M/M invocation worked as well as it did. But I also see the incident as ominous because it came on so suddenly and so early in the wedding countdown. If the pressures are getting to us this early -- with four and a half months to go -- what will be happening in August and September?

So now I'm back home after work. This time I'm trying my jyze luck at the dining table. Two a.m. I'm physically and emotionally worn out but I must jyze this jyze tonight. Or -- I don't know. I suppose I could put it off until tomorrow night, some of it anyway. (And I just hope Z doesn't wander in here again, unable to sleep and wanting to talk. It happened two nights ago just as I was preparing to get back to work on my big FF anniversary tripod refurbishment -- which I did finally manage to do, but not until two hours later, after five a.m. -- and sure enough, here she comes right now. I mean live. What timing!

"Hi. You still mad at me?"

"Just doing the jyze thing here. You still mad at me?"

"No."

-- She's gone into her bathroom. Usually she'd use the other one at night. If ---

[+1]

So then round two of the fight. Now it's the
hideaway a mere twenty-one hours later and I'm jyzing at
the desk. Two Friday-night bands are booming away in
different clubs one story down and only thirty or forty
feet apart, at times with a kind of quasi-synchronized
dissonance you could probably dance to if you were
exceptionally loose-jointed. And that's exactly what I
wish we, Z and I, could've done a little more of twenty-
one hours ago: that kind of fancy dancing.

Half past eleven. And I'm going at it literally in
the long cylindrical shadow of the orange plastic
"Millennium Time Capsule" which is temporarily standing
atop the printer to my left. If all goes well we'll be
filling that thing up and burying it in Betty and Kat's
backyard come late December. -- And I hadn't noticed
some of the smaller labeling on the box before. "Record
Your Own History!" it says at the top. And on the left
side: "For the Future!" And below the main label: "You
are making history right now!"

Well okay. Is this not positive reinforcement?

Before coming here tonight I mulled the situation
for a couple of hours at the WOC. Most of that took
place in the big whirlpool bath down in the former bank
vault in the basement. All but the first couple of
minutes I was entirely alone in there. The waterfall,
all seven or eight feet of it, was cascading away with a
strangely comforting roar. The ragged patches of froth
and foam kicked up by the waterfall were slowly drifting
around the edges of the pool as if in imitation of an
ancient Zen poem. Excellent place for in-depth -- about
four feet of that in the pool itself -- mulling. (This
is an old sybaritic habit of mine which I've only
recently revived. It reminds me strongly of the public
baths of overseas days. I hadn't tried one again until
I dinged my back last summer.)

I decided three different issues are involved in
the fight. One is the wedding. A second is money. And

44

the third is this jyze itself.

It all started right after not the previous entry but the one prior to that, Tuesday. On that night also Z emerged from her bedroom just as she did last night, only at three a.m. instead of two. This past winter she'd been having "insomnia issues" -- often stumbling out in the middle of the night -- but these had eased off recently after a visit to her naturopath (exactly what herbs she's consuming now I don't know, and it's probably better that I don't). My upside-down nightscoper hours haven't been helping matters, I'm sure, but as she points out herself she's struggled with insomnia on and off all her life. She thinks it's mainly "the mygs" -- stress -- that bring it on. And on this night the mygs swarmed around, as seems to be more and more the case, the wedding plans. We again talked in depth about guest lists, possible sites for the reception, so on and so forth. And she finally calmed down and went back to bed and I was able to put the finishing touches on the refurbed phallic FF anniversary tripod and then to mount it -- not sexually! -- but complete with a flotilla of goofily annotated balloons I'd laid in earlier -- on the coffee table in the living room (the seat of her armchair wasn't stable enough).

The next morning the FF display took her totally by surprise. The previous night she'd been displeased by my "distractedness," my declining her plea to come to bed right away, but ex post facto this magnificent lewd construction (mostly her own creation) excused all that. During the day she left a "5/5 Bouquet" here at the hideaway, five daisies and five of some other flower, a purplish one -- it's still here, the vase standing in the place of honor atop the filing cabinet -- and I thought everything was all right again. Our workout at the WOC went fine. She didn't get up that night, and she left me a note asking if I'd consider loaning her a portion of my deep reserves to pay off her credit-card debt (roughly twenty thousand bucks). She said she'd gradually pay me back with interest by picking up the full tab for our rent until the books balanced again at

some remote future date. Fine with me, I told her. In
fact, last summer I'd proposed a similar scheme, but at
that point, even though we were official "Deeps"
(domestic partners) and "engaged" (as we still are now,
both of those), she was nowhere near ready to consider
anything quite so binding involving such serious bucks.

Then Thursday noon she did lunch with Serafina and
had to tell her she'd be excluded from our wedding
proper, as opposed to the reception. And it was too
much for her. She broke down and wept when she called
to tell me about it. This is the woman whose umbilical
cord Z had cut for her first child's birth. She, Z,
also let fly with some boggling complaints suggesting I
was somehow to blame for the whole brouhaha, but I tried
to ignore them at the time. Then she left work early
and caught me still at home and brought up the same
complaints again, but this time in more explicit and
hard-hitting ways which I couldn't simply shrug off.

How's it my fault? Because I didn't want to have a
big wedding in the first place. That's the gist of it.
It wasn't enough that we compromised between what she
wanted and what I wanted, or that she later said she was
grateful for my "pushback" because she now thought
keeping the wedding small and making the reception big
was a much better way to go. Nor was it enough that
since then I've accepted virtually everything she's
wanted vis-a-vis the wedding. The idea to have the
ceremony in Olwen's backyard, for instance, was hers.
The idea to limit the number of attendees there to two
witnesses apiece was mine, yes, but even that came in
response to her expressed anguish over whom to exclude
from a much larger group. And she seized it eagerly at
the time. Yet now she was making me the villain of the
piece! (And not in the spirit of fellow conspirators.
She'd forgotten that this was the whole point of setting
things up as we did -- so she could deflect her friends'
cries of outrage by telling them the whole thing was my
doing. Now she was believing it herself!)

A wedding meltdown. Already. Serafina, the
fearsome "bantam fighter," had turned her right around.

(Oh those fun-loving D. sisters, who ever dreamed they
might bring so much high-grade trouble down on us!)

It was bad enough, our fight, that, as noted
earlier, she invoked the "Mokstraumen Measures" and we
brought out the sheaf of old agreements and she read
them out loud one by one all the way to the end. And to
my surprise, and I think to hers too, this clearly
helped. Just hearing all those achingly earnest vows
we'd come up with in lengthy negotiations during our
early "maximally turbulent" period -- and mainly at her
insistence back then -- seemed to have the effect now of
making us both realize this was something we shouldn't
be battling over.

And then last night. She disliked my failure to
respond immediately when she came out to the living room
at two a.m. -- other than to say I was doing my jyze
thing -- and I disliked her objections and especially
the indignant tone she couched them in. Worst of all,
she said -- arrrgh, the heck with it.

I'm not gonna lay this out in any more
chronological detail. It's just too damn grim.

It comes down to this: if I were to insist on what
I think is right in our dispute I don't see how it could
do other than ultimately break us up. "If I see you
jyzing I feel left out": those are the words I can't get
past. And her willingness to upend my plans (twice in a
twenty-three-hour period!) despite my having filled her
in about them in a general way in advance and having
asked her to bear with me now and again on those
isolated instances, all but inevitable over the long
run, when I've neglected to forewarn her about
specifics. She had even encouraged me to carry on with
this TJM project and assured me she'd never be one to
stand in its way. And much earlier she'd turned down my
suggestion that we do at least part of it in tandem-jyze
fashion as we did for the third part of "Jyze in Love"
two years ago -- the stress of it would be too much for
her, she said, on top of that from the job and, of
course, the wedding. So how can she complain now about
feeling "left out"? -- Because I asked her again last

night if she'd changed her mind about doing the tandem-
jyze thing and she said it's "unthinkable at this
point."

     (It's bugging me right now that I can't at least
frame this in a way that would give more of the feel of
the fight. She drives me nuts with her poor-me
accusations. "You're so reasonable and I'm a crazy
bitch. Now I've really blown it: I can't even respect
your art." -- And these aren't apologies; they're
accusations! I've driven her to them by being "too
good"! Yes! It's my fault that she's become the "crazy
bitch" she accuses herself of being! (Have I ever used
that "crazy bitch" term to her face? Not once! I don't
even think it!) -- And all the while tears are
streaming down her cheeks and her eyes are puffing up
and of course she's letting me know I'm responsible for
how she's going to look at work tomorrow.)

     I don't know what I can do. About the wedding,
probably nothing. About the jyze, she said it might
help if I put up a sign in the hall saying something
along the lines of "I'm jyzing right now but I love
you." Fine, I'll do it, and I'll also write down in
advance on our joint calendar in the hall exactly when
jyze will be in session. If this doesn't work I'll have
to abandon the plan to go at it at home at night at the
end of each J-week -- "closing it out at home before
bedtime." And I'll seriously resent being forced to do
that. To borrow her own words: it'll "ruin everything!"

     She took this afternoon off and came home right
after lunch. Didn't talk much -- obviously she was as
afraid as I was that the hostilities might restart.
Last night we almost canceled our plans for tomorrow
with Wei and Alison -- but in the end we hung in there.
I'm worried about what still might happen tonight. And
so I think it's best to stop this entry right here. And
to postpone the start of the next J-week one day, until
Sunday. The only time I could have at it tomorrow,
Saturday, would be after we returned home, and later in
the night after Z had gone to bed, but it's too soon to
risk trying that again.

[Got to Jyze It Up]

3

     Came boppin' out at sunset, boogied down the hill
and through the AQ to one of the few places other than
the hideaway where I knew I could set up shop indoors
without laying out some bucks. Though it's a clear
evening with a gorgeous sky, it's way too chilly for
outdoor jyzing. So I've hunkered down near the vending
machines in the waiting room at the train station. Only
a dozen other sitters in view (and not a single stander
or lier at the moment).
     I'm starting up a day late, as planned, which means
this is Mother's Day. And right here near the top I'll
say all seems to be going well again with me and Z. In
an earlier era of my life a jyze project like this one
might not've survived such a blustery storm -- just as
any of my earlier hitch-ups or serious shack-ups might
not've. Being a battle-hardened vet -- and we're both
just that -- can have advantages in both realms.
     So now it's catchup time. Get this jyze locomotive
back on track, chug chug wheeze wheeze. (Off and on
freight trains will be rumbling through, as one is doing
right now, just a few feet behind me, with the
soundtrack also featuring metallic shrieks and cries and
jounces.) (And I'll mention that I completely missed
the opening of the highest of the major mountain passes
last Thursday -- "the parting of a deep sea of snow," as
the caption for the front-page newspaper photo put it --
as a long line of cars snaked up into the high country
and the exceptionally onerous winter came to a symbolic
end, widely celebrated in these parts.)
     I think first just a plot summary of the past two

days. Later for the details, or maybe never if time's too scarce.

The reconciliation happened right away when I hit the sack Friday night, taking only a couple of hours to accomplish itself, and those including a celebratory copulation (by dawn's early light). This meant my sleep hours numbered about four, since I had to rise early for our afternoon outing -- "island arts & crafts tour" -- with Wei and Alison. Then, upon our return, a second wind allowed me to attend, with Z -- on spontaneous impulse! -- a showing of a Norwegian movie, of all things, at a north-end theater, with a stop for Scandi-style fish and chips on the way back. Then at home, finding June asleep on the couch in the living room, Z and I holed up in the bedroom earlier than usual for our routine Saturday-night read-in, with Z dozing off after about three minutes. Maybe an hour later I went out and awakened June -- her snoring was all but rattling the windows -- and went over the new draft of her paper with her, finally seeing her off sometime after four a.m.

Earlier today Z did brunch with Jess and Madge and then all three visited their coworker Nadine -- this is the woman who's undergoing chemo for an incurable brain tumor -- while I caught up on sleep. Later in the afternoon Z and I made a south-end provisioning run, first to the gas station, then the co-op, then the chain corporate supermarket and attached chain (different chain) corporate coffee shop. Back at home Z nuked herself some dinner and crashed shortly thereafter, at seven p.m., fixing to sleep through until morning.

(What's this? The station will soon be closing for the night? So early? But a man in an official-looking national-railroad uniform just came around with the news.) (And one of the trains listed on the "Arrivals/ Departures" board is still sighing and humming outside, cooling down after the long run up the coast. Hate to leave at such an intimate moment. -- It rolled in a couple of paragraphs back, the train, but the crowd's already completely dispersed, the noisy baggage carousel empty and shut down. -- And now the waiting-room lights

go off. Like a blink without its second half.)
*   *

    And so twenty minutes later it's once again the
hideaway. The rumble here is that of the building's
heating system -- sounds like roaring flames in a big
coal furnace with the flue door open, or maybe something
like the cab of an old steam locomotive that's on the
move -- but this is only when the system's turned on,
which tonight is the case maybe a third of the time.
Otherwise, when it's off, the Sunday-evening quiet is
even more complete.

    Yesterday's mail brought the news that I'm almost
four thousand dollars more solvent than I was a month
ago. This is the first big jump in my deep-reserves
account after many months of negative or lackluster
results while the market as a whole was zooming upward.
-- Zooming upward for those who have market holdings,
that is, yes. And it's quite an irony, no question,
that I now happen to be one who does. And so, aptly
enough on Mother's Day, I thank you again, ol' Mom, for
blessing me with those very same holdings (and you too,
ol' Dad, since you bought the life insurance that
eventually at your death laid most of the bucks on Mom
which she for the most part passed along at her death
almost twenty years later to us kids). And I beg your
indulgence, both of you, Maw and Paw, for how I'm about
to use this blessing. But yes, I think you'd approve.
(This month's gain all by itself, if sustained, will pay
for all my wedding-related expenses and then some,
unless the tab for the honeymoon flies out of control.)

    And then I suppppose I should also thank the
powerhouse U.S. economy. And all those who made U.S.
hegemony in today's globalizing "free market" possible.
So I do. I thank you, each and every one of you, and
never mind the centuries of slavery and genocide and
expansionist war-making and military strong-arming and
CIA dirty trickery, etc. etc., that cumulatively lie
behind a huge portion of it. (Do I rant? Very well, I
rant.) -- And I sure as hell hope, and it would be
excellent if each and every USAn did too, that things

51

will soon start moving in a direction that will favor
all those other countries and peoples who've been and/or
are being crushed by the present grossly lopsided and
unfair arrangements, which of course, when other kinds
of inducement fall short, are to this day brutally
enforced at gunpoint by our U.S. military. Or maybe
things already are moving that way and we just can't see
it? (Dream on, oh guilt-wracked radic-neoprag.)

And now a little more detailed rundown on how the
fight ended.

Friday night on arriving home I found Z had put up
a new sign. "Beware the Hydes of Jyze!" it said. And
in smaller lettering along the bottom: "Pee softly" and
"Stash da snacks." I'm supposed to hang the sign on a
chair at the crook in our L-shaped hallway whenever I'm
jyzing, thus ensuring she won't miss it if she wanders
out of the bedroom and starts padding toward the living
room (which is around the bend and past the kitchen,
which is separated from the dining/living area by a
waist-high counter which is itself L-shaped, as for that
matter is the whole kitchen/dining/living room or "great
room" (ha!) -- as for instance in that very fine film of
many eons ago starring a French actress who, a few years
after I first saw it, Lady V reminded me of so much:
yes, "The L-shaped Room").

If I detected a bit of undue grumpiness in the way
Z proposed this "Hydes of Jyze" scheme -- the J-slinger
is no Mr. Hyde with her and never has been! -- well, I
thought the sign was funny too and showed she really did
want to find a peaceable solution.

Admittedly I was still wary heading into the
bedroom at four-thirty a.m. Found her awake. A bit
sarcastic, perhaps, but not really hostile. "I hope
you're done jyzing for the night -- or should I turn my
back and put on my mask so you can do it with a
flashlight? Oh, and while you're at it, why don't you
use the flashlight for a butt-check."

It's unfortunate I didn't do just that. But
instead I plunged ahead with some much-needed
reacquaintance rutting and only afterwards did I check

out the H-zone -- even though she hadn't detected
anything untoward in checking the area herself earlier
by mirror -- and I spotted an outbreak higher up in the
asscrack in back than she's ever had one before. So
then I scrubbed myself down genitally, probably way too
late to do any good. So, yes, if the Big H is going to
nail me, it's going to nail me. Nor did it help that I
had a slight rash in my crotch from breaking in my new
jeans, and it certainly augured poorly that this rash
began stinging while we were still hotly in the act.

     What was good, though, was that Z didn't melt down
over any of the above. To me this suggests she'll be
able to handle our being jointly infected ("herped-up")
equally well if that's the way things turn out. And the
surprising increase in the pace of her outbreaks makes
this eventuality seem more likely than ever. They're
coming close to monthly now, probably triggered, again,
by "wedding mygs" more than anything else. Or at least
that's her theory. But it's also supported by both
docs, Karen and Lorraine, of mainstream and naturopathic
provenance respectively, and it's not all that often
they find something they can agree about.

     -- In any event, she's back on quarantine again.
And we're back to "plan B" sex, meaning nipple comes
primarily for her along with hand- or blowjobs for me.
Sort of like, say, a horny engaged couple of yore
resolved to save it for marriage. But we both believe
it's highly improbable we'll have to wait that long. If
things go as before, and they've always done just that
so far, she'll be on the H-rag a week maybe, give or
take a day or two. Which is still a pretty damn tough
span to wait out sometimes, and that's at least as true
for her (with her libido to burn) as it is for me. But
she's a rock on this and so far, again, we've always
managed to hold to the program.

     One other reconciliation detail. Along with the
sign on the chair in the hall she left a book for me on
my armchair: "Crying: The Mystery of Tears." It's true
I'm sometimes bothered that she cries as much as she
does, and that it's sometimes very obviously

manipulative (as she's not ashamed to admit; in fact she insists she's proud of this and what's more that it's a prime reason evolution gave us tears). But under most circumstances it doesn't bother me all that much. Ol' Mom, after all, cried fairly often too. -- It's just that I know I'd be crazy to react in a way that would encourage Z to do it even more.

What does bother me quite a lot, as I've told her over and over, is the kind of meltdown in which she turns openly hostile if not downright savage and starts blaming me for all her problems and seems to be welshing on important agreements. Later she'll usually try to play all this down as a mere "emotional outburst" not to be viewed too seriously. But it takes me a while to get over the really bad ones, and later when she wants to make new agreements like the one or more than one she's just broken, I sometimes find it much harder to do so.

-- But I'm going along with the agreements anyway and I'm assuming she will as well. I'm not saying her way's wrong and mine's right. I'm saying this is the nature of -- or it's one aspect of the nature of -- our struggle. And all those appearances to the contrary notwithstanding, I know it's a loving struggle and I believe it will continue to be that. All love's a struggle at times! Hear hear! -- But I still want it to be on the record that in our case I worry a lot about the potential explosiveness.

And that's gotta be it for now.

*

Back to Mother's Day for a moment. Today Z called Mama E. I was watering the plants at the time and didn't talk with her. But Z said Mama E was cackling over some new articles she'd clipped from her supermarket tabloids for me -- mostly sex-related stuff, Z said. "She's really getting off on sending you these things and I don't know why. I've never seen her like this before." To me it's a little odd that Z shows as much equanimity as she does over such kinky behavior by her own mother (harmless as it may be) in light of the way she, Z, insists that this same mother sexually

abused her as a child. I still don't know quite what to
make of this claim. And maybe I never will. But I
suppose I'll keep exploring the matter. (And if it
turns out it's too intimate for Z to accept my jyzing
about it -- "for posterity" -- I can always expunge it.
But I doubt this will ever be necessary. She's always
encouraged me to grapple in writing with the toughest
stuff and I know she does plenty of similar exploring of
my own abundant weirdnesses, and my family's as well, in
her journal as well as her poetry. -- How do I know?
Because she's photocopied many journal pages and poems
for me to read, just as I've done for her with jyze.
-- And yes, she's still writing in that journal and
still dashing off poems from time to time, but nowhere
near as often as before for either. She's said she's
hoping to get back to them both after the wedding. But
still not in tandem-jyze form for the journal. As she
put it: "I want to do it when I want to do it and the
way I want to do it. You savvy, Kemosabe?")

     Also earlier today she and I had planned to check
out a condo being shown open-house style a couple blocks
west of us on the hilltop. The price on the sign is
$129,000. That's peanuts compared with what's being
asked for similar-size places in other parts of town,
but for us the monthly payments (something like $1400,
or almost double our current rent) would still be steep
because of Z's high debt payments (and of course my low
income). By today, probably for that reason, she'd lost
interest in seeing it. But as soon as the weather warms
up and we're forced to open the windows so as not to
roast in our apartment, her displeasure with the exhaust
fumes coming in from the street and especially from the
driveway next door (where the guys like to work on their
cars and rev their engines and also to play lots of loud
heavy-metal music which she hates) (as do I, but not to
the foaming-mouth extreme she does) -- all this, yes,
may well revive her interest in moving. And other
frictions could arise. We have an agreement that she
won't bitch and moan about the fumes if I won't bitch
and moan about all the air cleaners roaring away in the

apartment. -- Surely a future source of conflict. But
for now why worry. I mean, we're still a couple of
months away from heat season (and I'm talking about a
couple of different types of heat season that will be
running concurrently).

[+2]

     The standard two days later, so still riding the
offbeat. And it's the hideaway again but this time the
jyzer's back to the armchair. He's not ready to venture
out again with the J-book just yet. Maybe by next
session his equilibrium will be fully restored and he'll
be good to go on the move.
     For today's items of interest start with one Zoelie
B. Who else?
     Today she didn't make it to the WOC for our workout.
She was busy updating her resume to apply for a new job
opening at the city, even though her boss, Dale, has
told her she's the only applicant for the assistant job,
which also happens to be the one she currently holds,
albeit on a temporary basis -- which has been the case
for close to a year now -- and she's said this is the
job she wants.
     (So why is she putting out all this extra effort?
She just "feels squidgy," she said, hanging out there in
the wind without another option. I said this reminded
me of her rationale for continuing to see those other
guys back in the first couple of months we knew each
other when she was supposedly, as she says now, so hot
for me. "That's exactly right, it's the same principle,"
she declared, "or lack of principle as I'm sure you see
it." But she laughed heartily too, meaning she may've
thought I had a point there.)
     She did drop by the WOC just to say hello before
going home (the weather was good and she decided to walk
-- "Got to get some exercise some way or other every
single day before September 25th"). And she called me
several times at home as I groggled through my breakfast

routine, once opening with a few bars of song. "Night
and day, you are da boy...." I think she's feeling bad
about the fight and wants us to get our "lim" back. I'd
like that myself. -- But wait, no. That can't be,
because I've already taken the position it's not gone,
the lim. Just needs a little recharging, that's all.

I haven't mentioned, by the way, it's now her
considered view that the real genesis of this most
recent battle was my telling her, as we discussed buying
the condo, about the only other time I almost bought a
house, when it was Lady S's opposition that quashed the
deal -- and eventually helped trigger our breakup. This
story gave Z the shivers because she thought I was
hinting the same thing could happen with us if she
misstepped in some way. Talk about twisting the meaning
of a story! (Or on my side, being less than optimally
aware of its possible multiple interpretations for her,
that also could be, no question, and I said so out loud
and she thanked me for it. She even said, "You know,
you're good. You're really good. I think your mother
must've really known what she was doing. You know, I
just wish so much I could've met her." (This being in
the aftermath of our Mother's Day talk about the
different ways our families influenced us.) -- But I
must add that the way she said this, with a quizzical,
head-bent look, it was as if she still thought ol' Mom
might've missed a trick or two and I might be trying to
put one over on her, Z, now with my "I should've been
more aware" talk. Could even be she's right on this
too.)

And: she spoke with Aida today, and Aida said she
had lunch with sister Serafina over the weekend and Sera
was now saying she'd be willing to do whatever Z wanted
regarding the wedding and she was mainly just pleased Z
and I had been able to reach an agreement "so easily" on
how things should proceed. Wow, some backtracking!
Flexibility even! -- And so it turns out the complaint
that served as the main declared (at the time) emotional
trigger for Z's meltdown last week amounted to nothing.
(But then again it's entirely possible, even likely,

the fraught weeks and months ahead will spur more such
flip-flops, and not just by Aida and Sera. -- I
neglected to ask Z about the current status of Aida's
plan to bring Z's former lover Kirk to the reception,
but that by itself could well induce a series of them.)
     And yet more on this dratted wedding that's
distracting jyze from so many other things it ought to
be tackling. Z says it'll be much easier for her to ask
her friends (except Aida and June and Betty) to miss the
actual wedding if we could delay the ring ceremony from
the wedding until the reception, as Max and Leah did
last week with theirs. Fine, I said, as long as I don't
have to give a speech. It's a deal, she said. -- And
Saturday, with Wei and Alison, we drove by the hilltop
garden club -- it's just eight or ten blocks from our
place -- and the three of us who hadn't seen it before
agreed with Z that it would make an excellent choice.
It's a large, century-old, three-story Victorian house,
grayish blue with white trim, gabled and turreted yet
not at all pretentious, rustic almost, with a big porch
on one side, surrounded by maybe three quarters of an
acre of well-kept lawns with lots of flowers and shrubs
and trees and a couple of arbors and even an old gazebo.
As of the Friday deadline the one applicant ahead of us
on reserving September 25th still hadn't come up with
the fee, so Z's now very hopeful we'll get it. And if
we do, I'll go ahead and make arrangements for our
honeymoon, which will start, by mutual agreement, on the
26th, the day after the wedding/reception, because we
have little doubt we'll be too exhausted to make the
long drive after the reception ends at five p.m. or so.
     And now, because I must be at the scope office by
eleven, it's potpourri time, kwikjyze type. First, I'll
happily report that my new jeans did shrink in the wash
just enough to prevent the bottom hems from dragging.
And up on the hill, a revelation: the internal lights
are now going on at night in "the castle" in preparation
for the dot-com move-in. For at least a decade the
lights on the top twelve floors (of sixteen) were shut
off, word has it; what I was seeing at night for the

past sixteen months was solely a matter of floodlights
shining in from odd angles and thus illuminating the
interior of the building from outside. And Z revealed
something touching: the reason I usually find my pillow
laid out vertically when I climb into bed is that during
the times she was without a boyfriend she arranged her
own extra pillow that way so she would feel less lonely
at night, and the practice became habitual during the
long period after she decided she was finished with men
forever (but then along came this LOML right here!).

And a news flash from the WOC: workout buddy Mitch
got taken in by an internet hoax. This has him
believing that some demento dude is going around
applying an arsenic/acid (LSD) paste to downtown pay
phones -- supposedly it could kill almost instantly --
and three city residents, he said, have already died but
the phone company is covering up the deaths. Mitch was
running around in a state of high excitement telling
everyone this story, adding (to me), "Man, I think the
world's coming to an end!" And when a limping one-eyed
two-hundred-ninety-pound muscle-beach ex-military lifer
gets that wild you feel the apocalypse just might really
be pending. -- But then since we know the apocalypse
actually is heading our way, in a decade or two or maybe
at the most four or five if not precisely on January 1
of next year, why should this be all that big a deal?

(Should note that Mitch lost his left eye at a
missile base in South Korea when someone switched on the
radar as he stood a few feet in front of it. This base
was just a few miles from the small city where Lady S
grew up -- except when she was living in her family's
other home in the big city.)

[+2]

Still working the offbeat. A good setting for it
too: the artiest bar in town, with some surprisingly
funky dance tracks pounding from the box. It's a
Thursday happy hour. Clinkety-clinks are happening too,

pool balls dropping, loud talk and laughter echoing.
And now a big groan from a pool ball not dropping.
"Damn damn damn! Fall you fucker! FALL!"
     Again I'd've liked to be somewhere outdoors tonight
but the weather is similar to what it was at the
downtown plaza last week, unpredictably drizzly and
cool. Cooler even: an Arctic system's been hanging
around for several days now producing a string of record
lows. I've gone back to wearing an extra layer under my
jacket and putting up the hood at night while waiting at
the bus stop.
     A heavy work night ahead. I'm halfway through the
first day of grand jury. Dinner's already bought and
sits in a plastic bag on the seat opposite: a packet
containing a tiny fliptop can of tuna and half a dozen
crackers, along with a bottle of mixed-fruit juice, all
from the downtown drugstore where I usually pick up
something to snack on at work if I manage to reach the
store before its ridiculously early closing hour of
eight p.m.
     So I'm back in the world. At least this is how I'm
feeling. South hill and the AQ/HQ are my primary turf
and I've had my head buried in them while playing
catchup and re-equilibration since the meltdown flap
last week.
     What's new out here in the world? Hot war in
Europe, the first there in fifty years, how's it going?
A supposedly errant NATO bomb hit the Chinese embassy in
Belgrade, presenting the Chinese government with an
ideal excuse to call forth massive anti-U.S. protests at
home. Antiwar opinion here and across the nation seems
to be building. But...the bombing continues. My sense,
however, is that NATO (and especially its hegemon the
U.S.) is already searching for an "honorable" way out.
     Meanwhile the Makah tribe over on the coast has
finally begun its renewed whale hunt amid a blaze of
media attention but the first harpoon toss missed. And
a few blocks to the north of where the jyzer sits now,
scores of "Star Wars" devotees are camped out in a
parking lot (some have been there for ten days) awaiting

next week's opening of the new episode -- "The Phantom Menace" -- amid nonstop bursts of megahype. And our local film festival is just getting underway, with some two thousand films scheduled for screening in half a dozen venues over the next five weeks or so. (But because of the difficulty of knowing in advance which films will be worth seeing as well as the inevitable long waits in line, often in the rain, for virtually every picture -- sometimes only to be turned away at the door because the house is full owing to the last-minute arrival of an unexpectedly large number of series ticket holders -- it's not likely Z and I will be attending even a single screening this year.)

In personal news there's this. First, it's official now: the garden club will be the site of our reception. Z's delighted and therefore so am I (and what's more I like the look and feel of the place, so I'm delighted all on my own as well). Z had intended to spend no more than five hundred bucks on the reception, but now because of the rental fee (she'd been counting on free use of a private home) she's doubling that. And I'm thinking maybe I'll kick in that half myself. Z had said from the start she'd pay for the reception, but now since I'll be cashing out the deep reserves anyway and the overall reception price has gone up, I might as well offer to do my bit. I'm sure ol' Mom would be pleased if some of her bequest went for this purpose.

Other personal items. For one, I wrote Z a three-page note explaining why I thought she was unwise to apply for a second job when she's trying to keep the one she's got now, and to my surprise she reversed herself after reading it. "I still can't figure out you white boys," she said in thanking me (her boss, Dale, being another cracker like me, except he's a red-headed one). And I left a mock letter, seemingly opened by me and very realistic-looking, its postmark coming straight from my rubber-stamp collection, in the stack of mail on the dining table; it was supposedly sent by a cousin of mine in Norway, "Bent S.," and it said he and twenty-three other relatives of mine would be in this area in

late September on their fishing boat and would like to
attend our wedding and were assuming they could stay
with us because they were sure we had plenty of room as
all USAns are known to have and they promised that
before docking in Jyze City they'd scrub off as much
mackerel stink as possible. It scored big.

The main event of the past few days was the
farewell party for Betty's good friend Wanda at an
Italian restaurant near the fairgrounds. It's part of
the same corporate chain where we dined with Z's family
last year in Centropolis and looks almost identical to
that other (franchise?) eatery, the walls crammed floor-
to-ceiling with photos showing aspects of Italian life
and pop culture so stereotypical that the place seems to
be a parody of itself. Meatballs and spaghetti, garlic
bread, tiramisu. It was also Wanda's birthday and the
restaurant staff serenaded her with "Happy Birthday" and
she blew out the candles on an impressive cake they
provided. The four of us gave her -- this was Z's idea
-- a "rainstick" (a dried cactus arm with cascading
seeds inside making, when it's moved, a downpourlike
sound) and then we all signed it on the spot with an
indelible marker. Kat was in exceptionally high spirits
and behaving badly at times, driving poor Betty half
mad. I tried to keep her, Kat, preoccupied with games
and crayon-drawing but Z said I wasn't helping much --
was mainly just ratcheting up Kat's excitement even
higher. It seems I'm getting a rep for doing this (with
Sera's girls and Aida's Charles also).

-- And must head myself on out now. "Got Work To
Do." (The old-school R&B tune of that name was playing
with fine timing until just moments ago, sounding so
good I stopped to listen and so it's -- ironically! --
delayed my departure for work by maybe two minutes.)

[+1]

To end the eighter some sanctioned jyze back on the
beat. At home on the couch in the living room at two in

the morning. The new "Hydes of Jyze" sign prominently
displayed on a chair in the hall. Z with a snack-stash
all set to go in the bedroom (or at least this afternoon
at the WOC she said she'd have one ready in there; but
when I arrived home the bedroom door was closed, as per
normal for the current era, so who knows if she followed
through on that).

Otherwise it's an ordinary night, except it's
Friday and so in-building noise and also street and
sidewalk traffic here in the hood are up a bit.
Probably the hookers and pushers are out and probably
the police patrols are beefed up too. (One night a few
weeks ago when I was driving home at two-thirty a.m. a
micromini'd Cawk hooker staggered out into the street
from a ramshackle open garage fronting on the sidewalk
just a block north of here and I had to veer into the
other lane to miss her and nearly collided with a big
SUV. Also caught a glimpse of probable pimp movement,
likewise Cawk -- to the surprise of my media-conditioned
mind -- in the garage.)

The president of the USA snuck into town today for
a fundraising luncheon. Z had to alter her own lunch
plans a bit because of blocked-off downtown streets. I
wouldn't even have known he was here if she hadn't told
me. She gets first crack at both local daily papers; I
rarely see either one until I arrive home late at night,
by which time many of the stories have been superseded
by the ones in the freshly arrived edition of the next
day's far-coast-megalopolis paper. And I like it this
way, because it makes skimming the local papers so much
easier and quicker when I'm finally able to glance
through them.

The undeclared air war goes on in the Balkans. The
longer it does so the greater the pressure on NATO (and
of course on the U.S. especially) to reach a negotiated
settlement. China is openly accusing the U.S. of
seeking world domination (and they're right, of course,
not that this aspiration of ours is anything new, and of
course they know that too). Meanwhile Congress is
reversing itself, it appears, and preparing to pass gun-

control legislation owing to public outrage over the high-school massacre last month. But it's mainly marginal stuff, just for show; gun trafficking will scarcely be affected. (And the debate over deeper meanings of the massacre continues, but public attention largely seems to be turning elsewhere. At the local level, though, I expect reverberations will continue for a long time, with "weird" nonconforming kids resembling the two shooters in this incident paying the price.)

Obvious stuff. But it's what's happening. This is how it is in the year of the millennial countdown.

And so back home. The news here is that Z's now "collaboratively" proposing I wear a Filipino barong dress shirt for the wedding and reception. Serafina's husband, Dak, will be traveling to Manila on business later this summer and he could have such a shirt made to order. And although I don't particularly like barongs and doubt she'll think I look good in one -- they're a lot like Hawaiian shirts, I'd say, worn with the tails outside the pants, and the wedding version is white with lacy white embroidery -- I do like the idea of wearing something Filipino, especially if I can come up with a pair of pants that would go with it, something more casual than the ones I recently bought, like say black hemp drawstring pants. (I tease Z that I'll go for the barong if she'll wear a Norwegian dirndl dress with special wedding rosemaling stitchery. She says she'd be willing to consider donning a piece of Norski pewter jewelry but that's about her limit.) (Actually, though, I'm not all that excited by the idea of ethnicizing the wedding, whether in a balanced way or not. But I wouldn't mind a counterculturish or neocounterculturish ceremony and I think that's what we'll probably wind up having, more or less, and the barong shirt might fit in with that.)

Score one for Aida, by the way. She's the one who persuaded Sera to reverse fields on her wedding demands. "Aida just told her," says Z, "that what she [Sera] basically was doing was trying to pressure me into breaking my word to you." It's not quite true -- as

noted before, Z did come around to preferring, at least
for a while, or in any case so she told me, the idea of
an "intimate wedding" -- but I guess it's close enough.

-- And then score one against Aida too. Yesterday
Z bumped into Kirk outside city hall. "Well, hello
there," she remembers herself saying, and he said
"Hello" back, but both kept walking, and Z said she
thought maybe Kirk had a slightly puzzled look, as if he
hadn't recognized her. A former lover! "Have I changed
that much?" she asked me, seemingly sincerely. (I mean,
how would I know? Photos? In that case the answer's
no, not much, except her hair's far shorter and, on top,
spikier.) Aida's slightly puzzling comment on the
encounter was this: "My two best friends in the world
and they can't find anything to say to each other!" And
so I ask: is Aida perhaps missing some important social
gland? She seems unaware of certain kinds of nuance --
impervious to them, one might say. But it's interesting
to know she's thinking so highly of Kirk so soon.
Apparently they're going at it hot and heavy -- or at
least Z tells me Aida says they are. I don't know Kirk
at all but I suspect Aida's acting out of a kind of
emotional desperation (like what Betty may soon be
facing with the loss of her friend Wanda: Aida in a
sense, as Aida sees it, and no doubt with some
justification, is losing Z). -- Or one could just say
Aida is trying to match Z, keep up with her, strike a
balance, and it's not exactly a coincidence that she's
doing it by partnering up with a former lover of Z's.

The first time the four of us meet should be...
interesting. I'm looking forward to it. Or I should
say: jyze is. Me personally, I'm not so sure.

One other note regarding Z's friends. It seems Wei
is now a bit miffed at her. Yesterday a friend of his
started joshing him about getting married. "How come,"
the friend asked, "I haven't heard anything about this
from you, Wei?" Well, it turns out Wei has been trying
to hush up the matter at work so as to avoid all the
predictable gossip and razzing. I didn't know this, but
Z did. And Wei did some digging and discovered that

this particular chunk of scuttlebutt came to his friend
via Nadine, Z's coworker with the brain tumor. Says Z:
"I figured I could tell her because she was dying and
she was scarcely able to talk. I wasn't even sure she
understood what I was saying!" But then under chemo
Nadine's condition improved considerably (alas, only
temporarily improved; the tumor's inoperable and Nadine
has less than a year to live even if the chemo works
optimally) and she started calling up all her old
friends at the utility and dishing with them for hours,
and now every last detail about Wei's wedding plans is
common knowledge there and probably throughout city
government and in numerous places beyond.

     (I can't believe Wei's really upset about this.
Yet I can sympathize with his desire to avoid having to
talk wedding all the time. It's a touchy matter between
Z and me too, not least because it's so old-paradigm
stereotypical that the woman should be openly excited
about the ceremonial hitch-up while the man's acting as
if he's being dragged into it against his will. Neither
of us wants to be perceived this way and yet we probably
deserve to be -- and I reminded her of those statistics
that show we're dead center of the middle class, that
is, prime boojie. I try not to act the predictable
role, I said, but obviously I won't always succeed. And
the truth is, as noted before, I'd much prefer to skip
all the ceremony and just run off to a judge and get it
done. -- But since that's not in the cards, I'll do the
best I can to enjoy it -- as in, say, jyzing about it.
Except, true again, even this can be a drag sometimes,
as I've doubtless mentioned before and am demonstrating
yet once again and in spades in this very paragraph, if
any of this even makes sense.)

     Going back to that incident with the prostitute
lurching out into the street, the community cop speaking
at our most recent block-watch meeting, Z tells me,
explained that most of the "sex workers" -- he actually
used that term! -- operating on the hilltop come from
other hoods and are transported over here in vans that
serve as their base of operations and also as compact

mobile bedrooms, a certain silver one and a certain
brown one being the major offenders in recent weeks (the
cop passed out photos of both, including close-ups of
license plates; when she got home, Z immediately posted
them on our bulletin board in the hall). Overall
hilltop prostitution seems to be easing off and I'd say
it was minor to start with (that is, during the time
we've been here), except down on the other side of the
high bridge, which to many is still known as "ho bridge"
(in part, but probably only in small part, because it's
named after the Filipino national hero -- and excellent
novelist -- whose first name is Jose). Maybe a dozen
times in my sixteen months on the hill I've stumbled
upon people engaged in a sexual act of one kind or
another more or less out in the open in that corner of
the upper AQ: in cars, in doorways, back in the weeds
and bushes.
       (Earlier today I altered a postcard for Z that
shows a kid sitting in front of a huge stack of books
poring over "protocols for marrying Zoelie B." By happy
coincidence the kid looks a lot like me at that age --
say about ten -- so on the back of the card I taped an
extra copy of an old photo of myself as a fifth-grader
that shows the likeness. Her note to me from tonight
raves about the photo and vows to post it in the "Family
Gallery" on the shelf by her desk at work.)
       -- And how about a few "plan B" sex tales? Plenty
of raunchy ones to tell! But no, best to leave those
for next time. Jyze has exceeded its page limit. (And
I've said virtually nothing about the setting here. The
large Christmas poinsettia growing like crazy ever since
I fertilized it (fish-based kind). The air cleaner now
acting as a footrest. The row of dusty old record
albums. The stacks of books and magazines and
newspapers. The balloons and windsock fish. The damn
good feeling I almost always get sitting here,
especially with jazz or blues playing on the radio,
although way down low so that the many day workers
around here, and one especially just down the hall, have
a better chance to rack up their beauty sleep....)

4

     Came boppin' out at two p.m. but not in the usual
way. It's Sunday and Z and I were bound for the street
fair out in the Yuke to resume the search for wedding
rings, among numerous other items. Kat was with us.
And then suddenly it was five hours later and Z was
dropping me off near my old edgeville digs before
swinging onto the viaduct to take Kat home. I walked in
to work by the same route I used to follow most nights
for the last year of the pre-Z era and the first nine
months of, yes, the Z era, but the pre-Deep part of
that, or rather of this, era. Blessed era!
     And now it's almost four more hours later. Break
time. But it can go only forty minutes tops because the
scoping job I'm thrashing away at must be ready by
morning. (If any unexpected difficulties arise I'll
have to take the last bus home and come back down in the
Z-mobile -- something I've done only three or four times
since our move to the hill.)
     So the same old conference room. It was just
starting to rain as we left the street fair -- we lucked
out -- and now big wind-driven waves are beating on the
windows here. My cheapo Russian-army pocket watch is
laid out on the table, its clamshell cover cracked open
(to reveal the startling incandescent-purple face with
its rococo Cyrillic embellishments). This watch is
tethered to my backpack and I haul it out at most once
or twice a month, usually for an occasion like this.
     -- And the break's already almost half over.
Obviously jyze won't be covering a whole lot of ground
here tonight.

And this on the day of the perigean tides. The highest and lowest tides of the year -- and quite a sight they were back in my ferry-riding days, all those clammers and fortune-hunters out sloshing around in the mud, surprisingly far -- hundreds of feet in some cases -- from what would ordinarily be the shoreline.

Yesterday Z and I made a run over to the north-hill market and stopped along the way to chat with brother Rob during his break. The only real news was that a postcard had come in from sister Barb and she and Keith are, or were when they sent it, in Bali. Neither Rob nor I had any inkling they were going on a trip. Could be his relations with Barb have become almost as bad as mine.

Z and I also hit the fuchsia show and bought a couple of specimens of a supposedly superhardy variety (the guy all but swore a death oath that they'd make it through next winter sitting out on our balcony). Z sprang as well for a red "bird duplex" -- a birdhouse with two rooms internally inaccessible to each other -- which appealed to her, and me too, because it resembles a Filipino stilt house. Now I have to come up with an unobjectionable way to attach it to the balcony railing.

Last night was Z's "date" with Cordell (from the utility) to see a jazz show at the symphony hall. I used the free time to catch up on work at the hideaway and also wrote to brother Jeff inviting him and Angie and their blended, so-called, offspring to the wedding. When I arrived home at the usual time I found the bedroom door open, a lamp on, jazz playing on the radio, and a bottle of wine chilling in an ice bowl on the bedroom armchair -- but all the ice cubes had melted and the lady herself was conked out in bed. (She'd also scattered her black lingerie about the area in artful disarray.) (I'd chaffed her a bit about this "date," which was an office-lottery prize she "couldn't kosherly refuse," and then she had the twisted notion I'd be waiting at home for her afterwards, eager to hear all about it.) Eventually I did succeed in waking her and some hot compensatory loving followed -- but again of

the "plan B" variety by necessity, sorry to say.
-- So back to work. With two minutes to spare!

[+1]

A dive out in the SQ (Scandi quarter). Way in back
by the pinball machine and the dartboard because here
the light is good and the crowd is sparse. Nonexistent,
in fact, within thirty feet or so. And just outside,
the Syttende Mai parade is still marching by. Cheers,
sirens, applause, a PA system identifying who's who.
Trombones blaring, majorettes strutting. If I stand up
I can see it all out a high window. But hearing it over
the roar of a large vent fan, blather of a TV, blare of
nasal country corn from the box -- that's not so easy.
No matter, though, because a bona-fide mini Norwegian
flag is sticking up from my shirt pocket (and three more
are stashed in my bag).
The Z-mobile is being tuned and its oil changed at
the lady's usual garage six or seven blocks down the
road. I intentionally set up the servicing for today so
I could be out here for the festivities.
Two years ago Z and I attended this same parade on
one of our early dates, and Kat was with us. In fact
that was the day Kat and I met. And she decorated my
khaki chucks with a black marker as we sat at the curb
just around the corner from here. It was instant hit-
it-off on both sides and helped seal the deal: Z was the
one for me. What's more: that was also the famous day
when Kat asked if Z and I were going to get married and
said she wanted to be the flower girl if we did. And in
September that's just what she'll be.
After dropping off the car I hiked up to the pan-
Nordic museum. Did a quick tour of the exhibits and
lingered a while in the gift shop, picking up a little
handbook on the Vikings, the four Norwegian flaglets, a
"Skanky Scandi" button, and a few other goofy novelty
items for Z, Betty, Kat. Something unusual: the shop
was full of neatly dressed Cawk twenty-somethings

speaking Scandi languages and sneaking glances at me
almost as if I were an emigrant homesteader who'd taken
on new life after breaking out of one of the museum's
history dioramas (presumably the group was in town from
the old country for the festivities). Then back outside
I found the parking lot had become a staging area packed
with kids -- not every last one blond and blue-eyed, but
most -- and many looked as if they could've flown in on
the same plane with the gang in the gift shop. But they
were all local grade-schoolers, it turned out, and the
nearby contingent of elders in traditional old-country
outfits were clearly locals too. A thought crossed my
mind: I've come to think of Norskis as all being either
tottering elders or hayseed younger folks. A direct
result, no doubt, of my childhood summers in Turtle
Rapids. But certainly my visits to the SQ over the
years have reinforced the impression.

As I walked up this way from the museum the clouds
darkened alarmingly and it seemed likely the parade
would be rained on if not canceled entirely. But maybe
twenty minutes later, after I'd taken shelter under the
pavilion at the central triangle -- an accordian band
was playing there before a crowd of two or three dozen
probable local Scandi elders, all but a few in
nontraditional but vaguely rural outfits (possibly
shipped in from Turtle Rapids?), as a single couple
kicked up their heels to a kind of "Ole Bones" polka --
just after I arrived there, I say, the sun burst through
a chink in those same roily dark clouds, and not long
after that, nothing but blue sky could be seen.

The mural in the triangle, I noticed, honors a
sister city in Norway and features a castle somewhat
resembling our marine hospital on south hill. But the
founding date on this real castle is almost a full
millennium earlier, at which point my ancestors were
probably scrabbling around in nearby peasant huts which
the muralist, however, has neglected to depict.

-- Big boom out there. Must be the summerfest
pirates -- a number of whom, as always, like to wear
historically incorrect horned Viking helmets. The joy

of marauding! Berserk warriors! How very USAn it is
(also)! And a few feet up the street stands a hook-and-
ladder firetruck with its ladder extended to the limit,
close to eight stories, and a big Norwegian flag (white-
frosted blue cross on a red field) hanging from the top
and flapping a bit listlessly. Always bugs me that the
country of my roots (a plurality of them anyway) still
sees fit to display a Christian cross as its symbol. A
crusader flag in essence.

     -- And now a flashback to yesterday, the Yuke
street fair. The high point there came at a booth
selling homemade hemp shirts and pants. I tried on
several of both (with that little scamp Kat sneaking
under the drapery into my changing booth -- that was a
high point all by itself -- supposedly covering her eyes
yet also dropping her jaw histrionically at certain R-
rated moments) and now I've got a whole new wedding
outfit. The barong is out, at least for a while, and a
cream-colored hemp shirt is in. Black dress slacks are
out, charcoal hemp drawstring pants are in (though
they're being "custom-tailored," since the last charcoal
pair in my size had just been sold, and we'll pick them
up during the hempsters' next visit to J-town over
Memorial Day weekend).

     As for the main quest, wedding rings, we didn't do
so well. Z was disappointed at the quality of the
craftsmanship -- couldn't find anything "distinctive"
enough (most of the jewelry-makers were either assembly-
line pros or green-finger amateurs turning out work at
roughly the level of sister Barb's efforts during her
early jewelry-making days on the road in Europe and the
megastate to our south here, where I was also living at
the time, which surely proves I know whereof I speak).
I did see some copper ones I liked, though, and I'm
hoping I can win Z over to that type of ring. At first
she didn't seem at all interested in any of them, but
afterwards, when we'd made the whole circuit of the fair
and come up empty, she seemed willing to reconsider.
Alas, by then the coppersmith with the best items (that
is, offbeat but not so much so that Z's friends with

more conventional tastes would be shocked) -- that woman
had packed up and left and we hadn't even nabbed one of
her business cards. So the search will continue.

All afternoon I carried the Kat scamp on my
shoulders and they're still sore today. We gorged on
hot apple dumplings, strawberry shortcake, and smoked-
salmon burgers, but not on buttered corn-on-the-cob; Kat
knocked our plate of three cobs onto the dirt floor of
the chow-down area before any of us had ventured a
single bite and we chose not to undergo another long
wait in line. And a bit later, while Z was off looking
at something else, Kat fell hard for a huge rainbow-
colored stuffed cat she spotted deep in an out-of-the-
way stall and begged me to buy it for her, twisted my
arm, promised to be good forever, and so I did; but only
after she'd agreed to kick in her three bucks of
spending money, which she then painfully unfolded and
flattened out and handed over one by one (my portion was
twenty-seven bucks, and those bills may've been even
more tightly folded). For no reason we could determine
she christened the beast "Rainbow Jack" and cuddled with
it the rest of the afternoon while absorbed in reading
her favorite mystery -- "The Babysitter Freaks Out" I
believe it's called, or should be in honor of what this
babysitter right here had to go through yesterday --
reading it, she was, for the fifth or sixth time.

Last night, by the way, I got hung up working on an
elaborate altered-art card for Z: "Blonde Savage" became
"Polapina Savage" ("The shocking TRUE story! How
Zoelie B. captured the HEART and SOUL of Glennar S.!").
I was chortling with delight every stroke of the way
because this is one of my best productions ever. (I'm
even fantasizing about putting together a display for
our reception: "Best of Z&G Altered Postcards." But it
probably wouldn't fly. Most of them, hers as well as
mine, deal with X-rated erotic or "private-language"
stuff. For instance: how many would grok the meaning of
the portmanteau word "Polapina"? And that's relatively
decipherable.)

(The hot news on the phone this noon was that Z,

while meeting with Aida during morning break, learned
Aida and Kirk had gone to dinner with Kirk's brother Ed,
the U.S. congressional rep for Jyze City and environs,
and we're not to say a word about it but Ed is thinking
of launching a run for U.S. senator. And Aida was
surprised to hear I'd proposed pooling the remainder of
my deep reserves -- what would be left after paying off
Z's debts -- with her, Z's, retirement account. "She
said she thought you were the type who'd want to keep
the money stuff separate." -- Which is typical Aida, I
must note, but never mind. The point here is I
apparently did myself quite a good turn with Z by
suggesting this. It seems to mean a lot more to her
than I'd've thought it would, if I'd thought about it at
all, which in truth I hadn't. It was strictly an
impulse move. "Intuitive." I just liked the idea of
our futures being pooled.)

    -- By now the parade's over, I'm sure. The crowds
have dissipated. (In fact a dozen or so paradegoers
have filed in here, most carrying telltale Scandi flags
and looking a little uneasy in this setting, clustering
at tables near the entrance and ordering soft drinks.
In normal times the place draws mostly hardcore alkies,
looks like to me. But still I wish we had something
similar to it on the hilltop within walking distance of
our apartment. We're way short up there on good indoor
jyze venues.)

    -- And if I want to beat the rush-hour traffic on
the way back I'd better be hoofing it down to the garage
and I mean right now.

[+1]

"The Prez Shopped Here" sign isn't up yet at the
only real bookstore (ORB). But he did, just last week,
squeezing it in along with what the papers called a
"somber" fundraising speech. He bought seventy-some
dollars' worth of books, mostly whodunits (it seems he's
as big on them as Z and Betty and Kat are), and bragged

74

a bit about the size of his personal library (seven
thousand volumes, he said). -- The question is, though,
whether this bookstore will remain in existence long
enough for them to make the sign.

     Well, maybe it's not quite that bad. But like all
indie bookstores this one's standing squarely in the
cross hairs of the digital revolution and it's already
taken several big hits. And developments in the past
few days suggest it's about to take another. First the
dot-com that's moving onto our hill -- whose main
business is internet book sales -- announced an increase
of their discount on certain bestsellers to fifty
percent; then just yesterday the major national
bookstore chains followed suit. If the indies did
likewise, of course, they'd simply go broke a whole lot
faster. (Also of possible relevance: the first wave of
three hundred employees of the dot-com has arrived on
the hill, with roughly six times that number still to
come. After months of rumors and hype and scouting
parties the invasion has officially begun.)

     So the ORB's basement cafe. My usual table in the
back corner next to a couple of elaborate old iron pumps
that've probably been obsolete for half a century or
more. Four p.m. I'm due to meet Z over at the WOC at
the standard time, just ninety minutes from now. (But
her spirit is hanging out right here. The table to my
left is where I sat when I showed up anyway for what was
to have been our first date, the one which she'd broken.
I did it to have a little talk with her ghost. And then
mailed Z a handwritten copy of some sparky highlights
from the dialogue. -- The fact is I'd already totally
flipped over her just from our talks on the phone.)

     -- And out in the world today we have some big
local news: the Makah have succeeded in offing their
first whale in seventy-five years. Local TV stations
carried the climactic moments of the hunt live -- I
missed them thanks to my upside-down hours -- and this
hunt is stirring up plenty of controversy, not least
because our city is both a major fishing center and a
major environmental center. And it should also be noted

that two other tribal nations, somewhat larger than the
Makah, and both quite familiar to me, are licensed to
kill, between them, over seven hundred whales this year:
Japan and, yes, Norway.

    Also it's opening day of the new "Star Wars" epic.
This too has been hyped to the max, though for the life
of me I still can't see why (but I do have some ideas
about it which I'll try to get into later since they
touch on the millennium). And peace negotiations
regarding Kosovo are said to be gaining, even as the
bombs keep falling (which they've been doing for about
two months now) and of course they're all still stamped
"Made in USA" and "Delivered by USA" and, bottom line,
"At crunch time this is how the USA does business --
dig it or die."

    At home Z and I are in a kind of lull, unable to
see much of each other because we're both so busy. She
scheduled an activity of some sort for every night this
week and two for both days this coming weekend (four in
all, that is, and all four involving me as well). She's
also trying to fight off a head cold she probably picked
up from Betty (and I thought it had nailed me too when I
woke up with a scratchy sore throat the other day, but
that seems to have cleared up). She's again saying
she's worried we're falling into a kind of rut, "post-
lim," the romance is fading -- but she's been worrying
about this off and on almost from day one, to the point
where we mostly just joke about it now (though still
somewhat seriously at times). And she wonders: are we
tumbling toward that mediocre reputed USAn average for
sexually active couples of two true consummatory "plan
A" copulations per week? That was part of today's talk.
I said I agreed it might've fallen close to that the
past month or two -- but mainly because she's been on
the H-rag so much during this time.

    -- And she's on a "be responsible" kick. At work,
at home. She's temporarily resigned, until after the
wedding, from the board of the county women's coalition
(yesterday I picked up their mail for her at the HQ post
office for the last time). And from now on, at Wei's

recommendation, she'll be paying all her monthly expenses in cash -- taking out a certain amount from the bank at the beginning of the month and that's it. No more use of credit cards. No exceptions. For real!

  -- And I must rush off. Can't even finish my root beer. (It's a new brand too, and not so tasty; could be that's why I've been sipping even more slowly than usual -- but then all serious jyzers do learn to sip slowly.)

[+2]

  If I work this just right I think I can avoid being pricked to death by the holly bushes. Alfresco this will be -- the weather's finally improving -- in the plaza of a big downtown skyscraper, and in the sun! What skyscraper it is I don't know, though the large sign anchored to the planter just to my right bears the name of a well-known international U.S. bank. Or is that just for a ground-floor branch office? Beyond that sign stands the main feature of this patio, the public art (it's required by law here in J-town, I'm usually pleased to say although not so much with regard to this particular case: a pair of sadly banal fifteen-foot-high green and red metal tulips).

  Thursday now. I'm on my way down to the hideaway and then the WOC. Bought a new set of gel pens at a downtown art-supply store. Picked a jyzing spot pretty much at random. The first one I went for, on a black marble bench at the foot of the big brown highrise kittycorner from here (another bank, I think; looks like about fifty stories) was just a little too chilly in the shade. The sun angling in through a gap between two other big buildings makes this spot where I'm sitting now just fine. (It's speckled brown marble. The holly bushes are trimmed square on a vertical line just above the inner edge of the planter ledge, probably to prevent people like me from getting too comfortable if we sit here. But if you go for a corner of the planter you can fit in nicely by hunkering down diagonally across it.

Only the upper part of my jyzing arm, well protected by
the green canvas jacket and two layers of shirt beneath,
is making contact with the holly leaves.)

   The gel pens were not cheap. But I need them for
drawing up the wedding invitation and also for my art-
postcard alterations. And I've had lots of scoping work
this week, so I'm feeling a little less worried about my
immediate financial situation. It now appears I'll be
able to hold out until the arrival of the next quarterly
check from the deep reserves. That should be around
July 1, and those funds should provide sufficient
booster power to carry me through July and maybe August,
depending on the extent of the usual summer scope-office
slowdown. -- But all this is really just illusion
anyway, habitual thinking and nothing more, because I'll
have to be borrowing a large sum regardless to pay off
the major wedding-related expenses coming up.

   And while on the subject of finances I should
mention that Z and I are continuing to explore ways and
means of investing what will remain of the deep reserves
after I've paid off her credit-card debt. June's said
to be an expert on such matters; the three of us are
supposed to be jawboning about this one of these days in
the near future. The main thing to note is that Z
continues to seem quite pleased by my willingness to
throw not just my fortunes but also my fortune, such as
it is, in with her. As she says herself: it calms the
anxieties she still has around men and money because of
her traumatic experience with Arvin during her previous
major, but in that case dramatically aborted, run-up to
marriage (and knock on wood for our own run-up except no
wood's in sight other than back in the holly stickers).

   She won't be meeting me at the WOC tonight. She's
home sick. It's just the sniffles, but yesterday she
got into it a bit with Wei and this left her feeling bad
and so she decided to take the day off. (The rift with
Wei is repaired now. And the details on that repair are
interesting. But best I let them go for the moment.)

   -- A shadow's about to fall across these pages.
It belongs to yet another big bank building, across the

street to the southwest, and also to another squared-off
holly bush dominating the next planter over in the patio
right here. (These hollies, every little prick brings
back the big row of holly trees -- not mere bushes -- at
the last rental house where Lady U and I lived in the
north end of this city -- the Marcelian involuntary-
memory effect being even stronger, I think, when it
involves not a hunk of madeleine but something that can
draw blood. But this jyze is not about Lady U memories
-- however prickly the ones from our last year together
especially may've been -- or better just to say were,
period -- so enough on that.)

*   *

Ninety minutes later and this is more like it.
Lounging under a palm tree in my swimsuit on a cabana
chair in front of a pool fed by a genuine waterfall.
True, the palm tree is fake and the waterfall is also
fed by the pool, on a loop. But the water of the fall
really is falling, closer to eight feet than seven I'd
now estimate, and it's shimmering too, and every few
seconds an airborne splinter flying out from it reaches
me way over here. The chlorine may be a bit thick in
the air -- Z wouldn't come in here without a gas mask --
but I don't mind it too much. Brings back childhood
days at the Gatewood public pool, it does, bloodshot
eyes and all. (As they urge upstairs: feel the burn!)
It's not quite the inner sanctum down here but it's
the anteroom to the inner sanctum, with the big round
vault door standing permanently open a few feet to my
right. (It's about seven feet high and two feet thick,
its inner side lined with glass drawers like an oversize
spice cabinet.) Where the vault itself used to be in
this former bank building -- is there any other kind of
building in this part of town? -- a warren of sauna and
steam baths can now be found (and it's said to get
steamy back there in more ways than one, especially for
same-sexers, though during my visits I've never
witnessed anything but the most decorous behavior).
(Just now padding in, a somewhat heavyset and
extremely busty Eurusan thirty-something, I'd guess, in

an almost incandescent chartreuse one-piece swimsuit.
I've never seen her before. Now she's sitting directly
under the waterfall, bent over, employing the cascade as
a back massager. I was doing the same myself maybe
twenty minutes ago.)

So I make a special effort to get down here and
only one of my buddies even shows up. That would be
Estella, and she was engaged in intense conversation
with a guy (could this be the new boyfriend she was
telling me about?) and I didn't want to risk spoiling
her action and then she apparently left with him.
Otherwise I saw not a single person I know by name.
About two-thirds of the faces were familiar (or in some
cases it was more the body) -- and this is about par --
but the crowd was small for a Thursday.

(I wonder what the woman in chartreuse is thinking
over there. Perhaps not too surprisingly her few
glances in this direction seem more wary than curious.)

-- Z and I are trying to stay trim for the wedding
(vain as we both certainly are about our bodies -- also
called our "fleshly correlatives," or FC's, in private-
language-speak). The locker-room scale here says I've
now crept about six pounds above where I want to be
(which is admittedly another five pounds above my ideal;
but at this stage of the game ideals are way too costly
to attain and then over the long run they'd be even more
costly to maintain). As long as I work out regularly I
don't seem to have much trouble staying, or paring back
to, within five pounds of my ideal. That ought to be
good enough. (And by the way, my ideal itself is now
five pounds above what it used to be -- 197 instead of
192 -- because I figure the workouts here must have
pumped me up at least that much. Or am I dreaming? I
can't prove they have, no. For that I'd have to submit
to a body-fat test and I'm proud to say I have better
things to do with my time and also with my FC. And why
bother, really, since I don't have a baseline test for
comparison purposes.)

So I wasn't able to get into it with anyone this
evening, as I was hoping to do, on the three hot

political topics of the moment. There's Kosovo, there's
the Makah whale killing, and there's the high-school
massacre. (The massacre has re-erupted as an issue
because of a copycat attempt, this time in a far-coast
high school, with six students wounded but all still
kicking as of last night.)

And on the phone earlier Z told me Betty's at her
wit's end over Kat's "bad phase." The other day the kid
popped her mom one in the arm -- first time she's ever
hit her. So Betty said she was glad I'd gone after Kat
for being a "smart-ass punk" last weekend (modified to
"smart-asp" when Kat professed shock at the language).
"She listens when Glen says something -- he's her be-all
and end-all." (Or was this Z speaking? She equivocated
when I asked whether those were Betty's actual words.
For some reason she's forever trying to convince me of
what I already know: that Kat and I are bonded at the
hip -- or the asp maybe.) But anyway: the giant stuffed
feline from the street fair, Rainbow Jack, scored big
with Betty as well as Kat. They both like to sleep with
him -- Betty says he feels so good lying on her chest
she has a hard time drifting off. (At which revelation
Z wondered aloud to Betty -- seriously -- whether it
might be time to run a personal ad.)

A quick description of this room. Artificial
potted palms in three corners, the waterfall in the
fourth, with the pool shaped like an arrowhead with
rounded corners and pointing toward the waterfall. Two
stainless-steel railings angle down into the water at
the back of the arrowhead starting about five feet in
front of where I sit. Gray tile floor and walls, two
different shades. Blue plastic tarp covering something
unsightly, most likely, in the corner to my right,
partially behind the grated door to the lobby. False
opaque green-tile windows. The jets turn off
automatically after twenty minutes and you have to climb
out of the water to push the button on the wall to
reactivate them.

The lady in chartreuse is long gone, by the way. I
was ready to smile at her in a tentatively friendly way

when she mounted those pool stairs -- shedding water
like the queen of naiads -- but our eyes never met.
     And...the warm moist gassy air, the slowly circling
foam and froth, the surprisingly comfortable chaise, the
lulling roar of the falls: it would be very easy to
drift off for a few minutes right about now....

                         [+2]

     Here's Z sprawled beneath a colorful flannel sheet,
her bare right foot sticking out in front of me as if it
were assigned to keep an eye on things down here. I
could almost clasp toes with her (her famous toes! -- at
one time six on each foot but since age six months just
five -- and all ten survivors at this moment admirably
pedicured and red-nail-polished as well).
     But no, for now it's enough just to be jyzing like
this. So I guess we must've worked things out all
right. I guess. One a.m. on a Saturday night. She's
even left the radio playing. ("Once I'm asleep nothing
bothers me.") And it's a comfortably warm night, with
the first truly hot (by local standards) days of the
year looming. Z's boldly planning to go sun herself in
our Filipino-themed hilltop strip park tomorrow morning.
     Earlier, after returning home from the five p.m.
showing of "The Dreamlife of Angels," we pillow-talked
for several hours right where she's lying now, with
extensive "plan B" canoodling interspersed. The talk
started with the Wei matter and branched out into other
work-related topics before zeroing in on the inevitable
wedding stuff. (The gist of the Wei matter seems to be
that Z's feeling uncomfortable with some of her new
managerial duties and dislikes having to ask him to tone
down the radical political stuff, especially since she
agrees with most of it. At least that's how I read it.)
     -- I'm sprawled in my old green armchair along the
back wall of the bedroom. Just a single small table
lamp is providing all the light in the room, and that
lamp perches atop the shaky end table at my right elbow

and makes the shadows in here dance when I move too abruptly. And Z's "Rat Lady" doll shields her, Z's, eyes from the lamp light. A dark-green plastic "stack rack" of towels and sheets stands immediately to my left (most of them washed and folded by me, as it happens, since it was my turn last), and atop that is the giant "The Troth & Nuttin But" Valentine's card I made for Z some fifteen months ago, and tucked in behind it is the three-ring binder containing the folder of "Moskstraumen Measures" we had to haul out a couple of weeks back.

Because Z was feeling sick Friday she canceled two of our engagements for the weekend -- including an afternoon meeting with Olwen to talk over wedding plans -- and then Betty canceled the third, saying she wanted to take advantage of this burst of good weather to tend to her garden (the soggy cool spring has put garden and yard work all around town way behind schedule). This in lieu of the "adult outing" we'd talked about launching in Kat's absence (she's off at swimming camp for the weekend; and before departing she threw a weeping tantrum for fear Betty wouldn't be there when she returned; and Betty assured her she'd be there but said if it ever happened that she wasn't and Kat was frightened she should call Aunt Zoelie and Subunk Glen and we were both pleased as punch to hear about that).

So as a consequence Z and I found ourselves with a rare totally unplanned weekend. And then today she was feeling much better (her main problem was exhaustion, she thinks now) and so off we rolled to see the film after all (at first she had also scratched that). Alas, for her it turned out to be another walkout. This time it wasn't so much the violence, which wasn't graphic at all, but, as she explained later, the way one of the female characters was "locked into" a degrading love relationship. (Back before my time Z even pulled a walkout at "Anna Karenina.") She worries each time that I'll think badly of her for doing such a thing, but on the contrary, as I've told her many times, I don't mind at all so long as she doesn't mind my staying in there to get my money's worth. And she swears that's just fine with her. (She always brings a book with her to movies. "I love to read in theater lobbies when no one's around and you can smell the popcorn and hear the music swelling behind the doors.")

     Afterwards at the indie fast-fish place overlooking the eastern shore of J-town's central urban lake -- and all lit up and looking unusually spiffy on the far side, the newly landmarked flying-saucer icon (where a huge crowd will gather at midnight on December 31, and we've agreed we'll be among them) -- we launched into an air-clearing talk about our relationship. It wasn't somber or overly serious but we still managed to salve several sore spots, mine as well as hers. She talked about how this is the longest, or very close to it, she's ever been in a relationship with a man, how the "calmness" and "stability" of it are just what she's always dreamt of and yet now that she actually has them she's discovering they sometimes worry her. Are we losing the romantic edge? Can she get along without her normal outbursts of "diva mode" high drama? Can I ("the stoic Norski") put up with her at those moments when she feels frustrated and must "vent" or "act out"? "Believe me, I'm well aware of what a bitch I can be." (She says this at least once a month, almost as if she thinks it's possible I could've forgotten it myself.)

     For my own part I tried again to explain how what she may be experiencing as a dwindling of my romantic interest is really just a reflection of a heavy stretch of nightscoping on top of the focus I've been trying to maintain on this jyze project. It has absolutely no other meaning, I assured her. And she seemed to accept this, at least for the time being, as well as my avowed belief we can still find plenty of ways to keep things interesting for both of us within a framework of relative long-term emotional stability (ta-da!). And I said even in the area of physical loving and the perceived fallback to the dread "two times a week" I think we're still pretty damn sexual when circumstances permit. (She'd also been complaining that I'm not being as "touchy" as in the old days, meaning in this case

physically affectionate in public, of all things. Me!
And she's the one who used to grouse over my being that
very way and to complain I was "slobbering all over"
her!)

       But onward. Take note of a couple of wedding
developments. First, after Z told me she sensed Jess
was hurt because I hadn't asked her to be my "second
witness" (Rob of course is number one), I called Jess
today and explained why I'd asked June instead -- at Z's
urging, in fact, but only after I'd told Z I'd prefer to
have Jess and thought her feelings might be hurt and Z
had assured me Jess was the one who could more easily
handle not being invited to the wedding proper and June
would have trouble with it. And Jess said she wasn't
bothered at all. (She's a stud. And she has the
studliest walk of anyone at the WOC, male or female, yet
her overall appearance is feminine in something quite
close to the traditional sense.) (She was speaking to
me on her cell while puttering around in their fabulous
garden. This was where she and Gwen had offered to hold
our reception, and I had endorsed the idea, but Z felt
she couldn't say no to Aida's offer. But then Z decided
Aida's place wouldn't be big enough if the weather were
bad, just as it turned out not to be big enough for Z's
graduation party on a rainy afternoon two years ago, nor
for that matter would Jess and Gwen's place be big
enough for the reception if it rained, so that's why
we've wound up at the hilltop garden club.)

       -- And regarding Aida, lately Z has been speaking
more and more -- telling me this "in strictest
confidence" each time -- of how "boring" her
conversations with Aida have become. All Aida wants to
talk about, droning on and on, is workplace politics --
and the workplace itself is one Z is largely unfamiliar
with except for what Aida tells her. Today Z agreed
Aida is probably punishing her in some sense,
consciously or otherwise, and not just for unwillingness
to talk about certain more intimate aspects of our life
together, Z's and mine, or for the purported fact that
I'm so much like Aida's ex, Tom, but also because during

grad school Z started cooling on the kind of family-
psychology-oriented thinking Aida goes for in such a big
way. By the time I came along Z was no longer interested
in starting a consultancy business based on that same
psychology training, as they'd been talking about doing
for several years. And another factor in their tensions,
I'd say, is Aida's increasing reinvolvement (again, since
her marriage broke up) with the Catholic Church, which Z
has no interest in returning to herself -- and thank the
cosmos for that!

Second nuptial development: as a wedding gift, Jess
and Gwen, along with Paz and Tobey, have offered to
provide all the wine for the reception. This seems to
prove not only that Jess wasn't hurt by my (seeming)
snub, but that she and the others are looking for ways
to help Z meet her goal of spending no more than a
thousand bucks on the reception (meaning they're helping
her try to look good in my eyes, since they think I'm
behind this economy drive just as I'm behind the keep-
the-wedding-intimate drive; and in a sense they're right
on both scores -- though I think Z's mostly pretty damn
pleased to be going along with me on both, in fact to
the extent she's now claiming they were really her own
ideas first but then she let herself be too influenced
by the concerns of certain friends -- no names given).

And a quick look at the status of some longer-term
stuff. What's on the fire? I have letters out to three
people: cousin Kar, brother Jeff, and surrogate-pop Jim
Q. The one to Jeff I sent just this week but concerning
the other two I've been awaiting responses for over a
month. Also I'm hanging on word from my lawyer Evie H.
about the divorce, but I shouldn't really expect
anything on that matter for ten to twelve more weeks
(especially since if it comes before then it'll be bad
news for sure). And for the past month I've been
awaiting a call from reporter Verna about contracting
for additional scoping work -- probably starting in
June, she said last fall -- but now, since I've reversed
myself and decided to decline her offer should she
actually make one, I probably ought to be the one doing

the calling to tell her just that. And I'm still on the
hook for making honeymoon arrangements.

   -- So...enough. Especially now that Z has shucked
most of her sheet and is lying there prone, wearing just
black "H-rag" briefs, her legs spread a bit in a
slightly knee-bent pose as I look straight up from
beneath her feet and take in her entire FC. And I'll
say it's looking mighty good. All the dancing and
trekking and aerobicizing and iron-pumping and stair-
climbing over the years, they've done the job. And it
all began with the massive amount of exercising she had
to do as a kid to learn to walk again -- twice! -- after
the follow-ups to those first, partly bungled foot
operations. And (what's more) the raw material was
exceptional to start with -- I mean, I've seen whole
boxes of photos from earlier eras going all the way back
to age three hours. Not that you couldn't tell right
now just by looking at her, by a kind of backwards
extrapolation. (Yup, all this male gazing has got my
gen set twitching. Not for the first time tonight, but
up to now I've had to be a monk for jyze.)

5

   No bopping out this time. Dragging out. Moping
over to the hilltop playground. For an hour slouching
on a bench under a tree, sipping on bottled frappucino
and trying to wrap a hand around the new turn with Z.
(Wrap a hand around a turn? This is just it. Trying to
jack myself up to the point where jyze can even delve
into it. Much of the time thinking I won't be able to
do it. Damning her for putting me in such a fix.
Unfairly damning her, granted, but under the

circumstances I've no choice.)

     What say now? Boy do I hate going at it like this.
But I'll push on anyway. Just got to. All the years
I've been eagerly awaiting the rollout of the TJM
project and there's only this one chance. "Can't go on.
I'll go on." (Repetition, yeah. Literary pilferage
too, most likely. Or at least that's the intention.)

     For most of the hour the park's been completely
empty. And on the finest afternoon so far this year.
Now a couple of Asian-looking ladies are batting tennis
balls against a wall and two Latino-looking dudes (or
Filipino?) are hooping it up. (Loud rims.) But what's
happened to all the older folks and little kids? Is
this park considered too risky for them even in
midafternoon? I can't believe it.
                         *

     Now I've laid claim to a picnic table next to the
wading pool (which is not yet, and possibly won't ever
be, filled). This in the northeast corner of the park.
The shaded bench turned out to be just a shade too cool.
And I'm noticing the truly hilltoppy feel of this place.
It rides the crest at our end of the ridge with long-
range mountain vistas opening up in all directions
(though most are partially obscured by trees and houses)
except due north, where the sixteen-story gray concrete
senior center blocks the view entirely, including that
of the old marine hospital two blocks behind it. We
have music too, from across the street where four
shirtless Cawk guys are reshingling a roof. Boom-box
hard rock: the neighbors must be real happy about that.
And the sun has turned all four shinglers a scary-
looking lobster-red, and now I'm thinking I'll soon be
looking like that myself if I don't return to the shade.
                         *

     Done. Right back where I started except one bench
over. At a moment like this I'm not pleased to be
thinking I'm all the way back to bench one, as in square
one, even if the metaphor's ridiculous and the bench is
actually bench two. -- But I am thinking it regardless,
yes. A return to my predicament prior to some twenty-

six months ago, pre-Z. But no point in going into it in
detail. Just flashing on the hassles of finding a new
place to live and moving out is enough to shiver my
timbers all the way down.

So has it come to that? I'm sure as hell hoping it
hasn't. But it's come to something. Just what, it's
still too soon to know. I suspect the nature of things
between us will be changing. Less closeness. More
wariness and withdrawal on my part, more fury and
histrionics on hers.

(I'm one bench closer to the sun here, yes, but
it's no warmer for that. The chill is only slight yet
still annoying. When I heard the forecast for the mid-
eighties I didn't bother to wear a henley under my
workshirt. Or rather I should say I gladly bypassed
that step for the first time since early last fall.)

Yesterday before the blowup Z and I took a late-
afternoon walk down this way to check out the garden
club a bit more closely. It's just one block east and
two or three south of here, near "the junction," the
hilltop's commercial center (such as it is). On Sundays
the club rents out its first-floor ballroom to a church,
and a service celebrating the Pentecost was going down
inside as we inspected the grounds, with everybody
inside wearing white (Pentecost is also known as
"Whitsunday" or "White Sunday," I learned from a flyer
on offer in a box outside). Baptisms were happening in
there. (And today is "Whitmonday," for those not in the
know, which until yesterday certainly included me.)

Z and I confirmed our satisfaction with that same
ballroom as the site for our reception. We also learned
that the building as a whole is headquarters for all the
garden clubs in the state. And the blocks around it are
full of marvelous residential gardens even though most
of the houses themselves are small and modest. Many
residents in the area are of Asian descent and most of
the gardens display an Asian aesthetic sense, usually
Japanese, with some featuring exemplary curved bridges
and carp ponds and exquisitely tortured bonsai trees.

And then we realized we couldn't stand so much

prosperity and went home and wrenched the whole thing
into jeopardy.

Or rather she couldn't stand it. And she
specifically said so. That was one of her two main
points, or perhaps I should say themes, and she's been
muttering about it off and on for weeks (and we've gone
through earlier cycles in which she pulled the plug on
her own previously declared happiness in a similar way).

In a word, she's fed up with everything being so
harmonious. She wants more excitement. "I want
conflict. I want Sturm und Drang! I crave it! I can't
stand all this peace!"

She wasn't joking. All her models for romance, as
she herself pointed out, involve fighting -- her parents
went at it like Siamese fighters every week or two if
not more often -- and she didn't hesitate to trot this
out as a justification for her own meltdown. She had
plenty of others as well.

To me it felt like, again, a betrayal. It was only
a few weeks ago she was telling me how delighted she was
that we'd found a way to get along without fighting.
She even grudgingly gave me some credit for this! Now
it seems what she was really trying to do at that time
was to convince herself she could put up with all the
bland contentment.

Some fighting, of course, is inevitable. Have I
not already acknowledged this to her? The question,
then, is, how much? What intensity? And must we
valorize it, glorify it? Is struggle the ideal or is
harmony the ideal? If it's struggle, we're in for a
very hard time. Even under the best conditions she can
be extremely difficult to get along with (she knows this
and admits it straight out: "I'm a bitch sometimes and
that's just how it is"). When we're struggling, though,
she's often off the chart. I mean things can turn ugly.
It's time-consuming too. It's high theatrics. It's
bloody (verbally). And I'm plenty unhappy about it.

At this point in the current round she still hasn't
pulled out all the stops but neither is she giving an
inch. "I am who I am." In a card she left on my

armchair last night she comes as close to showing a willingness to compromise as she's ever likely to. It says, among other things -- I have it right here -- "Yes, I wanna invent, paint a new [relationship] model for us and my attempts may sometimes be a little rude and crude." She signs it: "She who wants 'lim' more than the experts predict. With you!" But this is not very reassuring when she's just been insisting that what will bring back the "lim" will be a regime of conflict.

I warn her things are likely to fly out of control and tear us apart. To me this is a return to free rein of the temper -- assigning responsibility for one's own behavior to outside authorities. That is, we're once again talking Catholic/Protestant differences. It's also a matter of ceding control to her, because this is how she uses those nasty high theatrics: to get her way.

In response I can either pull back or fight on her terms. Or I could try to out-vicious her, justifying it her way as a matter of "losing it, yes, but that's how I really feel, and I am who I am, so what's wrong with that?" (And so if she really feels like shooting me, is she likewise justified in doing it? -- Because plenty of times she's said she feels like shooting me. Not to mention a host of other nasty actions she's threatened. And not just against me. Against the noisy guys next door, and against her friend Betty when she's an hour late for our meeting and hasn't called to let us know what's delayed her, and for that matter against just about everyone she knows for just about any trivial reason imaginable at one time or another. -- But if I bring up points like this or try to reason with her in any way about the whole "conflict" business she's championing she shrugs it off by saying I'm not hearing her, I'm just trying to out-argue her.)

The second matter she mentioned is really just an extension of the first. But it's doubly painful owing to the torments we've gone through concerning it before and the fact that over time I've allowed myself to believe she's gotten past it or found a way to live with it. In a phrase it's the "Story of O" thing again.

She's saying she wants more conflict in our sexual life
too. She wants me to be "pushier." She wants to be
"overpowered." She wants me to rough her up, to
manhandle her.

     And I don't know if I can deal with this. It's
Lady V all over again and it's a big part of what did us
in. (Two weeks ago Z was upset when I used that same
"did us in" phrase with reference to Lady S and the
house-buying issue, and she's heard me say similar
things in the past about the S/M and conflict issues
with Lady V, and yet she plunges right ahead.
Astounding. To me this means I can no longer regard
this matter as being anything less than crucial to her.)

     -- So okay, enough. I don't like jyzing this way
because, among other reasons, I'm sure I come off
sounding like I'm blaming everything on her and I think
she's the one who must do all the changing. The truth
is I know very well I must be "at fault" too. But in
just what way? And what can I do to change? Should I
start beating her up? In essence this is what she seems
to be saying I must do. ("I know it's politically
incorrect but....") -- Yet she also knows it's all the
fashion to be venting and even glorifying one's
"primitive aggressions" as being "natural" -- cf.
evolutionary psych, neocon branch -- or the product of
fascinating "perverse reaction formations." And having
been around this mulberry bush a time or two before I'm
simply not about to do what she's demanding. This isn't
how I love. I can't do it. I prefer not to! I refuse!

     So what happens next? We'll slug it out (verbally)
and probably at some point she'll give in. But it won't
sit well with her and the cycle will keep repeating
itself, perhaps with growing frequency and/or ferocity.
Can I live with this? Maybe. Depends on just how
ferocious she becomes and how long the interludes
between battles. And can I handle my own disappointment
over our failure to do better? Can I keep loving her
the way I want to? Can I keep accepting her love when
it makes such demands over and over and in the end I
must always disappoint her?

     Maybe we can both live with this. But we won't
have what we've been thinking we'd have. Is there any
point in trying to pretend otherwise? And: would
pretending in that way itself be a kind of love? If so,
would it be a worthy kind?

     Another note she left for me last night asked, "Are
you getting cold feet?" About hitching up, she meant.
And my answer: "No way!" A third note of hers asked,
"Can I lick your owies?" And my reply: "Sure, but
better not to 'ow' me in the first place."

     And then earlier this afternoon when the phone rang
twice, stopped for a three count, and started again --
her signal -- I didn't answer. She left a sad-voiced
message: "Now my feelings are hurted." And this to me
is utterly boggling. Does she expect to be able to do
Sturm und Drang any time she wants and yet never herself
get any "owies" back?

     -- And by the way, at one point in her demand for
"pushier" loving I did say something which stung her,
but again I wasn't about to hold back forever and let
her pull off such a one-sided assault cost-free. I told
her if she wants me to be "pushier" in sex, she'll have
to be less passive herself once she shifts into high
sexual gear; she'll have to be less caught up in simply
being done to and more willing to beam herself back from
her extended orgasmic kind of trance and occasionally
try what works best for me, and not in a spirit of
resentment ("If someone else did this for you" -- moving
her body in a certain way, say -- "then I'm not going to
do it"). Or to use the term she favors, she'll have to
stop being "lazy." She'll have to be more into
"mutuality" and "alternating" and "ratcheting." (And I
was surprised she didn't make a big scene over my saying
this. But she let it drop quickly.)

     -- And meanwhile the after-work crowd has begun
arriving here in the park. The merry-go-round is
spinning. (And I won't be meeting Z at the WOC, where
she'll probably be expecting me. But so long as she's
insisting her rages have priority over everything else,
I'll avoid doing public things with her. Until she's

willing to "ritualize" our conflict -- to set up some mutually agreed rules regarding places and times and manner of expression -- I'll be extremely wary about doing anything with her. So some big explosions could be in the offing.)

   I left an altered postcard on her pillow. The original card said "Bring out the animal in him" and showed some female models in leopard-skin lingerie; I added, "But beware! The animal you get might not be the one you want."

   (The animals I'm getting right now right here are ants -- lots of them. In my pants too, among other places. One crawled up as high as my left ear. Black ones, no bites or stings so far. And a moment ago a squirrel came sort of hop-hobbling up to within six inches of my right foot. I thought it might be about to leap onto my leg and so I twitched my foot, and the squirrel, gray and scraggly, jumped straight up in fright, about eight inches -- truly an impressive vault -- and then scampered off. But only about five feet. This critter's a vet. Now it's back to hop-hobbling down the line of benches begging for food. And I'm so hungry I'm tempted to do the same thing myself. -- But instead will head on down the hill.)

[+2]

   Real quick. Things can change fast. We've again dodged the whirling tornado (though some serious wrangling still lies ahead). Maybe we'll be able to keep dodging whirling tornados. At least I want to insist on continuing to believe we can.

   But more on that another time, possibly even tomorrow. Because the way things changed this time is Z got sick. Or rather a lot sicker, and fast. For a week she'd been battling the sniffles and yesterday something hit her that's now looking to be some sort of nasty twenty-four-hour flu. She's much better already. But late last night it was at its peak and this morning at nine I scraped myself out of bed after maybe three hours' sleep to take her to see her homeopathic doc, Lorraine. Then a stop at the east-hill co-op for snacks and magazines for the invalid while she waited all bundled up in the car, looking truly pathetic but also heartbreakingly beautiful, like the proverbial TB-struck heroine in the very kind of nineteenth-century romantic novel she'd refuse to read and she'd walk out of if it were a movie. By the time I hit the bed again it was one in the afternoon and I slept only until three. So I'm a wreck. And a heavy worknight lies ahead.

But what a splendid afternoon it is (anyway). I'm on the way in, perched halfway up the rickety old wooden staircase outside the leather shop. This is just a short block from the northern end of the high bridge, right across from the Natusan center, and the great orange-brick castle, now at least partially occupied by the dot-com, stands huge against the sky on the hill's northern prow just beyond and well above the far end of the bridge (it sports no corporate signs or flags, though, because the site's a historic landmark and the dot-com must jump through all kinds of municipal hoops before it can change anything about its appearance).

Down the side street to the west, across the traffic-clogged northbound lanes of the freeway (all vehicles there creeping along at roughly human walking speed right now), the bay glimmers silvery and the mountains lurk enigmatically behind a patchy veil of haze (it obscures all but the highest of the snowcaps). And also down in that direction a single flag ripples a bit, Stars and Stripes, jumbo size, atop the great gray concrete dome.

And in the Natusan center's parking lot across the street, large enough for maybe forty vehicles, there's only one: a rusty pickup with a "smoked salmon for sale" sign in the window. The driver's probably crashed out in the covered flatbed section while he waits for freeway traffic to ease off a bit.

As for current events, worldwide, the most notable new item is a USAn congressional report accusing China

of stealing America's most important nuclear secrets.
Chinese spies! Dangerous, inflammatory stuff, quite
likely untrue or only trivially true, but nonetheless
based on underlying dynamics that clearly matter a great
deal. It fits right in with the general effort by our
USAn ruling strata to puff up a major new enemy to
replace the fallen Soviet Union and justify massive new
military expenditures and Cold War-style social/cultural
controls. (Meanwhile the high-school massacre and the
Makah whale-killing are still reverbing, and the latter
to a degree few people would've predicted. These
matters also fit quite well into the underlying struggle
regarding those same social/cultural controls.)

     -- So jyze will have to make a special return
tomorrow. Today's a sick-out as of the end of this
paragraph. I'm on my way to the WOC to drop off an
article for Jay the juggler and then onward to grapple
with this week's grand-jury testimony. No time for
anything else. (But I'm feeling mighty relieved anyway,
I won't deny it. Dodged the whirling tornado, yeah.
The lady has apparently chosen to tilt the balance a
little more toward harmony.)

                        [+1]

     The waterfront streetcar just pulled out with a
feeble ringing of its bell. And now another one quietly
pulls in where the first one was, behind me. -- And the
Afrusan conductor tells me the number I see on the front
is for the route and not the car, whose number appears
on the side. 31. -- If only all urgent existential
questions could so promptly be answered! (He's taking a
cigarette break beneath the AQ-appropriate flying-eaves
streetcar shelter maybe fifteen feet to my rear.)
     Busy corner, right across from the AQ bus station
and the gray-tarp-wrapped easternmost of the two train
stations. A favorite spot of mine. A vent from the bus
tunnel opens up a few feet to my right, hidden behind a
concrete fence; a few steps farther on you can look down

on the tracks leading to the portal of the downtown
train tunnel. Often a long-distance passenger train
will be idling down there at this time of day, sometimes
as a lengthy freight rolls by on the mainline, or even
two freights heading in opposite directions, in which
case up here there'll be a whole lotta shaking going on.

     And I've got me a fine wooden bench. It's a pair
of gray planks, nicely worn and weathered, attached with
iron brackets to the concrete planter that serves, I
assume, as a safety barrier for runaway streetcars here
at track's end. This is just the reverse of that holly-
packed planter outside the bank skyscraper: here they're
welcoming you, not trying to prick you away. A kindly
little evergreen, about three feet tall, much like the
one holding forth on our balcony at home, stands just to
my left. I can even sniff it a little. And some
smallish pink flowers I can't name quiver in the breeze
on the other side. But if they're fragrant at all, the
same breeze seems to be blowing the evidence away.

     No ball game today. Traffic's light and the usual
row of souvenir stalls and food booths is absent. (If
it were up and running and the wind were blowing in the
right direction, which in fact it's doing at this
moment, you could sniff them and hear dueling bands and
maybe even snatches of the pregame show playing over
portable PA systems.) -- And a fluctuating crowd of two
or three dozen is awaiting buses or just hanging out at
the big stop with its long row of mangy newsracks
directly across the street to the south.

     So it's one day on, yeah. As promised. Z's still
staying home from work and I'm still sleeping on the
couch. Ooooh how she does love to groan and moan in a
low sickly voice and stagger around as if about to
collapse at any second and talk on the phone in a
pathetically immiserated way and in general make high
melodrama out of a little case of the flu. But actually
today she seems to be doing pretty well -- well enough
that we launched another cookie cruise to the east-hill
co-op this afternoon, which is why I'm running late now.
-- And I did overhear her cooing on the phone to Leola

about "how wonderful it is to have a man around the
house to wait on you hand and foot when you're sick."
(But then she had to admit I fall somewhat short of the
ideal, having failed to rustle her up a single real meal
-- maxing out with a plate of buttered toast, two
slices, which she then drenched with maple syrup.)

As for our reconciliation of two nights ago, that
seems to be holding so far. (Ding-dong, out pulls No.
31.) The reconciliation was easy because she said she
was taking back both of the previously noted "criticisms"
and I said I'd sure appreciate it if we could suspend
hostilities at least until the weekend and she said okay
to that. And very quickly we were both no longer upset.
And after all, the criticisms hadn't been anything new,
had they? The main thing is to know she can suppress
them at will. She can live with them. And if for two
days, why not for four, six, eight? Yes, why not a
whole J-week? So far at least they're not rising to new
levels and she's not back to demanding immediate changes
"or else."

When I failed to show up at the WOC Monday evening
she says she fantasized I'd been killed in one of three
ways: either I'd been shot by angry drug dealers in the
wasteland of the upper AQ, I'd been picked off by a
speeding SUV during one of my mad midblock cross-street
dashes in that same area, or -- here's the one that
startled me -- Lady S, alerted to my whereabouts by the
divorce notice Evie the lawyer sent out, had shown up at
our doorstep and shot me. -- Shot me? Lady S? Not Z
herself? (In truth Lady S is a woman of peace. Nor do
I believe she has any real cause to be angry at me, then
or now, by her standards or mine. And she'd agree with
this, I'm sure. If not always, at most times.) (Ding-
dong, a new streetcar arrives, and it's also signaling,
unawares of course, that I'd better get rolling myself.)

[+1]

Z-geist cafe. "Art & Coffee" says the sign

dangling almost directly above me. (As a drama plays out across the street, an older Eurusan gent arguing with a younger Afrusan gent as two Afrusan companions of that first Afrusan glower nearby in an old yellow beater car, and it's pretty obvious it's a drug deal gone bad. -- But they've cleared out already. The Eurusan started yelling at the top of his lungs in extremely hokey fashion, "I've been robbed! I've been robbed!" -- repeating this a few dozen times, briefly freezing sidewalk traffic before the matter got old and then got really old -- and then the other three reappeared and they all started talking again almost like long-lost buddies. -- Or it could be about scalped tickets for tonight's game. The sausage stall half a block down is already up and sizzling -- sniffable from here -- and game time's still about four hours away.)

So now I'm maybe two and a half blocks closer to the waterfront than I was at jyzetime yesterday, straight down the main east-west drag. If I stand up I can see the bench where I was sitting then: I just checked. I'm not totally sure but I think that same streetcar conductor from yesterday (No. 31) is sitting on it. I guess this could mean I was taking his usual seat yesterday -- and he never complained!

Today I'm holding down a metal chair painted silver, a round black metal table. I'm the only outdoors customer at the moment. Today it's chillier; my green jacket's loosely drawn around my shoulders. And some extra chills, sur-chills as it were, are coursing through me and something odd is happening in my throat when I swallow. Apparently the battle's back on to see whether Z's bug will nail me too.

Some satisfaction on the hike in. The meter cops were out slapping tickets on windshields all along the steeply curved hillside road next to the hospital where the dot-com employees are parking illegally, choking traffic and causing long backups, making it much harder for the locals or anyone else to get on or off the hill, whether by car or by bus. And only about a fifth of the occupying force is in place up there so far.

    Z's still hanging around home. With the holiday
weekend ahead she'll have three more days to recover.
Last night, while I was at work, Aida dropped by to
cheer her up. I knew about this even before Z told me
because on my chairside table I found a big chain of
discarded newspaper rubber bands Aida had put together
(one of her trademarks) slung around one of Z's hand-
painted mugs ("I'm trouble!", it proclaims, above her
own goofy markered self-portrait). They did the
intimate-talk thing, it turns out, and now Z's feeling
better about their relationship. And she knows a good
many intimate details concerning Aida's relationship
with Kirk, which continues to go well. (But even so
Aida hasn't introduced him to her parents yet and
probably won't, in Z's view, for a while.)
    I admit it makes me a little uneasy to think of Z
listening to Aida describe (in abundant physiological
detail, I'm sure, as Aida likes to do) getting it on
with a man who's a former heartthrob of Z's. What's
going through Z's mind as she hears this? What images
are sparked? (And Aida's sister Sera reported that
while visiting city hall on business she'd seen Kirk
hobnobbing on the elevator with the mayor himself.
Kirk's a high city muckety-muck now. And the papers a
couple of days ago floated a trial balloon for Kirk's
brother entering next year's U.S. senate race. -- To
all of which I say: big freakin' deal! I mean, does the
man have a button that says "Skanky Scandi?" Or how
about "Jeep. There's only one."? -- And last night I
made up a card for Z deploying the second of those
slogans (from a current corporate ad campaign). It was
a couple of weeks ago already that I had to remind her,
incidentally, because she'd somehow forgotten, that Jeep
was my childhood nickname. Whereas I remembered all
three of hers: Weezie, Lulu, Looney Tunes. But it's
taken this long to come up with a suitable riposte.)
    This afternoon Z and I did "talk serious" a little
bit. But I'd better hold off on describing it -- trying
to -- until Sunday night. No time to take that on
today. (The talk, however, was good. I'd say we're

almost certainly over this latest hump. But then again
we haven't gotten it on ourselves at all this week to
put matters to what I now can't resist calling -- and
why should I? -- the all-important hump test.)

     Today I'll jyze instead about -- what? Maybe just
keep looking around. As the ballpark crowds stream by.
Or this: moments after sitting down here I smelled smoke
and thought my bag might be on fire (it happened once
before, years ago, when I unwittingly set it atop a
smoldering cigarette butt) but then I looked behind me
and saw flames shooting out of a trash can at the end of
the block. Then a bulldozer lurched into view from
around the corner and the driver jumped off and kicked
the burning can over, spreading out its contents with a
shovel and stomping out the flames. Then the previously
noted dope/scalping spat started up and I forgot all
about the fire. -- And now big iridescent soap bubbles
are floating down from the windows of one of the lofts
above. -- Seven or eight stories of them -- lofts -- in
the old shoe-company building and in one of those lofts
I was once briefly planning to live. That was some
fourteen months pre-Z, just days before I hit on the far
superior B-2 digs a few blocks north of downtown, a
little over a mile from where I'm sitting now.

     -- Lots of red bricks around here. Concrete
sidewalk squares. Autos. Pigeons. Homewardbound
office workers swinging briefcases. Kids in baseball
caps holding the hands of grown men, presumably their
fathers or other close relatives, also in baseball caps,
all on their way to the game. Rippling awnings. Buses.
Cigarettes and ashtrays. Shadows of all these things
and of many, many other things, with quite a few of them
on the move. Prominent among these for me, a J-book
about to be snapped shut. -- Thirty this! -- Or twenty
it rather, because this J-week is not yet a wrap.

                         [+2]

     -- Sitting naked at the art table. Which is surely

a good way to be when you're sitting at an art table.

What isn't so good is I'm sick as a dog. A goose.
A Z-goose. Her bug. Now I've come to understand with
infinitely deepened empathy what misery she's been going
through for the past week.

As of two hours ago it's officially Memorial Day by
Gregorian measure if not yet by nightscoper upside-down
time (NUT). And a lovely night it is, the moon just a
shade gibbous, the feel of the night much different from
the ordinary Sunday night owing to the holiday and the
reigning sense, which will almost certainly turn out to
be vastly premature, that this is the day when summer
really starts.

(I just realized that, technically anyway, I'm not
fully naked. I'm wearing a ponytail loop, one of a
colorful new set I invested in months ago but didn't dip
into until today. -- And I've just taken it off so I
can be fully naked -- or "buck" naked, as some might put
it. Ready to romp if, say, one of those hilltop sex
workers were to stroll in the wide-open balcony door
after clambering up from the street via the dumpster.)

But no no no, no romping for me right now. Even
though for a long time Z and I have been going without,
probably the longest such stretch since we met. She was
on the H-rag for a week and then sick for another week,
and now that she finally might be juicing up again, I go
on the disabled list myself.

But otherwise things are much better. We've talked
them over at length. She's completely backed away from
the call for more "conflict" and she's saying I
misinterpreted her demand for "pushiness" -- she just
meant she wished I'd be lusting after her as often and
as fiercely as I did "back in the day" two years ago.

So then we talked about the double bind this puts
me in. After all, she's set up numerous constraints
since back then: don't wake her up when I come to bed,
don't come after her when we meet for dinner at home on
Tuesday and Thursday evenings (and lately we've rarely
even been able to meet on those evenings), don't do
this, don't do that. And our weekends have tended to be

scheduled to the hilt. And though most of this
scheduling has always been done by her, now comes my big
jyze project to tighten and toughen things even more.
Not to mention all the wedding hullabaloo.

Well, we'll see what we can gin up. At least the
issue seems considerably less vexed for the moment.

This weekend we mostly descheduled. Tonight I took
a two-hour bath. Yesterday we made a spontaneous many-
stopped trip all the way up to the far-north bookstore/
arcade, and tonight we did dinner at our usual Chinese
place near the hilltop junction. Meanwhile we've
secured our honeymoon reservations at the same ocean
resort we visited last year about this time (secured
them just this afternoon by phone, with Z doing the
talking for this second call since she's the one with
the credit cards) (this being a mutually agreed "special
exception" to her current self-imposed ban on credit-
card use). And I've consented to take on the tasks of
lining up music for the reception and finding out
exactly what's required to score a wedding license.
Both of these assignments I was already more or less
committed to perform, I guess, but now I'll no longer be
saying "more or less" or "I guess."

-- And what else can I tackle in my ridiculous
condition here? (Saggier and bloatier than usual too,
genitally speaking, this "buck" is, from the long bath
and also because I've got a fever, I'm sure, along with
the cold, sore throat, runny nose, achy muscles, stomach
pain, gas, diarrhea.)

Nothing else, that's what I can tackle.

Or just say I'm scratching this out at the center
of a semicircle of my own altered-art cards displayed on
the desktop. And that these cheer me up no end. And
that I have a month to come up with one Z would approve
of to adorn the cover of our reception invitation. (But
she was not pleased with my first suggestion: the sci-fi
mag cover "Journey Into Unknown Worlds" which I altered
for her by inserting "Marriage:" at the beginning. And
there's much more to this card, including a ponytailed
guy and a deep-cleavaged babe, both in fishbowl-like

space helmets, both emitting newly drawn-in word
balloons. Guy saying: "Z-goose babe, unless we act
right now it means the end of our separate worlds."
Babe saying: "But G-gander hunk, what can we do? We're
helpless!" And at the bottom a weird duck-faced outer-
space creature asiding to the reader, "Wotta slammin'
alien pair!")

[+1]

    Won't be able to end this J-week the way I'd like.
It's just too damn cold out there. And windy too. And
whatever else it might be, this bug that's laying waste
to me is not the twenty-four-hour flu (if there even is
such a thing) because it's now more than twenty-four
hours later and it's still ravaging away, kicking up all
of yesterday's symptoms and more and worse. I'm a fool
to be down here at all tonight. At the scope office.
Trying to play the hero, I guess. Except -- no choice
really. If Jyzer Ink doesn't get the job done, they'll
find someone else to do it. Pronto. Fact of life.
    -- So Z dropped me off at the curb down below. Now
the all-too-familiar setting of the conference room. At
least it's warm up here. The shivers seem to have
stopped. Or have they? No they haven't.
    Better wimp out and try my jyzing luck another day.
Like, for instance, unless it's just not to be,
tomorrow: start of a new J-week and also a new J-book.
Scope as long as I can tonight and bus home because Z's
gotta sleep. Though she did say she'd leave the phone
on and put it by the bed just in case I needed her to
pick me up. But no, I can't do that to her. And in
fact I told her this down by the curb. But I'd bet a
bundle she'll soon be, if she isn't already, lying in
bed with that phone by her hand. Probably won't even
undress. (Yup, I'm sapping out here. Illishly so.
What to make of this? Well who knows. Not me. Not
even close. -- Onward.)

BOOK B

[True at First Jyze]

6

Came dragging out. Schlepped jyzer self over here
to hillside strip park, the picnic table with a view.
"Spectacular." Yes it is. On the Fourth this seat is
to kill for. All that showy stuff a neck-twist to the
left. This on a cloudy late Tuesday afternoon, breezy,
chilly, but at the moment the sun's out and so it's just
warm enough to sit here in a jacket. (And through leafy
branches to the right, towering above tall evergreens
just across the street, the dot-com castle, as jyze
might as well dub it now, or let's make that DC castle.
And far below traffic's moving along pretty well in all
twenty or so lanes of freeway feeding into and out of
the downtown maw one hill northward.)

The unwell Jyzer G, he's a little better today but
nowhere near enough better. About the only thing he can
think of right now is that hot tub at the WOC. A slow
and easy hike down. Break a sweat in this chill and
he's meat on a hook.

First day of a new month. It's month seven of the
millennial countdown: seven, six, five.... In days the
number to go is 214, as shown on the city's official
calendar, a third copy of which now hangs on the unit
203 hall bulletin board to supplement the ones on the
walls at Z's office and my own jyze hideaway.

Got some bad news an hour ago, phoned in by Z.
Kiba-dog died over the weekend, victim of something she
ate in the garbage. Jess is taking it hard, blaming
herself for not making the trash can more dog-proof and
then not calling in the vet soon enough. She and Gwen
are both staying home from work today, accepting no

107

calls. Z suggested I leave them a voicemail (she's
sending over dessert in our name, to top off a dinner
Paz and Tobey are providing). But I demurred, saying,
"It's not me." Instead I'll do an altered card or maybe
even a wholly new one. (Three times Z and I have dog-
sat for Kiba and Cy, a total of at least fifteen days,
and Kiba and I have always gotten along well. -- So
naturally I'm also recalling the loss of Pogo when I was
about the age Kat is now. Likewise a small dog, but
more the Ty type, indefatigable, quick, lean but not
mean -- fox terrier, mostly, Pogo was -- and the only
living creature I slept with in the same bed all night
long on a regular basis until Lady S appeared in my life
some thirteen years later.)

So that's the lead story here. (And also Z's
fearing a showdown with Wei because he got into another
altercation with Rowena at the JCEJ meeting Z missed
because of illness last week. Z's saying now she thinks
Wei tends unintentionally to talk more sharply to
Afrusans. -- Oh the infinite complexities of our
diversity-celebrating lives!) (JCEJ: that's Jyze City
Environmental Justice, the group Z cofounded.)

-- Shortly after jyze set up here a longhair Cawk
dude dressed much like the jyzer himself (jeans, sneaks,
etc.) came hiking up the hill and eyed me a little
strangely, I thought, as he took a seat at a table under
the shelter a few yards to my rear. Until just moments
ago he sat there doing nothing and from time to time his
eyes seemed to be burning into my back. Finally he
stood and moseyed over to the point where the black
chain-link fence ends. A narrow grass ledge lies on the
other side of the fence; he trod along it until he was
about three feet to my left and then suddenly, while I
was focusing on this J-book, vanished. Dropped down
into the bushes presumably.

*

Turns out (just did a quick check) about five feet
below the edge a twisty and very steep path leads down
into "the jungle." I hadn't realized it was there.
(But I've always known "the jungle" has many entrances

108

-- as does any jungle, yes. How many ways out, that's
another matter.)
     The dude must've been thinking I could be a
plainclothes cop or, probably even worse, a social
worker of some kind -- parole officer maybe -- just
waiting to latch onto anyone heading down that path.
Unknowingly I'd been obstructing his plans all that
time.
     A few cars are parked in the lot straight ahead,
northward and slightly downhill, people sitting inside
gazing blankly out at the view. One driver's door is
open and a radio's blasting not-so-golden oldies as big
puffs of cigarette or maybe weed smoke emerge, almost as
if the car interior were on fire. Otherwise no one's
around. The bust of the Philippine national hero after
whom this park (along with the high bridge) is named
gazes down in this general direction from its perch
toward the upper (south) end of the park. The plaque
beneath the bust describes the man as "Patriot, National
Hero, Martyr and Genius." (Is this a benevolent country
or what, erecting a statue and naming a park and a
bridge for a leader of our vanquished enemy whom we went
on to colonize and are still neocolonizing today?) (The
man was also a medical doctor and, to repeat, a novelist.
He could treat the jyzer's flu and offer jyzing tips at
the same time. And in any case it's good to have a
statue of a man of Z's father's ancestry -- who to her
eyes looks a bit like him -- standing in a place of
honor so close to where we live. In fact it's one of
the main reasons we wanted to live in this hood.)
     -- The sun dips behind some thick clouds and
suddenly it's very cool in this spot with its high wind
exposure.
     -- But "hordes" of tourists will soon be arriving
in our town. A story in this morning's paper says so.
It seems we're the "it" U.S. travel destination for this
summer. (And over the weekend a building demolition,
meant to clear the way for a major expansion of the
convention center, went awry when the implosion turned
into an explosion, making for some terrific war-zone-

like photos ranking right up there with the ones coming
out of Sarajevo. -- And the other big local story,
starting last Friday, a twenty-two-year-old Afrusan guy
flipped out, killed his mother and a niece, then went on
a rampage up in the north end just a few blocks from
where Lady U and I used to live. Snapped under the
pressures, of course including those of J-town's ruling
liberal brand of racism: what else can be said? The
incident is generating lots of coverage but less fuming
law-and-order outrage than might be expected in the
aftermath of the high-school massacre. This could be
because the victims were also Afrusans.)

     And should mention this: if the jyzer's suffered
some sort of relapse, or moved into "the deadlier stage
two" of the illness (as Z did), it's probably because
she and I hit the folk-music festival at the fairgrounds
yesterday in chilly and rainy weather. Our intention
was to pick up my wedding pants from the hemp tailors,
but it turned out they hadn't finished making them and
so will be mailing them to us instead. Then, since we
were already at the fair, why not check out the jewelry-
makers for rings. And we did, a dozen or more of them,
but no luck. Under the circumstances I was afraid Z
would stress out a little (or a lot), but she didn't, so
in that sense the expedition was a success. And in the
end we wised up, deciding to forgo the chance to check
out another street fair farther north. Instead the
invalids putt-putted home and collapsed into bed for
tandem naps.

     -- And the jyzer's ready to do something like that
again right now but this time all on his lonesome, and
it'll be the WOC's hot tub he'll topple into.

[+2]

     It's First Thursday! I had spaced it out! -- So I
can set up here. Central square in the HQ. Usually
it's not the ideal spot for jyzing because so many
lonely and disturbed people hang out here, wards of the

numerous local missions and service agencies. Alkies
and winos, homeless drifters, migrant workers down on
their luck, psychos, vagabonds, alienated urban Natusans
and other Amerinds (many from Canada), drug seekers and
drug dealers, young toughs looking for a rumble,
panhandlers, misfits of just about every known variety.
Jyze-friendly they're by and large not. And those few
who are, they're likely to be way too much so. In
either case the net effect is jyze can't really do what
it wants to do.

     But today's different. It's artwalk! One day a
month booths and stalls go up, tarps and blankets go
down, artists and craftspeople and buskers descend from
the HQ's many low-income and loft buildings. Galleries
and shops set up well-guarded snack tables. If the
weather's good, as today, hundreds or even thousands of
downtown workers throng in, along with lesser numbers
from the city's outer hoods and maybe a few from the
burbs. Cops patrol in force, on horses, on bicycles, on
foot. Black mariahs rumble at select high-profile
curbside spots. The regular denizens accordingly make
themselves relatively scarce.

     And today I seem to be almost okay. Feeling pretty
good in fact. And being among, but rarely really one
of, the artwalkers always makes me feel pretty good all
by itself. -- As a streetcar rumbles by, bell clanging.
Through the trees up in that westerly direction stands
the ORB, the only real bookstore; straight south down
the bricked and tree-arched plaza I can make out the
corner of the massive gray blister of the concrete dome
(no game today) and a block in the opposite direction
the upper stories of the hideaway building; and a block
northeast, peeking through the crowns of still more
trees, the forty-plus stories of the great white tower
of guns'n'typewriters fame (because income from those
two products made by one man's company built it), which
this year is celebrating its eighty-fifth birthday.

     A fine area, yes, except for the high concentration
of unfortunates. At times it really is like being in an
internment camp of the downtrodden. It's a shame

society can't figure out a better way to arrange things.
This society, I'm saying. My society. Our society.
-- But then if it could, rents in the area would no
doubt skyrocket and most of the current crop of renters,
the jyzer included for sure, would be forced out. And
that process is in fact already well underway, driven
by the massive amount of new dot-com money flooding the
area; but certain ordinances regarding historic buildings
and also the presence of so many missions and service
agencies, and a few other similarly inconvenient social
factors, seem to be slowing things down somewhat for the
developers. And it would appear all those missions and
agencies have nowhere else to go. And of course that's
also true of the historic buildings themselves.

Pigeons strutting by jerkily, almost as if emerging
from hidden cuckoo-clocks. A few steps to my left a
crowd of female artwalkers is bombarding a spiffy trio
of uniformed firefighters with questions about the
upcoming Fire Fest, to be held right here, and laughing
uproariously at their replies, which I can't quite make
out because their backs are turned toward me. (If they
weren't, they might think I too am one of the
downtrodden. Or at least I hope so. Showing this kind
of solidarity is a big point of pride with me.)

Expanses of brick. Authentic cobblestones
underfoot. Imitation Victorian three-ball street lamps
overhead. And now the first slight chill as the sun
dips behind a cloud.

-- So there's big news. It appears the Kosovo
"conflict" is about to end. "YUGOSLAVS AGREE TO
PEACE." This after more than two months of heavy
bombing, much of it taking place in an area no larger
than the county in which this jyze is going down. In
order to save the Kosovars we've leveled many of their
villages in tried-and-true U.S. expeditionary fashion.
The worst part is that we'll now be able to proclaim our
policy a success and use it as a precedent to support
future "humanitarian interventions." It's not all black
and white, no, but there can be little doubt it'll soon
be portrayed as if it is.

112

     -- And beyond this it's an interesting day with
lots of things going on. Birthdays, anniversaries. At
one point Z and I had talked about meeting down here
this evening and hitting some of her favorite spots on
the artwalk circuit, but last night she sacked out late
and didn't sleep well and so she canceled for today.
     What've I been up to these past fifty hours or so?
Not much. No workouts, not much reading. Most of my
free time has gone to making up a set of "mourning
cards" for Gwen and Jess. Gwen called today to thank us
for the first card and the dessert we sent over and I
happened to be home to talk with her. She says she
thinks Jess will need another week before she can stop
beating herself up for failing to get Kiba to the vet
soon enough.
     Bongos hard at it. Hundreds of people milling
about. For a while a twenty-something woman was sitting
on the other half of my bench here. She wasn't
unfriendly but neither was she friendly, or only just
minimally so. Mostly she was preoccupied with a hand-
held electronic gizmo. Finally a couple of her friends
came up and she complained, "You got here too soon! I'm
playing a computer game!" Retorted one of the friends:
"Everything's 'too soon' for you with your idiot games!
You're addicted to that thing!" Then off they all went,
chattering happily. (The two who came to meet the woman
were both smoking -- addicted? -- but the woman wasn't.
She'd chosen a different poison. As has the jyzer.)
     -- Reminding him: media have been trumpeting the
news that in less than seven months, just about exactly
in tandem with the millennial rollover, the sun will go
into a season of intense sunspot creation. It will last
for some four months (that is, for the last third of the
projected lifespan of this TJM annal). Some experts are
saying that certain extreme but far from unthinkable
"sunspot events" could take down national power grids
worldwide at the worst possible time -- when, as a
largely different and mostly less credible contingent of
experts is saying, they'll already be sorely tested by
the Y2K meltdown, and this during the months when power

is most needed for heat (at least in northern climes;
and even there, and that includes here, it's less and
less needed for heat each year on average as the globe
warms up). -- And so of course the panicky ones will
jump on this. Just as hysteria over Y2K seems to be
calming, the survivalist set gets a new booster shot.
(Personally the jyzer sees all this -- except for the
global warm-up -- as a steaming heap of hooey. It's
millennial entertainment and little more. Well, and
grist for a lot of ideological mills, including, for
sure, this jyze one.)

Also interesting, but more interesting, astronomers
announce they've figured out the period required for the
sun to make a complete circuit of the galaxy. It's
roughly 225 million years. -- And in this jyze project
focused on temporal cycles we've serendipitously hit
upon what's probably the biggest of them all. Bigger
even than the ones in Hindu myth. The only possible
bigger one I can think of would be for the Big Bang
itself to roll out in cycles. (And why shouldn't it?)

And here's another fact jyze can't let go
unremarked: it's Chimborazo Day. Officially. This is
the mountain in Ecuador that pokes out farther from the
center of the earth than any other spot on the planet.
It achieves this notable prominence thanks to the
squash-down effect at the poles caused by the earth's
rotation and the consequent midriff bulge at the
equator, where Chimborazo is located. Its outward poke
exceeds that of Mount Everest by thousands of feet. I
had never known this until last night when the DJ on the
jazz station mentioned it, and now jyze has decided to
go with what she said. (The jyze fact-checkers will be
called in later.) (And I want to note the word "poke,"
deployed above, is also the street name for the hot new
male-potency drug which Z wanted me to try during my
foozly period in our first year together. But -- and
I'm proud to say this -- I didn't do that then and
haven't done it since (or ever). And in that period
I've been offered "poke" on the street any number of
times. -- Which in itself can't be a good sign, true.)

-- And now today's wedding dish.

First, as a preliminary note, Z and Wei have made
up. And Wei confessed to her, as he's done before, that
he's been testy lately because of his own wedding-
related travails; and we, Z and I, both know these are
much more trying than any we're facing, at least so far.
Alison has some fairly lofty inbred social notions which
translate into a lot of time-consuming work on occasions
like this. As I said to Z, "Just compare her house with
our apartment -- the same kind of differences apply to
the weddings." To which she replied, "No shit Dick
Tracy!" And went on: "But the really true poop here is,
Wei never had any illusions about what he was getting
into. I know because back in their early days he was
always moaning to me about it." And this also is true:
it's good to be reminded occasionally how relatively
fortunate we are in this respect. (Wei says we should
be able to find a wedding cake for three bucks a person
-- which still would add up to $600! I say why not buy
a bunch of supermarket cakes and stick homemade paper
"Z&G Forever!" flags in them? Why toss away $600 on a
cake? -- But all in good fun to be sure. -- And this
being the traditional prime wedding month we're moving
into now, June, the cover of the latest issue of our
favorite glossy far-coast-megalopolis lit-and-culture
weekly mag features a huge wedding cake maybe twenty
feet tall with a bride and groom standing on top looking
totally discombobulated, and last night I altered this
cover to make an unusually large card for Z, stripping
the groom of his pants and adding this note: "Could be
us if those hemp trou get lost in the mail.")

Meanwhile we've learned Kat's "uncle" Nick
(actually he's her widowed step-brother-in-law) will be
flying in for our nuptials. And that Z's regular
hairdresser will be taking August and September off to
care for her new baby, meaning we'll have to settle for
her green (in the double sense of being ecoconscious and
also fresh out of "alternative cosmetology school,"
according to Z) -- have to settle, I say, for her green
backup to do our do's. -- And yes, I do mean "we." Z's

now insisting I long ago agreed to let her hairdresser
spiff me up for the wedding. I have no memory of this,
but it's possible I did. In any case I'm eager to do so
now. Much better to eagerly comply than to give her
another matter to get squidgy about. (I'm trying to
hold to a vow here. It's not always easy. Don't want
to come off as a total pushover.)

     -- And yesterday was Mama E's birthday. I wasn't
around when Z called her, though, so I'll have to save
my congratulations until this weekend's planned longer
call. She's one year younger than the great white tower
over there. And still managing. Living alone. Back in
her period of high glamour (I've seen pix!) she had the
courage to follow her heart when she fell for a
dashingly handsome Filusan man twenty years her senior
in a city that did not take kindly to mixed marriage --
in fact it was illegal (they had to go out of state). Z
knows very little about her mother's ancestry other than
it's Polish and that there were numerous stopover points
for her, Mama E's, parents and their many kids in
various northeastern states, during one of which Mama E
was born, and that there are many, many relatives, both
here and in the old country. Z has never met most of
them and probably never will. (She keeps asking me if I
think she should look into the matter more deeply. I
say sure, if she'd like, but I don't want her to get the
idea that the extent of her knowledge about her roots
(on the Filipino side as well) will make any difference
in how I feel about her or think about her. (She fears
it's another one of those class things and it would
matter a lot to me just because of my work at Mother's
behest on Popeye's Chandler-Hutcheson genealogy.)

     (Quick note: we still don't have anything like a
fully resumed sex life. The past couple of mornings I
towsed (diddled) her but wasn't well enough that she
could do me. No tongue-wrestling yet either. And then
this: last night she said, "Won't it be nice that I'll
be coming off the H-rag just about when you're healthy
again?" But then this afternoon: "I'm not sure but I
think maybe I've got that prodomo feeling again." So it

seems possible we won't he having the compensatorily
superhot weekend we'd both been jonesing for, or at
least not one of the "plan A" kind.

     -- And now the sun's gone for good and the chill is
making me shudder a bit. And with the artwalk crowd
dwindling, the number of hardcore hostiles in the
immediate area is on the rise and space is limited. So
jyze is thinking yah, best to hit the road right now.

[+2]

     Time only for a kwikjyze holding action. And in a
setting both fine and Feiningeresque, sez I (breaking a
jyze rule by last-naming an artist), with tall buildings
slicing skyward on all sides, sharp angles, steel-and-
glass acutes and obtuses, and scarcely a sign of life
anywhere except for the occasional seagull flapping by.
And snapping flags, and rustling designer trees, and
nominal traffic sounds: honks, roars, jounces, squeals.
     This is about as far downtown as I'm going to make
it today -- or rather the bank machine one block to the
north is. I'll be meeting Betty, Kat, and Z at the
hideaway at five-thirty, or at least that's the target
time; and at my recommendation, based on reviews, we'll
all be seeing "The King of Masks" -- and I just hope it
doesn't turn out to be too scary or too heavy for a
nine-year-old. And because I didn't get away from home
until after three this afternoon the time squeeze is too
tight for a full jyze session. So with a nod from the
jyze gods -- who at times can be stern but hopefully
they won't be tomorrow -- this J-dude will return on the
offbeat to complete the session.
     Here's a sparrow. It can't believe a J-dude's in
action here. Nobody ever comes to this spot on weekend
afternoons. It's an outdoor plaza at about the third-
story level of yet another skyscraper bank, with a dozen
black metal tables arranged among small potted trees and
stone lanterns, each table having four metal chairs
attached loosely to its legs with bicycle chains and

small key locks (there's something bizarrely down-home
about these old-style security devices amid all this
high-tech splendor). The stone stairway to the street
is semicircular and facing inward, like an amphitheater
for very small beings -- but beings quite a lot larger
than sparrows, yes. Or you'd think so anyway, because
three sparrows are now hopping about on the steps on the
far side -- now four. And here come several more. It's
a conference of the sparrows!

     As I trudged by the ritzy steakhouse a block to the
east a stretch limo rolled up and two young couples
dressed to the nines stepped out, gawkily but with a
touching effort not to appear that way, and yet being so
solemn about it. My knee-jerk first thought was: a
pathetically young bride and groom and their "first
witnesses." But no, these were almost certainly high-
schoolers doing a fancy downtown pre-prom dinner. This
particular double pair didn't look to be urban or even
burban; no signs of piercings, tattoos, outrageous hair
or any of the other usual trappings. Small-town
innocents, it would appear, of the type even small-
towners might say they stopped producing years ago.
They could be anthropological curiosities, perhaps the
last of their kind for hundreds of miles. (Or maybe
they were morphing in from Turtle Rapids circa the era
of my own summer visits there as a kid. Which is to
say: maybe I was fantasizing or nostalgizing the whole
thing, or a big piece of it. Or then again, maybe not.)
     Earlier during the hike down I took note of another
unusual phenomenon. No fewer than five -- five! --
disabled shopping carts were strewn about in the grassy
off-sidewalk area in the upper AQ near the high bridge.
The scene brought to mind photos of burned-out hulks of
cars and tanks scattered along Gulf War roadsides. And
the nearest branch of the supermarket those carts came
from -- they all bore its name -- is miles away!
     Then in the HQ's central square I found the annual
Fire Fest in full swing, with a dozen fire engines
occupying a blocked-off street, several erecting, as the
crowd gasped and oohed, amusingly phallic telescoping

ladders like the one I saw at Syttende Mai -- and this
even though not a single Norski crusader flag was in
view. The area where I'd been doing the jyze thing on
Thursday was now fully carnivalized, with a barbershop
quartet of firemen performing on a special stage (a
number of hardcore locals had staked out a nearby
section of folding chairs, I noticed, and were giving
the evil eye to anyone approaching their turf, nor did
they seem to be enjoying the quartet). And the aroma of
grilling sausage and salmon inspired me to head over to
the ORB to call Z and suggest we do dinner at the fair.
But she told me Kat wouldn't be free until five, and the
fair starts closing at six, or at least the stall with
the aroma that inspired the call does (I checked). If
Betty's running as late as usual we won't make it.
     Also to note: billboards hyping a new clothing
store on the downtown glitz strip have been popping up
all over town. Timed to coincide with the pre-
Independence Day lull, they exhort us all to "Go 4th and
Shop!" Call it the new patriotism. (Well, okay, not so
new.)
     -- Gotta move on. (And by the way, the sparrows
fled long ago. The flock peaked at nine or ten. This
fall's conference of WTOers, if protesters who'd like it
to go away are included, will outdo them by a factor of
many thousands. That's what I hear.)

                        [+1]

     Some thirty hours later. Hoped to be doing this at
the scope office tonight but time was too short. Then
at home things got sidetracked by, first, early arrival
of tomorrow morning's far-coast paper (it showed up even
before I did) and then my extreme fascination with
several more new gel pens. Experiments. Worked up
tonight's card for Z, which is an old black-and-white
photo of an apparent biker-gang member slouched on a
stool at a diner counter, back turned to the camera in
such a way that you can't be sure of the person's

gender/sex/race, and a thought bubble added with lots of
G's and hearts in it along with the legend down below
"City Girl Can't Get Burban Boy Out of Her Head." -- Or
something better, maybe, if the jyzer's unconscious can
come up with it while he's otherwise occupied here.

It was the arrival of Wei and Alison's wedding
invitation the other day that scrambled our jets to the
paper shop today (where I bought the pens). This invite
is very tastefully done, using fine Asian papers tied
with fancy straw, maybe a little too froufrou for my
taste but what the hey -- or what the straw, yeah. The
text also refers to W&A's "wedding ritual" (isn't that
redundant?) and they leave out a couple of letters in my
last name, as Z pointed out, impressing me that she
would notice this. But without doubt we'll make plenty
of similar errors on our own invites -- probably lots
more if I wind up addressing the cards. Which I'm
pretty sure is, yes, "in the cards." (Look out, that
jyzer's on a bad-pun roll. Time to crack down on him.)

Mainly the arrival of W&A's invite served as a
wake-up call: this whole wedding business really is for
real. W&A are now about to enter their six-week
countdown. Z immediately declared we were entering a
new phase ourselves, and soon she came up with a lengthy
checklist of hitherto unconsidered (at least by the
groom) responsibilities along with a tentative budget.
I'll be looking them over tomorrow and letting her know
if I think they're okay. (I do. I know this already
without having seen them yet. Basically I'm going along
to get along whenever possible on anything wedding-
related. Since she's doing most of the work on this
ceremony which in any case is designed largely, by our
early mutual agreement -- she didn't even have to twist
my arm -- to appeal to her friends, the groom himself,
even though indispensable, is in no position to be
criticizing. She's already gently reminded him of this
a few times and he doesn't mind at all because, as noted
above, he agrees with what she's proposing.)

But today a surprising reversal. It suddenly
dawned on Z that her hub-to-be will be losing his

investment income when he gives up the deep reserves.
She wondered if it might be wiser for her instead to
take out a loan to cover the wedding expenses, including
his share, and then he could repay her on a monthly
basis. Since the interest on such a loan would be seven
and three-quarters percent and income from the deep
reserves has been averaging close to twice that for the
past several years -- yeah, that's probably not a bad
idea. We're now in the digesting stage on this. But
it's likely we'll go ahead with it. And what fine
irony! Instead of easing the stress on her we'll be
ratcheting it up! Her comment: "Shades of Arvin!" Five
thousand bucks was what she loaned that odious man right
before their engagement fell apart, and she never got a
penny of it back (despite suing him and winning in
court). "Yeah," this hub-to-be right here said, "but he
didn't offer to pay off your debts like I did. That
proves I'm a trustworthy guy. You said so yourself!"

     Ho ho. But it does seem she trusts me much more
now than she did, say, a year ago. Matters that
might've caused major freak-outs back then aren't making
a ripple in today's ever tougher trust-testing
circumstances. Our long swyveless period, just as one
example.

     -- And a word about last night's movie. It was
superb! Betty loved it (she was sitting on the far side
of both Kat, who was next to the subunk, and Z, and Z
told me she, Betty, was bawling at the end). Even Kat
said it was "really good." Since it's a Chinese film
about an eight-year-old girl adopted by a much older man
(who thinks she's a boy at first) we'd all been
wondering how Kat as an adoptee herself would react to
it. Betty called today to say the kid had uttered not a
single word about it since we'd parted outside the
theater. (What does Kat really think about the fact
that she was adopted? That her adopted mother is Cawk?
That her own mother and father were willing (or forced)
to give her up? That the country she was born in is as
agricultural and poor and war-torn as the China of the
movie?) She did seem fairly well absorbed in the movie

once she'd geared down to its un-Hollywoodish slow pace.
Much of the time she held the subunk's hand or rested
her head against his shoulder. That all by itself made
the movie worth seeing for him.

(From a series of articles in this week's papers we
learned Kat's school is seventy to eighty percent "kids
of color," is fifty to sixty percent reading at or above
the state norm, and has forty to fifty percent free- or
reduced-cost-lunch students: in all of which it's doing
better than most schools in the mostly POC south end and
worse than most in the mostly POW north end.)

-- And the news comes on, meaning it's time to put
a cork in the jyze. The Kosovo talks have broken off,
an authoritative voice is saying, and our bombing runs
are starting up again.

[+1]

It's raining harder now, and steadily; I can hear
it in the trees outside the window behind me and see it
slanting down through the cone of yellow light beneath
the street lamp visible outside the window to my right
(and from my angle nothing else is visible out there,
even when a car sizzles by below, as just now, with its
lights presumably on). I'm seated lengthwise on the
couch, legs drawn up into an inverted V to fashion a
jyze platform. It's a hairy one all right, this
platform, with an underlying meadow floor, as it were,
of whitish-pink epidermis, which of course would be just
as true were it made up of almost any other part of me.
(And off in the distance a red wooden Norwegian serving
spoon dangles blurrily on the side of the big bookcase
at about the six-foot level and I'm thinking it's
probably the only authentic Norwegian object I own,
unless the mini Syttende Mai flag now stuck into the
leftover Christmas poinsettia on the center coffee table
was made over there, which is doubtful).
Not only is the "Hydes of Jyze" sign propped up on
its chair in the hall but in a nod to redundancy I've

pinned the old "Jyzer at Work" button on my shirt. The
hour, again, is late. I've already doused the radio so
as to prevent another news disruption at four, just
minutes away. The fridge is humming with occasional
gurgles and gasps. Some of these grotesque sounds seem
to be new. Could it be that the numerous bags of frozen
fruit we've crammed into the freezer (they were on sale
at Z's co-op) are putting extra strain on the motor?
-- But this seems unlikely, yes. So maybe it's just a
matter of age. Are fridges old these days at age
eight? (Assuming here that this one went in when the
building went up. Of course it could've been used
already when they installed it at that time. From what
we've heard about the builders -- and this comes from an
actual member of the original construction crew who was
called in roughly a year ago to make some kind of
warranty repair -- we wouldn't put it past them to have
gone with all used or "hot" black-market appliances.)

   Tonight's excuse for getting to this jyzercise so
late in the day is that the jyzer was working up a list
of major expenses he's likely to face in the next year
and it took an alarmingly long time to do this. We've
decided to go ahead and borrow the money, Z and I have;
the only question now is how much. She's quite
confident she'll be able to secure an interest rate of
eight percent or less. She's constantly receiving new
offers from banks and loan companies wanting her to
switch her debt to them and offering incredibly low
rates as an inducement, though always with some nasty
strings attached. But as long as she makes the monthly
payments on time those strings don't turn into nooses.
Or so she says. And I'm thinking why not believe her.
If things go bad I can always fall back on the emergency
stash to cover the loan. Even if the stock market were
to collapse completely -- to flatline, as if that were
possible -- roughly a quarter of the stash would still
remain in place (the bonds part). Surely I'd be able to
cover eight thousand, which is the amount I've
tentatively decided to borrow. My aim is to get all the
way through this year and next before raiding the stash

again. I probably won't make it but I'll do my best
(but I'll also go wild for sure in the next couple of
months because I have so many backed-up everyday needs
as well as the madly proliferating wedding expenses).

-- So then today's nonevents or near-nonevents.
Just a few to mention.

For one, Aida has invited us over for the
celebration of Charles's graduation from elementary
school, which means the big meeting may finally occur
between the jyzer and Z's former sweetheart Kirk and the
jyzer will then be able to observe their interactions up
close and produce better-informed speculations about how
things really went down between them back in the day.

Another: the downtown restaurant against which Doug
T., our upstairs neighbor and the director of the small
pan-Asian museum in the AQ, launched a boycott
protesting its use of demeaning images of Chinese people
-- has closed its doors! Gone belly-up! It's a rare
political victory for the good guys!

Another: featured in a series on special high-
school grads in this week's paper was Z's god-daughter
Tess, who's deemed special by the paper because she
overcame the handicap of being on welfare (her mother is
Paula N., Z's friend from radical-therapy days) and also
fatherly sexual abuse (and it was extended exposure to
this situation, among others, that was making Z fear for
Kat back around the time we first met). (And Tess's
difficult life also made her a hard child to handle,
given to raging misbehavior; and eventually Z pretty
much tossed in the towel on helping Paula with her and
still feels bad about it.)

And finally, Marcus G. at the WOC declared (this
was the other day) that "all Filipinos have hot tempers."
When I questioned the "all," he defended his claim by
blaming the Spaniards -- "since they're so fiery and
they were there making the Filipinos angry for four
hundred years." Later I told the Z-woman about this
and she said she thought Marcus was right on both counts.
Her evidence for this was, first, that Aida loves to go
to Hispanic or Latino cultural events because she feels

much more comfortable there than at WASPy USAn ones, and
second, that another Filusan she knows at work likes to
call Filipinos "the Latinos of Asia," and this latter
notion I agree makes a kind of sense.

   -- Now I can see something out the window: a wedge
of gray sky. The rain is easing off and dawn is easing
in. And a train whistle is sounding, from a more
southerly stretch of the same tracks that go through the
downtown tunnel. These late-night whistles often remind
me of my student days in Mentoka Falls when I was living
alone a block from the depot and could hear the whistles
echoing down the coulees. It's a comforting sound here
just as it was there. -- And if jyze folds its tent
real quick a low-flying passenger jet won't have a
chance to blast that "train of thought," and maybe not
even the tent, to smithereens. Because that first
morning jet is due any minute.

7

   Found me a rock to sit on. Under a big old
evergreen. Corner of our street and the second cross
street to the north. Wednesday afternoon. Looming up-
close through the trees off to my left, the DC castle.
Across the street to my right, two long low apartment
houses that look more like misplaced small-town motels.

   Didn't come staggering out but didn't come bopping
out either. I'm still in the grasp of this grippe, or
whatever it is.

   Although a warming trend is underway, it hasn't
worked its way into the shadows yet. It's jacket
weather back in here. And look at all these pine
needles. Real nature stuff! Apart from the DC castle

with its sandy-orange brick outbuildings and seven-foot-
high black wrought-iron fence, and the two motel-like
buildings (but they're freshly painted and the dumpsters
by the sidewalk for a change aren't overflowing), it's
all hillside greenery out there. If I could see through
it, as I surely could've a couple of months ago before
the trees budded and leaves abundantly sprang forth, the
valley and the cross-lake freeway would be laid out far
below; and beyond that, a bit farther to the left, the
crowded but nondescript back side of east hill.

        (As here's another bus chugging up, passing me, now
squealing to a stop maybe a hundred feet to the south.
And a couple of hill-climbers trudge by, both breathing
hard, both Cawks and probably also new hill residents
working for the dot-com or they wouldn't be puffing like
that.) (Passersby might think I'm one of those dot-
commers myself, or more likely I'd be one of the locals
hired as minimum-wage temp groundskeepers under the dot-
com's much-ballyhooed new "mitigation program.")

        Z's feeling restless today. Called three times
within an hour to let me know this in various ways.
Plans to tie one on Saturday night, or so she says (and
does so fairly often -- says so -- but rarely gets truly
ripped). Sure does hope the H-outbreak's about over
(well, yeah, me too). I joke that maybe her
restlessness might mean she's starting to sense the
walls of matrimony closing in before they've even gone
up and she says, "Glen, that is just getting so old.
What do you think it means that you're so fixated on
this topic?" All once again in good fun though I do
believe.

        And she did have some dish for me. "Charles caught
Kirk and Aida kissing on the living-room couch and
wouldn't stop crying for an hour and a half." (Was
"kissing" a euphemism? I asked. She: "Maybe.") And
Z's now committed to helping stage Charles's graduation
party a week from Saturday, but since she'll have to
start at ten a.m. it means I probably won't be able to
attend. If I don't pry myself out of bed several hours
early -- on a Saturday! -- I'll have no way to get

there, since she'll be taking the car, and the party
will be over by three.

Z sees assisting Aida with this gathering as quid
pro quo for Aida's promised help on our reception in
September, but she, Z, would much prefer to be attending
the solstice parade and street fair out in her old hood
at roughly the same time as Charles's party. She'd
already talked with Betty about our doing that, so maybe
I'll fill in for her there. An efficient division of
labor as only befits a smoothly functioning prenuptial
duo. But this means I won't be meeting Kirk for a while
longer; and Z, of course, if he does show up for
Charles's party (that is, if Aida does decide the time
has come for her to risk introducing him to her family)
-- Z will be encountering him on her own. -- But
Charles's reaction to the "kissing" scene does not augur
well, in my opinion, for Kirk's being invited to
Charles's party.

Sez Z: "It sounds like Aida's going to be spending
more on Charles's party than we are on our wedding."
Hmm -- in my view that's something we ought not to feel
too badly about. (And then we went off on a comparison
of the celebrations associated with our own elementary-
school graduations. Neither of us had a party. Z's
parents took her out for dinner and I don't even
remember what happened with mine. Probably nothing; and
in any event I'm sure that would've been my preference.)

-- Pine needles are falling on the page as this
jyze goes down. Falling at the rate of, I'd guess,
several per minute. Sometimes they make a surprisingly
loud plopping sound. The big surprise, though, so far:
a platoon of spiders came rapeling down without warning
onto this same page, four small ones and then a larger
one I took to be the mother spider. I flicked them away
one by one with my index finger. Then I brushed off the
top of my head with my hand, discovering several more
needles but no new spiders, and put up my hood.

(All the buses are heavily loaded at this hour. I
can hear the diesel coaches roaring and groaning from a
block away as they labor up the steepest part of the

hill. The electric trolleys approach almost silently.
-- And this spot where I sit, I should note, is where
the grade levels off. It's where the hilltop proper
begins. I'm like a sentinel or a gatekeeper here. Or
to some perhaps more like a troll waiting in potential
ambush back under the boughs.)

Before leaving the house I called brother Rob at
work to check on a book. He told me his store will soon
be consolidated with the music outlet a few blocks to
the east. It looks like a bad move to both of us since
the bookstore part of the new dual operation will be
losing most of its drop-in foot traffic (and that may
be, by Rob's estimate, close to half its business). In
any case it's clearly another repercussion of online
bookselling, which must be why the castle right here is
at this moment looking to me more ominous than ever --
though the fact that the sun's no longer shining on the
side I can see could also have something to do with it.
I mean it's turned downright louche over there.

-- And for other news, international kind, it
appears the Kosovo agreement is coming together again.
Probably the media will have only a few more days to be
showing live footage of USAn bombs falling on Belgrade.
Then it'll be back to the delayed footage from Baghdad.

-- But I see my shadow has crossed the sidewalk.
And the shadow of my hood, taking on a fold like a
wizard's hat at the curb drop-off, is stretching out
into the gutter. Passing dot-commers stomping all over
it! So yes, it's time to roll on down to work.

[+2]

Blazing sun. -- Hey, this is different. I'm
filmed with sweat from the walk down! And fearing new
skin cancers too! (What, they'll grow on top of the
full-body complement that's already well seeded? -- But
no, wait, I've been a night worker for most of my adult
life. Pale is my problem and my predicament. And that
on top of the existential dilemma which paleness already

posed for me, as for any other Eurusan, from the moment
of my birth -- though it's true I needed maybe a decade
and a half to even begin to figure this out. And I
don't doubt at all, and I know Z doesn't either, that I
still have a long way to go.)

        Two days on, so Friday. Down below an engine is
rumbling. I'm assuming it's the usual one for this hour
and the train it heads is bound for my same old
ancestral grounds. Mine and Z's too. And in a sense
all of ours. -- We Eurusans, this is (so half of Z).
We latter-day Vikings and Huns and Angles and assorted
other nasty pale tribes such as, to be sure, the Poles.
(The inveterate punster Z referred to me the other day,
I must not fail to mention, as "my marital Polebearer.")

        -- It's not so comfortable here. The fence the J-
book rests on is too low. Northern end of the rail yard
down there, like an open sub-sub-basement in the shape
of a flattened horizontal bottleneck that lies about
thirty or forty feet below street level. The double set
of mainline tracks emerging from the tunnel portal a
block to the left (north) branches off into numerous
sidetracks for the station. That, the above-ground
portion of the western one of the two, stands directly
across the street to my right, its campanile clock, or
rather the one face I can see of its four, reading four
o'clock straight up. And I'm reminded I won't be here
long. It's workout day! I'm back into it! (And a set
of three freight engines, each in different livery
reflecting recent mergers, rolls by with a rumble of its
own and a high-pitched hum and some squeaky wheels
before everything's muted by the tunnel.)

        A small gray shed stands down there by the tracks.
It's not much larger than my old backwoods writing shed,
which is what I think of, knee-jerk fashion, every time
I see it. A certain degree of nostalgia is involved,
I'm not denying. But on the whole I'd rather be in Jyze
City. For sure. To hell with the backwoods! To hell
with militias and fundamentalists and a populace ninety-
nine-percent Cawk! -- And atop this shed here is a sign
bearing our city's official name. As far as I know

that's the only place around the station where the name
appears. It's the small towns that have large name
signs on the stations. This right here is the big time.
End of the line too, or some of the lines anyway.
"Terminal point." "The diesel stops here." (As the
steam engines did as well for many decades.)
     And a block straight ahead stands the newly
refurbed east depot with its wrapping off. Looks good.
Romanesque, clean red brick, cream-and-green trim.
Somewhat resembles the facade of the new ballpark --
which, by the way, from here is hidden, as is its
gigantic rolling birdcage, behind the dome with its huge
ripply Old Glory. A baseball game will be played in
there, in the dome, tonight. (Starting in a few weeks
all such games will take place at the new park. The old
dome will become last year's empty and hollow news.
Then next spring, BOOM -- gone.)
     And poking out from my shirt pocket is my new good-
luck pen. Commercially burned into its blond wood body
is the word "Jeep." And the Jeep slogan too: "There's
only one." I bought it from a Jeep dealer during
yesterday's northward shopping venture. I like it so
much I'm planning to spring for two more the next time
I'm up that way. I might even alter the slogan with my
own ancient woodburning kit (if it still works): "Not
the only one." Because whether they like it or not, I'm
one too -- a Jeep -- and fie on their trademark! (I
also bought a Jeep ball cap. I'm thinking I'll wear it
while jyzing at home as yet another tip-off for Z.)
(And I'll note that the personal use of "Jeep"
overrides the jyze-rules ban on corporate brand names.)
     A ton of work to do tonight. But I think I can
handle it. I'm feeling a whole lot better. (As Z
observed in this morning's note: "Ol' Pooshkin's got his
poosh back!" Yup, sure does. Only trouble is ol'
Peaches is back on quarantine again, though Z's now
wondering if the suspected new outbreak is just an
ordinary rash. I tried to take a look at it this
morning but I was too groggy to see much. -- So she had
to wank me off instead. The result was quite

picturesque after the long layoff, putting her in mind
of the "Old Faithful" card I sent her after the very
first such gusher of mine she witnessed (and generated).
"My technique's gotten much better since then, though,
don't you think?" Undoubtedly so, but I was so charged
up this time she scarcely had a chance to show it before
the deed was done.)

    -- And that's enough of this bent-over jyze. And
bent jyze as well, no question. (And what if Gramp
Perry had named his son Bent Perry, as he reportedly
almost did, instead of Glennar Perry? Then I'd be Bent
Jr.! I couldn't be Jeep anymore, from my initials; I'd
be Beep! (Funny I've never thought of this before.)
-- And this whole time the continental has been down
there rumbling and sighing and still is. Turns out I'm
the one moving on first.) (And as a final note I'll
just confirm, in case it's not clear from context, that
"Pushkin" is Z's latest pet name -- succeeding "Possum,"
"Oblomov," etc. -- for the jyzerman's male appendage,
and she likes to pronounce it the Russian way.)

[+2]

    Midnight in the garden of remembrance. -- And what
a struggle it's been to reach the point where jyze could
squeeze out those words.
    All afternoon Z was asking if something was wrong.
Was I mad at her? Displeased somehow? Not at all, I
said, and I honestly didn't think anything was wrong --
in fact I thought lots of things were right -- but later
I realized I was probably distracted ("at some level")
by the fact that this is Dad's death day. And then as I
was walking by the DC castle on the way down the hill a
rider in a passing car took a shot at me with a pistol.
That's right! True, his ammo was only water, but the
incident scared the shit out of me, and an hour later I
was still jumpy over it. -- And he did hit me, dead in
the chest, from about ten feet away. (It's happened to
me twice before, but not recently, and both times it was

near a university where you almost expect such things to
occur. And never before was it when I was on the move.
For a long time now I've been persuading myself I could
avoid danger on the mean downtown and south-end streets
by keeping alert and in motion. I think I'd even
convinced myself, more or less, pretty much. And so --
a vulnerability wake-up shot.)

     And thus it is I wind up in the garden of
remembrance. Seated on a stone bench just below the
symphony hall and outside the entrance to the bus tunnel
(which is closed now, its gates pulled down). A
passerby in a car (armed?) might easily mistake me for
one of the life-size gray statues of classical composers
scattered around back here in this little designer grove
of trees twenty or thirty feet from the street. The
trees, only ten or twelve feet tall, are underlit by
floodlights concealed in the planter groundcover. So
I'm underlit too. I'm also half-blinded and I seem to
be jyzing by light that's reflecting down off my chin.
"Jyze by the light of his chinny-chin-chin."

     Twenty feet to my right, across the main stairway,
a miniature waterfall cascades, one of several nearby.
They drown out most of the city sounds, motorcycles and
large trucks and souped-up sports cars excepted (and on
a fine warm night like this, even though it is a Sunday
night, that kind of noise is plentiful). And then
directly across the street to the west is the art museum
of "wedding of the century" fame. Past that, down
through the view corridor leading to the harbor, moments
ago I saw a jumbo ferry floating up looking like -- what
else? -- a giant wedding cake. Right there a cliche
even the J-town guidebooks strenuously avoid.

     And in my imagination a ghostly sailboat glides
along out there too. Exactly twenty-three years it's
been today. The phone call from thousands of miles
away, the "sailing accident." Or heart attack while
sailing. Or stroke while sailing. The end of a life
whose sailing hadn't been so smooth in recent years, it
must be said, and the beginning of a series of mysteries
that remain unsolved to this day. The old soldier --

sort of. Who died young -- as much young, actuarially,
as a USAn Civil War soldier who kicked off at age
twenty-five (in terms of percentage of projected
lifespan lived). "You give my death its meaning," says
the plaque on the wall here, speaking on behalf of
memorialized local soldiers to readers of the plaque.
-- And in a way I've been trying to do just that for
this death, my father's, ever since it happened: give it
all the meaning I could.
     I'd've been starting this entry a bit earlier
except for a small error of omission: I left the J-book
sitting on the desk at the hideaway. Probably another
effect of my being jittery about being "shot."
     -- Otherwise a fine couple of days. Today
especially. Z and I got our full-spectrum "plan A" mojo
working again, finally, at about eleven a.m. this
morning, and then again an hour later -- what a fine
double surprise! And she suffered no abrasions. And a
couple of hours after that I gave her an IOU for eight
grand and she gave me a check for that same amount and
that may be another reason I jumped a foot or three from
fright when the squirt gun fired: I was carrying that
massive amount of money on my person. Only in check
form, true, but still. The water could easily have
damaged it. (Except it was deep in my bag, well
protected in one of the waterproof nine-by-twelve
plastic envelopes I always carry with me -- and this J-
book often rides in one too.) (Z's mock-smoldering line
as she handed me the check: "You've been worth every
penny, big boy.") ---

                         [+1]

     Three flags flapping up there, each with its own
pole. Another one atop a hospital way up at the summit
of east hill, another atop the big gray dome (it's
rippling quite handsomely at the moment, the flag is,
framed for my eye by a section of iron-grated fence of
the east railroad station -- looks something like a huge

Siamese fighter hovering in a barred fish tank). But
that's it for flags. The only other one I've seen today
was the Norski mini planted in the poinsettia in our
living room at home; and a note from Z was spread out on
the leaves next to it: "Happy Flag Day!" And that's the
only mention of the holiday I've seen anywhere.

The flags here snapping as well as swimming: Stars
and Stripes, state, and...transit (had to pause while
waiting for that last one to stretch out to make the
logo readable). -- And who knew we had a transit flag?
Yet this refurbed depot is about to become transit
headquarters for the whole region. (Our No. 2 local
cybermogul, who also happens to rank No. 4 on the world
plutocrat list, sold it to the agency for one dollar, in
return, no doubt, for certain amenities and concessions
which will save him a fortune on his various new and
quite large buildings going up around here and elsewhere
in town -- and that fortune he's saving might all by
itself rank him pretty damn high on the plutocrat list.)

This time I'm sitting on a cement ledge with my
back to the iron-grate fence, the sun, the road, the
campanile. I can hear, and with my feet I can feel, and
with my glutes also can feel, a freight train rumbling
by down below. It might conceivably pass through --
eventually -- the town where I grew up some two thousand
miles eastward on this same mainline. Or before then,
no question, it could be shunted onto a very large
number of other mainlines or subsidiary lines.

Not much new to report. Well, one little story.

Preface it by noting that Betty and Manny did their
honeymoon at the same resort where Z and I will be doing
ours and they took Kat with them -- she was two or three
at the time -- and Betty's often talked about this since
Manny's death. So a few days ago, when Betty told Kat
that Z and I will be honeymooning there too, Kat's
immediate reaction was, "I want to go with them! Can I,
Mom, can I, please, please? You let me go when you
went!" And when Betty told her why she couldn't, Kat
started bawling and was inconsolable "for hours."

That's it, the whole story. Except Z and I are now

thinking we'll make a special trip down there later this
fall or next spring and take Kat with us. It will be a
"bespoke second honeymoon" for just the three of us (and
a break from the rigors of mothering for Betty).

        -- As for catchup, I'll try to do some of that
later tonight, after our workout. (And I want to note
that Z no longer writes "WOC" in her daytimer on days
when she plans to work out. That term was her acronym
for "work out - club" and jyze adopted it. Now she just
writes "W." But jyze is sticking with WOC.) (And last
week was the WOC's second anniversary. It celebrated
with an art show -- all paintings by members! Cake and
apple juice! Free refrigerator clips bearing the club's
logo, street address, phone number, and e-mail address!
We wound up with a dozen of the clips and a number are
already in use, mostly on frozen-fruit bags.)

                    *   *

        Not only is today Flag Day (still) but it's also
another extreme-tide day (along with yesterday and
tomorrow). The actual lowest tide of the year occurred
a little before noon today and either the highest or the
second highest occurred around seven this evening, just
a few hours ago. Now I'm sitting some seven or eight
feet above the water at the waterfront "pier park" as
the tide rushes out at the fastest pace of the year.
It's almost like watching a sink drain. (But the very
highest and lowest tides run on nineteen-year cycles and
we're only about two-thirds through the current one.
Today's yearly low of a negative 3.5 will be exceeded by
about a foot in eight years, I believe it is.)

        -- And now a blast of a foghorn (on a night
without fog) as yet another jumbo wedding-cake cliche
glides in, five layers of it this time or maybe it's
six, and not a single slice cut out of it yet so far as
I can see. (And if a slice were cut out, what would its
cost be? More than W&A's three bucks for sure. But
more than Pepe and Ramona forked over per slice for that
colossal wedding cake of the century? Maybe not.)

        The pier here zigzags, with a stainless-steel fence
and globe lights the size of beachballs, some yellow,

some white, all floating in the air about nine feet up
at each point of zig and zag. I'm midway between two of
them set about twelve feet apart and the lumens reaching
me are just right for jyzing. The lights of the western
part of town shimmer across the bay; a big blue-and-red
neon restaurant sign glows more impressively by the
minute at the end of the next dock south. A large flock
of gulls wheels overhead, veering north at the moment --
now east. And they're clearly not done veering yet
despite the deepening dusk. -- Meanwhile traffic
whizzes along on both levels of the viaduct half a block
inland, raised several stories on columns, with the
downtown skyline towering above that. ---
                          *
    Very touching. A young woman just came up and
asked if I was writing in a journal. "Well, sort of," I
said lamely, and then she asked if I'd like a poem.
When I hesitated she said, almost pleadingly, "It's
by --," and here she named a deceased USAn poet of some
renown who liked to spell his name in all lowercase
letters. "Well...okay," I stammered. "Sure. Very
good. I mean -- thanks." And she handed it to me and
hurried off before I could get my act together enough to
say something coherent that, who knows, might've ruined
everything.
    It's from "Sonnets - Unreality," it's titled "XII,"
and it starts out, "I have seen her a stealthily frail /
flower walking...." And a later line: "Across the
important gardens her body / will come toward me with
its hurtling sexual smell of lilies...."
    -- Certainly a fine gesture, not to say
provocative, not to say...stunning. And she, stealthily
frail indeed, and sexual too at least in appearance, and
sweet-smiled, and maybe young enough to be a college
student. And courageous too. A little moment of
literary and erotic grace. Serendipity. The girl --
young woman -- poetry sprite -- sure does know how to
make a jyzer's day.
    -- So I took a slow hike down this way. It's
something I used to do often back in my pre-Z era --

stroll the waterfront -- but have seldom done since. A
few times with Z herself but maybe not even once alone.
And not once ever -- here or anywhere, and I mean
lifetime -- was I presented with a sexy poem by a comely
stranger. Unreality indeed!

Otherwise things seem little changed down here.
The schlock level remains high. Wax museums and the
like. Horse-drawn tourist carriages. Boats, masts,
glimpses of ferries and big container ships on the move
in the harbor. Signs announcing points of historical
interest. "First regularly scheduled ship from Asia
landed here 1897." (The very next year we sent off our
warships to conquer the Philippines. How's that for
reciprocity? -- Or wait, was that 1898 or 1899?)

-- Well. I'm still sort of shaky here. First that
water pistol and now this. Wotta eighter! -- So then
how about some of that catchup. Though how far I'll get
I don't know. A sign says this park closes at eleven
and it must be near that now. "Trespassers will be
prosecuted." (Or it could be I looked utterly harmless
to her. And that in itself could be dangerous if others
see me the same way here or, even more, on the streets.
As maybe the dude with the water pistol did.)

Yesterday then. Sunday. I finally was able to do
some planting on our balcony. Got some dirt under my
nails and elsewhere. (One smaller ferry easing in right
now, one larger one rumbling out, and that one with its
open end at the back all lit up at water level. It
brings to mind the huge paddle-wheel steamboat Z and I
viewed up close last year back in Mentoka.) -- And I
saw our new next-apartment neighbors for the first time
out on their balcony a few feet away, two young Eurusan
dot-commer-type dudes who pretended not to see me. And
down below our balcony a mixed-race crew of six -- four
Asiusans and two Afrusans -- worked on shaping up the
building's front and side areas (yes, on a Sunday), and
I saw the Asiusan foreman looking up at the three
Eurusan guys (myself and the two dot-commers) and heard
him grump to one of his workers, "Hey, I thought they
said this was a Chinese place." (In fact, according to

our Chiusan landlord, Min, for the building's first five
or six years all nine of its units were occupied by
folks of Chinese or Filipino ancestry.)
    And going back to Saturday. That afternoon Z's
Eurusan friend from grad school, Lee M., drove in from
across the state to do some shopping and paid us a
surprise visit. Z was touched and a little bewildered
by this. "Why does he still want to be seeing me? I
don't get it, I just don't!" Nor do I, exactly, but
regardless I too was touched. The three of us wound up
visiting a sporting-goods co-op where he bought gear for
an upcoming weeklong bicycle tour and then we sat on the
deck of the coffee shop there chatting for well over an
hour. The good news is that his marriage is back on
track and he's functioning normally again, or so he
says. He explained what had happened with the marriage
-- Z had heard most of the story before but it was all
new to me -- and while doing so he said something which
she and I both thought was a hoot: "Even after many
years of marriage you keep learning new things and
discovering new mysteries about each other. It's true,
you'll see. It's like peeling an artichoke. But of
course you'll find there's a lot more variation in there
than in your average artichoke."
    After seeing Lee off at our place we turned around
and went right back up to the north end to meet a couple
of our workout friends from the WOC, Jay the juggler and
his wife, Melanie, to see the film "Limbo." They too
enjoyed the "average artichoke" marriage fable.
    -- Now a cool breeze is springing up off the water
and here I am wearing only a short-sleeve henley. And
it's after eleven and other than me the park's empty
(unless the poetry sprite is hidden behind one of the
big planter boxes, waiting to bushwhack me again: a poem
like a water-pistol shot to the heart!).

[+2]

    Another fine day. Quarterly tax day, and I mailed

off a check for three hundred bucks to the IRS -- and it
scarcely put a dent in my newly beefed-up account.
Tonight I did some pretty damn good scoping while
nibbling at leftovers from the surprise birthday party
of someone on the day crew (I'm not sure who; most of
the person's name -- except for an ending 'n' or maybe
'm' or 'h' -- had been eaten off the top of the cake).
Earlier I did some more planting on our balcony here at
203, thinking maybe I'd be out there jyzing tonight, but
it's a little too chilly now and also slightly drizzly.

On the way in I walked Z to her hilltop-council
meeting held in one of the outbuildings of the DC castle
(they've been invited to gather there, and at no charge,
as part of the DC's "mitigation program," which itself
was prompted mostly by the council's complaints).

And like all dates these days, or so it's beginning
to seem, today's is more interesting than most. But
first I should mention something about the date two days
ago. The arrival of the poetry sprite clearly
distracted me, because I neglected to point out in
timely fashion that the millennial countdown had reached
200. Now 198 days remain until the rollover. (And by
the way, Z and I have been thinking about throwing a big
and long-delayed apartment-warming party earlier in the
evening of that grand day, before heading over to the
fairgrounds for the fireworks at the iconic flying
saucer.) -- And I did notice today for the first time a
sizable show-window display of "Year 2000" noisemakers
and funny hats and other novelty items at the dollar
store I often walk by on the "high road" downtown. In
the next few days I hope to check that out more closely.

(What's new lately with fears about the vaunted Y2K
apocalypse? Nothing so far as I know. Fringe types
continue to rant about it, along with those who stand to
profit from it in one way or another, perhaps, say, from
a survivalist panic prompting the sale of huge amounts
of gear and grub and weapons and ammo. The public as a
whole seems to have decided the disruption, should there
actually be one, or for that matter more than one, won't
be much. I think they're -- we're -- probably right.

Any catastrophic disruptions are likely to occur, with
the usual horrible kind of irony, in countries which are
technologically "less advanced," which is to say better
prepared, in any number of important ways, though
admittedly not all, for the far greater horrors yet to
come.)

Finally, there was the night the elevators at the
scope building shut down, forcing me to miss my bus and
walk home at two a.m. (Actually one elevator was still
working, the freight car, but a janitor was using it to
pick up the recycling, as he told me, and he had the car
programmed to stop on every floor and that couldn't be
changed, and he was running late too because the regular
cars were down, so I wound up helping him load the
recycling bags on each floor in an effort to reach the
lobby as quickly as possible. By the time we got there
the freight car was jam-packed with those bags,
including some that contained wet garbage. I arrived at
the bus stop just in time to see my coach, the last one
of the night bound for south hill, pull away without me.
And several hours later, even though I washed up
thoroughly -- or so I thought -- Z was still able to
sniff the evidence of that elevator ride lingering on my
wrist (yuck!) when I climbed into bed.)

-- And the walk home that night was a little more
on the exciting side than I would've liked. I was hit
on maybe a dozen times in all, including several times
by panhandlers, twice by hookers, half a dozen by
dealers, and once by a looker (for dope) who was
thinking I must be a dealer myself. And other times I
worried about robberies or harassment by punks guarding
their turf. No poetry dispensers, though, on this
journey, and no water pistols either. And the sight of
the famous red-neon bread sign, still lit up at that
hour, was impressive as I crossed the high bridge.

And it's time to stop. For now. Must. Need some
sleep. (And I'd like to lay some good good loving on
the Z-woman, but likely I'm too far gone for that.)

8

An hour ago while crossing the high bridge I came
upon some fresh graffiti scrawled on a light pole near
the center of the span. It read, in slashes of bright
blue marker strung down the pole almost like a poem:
"Bitch! / You fuck / with one / Native / you / fuck /
with them / all!!!" At the bottom it was dated "Thurs
6/17": today.

Then under the freeway a blond Cawk woman burst out
of a parked van and strutted off, in tight jeans, spike
heels, and a scoopneck white top, reaching around to
adjust her underwear -- such amusingly exaggerated hip
swings -- and then, as a male voice inside the van
bellowed something I couldn't make out, she hung a hard
left and disappeared up a dirt path leading to a kind of
annex to "the jungle." (The van, by the way, didn't
look like either of the ones pictured on our bulletin
board. For one thing, it was blue.)

-- And now I sit beneath the giant green-and-gold
dragon mural in the pocket park in the AQ as a tai chi
group of a dozen or so moves through its slow mime-like
routine. They're out in the middle of the square next
to the small open-sided shrine with its flying-eaves
roof. Some rather harsh and tinny (to my ear anyway)
Chinese music plays over the PA as a male voice-over
issues instructions in what I believe is Mandarin. (One
possible translation: "Jyze to the left, jyze to the
right, stand up, sit down....")

It occupies just a quarter of the block, this park,
with streets to the east and south, the back of the post
office to the west, and the back of an eight-story low-

income residential hotel to the north (the dragon mural
taking up most of the outdoor wall space there). Rows
of small shops and restaurants line the far sides of
both streets at ground level, with four to six stories
of SRO apartments above and lots of cars parked or, in
several cases, double-parked down below. All the
buildings are made of brick, faded to mostly very
similar shades of red, and are roughly a century old. A
dozen medium-size trees poke out of the sidewalks
bordering the park and offer the only greenery in sight
except for a few small shrubs behind the shrine.

A couple of dozen men, mostly elders, sit on
scattered benches. They look as if they sit there every
day, weather permitting, and I'm sure I've seen many of
them before. Racially it's a diverse bunch, with most
or maybe all likely to be residents of nearby SRO
apartments. -- But half a block away another big yellow
crane swings above what will be a pricey ten-story
condo, and more new buildings like it are going up a
block or two to the west. It's the same story as in the
HQ: gentrifying somewhat hobbled -- but not enough! --
by the presence of social services and historic as well
as commercial and entertainment zoning.

I'm on my way in to work, of course, since this is
not a Saturday; but I can take my time because it's my
light week, meaning grand jury's not meeting, and
whatever work awaits me can be spread out over two
nights if necessary because I know Naomi's taking
tomorrow off. It's well after seven already, I'm sure.
I didn't leave the house until half past six and I
stopped in at no fewer than three markets in the upper
AQ in pursuit of a decent banana. It's just warm enough
to keep my jacket off. Z's working out at the WOC on
her own tonight because she missed last night, as I did
also since I knew she wouldn't be there.

First thing to note: the J-slinger got his pop back
again this morning after a couple of off days. When Z's
alarm sounded less than an hour after I hit the bed I
was almost instantly aroused, as if the pings alone were
enough to do it, as with a Pavlovian sex rat. For once

the lady was actually slower to rev up than I was. Just
a standard missionary mount, but the jyzerman had it
crackin', yes he did. The ejac was powerful and deep --
everything went so well I was unable to sleep for what
seemed like hours owing to the afterglow excitement.
And Z said: "You want to know something? If I were
still knock-up-able, that one would've done the trick
for sure." And a note she left on my armchair before
she left for work -- presumably alluding to her "Story
of O" critique from a few weeks back -- said, "I love
our sex life just the way it is!"

Saturday night, by the way, we'll be doing tandem
jyze. "Jyze on the town." (What town? J-town!) Z:
"You didn't think I'd let you be out there jyzing away
all alone on a Saturday night when young women are
running around handing out sex-invitation poems to any
letchy old average artichoke they happen to see?"

Yup, the story about the "stealthily frail flower"
at the waterfront park made quite a splash. "I can't
believe it! Are they really so brazen these days?"
She, Z, even asked me to bring the poem home so she
could show it to her friends whom she'd already told
about the incident. (I let word slip about it casually
-- or at least so I'd like to think -- right after she'd
told me about a sex-rap lunch she'd had with her
activist buddy Ryan V.) -- Or did she suspect I was
making the whole thing up to get her jealous? According
to her, no, absolutely not, she believed me. "I see how
the women look at you -- even the high-school chickadees
sometimes." Ooh, did I love to hear her say that! (But
how is it I always miss seeing them actually doing it?
Is she playing me here? Is the payback only beginning?)

(Right now a flock of grade-school kids are booting
around a soccer ball ten yards to my left, yelling at
each other in English though their mothers seated on the
steps closer to me are speaking what I'm fairly sure is
Vietnamese. And a couple of the mothers are carrying
paper bags from the same market where I finally found
the decent banana. The produce peeking out from their
bags, however, definitely out-exotics mine, at least by

traditional U.S. supermarket-produce standards.)
     -- Ryan, incidentally, is gay. Lately Z herself
has been reading a novel about young gay men on the
make. "Do you think they just have more sex hormones?"
she asked me -- with a straight face! Without even the
slightest cruel intention, she insisted! Ryan, as she
said, "is a real babe -- I don't have any trouble seeing
why he can get all the sex he wants" (as he'd told her
he can). In theory, at least, that's how she'd like it
to be with us too: all sex all the time. But in
practice these days she's mainly going for big weekend
flourishes and seems to feel a bit put upon if I ask too
much of her during the workweek. She's almost always
game for a quick dip or "plan B" nipple-tweak or two or
three but that's about it for weekdays. Although the
flourishy exceptions come often enough to keep me on my
toes at all times.
     And she admitted she thinks I'm "testing" her right
now. Testing the leash I'm on, she means. Suddenly I'm
feeling my power. She's pretty sure I think I've got
her all locked up. (Jeez, I should hope so -- we're
about to snap that lock closed and throw away the key!)
     When she talks like this, I tell her I think she's
describing herself at least as much as me, and at times
she acknowledges this is true. She's just about hitting
her limit: the longest time she's ever been monogamous.
She figures that's about two and a half years. This
might be linked with her current or anyway recent spells
of self-proclaimed "restlessness." I tell her I think
maybe she's recalibrating. Before our time together sex
had usually been a weekend thing for her and love didn't
necessarily have much to do with it and only in two
cases was a lifelong attachment looming, seemingly;
otherwise an unspoken, and sometimes even a spoken,
provisionality clause was almost always in effect. Now
she's putting it all together again under what for her
are emotionally new circumstances.
     (I do love the way she talks openly about certain
aspects of our sex life. We're both very direct about
it. Graphic. Pornographic, no doubt, if judged from

certain reactionary watchtowers of the culture wars.
And she's more into the visual aspects of it than most
women I've known. The other day when I knelt over her
while in the act, straddling one leg and lifting the
other as she lay on her side, she flashed on images of
that action all day -- as she said on the phone this
afternoon -- especially "the way you gazed hungrily down
at my pussy, the way it turned you on, the way it made
your veins stick out" (as she'd observed when I obliged
her request to pull out and "let me see it," which she
conceded she hasn't been doing as much lately but
insisted she still does like to do). "This time it felt
different," she explained, "like it was really long and
fat and bony and lumpy, all at the same time. That's
how it looked too. Sexy! Glistening with my juices!"

(Ryan asked her why she had cut me from the herd of
her pursuers. I pretended I was miffed by this: "Hey,
Ryan knows me! He shouldn't be asking a question like
that! It should be obvious why!") -- But I was pleased
by what she then told him: "Because he was the most
flamboyant." -- Flamboyance being, of course, a well-
known Norwegian trait. Well, but think of those
orgiastic Viking feasts. -- I mean, check out the
movie! -- Yes I'm talking about that old Hollywood
clunker "The Vikings.")

As for wedding news, Z's nephew Jacob called to say
he couldn't make it out for the ceremony. He served up
a number of flimsy excuses (the flimsiest of all being
that his eleven-year-old daughter Jillian -- his only
child -- just went through menarche and she's started to
resist him, talking back something fierce, and therefore
he's arranged to enroll her in a private school and
traveling with her would be difficult for a while). Z
was not mollified. "That's how it's always been with
Jacob. I'm older and so I do things for him; he doesn't
do things for me." Later in bed she briefly burst into
tears over this -- "You'll have your brother but I won't
have anyone from my family there for the wedding" -- but
she quickly recovered, saying, "Of course it's true I
moved two thousand miles out here so I could get away

from my family." And besides, she'll have scores of
friends at the reception -- maybe up to two hundred,
she's thinking -- and I'll have two or three at most,
other than those who were her friends first (and the
only one I'll have for sure, unless he can't get away
from work that day, will be Rob, so he'll be doing
double duty). And it should be noted the expense for
Jacob to come out here with Jackie and Jillian would
be huge, and they're far from wealthy.
     -- Birds are swarming in the trees here now,
including the one in whose shadow (if it were noon) I'm
almost sitting. Little birdshit splats are sounding at
a fearsome rate as close as a foot away as the steps
start to turn white. So I'm thinking I'll mosey along.
(But I'll mention I will after all be attending Aida's
party for Charles on Saturday. Z says it's important to
her, Z, that I do so. She'll be going early and taking
the wagon, but June will pick me up since she'd prefer
to arrive late herself. And I suppose June's thinking
in good Chinese fashion that she can somehow help me
save some face if Z's former lover Kirk shows up. At
this point we don't know if he will. Aida seems to be
playing it coy, and so I guess for that reason Z is too;
at any rate she hasn't asked Aida if he'll be there.)
     (And a couple of cops, both Cawks, are patrolling
the park and making me feel I probably shouldn't be
here. Like I'm some clueless European tourist --
utterly harmless don't you know -- thinking everyone's
squeaky nice around here just as back in Copenhagen --
that's how these cops are looking at me.) (And wow, the
beat in unison of hundreds of wings as a kid throws a
ball up into the tree! Like applause at the final
curtain! -- What, no bravos? No cries for an encore?)

[+2]

     The birthday party for Charles turned out to be
anticlimactic in more ways than one. The heavy rains
that had been forecast didn't materialize; that wasn't

146

the problem. The kids were able to take their swings at the pinata hung from the rim of the basketball backboard on the small cement court in back. The problem was that Charles himself failed to appear. He was in another of his infamous raging funks and remained shut up in his room the entire time I was there. And subverting the occasion almost as much, Kirk also failed to show. Most likely he wasn't even invited. Aida's ex, Tom (Charles's father who lives just a few blocks away), was present and so were most of the D-clan, including the highly traditional "senior D's" who basically run the family show from top to bottom, including its two foreign branches (the youngest son and daughter both being in the U.S. armed forces but half the globe apart: she in Germany and he in Thailand -- or maybe it's the other way around).

I shudder to think what kind of scene Charles might've thrown if Kirk had been there.

Still, the stress was such ("so myggy!") it wore Z out. She didn't sleep much beforehand and was ready to collapse at home afterward -- and soon did. She opted out of tonight's planned tandem-jyze session. But she still urged me to stick with it in the solitary form (as she sometimes recommends I do with movies and even with sex once in a while). And so it is I've come down to the HQ on my own. -- For jyze, that is, not sex or a movie.

Now, however, I've gotten lazy. Instead of setting up outside in the triangle -- where things are quite lively tonight, though it's still a little chilly for just sitting -- I've wound up in my office again. The brown armchair. As hip-hop music throbs up through the floor and literally tickles my feet via the hassock. Sole music, yuk yuk. (Even worse, I'm plagiarizing, because Z used the term first one night just short of twenty months ago when she was doing her journal thing alone up here, waiting for me. That was one of the entries she gave me a copy of, and in fact a framed copy of its first page -- very, very loving -- is hanging on the wall above my desk where I look at it quite often,

or otherwise I probably would've forgotten the pun long
ago. -- Or then again maybe not, since it was the
source of another term she uses from time to time:
"missing-toe music.") (And right next to that framed
journal page is an old blues album cover, also framed:
it shows a male cartoon figure whose head is a pork-pie-
hat-wearing planet Earth, and it's saying, with an
anguished look, sweat drops flying, "This World Is in a
Hell of a Fix!" -- and that's also a gift from her.)
     A story in yesterday's paper described the
renovation of the great white tower that looms far above
our building here. Seems the tower's become a hot
property with the dot-coms whose numbers are exploding
throughout the city and not just on the hilltop. The
story quoted several realtors to the effect that the HQ
is likely to be the happeningest place in town for the
next several years. Rents are going up fast; they've
already doubled at the tower and the rest of the area
can't be far behind. And our building is one of the
largest and most desirable in the whole district. It's
already home to a dozen or more dot-coms, including
three just in my corner of the second floor. The
predominantly -- almost unanimously -- young employees
of these companies are supposedly drawn by the infamous
HQ "edge," though I'm sure they'll take the amenities
too: sports, restaurants, live music, art galleries,
even bookstores (or they'll take them until their own
digital companies drive them out of business, right).
     If the rents double in our building I'll be gone
fast. Our best hope is that the building owner, who's
still the same octogenarian millionaire with extensive
real-estate holdings in several U.S. cities, is also
somewhat of an eccentric. (Being a former philosophy
professor he's almost bound to be.) He enjoys playing a
kind of Mother Hubbard role for strapped young people,
artists, immigrants, "tenants of color." During the
time I've been here he's never raised the rent more than
the year's COLA number. Then too, it could be that when
the dome blows and construction of its successor stadium
begins, the area will again seem less desirable for a

while. (And this week one of the dailies reported the
likely date of the dome demolition remains March or
April of next year.)

      In other news, a naval clash between North and
South Korea. "Tensions on the rise." But I've seen
enough of such incidents, including several during the
year I was living over there, to shrug them off, because
all parties involved need them to justify their enormous
military budgets and authoritarian methods of social
control (ourselves included to be sure, although as a
rule we try to do it in a less blatantly undemocratic
fashion if it's domestic and feasible). -- And today's
most interesting tidbit: it turns out the brain that
generated the special theory of relativity (among a few
other hypotheses of genius) really was different from
the norm. Structurally, that is. It sat in a jar for
decades -- an old apple juice jar, I think it was, still
bearing traces of the juice itself -- but lately a team
of scientists has been doing some slicing and dicing and
they've found an unexpected fold or two in the man's
cerebellum. (So I ask: if they were to slice and dice
my brain the same way would they come upon a hitherto
unknown jyze fold? Or maybe the lack of some
rudimentary folds without which one is helplessly driven
to jyze?)

      -- And so to be able to attend Aida's party we
missed the solstice parade out in Z's old hood with its
swarms of naked bicyclists. And today being Juneteenth,
we also missed an all-day reading of the newly published
posthumous novel of that very name (from perusing it at
the ORB, though, I'd say we didn't miss all that much).
And if Z had come along with me tonight, she might've
offered some pithy comments on a new book she's reading,
plugged by Ryan, called "The Male Body." (I did assure
her that her spirit would be present for this jyze
session even if her FC (fleshly correlative) couldn't
be, just like on that first night we were supposed to go
out when she broke the date via voicemail.)

      -- Well, I promised I'd return home earlier than
usual and now it's almost next-to-last-bus time. And I

might have to turn in early when I get there because
tomorrow's a big day: we'll have Kat. And by her choice
we'll be seeing a new version of "Tarzan" which just
opened yesterday. And tomorrow's also Father's Day.
And the last I heard, Z was making noises about hitting
the second day of the solstice street fair before the
movie. The idea is to conduct another search for
wedding rings. This, after all, is where we found our
"engagement rings" summer before last. And I don't
think I've mentioned it before: I'm still wearing that
ring. It's a five-dollar silver band from the flea
market and has stars and crescent moons punched through
it. And Z's still wearing hers, which is some sort of
fake black pearl which cost her twenty bucks, I think it
was. (She's lost the business cards for the makers of
the potential wedding rings we liked at earlier street
fairs. To her mind this means the cosmos doesn't want
us to get our rings from any of those people but rather
to find some new ones. I offered to break out my old
Viking runes to check on the truth value of that claim
-- a very good idea, she thought -- but then I couldn't
find them. Which to my mind meant we were even and
could move ahead without further ado on the ring hunt.)

[+2]

     -- Be it understood it's a Monday night and I'm
lazing out again. Or wussing out. And back at the
hideaway too.
     A miserable night, rainy and cold. We've returned
to the same kind of weather pattern we've been in for
most of the past year -- the La Nina type. And the
forecasters are saying it's likely this coming winter
we'll see much more of the same. Soggy, gray, cold.
-- And the truth is I often like this kind of weather.
Soon I'll probably be liking it again. I'm probably
even liking it right now. As I say, I just got lazy.
     -- So yesterday, to repeat, was Father's Day. And
suddenly, I think for the first time ever, I was on the

receiving end of it. And not just once. Twice!

First it was Z, surprising me with a present which
I found resting in my armchair after my Saturday-night
jyze session at the hideaway. She was awake again,
reading "The Male Body" in bed ("The penis chapters are
fascinating!"), so I opened the present in front of her
in the bedroom. The card said, "For the dad of Elgie
and the uncle of Kathryn." It was an art kit, three
small beanbag animals with plain white coverings and a
set of paints and craft items for decorating them. The
three animals were, and are, a tiger, a mule, and a
crab, and we agreed the tiger ("big cat") would be for
Kat, the mule ("Norski stubbornness") for me, and the
crab ("Do I even have to say why?") for Z.

(Z has what even she calls "crabby attacks" fairly
often, including, I'm sorry to say, one each yesterday
and today. Usually she blames them on hypoglycemia and
apologizes a few hours later, as she did with both of
these. The first one she also attributed to simple
boredom after hanging around at Charles's party with
little to do for almost four hours, and she implicated a
FOO as well: when she was a kid her mother used to drag
her to lots of parties, most of which involved numerous
big busty blond Polish ladies, at which there was little
for her to do except be stared at and yakked about owing
to her brown skin.) (FOO: that's acronymic, as I don't
think I've noted yet in this annal, for "family of
origin" and it's also shorthand for a psychological
insight about current behavior based on childhood
incidents. Z picked up the term in grad school a few
years ago and still uses it a lot. It follows by the
laws of mimicry and response that now I do too.)

Then when we took Kat home after "Tarzan" and the
street fair, she, Kat, presented me with two cards she'd
made at school. One's in the shape of a short-sleeved
shirt and has a glittery necktie on it, and Kat's
written in next to that, with an arrow, "Just kidding,"
because she knows neckties are not my thing. And to
make me feel better she's drawn in on the shirt a large,
extra-fancy pocket bearing a full complement of J-sticks

and other pens, just as my shirt pockets often do. The
second card's even more elaborate, employing several of
the pop-up tricks Z's taught her, with two miniphotos of
Kat herself attached and the male figure labeled
"Subunk." And both cards have lots of hearts drawn in,
and one says "I love ya!"

I'm still absorbing all this. At the time I
scarcely had a moment to think; Kat was urging me to
hurry up and finish my hunk of strawberry pie (homemade
by Betty with berries from their garden) so we could go
upstairs and wrestle. -- And I did hurry. Wrestling
with Kat is one of my favorite things to do. And how
fortunate it is for both of our sakes that her mother
and "aunt" will permit and even encourage such adult-
male/child-female physical goofery in our uptight age.
They believe, as I do also, that it will help make Kat a
"better-adjusted grownup" and it might even do the same
a bit belatedly for me.

Earlier at the street fair Kat was a sight to see
as she dashed around, hitting every last booth offering
kid-sized tie-dyed T-shirts (and there were plenty).
She herself was wearing a blue-and-white tie-dyed
pantsuit in which she looked terrific -- the vivid
colors of tie-dyes go extremely well with her own vivid
Mayan skin tones and flashing eyes and teeth and
abundant jet-black hair. She also bought a big hunk of
fudge and a yoyo with the ten bucks Betty had given her
to spend, and for the rest of the afternoon, except
during the movie when the theater lights were down, she
was constantly yoyoing, trying to make it "sleep" and to
"walk the dog." (At Kat's age I could do both of those
tricks and a number of others and so now I made a
gargantuan fool of myself trying to prove I haven't lost
the knack -- but for the most part I have lost it.
Which doesn't mean I've completely given up on refinding
it. Because an old dog can teach himself his own old
tricks -- of course he can! Even "around the world"!)

The movie turned out to be just okay, not the
animation masterpiece the reviews had led us to expect.
Again it was hard to tell how Kat reacted, if she did at

all, to the ugly-duckling/adopted-child aspects of the
story, with Tarzan adopted and raised by a family of
apes and in the end becoming their leader (but only
after taking one of his own grotesque human kind as a
mate). Zoelie has again been voicing concern that most
of Kat's friends -- selected by her from a school class
that's more than two-thirds "of color" -- are Eurusan.
But it's hard to find a way to broach this with Betty.
(And I should note that Z had another good excuse for
her little spell of crabbiness this afternoon at the
fair: she somehow picked up a nasty splinter in her big
toe. And the FOOs she's got around her toes, and
especially the two extra ones that were surgically
removed when she was an infant -- each from right next
to a big toe, one for each foot -- may be the most
powerful of them all.)

Today, incidentally, is the real solstice day. It
was celebrated over the weekend but the earth didn't
reach its greatest degree of southward tilt and reverse
directions until 12:49 this afternoon. At that time I
had just gotten up -- sleeping an extra hour or so
because I had to stay up late to perform a splinter-
removal procedure when Z's morning alarm went off -- and
I went over to the living-room window to see how things
looked out there at the big moment. It was gray and
drizzly then too, and the overcast was so thick and low
I couldn't even make out the houses clustered on the
next hill to the east. No one was in sight. Traffic
was light. The dog next door barked loudly a couple of
times and then went into whine-yip mode, I assume
because his night-worker owner was just getting up also,
like me, and the dog wanted to be fed or walked.

-- And I'll note Z's now regularly wearing an eye
mask in bed because she read somewhere that exposure to
light during sleeping hours can increase one's chances
of contracting certain kinds of cancer owing to the
pineal gland's role in melatonin production. She's
often worn a mask anyway to help in her long-running
battle against insomnia; she's just much more methodical
about it now. -- And I should be dead and turned to

dust by this point since it's only during exceptional periods such as our Mentoka trip last year that I sleep a full seven or eight hours in the dark. At this time of year I don't sleep in the dark at all. Nor do I wear a mask. On very bright days I might place a folded black washcloth over my eyes; otherwise I just press the back of my fingers over one eye and bury the other one (along with the socket, cheekbones, etc.) in the pillow.

So...the season we're in right now offers very little night for the incorrigible night worker to be working in, and as a "natural" owl it's when I find it hardest to work. And this factor too might have something to do with why I'm feeling super lazy tonight.

Also today, as another effect of the solstice -- really the major one, I'd say -- the sun begins ratcheting down the mountain peaks toward the millennium. It'll need about a nine-day "bounce" after it hits bottom at the winter solstice, but what's nine days after a thousand years?

As for news, not much to report on any level. Our bombing in Kosovo officially comes to an end and refugees start streaming back in. Congress winds up at an impasse in the culture-war battles over the high-school massacre and can't even manage to pass a perfunctory bit of legislation about it (no surprise there). South and North Korea remain as they were and so does the U.S. military presence there (and elsewhere -- many other elsewheres -- in fact many hundreds of them). A leaking pipeline causes a mile and a half of a newly refurbed stream to go up in flames in a burb twenty miles north of here, killing three kids and causing a lot of anguish for the many thousands who live near pipelines in this area. But the fuel is needed to sustain the burbs by keeping all those vehicles running, including an undeniable percentage that would still be needed even if mass transit were more widely available; if the fuel weren't transported in pipelines it'd have to be trucked in, vastly worsening the already fierce local traffic problems. (Trade-offs! Complexities! Simple slogans and rants and soundbites just won't do!

-- But they sure can be tempting, no doubt about it. So
at the very least, J-master, be concise in your use of
them. -- Or wait, what did I just say?)

Today Z talked with Aida. It turns out Kirk was
invited to the party after all, but Saturday morning he
called to say he was sick and couldn't make it. Z
didn't ask if he did this after finding out Aida's ex
(Tom) and his own ex of a nonmarital sort (Z) would be
present, but if that's how it went down, I'd say it was
a wise move on Kirk's part. The tip-off for him was
probably that ninety-minute tantrum Charles threw last
week when he caught Kirk and Aida "kissing" on the
living-room couch. I'd wager a tidy or even an
immaculate sum that Kirk (well known to be a pretty
smart guy) was sick only in a metaphorical sense. Good
for Kirk! (And I hope he proves as wise in dealing with
the thorny situation involving "double-dating" with Z
and me. It's bound to come up again one of these days,
and probably sooner rather than later.)

-- And time's up. Five minutes for the head, ten
minutes for the lazy man's shuffle up to the bus stop.

[+2]

Being bad again. Here I am sprawled out on the
couch in much the same way I was for the final segment
of last week's entry, dressed the same way (a henley
only) at about the same time (four a.m.) on the same
kind of night (rainy). -- And the five-day forecast
promises nothing but more of the same. It's right here,
four colored-ink weather panels on the back of the local
section of today's (by NUT time) afternoon paper, each
panel showing clouds and raindrops and cool temps.

But I'm celebrating anyway. Another pretty damn
good roll in the hay this morning (meaning I must
finally be rounding into shape again for real after that
weeklong "24-hour flu"). A fine movie last night,
"Eternity and a Day" (even Z liked it, sticking it out
all the way to the end despite the hard-to-read

subtitles which usually grump her out so much). Before
that, a successful surprise as I unveiled a bunch of
conception-day presents for her.

     Z was saying on the phone she thinks we've sort of
drifted into a solution for our main scheduling problem.
It didn't yield so long as we worked at it too hard, but
now we're there. I turn in late, we do pillow talk and/
or canoodle and/or shag after her alarm goes off (which
is when she as a lifelong lark likes loving best), I
sleep later into the afternoon. Seeing how hopeful she
was about this decided me on the spot to make it
official. My new bedtime is half past five a.m. for
sleep-hour-counting purposes, and I'll set my double
alarm for half past noon and half past one in the
afternoon. This'll cause some new scheduling grief of
my own -- especially in getting to my weekday jyze sites
early enough in mid to late afternoon -- but otherwise
it seems it might not be that bad. So then I ask myself:
why was I unwilling to stick with it when we tried the
very same arrangement the last time last summer? I
can't even remember. Was it because I lost too much
sleep on the weekends? That could again be the case
here. But I think Z's a lot more aware now of the
special scheduling needs of the night worker.
     We'll try it!
     There's one matter I want to get to for sure this
time so I'll take it up right now. A week ago I altered
a postcard for Z that started out as an old black-and-
white photo of a couple of swooning teenagers in a
tenement. It turns out the photographer is the same
Danny L. who went to college with Z and at one point had
a big crush on her -- the same guy I'd been urging her
to write last year on the chance he might still have the
contact sheets for the hundreds or maybe thousands of
photos he took of her. (She still has a few of those
sheets in her possession and many of the photos are
marvelous: the sultry sexy exotic glamour-babe going
through the paces, including partial dishabille and bold
seductive gestures -- they're so feministly incorrect
they come out on the other side, like parody, or close

to it -- yet they're still very, very sexy. Or true-
blue sex-positive-feministly correct, let's say.) And
talk of this led to mentions of various old boyfriends
of hers and wild incidents with them and between them as
they fought for her favor. This talk in turn left me
feeling bruised and beat up while trying not to let too
much jealousy show through (but not too little either).

        -- For Z's conception-day celebration I stopped by
the usual party store before picking her up at work on
the way to the movie theater. Came up with a balloon, a
pin-on ribbon, a yard sign, and a banner, all of which
say "It's a girl!" Also a couple of pink-bubblegum
"It's a girl!" cigars. And I did some inscriptions with
gel ink on a flashy glass "ruby" ring that cost me four
bits. All this, and a big bouquet of flowers too (from
the public market), was awaiting her when she ducked
into the car. "What in the world...." Before that
moment she had no conception at all -- ho ho,
unintentional pun -- of when her conception day was.
But when I explained how I came up with it she agreed it
was probably accurate, especially because it fell on a
Saturday night. Her parents, at least in later years as
Z was growing up, limited their "ootchimagootchi
moments" (that's a Z-ism from her teen years) to
Saturday nights. (Also she told me she's not sure they
were married at the time of her conception. They always
assured her she was legit, but this probably only meant
they were married before she was born. Whenever she
tried to pin them down on a wedding-anniversary date
they just laughed and changed the subject. As they
didn't tell her in those days but she eventually came to
realize, marrying back then was no simple matter for a
mixed-race couple in Centropolis.) (She also learned
later they either had to or maybe just found it easier
to go one state east to do the deed.)
        -- For kwikjyze items, I'll mention that Wei's
elderly father's visit to J. City has come and gone and
we didn't get to meet him, and I think Z's feeling quite
hurt by this. It made her realize she's not as close to
Wei as she was to Manny. Wei's been so caught up in his

own wedding preparations -- with Alison cracking the
whip because they're down to the final month now -- that
he's scarcely had time for anything else and he's been
testy at work even though he's back in a half-time
position now. He and Z have had several more run-ins
over alleged on-the-job political/racial insensitivity.
(Wei's father, incidentally, rode a bus round-trip from
and back to the main far-coast megalopolis, spending
altogether a day or two longer on the bus than he did
here. -- He's Chiusan, whereas his deceased wife --
Wei's mother -- was Japusan.)

As for our own nuptial preparations, Z's reversed
herself a couple of times on the reception invitation --
the "Marriage: Journey into Unknown Worlds" is again a
possibility if I'll agree to make some changes in the
wording for the cartoon bubbles -- and we've squabbled
again over the cake. For a couple of days it seemed the
daughter of Julia, one of Z's friends from work, would
be making it at a price of four hundred dollars, which
supposedly would save us a bundle. But that fell
through and we're now back to square (oven?) one. Z's
latest idea is to see if one of the community-college
bakery schools might be willing to throw something
together. And I have an appointment in the next week or
two to meet Z's "assistant hairdresser," the one who
I've agreed will be in charge of spiffing up my tresses
for the big day. And Z's said she wants to buy a big,
light-colored beach umbrella we can unfurl for the
ceremony in Olwen's backyard if the weather's as bad as
it's been recently.

-- So it's ten after five. Well past my old
bedtime but now I can keep going a bit longer if I'm not
too tired. Haven't mentioned -- what? Aida's plan to
tour Spain in August -- with Kirk! Z's surprising lack
of knowledge about male genitalia when she thought she
knew so much (and "Exhibit No. 1" did get hauled out for
anatomical inspection and experimentation and
confirmation -- poking, prodding, twisting, stretching,
stroking, squeezing, nipping, licking -- and enjoyed the
exercise thoroughly, this leading to the second "ootchi"

round of the day). -- And some canny advice on how to
appear lucky and thus become lucky. And the thought
that jyze is not paying enough attention to our very own
major local volcano. -- But it's been out of sight even
more than usual lately. (And there's still plenty of
snow visible on all the mountains when they are visible,
all the way down to the two-thousand-foot level in many
cases -- that is, the upper two-thirds to six-sevenths
are still white or white-streaked, and on these misty
days the black-white contrast often makes for a luscious
cinematic sight of the kind we Norusans notoriously
can't get enough of.)

9

   "Under the freeway / down by the AQ / on a
curbstone with my J-book / is where I'll be."
   Never thought I would be, and certainly not on a
day like this, but I am. For how long, we'll see.
   But oh how miserable it is! Rain is suddenly
falling in buckets, a chill wind blowing. Constant
jolts of tin are sounding -- almost like theater thunder
sheets -- from the ten lanes of traffic hitting
expansion joints on the freeway directly overhead.
   The foot traffic going by, trudging uphill, away
from downtown, even the ones with beach-size umbrellas
have soaked pantlegs. The foot traffic moving west and
downhill, however, is much drier at this point because
most have just parked in the big lot at my back beneath
the overpass, and many seem in a good mood despite the
wind and rain because they're bound for tonight's game
("We're talkin' 'the bigs' here, son!") and of course
it'll be played indoors in controlled-climate

conditions.

But then again lots of folks are very unhappy with the baseball club right now. A couple of days ago it reneged on a crucial clause in the financing deal for the new stadium and demanded that the public pick up a huge chunk of the club's hundred million dollars in cost overruns. The shockwaves are still bouncing off the mountains. We're talking major local issue here. But presumably most of the ones fuming about this wouldn't be going to the game anyway.

I'm a fumer myself but I'm still headed down to the old ballyard this evening. Our boys are in the midst of the last baseball homestand to be played there, this year or ever. After a long road trip starting next week, all home games will be held in the new stadium, with a gala grand opening scheduled for the middle of next month.

Meanwhile I'm leaning against a podiumlike concrete block, a foot square by maybe two and a half feet tall, bearing a plaque dedicating the "Colonnade." That's what it's called, the row of concrete overpass support columns, now that they're freshly painted. They number twenty-two in all (I counted them just moments ago) with half on each side of the street. The paint on fourteen of them is a bright orange, on the rest an even brighter yellow, and all now bear depictions in Chinese style of either carp or dragonflies. "A Symbol of Friendship" proclaims the plaque.

(There's a little more to the story though. The AQ undertook this project in an effort to spruce up its image in the aftermath of a widely publicized murder committed on the sidewalk about twenty feet from where I sit. A man who'd attended a game at the dome and was on his way back to his car was stabbed to death. He was a retired firefighter, a kindly, photogenic Eurusan, in from the burbs to see a game with his grandkids. Nor did it help that the murderer was a deranged Asiusan drifter who should've been behind bars at the time but had been released early. The media and the politicians were merciless. It's fortunate the AQ hasn't been bulldozed over in its aftermath.)

The parking lot behind me, incidentally, is one of
the ones I usually cut through on my way in. Not
only does this save time but on rainy days it keeps me
dry for a full block and slightly more, except for two
short open stretches between northbound and southbound
freeway sections.

And today's a kind of landmark in another sense:
just three months to go, to the day and almost to the
hour, until our wedding. Z left an easel-size piece of
paper covering my armchair with "3" written on it in
various ways (Roman and Arabic numerals, two vertical
lines scored with a diagonal, "trey" written out, etc.)
followed by exclamation points, with lots of hearts
mixed in. (Some of the people bound for the game here
today, I must say, are looking at me as though they
suspect I'm another deranged AQ drifter. Maybe this
pointed black thing in my hand is some sort of weapon?
Maybe they've never seen a J-stick before? Maybe it
looks like a lightly disguised container of Mace?)

-- And now the rain's stopped as suddenly as it
began (though some umbrellas are still up). Time for me
to join the promenade. (Looking up I realize you can
see a slice of the bay from here, straight down the
east-west street corridor. And I'm noticing the
Chinese-style street lamps, antique-looking red lanterns
on both sides of the main drag. And across the side
street is a very good and very large Chinese restaurant,
site of several lunches and dinners for me and Z back in
our early courtship days.)

*   *

-- Damn it's cold!
Probably I ought to stop right now. Drops of rain
finding their way in here, a little recessed alcove by
the northwest entrance to the old dome ballyard. The
facing benches four feet apart are sort of like those in
the back of a paddy wagon, I'm thinking, but a paddy
wagon would at least have a roof.

A few feet away, bearing the brunt of the elements,
the bundled-up masses huddle, pressing slowly forward

toward the entrance gate. Cops observe. Barkers bark
("Programs, getcha programs!"). Helicopters circle
overhead. Chitchat from the pregame show spews from
twin amps perched atop the newsradio van parked nearby.
Flags flap soddenly. Small trees shudder. City skyline
looms to the northeast. "Hotdogs! Hotdogs! Red hots!
Red hots!" Everyone's going in except me and the
barkers and the cops and the crew in the radio van and a
miserable-looking scalper who probably hasn't moved a
single ticket on an afternoon like this.

     And it's game time already. Right now. Roar of
the crowd as the national anthem soars to a close -- the
roar mostly coming from PA loudspeakers set up out here,
but there's also a slightly delayed echo, as it seems,
much fainter, that's the real thing. -- But excitement
anyway, absolutely. Images rear up of boyhood visits to
other ballparks in other cities (mostly just one --
Centropolis, north side, a mile or so from where Z grew
up -- a dozen games maybe, which is about twice as many
as I've seen in this one here). (But mostly I can think
only of the fact that I'm shivering. Literally. And by
the end of this J-week we'll be into July! -- And up
there a circling seagull. Such terrific clouds too, low
and gray in many shades and tumbling and roiling almost
like images from USAn World War II firebombing runs over
Dresden or Tokyo or, where I once lived, Matazaki.)

     -- And soon, BOOM. This'll be a big pile of
concrete chunks. (Word has it the arts community is
jockeying to schedule the implosion for the official
Gregorian millennial-rollover moment: midnight December
31. How fitting that would be! -- But it'll never
happen. In the divinely ordained sequence of sports
seasons football comes after baseball and if the
footballers who also make this dome their home qualify
for the playoffs, games might be played here into
January. That's what the contract says. And if the
team doesn't make the playoffs? But such a sad
eventuality might not be known about until too late to
carry out the prep work necessary to detonate the BOOM
at the millennial moment.)

[True at First Jyze]

[+3]

    -- Hope there won't be too many more entries like
this one where the gap between it and the previous entry
is three days. It means something's gone wrong. And in
this instance, yes, something has. A couple of things.
But neither's too terribly bad, in my view, and
therefore maybe I ought to reverse fields and say I've
lucked out again. Z and I both have.
    At this time last night, when jyze was supposed to
be doing its thing, I was fast asleep on the carpet down
there behind those two double-sashed windows with the
lights on and the blinds closed. That's the hideaway,
meaning "suite" 225, the office windows as seen right
now from one floor up through the balcony railing in the
atrium. I can also look straight up past several more
balconies to the glass of the skylight and see a misty
fog glowing pinkish-yellow from a blending of the lights
of the triangle and the uphill skyscrapers and tonight's
glorious full moon.
    I like sitting here at this hour. The display
fluorescents on the colorized and framed photos of urban
U.S. scenes from back in the days when this building and
the whole district surrounding it were young -- which is
to say roughly a century ago -- are turned off and the
overhead building lights are just barely bright enough
to jyze by. Tonight the furnace is working hard (the
blowers roaring) and I'm quite comfortable sitting here
in just jeans and a black henley, socks but no shoes.
No one's around. I've borrowed a chair from its usual
spot outside the manager's office twenty-odd feet to my
left. Pots hang on long chains from the balconies above
and also from this one, plentiful vines trailing from
the pots, a vast array of dusty philodendron leaves
visibly trembling in the furnace draft, some touchable
from where I sit. On the balconies of the three higher
floors a number of small trees grow, their branches
filling a good portion of the atrium space up there,
silhouetted handsomely against the glowing fog.

And I like the look of that office down there.
Jyzer Ink "world headquarters." It's bizarre, this
feeling I'm spying on myself. At any moment a frantic
jyzer could burst out of that door on his way to the
head or to the scope office or bus stop or -- who knows
where! (Other than the building manager, Trevor, I'm
not acquainted with a single person on this floor, but
once in a while one of them must see me sail out down
there. "Who is that masked man?" Of course they could
ask the same question about lots of other tenants, as I
often do myself. Social interaction between building
occupants here is not extensive.)

Next comes the story of the weekend. In a
nutshell: a donnybrook with Z Saturday night, an intense
reconciliation Sunday morning, a whacked-out back for Z
Sunday night, a trip to her mainstream doctor's office
(technically she's my doctor too) this afternoon.
Apparently the injury's only a "minor strain." But it
threw a big scare into both of us -- maybe an even
bigger one than the fight itself did (but I doubt it).

As noted before, Saturdays Z and I usually spend
together. But this time she and her friend Leola
scheduled an all-day shopping expedition focusing on the
proposed wedding shower for Z, scouting out sites and so
forth. I said I'd take the opportunity to run some
errands of my own, work out at the WOC, tend to various
matters at the scope office and here. She offered no
objection to any of this. But apparently it never
occurred to her that, especially with my new sleep
hours, it could take me until well into the evening to
get it all done. If I rise at two p.m., after all, it's
hard for me even to leave the house much before four,
and since I'm almost always traveling on foot I don't
reach downtown until close to five. (During Saturday's
expedition, by the way, I searched for prospective
wedding-reception invitation cards at the card cafe and
elsewhere, bought a new hooded rain jacket at the army-
surplus store -- for a price one-third of that for an
almost identical jacket at the sporting-goods co-op --
and discovered to my disappointment that the "welcome

2000" novelty items shown in the window of the dollar store around the corner from the scope office won't actually be for sale until early October.)

I did leave Z a note saying I'd be back between ten and eleven p.m. and also an altered postcard spoofing a movie called "Aida's Lovers" (the star of which even looks a bit like our Aida). But when Z found these awaiting her upon her return at six p.m., it turned out, she was not pleased. Somehow she'd imagined I'd be there too by then and we'd be "hanging out together" the rest of the evening. "My feelings were hurted and my abandonment mygs started swarming." Amazingly to me, she figured I was retaliating for her having breached our spend-Saturdays-together protocol by going off with Leola. And so now she decided she had to retaliate too, and drove up to the far-north bookstore/arcade and browsed there awhile by herself, figuring I'd be shocked to find she wasn't home when I got there. But then I missed a bus and didn't make it home until eleven -- ten minutes after she did, as she admitted later.

When I tried to open the door I found it blocked by our burglar bar (or actually it's hers; and I'll just note she's been using it to punish miscreant boyfriends since college days). She was furious. I was dumbfounded: first that she'd be upset at all, and second by the intensity of her anger.

-- But to cut this account short, I withdrew, she stewed, I proclaimed my innocence over and over, she said she wanted us to talk, we talked, I agreed to try to write better notes in the future (even though I'd intentionally not written the kind of detailed explanatory note she now said she would've appreciated, since I thought she might find it offensively untrusting), and the anger dissipated quickly after that.

So then yesterday -- day of the gay-pride parade, which we'd planned to attend but now scratched from our agenda -- on this day we instead conducted an expanded version of our usual weekend provisioning trip, picking up my new black shirt and a new "Hunk" pillow along the

way (Z insisted she likes the pheromones given off by my
foul old pillow and therefore will keep sleeping with it
anyway, but I decided I can no longer bear it myself)
and then henna kits for that same proposed wedding
shower. All this before hitting our standard grocery
stores.

   -- And in the midst of the fight, a visit from
June. Luckily she didn't arrive until one a.m., by
which time Z and I had struck a truce, and Z was
exhausted and more than happy to send me out to visit
with June, which I did off and on until four a.m. Good
talk about Aida and Charles, romance East and West, the
China v. Tibet issue, June's law-school escapades, and a
few grand-jury anecdotes, one of which I had to censor
carefully on the fly because it involved a Taiwanese
neighbor of June's in the burbs whom she knows
personally from her frequent casino visits.

   -- And that's gotta be it for now. (But I'd like
to jyze up here more often -- perhaps on the higher
floors as well. And if this bad weather continues I
might be doing it soon.)

[+2]

   Still on the offbeat. This time at midtown chain
burgers, a front-window seat. I've already eaten,
having snuck in my own peach juice and baked chips to go
with the two double-stacks. And I'm in no big hurry,
because I've already checked out my drawer at the scope
office (which is half a block south on the other side of
the street out there, the "very high road") and I know
tonight's job is quite short, only about thirty pages.

   But how long I'll be able to sit here I don't know.
A good long while, I'm hoping, because it's slow right
now and folks often succeed in hanging out here for
extended periods around this hour, especially when, as
tonight, uniformed security (an off-duty cop with a gun)
is not present. The staff doesn't like to come up to
the front part of the seating area and has no stomach at

all for asking people to leave, which can be perilous.

Then again I may be forced to take off on my own at some point because I'll need to use a restroom. To gain entrance to the one here you have to ask for a token at the counter and even then you may find yourself waiting twenty or thirty minutes because someone's shooting up inside and it's the only available restroom. Or it may be that I'll decide to take off because someone I know from the office shows up and wants to schmooze, though the chances of this happening are much slimmer.

So we're still caught in the same lousy weather pattern. Everyone's griping about it. And it will likely continue at least through the weekend. The front-page banner headline of this afternoon's paper: "HOLIDAY COLOR: COOL GRAY."

Otherwise the news of the world looks generally good, at least from our current local and national perspectives. The booming U.S. economy has led to a revised estimate of overall tax revenues for the government amounting to a gain of a trillion dollars over the next fifteen years. This is on top of the big gains foreseen as recently as half a year ago. In essence the future crises which conservatives have predicted for Social Security and Medicare can now be made to disappear with a wave of the hand.

Is this boom really happening? There's just got to be a catch somewhere. Yet this week we learned three of the four richest people on earth live right here in Jyze City, along with a good many lesser billionaires (including the CEO of our new hilltop dot-com at the marine hospital). Suddenly more and more references are popping up to this city being "world class," "the city of the future," "co-capital of the cybereconomy," so on and so forth.

Or consider the headline in the night final: "RATES RISE; MARKETS SOAR." After a month or so of idling in place the leading indexes are again close to record territory. Even on a day when the fed raises interest rates to counter inflation the markets are ecstatic because the fed also announces its "bias" regarding future increases is "neutral," as opposed to its earlier expectation that rates would continue rising. It's one more sign (among a seemingly unending parade): Wall Street is running the world. (So what else is new? But it would appear to be more true than ever before.)

So maybe I'll try to come back to that topic. "Jyze Philippic of the Week" -- certainly it would make a good candidate. Meanwhile a word about my own personal life, utterly mundane though in so many ways it undeniably is. (Because I must.)

Today Z went back to work after taking two days off. Her plan was to put in a half day at most but she hung on longer than that, returning home at three when her back started aching again. Her boss guessed the cause of the injury was basically "wedding stress," but everyone agreed Leola should take a big chunk of the blame for "making" Z ride in the car for long hours during Saturday's wedding-shower expedition. Henceforth Z will again be using a seat pillow whenever she rides in a car, and especially if it's Leola's car.

Only June has been sufficiently solicitous about the retweaked injury, Z reported unhappily. And Olwen to a lesser extent. No one else returned her calls announcing the injury and elaborately describing its nature and effects. Aida, though, had an excuse: she's sick. Apparently she's the latest victim of the same bug that's taken down the rest of us. (And Aida's just "shrugging off" the Charles graduation-party fiasco.)

Otherwise I've been Z's main support. And I have to say it hasn't always been a picnic. Admittedly I'm far from the ideal caregiver. And her way of being an invalid is close to the opposite of mine. She dramatizes a lot, to the point where it's hard to tell what's real and what's not. She says this comes from her "Polapina tradition of expressiveness about feelings" as opposed to my alleged "Norski stoicism and dourness." And she agrees our sibling positions also have something to do with it: my being, although the eldest, just one of four sibs who had to be cared for, her being in effect the one and only (half-sister

Camilla having moved on before Z was one year old).
-- But in truth it wasn't all that hard for me to put up
with her "sick persona"; it was more just a matter of
bogglement at its characteristics (even though I've
certainly seen them before). The moans and groans and
grunts as she hobbles about, the outbursts of wholly
indecipherable Tagawocky. -- Today when she arrived
home from the office her first words were, "Ah, now I
can start groaning out loud again! It's so hard being a
stoic! How do you do it anyway? Will you teach me
someday?"

      -- And I'm guessing I've been here just about long
enough. No one's pressuring me to go, though; it's all
internal, and I'm not talking only about my bladder.
Might even be related to the "stoicism" thing, who
knows. Don't disturb others if you can avoid it; try
not to make a nuisance of yourself. Is this really so
terrible? Because I mean it's either I do it this way
or I lead a whole different kind of life -- neither a
jyzer nor a nightscoper nor a partner of Zoelie B. be.

                    *   *

      An hour later up in the scope office. Soon I'll
have jyzed this millennial jyze in every last chair in
the conference room. Or maybe it won't be all that soon
if the weather turns better within, say, the next couple
of weeks, that is, by mid July, as it often, though far
from always, does.

      This time I'm holding forth from the head of the
table and facing south. The usual upright checkerboard
arrays hang outside to my left -- something like
pointillist geometrical versions of the northern lights,
say -- and way up there a dramatically underlit U.S.
flag is frantically aflutter. A moment ago a helicopter
buzzed by, probably headed for one of the east-hill
hospitals; its flight path, well below the tops of the
tallest buildings, brought to mind those futuristic
model cities in which everyone gets around by helicopter
or flying automobile instead of ground-hugging
automobile (or do I say this just because I've been
thinking too much about all the recent assertions that

this is the city of the future?).

A couple of small yet crucial personal matters I
wanted to mention. One is I'm already unhappy with my
new sleep regime. It could be I don't rest as well if I
go to bed much after dawn -- though lately the days have
been almost as dark as the nights, so how would I know
for sure? But days are noisier too no matter how dark.
And I miss being able to fall asleep with Z in my arms
(or as it happens just as often if not more, me in Z's
arms from behind -- "spooning" -- with my ever longer
hair pulled under my head so it won't tickle her face
and then directed upwards so it won't tickle mine).

Obviously this is another of those tricky trade-off
matters. If I go to bed at three-thirty or four a.m.
it's not easy for me to engage in the pillow talk she
likes so much when her alarm goes off an hour or ninety
minutes later, and I'm also less likely to be interested
in loving, although it's true I'm better-rested and
therefore actually more likely to be able to function on
all cylinders if I can just get myself started. It
usually takes considerable effort for me to rouse myself
after I've been asleep for an hour or two -- whirling
around the depths in a deep-REM state. Yet I can do it
and on balance I think I'd prefer to discipline myself
that way rather than the way I have to do it with this
new regime.

-- But first I should give it more of a chance.
Obviously I'm not yet fully adjusted to it. And by the
time I have fully adjusted I'll suddenly need to be
rising earlier again during our trip to the country fair
with Kat and Betty at the end of next week. (And in any
event I don't want to sound like I'm whining about this
sleep stuff. This life I'm living is the life I want,
damn it! The drawbacks are minor! Remember that, J-
slinger! -- And I usually do. But once in a while the
perfectionist demons start drumming up a storm in my
head.)

A few other things. First, back to politics. It's
ironic that in the past week the U.S. Supreme Court, in
a series of decisions favoring states' rights to an

unheard-of degree, has revealed itself to be every bit
as activist as the famously liberal court of a
generation back, but of course this time in the opposite
direction. Leftists who aren't big-government liberals
might not find these decisions too threatening, though,
because they increase local and state control in the way
many ecologists, for example, favor. But I worry about
the effect in highly conservative or reactionary areas
of the country where minority rights historically are
not protected by local and state government. It seems
like every week or two the Supremes are sending another
signal to Cawk supremacists: "Go for it, boys and girls!
Now's your chance! We've got your back!"

Locally here the baseball team's demand for more
public money has incited an uproar and appears doomed.
Good things can happen! (But stay tuned.) And the
mayor's task force on the arts has come up with a series
of proposals that don't look too bad if they can
actually be implemented, though any chance of that
occurring is a long way off and far from a sure thing.
And the amount of tax money to be earmarked for the arts
looks much too small -- just one percent. A number of
less wealthy cities tax themselves at twice to three
times that rate for this purpose.

And returning to the globalization theme, a new
essay on the topic I came across has me persuaded even
more than before that the term is synonymous with
USAnization. Economic global domination has followed in
the wake of the virtually unchallenged military global
domination that emerged almost a decade ago with the
collapse of the Soviet Union. Can anything be done
about it?

The overriding U.S. view of this situation seems to
be: let's get ours while we can. If this means global
catastrophe -- through ecological devastation and
exploitation of the poor and the weak -- why, we'll
worry about that later. In fact we'll be in far better
shape then because we'll be even more firmly and
brutally in charge. -- But even so I'm perversely
optimistic. Not everyone is waiting until later. These

problems are new to the globe in at least some ways and
they're largely a result of what can be regarded from
certain perspectives as successes. Intelligence, once
focused on them, can alleviate them and in some cases
solve them. The main problem is getting intelligence to
focus on them sooner rather than later -- while much of
the pain and devastation can still be avoided.

What's this, I've become a pollyanna? Hardly. I
recognize the extreme difficulty of the task and the
high risk of failure. I just can't see any alternative
to (1) believing that human intelligence will eventually
prevail and (2) trying to make that happen. If there is
such an alternative, I hope someone will figure out what
it is before it's too late (ha).

[+1]

Back on the beat -- meaning off the offbeat -- even
if this is the latest start ever. But it's the 1st of
the month and I can't miss it. All right, technically,
which is to say Gregorianly, it's not the 1st anymore,
it's almost five hours into the 2nd. But by Nightscoper
Upside-down Time (NUT) it's still the 1st until I go to
bed. And that means for me the 1st still has about,
say, forty-five minutes left to run.

It's raining and has been for most of the night.
The clouds are so dark dawn's not even visible yet. And
meanwhile the new trifecta is in place: jyze sign up,
"Jyzer at work" button on, Jeep hat also on -- just in
case. The pink and black "It's a Girl!" yard sign -- so
amusingly drawn with its smiling baby face onto which
I've painted a tiny heart-shaped "G Loves Z" beauty spot
-- still rises above Z's chair. The end-of-month bills
are all paid, including the first fifty-dollar monthly
installment on the loan repayment to Z (just 140-some
installments to go). The newspapers are read.
Tonight's altered postcard is ready: a Japanese design
for a matchbox cover showing an elephant holding a big,
dazzlingly lit match aloft with its trunk, to which I've

added the words "BEST MATCH EVER!" -- and then down in
the corner the paste-on face of Myg, Z's amygdala
character (the amygdala of course being the part of the
brain, or two parts actually, in charge of anxiety and
fight-or-flight reactions) -- Myg saying diabolically in
a tiny white cartoon bubble, "Now that's scary!"

    -- And speaking of scary, today starts the month in
which the No. 1 scary soothsayer of the millennium, the
infamous medieval French guy Z refers to as "Nasty-doom-
us," predicted "the Great King of Terror will fall from
the sky." (What do I know from this soothsayer?
Virtually nothing, other than that apocalypsians of all
stripes love to quote him at you. And for years it's
been just about impossible to enter a bookstore without
running into something written by him or about him, or
more likely lots of such things, and that's never been
more true than it is right now.)

    And for many people today is the first day of
Fiscal Year 2000. So shouldn't big celebrations be
breaking out in all the financial districts, the
boardrooms, the planning departments where fiscality is
basically all that matters? In a country whose business
famously is business, in which megacorporations and Wall
Street run the show from top to bottom, shouldn't this
be the most important millennial date of them all? But
I've yet to come across a mention of it anywhere. For a
while I was even wondering if I was confused about what
a fiscal year is or how it works. But then I did find
at least one confirmation: yes, for many people FY 2000
begins today. But nothing about it being a big deal.
Odd. After all, to whom do numbers matter more than
accountants? And doesn't that apply to calendrical
numbers as well as financial ones? If not, what the
heck is this whole Y2K thing about?

    (Comes to mind a startling sight yesterday
afternoon. Rounding a corner downtown I saw several
fire trucks parked in front of that same dollar store
that had the "Welcome 2000" banner in one of its
show windows. Now all those windows were knocked out
and big black tongue-like burn marks scarred the

building above them. The interior of the dollar store
was an ugly soggy stinking burned-out mess. -- The work
of the Terror King, some just might be saying. Or
perhaps the culprit could be a customer who was even
more disappointed than I was by the unavailability until
October of the promised kitschy millennium novelties.)
     -- When I came in tonight I found a "BUS PASS!"
sign taped inside the front door. This refers to the
fact that I once again forgot to take the pass with me
earlier in the evening, just as Z forgot to hand it off
to me. (And this trait of hers that she does something
about things that aren't going the way we think -- or
sometimes just she thinks -- they should, I like it a
lot even if it does at times make me scramble when I
don't really want to be scrambling.)
     This past morning's altered postcard for her was a
reduced-size copy of the poster for the movie "Christmas
in July" showing its old-timey Hollywood B-movie stars
(one "as 'G'" and the other "as 'Z'") in loving ecstatic
embrace, with the words added, "A True Love Story That's
Only Beginning!" Oh I do go for this corny stuff and
the cornier it gets the more caught up in it I get.
     Tonight I checked out the cards for sale at the
art-museum store, which was open late because this is
First Thursday. It was also opening night for the much-
hyped Impressionism exhibition and big crowds were
swarming about. To my surprise I came up with a dozen
new cards. I've laid in so many now I've had to conduct
a triage operation on the old portable file box I've
been stashing them in. I keep it hidden behind the
black armchair where I'm sitting now.
     -- And finally I can say it. I just looked up and
saw the first light. So here it is: all of tonight's
jyze, I hereby declare, is indeed true by that same
light. I'd even say all jyze is true by first light or
for that matter any light. And it's certainly true at
first jyze -- that is, before time and circumstance and
critics and revisionists can get at it, and I include
here the critics and revisionists roaming about in the
brain of the jyzer himself. (The title "True at First

Light" is said by at least one far-coast-megalopolis
critic to be the one good thing about the new
posthumously released book by the internationally
acknowledged American fictionmeister whose work however
has pretty much gone out of fashion in recent years,
including for this same jyzer.)

[+1]

     -- And now I've just about completely screwed up.
Left myself only twenty-five minutes for this coda. I
was having too much fun putting together another of
these damn altered cards.
     Z, I'll say first, is much better, but we're
holding off on resuming full sexual relations until she
can see her regular doctor early next week. Right now
she can't "arch" without fear. I definitely don't want
to see her developing anything even remotely approaching
the kind of back troubles Lady U suffered from. (Z also
"can't bend" and therefore can't go down on me either.
I tried to compensate by "going up" on her as she lay on
her back in bed yesterday morning, my knees straddling
her chest, but that didn't work out too well either.)
     Nonetheless it's been the week of the "love-wanga."
She's liking me again. It took a while, though, to
escape from her glower list for having "abandoned" her
last Saturday night.
     And July 1st was my deadline on production of the
mock-ups for the reception invitation. Today, only a
day late, I presented her with five of them, including
one fashioned from a vintage Krazy Kat "Wedding Bells"
movie poster and another from a doctored romance-mag
cover (along with altered music cards for "Let's Do It"
and one other I'm spacing out right now). In the end
she agreed "Marriage: Journey into Unknown Worlds" is
the best and she's willing to accept it rather than try
to come up with something better herself. (The
caricature of us drawn during Ramona and Pepe's wedding
reception is no longer even thinkable to her because "it

makes you look too good relatively speaking.")

Zipping right along here. -- Next I'll mention a joke cracked by one of the "S&M girls" (Sally and Marcy) from the halfway house. I see them on the bus from time to time, and last night they were counting down the days until their release in September. "We've got sixty-six days until we get out," Sally quipped, "and you've got eighty-five days until you go in." (Marcy hasn't been talking much lately. She met a guy on the bus and they now spend most of their time giggling and smooching.)

This room here, June mentioned it seems to be shrinking and we finally figured out why: it's because the plants are growing so fast. It's true, and several have become huge. The fish-bone fertilizer I dose them with seems to possess almost miraculous powers. It would be interesting to know what percentage of the livable space these plants are occupying. Soon I might have to do some serious pruning just so we can keep moving around unimpeded. Or better to say "in a way less impeded," because "un" is no longer within reach.

First light again. The jyze truth is revealed yet another time right here and right now (as an early-bird chorale blares). I'll be back in these pages in ten hours or so but it'll be a new chapter -- this one, No. 9 No. 9 No. 9, now becomes at the very least yesterday's jyze. Which is to say first jyze no more.

10

Came doddering out this time, hand in hand with the bad-back invalid. Earlier while I was asleep she drove over to a medical-supply house and picked out a couple of back-support items. One's a new cushion for the car

seat ("not as hard as the last one" -- that is, the one
that may've protected her back but knocked mine way
outta true when I heedlessly plopped down on it one day
last summer while jumping into the car). The other's a
light blue wraparound tube that looks amusingly phallic
when it's straightened out and hung from her groin (as
she demonstrated) and also like a skinny pastel inner
tube or a beefed-up hula hoop when it's tied around her
waist, as it is now.

I'm gazing at her as she browses along the far wall
of our hilltop branch library. Black capri-style pants,
a gray sweatshirt, the inner tube. My beautiful babe.
My intended. My "bann'd one -- bann'd in J-town" (as
in wedding banns). -- And during our stop on the way
here at the little coffee shop across the street (the
one with the nightscoper-unfriendly hours) the woman
behind the counter blurted, "So, is this the lucky man
you're going to be marrying?" It seems Z and her friend
Sylva stopped by there for coffee the other afternoon
and did an unintended secular banns thing, that is,
announced the marriage to "the community." "I guess
maybe we were talking a little too loud," Z explained.
In any event no one's stepped forward so far with an
objection to the hitch-up. Or if someone has, I don't
know about it. (And then there's Aida to consider. Has
she? And what about Kirk? For that matter what about
Lady S? How far has the word spread?)

Surprisingly it's a little sunny out there today,
although big gray clouds lurk just offstage in all
directions as seen from the hilltop. But this sunniness
is apt, because today Sirius the Dog Star appears in the
heavens and the Dog Days of summer officially begin. In
real life (as opposed to mythical/astrological) a couple
more days of rainy weather are expected in these parts,
covering both holidays (the 4th is tomorrow, Sunday, and
so Monday of course is observed as a holiday), and then
a warming trend will follow. Again the timing is good,
because with the July Fourth holiday I instinctively
think of "core summer" setting in. This year I'm
dedicating core summer (which to my mind ends on Labor

Day weekend, which falls late this year) -- dedicating
the core, I say, not just to jyze but to whipping myself
into the best physical shape possible. "Marriage
shape." Five workouts a week. "No exceptions."

      -- Now Z's sitting across from me at this classic
library table of sturdy and thickly varnished oak.
She's culling a stack of maybe two dozen whodunits down
to five or six to take home. Yes, the bride-to-be truly
does relish "the mysteries," and especially those
authored by women, or even better, feminist women (good
for her!).   -- Also at our table are two Asiusan men: a
youngish one in flowery pants and a Homer Simpson T-
shirt (a moment ago he was flipping rapidly through a
stack of men's fashion magazines but now he's snoring,
chin pressed against chest even as he continues to sit
up impressively straight); and a grandfatherly one who's
peering at a basketball-size globe he's holding in his
hands up close to his face, like a melon he's checking
for defects; and it's the big red splotch of China he's
peering at. His grandson's over in the children's
section and comes trotting back every now and then with
a question or a triumphant observation (delivered in
English, but so far I've heard nothing other than grunts
from the grandfather, who's a touchingly kind-looking
fellow, almost a stock Hollywood Chinese grandfather,
except -- does Hollywood even have one of those? Evil
stock Chinese characters, of course the studios never
run short on them).

      There's news. In fact: an earthquake. A real one,
epicentered about seventy miles south of here but strong
enough at Richter 6.8 to sway the downtown highrises of
J. City. Z was lying on our couch reading when it
struck a little before seven last night and she felt it
-- for about a minute, she says -- and watched the
plants undulating and wondered if the high bookcase
behind my armchair might topple. But it didn't. Today
we reviewed our "earthquake plans" -- nothing too fancy:
we'll return to our apartment no matter where we might
be -- and decided, at her insistence, to lay in some
emergency provisions, including bottled water and extra

canned and jarred food. And these would also serve us
well at millennium-rollover time just in case.

I didn't feel the quake. At the time I was
browsing at the ORB and I think it went entirely
unnoticed there. But if ever there were a place to be
buried beneath falling books during a quake, that's it.
And what a way to go! It rises to the top of my list of
preferred-demise scenarios. Its likelihood also seems
high, relatively, since I spend so much time sitting in
the black armchair under my own killer bookcase.

Had this quake been a Richter magnitude or two
bigger the French-soothsayer freaks would be nyah-nyah-
nyahing for sure. No doubt this is how the canny old
prophet stays in business so many centuries after his
copyright ran out. When you predict a disaster in such-
and-such a month of such-and-such a year, you can be
pretty damn sure there'll be one -- somewhere. Maybe
even right here in J-town.

Today's other big news is another all-time high for
the stock market. It's the first in seven weeks. I
guess some people were starting to feel miffed. The
U.S. economic juggernaut keeps rumbling right along.
It's truly frightening to me. Just the side effects of
this consumption-driven prosperity will almost certainly
prove the French soothsayer correct on a worldwide scale
within the next half century or so if not sooner. I'll
even venture to predict this myself. Jyzer-doom-us!

-- Z returns from the restroom and whispers, "I've
been in a lot of libraries in this city and I think this
one has the worst amenities of any I've seen. It's
amazing they've let it stay like this for so long."
It's housed in a single-story, low-ceilinged fifties-
style storefront, with seating for a couple of dozen
people at most. The good news is that it'll soon be
replaced by a much larger building, newly constructed,
as a result of the recent library-bond passage (which
will also pay for a new downtown library, to be designed
by a red-hot "radical" Dutch architect whose work leaves
me cold -- and all this yet another reflection of the
city's recent cyberwealth efflorescence).

    But the light-rail station which was to be built
almost directly under this library right here -- or
rather, the area was to be prepped for a station to be
built later -- is now in doubt. The rapidly rising
cost of the system will force cutbacks in the original
plans. This part of the city (being among the poorest
parts, with among the largest "of color" populations,
and therefore among the most in need of help) is by the
usual logic of oligopolistic power politics among the
first to suffer from such cutbacks.

    -- Z's just gone off to the small hilltop corporate
supermarket to pick up a snack. She's left behind her
"inner tube," which is stretched out across a jumble of
books with her shades riding the shaft near the end
(giving it the look of a hip young powder-blue python).
She must've noticed, as I also did, that the clouds have
moved in and rain seems imminent. Almost certainly our
plan to continue this session in the park will have to
be scratched. (I just nodded sort of conspiratorially
to the woman from the coffee shop. She's a politically
active Cawk lesbian -- wearing a handsome lefty-looking
black beret -- and probably doesn't have too high an
opinion of hetero marriage and no doubt detected a
certain dissonance -- an amusing one, I hope -- in my
reaction to some remarks she ventured back at the coffee
shop about the nature of marriage in general.)

    -- But the week ahead looks to be interesting. We
have June staying with us for the weekend. We have the
fireworks and the holiday and no other plans at all
until Tuesday; we can just kick back (Z wants me to read
"The Male Body" while she still remembers what the many
brightly colored blank post-its she's feathered it with
are referring to). Then midweek comes my big showdown
with the nuptial hairdresser -- or our preliminary
mutual sniffing-out session, I should say, since the
shearing itself won't occur until mid September. Then
on Friday we'll drive down to the country fair with Kat
and Betty, shacking up for two nights at a nearby motel.

    One other millennial note. I keep coming across
articles on efforts to counter the Y2K problem, and

although they're all generally positive, saying most of
the problem has been eliminated at least in this
country, their cumulative effect is probably negative
because they make the problem look so massive. And why
do we need to be beaten over the head with the fact that
it's being solved unless it actually remains a serious
problem? (But I myself believe it's being solved and
most polls say the USAn public as a whole does too,
except for a mere "small minority" -- numbering in the
tens of millions, true -- of weirdos and fanatics.)
(In one of these articles I found an explanation of the
distinction between "Y2K compliant" and "Y2K ready."
The first means a computer can work with dates for 2000
and beyond; the second means that at rollover time the
computer's clock will reset itself back to the last year
with the same sequence of days and dates. And since
2000 is a leap year, the last previous year fitting this
description would be 1972, or twenty-eight years ago.
And since twenty-eight years just happens to be the
length of a full Glennarian cycle or stage, I couldn't
help but be amused. -- But not to worry, I won't be
delving into Glennarian calendrics again as in previous
jyze annals -- not if I can help it.)
     -- Z returned to the library in the middle of that
long parenthesis. She hasn't said anything but I can
see she's getting restless and so yes, I think we'll be
moving on soon. She's already tied on her "inner tube"
and is modeling the back side of it for me, wiggling her
hips also, as if to say, "If you want some of this later
when we get home, J-man, you'd better follow me pronto."
(But we're not forgetting the bad-back sex embargo for
one second, no we're not.)

[+2]

     Jyzing on instruments now as another long holiday
weekend sputters to a close. And I'm tired, sick, and
hurting. The weather's finally improved and in theory I
could be sitting somewhere down in the HQ triangle

squeezing out this entry, but it seems I just can't
transport myself the hundred steps from here to there.
It's taking all my energy to resist the temptation to
declare a jyze exemption and cancel the session.

Tired -- from losing too much sleep to yet another
fight two nights ago and to extended but also extremely
cautious reconciliation rutting this morning.

Sick -- from what appears to be a relapse into that
same nasty flu/cold (featuring four powerful sneezes in
rapid-fire succession at a chain bookstore earlier
tonight -- so explosive they nearly had me doing a
series of backflips, or so it seemed to me -- along
with the usual coughing, snuffling, feverishness, and
achiness, all of which started to appear on fight night
and have gradually worsened ever since).

Hurting -- from what's most likely a sprained right
foot, suffered when I stepped in a hole in the sidewalk
as I was carrying Kat on my shoulders on our way over to
the hilltop strip park to view the fireworks (luckily I
was able to tumble into some grass and to break Kat's
fall by catching her with my stretched-up hands and
forearms, at the cost of skinning my elbows a bit -- and
even more luckily, Betty and Z had gone ahead to search
for a spot to lay out our blanket and didn't witness the
incident) (because neither Kat nor I would want to have
to give up our shoulder-rides just because of a little
spill) (Manny's brother Reuben was a few steps ahead of
us but was distracted and seemed to think we were just
goofing when he turned around to see us sprawled on the
grass laughing hysterically).

So Z and I must've made quite a sight as we crossed
the high bridge on my way in tonight (she accompanying
me partway for the exercise) -- Z moving cautiously in
her "inner tube" and me limping pathetically. But I do
recognize the nature of the injury from the numerous
similar sprains I've suffered before and I know what's
best is to walk on it as quickly as possible. That and
icing down the injured joint until the swelling subsides
and then soaking it in hot water, and that's what I did
at the WOC tonight, and that helped a lot. Now it's

stiffening again, and it'll be bad in the morning, but I
think in two or three days I'll be fine. (Except for
the bug, maybe. But I'm hoping this is just a minor
relapse. Surely I ought to have built up some
antibodies over the past month to rout this thing.)
     The fight was preposterous. Saturday night and
Sunday morning Z threw a series of minifits, I'll call
them (surely not for the first time), because she
thought I wasn't responding passionately enough to her
amorous attentions, despite our earlier agreement about
avoiding sexual exertions at all costs because of her
vulnerable back. The minifits were so out of proportion
to the alleged offense that I "withdrew," upsetting her
still more. Yet I feel I have no other choice when she
acts this way, because I can't be letting her think she
can manipulate me with tantrums and I don't want to go
head-to-head with her when as far as I can see the only
real issue is the overreaction itself. And this time,
at least, she came to her senses fairly quickly and even
admitted later on I'd been right to react the way I did
and thanked me for not letting her aggravate the injury.
Today she said it was all just a matter of horniness
overriding her better judgment. I'd say it was more
general frustration -- from the way the bad back impedes
her movement -- combined with anxieties about the
wedding and various other matters, including the news
that her friend Nadine's chemo has failed and her tumor
is growing again, meaning the end is near.
     The fireworks for the Fourth didn't seem all that
great from our vantage point, just as they didn't last
year (but we'd pretty much forgotten about that earlier
disappointment). In part they appear to fall short
because we're seeing them from so far away (roughly
three miles); in part it's because the natural scene
itself is so spectacular it takes away from a smaller
spectacle staged within it. But it's still fun to
watch. A crowd numbering well over a thousand -- maybe
more like two thousand -- gathered in the blocklong
strip park, many of them picnicking there for hours
beforehand. We wound up sitting between a pair of

dueling portable barbecues, hot dogs to the left and burgers to the right, with Z donning a face mask because of the smoke (she always carries that mask with her in her bag). And the low cloud cover helped by providing greater darkness and reflecting back the glow of the explosions. And it didn't rain!

[+1]

An offbeat note. Today is what I'm going to call Far Out Day. At ten p.m. -- which is about two minutes from now -- the Earth reaches aphelion. It's the point in its slightly ovoid orbit at which it's farthest from the sun -- about three million miles farther from it than it is at its closest point, perihelion. Oddly, in this era aphelion falls in the middle of summer and perihelion about six months later in the middle of winter (they gradually cycle around the yearly calendar over a period of millennia). Presumably the summers in this hemisphere are a little warmer and the winters a little colder when aphelion and perihelion are reversed -- that is, the weather is a little more extreme -- whereas in the southern hemisphere the opposite would be true. And this year we'll be approaching perihelion -- plunging toward the sun, in a manner of speaking -- at about the same pace as we're approaching the millennium-rollover date, which falls a few days before perihelion (just as the rollover itself falls some ten days after the winter solstice).

Complicated stuff! And while I was laboring my way through that paragraph the Earth did indeed pass through aphelion (assuming my watch is about right and the almanac knows what it's talking about) and "changed directions"; it's now starting to move closer to the sun again. And it's also starting to slow down in its orbital speed, which peaked at the moment of aphelion. Which means that between now and January the speed will be gradually decreasing -- we'll all be going down slow -- even as we also move from far out to far in.

Why isn't Far Out Day more widely known and
celebrated? Well, maybe because aphelion itself wasn't
known about before the invention of powerful telescopes.
That is, the knowledge came too late for it to be
incorporated into any of the major calendrical systems
which arose out of the major religions and then evolved
into the ones we use today.

Meanwhile I'll say that as I walked downtown, gusty
winds were blowing and big inky clouds were tumbling
overhead against an almost incandescently blue sky. Our
spell of fine weather -- some thirty-six hours straight
of it -- appears to be coming to an end. But most of
the rest of the country is roasting in one of the worst
heat waves in years, so best not to kvetch too much,
especially since the real roasting on a worldwide scale,
as we all know or certainly should know, is only just
beginning. (Do I repeat myself? Yes. Got to on
something so important. Will do it some more for sure
as this annal goes along.)

[+3]

Another jyze breakdown. But just a temporary one,
I do hope, since here it is groping its way back into
being, a new riff or series of riffs. In a motel five
hours south of J. City. At something like five in the
morning.

Z's asleep in the bed right next to me. She's
wearing a black sleep mask, a red utility "Talk Trash to
Me" T-shirt, and the blue "donut," as we're now calling
it, lying on her stomach with her head turned away from
me, her face pressing into the pillow which is cradled
in her left arm. A small patch of the small of her back
shows above the white sheet which is drawn around her
hips. She's all but kicked off her thin pink blanket;
it's bunched around her ankles. (One of the advantages
of being a night worker is you're much more likely to be
exposed to touchingly intimate scenes like this.
Several times in the past I've watched with fascination

-- or voyeured, could say -- as she began lightly
caressing her nipples in her sleep, with her fingertips
and/or the middle of her palms.)

     I took a long nap after we arrived at ten p.m.
Upon awakening, with Z sound asleep, I read yesterday
morning's papers -- well, no, first I stole barefoot,
slowly and carefully, across the asphalt parking area of
our motel to buy a can of root beer, it turned out, from
one of the three vending machines humming away --
glowing brightly too -- over by the office. A trio of
college students staggered by across the street,
laughing and goofing, but otherwise it was utterly quiet
out there even though we're near the center of town. In
here I can make out only the hum of our air conditioner
on the far side of the room, its overly strong fan
action intentionally blocked by one of our two red
armchairs (at Z's request I moved it over there). I'm
sitting in the other one.

     Jyze not by first light but by the soft silvery
lumens of the bedside lamp. (Now a truck's rumbling
outside and I think it's picking up trash. So first
light's probably not too far off. Or could the trash
crew have heard about Z's T-shirt and resolved to have a
little chat with her? -- Oh, and while outside I did
detect one other sound: a train whistle. And it sounded
familiar. More than likely it was the same continental
run I've been aboard several times myself while passing
through this area, or at least it came from the same
kind of diesel unit. And that means it's also the same
kind of whistle we hear back home on the hilltop when
the wind's blowing from the west or southwest.)

     Because we stopped twice so Z could loosen up her
back and a third time for dinner at a restaurant with
dismally slow service (and equally bad food), the trip
down took almost eight hours. That's a bit much even
when you have a Kat along to provide endless diversions.
She wrestles in the grass with Betty, reads aloud from
her latest volume of "The Babysitters," smears pink
bubblegum on her face, plays ferociously at the slap-
hands game and "scissors, paper, rock" with me and Z.

She's also in a surly mood part of the way and Betty has
to discipline her by threatening to reduce (by one buck
for each failure to obey) the twenty dollars she's been
promised as spending money for the fair tomorrow. But
most of the time she's a delight and I'm able to forget
how tired and cranky I'm feeling myself after working
downtown until five a.m. last night, four hours later
than usual.

Maybe two or three times in a year I'm hit by an
avalanche of scoping as heavy as this week's. In itself
it wouldn't have been all that bad except for the fact
that I needed to compress five nights' work into three,
since this trip is taking away the usual Friday
worknight and the Sunday safety-valve night. And I'll
still have to grind out the last seventy pages or so on
Monday night, or maybe late Sunday night if we make it
back early enough. Thursday night's grand jury turned
out to be a lot tougher than usual.

But I'll say right now it's been one of the best
weeks ever for G&Z. The scoping overload hasn't
affected that at all. Neither has the fight or Z's
gimpy back or G's gimpy foot and flu-relapse scare (now
at least seemingly over). Z's said it several times in
different ways, including in these words, and I quote
them with much pride: "I've never been so happy in my
whole life." She used to fear that saying such things
would provoke the anger of "the goddess" but now she's
decided this kind of fearful thinking itself might upset
a truly divine being; and I believe that, yes, she's
much better off seeing it that way, and so are we.

-- The naked jyzer. Right here. J-book balanced
across my right thigh and "ol' Pooshkin" nestled just
below the book's left edge, veiny and loosey-goosey from
the heat. Looking quite smug and deservedly so because
this week the old member has done itself proud. And so
has old Peaches. Was it all the result of our scholarly
study of "The Male Body"? I say no. I say it's the
love-wanga pure and simple.

-- Need some more sleep though. Z's tossing
restlessly -- it's well past her normal waking time.

[+1]

Same place a day later but maybe ninety minutes
earlier in the wee hours. Just a kwikjyze, a few
essentials. Again some hot and yet almost motionless
a.m. lovemaking (our farthest-south copulation ever). A
bus ride out to the country fair in the early afternoon,
and the fair lived up to its billing (mother of all the
sixties-born Renaissance Faires, set in an authentic
forest, winding paths lined on both sides, between huge
tree trunks and abundant shrubbery, with colorful tents
and banners and elaborate wooden booths of ancient
vintage). And the fair offered up all we'd hoped for
and more: a set of wedding rings, a wedding dress for Z,
a flower-girl dress for Kat (along with a pair of
gossamer blue angel wings), and a fabulous brass
Buddhist-inspired bell-bedecked good-fortune shaker
which we'll keep handy at all times all the way to the
wedding and, yes, why not cop to it, even beyond,
possibly even all the way to the end (and then we went
back and bought a second shaker, similar but not
identical, as a wedding present for Wei and Alison).
-- Oh, and I bought Z a primitive-copper "Sweetheart"
pendant and one saying "Celebrate" for both of us.
It was a hot day and Z (like a number of women --
though in percentage terms a very small number) was
inspired to doff her jersey and go bare-breasted in
traditional free-spirited sixties style. This all by
itself made the trip worthwhile. And at the same time
she was in truly zesty and vivacious form such as I've
rarely seen, and I've seen quite a lot of both (just
from her I'm saying).
Details on all this -- and more! -- much much more!
-- coming up in the next volume, I swear it. But now,
bed. And tomorrow at noon we start the long drive back.

BOOK C

[A Hitch in My Jyze]

                           11

        In "the jungle" more or less. Technically I think
this would qualify. On the prow of our hill, just
across the street from the grand old DC castle, sitting
atop a fence that borders the sidewalk and marks off the
start of the greenbelt which is also "the jungle." A
couple of feet to my left stands an impressively aged
wooden utility pole. A nearby dirt path leads down into
the shrubbery, and the shrubbery grows high enough here
that it blocks my view of the Asian quarter immediately
below, though not of the high bridge or the downtown
skyline or the bay or the mountains to the east.
        A fine spot for jyzing. And it's a fine day!
-- And it should be, because as of yesterday we're into
the "hot core." And the forecasters are saying summer
this year will likely extend a few weeks beyond the
norm, which means that by the time this jyzathon reaches
its first climax (that is, if all goes well, on our
wedding day), it should still be with us. (But even
with the weather odds turning in our favor, z still
thinks we should prepare for the worst with not just one
beach umbrella but a whole rack of them and they must be
cream-colored "to reflect the dignity of the occasion."
A big expense there! And what if "the worst" includes
high winds? Not to mention the truly worst: an
earthquake. Or nuclear war. Or early onset of
Y2Kalypse or the real apocalypse of global roasting.
        -- And I just noticed: from this spot I can peer
straight down the old "very very high road" downtown,
and floating at the far end of it, just about wide
enough (but not quite) to be mistaken for a skybridge at

                          191

roughly the twentieth-story level between the city's two tallest buildings, is that same iconic flying saucer spinning out the myth of eternal technological progress. Yes! -- And flags are flapping at the apexes of several big towers, I see, and construction cranes are perched here and there in the downtown aviary, and some skinny gray clouds are slowly advancing from left to right and partially obscuring the mountains, and the sun is about to emerge beneath the branches of the tree to my left.

And I sniff earth and flowers mingling with the usual city smells. And gulls are soaring, circling. And an Afrusan dude carrying a beat-up gym bag just emerged from a path leading up from the lower circles of "the jungle" and awkwardly stepped over the fence twenty feet down rather than pass close to me here where the path joins the sidewalk. And an Asiusan dude is sprawled across the front seat of a shiny orange low-rider car a few yards uphill watching the All-Star baseball game on a portable TV and the passenger door's open and I can hear the play-by-play. And farther uphill in the strip park a troop of Eurusan drifter dudes has pretty much taken over the area (under the stern gaze of the statuesque Philippine national hero) and that's why I'm down here now instead of up there.

"Hot core" summer. In this city it's a lot different from the season immediately preceding it and so it's very noticeable. It usually arrives abruptly, not gradually. And it's a joyous time because it's been awaited for so long. Here you get to wear summer clothes for only a short spell, so you'd better seize the opportunity -- that is, if you have any summer clothes. And if you don't, you can summerize what you do have by rolling up sleeves, baring midriff, chopping off pantlegs. And many do. Meanwhile the downtown sidewalks are crowded with tourists clutching maps and waits are much longer at coffee shops and restaurants. For a short period the draft emerging from the transit-tunnel entrances is relatively cool, not relatively warm, compared to the surface air. Doors and windows are propped open and you can hear interior sounds. Last

night, from the scope-office windows, I saw people
partying beneath the stars on a third-floor rooftop far
below, and in fact I'd never seen anyone partying there
before.

So what's going on in the world? Not much. Or
rather: not much up there at the requisite media feeding
levels. No new wars this week, no big new natural
disasters, no hot new scandals. At lower levels it's
just the same ol' same ol', of course: millions dying of
AIDS, rich-poor gap ever widening, a billion people
barely surviving, nukes straining for immediate release,
global roasting flaming ever higher, species extinctions
piling up, resources dwindling, oceans acidifying,
grasslands desertifying, aquifers drying up, so on and
so forth. (And lots of folks trying to do something
about all this too, and maybe even making some headway
here and there. Just yesterday the final installment in
the far-coast paper's big Y2K series left me feeling
even more confident we'll get through the rollover with
no more than minor disruptions, not just in this country
but worldwide. which is to say -- admittedly not for
the first time in these pages -- we might have to wait a
few more decades for the true apocalypse.)

-- And then twist the focus way down to our
personal lives. What's happening at home? Well, Z and
I are wriggling back into harness in the aftermath of
the country-fair road trip. Yesterday morning I
surprised her and also myself with some frisky doings in
bed despite exhaustion from the long drive on Sunday and
then working late that night. And she, though also worn
out from the drive, was pretty frisky herself (as she
quite often is in the morning). -- And it was good!
(Nonetheless she's decided to cancel the trip we'd been
planning to make to the eastern part of the state to see
Lee M. in late August. The hours on the road for that
would be about the same as those for the country fair
and she doesn't want to risk jouncing out her back again
at such a crucial time.)

The triumph of our new wedding rings -- eight bucks
apiece! -- lost some of its glitter when Leola pointed

out that copper rings, and especially cheap copper rings
-- even if they're authentic "primitive" copper and
even if they really do have strong antimicrobial powers
just as Vida the jewelry-maker assured us they do --
these rings of ours would, Leola said, before too many
weeks or months (more in winter, fewer in summer), turn
our fingers green. Now Z wants to line the inner loops
of the rings with a thin layer of silver. I said I'm
perfectly willing to go greenfinger as proof of my
devotion. Z said she's not. But what we'll actually do
remains to be seen. (And besides, the real triumph of
this trip for her was the public baring of her breasts
before a captive audience in the tens of thousands. No
one can take anything away from that. I asked Kat if
she was surprised to see her aunt do such a thing.
"Nothing she does," Kat cried, "can ever surprise me!")
     -- One other new wedding development. Z now has
hung my outfit and the tunic she'll be wearing as part
of hers on adjacent hangers facing flat against the
stacked bedroom storage cubes. "I realized it's time to
get serious about color coordination and things like
that" -- for her dress, she means. Kat and Betty will
both be wearing red or purple velvet outfits. Kat
modeled hers for most of Saturday afternoon at the fair
and looked ravishing in it. (I also should mention that
my hemp pants arrived in the mail late last week and
look about as expected.) (Will I ever wear them a
second time? I doubt it.)
     Wei and Alison's countdown, meanwhile, has shrunk
to ten days. Unbeknownst to them Z has now taken to
shaking twice daily on their behalf the brass Tibetan-
style "good fortune" noisemaker we bought for them at
the fair (we'll be presenting it to them at the wedding
itself). She's so pleased with the way our own
preparations are going that she's saying we can hold off
on deploying our very similar G&Z shaker until after
W&A's big day.
     -- And I see more clouds shouldering in. And some
majestic late shafts of sun are angling down out over
(and onto) the water, looking like huge escalators or

ramps extending from a mother ship. "This is it, Earth
people, the rapture! Last chance! Our forecasters tell
us that by the time of our next visit this planet of
yours will be a cinder!"

     -- And I've been sitting on this wooden post far
too long. Now I too am thinking about how backs go out
and you must wear big blue "donuts" when they do.
(Meanwhile as I spin around I notice the parking lots
have emptied out at the castle and also up by the strip
park. All three were full when I arrived here. In
today's jyze I've taken little notice of the traffic
sounds or fumes or flashy glints but traffic has been
the main thing happening around here for the whole
session. In fact I could make that a general statement
for the hilltop as a whole for most hours of most days.
In just three months the workforce for the dot-com
that's taken over all but the basement and first floor
of the castle has grown from zero to the full complement
of two thousand. The hood is going fast.)

                        [+2]

     Well but ain't this a trip! Such a raucous
cacophonous jumble: a bagpipe, a tuba ("Take me out to
the ballpark"), rumble of bus engines, a Dixieland band,
music from radios and boom boxes, scores of voices,
horns, barkers, clatter of hundreds of feet marching by
just an arm's length away at my upper visual periphery.
So much is going on they all ignore me down here (except
for one woman who said, "Hello, you," tapping my knee
with her toe, and I can't think who she is -- works at
one of the downtown chain bookstores maybe).

     -- It's opening day for the most expensive stadium
ever built anywhere. The "Taj Ma Ball," some are
calling it. "Ballpark of the Next Millennium." On the
radio at home I heard about huge crowds milling outside
the gates and that was about three hours before game
time. Now about two hours later I'm sitting on the
sidewalk by one of the team store's show windows, my

back pressing against glazed bricks that are part of
the stadium facade, and the place is a total madhouse.
     Crammed into my bag here are a dozen ad-packed
"collector's items" that hawkers are handing out for
free. Scalpers are everywhere (two hundred bucks seems
to be the going gouge) and so are fans frantically
seeking tickets, many carrying hand-lettered signs: "I
need two!" (Here's a flatbed truck creeping by with a
working rock band aboard -- whew, loud!) (And planes
are circling up there towing messages -- I've never
before seen so many in a single air theater, as it were.
As I walked in from the hill I counted five.)
     (It's getting even more chaotic. A guy I rode the
ferries with years ago just came up -- Bart. I'd
forgotten his name. Khaki shorts, T-shirt, curly red
hair, Hollywood shades. "I'm pumped!" He surfed the
internet to score his ticket, seventy-five bucks.)
     -- Sheez. Help! I'm being trampled! I'm now
pressing myself against the base of the window
lengthwise, leaning back against a foot-wide brick
column that extends out from the wall. The thighs of
Jyze City are parading by. The feet. The footwear.
The hairy calves. (And inside the window stand row upon
row of painted and autographed baseballs, individually
spotlit like huge diamonds and probably worth millions.)
     -- Meanwhile a bit of amusing news. Just as Z
starts hinting I ought to check with Evie about how the
divorce is coming along, a letter arrives from Evie's
office. As I open it I'm wondering: does this mean
they've found Lady S? Then I unfold a legal document
referring to a court date for a criminal trial. Holy
shit, they've nailed me! -- But no, it turns out Evie's
office has mistakenly sent me someone else's notice. So
naturally the question arises: what did they mean to
send me, if anything? Tomorrow I'll stop by there and
try to find out.
     (It's not letting up. Toss a mariachi band into
the mix. Baby carriages. Huge motorcycles revving on
the sidewalk. Fanny packs galore and belly packs too.
Oh what a spectacle, baseball fans!)

[A Hitch in My Jyze]

     -- It's a good thing, I'm thinking, that I'm
feeling good. My sympathetic back pain (actually caused
by, I suspect, the deep bucket seats in Betty's car) is
gone, and so are my various other afflictions of recent
weeks, including most of the right-groin pain, which
this jyze might not even have mentioned before (for
shame!). And Z's back seems much better, although she's
still wearing the "blue donut" in bed per doctor's
orders. (The past couple of nights, I'm reminded, we've
had some lively pillow talk, about Aida and Kirk and
"tough love," among other things -- but what am I
thinking of, I can't go into stuff like that now. I'm
due to meet Z in roughly thirty minutes about six blocks
from here. So later maybe. Or not.)
     A steel band too. Hot-dog smells. Peanuts and
popcorn (but no crackerjacks in sight so far). Souvenir
programs. Jerseys bearing player names and numbers on
highly unathletic-looking bodies. Dozens of mouths
munching seemingly almost in sync. Excited kids in
partial or complete miniature baseball uniforms.
"That's the one I want!" -- Some guy lunging at the
window and pointing at a particular autographed bat in
there, meanwhile kicking my foot. ("How's the weather
down there?") I can say this: it's far, far, far too
noisy to be able to hear "the roar of the crowd."
     I just inherited a special ballpark edition of this
morning's paper, heedlessly tossed by someone. It
flapped down from nowhere like a giant origami bird.
The effrontery! Snuff the jyzer! Paper him over!
     (Helicopters are thwacking, though, and I can hear
and see them. Dueling TV networks. Even the nationals
are here. The sports big-wigs being carted about town
for days. The limos of unprecedented length. And ooh
lots and lots of cops -- but just another minor warm-up,
everyone's saying, for this fall's anti-WTO protests.
"Anybody have tickets? Tickets? Help, tickets?")
                    *   *
     Hideaway. A kwikjyze postscript far, far, far
(only about nine blocks actually, but the walls here are
thick) -- far from the madding madding madding...(whose

197

roar I finally did hear but not until I was about to
open the street door here).

Z was looking exceptionally fine in her long black
hemp skirt with the slit up the front and the scoopneck
white top and the colorful Guatemala jacket, all among
my favorites, as she swung into Z-geist ("Ooh, hey, you
with anybody, Big Guy?"). We discussed the five topics
on her agenda -- scrawled out on a yellow five-by-seven
notecard in standard Z fashion -- as we walked to the
ballpark so she could get a firsthand look at the over-
the-top craziness I'd been telling her about:

(1) Even though Sera's not too happy about the
wedding arrangements, her husband Dak is insisting on
providing a roasted pig for the reception (and I agreed
-- as maybe Z thought I wouldn't -- we can't say no).

(2) Vida said on the phone she can line the rings
with silver, though she's never done it before, and Z's
willing to pay the difference in cost for both of us
(and so I agreed to this one too -- why the hell not --
though we'll no longer be able to boast we scored our
wedding rings for under ten bucks apiece, tax included).

(3) Wei has requested use of a shelf in our fridge
to store bags of cherries destined for W&A's reception
(and of course I assented to this but advised wait-and-
see on the actual shelf cleanout since that job would
fall to me and would be a fairly big one requiring major
mutual decisions on what should be tossed).

(4) Z wants me to take a quiz which she took
herself for some "ethical-values group" (and once again
I agreed to do it, with the quid pro quo that she'd
promise to listen to my "ethical critique of the values
of the outfit that created the quiz" (if, that is, I
have one, and I suspect I will), and she said fine).

(5) Lorraine, Z's naturopath, pointed out that Z's
sleep problems stem from not just wedding tensions but
also the fact that she's essentially been on probation
for the past year at work while waiting to see if her
new job will become permanent (and I definitely agreed
on this one -- then joshed her, Z, that being engaged to
marry is a form of probation too, sort of, especially

after her previous disastrous experience with it, and
for my saying this she exacted revenge by not letting me
hold her hand for a whole block).

And why not, while jyze is at it, a few words about
the pillow talk I skipped over before. In a nutshell I
learned Aida still regards Z as a "zole [soul] sister"
and Z is much touched by this as always, perhaps even
more so as she comes to realize that in some areas their
differences are far greater than she ever suspected.
When Z mentioned the women going topless at the country
fair, Aida immediately objected, "What about Kat!" Z
decided not to reveal she herself had been one of those
women. Yet she's told several other people about it at
work. Her comment to me: "Aida doesn't really get my
wild-woman side. She never has." (She's not telling
the Confucianly proper June either -- though both June
and Aida are sure to learn eventually.) (To me it's
hard to see how Z could think of someone with such a
prominent prudish streak as a "zole sister." But it's
also hard to see how Aida, a drama-department/theater
person, could be so conservative in certain social
respects. I often feel it's a role she's playing which
could profit from a lot more rehearsal time. Of course
staunchly old-church moral is the way her whole family
is, but -- no, I still don't get it.)

Also I learned -- confidentially -- the estimable
Kirk is planning to go back to school in pursuit of a
Ph.D. in economics. A cousin of his who's hit it big in
cyberstock has set up an education fund for which anyone
in the extended family qualifies, age being no barrier.
("It's like hitting the lottery," said Aida. "Looks
like white privilege to me," said Z.) For Aida this new
plan puts the whole relationship in jeopardy, because
she's sure Kirk will choose to attend some snooty
eastern school and Aida balks at the prospect of leaving
her extended family behind, even if only temporarily. Z
advised her that if she's really serious about Kirk she
can find a way, but Aida still seemed doubtful. (And
last week Aida had a long talk with Kirk's older brother,
Ed, the congressman, on the day before he went in for

his heart-valve operation. Aida clearly enjoys taking a
turn or two in the political limelight -- and this is a
much more expectable outcome of her drama orientation,
I'd say.)

     The other major pillow-talk topic was "tough love."
I was telling Z I thought maybe she was again being
overly strict with Kat, especially when upbraiding her
and warning her to expect a "Filipino pinch" because she
wasn't obeying her mother. Z agreed she really
shouldn't be acting on Betty's behalf in that way --
making Betty look bad, as if she's unable to handle Kat
on her own -- but says she sometimes just can't help
herself. "My daddy was super strict and now I feel
showing respect to your parents is crucially important.
I believe in tough love with kids." I told her I
thought she might do better to take Kat aside and talk
with her privately about such things rather than
castigating her in front of others. (She never does it
for long, but she does do it fairly often. It's become
part of her basic persona with Kat: the loving-but-tough
auntie. Yet she doesn't really want to be viewed that
way and often expresses dissatisfaction with it. I also
suggested she try to be physically closer with Kat,
touching, embracing -- as Betty certainly is -- but Z
finds this hard, just as she does with me unless we're
in bed or some other private place. She just didn't
grow up that way. And she loves to step into that hard-
ass Centropolis persona. At heart, though, she's a
teddybear -- just don't ever tell her I said so.)

                        [+2]

     Now the far-north bookstore. Z and I are out
living it up on a Saturday evening.
     She's off browsing somewhere. For this abbreviated
jyze session I've been granted, after some tough
negotiations, until seven-thirty, a bit more than half
an hour from now. (I've already blown almost that much
time on scanning today's paper while gobbling down a

plate of pork fried rice.) We've come from an afternoon
of Scrabble with Olwen, who's not only Z's longtime
friend but also the certified Sufi minister who'll be
marrying us, and her son Trent, who will assist with the
ceremony. (In an amazing come-from-behind burst Z won
by two points over me and four over Olwen, with Trent
trailing badly, which was only fitting since he skunked
us all last time.)
        And the rain's back. What bizarre weather this
year. On the night of the ballpark fireworks a big
storm rolled in to provide some celestial augmentation,
thunder rumbling and cracking, seeming to shake the
scope building as I worked, and lightning flashed
spectacularly all night long outside the windows at home
-- first time I've seen anything like that since we
moved to the hill -- in fact since my move with Lady U
to Jyze City. And a new long-range forecast is out,
even more authoritative, confirming earlier predictions
of another La Nina winter, extremely wet and dark and
cold. In its unusualness, anyway, it seems apt for the
millennial-rollover period. But the effect on an
outdoor wedding in late September might not be so good,
and that was one of the major topics of conversation
during the Scrabble game. Maybe I'll need to empty out
my cedar boxes so we can use them to shelter the candles
during the ceremony -- seven candles for the seven other
spiritual traditions recognized in a Sufi rite (at least
as I understand it so far, and that's admittedly not
very far).
        -- As the music starts up here. A trio, sounds
like (the stage is around the corner). Not bad.
Rocking the old bookstore. "Live R&B with dancing."
This is the other reason we came here tonight, besides
the new load of used whodunits Z was hoping to score.
        But there's big personal news. I'd been thinking
Lady S might've raised some objection to the dissolution
-- why else would Evie be trying to contact me before
the end of the mandatory waiting period? -- but it turns
out the waiting period was shorter than I had recalled.
Evie's paralegal, Gina, apologized profusely for the

mix-up that had me receiving the notice for one Thanh
T.'s trial on a car-prowling charge, as it turned out,
and she located the paper I was supposed to receive
saying the search had been unsuccessful, which by my
lights means it was successful, and therefore we can now
go before a judge and complete the "disso process," as
Evie calls it. Barring some last-minute glitch, that
will be happening this coming Tuesday afternoon.

        Z was delighted with the news when I passed it on
to her as she pedaled on a stationary bicycle at the
WOC. "You want to celebrate? Aren't you excited?"
Mainly relieved, I said -- and let's hold off on the
celebrating until the disso's official.

        -- Wow, the time's gone by fast. Z sneaks up from
behind and whispers in my ear, "You've got exactly two
more minutes, Mr. Jyzeslinger." (The trio now has
conjured a silver-throated warbler -- very fine. And
very sultry. And sounding more than a little like a
certain Zoelie B. when Zoelie B. warbles, which she
still does do once in a while, mostly when she slips in
to wake me up on weekend afternoons.) (And lately she's
talked about joining a class on jazz singing with Leola
"after things settle down," meaning maybe next summer.)

        And I'll have to save the other stuff, of which
there's plenty, for later, possibly tomorrow. The
north-hill grocery closes at nine; that's the real
reason for the squeeze here. And getting to north hill
could pose some navigation problems because "The Bite of
J-town" is going down at the nearby fairgrounds tonight
and the size of the crowd for that could double or
triple the one for the ball game the other day.

[+1]

        -- So there I was quietly licking my vanilla yogurt
cone in a corner at downtown chain burgers when a riot
broke out. Luckily I was sitting near the back door and
was able to exit that way along with scores of other
customers as the tac squad rushed in through the front

202

entrance. They came on fast in ranks of two, all in
blue uniforms and black helmets, moving bent over and
low to the ground with shields raised high, similar to a
grimly determined football team charging down the runway
onto the field.

The streets outside were thronged with young folks,
mostly non-Cawk, and cops, mostly Cawk. Patrol cars
were zooming up, red and blue lights flashing; the
equestrian squad was galloping up one main street and a
bicycle squad was zipping down another. Kids were
running off in all directions, in a few instances with
cops in hot pursuit -- but luckily not in the direction
I found myself going. Traffic had come to a standstill
as the crowds swarmed into the streets.

I don't know for sure what caused it. As a bunch
of us were looking back at the scene from a block away
one guy said someone had jumped over the counter and
taken a swing at the manager, but then someone else said
a pair of plainclothes cops had tried to bust a dude
waiting in line who had assaulted someone outside "The
Bite" ten blocks to the north, and the lines at the
burger joint were unusually long and tempers fraying
anyway. And the young folks were congregating downtown,
as they always wind up doing on "Bite" weekend (which is
basically a promotion for posh restaurants), because the
fairgrounds, where admission is usually free, charges a
steep entrance fee for "The Bite" and most of the kids
can't afford it and so they hang around outside the
grounds until high spirits and/or old feuds cause some
sort of incident and the cops start cracking down,
chasing them southward into the downtown core and then
maybe farther into the south end of town where most of
them live and some possibly are our neighbors.

I'd already finished my night's scoping and was
taking a break before setting up somewhere outdoors to
follow up on yesterday's bookstore entry. Now I've
returned to the scope-office conference room just to be
on the safe side, and also because it was a little
chilly out there and I left my jacket at home today.

This is the fourth or fifth of these minor "riots"

I've witnessed in this city. The veteran. Didn't panic
at all -- even stepped back inside for a moment to help
a couple of smaller kids who went sprawling when some
big guys thundered by. But even so I was worried: I've
never been so close to ground zero before and this was
potentially the most explosive of the incidents I've
been present for simply because so many people were
involved in such a small enclosed area.

So jyze was "out in the world" with a vengeance
this time. And the incident left the jyzer himself, no
doubt like lots of others involved, itching to see a
little vengeance wreaked upon a system whose injustices
make racially related blowups like this one almost
inevitable not to mention predictable. I mean, the tac
squad was already in place nearby just itching to launch
an operation -- or maybe a better word would be ambush.

Oddly enough I'd been intending yesterday to note
the big economic news of the day: our local software
megacorp became the first in history to have its stock
valued at half a trillion dollars. What's more, the
personal wealth of its CEO reached a hundred billion
dollars. That latter figure is equal to the combined
net worth of a good chunk of the country's population --
is it forty percent? Sixty? Either way it's obscene.
And yet it's accepted by society as a whole almost
without a peep of protest. (And in the papers today
another story about the outrageous mansion-building
shenanigans of our local plutocrats. This time one has
filed suit against a neighbor plutocrat because dust
rising from the latter's construction of a twenty-four-
car underground garage for his mansion has made the
former's Olympic-size swimming pool "unusable.")

Meanwhile the nation's economic expansion rolls on,
now in its record ninth year. For the last two months
inflation has been zero. No one can explain why
everything's going so well economically at this
particular time. Pundits generally credit the delayed
effect of computerization and the growth of the internet
and this analysis seems to be achieving some sort of
acceptance, but it obviously doesn't go far enough. And

so I innocently ask: why is it economists don't want to
chalk it up to the worldwide U.S. economic hegemony
that's resulted from the collapse of its only superpower
rival more or less exactly nine years ago? Might that
not have something to do with it?

(And how about this. Despite all its wealth and
power this country ranks only third in quality of life
according to a UN agency's latest research, with
woebegone Japan a fraction of a point back in fourth
place. And the first two? Canada and -- Norway!)

In another odd development, on Friday Gene, the
former Air Force pilot at the WOC, offered to fly Z and
me down the coast to our honeymoon resort in his private
plane. I believe this is the first time I've ever had a
chance to fly in a private plane. Gene's some sort of
stockbroker now and like lots of others in his field
he's been raking it in big-time recently. (Is this not
just a speculative bubble we're in? You hear it
constantly argued that it is but you also hear that same
argument constantly pooh-poohed from all sides,
especially by people who have a lot of skin in the game.
There's no way to know the truth, of course. Nothing
unusual here. Except for me, that is: because this time
I'm part of it. I'm benefiting from it directly in my
deep-reserves account. "Inherited wealth." And if the
bubble pops I'll be hurt for sure. -- Yes, but then
I'll just be back to the old status quo, which always
worked fine for me, so what do I really have to moan
about? Absolutely nothing, that's correct. In terms of
my personal financial life I'm talking, but of course
it's equally true pretty much across the board owing to
my status as a lifetime member of Team USA and the Pink
Privilege Club (male branch), among other causes.)

I thanked Gene but said I didn't think Z would go
for the idea and mimed wide-eyed, hand-waving panic.
"Well, we could blindfold her," he joked. "You'd have
to blindfold me too," I said. And though strictly
speaking this may not be true, it's close enough.

And while on the subject, today's wedding update
includes a relapse on number of attendees (quickly

overcome) and a new decision on clothes. Z was so
bothered by Sera's little shudders of "rejection dismay"
when Z was talking with her and Aida about the reception
that she decided to ask me if I'd agree to restoring the
wedding group to its original projected size. She did
this with some trepidation, probably because, again,
she'd come to believe her own cover story which fingers
me as the culprit who insisted on the limitation. I
said I'd go along with whatever she wanted, but wasn't
she forgetting all the headaches she'd had earlier in
trying to limit the size of that larger group? If she
let Sera back in, what would she tell the senior D.'s,
Jess and Gwen, Wei and Alison, Gerry and Leola, Paz and
Tobey, Lee M. and his wife -- on and on and on. A few
hours later she'd decided to stick with the smaller
group -- "And this is absolutely the last relapse."

    I like what she's doing with her wedding outfit.
Suddenly she's afraid the red velvet dress would look a
little too froufrou or chichi or just plain predictable.
She takes great pride in being thought a bit or even
quite a bit provocative and outrageous -- witness the
improvised topless act of extended duration at the
country fair, among a good many similar capers over the
years. So now she's decided she wants to wear her
smashing Guatemalan jacket over the dress. And when
Olwen said the ceremony would provide little of
substance for Kat to do, Z felt confirmed in this
decision.

    For a day she was intending to go with Leola and
Aida to pick up the dress at a fair at a certain upscale
mall way out in the eastern burbs, but then she learned
that this fair charges a thirty-five-buck entrance fee.
Now she's decided to do it by mail. Z's new watchwords
for the wedding are "simple, easy, relaxed, and cheap --
because what's the point if we don't both enjoy it?" (I
definitely appreciate this approach -- but I still
suspect lots of frenzied days lie ahead. As Wei put it
on the phone to Z today, "I'm learning I'll have
excellent grounds to feel extreme sympathy for you in
about eight weeks" -- that is, when our countdown will

reach the same stage his and Alison's is in now. -- But
they did find room in their fridge for the bags of
cherries, meaning my decision to delay cleaning out our
bottom shelf was a wise one, impressing Z with my
"Norski sagacity.") -- And I intend to apply that same
trait to her decision that yes, I should go ahead and
empty out the two cedar boxes (one of tools, the other
of old clothes) for use in the ceremony in Olwen's
backyard. (And just tonight I started reading the book
of Sufi love poetry I gave Z a month or two back --
Olwen suggested we pick out a couple of poems for her to
read at the ceremony. Some real good stuff in there I
gotta say. And therefore: more hard choices ahead.

     Oh, and the license. Wei went in to score his and
was told that, even though Alison had signed the form
he'd brought with him, no license will be issued unless
both parties are present at the licensing office; and
yet if you apply by mail only signatures are necessary
(that makes sense all right). How much it costs we
don't know yet, because Z forgot to ask him. But
already my task is simplified. (At the same time I'm
starting to feel anxious about choosing the music. I
heard Z mention to Aida on the phone that I'm the go-to
guy on music and it suddenly became much more real for
me. -- And I'm wondering: does brother Rob's employee
discount apply at the company's music outlets?)

     (This is going down at a corner desk in the
conference room, by the way. The desk showed up here
unexpectedly last week, displacing my computer cart to
another corner. No one bothered to leave me a note
explaining the change or any of several other similar
shifts and revamps not worth specifying here, except to
say this is all so typical I can scarcely get upset
about it, even though I'm pretty sure I'd like to or at
least should. But to hell with it.)

     Today Z came home in tears from a farewell party
for the rapidly deteriorating Nadine. (It was too early
in the afternoon for me to attend and I don't know
Nadine anyway. But Alison was there with Wei -- another
of Nadine's former coworkers -- and so I felt bad

regardless.) But Z also said she was newly appreciating
our relationship. "The truth is I was happy before I
met you -- now I'm euphoric." And then later: "I didn't
just settle for you, you know. You're IT! You're THE
ONE AND ONLY!!!" -- Aida, in trying to figure out
what's happening between her and Kirk, asked Z what it
was that made the two of us get along so well and how
could she, Z, be sure it was for real. Z told me all
she could say was, "It's a miracle." And: "I couldn't
tell her what the secret is because I don't know.
-- But the good sex helps for sure, I did say that. But
no details!" (It's been continuing good sex, I want to
note. And I say she's right: it's all miraculous pretty
much across the board, and beyond that nothing truly
useful can be said about it, though I'm sure jyze will
keep trying to come up with something, or even many
things.) -- Aida has fears about Kirk, Z says, because
he's still involved in a divorce, his wife's calling and
trying to reconcile with him, he'll soon be going off to
grad school and -- surprise, surprise -- he "doesn't
want to commit." He's sleeping over most of the time
when Charles is with his dad but not when Charles is
home with Aida, and that too is making things awkward.

[+1]

     Finally a night warm enough to hit the 203 balcony.
And dry enough -- I can even see stars up there. And
scattered yellow lights on the hill on the far side of
the valley -- streetlights, I suppose, because they're
all the same color, except for a few. And here's our
very own streetlight maybe forty-five or fifty feet
almost due east and about thirty degrees up from where I
sit, its reflections glistening on the trolley power
wires. In the row of old two-story houses and newer
two- and three-story apartment buildings on the block
across the street not a single light shows. Only
occasionally does a car pass below, maybe once every
seven or eight minutes on average, and often at high

208

speed. Once in a while I can hear individual engines --
big trucks mostly, sounds like -- on the cross-lake
freeway hundreds of feet down in the valley to the east.

     This is the first time I've sat out here in my old
redwood chair. I'm finding the accommodations a little
tight, with the sliding glass door to Z's room just
inches to my right and one of the four big flowerboxes
lining the railing even fewer inches to my left, the
starlike red blooms of one of the hardy fuchsias planted
there leaning over to brush the top of the J-book cover.
Another flowerbox rests at my back (featuring mostly
geraniums, marigolds, and lobelia) and the four-foot-
tall potted evergreen stands directly in front of me,
leaving barely enough room to squeeze my splayed-out
feet in between the chair and the pot. This balcony is
no more than eight feet long and maybe three and a half
feet wide and the chair faces sideways, not out toward
the street and the view, because only this way is there
enough legroom to sit in it at all. A globe light the
size of a bowling ball is attached to the wall between
Z's door and the living-room door and illuminates the
area quite well, including these J-book pages.

     When I arrived home tonight I found the apartment
door cracked open and chained from inside. I had to
call Z's name maybe eight or ten times, turning up the
volume a notch for each, before I was able to rouse her.
Our bed's only about ten feet from the entranceway and
the bedroom door was partially open -- I could see a
sliver of it through the gap permitted by the chain --
but she had her earplugs in and the air cleaner turned
up high, specifically to block out noise. The last
"ZOELIE!!!!!" was probably loud enough to wake everyone
in the building if not a good chunk of the block.

     When she finally came over to the door she was
wearing just her blue "hula hoop" (her preferred term
for it these days). And wotta lovely sight she was!
And laughing like crazy even as she exuded apologies.
She vowed to put up a couple of signs reminding herself
to take the chain off the door when she goes to bed.
It's surprising I haven't been locked out before. In

fact, that it would happen now might even be a sign
she's feeling more comfortable living here. After last
year's break-in across the hall (in unit 202) she feared
human intruders as well as auto fumes spiraling up the
staircase from the garage and so refused to leave our
door to the hall cracked open -- secured only with the
chain -- even on the hottest nights.)

     (The hood is gentrifying all right, but it can
still be a pretty wild place. One of the women on the
bus tonight was talking about a guy who got shot outside
her work-release house this past weekend -- and that's a
few doors south on the street immediately behind us.
(The cause of the shooting -- no surprise here -- was
rivalry for a woman locked up inside.)   June's decided
she'll look for her in-city condo over in the lower
north-hill area on the far side of downtown because, she
says, "There are still too many poor people where you
live." -- And this reminds me: a story in tonight's
paper reveals that our average monthly hilltop rent now
falls only ten bucks short of that for the city as a
whole, which is a big jump from what it was when we
moved in. And I'll mention too I haven't heard the
next-door dog barking at night since Z anonymously sent
its owner a copy of the city regulations about animal
noise a few weeks back.)

     -- And this is another interesting day. It's the
last day I'll be a married man after a run so long it
amounts to three-quarters of my adult life. (I'll admit
that lately I've been neglecting to add the proviso:
unless Lady S really did go through with divorcing me
before as she said she would and I simply wasn't
notified.) In a more important sense it's the end of an
even longer run -- say ninety-plus percent of my adult
life -- that began the day I first met Lady S when I was
just a few months out of college. True, for most of
those years I was with others, but over the long run the
relationship with her has proven to be the most
important of them all -- up until now. So I raise my
glass in a toast to it (or bottle rather -- of grape
juice). An amazing woman, that Lady S. And yes, I'm

serious.

     Then there's Zoelie B. Without Lady S no Zoelie B., I'm quite sure. And without Zoelie B. no life at all (life as in "get a life") for me here in my Third Glennarian Stage and certainly no crowning love glory (sorry for spewing such sappy stuff but not for believing in this hitch-up as I absolutely do -- and now I'm unleashing declarations of absoluteness!). (If my math is right, I'll be unmarried for a grand total of sixty-seven days before starting in on the next one. In her nightly note left on my armchair inside, held in place as always by the "I lub you!" rock, Z asks how we're going to celebrate my new status tomorrow evening -- but also says she doesn't want to miss her block-watch meeting. Probably I won't really be in much of a celebrating mood anyway. I imagine I'll be feeling sad even if also plenty relieved.)

     And Z's saying a new era is underway. "We're starting the countdown to putting a man and a woman on the moon -- our honeymoon." That's the new voicemail message she's running on our phone. (It's alluding to our "Marriage: Journey into Unknown Worlds" wedding theme, and also to another anniversary coming up tomorrow: the thirtieth for the first moonwalk.) And she and several of her friends at work have formed a "shape-up pool": each will kick in five bucks a week and the one who loses the highest percentage of weight by September 20th will win the whole pot. Not that Z has any chance at the prize -- she's already almost on the edge of scrawny. But she's determined to take off a pound or two or even three. So I've now assumed the added prenuptial duty of tackling her if I see her reaching for a bag of cookies or opening the freezer door and pulling out the Neapolitan soy ice cream.

     -- And I see the sky's starting to turn a light indigo blue on the eastern horizon. Or above it, rather, since a band of faintly orange and brown haze on the horizon itself is blocking out the mountains whose silhouettes would otherwise be visible. And traffic's picking up too, not so much on our street here but on

the freeways. Yet the stars are still visible in
sectors where the streetlight glare can't reach, and our
block still sleeps (or maybe lies there awake in the
dark wondering who the heck that was who woke them up a
few hours ago by yelling "ZOELIE!!!!!" or "SOLELY!!!!!"
or "SLOWLY!!!!!" or whatever the heck it was).

The last full day of the Lady S era (technically
speaking) was a fine one. Beautiful weather. Another
splendid five a.m. round of rutting which Z said she was
flashing back to all day long, as I was also (but will I
still be such a stud when she stops wearing her "hula
hoop"? Seriously. When I no longer have that bizarre
obstacle forcing me to bust some moves I'd probably
never dream of busting otherwise?). Also I did her a
big favor and hauled some disks for her malfunctioning
computer up to the repair shop in her old north-end hood
(her machine's more than five years old, ancient by
computer standards, so the repair people wanted to see
all the software she's using). And then I made her a
splendid -- sorry but I just can't be modest about it --
yes, a splendid altered postcard and left it in the
usual place on her pillow before hustling down to meet
her at the WOC. After she left for home I put in a long
workout and jac soak and then rearranged parts of my
office for a couple of hours before heading home myself.

(Last week I met Caleb, the twenty-something
Eurusan -- a dot-com worker but of course -- who shares
the next-door unit, the same 202 mentioned earlier,
with, it turns out, his girlfriend, not the guy I saw
him with before. Their cat, Doobie, is crouching on the
edge of their balcony at my back right now. Gray and
white, long quivering whiskers, killer eyes. Doobie's
existence has forced us to give up our plans to make a
bird haven of our own balcony, with the new red
"Filipino duplex" birdhouse at its center. Doobie
could easily jump over here. -- Caleb was standing
right where Doobie is now, by the way, when I met him.
And I must say: he could jump over here too. Yeek! A
techie invader! -- No, in truth I was surprised to find
he seemed to be a passably normal and even somewhat

friendly person. The few other times I've seen him down
in the garage -- not knowing for sure who he was -- he
was distinctly unfriendly in what I would call typical
techie fashion, with glowering squinty red eyes as if he
hadn't been outdoors in weeks. -- But yes, I'll admit
that last phrase could just as easily, or probably more
easily, apply to a nightscoper such as myself. -- And
we're dying out, my nightscoper kind, and his dot-com
kind sure as hell isn't, and just how does all that, I
ask, in the long run, compute?)

     -- Some lovely blues out there now and I'm noticing
the big evergreen across the street so prototypically
(for the region) silhouetted against them. -- And I'm
thinking how happy I am to be able to jyze like this --
or just say to have my life going along like this. How
lucky I am! How much I want to make the most of this
blessed -- what? -- but yes! -- turn in my life. Wholly
unexpected opening. Whatever it is, it's here and it's
real. It's happening. So go with it. Ride it. Do
whatever it takes. Don't look back, or at least not
anytime soon. (Other than, that is, the day or two per
J-week, or once in a great while three days per J-week,
when it's required by this year's TJM jyze protocol.)

12

     Now the 203 balcony in the afternoon. Exact same
spot as the last installment. But this round just a
brief holding action. Heavy work night awaits.
However: the deed is done. For the first time in many a
moon I'm an unmarried man. Or I should say: an
unmarried man for sure.
     The street. A bus. The mountains. Birds. Haze.

The kids playing on the sidewalk (just yesterday Z said
their racial mix reminded her of her own childhood days,
and she immediately burst into tears. She's so labile!
-- Which of course is just another way of saying she
feels things deeply and often expresses those feelings
openly and directly and powerfully and movingly. And
these are among her very finest qualities even if not
always the easiest to deal with. -- Just like my
mother, yup.)

So: Evie the lawyer was "nervous" because the judge
is "such a Mormon." But he asked me no questions and
didn't seem to notice how I was dressed (in white shirt,
brown "slacks," and courtin' shoes) or the fact that I
was bathed in sweat (it was a very warm day!). Nor was
he bothered that Evie had left an important affidavit in
her office. "Drop it by the next time you're in the
neighborhood," he kindly suggested. And that was pretty
much it. The whole hearing took no longer than five
minutes. Back out in the hall I wrote Evie a check for
$650 and we went our separate ways. As was only
appropriate on "Disso Day."

Whoooee!

A few minutes ago I put the finishing touches on a
"King of Jyze" card for Z. Jyze is just so darn much
fun. I'd almost forgotten this wondrous truth during
the four-month downtime. Anyhow -- gotta go.

[+2]

Down in the valley -- but not all the way down.
The gulch a block south of here is as low as it gets,
right at the northern base of our hill, with the high
bridge suspended far above. I'm sitting on a fencepost
at a woebegone and yet most excellent corner, facing
straight toward the hill.

It's all green up there from this angle, I can now
report, except for that same orange-brick DC castle in
all its magnificent sixteen-story many-setbacked
complexity (and faintly visible almost directly above it

right now, a semiglobe of moon seemingly slicing through
a pure blue sky, sort of like the hull of a boat or
maybe a water-skiing disk seen from underwater).

This fencepost here is even smaller and less
comfortable than the one I got to know intimately one J-
week back. But it beats the immediate alternatives. I
was hoping to hunker down on the front stoop of the food
bank a hundred yards north of here but the homeless guy
with the growly dog and the grossly overloaded shopping
cart is once again claiming that spot.

So this will be another quick holding action. It's
proving to be an unusually hard pull of a workweek and I
also want to stop at a downtown emporium (or more than
one if necessary) to pick up a pair of khakis to wear to
Wei and Alison's wedding tomorrow. (It's to go down
outdoors in their local "pea patch" community garden and
the forecast is for a sunny day, lightly breezy, not too
warm. But the ceremony will be fairly lengthy: a
Catholic priest will be doing the honors and his words
will by and large be the standard ones, we're told, and
then W&A will be adding some of their own, scripted by
them in advance. Then at the end Z and I are planning
to give a good long shake to the Tibetan "good fortune"
noisemaker before handing it over to the newly wedded
pair -- who presumably will find some use for it
eventually if not right away. -- But as much as we will
for ours? Or perhaps more? Stay tuned, jyze fans!)

So far being certifiably single is working out okay
for me except for one thing: as is probably the case
with many other guys in my shoes I'm finding it tougher
to get laid. But then yesterday Z was obsessing over
her big job interview, and this morning she was
perseverating over Big H "prodomo" rumbles, and in
neither case did I have the gumption or the energy or
the raging need to try to thrust on through regardless.

(From time to time some of the usual denizens of
this area are happening by -- staggering in some cases,
not to mention lurching, reeling, stumbling, wobbling --
and some of them appear to be wondering what I'm doing
here. The Natusan center's just up the street, a patch

of "the jungle" (a/k/a "the rez") is to my right, a tong
headquarters is directly across the street, and
kittycorner is the large warehouse -- graffiti yet again
freshly painted over -- in whose doorways I've several
times inadvertently surprised hookers and johns hotly in
the act (blowjobs only, though, so far). -- And at my
back, behind a chain-link fence and maybe thirty feet of
not-so-green greenbelt, sixteen lanes of fume-spewing
freeway traffic finally starting to move at a decent
pace. When I arrived in the area they were just
creeping along, as is often the case at rush hour, this
time at slightly less than my normal walking speed.)

     Z thinks her job interview went well. "I told them
the leadership institute had changed me a lot. One of
them said, 'It was noticed, yes.' I mean she said this
like" -- Z here going into her severe-Russian-professor
imitation -- "very, very seriously!" But for a while
yesterday she, Z, was noticeably agitated about the
whole process, feeling she must've screwed up some way
or other. And then at the WOC she melted down a bit,
grumping about how I "never" ask for her help the way
she asks for mine. "It's so unbalanced! Sometimes I
can hardly stand it!" But in bed this morning she
apologized and acknowledged we're close to perfect for
each other in just about every possible respect and so
what's the point of getting worked up about such truly
minor quotidian beefs? (Then the talk veered off into
the matter of other women I've known who saw therapists,
threw heavy, sharp-edged objects during fights,
attempted suicide in their formative years, among other
vibrant topics.) -- And she should find out any day now
whether she got the job.

                              *

     (Some Cawk guy just tried to hit me up for four
bucks because his car was supposedly towed and impounded.
That's how short he is on the fifty-five dollar fee --
so he says. The fourth or fifth time someone's tried
that scam on me in our eighteen months living on south
hill. As I wearily told him. He just shrugged and
walked away. (I should also have mentioned that he

needs to update his pitch: the towing/impoundment fee's
up to eighty-five now.) -- And hostile glances from a
couple of Natusan guys and a bored come-on from a
Natusan woman who's probably hooking, maybe for one or
both of them. Just could be they all think this is
their turf because of its proximity to the Natusan
center or possibly because it was their ancestors' turf,
along with, of course, the entire rest of the region
and the nation and the continent, for thousands of
years before we Eurusans forcibly stole it from them,
in this case here, a century and a half ago.
-- Meanwhile they've already moved off down the hill.
And I notice some early arrivals for tonight's ball
game -- this area offering probably the closest free
street parking for the new stadium -- free but hardly
without risk. Nearby curb gutters are all deeply
pebbled with shattered car-window glass. From what I
hear it makes good aquarium "gravel.") (At the block-
watch meeting Tuesday night, Z told me, the police rep
said crime is down by half in our hood over the
previous two months, although it was up by a quarter in
April -- all this as compared with a year ago. I'm not
sure but I don't think water-pistol assaults count as
crime in the police statistics, and no doubt you'd have
to be a pretty stern law-and-order type to think they
should, but -- yeah, maybe that's not such a bad idea.
-- Naw, just goofing.) (And by the way, Z said she was
the only person of color and the only renter present
for the meeting. All the others were Cawk property
owners. "But I said some really good things," she told
me, "and I think you might even have agreed with a
couple of them.")

    As for my own wedding news, Z's dress has arrived,
but she's been persuaded it would be bad luck to let me
see it before the ceremony. Aida has suggested that
she, Betty, and Kat also wear or carry, as will Z
herself, some sort of Guatemalan clothing item or scarf
or folded cloth as a kind of wedding-theme thing and Z
seems to like the idea. She'll see if she can come up
with something appropriate at the flea markets in the

next couple of weeks. (Today she's taking the afternoon
off with several friends, including Leola and Ramona --
she of the big art-museum wedding reception earlier this
spring -- and they're off shopping somewhere out in the
burbs, I don't even know for what.)

And today I talked with brother Rob, returning his
call from yesterday. He's received a card from Jim Q.
hinting he'd like to be invited to the wedding, meaning
he apparently didn't receive my letter of roughly two
months ago. So I'll have to write him again, and it
looks as though I could be gaining a third "witness" at
the wedding (and thus match Z's witness count).

Rob also said he's been diagnosed with malignant
skin cancer on his nose. The growth will be removed
next week and everything should be okay, but for the
rest of his life he'll need frequent checkups. He
speculates that I'm probably vulnerable on this score
too and I'm sure he's right, although my years as a
night worker have markedly limited my exposure to the
sun. Nonetheless I should probably go in for some sort
of checkup. But most likely I won't do that unless the
same thing happens to me that happened to him: a mole
starts bleeding and won't stop. (He says it's like an
extremely bad pimple -- "worse than the worst teenage
nightmare.") (And by the way, in three weeks he'll be
leaving for his Mentoka vacation. And -- what I
should've mentioned first, certainly ahead of the Jim Q.
news -- Rob's employee discount does apply at the music
outlets.)

-- And I'll likely be wearing the pattern of this
fencepost -- rings and whorls like a huge fingerprint --
on my heinie for the next week. Z just might find it
sorta kinky. Certainly I would if her heinie were thus
adorned.

[+2]

How thoughtful of the art museum! They've left
four black metal tables standing on the middle landing

of the grand staircase outside the cafe. Even better,
one of these tables is surrounded by three black metal
chairs. They're not even chained down! -- Obviously
this is an oversight for which heads could roll,
especially if someone makes off with the chairs tonight
(or the tables -- but for what it's worth I could barely
budge this table here when I tried to move it a few
inches to catch the light better).

It's somewhere around eleven p.m. Just an
occasional figure passes by on the sidewalk outside the
stone fence, only head and torso visible, something like
a legless silhouette bumping along in a shooting
gallery. When I first sat here, the moon, now within a
few degrees of being full, seemed to be balanced atop
the roof of the seven-story building across the street
to the south, but it's already dropped out of sight --
unless I lean back, in which case it seems to return the
favor by peeking out at me above the roofline, just the
upper half of its glowing bald bad-complected pate
(we've got a goofy selenotic up there!). -- And on the
fifth story of the same building another legless human
silhouette's been moving around inside a lighted window
-- until just now, as I glanced up, the light went off
(and now the moon peeks out again -- and the peeping Tom
down here, myself, as I suspect the person inside that
room up there suspects I am, twists to face in another
direction).

This is serendipity, as if someone's going around
downtown setting out chairs and tables in hopes an
aspiring jyzer will happen by. But on the other hand
shops are closing up early. Tonight it's my cone shop
-- referring to downtown chain burgers -- whose hours
sign by the door says it's open until eleven every night
-- but tonight when I arrived there at ten-thirty the
interior lights were off and the doors locked. Perhaps
another riot broke out earlier in the evening, like the
last time I was there? In any event I'm still feeling
deprived after looking forward to that cone all week (as
has been the case for at least a decade, I allow myself
just one per week -- no change in that).

And earlier another shop was closed because of a
local parade in the Asian quarter. I couldn't pick up
my usual brand of banana. But on that one I found
another source and it doesn't seem to matter much -- as
far as I can tell up to now, maybe ninety minutes post-
consumption -- that the brand's different.

At the last moment Z decided she couldn't take the
time to walk down with me to see the parade. The
chicken she was roasting was not yet ready to come out
of the oven. And June was there, sticking around much
later than usual to taste the chicken because it's so
unusual for Z to be cooking anything at all, much less a
whole chicken (free range to be sure -- or rather if the
label's to be believed).

(Now the moon's showing again. Very odd. It would
seem to have developed a hitch in its orbit -- a hitch
of another kind, I'll note, from the type that's been
dominating this jyze for the past three months and no
doubt will continue doing so for at least two more. But
unless the building's on the move it must be a simple
matter of angles and perspectives. Either that or I'm
moving myself -- significantly fidgeting, say -- and
don't know it. Or the earth is moving and I don't know
that. Or I've become part of some new kind of active-
art presentation curated by the museum. Maybe that's
why all the furniture's out here at this hour? Is a
film crew perhaps hidden up in the trees somewhere?
Smile Mr. Jyzeman! Action! Jyze away!)

*

-- And a chill wind just sprang up and I donned my
jacket. I've become wiser: I'm carrying it with me now
at all times, even on journeys when it seems unlikely
jyze will be bounding into action. Even in the "hot
core" of summer most of my normal nighttime outdoor
stomping grounds can be quite chilly, especially if the
wind's coming off the bay.

And now the moon is rising above the roof edge, as
if it's been making a takeoff run in extreme slow
motion, preparing to jump the gap to the roof of the
slightly taller building next door to the west. And an

alley has suddenly appeared between these two buildings
at the bottom of a perfect geometrically shaped abyss
seven stories deep on one side, eight on the other, all
of it lit up by direct moonlight. (Of course it's
possible I just didn't notice its existence before.)
     -- A few words about Wei and Alison's wedding. The
winds were a little frisky at the pea patch, the sky was
gray, drizzles had crept into the forecast, but the
ceremony came off dry and "without a hitch" (except for
Alison's tears -- and after a bit, Z's too -- as Wei
read his self-composed vows). We attendees, a couple of
dozen strong, gathered in a semicircle around the
principals in a small outdoor meeting area at the center
of the patch, with the presiding priest proving to be
laid-back and surprisingly humorous. The patch itself
was at climax stage or close to it, aburst in some cases
to human-head height and above with glorious blooms of
many colors, which everyone agreed was kismet at work
and the very best kind thereof. At the end we all
joined hands in a big circle and the newlyweds invited
us to pray aloud, individually, one at a time, for the
marriage -- or silently if that was one's preference,
and I'll admit I was grateful for that escape clause.
But Z and I decided that when our turn came it would be
the ideal time to shake the "good fortune" noisemaker,
and so we did, with me doing the shaking as she
exclaimed, "May these auspicious bells always ring out
joy for you," or something to that effect. And then I
chimed in, perhaps just a bit lamely, "Hear hear!" (Or
was it "Here here!", as in "Me next to her here too"?)
     Then a short drive up the hill to W&A's house for
the reception. Sixty or seventy people showed up, and
the sun did too, meaning we could use the outdoor tables
and seats and the toasts and cake-cutting could take
place there, in the patio of their backyard garden,
fifteen or twenty feet down the steep hillside from the
house. Most of the afternoon I nibbled on cherries and
chatted with members of Z's (and Wei's) book group, who
tended to gravitate together just as they've done at the
two other weddings of group members we've attended in

the past year. All afternoon Z and I were the
recipients of various forms of joshing "You're next!"
warnings. (And indeed we are: exactly two months to go
as of today.)

    I was very touched that for this important occasion
Z wore the miniature-jyzebook earrings I made for her
some twenty months ago as a Christmas gift. Several
people read them, or tried to, she told me, and one
she's known at the utility for years commented, "This is
so mushy! You two are just perfect for each other!"

    Wei's friend Dougal, while smoking what he insisted
was a marijuana "splyb" (it was actually a cigar
stogie), gave an amusing stonerlike toast he called "A
Joint Epithalamium for Wei and Alison." He'd known Wei
longer than anyone else present, and later he told Z
that back in their college days Wei was "a very straight
engineering nerd." (Two of the passages read aloud at
the wedding were, at Wei's instigation, from renowned
Latin American revolutionary thinkers.)

    At the end we were directed to a guestbook to sign
and then given a memento, a heart-shaped rock wrapped
with a best-wishes statement from W&A. I'm just hoping
Z didn't get any big ideas from this. But if she did,
so be it. -- And she did say she'd had her eyes opened
by how little difference all the fancy catering made --
the affair was over in a couple of hours and certainly
it would've been just as enjoyable if they'd served two-
dollar-a-slice cake instead of the four-dollar kind.

    (More and more I'm reminding myself this wedding is
mostly for her -- I've already had my shot at the full-
scale deal and also at the minimal-scale deal and she's
never had a wedding at all -- and so I should defer to
her preferences as much as possible. But I think it's
better not to make a blanket statement about this to
her. Because if I did, it would be "Weezie bar the
door!") (Her half-sister Camilla used to call her
"Weezie" before she, Z, changed her name from Louise to
Zoelie.) (Did jyze cite this fact before in this annal?
I don't think so. If it did, please forbear!)

    -- Moon's gone now, flown off behind that taller

building. Abyss-like alley across the street's pretty
much gone too, seemingly. And a gang of skaters has
appeared, and they're loudly doing all they can to
convert the stone walkways and low fences of the hill-
climbing museum patio into instant classical ruins (but
apparently making little headway so far, other than on
my eardrums). -- And I'll note that when I skedaddle in
a moment here I'll be a good scout and leave the table
and chairs in a condition at least as good as when I
arrived. -- And should also mention this: a few months
back, at a table on just the other side of the large
window a few feet to my right, Z and I were feeding each
other slices of tiramisu from Ramona and Pepe's seven-
tier wedding cake as that fabulous fifteen-piece band
blasted away two levels below on the grand staircase.
    Now it's dark in there and all the action's out
here and the skaters are it. Wham! Crash! "Look out!"
-- And the jyze part of the scene is moving on.

[+1]

    -- And it's a whole lot like last night. The
hour's the same, the part of town is almost so -- about
two and a half diagonal blocks northeast of the art
museum. And again the moon's up there shining
gloriously, even closer to doing "the full moonty" (Z's
pun that I'm stealing from this morning's armchair
note), and again I'm bummed out because I've been
deprived of my weekly vanilla softie cone for the second
night in a row. The cause of tonight's deprivation is
different, however: a malfunctioning softie machine.
Ooh-ooh-ooh, the disappointment! The insuppressible
frown! The pathetic little whimpery groan! (Not
feigned! Real!)
    So now I'm sitting in a kind of cartoon hall of
mirrors at the downtown central plaza. Almost directly
above me to the north hover three large glowing floor-
to-ceiling-size renderings, one each of Donald Duck (who
qualified for Social Security last month), Mickey Mouse,

and Minnie Mouse. Reflected in the glass windows of the
coffee shop to the south, on my right, across a sea of
completely unoccupied tables with their chairs chained
tightly to them -- that's why I'm sitting on the stairs
here -- I see the same antic cartoon trio, but amusingly
fractured and distorted. Yet all three can still be
seen to be grinning with wide-open dinosaur-like mouths
whose interiors are all the same shade of purple.

I'm tired. My calves and thighs -- the latter
especially -- are aching. I almost gave up on doing the
jyze thing tonight. Then I came upon this excellent
site, which I hadn't noticed before because it's blocked
off from where I usually sit roughly half a block to the
south, out in the plaza. It's been years since I've
been up in the big arcade building rising behind and
above the cartoon panels here.

I'm not sure if staring at the moon last night did
it to me, but all day today I've been compulsively
trying to perform the mental exercise of imagining the
universe "upside down." Of course it's just a matter of
convention that we think of it as being right-side up.
-- And then there's the question of which direction we
as a planet are headed in. Earth's orbit has us going
in one direction, the solar system is charging off in
another direction, the galaxy in still another one.
Where was the planet twenty-four hours ago? Where was
I? Where was anyone? Where was time itself? Is
relativity relative to the center of the universe or is
that also moving and therefore relative to something
else, for example the site of the original big bang, and
was that site itself on the move pre-big bang in some
predecessor universe? I mean, no wonder scientists
freak over uncertainty! -- And so, I ask, shouldn't it
be okay for jyzers to do so as well?)

But never mind all that. Because I've got some big
news. We're back to square one on the wedding site.

This afternoon I called Olwen. My main mission was
to inquire whether the addition of Jim Q. and possibly
his partner to our wedding party would make it too large
for her backyard. To my surprise she used this opening

to reveal she'd rather not have the ceremony there at
all. It seems that, as a sufferer from multiple-
chemical sensitivity, she's been worrying a lot about
the long-term effect of having people present who might
be wearing fragrances and deodorants and who might go
into the house to use the bathroom. She suggested the
hilltop garden club might make a better site.

    I knew that would never fly because we've rented it
for only a certain number of hours and also Serafina and
Adele and some others who won't be invited to the
wedding proper would be there readying the place for the
reception and matters could become quite awkward. I
said Z had suggested Betty's backyard as an alternative
and Olwen thought that might be all right, but the pets,
including the cats, would have to be leashed up inside
(not just locked up; she was adamant about that) and
she'd need to check out the backyard for other odors
and chemical presences before giving her final okay.
(She knows Betty, by the way, and was a longtime friend
of Manny, who was a member of that same radical-therapy
group along with her and Z and Z's ex-fiance Arvin. She
asked me where Betty had finally decided to dispose of
Manny's ashes and I had to admit I didn't know for sure,
although I suspected it was at "Manny Lake" since we've
gone there on his death-anniversary days. But it turns
out they haven't been disposed of at all -- they're
sitting in an urn on the mantel in Betty's living room.
They've been stashed there all along as we played
charades and various other games -- hide'n'seek included
-- and I never knew it. From the very get-go Manny was
joining in the fun, concealing himself right there under
everyone's noses.)

    (And this brings to mind the fact that Kat's been
off at camp for a week, her first prolonged stay away
from home on her own. At first Betty was vastly
relieved to have some time to herself but after a few
days she was lonely and Z worried she was hitting the
sauce and/or the weed. Betty used to be heavily into
smoke -- before becoming a nurse -- and Z wonders if she
might've been, and thus might still be, an alcoholic

too. But, despite their closeness in other ways, she
doesn't feel she can ask Betty certain kinds of intimate
questions. Nonetheless she was and is still worrying,
although Kat's back as of yesterday. Kat sent just one
postcard from the camp and it said she was ready to come
home "but not quite yet," so we're guessing her stay
went pretty well.)
       -- After talking with Olwen I called Z at work to
break the news about the wedding site. She was as
surprised as I was but she reacted quite well, to my
mind, looking right away for practical solutions. One
possibility would be Aida's backyard, she thought, but
I said I had my doubts about that (for one thing, the
expansion of the cement basketball court currently
underway -- up from half court to full -- occupies a
large part of it and may not be ready in time) (Aida
decided to go ahead with the expansion when Z told her
we'd chosen Olwen's backyard as the site because of the
chemical-sensitivity issue). Well then what about Jess
and Gwen's garden, she asked. And of course that was
the spot I'd preferred from the start, so I said I could
go for it -- not wanting to sound too enthusiastic much
less triumphant -- and Z said she could too and is
supposed to be calling Jess about it tonight.
       I also brought up the matter of an honorarium when
I talked with Olwen. She said her services would be her
wedding present to us. I said we'd still like to do
something for her. She said she'd see what she could
come up with.
       Other wedding news -- sure, why not, while jyze is
circling the area (as if it's ever circling anywhere or
anything else for more than a moment these days). At a
flea market Saturday night while we were waiting with
Wade and June for the theater to clear to see "Xiu Xiu:
The Sent-Down Girl" (which was awful) Z chanced upon a
kind of "slip-dress" which she felt would serve
admirably for a slip beneath her wedding gown. It's a
bit long, but June's offered to alter it. And I'm not
allowed to see it either: the bad luck provoked by that
would equal or exceed, because of its more intimate

nature, that of seeing the dress itself. Z's also
trying to come up with the traditional "something old,
something new, something borrowed, something blue." And
she's asked if I'd approve of her not wearing a bra
since she's already saddled with "too many layers."
Fine with me, I said, as long as she didn't think it
would bring on more bad luck. What might really stir up
the demons, she replied, is my making fun of hallowed
traditions. But she was nuzzling my ear and had a hand
in my crotch when she said that. (Lucky me!)

And then the cake news. Adele recommended a bakery
on the hill, just six blocks or so from the garden club.
Z called, assuming it was a Japanese place (Adele being
Japusan), and negotiated a deal for an "uve" cake for a
very respectable price (roughly a third per slice of
what Wei and Alison paid) and later she found out it's a
Filipino bakery and "uve" means -- what was it again? --
sweet potato or something (not "shaped like an uvula,"
as I'd guessed). (Perhaps I should note here that Z's
always copped to having vast gaps in her knowledge of
things Filipino.) Anyway it's supposed to be tasty, uve
is. And I'd already decided to raise no more objections
on the cake -- if she wanted to spend eight hundred, a
thousand bucks on it, fine. So now she's planning to go
to the bakery with Aida and see if she can bargain them
down further -- Aida's a demon at bargaining -- or at
least coax them into providing a peach filling (they'll
do raspberry or several other fruits and berries but not
peach, the woman told Z on the phone).

-- God, I can't write another word about this
wedding stuff. Especially not with Donald, Mickey, and
Minnie looking on so mirthfully and in duplicate, in
fact triplicate if I include the reflective high glass
façade of the building farther down the sidewalk. (Why
no Daisy Duck here? It's a puzzle. Maybe she stayed
home to plan the wedding?)

-- But I should mention, and very seriously, that Z
is again on tenterhooks about whether she'll be selected
for the permanent job. Dale's promised to make his
decision this week before he leaves for a month's

vacation. Z's been trying not to think about it but
that's turning out to be not so easy. She's assured me
she no longer cares whether she lands the job, but if
she doesn't, she won't be applying for another one, at
the city or elsewhere, until well after the wedding. Up
until the past few days I was all but certain Dale would
choose her, but now I too am starting to wonder. Why
would he be delaying this long unless he were seriously
considering someone else?

    -- Moon's gone again. Duck and mice not. Me, yes,
waddling on.

[+2]

    Yup, it would've looked great from here, the
eclipse. I know, because last night at about quarter
past three I opened the south-facing blinds and checked,
just to be sure it would be visible from the dining
table tonight. And there it was, the moon -- that
again! -- huge and glorious, floating just to the left
of the chimney atop the peaked roof of the two-story
house next door. At that point I was worried about
forecasts mentioning "possible showers" tonight, though
those were called off later. And at 3:22 a.m., about
seven minutes after I completed my check, the actual
umbral part of the eclipse began. It lasted more than
two hours. And according to those who saw it (for
instance, Gene the pilot at the WOC, who raved on and on
about it earlier this past afternoon) it was spectacular.

    In short, the eclipse got eclipsed, at least as far
as jyze goes.

    How bizarre it is that after all these years of
living under the spell of NUT time I should fall for it
as if it's real. By NUT time, the 28th didn't begin
until nine a.m. today, meaning halfway through my
sleeping hours. The almanac said the eclipse would
begin at 3:22 a.m. on the 28th. Two calendars I checked
agreed. By Nightscoper Upside-down Time this is the
28th right now. But by regular Gregorian time it's (of

course) the 29th.

So it goes. -- And because I don't ordinarily see
our local papers until near the end of the day (the NUT
day) when I get home from work, I couldn't be alerted by
them (and I missed the alerts anyway: I must've skipped
over them last night right while the eclipse was
happening). And then today I reminded several people, Z
included, to keep an eye out for tonight's eclipse. Not
until I arrived at the WOC did I start running into
people who thought it might've already come and gone.
Some even looked at me a little funny, I thought.

Nor was that the only calendrical screwup that
flapped into view today. For some reason it was
engraved in my memory that "Gotcha Day" for Kat, the
anniversary of Betty's picking her up in Guatemala as a
four-month-old adoptee, was this same day, July 29th.
Actually it's June 29th that's the real "Gotcha Day" and
so we missed it just as I missed the eclipse, except
with "Gotcha" the gap's a full month. Or at least this
is what Z's telling me now. She forgot it too, and no
doubt for similar reasons. And Betty probably figured,
for very good reason, that we already had more than
enough on our minds and chose not to remind us.

-- Well, it was out there tonight, the moon, for a
while, somewhat veiled, and the veil was brownish too
(just as last night), as if an eclipse really were
happening (as it was then -- the penumbral part). Now
it's disappeared entirely, the moon has, I suppose by
dropping below the roofline of the next-door house or
ducking behind the tower in the next block, sort of like
that bald-pated building-top peeping selenotic across
the street from the art museum night before last. (I've
devoted almost all this week's jyze to moon-watching --
like some drunken would-be versifier of the pre-electric
era, back when the state of the moon still mattered a
lot, and especially to night workers.)

And the latest on Z's job situation. Yesterday,
after Dale invited her out for lunch tomorrow, she was
sure he'd done this to lure her away from the office
before telling her the bad news (even though he'd said

the purpose was to show his gratitude for the excellent
work she'd done on a certain campaign a while back).
Then this afternoon when I met her at the hideaway she
revealed the latest twist: she's now been called in for
yet another interview regarding the job. The panel
approved two finalists, and because Dale's leaving
Friday for his month's vacation, that interview must
take place tomorrow, just an hour before she'll be going
out for the previously scheduled lunch with Dale (and
how will that look to the other finalist?).

    So -- tenterhooks to the max for Z. Tonight when I
arrived home she was still up; she opened the apartment
door just as my hand was reaching for it. Turned out
she'd been sitting here in the living room by the window
waiting for a dose of melatonin to take effect and saw
me down below on the sidewalk as I came walking up from
the bus stop. Then she flipped through the newspapers I
brought in. Then she and I rolled around on the bed for
a while, but nothing too sexual could take place because
the prodomo proved out this time: she's on the H-rag
again. (Chocolates she blames this round on, along with
stress over the job and, not least, the wedding.
"NSDT," she'd say -- addressing Dick Tracy as she quite
often does.) At one point she suddenly stopped rolling
and after an unsettling moment of staring into my eyes
as if I were a stranger said this: "Give me just one
paragraph about why you love me -- who I am to you, this
person you're about to marry." -- So I described the
provocative effects of watching her wiggly walk in her
therapeutic powder-blue "hula hoop," and that,
surprisingly enough, seemed to do the trick all by
itself, at least for the time being.)

    She did talk with Jess about hosting the wedding at
her place. Jess thought it would be fine, but because
so many people would be involved -- roughly twenty --
she wanted to talk with Gwen before making it final.
(And she said they were again outbid on a piece of
land. "There's too much goddamn cybermoney chasing the
good parcels." -- And this matters because they're
postponing their commitment ceremony until they can do

it on the lot where their new house -- built by Jess to
be sure -- will go up.)

    -- And now the only glowing object in the window is
the reflection of the light-fixture globe hanging over
the table here. Indeed that globe appears somewhat
lunar except that the fixture itself is also reflected
and that looks more like an undersized conquistador
helmet. And I'm thinking I might as well put an end to
this eighter of bobbles and revelations about missed
opportunities. -- Or maybe just lighten up, J-dude, and
call it a good run of moonjinks.

    No big deal in stopping here: a new J-week will be
starting up in just a few hours.

13

    Down in the valley at the corporate supermarket.
Hunched over a table in the attached chain coffee shop.
Yes, I'm paying for this. But it's worth it because
"The Book of Love" is playing on the sound system.
Rollicking good fun and it might even make acceptable
reception music.

    Out the window a view of south hill from the inland
side. Down this far not much hill is left to see, but
at the other end of the valley a number of downtown
highrises poke up in the gap, with our extreme-northern
part of the hill to their left looking big and foresty
(and the back side of the DC castle rising serenely
castle-like, as is only right, above it all).

    Up closer, in fact much closer, lots of folks
heading in and out of the main supermarket entrance just
outside. Quite a variety too, young and old, mamas with
little ones, grampas with walkers, a racial mix in which

we of pinkish hue are a distinct minority (roughly at
the same ratio, I'd say, as we are in the world as a
whole: one to six, innit?). The outdoor bench across
the way is occupied at the moment by another pinkish man
of roughly my vintage: a sprawled-out drifter wearing a
heavy and astoundingly ragged winter coat on a warm
summer afternoon. He and I are like twin alien greeters
for the shoppers, one on each side. And here's a clerk,
not pinkish, or at most partly so, pushing an impossibly
long train of glittery chrome shopping carts -- the very
type of cart frequently seen parked on the sidewalk or
sprawled on its side or upside-down in the grass at our
end of the hill, often with this market's plastic name
plaque in view. -- And a pause right here to consider
how much effort it must take to wheel those carts on
foot all the way up there. Meanwhile I'll be hitting
the head.

*

    Seems like about once a month or so I make it down
to this market on my own. Usually it's a Tuesday or
Thursday afternoon, and the Z-mobile must be available.
The proximate cause of the trip is almost always the
same: the cereal milk has run out at midweek. (If this
happens near or during the weekend, Z and I will launch
a joint provisioning run which ordinarily takes us to
the other end of town.)
    -- Here's another excellent tune: "Peanut Butter."
How good it sounds! And how apt it is, for peanut
butter is on my expanded shopping list for today! --
along with milk, bananas, tuna, crackers, cinnamon-
raisin bread, and corn toaster muffins. (Call me Mr.
Bland, as indeed Z often does, particularly in this
context. And she's far from the first to do so.)
    And now today's news briefs.
    First, Z thinks her interview went well. And one
of the higher-ups who was on the panel for the earlier
round said she'd been "exceptional" in that audition.
"You're so spirited!" (My ebullient Deep.) Dale will
be making his choice by noon tomorrow and he gave her no
clue what it would be -- regulations say he mustn't --

232

but Z thinks her chances are good. (Her view on the
selection process, voiced over the phone an hour ago: "I
know our whole system is based on competition, but I
still hate it. I swear to god this is the last time
I'll go through an ordeal like this.")
     And on the wedding front, two items. First, Gwen's
granted her permission and so the ceremony will take
place in her and Jess's garden. Since this was my top
choice all along, I'm delighted. (Yes, I'd be more
delighted with a judge's chamber, or better yet no
setting at all, but...get real, Jyze Guy! -- And I did,
long ago. Because given our USAn cultural conditioning
on marriage it's totally unreal to think you can just
mail it in and that's that.)
     -- Second, Z's now leaning toward a bakery out near
Betty's place for the cake. It garnered glowing
recommendations from Betty and two other friends, it's
less expensive (buck and a quarter a slice!), it will
deliver to south hill, and best of all it will provide
peach filler. For some reason Z's adamant about having
the filler be peach, just as she's firmly set on what
she's now calling "the Mayan-heritage theme" for
accessories (to honor Kat and also, not at all
incidentally, maybe boost Kat's tepid interest in her
own roots a bit). As we go along, she, Z, is becoming
braver and braver about making the outre choice even in
such a tradition-saturated realm. Fine with me!
     And a third item, just for the record. I've
assured her at some length she needn't worry (ha!), I'm
right on schedule with both the invitations and the hunt
for danceable reception music. "Hey, didn't I tell you
I'm on this?" Today she reiterated that even though the
reception will be in the afternoon, danceable is a must.
Everything gohn be funky -- or else!
     -- But onward to the shopping. And then home
lickety-split to meet Z for an hour or so before I take
off for work. We'll be doing Thursday dinner together
for a change. I might even present her with a surprise
dessert if I can find something here she'd eat, which
admittedly is a long shot.

[+2]

Good news, bad news.
First the good. Z got the job. Dale took her
aside yesterday, Friday, morning and gave her the word,
though it won't be official until all the higher-ups
sign off on it. It was a close competition, he told her
-- "invigorating, eh wot?" -- but the other finalist
"just doesn't have the right skill set." Also, like
Dale himself, he's a Eurusan male, and all the other
supervisors except one are Eurusan males, and that one
is an Afrusan male. Too much maleness around,
especially considering that the director of the utility
is a female who's on record as wanting more women in
management, and rightly so. And -- Z gets a hefty raise
too. This she hadn't even known about before. And --
for the month Dale's away Z will be acting boss. "It is
September 25th you're getting married, right, not August
25th? If it's August 25th I'd better look for someone
else!"
The bad news is truly bad, but apparently not as
bad as it first appeared. When Z arrived home from the
WOC around seven she tried to phone her mother back in
Centropolis (as jyze will continue calling it in the
Mentoka tradition) to tell her about the promotion. No
answer. She kept trying every twenty minutes, and after
another hour without an answer she started to panic.
Mama E almost never goes out at night, and for the past
week we'd been reading about one of the worst heat waves
of the century baking that part of the country. Z was
imagining her mother passed out on the floor in her
apartment, which has no air conditioning, with hours and
even days going by and no one checking on her. Z
decided to try one more time and then call 911, because
she'd heard on the news that city workers were being
deployed to knock on the doors of seniors who weren't
responding to phone calls (dozens have already died).
On this last attempt she did get through, but it
was Mama E's friend Tito who answered. He told her El

(as he calls her) was in the hospital: he'd come back to
the apartment, where he was staying with her for a few
days (which was news to Z: he lives in Canada), and
found her passed out on the bathroom floor. He tossed
cold water on her until she revived, then took her to
the hospital. The doctors thought she'd be okay, he
said, but she'd had a temperature of 105 upon arrival
and they wanted her to stay overnight for observation.
-- All this coming in bits and pieces because Tito,
who's something like ten years Mama E's junior, has a
heavy Greek accent and was operating under instructions
from her not to tell Z what had happened. (Mama E
doesn't like to impose on Z and also fears Z will take
matters into her own hands and force her to move to
another apartment, one with air conditioning and
elevator access, or even possibly to come live out here.
And there's a moral angle too: she doesn't like her
daughter to know she's having relations, or the
appearance thereof, with a man she's not married to and
who likes the horses a lot, which she does also.)
     Z was able to get through to the hospital right
away and received reassurances from the night nurse on
duty that Mama E, who was asleep at the time, appeared
okay and was being seen by her regular doctor who would
be accessible by phone in the morning. But she, Z, was
still in panic mode and unable to reach Aida or Betty or
anyone else who could comfort her, including, of course,
me. So when I came in at the usual time I found her
dozing on the couch in the living room, and after
filling me in (briefly) on the news she lit into me for
my cussed independence, demanding that I devise some way
she can communicate with me in an emergency. And then,
when I showed signs of resisting, she threw a fit and
stomped out of the living room and into her room,
slamming the door -- though in a way she later called
"fairly low-decibel for me, wouldn't ya say?"
     -- Nothing unusual here. Drama! Temperament!
Tantrums and fits! Within an hour or so she'd calmed
down and by this afternoon she'd come back to her senses
enough to remember why we've set things up the way we

have regarding communications. Not least, she recalled
how much she appreciates her own hours of freedom and
"unreachableness." We wound up spending most of the
afternoon and early evening together and getting along
fine.

During that period we also talked at length about
the situation concerning Mama E. Part of the reason it
makes Z so frantic, she's quick to say -- but also very
tearful in saying -- is that she, Z, wasn't present when
her father died. She had little money at the time;
she'd already returned to Centropolis once when his
condition had worsened, so for his relapse roughly a
month later she had to choose between going there again
to see him in the hospital or returning later for yet
another hospitalization or possibly for a funeral; she
certainly couldn't afford to go back twice more. Now,
of course, things are different regarding her financial
situation. And even though it appears Mama E has dodged
the bullet this time, Z wants to fly back to be with her
for a few days and to do what she can to improve her
living conditions. She can't trust Tito to do it and
she certainly can't trust her mother to do it on her
own. But except when in high dudgeon Z's usually
realistic and admirably accepting, I think, that her
mother won't live forever and that Z's own influence on
her in her remaining time may be sadly limited. Z's
already sending her money and she'll be sending her more
now with the new raise kicking in. She'll talk with
Tito, with the doctors, with Mama E herself -- try to
nudge her into accepting more sensibly her increasing
limitations of advanced age.

Z tried to enlist her nephew Jacob's help, but
Jacob told her he's too busy. He couldn't even manage
to find a way to go out to Mama E's place (it's just a
thirty-minute drive, but he's never been there) to make
sure an air conditioner (which Z would pay for) is
properly installed and working. Mama E did a lot of
grandmothering for him, but she's not his blood
grandmother and he appears to feel little family
obligation (he won't be coming out for our wedding

236

either -- this hasn't changed -- and the situation as a whole with Jacob still upsets Z a lot, because he's really the only candidate besides her mother if she, Z, wants to have family present for the ceremony, as she surely does. Her half sister Camilla (Jacob's mother) and Camilla's half sister on her own mother's side, Merry -- not a blood relative of Z's -- are both considerably older than Z and neither's in good enough health to make such a long trip).

Right from the start Z said she wanted us to go ahead with the wedding no matter what happened with her mother. "If she dies or is in critical condition I think we should cancel the reception but not the wedding itself. I want it to happen now. I want us to be done with this." And, as is usually the case when something bad happens to her, she feels God must be punishing her (or the gods or the goddess or just the cosmos: she's not at all picky on this). On the way home last night before calling Mama E the first time, she'd even been thinking she was feeling too happy because of the promotion and the raise and the way our relationship is going and the upcoming wedding is looking; therefore she was due to be punished. (My comment on this: "Yeah, sure, the deities care about us. What hubris! That's what they want to punish you for, your hubris!" -- And she seemed to appreciate the notion. Could it be, she asked, that I was starting to think like her?)

So today, since it was the day of the big downtown torchlight parade (the summer festival's underway and the truly fine weather has finally arrived just in time for it -- the six weeks or two months everybody around here lives for, including those with vacation homes elsewhere -- and I ran into Roger the self-proclaimed mystic who lives surreptitiously on the fifth floor of the hideaway building and he said his intuitions are telling him the weather will be good into November this year) -- because we, I say, Z and I, belatedly realized downtown would be jammed with roughly a third of a million paradegoers, we decided to drop our previous plan to hang out at the hideaway for a few hours and

then hit one of the local jazz & blues clubs for dinner
and a show during which we could boogie down a bit
(depending on her back).
    Instead we tended to business and visited the two
bakeries still remaining on our wedding-cake list. At
both we looked through "display books" of photos of
fantastic cakes, not one of which I'd ever agree to have
at any wedding of mine except under extreme duress.
That happens to be the situation obtaining here --
extreme, no question -- and guess what? That's okay!
Let us eat whatever cake we wind up with! We liked the
people at both bakeries (the proprietor at Betty's
bakery was also ethnic -- not Z's kind, though, as at
the Filipino bakery -- but his first name happens to be
the same as Z's father's, Vincenzo, which of course is
also the source of the "Zo" in Z's own name, so she
feels he's "almost like a relative"); and although while
at the Filipino bakery we decided to buy sample cakes
from both bakeries, in the end Z preferred to keep
things simple, and because "Vinnie's" (as we're now
calling it) is far better on price, ingredients, and
indulging weird customer requests, we'll go with that
one. Now we just have to come up with the specifics for
the cake: flavor, size, shape, color, filling, icing,
toppings, etc.
    After that we swung a wide circle around downtown
and sped up to the north end to see "A Midsummer Night's
Dream" at the bargain theater, stopping along the way at
a fancy new upscale nursery in our never-ending hunt for
edible "nasties," or nasturtiums (which Z loves to
sprinkle on salads and -- maybe -- our wedding cake).
We also bought half a dozen new house plants, all on
irresistible sixty-percent markdown. Two will take up
positions on the big living-room bookcase where the
former plant occupants have recently expired -- one of
the deceased being a geranium which I'd nursed through
almost the entire span of the Jyze Age up until a few
weeks ago.
    The movie was typically bardian, with spasm after
spasm of gorgeous language, but not much else good could

be said about it except for the excellent midsummer
timing of its appearance at the theater. In fact what I
consider the real midsummer's night is coming up next
week (August 7, two days later than usual this year but
still the exact middle of the Gregorian or "Common Era"
1999 season called summer); and then, of course, begins
the increasingly steep and perilous downhill run to the
autumn equinox; and the wedding will be two days after
that. (In the era of bardian flourishing, I should
note, midsummer's night was deemed to fall on the day of
the summer solstice, or roughly June 21. I learned this
from a review of the film I read on a lobbyboard while
in line at the theater. The review also confirmed that
New Year's Day fell on the spring equinox, roughly March
21, in that era, prior to the major Gregorian adjustment
of the Christian calendar. Since the dome implosion and
the TJM project climax -- "the true millennium" -- will
take place at roughly (very) the same time next spring,
this may turn out to be a good fact to know.)

     -- And on the way back home we stopped at the
glitzy new co-op grocery on east hill. Z's decided to
start going there regularly, switching her main co-op
allegiance, because it's quite a bit closer to us and
it's open 24/7. It's also very expensive, so I'll keep
shopping at the much cheaper markets which I've been
patronizing all along, meaning our travel time and CO2
production for provisioning runs will increase
substantially.

     Then Z dropped me off near the high bridge so I
could hoof it down to the hideaway and pick up this J-
book, among other things, since I'd left it down there
Friday thinking we'd both be going there tonight, as
originally planned. On the way in I hit the tail end of
the torchlight parade. This was at a visually
interesting spot where the course angles around a couple
of sharp corners with a fairly steep downhill block in
between, before making its way to the official endpoint
four or five blocks farther south in the dome parking
lot. "The parade comes around the corner onto your
block": that's what it felt like from my vantage point.

Majorettes, a twenty-four-legged dragon, colossal
floats, beauty queens in convertibles, antique fire
engines, madcap clowns, a couple of snazzy marching
bands. Applause, laughter -- and the noise, the drums,
the tramping feet, the trumpets and tubas and trombones.
It's all from another era now -- nostalgia to the max --
and maybe you even forget that sort of thing exists
until you happen upon it as I did. "And then it's
gone." -- And the crowd breaks up in no time at all,
dissolving into the streets in the parade's immediate
wake, becoming its own chaotic procession that's at
least as deserving of comment as the parade itself.
-- But jyze won't be rising to meet that challenge
right now, no. Maybe later. Or more likely not.
     The triangle and adjoining parts of the HQ
entertainment zone were as hopping as they ever get.
Volumes up high everywhere -- I could scarcely focus my
eyes during the few minutes I was in the hideaway. The
undulating flesh on display on the sidewalks down there
on warm summer weekend nights -- you forget about that
too. (Honest you do. Or I do anyway. Although I'm
remembering it right now, true enough. But only in
service to jyze demands that can't be denied.)
     -- And then home and I found the Z-woman conked out
in bed with a note on the closed bedroom door saying
she'd taken two sleeping pills just in case. And then
to the black armchair, where this has been going down
ever since. Until this moment.

[+3]

     A big boomer of a thunderstorm, totally unexpected
(at least by me), some sharp after-rumbles still
sounding right now and a light rain still falling. I
sit sideways on the couch in 203 -- in the afternoon! --
looking out at odd yellowish cloud formations far to the
east. The balcony door's wide open, the fans and air
cleaners are all whirring (Z leaves them on and so I do
too, unless one happens to be blowing directly at me),

and a cool natural breeze laden with rain-sniff is
wafting through the room almost as noticeably as
fragrance from a baking pie -- a peach pie, say. Fruit-
juice sweetened. Because that's the only approved kind
around here right now.

    Some of the early thunderclaps (preceded by
lightning bolts so vivid they lit up the farthest
corners of the apartment where sunlight never reaches)
were violently loud, setting off numerous car alarms on
the street below. Soon fire engines were racing by,
first headed north, then south, like keystone cops on
the noontime comics I loved to watch as a kid. And it
was dark enough out there for late dusk. This started
around two p.m. and only now at quarter to five is it
letting up. Overhead the gray of the clouds is still
quite dark and at times the rain suddenly intensifies,
but the thunder sounds much farther off (recalling the
receding drums of the torchlight parade) and the
lightning is barely visible and the general atmosphere
somehow much brighter.

    -- Though now (this minute! this five seconds!)
the intensifying rain is turning into hail. Pings and
ponks and cracks. It's not a sound you often hear in
this city. Hailstones the size of frozen white peas are
bouncing off the windows and the streets and the cars.
A few larger ones lie scattered on the balcony deck like
somewhat shrunken mothballs. -- But it's easing off
already. Though every few seconds you hear the thonk of
an unusually large stone hitting something.

    This bodes ill for tonight's scheduled block party.
Will the storm blow over by then? The street below is a
river at this point, cars plowing by like speedboats.
When I talked with Z on the phone an hour ago she said
the block party had no indoor backup site lined up as
far as she knew. Sheez -- the cherry pie and hotdogs
and Filipino "uve" cake in the fridge, we might have to
eat them all by ourselves. (Z felt ethnically
honorbound to buy a large "uve" cake, especially since
we stiffed them and went with Vinnie's instead on the
much larger reception cake order.)

My original plan was to ferry over to the storage
unit today. It's a good thing I got lazy about that.
-- Or not lazy, really, but I suffered a twinge of
jyzer's conscience. I can visit the storage unit
anytime but only once a year is there a block party.
And I missed last year's (which was a first for this
hood, a product of the gentrifying process running smack
into the high crime rate; now it will be fascinating to
see whether any of the newly resident techies show up).
And: Z helped organize this year's party just as she did
last year's, and she wasn't happy I missed that one.
Therefore, QED, I should attend this one.

I do see a couple of patches of blue sky now. And
the rain and hail have completely stopped.

-- Yesterday Z called her mother to say she'd be
flying back for a visit and wanted to know which weekend
would be better, the 15th or the 22nd of this month.
Mama E said she had a strong premonition Z shouldn't fly
during the period from the 16th to the 21st and she was
insistent about it, thus quashing at a single stroke Z's
potential plans for both weekends (since she needed to
set up a five-day itinerary, leaving on a Thursday and
returning on a Tuesday, and she'd told her mother this).
So they settled on the weekend following those two, and
Z went ahead and made the reservations, including five
days at the same hotel we stayed in during our visit
last year. Only when she called to tell me about all
this did she realize -- because I gleefully pointed it
out (well, if not exactly gleefully, then at least with
a sadistic chuckle) -- that she'd be gone for my
birthday.

Since then she's been frantically apologizing and
I've been having a grand old time ragging her. Imagine
how she'd hit the roof if I forgot her birthday! (She
admits this.) -- But still, I must concede it's
entirely understandable such a snafu could happen. And
it's important that she go, and she can't really put it
off for yet another week because that would encroach on
wedding-preparation crunch time. She could defy her
mother's "premonition," but we both suspect that's just

a cover for something her mother wants to hide.
Possibly Tito will be staying at her place until then
and she's too embarrassed to tell Z about it. Possibly
she and Tito have a racetrack agenda. Best not to push
too hard on this. So that leaves my birthday weekend.

She vows "major reparations." I tell her there's
no need, and I mean it. I even kind of like the idea of
a solitudinous birthday. Or as I told her, if there
were ever a good year for me to have a wide-open
bachelor's birthday, this is it.

(But here she is now, home from work.)

*

(A bit more jyze while she showers.)
-- Going back, on Sunday morning during my sleep
hours Z and Aida went off to the Filipino Pista
festival, returning together at three, surprising me.
"You naked in there?" I was. Pulled on shorts and a
henley. "Not the black shorts!" barked Z when she came
in and saw me. "Those're obscene!" I meekly changed to
the red ones. Then the usual strange mix of hilarity
and awkwardness with Aida. At one point as we sat in
the living room, our legs propped up on the coffee
table, she piped up with, "Gee, Zo, I wonder how he'd
look right now in the black shorts." But then in
response to Z's comment about how their friend Jamilah
seems to think Z and Aida were much closer before I came
along -- Z tells me privately that's not so -- Aida gave
a weird laugh and said, "It can cause big shifts in a
friendship, you know." As far as I'm aware it was her
first open acknowledgment that she thinks this has
happened with her and Z.

But I no longer believe Aida's hostility toward me,
however deep it may go, is the main reason we don't get
along so well. We're just unsimpatico. Simple! She's
even got her kid wearing a run-with-Jesus bracelet. And
it's not ironic. -- So I'm not all that troubled
anymore when I sense those negative vibes coming from
her. And on Sunday this allowed me to say it was fine
with me if the two of them, Z and Aida, want us to
double-date, thus finally introducing me to Kirk, Z's

former lover and Aida's current one. But even then Aida
didn't catch on to my joking about it, "the need to
strike a balance here." (Z has all these former lovers
in this town and I have only Lady U -- and most likely
she's moved back to her home state anyway -- so I need
to come up with some way to keep her, Z, from pounding
away at me with unrequited in-the-flesh evidence of her
worldly past.) (And the latest word is Kirk won't be
doing grad school until year after next and then he'll
probably stay right here to do it.)

(And this note. For the final act of the weekend,
Z walked all the way downtown with me and I cajoled her
into trying out the whirlpool at the WOC. Her back had
started acting up again -- simply because of the stress,
she thinks -- and therefore she overrode her antipathy
to chlorine. But only briefly. Yet even so it, the
whirlpool, may have done the trick, because yesterday
and today her back's been pain-free. -- Not that she's
conceding anything on the toxicity of the chlorine.)

(And this too. After Aida left, Z told me several
things I've never heard from her before, all of them
related and all in one big blurt: "The truth is, while I
was growing up and living in Centropolis my Filipino
heritage never seemed that important to me. It was only
when I got out here and especially after my father died
that it did. And that's strange to me because my father
was first generation. He didn't leave the Philippines
until he was eighteen! -- And you know what? I still
find it hard to last very long at these festivals like
Pista. Too many people! Too much repetition! I was
ready to leave an hour before I could tear Aida away!")

[+1]

It's vacation month. It's the week of the big
summer festival. It's the hot core of the "hot core"
and the doggiest of the Dog Days. I just don't want to
be doing anything. My brain's lying out on a beach
somewhere -- and wouldn't it be fine if it happened to

be the one at our honeymoon resort and the wedding
countdown were already fully counted down and out!
     -- But also here I am holed up in the living room
at something like quarter to four in the morning. Cool
winds are rattling the blinds, occasional raindrops are
tapping away at the windows. Some fine old trad jazz is
playing on the radio -- "Blues My Naughty Sweetie Gives
To Me." (But not mine to me! -- Well, not too often
anyway. And then only just enough to keep things
interesting. -- Well, no, I lie. A little more often
and a little more pressing than that. Especially when
she has some major 'tude on, as has been the case quite
a bit more than usual, I'd say, these past few weeks.)
     Wandering thunderstorm cells left over from
yesterday's blockbuster storm, that's what those are out
there. I've glimpsed a few lightning flashes off in the
distance and heard a few faint tin-sheet-like thunder
rumbles. They'll be talking about yesterday's natural
fireworks for a while. They sure were doing that today,
and just about everywhere I went. -- This as the fleet
chugged in and the sailors in their dress whites swarmed
onto the city streets, with whole shiploads clustering
outside the clubs in the HQ triangle as shore-patrol
vans lurked nearby, engines idling, ready to pounce.
     The block party was a go after all. The weather
cleared just in time; when we arrived, hilltop
volunteers were wiping rainwater from the half-dozen
tables and nearby chairs and rolling out four portable
barbecues from a garage (I became one of the rollers).
I got to meet several people Z has told me about from
the neighborhood group, including Matt B., a/k/a
"Zonker," the longhaired blond apartment-house owner
who's a near double for the cartoon-strip character. Z
and I barbecued hotdogs. An eight-member Afrusan Girl
Scout drill team performed admirably. We made the
acquaintance of people living in a number of the old
houses on our block and the one to the north, some
Asiusan, some Eurusan, one Afrusan, most of their houses
built around the turn into what will soon be the
previous century. One retired Cawk couple provided a

tub of homemade ice cream. Tomoko, their boarder, an
art student from Tokyo, sat with Z and me for a while
and I broke out some of my cobwebby Japan tales for her.
I tried a slice of the purple "uve" cake which Z had
bought as one of her contributions to the potluck and
didn't much like it, nor did she (it was ninety percent
icing, I'd say, with tiny crumbs of cake stuck to it
here and there); and this reaffirmed our decision to go
with "Vinnie's" for our wedding cake (and I learned most
of her father's Eurusan coworkers called him "Vinnie"
also but to his Filipino pals he was always "Zo," just
as Z herself is to many of her friends, Aida included;
she'd never mentioned this about her father to me
before).

I couldn't stick around to party's end. But when I
left all was well, and Z and I had survived, with no
apparent damage done, the airing of our opposing views
on gentrification. In essence, despite her general
radic-lib politics, she stands with the property owners
and especially the apartment-house owners such as
"Zonker" on this issue: they want property values
protected and crime cleaned up and apartment demand on
the hilltop increasing, and therefore they basically
support the dot-com invasion. I stand with the renters,
who'd prefer the hood to stay the way it is as much as
possible (so we're the real conservatives?) and
especially we don't want property values and rents to
keep zooming up so that the most income-challenged are
forced off the hill and maybe out of town. But such
matters quickly become complicated and this is not the
time to delve into them, although we did do just that
for the better part of an hour at the party. (And not a
single dot-commer showed up, by the way.)

The entire time of the party fabulous cloud
formations were rolling across the sky -- the blocked-
off street offers panoramic hilltop-corridor views to
both east and west -- and then walking across the high
bridge I was treated to a spectacular big-cloud sunset,
lots of dramatic shafts of sunlight and glowing silver
cloud linings and vivid colors and quickly shifting

shapes, all on the grandest of scales. Sublime for once was truly the word.

Earlier Z called Vida about our rings and I talked with her briefly. She'll be bringing them to town next Tuesday and that will likely lead to another postponement of my trip to the storage unit which I had reset for that day.

And tonight...tonight I'm again a happy camper. Earlier I came up with the words for certain crucial cartoon bubbles on the reception invite. I also found myself on a multicard roll for the first time in weeks, churning out three new altered yuk-it-up masterpieces for Z. And I've been holding to my vow about working out. And I'm keeping up pretty well on periodical reading. And tonight or more likely tomorrow Z will be coming off H-rag quarantine and we can start celebrating carnally again, that is, "plan A" fashion to the hilt (if also with caution owing to her gimpy back).

So far this Book C of TJM hasn't touched a whole lot on world news. Ignoring it feels good but I'm also bothered by its absence; I swing back and forth. At times I wonder: am I being irresponsible here? To kick back and ignore the jyze rules -- will there not be a major price to pay? Am I not letting this hitch-up cause a different kind of hitch in my jyze?

So just to abide by the letter of the rules, a single item. To wit: earlier this week one of the new breed of day traders flipped out and shot a dozen people, including his own family. It happened thousands of miles from here but it's a media natural for this area and this era. Several WOC members are day traders and many more invest with one or more than one. It's all part of the brand-new cyberworld in which I just can't work up much interest even as it threatens to take over my own neighborhood -- not to mention the city, the country, the world.

And that's it for the letter and the rules. For now.

Meanwhile this on wedding-related news: Wei and Alison are back from their honeymoon. Z was telling Wei

about our conversation the other day with Aida regarding
Kirk. Wei's been a believer all along in maintaining
friendships with former lovers, including in his own
case one Dorene, who was apparently doing some
videotaping at his reception, and at his request,
although I never met or even noticed her. He and Alison
have had numerous squabbles over this "vexed proclivity"
of his (and the term is also his). And now that they're
married Wei says he sees things differently: "I feel
Alison should come first now." Z's reaction was
immediate: "You mean she didn't come first before? No
wonder she was so upset!" That was my reaction too,
pretty much. The exclusive focus: in the absence of
mutual agreements to the contrary, Deeps and partners
and spouses should be able to count on it. Certainly
I'd like to myself. And Z's made it very clear she'd
like to as well. A couple of good building blocks to
have in place at the very start of a long-term couple-
up, no doubt about it: on this we're agreed.

    Z also mentioned, by the way, that she wouldn't be
at all surprised if unconscious resistance to our
marriage lay behind her mother's heat-prostration
episode. From the time she was a little girl Z was told
she shouldn't marry; she should stay with her mother and
take care of her. "No man will ever want to marry you,"
her mother would say -- not in an openly cruel way, but
more as a warning she should be realistic (owing to her
extra toes, her racial mix, the absence of fine clothing
because the family couldn't afford to buy it for her and
so forth). All this led to much grief for Z --
psychological weirdnesses, especially in her late teens
and early twenties, including the suicide attempt at
nineteen -- and eventually forced her to move to another
region of the country -- here. This is what she says
herself. And then at least in part for the same reasons
she always had trouble maintaining a relationship with a
man for more than two and a half years tops. In fact
she's very close to that limit with me already and we
haven't even gotten to the really serious part yet --
I'm talking about the part where a lot of sacrifice will

be called for on both sides -- though it's closing in,
yeah. Crunch time. Never-ending kind of crunch time
maybe. -- Naw, just playin'. Or call it jittery
prenuptial hyperbole.

So now she's saying her focus for the next two
months will be on two matters: Mama E and the wedding.
(Hey, no wonder she forgot my birthday when making her
travel plans!) Meanwhile she's suddenly the acting boss
at work with an entire department depending on her to
make the tough calls (to the limited yet still worrisome
extent any are likely to arise in the traditional siesta
month of August). And just today the official
confirmation of her promotion came down.

And yet, here's something she said on the phone
earlier today (by NUT time): "I don't want to be
thinking about it too much for fear the goddess will
take offense" -- the vengeful deities are baaack! --
"but I'm really happy right now. I feel like we've
dodged a bullet with Mama. I got the job. The wedding
arrangements are looking good. It's like this is one of
those miraculous periods...."

That's verbatim, or pretty damn close to it.

-- It's staying dark later these days -- of course!
We're forty-some days past the solstice -- and as of
yesterday exactly 150 days from the millennial rollover.
So there's that to think about too. And for another
matter big cosmic events will be happening in the next
ten days: horoscopists of all persuasions are seriously
aflutter over this. Rare planetary conjunctions, meteor
showers, an eclipse of the sun. -- And I just
remembered, today it was announced that snowfall for the
past year on the great volcano occasionally visible far
to the north from our hilltop has reached ninety-five
feet, the largest "verifiable" amount ever recorded
anywhere in the world. That's snow deep enough to bury
a wedding cake the size of a ten-story building!

-- And bedtime is here. Gobble some supps & vites,
wash up, strip, go for the prize -- in fact it's already
starting to happen all on its own, and verifiably by
gen-set twitch count -- quarantine or no quarantine.

14

Coming down off the hill on a time-crunch
afternoon. I'm running way late already. Now this --
squeeze off a little J.

Gray afternoon too. The thunderstorm pattern seems
to have moved on but rain is in the forecast for today
and the four days following. Cooler temperatures as
well. It's quite possible we've already seen the last
of our summer. Not likely, but I can testify it's
happened here before -- a week or two when rain wasn't
threatening and that was it for the "hot core." At
least I can still be sitting outside jyzing this jyze.
And wearing just a single layer of clothing (above the
waist, a black short-sleeved henley, for the record,
since the color of the short-sleeved henley is usually
my only clothing variable this time of year).

Glimpses through nearby trees of the bay, the
downtown highrises, the freeway, the stadiums. I'm
holding down a spot on the cement fence along the front
prow of the DC-castle grounds, across the street from
the post (literally, and in two senses) of a few weeks
back. A black iron picket-like fence stands behind me,
then a hundred feet of grass, then two levels of parking
lot, one gravel and one paved, then the castle in all
its orange castellated magnificence.

Z arrived home early after a dentist appointment in
the AQ. At two she'd called from the office with more
bad physical news: now her left hip was bothering her.
Yesterday she detected a new herpes outbreak, so she
couldn't come off quarantine after all. She's still
having trouble with her back and her knee (the right

one), and she's only recently recovered from a bout of
foot pain (also the right one). "I'm getting old,
there's just no denying it." Or could it possibly be
prenuptial stress that's doing it? In the space of less
than an hour Aida, Leola, and D'Arcy, apparently acting
independently, took it upon themselves to remind her:
"You've never been married before! You gotta cool it a
little!" (That's Z quoting D'Arcy.) But in fact she's
gone through virtually all of the prenuptial drill
before, with Arvin, and her health deteriorated then
too. Big stress-related gum troubles struck, among
other disasters which she can't specify ("I know there
were others, but that's the one I remember"). Today she
told the dentist about all this and he inquired, "You do
want to get married, don't you?"
    The way she talks about her aches and pains and
links them with hitching up, I suspect some people must
think I treat her badly. Manhandle her even maybe.
(She's mentioned for the first time she thinks our bed
might be causing some of the aches. She's now convinced
the blue "hula hoop" has been helping her in that
regard, compensating for the body warpings caused by the
ravine at the center of our double-deck futons. Last
night she tried going without the hoop and she thinks
this might've led to the hip pain.)
    Meanwhile she's unable to do her share of the
chores, including the vacuuming and general apartment
cleaning. I try to cover for her but the mess is
gradually worsening to the point where she wants to hire
a "cleanup person" for regular visits. So far I've been
able to dissuade her from pursuing this further. Best
she should just try to relax when she's home, I say, and
not worry so much about every little thing. But I know
such a laid-back approach will never work for her --
because, as she says herself, her "mygs" (amygdala
secretions, i.e., anxiety or stress attacks) just won't
let it. (I can never forget the snooping and pilfering
Lady V and her friends used to do when cleaning other
people's apartments for money and I shudder to imagine
someone let loose in ours -- and most likely this

cleanup would be happening while I was trying to sleep.)

The remaining seven weeks, as of tomorrow, of wedding countdown could turn into a real nightmare. I'd better prepare myself. But just how does one go about doing that in a situation as fraught as ours?

-- And now a few splintery drops of rain. So to hurry this up even more:

Yesterday I was awakened at eleven-thirty a.m. by the ear-splitting shriek of warplanes practicing for the big summerfest show this weekend. Same thing today, and then tomorrow and again Sunday they'll be doing the actual performances at about the same time and following the same routes. We have a great view of the planes from our living-room window, like it or not. And of course we both hate it. For me it brings back Gatewood days at their worst, the festivities at the naval air station with the jets roaring a few hundred feet above our first house there as they landed and took off -- not to mention the regular year-round outbursts of weekend-warrior activity. (And I should note that my bed-headboard noise machine in unit 203 is utterly useless against the summerfest jets -- it's like trying to mask exploding cherry bombs by turning on a bathroom faucet.)

Meanwhile I'm still grumped out because the far-coast newspaper never showed up last night. As Z learned this morning when she called to complain, they suspended our service for alleged failure to pay a bill on time. They did receive the payment the very day they suspended us, but they "forgot" to reinstate service. What's more, I'm convinced they failed to credit one of our earlier payments, but to prove it I'd have to go through all sorts of contortions, and I might be wrong. And I guess I'd better say it's still my bad, because I'm the one who's responsible for paying that bill. So the hell with it.

-- Now I'm finished. Can't linger any longer even though the rain has held off. (And here's a traffic chopper hovering noisily overhead and slightly to the north, probably observing an accident or a jam on the freeway out of sight down below. Flap-flap like a giant

pigeon or normal pterodactyl. I can even feel the
breeze from its rotors or at least imagine I can.)

[+2]

    -- A bit of life in the HQ triangle tonight. Must
be because it's still summerfest weekend. Here's a pair
of chichi couples strolling by, both of the women in
spike heels and little black party dresses, low-cut and
short-skirted (and these women are long-legged and
sauntering perilously on those heels and frightfully
young, scarcely out of middle school, or so it seems to
this letchy old reinstated bachelor jyzer right here).
    From a certain angle this same jyzer could almost
be taken to be the bottom figure on the roughly eighty-
foot-tall totem pole that dominates the triangle. His
bench sits directly in front of the pole, no more than
six feet from it, and he's got the whole bench to
himself. Five-globe Victorian lamp fixtures stand atop
posts rising maybe twelve feet within a foot or two of
both ends of the bench, and big double wooden
flowerboxes hang from both fixtures, and all four boxes
feature long trailers of hardy fuchsias (they're
pinkish-red too, just like the ones in the flowerboxes
back home on the unit 203 balcony). And a live blues
band is playing at the saloon which the jyzer's facing
obliquely across a fifty-foot span of bricks and
benches, and that saloon's the center of the action here
tonight with a dozen patrons dawdling in its sidewalk-
cafe section and a couple dozen more local drifters
hanging about nearby on this sweet balmy Sunday evening.
    Summerfest's all but over and I (enough for the
jyzer as third person!) am delighted that it is, if only
because the warplanes will no longer be messing with me,
waking me every day several hours before my normal time.
Four days straight they've done that, including today.
It's become an annual low point of my nightscoping life.
    (Just as expected, I'm being bugged quite a bit by
some of the drifters mentioned above. But the presence

of a fairly large crowd -- cops too, at times -- means I
needn't be too concerned about the drifters or any other
potential interlopers.)

I'm feeling good but Z isn't. When I left home she
was soaking her bad left hip in the bathtub, using my
old bathboard to prop up one of the whodunits she's
poring over these days, and even more avidly than usual,
in an effort to keep herself distracted. Earlier this
afternoon as I read the paper in the living room a loud
cry came from her bedroom: she had bent over to reach
for something and a sharp pain nearly toppled her.
After that she was taking ibuprofen and moving very
slowly and carefully as we did our fortnightly Sunday
provisioning. We also stopped at Lorraine's to pick up
herbal medicine of some sort but it turned out Lorraine
had left a voice message for us at home just after we
left saying she'd run out of the very herb Z was seeking.
A bad moment for Z followed, weeping, gnashing teeth,
"Everything's going wrong!" But the moment lasted only,
yes, a moment. I tried to cheer her up by admitting that
for the most part it's my fault, this chain of injuries
and outbreaks. By resisting her proposal to bring in a
cleanup person for the apartment I'm all but forcing her
to become anxious and overextend herself. Oddly enough,
it worked. Not that I think it'll keep doing the trick
for long.

While in the bathtub Z was reminded of a story I'd
never heard before. When she was eight or nine, she
briefly became friends with a blond Eurusan girl roughly
three years younger named Bonnie. Bonnie lived in the
relatively fancy apartment building a few doors down the
street. One day she came over to play and for some
reason wound up naked in the bathtub. "I just remember
how much she looked like this pink babydoll I used to
have -- and her girl parts. I really got off on
splashing water on her. I can still see her in that tub
so vividly." -- And after that, Z said, Bonnie's mother
never let her come over to play again. "I didn't
understand that at all. It hurts to this day!"

Also: the J-town Sunday paper features a three-page

spread on the very fine Filusan protojyzer who wrote
"America Is in the Heart." One of the residential
hotels in the AQ is mounting a permanent exhibition
celebrating his life, including a new mural, and on the
way down today I stopped by to check it out -- but it
turns out the opening is later this week. But this is
the man, a decade or so younger than Z's father, whose
life resembled his in many ways: ill-paid hard migrant
labor in the fields and canneries up and down the coast
and in Alaska, horrible housing, vicious discrimination,
a period as a personal servant and cook for a wealthy
Eurusan family (in Z's father's case the family took him
along when they moved to Centropolis). Z can't read
more than a paragraph or two of any of this writer's
works without choking up and declaring she can't go on
with it, it's just too painful.
     -- Meanwhile crazy things are happening in the
triangle. I mean right here. A loud tinny WHOMP: an
auto accident in the alley at the back of the small
parking lot across the street to the northwest. Smell
of smoke, fire engine, flashing lights. -- Then an aid
car, also flashing lights and a whooping siren, and it
pulls up at the bus stop right in front of me to tend to
a guy lying motionlessly on the sidewalk over in front
of the convenience store. -- And a police car noses
onto the sidewalk in front of the big building at the
corner to my far right -- that's the hideaway building,
folks! -- to chase away the dozen or so remaining
aforementioned drifters sprawled on the steps beneath
the high rounded stone arch of the front entrance. "The
park is closed!" the cruiser's loudspeaker reminds us
all. But they're not aiming that announcement at me
over here or at any of the folks standing outside the
saloon. I suppose it's not irrelevant that we're all
Cawks and these front-step dudes are all drifters of
color. Most of this latter group also appear to be
drunk or high and some are hurling nasty remarks at
passersby -- not exactly a quorum of model second-class
citizens. The sad truth is if the authorities let too
many of these guys do their thing too often in the

triangle there wouldn't be any nightlife at all down
here and many of the clubs and various other businesses
would fold. But then another sad truth, much more
important, and so obvious jyze is almost embarrassed to
keep harping on it, is that racism is still alive and
well in this mostly Cawk city and most of that racism
comes from -- surprise! -- us Cawks. And of course I'm
looking at some of it right here and scratching my chin
and not really doing anything about it -- except
scratching out this jyze with the other hand, yes.)
(Not to say it's likely to make a big difference here or
anywhere, jyze. But how fine if it could.)
     -- A voicemail message for me this afternoon: it's
cousin Kar saying he and Kerani will be in town tonight
and they'd like to get together with us. I'm wondering:
is he just being spontaneous or is he intentionally (or
unconsciously) dissing the cuz? It's this way virtually
every time: with an absolute minimum of warning he
descends from the jet-setter skies and expects everyone
to shove aside all other plans for the rare opportunity
to party down with him and his main squeeze of the
moment. But -- that's Kar. It's all right, I suppose.
I just don't usually respond to it -- for the simple
reason that by the last minute when he calls I usually
do have other plans. (Z is amused by our low-intensity
feuding. "How long has it been going on like this
between you guys?" -- referring also to brother Rob, who
reacts to Kar's antics pretty much as I do. "Eh, since
at least college days." -- So what the heck, it's not
like we're shocked or anything.)
     What else is happening? Last night we joined Gerry
and Leola and several of their relatives at a live
theater event. I didn't think much of it -- can't even
recall the play's name. It's about a recent nasty far-
coast big-city racial conflict much like the ones that
break out all too often right here in J-town. I'd been
forewarned about Gerry's fundamentalist relatives --
"Best to go easy on the irreverence," as Z put it. And
they're Afrusans! But we scarcely had a chance to talk.
(It was odd returning to that theater because the last

time I was there Lady U was one of the performers.)
-- And for the second time this summer I dressed up to
the max, including my courting shoes, and then it turned
out one of the four cast members was wearing exactly the
same brand and model and color (black) of shoes I was.
From our second-row seats we had a perfect up-close view
of them as he sat on the front edge of the stage for
long periods. For some odd reason seeing your own shoes
on stage makes suspension of disbelief very difficult.

     Today I ordered a set of color photocopies of the
"Journey into Unknown Worlds" card. Next comes the
alteration artwork. Also I'm finishing up the Turtle
Rapids file for Rob to take along on his Mentoka trip
next week. (I'm focusing on "ancestral glimpses" and
the Silver Mound story -- truly a fascinating tale even
without the fictional embellishments I've applied to it
in the past. -- And the "celestial crucifixion" is
coming up, just three more days. They're even saying
this might be the apocalyptic moment itself, terror
reigning: so give the canny medieval French soothsayer
who predicted it -- this would of course be the very
same "Nasty-doom-us" mentioned before -- give him some
credit, yes, for being off by just a few days at a
distance of several centuries. As a pundit of sorts he
was definitely a cut above the pack.)

     -- More sirens. What now? More drunks too. And
the J-stick's running low on toner anyway, as it were,
so it's time to move on, and fast. (Panicky-looking
dudes of color running through the triangle, never a
good sign.) (And it's sort of distressing that I wrote
"toner" there and only afterwards realized what I'd
done. The digital demons are seizing my mind!)

                    [+2]

     Got me a seat under the shelter across the street
from my usual midtown bus stop. The transposition is no
big deal -- it's just that no seats are available over
there, only hip-high aluminum bars to lean back against.

And over here, right in front of the main post office, I
have a full view of the blockwide glass front facade of
the symphony hall. Its big electronic marquees on the
second-story level at both ends of the building are
turned off for the night, but the indoor lights glowing
above the entire length of the main concourse are still
on. They're rose at the bottom fading up into purple at
the third-story level, somewhat like a giant mood ring
stretched out flat for hundreds of feet. It's designed,
it would seem, to look like a sunset, as if you're
seeing right through the building, especially if you
happen to be doing this during the hours around sunset.
-- And what a contrast between the folks waiting at the
bus stop outside and the symphonygoers mingling on the
other side of the glass just behind them, taking no
notice of the riffraff a few feet away. This isn't the
case right now, of course, because no one's inside at
this hour except maybe a few janitors and guards. (The
clock in the post-office window, which is usually fairly
close to correct, says it's 12:05 a.m.) But earlier in
the evening the class contrast at those windows over
there is almost always glaring, during both the preshow
period and the intermissions, which are the worst.
     -- I thought this entry would be going down in the
Yuke (University quarter, or UQ) and earlier in the day,
but things happened. Then I thought the venue would be
the central fountain at the fairgrounds near Rob's
workplace, but more things happened.
     -- The main surprise was that brother Jeff rang me
up. First time I've heard his voice since we saw him, Z
and I, during our "Deep Roots Road Trip" almost a year
ago. His ostensible reason for calling was to let me
know he and Angie would be unable to attend the wedding.
(He said he'd just stumbled across my invitational
letter from several months ago in the clutter on his
desk. "It sort of fell out of a pile. That was a wise
thing you did, writing the phone number by the return
address on the envelope. I asked myself, hmm, did I
already call Glen about this? Hey, maybe I didn't!")
     But then when he revealed the reason for their

being unable to come -- a severe financial crunch -- I
sensed another motivation for the call itself. It turns
out they've moved, though the new house (rental) is only
a block away from the old one and not that different
from it. But Jeff's also quit his side job as a real-
estate salesman -- "There was just no action; I've made
virtually nothing from it" -- and he's been unable to
sell either of the condos he built. And with the loans
he took out for their construction coming due he has no
choice but to sell his beloved farmette. It was a shock
to hear him say this and to realize that the bravado
with which he'd been talking earlier was exactly that --
and also a cover for some real pain. Afterwards I
realized a certain nervous quaver I thought I'd heard in
his voice from the start might've meant that his real
reason for calling (or say, an additional reason) was to
ask for financial help or hope I'd volunteer it,
possibly offering to reinvest my deep-reserves legacy
money from Mother in the farmette. (The ad putting the
place up for sale is appearing this weekend.) But if
that's the case, he didn't have the heart to actually
ask, nor did I mention the possibility myself. Because
there's no chance I could help him out that way.
    It's sad. The farmette is his life's dream and
he's put many hundreds or even thousands of hours into
rehabbing it. I well recall him vowing he'd never let
go of it no matter what. He was sure he'd always be
able to scrounge up a way to keep it. Now on the phone
he was saying it no longer meant as much to him, and he
was admitting this was largely owing to his own
subdivision of the adjoining property and construction
of the condos there (even though he'd assured me when
they were going up that he'd located them so they
wouldn't impinge in any way on life at the farmette).
Of course he's still attached to it, he admitted, "but
I'm over the big part of the hurt."
    Rob too was shocked when I called him with the news
right afterwards. He'd had no inkling about any of it;
in fact he'd been hoping to stay at the farmette during
his Mentoka trip next week. -- But otherwise Rob seems

to be doing well. He's still wearing a bandage on his
nose over what will be an inch-and-a-half-long scar ("in
the shape of an upside-down question mark"), but the
procedure was apparently a success. I'll be seeing him
Thursday afternoon to deliver the Mentoka file I
finished putting together for him last night. (Jeff's
only word from sister Barb since her Bali trip was a
postcard with a short message saying Keith had bought
some land up in the mountains and they were delighted
with it. Rob hasn't heard from her at all.)

    And then Z and I drove up to a craft shop near Z's
old turf to check out our rings with Vida, who was in
town to pick up supplies. She's not finished with the
rings yet, but the silver linings are in and Z wanted to
see how they looked. Vida was pleased with them herself
but I could tell Z had some doubts, and later she
admitted as much. "I didn't want to be a whiner, but
you know what? I'm going to be wearing this ring the
rest of my life! So I'll call her again tomorrow." It
turned out she was also worrying about her mother, who's
been losing lots of weight lately. Mama E's going in
for a blood test and the results should be back in a day
or two. Z also remains afraid "Mama'll try to find some
way to sabotage or upstage the wedding. But I still
want to go ahead with it no matter what." (This as I
was picking out paint markers for working on the
reception invitation tonight. She wants to photocopy
the final version Thursday.) And she said (again) she's
intentionally moderating her expressions of happiness
these days to propitiate the goddess, et al., but she
wants me to know she's happy "beyond anything I ever
dreamed of." -- This despite all outbreaks, stress,
injuries, pain, stomach aches, headaches, and also
despite the fact that when she was saying this last
night her cheeks were still tear-stained from a "vent
bawl" (or what was it she called it?). Last night she
even paid a second visit to the chlorine-saturated spa
at the WOC in hopes of easing her hip pain. -- And she
admits to being mighty horny herself these days, just
like me. "I can tell," she says, "because all the time

I'm obsessed with how cute you look walking around the
apartment naked." And of course we make all the usual
jokes about saving it for marriage. (Her note this
afternoon was signed "S.W.C.H.S.T," with a footnote for
decryption: "She Who Craves Her Sweetie's Touch.")
     -- But the bus is due any minute. (They roll up
fast at this time of night with the streets virtually
empty. And sometimes they don't wait until 1:15 to
leave as they're supposed to. "All 1:15 coaches are now
clear to leave the CBD" -- this announcement from the
bus radios and onboard loudspeakers reverbs in my
nightmares. But it's the last run for many of the
drivers and the sooner they return the bus to the barn,
the sooner they can go home, and their pay isn't
affected. Is it even slightly surprising that every now
and then one of them yields to temptation and pulls out
a little early, and this seemingly always happens when
I've just arrived at the corner across the street, I'm
waving, yelling, dashing across -- the bastards!)

[+2]

     Home and the couch -- the end by the balcony door.
Roughly quarter to four in the morning. The radio's on
very low and the fan by the door's spinning and the air
cleaner over by the art table's whirring -- three
different kinds of hum, like a barbershop trio, I guess,
or a quartet if I join in -- "Hmmmmmmmmm" (now I've done
it, but only for a few seconds) -- and beyond this for a
soundtrack there's nothing. Just moments ago I did
angle open the blinds to make sure it's still overcast
out there, and it is. Tonight the Perseids are supposed
to hit their peak. I don't know whether they're
actually doing that, or if they've even shown up this
year, because I've heard nothing and read nothing and
seen nothing about them. The skies have been overcast
for the past several days. But I do know that in
Gregorian terms we're now almost four hours into Friday
the 13th. So look out. (And I'm naked too, though

maybe only Z would think I'm looking "cute" like this.
Yeah, and maybe not her either, right. But it's not
warm enough to sit outside without getting dressed again
and putting on a jacket -- I'd been thinking jyze might
want to revisit the balcony -- and in here it's close to
tropical.)

So yesterday has come and gone. An assertion hard
to refute! But the yesterday referred to here is the
one that was supposed to be truly horrific to the point
of being the very last of the last of days. "The
Celestial Crucifixion." And also "the last full solar
eclipse of the millennium." -- Or no, now that I think
about it, it's a different yesterday I have in mind --
yesterday's yesterday, which is to say the day before
yesterday. In any case none of that bad stuff happened.
-- And it was the day of the new moon too. Again.
Rolling around with true lunar-calendar near precision.

There's good news (as I pause first, though, to
shut off the radio news just coming on). Z's mother is
okay. The blood test turned up nothing bad. She
couldn't even tell us what it was looking for. But she
did pass along a touching story (I listened to the
message) of how, when Tito escorted her to the doctor's
office, the doc heartily shook his hand and declared him
a hero for saving Mama E's life. Now Z's gearing up to
fly back there and do all she can to assure herself that
nothing like this will ever happen again.

The national news grabbing attention these past few
days is yet another incident of hate-related gun-toting
violence. This time it involves a local and even a
personal angle of sorts -- in fact of two sorts. A lone
Cawk male shoots up a group of kids at a Jewish
community center a thousand miles south of here and then
offs a Filusan mailman. And the killer grew up around
here and lived here until recently, and just last year
Z's friend Irene came into contact with him at the
mental-health facility where she works. He's middle-
aged, a pink-supremacist militia type. "Christian
Identity." Pathetic man. And sorry to say, our local
woods are full of them. In fact the particular woods he

comes from happen to be just a few miles from the ones
where I lived for seven years up until the year before I
met Z, and I can confirm a whole lot of people with
his kind of political views and hatreds live out that
way. And I'd like to believe that this heinous act --
and the many others similar to it over the past decade
or so -- are driving this country's far right ever
deeper into isolation. They're starting to look so bad
from the mainstream and even the standard horrific-
enough right-wing viewpoint that I'm fearing the FBI
will soon be sending out agents provocateur attempting
to make the left look equally bad, just to maintain the
national equipoise, so to speak, which of course the FBI
is always quite concerned about.

    I've had plenty of time to think about such things
the past couple of days. Mostly I've been caught up in
screamingly tedious detail work on the "Journey into
Unknown Worlds" wedding-reception invite -- first making
it, then having it copied. Little things going wrong
and forcing maddening redo's -- especially in lettering.
Smears. A word or letter accidentally left out. Colors
not picking up on the copier or picking up too much.
It's all reminded me one more time why I didn't try a
little harder to become a visual artist (or for that
matter a musician) despite strong adolescent-years
interest in both. Writing and editing (revising) may be
full of busywork too but they're rarely tedious to me.
Words make the difference. (And thus jyze arose.)

    Today Z took the mock-ups in for final printing.
It was supposed to be an overnight job but I found the
boxes of color photocopies on the dining table when I
arrived home at 1:40 a.m. In a note she declares
herself pleased with them despite the reddish skin tones
and the missing right vertical borders on half the
cards. I'm not so pleased. I've been kicking myself
for not being there with her to walk the job through.
Now I'll have to add a border to all those cards by
hand, and that means redoing the other three borders on
all of them as well because otherwise the colors and
textures will clash too much.

Yee-ha! -- But I still like the idea of this card.
The execution of it is just fair. Guess I'll have to
settle for that. (But it coulda been a champeen!)

Today I drove over to north hill to lay the Mentoka
material on brother Rob. We had a chance to talk for
twenty minutes or so during his break. He was still
wearing a small bandage on the left side of his nose --
meaning I couldn't see the question-mark-shaped scar,
which I was perhaps a bit morbidly curious about -- but
otherwise he looked fine. Mostly we discussed Jeff's
situation. Rob's just as upset and concerned about it
as I am, and he wanted to know everything I could tell
him since he'll be dealing with the matter in person
next week. And in the end I'd say it's as mysterious to
him as it is to me why Jeff keeps screwing up
financially like this.

Rob happened across a book he thought I might like
and kept it on hold for me: a collection of new
translations of Tang poets. He was right: I bought it
(using his discount) and started poring over it on the
bus trip home tonight (setting aside the talented but
annoyingly hyper-religious Sufis). He also presented me
with a clip of the very same newspaper review I'd cut
out for him, about a newly rediscovered English diarist
of the early nineteenth century. And he told me Zach's
working as a cook at a camp up in the mountains this
summer. He pulled straight A's spring semester and he's
still thinking about majoring in Chinese, but he's doing
so well as the acting chief cook -- he started as the
assistant but the chief quit a few days after Zach
arrived -- that Rob wonders if he might decide to become
a chef. Chefs are smoking (or say fricasseeing) hot
these days.

And lots of little stuff. Blueberries, for
instance, have suddenly leapt to the top of the healthy-
food list; turns out they're more beneficial than even
broccoli sprouts and garlic. For me this is an unusual
bit of positive health news, because I've been gobbling
blueberries all my life, and never more so than recently.
Rarely does a day pass when I don't put away at least

half a cup's worth. -- And this reminds me: the
blackberries growing wild on and around south hill are
finally ripening. Today while walking in at dusk I saw
eight or ten street dudes plucking away at them like a
sad vision out of "The Grapes of Wrath," including,
near the freeway overpass, several brambly patches which
must absorb massive amounts of toxic exhaust fumes.
(And I noticed four new makeshift encampments down in
the portion of the greenbelt visible from the high
bridge. Yesterday a uniformed cop on the bridge was
peering down that way with binoculars, but I walked on
the other side of the road to avoid him and so couldn't
get much of an idea what he might be peering at or why.
But for some reason the scene reminded me of a French
movie I can recall nothing else about. Maybe it was the
almost farcically odd way the cop bent down as he
peered, one hand on his non-weaponed hip and his elbow
on that side sticking up almost as high as his head.)
     -- More to say, but I'll have to let it go. Time's
up. I vowed to hit the sack by five and we're just
about there. (Z's note said, "I miss you!" -- We've
been unable to make most of our usual connections for
several days straight now.)

15

     First time for me in this particular park.
Outdoors, that is. A square picnic table under a tree,
with tennis courts to the right, a sandbox to the left,
a reservoir in back, a golf course straight ahead -- as
a swarm of hogs of the motorcycle type roar by on the
street between here and the golfers. Zoelie sits across
the table reading a Japanese whodunit -- but now just as

I write those words she stands and walks around the
sandbox to a park bench with a back, as she alerted me
earlier she might do. Sensibly enough she's hoping that
bench will offer better back support than the backless
bench here. (She departs silently. I say, "Bye." She
turns and puts a finger to her lips with a mischievous
little mock glare: "Sssssh!" She's reminding me it's
jyze time and talking's forbidden. To be sure, she's a
lot stricter about this than I am. But I'm grateful
anyway, no question, that she's willing to treat the
matter seriously and yet at the same time lightly and
humorously.)

It's a Saturday afternoon and we're in the midst of
touching up and addressing the invitations. Last night
it took me several hours to redo the borders on sixty of
them, with ninety still to go. The city printing office
did a lousy job: clipped off a border on half of them
(somehow thinking they were doing us a favor), leaving
the border white on the other half. -- But I've
mentioned this before. It's just bugging me a bit right
now, there's no denying. Not that I'm saying anything
about it except in here. In a way I even like the idea
that I'm applying a personal touch (or touch-up) to each
and every invitation. I just wish the labor itself were
a bit less stultifying. But what the hell. It's
celebration time! We're getting hitched!

So a break from the invitations. "Jyze walk." I
noted the session itself on our main calendar well in
advance, as I'm trying to do with all the ones falling
on a Saturday or a late evening at home. If Z sees it
on the calendar in black and white (actually red all
over this time) it seems to become more legitimate for
her -- quite aside from the matter of being forewarned.
(The other night the "Hydes of Jyze" sign was posted but
she didn't notice it and came wandering in anyway, as
she's wont to do, naked except for the blue hula hoop
and the black sleep mask pulled up as usual a fraction
of an inch so she could see the floor, switching off the
lights one by one as she approached -- high drama, and a
pleasing and touching sight as well as a sexy and at

times comical one. Her excuse for the "unforgivable
interruption," as she called it with tongue firmly in
cheek, was that she'd forgotten to check our calendar.
So today she's making amends by being super careful
about observing the so-called jyze ground rules, which
she herself asked me to draw up in the first place.)

So we walked all the way down here. This is the
main park on the hilltop, probably about two miles south
of our apartment. Half a century back it was one of the
largest parks in the city, but politicos have whittled
away at it over the years, with the residents of the
area (mostly Asiusans and Afrusans, with Latusans --
Hisusans? -- on the rise lately) lacking the clout to
halt the process. Some local groups are trying to
rectify this now, seeking public facilities on a par
with those provided for the wealthier (mostly Eurusan)
districts to the north. Of course they've got their
work cut out for them. And "them" is us, among others,
since as Deeps (domestic partners) Z and I are a single
unit of sorts, and soon will be even more so as spouses,
and Z is working with a couple of these groups. And I
support their aims too, of course, but prefer to use my
time differently (admitting this in a sense is nothing
more than the classical Cawk copout -- but I know if I
tried to do the politics I couldn't do the jyze and then
the politics would lose much of its meaning for me and
so would a great many other things).

On the way over we walked by the garden club. From
well up the street we could see an event was taking
place there -- cars pulling in and disgorging snazzily
dressed passengers, people standing on the porch gabbing
with drink glasses in hand -- and it turned out to be a
wedding, an Afrusan couple, mostly Afrusan crowd, with
the ceremony itself being staged by the gazebo in the
side yard to the north, bridesmaids in skimpy black
dresses giggling as their high heels sank into the turf.
The place looked good (but for our reception -- exactly
six weeks from today, and at about the same hour --
we'll try to do a better job of policing the grounds
(Wei will be in charge) and we'll try to remember to

take the "Hall for Rent" sign down from the window by
the main entrance. And I expect these things will
indeed happen because Z already has them written down in
her "wedding to-do's" notebook which goes everywhere she
does (including, she tells me, all restrooms).

Next we stopped by the branch library where Z
picked up a few more whodunits. How she can chomp
through those things! (I spotted a lost set of keys on
the rug in the tiny children's play area and turned them
in just as the mama who left them there was about to
leave the building, and for this she effusively thanked
me to the point where one of those telltale good-boy
blushes crept into my face, for which Z ragged me
mercilessly afterwards.) She, Z, is also wringing a lot
of mileage out of the doctor's warning, in writing, not
to strain her back -- an official doctor's excuse to do
no vacuuming (Doc Karen reportedly got a good laugh out
of providing this) -- but here's Z not hesitating a
moment to haul a pack of books for miles on that same
back. The walking's supposed to be good for her,
though, and maybe she thinks the book-carrying will just
add to the effect. Meanwhile I'm in charge of vacuuming
for the duration. I told her I'd put it on the calendar
for the first open weekend date: April 24th of next
year/decade/century/millennium, right after this jyze
annal is slated to end. And that's only a slight
exaggeration as far as open weekends go. But she wants
me to be "as collaborative as a crazed jyzeslinger can
possibly be" on keeping the apartment "reasonably clean"
and I assured her I will.

(She couldn't stop chuckling as she addressed our
bizarro invitations. "Oh, I wish I could be there to
see Camilla's face when she opens this." -- That's her
half-sister she was referring to, not one of the several
other Camillas and Camilles she knows at work.)

(And looking back to my left I'm surprised to espy
a portion of downtown skyline through the high chain-
link fence atop the grassy reservoir wall. Either the
hill runs slightly to the northeast or the downtown is
slightly to the northwest, but from here I'm looking

obliquely off the side of the hill, with the crown or crest where we live jutting up to the right of the downtown view. -- And a flag's waving by the fire station at the end of the block here and rock music's playing, tennis balls ponking, kids screaming as they ride the park swings, a jet roaring overhead, auto traffic sizzling by -- view of a golfer in white shorts and T-shirt frozen in his follow-through across the street, the club angled over his head for what seems an eternity as he watches the flight of the ball -- this directly behind where Z sits with one leg propped on the bench, her book resting on her thigh. Z looking exceptionally alluring I must say in black capri-like pants, a white top, blue raincoat. Ooh, and those ever fabulous eyes and lips and cheekbones. My wife-to-be right there. Yo honey, you missing me yet across our little patch of weedy fairway, so to speak, with its own boxy sandbox trap in the middle to keep us honest?)

   -- This Japanese mystery she's reading at the moment, I spotted it on the remainder table at the ORB and bought it for her for five bucks. If the blurbs on the cover can be believed it even possesses redeeming literary value. "Hey, here's one we both might go for." (Joke joke, and not much appreciated when I foisted it on her.) -- Reminds me, though, today's what used to be celebrated as V-J Day, or at least I think it is. I've seen it described as falling on the 14th and the 15th both -- probably because of the time difference, I suppose, like my own conception day being on both the 7th and the 8th of December. And the murder of the Filusan mailman last Tuesday, that fell just two or three days short of the anniversary of the U.S. fleet's capture of Manila just over a century ago. More than a mere glint of irony there, as Z rightly pointed out. -- And her father was born on a nearby island in the Visayans just a few months after Manila fell.

   Walking up here we passed the Filipino buffet restaurant where we would've set up camp had it been raining. -- But now she's returned over here and she's cold and pressing her back against my left side to

partake of my "remaining heat, if any." Very funny! In
any case I'm taking the hint.

[+2]

I've left myself only a bit more than an hour. And
for this dubious setting that's probably more than
enough. I'm hunkered down on the boarding ramp at the
streetcar stop just a hundred feet east of the only real
bookstore (ORB). The last car of the night clattered by
a few minutes ago. I'm facing the bricks, cobblestones,
benches, street lamps, pagodas, totem poles, fire
memorial, glowing white lights strung in trees -- all of
the historic quarter's central plaza (and through the
leafy crowns of the trees, scattered highrise lights,
most noticeably those of the great white tower, making
for a kind of pointillist impression of itself). My
toes are dangling inside the usual black-and-white
chucks a few inches above one of the streetcar rails. I
see them wiggling down there (the chucks).
It's Monday night at what the two previous jyze
annals before last year's dubbed the south pole (but
with south hill being south of here as well as east,
that name's no longer apt and hasn't been for eighteen
months: our Deep time). Not much action tonight. Free
blues jams at three of the dozen or so clubs with live
music, and I can hear two of the bands playing
simultaneously just around the corner, though I find it
all but impossible to focus on both at the same time
(maybe sort of like an aural version of a rabbit/duck
optical illusion).
Engines. A few autos go by. I got squirted again
up at the corner -- rambunctious frat boys from the U
this time, or so it appeared to me. The usual motley
assortment of HQ drifters and tough guys is loitering
near the clubs, but it's fairly quiet over here. (A
Cawk woman roughly half my age just came up carrying an
almost pristine rolled-up sleeping bag. My first
thought was: is she about to hand me a brazen sex poem?

But no such luck. "Can you tell me," she asked, "where
the women's shelter is?" I couldn't. I directed her to
the nearest mission I know of, half a block west, but as
I mentioned to her, it's coed. To which she replied
quite sensibly, "Well, that's a start, I guess.")
     A little bit of news, and it's disappointing. Jess
and Gwen have let Z know they won't be attending our
ceremony even though it's being held in their yard. The
reason Jess gave is that they don't want to be
contributing to the "pressure" -- if they attended and
others weren't invited, those others would be resentful.
Or maybe they were just hurt not to be invited in the
first place back in the days when the wedding was to be
held at Olwen's. I'll admit I'm hurt myself that they
won't be present. Z says she tried to talk Jess into
changing her mind -- "I gave it my best shot." She
suggested I call and try it myself. But after mulling
the idea I've decided not to. I'm thinking it's best
just to be resigned to this thing going down however it
does. (But I will say this is an excellent example of
why I dislike formal weddings. Part of what's always
involved is this hierarchical bit of who's "best man,"
who's second best, so on and so forth. The
"exclusionary sorter" Z hates so much in other contexts
is built into it.)
     Ah well. The process is grinding right along now.
Can you entirely escape your own culture's obsolete
protocols and conventions? Not likely. -- But yes, I'm
celebrating regardless. Of course I'd be celebrating
just as much if we had no official wedding and reception
at all. More, almost surely. (I could tell Z suspects
I'm holding her responsible for all this ritual nonsense
we're facing. I'm trying very hard not to show even a
tiny trace of that kind of attitude. And if it weren't
for her suspicions I'd think I've been succeeding
admirably.)
     As for the narrative of the interim (since last
jyzetime, I'm saying), it comes down mostly to my
working on the invitations to repair the bad job done by
the photocopy crew. It's been, at best, a kind of

purification exercise, with way too many hours going to
it. -- But on Saturday we walked back home from the big
hilltop park, stopping first at the Chinese place near
the junction for dinner (Z was suddenly very hungry, and
since we were there I went for the bell-pepper beef even
though my breakfast was still digesting) (she ordered
the sweet-and-sour pork as she almost always does) and
then an impulse stop at the small hilltop supermarket to
buy "Freshly Picked Local Peaches" on sale for the
bargain price of seventy-seven cents a pound, as the big
sign outside brightly proclaimed. Later in the evening
Betty and Kat dropped by briefly, on their way home
after seeing "Tarzan" again; soon every chin in sight
was dripping peach juice. (And again I sensed the gap
between Kat and me is widening. If so, I can probably
do nothing about it. In any case I'll bide my time
before attempting to remedy the situation. Certainly
I'm available for her if she wants me to be -- and just
as important, or more so, if Betty wants me to be.)

     Sunday, newspapers, then a movie with Z. A good
one too, French, "An Autumn Tale," which tells a love
story much like our own in some ways, not least the fact
that two of the female lead's friends write a personal
ad for her without her knowledge just as Jess and Gwen
did for Z. What's more, the male lead is a dead ringer
for my father in his midcareer days, right down to a
number of his quirky mannerisms -- especially those of
"the old roue" type, as Mother would say.

     (Even more than usual I'm keeping a wary eye out as
this jyze goes down. Lots of folks passing by, slinking
about, hustling, panhandling, looking for an easy mark
to hit on. Only two more brief interruptions so far,
though: both times a guy asking for a smoke. Because of
the post-it folder and other items in my right shirt
pocket, people often assume (wrongly!) I'm carrying
cigarettes. -- And here's a city worker popping up at
this unlikely hour to water the flowerboxes. They're
hung high on the lamp posts and he's dragging a hose
from post to post, with a special ten-foot-long
attachment at its end which hooks onto the boxes. He's

wearing a yellow slicker with the hood up and it's easy
to see why as the water cascades down. But people who
encounter him in his dripping slicker as they emerge
from the clubs must be confused for a moment -- "Holy
Toledo, Mabel, we'd better make a run for the car; looks
like a gully-washer's a-brewin'!"

And this coming Saturday is yet another big
calendar day, the GPS "dress rehearsal" for Y2K.
-- GPS, that's me, yes, but it's also the Global
Positioning System; and that GPS -- and maybe this
flesh-and-blood one right here as well, who knows --
could be going haywire by the time Saturday rolls
around. Why? Something about an upgrade to the
worldwide system, I'm told, but I don't really know,
other than the number of weeks since the last such
upgrade is 1,024, or exactly two to the tenth power
(or by another measure, a "millennium of weeks" with two
true or non-baker's dozens to spare).

I pull out my trusty pocket watch and see it's
quarter to one. Leaves me just enough time to stop by
the hideaway to fetch my dirty laundry before heading up
to the bus stop. (Also I could point out that my lucky
"Jeep Jyze" wooden pen has been poking out of my left
shirt pocket this entire time, protecting me with its
talismanic powers. -- Maybe I didn't mention it before:
I woodburned in the "Jyze" part. -- Not that I'm
superstitious. Unless having fun with it also means
you're hung up on it.)

[+2]

Beneath the designer trees in that other triangle
that's big in my life in the current era, the downtown
central plaza. A balmy summer evening that's already
starting to turn chilly in this particular spot, and I'm
on my way in to work and I'm running late, or soon will
be. As frequently happens I got caught up in doing this
and that -- reading, altering cards, browsing at the big
chain bookstore right across the street here -- (and now

a tiny yellow leaf lands on this page, skids along and collides with the J-stick as if it might be carrying a message from the jyze gods -- a leaf half the vertical width of one of the ruled lines here and twice that same width in length, so roughly four times as long as wide -- a fine little leaf, a darker brown at the top, vulvar in shape, I'll say, and still hanging around by the gutter between pages right now but lying on the facing or verso page, slightly higher up than where I'm jyzing on the recto page -- and meanwhile my left hand is holding down that verso page because a stiff breeze keeps trying to blow it across and shut down this entry -- and yet the insouciant little leaf just sticks right there as if it has tiny hooks on its underside, say like gekko feet, and maybe it does).

I'm facing north, toward the thundering wall of water and the arcade building at the wide end of the triangle (Donald, Mickey, and Minnie are still hanging around up there, I know, but except for a faint purplish neon glow high on the arcade wall, the coffee shop on the corner blocks them from my view). All but two or three of the two dozen benches under the trees here are occupied by the usual folks sent out nightly from central urban casting. Flowers are looking good overbrimming the half-whiskey-barrel-size cement planters scattered here and there to deter joy riders and terrorists, among others. And down on the tiles -- squares and rectangles of various sizes, colors rose and gray -- scores of little yellow leaves, almost all vulvar in shape, are scudding about. (My left thumb is now pinning the original interloper leaf against the verso page just in case its hooks fail, until I can turn this page and trap it for good.) -- And here comes a scruffy flock of grazing pigeons. They're maintaining strict separation from each other sort of like soldiers on patrol, pecking jerkily as the leaves skitter and swirl beneath them, no doubt causing them endless distractions and confusions.

Or are they eating the leaves? The little vulvar ones? I can't really tell. Maybe they are!

     -- Out in the real world a natural disaster has
struck, an earthquake killing thousands in Turkey. And
those two depraved teens who murdered a drifter up in
the north end of our city are going on trial, and one is
quoted as saying -- it's the banner head in this
afternoon's paper, blaring out from all the downtown
racks and being hawked on various busy streetcorners --
"THAT'S ONE LESS BUM ON THE FACE OF THE EARTH." (And
so do I have a plan for a better society that would put
an end to this kind of outrage? Damn right I do! But
am I certain it would work in the face of intense
opposition from the united ranks of the powers that be,
the cumulative corporate vested interests of the status
quo? Hell no! Does that even matter? -- But it's a
good reason to dig in for the long haul, yes. And just
hope it's long enough that some serious changes can
somehow be made to go down at some point enabling it,
that same long haul, to last a little longer than looks
likely now; and during that bonus period perhaps a few
more serious changes can be wrenched into place to
stretch things out still further, and so on.)
     And then my own puny news. Today it's all good, so
I don't want to let any of it slip away unjyzed.
     First, every last one of my personal wedding and
reception invitations is in the mail -- all eight of
them (compared with Z's hundred forty plus). The
advantage of sending out so few is that I can add some
personal touches to each one -- for example, having the
cartoon figures on the "Journey into Unknown Worlds"
card refer to that particular invitee by first name in
the figures' speech bubbles. -- And already the early
reviews of the invites Z sent out are coming in.
Everybody loves them, she says, while cheerfully
conceding that anyone who didn't would probably clam up.
"Delightful!" was Wei's remark. "Typical Zoelie and
Glen!" raved Leola. Even June found hers to be "very
colorful," though her real reason for calling was to
check with Z to be sure she, June, had caught the
nuances of the speech-bubble dialogue (because June is
very good at the strictly rational English-language

stuff but USAnese idioms and slang still give her fits).
     Second, Jess has reversed herself: she and Gwen
will be attending the ceremony after all. Z took Jess
out to lunch yesterday. "I said to her, 'Okay, now what
the heck's going on here?'" Possibly Z hadn't really
given it her best shot the day before (as she'd told me
she had) because this time Jess caved quickly.
     Third, late last night Papa got his (ta-da!) pop
back. Z came off the H-rag incapacitated list yesterday
evening before I left for work, but as soon as we were
able to confirm her healed status Papa did the opposite
of rising to the occasion. "I think Pooshkin is just
very, very cautious," Z observed, using the most recent
of her penile pet names for the first time in a while,
"after being rejected for so long." Geez, how
embarrassing. It never stops being embarrassing! But
this a.m. all was good again. (Why? Maybe just because
I was so tired I'd already written myself off again
until tonight. But then she had other ideas. And the
moxie to put them vigorously into play.)
     -- And enough. Some good stuff still remains
unjyzed, but the chill's getting to me. (It's J-town's
coolest summer in forty-three years, the paper says.
Local denialists on global roasting are trying to make a
big deal of this, but all they're really doing is
showing (A) their ignorance on the science or (B) their
blind commitment to their own fantasies and/or rabid
power-grubbing market-fundamentalist ideology.)

                    *   *

     A note from the bus stop, just to be sure this
makes it in. The new edition of the alt-weekly is out
and here's what the cover says: "SHUTTING DOWN J-TOWN /
The fat cats of the / New World Order are / meeting here
in November / and activists are preparing to greet them
with / the Protest of the Century."

                         [+2]

     -- Just back in from clipping the spent blooms on

the balcony at twenty to four in the morning. Before
that I watered out there with the long-spouted brown
pitcher. Usually I deploy the green juice pitcher too,
one pitcher in each hand, but tonight I just hit the
squeakiest of the unspent blooms.

While watering I saw two mysterious fellows pedal
by on the street two stories below, and because our
balcony light serves as a kind of spotlight with the
other building lights off and any movements I make cast
shadows down in the street, they both noticed me -- I
saw their eyes flick up. Drug couriers, I'm thinking.
Those bikes are cheap (free, really, since they're so
easily heistable) and probably better than cars for
steering clear of cops and, if spotted, eluding them on
the narrow hillside paths found in abundance up here.

So it's 203 jyzetime again. Sign's up, cap's on.
I'm back on the couch, basking in the gentle cross-
breeze flowing between the dining-area windows and the
open balcony door. Once in a while the blinds rattle a
bit and the leaves of the big peace lily on my far-left
periphery wave a bit, though feebly. And twice I've
heard the sudden rapid acceleration of a police cruiser
down below, possibly taking off after a bicycle courier.
Otherwise it's an unusually quiet Friday night for
midsummer -- or late summer, really, I guess, since
football teams are already practicing and back-to-school
ads are fattening the papers and little brown leaves of
many shapes and sizes are skittering about and not just
at the downtown central plaza. (I couldn't help myself,
I taped Wednesday's interloper vulvar leaf into the J-
book right where it landed. First time I've ever done
anything like that. -- Possibly I did it because I've
fallen thoroughly under the spell of the Tang poets in
this new collection Rob laid on me. While in their
thrall I find everything around me charged with a new
interest and at the same time I become the worst kind of
sentimental fool. And so I probably ought to be doubly
on guard against all the nastiness out there in the
streets, the executive suites, the pulpits, the malls.
And against all the nastiness that's doubtless lurking

in me too for that matter, sure, why not. Though I'm
not ready to cop to anything specific just yet.) (But
perhaps I should mention that both probable bicycle
couriers looked Latino. And why do I say "probable"?
Do I really understand the odds that well? Could these
dudes have been a couple of sub-minimum-wage baker's
helpers pedaling in early to work? -- Not that I want
to be too willfully naive either.)
     This was girls' night out for Z. It was the last
one before the wedding (ours) and I gather it focused on
her, though I haven't heard any details yet. She
usually comes in a little snockered on such nights and
falls right into bed, but this is the first time in
quite a while she hasn't even hauled out the "I lub
you!" rock and put it on my chair (which she ordinarily
does even if she's too wasted to write a note). When I
came in I found her purse and bag and backpack all
unceremoniously dumped in the middle of the small
clearing at the center of the "great room" here and her
clothes scattered on the hallway rug. -- And it was a
tough night at work for me, pushing out a 210-page
grand-jury rough in under five hours, jamming into
overdrive for the last hour so I wouldn't have to head
back in again at two a.m. in the Z-mobile.
     And now some wedding jyzebits. Best among them,
Z's going along with my new idea to raise a miniature
solar system atop Vinnie's cake with two planets at the
center labeled Z and G. I'll put it together myself and
I'll try to make those two planets look as if they're
orbiting each other with massive bolts of lightning
flashing back and forth between them. And the planets
will be red and blue to match the blueberries and
raspberries that will be studding the frosting of the
cake (whose filling will be, yes, peach). I also
proposed adding small "astral bodies" for each of the
reception guests -- thus making them all part of the
grand G&Z system -- but in the end I had to agree more
than a hundred of those sticking out from the cake would
be a bit much. Nor did Z go for another idea of mine --
tongue-in-cheek kind -- that we arrive at the reception

in old-fashioned bubblehead space suits like the ones
worn by the Z and G figures on the invitation. I happen
to know the party store near the fairgrounds stocks such
costumes year-round deep in its back room.

And a note on our "surfeit" discussion. Z used the
word to describe how she felt the other day when she was
locked in a conference room for several hours with two
"really good-looking" Jewish men, both of whom reminded
her of her beloved deceased Jewish brother-in-law Ben
and both of whom were trying to hit on her, sort of
taking turns as she explained it. These were the kind
of guys who, she said, might've had her "aching with
longing" back in her pre-G days. But now she noticed
she was feeling no longing at all -- or so she said --
because, as she explained, our conjugal activities that
same morning had left her "feeling surfeit" (pronounced
her way, which is very likable for its intimation of
destiny at work and then some: surFATE). Later I said I
was surprised just one little roll in the hay could have
that much effect and she said, "No, no, it's the whole
gestalt." And so I've been having fun with the terms on
my altered postcards ever since: "surfeit," "gestalt,"
"aching with longing," several others. (I can't stop
doing these cards and don't want to. They're an
addiction now but a sweet one.)

Also this note: The article about the anti-WTO
"Protest of the Century" is quite persuasive: looks to
me like it's gonna happen and it's gonna be big. But
whether it'll make any real difference is something else
again, same as before. But then again is there some
better way for the essentially powerless to create some
positive change? In any case, Z and I are agreed: we
just can't participate in the preparatory stages, or at
least not until after September 25. And Z's let me know
in no uncertain terms that she's not ready to go to jail
over WTO, and I assured her I'm not either. Her
comment: "In my condition I'll be lucky to be able to
march a few blocks without collapsing. But I'm sure as
hell gonna try as long as it seems reasonably safe."

And this: tomorrow at one minute before three p.m.

J. City time the world GPS system resets. It's expected
to wreak a good deal of havoc, especially among ships at
sea -- seriously -- and thus to offer a foretaste of the
massive Y2K disruptions that will allegedly, according
to some, and despite all the ongoing remediation efforts,
take place a little more than four months down the pike.
Oddly enough, tomorrow afternoon at about that same hour,
3:01 p.m., Z and I and Betty and Kat will be boarding a
"ship at sea": we'll be going out for a boat ride on our
city's major urban lake. Z was the high bidder on this
ride a while back at an office charity raffle, just as
she was last year, though this year the boat's a
different one (Madge I.'s) and the ride will take place
on a different body of water. So: is it possible a
reckless cyberzillionaire in a yacht will run us over
while he (or she, to be sure, though I think most social
analysts would agree a female in this role is much less
likely) -- when he/she attempts to recalibrate his/her
GPS-based navigation equipment?
        -- And this means I'll have to be getting up in
just seven hours. So I should turn in now. But first,
just because I haven't come right out and said it in
these pages for a while, I'll note I too am dazed with
happiness these days and I'm as preposterously gone as
ever or probably even more than that on this fabulous
Zoelie B.   -- And would the Tang poetry gang approve of
my coming right out and saying this in so many words --
but not one more or one less? And not even a hint of
indirection or subtlety in them? I have no doubt they
would. (And Sunday I'll be doing the vacuuming on Z's
behalf. I'll be subbing for her. This has been the
other main subtheme of the week, working out the exact
details of what needs to be done regarding cleanup as
opposed to what merely appears to need to be done but
can be put off another week -- or better to say five
weeks, since that happens to be how long we have to go,
as of this Gregorian day we're in right now, before the
wedding. Or give it one more week beyond that to get us
through the honeymoon. Then madly hoover away to one's
heart's content. Or both hearts' content!)

BOOK D

[A Jyze Epithalamium]

                          16

    Plucking wild city blackberries stains jyzer
fingers and tongue purple.
    Just felt compelled to open with that.
    Z walked with me as far as right here and then
headed back across the high bridge. I rounded the
corner and discovered the blackberry patch along the
north side of the Natusan center was loaded. Gorged
myself for fifteen or twenty minutes, leaning out over
the edge of the steep hillside drop-off, my backpack
still riding my back because this isn't the safest place
to leave something untended on the ground -- even a
backpack as duct-tape funky as mine.
    And now perched on yet another post. Just moments
ago the sun completed its vanishing act behind one of
the jagged peaks to the west, roughly in the middle of
the range from north to south and almost exactly where
such acts were occurring back when this TJM project
launched. -- And as I glanced out at the vista just
now, fireworks began bursting into view above the new
ballpark. Only a few, mostly incandescent greens and
yellows. I don't know if they're celebrating a home run
or a victory or just what. But I do know a game started
down there at five p.m.; and to avoid the resulting
congestion Z and I took the great-circle route for our
usual Sunday-afternoon provisioning run. Then on the
way back we stopped by briefly at the hideaway during
one of those peculiar periods when a game's underway
and traffic in the area's much lighter than usual, both
foot and vehicle, because the game crowd has nabbed all
the parking spots. (And now I glance again at the

                          283

ballpark and see the lights are on and the field's illuminated. Late at night, as viewed from the bus on the high bridge, the lit-up field -- and at my homecoming hour it usually is still lit up for cleaning after night games -- looks even more jewel-like.)

And peering in the other direction, slightly more than half a moon floats above the DC castle and its shaggy green hilltop surroundings. And a rosy haze, shading into dark gray at its base, obscures the mountains to the east -- or rather obliterates them, I think. Or is some part of what I can see over there gray rock instead of gray haze?

Car lights flicking on now on the bridge. A bicycle whizzes by on the sidewalk, startling me. So far no one's appeared on the path at my back leading up from "the jungle," often called "the rez" in this area (but just as I say that a pair of men -- both suitably Natusan-looking, in jeans and baseball caps -- head down it; possibly they were partaking of the blackberries not far from where I was doing that myself).

While Z and I were out, Rob called from Mentoka and left a short message. The trip's going well, he said, and he'll fill me in on it when he returns later this week. And at just about the same time, as it happens, Z will be leaving, bound for the very Centropolis airport he'll be coming in from. And that airport is about ten miles from where I passed most of my formative years -- and the same's true for Z and her own formative years, except her ten miles were in a different direction, southeast from the airport as opposed to northeast in my case (we actually measured this on a map before our trip to Mentoka/Centropolis last year).

(Wow -- suddenly wisps of cloud are lighting up a rosy orange hue in a horizontal V shape above the castle, with the moon like a small globular light right at the base of the V -- or at second glance it's more like a glowing ball impaled on the tip of an arrowhead pointing west. -- Those clouds are so insubstantial I hadn't even noticed them before. And twisting around I see the central part of the sunset ain't half bad

either: lazy swaths and pools of gold floating above the
sharply silhouetted mountain skyline.)

    -- But fine as this scene is, it's probably not
such a hot idea to linger here as dusk settles in. Jyze
will pick up again somewhere down below.

*   *

    Namely the hideaway. Having just discovered three
itchy spots on my left arm caused by blackberry
prickings, with angry little red rashes breaking out
around all three. And I know just why this is happening.
I'm not allergic to blackberries, but their chemical
composition is such that it hoodwinks my body into
calling a poison-ivy alert. Only after twenty-four
hours or so will it realize this isn't poison ivy and it
can afford to relax. -- And worsening the reaction, my
arms are sunburned from yesterday's boat ride and this
makes them sweatier and the saltiness of the sweat makes
me more aware of the rashes and I absentmindedly scratch
them and they spread.

    Also I dropped the vacuum cleaner on my right foot
this afternoon while trying to get at a tricky corner in
the bedroom. For a few minutes I thought I'd broken a
toe. Gradually the pain eased off, but the thing's
still aching some. I had to arrange my sock just-so
inside the shoe to avoid scraping the bruised and
slightly lacerated area while walking. (But I didn't
mention any of this to Z. She's taking all such minor
accidents extremely seriously these days, seeing them as
still more signs the gods are out to get us for being
too happy and for supposing we can pull off a wedding
hitch-free, so to speak.)

    -- And in fact things do seem to be going quite
well on the whole, including wedding-wise. But this
doesn't mean we've had to do completely without bad
moments. "By the time September 25th arrives," Z asked,
and not rhetorically, "do you think I'll just totally
freak out?" "Well," I said, "maybe not totally. Maybe
a couple of ninety-percenters just to keep things
hopping?" Or something like that. (She did laugh.)

    This weekend she came up with a couple of sixty-

285

percenters, I'd estimate. Maybe even seventy. One
arose from some new revelations concerning her mother
and the other from a new episode in Betty's unending
battle against lateness. -- But time's short and the
grand-jury corrections are waiting. So maybe I'll try
to tackle the freak-outs later.

Meanwhile a few items from today.

** The lead story in both local papers reports
that computer software has replaced aerospace as the
state's leading industry. The real shocker is the size
of the average annual salary of a software worker in
this state. It's $270,000. Yes! CQ! That's four
times the average for an aerospace employee and almost
ten times the average for all workers. "Should I feel
ashamed of my salary now, do you think?" Z asked earlier.
"Hell no!" I said. "Those numbers are obscene! I'd be
ashamed to be making a tenth that much!" "But they're
saying that's the state average." "Exactly!" (Or would
I suddenly think I deserved every penny? Maybe. Should
a software worker outearn a nightscoper by a factor of
thirty? -- Airy speculations here.)

** And I should just mention I was indulging in
similar speculations as I passed a long line huddled
outside one of the missions on my way in (a mission with
an oddly bright and attractive and almost festive neon
sign in three colors hanging above its entrance). This
made me feel even more ashamed for my country, my state,
my city. It also brought to mind the sobriquet that the
French have started using for the U.S. We're not just a
superpower anymore, we're "the hyperpower." (Given the
way we use this power, I'd say hyper in another sense is
just what we should be called -- nervous and agitated --
and in that same sense it's the way everyone else should
be about us. -- But no ranting!)

** Gwen left an RSVP voicemail for the wedding and
included a compliment on the invitation artwork. I
called her back later and was able to tell her "live"
how pleased I am she and Jess will be attending the
ceremony and it'll be held in their yard. I don't think
she could possibly doubt my feelings about this now.

(But Jess's full "parental unit," including her ravingly
demented gramma, is visiting at the moment -- for two
weeks! -- and staying at the house, or rather in their
own RV parked in the driveway a few feet from the house,
so Gwen has much else to be thinking about. And Z is no
longer living half a block away to offer both Gwen and
Jess an easy place to retreat to, as during the "unit's"
most recent prior visit two years ago.)

                    *   *

     Wrapping it up at the scope office.
     So the latest on Mama E is this. Last fall she was
robbed of nine hundred dollars -- or at least that's
what yesterday's letter says. Supposedly she had just
withdrawn the money in cash from the bank to pay her
monthly expenses and the robber saw her do it and
followed her to the bus stop, where he brandished a
knife and forced her to hand over the cash. She didn't
tell Z about this at the time, the letter says, for fear
of upsetting her. (Most likely Mama E wouldn't've told
her now either except she was under the mistaken
impression, it turns out, that Tito had earlier let
something slip about it to Z on the phone.)
     Nine hundred a month in expenses? Hmm. As Z
noted, "Sump'n hokey there." Her guess is Mama E lost
the money either on an uncollectible loan, probably to
none other than the heroic rescuer but also notorious
gambler Tito, or on playing the horses herself, or both.
     A phone call to Mama E followed. After a period of
wrangling and gnashing of teeth Z suddenly handed me the
phone and spun around to glare out the window. All I
could do was tell Mama E it's not a good idea to be
paying bills in cash -- as of course she already knows.
Something falsely cheery in her tone hinted she wasn't
being entirely straight with me, and I suspect she knew
I suspected this and was grateful I wasn't pressing her
harder to come clean. It was almost as if she and I
were colluding to play down the incident as much as
possible to keep Z's visit from being derailed.
     Afterwards Z broke into sobs. "If you had any
idea...ever since I was a kid I've had this feeling I'm

helpless to do anything about my mother...." Now I
tried to assure her I believe she's doing a superb job
on relations with her mother and she's doing it under
extremely frustrating conditions. And I really do
believe this. And the assurance seemed to work, because
after a while she perked up and decided to try sending
Mama E small amounts of cash in the mail (which she
picks up once or twice a week at a post-office box).

A second freak-out stemmed from a misunderstanding
over the starting time for the wedding ceremony. Z was
upset because Betty was forty minutes late for
Saturday's boat ride and also because this sort of thing
is typical for her. It drives Z, as an ABE type (always
be early), straight up the wall; as we wait for Betty to
arrive she starts muttering, then cursing, then vowing
escalating forms of revenge. I've seen her go through
all the stages on this at least half a dozen times. So
yesterday while deep into the revenge stage she decided
the wedding would start on time "no matter what" and
also decreed "if she's not there by one-thirty, that's
it, we're starting without her and Kat. That's just how
it's gotta be." I was trying to talk her into cutting
Betty a little slack, and soon she was coming after me,
accusing me of being on Betty's side instead of hers.

But in fact in saying she'd wait until one-thirty
she was already cutting Betty some slack, because for
months the ceremony's been slated to start at one sharp.
I'd forgotten this. She forcefully reminded me. And I
recalled then that the fastidious Nick, who'll also be
attending the wedding, will be staying at Betty's place
on that day; and we agreed to delegate to him the task
of shepherding everyone to Jess and Gwen's yard on time.
(And as soon as we hit on "the Nick solution," the storm
blew over -- this in the parking lot at the natural-food
chain store way up north, and with the car windows
rolled up because Z's voice was getting just a bit loud,
and mine too most likely.)

And finally the boat trip itself. This was
something I'd always wanted to do -- explore the
shoreline of our largest in-city lake -- and I'd never

been aboard any of the houseboats there either. Madge
I., our host, shares a fine specimen of such a floating
abode with her sister. (Madge is lesbian and as butch
as they come -- she's a retired military lifer -- but
also very likable, at least to me, though Z thought she
was in a bad mood yesterday, and Madge later confirmed
this: her horoscope had warned her to be alone on
Saturday, the very day we were seeing her, but she felt
she couldn't let us down, and especially not that
adorable little Kat.) The best moments out on the lake
came when Madge cut off the engine of her small
motorboat and the five of us drifted just outside the
takeoff lane for float planes and watched several of
them roar by and struggle skyward as the cloud of mist
kicked up by prop backwash -- hundreds of feet long --
drifted over us very refreshingly on an afternoon that
had turned sunny and quite warm. (And by the way:
although we saw lots of fancy "ships at sea" of the
yacht type, none came closer than twenty or thirty yards
to our boat, nor did any of their wakes rock us more
than slightly. And in similar fashion I, despite my
initials GPS, personally felt no significant internal
shifts at all as a result of the official GPS reset.)
    However, in less than six hours the sun moves into
Virgo. So look out. Talkin' my sun sign, New Agers.

[+3]

    A day late and I'm also running late today. My
first thought was to hang out at the waterfall park in
the historic quarter (HQ) this afternoon, but it turns
out they really do close the gates there before six p.m.
So I went on to the hideaway and got some J. Ink
busywork out of the way and then hiked two blocks up the
hill to the grassy municipal park, also known somewhat
anachronistically as "muscatel meadows" (these days
drugs other than cheapo wine are far more appealing to
many of those who hang out in the "Drug Free Zone"
designated by the sign standing right behind and above

me at this moment, its middle word aptly X'd out with black spray paint -- presumably by private enterprise, so to speak, not by a mischievous city worker from the parks department).

I'm perched on a low cement fence facing a complicated five-way intersection that's a favorite of mine. Sun's still shining brightly on the middle and upper stories of the old brick buildings across the street to the south (up to a dozen stories tall, these structures, and now serving mostly as low-income housing) -- but down here in the shadows it's cooling off fast as a breeze rises off the bay and therefore I've just donned my shirt-jac over my tight red henley ("muscle shirt," Z calls it, then quickly adding, "no flattery intended" -- but tweaking a triceps as she says so -- and following up with, "As of this moment this is my favorite above-the-waist G-man body part, especially this little lump right here." -- All this going down when we ran into each other on the high bridge, she headed home much earlier than expected after a dinner engagement canceled at the last minute, I headed in.)

Straight up another street I see, a mile or so to the southeast, the DC castle commanding the green heights of south hill. Down a third street stands the clock tower of the railroad depot with the domed stadium looming massively behind it in all its stupendous concreteness ("biggest freestanding concrete building in the world"). And a portion of the new ballpark's huge retractable roof is also visible, sticking out to the east from behind the dome, meaning the playing field's uncovered at the moment (no game tonight). Just across the street here, to the west, is a small sculpture fountain -- dry for years -- and behind it the green neo-Victorian arches of the entrance to the HQ station of the underground, with the graceful spire of the great white tower rising far above the arches just on the other side. (That tower, to repeat, was built by a Cawk mogul who made his fortune off gun and typewriter sales -- what a combo! -- and for half a century it was the tallest building in the western half of the continent.)

Back under the trees behind me the park benches are crowded with folks well mixed racially but certainly not classwise or genderwise. Same's true of the crowd on the grass, which right now is about as dry as it ever gets, meaning rain-free. Gulls and pigeons patrol the few areas which humans haven't claimed. -- And I should note my and Z's much-admired Filusan protojyzer, the one whose horrific early life was so much like her father's, used to partake of the vino quite regularly in this park roughly half a century ago.

Half a block north stands the nastiest bus stop in town -- the one where my gym shorts got ripped off a few months back. These days it's so bad over there I'm avoiding it entirely when I catch the last bus home down in this part of town, instead hiking two blocks farther north to the stop in front of Z's building. -- And looking over my right shoulder I see the dozen-story-tall gray-stone municipal building, I guess it's called, where Gail and brother Rob were married about ten years ago while I served as first witness (a clerk was the second); and towering above that edifice in the next block up diagonally, the tallest building within two thousand miles or something like that, a dark brown/ black modernistic eyesore if ever there was one.

And so with the setting firmly established I probably ought to say that's enough for now and mosey on up to work. But no. There's much to mention first -- though nothing of earthshaking importance really. The fed boosts interest rates by a quarter point, for instance, and the stock market celebrates by hitting another record high. Worth a mention? There it is.

But I messed up by not bringing my heavy green sweatshirt along for this J-session. I thought about it -- it's hanging on the hat tree in the hideaway -- but the thought was nah, no need; the shirt-jac would be enough. Now I'm about ready to concede the chill's too much for me. -- Okay, well at least work in the fact that this is the 25th of August and therefore the wedding is now exactly one month away. And day after tomorrow Z leaves for Centropolis to visit Mama E. And

three days after that, my birthday.
     -- Dusk now. Lights coming on. Neons.
Streetlights. The northern face of the four-sided white
clock near the top of the west-depot campanile
materializes like an unusually pristine full moon or
maybe, if I squint a bit, a fuzzy white peach, looking
sprightly indeed against the rose-tinted sky. And even
if I weren't shivering from the cold breeze I wouldn't
want to stay here now -- the rowdies are starting to
rule as the main mass of low-income folks heads back
inside and the sidewalks drain off the last surge of
nine-to-fivers, many hurrying down to the dock to catch
a ferry back to their upscale suburban-island redoubts.

*   *

     Now at the hideaway with my jyze hat on. Turned
out only an hour's scoping awaited me tonight. And it
actually is full-moon time, or almost, as I noticed
while walking back down here. It was hanging above the
skyline fairly low to the southwest, very bright, and I
couldn't see anything missing from it even though it
officially lacks one day for fullness, or so my calendar
says. While ambling along I was thinking this particular
moon has a reassuring old-fashionedness to it and at the
same time a kind of unspoiled wildness -- all cratered
and beat up -- even as it hovers up there so mildly.
Antiquated moon: it just doesn't get much press these
digital days. Doesn't seem to be inspiring a whole lot
of poetry either. Nothing even close to what it
prompted, for instance, in the Tang or high Sufi times
on which I've been focusing lately.
     What's new otherwise? Well, first of all, Z pulled
off a kind of coup. Yesterday, after we'd witnessed
another dangerous incident with a trolley pole breaking
off right in front of our balcony (if a car had been
tailgating the trolley, as they often do in this stretch,
the driver might've been garroted), Z called the transit
agency to complain. She actually managed to reach the
person who deals directly with repair crews, and he told
her they can't do much about the physical problem itself
(which would require a road resurfacing), but he'd check

292

into the possibility of imposing a go-slow order for our
block. He said it's mostly the new transit drivers who
have problems there. So then maybe twenty minutes after
she told me all this on the phone I saw a repair crew
pull up outside. Wow! And they went to work on the
wire itself. Incredible! So I called her back and left
a congratulatory voicemail, and later she returned my
call to do some well-deserved crowing. "See, I'm just
like your mother, I can make things happen too." -- And
that's true, there is some likeness there, but my own
thought (not for the first time) was what a dynamite
investigative reporter she'd've made.

Since then, however, several more bus poles have
jumped the wire at the same spot. The first came
roughly ten minutes after that second call. So an
opportunity still exists here for additional savvy
complaints. (And if they eventually do lead to service
improvements? For once we won't simply be aiding the
gentrifiers -- because what do they care about trolleys
and buses? And besides, many of the ones living on the
hill and working at the DC castle can just walk over
there or maybe roller-skate over or for that matter fall
out of bed and simply roll over, as in log-rolling.)

-- And the loving's been good. Three mornings in a
row I've had hyper-pop, I'll say -- with a nod to those
randy French -- though today Z had no pop at all herself
after crashing unusually late and also after 'gasming
over and over yesterday morning while moaning again and
again "Ooh it's so sweet, it's just unbelievably sweet,
ooh ooh, yeah, like that, ooh ooh yeah, again...." (and
in this morning's note she apologizes for today's "bad
bedside manner").

And then June. She's in the midst of a four-night
stay in Z's room as she prepares to start her second
year in law school. Next week she'll again be staying
with us four nights before her dorm room finally becomes
available. And I like having her around. Last night
she and I had a good time rapping about her sagacious
ancient clansman Confucius (born twenty-five centuries
ago) whose birthday falls either three days before or

twenty-eight days after mine, depending on whose
calendar one believes. And this morning I found a check
for $110 lying on my chair with "Wedding Wishes" written
in the "For" line. How she hit on this number I don't
know, but she's said it's to cover part of my wedding
outfit -- and it will actually pay for the entire shirt
plus I'd say the bottom foot or so of the pants (more
respectful, maybe, to put it that way than to focus on
the upper part of the pants, because June, though lots
of fun in many ways and quite good to look at too, is a
very proper and upright person and extremely loyal to
her friends, or of course Z would never allow us to
spend so much time together alone).

Final jyzebits:

(1) Yesterday afternoon I saw no fewer than eleven
women carrying sun parasols in the AQ. I counted, yes,
after spotting an early cluster of five on a short
stretch of sidewalk. This was the most ever for a
single AQ walk-through by me (they rarely appear
elsewhere in the city as far as I know).

(2) A big sign went up at the WOC announcing "End
of Summer Specials." It made the changing of the
seasons hit home as I pumped iron directly beneath it,
the words looming obliquely and partially cut off so the
sign seemed to say "End of Sun" -- and let's hope it's
not the end of either of those, summer or sun, because
on 9/25 we'll be needing both.

[+2]

In about twenty minutes Z's supposed to be calling
from her hotel. She said she'll be setting the alarm
for roughly her usual time, six a.m., and that'll be
four here. She's been gone less than a full day -- Wei
kindly picked her up at seven this past morning (or late
last night NUT time) and drove her to the airport -- and
she and I talked briefly around three p.m. Centropolis
time when she arrived at the hotel.

I've just opened one of the four envelopes she left

for me, one for each night, and it contains a nifty art
postcard showing a number of antique watches, to which
she's added cartoon-bubble phrases as if the watches
were conversing with each other: "How long she gone?"
"When she back?" "She back soon?" "Yep, she counting
da minutes!" And on the back of the card: "Mmm, miss my
babe," and signed with a heart packed with X's and O's.

　　Hey, we're in love! We're about to tie the knot!
(I hid a card every bit as mushy in her suitcase --
which she found and opened and replied to even before
she left.)

　　And here I sit in my prim and proper red shorts
(June could be wandering out at any time) beneath a
flowery weinie-shaped "Happy Birthday" balloon about
three feet long and I'm gazing straight ahead at a
vaseful of yellow birthday daisies and a "My Birthday
Boy Toy" sign, all of these also Z's doing before her
departure. Jazz is playing softly on the radio to my
right. Fans are whirring. The balcony door's wide open
and some fine fresh night air is drifting my way.

　　For wedding news there's this: sixty-some RSVPs
have come in so far. (They're RSVP-ing only if they're
planning to attend.) And one was from Jim Q. I haven't
gotten back to him yet, but an enclosed note says he'd
like to take us out to a jazz club while he's in town.
One glance at her daytimer and Z said that would never
work for her. Jim's presence, presumably with his new
partner at his side although he doesn't actually say so
in the RSVP, could complicate matters considerably --
but the phone's ringing ---

*

　　-- We went on a long time. And she hit me with
some surprising news which could have a big impact on
our lives, but I'll leave that for next time when I can
hope to be a little more coherent than I am right now.
I'll mention this, though: I finally finished reading
the book of Sufi love poems. A couple of them may wind
up being part of our wedding ceremony, but by and large
they just don't do that much for me: to my taste they're
far too obsessed, even if divinely so, with divinity

295

itself. And I'll note that all week Z was bringing home
little space-suited figurines as candidates for
straddling the Z and G planets on the orrery atop the
wedding cake ("orrery" being a fancy term for a model
solar system). For the moment they've taken over the
back half of the dining table. But I don't see even a
single semifinalist among them. The truth is they're
nowhere near hokey enough.

[+2]

-- As the minute hand sweeps past the "12" into the
opening moments of the Gregorian version of my big day.
And where do I find myself? The scope-office conference
room! (The Nightscoper Upside-down Time (NUT) version
of the day doesn't start until nine hours from now.
-- Or since we're still in Daylight Savings Time, I
suppose that should be NUDST.)
     Earlier tonight June and I did dinner at a
restaurant she picked out. It's black southern style,
Afrusan owned and run -- terrific -- not far from the
new co-op on east hill -- and I indulged in a strawberry
shortcake for dessert. It was huge and wonderful: home-
baked shortcake, real whipped cream, big fresh juicy
strawberries. It took me back to the birthdays of my
childhood to a degree unmatched in all the years since.
     Last night June and I went down to the art museum
thinking we'd check out the all-night last hurrah of the
Impressionism show (which Z and I had previously planned
to do on that night), but a late publicity barrage had
drawn a huge crowd, with the line stretching four
abreast for a full block and disappearing around the
corner. Through the windows along the grand staircase
we could see the interior was jam-packed like a theater
lobby at intermission for a hit show. We decided to
just keep on walking and wound up at the digi-cafe in my
old hood and had a nice relaxed talk there.
     In June's view -- and of course I agree -- Z and I
are extremely lucky to have found each other. Our

eccentricities and unorthodoxies mesh well, she thinks, and we're both very good at overlooking whatever we might see (and much of the world might see, for that matter, I suppose, if it had any reason to look) as each other's flaws. She also thinks Z needs to learn how to rein in her emotions a bit now owing to the importance of her new job, and I'd say she's definitely right on that one, and she, Z, might as well start in on the task at home. (It's almost as if June and Z are sisters, or actually I'd say it's more as if she's a part of Z. This is what marrying Z means. I'm marrying June too, and Aida, and Betty, and a number of others to a somewhat lesser extent: that's just how it is and it's fine with me. Or more than fine: it's a trip!)

The Z-mobile's parked down on the street. I'll try to come back with the jyze later at home and I don't think I'll be waylaid -- June has to go to work bright and early -- but she is staying over again, and tomorrow night as well, and you can never be sure what will happen with her. Just like Z she'll wake up in the middle of the night and wander out -- but in a robe; never, never naked, or at least not so far -- and she'll start talking and sometimes it's hard to shoo her away.

-- And so what else can I say on this special occasion? I'm a year older. A year wiser also? That would be a serious stretch.

But I'll be back. Technically when I wake up it should be a new jyzeday (by NUDST time) and thus a new jyze chapter, but it seems more natural to extend today's entry through the rest of the Gregorian day.

*   *

Twenty-two hours later and I'm right back where I was last night. A rush job on my birthday. So it goes. It's not even the first time it's happened.

-- Last night when I arrived home June had long since gone to bed. I found a note from her on my chair saying Z had called at 12:10 to wish me a happy birthday. "And June wishes you happy birthday too." At Z's behest she had set out Z's presents for me on the chair along with a couple of cards. I opened them all immediately.

297

One gift's a novelty-store ring in the spirit of several
I've given her before, with "Da angels sent you" inscribed
in yellow gel on the top and lots of Z's and G's on the
side facets. The other gift's a fine old wooden pen box
with a flower pattern on top, gold on black, with little
G's and Z's added to the leafs of the flowers, and
handwritten notes inside and on the bottom. Inside:
"Whether near to me or far / it's no matter, darling,
where you are / I think of you, G-duck, night and day"
(she sang "Night and Day" for me at her Christmas-gift
mini-concert-for-one last year). And on the bottom: "Z's
love for G is bottomless -- and topless too" with a nifty
kwik-sketch nude self-portrait.

     At about four (talking a.m. here) I lay down on the
bed with the phone at my side. A short nap. I figured
if I truly did fall asleep, which seemed unlikely, the
ring would awaken me for her scheduled four-thirty call.
Moments later, as it seemed, I woke up with a start and
saw it was 4:35. I found two voicemails left by Z at
4:31 and 4:33. "Birthday boy, where are you? Did you
leave the phone turned off tonight of all nights,
birthday boy? Are you being bad, birthday boy?"

     As it turned out, the phone batteries were low,
making the ring too feeble to be heard from a distance
of roughly eighteen inches. I was lucky I happened to
have my hand on the receiver when she tried to reach me
a third time at 4:40 or so. This time I could feel the
ring and also just barely hear it, but I wouldn't've
thought it was a ring at all without the tactile
dimension.

     The big news is that Mama E is now saying she's
ready to consider moving out here. It could happen as
early as next March when Z and I are tentatively
scheduled to travel back there. Or at least on the
first day of Z's visit Mama E said she'd be ready to
move by then. But then the second day, Saturday, when
Tito was present for dinner, Z could see he was
surprised when she, Z, mentioned it, and then he and
Mama E exchanged looks in a way Z interpreted as meaning
maybe Mama E had been stringing her along a bit. But Z

was worrying anyway -- how would her husband-to-be feel about all this, having a mother-in-law move nearby almost before the honeymoon was over? And so I reminded her I myself had proposed such a move by her mother and encouraged it from the start.

But by the end of dinner Saturday night Z and her mother had gotten on each other's nerves so much they decided not to see each other Sunday. And Z said "the mygs are flying again," meaning she was undergoing anxiety attacks over the large amount of money she was spending, because just in the short time she'd been away she'd used up half the projected proceeds from her raise for the entire next year. And today she spent another big bundle on a hearing aid (before now Mama E's never been willing to wear one, so apparently the heat-prostration episode has affected her in multiple ways). Also, Z left me another message saying Mama E was driving her bananas just as she always has and "I want to be sure you understand that if she does come back with us next spring we'll be finding her a separate place up in the north end somewhere and she'll never, ever, EVER be living with us.")

Tomorrow afternoon I fetch her, Z, at the airport at two o'clock. And then the wedding countdown starts up again after the five-day-plus hold, and this time with a good deal more urgency. So I want to say right here I'm as ready as I know how to be for any and all kinds of craziness in the days and weeks ahead.

*

A couple of interesting phone calls came in this afternoon. The first was from brother Rob. He's been back from Mentoka since Wednesday but waited until my birthday to ring me up, and now he's holding off again until we meet next Monday to fill me in on the details of his trip. The main news is that the farmette's officially been sold. He and Gail slept there on the last weekend it was still Jeff's property -- and Jeff and Angie couldn't bear to go out there with them.

The other caller was Jim Q. "Well I don't believe it, I've finally gotten through." And except for an

299

occasional slightly peeved tone and a sarcastic question
he tossed out at the end -- "So tell me, is there anyone
who answers phone messages up there?" -- he showed no
sign of the ire he'd be perfectly justified in feeling
at my poor record of communicating with him. He'll be
coming up Wednesday three days before the wedding and
staying for five days and he's proposing a bachelor
party of some sort, perhaps taking in a ball game at the
new stadium or hitting a jazz club or maybe even both.
He might be bringing along Nancy, his current inamorata,
I guess -- he talks as if I know all about her; in fact
I know next to nothing, and I didn't think asking about
her would be too wise at the time -- but it depends on
the state of her health: she's recovering from a heart
attack. His main concern was to know what he should
wear for the wedding. I told him I'd be decked out in
"a sort of New Age hemp outfit" ("Did you say 'hemp' or
'hip'?") and that yes, dark pants and a white shirt
would be fine for him. Would a starchy white shirt be
okay? he asked. No problem with starch, I said, but
he'd have to go easy on the aftershave and deodorants,
and then explained about Olwen. His own health has been
good, he said, except for nagging problems with his hips
(or did he say "hemps"?), a couple of muscles that get
pulled very easily.

     So the wedding party's just about set now. The
only remaining question is whether Frank and Terri's
son, Tarik, will be joining it. Or maybe Z knows the
answer on that but hasn't told me yet.

     My last birthday as a bachelor. Other than those
phone calls and a few words with the comically sleepy-
eyed June last night I haven't talked with a soul all
day. And it seems to me this is utterly appropriate.

     I guess what I'm saying is this time apart from Z
really has given me a chance to gain some perspective on
things, and now those things are looking even better.
I've examined all the weight-bearing walls and columns
of the new dwelling we'll be moving into (matrimony) and
everything looks solid to me. I'd say I'm wildly happy
but I don't want to suggest I'm utterly out of touch

with reality. Still, I'm pretty damn pleased with just
about everything and I believe I'm also in touch with
reality at least a decent fraction of the time. Of
course I also know things could change at any moment and
eventually everything that could go wrong will, most
likely, though if we're lucky maybe not too badly wrong
and not too soon. To limit the wrong-going, as it were,
as much as possible would be an admirable and realistic
and even achievable goal, I'd say, and I'm gonna go for
it, and certainly not at all in a driven or obsessive or
too straightforward way. (Not quite sure why I'm even
saying any of this, actually, except I feel I ought to
be coming up with something big-picture-like at the end
of my big day.)

17

    Found me a seat in the sun -- though as soon as I
sit down I realize it's not quite in the sun, because
I've dipped most of my FC (fleshly correlative) into the
shadow of a small tree I didn't even notice before
that's standing across the street. And I can see more
sun glinting off the bay and extending outward in a long
corrugated corridor with, at its far end, a set of
cloud-swathed peaks presiding just under the sun itself.
    This is the next streetcar stop west of the one by
the only real bookstore (ORB, yes), the steps leading up
to the platform. Lots of activity here -- autos roaring
by on two layers of the viaduct just behind and above
me, a streetcar rounding the bend with a metallic
screech and gliding by a few feet away, more heavy rush-
hour vehicular traffic surging along the waterfront
highway, tour boats and freighters and tugboats with

barges plowing by just offshore, a ferry pulling in with
a toot on its foghorn at the dock a block to the north.
And bicyclists streaking by on the bike path, and
skaters out there too, joggers, power walkers, dog-
walkers, health-minded (maybe) workers hoofing it home
or wherever it is they're headed.

I'm on my way in to work. Z's back from
Centropolis, the extended birthday celebration is all
over, we've rounded the bend into September with a
metallic screech or two of our own. Suddenly it's not
tourist season anymore, although Labor Day falls late
this year -- it's still five days off -- and so there's
some ambiguity. But the air's crisper, the sun angle
feels autumnal, the crowds in the HQ triangle and
elsewhere in the tourist zone are suddenly much smaller.
And everyone, it seems, is back from vacation, including
Aida (from Spain and also Germany, where she saw her
youngest brother, Angelo, a U.S. soldier stationed there
with his wife and kids -- I met them all in their visit
here last year), and Betty and Kat (from Gramma's house,
I think, in a small town two counties south of us here).

September -- the month of months. Marriage closing
in with a nerve-racking yet sweet inexorability.
(Here's a punky blond guy, almost Nazi-looking, wearing
shiny black military clodhoppers and lederhosen, being
tugged along on a leash by a no-nonsense black-and-white
cocker spaniel. And here's a woman in a bright orange
sun dress carrying a heavy box, resting it on the
platform, even saying hello to me, though a trifle -- or
more than a trifle -- warily. Not that I hold it
against her. Lots of homeless dudes hang out around
here, some inebriated and some flying high on who knows
what and a few quite nasty; one of the largest missions
is just a block up the street. To her I'm probably one
of them. I don't doubt I look the part. Nor do I wish
to look any other way when I'm down in the HQ.)

I'm running late, as usual these days, and it's for
a familiar reason: I got caught up in altering a
postcard for Z. This one is a reduced-size lobby card
for the ancient Hollywood clunker "Tarzan and the

Leopard Woman." This morning I was Tarzan in bed -- she
called me that because of the way my hair was flopping
around as I hovered above her while engaged in some
"plan A" jungly juking. -- The third round of same,
more or less, since her return yesterday afternoon.

A fine homecoming. I timed it just right at the
airport -- that's one thing I wasn't running late for --
and came hustling into the waiting area just as her
plane nosed into the gate. Mr. JIT, just in time, she
being Ms. ABE, always be early -- to repeat, for sure,
and aptly enough, since this black/white contrast is one
of the prime descriptors of our matchup.

On the way home we stopped at a discount mart so
she could nab a certain T-shirt before they were taken
off the floor, and while we were there she also treated
me to a "birthday berry sundae" because she'd been
jonesing for one of the hot dogs on offer at the same
stand. Then home and to bed. (Rumble rumble screech
screech, another streetcar -- it's fun to watch and
listen to them lurch around the bend, yes it is; and
then they roll up an arm's reach from where I sit.)

-- Now the page I'm jyzing on lights up as the sun
dips under the crown of that same little tree mentioned
earlier. Illumination! And the message is: time to go!
(But this note first: the new hearing aid Z bought for
her mother cost twenty-five hundred bucks (before tax).
And that was only about a third of the total amount she
spent on the trip. -- But I talked briefly with Mama E
on the phone and she seemed quite pleased -- couldn't
stop thanking me for this and that, though I basically
had nothing to do with any of it -- and confirmed she's
ready to move out here. "Is that okay with you, Glen?"
"Best news I've heard in a long time! And this has been
a heckuva good-news year!" "Glen, you sound like you're
off your rocker just like me!" -- We still goof with
each other pretty damn well, I'd say, all things
considered.)

                    *   *

-- A blade of waning moon hanging out there
directly above our tiny slice of lake. I'm looking at

it now from the funky black armchair. Sparkling bright
near-crescent moon on this crisp fresh-aired breezy
night. Tomorrow afternoon it enters its final quarter.
And in a few more days it goes dark -- but then from the
darkness will spring forth the new moon and this time
it'll be our marriage moon, waxing to fullness on the
25th, our big day, as noted at least once in every
goldang jyze entry -- it must be jyze de rigeur!)
     -- I haven't taken note yet of another burst of
bizarre prenuptial weather. Monday evening as I was
pounding away on the birthday rush job a second rare
August hailstorm was roaring along the far side of the
lake, spawning funnel clouds and tossing off vast
numbers of "golfball-size" hailstones (and in the burbs
over there "golfball-size" is for sure an apt
descriptor). They piled up several inches deep in
places and for a few hours had the area looking as if a
blizzard had hit. Some folks even brought out snow
shovels or little home-size snowplow tractors (I've seen
pix). And the crops on a number of truck farms in the
area were wiped out, including most of the flowers sold
by certain Hmong families at the public market (a
bouquet from one of their stalls stood on the desk next
to mine at the scope office as I worked tonight and now
holds forth on our dining table).
     I got a big scare myself last night. As I was
walking up the sidewalk to the entrance lobby of 1511 a
loud crash ripped through the bushes to my left --
they're planted several feet above sidewalk level in the
embankment that separates our building from the driveway
next door -- and before I could even react a huge dog
jumped down right in front of me. At first I thought I
was being attacked -- it was like a movie scene in which
a black panther pounces from a tree limb on someone
(Tarzan?) walking the jungle path below -- and then the
mutt came up with tail wagging and tongue hanging out,
eagerly nuzzling my hand to be petted. My heart was
pounding like crazy for I don't know how long after
that. A shiver still rattles my spine whenever I think
about that beast bursting out of the bushes. Yikes!

One of the scariest moments of my life -- right up there
with the techie drive-by water-pistol assault a few
months back. (This is the same neighbor's dog that does
all the heavy-duty barking.)
     And finally, a handful of wedding jyzebits. Our
first official wedding gift of the wedding season itself
came in -- despite the words on the invitation abjuring
them -- and it accompanied a funny letter from Justine,
mother of Z's cousin Jacob's wife Jackie, the very same
Justine who sent us the first preseasonal wedding gifts
-- the two terrific hand-painted wooden cigar boxes (she
did the painting) -- that arrived shortly after we met
her during our Centropolis trip last year. Now she
congratulated us on daring to be different in our
invitation and included two "Jacksons" (twenty-dollar
bills) to buy finger food for the wedding (the reception
invitation also suggests everyone bring his or her own).
"I do wish both of you two astral bodies the best and
I'm sorry I can't be there to orbit with you at your big
gala. May you spin together forever, happily...." ("A
handful" of jyzebits here turns out to be just one.)

[+2]

     Well, I gave it my best shot, but the only part of
the outside world jyze will see tonight is the same old
conference room at the same old scope office.
     Almost did the jyzing first -- a couple of hours'
worth, I was thinking -- but something about one of the
jobs lit a flashing yellow caution light, and a good
thing too: on a per-page basis, scoping it wound up
taking three times as long as the average deposition.
     So it's a Friday night. And it's fairly warm out
there. The good weather's back for what everyone's
saying is probably one last round. (But surely
everyone's wrong. Even if this turns out to be the
exceptionally bad La Nina year that's widely predicted,
several more rounds of good weather should be in store.
And if we're lucky, one of those will roll in just

before or on the 25th. But we saw a long-range forecast
predicting the rainy season will start "toward the end
of the month" and so we're back to thinking we'd better
rent some sort of tent or shelter just in case. And
I've been delegated to look into that.)

     -- But it dawns on me now that since we're past
midnight we're into the 4th of September by Gregorian
measure. I was writing about things happening on the
3rd (which was also opening day for the end-of-summer
fling at the fairgrounds, the major "arts festival" in
these parts; and it looks like this year I'll be missing
it yet again -- it runs through Monday, which is Labor
Day -- and though I usually say I'm skipping it because
I hate to fight the crowds, which is true enough as far
as it goes, the main reason is I just don't care much
for arts festivals -- and that's why I was so surprised
to discover I did enjoy the country fair this summer,
and I was doing so even before Z went into her topless
act for the multitude).

     The 4th is an important day too. It's Barb's
birthday. My estranged sister. Does she feel any pangs
about our estrangement? I wonder. Maybe not too many.
I think about her quite a bit but it's usually not with
any pangs of my own, or maybe I should say it's usually
with a kind of puzzlement pang. How is it possible she
can be the way she is? I don't very often wonder about
what I might've done differently to be able to get along
better with her. I used to do that a lot, and once in a
while I still do it some, I suppose, in a kind of
impersonal fashion having more to do with figuring out
how to jyze about the situation, or simply how to see it
as deeply as possible -- but now for the most part I
find myself feeling grateful I don't have to deal with
Barb on this or that or any other particular issue.

     And the 4th is Jess's birthday too. On that very
day two years ago I took advantage of the coincidence to
anoint her as my surrogate sister but I doubt she even
remembers it. I've missed seeing her at the WOC this
summer -- she takes a leave of absence during the months
she bicycles outdoors and doesn't need the WOC's

exercycles -- and in other ways Z and I have also been
seeing less of her and Gwen, probably just because we
now live about seven miles apart rather than the one
block apart of two years ago when Z was their neighbor.
I used a gold marker to ink a fancy monogram on the
deluxe black wine sleeve Z bought for Jess's birthday
present. I didn't hear from either of them, Gwen or
Jess, for my own big day. This really isn't surprising
or to be anguished over (and especially not with "the
unit" in town, raging granny included, and parked in the
very driveway where we're hoping to be married,
according to the latest plans as I understand them).
      -- But it's leavin' time.
                    *   *
     Now at home again about an hour later, looking out
on an even more emaciated shred of moon that's further
obscured by some sort of mist or haze. For solace
there's a cool breeze, jazz, newspapers, magazines, a
mug of cherry cider. And sitting on the dining table is
a large box containing the orrery, the model solar
system we'll be affixing to the top of the wedding cake.
Z picked it up at a downtown emporium tonight after her
workout. I'm delighted because the thing looks good and
will save me a whole lot of work. But a dispute may
loom on whether the entire solar system goes atop the
cake, as I'd like, or just a two-planet system, planets
G and Z, sticking up sort of like huge lobster antennae,
as Z seems to prefer.
     That's the other significance of the 4th. The
wedding is now exactly three weeks away.
     And Z's getting frazzled. She admits it and in
fact takes pleasure in dramatizing it and even in
telling me she just might be "testing" me in doing so.
(If that's what she's up to, I wish she'd stop. But if
it's something she just can't help doing, fine. And I'd
say the latter interpretation is far more likely, even
though she might disagree.)
     "Money mygs" are a big part of this. Yesterday
she was dinged by an unexpectedly large $600 car bill.
(I don't imagine the bill shrank any from her telling

307

the mechanics she needed everything fixed up just right
in preparation for our upcoming honeymoon trip.) The
three-thousand-dollar "advance," as she calls a loan she
obtained through a credit card just recently, is already
almost gone. "I can tell from looking at my checkbook,"
she said, with a kind of puzzled frown which I found
very mysterious. Now she declares she's tempted to
start cutting corners. "Remind me again, how much were
those blueberries and raspberries for the cake going to
cost?"

Then we have a whole different set of mygs
galvanized by the question of which friends to exclude
from the short list, the one for the ceremony itself as
opposed to the reception. Sera's still smarting from
her failure to make the cut. She told Z this, again,
when they met for coffee today. And she said Z and I
may have to wash dishes after the reception because they
(the organizers, of whom Sera is the chief) can't find
anyone else to do it. And her two daughters are miffed
that they can't be the flower girls (as they were at
Ramona and Pepe's "wedding of the century" last spring)
(that phrase is used for all big events these days,
including the upcoming WTO protest: "It's the X of the
century") and so they've been given the job of passing
out chocolate kisses at the reception. And Dak, Sera's
husband, won't be there at all; he's leaving on an
important business trip to Manila on the 20th. And what
about the pig he offered to roast for the reception? It
hasn't been mentioned lately. Probably the pig is out.

Z's been trying to keep secret the fact that the
ceremony will go down in Gwen and Jess's yard. To my
mind this is a bad idea and in the long run will result
in even more hurt feelings. She's also decided to let
Paz come and take pictures -- black-and-white only. So
that's one more person who must be sworn to secrecy, or
two more, since of course Paz will tell her partner,
Tobey, and perhaps bring her along as an assistant. And
Z's still obsessing over Betty's habitual lateness. "I
will not let this ruin my wedding!" Again I had to
swear my support for her plan to start the ceremony no

more than thirty minutes after the scheduled tip-off,
I'll call it, of one p.m. At lunch with Aida today Z
burst into sobs over this. Aida assured her she'd strew
the petals herself if Kat didn't arrive in time. I
repeated my sage advice that she, Z, phone Nick as soon
as possible and put him in charge of escorting Betty and
Kat to the ceremony on time. She vowed to do it.

    But she's still feeling her life's a shambles. "I
can't wait until the honeymoon," she says, and often.
-- But actually, as she also says, and almost as often,
she's enjoying the agonizing and kvetching. But still
it frazzles her so much she keeps popping kava kava and
various other dubious herbal remedies (and here she is
now, so I'll stop -- tonight's not an official jyze
night, after all -- the sign's not up, the hat's not on,
I'm not wearing the button -- I'm triply remiss!).

[+2]

    A bit of an experiment. I've taken up position
(hunkered down, really, on this windy night) in one of
the octagonal brick open-air ramparts near the base of
the big federal office building. Eleven p.m. give or
take. Fog's rolling in -- ferry foghorns are blasting a
few hundred yards from here -- and if I tilt my head way
back the top floors of the half-dozen nearby highrises
are only intermittently visible if at all through
streaming mist. I jyze by the lumens cast from a big
white globe light marking the entrance to the
underground parking garage for federal workers about
twenty feet up the steep hillside. End-of-summer
partyin' folks stroll by on the sidewalk about ten feet
below, including, right now, a trio of hardy student
types, probable frat subcategory, two of them shirtless
despite the chill. Across the street on the next
building to the north an orange neon sporting-goods sign
glows brightly, causing the leaves on the tree just
uphill from it to reflect the light and thus appear to
be aflame -- making it, to my mind, "the burning tree

of jyzefire" -- or why not make that "jyzefyre."
     It's the middle night of the long Labor Day
weekend. And I can't deny it: I'm glad to be getting a
few hours' respite from the wedding pressures. It can
be a little tough hanging out with Z for long periods
these days. She's well aware of this but sometimes just
can't help herself. -- But as another sign that she's
trying, tonight before we parted outside the WOC (it was
my idea, proposed well in advance, for us to go there at
such an unusual time and mainly in hopes it would help
her work off some steam) -- tonight she proposed that we
each wear the other's pendant: I would get "Sweetheart"
and she "Celebrate." And so it is. We swapped them on
the spot.
     She says if I think she's hard to put up with now,
I should've seen her during premenstrual times in her
late teens and early twenties. Or any other times
during that era, for that matter: her "flipped-out
phase." She calls it that herself. And I believe she's
being pretty much literal about it. I also have much
more sympathy than I did earlier for what Arvin must've
gone through during the tumultuous months of their
engagement. I don't doubt her wiggy behavior then had a
lot to do with the breaking-off of the engagement just
days before the planned date for the wedding. (Exactly
how close they came to it Z now insists she can't
remember. It's all a blank.)
     -- None of which is to say I think we're in trouble
or I relish life with her one bit less. It's just
fascinating to watch all this unfold. And it's keeping
me on my toes for sure.
     Such drama! A burst of sobs one moment, a
proclamation of wild and crazy love the next, a fierce
interrogation over a triviality (sez I) right after
that. Screams coming from the next room: "I can't take
the pressure!" Double-edged remarks: "You're being such
a fucking good sport, I can't stand it." Impossible
questions: "What happens if you suddenly stop loving
me?" Intentional provocations: "If you really cared you
wouldn't let me do this!" I'm accused of being on

everybody's side but hers. She proclaims she's wildly, impossibly happy, "the happiest I've ever been in my whole life." She insists she should be treated like a princess because, after all, that's what she grew up learning to expect and furthermore that's how all her other men have treated her, most notable among them her father and her brother-in-law Ben, so why not me? She declares herself to be utterly miserable. She reminds me that after the Arvin fiasco she'd expected to remain an independent single woman forevermore and she pronounces interdependence and mutuality and reciprocity to be nothing more than "boojie patriarchal scams" (though usually she's big on all three, and especially reciprocity). She demands that I pull aside the legs of my loose hemp shorts so she can scope out "your N'dow package" and then feigns taking a photo of it: "Click! For the wedding memory album!" -- And mostly we're laughing through all this. Usually it really is fun. But I do feel I'm walking on eggs at times and doing that can get yucky, yes, and yolky and albumeny too (not to mention all that nasty cholesterol).

A big eighter coming up. Tuesday Vida delivers the completed rings. (Z's already promised me she'll hold off until after the wedding to ask for further changes if she still finds her ring inadequate.) Thursday, which is a massively auspicious day by some people's reckoning -- it's 9/9/99, a numerologist's dream -- we'll be going in to acquire our wedding license. (I'm the one who suggested the date. She had to do some juggling because she already had a mammogram slated for that afternoon but she agreed we ought to seize on anything that looks propitious.) And next weekend we show Vinnie the baker our final design for the cake.

The orrery she came up with looks great. She's signed on to my plan for mounting the thing atop the cake with the Z and G planets included and on a somewhat larger scale than, and well above, the others, so it's actually a compromise. We -- I -- even get to paint the planets. They're impaled on the tips of stiff wires projecting up to several feet from a bright yellow solar

hub just like a miniature version of something you might
see in a planetarium -- if "miniature" is the right word
for a fabication with a wing span of close to seven
feet. There's also a little motor that sets the whole
system slowly spinning. For that matter there's a
projector that beams star patterns onto the ceiling --
constellations is the word -- but we probably won't be
able to use that since the reception will be in the
afternoon and the many-windowed room can't be darkened
enough and the ceiling is fairly high and it's white.
     -- Oh: and tomorrow I'll go with brother Rob to buy
the music for the reception. Z and I picked out a dozen
or so CDs yesterday and put them on hold. Most are
oldies -- doo-wop, funk, soul, classic rock -- and
there's also a vintage Polish polka collection in which
one of the accordionists might even be a relative of
hers (well, he has the same unusual Polish surname her
mother did as a maiden). At one point Z was saying we
should save money by having Leola and Gerry provide the
music from their massive soul collection, but I just
couldn't see asking them to do that. Z agreed to spend
fifty bucks from the wedding money, so I'll kick in the
rest. And Rob was planning to buy me a couple of blues
CDs for my birthday -- that's why we were scheduled to
meet today in the first place. I'm sure he won't mind
switching those CDs over to doo-wop.
     -- Partiers out there, meanwhile, on both sides of
the street. Lots of them are spilling over from the
end-of-summer fest a couple of miles to the north.
Tonight's probably the last big summer partying night of
the year -- last big official hoedown, for that matter,
before the millennium rollover. Unless WTO counts. And
why would it not? From everything I've read it could be
the biggest of them all. -- And it's not just chilly
out here tonight, it's cold. No more bold shirtless
probable frat dudes juggling beer cans have appeared.
Whoops and hollers, though, have been plentiful, as have
boom-box cars, honks, squealing tires, poppety-popping
motorcycles. And huffs and groans as groups climb the
hill, passing within a few feet of the crazed hunched-

over jyzer in his bizarro protected rampart. -- Who
doesn't really know what time it is, his pocket watch
having inexplicably stopped ticking.

[+1]

     -- I'm able to finish off this eighter at the
waterfront chain burger joint because on holidays it
stays open an hour later than usual. Lots of folks ride
ferries on holidays -- especially the last day of a long
holiday weekend, as today is -- and this franchise is
part of the state ferry dock. Most of its customer base
is captive: the hundreds of people waiting in cars to
board ferries. It hikes its prices accordingly. That's
the main reason I usually walk seven-tenths of a mile
north to the downtown franchise of the same national
chain rather than just two-tenths or so west to this
one. That and the fact that I like to rack up the
exercise, which in turn makes me feel better about
eating the cone.
     This is just about the last place around where the
holiday still seems to be in progress, and even here
it's sputtering. Only two large booths are on offer in
this restaurant (sic!), and usually both are occupied,
but now I've got the largest one all to myself (along
with the clam-dinner leavings of the previous occupants,
probably smuggled in from the fish-and-chips place half
a block up the waterfront -- but I'm still relying on
these leavings, suitably arranged by me to resemble a
single meal, to help persuade the staff I'm a big-time
patron worthy of being allowed to stay on in this booth
a good long while). And the other large booth's empty.
And to my left through the picture windows I see a
lengthy line of cars climbing the hill after
disembarking from the jumbo ferry that just arrived.
     So at two this afternoon I took off on foot for the
record store by the fairgrounds. For the first time
ever I hiked up and over east hill (reminding myself of
the hike up and over north hill on the way to meet Z for

313

the first time). As I neared the fairgrounds,
approaching from the southeast (the look of it from that
angle much different now with the bloblike music museum
rising in the shadow of the golf-tee-cum-saucer icon),
the sidewalks were suddenly crowded with fairgoers and
the air full of cacophonous live music coming from
several sites within the grounds. I timed it just
right: my pocket watch (magically working again after I
gave it a stern shaking) said two minutes to three as I
crossed the last street and heard Rob hailing me from
behind, where he'd just stepped off a bus.

Incredibly to me, the store had failed to hold the
CDs we'd given them for that purpose on Saturday. Rob
says they're notorious for this kind of screwup. He
went off to browse in the classical section while I
tried to round up by memory alone the selections we'd
made Saturday. The total bill was around ninety bucks
-- and it would've been thirty-some more without Rob's
discount. I did manage to find the two CDs Z picked
out, the polka disc and a collection of soul hits;
that's the important thing. (As hoped, Rob made two of
the doo-wop collections his birthday gift to me.) ---
*

At that point a cleanup worker came into view --
scrubbing down tables and suspiciously eyeing my decoy
clam dinner from their rival chain -- and I figured it
was time to move on. Then while passing under the
viaduct on my way back to the hideaway I had to make a
wide circle around what appeared to be a major drug
bust, with six or seven police cars involved. Walking
over earlier I'd been approached in that same area by
one of the bustees whose "America's Team" jersey I now
recognized (could any apparel be more apt?). "You
straight?" he inquired then. "Need anything?" As far
as I can recall it's the first time anyone's ever asked
me if I'm straight. Just might be the imminence of
wedlock that's causing so many different kinds of
weirdness to happen to me and around me these days.

-- So back to seeing Rob. At dinner he told me
about his Mentoka trip, regarding which I took quite a

few notes just in case my plans for a fictional Mentoka
series ever lurch back to life. We also speculated
about the likelihood of son Elgie's looking me up
someday (Rob thinks it's greater than I do). About Z he
said, "Everyone thinks you've really struck gold with
her" -- and by "everyone" I assume he means Jim Q. and
brother Jeff and Jeff's wife Angie as well as his own
wife Gail. He said Jim mentioned (on the phone)
"finding some way to get Glennar and Barbara reconciled"
and that he, Rob, replied that he, Rob, probably ought
to steer clear of a project like that (I agreed, of
course) -- but I stood forewarned, Rob said, that Jim
might be broaching the matter with me.

  Rob also inquired if it would be okay to bring
along Emily, his daughter, to the wedding, and I'm
anticipating some grumbles from Z about that. And I'll
have to be calling Jim too, because if Jim does show up
with his current partner Nancy, Rob won't be able to put
them up at his house now with Emily visiting for the
week and using the spare bedroom. -- As I told Rob, and
continue to believe with ever-greater conviction, he
and Gail hit on the right way to hitch up: just the two
of them and the required pair of witnesses before a
judge. If you want to celebrate with "the tribe," as
Z's often putting it these days, then do it serially
over a period of weeks, couple by couple, person by
person, maybe even small group by small group. But of
course we've already gone way past that fork in the road
(and I don't think Z really wishes we'd taken it).

  At five-thirty Rob and I walked downtown so he
could catch a bus home. It was the same route I used to
travel several times a week when I lived alone in the
area and hiked up to the "north pole" on provisioning
expeditions. Already the hood's character has changed
considerably because of new construction involving
several huge upscale apartment and condo buildings. One
of the smallest of these, just now topping out at eight
stories, stands right next to my old building. As Rob
pointed out, it would've been virtually impossible for
me to go on living in B-2 -- sheer hell if I'd tried it

-- because the construction taking place only a few feet
away, literally on the other side of my hallway wall,
would've made daytime sleep impossible. And when I said
it's true that, though I still sometimes miss certain
aspects of my "one-man odd couple" life there, on the
whole I'm a helluva lot happier now, he said that's just
how he thinks of his own period of living alone after he
and Marcia divorced, before Gail reappeared in his life.
(While in Gatewood he looked up Steffi, the big love of
his high-school years, and the three of them -- Gail
included! -- had dinner together, in fact at a
restaurant where he used to bus tables back when he and
Steffi were an item. That's something I don't think Z
and I could do if we ran into one of my old high-school
heartthrobs -- Cindy, say. I know I for one wouldn't
want to try. -- And Rob says from what he's seen I
serve as an "anchor" for Z in much the same way he does
for Gail. And he thinks Mom and Dad would've been proud
of us for this, especially given some distinctly
unanchorlike behavior by both of us -- and me in
particular -- in earlier eras.)

18

     Not the ordinary opening gambit. But it's apt that
the first day of school finds me bivouacked at my
favorite cafe out in the Yuke. True, the first day of
classes for most students here is still weeks away (a
large number of foreign students taking crash courses in
English being among the exceptions). The cafe is only
about a third full. But then again, for me this isn't
any usual post-Labor Day "real start of the year" either.
All that's on hold until the end of the month. But it

is the first day for classes at city schools. And Z
told me she was moved to tears by the emotional scene
she witnessed at one of our hilltop bus stops as parents
greeted their homewardbound kids.

     -- She was out from work early so she could meet
with Vida, the ring-maker, at our place. But the phone
rang at half past four, thirty minutes after the
scheduled meeting time, and it was Vida saying her car
had broken down on the freeway coming in and she was
stuck in a parking lot way up north near the city limits
(the car had been towed to a garage nearby; and her
parents, visiting from somewhere far off, and her son
were with her). Since they'd be marooned in that area
at least two more hours I proposed that we drive up to
meet her there and pick up our rings.

     And that's what we did. Vida, resplendent in
jewelry she'd made herself, bespangled and bedecked,
laid out her bag on the hood of the Z-mobile and brought
forth the rings and also two new pendants I'd ordered
(one inscribed "Zoelie B." and the other "Jyze"). In
finished form, including liner inscriptions ("Z&G" on
mine, "G&Z" on hers, per Z's specification), the rings
looked even better than I'd expected. Z seemed pleased
with hers (though she's not usually exuberant about such
things and wasn't this time either). Mine didn't fit so
well; at some point I'll have to tighten it somehow.
But I still like the ring. And I feel plenty fortunate
to be with a woman who goes for the unorthodox every bit
as much as I do or, often, more. (To her my ring seems
"sort of Viking like," she said, "you know, big and
rugged and primitive, like, GRRR....")

     Vida brought along her ring-snipping tool but as it
turned out we didn't need it. Last night I managed to
pry off my star-and-crescent engagement ring. It took
about half an hour and my finger's still looking a bit
misshapen and bruised. Had I not succeeded in wrenching
it off almost by accident a week ago while talkathoning
with June (and fussing with the ring by longstanding
habit in such situations), I probably would've given up
last night.

     And so that's why at this moment the ring finger of
my left hand is ringless for the first time, other than
last night and the night with June, since Z and I found
the engagement rings at her neighborhood flea market on
my birthday weekend two years ago. "I don't know if I
should let you go out in the world alone," she said
while dropping me off an hour ago, "in this state,
ringless, a newly confirmed bachelor, and wearing your
black 'Stanley' muscle shirt." (Earlier she'd said,
"Don't think just because I don't say it very often I
don't realize what a catch you are. It's just I don't
want it to go to your head." And I said: "So where do
you want it to go then?" And she said: "Ooh, ooh, maybe
we should go fuck right now." -- But just playing of
course. At that point we were on our way to meet Vida.
And she loves to "shock" me like that, Z does, and I
love to play "unshockable" right back -- though once in
a while I might try to return the shock with a little
something extra on it just to keep her honest, and once
in a very great while I might even succeed.)
     The big week of prenuptial preparations. It's
exciting. After finishing up with Vida and the rings we
stopped for dinner at a gourmet burger joint that's Z's
longtime favorite in all of Jyze City. For much of the
time there we were exploring the deeper implications of
a phone message Z received from Aida asking again if she
could bring Kirk to the reception. Z has already said
no to this twice. "Why does she keep asking? What's
really going on here?" And she filled me in on the
latest additions to the list of reception attendees.
RSVPs are now up to about a hundred and twenty, with
almost fifty arriving over the weekend and today.
     The other main topic was a question I'd asked her
last week. "For some reason," she said, "I can't get it
out of my head." It was simply inquiring into how she
thought she'd be different had she been born into a
society as racially diverse and integrated in at least
some senses as J. City is today (especially for
Asiusans). Her basic "choosh" is she would've been
"less insecure." And what about me, she asked. I

admitted I might've been less attracted to people who were racially and/or culturally different from me -- but only as a generality. I don't doubt I'd still have been besotted with a certain Zoelie B.

And so here I am stomping on the old turf -- "old" as in four homes removed, meaning four residences back in my life. This cafe didn't exist when Lady U and I first took up living in this city just five blocks west of here, but the dance studio where she rehearsed did, and if the signs outside are up to date, it's still located directly above where I'm sitting now. -- Are you dancing up there as I jyze down here, O ghost of Lady U? -- But no, I'm not "going there," not in person and not jyzewise either. That story's over, and even as a tale told in deep retrospect it's certainly not for now. ("Now" being, I should note, the 250th day of the last year of the Gregorian decade/century/millennium.)

[+1]

Well, here's a bit of serendipity. Since it's a mild night I thought I'd stroll over to the public market to welcome in what some are calling the luckiest day of the twentieth century. I had little to do at the scope office and certainly nothing better to do at midnight on a Wednesday night. So I've done that, ambled over, just four blocks, and now I'm sitting almost directly under the big market clock. Both the clock and the sign next to it are lit up in bright pinkish-red neon which shimmers in reflection here and there on the wet bricks of the street and the windows of a row of parked vehicles. In fact I can read the time on that clock reflected in the passenger window of a gas-guzzler silver SUV standing maybe ten feet in front of me. Five minutes before midnight, it seems to say, but the mirror effect means it's actually five after. It's a lucky new day!

And making it doubly lucky, I'm now leaning up against the swollen belly of the big brass pig that

guards the entrance to the main arcade. It's the size
of a shockingly obese small pony or, why not, a 4H blue-
ribbon porker. Later on I just might mount it and
scratch out some jyze piggyback -- which will be a first
for sure.

    Says the sign right in front of me: "The Market
Foundation Piggy Bank makes wishes come true." I've
already dropped a dime in the slot on the pig's back.
And my wish is that the marriage of G&Z, for which we'll
be obtaining an official license in about fourteen
hours, will prosper from the get-go and forevermore
thereafter. And since the wishes don't appear to be
limited in any way, here goes another dime -- kerplunk!
-- and this time I'm asking for prosperity for the
whole damn world (of the sustainable kind to be sure --
but isn't that redundant? Is it really prosperity if
it's not sustainable?). And here's my last coin, a
quarter -- kerplunk! (again but with a little more aural
substance to it) -- pleading for safe resolution of the
terrible planetary crises looming before sustainability
can even be considered a real possibility.

    Pretty corny, I'm not denying. Also a whole lot
sententious. Worth even less than hog slop. But
heartfelt and amply brain-processed all the same.

    -- What's good about this spot is that it's safe.
Janitors and cops and delivery folks are working nearby.
The lighting is good too. The smell, however, is not so
good. About twenty feet to my rear is the notorious
stall where tourist crowds gather during the day to
watch fish flying through the air, and the remains of
the day's tosses still stain the ice in the bins back
there as well as whatever breezes blow this way.

    And a few couples and other nightlife permutes and
combos occasionally pass by. Probably half a dozen bars
and clubs and restaurants within fifty yards of here
remain open at this hour, including the bistro a level
down across the slanting brick alley; through the window
there I can see candles flickering in jars on a dozen
tables (at one of which Z and I dined last winter, and
all I remember about that is we decided not to go for

the "Special Market Porkchops"). And from these
passersby here I've drawn more than a few puzzled looks
and raised eyebrows, but so far not a single comment or
at least not one whose words I could make out.

And then there's this. We need a good news day
because yesterday was a bad news day. It came in waves:
three of them. Or from Z's vantage maybe four. Nothing
too terrible in any of them for us personally, but for
others close to us, maybe so. I suppose it'll be a
while before anyone really knows for sure.

First, and mildest, Z's "feelings were hurted" when
Aida told her the senior D's might not be attending the
reception. It seems their regular Saturday rosary
conflicts with it, taking up exactly the same three-hour
stretch. These are the people Z has regarded as a
second set of parents for much of her adult life. And Z
thinks some payback may be involved: we didn't invite
them to the ceremony itself, so they won't attend the
reception. (And I should mention this talk with Aida
also produced a morsel of good news: she's "finally okay
with," in Z's words, "Kirk's not coming.")

Second, Z's friend Leola, who was supposed to be
hosting the henna party for Z a week from Saturday, has
been plunged into a world of hurt in her marriage. By
happenstance she was home during her normal work hours
to answer the phone when a call came in from an airline
saying "the reservations to Rio for Gerry J. and Arlette
X" would have to be changed. A big confrontation
followed and the jig's up for Gerry: an affair's going
on. He's confessed. Leola cried on Z's shoulder "for
hours." Gerry and Leola may be headed for divorce
court.

Equally bad or worse, number three: Tobey at the
utility received an e-mail saying Jess and Gwen have
broken up. As of earlier tonight nobody knows anything
more about this; neither Gwen nor Jess was reachable by
phone or e-mail or knocking on the door at their place
-- which of course is where Z's and my wedding ceremony
is supposed to take place two weeks from this coming
Saturday. (That's seventeen days from now by NUT time!)

-- So obviously big changes could be in store for the
ceremony site. It might switch to Aida's backyard or
Betty's or Wei and Alison's or one of several parks or
the arboretum or some other spot yet to be determined.
But we refuse to let anything stop us.

Finally, maybe worst of all (ha ha), Z learned her
duties at work will henceforth include supervision of
the Filusan bombshell Gloria G. Dale's washing his
hands of her. "This is why you got the job," he told Z
on the phone, goofingly to at least some extent (he's
now officially on vacation in the megastate to the south
but still checking in from time to time). "You're the
only one who can handle her."

-- But it's ten to one now and I still haven't
mounted the porker. A moment ago a bearded janitor came
by, scraping gum and other sticky items off the market
floor tiles. He's gone now. Three or four folks are in
sight but for the most part that's been true all along.
Simple fact is I won't be able to do this unobserved.

Here goes nothing.

*

-- Good solid pig. (As I just told a bypasser, who
laughed and said, "And I don't think he's going anywhere
either.") My knees are propping me up, pressing against
the back of the porcine ears. This bronze is slippery.
And my J-stick picked a good time to run out of ink --
but a staunch J-slinger always carries a backup. And I
feel a literary reference coming on. "A Voyage Around
My Room," wasn't the author riding a hobbyhorse while
writing? Or how about this: "When you wish upon a pig,
makes no difference what's your gig...." (But here's a
surprise. My bad groin which I'd thought had completely
healed is aching from the wide spread of the mount. But
even so I feel good luck osmosing up into me. And the
silver SUV has left so I can't tell the time from here
but I know I'm cutting it close on the last bus
considering that the bus stop is three blocks away.)

So much for the wild ride at the start of the
luckiest day of the century. But more craziness lies
ahead -- hey, a hitch in time saves 9/9/99! Or no,

reverse that. Or anyway: sooey, sooey! -- Over and
off. Pig out!

[+1]

-- Now only a few hours left in the fabulous lucky
Gregorian day. And I'm being courageous again, even
reckless. On a cool and maddeningly blowy Thursday
evening I'm sitting outside the office where we
purchased our wedding license this afternoon. It's the
county administration building, right across the street
from the county jail (to which a windowless skybridge
leads from this building here, seven stories up and
almost directly overhead -- so, in theory anyway, you
could buy your wedding license and go directly to jail
without passing "Go" or anything else).
     Right now it's hard enough just holding down the
pages of the J-book. The jyze is coming in little
spurts between boisterous gusts of wind.
     If I lift my head I'm looking directly at the two
tallest buildings in the city. They tower across the
street from each other just a block to the northwest, a
total of something like 140 stories if one building were
stacked atop the other, and right now both are brightly
lit up from top to bottom, and only slightly above them
puffballs of cottony gray cloud are stampeding
southward, with half a dozen searchlights casting
laserlike yellow beams up into and in some cases through
them in shifty eye-catching patterns that resemble a
glamorized Hollywood version of a World War II air raid.
     This morning's Jyze City daily emblazons "No. 9,
No. 9, No. 9..." across the top of the front page, just
as does a card I made for Z well before seeing the
paper.
     If those clouds up there went away I might be able
to gaze at a skinny crescent of new moon -- the marital
moon. Supposedly it first appeared this afternoon at a
little after three while we were filling out forms in
the office right here. And is that auspicious or what?

Z wore her sexy slit black skirt along with a black
jersey and also left her normally spiky hair unmoussed,
all, she said, just to please me (though the truth is I
like her hair just as much when it's at its moussed-up
spikiest). Her mammogram took less time than expected
and she arrived home almost an hour early to pick me up,
finding me naked and just starting in on breakfast (I'm
rising around one p.m. these days). For the trip to
score the license I dressed in jeans and a khaki shirt:
nothing too formal. She was teasing me for being
grouchy, but in truth I was just trying to wake up.

So it was quick and simple. We'd both expected
long lines, but only one other couple was present and
they weren't Chiusans. On this propitious 9/9/99 day
apparently everybody else expected long lines too and
came early to beat them. The clerks were very pleasant
-- as Z commented, of all city employees their jobs are
probably the most enjoyable. Fifty-two bucks we paid.
I wasn't quite sure of the birthplaces of my parents
(some minor questions arose concerning both after their
deaths) but regardless I took an oath that I was telling
the truth, as Z did also. I didn't have to show the
divorce papers that cost me a total of twelve hundred
bucks to obtain, nor did I expect to, although I brought
them along just in case. (Z had to swear, as did I, to
have revealed to her prospective spouse -- to his spouse
for me, yes -- the existence of any sexually transmitted
disease. This surprised her. Did genital herpes count?
Could I go for an annulment by claiming she'd failed to
inform me? -- But of course she'd informed me long ago,
in fact shortly after we met, and with a dramatic
weeping four a.m. telephone call I'll never forget.)

We now have sixty days to do the nuptial deed. In
a rainproof plastic envelope right here in my bag I'm
carrying the official papers for Olwen to sign when the
deed itself goes down. And we're required to sign them
too at that same time.

Then we went home -- or no, first we stopped by my
primary corporate chain supermarket. How thrill-packed
almost-married life can be! (Z often comments to this

effect. She's pumped. This is the first time around
for her -- as it seems I can't mention too often in
these pages -- and it's all new and startling and scary
and exciting and disappointing too, sometimes, though I
do the best I can to make it as terrific as possible for
her as well as myself, and she does likewise for me, I
have no doubt.) -- Then home, and Z was tired and
wanted to take a nap before going out for her evening
engagement, and so naturally I did too. And we both
got naked. And lo: a not-so-prosaic almost-married
consummation ensued with a bottom-scraping gusher of an
ejac for the J-slinger (which of course was for her as
well and also in her, happily, as we moved back to
"plan A" mode) (and she meanwhile unleashed her usual
astounding barrage of 'gasms). -- And then we both
napped a bit while remaining genitally conjoined and
that too was delicious.

The evening engagement for Z was Jess's birthday
dinner. This was to be a subdued, limited gathering
because the rumors have proved true: Gwen is involved
with someone else. Almost more startling, this person
is male. What's more, he's wheelchair-bound and at one
time was a patient of hers (she's a physical therapist).
She's had boyfriends before, true, but those were before
she met Jess -- and that was about seven years ago.
Tonight's get-together is slated to be all lesbians (Z
excepted, although, as she's not shy to say, she might
easily have gone that way herself) and includes Madge I.
with whom we took the recent boat ride and Z's and
Jess's work associates Paz and Tobey, who are throwing
the party at their house (so they can introduce everyone
to their new dog, Roxie, a German shepherd they're
depending on for protection in their run-down -- but
also rapidly gentrifying, like ours -- hood).

No doubt I'll be getting an earful about all this
later, so I'll drop it for now. -- And in fact I think
I'd better run along to the hideaway while I'm still in
one piece. If this cold wind doesn't tear me apart it
might topple me over onto the concrete sidewalk where
I'll shatter into ice shards. It's a straight shot down

the hill, three and a half blocks, past city hall, past
the municipal building, past the police station, and, if
I go by way of my preferred mom-and-pop store, past Z's
utility building. And by the time I thaw out down there
I'll need to hike most of the way back up here to catch
the last bus.

[+1]

     The usual Friday-night cacophony. It must mean I'm
once again holding forth at the hideaway, and that's
exactly right. It's an exceptionally light week
workwise with Naomi out of town for most of it and so
I'm trying to squeeze in a little more jyzing than
usual, going to an every-day schedule for at least a
short while. Two bands are thumping down below, my fan
is buzzing quietly up here as the Jyzer Ink license
flaps lazily and the kitschy little Uncle Sam doorstop
props open the door (or rather prevents it from opening
still farther under pressure of the breeze from the fan,
which is set up on the filing cabinet right next to it
for the purpose of blowing stuffy air out of the room).
     It's a special Friday night too. Haul out the
ram's horn. As of Sunday, Jewish year 5760 got
underway, and tonight begins a ten-day period of
reflection and remembering and I'm thinking maybe I'll
ride piggyback on it, as during last night's market
porker mounting, for at least some of those days. A bit
of sober private thought about the life gone by and the
meaning of the nuptials just ahead -- which, in fact,
will be taking place on the Jewish day of celebration
following all this soul-searching, Sukkoth, which also
falls on the magical 9/25 date this year. -- And then
today, Rosh Hashanah, is held to be the birthday of the
world, so this too is an occasion for celebration.
     Yayhoo! Roll out the Rosh Hashanah hosannas!
     What's more: today by Gregorian count is (for it's
a few minutes past midnight) the day of the wedding
haircut. Two haircuts, in fact (again), because Z's

will be taking place in the same shop at about the same
time as mine. And I'll say I'm as prepared as I can
ever be for this shearing. The dry run a month or two
back somewhat boosted my confidence about it, at least
to the extent I'm no longer fearing a sartorial atrocity.
How much it'll cost me I don't know but it's sure to be
by far the most expensive haircut of my life.

    Z's been cracking a lot of Samson-and-Delilah jokes
lately. And I think I just ought to say in light of all
the disasters visited upon her this past week her
spirits are holding up much better than expected. I
think she's surprising herself too, and I know (from
talking with June on the phone this afternoon) she's
surprising a lot of her friends, and not least those who
knew her at the time of the Arvin engagement. -- June
herself sounds more upset about the Gerry/Leola and
Gwen/Jess shockers and is also mightily "P.O.'d" (a
favorite term of hers) at the senior D's for their
ambivalence about attending our reception. She even
grumps about Z's extended family back in the heartland
for failing to dispatch a single representative to the
ceremony. Heads would roll for this in the land of
Master Kung! (June's savvy advice to me: "Remember,
Glen, winds blow, the mountain is unmoved.")

    And because of limited time I'll again put off any
further dish on the shockers. Enough for now just to
mention that the wedding will still be held as planned
at Jess and Gwen's place, but Gwen won't be there and
it's not her place anymore either (and actually it never
was, it turns out, in strict property-owning terms):
which is to say she's outta there. She's history. And
so far Jess seems to be taking the loss admirably well.

    -- And it's been a fine day for me. Full of
unusual events, but I've been no more than lightly
brushed by them. By coincidence I was included in a
street scene being shot outside the entrance to the ORB
for a TV show. I saw a vehicle accident, a warehouse
fire, a stalled train (in the old tunnel), and a massive
downtown traffic jam caused by road repairs -- all just
during the walk in. I also saw a huge crane being

mounted above the excavation hole for the "millennial
tower" across from the WOC -- the first thing the crane
will do, a fellow knotholer told me, is haul up the big
"steam shovel" from way down in the hole. "Ya didn't
think they were just gonna leave it down there, didya?"
     -- But yikes it's time.

                        [+1]

     -- Bantering at the hair salon. Sunny day, the
door's wide open, light sweet folksy music's playing.
Z's being shampoo'd. "So, are you having a good day?"
Jackie asks her. "No, I'm not." "Oh? Why not?"
"Because we're just two weeks away now, as of today."
     Mine's already done. Just a trim behind, but in
front I now look like one of those receding-hairline
guys I never wanted to be but always suspected I would
one day become. (Now Z, on her way back to the cutting
floor, says to me, "She made your temples look nice."
"Oh yeah? My temples? Really?" "Very distinguished,"
confirms Jackie. "Distinguished! Well! Distinguished
from what may I ask, or whom?" Repartee. Barbershop
style could say. Not that I've been around many
barbershops in recent decades.)
     Pressed under glass on the coffee table here are
two large bird molas, one quite a bit like the one
hanging on the wall at the hideaway. The rest of the
art on display is much the same type -- ethnic and
"outsider" and counterculturish. And Z's been coming
here for years. It's one more clue as to why she and I
get along as well as we do. -- And that's pretty damn
well, yes. Though of course not always. Like last
night and this morning, just for a couple of instances.
She's been in a bit of a foul mood, to the point she
openly cursed out the lady motorcyclist who as of a few
weeks ago lives upstairs in 301. "Eat shit and die,
motherfucker!" Of all Z's oaths -- and she has a
bitchin' repertoire -- that's her favorite, as she
confided on the way here. -- But the motorcycle was

roaring out the garage doorway amid clouds of black
smoke at the point she mouthed those foul words and the
motorcyclist couldn't possibly have heard a thing -- or
could she?)

They're talking about that incident right now.
Much hilarity. Personally I think we were lucky to get
out of it unbloodied. But then I'm one of those
sheltered and hypercautious burban types, even though at
least partially reformed and reborn.

-- An interesting little coincidence revealed
itself this morning. I showed Z the two short poems,
one Sufi Persian and one Tang Chinese, which I thought
seemed suitable as a kind of benediction for our wedding
ceremony. Olwen, our "officiant" (that's the term on
the license), happened to call shortly after that, and Z
read them both aloud to her. Afterwards I asked Z for
Olwen's reaction to the Sufi poem especially. "She said
she can't very well turn it down -- she's named after
the poet, you know. Her Sufi name is Hafiza."

-- And now we roll on. (My head feels good, I'll
say. Or my scalp. Jackie's talented fingers working
the shampoo in deep did it. But at forty bucks per
would I ever go for one of these on my own, just for
standard maintenance? Instead of cutting it myself for
free? Not too likely.)

*   *

On second thought, and first sustained glimpse
really (being too queasy so far to go beyond a glimpse),
I'll say this haircut isn't really all that bad. After
leaving the shop I didn't bind myself up into the usual
ponytail. Soon Z was calling me "Rod," for a certain
longhair classical rocker whom I happen to know she
intensely dislikes. Thanks a lot, Z! But in truth I
don't think Rod looks all that bad. It may be my
imagination but suddenly many more eyes seem to be fixed
upon my coiffure, for good or ill, as I stride along out
there in the real world.

Right now I'm wondering just how horny I am. Last
night I was the one who exercised the sexual veto;
tonight, most likely (but not certainly) in revenge, it

329

was Z's turn. This was during a nap after our many-
stopped drive back to the hill. So then I got up a bit
abruptly, but trying to project ambivalence about the
deeper meaning of the move. And it's gone on from there,
superficial sparring. Not a good night for us but not a
disaster either. I'm hoping we can clear all this up
with a good rousing prenup shag in about fifty minutes
when I go back in there (jump back into the ring "with
my spirit way up high," as in "Empty Bed Blues").

It's now ten after four in the a.m. The Sunday
far-coast-megalopolis paper just arrived with a
tremendous skidding thud: the new delivery person is the
first we've ever had who tosses the heavyweight Sunday
edition, or attempts to, in traditional paperboy style
rather than running it all the way up the walk to the
door and simply letting it drop, which is usually loud
enough by itself (unless it lands on one of the lobby-
patio potted plants, as has happened at least once).

After arriving home and rising from the nap it's
been a good night at least for catching up on periodical
reading. This is especially true for me since I've been
able to devote several more hours to it than Z has. (I
notice I must do a whole lot of skimming these days to
stay anywhere near what I consider current.)

And of course I should see to the promised dish.
And this even though there's really not a whole lot new
to add.

Gerry and Leola are back in their original high-
plains home state this weekend for a long-scheduled
school reunion. They're also supposed to be deciding
the fate of their marriage. My guess is if they're able
to make such a trip together under such trying
circumstances they'll also be able to salvage the
marriage. Leola, Z says, is setting a couple of
conditions of a basically materialistic nature. For
one, Gerry must pay for the new SUV Leola has her eye
on. For another, he must take her instead of Arlette to
Rio. At this second one especially I'm agog. Who'd
want to be in Leola's shoes for a trip like that? Or
maybe Leola relishes the punishment such an itinerary

would surely constitute for Gerry. She's also making
all kinds of noises about divorce lawyers -- weighing
which one could squeeze the most from the treacherous
old fessed-up two-timer -- and she's thinking about
returning to live in her old hometown (just a few miles
from his) because her alimony payments would stretch
much further there.

      With Gwen and Jess it's more puzzling. Others
claim they've been detecting signs of trouble for
months. Suddenly G&J were postponing their plans to buy
land together and to hold a commitment ceremony and they
weren't wearing their matched leather jackets at the
same time and they weren't raving about the $2500
matched rings they had on layaway. And people were
seeing less and less of them. Apparently Gwen's
involvement with her paraplegic male patient was
deepening over this period, although it's not clear when
Jess learned about it. But last weekend (Labor Day)
Jess went off by herself on a planned camping trip and
for the entire period she was away Gwen had the guy
staying with her in their house, and when Jess returned,
a couple of neighbors remarked to her on his presence.
Gwen had told her nothing about it and at first denied
what the snitchy neighbors had said to Jess.

      It was the lying that did it. And when Jess
confronted her, Gwen, who's eight or nine years younger,
started spouting a standard bunco line for busted
betrayers: "I don't know who I am anymore, I need to get
away on my own for a while." And since this is Gwen's
second infidelity, Jess had had enough. "That's it,
you're outta here" -- those being the actual final words
as she reported them to Z and the others at her birthday
party Thursday night. The next day she had Gwen sign a
batch of papers rescinding various agreements they'd
made, and again that was it: bye-bye sweetheart.

      And unlike the first infidelity go-round with Gwen
five years ago, when Jess nearly went mad with rage and
grief -- to the point of cutting off all her hair and
shaving her skull -- this time she seems in good control.
She didn't hesitate to say she still wants our ceremony

to be held in her yard, and she's been going ahead with
other previously scheduled commitments, both at work and
socially. But this was a nearly eight-year relationship
and Jess is staying on alone in the house where she and
Gwen lived together for most or maybe all of that period,
so I'm sure she'll be hurting plenty.

        (What's all this to do with us? Maybe it shouldn't
be much. In a sense Gwen and Jess introduced me and Z.
Z's close to them both, especially Jess, her work
associate. I regard them as friends and enjoy their
company, and at various times both have helped me out in
one way or another in my struggle to win Z's heart and
mind and keep them won -- sure, I'll say it like that;
why not? -- and...well, that's enough. Gwen's probably
history now for Z just as she is for Jess and so most
likely for me too. And that's sad.)

[+1]

        Maybe this'll work after all. I didn't give it
much of a chance when I was walking down here, or at any
other time after sundown over the past several months,
but now that I'm here not another soul's to be seen
within fifty yards except the upper-crusties dining at
the fancy seafood restaurant a few yards behind my back
(a whole row of them, a dozen window tables, all
occupied, many of the diners gazing out in this general
direction) and like museum dioramas of aristocratic life
at the court of Louis-the-Nth they're all behind glass
and stuffed (and what's more, stuffing themselves,
though of course in genteel fashion).
        This is my favorite corner picnic table at the
overlook park by the public market. I'm facing out into
the inky darkness on a warm starry night as traffic
roars by on the viaduct out of sight a few feet to the
west and some thirty or forty feet down. Lights of the
waterfront container yards glitter to the southwest and
the downtown towers shimmer to the southeast as well as
the east and the northeast too, directly behind me. A

332

few groups of people are gathered at various spots in
the park, most of them Natusans, I'd guess, a dozen of
whom are sprawled on blankets on the grassy knolls at
the park's center. Behind them stands the northern end
of the market, now closed for the day, the arcade
looking desolate with all the lights on for cleaning and
the booths and stalls empty and no one in sight.

Looks as though I won't be bothered over here.
Good deal. (And now cometh a ferry gliding around the
point and into the harbor. "Floating wedding cake" --
more apt than ever! And a train's emerging from the
northern end of the tunnel down below; I hear and feel
its engines and also hear its bell. -- And a klaxon
sounds on a tour boat easing by just offshore.)

Earlier today Z and I were walking on the beach
near that same point the ferry just rounded. This was
after finishing our fourth major wedding chore of the
week, which involved meeting master-baker Vinnie to firm
up the plans for the cake. To my eyes the real cake
(even if it's still mostly imaginary) looks almost as
big as one of these floating cakes I'm seeing now.
It'll be chocolate with peach filling, with three
different tiers including one elevated on stilts, and
atop that one the orrery will be spinning. Or maybe not
spinning: just suspended in place, because it turns out
the batteries are only for the starry light projections
and not, as I'd assumed, for a planetary spin engine.
Too bad! But Vinnie said it would be no problem baking
the top tier with a large hole at the center, angelfood
style, to accommodate the solar hub for the planetary
system. The system itself consists of plastic balls of
various shapes and sizes riding one to three and a half
feet out from the hub in all directions on stiff wire
spokes (except downward into the cake, of course).

Vinnie's eyes lit up at the sight of the orrery,
which we brought along to show him. He asked right away
if we'd agree to have photographs of the finished cake
taken for his display book. (He's a short Latino-
looking man with a mustache, probably around forty, very
friendly and easy to work with.) And the cost is just

$245 for a 140-piece concoction, for a savings of over
$300 compared with the bakery Wei and Alison used.
(Dish! Dish!) Vinnie had baked up a small sample cake
for us and Z and I both found it plenty tasty enough.
(And then we had to stop at the co-op right afterwards
to buy a piece of roast chicken at the deli solely to
head off a potential hypoglycemic attack which the sugar
in the cake, Z felt, was threatening to bring on for
her.) The only disappointment was that the icing will
be, like the cake itself, chocolate, not blueberry,
which Vinnie can't do. He could do blue dye in standard
white sugar frosting, but Z nixed that because the dye
might be toxic (though she didn't actually say that to
Vinnie); and I told her it was enough for me that we
could have the orrery on top and the rest was just, yup,
icing on the the the -- yes.
     And then we did the leisurely beach walk. It was
another warm and sunny afternoon -- we're into a good
late-season stretch here and crossing our fingers it
will continue -- and lots of sunbathers were out. The
beach is narrow (and pebbly and even stony in places)
and the tide was closing in on its high for the day,
shrinking the boundaries still further and making the
place feel thronged. Urban beach: folks of all kinds
and ages and body types and sizes (and temperaments too,
no doubt: we had to dodge two separate fistfights). The
view from there of the islands and the mountains is
almost as good as the one at the marina up in the Scandi
quarter. Fishing boats and freighters and tugs towing
barges were chugging by along with lots of pleasure
craft including several magnificent (but gliding not
chugging) sailboats ol' Dad would've salivated over.
     (A hunchbacked lady of uncertain age scuttles by.
Right here at the overlook park, I'm saying. So-called
bag lady, I guess, complete with a real bag almost as
big as she is (and unmarked). She's tidying the place
-- even went after the lid from my bottle of berry juice
on the next bench seat until I asked her please to leave
it. Is this a self-appointed task, I wonder, or is she
one of the downtown low-income folks I've read about who

334

have contracts with the city for street and park cleanup
-- i.e., in a sense one of Z's "fellow" city employees
and therefore a public servant, and so in theory I'm her
boss? -- As I like to say to Z regarding herself, but
only, for sure, if her mood seems right.)
     This is fine -- jyze going down mainly thanks to a
viaduct sodium street lamp, by the way -- and looking
now at a crane swinging above one of the floodlit white
cruise ships parallel-docked up at the pier three blocks
to the north, just down the hill from my old B-2 digs --
but I'm thinking I ought not press my luck too far. And
I need to take a leak, I do, I do. -- And besides, the
park officially closes at ten and we're well past that.
                    *   *
     So now the hideaway. I think I'm doing okay thus
far in my Rosh Hashanah quest for repentance and prenup
spiritual renewal, even while acknowledging I still have
a long way to go in the remaining eight days. What
makes it okay is that so far I haven't hit upon much of
anything I feel urgently requires repentance and this
failure does indeed give me a feeling of spiritual
uplift. Hey, I'm doing pretty damn well here! Main
thing I ought to be feeling is gratitude, I'm thinking,
the broadly generalized kind to start with and then
later I might try to spell out some particulars, such
as, just for starters, having this hideaway office as a
secure retreat at times of runaway wedding stress.
     Z's been reading James H.'s latest alternative-
psychology screed. It's making her more aware we
haven't been together very long in comparison with a
good many other couples she knows. Our two and a half
years are as long as she's ever been with anyone --
slightly longer than, she thinks -- but of course
they're still only a small fraction of the time we've
been alive (slightly smaller in her case than mine). So
instead of seeing our time together as being very long
she's suddenly seeing it as very short. "Who are you
anyway? What were you really doing for all these years
when you didn't know me?" It's a shake-up. Life with Z
is full of such shake-ups and that's one more reason

it's so often so good for me (and one more reason why I
think aging might be less of a trauma for us than for
some: constant shake-ups also mean constant renewals.
One might even say it's Rosh Hashanah 365 days a year).

While walking on the beach we talked about these
things and many others. How lucky we are. How
fortunate. How preposterously well suited for each
other, even with, and perhaps in a sense because of (but
not always), our massive differences. How much we truly
believe all the hokey loving banalities which are such
an undeniable pleasure to mouth to each other over and
over. How much we truly and sincerely do vow never to
let things go stale -- instead we'll go ever deeper and
at the same time ever further afield while nonetheless
remaining inseparably tethered up. And she talked about
her growing realization, during her difficult times with
the D-clan over the past few months, that perhaps she's
subordinated herself to others too much. "I'm wondering
if maybe I bent too far in an effort to get along. I
need to rethink all this. I became a sort of handmaiden
to Serafina especially. I'm going to try to view all
these things that've happened lately with them as what
the leadership institute used to call 'a major AFLO' --
another fucking learning opportunity."

Tonight she met Aida at the hilltop Filipino buffet
to talk over wedding matters and also just to schmooze.
She returned home right before I left and so treated me
to the latest dish on Aida and Kirk. They're getting
along well and he's now demanding she install a bigger
bed ("king size of course") and also insisting she let
him sleep over even on those nights when Charles is home
rather than staying with his father or grandparents.
And according to Z, "Aida really does like you, you
know. She thinks your idea for the planets on the cake
is really cute." My own view is Aida just barely
tolerates me. But now that she has Kirk she has less
reason to think of me as a villain -- the one who
snatched Z away from her and left her bereft and with
way too much empty time on her hands. So at least it
might be true to say our relations have bottomed out and

are heading back up. Certainly I hope it is.

   Aida's explanation for her sister Sera's bad
behavior of late is that she's highly upset about the
likelihood of an upcoming move back to the Philippines
(where she grew up to age eighteen, just like Z's
father). It's either that or a marital breakup, because
Dak is determined to move there and set up a microbank
(he'll be doing the spadework for it during his visit
there starting on the 20th -- the one that's deprived us
of the roasted pig -- and according to Z his parents are
wealthy enough to finance the entire venture and it
won't really be all that "micro" except in the size of
the individual loans as opposed to their cumulative
sum).

   -- And Z's decided to transfer, chiefly to Wei,
some of the reception duties originally assigned to
Sera. Among others, the grounds cleanup, the
dishwashing, and now the final merging of orrery with
cake -- they're all his. And Z says we shouldn't feel
too bad about this, because she had volunteered our
services in a similar way for W&A's wedding, even if he
and Alison chose not to make much use of them. (We
drove by the garden club because of the possibility --
no longer an issue now -- that we might need to hold the
wedding itself there. It still looked okay, but not
nearly as good as it did before. The reason is simple:
the headquarters of the state association of garden
clubs has allowed its lawn to turn brown -- and not in
an ecologically aware fashion! They've simply neglected
to water it! The flowerbeds too! In several places
they're looking bedraggled and forlorn!)

   I want to note, also, today's fine sunset, again
viewed from the south-hill high bridge, in which the sun
sank directly behind the massive mountain with the
double summit. At one point rays were shooting from the
outsides of both summits as well as from the notch in
between, all through a reddish-orange haze. -- And this
was quite a shift in just a few days from the next big
peak to the north. Ol' Sol's going south on us and it's
moving fast!

[+2]

       -- As a parasail soars and swoops out over the bay.
This being viewed from the exact same lucky spot but two
days later and three or four hours earlier in the
evening. The two couples with whom I share the table
are in agreement -- all four heads nodding at once --
that it'll be a fine sunset about an hour from now
thanks to the jagged cloud streaks hanging just above
the mountains. Both couples are from somewhere on the
upper far coast -- they're talking now about how
"reasonable" the property values are out here. I'm sort
of half listening in -- don't really have much choice.
Says the apparent alpha female of the bunch: "I don't
think the prices are that outrageous. I mean if you
live right here in the city." -- And now they're all
turning southward, admiring the volcano, which from this
angle seems to loom above the two stadiums almost as if
they were foothills to it, one on each side.
       Dazzling corridor of sun on the water, an inbound
ferry just now breaking through it. Once again the
corridor leads directly toward the mountain with the
twin summits. Today, I'm thinking, that mountain can
symbolize my two brothers. Jeff's birthday is today,
Rob's is a month from today (or is it a month from
tomorrow? -- I'm always confounding the actual
dates and having to look them up).
       Our tourist couples have turned their attention to
the traffic noise emanating from the viaduct. "Why
don't they just cover it up -- make a tunnel of it?"
Well see, folks, we'll do that just as soon as the
earthquake levels the viaduct. That's what we're
waiting for. It's much cheaper that way. Okay? We're
cheap out here. -- I as a quasi-local sometimes feel an
impulse to enlighten tourists about the local ways. Not
this time, though; I'm keeping all comments to myself.
-- But about many of those same local ways I must admit
(again, to myself only) I'm flat-out ignorant, or close
to it. For instance, what stories do these two totem

338

poles here tell? Dunno. Don't have the faintest.
Unforgivable, especially considering how often I've
hunkered down in this very spot over the years.

A marvelous stretch of weather. At the diagonally
opposite extreme of the country right now, though, it's
terrible. Truly. Headline in the evening paper:
"MONSTER HURRICANE AIMING AT SOUTH." If it follows the
predicted course, damage will be catastrophic. Then the
arguments will intensify about whether this particular
storm is a product of global roasting. In fact they
already have. As if it matters to the larger "debate"
about whether global roasting is happening. I tell you
it's happening! And you'd better listen, all of you!
Or else!

-- On Jeff's birthday I mailed him a brief birthday
note along with the official wedding invitation I told
him a few weeks ago I'd be sending. These went out from
the post office in the AQ, as did the poetry package for
Olwen. I also bought another sheet (the last one they
had) of the Year of the Rabbit postage stamps. I
arrived there late and the lines were long; otherwise
I'd've made it here half an hour earlier and I probably
would've had this table all to myself (as I do again as
of a few minutes ago when my tablemates headed for the
seafood restaurant -- in fact they're now, already,
sitting on the other side of the glass about thirty feet
due north of this table and what's more they're sipping
wine -- and we're seemingly pretending we're total
strangers now -- or at least they haven't waved. Nor
have I, though I was briefly tempted to. -- As if any
of this matters. -- But it all does, that's the thing.
Of course it does!).

(A sleek yacht is gliding by -- actually a tour
boat. A super-jumbo ferry is replacing a smaller one at
the state dock. Haze all along the crest of the
mountains is glowing orange as the sun sinks halfway
behind the southernmost slope of the twin summits and
suddenly our park here is unbedazzled and disenchanted
-- all the grimy urban details jump into focus as if a
blanket of snow had instantly melted and evaporated --

or as if some mischievous deity had snatched it away
like an immaculate sheet from a funky mattress. -- And
now it's gone, the last bit of glowing rim and the last
of the triple rays as well. But the twin peaks are
spectacularly backlit and the streaky clouds are
horizontal dazzles of orange and red, with most of their
former raggedness somehow planed off -- as if, to shift
metaphorical tools here, they'd been restroked with a
much finer brush.)

     Z is wonderfully happy and excited these days.
This all by itself would be enough to make going through
all the wedding preparations worthwhile. And she's
telling me she's happy, and she's doing it often, and
that's somewhat new. There were times in the past when
I almost had to beg her to say a good word about our
relationship. (She's getting back into the swing of the
altered-card game too, leaving me a new one most days
and sometimes two a day. And they're funny. This
morning's worked a nautical twist on my saying to her,
as we lingered in bed, "Ooh, I do like those testicle
tugs": she drew two tugboats towing a couple of asteroid-
size spheres with sharklike sperms swarming on their
surfaces (presumably inside too), each sperm shaped like
an upside-down lowercase "g".)

     As clouds turn pink-shading-to-purple above the
southern volcano, the peak itself fades into gray haze
and now is barely visible. But the lights in the
container yards come on and a dozen huge orange cranes
spring into new prominence. -- And a bit of chill in
the wind encourages me to don my long-sleeve khaki shirt
which I've been carrying in my bag. The restaurant, I
see, is packed now. My former far-coast tablemates are
completely engrossed in chowing down (no more yakking
for the moment). Meanwhile the grassy parts of the park
are suddenly missing half their blanket sitters. Have
any of them shifted over to the restaurant? I highly
doubt it. And the street lamps are on. And yes, I
smell grilled salmon. And I imagine everyone else out
here does too and would love to have a plate of same
along with some wild rice and cornbread with butter

and/or honey. And doesn't the restaurant owe us for
providing all this authentic local color out here?

Z jokes I'd better be ready, she's about to become
"massively dependent." She'd been scheduled to speak at
a conference on recycling in the nation's capital in
early November but she suddenly felt she didn't want to
go there alone so soon after the wedding -- I couldn't
go with her owing to my job commitments -- and so she
wangled Dale's permission to have David take her place.
It'll be David's first speech to the association and, as
Z said, "He'll be shaking up the ol'-boy network for
sure" -- David being one of Z's proteges and an Afrusan
by way of the West Indies with massive dreads and truly
colorful threads which he wears to work every day as a
matter of principle as well as preference (Z tells me).

Today's also primary election day. I haven't tried
to keep up with it in here, but the city council could
shift a bit further leftward (hooray!) and so Z's crowd
has been involved in the campaigns -- though not as much
as I would've expected. It could be that their interest
in political activism is starting to wane. If so, I
don't think anyone would deny they've already done
themselves proud and then some over a period of decades.

-- And surprise: here's the moon hanging roughly
twenty degrees above the horizon and seemingly directly
over the middle of the bay. Apparently it snuck out
there using one of those slow-moving black clouds for
cover, like a guerrilla inching in closer behind a
movable shrub. The marriage moon -- first real sighting
of it for me. A fingernail crescent suspended mostly in
streaky horizontal black clouds like charcoal rubbings.

Yesterday, by the way, a back order came in for
Naomi and therefore I had to scratch my plan to do the
jyze thing every day this week. At the end of her
voicemail she added, "Incidentally, Glen, I'm not sure I
understand the message on your answering machine. Could
it be you're about to get married?" So I had to leave
an explanatory note for her in the office safe on top of
the night's transcript. I don't want Naomi to feel
obliged to do anything for us. Years ago she and I hit

on a friendly but arm's-length and almost impersonal way
of relating that's worked well for both of us and I'm
hoping we can keep it just as it is and I don't doubt
she is too.

(And I see the far-coast couples are gone from the
restaurant; their table is empty. If they did dessert,
I missed it. Nor did they drop by the table out here to
say goodbye. Our brief moment of crossed paths appears
to be over.)

*   *

-- It's late now. Very late. A couple of months
ago the morning's truth at first light would've turned
to humdrum nonsense by this hour. And I guess I'd have
to say I'm being bad -- a bad lover. I've had no pop
the past two mornings. Or it's actually not that I've
lacked pop; it's just that my timing's been off. I'm
trying to do a lot these days. Too much? Maybe so. At
times. Seems it's all but inevitable when you strive to
walk the crumbling edge as a good J-slinger generally
should do during a crucial stretch in a serious jyze
project. And I'm striving to do that! (Conceding
however what's an edge to me might not be to someone
else -- to lots of folks, I suppose. Might just be a
featureless patch of flatness -- and what's it to ya?)

Oooeee how this boy's mouthing off tonight! (As
the withered and half detumesced old birthday weinie
balloon sways in the breeze overhead, still attached to
my chair by a six-foot-long blue ribbon.)

A little ex post facto I learn a big fire was
burning up in the mountains and that accounts for the
orange glow of the "mist" and of those fractal rays
shooting out from the sides of the twin peaks and
through the gap in between and I'm once again made
mindful of certain paradoxes of aesthetics, among other
things. And a rare September smog alert was posted
today -- also the first this year. It was smog the
southern volcano was fading into tonight.

And I haven't mentioned June's visit here at two
a.m. Monday night seeking help on a paper for law
school. She's now living in a dorm just a mile to the

north and can come over for short periods at odd hours.
The paper was about a sex-harassment case -- June in her
pink shorts and me in my red ones, a hot night, lots of
yuks (especially walking her back to her car at three-
thirty a.m. as a couple of passing vehicles slowed,
probably wondering if she was a hooker and I her pimp or
more likely her john just finishing up -- because I
still often see hookers on the street here at that hour,
although it's true their numbers seem to be dwindling
lately as gentrification powers ahead). (And that night
was when June told me what I should've known myself:
that in Chinese lunar astrology the Year of the Rabbit
is highly propitious for marriage. Which is why I then
went out and bought the sheet of Rabbit stamps mentioned
earlier -- not for mailing purposes, but for attaching
to the back side of my altered postcards for Z.)

      So I'll cut it off here. See what kind of pop I've
got tonight. And if little or none, then best to go to
"plan B." Because we both be needing some skin.

19

      Stopping briefly to lay down a few jyze licks on
the way in. Upper AQ, a narrow cement staircase outside
the side entrance to a big warehouse -- "the gray one."
Like the blue one behind it and the green one kittycorner, it's being refurbed (all graffiti have recently
been painted over on all three warehouses, I notice).
And it's already stuffed half-full with cyber product
(which appears to be deluging the district, much of it
no doubt bound for or in one way or another emanating
from the big-time dot-com at the DC castle.
      I thought I'd sit on the steps outside the food

bank just across the street, but right now they're being
tended to by a matched pair of small bundled-up Asiusan
women with brooms. Too bad, because the homeless
Eurusan man with the dog and the grocery cart who often
takes possession of those steps in the afternoon isn't
around today. It's a one-story wooden bungalow, more
like a shed, gray and desolate-looking, with a covered
area in back where people rummage through bins of
donated goods, but it's almost always closed at this
hour.
     Or I'd like to sit on the front stoop of the church
right next to the food bank, but lots of people are
going in and out there. It's a handsome old two-story
brick building, dark brown with a green roof, with signs
in Chinese and English on both sides of the entrance and
an ancient white-painted coal chute down at sidewalk
level behind one of the doughty evergreens which both
demonstrate and embody an aesthetic concern highly
unusual for properties in this area. (And through the
narrow gap between the food bank and the church, right
behind them, flashes of freeway traffic moving fairly
quickly for this hour: maybe close to ten m.p.h.)
     -- These women with the brooms are bundled up
because the weather's taken an unexpected turn (and in
fact an unpredicted one as of last night), becoming
overcast and chilly. It's almost as if the glorious
days of the past week had become an embarrassment for
our entire region in light of what's happening on the
other coast. There the massive hurricane mentioned
before is raging just offshore -- they're saying it's
the most dangerous storm of the century -- and millions
of residents are evacuating, with the latest forecasts
calling for the main body of the storm to make land late
today.
     At home the news is good on the consummatory front.
Ol' Poosh did show some pop last night. And Z was
especially loving, at first trying to keep quiet
(because I'd left her a "Doggone Tired" card citing our
long-winded late-night updates on nuptial doings as a
cause of my in-vag foozle yesterday) but then casting

aside all constraints. Or at least many constraints;
if it had been all, the whole hood would've been
shaking. On the phone this afternoon she confessed to
feeling "mellowed-out all day." Even to the extent
she'd decided not to file a complaint about the
construction going on next door. She had checked and
they don't have a permit. And she especially dislikes
all the loud racist and misogynist and generally ugly
and hate-filled far-right trash talk coming from the
workers, including the owner, all of whom are Cawks.
But we'd be sitting ducks for retaliation and wouldn't
really accomplish anything by complaining, other than,
probably, to stir up their ire still further. And we're
already going after them for their loudly barking,
unleashed dog (whose name is Mikey, we've learned),
their illegally parked vehicles (blocking our sidewalk
entrance), and several other somewhat lesser concerns.
     Meanwhile the word is Jess is looking pretty bad.
The breakup's hitting her now. And Leola's still
demanding all kinds of consolatory attention from her
friends at work, but it appears she'll be caving to
Gerry. Z's again grumbling about how narcissistic and
materialistic Leola can be. "It's as if all she cares
about is being the center of attention and being sure
she gets her new deluxe SUV." Z figures she, Z, ought
to be the center of attention right now and doesn't want
anything to mar the happiness and excitement of these
final prenup days. (Well sure!)
     -- As a trio of saggy-ragged Afrusan street dudes
saunter by. Not too hostile though. Nor did they try
to peddle or push anything on the jyzer, though at first
he was sure they were about to. Instead they were
talking football with lots of loud laughter and big
physical gestures and imitations -- "tiptoe down the
sideline" (as through the tulips) for one.
     A wedding present arrived from Amalia M., former
city councilmember and mayoral candidate -- and she's a
Filusan -- several of whose campaigns Z helped out with.
It's a tape: dance music from "The Buena Vista Social
Club." Bizarre. And when I called the car-repair place

to tell them I'd be bringing in the Z-mobile tomorrow,
the guy said, "Ah, would you be the new husband?"
     (Here's a pigeon practically pecking at my toes.
And once again a crane is swinging overhead, this time a
blue one boasting a curiously pristine-looking U.S.
flag. An ancient loadless forklift jounces noisily by
on the street. One of a trio of presumably Chiusan kids
presses the buzzer at the locked church entrance and the
door cracks cautiously open at first and then swings
wide and the kids scoot in. -- And I see the church's
street-level side windows are barred but the front ones
aren't, almost as if they assume that no one would dare
to make a frontal assault on a house of worship.)
     And: it's the 15th of the month, quarterly tax day.
My next stop is the post office to mail the IRS an arm
and most of a leg. (Naw, it's really not that bad.)
(And just one more note: 25 minus 15 is 10, so we're now
into serious countdown territory. 10, 9, 8....) (Well,
and this: Z started the serious countdown on the
calendar in her room at 15, I noticed. That was Rosh
Hashanah, the day after we got the license. She wrote
the numbers with a sparkly purple kids' marker, her
favorite kind.) (And, finally for sure, this: her
interest in Jewish holidays and Jewish ways of seeing
the world -- and Jewish men -- came from the same Ben
or Benny mentioned before, the twenty-years-older
brother-in-law she idolized.)

                          [+1]

     Here's a decent spot for some next-day follow-up.
It's the waiting room at the repair garage in the Scandi
quarter. But it's the industrial-wastelands sector
thereof, and after walking several blocks looking for a
suitable jyzing spot I headed back here. I came across
one other possible venue, a tavern, but the Eurusan
geezer gang inside was taking up most of the seats and
it appeared chitchat might be hard to avoid. Also I
passed by a couple of roadside boulders that looked

pretty good for perching on, but by that time I was
thirsty and jonesing on the soft-drink vending machine I
thought I remembered standing outside the restroom door
here. Turns out, however, it's not there now and
they're saying they've never had such a machine anywhere
on the premises. Odd. In my mind's eye I can still see
it humming away over there. Am I perhaps moving into
the next phase of my own prenuptial flip-out?

   No problem, though, because the boys in back (all
Cawks just as always) gave me a small paper cup of
water. And the perch here is definitely comfier than
either of those boulders -- it's a small gray armchair.
And to my right a worthy picture-window view. A
sidewalk, four lanes of a major road, another sidewalk,
a chain-link fence, and then some shrubs and small
trees, lots of weeds, several old one-story wooden
outbuildings, a half-full parking lot, trucks,
dumpsters, and at the center the largest building
around, home to a galvanizing company. It's just two
stories, but its open garage-size doors in front reveal
a kind of nineteenth-century industrial-revolution
vision of men (all Cawks) laboring over machines, with a
couple of soldering torches throwing off some undeniably
twentieth-century incandescent sparks. But even so,
"Satanic mill" is a term that's hard to push away.

   Just outside the door here (I've got the waiting
room to myself) I can hear the estimable Russ soothing a
customer on the phone. Yesterday I was one of the ones
he was talking to that way -- and he was remembering not
only what needed to be done on the car (no doubt he'd
brought up our screen on his monitor) but also that Z
and I would be taking it on our honeymoon. Today when I
presented myself he again greeted me, "Aha, the new
husband -- in the FC!" But no, he said "flesh." ---
               *   *
   -- They finished that up fast. And I probably took
longer than I thought I did to scope out the hood (and
I'm realizing now I failed to mention it's within a
block or two of the ship canal and fishermen's terminal
and everywhere you go in the area you see thickets of

347

masts sticking up and occasionally pilothouses and the
upper reaches of superstructures and electronic rigging
of larger vessels that in some cases almost seem to be
docked in people's backyards -- and also lots of worn
and flaking paint on the houses and other buildings,
which gives the hood as a whole a fine weathered
seagoing wabi-sabi feel).

Z's been taking her car to that garage ever since
-- (but now she walks up down below -- I'm back at home
-- "who dat guy up on da balcony?" -- and I'll sign off
for the nonce and greet her at the door, which I rarely
have a chance to do) (and when I do I usually blow it).

*   *

About ten hours later. Nonce over. During which
I've walked into town, done a night's scoping work,
returned home on the last bus, and now I'm back on the
living-room couch, this time facing south for a change.
Sighing a little. Things are starting to get...a bit
baroque, yeah. Freaky. Twisted. Disquieting. (Not
for the first time, true, on any of these. Nor can I
say the development in general is unexpected, except in
a few of the particulars.)

Start with a simple observation: this is the very
last J-week in which I won't be a married man. Of
course this is assuming once the marriage happens it'll
take -- and that's exactly what I am assuming. Or
alternatively, or in addition, it's my last J-week as an
official domestic partner ("Deep" -- the papers we filed
with the city some twenty months ago say so) and also my
last as a "confirmed bachelor."

Out in the world, the far-corner hurricane looks to
be less catastrophic than expected. It's already been
pushed out of the headlines by a mass murder involving a
church group in a southwest state. Meanwhile another
crisis ratchets up in East Timor -- looks like the UN's
going in. Here in J. City most of the more progressive
candidates have survived the council primary.

And a bit of good news for me: Naomi has found
"reasonable" my proposal that she pay me a nickel more a
page. This amounts to a raise of about seven percent on

deps and maybe two and a half percent overall, since
Jyzer Ink makes most of its money on grand-jury work. I
was a little disappointed she hadn't proposed such a
boost herself. But I didn't want to embarrass her too
much over her failure to do so, so I waited to bring it
up until the status of the firm's overall rate hike was
clear. Her defense is that it's "a two-steps-forward,
one-step-back kind of thing" -- but evidently she
believes the net of one step forward is enough to
justify paying me the extra nickel.

     She also wished me well in my marriage -- "as much
happiness as I found the second time around." And she
assures me it is a big deal (contrary to what I wrote in
my note to her). And I'm pretty sure she's relieved not
to have to deal with it, meaning my own deal, anymore.
(The whole time we were talking, Larry -- the big deal
she was referring to in her own life -- was standing
poker-faced just out of earshot, I assumed, by the
office door. Two of the cases I scoped tonight involved
his interrogation of witnesses before the grand jury.
My guess is he's still as suspicious of me as he was the
day we met a dozen years ago, but he tolerates me
because the FBI has cleared me several times -- each one
inexplicable, no question -- and maybe even more because
Naomi vouches for me and doesn't want to lose me.)

     -- What's troubling me right now, an hour ago Z
padded out of the bedroom, unable to sleep and in a
grumpy mood. In a matter of minutes she managed to irk
me in at least three different ways. First, she said
June's "pushing it too far" (June left a message saying
she's coming over late tomorrow night so I can help with
her resume update). Second, she razzed me about being
more interested in reading the newspaper than talking
with her (true enough, at that moment, especially given
the disagreeable way she was speaking; but at least I
was trying to suppress it). And third -- by far the
most painful -- she announced that "after the wedding"
she won't be doing any more postcard alterations for me.
Evidently they've become too stressful for her -- she's
feeling pressure to match or outdo the ones I make for

her. The plain implication is she'd prefer not to be
receiving these cards from me. And this stings. Since
they take a lot of work, I'll stop doing them if I feel
they're unappreciated. On the other hand I don't want
to simply be retaliating. So I suppose what I'll do is
tell her I'll suspend them for a while and wait to see
how things shake out when our lives have returned to
something more like normal. -- And I'll do this with
majorly mixed feelings, because I enjoy altering the
cards but of course these days I'm also in an ongoing
and ever-deepening time crunch of my own. Certainly I
can use the card-prep time on other things. (Now to see
if I can make the change without stinging her too much.)

     Earlier tonight upon arriving home she proposed we
take a quick nap. I was so tired I was hesitant to do
it, thinking I might have a hard time getting back up
and off to work -- might really conk out. But after a
little chitchat we segued into a shag session and to my
surprise I discovered I again had some serious, yup,
pop. The timing here is good -- it's taking away one
possible source of stress. That would be true at any
point, of course, but it's especially important in this
period of prime wedding countdown. (And she said her
back felt fine -- "completely back to normal.")

     Earlier today Olwen, a/k/a Hafiza, called to say
she likes the "Hemispheres" poem and has found a spot
for it in the ceremony. Even better, to my mind, she's
crazy about the collected Tang poems and also wants to
include one of those (Sufism takes great pride in being
eclectic in this way -- though my hunch is it's just as
convinced in the end of its own superiority as any other
religion; I mean, how could it not be and still be a
religion?). Our talk was a little awkward -- also par
for the course with us -- but regardless I felt pleased
about the kind of friendship we're developing. (Z, by
the way, ran into Olwen's former boss and in the course
of talking about Olwen's "retirement" he mentioned that
Olwen was busier than ever these days, and one of the
first things she was doing was "conducting a marriage
for a very dear friend." "That's me!" cried Z -- and

she really was delighted to know Olwen would describe it
that way to this man. -- And I told Olwen this story,
only to have her inform me she'd just heard it from Z.
"But a story like that," she added, "is worth hearing
several times even in a single afternoon." And
punctuated this at the end with a double dose of her
excellent honking chortle.

    Z, meanwhile, is obsessing over the way Leola's
acting so self-centered, wanting to talk about nothing
but the fraught situation with Gerry. She, Z, is afraid
it will ruin the "henna party" -- equivalent of a bridal
shower, to be attended by her closest friends -- on
Saturday. She's also worrying about what to wear under
her wedding dress, and should the pantyhose go inside or
outside the undergarment? Cards have come in from her
half-sister Camilla and from Uncle Joe and Aunt Clara,
her mother's sister and brother-in-law, back in
Centropolis, both cards containing checks, and these
have taken some of the sting out of the near certainty
none of her relatives will appear in person at the
wedding next week. Some of that gift money we'll be
spending on a discounted "Rhythm & Roll" boxed set; Z
found it on the internet (so we're consuming even as we
criticize -- but this is basically how it must be across
the board, period, so what the hell). This boxed set is
the one I've been searching for in so-called brick-and-
mortar shops ever since I heard it playing at the
franchise coffee shop next to the corporate supermarket
down in the valley; it should take care of any remaining
concerns about music at the reception. (Brother Rob
will likely be in charge of keeping the music going.
Wei could do it too but he's already overloaded. The
sound system itself will be Aida's.)

    What else? Serafina sent out a lengthy e-mail with
detailed instructions for the reception crew. Positive
RSVPs are now up to the mid 130s. Jess is saying we
should do the ceremony under the arch in her garden, not
on the cement driveway area, and I agree, but for some
reason unclear to me Z is dubious about this. She also
doesn't want to be bothered with renting a canopy in

case of rain -- she's now back to thinking large
umbrellas will be fine, and if the rain's heavy everyone
can move into Jess's kitchen while we do the ceremony on
the small covered back porch outside the kitchen door.
(I have to say the basically improvisatory quality of
this setup for something so important to her -- and me!
-- doesn't sound like Z at all and I'll be surprised if
she sticks with it.)

Z's friends Terri and Frank arrive from Lahontan
early Saturday morning, only a little over twenty-four
hours from now. So we're truly about to move into the
final stages.

(And even if I'm probably making it sound as if
everything's frantic and everyone's cranky, in fact for
the most part we're having ourselves a real good time.
Z's laughing a lot and so am I. There's truly an
abundance of rich material for humor here. One small
example: perhaps in lieu of being able to clean up the
apartment for Terri and Frank, or possibly as a kind of
nominal or symbolic cleaning act, Z poured massive
amounts of liquid soap on all three of our kitchen-sink
sponges but then got caught up in other things. Not
knowing she'd done this, I turned the water on with one
of those sponges under the tap and stepped out of the
kitchen to answer the phone (it was June calling);
moments later I was startled to see something like the
head of a giant cauliflower rising well above the level
of the countertop. It was a huge mound of soap bubbles!
It took ten or fifteen minutes of crazed squeezing to
get the soap out of one of the sponges (we had no spares
left) so I could clean up all the rampaging bubbles and
then rinse off the counters and stove. "Sorry Zoelie
honey, no nipple action tonight; my tweaking muscles are
all worn out....")

And all this week Z's been mesmerized by a
miniseries on public TV about a mixed-race family. It's
the first time she's seen the kind of biracial issues
she grew up with even mentioned on national TV, to say
nothing of the kind of detail and depth this series (ten
hours of it) is going into.

[A Jyze Epithalamium]

[+1]

Here's our local urban waterfall. It threatens to
spray little droplets all over this J-book if I don't
shelter the pages just right.
It dominates a corner lot next to the main HQ park,
with a high iron grillwork fence guarding the street-
facing sides, medium-size trees and thick shrubbery
standing just inside, tables and benches scattered among
smaller trees farther in, and large gray and brown
boulders stacked twenty feet high along the two inner
walls. A stream about eight feet wide pours over the
top of those walls at the corner where they meet and
cascades down a rocky concourse to the inner patio,
which is several feet below street level. The patio's
made of red brick and adorned with black iron tables and
round pink granite planters bursting with flowers,
mostly bright red and white New Guinea impatiens.
Blue sky fractured by tree limbs. The upper three
apartment stories of a commercial building rise right
behind the northern inner wall. The windows there are
the kind that swing out horizontally, and many of them
are open right now, and people could lean out -- jump
out -- in theory could dive into the pool at the bottom
of the falls. It would be highly hazardous though.
(And cool misty splinters from the falls caress my
cheeks as I look up at those windows -- blur the jyze
too here and there, but only a little.)
I like this spot. Tourists know about it and a few
are always around -- as now, a couple taking a photo, he
of her, and my left shoulder is probably included --
they're Dutch if I'm not mistaken, but tall blond Cawk
Europeans for sure -- and at noon it's crowded here, but
afternoons it's generally quiet and restful, truly the
"urban oasis" the laminated brochure displayed on the
table proclaims it to be. And according to a figure
penciled in on the hours sign it's now open until 5:45
-- summer hours. The rest of the year it's five
straight up. And it was close to five when I passed by,

so I didn't think I'd be able to sit here. Oh happy
happy day. -- Though I'll be asked to leave soon, I
expect. (And would need to anyway, because it's another
heavy worknight. So heavy, in fact, I've already
decided to put some of the work over until Sunday night,
or I couldn't be here at all.)

Z won't be meeting me at the WOC tonight. She has
physical-therapy and beauty appointments. At physical
therapy they're literally stretching her out on a rack
to relieve pressure on her cervical spine which they're
theorizing is causing her shoulder pain (I have to be
careful not to give her sudden squeezes these days --
especially after a don't-know-my-own-strength embrace in
bed the other night). She's never been stretched on a
rack before -- not literally -- but finds it relaxes her
into a strangely pleasant "hyper-meditative" state and
at the same time sees it as being nicely symbolic of
what the overall wedding preparations are doing to her.

Her friend Nadine, the one with terminal brain
cancer, has been moved to some sort of hospice this
week. Z's been told it means the end is very near. She
was hoping to be able to pay her a visit this afternoon,
but her schedule may have been too tight.

The marital moon reached its first quarter several
hours ago, meaning it's halfway to full (lunar math is
loony). I searched the skies for it on my way in but
without success. (And looking up now I see, in sharp
silhouette against the blue sky, a row of avian odd
couples perched motionlessly atop the west wall: four
gulls and four pigeons, perfectly alternating as if
they're mixed pairs waiting for the signal to start
their act -- sort of like a square-dance octet, I'm
thinking, just before it moves onto the floor to form
the square and the music strikes up. (Well, but what's
the deeper meaning of all this, please, Mr. Jyzeman?)

-- Uh-oh, here's a guard in uniform. Asiusan, I'd
guess Japanese descent. Closing time, he says, firmly
but not unkindly, which is a surprise since he probably
sees me, and rightly so from the perspective of the
international tourists, as local street riffraff. ---

[A Jyze Epithalamium]

[+1]

      -- Now sitting sideways on the couch at home, fully
naked this time, facing north, my back to the lamp and
the big peace lily, looking out into blackness to my
right because the streetlight there flamed out night
before last and my angle of sight is just above the
outdoor lights of the building across the street and the
ones speckling the in-city hills to the east -- and this
on an uncommonly warm Saturday night at three a.m. with
Z sprawled coverless atop the sheet in our bedroom, but
wearing tight pink H-rag "unners" (she's afraid a new
outbreak is on the way). This on the first day of my
last bachelor weekend ever (as Jay at the WOC reminded
me earlier before offering, tongue-in-cheek to be sure
-- I think -- to take me out to a burlesque joint for
"one last and final really good time"). ---
                              *
      -- Did I have a train of thought going there? If
so, it got sidetracked or more like derailed. Z
wandered in still wearing just the same "unners" and we
had a nice little mushy three a.m. talk and now it's
four a.m. and we're both in the bedroom. She's reading
on the bed, I'm doing my jyze thing in the armchair.
      Building up jyze steam. Sometimes it's a little
tough. But there will be only one such night as this!
      Terri and Frank's flight arrived ninety minutes
late this past morning and now they're on the road
again, staying tonight with their friends Fred and
Eleanor (all names guaranteed real) in the first burb to
the south before driving cross-state to see their son
Tarik (Terri is of Lebanese extraction -- a Lebusan!),
who hosts a show on public radio over there and because
of weekend station staffing problems won't be able to
attend our wedding. Earlier in the evening, after Z and
Terri returned from the henna party, the four of us went
out for sandwiches at the ORB cafe and then took a
"tour" of my hideaway office -- all ninety square feet
of it. (And I'll mention that Terri and Frank have been

355

cracking wise from the first moment about the other time
they were out here for a Zoelie wedding -- the one that
was canceled at the last moment -- except that it wasn't
a Zoelie wedding then, it was a Louise wedding, because
she was still a year short of changing her name (and the
failed wedding was part of what spurred the change).
And I learned something new about that traumatic time:
before everything came crashing down, Z and Arvin had
signed papers to buy a house. Z had entirely forgotten
about this but Terri and Frank reminded her. They had
been promised a tour of that house, but it never
happened. It was on the far side of the Yuke, it turns
out, the house, just a couple of miles from where Lady U
and I were living at the time.)
     While Z and Terri were at the henna party -- which
ran two hours longer than planned, until after six --
Frank was more or less stranded here. I didn't get up
until two, but after that he and I talked nonstop until
the ladies returned. Also, because he's a skilled home
handyman, I asked for his help in figuring out a better
way to attach the Z and G planets to our wedding-cake
orrery. And within maybe twenty minutes, using a
hacksaw, a pair of pliers, and a handful of old wire
hangers, he'd come up with one.
     Only eight people showed up for the henna party.
Ramona and D'Arcy were out of town, Jess was down in the
dumps over the breakup with Gwen, June had an important
job interview, and Aida had to watch Charles, so their
absences were all more or less forgivable. Sera's
wasn't -- and her failure even to call and say she
couldn't make it was worse yet. Z's not taking it too
badly, though. She seems to be more troubled by hearing
how expensive the henna-lady's services were. -- Leola
did not obsess on Gerry, by the way. And Adele put in
an appearance even though she'd been banged up a bit in
an auto accident a few hours earlier. The main present,
other than the henna-lady's labor, was a gift
certificate to the woman-friendly "erotic" store on east
hill. A portion of the party was videoed and someday
I'll get to see it, Z assures me, including a section in

which everyone grilled her about what kind of guy I
"really" am. "So what did you tell them?" "I just
told them the truth. I'm a very truthful person. You
should know that." (She loves to goad me with this
line, always delivered deadpan followed by a sudden
crooked mischievous grin and sometimes a mock grope
thrust.)
     So now her henna applications are almost dry and
the mudlike coatings are starting to peel off, revealing
orangish-tan patterns underneath like contoured lace
nets on her wrists and one ankle. The latter design
features a large and flourishy "G+Z." Z wishes the tan
was a little darker ---
                              *
     A touching few moments in bed just now. I felt it
coming on: pure mush. And fully indulged the impulse
(it was me I felt it coming from, not her; from her I
felt a need for just such pure mush to be supplied by me
in this very special moment; but maybe I was projecting).
-- But how thrilled I am, how lucky I feel, how good
it's been and is and I know will be, how I'll love her
forever and ever, how "We've got game, grrrl!" (And
this despite the fact that she doesn't really care all
that much for doo-wop. That startling revelation came
when I played cuts from our reception CDs for her
tonight for the first time. And I've got a whole lot of
doo-wop, strangely enough, in my burbified Cawkazoid
soul. As she said: "I could see right away it makes you
very, very happy." And then pleased me even more by
adding, "So how could it not make me happy too?")
     -- And it may be too much to keep this going right
now. I think I need a different setting and also a
different frame of mind. Z's trying to sleep but she's
"got da shpilkes" -- is very restless -- and she's
occasionally emitting odd little groans (now wearing her
red bathrobe because according to her a chill has come
in on the breeze, easily detectable by the tropical half
of her blood even if not so much by my unmixed northern
kind, or rather my all-northern, relatively, mixed
kind).

[+1]

    Tonight, some twenty hours later, I'm determined to
put in my two or three cents' worth but it probably
won't be much more than that. I'm down at the scope
office now (the receptionist desk this time, looking up
at the clock, which says twenty to one), and when I get
home I doubt I'll be able to do any jyzing. Chances of
interruption will be at a probable all-time high.

    Not much new to report. As of sundown tonight
we're into Yom Kippur, the main day for repentance, but
I've discovered that even though I've scarcely even
begun with the repenting, I already feel I've done
enough.   -- And just about every day of the year, or
certainly a large number of them, is a holy day
according to some religion, and each with its demands
for confession and repentance and the like. Best not to
set too many precedents here. I mean, at heart I'm a
pagan infidel. (And every now and then I still wear a
button on my shirt that says, in inflammatory Gothic
font, "Heretic," just to remind myself.)

    -- So on this day (a Sunday, day of rest, day of
worship for at least one of those religions whose talons
I like to think I've eluded) -- on this day we did our
last scheduled premarital shopping trip, Z and I,
hitting the usual three grocery stores plus the usual
big discount mart and -- a first for us -- a franchise
arts & crafts superstore, not too far from us just off
the south end of the hill, where I stumbled across a
couple of grapefruit-size styrofoam Christmas-tree
balls which I'll be painting up as a superior set of
planets G and Z for the wedding cake (maybe with a sign
to implant nearby saying "Outer Space This-a-way").

    And at the end of the trip we brought all the stuff
upstairs and I repacked the freezer and then Z walked me
down to the north end of the high bridge by way of the
strip park and the statue that reminds her of her
father's authoritarian side -- "but not his class
background!" -- and then I walked straight to this

office and since then it's been nothing but scope,
scope, scope.
    That's it. At some point I'm still hoping to
squeeze in details about today and yesterday. But as
things are looking now that point might never arrive.

                        [+1]

    Plunking myself down on the new covered footbridge
leading over the west depot's rail yard. An event's
going on at the dome maybe five hundred feet to my left
-- home show, boat show, I don't know what -- and to my
eyes the old dome's looking sort of pale and bleached-
out right now, as if it's just learned it has only about
six months to live. And the execution order's in fact
been signed; it's just not known on exactly what date
the deed (implosion) will occur. But first there's one
last football season to be celebrated or more likely,
from what the sports freaks are saying, anguished over.
    A lovely evening. If Yom Kippur ends at the hour
it began, at sundown, it's down to its last half hour.
The sun's already dipped behind the six-story apartment
building on the far side of the huge dome parking lot
but it's still making the reddish-brown bricks of the
quarter's historic buildings glow warmly. I'm wearing
just a short-sleeve red henley (and the usual jeans and
black-and-white chucks) and still feel a little too
warm. That high-pressure ridge is hanging in there
somewhere just off the coast. Five more days is all we
ask of it. -- Or why not ten more so we can have us a
glorious honeymoon too. (On the phone this afternoon
brother Rob said he thinks we'll luck out on weather.
"But you took a big risk picking a date so late in the
month. Three weeks earlier your odds would've been much
better." No doubt he's right -- but that's not the way
it felt to me. Ever since arriving in this burg I've
always had the gut feeling that September and early
October will be the best months weatherwise. Could be
it's a kind of reflex Z and I both acquired during an

earlier phase of life in Centropolis, a city with a
whole different kind of climate.)

    And now -- already -- sundown has fully set in.
First the old brick buildings stopped glowing, and then
the top of the clock campanile above the station dimmed
out, and then the pyramid atop the great white tower did
likewise (it's poking up a few degrees to the left of
the campanile but several blocks to the north), and then
the topmost stories of the ultimate black tower lost
their gilded glitter (it's poking up farthest of all, as
always, between the campanile and the white tower but
well up the hillside, which adds a couple of hundred
feet to its height, making for about a thousand in all).

    So it could be my chance for symbolic repentance
has faded out also. But that's okay, because I never
did come up with anything I was sure would be
appropriate to offer along the lines of reformed
behavior. Either that or far too many things. The
effect is pretty much the same either way.

    Crossing the high bridge I couldn't tell exactly
which peak would get to impale the old life-giving orb
tonight. Maybe Mt. -- XXXXXXXX. (If the jyze rules
didn't relieve me of the need to name it, I'd have to
look it up. And I used to know what it was. Which is
to say: jyze has the effect of allowing me to utilize my
strictly limited memory banks for other things.)

    Here and there folks are hiking through the parking
lot, all going in more or less the same direction:
south. Behind me construction workers are still hard at
it, well after the usual quitting time, jackhammers
almost harmonizing, trying to complete some road repairs
before that same high-pressure ridge dissipates (Z and I
are not the only ones hoping it'll hang tough).

    Now bells, a deep rumble, and a clutch of switch
engines rolls under the footbridge. Five of 'em hitched
together -- hitched, I say: I'm seeing hitches
everywhere! -- the first two orange, the last three
green (livery of the two lines that merged a few years
back). And when I look around to check out the livery I
see the big yellow construction crane atop the east-

depot extension is still swinging ponderously about.
That odd-shaped new building -- it looks something like
the front end of a diesel locomotive made of green glass
-- is startlingly large for its setting. It casts its
shadow over much of the AQ and blocks the view of the
southern volcano up the "high road" corridor. In short
(or tall) it's breaking the low-rise spell of the whole
area, over which the brick campanile used to hold sway.
Before long many more overgrown buildings will be going
up between here and downtown -- in fact this will all be
part of downtown, an extension of it, after decades of
being "underutilized." The city planners have so
decreed. Or so I hear through the city employees'
grapevine by way of Z. (I'm just so much better
informed on all things municipal since meeting her.)
    Well. The twilight glow is now fading too. Little
embedded anti-slip-and-fall lights have flicked on all
the way down to the bottom of the staircase, including
one right between my feet which I could conceivably use
to jyze by as full night seeps in. But I want to move
on soon -- go work out and then come back for another
appearance in these pages, but at a different venue.
    This afternoon I stuck around the house until quite
late -- past six. I thought I'd given up altering those
cards for Z for a while -- for the extended nonce noted
before -- but I found myself back at it again. I can't
resist them. And the whole time I was listening to the
new CDs, trying to form an idea of what's usable for the
reception and what's not. But it turns out Sera has
asked Leola's husband, the baaad baaad Gerry, to tend
the CD player at the reception (she forgot to mention
this in her e-mail instructions which Z printed out for
me) and therefore my efforts have been wasted. But on
the other hand my ass is covered. Gerry's out of town
right now, but when he returns later in the week I'll
call him and see if he has any good danceable stuff he
can bring (I know he does). And I'll designate a few
cuts to play on the CDs I've got, mostly golden oldies
from Z's and my high-school days which we were dancing
to at the same time just a few miles apart but never

knowing it (we ought to be able to milk that happy coincidence one more time for this truly special occasion). "Only You," "Earth Angel," other doo-woppy stuff -- which, shock of shocks, she doesn't even like all that much! Doo-wop, that is. She explained this further on the phone today. "That was exactly the kind of thing I thought I'd never get away from in high school." -- Because she felt excluded, I guess. And also because she wasn't allowed to date. And when she and some girlfriends slipped over to the huge nearby all-male high school and did dance to this kind of music, "the boys poked us with their dicks and were just total jerks." (Though not all of them. There were a couple she could've gone for in a big way if her father hadn't kept her in line with an iron hand.) (She loves to tell me stuff like this. "Does that make you ragingly jealous, I hope?") (And I should note she also told me on the phone today that the "Rhythm & Roll" boxed set has arrived, so this means my ass as the kingpin of the music overseers is doubly covered.)

　　-- Sky's darkening but it's still blue, nary a puffball or a scudder-cloud in sight, building lights on and looking lovely against that backdrop, especially the underlit pyramid atop the great white tower and the one visible clockface atop the campanile (though the microwave relay dishes lashed to the roof up there sure do uglify it at the very top). (And a freight train's rumbling through now, whistle blaring, footbridge shaking under me -- one of the little footlights is flickering -- seems to be shorting out -- makes me wonder if the whole footbridge could collapse.)

　　Jim Q. called this afternoon. He'd been unable to reach Rob for the past week, and day after tomorrow he's flying up -- without Nancy -- and his accommodations still aren't set. So we're in the process of dealing with that, as well as deciding what we'll be doing together for a "bachelor blowout" sometime before Saturday. -- But more on all this later.

　　A fleet of old wooden baggage carts is parked along the back side of the station. Antiques with big wide-

spoked wheels. Who knew they kept them around? Lights
have flicked on down there. Jyze could be jotting away
as I sat atop one of those carts -- maybe. At least I'd
like to give it a go one of these days. (And blocked by
the covered part of the footbridge this whole time, I
see as I rise to survey the scene "once more just once"
before packing up, a gibbous slice of moon hanging over
the dome. "There's a moon out tonight -- let's go
strolling" -- a doo-wop sample right there. And
Saturday's the Chinese Moon Festival, have I mentioned
it before? Another reason we picked the date. With so
many celebratory aspects to it it was just too perfect
to pass up merely due to a high risk of bad weather.)
                    *   *
     Carrying on four or five hours later at the
hideaway. Well, it's a couple of minutes before
midnight to be exact or rather almost exact. And right
back into the jyze hitch chronicle. Where was I?
     Start with this. Today is wedding weigh-in day.
In Z's case it was official: the women in the pool all
weighed themselves and the one who achieved the biggest
reduction in percentage terms over the past six weeks
will win the cash prize of a couple of hundred bucks.
On the phone Z proudly told me she'd lost the three
pounds she'd been hoping to, but the numbers on the
others weren't in yet. (Trouble is, all this is self-
reported by honor system.) I wasn't part of that pool,
nor did I actually weigh in, but Z mentioned yesterday
at the discount mart that she thought I'd put on a
couple of pounds lately. And Rob asked, back when I met
him at the bookstore last week, "Are you still working
out?" I suspect his message was the same. Actually I
think I'm within my normal ten-pound fluctuation pattern
(five pounds below or above the norm) but maybe up in
the high end, so this week I suppose I should fast a
bit. I don't want Z to be thinking I look porky at the
wedding. (And I don't think she does think I look
porky. She still likes me to walk around naked in the
apartment and still says lots of flattering things
despite her own self-proclaimed reluctance to do so for

fear I'll get a big head. And during that same trip to
the discount mart she'd raved, "Mmm, mmm, mmm, Stanley,
you're looking so sexy today in your black muscle shirt"
(meaning shrunken henley). And a bit later, when we
spotted each other after separating for a while in the
store, she came up and said she'd seen me from a
distance and "You still look so good it makes my pussy
twitch and give a little squirt." -- And exactly where,
I asked, did that squirt issue from? And she said it
was from "the squirter" right at the entrance to the
vagina (or the exit to the vulva, I suppose). -- And I
mention all this because she's had lots of studly dudes
chasing her -- and a good many catching her -- over the
years and sometimes I don't feel so confident I'm
anything special to her. So I like it a lot when she
makes me feel I am. And if having a big head is the
price I have to pay for this, I'm willing to do that.)
     Lately, sorry to say, we've had almost no sexual
contact. I'm not entirely sure, but I think this is for
the same reason I'm not supposed to see her in her
wedding dress. It's a twist on the old superstition
that it's bad luck to look upon the bridal outfit before
the ceremony. Thus a few days ago I found all the
plants moved from her room to the dining table and a
note forbidding me to go into her room anymore for
watering or any other reason until after the ceremony.
And she's still saying she fears a herpes outbreak is
imminent and she's wearing her H-rag "unners" to bed,
but unlike all the other times this has happened she
isn't asking me to do a butt-check. So I have a feeling
a kind of low-profile ritual purification is underway.
And that's fine with me. It's probably good if we can
build up a little extra charge for the honeymoon. (But
personally I'm already feeling well prepared on that
score. There's no physical need for anything extra.
But emotionally I suppose it can't hurt. True, it's
submitting a bit to the old patriarchal symbology of
marriage, as she might like to put it -- but if she, a
dues-paying feminist (I mean literally and what's more
twice over since she's a member in good standing of two

different feminist groups) -- if she's willing to so submit, I say, why shouldn't I be?).

An interesting note for future melodrama. Today on the phone Z told me that, as a way of thanking Aida and Sera for their help with the reception, she wants to take them out to the same southern-style Afrusan restaurant June took me to, and she wants to do it in couples fashion for some reason, and so she asked if it would be all right if Aida brought Kirk. "It'll be after the wedding so you won't have any problem with it, right?" "Okay, sure -- why not. Let's do it." (But I'm wondering how she'd like being in my shoes. Not very much, I bet. What if one of my old news-game buddies, say, came into town and called to ask us out to dinner and casually mentioned he was now heavily involved with Lady V and he'd be bringing her along? -- Ooh, that would be a toughie all right. For Z and just possibly for me too.)

And Sera is now complaining her invitation for the henna party came in late and she's implying it's somehow Z's fault, even though Leola and Adele handled all that. Sera is revealing herself to be a first-class pain in the ass (as Z's friend Manny, once the housemate of them both, always thought she was, and more than a few other people have too -- not for nothing is she widely known as "the bantam fighter"). But what's most important, and also revealing but in a very good way, Z is coping with all this quite well and for the most part without getting too upset.

(Betty, I can't help but mention, has been asking Z a lot about how our sex life is going and panting to get some juicy details. Z figures Betty is really feeling the loss of Manny right now -- being reminded repeatedly of their wedding. -- And June's been barred from coming over again until after the honeymoon. The announced reason is that I need some space -- and that's true enough, though I never made much of it with Z or anyone else. Actually Z's the one most bothered by June's visits, and for understandable reasons. June knows this too. Just for instance, time I spend talking with June

is time I don't spend dealing with wedding snags. And
June is an attractive woman who reminds me more than a
little, as Z well knows, of Lady S. So June and I just
laughed it off when we talked briefly on the phone today
when she happened to drop in at Z's office while Z was
talking with me. -- Well, didn't "happen to." She was
there because Z had told her she, Z, would help polish
up the paper I was supposed to look at last night before
Z unilaterally canceled that visit.)

[+1]

     -- A free hour before I go home. I was intending
to set up for this jyze session at a special place --
the toes of the huge "Hammering Man" statue by the front
entrance to the art museum -- but when I arrived down
there a moment ago I discovered the moon wasn't visible
from that spot. And "Hammering Man" wasn't hammering
anyway ---

*

     Oops. At that point a beefy Cawk security guard
ran me off from the stone table where I'd taken a seat
by the symphony hall, next block up the hill from the
art museum, in the war-memorial area by the entrance to
the bus tunnel. The guard informed me "the building" is
off-limits when it's closed. "Well, okay, but does the
building end somewhere?" I asked, trying to sound
easygoing -- after all, we were standing well outside
the building. "Uh..." -- but he was stumped only for a
second. "At the street. It ends at the street."
     The street? Even the public sidewalk is part of
the building? Not frickin' likely. Of course the
antivagrancy laws say you can't sit or lie on the
sidewalks anywhere downtown. But this was a private
security guard. -- And actually only my feet are now on
the public sidewalk. I'm sitting on the low stone wall
surrounding the pool at the bottom of the small
waterfall course flanking one side of the steps (nine or
ten of them) leading up into the garden of remembrance.

So the beefy Cawk dude might be back at any moment to run me off a few feet farther: into the gutter.

Meanwhile the moon has ducked behind the big condo building so I don't need to be here anyway. But now I want to stay on so I can carry out my tiny act of defiance.

The moon should be about three-quarters full on this date and by golly it is. (There's that confusion with quarters and fullness again. If the "first quarter" moon is actually half full, the one we're seeing tonight would be half of three-quarters or the "first three-eighths" moon, correct?) And when I first saw it tonight as I ambled down the hill it looked large, bright, and harbingery. I hadn't realized I would want to sit within view of it for tonight's jyzedown, but suddenly that became imperative.

(So far so good. I'm probably not visible down here from the guard's usual post. But he or someone else might be making rounds -- I often see a guard doing that on the inside as I await my one-fifteen bus on the uphill, "high road" side of the hall. It's quite clear none of these security personnel have received any charm-school training, not to mention lessons in arts-friendliness. Same's true for the guards across the street at the art museum. Of course! We're talking big bucks here! Big important institutions! Like banks but with at least marginally better reps though not for much longer if this kind of treatment continues and starts spreading down the high-culture hierarchy.)

(Little airborne water splinters are hitting me in the back and even flying over my shoulders to land on this page, just as at the waterfall park and the WOC whirlpool. Maybe I should break out my foldable umbrella. -- Which reminds me: Jess says a tarp or canopy won't work for the ceremony. She's already decorated the porch and anything rigged up on the driveway next to that -- which in her most recent view is the only possible outdoor site -- would detract too much from her decor. So we'll just keep hoping for the best, and if those hopes fail, we'll improvise, perhaps

with some people standing outside in raincoats or under
umbrellas and some standing inside in the kitchen with
the windows and the door open. It could be extremely
odd for a wedding ceremony. But then again, is that
necessarily bad? Does it not make the occasion even
more memorable? -- And Jess is looking so poorly these
days -- pale, drained, almost shockingly grim at times
-- that a group of her friends are scheming to drag her
to a shrink who'll prescribe powerful antidepressants.
To my knowledge there's no sign at all of the kind of
dramatic reconciliation that took place after the last
G&J breakup five years ago.)
     -- But the news about the weather is mixed. The
first forecast specific to Saturday is in and it calls
for morning fog clearing by afternoon (Z got it off the
internet this morning and left me a note about it). But
later on the phone she said someone at work saw a
forecast mentioning possible showers on Saturday. So
we've got dueling forecasts. And around here such face-
offs are quite common. This one could easily continue
right up to zero hour.
     Most of my afternoon went to applying another coat
of paint to the eleven planets of the orrery -- that
includes super planets Z and G -- and the evidence still
clings to my fingers: little flecks and patches of
paint, and probably in all ten of the colors I used (Z
and G are the only two of the same color: purple). Wei
will be picking up the fully fledged orrery at noon
Friday (he called today to let me know) so I still have
time to add some detail, cloud streaks and whatnot.
Maybe a few craters here and there? Massive planetary
storms? (I wish I'd thought to ask Kat to help. It
would've been the perfect thing for her. But I've sort
of given up on maintaining high-level relations with Kat
during all this prenup commotion. Moreover, the sad
fact is she's just not showing much interest in the old
subunk these days. Hopefully it's a phase she's going
through and the phase will soon end.)
     While painting planets I also listened to the
"Rhythm & Roll" boxed set all the way through. I

wasn't as happy with it as I'd hoped to be. So I may
bank on Gerry's CDs more and the boxed set less. And
this might not be a bad idea anyway, because yesterday
when I stopped by the corporate chain coffee franchise
in the triangle I heard the same boxed set playing
there. They're not selling it but maybe -- or even
probably -- they're showcasing it in all their shops as
a matter of policy and it's being widely heard. People
will walk into our reception and say, "Is this Glen and
Zoelie's reception or is this a corporate chain coffee
franchise?" Or simply, "Have these folks no shame at
all?" (But maybe we'll use one of those cuts for our
first dance, the one for the bride and groom only. I
like the classic version of "Only You." But Z might
not; she didn't go for it right away when I proposed it
last night and played it for her. In fact she quickly
said, "Could you please turn that thing down?" But she
was distracted at the time by another splinter -- a real
one, wooden, this time in her thumb. And she was
displeased with me because she thought I wasn't being
sympathetic enough about her suffering. I on the
contrary thought I was being just exactly sympathetic
enough. I'd even say Z's touchiness meter has reached a
previously unseen red-zone level. -- Today she visited
Lorraine, her naturopath, and came home with a new array
of herbal medicines that's supposed to keep her from
freaking out during these stressful final days. Mygs
zinging about everywhere! -- And when she's momentarily
calm, relatively, Z attributes the improvement to
previous massive herbal dosages, so I'm not raising any
objections here to the new stuff. -- Also Z brought
home a bag full of highly fragrant garlic bulbs:
Lorraine's wedding gift to us. At my suggestion we're
keeping it out on the balcony, as far from the door as
possible. So far neighbors have said nothing about it.)
     -- I have a hunch my back is thoroughly soaked.
I'm wearing the same long-sleeve black cotton shirt I've
been using as a light jacket for the past several weeks.
I could take it off and check. Or I could just continue
as-is a bit longer and then it'll be time to go anyway.

[The Jyze Millennium, Part I]

     A huge earthquake hit Taiwan yesterday. Deaths are
up to fourteen hundred and climbing. It's not far from
June's old stomping grounds and some of her family and
friends could be affected, but so far I've heard no news
on that.
     And then this note: it was 101 years ago today
(just as U.S. armed forces, including one of my Norusan
great uncles, were launching a war to smash the Spanish
and wipe out indigenous independence fighters in order
to colonize the Philippines) -- 101 years ago, I say,
that the body of another of my Norusan great uncles, the
gonzo boozer and petty thief Roar, along with those of
Sadie and her son little Petie, were found on an island
near Wachute in Mentoka. Possibly a love suicide and
murder but the coroner ruled it double-murder/suicide.
And Sadie an Afrusan and Petie biracial, though Roar was
not his father. And lots of ol' Mom's ancestors
slaveholders. And lots more shameful behavior yet to be
noted in this or any other jyze annal, especially on
Dad's side, including centuries of Crusader and Viking
rape and pillage throughout Europe and the Mideast.
     I got bad blood mama.
     (Worsening droplets -- I'm outta here. And not a
moment too soon. -- But jyze has at least tangentially
tackled this bad-blood business before. And there's
plenty to go around in this town, in this state, in this
country, and especially in the Cawk cohorts of all of
same. No need to hit too hard on it when it's all
around us and in us, am I right? Well of course I'm
not, but -- STOP FOR NOW.)

                         [+1]

     A gorgeous night. The moon and the harbor. The
empty market. The good-luck spot -- I came back for a
second hit. This time I'm here a little later and the
weather's a little cooler and I have the whole park to
myself. Presumably they've already done the sweep to
kick everyone out -- or is it self-enforcing by now?

[A Jyze Epithalamium]

    This is the night of the equinox. It's still about
five hours off -- it's falling very late this year --
but I'm feeling it already. This evening the sun set as
close to due west as we'll see it this year. The earth
is in balance, so to speak, with the amount of daylight
everywhere about the same (twelve hours and eight
minutes, is it?) -- and sunset as close as it gets to
due west just about everywhere too, except up toward,
and down toward, the poles (how one can know what's
truly up and truly down I'll once again leave for
another time to ponder). Autumn is officially arriving
and so is the reign of Libra, the sun sign following my
own (and this is just about the only way the western
zodiacal business has any real meaning for me: it allows
me to feel I'm still vaguely in contact with my birthday
up to three weeks and a few days afterward, making both
August and September, or most of it, the months it
occurs in). (Virgo I'm talking about, yeah.)
    -- Big screech of train wheels down below as they
grind around the sharp bend heading into the tunnel.
    When I left the WOC at seven-thirty tonight I was
struck by how dark it was outside. Not pitch dark but
dusky dark. It was the first time for that thought this
year and it happened spontaneously on equinox night.
-- Of course subconscious or unconscious forces could
well have been at work. (And I concede the same when Z
suggests maybe I'm unknowingly feeling a ton of
premarital stress "down deep." Sure, and why wouldn't I
be? Isn't this just about my very best chance to do
that? Or my very last chance anyway? I hope so!)
    That moon glowing directly above the harbor, it's
spectacular. The evergreens here in the park are
casting sharp moon shadows. It's almost too bright to
look at; you glance away and see a glowing blue globe
elsewhere up there against the dark, moving as your eyes
do, thanks to retinal seleno-shock. The cones, the
rods. A big clamshell button holding the sky in place,
and like many clamshell buttons it's not quite perfectly
round; it's a sliver or two short of that in the upper
left quadrant. -- Down below, the water of the harbor

is just slightly aripple and it's attractively streaked,
as almost always, with the bright lights of the docks
and shipyards across the way and to the south; but
tonight the moon is far outdoing all those other
attention-grabbers.

Today's also notable for its relation to year's
end. The millennial countdown has reached its last
hundred days. I was expecting some big whoop-de-do over
this but so far haven't run into anything like that.
But then I've got other things on my mind (and haven't
had a look at today's local papers yet -- rarely do
before I arrive home -- and in a way this is usually a
blessing, because I see the day itself uninfluenced by
any media. Directly, that is. And the far-coast-
megalopolis paper is an exception, but a qualified one
because I see it in the early a.m. of the night before:
by the time I'm up and about the next day (by
Nightscoper Upside-down Time) it's like old news,
meaning yesterday's news; and by NUT time that's just
what it is. During the day I'm usually not directly
exposed to fresh news except what I glimpse at newsracks
or hear about via the grapevine, most often at the WOC.
Of course like any sane person trying to minimize
unnecessary distraction I avoid all contact with the
internet except that which can't possibly be dodged, and
even that's almost always through Z's printouts which I
see when I arrive home. On the computer at work I can
usually ignore it completely, and do.)

Nobody around. This is so strange. Most of the
windows are dark in the big apartment buildings in the
market area, and for that matter in the smaller ones as
well. In the large downtown highrises they're lit in
either scattered fashion or in banks, whole floors or
groups of floors -- the combined night-worker/janitorial
light festival as we present it to our Jyze City
compatriots seven nights a week all year round with very
few exceptions.

(And suddenly now the first human encounter of the
evening. A drunk, probably mid thirties, Cawk, worker
clothes, pants of one leg wet, probably with urine but

maybe with beer since he's carrying an open can of same.
He starts out slurrily, "You know what happened to me?"
But I stand up menacingly and say, "I'm real busy here,
man, really," and to my surprise he immediately
continues on his way, almost as if he's just remembered
an urgent appointment. -- I'm sitting sideways so I can
observe all approaches, looking halfway back into the
park, halfway out at the harbor, but actually facing
directly toward the market sign and the downtown core.
-- As now a guy on a bicycle whizzes up and props
himself against the wall maybe fifteen feet to the
north; he's gazing out at the bogglingly beautiful
harbor scene.)
      -- So Jim Q.'s in town. He made it, no major
glitches. We'll be getting together tomorrow night for
dinner with Z, Friday night for a ball game with Rob and
possibly Wei. (And from the look of the docket up at
the scope office I'm guessing I'll have a fair amount of
work to do on both of those nights, but nothing
overwhelming. As of now I'm fully caught up.)
      Also nothing of great moment in the way of other
wedding news. All seems to be going smoothly. The
weather forecasts are still dueling. The last-minute
RSVP confirmations for the reception are just about
balancing the cancellations, meaning we're holding firm
at about a hundred and fifty attendees. Z wants me to
come up with a box for Rob to hold the rings in. I'm
still working on the orrery, painting some corny red
hearts on the purple Z and G planets and trying to mount
some bright yellow lightning bolts (cut from a plastic
sheet) so they appear to be flashing between those same
two crucial planets. (As I hear a hose go on. It's
around the corner, out of sight, but I can actually
smell the water. I'm guessing they'll be hosing me out
of here within a few minutes. -- And this spot could
use a good hosing irrespective of my presence. The
litter's not too bad but the whiff is. Urine, beer,
rotten food, stale sweat from some old rags -- all built
up during just one day, I presume. -- But I do like
these thick wood-plank tables. Lots of carvings in

them, some quite ambitious. In fact just past my right
elbow there's a lightning bolt approximately the right
size (a foot) to shoot the interplanetary gap between
planets Z and G. -- And maybe the hose-down worker is
going in the other direction. No further sign of him so
far. If he's taking the long way around he might not
reach here before dawn.) (Could be we're talking about
a female hose-down worker too, yes, or for that matter
someone of ambiguous sex/gender, but the two possible
hose-down itineraries would still be about the same.)
     Lots of little wedding anecdotes and details I'd
still like to pass along. Razzing at the WOC. Marcus
bellowing in to me from outside the gate of the noisy
whirlpool: "There's no getting out of it now!" On the
second floor Z and I encountered Willis E. (former Black
Panther and our hilltop hood's current rep on the county
council) panting away as he jogged on a treadmill and Z
invited him on the spot to drop by the reception. And
here's his verbatim reply: "I'd love to but I have a
funeral to go to." And here's mine to him: "Hey, that's
okay -- it'll probably be livelier than our reception
anyway." And here's Z's remark to him (after she gave
me a scrunched-up "huh?" look): "Don't mind him, Willis,
he's just going to be my weird husband."
     -- And lots more. The ones just mentioned barely
scrape the surface. But now I'm realizing it's not a
hose-down worker I'm hearing, it's the park sprinkler
system. And the reason I can smell the water is that
clouds of sprinkler mist are drifting this way and they
seem to be growing bigger and denser as the night air
chills them. And this is causing them to condense right
here on the J-book page. So I'm moving on.

*   *

     -- About four hours down the line. Just a
postscript as the momentous seasonal crossover is about
to happen. Just about --
     NOW.
     Day after tomorrow (considering we're officially
into Thursday) is hitch day. Better get right back to
work on those lightning bolts.

374

20

     Can't open this one the way I'd hoped to. And I
suppose it'll be pretty much the same story for the rest
of the J-week. The crucial J-week. Stuff will be
coming up all the time and even when it's not I'm likely
to be frazzled and distracted, worried about this or
that, just as I am right now (and this sentence itself
is a good indication of it) (and what's "it"? -- I don't
even know anymore and don't want to go back to figure
it, that is, "it," out).
     Thought I'd take a leisurely stroll over to the
garden club this afternoon. Give it one last once-over.
Set the scene for Saturday. Ha! Fat chance!
     For one thing, the garden club would offer no place
to jyze. It's raining out there. On equinox day the
weather has shifted to our customary fall mode: chilly
and wet and blowy. Maybe by Saturday afternoon it'll
have cleared up and maybe it won't (or probably it won't
-- though yesterday afternoon's paper says it might, and
yesterday morning's paper says it will). But for right
now, forget it, I shouldn't be going over there even if
I could.
     And I can't. Jim Q.'s due here in about an hour
and Z even before that. And a couple of calls might or
might not be coming in. I'm trying to let Wei know the
bachelor jaunt to the baseball game tomorrow night is
off -- we couldn't score tickets. Our lousy sub-.500
club has unexpectedly sold out its last three games of
the season! The best we could do was come up with three
widely scattered single seats! And we are four! Triage
(in more than one sense?) would be necessary!

So instead we'll go for a restaurant and maybe a jazz club. But jazz might start too late for me -- what if I have to work? And does Wei even like jazz? If he does, I don't recall hearing about it or seeing evidence of it.

Oh well, onward ever calmly. Leola's supposed to be calling me to talk about music for the reception. Gerry's the one who'll be handling it, but he won't be getting back into town until, as it now turns out, noon Saturday, just hours before the reception begins. And are Gerry and Leola even speaking to each other? But no matter -- if all else fails we can just go with the "Rhythm & Roll" boxed set and the doo-wop CDs. Their combined playing time is roughly double the reception's scheduled span of three hours (three to six p.m.).

Other calls might come in too, but for now the phone's strangely silent. When I rolled out of bed today I quickly found myself behind the eightball because two more than that number of messages -- ten! -- were backed up for me to listen to. By the time I'd finished, the breakfast hour was almost over and it was time to start painting planets again (or actually at this point the wires holding them up, and specifically the white hanger wires supporting planets Z and G -- they needed to be blackened so as not to be more conspicuous than the planets themselves) (even in Noh where the puppetmasters' mastery is meant to be visible, everybody wears black). I also launched a search, eventually successful but not before I did a lot of sweating, for Popeye's antique wooden box which I thought would be perfect for the rings (and it is!) (size of half a stick of butter). And I talked with Z, who was surly, muttering in Tagawocky at times, refusing to explain what was up -- but let it go, got to forgive just about anything at this point, and of course the pressures on her are at least as great and probably a whole lot greater than those on me. (I suspect what's riling her most right now, though, is the question of why her office seems to have no party planned for her.)

I did come up with a good card for her last night,

and solved some tough design problems with it in a
surprising deep-concentration jiff. It's a scaled-down
lobby poster for the movie "The Vikings" and it shows a
blond woman being borne aloft by a rowdy band of ---
*   *

     At that point the building fire alarm went off.
It's a high-pitched WHEEEE that's intolerable for more
than twenty or thirty seconds without earplugs. So I
jumped into my clothes and got out of there fast, even
though extensive experience with prior false alarms at
our building and also the lack of any burning smell told
me there was no real rush (and I paused to take a whiz
and to pack up my rucksack, making sure this J-book was
in it). I checked out the hallways on all three upper
levels and found no sign of a fire. Same was true of
the garage in the basement, but something was unusual
there: Mikey, the big black dog from next door, was
trapped inside. I let him out and then waited for the
fire engine's arrival, which took about ten minutes, it
seemed, as the in-house alarm kept WHEEEEing away.
     Finally the truck rolled up outside and since no
one else was around I found myself the spokesperson for
the building. Two yellow-suited, fully equipped
firefighters investigated upstairs while I stayed with
the two officers who were checking out the main alarm
box in the garage. Only when the firefighters came back
down did one of the officers spot the cause of the
alarm: the small red pull-box by the main garage door
had been activated and in an unusual way so that it was
jammed and hard to turn off. At that point it dawned on
me what probably had happened: Mikey had hit it with a
paw while standing on his hind legs trying to get out.
The fire crew agreed that must've been it -- no one else
was around inside and the pull-box couldn't be reached
from outside. And just then Mikey came innocently
trotting up the driveway almost as if he were turning
himself in. "I'll need your name and number, please,"
joked the chief. -- An unusual cause for a fire alarm,
he said, but not unprecedented. (And later I learned
Mikey had been loose all day and Z had called animal

377

control about it. And when Jim Q. and I were sitting
out front in his little white rental car while awaiting
Z's arrival, Mikey came trotting up again to check us
out through the partially open passenger-side window,
his snout sticking in through the window gap, whiskers
aquiver and nostrils energetically sniffing.)

So now it's no longer the Gregorian day in which 99
days remain in '99. We're forty-five minutes into the
Gregorian day before the wedding. The three of us -- Z,
Jim, and I -- went out to dinner and then Z dropped me
off downtown, around eight, and except for an hour's
"magic carpet" nap on the conference-room floor I worked
right up to the time of starting this entry. If I
could've gone without that nap I'd have a decent jyze
hole here. But no.

Jim's looking about the same, and at age seventy
that means he's doing all right -- though he's always
looked his age or more in the decade or so I've known
him. It's been a couple of years since I last saw him.
I still like the man and get along well with him -- feel
toward him as if he were a favorite uncle. From time to
time during our dinner with Z Mother momentarily seemed
to materialize in the empty seat at our four-chair
table. Brother Rob and I were Jim's champions right
from first meeting him -- at a time when Barb was trying
to persuade Mother to drop him -- and I think he's
always remembered that and been grateful for it.

We did talk briefly about Barb while waiting in the
car for Z. Jim had spoken with her twice over the past
week, trying to persuade her to come up for the wedding.
Thank the divines she'd said no. Then again she'd
falsely led Jim to believe I was the one who put an end
to our relationship -- unilaterally! -- so I had to give
him my version of the story, though I managed to impart
most of it in thumbnail form. Jim himself had gone
through a ten-year estrangement from his own sister, so
he was sympathetic enough, but at several points he was
also a bit more moralistic than I liked. It's just a
tone he sometimes takes, and I've heard it from him
before regarding my jyzing, medical care, allegedly

neglected paternal or "career" duties and so forth. And
he drops it fast enough so that it doesn't cause a
serious breach between us. And basically I agree with
him: it's a shame Barb and I should be "feuding" like
this. But at present I'm not prepared to make any more
efforts to repair relations with her -- for the simple
reason that I've seen no sign anything would change if I
did. Later, who knows, maybe I'll feel differently
about it or she'll start acting differently.

     -- And that's all I can do for now with the jyze.
Don't even like to be thinking about the sorry state of
affairs with Barb at a time like this, so I won't say
anything more about it. Whether I'll be able to go into
other matters later when I get home, however, remains to
be seen, and that's true for a good many other things as
well. (It's still raining. The forecasts for Gregorian
tomorrow -- meaning Saturday, since we're past midnight
on Thursday -- are still dueling. -- And I laid out a
hundred bucks even, tip included, for the dinner tonight.
The strawberry shortcake was again very good, but not
quite as sensational as the first time, maybe just
because it lacked the element of surprise.)

[+1]

     Here's the gazebo at the garden club. I made it
after all. Friday afternoon, and tomorrow's the
wedding. Twenty-four hours from now -- it's roughly
four p.m. -- the joint'll be jumpin' oh yes it will. We
might even be cutting the cake by that time. But today
no one seems to be around -- though a hose is coiled
outdoors in the other side yard, to the south of the
building -- and aptly autumnal maroonish leaves are
scuttling across the gray wooden planks of the gazebo
floor. And of course at any moment I could be run off
from here too, just as I've been chased from a number of
other jyzing spots in recent weeks. A man working in
the elaborate garden of the house next door eyed me
suspiciously while I was poking around in the yard and

peeking in the main-floor windows. But I'm somewhat
hidden here in the gazebo and I'm not up to any obvious
mischief and I'm hoping he and any others wondering
about me might just act as if I'm not here -- ignore me.
     And if they don't, if one or more challenge me,
what I'm doing here, and I answer, "My wedding reception
will be held here tomorrow," will they say, "Sure, and a
Martian spacecraft will be landing on the premises any
moment, so I'd advise you to get the hell out"?
     An old 1890s-style wooden gazebo, hexagonal, cream
colored, with interior benches, open to the elements
except for the low conical roof. The structure stands
at the back of the north side yard, which is bordered
with shrubbery and small trees and flowerbeds on three
of its own sides, with a large lawn (not looking too bad
now thanks to the rains of the past few days -- a
mixture of green and brown, late-summer style -- and a
low white iron-grill fence running along the sidewalk in
front. People walk by from time to time out there,
mostly Asian- or Latino-looking, including some kids
probably on their way home from school. Local traffic,
bicycles, vans and pickups, a yellow school bus. Across
the street, two single-story wooden homes and a larger
one, all appearing almost as old as the garden club
itself -- which is to say, close to a century. The club
building is wooden also, three stories, light grayish
blue with white trim, and a big Victorian-type turret on
the second and third stories in front and a smaller one
toward the back near me, and a first-story porch running
the length of the other side and looking out on a larger
side yard containing one big old tree and a small pear
orchard and lots of flowerbeds, most of which look much
better than they did two weeks ago. This yard here is
half the size of that one and more secluded. This is
probably where our wedding ceremony would've taken place
if the arrangement with Jess had fallen through.
     I'm on a rather tight schedule today, no question.
By seven I must run several errands (hiking or maybe
busing into town first), stop at the WOC to shower, and
make my way up to the appointed jazz club in my old hood

to meet "the boys" for the bachelor blowout.
     -- Just before I left the house, a fairly serious
meltdown by Z. She drove all the way out to Betty's to
fetch the flowers Betty picked this morning and then
discovered she didn't have Betty's house key on her key
chain. The flowers stood in pails just inside the door
but she couldn't get at them. By her own account she
bawled all the way driving home. But I didn't know that
at the time, and when she came in and announced she'd
been unable to pick up the flowers because she'd
misplaced the keys, "So fuck the fucking flowers!", I
wondered aloud if she could try again later (after
Betty'd put in all that work picking them). She started
crying again. "You think I'm a horrible person!" It
took about thirty minutes to patch it up. And first I
had to listen as she sobbed out weeping, hysterical-
sounding voicemails for Betty and Aida. So before
leaving I asked (tongue-in-cheek!), "Would you mind
calling Betty and Aida back and telling them someone
else was beating you this afternoon, it wasn't me?"
"You're trying to jolly me up!" she charged. "Damn
right!" I cried. -- And to my surprise this effort did
seem to help a bit. She excused herself to the bathroom
and a few minutes later came out noticeably more pulled
together. (Hopefully most of the puffiness around her
eyes will have subsided by tomorrow. Unless, that is,
we have a repeat meltdown or two before then, which
seems quite possible.) (Can we survive this wedding?
Durn tootin' we can! Things may look a little chancy
right now but overall they've been much better than I'd
expected. And I think she might say the same, though
maybe not anytime soon. Maybe in a month or two.)
     While she was away I tried on my wedding outfit.
I'd forgotten how loose the fit was on the shirt. I
could lift weights for a hundred years and not fill out
enough for the shoulders (and I think of my shoulders as
just about my most troglodyte parts). I tried three
different types of undershirts, two bought especially
for this occasion in a spasm of overpreparedness last
spring, and decided to go with the V-neck (for the first

time in my life -- and I'd bet the last time too). The
fit on the pants is fine; I haven't gained any
perceptible weight in the waist (so take that, Z-goose).

All day I've been suffering from a strange
prenuptial bleariness. I'm sure it's not all owing to
my rising at eleven o'clock this morning, two and a half
hours earlier than the current norm. Tension yawns,
could it be? Tomorrow I'll be debedding even earlier,
ten-thirty -- equivalent of three a.m. for a right-side-
up person -- and we'll be leaving the house at half past
twelve, with June picking us up and doing the driving.
I'm figuring a mix of caffeine and adrenaline will power
me through the day.

Last night I put the truly final touches on the
orrery and today at noon Wei hauled it off. It looked
frightfully flimsy with the outlying planets protruding
in all directions from the big cardboard box and the
smarmy planets Z and G bobbing overhead like the
antennas for a giant-size bee costume. We had to turn
the box sideways and bend back the wires for certain
planets to maneuver the contraption through the various
doorways. I couldn't tell what Wei thought of it, but
he wasn't raving, and I've always held his sense of
humor in high regard. So maybe it won't be a big hit.

For tomorrow's weather we now have a forecast of
temps in the sixties, scattered showers in the morning,
possible sun in the afternoon. Olwen's adamant about
not doing the ceremony on Jess's porch in case of rain
(Jess is insisting it be there; we've deputized June to
deal with Jess on this matter tomorrow, if necessary)
and today Z went out and bought an eight-foot beach
umbrella with a stand just in case. It was one-third
off, she let me know, possibly because I'd been trying
to warn her about the need for a tarp for the past week
and had finally given up when she said she didn't care,
she wanted to go with the flow (not to the extent of
standing in a downpour, though, it turns out). And: she
didn't say one-third off what. And: I didn't ask.

-- Well, I suppose it's a good omen I still haven't
been eighty-sixed from the gazebo. The trees are

filling up with birds and they're chirruping like
crazy at the moment and the sun is even showing signs of
breaking through the clouds to the west. No spectral
figure has arisen through the gazebo floorboards to
caution me against going ahead with the wedding (and of
course if one did I'd tell it to take a powder -- I'm
down with this hitch and I mean all the way).

*   *

    -- The digital clock on the receptionist's phone
here in the scope office says it's "Sat 25." So it's
here. The big day! The Feast of Joy! The Moon
Festival! And according to the almanac, the 483rd
anniversary of what's widely thought to be (but how on
the gods' green earth could anyone really know for
sure?) the first European encounter with the Pacific,
which was christened on that day the "South Sea" and
claimed in the name of Spain -- as the Philippines were
also by another Spaniard soon afterward, of course,
setting in motion the long chain of events leading to
(among a few other things) today's big event.

    I used to pound it out on the piano in the basement
in my early teen years, that happy little show tune
(wasn't it from "My Fair Lady"?): "I'm getting married
in the" -- that one. The ding-dong bells they -- yeah.
Boppin' over to Jess's house we gonna go and there do
what all agree must -- yup. (Only to find rain falling?
As of two hours ago, brother Rob the excellent lifelong
amateur meteorologist was rating it a toss-up. "What do
we do if it's raining?" he asked with true concern in
his eyes. "We improvise." "That's it?" "That's it.")

    -- So here I've been presented with another small
jyze hole, unexpected, and it's already a third used up.
Tonight's scoping corrections took just under ninety
minutes for 157 pages and I budgeted two hours because
of the high chance of blunders with the new forms the
office is requiring to conform with recently revised
state regulations, making for a total of eight forms per
job now instead of four. But I messed up only once and
that was fairly minor.

    Rob, Wei, and I arrived almost simultaneously at

383

the jazz club and Jim Q. came toddling in just moments
later (his bad right hip forcing him to take small
careful steps). We snared good window seats in the
nonsmoking section and for the first hour or so we were
the only dinner customers in the place. The talk was
livelier than might've been expected, with Wei
apparently taking it upon himself to keep the ball
rolling and doing quite well at it. We talked taxes,
baseball, WTO and millennium foofaraw, ungodly techie
salaries and stock options, Sandefjord family genealogy,
East/West contrasts and comparisons, and of course tips
on marriage (and I kiddingly called on Wei for advice on
marriage to a woman of a certain not-too-terribly-
vintage age who's never been married before -- Alison
being another example of same -- and he said rather
gravely I should be aware there will likely be times
when she feels her identity is being eroded by the
patriarchal nature of the institution itself) (I wish I
could produce an exact quote -- it was very cautiously
worded and both intentionally and unintentionally
hilarious). And the music was better than expected.
All but one of the musicians were young guys with short
hair -- a new jazz generation. And a very capable one,
I'd say. Guy in a red shirt thumpin' away at a string
bass, drummer in a brown shirt hunched over his kit.
Rob seemed impressed. (He knows the standing
of many local bands from years of selling their records
and tapes and CDs.) I was reminded of the time Dad took
the family to hear a certain legendary trumpeter after
my college graduation -- or was it the year before?
    I liked it. My bachelor party I'm talking. Far
freakin' out. "Last night of an era." A ritual, have
some fun, play with it, bookmark it.
    In the end the other three split the check and I
picked up the tip. But I felt bad for Rob and even more
so for Wei, since I invited him in part as a gesture of
thanks for all his help with the wedding. So somehow I
should repay the forty-five bucks he had to lay out for
dinner and drinks (and I told him I'd be doing that).
    (From time to time bypassers and street people

pressed their noses against the windows and the glass
door of the club just as I often used to do on Friday
and Saturday nights toward the end of my walks home to
unit B-2 from the hideaway or the scope office. But
before tonight I'd never been inside. Nor did I realize
back then quite how pathetic those standing outside
might look to those sitting inside.)

      -- And now the last bus home. I've been feeling a
little badly because I have nothing to present to Z as a
memento of this highly special night. We talked about
giving each other wedding gifts and decided against it.
But an urge is upon me. But...to do what? -- And then
there's the old Scandi custom of a gift for the bride on
the morning after the first night of marriage. That
we'll probably skip too. But if I could come up with
something good real fast (but not too good, so as to
make Z feel bad if she hasn't thought of doing
something herself) I absolutely would.

                     *   *

      -- Just heard the far-coast paper arrive. It's
starting to show up earlier again -- the three a.m. news
hasn't even come on yet. And I'd go get the paper to
check out the headlines for what will be the third and
I'm sure the best by far of my lifetime wedding days,
but I'm afraid I'd awaken the bride. And I've already
awakened her once, shortly after I came in, so she could
get a glimpse of the gorgeous full moon. I couldn't
help myself. And she did glimpse it, because all she
had to do was roll over and slide down a little toward
the foot of the bed and pull up her sleep mask half an
inch or so and there it was, visible through the blinds
I'd just canted open. It was floating gloriously a
little above the peaked dormer roof of the neighbors'
house (the bad guys), this time to the right of the
chimney, fetchingly framed by the ferns arrayed above my
clothes cubes -- ooh such a spectacular wedding moon!

      And then back to sleep she went. Beauty sleep.
The bride's been in seclusion all night, having turned
off the phone shortly after I left, I gather, or at any
rate early in the evening. Phone messages for her are

stacked up from here to eternity but I won't be
listening to them. In her wisdom she chose seclusion
for this evening; I'll respect that wisdom. I can say
this with full sincerity because I'm a frequent
practitioner of seclusion myself and she knows it well
(and sometimes counts on it even a little more than I'd
like, but never mind about that).

It's gusty out there. As I was walking home from
the bus stop the southern half of the sky, swept
entirely free of clouds, was all glittery with stars.
Up north hung a massive but seemingly immobile cloud
bank. -- And now the moon's slipping from puffy little
cloud to puffy little cloud. I even hear things being
blown over, tumbling around in the street -- probably a
plastic trash-bin lid or two. Little whistles of wind
from the eaves. Has the massive cloud bank perhaps
become mobile? And if so, what might this portend?

A poster, a card, and a note were waiting to greet
me on my chair after I showed Z the moon. The note
thanks me for making "da truly cool cake thang," by
which I presume she means the enhanced orrery (she's
often belatedly thanking me in notes like this, even if
she's already done so in spoken words -- as again in
this instance -- because she recalls her insight about
me that I "like to be appreciated" -- hey, who doesn't?
-- and lots of times she can't remember if she's
already done the deed: her short-term memory for such
things for some reason not being so good).

The card is teasing me for my remark this afternoon
which brought on the meltdown. It shows a print of the
iconic "Nighthawks, 1942" diner scene, and she has the
man sitting next to the woman at the counter saying, "I
was just offering her a suggestion." And on the back
she writes, "Your high-drama bride is infinitely happy
she's marrying you." (She missed the kind of pun she
usually goes for, turning "happy" into "Hoppy" to honor
the artist: shows her stress level is still high.) (And
mine? You betcha, very high. But I'm cool too, or
trying to be and even more trying to appear to be when
Z's around. "The designated anchor." -- And in the

back of my mind wondering if I can wring a short groom's
speech for the reception tomorrow from the Spanish
"South Sea" claim anniversary and the Chinese Moon
Festival/Sukkoth Feast of Joy and maybe the Rosh
Hashanah repentance thing too and perhaps something
Norski (but what?) (make a play on "Skanky Scandi" while
doing a skanky ska with the button pinned to my wedding
shirt?). -- And Wei's final words of advice to me
outside the jazz club were, "Don't stay up all night
working on your speech for the reception.")
    And the poster Z left on my chair is for a local
drama group's upcoming production of a play called
"Derailed Desires." It shows three women about to
board a train, looking off at something down the
platform, and Z has the one with raised eyebrows and an
appraising look saying, "Whoa -- hope dat boy's ready
for a wild honeymoon!" And the subtitle of the play is
"A one-way ticket to SHAME."
    So once more it's clear why this is the woman for
me. -- I just wish I could come up with something as
good for her on such a landmark night. Or anything at
all. But it's already past my bedtime and I don't want
to be breaking my brain over this. I have no choice but
to ride on my laurels. Cash in some chits. And on
wedding eve! Or by Gregorian measure early wedding day!
-- But I think of all those girls'-night-out occasions
when she came home snockered. On the night of my
bachelor blowout I've at least got a decent excuse.
    -- And last thoughts? Any of those?
    I'm thinking.
    -- Well, I could say all this buildup has been a
lot of fun. And it has. But I'd still prefer hitching
up in a simpler way. Yet...one reason life with Z
delights me so much is it's constantly cajoling or even
on occasion jolting me into doing things in new and
different ways. (Of course it is!) -- So I'm
blithering. Don't want to give jyze the hook just yet,
I guess. -- Could mention that a present from cousin
Kar came in, a couple of silver candlesticks, and a note
apologizing for being unable to "arrange" to attend the

wedding, adding he might be up in January. No surprise
there. And Rob tells me he's gotten a couple of notes
from formerly "lost" cousin Ron H. this week with no
mention of coming out, so scratch him too. We're down
to the hard core: me and Rob, with Jim Q. and Gail and
Emily as in-laws, as it were. And I'm grateful to them
all, and it's just fine with me that this is how it is.
At another stage of my life I might've felt differently,
but not now. This is my world right here.

...And somewhere in the space between the end of
this sentence and the number with the plus sign in
brackets announcing a new day, "my world right here"
will be officially merging with that of the fabulous
Zoelie B.

[+1]

'Twas a great day. And I mean it really was.
Everything came off brilliantly with just one hitch --
and that's the one represented by the "Z&G" ring on my
finger and the matching one on Z's (who's at this moment
sitting atop the bed, just across from where I'm holding
forth in the green armchair, her back propped against
the headboard, engrossed in a mystery, winding down for
sleep -- this in our usual 203 bedroom, on what's now
our marital bed, because it's not until early tomorrow
afternoon that we leave for the coastal resort and the
official honeymoon).

The jyze of a newlywed. Right here. Never before
seen on this earth. (This kind of jyze, I'm saying.)
-- And as yet it's an unconsummated marriage, I should
note, though we canoodled some and the bride showed she
can still fire out those skyrockets and roman candles on
extremely short notice -- but the session quickly
devolved into a tandem three-hour nap. It was a long,
intense day, and it was capping off a lengthy series of
long, intense days. And this, after all, is a Stage III
alliance (but early Stage III, I'm not forgetting).

The weather cooperated splendidly. Towering cumuli

(super-duper type) were floating about here and there
like stately white cruise ships but seemed never to
block the sun. One of the best moments of a day loaded
with them (more so than any prior day in my life, I'll
go ahead and testify, being already sworn in) came when
Z slipped into this room to wake me up at ten-thirty
a.m. and I saw the telltale row of sunny dots glowing on
the translucent Chinese screen in front of the window,
cast there through the tiny string holes in the blinds.
What, sun so early? Well before the forecast "possible
afternoon sun"? Right then the feeling grabbed me and
it never did let go: this day would be sensational.

So I had two hours to do breakfast and shower and
shave and dress and maybe even flip through the papers.
Z, the lifelong lark, had already been up for hours, of
course, and was ready to go except for the dress itself.
She made numerous calls to check how people were doing
or just, as I overheard her saying to Terri, "because I
need to be entertained!" The one downbeat moment came
when Jess called to say she couldn't bear to attend the
ceremony itself because she knew it would make her feel
too sad (after losing Gwen so recently and just at the
time they had originally planned to hold their own
commitment ceremony). Z handed me the phone and Jess
said we should respect her, Jess's, needs and I agreed:
she should do what she had to do and if she had to be
elsewhere during our ceremony, we would understand; but
in any event I wanted to be sure she knew we would miss
her plenty (and Gwen also, of course, but it seemed best
to keep mum on that).

June picked us up right on time at half past twelve,
and it was clear she was proud to be playing such an
important role in the ritual (and she looked wonderful
in a velvety purple dress and she and I felt a special
bond during the whole day, perhaps in part because she'd
paid for roughly two-thirds of my wedding outfit, shoes
not included), and later she pronounced us to be brother
and sister and gave me a real all-out hug for the very
first time -- and while we're away she'll be dropping by
to pick up our mail and, yes, water the plants (but

moderately, she promised!).

    It's all superlatives here. Jess's garden was in
late-climax shape -- a tribute to, and a sad reminder
of, Gwen's green-thumb artistry. ---
*

    -- Just tucked in my new wife. Love, honor, obey,
cherish, support, serve, prop up, tuck in -- all that
and more. Way more! "I'll be right here, now and
always and forever." We're giddy with our good fortune.
Out of all those people attending the reception how many
would've predicted back in the early days we'd end up
going the connubial distance? -- Well, Kat did, it's
true -- in fact on the very day she and I met.

    I think it's understandable jyze is all but
overwhelmed by the task it's presented itself with
tonight. It's gonna hafta wax sketchy and
impressionistic. Hit a few high points, maybe even a
low point or two if any can be found.

    Olwen set up her table of readings and candles in
front of Jess's small shed with the wooden yellow-
crescent moon nailed onto it (of no significance
whatsoever to the ceremony or anything else as far as I
know, except it was right in front of me and I kept
staring at it as the rite proceeded and wondering why it
had needed so many nails to be held in place) (dopey but
true) -- Olwen assisted by son Trent in white shirt and
jaunty black Irish bowler. Altogether fourteen people
were present, and the one major glitch was that Nick
wasn't: somehow Betty had gained the false impression he
was invited only to the reception (and to compensate
we've invited him, along with Betty and Kat, to a
special brunch tomorrow before we hit the honeymoon
trail). On my side were Rob and Gail (in straw hat and
purple dress) and Rob's daughter Emily, Jim Q., and
June; on Z's, Aida and Terri and Frank (usually creeping
about with a camera) and Betty and Kat. At the start Z
stood at the far end of the garden and then she walked
up the path with Kat strewing flowers in front of her
and ooh ooh ooh such a heart-stoppingly gorgeous live-
action picture it was and I know I'll be replaying the

390

tape of that in my mind forever. (Gush! Gush!)

    The ceremony consisted of candle lighting (one for
each of the major religious traditions), readings
(again, one from each), and the vows. The wind was a
little frisky and several of the candles soon went out
and after a couple of quickly failed relightings we had
to leave them that way. Olwen read well -- with a
poet's feel for the shapeliness of the words as well as
a believer's feel for their meaning -- and I was touched
by our eye contact as she recited the poems I'd provided
to her and I was delighted to have a friend of ours
doing the honors (and tears were flowing -- Z's a couple
of times, Terri's, Betty's, Aida's -- and mine briefly
during the Tang-poet reading, but then suddenly I was
euphoric again). The only disappointment here was that
for some of the group the words were hard to make out at
times: Rob said he caught only a third to half of them.

    For the vows themselves we knelt on large pillows
-- the two cushions from our sofa, actually, covered by
Z's Nepalese dragon rug -- and placed the rings on each
other's fingers after Rob slowly and carefully extracted
them from Popeye's old wooden box and slid them off
their cloth loop and presented them to us. A series of
questions to each of us followed by "I do," "I will," in
one instance "I will and I do." (And I was wearing, by
the way, at Z's last-minute request, a copper Guatemalan
necklace which had somehow played a role in Betty and
Manny's wedding.) And then the prescribed "you may"
kiss. Then another, to make up for that comically
awkward first one.

    Short and sweet -- no more than thirty minutes in
all. With perfect timing Paz and Tobey arrived with the
camera equipment just as we finished up (it turned out
they'd been waiting outside the high wooden garden
fence) and for the next forty-five minutes or so we
mixed picture-posing with paper-signing. Jess returned
from her walk with Cy-dog, and she sort of hid out at
the far end of the garden looking heartbreakingly
forlorn -- begged off from joining the group for photos
or anything else. Jim Q. asked our forgiveness: he

would be forced to miss the reception in order to fly
back home to be with Nancy, his new partner, whose
nurse, he'd learned earlier that morning in a panicky
call from Nancy herself, had without warning taken off
for the weekend (Nancy suffered a minor heart attack a
month ago -- she's about seven years older than Jim, I
learned today, just as Mother was). And then in a happy
surprise our "limousine" showed up and it was Leola
driving her sparkling new white deluxe SUV which she had
just picked up at the dealer's the night before. So in
a way she was able to attend the ceremony after all, and
she did it with considerable grace, showing no trace of
resentment over being "snubbed." (And later Gerry and
Leola seemed to be getting along well -- it was touching
to see them slow-dancing to one of their favorite high-
school tunes after all the troubles they've gone through
recently -- and Gerry arrived in plenty of time even
though his flight was an hour late and he was a dynamite
DJ and even helped sweep the hall afterwards.)
     We arrived at the garden club ten minutes before
the reception was due to start at three. It was a
beehive of Z's friends finishing up the preparations,
with the four D-clan girls -- all between ages five and
eight -- scampering about in identical white dresses,
each by herself a picture of adorability and the sum of
all four way off any known chart of same. The cake had
arrived on schedule and stood on a table at the head of
the hall with the orrery solidly in place, planets Z and
G quivering magnificently overhead as the lightning
bolts surged between them, and white stars and moons
adorning the icing on all three layers -- all in all it
looked a little or probably a lot corny, true, but still
spectacular. (And yes, Wei informed me, Vinnie had
taken pictures of it for his cake display book.)
     After that the whirl. Three hours, about a hundred
and fifty people present at the peak, and Z and I tried
to schmooze at least a little with everyone. (I
neglected to mention one other glitch: Mark, husband of
Z's deceased friend Julie K., couldn't come because
their son Ben took sick at the last moment.) It turned

out I felt quite comfortable with the crowd, all but a
handful of whom I knew at least slightly, and I was able
to kick up my heels pretty good and make a few
spontaneous remarks in my "speech" which seemed well
received (got some laughs anyway, especially the "Skanky
Scandi" line) (everyone thought I was kidding when I
said I'd forgotten to wear the button, but that was the
truth) -- this during the round of toasts and the cake-
cutting ceremony. Aida was the toastmaster and she kept
her remarks short and wasn't too demanding with the
crowd. Brother Rob read a quote he'd come up with some
months ago and saved for the occasion. (He gave me a
copy of it but it seems I've misplaced it somewhere.)

The oddest moment of the day came during the toasts
when Z's irrepressible Filusan-bombshell workmate Gloria
G. suddenly came forward with a tray containing hundreds
of coins, all quarters, and gave a little speech about
Filipino traditions, and then stuffed our clothes with
folding money, and several others followed suit as most
in the crowd looked on somewhat perplexed if not aghast,
and eventually quite a few other people who'd probably
never dreamed they'd be doing such a thing felt obliged
to cough up some bucks. With all the bills sticking out
of my pockets and the open collar of my shirt, Z said, I
looked something like the Jolly Green Giant layered in
leaves. A few minutes later June "fleeced" us in the
kitchen and totaled up all the bills: hundreds of
dollars, I forget exactly how many. Certainly it was
enough to pay for a large chunk of the wedding.

After the toasts, dancing started, first with Z and
me staggering about to "Only You." Later I proved to
her I don't have the faintest idea how to polka. I
danced three straight git-down-funky cuts with Rose F.
and her comment at the end was, "I think we just bonded
for life!" For much of the afternoon the dozen or so
kids present were playing out in the side yards,
including in the gazebo where I'd been jyzing the day
before. People stood on the long porch, sat on the
railings -- the sun was warm and the flowers mostly
picturesque, the side-yard orchard beckoning, quite a

few pears still adorning the trees, and I actually
espied one in the act of falling. Kerplunk! -- Oh, and
again I've failed to note a high point: the four
adorable ones performed a kind of kiddie shivaree, a
song complete with doo-wop steps and movements,
meanwhile making the letters of the word LOVE with their
arms -- and Sera intently directed them, kneeling on the
floor in the middle of the ballroom, as a couple of
toddlers wandered out to join them. It was hilarious.

I was just so pleased with it all. The crowd was
mostly working folks, and it was as racially diverse as
they come -- as a crowd can be, really -- and even
though most of them started out as Z's friends, I felt
strong ties with many. And Z was wonderful (it'll be a
trip to see the photos and the videos, of which it
seemed several were always being taken). "The radiant
bride" -- and that she was. In white, with sixties-
style platform dancing shoes. She worked the room so
easily and so vivaciously. So many people love and
respect her! The woman is so charismatic! (Two people
actually said this to me.) In an important way the
reception was a tribute to her, the fruit of a lifetime
of caring intensely about her friends and coworkers.
Her boss, Dale, attended (and danced up a scandalously
rowdy storm) and her coworkers presented her with a
number of gifts, including a check for several hundred
bucks and a stereo sound system (Leola was the big force
behind that) which we'll probably set up here in the
bedroom. Dale and I had a good talk -- it was the third
time he's told me he thinks I'm making a big difference
in Zoelie's life and he admires me for it and wants to
know my secret (and each time I've been almost
blushingly proud to hear him say that).

I could mention a lot of names. Lee M. of "average
artichoke" fame, he drove three hundred miles this
morning to spend a few hours at the reception. Craig A.
and Spencer, the two gay guys from the utility, and Ryan
V., the younger gay environmental activist: their lively
and shamelessly campy and funny presence meant a lot.
Wei and Alison making us promise to go "dancing and

arting" now that all four of us are officially in the
hitched state. Wes P. from Z's book group: I was
startled to hear myself blubbering absurdly to him about
how he and his new wife must get together with us.
Bitha the dot-com millionaire with her adorable (again!)
adopted Chinese daughter. Paula N. who can't be
physically touched: more tales of her tribulations. Lou
G. who gave us a boat ride, Madge I. who also gave us a
boat ride (during the past two summers I mean, these
rides) (and Madge was treating me like a long-lost buddy
and presented us with a Japanese ukiyoe-style cloth wall
hanging because I'd perhaps a bit too extravagantly
praised one much like it displayed on her houseboat).

    -- Well, okay, enough. Or almost. I have to
mention Fred and Eleanor W. we occasionally see movies
with, Cassie B. who swore she recalled my byline from
way back in newshound days, Tina whom I met at one of
Z's pharmacies but I didn't recognize her now because
she'd cut off her dreads since then, the sweet-smiled
David M. who'll be delivering Z's speech for her at a
regional convention she has to miss for our honeymoon
(he still has his own dreads and he's six months into
his own new marriage and is still euphoric and not at
all shy about saying so), Manny's brother Reuben who's
still spinning Kat flawlessly several feet off the
ground (and I have to concede she seems to love his
spins more than mine), Roy the utility unit boss and
Cordell who took Z to the jazz concert whose tickets she
bought at an office charity auction. -- And I can't
fail to mention another high point: the line dance Sera
(you gotta give her credit!) organized, the funky tunes,
people pairing up with whoever was at the top of the
line opposite and strutting their best stuff in tandem
down the gauntlet -- just about everybody having a
marvelous time then and the whole afternoon and telling
us so and you knew they meant it because you'd seen
plenty of evidence of it even discounting for the ultra-
rosy lenses you knew you were seeing it all through.

    -- At six the cleanup. Lots of people pitched in
so it didn't take too long. June drove us home, her car

loaded down with flowers, gifts, cake, food (and I should've mentioned the potluck "finger food" worked out well too: a row of tables lined one whole side of the hall and they were piled high with goodies of all kinds, from Filipino adobo to Chinese candies to a bowl of cherry tomatoes fresh from someone's garden; and the hall was festooned with fresh flowers cut from half a dozen different gardens, including Betty's -- they did finally get there somehow). The big hug from June, that was another high point. "Glen, I am so happy for you and Zoelie!" And later Gerry drove all the way across the lake and back to bring us a loaner CD player for the honeymoon trip to the resort (it runs off the car's lighter). And here at home we opened the dozen or more gifts people bestowed on us despite our request that they not do so. And reviewed the day, trying to digest it, both of us stunned at how well it went and feeling ecstatically pleased to be officially hitched. Period. That's how it was and that's how it is!

    And here she lies, the wife. Stretched out prone beneath the sheets, sleep mask and back-protecting blue hula hoop on, one surgically reconfigured foot poking out quite fetchingly right in front of me, probably just to show off that henna'd ankle (or the copper-colored toenails she had professionally painted last week to match the rings -- I definitely shouldn't fail to mention those toenails). It's close to five a.m. now and I'll soon be joining her in bed. (The wedding moon shining outside most of this time, casting its own little chain of somewhat fainter dots on the Chinese screen -- "Festival of Joy" well underway.) The alarm's set for ten-thirty and we're due at the same southern-style Afrusan restaurant for brunch an hour later and we'll make our honeymoon getaway from there.

                        [+2]

    The moon, the moon, the honeymoon moon. It's rolling along so splendidly it's hard to feature, oh yes

it is. But jyze is trying to do it anyway. Feature
this! Marvelous weather, luscious loving, superb digs
-- and an astounding story to top it all.

   Two days post-wedding now and here's the front room
of our honeymoon suite. Z's breathing steadily in the
bed a few feet to my left. She wanted to stay up later
-- "to go by your schedule this time for a change"
(meaning not just tonight but for the whole five days)
-- but both last night and tonight she was unable to do
that. Last night, in fact, we both hit the bed about
nine p.m. and didn't awaken until this morning, some
fourteen hours later in my case, a couple fewer in hers.
But tonight she said she wanted me to do my jyze thing
in the same room even if she couldn't stay awake, and so
here we are.

   This going down in the back corner of the room at a
small table bearing an ancient fluorescent desk lamp
reminiscent of the one which stood on Popeye's desk when
I was a kid. The bulb hangs directly over the J-book at
a height of about ten inches. The two detachable
speakers of our new CD player -- which we haven't used
yet and probably won't until we get back home because
it's so quiet up here -- are standing on the edge of the
table to keep the light out of Z's eyes. Through an
open vent by the side of the single large double-sash
window I can hear the roar of the surf a few hundred
yards away across the dunes. Two vintage tiltback
armchairs sit side-by-side before the window, which
looks straight west and during the daylight hours
commands a broad view of the beach through the tall
trees surrounding the house except directly in front. Z
and I, after a full day outdoors, sprawled in those
chairs reading and drinking wine for a couple of hours
this evening, starting just before sunset (which was
lovely in an understated way, charcoal pink at the
horizon with a few darker gray horizontal brushstrokes
just above). -- And we nibbled on pate'-smeared
crackers from the bountiful picnic basket Nick and Betty
and Kat packed for us.

   -- And by the way, this marriage has already been

fully consummated and not just once. That's right,
twice. Within twelve hours! Right here in this bed!
-- And a funny, even slightly scary story attaches to
that too, related to the confetti-size metallic glitter
Kat deposited down the front of Z's dress (and then my
shirt as well) just before our departure for the coast.
This by the dictates of tradition because she'd done the
same as a three-year-old at Manny and Betty's wedding in
a caper that's lived on in family legend. -- But maybe
before I dig more deeply into the glitter story I ought
to start back at the beginning and do all the drama-
building I can (which, because I'm working on a glass of
fancy wedding-gift bourbon after glugging down several
glasses of wine, may not be much, and will surely be
increasingly sloppy not to say sloshy).

My sleep hours Saturday night after the reception
numbered about five, ending at ten a.m. When I climbed
into bed Z welcomed me with a snore and that was it --
on our wedding night! And was I ever glad! We were two
totally zonked postnups of the freshly minted variety,
no question about it. In the morning we had just enough
time to pack up and drive over to the restaurant, where
the other three were awaiting us, and the delay on a
table was only a few minutes. Unfortunately Kat was in
a snit over an incident that happened the previous night
(the adults had vetoed the video she wanted to watch in
favor of their own choice) and for the first half of the
meal wasn't speaking to anyone. A table for five right
by the open front door, trad-jazzy music playing,
breakfast fragrances wafting about almost visibly, Nick
in exuberant good spirits (and by coincidence he and I
were wearing identical black cotton shirts) -- it was a
jolly time, and especially so after Kat perked up. The
warm homemade biscuits with strawberry preserves were
outstanding -- twice we called for a new basket. Nick
told funny and alarming tales of his recent experiences
as a high-school English teacher.

Afterwards lots of hugs where our cars were parked,
bestowal of gifts, strewing of glitter, a last-moment
incident with Kat diving into the front seat on our laps

and refusing to leave until finally Nick and Betty had
to drag her out, half stripping her in the process (and
as we were leaving the restaurant she had demanded
Nick and I take off our shirts so she could compare our
muscles, but we had to let her down) -- and we were off.
Tears were rolling down Betty's cheeks -- no doubt as
memories came bubbling up of her own honeymoon trip with
Manny and Kat to the very same destination.

A brief stop for gas and another at the nearby
east-hill co-op for red-flame grapes and other snacks
and then a four-hour drive in fine fall weather, taking
the freeway seventy miles south and a serpentine state
road west through the woods to the coast (with scarcely
any traffic until we came upon a ten-car caravan of
spiffy antique vehicles and had to crawl behind them
through the hills for the last twenty miles) and then
the southward jaunt down one side of the bay and the
turn northward up the peninsula (which is long and
straight like a very thin finger and points due north)
and up about a third of the way and across to the ocean
side half a mile south of the main peninsula town.

The resort is set in a grove of huge old evergreens
just off the beach, separated from it by a grassy duned
strip a couple of hundred yards wide. The main house --
"the lodge" -- is a reddish three-story wooden structure
which a card on the desk here says was built over a
century ago as a "family beachside retreat" for a U.S.
senator from the next state south; it's surrounded by
half a dozen small cabins and several vintage trailers
which are also rented out. Everything about the place
is old, comfortable, and artsy-craftsy in an
unpretentious way that we both find delightful. We have
suite number 6 which takes up the southern half of the
garreted top floor of the main house, with the ceilings
slanting down to the side walls. The suite consists of
two bedrooms separated by a large kitchen and a small
bathroom. Homey touches are everywhere. On this desk
alone (where I'm jyzing) there's a small globe, a potted
begonia, a sculpted bowl of shells, an Indian-weave mat,
and a row of well-worn books, including one called

"Oysterville" describing a small nearby community; and
lying atop the row of books is a spiral tablet in which
previous occupants of the suite over the past few years
have written comments about their stay here and in
several cases, including that of the couple who preceded
us, drawn elaborate sketches. Brightening up the walls
are a number of watercolors and acrylic/oil paintings of
the beach, the house, and the room itself, along with an
assortment of posters and textile hangings. Many of the
people who come here are artists and some swap samples
of their work for a week or two's stay -- and on that
detail hangs the astounding tale referred to earlier.

*

     -- So then I had to take a break. And now I'm
thinking I should fill out the chronology first (just
because I don't want it to seem anticlimactic or to
forgetfully leave it out entirely) and save the
astounding tales -- two of them, actually; I've decided
the second is almost as astounding as the one already
referred to -- save them for last.
     Upon arrival we were met at the front porch by Sid,
the white-bearded, South African-accented man in his
seventies who with his wife Laila has owned and run the
place for decades. (Or possibly I misheard and they're
Australian, as Z thinks she recalls.) A charming pair,
and far from your ordinary innkeepers. The common room
downstairs is full of books and art objects, writing
tables, dictionaries, a video movie collection, literary
and political magazines addressed to the owners. Sid
and Laila congratulated us on our marriage but nothing
too elaborate or overdone: just a small card welcoming
us with a few words written in by hand. A windowed
porch occupies half the front (west) and most of the
south side of the house, and it too contains an
intriguing variety of driftwood pieces, old chairs and
couches, plants and sculptures, and two people were
sketching there when we came in -- quite possibly the
ones who had this suite before us (the rooms were still
being cleaned at seven in the evening when we arrived --
a "misfire of sorts," Laila confessed later,

400

apologizing).
       We took a walk on the beach while the rooms were
being readied. Only two or three other people were out
there, widely separated, and just a single auto (the
beach to the north is open to vehicles after Labor Day,
and the rest of it to the south all year round).
Memories fluttered back of our first and only other
visit to that beach some sixteen months ago (when we
stayed in one of the trailers here) -- of flying a kite
and tossing a frisbee with Kat and Nick.
       After an hour or so we returned to the house and
the room was ready, but we stuck around only long enough
to unpack and then took off for town so we could make it
to the market and a certain diner before they closed (Z
was jonesing for a burger like the ones we feasted on
there last year). It turned out the diner -- in a
spruced-up old caboose -- had already closed, alas, and
worse yet, the closure was permanent; the place looked
forlorn with a "for sale" sign flapping by the entrance
even though flowers were still thriving in the deck
planters. Z was tempted to start nibbling on the
nasturtiums which grow abundantly in the area; she loves
them mixed into a green salad. But we wound up at the
only eatery we could find open nearby, which is also the
area's pride and joy, an upscale inn which boasts a
many-starred restaurant. We dined in the bar there,
just sandwiches. Stained-glass windows and good music,
prices not too outrageous. And behind the bar the only
person of color we've seen in the entire town so far: an
affable young Afrusan dude who's also a published poet.
       And the walk back, down side streets lined with
oddly undersized, low-riding houses (first floor usually
flush with the ground), many proudly announcing their
age with plaques hung on the buildings themselves:
mostly from the 1880s and 1890s. Lots of flower gardens,
hanging boxes, windsocks (on the main street downtown we
saw several kite shops; the beach here often hosts
national and international kiting competitions).
       Up to the room -- for a nap. But almost
immediately the marital act. Long and good marital act!

G comes with groans of joy! (Z comes with groans of joy
too, many times, as almost always -- but she can't let
herself go vocally as much as she'd hoped she could;
the house is just too quiet.)
     -- And then afterwards as I, this husband-person
right here, rise to fetch some drinks, Z notices an odd
red/purple splotch on the lower left side (as it hangs
down still somewhat tumesced) of my consummatory organ.
At first it looks to her like a scrape or abrasion or
possibly a rash -- maybe even a herpes outbreak. On
closer examination I tell her I don't think it's any of
those things but I don't know what the heck it is. Not
a broken blood vessel either -- the red is a little too
bright for that. -- And only after several minutes does
it dawn on us it might be Kat's glitter "melting" from
contact with Z's vaginal juices. Then we start noticing
glitter all over the place -- the rug, bedspread,
tabletop where our clothes wound up -- and even a few
pieces caught in our pubic hair. And the red of one
such piece and the purple of another appear to match
those of the colorful two-tone splotch on ol' Poosh.
Which means, Z suddenly realizes, she's probably hosting
at least two pieces of the stuff inside ol' Peaches.
     She didn't panic over this. In the morning we even
performed the marital act again, though this time much
more cautiously. Then for much of the afternoon as we
explored the town on foot, and later along the beach
boardwalk as we slowly made our way back to the lodge,
we cracked wise about glittery metallic robot fetuses
and searching for "glitter douches" at the drugstore.
-- But in the past, well before I knew her, Z's had
terrible trouble with fibroiditis and so is planning to
undergo a full exam when we return to the city.
     That's one tale. (And I'll note we indulged in a
big three p.m. breakfast in town just as my coffee
craving was about to take me down. Many of the shops
are closed with the end of high tourist season almost a
month in the past now. The far-coast-megalopolis paper
is nowhere available, but the Jyze City morning paper
can be found albeit at double the city price. Z swore

she'd never before seen me eat a bacon-and-eggs
breakfast (though I know she did -- during our trip to
the country fair less than three months ago -- and
eventually persuaded her). And in the center of town we
ran into a former work colleague of Z's from the
utility, Harry L., in his motorized wheelchair -- he was
director of city services for the handicapped, I think
she said, before his recent retirement -- and for the
first time she introduced me to someone as her husband.
And she did it, I thought, quite naturally, perhaps in
part because only moments earlier we'd been practicing
tongue-in-cheek for just such an eventuality.)

(By the way, I had several drinks at the pub last
night -- my usual brand of bourbon for special occasions
-- and Z said it made me voluble and "forthcoming" to a
degree she'd never witnessed before and she loved it.
And now I'm into my third drink tonight, on top of the
wine, and feeling even more loosened up -- not that I
think I'm all that tight at other times, necessarily,
but rather now I'm saying to hell with it, let it all
hang out wherever it wants to hang and however purplish-
red and glittery it may be. I know I'll regret it later
but I have no other choice if I want to keep cranking
out the jyze. And I do want to do that.)

Any other small items before turning to the second,
even more amazing yarn? -- All day Z was grumbling
about a tree-topping crew which was working nearby.
Tearing up the trees, making lots of noise, releasing
lots of pollution -- too much! And the "maid person"
for the resort drives an old beater car which sounds
like a cement mixer and spews clouds of black smoke –
and until that beater engine's shut off poor Z's shaking
as if to fly apart at any second. I tell her I'm
wondering if she's as ready for backcountry living as
she likes to think (during our walk she talked about the
possibility of buying this or that cute little century-
old house -- and lots of them are for sale). And she
says very fetchingly: "The truth is nothing could drag
me out of Jyze City and you damn well know it. So: you
got a problem with that, Mr. Spouse?"

(And the surf, it just keeps on a-roarin'. Ooh
such fun it was and seemingly downright profound to sit
on a driftwood log observing the nearby squiggly lines
in the sand, ever-shifting patterns of graceful foam-
crested curves formed by the waves as they eroded the
cuneiform languages ("chicken tracks") left by a big
flock of gulls which had wandered by headed north -- and
then a pair of big cavorting mutts explosively scattered
the gulls. And the best spot on the boardwalk was a map
under clear plastic showing the location of hundreds of
shipwrecks in this area and southward, with one of the
two lighthouses standing on the promontory in between,
and probably visible from the window here when they're
in operation, as they haven't been so far to our
knowledge during our stay -- but that closest one is
picturesquely visible from the beach in daylight and
I've found myself gazing at it almost obsessively as if
it holds some secret for me or us.)
     -- My snoring wife. She does know how to do it,
especially when she's had a drink or two. -- This
"hub'n'wiff" thing, we're still feeling our way on it,
and again especially she, but me also, for real in part
but also because I don't want her to be thinking I'm
jaded about marriage just because I've been there (here)
a coupla times before. And she's already saying she
wants to come back to this same suite for her heavenly-
year birthday celebration eighteen months from now --
though she and Leola have agreed to celebrate theirs
together -- and I'm chaffing her for the way she's
always got to be leaping ahead to plan the next big
occasion even while still whooping up the current one
(the big one of her lifetime, arguably, and I'll
immediately add it's the same of mine and never mind
about those other aforementioned two).
                              *
(And I in my black sweatpants. I in my "Zoelie B."
pendant. I who've just poured myself another one, yee-
ha! And it wasn't easy because I could barely stand up
straight to fetch more water. I'm one hell of a happy
camper or I guess I should say lodger or resorter. One

hell of a lucky one too. That's right. And majorly
intoxicated for sure, and it's utterly apt, because I am
just that and more and in a trans-alcoholic sense, I'm
stone gone on loving this woman -- who's still snoring,
but so tenderly now, little come-hither snores, but not
to worry, jyze fans, I won't yield, I'm staying right
here until the full story's in the can. Of course I've
already given away much of what it's about but never
mind -- the details please, Mr. Spouse.)

All right. So when we first walk up to the outdoor
porch of the lodge here, I notice two sculptures, both
busts, men's heads, and I like them. The next morning I
point them out to Z as we're leaving to get coffee and
she says, "That looks like Marie T.'s stuff. You know,
the one who did me." She takes a closer look and is
convinced, it must be Marie T. Just then Laila, Sid's
wife and co-owner, comes out (we've rung the bell on the
front desk), and the first question Z asks is about
those sculptures: are they Marie T.'s work? Why yes,
they are! Laila's delighted that we would recognize
them. It turns out Marie's a regular visitor here, and
for the past several years she's been bringing a group
of kids down for a week's stay which she pays for in
trade with one of her busts. Z tells Laila she's been a
subject of Marie's work herself and knows her well.
Laila says there's one more work of Marie's in the
kitchen of her and Sid's personal quarters at the back
of the first floor and it's her favorite of them all.

Well, it's pretty damn obvious where this is going.
I say, as we walk back to see this other statue,
"Wouldn't it be a trip if it's the one of you?" -- and
of course it's just that. There it is standing on a
pedestal atop a table in the middle of the kitchen, the
focus of the whole room, which is quite large and high-
ceilinged. The easily recognizable face is up at about
the six-and-a-half-foot level. "Why, I talk with her --
I mean, with you -- all the time!" gushes Laila, who's
as stunned as we are. It's almost embarrassing --
you could say Z's soul has been hijacked and is serving
as a kitchen goddess -- but Laila handles the matter

just right, says all kinds of flattering and caring
things, stands Z on a chair next to the bust (which is
an approximately life-size head-and-torso about thirty
inches high), admits other people have said the statue
resembles Laila too (and it does -- she's a shorter,
older, somewhat less "exotic"-looking but still very
pretty version of Z, maybe more as she'll look at
Laila's age), and then says Marie has written out by
hand the story of how she came to sculpt this particular
bust and she, Laila, wants Z to read it. The story
appears in the flyleaf pages of a cookbook because
that's where Laila figured the words would be longest
lasting; and the lower part of the bust itself (the
actual bosomy part) was serving as a bookend, among
other things, for a row of cookbooks, including the one
she'd referred to. And Laila pulled it out and gave it
to us to take upstairs, and later Z and I read Marie's
account, which goes on for seven or eight pages and is
impressively well written, and it tells accurately, Z
says, how she and Marie met and describes Z in a fashion
so flattering she was all but sobbing when I read it
aloud (with pride to be sure), using terms like "fierce
intellectual presence" and "strikingly beautiful" and
"mischievous eyes" (some of the very terms I used for
her myself after our first meeting!) and said also she'd
again run into Z recently, a dozen years after doing the
sculpture, and she still had those same qualities.
     So isn't "astounding" the right word for this? A
pair of newlyweds arrives at a far-off resort for their
honeymoon and they find a bust (or a "torso" as Marie
also calls it) of the bride herself more or less
presiding over the place, a complete surprise to both of
them, just as the bride's identity as the subject of the
sculpture is a complete surprise to the resort owners?
And this bust/torso -- and the description of it by the
artist herself -- so well represent the bride, the new
husband immediately feels he's in love with it just as
he is with her (well, but of course not in exactly the
same way, but still -- in something like the fleshly-
correlative way, I'll say, if the FC were set in stone).

[A Jyze Epithalamium]

    And the backstory on this, a dozen years ago Z,
when she was working as an energy-conservation inspector
for the city, did one of her inspections for Marie T. A
short while later Marie tracked Z down by phone at the
utility and said she'd been much taken with her and
wanted to sculpt her. Z agreed to sit for her. And the
very first time I visited Z's apartment a few weeks
after we met I saw a framed acrylic-crayon sketch for
the resulting sculpture hanging on the wall above her
bed -- it's now mounted on her bedroom wall in unit 203
-- and later still I saw photos of the bust/torso itself
and was blown away by both. And for a long time that
framed sketch done by Marie served, along with Z's
college-graduation photo with her parents and the
contributors photo for the "12-PAC" poetry collection
and then later the contact sheets shot by the celebrated
Danny L., as my main images of the person she'd been in
earlier years. Those Z's in a sense merged with the
live one; they gave her a depth of history and being she
might not otherwise have had for me.
    Astounding. Truly. Flabbergasting. And I'm
loving it. Even more than Z is. In fact she's
naturally humble (though also vain of course); she
already seems to have forgotten about it or to be taking
it for granted as a kind of strange coincidence. Not
me. I'm seeing this as a fabulosity of the highest
order. Can't help it. Clearly, if also maximally
unclearly, jyze is going wild over this. -- But must
stop now. Can't possibly say anything more.

                        [+2]

    It's over this soon -- the actual physical thing, I
mean. The honeymoon. Tomorrow morning we finish
packing and head back to the city. (But the
metaphorical honeymoon, no reason we can't keep it going
for a good long time. That's my aim anyway, corny as it
may -- no, does -- sound. I haven't asked Z about what
her aim may be in this regard or even said anything

about the matter to her yet, but I expect she'll go for
it too.)

     Tonight I'm holed up in the back bedroom of suite
no. 6. It's just about midnight. Knowing someone's now
occupying the suite below ours as well as the one across
the hall, I've been creeping around on tiptoes. The
house rules say something about "no unnecessary noise"
after eleven and the floorboards up here creak something
fierce (the steep wooden staircase between the second
and third floors something even fiercer) -- one of the
joint's most endearing features. The numerous creaks I
set off regardless, even when tiptoeing, I consider
necessary: creaks of a jyze ninja.

     As we hurried through the darkening back streets to
the restaurant at the same many-starred inn for our big
blowout dinner tonight it occurred to me this day has a
news peg I'd lost sight of in all the excitement: as of
four o'clock this afternoon we've now been together
exactly two and a half years. It's a significant number
because in our talks over this entire period Z fairly
early settled on it as representing the outer limit of
the time she'd been involved, ever, with any one man.
Tonight, though, she didn't seem much moved by my
mentioning this -- probably because we've been talking
for the past couple of months as if we'd already passed
the barrier. (But it did get us to bantering a bit at
dinner about former lovers. Briana T. came up for the
first time. And I proposed a toast to all her "majors"
-- Marty, Gabe, Terry, Rodney, Brian, Arvin, and Jerry
II -- several of whom had two-year shots at her and,
fortunately for me, botched them.) (And by the way,
she's now insisting Kirk was never a major.)

     Crab for her, baked halibut for me, three drinks,
two tiny berry cobblers ala mode, well over a hundred
bucks shelled out. But who was squawking? I liked the
room, which with its Victorian decor reminded me of
dinners with Mom and Dad when they were visiting the
young jyzer in his college-days incarnation. Z might've
winced a few class-related winces but she also handled
herself with admirably stylish aplomb. And I tried not

to disappoint her expectations, complicated as those
undoubtedly were (and are!), and felt I did okay.
-- Then again none of this really mattered because we
were still flying on full tanks of newlywed euphoria
(even after four days of nonstop togetherness and all
those preceding weeks of prenup tensions).

   One setback, though. At a downtown deli where we
were doing a late lunch she returned from a restroom
visit and said, "Don't panic, but I'm spotting." We
joked about how this must've been a result of all our
heavyweight whang-dang-doodle, including a round just an
hour or so before that, and also an extended session the
night before which involved relatively acrobatic (for
us at this stage in our conjugal careers) maneuvers and
some fairly strenuous thrusting (for me in unfamiliar
wham-bam mode because she likes it and was urging it,
and we'd both temporarily lost sight of our vows to keep
things restrained). But in truth we're both still
worried that one or more of those pieces of glitter
might be cutting her up and we've decided to put off any
more true humping until after she can get herself looked
at back in J-town. -- But have kept on joking about it
all anyway, because why not? What else you gonna do?
She came up with the best one, something about the irony
of a woman with a certificate in toxicology now walking
around dripping toxic wastes from her own vagina (this
sounding only slightly less crude in her version).

   Today we traveled basically the same loop we did
yesterday, hiking into town via the main drag, trekking
back along the beach ("The World's Longest," according
to the sign above the main entrance). After lunch Z
bought two huge bags of freshly made saltwater taffy for
her coworkers and we foolishly hauled those all the way
back by foot, with a large part of that trek on sand.

   (When I first took notice of this back bedroom, two
of the posters mounted on the walls caught my eye in a
special way. Briana T. long ago gave me a copy of one
of them; a copy of the other had ridden the walls in
most of the places where I lived with Lady U because it
was a favorite of hers and of her mother's as well.

-- The past, I'm not denying it. It's still there. But
suddenly it looks even more museumlike than it did, say,
a week ago. Marriage, I shouldn't be too surprised to
discover, seems to put everything in a whole new
perspective.)
       -- Lots and lots of details I'd like to jot down.
The great weather! The only smudge on it was some
morning fog today, but it burned off as we walked into
town. And beach descriptions. Birds. Kites. Local
yokels and local sophisticates. Our second viewing of
Zoelie B. the kitchen goddess (for photos and a video
with Sid and Laila and the "maid person," Sammy, who was
dying to meet the model herself after Laila told her the
tale). The canoodling here, there, everywhere. The
spectacular driftwood. The foot massages (my fingers
working on her feet) as we read side by side in the
armchairs facing the window and the sunset (these
massages reminding her of, but of course remaining far
inferior to, the ones her daddy used to give her as they
watched TV). The hundred different ways I feel almost
shockingly close to her (proud of her, tender toward
her, lusty for her, inspired by her, awed by her). And
colossally fortunate to have her, yeah for sure. (I
admit it: I'd never realized a new husband could be
thinking so over-the-top like this. Or at least not
that I can remember.) -- And how I love wearing this
big copper ring with "Z&G" inscribed on the inner lining
("ZAG" and "GAZ" is what Wei came up with when he tried
to make out the inscriptions -- and at some point I
expect we'll be trying to make something more out of
that misreading).
       -- And so, end of honeymoon. That is, the
initially scheduled part. And end of this volume: the
fourth of the projected TJM ten. Take a few days off
now to prep for starting up the centerpiece, middle
three volumes, kickoff of the big civilizational
countdown -- or simply call it the continuation of the
long honeymoon. -- In any case for me it's obvious the
real centerpiece is already in place and no mere
millennial blowout could possibly compare with it.

BOOK E

[Jyze Postnup]

21

Here begins the new married life, workaday aspect.
I'm hunkered down on the grated lid of a window well at
the Natusan center. Late sun shines through the low-
branched trees hugging the building. Straight ahead
through some different branches I see the lime-green
railing of the high bridge and the lower stories of the
DC castle. Down below, vehicles whizzing along on
several tiers of freeways. To the far right, a mile or
so distant, the huge structures, one domed and one
movable-roofed, of the two stadiums.

Moments ago the postnups walked hand-in-hand across
that bridge and then after a mushy farewell at the
northern end the new wife ambled back the other way.
She didn't know the recidivist husband was planning to
set up a jyze operation quite so soon. But then he
didn't know it himself. -- This area being a bit risky
because, as noted previously, numerous denizens of "the
jungle" and "the rez" hang out around here and the
hillside below. And the blackberries are still
plentiful. And on any day of the week other than Sunday
the office whose windows open just above my head would
be occupied, but now it's not; I'm on my own.

As of today the honeymoon's officially over -- Z
goes back to work in the morning. But we're still
saying we'll do a week's honeymoon anew every week. No
exceptions! And for the past few nights narrowing
crescents of our marriage moon have been scything across
the night sky in ultra-slow motion and they'll likely be
doing so for a couple more nights before that particular
moon is gone for good. Nonetheless we must already

concede that in Gregorian terms, even if not by those of the lunar calendar, it was last month we got hitched.

Today also the baseball regular season comes to a close. For sure we're into autumn now. Leaves carpet the ground under the trees here, and not just those tiny vulvar leaves of six weeks ago. Rather your archetypal local array of autumn leaves, including some truly big ones from -- no surprise here -- the many bigleaf maples in the area. Soon you'll be able to push all the leaves, or anyway a lot, into a huge pile and jump in.

Meanwhile I have some news of literally earthshaking personal import, or it certainly could become that -- and not just personal either. A story in Saturday's paper reported the discovery of a probable earthquake fault line running under and through south hill. A seismologist caught in a traffic jam last summer on a section of the freeway I can see from here -- the north-south portion that runs along the west side of our hill -- noticed a suspicious geological outcropping in the hillside greenbelt area (which is not visible from here). That rocky formation protrudes on an east-west line closely paralleling the street which passes just three houses north of ours. Initial testing confirms the configuration could have been caused by tectonic forces. Whether it actually was is still a matter of dispute, and much more testing remains to be done, but a number of seismologists now believe we're talking about a "new" branch of the major Jyze City fault. That fault is active and so this part of it probably is also. Just when its last activity might have been, the article doesn't say, nor is there any indication yet of when the next big shake might occur. But I'm sure we'll be hearing lots more about all this.

Nobody's panicking though. This is earthquake country; the risks are well known in general even if not in every last particular (like, say, those involving our potential new south-hill branch fault). And although Z and I might not stay in our present apartment too much longer, it's likely we'll still wind up living in the same hilltop hood or very close to it. It's home. We

dig it. We're sticking with it if we can and never mind
the odds on a quake taking us down -- maybe way down
into the abyss itself -- although the article does say
this appears to be the kind of fault line that grinds,
not the kind that opens abysses.

    But the specific building we're in, that's probably
history for us. Or at least the chances of its being so
seem to have increased substantially. That was the
other bit of startling news awaiting us when we arrived
home from the coast, and this item was literally taped
to our 203 door. It was a hand-printed notification
from the landlord, Min, of a walk-through building
inspection as part of a bank appraisal. To us this
implied the building was about to be sold (and oh what
an eyeful the appraisers must've gotten when they hit
our wedding-shambled digs on the 29th, while we were
away); and confirmation of the likelihood of a sale came
a short time later when Z opened an old e-mail message
from Matt B., alias Zonker, owner of one of the motel-
like apartment buildings just up the street, saying our
building was on the market again and he was interested
in buying it himself and wondering what we might know
about it. (We know plenty, but we couldn't reach him,
and it was probably too late anyway; his message dated
from mid September and had been shunted aside by Z
herself during the chaotic wedding run-up.)

    (And what's the impact of news item No. 1, the
probable fault-line discovery, on news item No. 2, the
probable sale of the building? I haven't really stopped
to consider this. But here's my first choosh: it's
likely not much. Temporary at most. The buyer might be
able to swing a slightly better deal. -- Because
virtually every building in this city would be affected
by a major quake along the main Jyze City fault, and the
market long ago discounted for this fact (or chose to
ignore it). And another point to be noted is that
people's memories on such things tend to be very short.
I know this from my time in Jyzer G city number 2/7
where quakes are even more common than they are here.)

    -- So yes, I'd say the chances are still high we'll

soon have a new landlord and no doubt even higher that
he/she/they/it will be jacking up the rent. I'm
guessing it'll happen before January 1st. Which means
we'll be part of a wave, because it's the same story
right now all across the city: huge increases, with
rents and security deposits doubling, even tripling.
And the wave's arrival on south hill has been widely
predicted for many months owing to the dot-com invasion.

So here it is. Any minute now. The bankers are
already doing their thing. Damn the fault lines, full
speed ahead.

And speaking of fiscal institutions, there's one
other matter to mention. As of day before yesterday
we're into the new "budgetary" year, and its Christian
number is 2000. Just how "budgetary" differs from
"fiscal" I don't know, but apparently this is another
way of counting and labeling by which the rollover has
already occurred and the new millennium is upon us.
Yayhoo! -- Not that anyone seems to be paying a whole
lot of attention to this milestone, if that's what it
is, any more than they did with the new fiscal year back
on July 1. As far as I'm aware, both of these
ostensible preliminary rollovers have received zero
media play.

Z devoted most of today to writing thank-you notes
for the people who worked on the wedding and reception
and the ones who -- contrary to instructions! -- gave us
gifts. Tonight after work I'll be adding a quick
drawing and/or a few words to what she's written on each
card. Yesterday we saw a movie ("Earth") and appeared
in public here in J. City for the first time as a
consummatedly married and honeymooned couple, joining
the promenade of strollers on the east-hill commercial
strip. Friday night I worked at the scope office while
she decompressed at home with untrammeled mystery-
reading and "schmoozy" phone calls to Aida, Betty,
Olwen, Leola, Jess and others: that is, all or at least
many of the usual prime intimates.

The last day at the resort was very fine. We slept
late and found a note from Sid and Laila inviting us to

stay on an extra day at their expense. We couldn't do
that, but we assured them we'd be back and said we were
assigning an additional duty to the Zoelie B. kitchen
goddess: watching over their health and prosperity as
well as their culinary pleasure. Then we went gift-
hunting in town. After we left one of the many kite
shops the owner came running out with a miniature kite
as a free gift for us as "The Honeymooners" (he'd
overheard us comparing ourselves to Ralph and Alice from
the old TV show of that name). At one of the museums Z
splurged on a small yellow Japanese hand-painted kite --
size of a sheet of typing paper -- which we'll hang
above the art table as a honeymoon memento. And I
bought a six-inch wooden model of the lighthouse that so
intrigued me and that will serve the same memorializing
purpose at the hideaway. A last stop at the market near
the lodge for travel snacks and cornflakes -- Z had
noticed my favorite cereal was on deep sale and I sprang
for half a dozen jumbo boxes -- even on our honeymoon!
-- and then an easy and fast drive back to the city
retracing the same route we'd come out by, finding the
autumn coloring of the trees, especially along the state
highway, significantly advanced after just five days.

     -- And now the new life. But I must say once again
we did pick a doozer of a wedding date. The fine days
are still rolling themselves out!   -- And there's news
in the larger world too, beyond J. City, but I can't go
into that or anything else right now. Sun's down, the
chill factor is deepening: time to move on. (And while
I've been jyzing away five drifter dudes, all probable
Cawks judging solely by appearance -- three normally
grungy singles and a truly scuzzy Mutt'n'Jeff pair --
have clambered out of the bushes hugging the lip of the
hillside only about thirty feet away. To my surprise
none of them noticed me. It seems that back here under
the trees I'm better hidden than I realized. I'm part
of the scenery, my brown henley perhaps serving as
woodland camo of sorts as well as the street kind.
-- So I may return here someday, weather permitting, on
another afternoon when the center's closed.)

                    *   *

-- Later, some jyzey follow-up.

First a word or two about the postnups' sex life.
For the opening eight days of matrimony it's been feast
and then famine at the "plan A" level. At this point
we're still abstaining until Z goes in for inspection on
Tuesday (day after tomorrow) to see what effect, if any,
the glitter injection has had. This is fine; we're a
mature, experienced marital unit, yes, and we can delay
gratification if necessary (and truly it's not as if
we've never done that before). And neither of us thinks
Doc Karen will find anything seriously wrong. But I'll
note that even with lots of scrubbing I haven't been
able to completely efface the red and purple "glitter
stripes," as we've dubbed them, from my "gen set" and
nearby areas. They're faded but still quite conspicuous
and they're right where they were. And this fact has
stiffened, I'll say, our abstinence resolve whenever the
hormones have urged us to abandon it.

Feast or famine. Owing to Z's H-outbreaks if
nothing else, this polarized pattern will likely be with
us the rest of our days. The only question, really, is
how deep and how long the famines, or conversely how
frequent and lengthy, and rich, and deep too, and doozly
but hopefully not foozly, the feasts. And if they're
anything like what they've been so far, and especially
lately, or just say over the past seventeen months, I
think we'll be fine. Or better than that. And I think
she'd agree. (And I'm actually talking about both plans
here, A and B, along with any additional ones that might
take shape later on. They're all good!)

This may be an apt place to note that while on east
hill to see the movie Saturday night, Z and I visited a
porn shop together for the very first time. This is the
one catering mostly to independent women and lesbians
for which the attendees at the henna party gave Z a gift
certificate. In fact neither of us had ever checked it
out before. It's small and yuppie-ish, as Z said, and
surprisingly tame; she seemed even less impressed than I
was. Aside from a few videos it offered little in the

way of hardcore porn (and Z and I have never seen any
porn together either, whether via video or magazine or
cinema or live -- not even via internet). The shop's
tabletop displays of colorful dildos, many made of glass
and seemingly intended mainly for decorative purposes,
were about as erotic, we agreed, as tablefuls of
glassware at a department store. "Been dere, done dat"
seemed to be Z's general response, clearly referring to
a time well before I came along. In the end she swapped
the certificate for a lavishly illustrated book about
breasts (human female kind) and several packets of
putatively erotic bubblebath. And it didn't take long
for her to find the book, which is supposedly popular
these days with high-school and college grrrls and
wymyn, boring. "This is basically just a rehash," she
observed, flipping through it in bed at home, "of all
the stuff we were saying twenty years ago." Looked
pretty much that way to me too. (But this didn't stop
me from paging through it again a bit more lingeringly
after she'd fallen asleep. Just on impulse mind you.)
     -- On the D-clan front, a number of new
developments. First, Z's still trying to come to terms
with her disappointment at the senior D's' failure to
attend the reception. They sent us a boxed assortment
of fancy Filipino snacks with a perfunctory good-wishes
card and that was it; in the end they decided to join
their church group for its weekly Saturday-afternoon
meeting. And Z's been a regular at D-clan gatherings
ever since she first arrived in town. She thought she
had a kind of surrogate family in the D's but now she's
wondering if the ties all along may've been shallower or
more one-way than she ever imagined.
     In a sense the same thing goes for her ties with
the two older D-family daughters. She's doing what she
can to repair those, but she's also recalling she's
often been advised not to let herself get caught between
Aida and Sera. At the reception Aida told Sera that
Jess, Leola, Paz, and Tobey had attended our wedding
ceremony, though this wasn't strictly true (they all
arrived after it ended), and Sera supposedly freaked

over this (false) news and was still unhappy enough to
be grousing about it during Z's "schmooze" call to her
Friday night. Z's theory is that Aida is goading Sera
about such matters, perhaps unconsciously -- but Aida,
three years younger than Sera, has a long history of
this kind of "oops" blurting (I've witnessed numerous
instances of it firsthand, several almost certainly
intended to make me look bad, as Z agreed at the time).
And Sera herself, though much like Aida she can be
charming and funny and very likable when she wants to
be, is also widely known as a top-tier controller type
and is not shy about putting her own siblings down
publicly in fairly blatant ways, and Aida most of all.

     But still, Z's trying to make amends. In the next
few weeks we'll be taking Sera and Dak out to dinner and
a play to show our thanks for Sera's splendid work on
the reception. And after that we'll be doing a dinner/
movie "double date" with Aida and Kirk. Z asked if I'd
mind if she dropped her insistence on avoiding them as a
couple now that the wedding was over and I said not at
all; in fact I thought we'd already agreed on that. And
Aida, Z reported, was "thrilled" to hear about this new
"green light on Kirk"; she'd apparently thought the ban
was permanent. (Meanwhile Aida's having more trouble
with Charles, and her relationship with Kirk is the
likely cause. Last weekend they took Charles to a movie
and after Kirk left that evening Charles lost it and
started bashing the door of his room with a baseball bat
-- did it, Aida said, twenty or thirty times (the door
had to be replaced). Charles is almost Aida's height
now and at age twelve -- his birthday was the day of our
wedding -- he's about to "go teenage-al," as Z put it
(no, not "teen angel" as I at first thought she'd said).
Z and Aida are so close that Charles's development over
the next few years could significantly affect our lives,
for better or worse, mine obviously included.)

     -- And I'll mention I'm wearing my "Jyze" pendant
while jyzing. It's a first. Z noticed I had it on -- I
was no longer sporting the "Zoelie B." pendant that
looks a lot like it -- and she seemed to stifle a

miffed-type comment. I was glad she could do that. And
she asked if she could hang on to the "Celebrate"
pendant, which is also part of the primitive-copper set
Vida made for me, and keep it on the little jewelry
shelf in her bathroom, and I said fine. She liked the
way it seemed to work for her, she said, during the
wedding run-up; she even took to rubbing it like a
rabbit's foot at times when she started to feel frantic
about something. And she promised to let me wear it
occasionally too, but I must ask first so she'll know in
advance if it won't be available for her "to help get me
through any really heavy incoming doo-doo." (I'm not
making this stuff up. This is jyze postnup, how it is.
And I like it!)

[+2]

     While stopping by a soup kitchen on an overcast
evening. -- Or at least I was intending to make that
tonight's lede until the overcast started squeezing out
raindrops. This was up at the municipal plaza where
hundreds of hungry people, many homeless, line up every
night for a free hot meal. And they're probably still
doing that right now, with the servers ladeling out the
soup (more like a potato-laden stew) under a tent and
everyone else out soaking up the liquid sunshine. In
any event: no shelter was available for the jyzer to do
his jyze thing up there, so I've headed down to the
hideaway instead. Some other night for getting down up
close with the grub line.
     Today's good news is that Doc Karen's probe for
lost glitter came up empty. Z called me about it: "I'm
cleared for humping!" Some signs of abrasion were
evident, the doc said, but those looked more like "the
natural result of a joyous honeymoon -- certainly
nothing to worry about." So tonight we'll see what we
can do to make up for the honeymoon and post-honeymoon
joys lost to our self-imposed glitter quarantine. (And
I loved this: earlier, before going in for the probe, Z

left a note on my chair at home saying she was "hoping
for a clean bill of pussy from Doc K.")
     Meanwhile some other jyzey newsbits.
     First the world. I've pretty much neglected the
big picture over the past couple of weeks. And it's
been an interesting time out there, with most of the
headline stories coming from East Asia. October 1st was
the fiftieth anniversary of the communist takeover of
mainland China and so lots of ink has been spilled on
conditions in China today and its place in the world and
the United States' relation to it. Of course much of
the analysis appearing in this country is hostile,
reflecting the usual racist assumptions and ideological
biases and historical amnesia -- but even to see how
these play out can be fascinating in its own way, with
free-market fundamentalists, as an example, salivating
over, yes, the huge market of communists over there as
it grows ever bigger and ever richer -- though in terms
of per-capita GDP it's still a small fraction (under a
tenth) of the richness here.
     Also an unlikely story broke about a massacre of
hundreds of Korean civilians perpetrated by U.S. troops
during the Korean War. I don't mean it's unlikely it
happened; I mean it's unlikely that such a revelation
would be occurring after such a long period. I don't
doubt at all that massacres like this one were common.
Lady S and some of her Korean friends used to talk about
them when she and I were living together in Korea --
about tens of thousands of Koreans dying that way. Of
course this report, except in its gruesome details, was
little different from many others concerning the U.S.
military's behavior in Vietnam, in the Philippines, in
the U.S. itself over the centuries of the "Indian wars."
It's ugly, it's horrible, and it's -- us. -- And now
what? We'll go on doing essentially the same, that's
what. Most likely. In fact we're doing something much
like it in Iraq at this moment and have been for years,
intentionally starving thousands of children in an
effort to impose our will on the dictatorial regime
controlling so much oil there. (And can average U.S.

citizens do anything about this? Well of course we can!
It's a free country, isn't it?)

    One other big story: a serious nuclear accident in
Japan. For a day or so it was threatening to become
another Chernobyl or worse -- a "criticality event." In
the end it was brought under control, with potentially
lethal exposure limited, authorities say, to "only" a
few dozen people. And in all the coverage I saw, the
related and even more urgent issues of accidental
detonation of a nuclear weapon or of outright nuclear
war, accidental or otherwise, were never even mentioned.

    -- And then it's another day and new outrages are
already pushing the ones just noted off the front pages.
And you do have to think about these other matters as
well. Because if you don't, you might not be able to go
on at all.

    Z and I, yes, we're going on. We're just ten days
into being hitched! -- But it's officially official
now, because Z, during her lunch break yesterday, took
in the papers signed by us and Olwen on our wedding day
and registered the marriage with the state and later
brought home a notarized copy saying it's for real. She
also brought home a new button for me which at this
moment is pinned above my left-side shirt pocket:
"That's so Millennium" (the absence of an exclamation
point at the end making the tone sardonic, innit?). And
photos have started fluttering down upon us, including
the official ones taken by Paz with Tobey's help. I
haven't seen Paz's work yet, but she's a pro and I don't
doubt it's good. However, Z tells me that in the
pictures in which I appear she can find no trace of that
"sultry rockstar look you used to have down so good."
(I explained it must be because Paz is always telling me
to relax and lighten up for the camera and so I come off
looking lightweight and dorky and phony to boot.)

    Meanwhile we've run the first post-wedding gauntlet
at the WOC, enduring a cascade of mixed congratulations
and razzing from various friends and acquaintances there
(none of whom we invited to the reception -- with the
exception of the casual verbal invite to Willis E. as he

jogged on the treadmill; and he assured us yesterday he really did have to attend a funeral the afternoon of the 25th but he'd heard the reception was "the dopest ever.") -- And an interesting coincidence: in telling Jay the juggler the kitchen-goddess story we learned that he'd gone to school with Marie T., the sculptor, and he and his wife Melanie have visited the resort several times and know Sid and Laila quite well (as does Malcolm the diversity counselor, also a WOC member, who even recalled the statue itself but said he'd never recognized it as being Z; like others, he'd thought it was Laila from a few decades back).

Sunday night, by the way, another one-two punch awaited me at home. First Z left a note on my chair saying Min had called to announce he'd be coming by late the next day with an electrician to do maintenance work on the wall heaters. I wound up putting in several hours that same night and the next afternoon on straightening up the place (since in effect Min was giving us a chance to redeem ourselves after his shambolic walk-through with the appraisers while we were away). Also Z left out a hand-drawn finances sheet showing her credit card debt is up to 29K (on top of school debt of around 60K) and asking for my advice on how to deal with it. "Are you ready to advise me, Mr. Spouse, in your debtless way? Because I'm ready to be advised." We've agreed to talk about it this weekend.

-- And now time's running out. This office is little changed, I want to say: it's still the fine hideaway it's always been. (I never can quite get used to having it available 24/7.) And note this: after running into Mad Mitch of the WOC on the street the other day I brought him up here for a "tour"; and while sitting -- massively -- in this very chair he recited from memory a poem he said was his own work about the warships mothballed over in port jingo on the peninsula (and I'll be seeing them up close when I hit the storage unit on Thursday, weather permitting). Oh, and he told me I'm looking good -- "Obviously being married suits you a lot better than being about to be married."

[+1]

     -- Next night now, coming up on four a.m. Trees
shaking and rustling restlessly outside the wide-open
dining-area window: they sound as if they're inside the
room. Z usually closes that window at night and I just
leave it that way when I arrive home, but tonight she
left it up all the way in hopes the air cleaners would
push out the bad air coming in from the hallways and
stairwell. The shampooers were at work out there
earlier, presumably as part of the effort to make the
building more presentable for potential buyers -- and
perhaps also to compensate for the effect of the
discovery of the probable fault line. (Would the owner,
Min, do this for someone he's already sold it to? I
doubt it. He certainly hasn't done it for his tenants
before now, or at least not in the time we've been here.
Or at least not to my or Z's knowledge. And from the
extent of the whiff earlier today I think we would've
known any other time as well.)
     Z also left a big handmade cardboard key attached
to the knob on the outside of our 203 door. Written on
the cardboard: "No more key screwups!" That's because I
found her keys dangling there when I entered the foyer
at the usual time last night. She also said she got a
chuckle from the way a note I wrote her later about this
ended: "Any fool could've walked in and stolen my stash
of cornflakes!"
     She's up right now, or was until a few minutes ago.
This is one of her worst insomnia nights in a while.
She thinks it may be because she's stopped taking the
magical herbs she was ingesting by the wagonload during
the wedding countdown. Three separate times she's
wandered in here. I'll confess it can be a bit
exasperating when I have so much I need to tend to
tonight so I can make the peninsula trip tomorrow. But
we're newlyweds; I certainly don't want to be getting on
her case about such things this early. So I try to be
understanding, yes. Treat your Z-wiff right! (The

first visit she sat on my lap right here in the black
armchair as I was trying to flip through the paper. She
was naked except for the blue hula hoop. We joked about
how her sexy aroma sure did beat that of the carpet
shampoo. (She said her own natural sexual fragrance,
when it hits her unexpectedly, always reminds her of her
mother because she slept with her mother for so many
years, until she was almost twelve.) -- But lack of
sleep and two hard scoping nights have left me feeling
decidedly out of musth.)

      -- And then there are our wedding and reception
photos. She's sorted several sets of these into stacks
which are scattered over the couch and dining table and
various chairs right now, all weighted down with cups or
other heavy objects, as she tries to decide which photos
should go to whom. She's also putting together a batch
for a special small two-ring "My Wedding" binder -- "I
know you think this is very uncool" -- and she'll carry
the binder with her to show people at work. Truth is
I'm pleased she likes the photos enough to want to do
that. Or is she perhaps admirably lacking in vanity
about them? At one point she showed me a photo in which
she thought she looked "like a portly middle-aged woman,
you know, 'full-figured' and totally out of it" -- and
started weeping. So then I pulled out picture after
picture in which she looks fabulous and before long she
brightened and said, "Well, sometimes I'm just
photogenic, that's all." -- And she wasn't trying to
rub it in either or making any invidious comparisons.
Just the facts, sir.

      Because then there are the photos of me. But never
mind, I've already discussed those. (She did point out
a few she "sorta" likes -- "pick of the subpar litter"
-- and that, as the quote marks indicate, is a quote.)

      What news I haven't mentioned? Gerry's off to Rio.
In the end he didn't buckle; he didn't take Leola with
him. He did write her a long letter dealing with all
the issues she raised and saying he still thought they
could work things out, but she's furious anyway. His
only justification for the trip is that he needs to be

alone for a while. Even his own sister is on Leola's
side, Z tells me -- but then this is the same sister who
warned Leola back before she married Gerry that he was a
loner and she should dump him. Leola stayed at a hotel
for the last night Gerry was at home and she's planning
to move in with a friend when he, Gerry, returns in two
weeks. She's again making noises about seeing lawyers
and getting appraisals on the furniture and whatnot.
She told Z she's the angriest she's ever been in her
life. (Z worries Leola will forget to take her blood-
pressure meds and have a heart attack.) -- But I still
find it hard to believe a permanent split is in the
works. The two of them fit together too well, I tell Z,
with their smoothly complementary strengths far
outweighing all the alleged flaws and weaknesses. And
their "conjoined" history goes back so many years!
-- Not that considerations such as these have ever made
much of a difference in my own life, I must acknowledge,
with Lady U or anyone else. If your time's up, it's up:
that's always been my view. But of course it's not so
easy to know whether it's up at the time itself. In
fact (fact!) it's impossible. Retrospect is much easier.
     And Betty and Kat have returned from the farm.
They had another wedding to attend back there, a
traditional type in which, as Betty said, "everyone and
everything was white" (and Z had to bite her lip, she
told me afterward, to avoid pointing out that Kat was an
extremely obvious exception) (and then I had to tell Z
-- I just couldn't prevent myself -- I thought Betty
probably figured the exception was so obvious she didn't
need to mention it; I mean, why else would she even
bring up the whiteness thing? And Z conceded this could
be true, "But now I'm having to bite my lip again," and
tears started leaking out. And I immediately came to my
senses and said, "Well, I'm thinking maybe I should be
biting mine too. I wish I'd been doing that the whole
time." And before long all was pretty much good again.
I think.)
     -- But it's time to go. Too tired to carry on.
Good night.

[+1]

For shame. But yes, I've canceled the peninsula run. Again. And on a day that's ideal for it, with even the weather turning out just right: cool enough for the long hill climb to the storage facility on the far side yet not too cool and not at all rainy. But if I'd gotten up at my ordinary time I couldn't've made it back to J-town until too late to handle the full docket of scoping work I already knew I'd be facing tonight. And if I'd instead wrenched myself up early enough to catch the prior boat I'd've been too tired by the time I returned to take on that same docket. And so when the alarm went off at ten-thirty (a couple of hours early) I mulled the matter for about fifteen seconds and then punched the radio off and went back to sleep.

So now I'm opting for the next best thing. Surely it's the jyzey thing to do. I'm perched on a bench in the lobby at the state ferry terminal, with the toll booths to my left and the ten-foot-high four-sided glass-cubed clock to my right in the middle of the lobby (it used to stand atop the building before a rampaging ferry demolished the whole dock many decades back). In Roman numerals the clock says it's VI almost straight up and down. And the commuters are still trudging by, scores of them, many in business suits, although the main homebound rush is long over.

It's a familiar scene all right. I was thinking about it as I was walking down. During my peninsula years I made the cross-sound commute close to two thousand times -- that number still astounds me so much I recalculate it every time it crops up anew just to be sure -- and on most of those trips I passed through this lobby twice, once going in each direction. I sat on the benches, the ones right here when the gates were temporarily closed but usually the ones in the main waiting area on the far side of the pay-booth gates, for many hundreds of hours cumulatively, and sometimes for up to five or six hours at a time on the worst fogbound

428

days. And I was always fond of that commuting life.
For a jyzer who also likes (and needs) to read, the
hardships often seemed more like advantages. (As now
swarms of citybound commuters are thundering by, having
just disembarked from a super-jumbo ferry arriving from
the main burban-fortress island. A small portion of
them are night workers and I've dimly recognized
several, but no one's spotted me so far.

   Through the upper windows to the right I see puffy
gray clouds tumbling along just above the tops of the
highrises. Through the waiting-area windows to the left
I see a corridor shining on the water with the hills of
the peninsula and the entrance to the twisty Z-narrows
over there just barely visible in the mist at corridor's
end. A moment ago I watched a heavily loaded passenger
ferry, its outside back deck crowded with men in suits
(no women), chugging into that same corridor, its wake
making the shine wiggle sinuously.

   Coming down I was struck by the unusually high
level of street activity: the motion, the color, the
crowds, the endless eye-catching variety of just about
everything. The HQ triangle and environs once again
were thronged with "First Thursday" artwalkers gawking
at outdoor displays and spilling out of galleries,
wineglasses sparkling. The waterfront was a sun-
glinting dazzle at rush hour, featuring bikers, joggers,
walkers, skateboarders, vehicles of all sorts, including
horse-drawn carriages and streetcars and motorized
wheelchairs, three layers of highway (all congested),
big freighters (one departing with tugboats pressing
against it like the proverbial nursing piglets) and
ferries and tour boats rumbling by offshore and tied up
at the docks, helicopters buzzing overhead, jumbo jets
soaring -- a fabulous urban-hive scene. And nearing the
triangle I also ran into a long line of teens and twenty-
somethings, most dressed in black and many with their
faces painted into black-and-white masks, waiting to see
a currently red-hot band at one of the clubs. Two of
the band's gaudily painted tour buses were idling in the
street, offloading equipment, sparking a frenzied and

all but impassable fan-rapture scene.
      -- "Last call.... Last call.... All Aboard."
Feet suddenly thudding. The words of the announcement
setting my own heart to racing for a moment. How many
scores or more likely hundreds of times back then did
they prompt me to start moving fast or faster? The
worst were when you heard them just as you were entering
the building and you had to sprint up the long ramp
carrying a heavy pack (as I almost always did in those
days, much heavier than it usually is now).
      -- And I hope I didn't put myself on Z's bad side
by failing to love her up enough during her insomnia
spells last night. To make up for the possibility that
I did, this afternoon I drew up a schmaltzy "The October
Buzz at the Honeymoon Resort" card for her. It shows a
flock of seagulls wandering on the beach and lamenting
to each other the unexpected absence of "that torrid
vintage couple from Jyze City." She also left me a
frazzle-faced note this morning (the kind with a
squiggly line for a mouth) saying she's again sensing
prodomo tremors and needs a butt-check.
      What else? The real-estate company holding the
lease on the DC castle sent every resident of the north-
hilltop area a four-page letter, single spaced,
explaining what they're trying to do with the property.
It's an impressive piece of PR work, in a way, although
as Z pointed out, and with well-justified scorn, only a
small minority of hilltoppers would even be able to read
it (especially considering that many can't read English
at all). But still, if the company follows through on
all their plans and promises, the hood will have little
to complain about -- the property owners, that is. The
renters will of course be paying more, but even many of
them may not be too unhappy to do so, I must admit, if a
safer, more upscale hood is the result.
      As for those who can't afford to pay more, they'll
obviously be a good deal more unhappy. Which is to say:
it's the same old story. It's what "progress" is all
about. And I'd like to offer some remedies for its many
drawbacks, but that would take a whole lot more than

four single-spaced pages. (There are the small,
individual, person-oriented drawbacks and then there are
the big systemic local, statewide, regional, national,
and global ones. Of course they're all linked. Can
they be delinked and mitigated in time to prevent global
catastrophe? This looks less and less likely. -- But...
enough. Another preachy spiel coming on.)
     Crossing the high bridge I was startled to see a
cleanup crew, including a grumbly smoke-belching yellow
bulldozer, hard at work in the city-owned portion of
greenbelt "jungle" or "rez" on the hillside below the
Natusan center -- the very area I was looking out at
earlier this eighter from some thirty feet away. A good
third of the weeds and shrubbery had been bladed back to
bare ground and all the makeshift campsites except one
-- a kind of token maybe -- razed. My guess is that
this is part of the last-minute J-town "prettification"
campaign which WTO opponents have been predicting.
     -- But time to get to work. Zip over to the
hideaway to water the plants and pick up some grub, hit
one of the mom-and-pops on the way downtown for a cold
can of peach juice (or even better, guava, if they have
it, which they often don't), and then the grind.

[+1]

     Again it's four a.m., this time on a Friday night
by NUT reckoning (Gregorianly it's Saturday the 9th).
And again I'm catching myself at a bad time because the
Z-wiff is going through another insomnia spell,
wandering in and out, ignoring the "Hydes of Jyze" sign,
and this time I'm being openly grumpy about it. She's
not in a real good mood herself. Suddenly she's caught
up in a crunch period at work, much as I too have been
in my own bailiwick (except the crunches themselves are
of vastly different kinds to be sure). And now Min's
announced yet another walk-through of all the units next
Tuesday and we're both unhappy about this. It adds more
pressure to a weekend already overpacked with chores and

commitments. And the cleaning kind of pressure sets Z
off more than most other kinds. It's the old cultural/
patriarchal/phallocratic guilt thing directed at women,
as she quite often points out. I tell her we don't have
to cave to it. And she tells me, "Easy for you to say
when it's a cave you've never spelunked."

But never mind, best to call this an early case of
routine minor marital friction and give it the boot.
And presto -- it's gone. I mean, our twenty months of
practice as Deeps ought to be good for something.

-- In a few hours the new moon rises. But the old
marriage moon is hanging around anyway, if only in
symbolic form. It turns out the miniature kite which
the shop owner ran out into the street to give us shows
an animated moon against a backdrop of stars. I added a
cartoon speech bubble for this kinky-looking man in the
moon -- he's saying, "Call me Honeymoon Moon! September
26-30, 1999," and hung the kite on the big bookcase in
the hall opposite our front door. It sports a two-foot-
long double yellow tail made of tightly folded crepe
paper; maybe I ought to add something referring to that
-- how we're now twisting slowly in the wind together
forevermore (alluding to the kiri ribbon I sent Z when
she broke our first date, saying it was meant to remind
her how she'd left me twisting in the -- yeah). But
nah, too much work. For now. Maybe another time.

This morning she did something unexpected that
truly touched me. She was amorous upon awakening but I
was so wasted I couldn't respond at all. I'd even given
up the ghost an hour early and crashed without taking my
vites & supps or setting out my frozen fruit to thaw.
Heavens to Murgatroid! Well, she noticed this, and when
I arose I found a dish of fruit thawing in the fridge
with a note saying "Jyzeman too fried?" I mean this
involves my daily bowl of cornflakes. We're talking
major significance here, depth upon depth of it
(reaching even to the remote era when ol' Mom used to
leave fruit out for me for breakfast because in those
days I tended to be grossly constipated at fairly
frequent intervals) (and possibly would be that way

again now if not for the daily breakfast fruit hit, and
especially those blueberries).

    In return I tucked my ceramic owl (the one I
originally gave Dad when I was in college) beneath Z's
white comforter with its head resting on her pillow and
a narrow paper strip featuring a vertical row of "Z!"s
issuing from the bird's beak and stretching down about
two feet on the comforter. I'm that owl; there's a big
"G" on its chest. A couple of nights earlier I'd left
the same owl perched atop the far-coast paper on the
chair here, a bright red label tied to its neck saying
"Your owl hubby loves you madly!" (And that label was
still in place for today's owl encore.)

    Schmaltzy and smarmy and corny and gooey and sappy
and soppy and mushy, no question. Continuing a great
tradition! Makes life worth living, that's what.
-- And as a corollary, say it can also make some of
those moments of routine marital friction a bit easier
to finesse.

    -- Meanwhile today for the first time in months I
packed the contents of my backpack, including this J-
book, inside a plastic bookstore bag acting as an inner
liner to help guard against rain damage. And broke out
my fold-up umbrella. And wore my old forest-green
canvas work jacket with the attached hood. And needed
all three forms of protection while hiking into town
this afternoon. The season of dread is upon us. -- But
the paper says the La Nina effect appears to be
moderating and thus this winter may not be as severe as
forecasters had been warning, though it'll likely still
be colder, rainier, and especially snowier than usual.
-- This from a front-page story running above the fold.
Who says weather no longer matters in the digital age?
But then we are talking the primitive and wild "far
upper corner" here, by standard USAn reckoning.

    -- And I'm now thinking this has been a kind of
buffer week for me. I've needed a week not just to
catch up on missed scoping work but also to come down
from the clouds and the frazzle/dazzle of the hitchfest.
In the weeks ahead I want to focus hard on this TJM

project right here and also on keeping myself in decent
husbanding shape. It could also be I need to work off a
bit of wedding gastronomic overindulgence. And beyond
that, Z and I are talking about reducing our calorie
intake by ten percent, maybe even twenty, so we can live
longer like the rats in certain experiments we've been
reading about lately: live for another century or two,
say. (But not talking seriously, of course. I mean a
regimen like that of the rats sounds way too demanding
for even the short haul, like twelve hours.)

The word is Gerry called Leola from Rio to say it's
been nothing but rain, rain, rain down there -- and
downpours the likes of which no one's ever encountered
here. Meanwhile she's seeing a lawyer and when Gerry
returns she plans to meet him at the door with a list of
demands, maybe even with the lawyer at her side if he's
willing to risk it (and irrespective of that, she told Z
he's "really cute"). One of those demands will call for
intensive marital "couples counseling." That puzzled me
because I thought Gerry had already agreed to it in his
letter. "Don't expect me to explain," said Z. "My job
is just to sit there listening and nodding."

Five a.m. now. The radio says so. On Saturday and
Sunday mornings public-radio news comes on an hour later
than on weekdays. -- Flick! It's off. (But its
national news team is touring the country to celebrate
an anniversary and they hit our town today. Tonight's
paper provided the very first photos I've ever seen of
the news entoners whose voices are such a big part of my
life. The two men are not at all as you'd expect:
they're just tired, straight-ish, average-looking guys,
I'd say, in appearance sadly far from authoritative.)

Sera sent us a refund on the wedding. She used
only three hundred of the five hundred bucks Z advanced
her. I hinted that maybe some of the refund should go
to the husband-person, but Z didn't take to the idea,
and since I'm sure she spent a lot more money than I did
(though not in proportion to our incomes!) I'll say to
hell with it. A fortune well wasted and therefore
scarcely wasted at all. -- And today she came home with

a nice new brown raincoat paid for (in part) by that
refund. Leola needed to go shopping to make herself
feel better after Gerry's call and Z agreed to accompany
her and couldn't resist the consumption impulse. "I
needed to reward myself," she explained, "for surviving
the first four days of this week" (at work, she said she
meant, when I asked for clarification).

     And when she wandered in earlier to shake our brass
Tibetan Buddhist good-luck marriage noisemaker from the
country fair -- this item is now known to us for short
as "the twanger" -- she couldn't find it, and after a
while I joined the search and it still came up empty.
Did Min or his electrician or a potential buyer or a
banker on the inspection team, she mused, steal the
thing during a walk-through? Well maybe, I said, but I
doubt it; most likely they'd all see it as a worthless
piece of junk. But I didn't fail to remind her this is
the kind of suspicion we might be arousing nonstop in
our own minds if we were to hire a housecleaner, as she,
Z, is still hounding me (sweetly for the most part) to
do. And I don't care, housecleaner or no, we're both
still so cluttery and shambolic we'll always be
misplacing and losing things.

     -- But this doesn't mean I think we're not lucky.
We're as lucky as they come. (Knock knock knock on woo-
woo-wood -- and doubly woo-woo it is, more than ever!)

[+2]

     Don't really want to be doing this now and don't
want to be doing it here but I'm stuck. At the scope
office, a few minutes before midnight, the conference
room, power seat at the north end of the table. Rank
upon rank of windows stacked outside across the street,
forty-some stories' worth; Old Glory rippling half a
block farther east, far above the horseshoe-shaped
entrance drive to the fancy hotel.

     A janitor just traipsed through on foot, the latest
new guy, short and stocky, friendly, Latusan, fluent in

lightly accented English offered in a somewhat squeaky
high-pitched laughing voice that's very likable -- and I
already know he pushes hard to get his work done in less
than the allotted time so he can sneak off to read
discarded newspapers in the hidden alcoves along the
main hallway. Which is to say: he's my kind of guy for
sure.

June will be dropping by at 203 later tonight for
an editing session and therefore I might not have time
to jyze there as per the usual practice at J-week's end.
And it's not really worth walking over to the hideaway
now, considering I'd lose a quarter or more of tonight's
remaining downtown time in doing so (meaning before I
have to catch the last bus). And worse still I'm
stewing because the scope firm's new noticing
requirements are suddenly causing me all sorts of grief,
roughly tripling the amount of time I have to spend on
notices -- and I've had over a month of shakedown voyage
on them, so things are not likely to get much better
with more practice. I can either absorb the loss myself
or ask Naomi to pay for it, all or part, thus hitting
her up for a raise (in effect) for the second time in a
couple of months and risking nudging her into doing her
work a different way or with a different scoper. I
don't like either option, obviously, and that's why I'm
stewing. That and sheer exasperation, because notices
have always been my least favorite part of the job.

An hour from now I'll have shrugged this off, or
anyway I sure hope so.

So I'm here. And I can report it's been quite a
day -- two in a row -- but today especially. Good old
Kat: first she does another peeping Tomasina on me as
I'm dressing in the bedroom at home, then at the
hideaway she stumbles upon a binder containing some
pages from one of my old photo albums showing me and
others stark naked (or if not always starkly so, still
naked enough). I'd forgotten all about those pages
being in there; I removed them from one of the albums
before showing it to Z shortly after we met. -- Nothing
hardcore or anywhere close to it, but still. The kid

erupted in hoots and whoo-whoos. I asked her to do me a favor and not mention those photos to anyone and she said she would do that (do me the favor) but the chances she'll hold to it are slim. Several times during dinner at the hilltop Chinese place with Betty and Z she started to say something about them, I think, before I shushed her up. And at home earlier she did go rushing to Z to say, "I saw Glen's thingy! I saw Glen's thingy!" But Z was cool: "Eh, big deal, I see Glen's thingy all the time. What else is new?"

So now Betty will be hearing all about Glen's thingy and maybe also that he's showing Kat whoo-whoo pix. Good heavens, what next? -- Just hoping Betty's as cool about it as Z proved to be.

Kat was in my charge all afternoon because Z's mygs were flying again over work and she needed to be alone. I hit on the idea of taking Kat to the arts & crafts superstore, which she said she'd never seen before (but it turned out she had, many times, though I didn't learn this until Betty told me; Kat for some strange reason kept it to herself). She's a great wheedler; like a classic sap I wound up buying her half a dozen items, including a round wooden box, a wood-paint marker for writing on the box, feathers to decorate it with, a couple of incandescent pencils, and a tube of revolting vomit-green squeeze candy. (And I bought several cheapo postcard display stands for myself and Z and came across dozens of do-it-yourself items I might go back for later, finances permitting.) Then I took her to see the new baseball stadium and stopped by my office to drop off a case of fruit juice, and she begged me to let her see the pictures of my family and former girlfriends -- and then while I was distracted she pulled out that other binder at the end of the shelf and "whoo-whoo-whoo-whoo-whoo!" (I'd also planned to take her to the natural-food chain store but by then it was too late; Betty was already back at our place after seeing the play. We called Z from the outdoor pay phone in the triangle as a number of unsavory characters leered at our gorgeous little pre-Lolita.) -- And I haven't even

mentioned our "wrestling" session on the bed at 203.
Have I ever had a more intensely physical nonsexual
(sic, right) relationship with anyone? -- Maybe with
brother Rob back when he was around Kat's age.

   And a few words about last night's party. Linda,
one of Z's coworkers, threw it in a fixer-upper house on
the lake side of east hill. Linda got married a few
months ago; this was a kind of second reception for
friends who missed the first one and also to introduce
the couple's new home. Z said she wanted to attend
because Linda's in another division of the utility where
Z would like to know more people; it was as much a
business as a pleasure thing. Everyone brought desserts
and I dug into several of them. And everyone was
Eurusan, which was a surprise to me but not to Z; that
part of the utility (resource conservation), she told
me, is notorious for it. Rawly repainted rooms (purple,
red, black), dubious neopunk wall hangings verging on
neofascist. And the promised dancing never happened.
And that other newly hitched pair were squabbling the
entire time despite all their off-color double-entendre
jokes, some of which sounded, Z and I had to admit to
ourselves later, a bit like some of ours.

   Cutting it a sliver close here. Buffer week coming
to an end. Serious rededication dead ahead across the
board. And lots of thank-you messages still to tend to;
Z's displeased with my stalling. And not to forget
we'll again be honeymooning anew this coming week as
well as winning the wedding lottery yet another time.
-- And though she left me an amusing card about it, I
never made anything of the fact that yesterday was Leif
Erikson Day (which always makes the papers here, of
course, in this whitest and Scandiest of USAn cities --
except maybe for a certain one just off the "wild west
coast" of Mentoka where a number of my relatives have
lived and probably still are living their
quintessentially white-bread and -bred USAn lives) (and
of course while growing up I also ate and drank far too
much and too deeply of that whiteness stuff -- the white
koolaid, yeah).

22

This bench, I don't think I ever noticed it before.
I've probably sat on it or stood nearby, but always when
the crowds were so thick the bench itself became
invisible. Today, however, the crowds are not thick.
Except for one drifter lurking about beneath the strip-
park shelter a couple of hundred feet up the hill (and
playing his boom box so loud I can hear it clearly down
here) no one's around.

The parking lot behind me is full, and I'd guess
most or all of those cars belong to dot-commers working
in the DC castle just across the street. It's not quite
quitting time yet, although traffic's already heavy on
the freeways down below. And the overcast is breaking
up to the west where splotches of blue are slowly
expanding, streaked horizontally with gray across their
midriffs. And the flag atop the great concrete dome is
flapping vigorously even though the wind isn't too bad
up here -- it's from the south and therefore the hill
itself shields this area.

Yesterday I got lazy again. All day long I kept
delaying the start-up of this new jyze eighter and
finally I said to heck with it, I would take the day
off. After all, it was a holiday: Columbus Day. Best,
I figured, not to honor the anniversary of the
emblematic Cawk invasion of the continent with a jyze
session. In addition I had a lot of apartment cleanup
to do in preparation for Min's inspection visit today
(his third in the past two weeks).

Today I wanted to be out of the apartment when Min
and crew arrived, so I drove down to the south-end

branch of my primary corporate supermarket to read the paper at the attached chain coffee shop and tackle some of the provisioning I wasn't able to do Sunday. On the way there I stopped at an auto-supply shop. That stop was made necessary by a mishap on Sunday while I was out with Kat and failed to put the cap back on the gas tank after fueling up at the hilltop station (right across the street from our garden-club reception site). Probably I left it atop the car roof and it fell off at some point as we drove down the steep and twisty road on the west side of the hill en route to the HQ. Later that evening we returned to the gas station to look for it, but it wasn't anywhere around and the guys behind the counter claimed to have no knowledge of it and were just as surly as they'd been the first time we were there. It was probably their over-the-top creepiness with Kat during that first stop that distracted me and caused me to forget about the cap in the first place. (But it gives Z one more matter to bring up at our neighborhood meeting. She's had some bad experiences with those guys herself.)

Today's of note for one other reason (at least one!). Demographic experts say this is the day when world population will reach six billion. Not yesterday, not tomorrow, but today. Just in the past century it's more than tripled. Every forty-eight hours or so it grows by half a million, a number only seventy-odd K short of J-town's population (burbs excluded). Yet the alarm over population growth has all but vanished in recent years. And this is truly absurd. But most of the increase is taking place in what might be called "less overdeveloped" parts of the world and even there it'll supposedly come to a halt by the year 2100 when world population is projected to reach twelve billion. This assumes prior calamities won't cause a population crash. A very shaky assumption indeed.

(I'm being hit up for smokes and spare change now -- three times in just a few minutes. They're popping out of the bushes, all kinds of dubious dudes who no doubt see me as equally scuzzy except for my

misleadingly cigarette-pack-shaped shirt pocket. -- And waddaya know, here's some sun angling in!)
     -- So I'll mosey on. I'm losing my concentration. Kids playing, a car blasting hip-hop...and a yakkety-yakky Cawk elder has just joined me on the bench.
*   *
     Later. After another frustrating night at work. I wish it had been otherwise and I'd like to shrug it off and so -- will try. Certainly jyze would prefer to focus on something else. It's just the thing with the notices again, but tonight it came on top of yet another unexpectedly large workload. Wotta week. Two in a row! I wheel the computer down the hall, crawl around the printer room hooking it up, whale away at it for five and a half or six hours. At break time pop down to midtown chain burgers for a couple of double-stacks and then back at the office chop them up into nice manageable sixths so my keyboarding fingers won't grease up too much as I scope ever onward while chowing down.
     -- But enough already. I come bearing updates!
     First, Gwen and Jess. Is a reconciliation in the works? A first hint of this came when Tobey mentioned something to Z about Gwen dropping by to see Jess at four a.m. Z wasn't able to learn more, though, and that single tantalizing clue hung in the air for several days despite widespread efforts to augment it. Then yesterday came word the separated pair are "talking." But could Jess accept Gwen back again after a second betrayal? As Z observed, "How could she not be wondering all the time when it would happen again?" And then her follow-up: "Nothing like this could ever happen to you and me, though, right, G-hub dear? Because we're always going to be good, right?" And my reply: "Define 'good'." (Same as it says on one of my Christmas buttons she likes.) To which I hastily added: "Joke! Joke! I know in my bones we're gonna be hi-fis forever!" And she: "Okay. Good." Me: "And that 'good' right there needs no further definition." (All dialogue guaranteed verbatim.))
     The other news of note, and it's upsetting indeed,

441

is that Mr. D, Aida and Sera's father, has a "large
growth" on his face which is being biopsied. For the
past week the family's been able to talk about little
else. Mr. D surely knew about it weeks ago. Z suspects
this is the real reason he and Mrs. D chose not to join
us at our wedding reception: Mr. D doesn't want to be
seen in this condition. Furthermore, if they really did
attend their Saturday prayer group instead of the
reception, they had something truly important to pray
about. Z's also inclined to chalk up a lot of her own
recent troubles with Aida and Sera to family tensions
arising from, although this was unknown to her at the
time, Mr. D's emerging health crisis. Even if other
causes for the tensions exist (and of course they do),
she now has a good excuse to override all of that and
mend relations with everyone in the family. And I think
she's quite determined to do this, and I've said I'll
help her in any way I can.

When we saw Betty on Sunday, I also want to mention
-- with a shift of tone here for sure -- she said she'd
met Kirk a while back when she dropped by Aida's place
for some wedding-related reason. And according to her I
have nothing to fear from him; he won't be able to
snatch Z's heart away from me. "He's just a little
round turkey," Betty reported, "with a stiff rod stuck
up his spine." Her manner of saying this was way past
comical or otherwise I suppose Z might've been a little
offended; after all, we're talking about a former lover
she was once gaga over. But she just chortled and kept
completely mum about that "stiff rod." And normally
that's the kind of thing she'd leap on -- verbally at
the very least, correct. Instead she added with
impressive savoir faire: "And don't forget, he's the one
who dropped me."

Z's been very nice to the G-hub the past few days.
Apparently it's because he -- I, this G-hub -- "stepped
into the lurch" and did all the cleaning she was too
myg'd out to do. Also I plied her with "plan B" nipple-
tweak "immunity boosters" the past couple of mornings --
and both times she left me in a highly tumefied or

442

"ithy" state (from "ithyphallic"), "vulnerable to blue
balls" (as she herself observed later with, I'd say, a
fine mix of merriment and rue), because she had to hurry
off to work (and she's still on the H-rag anyway).

Tonight she left me a funny drawing in her "XXX-
rated Marital Love Manual," the first new entry she's
made in weeks. It shows "G's bod" and "Z's bod" (both
naked) (and yes, "FC" seems to be out for her now and
"bod" back in). Labels describe symptoms from the past
week or two and arrows point to the requisite sites:
nipples "well immunized," her face displaying
"sculptural integrity," her back and shoulders "vacuum
free," my head hair "growing back" (after the prenuptial
scalping), my butt "ongoing admirable," my brain
revealing "gas cap overload," my phallus "well ithy'd"
(yay!), and both of our hearts showing "strong beat."

And the last faint traces of the wedding-shower
henna patterns on her ankle are gone as of tonight.

[+3]

Interesting times, curse the fact (but not if
you're a jyzer).

Today I've managed to bundle myself down to a bench
in the HQ triangle. Again it's the isolated one at the
foot of the totem pole, looking toward the bus stop and
the saloon and the pizza place, the northernmost acute
angle of the triangle, and then straight up the old
"edge road" except at a slightly oblique angle allowing
me to see only about six blocks, roughly as far as the
art museum (but I can't actually make that out because
it's dusk and the streetlights are glary). -- Most of
the other benches run along the far side of the 'rangle,
with a double-sided one just across the sidewalk from
the entrance to the hideaway building (and the trunks of
a row of good-size trees, their canopies still mostly
green, are interspersed among the benches). -- And
several more benches stand under the old glass-and-iron
pergola some thirty feet behind me (there you're

protected from rain if the wind's not blowing too hard but at night it's too dark for jyzing and at almost all hours numerous local drifters of the highly distracting if not totally disruptive type hang out under there).

I've wound up allotting myself about an hour. The usual thing. I'd hoped for two hours, but then I hung myself up browsing at the ORB and, before that, doing some early Christmas shopping at the wooden-toy shop (bought two animated clocks there, my intention being to repaint them as gifts for Z and Kat/Betty -- these are colorful kids' clocks with goofy moving parts and figures, sort of like old-time cuckoo clocks but much more complex, and yet not too expensive).

Strong woodsmoke fragrance in this spot, surely not coming from the wooden-toy shop but from exactly where I don't know. But no question it's still seasonally apt -- could even be burning autumn leaves I do believe but maybe with a big batch of green ones mixed in.

And I want to mention this: it was exactly a century ago this month that the totem pole at my back first went up. It was stolen from a native village about a thousand miles to the north and hauled all the way back here. By whom? Essentially by a rowdy raiding party from the all-Cawk Jyze City Chamber of Commerce, that's who. (Or to be a stickler, the pole here is a replacement for that one.)

-- And for me it turns out this is another buffer week. It's next week I'll be applying proboscis to grindstone on the TJM project and some others as well. This week I'm just too damn busy to do it.

The big news for me and Z today is that our fate at 1511 and No. 203 has apparently been sealed. But before going into how so I'll mention a military coup's occurred in Pakistan; the bellicose U.S. Senate has rejected the treaty banning nuclear testing already signed by this country and virtually all others in the world, effectively killing it; and a great sports hero of my youth has died of a heart attack (drawing massive commentary in the media and also among my more jockish workout pals at the WOC, and in the latter case -- and

probably the former as well though not when I was
listening -- most of it focused on the hero's boast
that he'd slept with twenty thousand women; and if I'm
right that works out on average to a copulation with a
new partner every twenty hours or so for his entire
adult (sic) life).

And today is Rob's birthday. I called to
congratulate him and we had a chance to talk a bit for
the first time since the wedding. About which he
commented, "Everything was just perfect -- the ceremony
itself, the reception, even the weather. Everyone
thought so." (And it's true we keep hearing this and we
think it ourselves -- "it was the dopest!" (and the
wackest too!) -- but I suppose anyone who had a
contrary opinion would keep mum about it.) Rob and Gail
received a thank-you note from Jim Q. saying
everything's all right with him and Nancy (somehow Rob
hadn't heard the reason for Jim's sudden departure; I
had to fill him in on it). He, Rob, is busy this
weekend but we'll be meeting up sometime next week for
our annual one-on-one joint birthday celebration, quite
a bit later than usual this year because of the wedding.

-- And so the news on the apartment. Last night
while I was at work Thuy from upstairs dropped by to
deliver wedding gifts -- she and the kids were sick, it
turns out; that's why they missed the reception -- and Z
got an earful about the building and many other matters
as well. In a nutshell, the building's been sold and
it's slated to be condoized, with prices for individual
units expected to start at 150K. Exactly when this will
be happening Thuy doesn't know, but she met the "Yuppie
couple" who are buying the building and learned they
intend to "cosmeticize it first" (Thuy's term; she used
to work in real estate), putting in parquet floors and
granite counters and "faux wood-burning stoves"
(probably gas operated, she suspected), and thus we know
we'd have to move out for a period while they did all
this even if we decided to stay on for the long haul and
were able to swing a condo purchase financially, and our
prospects on both of the latter scores are poor. And so

we're almost certainly outta there, and probably for
good, maybe even before the first of the year. And if
not before, soon after. And so, yes, most likely well
within the span of this TJM project. But then I should
look on the bright side and say at least such a move
would generate some juice for the last third of the
project in case Y2Kalypse and the WTO protest and the
Jyze City earthquake, among various other plot-churning
kinds of potential events, fall through.

(And the minute hand's already crept all the way
around on my pocket watch. A full hour's gone by! And
I've been hit on by too many panhandlers to work up a
full account. So I'll have to do some backing and
filling later, or at least try.)

*   *

-- And it's later and I'm back and ready, yes, to
fill.

(Be it noted on this day I wore my first Halloween
button of the year -- "Killer Costume," it says -- fully
apropos because I was of course decked out in my usual
rags -- camo for the night streets -- and at the scope
office I successfully fought off the first urge to dig
into a bowl of brightly packaged Halloween sugar.)

And it's been a hot couple of days for sexual
loving. Even with a heavy work schedule Z's come
roaring off the injured list. "We hump!" she was
crowing on the couch yesterday afternoon. "We hump! We
hump!" Thuy had noticed it too; she came right out and
told Z -- taking her aback -- "I know you two have a
very active sex life." Of course Thuy sleeps directly
above us, so if anyone would know, she would, along with
Aboula and his wife directly below us. (But still it
was surprising she talked about it so much. She and
Doug hardly ever get it on anymore, she moaned to Z --
they don't even sleep together, but rather each sleeps
with one of their two kids -- and the kids are so
"wild," she said, that none of the relatives will watch
them long enough for mom and dad to carve out an amorous
evening alone together -- and so Z figures Thuy is
probably just super-horny. "She was looking at your

446

books and she said, 'There sure are a lot of books about
passion and desire here!' And she said she thinks
you're so nice. I think she really likes you!" -- And
why is it Z always sounds so amazed when she discovers
one of her friends might have a positive thought about
me? Surely it couldn't be because she suspects they
have poor taste in men?)

     But I gotta like my pop these days, I do, I do.
And two mornings in a row it's been there when I thought
it wasn't. Each time the arousal came about an hour
after I went to bed feeling very tired, dozed a little,
then woke up to talk a bit with Z before she arose. Z
was surprised herself, and of course she said so. "The
way your sexuality works is still a big mystery to me."
(Yeah, and then there's the world-class mystery-miracle
of hers. Which brings to the fore a major reason we
have such a good time together: we can't figure each
other out. We've agreed about this almost from day one.
And it's true of a lot more spousal sectors, I'd say,
than just the sexual ones.) -- This morning's rutting
she called a "soothing fuck" because she'd upset herself
talking about our financial situation and the need we'll
likely soon be facing to find a new place, and oddly
enough that happened to be when I found myself turning
on. -- And I guess it really was soothing for her, but
certainly not immediately, because she burst into tears
right afterward. But a couple of minutes later she was
hooting with glee. ("Such elegance! Such mischief!
Such fierce intellectual passion!" -- I'm thinking of
what Marie T., the sculptor of the kitchen goddess,
wrote about Z in the cookbook.)

     And one other financial note. She was startled to
learn my deep reserves total only 60K. For some reason
she'd been thinking all along it was a hundred! And the
difference is significant, at least to her mind, because
the hundred would cover her combined credit-card and
educational-loan debt, but the sixty would fall far
short on the combo. -- And so, she concluded, we'd
probably have a hard time lining up the financing
necessary to purchase a house or a condo. (Though I'm

not at all sure this is true. And she's planning to
look into the matter further.) -- Then this afternoon
(she came home early after finishing her final
facilitating job -- for a big citywide meeting -- and is
also taking tomorrow off) we started kicking around the
topic of what kind of place we should look for. She
wanted to make up a list of our priorities. So we did
that. For me it's mainly a matter of keeping the amount
I pay for housing, whether rent or mortgage, at $400 a
month or less; all other priorities are secondary. For
her, security's more important, as is having an in-unit
washer/dryer and off-street parking. But I think she's
much less particular than she was a couple of years ago
during our first apartment hunt. (One possibility she
mentioned today is a rental house owned by Dak and Sera
across the street from a small Buddhist temple in a
quiet hood about eight blocks off the hill to the
northeast. And wouldn't that be something after all
we've gone through in the past few months with Sera:
having the "bantam fighter" as a landlord! -- Or maybe
she'd delegate the task to her sister Aida? Bring in
nephew Charles as the baseball-bat-wielding enforcer?)
     And then the ongoing tales. In kwikjyze form:
     (1) Gerry was due back from Rio last night. Leola
was planning to confront him with a list of demands
she's been fiendishly working on since well before he
left. But no one knows what's happened, or whether the
"so cute" lawyer was at her side, because today Leola
didn't show up for work, nor was she answering her phone
or replying to e- or voicemails (Z tried all three).
     (2) Jess and Gwen have been conducting all-night
"exploratory talks" (that's the going term for whatever
it is they're really doing all night) but Jess is still
saying a reconciliation won't happen. She's also saying
she's planning to sell the house before next May because
she can't afford to keep up the payments on that, along
with those on the SUV and various other debts, by
herself without Gwen's help, in part because she, Jess,
took a voluntary pay cut to get out from under Dale
(thus freeing up the job Z now holds). Jess invited us

to come live in her basement if we need to -- as long as she has the house -- but Z and I both dread the idea of moving twice. (I dread the idea of moving even once. But here we go again. It's the fate of those who try to, or have no choice but to, buck the preferred cultural way of home and property ownership.)

(3) June reports her oldest son, Adam, is switching jobs again -- after barely settling into the one he's now giving up -- because he's been offered stock options with a company that's going public. High tech, Silicon Valley -- talk about the USAn dream. It's the rage of the land. June is sure he'll soon be rich. (And she says she'll apply her mind to solving Z's and my financial problem regarding housing. But the only suggestion she's come up with so far is that I stop buying books and magazines and we drop our subscription to the far-coast paper. And I think she's serious. So I'd say this doesn't augur well for what she might come up with for her next austerity tip on housing.)

(4) The sad Nadine story. She died last week. Z says, "I hope you won't think badly of me if I don't go to the memorial service. I just can't bear the thought." The truth of the matter is she never was all that close to Nadine but she was trying to be there for her at the end because Nadine looked up to her and had so few friends. And Z just took on more than she could handle. -- And that she does such things so often is to me one of her most admirable traits, even though it means she sometimes spreads herself much too thin and this can cause, among other worrisome effects, major myg scramblings.

-- And I can't lay down the J-stick without mentioning the new moon. It was hanging at midlevel in the southeastern quadrant as I walked across the high bridge early last night, its slicing sickle representing so well the transitoriness of all things. Off with their contemporaneity! In short, it was a fine moon, a very fine moon, but still, I can't deny it, my sappy thought was this: it's not our wedding moon anymore. Yes, true.

[+3]

        Couple of odd things. Sunday night about ten p.m.
finds me at the art bar. The current bartender's a
longhair blond Cawk guy in a sleeveless white T-shirt
and a fancy white cowboy hat -- he's lanky, he's cranky,
he's got U.S. southwest written all over him -- and yet
when I ask for a diet cola he gives it to me for free,
saying perhaps a hint dismissively, "I don't take money
for no soft drinks." Huh? Well all right! This could
make me a regular again!

        Another odd thing: I have a couch to myself where
never a couch was before. It's toward the back, right
next to the raised and fenced-in section enclosing the
two pool tables, and it's even equipped with its own
table lamp. The lamp's a little dim but still -- very
handy! A jyzer can be quite happy here tonight.

        Eight or ten younger folks, all Afrusan, all but
one male, are slouched against the wall or circling the
pool tables with cues at the ready. I, this pink G,
suspect I out-age any two of them combined. But it
doesn't matter. Mainly they're talking football -- the
walloping endured yesterday by the local U as well as
the one suffered today by the local pros. (And someone
says, "Here comes the alley cat," and a glamorous long-
legged Afrusan woman comes prancing around the corner
wearing a smile bright enough to light up the whole area
-- outshines my poor little table lamp, I gotta say, by
a whole lotta lumens.)

        No work at the scope office tonight. Central-plaza
chain books was almost empty when I stopped by for a
little browsing there. No line to speak of at downtown
chain burgers where I made my next stop to score my
weekly Sunday-night cone. And here the entire middle
section of the room is deserted and just two or three
bar-birds are perched at the counter up front.

        (Now it appears a band's setting up on the top
level. "The alley cat" is part of it. Or maybe it's a
DJ operation, it seems now.)

And I come to this jyze tonight bearing what may be very bad news. When Z went in for her ultrasound the technician spotted some growths which will require biopsy. Z's not sure whether they're uterine or ovarian. He described them as "probable cysts" and told her he didn't think they looked menacing but they should be checked out regardless. At this point Z doesn't seem too worried and so I'm trying not to be too worried myself or at least not to act as if I am when I'm with her. For the most part I think I'm carrying it off all right. A brief bad moment, though, occurred this afternoon. Last night when we performed the marital act ("conjugated the F-verb") I was less than maximally "ithy" except toward the very end, and other than that one time we haven't gotten it on at all since Wednesday, right before she found out about the cysts. And then this afternoon she said suddenly, out of the blue, "So, does it turn you off to think of those cysts in there?" When I replied hesitantly -- "Well, I mean..." -- she burst into tears. She loves to burst into tears! -- But soon pulled herself out of it this time and fortunately didn't pursue the matter again.

After what she went through with fibrocystitis ten years ago she must be plenty concerned. And I don't have many happy memories of the period five or six years ago when Lady U and I -- but especially she -- endured the biopsy of a lump in her breast. So now I'm crossing my fingers (except the J-stick-holding ones, and those I'll cross later) and hoping for the best with the Z-wiff. -- For how long before we know the results I'm not sure. A week, two weeks?

(Yup, it's a disco setup. And it appears a door charge is imminent. Therefore I'll probably be moving along shortly. Either that or risk being moved along by the wrangler bartender. I should've known this whole scene back here was too good to last.)

-- Otherwise what? I've been churning out thank-you cards at the rate of three or four a day. Last night we saw a bad but interesting play at the fairgrounds. Friday we made a north-hill provisioning

run and stopped along the way to see Rob and pick up the
book on the Mayans we ordered for Betty and Kat (but
we'll read it ourselves first). The shock of knowing
we'll almost certainly be forced to move out of unit 203
before much longer -- but still not knowing exactly when
-- seems to be wearing off. Already I'm feeling
resigned to it, although I continue to nurse a faint
hope we can hang on into May or June. The truth is jyze
is dreading the thought of grappling with another move.
Two moves in the first five annals of the Jyze Age --
that's enough for the whole damn age and then some.

     -- So maybe I'll just leave now. "The alley cat"
calls herself a "discologist," I'm hearing, and is quite
friendly and without question fine to look at as she
struts about in her tight powder-blue jeans and candy-
apple-red spike heels. (Just like me, the whole pool
section is in thrall, the games there slowing to a
fraction of their former speed and intensity. I'd wager
felt's being ripped by errant cues.) And my legs are in
the way of people trying to visit -- or storm is more
like it -- the discologist's booth.

*   *

     Now the scope office a few minutes later. It's
quiet up here too, and likely to stay so, although not
as quiet as it used to be on Sunday nights. In fact I'd
forgotten the janitors would be on the job tonight
(Friday has now replaced Sunday as their night off, to
go with Saturday night). Otherwise I probably
wouldn't've come up here at all. But it's only a few
blocks from the art bar, and I recalled the jumbo bags
of Halloween candy stashed in one of our reporter rooms
-- eventually to be distributed into small baggies to be
attached to completed transcripts with the scope firm's
compliments -- and I figured what the heck, it's not
until tomorrow that I start the latest new campaign to
live right, so why not pig out tonight? Or at least why
not sample the wares so I'll know what's being given out
in my name (so to speak -- one level removed -- because
in fact few of the firm's clients, other than Naomi's
husband and the rest of the prosecutor gang at the U.S.

452

attorney's office, know I have anything to do with it;
and of course that's the way I want it to be and no
doubt the way the scope firm here prefers it as well).

But now I'm thinking the sound of the approaching
vacuum cleaner I was hearing a paragraph back was coming
from one floor up. Until they actually burst into your
office it's sometimes hard to tell what floor they're
on: this one or the one above or the one below (they
don't always do them in the same order, depending on
whether tenants are working late and no doubt other
factors unknown to me).

(Now noticing my wedding ring. Already it's
looking worn in a couple of spots, but then it's
supposed to look worn -- just not this worn, with a
flattened squiggle of gray solder, I guess it is,
showing through where the loop is joined. And I'm still
not really accustomed to the heft of the ring or its
looseness. If I push up hard on the palm side of it
with my thumb, a gap of close to a quarter of an inch or
so -- say it's three sixteenths -- opens between the
skin of my finger and the inner surface of the ring.
But I still like this ring a lot and like even better
what it stands for. That's right! And even the size
has its uses: for this ring, unlike its various wedding-
type predecessors I've worn over the years, I can easily
slip off if I want to, and it definitely gets in the way
when I'm pumping iron or doing pull-ups. -- So will I
lose it because I'm frequently taking it off and putting
it back on? A possibility. So best to be real careful
on that, no question.)

And as always out here in the world -- but
especially in this millennial year -- all kinds of
fascinating things are going on. It's October and so,
as is almost traditional, the stock market is falling
precipitously, with this past week being the worst in
ten years in percentage terms. The presidential primary
campaigns are heating up, and just yesterday the leading
candidate for the more rightward of the two major
parties (both of which, in my view, are well to the
right), the insufferably arrogant and intellectually

lightweight son of the previous president, was in town
and dropped by Kat's school for a photo op and Kat got
to shake the great man's hand (and as of last night she
was still refusing to wash that hand). State and local
races are firing up too, with the burning issue of the
moment a statewide initiative requiring a vote of the
citizenry on any new tax proposed at any level of
government as well as a sharp rollback of vehicle taxes
(which are high in this state to make up for the absence
of a state income tax). This is crazy yahoo hard-right
let's-cripple-the-government stuff but because it would
mean an immediate windfall of several hundred dollars
for most vehicle owners it's wildly popular everywhere
in the state outside of Jyze City, or at least it was
until the campaign against it revved up and specified
the major cuts in services it would entail. (The latest
poll says its support has dropped from 60-32 to 52-41.)
The election is only two and a half weeks away.
     What else? The big WTO conference, set to convene
six weeks from tomorrow, is already drawing substantial
media coverage nationally and even internationally as
well as locally. The debate is intense and in my view
neither side is getting at the true core issues. And
then there's the constant drumbeat of stories about the
millennium celebration and the Y2K problem, which is
starting to look potentially a bit more serious than has
been the case for a while. And there's our very own
hilltop dot-com (the one occupying the DC castle, yes)
announcing a massive new expansion in its drive to
become "the shopping bazaar of the internet" -- moving
way, way, way beyond mere books. (And earlier I
should've mentioned this: debate is continuing hot and
heavy on the nature of the planned J-town light-rail
system, with a final decision on its route and station
locations due the middle of next month.)
     And then we have our city council race. Here
several of the major issues touch Z and me directly, and
especially the ones regarding housing: steeply rising
rents and security deposits, metastasizing evictions,
low-income workers being forced out of the city. Yet

it's just about impossible the election will
significantly impact matters like these. Again the
problems are systemic and they're not just local; many
can be dealt with only at the state and/or national
levels. But nothing like that's about to happen either,
at least not unless the rules change on campaign
spending. And that's not in the cards this year and
probably not for a long time, if ever. More likely the
legal form of corruption at the heart of what's left of
the democratic system in this country will just keep
spreading and deepening. On this crucial issue the only
real hope is, sadly, at the local level.

And with all that out of the way, back to the more
personal stories.

First I'll say there's nothing new to report about
Gerry and Leola or Jess and Gwen.

The latest about Aida and Kirk is that he'll soon
be traveling in Italy for two weeks and she won't be
able to accompany him, though he wanted her to, and in
any case our double-date dinner/movie with them has been
put off until December. Z says, I think echoing Aida,
that Kirk now seems to be "antsy" about potentially
finding himself at the same table with Aida and Z at the
same time -- maybe he fears Z is out to get him because,
as she's mentioned to me several times, he's the one who
broke up with her, supposedly because he was a hardcore
rationalist labor organizer with strong Marxist leanings
and in his view she was turning woo-woo spiritualist.
But now he's the one who's attending church on Sundays
and wearing a suit and tie to work (where his boss is a
real-estate developer), so maybe he's afraid she'll razz
him about all that or in some other way try to make him
look bad in Aida's eyes. (This much I know: I wouldn't
want to be on the opposite side from Z in any kind of
tense emotional situation -- unless, that is, I believed
she loved me. Which thank the spirits-that-really-
matter, woo-woo or not, I believe she does. And I
seriously doubt Kirk could believe she still loves him.
But then -- who can really know what Kirk believes or
feels? Not me, folks! I say Kirk is who he is and

that's that and let's move on to the next jyzebite.)
     Our other double date actually took place last
night -- a week earlier than expected -- and this one
was with Dak and Sera. We paid for the whole thing as a
way to thank them for all the hard work they, or rather
mostly Sera, put in on the reception. The evening went
well enough but not smashingly, and I'd say that's
because I just don't have much rapport with Sera. She's
like one of those unidimensional girls in high school
who cared about nothing but student-council politics.
In her current job she works closely with the mayor's
office (sometimes including Kirk) and so she talks about
little other than city politics, and mostly the mayor's-
office version of those. After the play ("Golden
Child") we hit a nearby coffee shop where we happened to
run into two more city workers and the three of them
gabbed about insider politics virtually nonstop while
Dak and I and even Z twiddled our thumbs. Dak's warmer
than Sera, I'd say, very friendly, yet seemingly little
interested in anything but his own projects (real estate
and microbanks); he goes through the motions of being
sociable in a likable way but even as he asks good
questions about such things as jyze, for instance, his
heart somehow seems to be somewhere else. (Fancy that!)
     We started out the evening at a Thai restaurant
right across the street from Rob's bookstore. Owing to
babysitter problems and traffic snarls Dak and Sera
arrived almost thirty minutes late and we had to chow
down quickly to make the play. This was at the new
fairgrounds theater a couple of blocks up the street,
the replacement for the one Lady U used to perform in,
but even so I couldn't help but frequently be reminded
of her. Along with "Indigenes," in which she appeared
-- frequently naked -- eighteen years ago next spring,
this was one of her former company's very few
productions with a largely Asiusan cast. The play
itself, though, with its focus on the tensions between
Taoist/Confucian and Christian ways, reminded me
strongly of my days in Korea with Lady S and her family.
-- And I'm glad Z saw it because now I have something

concrete to refer to when trying to explain to her my
view of what went wrong between me and Lady S. (I'm
sure the matter will continue to come up from time to
time: Z knows how important it's been in my life. And
she's several times expressed an eagerness to meet
Elgie. -- And I think she understands it's crucial
that she be partisan in my favor on this matter, as well
as on the continuing dispute between me and sister Barb
that grew out of it, rather than being knee-jerk pro-
Asian or pro-feminist or anti-Eurusan-male -- just as
she asks me to be partisan in her favor regarding her
ongoing struggle with Dale at work and with various
other troglodyte Eurusan males and condescending
suburbanite Eurusan females, and so on.)
     Ooh but this is getting heavy. And it's almost
last-bus time. So -- full stop right now.

[+1]

     A true kwikjyze. How much can I squeeze out here
at the hideaway before it's time to go home? For sure
it won't be a lot. No more than thirty minutes' worth.
     It's Monday, my easy day. I dawdled at home late
into the afternoon, browsed for an hour or more at the
ORB (maybe closer to two hours), didn't drag myself into
the WOC to start the new Right Living workout campaign
until almost half past eight. But I did start it.
There's no turning back now.
     It's getting to be serious Halloween time. All day
I've been wearing an "antiqued copper" pumpkin pin Z
gave me last night. The fence surrounding the sidewalk
cafe at the saloon in the HQ triangle is hung with
Halloween-themed beer ads. (And people were sitting
outdoors there at eleven p.m. when I walked by on the
way back from the WOC: we're into another good-weather
streak these days.) Wei and Alison have even invited us
over to carve pumpkins on Sunday -- we're trying to
reactivate our "do things together" friendship after the
long double-nuptials hiatus -- but to my surprise Z

doesn't want to go. "I'd just sit there watching the three of you carving." This puzzled me. Why couldn't she carve too? But when I asked exactly that question, she just shook her head and said, "I don't wanna. Okay? I just don't." And that settles that. Which means we'll probably not see W&A until Thanksgiving, when we'll be doing the holiday dinner at their place (as we've done each of the past two years -- which is to say, all the years Z and I have known each other).

And the likely outcomes of the crises in the Gerry/ Leola marriage and the Gwen/Jess domestic partnership are now in view. Z had lunch with Jess today and talked at length with Leola. -- But should I save the details until my J-weekly down-home (also up-home) close-out? Yes, I think so. Because I have some stuff I'd better tend to real quick before I head for the bus stop.

*   *

-- Now down-home/up-home four a.m. The stink in here tonight, I finally figured out, is coming from the wedding flowers Thuy gave us last week (with the best of intentions, I'm sure). Otherwise all appears normal -- except for the fact that this will soon be our ex-home and I'm starting to actually see it that way. Which means everything appears strangely different, almost as if the place is a reproduction of itself, like a museum diorama. Soon I suppose we'll be thinking of this apartment, Z and I, mainly as the residence of our touchingly innocent Deep period. In essence we're just waiting for the other shoe to drop: to find out exactly how much time we have left in ol' love nest number 203.

And it feels different in other ways too. For one thing, why worry a whole lot about keeping the place up if the new owners will be remodeling regardless? In that sense living here becomes less -- something. Less personally meaningful, I guess. It's less like a home and more like a motel suite. But on the other hand I suppose it could also become more interesting. "Jyze it up while you still can, before it's gone forever."

There's another kind of change as well. Last night we used the heavy comforter on the bed for the first

458

time since last winter. The days are fairly warm but
the nights are becoming much chillier, especially on the
hilltop. When I hop off the last bus my breath looks
rock solid, as if I were exhaling jagged slices of
grayish-white slate which ought to immediately fall to
the sidewalk with a clatter (but don't!).

Doc Karen called Z today and told her that nine
times out of ten the kind of ultrasound reading she
received turns out to be nothing at all. A D&C is still
called for, though, because the membrane of her uterus
is twice the thickness it should be, which is to say
it's about the normal thickness of a premenopausal
woman. Karen advised her to take three or four
ibuprofen half an hour before the "procedure" and said
she should be able to go back to work afterwards. The
appointment is for a week from tomorrow.

Z's still showing no signs of panic or even of
great concern. But she must be worried. This is Z!
She's the anxiety queen! Her mygs are the baddest! So
I'd say down deep she's probably fearing she's being
subjected to divine payback either for being too happy
in our relationship or for being too sexually
"promiscuous" in earlier years, or, more likely, both.
And no doubt a few -- or many! -- other things too.

Tonight she drew me a nifty cartoon featuring "the
maverick vagina" and left it on my armchair beneath the
"I lub you!" token. The vagina is saying, "Well, after
seven years G was quite a shock and maybe I've
overreacted." And out of the other side of its mouth:
"Am I regenerate or degenerate?"

This morning, by the way, we did lay to rest,
literally, the suggestion that ol' Poosh was "turned
off" at the prospect of visiting the real (but of course
still maverick) vagina in its current state. A rousing
quickie lay -- and she almost slipped away before I was
fully pumped to make my move.

-- And while I'm thinking of it, the neighbors in
the next-door house to the south do seem to be better
behaved these days, quite possibly as a result of the
note Z sent them (signed "one of your neighbors"). Thuy

also mentioned the improvement. On the other hand the
trolley poles are again going awry and just as often as
before if not more so. Yesterday alone the repair crew
had to come out three times to fix a major break. (They
walk around on top of the bus almost at the level of
this window behind me here as I jyze. From the balcony
I can talk with the crew in just a regular speaking
voice and have done so several times -- they're not much
more than twenty-five feet away. Even they regard it as
comical that they're deployed here so often.)
     And then finally the two ongoing soaps.
     With Jess and Gwen it's definitely quitsville.
Jess told Z that Gwen's involvement with her patient
actually began a year ago and she and Gwen had fought
over it numerous times before but kept it to themselves.
Matters worsened considerably when Jess caught Gwen in a
couple of minor lies about him, and then came the big
lie of the weekend when Gwen snuck him into the house
while Jess was away: that was just too much. Gwen and
Jess have talked a lot in recent days and Gwen has even
agreed to see a therapist if Jess would first tell her
there's still a chance they might get back together
someday, but Jess says she just can't do it. She's only
willing to say they'll always be friends -- but she'll
never be able to trust her again. (How fair this
account is to Gwen I have no way of knowing and neither
does Z. But Jess was Z's friend well before either met
Gwen, and Jess and Z have worked together at the utility
the whole time, so Z's loyalties clearly lie with her
and therefore mine pretty much must also.) Meanwhile
Jess is in deep financial trouble because she's paying
$1700 a month on the land -- bought earlier this year as
the future site for her home with Gwen -- as well as the
mortgage payments on her current house. So that house,
as we'd heard before, will soon be going on the market.
This is sad for many reasons, not least -- for us --
because we probably won't be able to return to the spot
where we were married. We likely won't even be able to
see it; the fence around the yard is too high. (Well,
and so there it is again, the mutability of all things.

The city -- any city -- is a work forever in both
progress and regress, so forth and so on -- and just
remember, I tell myself, how lucky Z and I have been to
meet and to have these two and a half fabulous years
together: focus on that, hope for the best, keep on
keepin' on and, what's truly crucial, keep on jyzin'.)

    As for Leola, Z just shakes her head, rolls her
eyes, and at best chuckles. It seems Gerry was a
sweetheart all weekend, taking Leola out to a movie
Friday and dinner Saturday, engaging in a long heart-to-
heart talk with her Sunday, agreeing to more of all the
above in weeks to come -- and it appears Leola's about
to buckle. Give the poor ramblin' man one (more) last
chance, yup. -- And I for one am pleased. I don't
understand why Gerry needs to get away from Leola as he
does, nor why he actually tries to do it for short
spells, nor why she lets him do it to the extent she
does (she must) and also to the extent he does, but I've
never been able to see him as a bad guy. And when he
was dancing with her at our reception he sure didn't
look like a man who wanted his marriage to end. Nor did
she look like a wronged woman heading for the exit.

    And that'll be it for tonight. I'm yawning wide
enough to gobble up a bobbing Halloween apple in one
bite. But -- no apple's abob anywhere in this joint!

23

    Came gamboling out of 203 only to find the car had
a flat tire. Well, no, that wasn't quite the sequence.
First, as I was doing a whirlwind cleanup prior to
leaving I happened to catch a glimpse of Z arriving
home, pulling her wheeled backpack along the sidewalk

down below (and I, wearing just those notorious black
shorts, boldly stepped out onto the balcony to wave to
her). Then, when upstairs, she told me the car seemed
to have a flat tire. "Driver-side front?" I asked, and
she nodded (we've been having a problem with a very slow
leak there). So then, hauling the heavy box of dishes
she needs to take to tomorrow's JCEJ training session, I
"gamboled" down to the garage with her. I'd thought the
"flat" was probably just a matter of the tire being a
bit lower than usual on air and we could drive to the
gas station, but no such luck. It was a real flat.
(JCEJ: that's her environmental-justice group.)
     So did I roll up my sleeves and heroically change
the flat tire as a truly good new husband would've? I
did not. We decided to wait until the weekend to deal
with it -- between now and then she'll use a city car
for evening meetings, as she's entitled to do as a perk
of her new job -- and I just kept on gamboling.
     Not far though. Only three and a half blocks.
I've taken up a newly available position at the
intersection at the south end of the high bridge (the
higher end). The same city crews which razed the
homeless encampments and cut down the shrubbery in the
jungle/rez have been at work up here too, whacking back
the blackberry patch on the southeast corner in a ten-
foot-wide swath, and this has revealed a two-foot-high
metal box of some sort, presumably related to
underground wires in the area, and I'm perched atop this
box out in the middle of the cutover swath. It offers a
slightly different angle on the usual panoramic city
view, and since I'm facing due north I can look east as
well as west and thus scope out both of the major
mountain ranges. The main cluster of downtown highrises
stands straight ahead and to the northwest across the AQ
valley. And a golden haze embraces the mountains to the
west as sundown approaches, but the sun itself is out of
sight, blocked by the hillside -- and it's now setting
well to the south, the sun is, of the southern end of
those same mountains -- "well to the south" meaning
several sun widths -- and racing day by day yet farther

south across the plain down there toward its immediately premillennial turnaround point at the instant of the winter solstice (and we're not forgetting the perihelion "Far In" turning point will arrive about two weeks after that, three days post-millennium as I recall).

Such a fine day it is, I just had to jyze outdoors. How many more chances to do this will there be? Maybe none at all before project's end. At best two or three.

In my hooded green jacket over a heavy black outer shirt and a heavy long-sleeve henley I'm just barely warm enough. The metal of the utilities box is quite cold; and since it has two raised metal bands in the shape of a plus sign right in the middle of the lid I'm sitting on, you could say this box is serving up cold-cross buns. (Rim shot please!) -- And already as sunset gets underway I'm growing chillier. I did bring along a sweatshirt and I could put it on right now. (I'm noticing the green leaves among all the chopped brown shoots. Some sort of ivy, I'd say, because they look like the swedish ivy in front of 1511 and the two adjoining houses except the borders of the leaves here are red instead of white. Poison oak it's not; that's the first thing I checked for in the area before venturing out into it.)

-- As dusk deepens. The mountain silhouette is sharper now against the band of gold and here I'm already jyzing mostly by streetlight. And male voices are audible in the greenbelt behind me (it parallels the street as it mounts the hillside west of the DC castle -- whose display lights are now turned on, making it visible through the trees like a craggy sandstone cliffside or even a huge pueblo roughly 180 feet high). The rustlings in the bush sound like those of megafauna because in fact large mammals of the human kind, and quite possibly the predatory human kind in some cases, are making them, which is only fitting in survival-of-the-most-predatory USA (but still very sad). I'm a little removed from the main walkway here -- off in the deepening shadows -- so I'm thinking I'd probably be wise to mosey along right about now.

[+1]

     Some backbeat follow-up. Just a few things I'd
like to mention.
     For starters: a very fine roll in the sheets this
morning. It left both of us reverbing with eroticized
afterbliss all day. This one I initiated, waking her up
with the slow light back caresses she likes so much, a
few minutes before her alarm was due to go off. It's a
mystery (it always is these days) why I was so turned on
this morning as opposed to some other, although the fact
that for a change I slept a full eight hours the night
before could've had something to do with it, as could
the fact that I'm now hitting the rack later than ever
before in the Zoelie B. era: twenty to six as the target
time (but this is subject to change at any point; as
mentioned so often before, my sleeping hours appear
to alter in an almost predictable, cyclical way as a
function of the Grass Is Always Greener rule -- or maybe
I should call it the ZZZZs Are Always Deeper rule).
     The fuck. The fuck's the thing. "I'm swimming,
I'm swimming" -- it's only the second or third time
she's moaned out those words while in the act (in my
presence, I'm saying, of course). And afterwards: "That
was the kind of fuck about which if we'd met a little
earlier I might've said, 'I'll be surprised if that one
doesn't knock me up.'" -- And all day such compliments
from her: "big sexy guy," "studmuffin," "the mouth that
launched a thousand oohs." Playful stuff, lots of spin
on it, but still: truly meant. I'm convinced. -- And I
reciprocate, of course, and try to outdo her in hopes
she'll want to outdo me right back, and often she does.
And on it goes.
     Whooeee!
     Other quick bits about today. Well, it turns out
the specific deal between Gerry and Leola is that
they'll confer every Sunday to see how they're doing on
their list of sore points (mainly Leola's, I gather),
and if they can't agree they're making progress, they'll

see a "couples counselor" together. An entirely fitting
conclusion to their crisis, I'd say, if a conclusion it
truly turns out to be.

     And: a copy of Olwen's wedding service arrives in
the mail. A stickie note points out that the word
"serve" was not included on the list of Z's vows, but
it was included on mine. What? Corruption! Foul play!
But later on the phone Olwen says the Sufi ceremony is
written that way -- "serve" is for men only, not women.
(For weeks Z and I have both been joking we have no idea
what we agreed to in our vows. Turns out to have been
truer than I, at least, imagined. Not that I think it
really matters other than for goofing purposes.)

     And: Z's been talking lately about not being able
to afford our tentatively planned Mentoka/Centropolis
trip next March. Only now with all the September
credit-card bills in is it finally dawning on her just
how much she spent during the emergency trip to see her
mother in August (close to 10K). Meanwhile Mama E seems
to be backing away from the plan to move here. She's
saying Tito wants to live with her permanently (and he's
pounding away on the "I saved your life" theme to get
her to agree to it) and the implication is that if she
did agree to it (which she's not doing yet) they would
stay right where they are. Realistically speaking how
long that could last I don't know, but Z seems quite
willing to accept it. It's almost as if she's so fed up
with her family for not sending anyone out for the
wedding that she's saying if they're not interested in
her, she's not interested in them. But I don't think
this will last, because the truth is she is interested
in them -- a bunch.

     -- And I'll mention quickly my recent sense that
suddenly the city's getting its act together. This is
prompted by a number of small observations and they
don't necessarily add up to much, if anything at all.
But in the last week I've noticed the light at the very
top of the great white tower has been turned on for what
I think is the first time in years (it's like a huge
old-fashioned lightbulb, clear glass). There's also a

new light atop the west rail depot and all four clock
faces on the campanile are lit up at night and showing
the same time (and it appears to be the correct time!).
The refurbished east depot and the new county office
building across from the west depot are both open for
business as of this week. The new digi-plutocrat
buildings behind the east depot have topped out. A
large crane is up and in action above the completed
basement foundation for the "millennial tower" across
from the WOC and Z's utilities building. -- And much
more. And I'm playing down a few contraindications I've
spotted here and there. Cities are complicated! -- But
I've got this feeling big doings are ahead....

[+1]

     Aboard. I must say I timed it pretty damn well,
arriving just seconds after the ferry worker swung open
the gate for foot passengers. Nor was there any wasted
motion hiking down here from the hilltop -- and that
included a quick stop at the east-depot market on the
way for some grub to take along on this field trip.
Small package of fig bars and a can of peach juice, both
open already, right here on the booth tabletop. Buy
them at the ferry canteen and you pay two or three times
as much and they're probably sold out of both anyway.
     The klaxon brays and we're starting to move. A
very smooth start. I'm up toward the bow, port side,
and on the starboard side the white superstructure of
another ferry, still docked, slides away; on this side
nothing at all slides away because everything's blankly
gray out there: fog. Very thick fog. Yet we're leaving
almost on time. This would suggest it's probably clear
on the far side and most of the pond in between.
     The horn's sounding quite a bit, every thirty
seconds or so. Visibility is very slight -- appears to
be zero. It's symbolically just right for a ride back
into the past. (But the gray out there is exceptionally
bright, I'm realizing now, enough so to cause the

466

boothbacks to cast sharp shadows. The presence of so
much light means the top of the fogbank can't be too
much higher than -- maybe it's even a little lower than
-- the highest point on the vessel.)

The banner headline on today's far-coast paper
lying on the tabletop here says the FBI is warning that
the militias -- that is, our own homegrown right-wing
USAn terrorists -- will be stirring up big trouble
around the millennium.

Only about a dozen people are in sight in this
forward section which seats hundreds. None look too
worried about the militias or anything else -- not even
the fact that we'll likely be arriving at the transit
port way behind schedule. Right now we're chugging
along at a speed maybe one third the norm for full-
visibility days.

So far I've recognized just three people: two ferry
workers and the third a passenger, an elderly Afrusan
man in pressed blue denim, meaning the kind that shows
creases. But then in terms of the daily schedule this
run is about as distant in time as it could be from the
ones I regularly rode for all those years: it's midday
as opposed to early evening or early morning.

Two nearby riders are talking on cellphones at the
moment, a woman who sounds like an attorney and a man
who appears to be some sort of construction contractor,
both yammering away loudly and obnoxiously. Earlier
several others a bit farther away -- but still nowhere
near far enough away for my money -- were doing the
same. Although cellphones were around during my
commuting days too, they're obviously much more common
now. They must drive the sleepers nuts. (Reminds me of
my time in Korea: when phones are new, people distrust
the technology, perhaps unconsciously, and talk loud.)

A fortyish Asiusan couple is sitting in the window
booth directly across the aisle, quietly conversing in
mixed English and Japanese. In looks they remind me of
the married couple who owned the small Japanese market
Lady U and I patronized near the old home port -- and
also, just as in their case, her voice is considerably

467

deeper and huskier than his. (But I'm almost sure this
is not that couple.) ("Say hello to 'Nora,'" Z teased
me as she left for work this morning, using the name she
adopted for Lady U from a cartoon character. She still
calls it "Noraland" over there -- or over here now, I
should say, or almost. And it's getting to the point I
sometimes think of it that way myself: Noraland.)

(A snore starts up in a booth behind me -- a man
dressed in black is stretched out with his face pressed
against the boothback to shield his eyes, his feet
sticking out into the aisle. A familiar sight, a
familiar sound. -- As is the beeping and whooping of an
electronic game just outside the canteen maybe fifty
feet aft of us here.)

A couple of gulls are flapping around a few feet
above the bow. -- And the sun's shining in now --
flickeringly -- and I can see houses through the mist on
the far side, very close by, as we move into the bay
preceding the twisty Z-narrows (as I began calling them
for their shape long before I knew Z) on our way to the
inlet. It was just a few hundred yards from here, on a
morning far foggier than this, as it turns out, that a
ferry I was aboard bumped head-on into another one --
the only such collision in the history of the system.

(Speaking of collisions, Wei and Alison were
involved in one yesterday. Wei made what he refers to
as an "ill-advised U turn" and smashed up Alison's car.
Apparently no one was hurt, but beyond this Wei isn't
revealing much, or at least not so far (Z saw him at the
JCEJ meeting last night). The silver lining here is
that they probably won't be worrying too much about our
-- Z's -- turndown of their pumpkin-carving invitation.)

For the first time I'm hearing a little rattling as
we accelerate a bit for the last part of the voyage, up
the inlet -- and though the sun's still present, the fog
seems to be closing in again -- neither shoreline is
visible -- and it's darker now -- and we're also slowing
down again. -- And I see I was wrong, we're still in
the twisty Z-passage, going around the last bend,
because suddenly the fog is thinning again and turning a

bright misty white and the sawtoothed evergreen treeline
along the shore is reverse-fading into view.

Now the inlet itself, and it's nearly fog-free.

Some fall colors showing up out there along the
heavily wooded shorelines. The mix of evergreens and
deciduous trees is still very easy on the eyes. (Atop
south hill earlier this morning I noticed that the row
of infrequently driven cars along the back line of the
parking lot of the largest of the apartment houses was
nearly buried beneath fallen maple leaves, an eye-
catching harvest-time palette of yellows, oranges,
reds.)

Through the starboard windows the hills of jingo
city are coming into view, crowded with houses and
trees. within fifteen or twenty miles resides one of
the largest collections of nuclear weapons on earth.

-- But I do like these ferry rhythms, yes. Slow
and easy does it. Relax, you're not going anywhere for
an hour or, as today, closer to two. The low rumble and
vibration of the engine, the soporific effect. The
stateliness and innate dignity of the journey with its
generally steady speed and slow smooth turns. It's
almost as if I'm still lying in bed -- and in fact on an
ordinary day I'd be doing just that right now. Half an
hour or so to go until the later of my usual current
wake-up settings sounds the alarm at 1:40 p.m. (the
first alarm, at 12:40, almost always fails to roust me).

Here's the "now arriving" announcement. we're in
the big long slow final turn. The gray row of U.S. Navy
vessels, the jagged mountain peaks moving in so much
closer than they would've been at the start if the fog
hadn't totally blocked them out. No surprise, this, of
course, yet -- surprise! They're so big! So craggy!
And it always was a surprise, every trip, if the
mountains were visible at all.

*   *

Here's another surprise, at least to me. It's now
six hours later and I'm back aboard a ferry bound for
the city. This time it's one of the new high-speed
passenger-only boats, but one that's crippled by a court

469

order limiting it, along with its sister vessels, to a
very low speed because of shore-erosion problems caused
by their wakes and bow waves. The irony is that the
previous class of passenger ferry had the same problem
and this new class was supposedly designed to avoid it.
And I don't like this vessel any more than its
predecessors; the ride's so much more comfortable on the
big old clunky auto ferries. (I know how this one rides
from a previous trip early last spring prior to the TJM
launch. Right now we're still idling at the dock.)
     I thought I'd be jyzing at the storage unit. It
was a fine afternoon for it, plenty warm even with the
garage door pulled all the way up. The table and chair
were ready and waiting even if a bit dusty. But I
decided to tend to business first -- mainly looking for
certain old family papers -- and got caught up in a
couple of files I'd never opened before because they
were mislabeled as being part of Dad's voluminous
financial papers. The actual contents turned out to be
mostly correspondence between our family and his,
hundreds of letters, including several of my own to Gram
and Gramps from childhood years. Two hours passed in a
flash as I pored over these letters and suddenly the sun
sank behind the hill and it was time for me to move
along if I wanted to catch the 6:20 ferry back to J-town.
     (But here we go. They're untying the ropes.)
     And by the way, I didn't catch that 6:20 boat.
Came within fifty feet of doing so, but then, just as I
hit the bottom of the ramp, the gangway at the top
started rising and the red "Departed" sign lit up. I
could've made it if I'd realized just how tight the
timing would be and more or less sprinted across the
dock and up the ramp. But I heard one of the workers
radio ahead that one more passenger was coming -- and he
was looking straight at me when he did that -- and
though I wasn't sprinting, I was trotting. So I guess
the captain just ignored the message. And maybe that
was because he didn't recognize me, as he might've done
in my years as a regular.
     (Most hateful about these passenger-only ferries,

as everyone says, is the excessive air-conditioning.
They designed these boats for southern climes and so
they lack intermediate settings: it's high tropics or
nothing. And the interior air must be freshened
somehow. Thus the arctic blast you can't escape.)
    -- The home port itself got to me a little bit more
than I thought it would. I took a different bus route
this time, passing along the shoreline and then up to
the farthest east of the malls before circling back to
the storage place near the high school. Along the way
we passed a number of businesses I hadn't seen since the
era when Lady U and I patronized them, including our
favorite Japanese restaurant and the discount mart where
(by default) we did a lot of our shopping. For some
reason I was reminded of how high our hopes had been
when we first moved over there and then, of course, of
how they were dashed, or maybe I should just say how we
let them slip away. I'm extremely lucky the way things
have turned out with Z -- for sure I wouldn't want to go
back to that prior life even if I could -- but this
doesn't mean I can't reexperience for a moment how
devastated I was when it came to an end. And at several
points during this visit I did reexperience it. (One of
them was on the bus going back in when I suddenly
realized that tomorrow, the 22nd of the month, will also
be the 22nd anniversary of the day Lady U and I met.
Somehow I'd totally spaced it out before then.)
    Rolling up the garage door of the storage unit,
it's always like opening a time capsule. This time I
was reminded of reentering a relative's room that was
closed up tight at his/her death. The unit is literally
packed to the rafters with the detritus of the six-year-
plus period when Lady U and I were living ten miles down
the road. My old mountain bike, looking almost
comically odd, perched precariously atop the loft at the
back. The windsocks that fluttered from the eaves of
our veranda now hanging limply from a rafter in a spot
where the wind never reaches. Lots of our emergency
gear for storms is in there too -- a couple of kerosene
heaters, gas lamps, a small generator (broken), bundles

of blankets -- and all those seem especially useless
given my current life, except of course they could serve
as a form of insurance against Y2Kalypse (some people
are still saying the worst-case scenario would be
something like a typical three-day winter storm in which
the power stays off just that long, and not only here
but possibly throughout the country -- but I think both
the local and the national version of that scenario are
highly unlikely). -- So perhaps I should offer to let
Wei, who's convinced we're facing a catastrophe, borrow
that gear. Or rent it to him for the nonce.

        -- Now we're scooting across the open water of the
central sound with the boat's bow high in the air.
Today's ride is turning into a rough one -- we're
skipping at times, maybe after hitting submerged logs or
maybe because the boat just rides the waves this way, or
of course maybe both.

        The deja-vuiest moment of all came as I stood at
the top of the ramp in the old home port while a packed
foot-ferryful of shipyard workers and other locals filed
by just a few feet away. Many familiar faces, even more
familiar types. What a scruffy lot they are! Not that
I don't fit right in with them even now, at least by
appearance. But by and large these folks don't like
city people, they don't like urban culture, they don't
like books, they don't like government, they don't like
minorities (even the few who are minorities themselves
don't, at least in my experience) -- just a whole lot of
cussedness and hostility and resentment and
provinciality there. And yet these are some of the
best-paid workers in the country -- the world -- and
it's our government that's paying them.

        -- As we pull in. There's the Jyze City skyline --
looks mighty good to me.

                              [+3]

        Yesterday I tried to do my jyze thing up in the
Yuke. But before I could even unpack the J-book it was

                              472

announced that the cafe I'd gone to was shutting down
for the day "for painting." No sign on the door about
this, no indication from the server at the counter where
I bought my coffee (luckily it was in a paper cup I
could take with me). Nothing. So I said to hell with
the jyze. Then I had to wait outside for almost forty
minutes until Z appeared. I couldn't go looking for her
a couple of blocks up the street where she was shopping
because in the meantime she might've started back down
by any of several alternative routes. And in fact she
had done just that: she chose the road next to the
campus so she could check out the fall colors (and
brought me three perfect maple leaves ranging from
blazing yellow to deep red, with even more intensity in
the colors than we've been seeing on the hilltop). Then
we tried a new franchise of a national-chain corporate
diner for supper and the service was so slow Z canceled
her order and eventually the manager picked up the check
for what little did arrive.

   After that, "Jules and Jim" at the theater across
from U-books. It was emotional for me. I was back in
the world of Ladies S and, especially, V, whose first
language was French, as was a large portion of her way
of being in the world. I said nothing about any of
this, though, and none of it really mattered because Z
didn't much like the movie anyway. Why, I don't know.
As a rule she just doesn't go for artsy romantic movies
set in high patriarchal days, and that's doubly or
triply true if they're subtitled and slow-paced and the
male protagonist, or in this instance, crucially,
protagonists, a rivalrous pair, cause the female
protagonist to suffer. The exceptions have been few.

   And then home for a night of reading, in my case
first the newspapers in the green bedroom armchair
(reading them in bed is too awkward) and then a stack
of reviews and magazines in bed (they're more
manageable). Z dozed off quickly, worn out from a day
that started for her at five-forty a.m., as most of them
do under our current regimen.

   Friday on the phone she told me she thinks we

should have more "serious face-to-face conversations."
Fine with me, I said, and meant it, although in truth I
think we already have plenty of "serious" conversations
even though we usually conduct them in a casual manner,
improvisational and ad-lib and maybe even with some (or
much) goofing mixed in. I'm not one who believes
important things get said only if you try to say them in
a serious or formal manner and setting; if anything I
think the reverse is more often true. But of course
once in a while you do have to do the "serious" drill --
and when you do, and it's Zoelie B. you're doing it
with, you'd better take it pretty damn seriously.

     This afternoon and evening I finally finished off
the last dozen of the thank-you cards (though I have yet
to do the ones for my own invitees: Rob and Gail, Kar
and Kerani, Jim Q.). The way I get when I'm doing "art"
-- all these thank-yous are altered postcards, each one
different -- often reminds Z, so she told me, of a kid
she used to have a crush on when they were both about
five years old: a neighbor of hers, a little Cawk kid,
Harvey. "Sometimes I wish so much I could talk with
your mother. I'll bet the way you were with her when
you were working on your drawings and stuff at that age
is just the way you are now" -- which I do believe is
true, yup, and especially the way I went running to ol'
Mom with each and every new production seeking her
praise. Dad not so much, although I don't recall him
ever reacting unkindly. But he didn't light up the way
Mom did -- and once in a while Z does too. (But not as
much as I'd like. And I complain about this!)

     Also yesterday before heading up north for shopping
and the movie we stopped by at one of the hilltop gas
stations (soon to be under new corporate ownership; it
seems they're all changing names these days just like
the banks did earlier) to have the newly repaired flat
tire mounted. The repair guy found the villain: a tiny
inchlong finishing nail. Taking this tire in was a "guy
thing," Z decided; but then she spared me and instead
called in her auto service to do it Saturday morning as
I slept. This cost her nothing since it's covered by

the yearly fee she pays -- and she knew I hadn't been looking forward to grubbing around in the garage all afternoon. And an amusing note: the driver for the auto service turned out to be a woman who looked so much like Madge at the utility that Z initially hailed her loudly with "Madge, it's you!" before realizing her mistake.

The night before that, it being Manny's birthday (and the day before Nick's), Z and I took Betty and Kat out to an up-and-coming local gourmet burger joint on east hill to celebrate the occasion. It was my job to keep Kat entertained while Betty vented to Z about Manny's younger brother, Reuben, who's imposing himself on them more and more these days, and whose estranged wife is reportedly about to descend from afar for a reconciliation attempt and will probably, given past experience with these two, also descend on Betty and Kat, invited or not. During the meal Kat got a bit wild (possibly because I was overdoing the "entertainment") and wound up smearing barbecue sauce all over her hands and arms. Betty sent her off to the ladies' room to wash it off, but when she came back much of that sauce had somehow wound up on her face, resembling war paint. "Look, look!" the girl cried excitedly. "Isn't it like a real Indian?" A classic moment, because of course a real Indian is exactly what Kat is: indigenously Mayan/ Guatemalan. We were all agog over this.

(Afterwards Z asked if I think Kat needs counseling. I was startled. No question the girl (grrrl) is full of herself -- from being spoiled half to death, including by us -- but she's still a great kid and in my view she's doing just fine with her "cultural and class adjustments." -- Or do I think this just because she and I are so well "bonded"? And as proof of the bonding I offer this: not only did she confide in me that she'd seen Jared's boxer shorts through a hole in his pants, but also that she'd told all her grrrlfriends about what she'd gotten a gander at when Subunk G was changing clothes in the bedroom a few weeks back and she snuck in behind the screen.)

We also learned that Betty's friend Wanda who moved

to the desert southland last spring and quickly met a
guy and fell in love with him and moved in with him and
his kids, apparently is suffering a relapse of the
cancer she thought she'd beaten several years ago, and
her new man has vowed to stick by her no matter what.
-- And to our surprise, Betty's joined a neighborhood
political group that's planning to participate in the
"actions" against the WTO next month by hanging huge
banners on various bridges and walls in their part of
the city. -- And we learned that Betty told a carful of
Kat's grrrlfriends about Aunt Z who doffed her blouse
and went topless just like the hippie girls at the
country fair last summer, "and her nipples pointed up
just like theirs did." (This puzzled Z and she asked me
about it. Yes, it's true, I said, they're perky almost
like a teenager's and of course the fact that she's
never nursed a kid or been pregnant could have a lot to
do with it.) (Was she putting me on with faux naivete?
Quite possibly. It's not unheard of that she fishes for
compliments this way. "Why do you think those men over
there were looking at me like that? I just don't get
it. Did I do something strange?" Ha! -- In any case,
I told her she should check out the photos of nipples in
her wedding-shower gift book on breasts if she didn't
believe me, and she said she would do just that.)

     A full moon last night, visible in the misty sky --
but again for me it carries nothing like the charge of
last month's wedding moon. Also yesterday the sun moved
out of our nuptial sign and brother Rob's birth sign,
Libra, and into Dad's birth sign, Scorpio. And it turns
out that some flashing greens I saw in the northern sky
when I came home at the usual 1:30 a.m. hour Friday
night weren't lightning or wandering searchlights boring
into fast-moving clouds, as I thought they must be at
the time, but a rare outbreak of the northern lights.
Rare for this city, that is, and especially for being
visible above the lights of downtown. The papers said
the last such display seen in J-town was eight years
ago, though I've personally viewed a couple of others
during that period in the skies above the peninsula.

[+1]

So now it's the night of dread. Tomorrow Z goes in
for her "scrape." I've been trying not to think about
it too much all along but I'm plenty worried. Betty
says it's "just a routine thing, nothing to get upset
about," but that's the reassuring nurse talking (and we
both appreciate it too -- but still).

As Z points out in one of several notes she left me
tonight, she's been "stoic" about the situation so far.
"What's my reward going to be?" she asks. She deserves
one, yes, and presumably she'll receive one: the reward
of feeling good about herself for having acted
courageously. (Am I being an idiot here? Quite
possibly yes. Nor am I ashamed to admit it. Maybe, as
Z would probably say, it's just a typical Norski thing,
the "glorification" of stoicism. -- In any case I'll
shower her with words of praise and then I suppose I'd
better be thinking about what else I can come up with as
a reward. But I wonder: should the award be bestowed
under "plan A" or "plan B"? And how long will we be
required to wait for the award ceremony?)

She might wander in from the bedroom at any time.
If she does, jyze will call it a night. -- And if it
turns out the "scrape" reveals something's seriously
wrong with her, jyze might have to call off its whole
TJM project. -- Or no, maybe it won't have to, but
quite possibly I'd feel it should. I the jyzer. Which
is not a happy thought, no.

One of her messages says she noticed spotting again
today and this scares her. Only once before in the past
couple of weeks has it happened, and not at all prior to
that in the entire time we've been together, but she
wonders if she might've missed some occasions because
she can't see detail that well without her glasses and
she's rarely wearing glasses when she undresses or uses
the toilet. But I can see detail all right and I
haven't noticed any evidence of spotting in the sheets
or in her "unners." So I think it's been light at most.

And we did make the double-backed beast this morning and went at it fairly rambunctiously, much as we'd done right before the one other time she noticed spotting.

Of course it's useless torturing ourselves over this now. We'll know the score soon enough. (Exactly how soon, though, I'm not sure. A week? Two weeks?)

Another of her notes said, "G-hub be way way sexy today -- Z-wiff din wanna leave," referring to her brief drop-in at the apartment this afternoon to pick up something as Leola waited for her downstairs. This too is probably in some way a reflection of her fear. It's also a reflection of how special she is, that she'd write a loving/sexy lighthearted message like that at such a time.

All this on the day when we've been hitched exactly one month. And the year of the TJM, I'll point out, is four days into its second six months. And the millennium countdown has dwindled to sixty-eight days.

In yet another of her notes Z mentions that Jess has asked if we'll house-sit for her over New Year's. This would be a big comedown indeed after all our notions of organizing some sort of millennium-rollover extravaganza. But as of now we have no plans at all for the big night. Well, no, we'll be attending the midnight fireworks at the fairgrounds. But we have nothing for earlier in the evening. And we can do the fireworks whether we're staying at Jess's place or at home. And I like house-sitting, and I like Jess, and it seems Z is willing to do it. After injuring her foot the last go-round (also for Jess, and for Gwen too then) Z vowed no more holiday house-sitting. But her note says it would be okay as long as I'd help her remember to wear clogs to protect her toes.

-- I'm sitting on the couch. A few loud thumps overhead remind me that Doug and Thuy and kids are still hanging on in 303. The word is the contractor hired to remodel the house they've bought about two miles south on the hill has quit in disgust over Thuy's frequent changes in what she wants done with it. According to Aida, the house is now sitting there "gutted" and the

family will be stuck here at 1511 for several more
months if not longer. Meanwhile Z is expressing new
interest, surprising to me, in our staying on in 203
after the building goes condo. I have my doubts that we
could afford to do it -- without question I'd have to
invest all my deep reserves in it -- but I'd be
delighted to live here permanently. How much, though,
should we be willing to pay? And what kind of
assurances can we get that the building itself is
structurally sound -- especially considering that one of
the contractors who built it told me (when he was here
last winter on a repair job) that it was a shoddy piece
of work? But then how many nonshoddy pieces of work are
available in J-town these days (or for that matter any
other days)? And what is that "shoddy" relative to?
Anything within our potential price range?

     -- Last night June came over. She was lying right
here snoozing when I arrived home, and she went back to
snoozing while I edited one of her papers for law
school. After we'd gone over that together we had a
good talk for an hour or so before she went home at five
a.m. She waxed all emotional in telling me how much our
talks mean to her. I was touched by this, and also by
her determination to hang in there at law school despite
her disappointment with her performance so far. And
she's also fiercely vowing to keep working full-time for
the city while attending school. In the past week she's
fallen down twice from sheer exhaustion (she showed me
the scabs on her knees) (and she has very "well turned"
knees and legs too, I must say -- or anyway am saying,
maybe just because I can). And she makes an interesting
point: she says she needs to stay with her city job no
matter what so she'll have an excuse for not doing
better at law school; otherwise she couldn't take being
seen as such a mediocre student. She's realistic enough
to know she'd stand little chance of being "law-review
caliber" given her "handicaps" in language, culture,
race, age, gender. Whereas she thinks Z, by contrast,
is nowhere near realistic enough, especially at work:
"She tries to fix everything immediately! She needs to

be more patient! She is too emotional!" -- But she,
June, had some good news too. It appears her son Adam
(the older of the two) is about to strike it rich via
stock options, with two well-financed start-up high-tech
companies engaged in a bidding war for his services.
And June herself has decided to concentrate on
intellectual-property law in the high-tech field. (This
wouldn't impress me a whole lot if anyone else were
doing it, but June's the exception. As she is for a
good many other things. And even so I have to bite my
lip sometimes to keep from blurting, "why in the world
are you trying to do all this?")
       -- But I hear stirrings in the other room and it's
late so I think this will be the stopping point for this
week, an abrupt one but it can't be helped, and won't.

24

    Came bopping out into the wind and rain and just
kept going until I landed here: at the ORB cafe.
Streets plastered all along the way with leaves yellow
to orange to red, the yellows predominating. Brother
Rob says the trees are turning much later than usual
this year -- all except the maples. And down in "the
jungle/rez" I could see whole areas sectioned off with
bright yellow crime tape. Where once trashy homeless
campsites stood there's now only trash.
    I'm just a little soaked at the moment. The back
corner table by the big iron pump. Nor am I paying for
any food or drink. Here you can get away with it once
in a while if you're not too overt about it, especially
if you prominently display on your table a couple of
items you've bought upstairs moments earlier, and I'm

doing that. At this hour, though, I doubt I'd be
challenged anyway. Half past six, and tonight's reading
in the next room probably won't be a big draw. (I saw
the new owner of the jazz record shop standing in the
rain on the staircase leading down to his basement digs
and he nodded to me as if I'd really come in to browse
all those times I'd merely meant to. He looked forlorn,
conveying the sense that business is abysmally bad now
with so many vinyl records and CDs being sold over the
internet. And that's probably exactly how it is. He
may peddle items on the internet himself, but it's
likely becoming prohibitively expensive to maintain his
physical "brick-and-mortar" shop. He might as well
store the merchandise in his basement at home. And what
a shame this is, or at least seems to be right now. A
few decades down the road, who knows, all direct human
contact, if any such is even possible by then, might
seem shameworthy in a similar way.)

Alison left a message saying she and her "group"
(I'm not sure what the group is) will be praying for Z.
Z seemed surprised by this, as if she'd succeeded in
convincing herself that her situation isn't serious and
Alison's message was destroying the illusion. But last
night she couldn't sleep and did break down for a while.
"I deserve to be indulged on this after keeping up the
stoic front all day at the office." Soon we were
laughing, though, making jokes about her old boyfriends'
"spoors" still lurking on various items she's had for a
long time such as her red "courting couch" which opens
into a bed. (What brought this up: in changing our
regular bed and turning the mattresses -- actually
futons -- she'd noticed a faded splotch of what appears
to be menstrual blood on the old maroon futon which
"Nora" and I once shared.)

It might be as long as ten days before we know the
results of "the scrape," also called "the probe." And I
think we'll get through this "period of the scrape I'm
in," as Z described it, without too much grief. Last
night she seemed more concerned about a rift that's
opened between her and Rowena, one of the JCEJ people.

Z did come home from work early after seeing Doc Karen,
but she wasn't in pain; she'd taken several ibuprofen
(as instructed) before going to Doc K's office and that
turned out to be enough. She went to her JCEJ meeting
last night and to her own office this morning. I saw
her briefly before leaving the house and she seemed in
good spirits. (Her note last night mentioned she was
feeling "cranky," but she attributed this in part to the
Rowena incident and in part to the "post-wedding
letdown" associated with no longer being the center of
attention among her various groups of friends. Wei's
the only one she's told about "the scrape," and he
obviously told Alison. -- And Z was a bit displeased
because Wei seemed to be taking a "neutral" stance
regarding the Rowena business. But Wei himself had a
run-in with the formidable Rowena a couple of months ago
and Z pretty much sided with Rowena on that one, so she
had to acknowledge it's at least partly an instance of
what goes around comes around.)
    Today's the three-hundredth day of the year.
Sixty-five to go before the "biggest celebration in a
thousand years," as I saw it referred to in a newspaper
article. Excitement's building for sure. At the same
time the WTO meeting here -- just a month away -- is
drawing all kinds of media attention and the city's
consumed with preparing for the event. Y2K concerns are
building too, including for me; the past few days I've
been thumbing through old computer manuals in search of
some way to reassure myself -- just as a precaution,
mind you -- that my own puny Jyzer Ink operation won't
punk out on me. (No luck so far.) Meanwhile it's
Halloween week. And with the election just six days
away, political campaigns are charging into the home
stretch. Despite a massively funded effort to derail
our state's colossally foolish antigovernment
initiative, it appears it will pass. Its lead in the
polls is shrinking, but probably nowhere near fast
enough.
    And this should be an interesting weekend.
Saturday night we'll be attending the fundraising party

and dance thrown by the Filusan city workers association, and it appears the redoubtable Kirk M. will be there with Aida (and so will Z's new "managee" at work, the even more redoubtable Gloria G.). The latest word is that Aida's no longer interested in marrying Kirk, but I suspect that's just one of her mercurial moods speaking. (And she's seeing a counselor about ways and means of handling Charles, and everyone's relieved about this except Charles himself, because he's being dragged along to the sessions and hates them and starts "acting out" the moment they're over -- almost a textbook case of psycho-iatrogenic behavior, innit?)

And finally I'll mention I had a couple of drinks with brother Rob yesterday in belated celebration of our birthdays. We met at the hideaway and I showed him what I've been up to lately and he went through the box of wedding photos and some other items. He was quite taken with the color photocopy of the daytimer cover I made for Z last Christmas -- he was seeing it for the first time -- and I was pleased by that. Then at a nearby bar I spun out extended versions of the two big honeymoon stories -- "Buried Glitter" and "Kitchen Goddess" -- and we talked at length about brother Jeff and sister Barb and the stash of family letters I discovered at the storage unit the other day, several of which I'd brought along to show him. Currently Rob's disappointed with Barb because she hasn't replied to a long letter he sent her describing his Mentoka trip in August. "I always worry she'll be offended by some little thing." (Et tu, bro Rob!) We both wondered if her failure to reply might have something to do with my wedding and Jim Q.'s importuning her to come up here to attend it with him (as is true of so much concerning Barb, we'll probably never know what's really behind her actions or reactions or inactions). The last part of our very enjoyable gabfest went down as I walked him to his bus stop on my way to work. We also tentatively agreed to get together for dinner along with "the wives" at 203 on Christmas Day (Z had already approved the plan); and as he pointed out, it'll be the first time he and I have ever been in

a foursome where we're legally married to the other two.
     -- And now the onward trudge to work. Here in the
ORB cafe it's remained quiet this whole time and I
haven't been challenged as the freeloader I undeniably
am. Therefore I might try the ruse again sometime -- at
a different table, to be sure -- say when my funds run
low during the bad-weather months fast approaching.

[+2]

     The wind was blowing in the right direction and so
as I walked down off the hill today I was escorted by
flocks of tumbling and scraping leaves. -- Against a
gray backdrop and with a surprising roar coming from the
double line of trees, a slight drizzle serving as a
damper on those cymbal-like dead maple leaves (or say
they're like the stretched skin of drumheads). And yet
all along the route flowers still in bloom were hanging
in there bravely -- especially considering that on this
very day it's been announced their ancient genetic
secrets have been decoded and we now know how it was
that the first flower appeared on the planet. (And can
the secret of consciousness be far behind? Well, maybe.
But the story of the differentiation of the sexes isn't.
That was supposed to be announced today too, but somehow
I've missed it so far.)
     A fine day. An exciting day. And a full day: in
just eight minutes I must head over to the WOC (where Z
will be meeting me for only our second joint workout
since before the wedding).
     And so I'll mention that today's the seventieth
anniversary of the stock market crash of 1929. The
current market, after a month or two of "corrections,"
has been roaring upward again in recent days, spurred on
by an announcement that U.S. economic growth has been
greater than expected and now it's all but certain the
overall long-running expansion will qualify early next
year as the longest in the country's history.
     Other matters of interest to mention, most notably

a shoplifting incident in which I was the suspect. But
no time to get into that now. Somehow I'll return later
for an encore but I don't know how much later: the
weekend looks busy too. The Filusan dinner/dance (but
without, as we've learned, former Z lover Kirk in
attendance -- seems he's gone off to Italy a few days
earlier than expected). Trick or treat. Time change.
All kinds of craziness on the docket!

[+1]

     Can't resist putting in an appearance here in the
hour that exists twice. Sixty minutes ago it was one
a.m. and now it's one a.m. again. The clocks even say
so, including the one on the stove, and in fact that
particular one's been providing standard time ever since
we moved in -- because we moved in during standard time
and we've never been able to figure out how to change it
(most likely the reset mechanism's broken).
     Cheap thrills and deep space/time mysteries -- what
a combo! (As aids in easing our way down the twisty
path, I'm saying.)
     Just finished reading a long think piece on
"Buddhism and Poverty." Z came across it last week and
liked it so much she distributed a batch of copies to
her PMS friends (that's printed material syndrome), and
it just happens I'm on that list. I like the article
too, and in fact try to live my life pretty much as it
recommends, but even so I see one major flaw in it for
which I can imagine no easy fix. To wit: if everyone in
a particular nation lived by those precepts, the nation
would soon become considerably less technologically
sophisticated than a nation guided by, say, dog-eat-dog
capitalist/consumerist/neoimperialist principles and
would almost inevitably fall under that "more advanced"
nation's domination. In fact that's a pretty good
thumbnail description of what's been going down in much
of the world for at least the second half of the
millennium now ending, along with the clashes between

the "more advanced" nations themselves seeking absolute
top-dog dominator status, top of the top. Of course the
aforementioned principles, while more successful in the
short and medium run (in Darwinian terms as applied to
nations), may well soon lead the entire human race into
an extremely dark era if not to extinction (and have
already resulted in the extinction of many other species,
of course, in just the last decade or two, and at a pace
that's rapidly accelerating).

So what's to do? Dunno. Guess maybe we'd all
better be thinking on it a bit more and real soon too.

And in the meantime, even as the cataclysm edges
ever closer, more jyze of this special intercalary hour.

Z's asleep. Before she drifted off we engaged in a
fairly rare late-evening (for her) shag session.
Possibly owing to the three drinks I downed at tonight's
Filusan dinner/dance (actually it was a fundraiser for
the regional Filusan newspaper, it turned out) I found
I had no pop at the end, although I had plenty of prepop
all the way up to it. And we got a large charge from
the "session" regardless -- just as we did earlier from
the dinner/dance, except, again, toward the end when the
entertainment (much of it in Tagalog) itself had no pop
for either of us. And so we snuck out early, before the
dancing even started, and even though I'd promised to
save Gloria G. a dance and Aida had promised to save me
one. (This was downtown in the ballroom of a fairly new
highrise hotel up near the freeway on a blustery, rainy
evening, and Z wore her sensational Halloween skeleton
stockings and a very short black skirt to show them off
to best advantage and then had to change out of the
stockings midway through the evening owing to the
appearance of a big ugly run. -- But she'd expected
something like this might happen and come prepared with
a backup pair of red fishnets (also sensational!).

Aida showed up ninety minutes late for the dinner
and left after less than an hour, even before we did.
As she explained briefly to me, her life is "just too
full of stresses and pressures right now." Most of
these I knew about before -- counseling for herself and

Charles, fear her father has cancer, conflicts with a
new boss at work, disputes with Tom (her ex), the
ongoing struggles with the troublesome Kirk -- but I did
hear about a new stressor later from Z: Aida has a
housemate now, a paying one, a young woman, living in
the basement "suite," and apparently her presence is
sparking even more bad behavior from Charles.
Nonetheless Aida will be throwing a birthday party for
herself two weeks from today and Z and I will be
attending and by then Kirk will be back from Italy and
presumably he'll be attending too. The long-delayed
all-principals meeting will happen one of these days,
it's just bound to. Or not. (Who cares? I do! It'll
be a hoot to rub up against one of Z's prime "spoor
carriers," to deploy one of our going terms. This is
how I'm looking at it now or at least trying to.)

        In a room packed with a couple hundred banqueters I
surprisingly knew maybe as many as two dozen people.
Among these were Sera and Dak, the voluptuous and
tempestuous Gloria G. and her Cawk fiance' Bud (may the
gods help him -- but her too; he looks twice her age and
highly irascible if not downright mean), the excellent
journalist and fiction writer Palmer D. (who sat at our
table but on the far side, beyond any hope of extended
conversation in such a noisy room), the politician Sylva
S. who represents our district in the state house, and a
number of others I met at the wedding or at other
functions but whose names and thumbnail IDs (as provided
back then in whispered form by Z) mostly didn't stick.
        One surprise attendee was our downstairs neighbor
(in 102) Ciro, who's recently been appointed 1511
building manager. He passed along some new info flatly
contradicting what we'd heard from Thuy about the sale
of the building. Min, the current owner, has assured
Ciro that the building isn't about to be sold and he
needn't be looking for a new apartment or even be
worrying he'll have to do so in the future. But then it
was hard to understand what Ciro was saying owing to his
strong accent and that same noisy room -- the band
playing nearby and everyone trying to talk over the

music -- Ciro was leaning down between Z and me -- and
in the end Z said she would call Min on Monday and try
to extract the straight scoop from him. If I caught
Ciro's drift, the bank might've uncovered some problems
while doing its appraisal -- but then I also thought I
heard him say he'd learned all this "last year" -- so
who knows.

        -- And now my phantom hour is almost up. No point
in starting into all those matters I cued up yesterday
for today's jyze. Instead I'll come back tomorrow with
the Halloween entry -- since NUT-wise we're still in the
30th -- and I'll also try to touch on the cued items
then (or some of them anyway -- given the fact that the
real cue, or queue, of such items is endless, as always
-- however trivial most of them may be -- so nothing to
be ashamed of in falling short on that task. Or at
least not in theory. In actuality, however, I should do
better and this belief of mine is almost always harder
to suppress than I'd like).

[+1]

    The view from the seventeenth floor! -- But with
one curtain closed and my angle on the other window so
oblique I can't make out much of what's beyond it. Of
course I know that scene out there quite well
regardless. But as for actual visibility, there's one
corner of the pyramid-like roof atop another big new
highrise hotel and a few scattered and unidentifiable
glinty lights (reflections of cross-street interior
lights from the bank-of-whatever-its-name-is-today, I
presume, on darkened windows of the stately old many-
starred hotel) and that's about it.
    But it's Halloween. Trick-or-treat night. And
down in the HQ triangle a radio station had set up a
stage and a couple of tents and driven its broadcasting
van onto the cobblestone/brick plaza and when I passed
through the area an on-the-air party was roaring along,
with DJ patter and music amplified horrifically and

crowds of costumed (intentionally or otherwise) and in some cases masked or face-painted celebrants gathered round and a group of dancing girls in scanty outfits huddled shivering and goosebumpy in a corner of the stage. And then after I hiked up to the "very high road" and hit midtown chain burgers for my lunch, another swarm of goblins, witches, and aliens came a-vamping in. -- All in all pretty tame, true. But not your ordinary night either. (And at downtown chain burgers, which I also visited for a cone, business was so slow they didn't bother to put the country music on the PA to drive away the so-called undesirables (it still works on me, I know that).)

I considered setting up shop in a bar, maybe some new place. A few candidates do exist in the area. But no. This right here is much more comfortable. And I was thinking I might need a nap, and that turned out to be the case. A forty-minute carpet-drooler (I'll call it, owing to the yucky silver-dollar-size spittle spot I produced) behind the conference table, with the chairs on the door side of the table tightly packed to screen my fallen body. Eek, a highly realistic corpse! They must take Halloween very seriously around here!

This year the holiday happens to coincide with Reformation Sunday, the 482nd anniversary of the rebellious presentation of the ninety-five "theses" by the highest Lutheran honcho of all time, the fanatical antisemitic eponym himself. I was reminded of this by an article announcing that Catholics and Protestants are finally burying the hatchet on some obscure doctrinal difference having to do with the Reformation. Fascinating stuff: to think people could still care so much about such things. Yet a thousand years from now this "rapprochement" might be seen as the only notable event of this entire benighted year. (And for Z and me obscure Catholic/Protestant psychological differences can matter a whole lot at certain times, so what am I really trying to say here?)

-- So I'll go with this instead: just today we applied our new tabs to the license plates on the Z-

mobile. They're a bright silver and they bear the
number 2000, and when we first saw that number displayed
on our back bumper it hit us both that we're really
almost there now. And for me as a jyzer one of the
biggest challenges ahead is finding a way to keep alert
to the fact that it's happening in a great many other
ways as well and not just taking them all for granted.

    We'll be house-sitting for Jess when the rollover
moment occurs, that much we now know with near certainty
(Jess will be traveling with her "parental unit," raging
granny included). Otherwise we're wide open. I'd like
to attend the big midnight celebration with fireworks at
the fairgrounds, but how wild will it be? Since brother
Rob works nearby, he might have the best choosh on it,
and he told me the other day he's concerned about gang
activities. That strikes me as overblown -- crime's
plummeting these days and the streets are unquestionably
much safer (but then the HQ triangle seems to be an
exception and the fairgrounds might be another one and I
shouldn't forget the fairgrounds-related riot I was
nearly caught up in at downtown chain burgers back in
July) -- but but but. We might be mulling this one all
the way to the evening of December 31st. Odds are we'll
just stay home (even if we're at Jess's) and watch the
celebrations on the tube and brace ourselves for
Y2Kalypse just in case (because this new wife of mine
sure does like to worry about every little thing and
always be prepared for the worst and -- what's more --
staying up much past nine or ten p.m. just isn't her
thing at all -- not even when the mygs are swarming).

    Today, a fine day featuring magnificent clouds
(like galleons! like cathedrals! like rollicking
badlands of the sky!), we drove up to the north end to
visit Olwen and Trent. For once the four of us didn't
play a board game but immediately joined hundreds of
other Sunday strollers for a "Manny Lake" promenade.
In honor of Halloween Z was wearing a "Ghouls will be
ghouls" button. I had more chances than usual to talk
one-on-one with Trent and truly enjoyed doing so, since
he's the only person I know at present with tastes

sufficiently twisted that he reads many of the same
periodicals I do. The main focus today was on the hokey
neoconnish claims of the so-called evolutionary
psychologists (to us, evolutionary psychos). Trent also
told a funny story about trying to obtain a bathroom
token at midtown chain burgers at a particularly
desperate moment ("imminently emergent in an explosive
way"). -- And in January Olwen will be reading her
poetry at a big corporate chain bookstore near the U.
I've already decided I'll make that occasion an
exception to my rule about avoiding all readings.

The cover of the indie weekly's special Halloween
issue shows a green Frankenstein's monster getting it on
with an Asian-looking female mummy, with the monster
seen mostly from behind as the mummy wraps her arms and
legs around him. To Z's eye the two looked a lot like
us. The monster "has your long face, your big shoulders
and little buns, he even has your hair when it gets back
to its normal state." Cheee, did she imagine I wouldn't
be flattered to be likened to a Hollywood idol?

-- And then there's that one-in-ten chance that
serious troubles might lie just ahead regarding "the
scrape." We're not doing too badly at suppressing it as
a topic for talk or open worry, but behind the masks,
well.... I'm goofing with her more than usual, I think,
possibly in hopes of keeping both of us distracted. Of
course to her my antics likely seem strained or phony
and probably just make matters worse. And then Friday
on the treadmill she misspoke while lobbying for my okay
to contact her former hotshot lover Bradley P. (not her
coworker Bradley L.), saying it would just be "a
platonic affair" when she meant to say "platonic
friendship." Hmm, a platonic affair, sounds a lot like
a series of friendly fucks. At any rate we're just
sliding by day to day as we await the results on "the
scrape," saying we'll hold off until after the facts
shake out to worry about anything truly alarming. This
isn't really her style, so she deserves a lot of credit
for going along with it regardless. (And I hereby vow
I'll do better at seeing to it she gets that credit.)

    For me the stoic approach and sliding by day-to-day
is pretty much the norm. I try to do most of my
worrying in private and if there's any way I can
suppress it without freaking anyone out in the process,
I go for it. Most of my adult life I've lived from
paycheck to paycheck and that's been good training for
this approach. (Just tonight I made a special trip up
here to fetch my fortnightly Jyzer Ink check so I'd be
able to pay my three rents tomorrow. But I still have
some cushion in savings -- about $2800 at the moment, or
enough to cover close to three months' expenses -- or
I'd be having a lot more trouble suppressing financial
worries.)

    -- A few words about the drugstore incident on
Friday. It fit right in with a well-established pattern
in which I'm suspected of shoplifting by overzealous
guards who alert on my big beat-up backpack and my
streets-compatible nightscoper way of dressing (and
being unshaven on many days). The guard at this store
has been shooting suspicious looks at me for weeks.
This time I picked up a copy of the "Millennial
Prophecy" issue of one of the newsweeklies and then was
poking around in the deodorant section while the guard
lurked nearby, going up and down parallel aisles and
peeking over display racks as if we were characters in
a French farce. I was conscious of him but trying to
act normally. But the deodorant I was looking for, the
unscented version of the cheapest brand, seems no longer
to be available and I was checking other unscented
types, lifting them from the shelves to read the labels,
even taking off the cap to sniff them when possible.
I'd just picked one of these brands to buy and was
leaving the area with a container of the chosen stuff in
my hand when the guard came rushing up. I surprised
him, walking right past him as if I hadn't noticed a
thing about his casing me, but he turned and followed
and called for me to stop just as I reached the juice
cooler (I was after my usual can of guava or peach juice
for the office). "I want my deodorant back!" he
demanded. "Huh? Why?" I still had it right in my hand

along with the magazine and showed him. "Here it is --
why do you want it?" "Not that one. The other one. I
saw what you did." "There is no other one." -- So then
we got into it a little, though not with raised voices.
I didn't like the way he was following me around, he
didn't care whether I liked it, so on and so forth.
Finally I offered to let him look in my pockets and
check my bag and he started backing off. -- And I went
further: told him I come in that store a lot, I'd like
him to know me, my name's Glen, I don't steal stuff, I'd
like to know his first name, let's shake on this -- and
we did. His name? Brad. As in Z's Bradleys.

     Maybe every six months or so something like this
happens. Sometimes I see red at the moment of being
accosted but I've never actually gone off on any of the
guards or taken retaliatory steps. Basically I'd say
this is because I sympathize with them: minimum-wage
workers doing a thankless job that can get nasty fast.
And for sure if I were in their shoes I'd be suspicious
of a guy like me. I might even take special pleasure in
nailing a Cawk oppressor (because the guards are almost
always Afrusan or Latusan these days, including this
Brad, who could be either or both).

     -- And time's just about up for now. But I can
still mention this: the storage place across the sound
is bumping up the rent for my unit by an additional six
percent, making the total increase for the year about
fourteen percent. And a computer company has settled a
lawsuit regarding a glitch in all their laptop models
going back fifteen years, and I happen to have one of
those models (it's seven or eight years old). The
settlement is for a billion dollars. Of course I'll
probably never see a penny of it, and in fact I've never
had any trouble with the laptop, although it's so slow
and ergonomically poor and the keyboard's so small I try
to avoid using it if at all possible. -- And my fear
has been confirmed: Juana, the Latina short-order cook
at midtown chain burgers who's so friendly and always
puts extra tomatoes on my double-stacks (to make up for
the cheese which I ask her to leave off) has quit. And

no one knows where she's gone. One guy who used to work
there thinks they (we USAns) might be deporting her.
"She's illegal, man. Didn't you know that? They all
are." (And he and I aren't doubly illegal? We and our
kind who both make the lousy rules and also break them?
At the international level I'm talking about. As in our
so-called proxy wars in Central America, Africa, the
Middle East, and Southeast Asia, just as examples.)

[+1]

     -- Could be I'm trying a variant of the old nap
routine as a way to resolve my sleep dilemma. Again
I've just crashed on the carpet here in the conference
room. During the commuting years I did this almost
every night for eighty minutes or so. "Magic-carpet
ride." But it probably won't work now as a long-term
solution. Back then I'd usually start the nap a little
after two a.m. when the chances of being disturbed were
close to zero. If I were to do regular naps now I'd
have to start at ten or eleven p.m. when the janitors
are still at work and guard patrols are more frequent
and reporters occasionally drop by the office. The past
two nights I've been lucky no one's come in.
     No news yet on "the scrape" results but otherwise
it's been an interesting series of days. Now we've
reached the second of the Days of the Dead -- All Souls
Day -- and it's also election day. Most of the results
for that are probably in already, but so far I've heard
nothing about any of the ones that matter to me and/or
the Z-wiff.
     The hot media news both yesterday and today, at
least before the election results started coming in:
another locally made jetliner crashed. It plummeted
into the sea, killing hundreds -- and this one's likely
to cause big trouble because the circumstances closely
resemble those of an earlier crash which took place
seven or eight years ago -- and that plane just happened
to roll down the assembly line in a northern Jyze City

burb right after the plane that went down yesterday.
And around here this is big, big news. It could portend
a crisis for our second-largest (and by far most
arrogant and dangerous and imperial) local industry.

Last night our local pro gridders played on Monday-
night football on national TV. When Z and I were at the
WOC the game was showing on at least half a dozen
screens but not drawing much attention -- probably
because most of the WOC's prime jock types were at the
game itself. If you stood just outside the front
entrance you could easily hear the roar of the crowd
live from the dome because the wind was blowing from
that direction.

(Also at the WOC, two new posters. One celebrates
the club's selection by a fitness magazine as among the
"top ten in the nation" (wotta crock!); the other warns
about a new wave of locker break-ins and says "the FBI
is on the case" (oh sure). Z asked at the front counter
about the break-ins and was told eleven have occurred
in the past few weeks, all but one in the men's locker
room. We've been advised to leave our valuables at the
front desk, but I never carry any with me into the WOC
(I leave them at the hideaway) with the exception of my
wedding ring and whatever pendant I'm wearing (it's been
mostly the "Jyze" one lately). Would anyone actually
want to steal this funky little ring? (Or big ring I
should say: funky chunky hunky ring.) I'm almost
curious enough to keep leaving it there just to see what
happens. -- But better not, right.)

Tonight I returned to the downtown drugstore for
the first time since the "shoplifting" incident and gave
security man Brad a big greeting. To my surprise he
smiled back almost as if I were a long-lost friend.
Then he followed me through the store in the usual way.
Gives him something to do, I guess. Or maybe he now
sees it as less risky than following someone else.
-- But in any case, if he ever suggests we swap jobs
just for the fun of it, I still intend to say no.

-- For a couple of days it seemed Jess and I would
be stepping out together on Thursday night. She had

asked Z to accompany her to the art museum's "USAn
Century" photography show but Z had other plans and
offered me as a substitute. Okay by me, as Z knew it
would be; but then Jess herself backed out. She feels
her new dog -- she onomatopoeically calls her "Erfa"
because her bark sounds just like that, with an odd
little uptick at the end as in the currently popular
version of preppy-speak -- Jess feels Erfa isn't ready
to be left alone those extra hours just yet. Erfa's not
a puppy either; she's a six-year-old stray from the
pound. So on the phone today we agreed to get together
to see a movie or have a drink sometime in the next week
or two. But I'm guessing it won't happen. It's all a
bit peculiar, because as much as we like each other --
and I think she really does like me -- we don't have
that much to talk about and things quickly turn awkward.
-- The latest twist in her breakup story, by the way, is
that Gwen's still trying to engineer a reconciliation --
she left a big bunch of flowers at Jess's front door
last week -- but Jess is still hanging tough. And I
learned the fate of their $2500 matched engagement
rings: Jess buried them near Kiba's grave in the
backyard. She has a marked dramatic streak just as Z
does and I suspect also a hidden dark side (maybe
violent) something like Lady V's. This is one reason I
think she and I might be able to break through that
awkwardness if we had a chance.

     Also I convinced Z we should agree to house-sit for
Jess at New Year's even though the number of days to be
covered has now expanded to six. Earlier today Z
bridled when Jess requested the extended stay. Later on
the phone with me she executed a quick one-eighty when I
reminded her Jess had come through for us in the crunch
in letting us use her place for the wedding despite the
Gwen breakup imbroglio. I greatly admire this quality Z
has of being able to rethink things on the move, as it
were, keeping her mind open. (On the matter of where to
go for Thanksgiving I left it up to her to decide what
we'll do, and she's decided we'll spend most of it with
the D-clan. It seems to me we've been slighting Wei

and Alison a bit too much lately and here we are doing
it again, asking them to understand our needs after we'd
already agreed to join them for Thanksgiving dinner.
-- But evidently the situation's grim with Mr. D.
Aida's going hysterical over it at times, Z says, and
this is reminding Z of her own father's final months and
weeks, about which she's felt badly ever since because
she chose not to spend more time with him at what turned
out to be the end, although she had no way in advance to
know it would be that. And Mr. D has long been a kind
of surrogate father for her. June says the tumor is
visible on his cheek and neck and Z is still assuming
this is why he and Mrs. D didn't attend our reception
and it seems to have helped her overcome most of her
disappointment regarding that.)

[+1]

   -- It's last night all over again. Same chair,
same hour, same computer on a cart at my back (Jyzer
Ink's computer, the one I'm most nervous about for Y2K
reasons). I'm even wearing the same jeans and hickory-
striped workshirt and sporting the same humongous pimple
on my lower left cheek (which I don't think I mentioned
yesterday): it's riding my jawbone like a machine-gun
bubble on an old B-24 fuselage. I knew I shouldn't have
gorged on those bowls of leftover Halloween chocolate.
And I've just risen from another short early winter's
nap -- an immaculate nondrooler this time.
   When I arrived home last night Z was still up,
unable to sleep, and stayed that way for another ninety
minutes. The election results were what did it. "The
city council is all white people now," she groaned --
actually not true since one holdover is Afrusan, but
close enough. Three of the four moderately liberal
Eurusans supported by downtown corporate forces won.
The three "candidates of color" Z backed -- two Asiusan
men and a radic-lib Afrusan woman -- all lost. But the
council will still lean more to the left than it did, I

believe, and I don't foresee any major disasters there.
Statewide, though, the antigovernment initiative won
big, meaning all tax increases at every level of
government must be put to a popular vote (this is
assuming the proposition measures up constitutionally)
and government services will undergo significant
cutbacks because of revenue lost through reduction of
car-registration fees to a flat thirty bucks per
vehicle. In the absence of a state income tax the
registration fees were an important source of funds and
a relatively progressive form of tax.

   -- Old Marcus, the WOC's resident token Afrusan
right-winger, was chortling over all this. In his view
the "shake-up" caused by passage of the antigovernment
initiative will of course be highly positive. His own
daughter's likely to lose her government job; he
couldn't resist calling her immediately with an "I told
you so." "I warned her she should get involved if she
didn't want it to win!" He seemed surprised I wasn't
more upset than I was. I talked pendulums and tides
rather than risk spiraling off into another political
donnybrook with him. But for the state as a whole I
think the results could be even more damaging than those
of the big antitax initiative in the megastate to the
south some twenty years ago.

   And today was newsy in other ways. A man "went
postal" in Z's old hood, shooting up a business office,
killing at least two and wounding several others, and
for most of the day it was the lead item on the national
news. The northern half of Jyze City was in a state of
siege with the gunman remaining on the loose for several
hours. Z herself was affected: she was responsible for
making sure no utility crews went into the locked-down
area. -- When I heard the first report on the radio
while I was still in bed this afternoon, my reflex
thought was that Jess had freaked out.

   Meanwhile the typical November storms are rolling
in right on schedule. It's rainy, it's cold, it's dark,
it's blowy. And I'm still waiting for the arrival of
the new check card that was supposedly mailed out a week

ago (my old one has expired as of October 31st). And I
learned from the HQ business paper that the cops will
be doing their best to protect us valiant and hard-
working HQ business owners during the WTO meeting (I
hadn't realized it, but the opening ceremonies will be
held at the huge new exhibition hall between the doomed
old dome and the brand-new luxury baseball stadium).
And this morning I again crashed out on Z -- did I
start crowing too soon about my latest studly revival?
-- and now she's launching a campaign for me to get
more sleep on a regular basis. But it also feels like
punishment, this campaign, or at least a threat of it:
she'll withhold herself, no pillow talk but also no
loving until I can be fully into it. She's definitely
capable of an act so dastardly -- but then I am too
(well...maybe). Meanwhile I'm trying to sweet-talk her
into being more relaxed about the occasional friction
naturally arising from our extreme owl/lark conflict.
    (For the past couple of pages here I've been
nibbling from a bag of microwave popcorn. It's the
first one I've nuked up in years, since the scope firm
changed offices. Greasy yellow left hand. Crumbs. Now
must clean up the table before I go. Fingerprints all
over the place. Carpet's a mess too, I see. Therefore
must shut down this jyze a few minutes early.)

25

    Get to start off with a hit of good news. Z called
a while ago and said she'd talked with Doc Karen and the
tests showed nothing wrong with her. "They couldn't
find anything." But the doc is still concerned and
wants Z to see a specialist and possibly undergo a full

D&C just to be sure nothing's there except for an
"unusually youthful uterus." "So maybe," I said, "it
started swelling up in anticipation the day we met, and
it's stayed that way ever since?" "That's exactly
right!" she said. "That's why I want to have a second
opinion from Lorraine before I let them go in there and
do a heavy-duty scrape." -- Because, well, no one's
saying mainstream medicine's a complete and total scam
or anything like that, but we do want to keep in mind
its built-in economic incentive to foist on patients the
maximum possible number of tests and prescriptions and
surgeries and hospital stays (and much, much more!).

    -- And here I still sit at home, naked as the day I
was born (but cleaned off some compared with back then,
most likely, although also considerably hairier pretty
much from top to bottom, at least judging from the baby
pix I've seen). And yet I'm anxious to get going. It's
after seven p.m. already -- 7:03. (If I try to picture
a naked Cawk man sprawled in a black armchair under a
glowing reading lamp, J-stick in hand and J-book in lap,
I come up with nothing that's not ludicrous.) It's
artwalk day and I'd thought of trying to squeeze out a
few pages in one of the studio clusters near the
hideaway. Clearly that's a scrub now. I reveled too
long in catchup reading and altered-card touch-up (and
also did a new one showing a certain famously lippy rock
star stretched out prone on a bed, head raised; he's
peering up at the camera and asking, "Hey Boss, okay if
I serve you in a sultry way?" A footnote says, "See
'serve' clause in GAZ & ZAG wedding vows").

    For news there's the casualty count from the big
typhoon in India (maybe ten thousand dead, more than a
million homeless) and the aftermath of our own little
unrandom mass shooting yesterday right here in J-town
(the perp is still at large), not to mention the ongoing
reverbs from the election. And there's Mad Mitch's
prediction: on Vets Day one week from today -- which is
to say the last day of this J-week -- a powerful
earthquake just off the coast will cause a tsunami to
roll in through our harbor and inundate the lowest-lying

portion of the city, meaning the area where the WOC is located, along with my hideaway and the ORB and also Z's office. How does he know this? A girlfriend of his saw it first in a dream; then he mentioned it to certain "alien spirits" he keeps in touch with and they said it all checks out. (The gang at the WOC is afraid Mitch is losing it for real, i.e., whatever little he had left of it. Even his fellow shrapnel-carrying vet Marcus -- both of them one-eyed as well -- says he's afraid of what Mitch might do. The man is into guns in a big way. He's also 285 pounds and undoubtedly the strongest man at the WOC if not in the entire city. I run into him from time to time wandering around the Asian quarter, where he lives in an SRO hotel room (sort of like a monstrously beefed-up Travis B., the right-wing nutcase in "Taxi Driver"). A few weeks ago I invited him up to check out the hideaway, but that was before I realized how truly loony he is. Supposedly any day now he'll be bringing me a copy of a physics paper he wrote which he insists cracks the unified-field problem.)

This morning Z came back into the bedroom shortly after getting up (that is, shortly after I'd gone to bed) and called me a genius. She'd written a card to Wei and Alison trying to explain why she pulled the rug out from under our plan to do Thanksgiving together at their place. On my first reading it sounded a bit raw, as if she were miffed at them for being hurt or upset by our withdrawal. So I stayed up an extra thirty minutes and wrote an alternative message for her to send them, or at least to refer to in doing a rewrite of her own. And she did do a rewrite, coming up with a whole new card which she proceeded to show me. She thinks I'm a whiz at southern USAn "graciousness," or in other words knowing the proper manners of the ruling class. Usually she doesn't speak so highly of this alleged trait, but today she did. It's nice to think she believes her husband can be good for something in addition to top-of-the-line rutting: that's about the best spin I can put on it.

The other bit of news is that Jess is planning a

final meeting with Gwen at which she'll return her ring
(after digging it back up from its backyard grave) and
also repay some equity she's now conceding Gwen has in
the house. Today she asked Z: "Do you think it would be
good to schedule it for the fifth anniversary of the day
she ran off with the other woman?" (Would anyone be
surprised if this final meeting turned into a dramatic
reconciliation? Not me or Z.) -- And regarding our
agreement to house-sit for all six days leading up to
the rollover, Z said, "She knows you're her bud." (I
hope so. I'd like to get closer to Jess. But I still
doubt it'll happen.) -- And the three of us will be
doing dinner and a movie together next Friday, which is
also the day, according to Steve from the WOC (citing
Mad Mitch), when the earthquake/tsunami will hit. My
meeting Jess alone is out, at least for now.
    -- Put on some clothes, that's what I'll do, and
then set off down the hill. Z's attending some sort of
city political meeting tonight -- exactly what's
involved I don't know, but it's going down at one of the
big hotels and she's wearing her best exec-style power
pantsuit for the occasion. (And yesterday's J-town
afternoon paper ran a letter written by the Zonker-like
landlord who lives a block north of us, Matt B.,
defending the dot-com's lease of the old marine hospital
a/k/a the DC castle. It's not half bad. From a
landlord's point of view he scores some good points.
But then why would a landlord oppose gentrification in
his own neighborhood if it leads to vastly increased
property values and enables him to charge much higher
rent? It's a given. And he fails to grapple with a
number of important social-justice issues -- that's also
a given for someone with his quasi-libertarian views.)

*   *

    In follow-up I want to mention it's not a good
night for standing in line waiting for a bed at one of
the local missions. Cold. We're moving into the season
in which clear days usually mean cold nights. (But this
was an unexpected clear day, sunny, after a forecast of
rain and gloom, and thus especially fine as long as the

502

sun was up.) A double line was running down around the
corner at the first mission I walked by, bedraggled,
bundled-up folks, downcast eyes, the kind of scene that
makes you think if only the tube would show footage of
such deprivation on a regular basis, public shame and
outrage would spur a prompt fix. Ha! A flashing
reflexive thought, utterly absurd, that's correct.
-- And a similar scene up in the glare at the muni
plaza, even longer lines awaiting a ladel or two of
whatever they were serving at the soup kitchen at eight
p.m., and likewise at the mission down across from the
ORB, except there the ladelings take place indoors and
are preceded by a bout of religious indoctrination and
thus, although people can eat in relative comfort, the
mission serves far fewer meals. Or so I'm told.

Meanwhile I notice the storms of November have
stripped completely bare the row of maples in front of
the Natusan center, so splendidly colorful just a week
ago. And the mess left by razing the homeless
encampments down in "the jungle/rez" has been cleaned
up; even the yellow no-trespassing tape is gone. Is
this part of the Potemkin-like beautification campaign
for the WTO gathering? That's what everyone's saying.
Elsewhere you see similar signs the city is sprucing
itself up for the visiting dignitaries. And if this
comes at a high cost to certain beleaguered segments of
the local population, well, that's life in the naked --
yeah. Spokespersons for the homeless warn of upcoming
"street sweeps" like those preceding other world-class
media events held here in the past decade or two (parts
of a couple of which sweeps I witnessed firsthand). A
police captain is quoted as saying that if the jails
become full to bursting at such times it's not because
anyone's being targeted but simply because a lot more
cops are on the streets making arrests. (So does this
mean they're on the streets making arrests in all those
north-end gated communities? I don't think so.)

And a final note just for the helluvit: the
billboard at the foot of the south-hill high bridge has
made its monthly metamorphosis; now it's an ad for milk.

[The Jyze Millennium, Part I]

"Want strong bones?" That's the query.

[+2]

     It's early in a Saturday evening and we're on a
used-book-buying mission up at the far-north arcade.
"It's my ideal date," Z assured me. But it turns out
the sale isn't storewide after all -- we both misread
the flyer -- but rather the kind in which thousands of
sale books are laid out on tabletops pretty much at
random. If you're looking for anything in particular,
forget it.
     At this moment she's off hunting for something
fairly general: children's books that might make good
Christmas presents. We already did dinner over in the
restaurant section of this vast unpartitioned space --
it's all on one floor -- and now I've moved to a quieter
spot well past the sale area, just ten feet or so from
the giant floor chessboard (the chess pieces themselves
-- about a third human size -- conspicuously absent).
Judging from a sign standing by my elbow, this table on
which I'm jyzing is where the "community guestbook" is
usually located. But it's nowhere in sight. Did
someone rip it off? (We are talking the burbs here.
We're several miles north of the city limits. Best to
keep a close eye on our possessions in this wasteland.)
     Got me a full hour to trip the jyze fantastic.
That's the Z-woman's promise.
                          *
     -- A larger table just opened up. It's over behind
the elevator shaft and stairwell on a kind of promontory,
right by a wall of two-foot-square windows looking down
on the jam-packed parking lot and the ceaseless four-
lane-highway traffic half a block to the south. -- And
on the other side of the wrought-iron railings
surrounding the stairwell, maybe fifty feet away,
throngs of bargain-hunters are pawing over those same
tablefuls of bargain books.
     Just as we were sitting down at that first table, a

504

woman Z hadn't seen in "at least ten years" came
bustling up. She had been a classmate at some sort of
weeklong training conference. "Why is it they recognize
me and I don't recognize them?" Z asked me afterwards.
It's true it happens a lot. She thinks her memory must
be failing, but I say it probably happens for the same
reason Marie T. was so struck by her and wanted to
sculpt her: in looks and otherwise she's one of a kind.
"Extremely striking." "Memorable." She always pooh-
poohs me when I say such things to her but usually not
all that strenuously. She knows I speak the truth.

Today she's taking the lead on lust. That's
because she thinks it's Sadie Hawkins Day. I suspect
she's confused it with Guy Fawkes Day, which is what it
really is, but who wants to complain? And besides,
Sadie Hawkins Day I'm pretty sure falls later this
month, so that means we can have two such days almost
back to back -- not to mention belly to belly.

As we walked in here from the parking lot I said
something about coming up with an "alt-romance origin
myth" in honor of this (bonus) Sadie Hawkins Day, one in
which she was the pursuer and I was the pursued, and she
whooped, "Oh yeah, baby, what I want is a vagina-ful of
this!" -- and grabbed my crotch. No one was around at
the time, but if the mall's bank of security screens
ever has human monitors they might find it worth a
replay or two -- the shocked look on my face especially.

-- And the PA has just declared this is singles
night and dancing will be part of it (as we knew), but
if you're married -- that's us! -- you're barred from
the dancefloor "unless you take off your wedding ring
first." (In fact as of tonight we're six weeks hitched.
And we're both still wearing our rings.) (And it's also
Midautumn's Night, I should note, exactly halfway
between the equinox and the solstice.)

Warm day, a little rainy and gusty. A fine evening
to be indoors in a happening joint like this. And yes,
I'm serious. Some merry zydeco playing right now. Hum
of many voices. Dinnish clink of glasses and silverware.
"Echolalia" to beat the band -- just as at the big

Filusan dinner at the hotel last week, or close to it anyway.

The banner headline news: court declares our local software behemoth to be a monopoly. This is the major Justice Department antitrust case that's been in the works for a couple of years. Over that time the local buzz about it has of course been substantial. We're talking about the home team here. The main engine of the local boom, the prime incubator of our zillionaires. "CEO is defiant" (the subhed). Will the company be broken up? Will its stock crash and all those plutocrats deflate into paupers? Not too likely -- but dire consequences are possible. Just as an example: a large number of local "smallholders" could be badly hurt, and our friend Betty and her daughter Kat are two of them: Betty's invested most of the funds intended to pay Kat's college costs in that same stock.

First the local baseball megahero asks for a trade, next a second locally made airplane falls into the sea, now the local tech genius is declared to be a crook. What next? (We hope what's next is the WTO comes to town and is chased out immediately by tens of thousands of protesters. And then when the millennium rolls over, all computers owned by USAns making upwards of ten times the median U.S. income freeze for all perpetuity.)

Well, but never mind. Such absurd adolescent fantasies. And yes, I'd like to indulge in more of same regarding the gene-splicers, the bomber-makers, the evolutionary psychos -- whole hosts of others! -- but no. Best to stick with celebrating the TJM program here. (So maybe just an occasional political digression to keep things grounded? Well all right then!)

-- And now pressure. "How much longer?" Z's wondering. She's ba-a-a-ck! Already! And she's hot to boogie. The woman sure does like to shake that thing. And for sure I don't want her to go do a Sadie Hawkins grope, however mistimed, on someone else. -- But perhaps just a little more jyze here first (as she drags over a big armchair from twenty feet away after another lady commandeered the one she, Z, used before and I let

the lady get away with it because I thought Z wouldn't
be wanting it again). And she says: "I know I'm a
little early, sweetheart. You've still got six minutes.
That's what that clock over there says."

First real quick item, she's made an appointment
with a gynecologist for the day after Thanksgiving. So
the tension regarding the state of her conjugal zone
will be lasting a while longer. And my bank is now
admitting my new check card is probably "lost in the
mail" and they're saying they'll send me another one and
it should arrive in a couple of weeks. And so for that
time I'll be depending on Z for cash -- and that's fine,
it's one more way it's good to have a mate and I enjoy
having things like this to point out to her during her
not infrequent agnostic moments regarding marriage
(though of course she's usually just playing).

-- And we're at the limit. As the actual dancing
and the actual live music get underway and the crowd is
seriously growing and Z's shaking that same thing right
now about a foot from my nose, with her arms undulating
above her head -- "Ooh baby, come on! Let's get it on!"

It's a Midautumn Night's Dream!

[+2]

Danged if I'm not stretched out in and well beyond
my armchair at the hideaway.

What's happening right now? The hot topic
everywhere I go is still the software decision, the
judge's "ruling of fact." What does it mean? Nobody
really knows, but the way the outside world sees it, our
town is suddenly taking its lumps. A story in the far-
coast paper delivered to our door late last night says
it straight out in the headline: "High-Flying Jyze City
Comes Back to Earth." The rest of the tech world -- the
competition -- is chortling, of course, but in my view
probably too soon. The deeper import of the decision
may be that our national rulers have decided to rein in
the internet and its running dogs, including the

507

employers of a good many of those out-of-town chortlers.

   In a sense the internet is causing the grand
cultural shake-up promised by the sixties (and many of
its high-stakes players seem to see it exactly that
way). The suggestion now is that the old establishment
will redeploy the old way of running the country and
also the world in an effort to quash these upstarts who
are threatening their power. I admit I'm seeing things
a bit this way myself. It's near coast versus far
coast, new ways versus old.

   More than ever it's easy to see now how those
villainous antiprogress people (as mainstream culture
painted those of us who opposed building ever more
freeways and highrises and malls, say, or producing ever
more processed food and fancy consumer goods) -- easy to
see they/we had some legitimate points. What does it
mean now to be in favor of progress? Who's really the
"most progressive" candidate? The one who favors gene-
splicing, cloning, the merging of human and computer
"consciousness"?

   These are among the hottest issues of our time.
They've been hot for years and they'll probably stay
that way for many more. Is it progressive to favor
ever-expanding production of material goods? So on and
so forth. -- Where do we go from here? How do we make
sure we can keep going at all? How do we stop the
headlong race to the abyss?

   All right, enough of that. Again. For now.
Because these things matter!

   -- And our local world is still trying to come to
grips with the meaning of the statewide antigovernment
initiative. What services will be cut? Screams and
howls of pain -- of incomprehension. J-town bus service,
to be cut by a third. Ferry sailings, the same or more.
Inspections of industrial plants, restaurant kitchens,
all to be deeply cut. It's a disaster but the true
extent of it is only beginning to reveal itself. An
election must be held every time government at any level
proposes levying or increasing a tax (and the same for
fees, no matter how trivial -- to charge a nickel more

for a school lunch, the electorate must be consulted).
And elections are expensive! -- A great victory for
the right wing, the antigovernment libertarians as well
as the out-and-out reactionaries.

        -- Okay, enough for that too. The pendulum swings,
a step forward and a step back, the majority rules and
in this state the majority is even Cawkier than in the
country as a whole and the Cawk majority everywhere is
feeling threatened and will be feeling more and more
threatened as its relative size shrinks. It's riddled
with guilt over its centuries of racist and militaristic
expansionist power-mongering and it fears that
retribution (well deserved!) is headed its way if it
doesn't crack down even harder. How can this Cawk
backlash be dealt with? At this point it seems no one's
even thinking about the question.

                        *   *

        Following up in the black armchair at home, I'll
start with the new red liner bag tucked inside my
backpack. Z gave it to me thinking it might be close
to what I was looking for months ago to help protect J-
books and other valuable items from water damage. And
it is! I think it was originally the cover for a
sleeping bag. Maybe it's not waterproof but it seems to
be water-repellent enough. A bright rayon, almost
silken: it reminds me of a colorful kimono liner or a
teddy, some sort of sexy undergarment.

        Meanwhile Z and I have all kinds of plans.
Thursday, Vets Day -- assuming Mad Mitch's earthquake/
tsunami doesn't hit before then -- we'll be seeing the
Japanese anime' film "Princess Mononoke" with Betty and
Kat (it appears we'll be skipping the Polish filmfest
this year). Saturday it's Aida's birthday party, Sunday
it's dinner and a movie (not Polish) with Jess. And the
following days and weeks all the way to the rollover are
equally crowded if not more so. (At one point we were
planning to see my man Henry F. -- a/k/a Taj -- at a
jazz club with Gerry and Leola but for complex reasons
that had to be canceled.)

        I was stung a little bit by Z's reply when I told

her, after she asked, that no, I didn't find the
invitation Aida sent out for her birthday party all that
cute (it bore a photo of Aida at age four or five in a
formal white dress). "Isn't it something," Z said, "the
way the two of you go after each other." Huh? My jaw
dropped the requisite big-jawed-Norski foot. Shock.
For one thing: how is it Aida's been going after me?
Lately, I mean. Is there perhaps something Z hasn't
told me about? She danced away from my inquiries about
this. But I did tell her I don't appreciate her
treating the matter as being symmetrical after all the
grief Aida's given us -- both of us -- over the past two
years plus. But Z, it's clear, no longer wants to look
at things that way; one of her means of keeping Aida as
her best friend will be to postulate a flat-out
incompatibility, equal on both sides, between Aida and
me; it's as simple as that. And upon reflection I've
decided I can live with it. As I've done a couple of
times before -- and in the end failed at it, obviously
-- I'm vowing to myself to keep any problems I have
with Aida to, yes, myself.
     -- And I'd better add this: I need to be reminding
myself that for Aida it's a time of great stress because
of her father's illness. Only a few days ago did she
hear him acknowledge for the first time that he knows
what's wrong and give it a name: lymphoma. This was at
a session with a Chinese doctor whose name Z had
obtained for him from Lorraine, her naturopath. This
family emergency no doubt also has a lot to do with the
slow pace and bumpiness of Aida's relationship with
Kirk. -- But Z thinks otherwise; in her view that's
just the way the two of them are, not inclined to jump
into things with both feet (unlike us -- as she says now
-- although back in our early days I had to do a lot of
persuading to get her to make even the tiniest of leaps;
and at the same time Aida was trying to talk her into
leaping in the opposite direction: away from the jyzer).
     At work Z's been involved in a number of "testing
incidents" with the incorrigible Gloria G. As Z views
it, unconsciously she may have agreed to become Gloria's

supervisor "to see if I've finally learned how to handle
the flash-fire Filipina temperament." (She meant the
one in herself too, I'm pretty sure, but she didn't come
right out and say so and I didn't push it, sensing she
might be close to a flash-fire moment of her own
regarding the Aida issue; and no one who knows Aida even
slightly would deny she too has that same kind of
temperament. -- Not that we're stereotyping Filipinas
here. Not a bit of it! We're making observations about
individual character and we're informed in doing so by
experience and knowledge of cultural differences and
their many forms of expression, yes we are. Right, Z-
goose? As with your own plentiful insights regarding
Norskis and Cawks and male-persons and race-blind
suburban upper-middle-class environmental and feminist
persons of colonial-settler pinkness, yes? -- Ooh, the
lenses, the lenses, we must never forget to click the
lenses into place!) (And I do mean that sincerely, yes.
And I believe she knows this and appreciates it.)

[+2]

    Starting out this one behind a head-high wall of
banker boxes stacked atop the conference-room table.
It's early and people are still coming in and out of the
scope office and this makes me a little uneasy.
Technically I suppose I shouldn't be jyzing here. As an
"independent contractor" I have no rights or at least
none of the type of rights employees have -- or should I
say "privileges" instead of "rights"? Either way I
ain't got many -- except de facto, when no one's around
to care what I do. And fortunately that's most of the
time.
    Owing to the Vets Day holiday tomorrow, grand jury
is meeting only once this week and so I'm hoping I'll
have less work than usual for a heavy week. But I can't
be sure about this until tomorrow night when I'll learn
whether Naomi was able to come up with some other job
for tomorrow (holiday or no, many people will be

working). Meanwhile Z and I are already committed to
see "Mononoke" tomorrow afternoon with Betty and Kat,
substantially reducing my potential scoping time, and
therefore I'll need to get a lot done tonight just in
case Naomi lands a big job for tomorrow. And that means
I can't go for very long with the jyze here. (But
that's all right, because I can carry on with it at home
later and maybe again tomorrow.)

On the jazz station's hourly news headlines I heard
that in a speech today the president of the USA said he
foresees no major Y2K problems occurring on January 1 or
for that matter at any time. We're being soothed and
calmed and reassured. No panic please! He does allow
as how some minor problems may occur -- little glitches
here and there. Z, meanwhile, as our designated tsuri
(worrier), is moving ahead on preparing a basic
emergency stash, "just in case." Our many flashlights
are ready to go and we're working on the radios and the
cans of tuna and the water jugs, of which she wants to
have a dozen or more in place. Last weekend I bought a
couple of gallon jugs of drinking water at the corporate
supermarket for eighty cents apiece (the shelves were
nearly bare). This was at her behest, but I felt bad
about it anyway and afterwards convinced her we can
store tap water in my empty plastic gallon milk jugs for
the rest of the stash. After all, she's part of the
utility that supplies this city and much of the
surrounding metro area with water; does she not think
it's good enough for her and me even in an emergency?

Another news headline passed along a "D.C. sources"
leak that the feds are definitely seeking to break up
our software behemoth. (I was amused by a tidbit in the
Jyze City morning paper's main gossip column about the
behemoth's CEO, who also happens to be the world's
richest man, stopping by for a burger at the fast-food
joint I sometimes visit myself just half a block from
brother Rob's bookstore. While a reporter conducted an
interview with the CEO in a booth there, a panhandler
passing by outside recognized plutocrat #1 and pressed
himself against the window and demanded spare change --

without success, I'm sure. Could be the panhandler's in jail now and soon will be headed up the river, possibly for life. Or then again he might be well on his way to becoming a national celebrity with a million-dollar book deal and now they're looking for a suitable ghostwriter. (If they call me I'll have to decline and explain that jyze already has me locked into an exclusive lifetime contract.)

It's the 10th. Today is Aida's actual birthday, I learned from Z, who had lunch with her. Aida wants us to arrive a little early for the party on Saturday, Z said, so I can move some furniture around for her. "What about Kirk?" I asked. "Isn't he into heavy lifting?" "I'm not even sure he's coming," she said. Bizarre. What kind of romance is this? -- But I'm glad my own romance is going well enough in its early postnup stage that the Z-wiff can volunteer the G-hub's services in such a matter without first asking him -- yes I am. Because in the long run this faith of hers that she can count on me will surely work to our advantage.

Last night Z learned her mother will soon be facing cataract operations on both eyes. Z will have to pick up the portion of the cost not covered by Medicare. Of more immediate concern to her, there's no one to accompany Mama E to the doctor's office for the operations. She, Z, doesn't want to ask the utterly unreliable Tito to do it. She wishes she could go herself and feels guilty she can't; but she's just not in a position financially or temporally to be making frequent four-thousand-mile round trips. This will be tearing at her in the future. She apologizes to me: "You didn't know you'd be marrying someone who has her mother as a dependent." But that's not true; I did know. She told me all about it. And I assured her then I could handle it and I still believe that. -- Z's also saying now she might accompany me to Mentoka/Centropolis next spring after all. She promised her mother we'd be visiting "as soon as we can" to celebrate the marriage with her and this would be the perfect opportunity. But Mama E has also said she'd be moving out here next year,

and now she might be backing out on that or trying to
delay it for a while; we just don't know. But she's
said she'll be thinking about what she wants to do and
will fill us in on her decision by the end of the year.
     What else? Well, this morning one of the vanity
lightbulbs in the bathroom exploded as Z toweled off
after her shower, possibly just because she was looking
so good today. Luckily she wasn't hurt. And last night
she came in muttering because the lock for the garage
"pedestrian door" wasn't working, the building's lobby
door wasn't closing properly, and the dumpsters were
overflowing again. She called Min and left a message
reporting all this and afterwards said, "I thought I did
quite well at not sounding furious." She's well aware I
still feel it's not a good idea to be complaining so
much. But at this point it probably doesn't matter a
whole lot whether she does or not. Any day now we
should learn whether the building's been sold. (And if
it has been and it's not condoizing immediately, we'll
probably be hit with the big rent increase we've been
dreading for months.)
     In less than three weeks the WTO shindig gets
underway. Preparations are mounting at a rapid clip.
The president himself (USAn) will be popping in during
the conference to deliver a speech. Several supreme
leaders of other nations will also be showing up,
possibly including the charismatic cigar-chomping Cuban
so-called "El Caudillo." Hospitals are being readied in
case of terrorist attacks involving weapons of mass
destruction, whether gas or bio or high explosives or
even a "suitcase nuke." ("Admittedly the chances of any
such incident happening are quite small," says a member
of the event committee, "but they are real.")
     And yesterday, the 9th, was the tenth anniversary
of the crumbling of the Berlin Wall and, symbolically,
the collapse of the Eastern Bloc and the supposed
triumph of the West in the Cold War. It didn't draw the
kind of play it might've. Why is this? Another big
mystery. Is it that the Cold War was largely a sham all
along and everyone's always known it? Is it that the

U.S. is secretly ashamed of its consequent "sole
superpower" status and what it's making of it? -- Is it
that we all expected, consciously or otherwise, that
things would be wonderful if only those Bad Guy Commies
would go away but then when they did, nothing much
changed in most of the rest of the world? Is it bad
conscience because deep down we know those Evil Reds
were actually trying to do something admirable and our
own antagonism to them played a big part in their being
unable to do it and helped lead to massive amounts of
misery and millions of deaths, many of them at the hands
of our own armed forces in remote countries such as
Korea and Vietnam and Iraq? Is it because deep down we
know we won the battle at the cost of losing the war --
making all but inevitable the uninhabitability of the
earth for human beings? (From militarization,
overproduction, nuclearization, overpopulation -- but
stop the list right there because it's close to endless
and I've just gotta get back to the scoping -- must do
my bit to keep those wheels of USAn justice turning.)

[+1]

      A slight change in plans. Now it's a day later and
jyze is once again ready to go at it in the very same
spot. The big stack of banker boxes is gone but
everything else seems about the same. Here's J. Ink's
trusty old computer resting on its shaky cart in the
corner under the spreading branches, none looking
particularly healthy, of a six-foot-tall potted tree.
At the far end of the room, tilted upward at a jaunty
angle on its tripod, stands the red telescope with which
the day crew checks out the fleshly correlatives
displayed on the rooftops of nearby shorter buildings
during the warmer months (focusing mainly on male FCs,
presumably, since the day crew is, by firmwide consensus,
composed entirely of straight women and gay men) (I used
to be the one known het-male exception, back before I
was induced -- forced -- to go independent contractor).

It's rainy and blowy out there. Annoying weather
to be walking around in. Extremely puddly. An umbrella
does you little good and the same goes for boots.
(Yesterday afternoon about three o'clock, I want to
note, it was about as dark as I've ever seen it in this
town during daylight hours. In many places the
streetlights came on.) -- But wet and wild though it's
been and is, Mad Mitch's earthquake and tsunami have not
come to pass. Looks like Mitch joins the honorary
"Nasty-doom-us list" of failed millennial prophets.

   Just fifty days until the rollover. We're starting
to hear more about the parties and celebrations planned
for here and around the world. Z brought home a
pamphlet listing various events scheduled around town
for the final week of December. The mayor has announced
a celebration in which huge wood-and-paper "sculptures"
will be burned -- supposedly something truly spectacular
befitting J-town's stature as a leading arts city, an
imaginative, cutting-edge kind of place. (Apparently
it's artwork specially created for the occasion. Beyond
this little's known so far. It would appear they're
trying to maintain or build suspense about it.)

   But never mind all that for now. Fifty days,
surely there'll be plenty of time to catch up on such
things. And in the eighteen of those days remaining
until the WTO convenes I should be able to do at least
minimal justice to the preliminaries for that particular
event. And in the two weeks remaining until
Thanksgiving, enough time for a few burblings about
turkey day but of course. (And I shouldn't leave
Christmas off the list. Day before yesterday I saw my
first Christmas tree of the season. It was a miniature
live one decorated with dangling golden hearts and it
was slowly spinning atop a turntable in the window of a
midtown flower shop occupying a very small storefront at
the foot of a very tall building. And just today at my
usual midtown drugstore I heard my first canned
Christmas music -- and Brad the security guard was again
nowhere in sight. Has he perhaps been let go for not
making his pinch quota? If he'd succeeded in nailing me

would he still have a job?)

     Earlier this afternoon we actually did make it out
to see "Princess Mononoke." This was at a fancy new
multiplex up on the fifth or sixth floor of a recently
opened shopping arcade on the main street -- "glitz
strip" -- in the downtown "retail core." So I can try
to say something about all that too -- when I'm back in
203. Because it's bus time right now. Can't dawdle
another second.

*   *

     -- Four a.m. just blinked in on the radio digi-
clock. Off with their news! Now a steady tapping of
rain but I note the wind's died down. And I have to
risk alienating Z to do this, so the jyzeburst won't be
long and it won't follow any secondary bursts very far.
"Hydes of Jyze" -- the sign -- is not up.

     Twenty minutes ago she wandered out to the kitchen
to toast herself a waffle. She has the sniffles and is
surprised I haven't succumbed to them yet myself (as am
I). I in turn was surprised to see she was wearing
"unners," which she usually does in bed only when she's
trying to convey the message she's sexually unavailable,
on most occasions because of either "prodomo" tinglings
or an actual Big H outbreak. But I guess this time it's
because of the cold or flu or whatever it is. -- And
she was muttering about a "boys versus girls" thing
developing at the office over the question of who does
and who doesn't get to work overtime. This is arising
out of her conflicts with Gloria G., who wants more
overtime and is accustomed to having plenty of it but is
being denied it now on Dale's orders, probably because
of the anticipated budget shortfall owing to the victory
of the antigovernment initiative (though it may just be
a matter of an overspent division budget). Now Z's
discovered that several division males have been
approved for overtime at the same function which Gloria
wanted to work. Z suspects the males are gaining
approval either because of an old-boy network ("though
probably the unconscious type") or a tendency to favor
"breadwinners." -- But after a while I had to remind

517

her a second time I was hoping to get down with the jyze
for a bit before bedtime.

       She also said she might need to see Lorraine again.
She suspects her insomnia thing is coming back. She's
in there right now trying to read herself back to sleep
with one of Kat's Harry Potter books. (They're all the
rage these days, occupying the top three spots on the
bestseller list, but after some quick scanning I've
confirmed they're not for me.) (And I can't fail to
mention this: Z said she'd heard on the news that the
sun set today for the rest of the winter in Tromso,
Norway. "Does that mean in your heart of hearts you'll
be going into hibernation now, dear?")

       "Mononoke" was splendid -- a kind of ecocrisis
cautionary fable. It reminded me of the stories Lady S
used to write about the animal kingdom. Afterwards
Betty asked if I could explain the symbolism and how it
related to Japanese myth. Other than fumbling out a
few words about Shinto and Buddhist animals and the
Peach Boy I had to admit it was all a gorgeous mystery
to me. ---

PART II

[Jyze of the Far In]

BOOK F

[The Battle of Jyze City]

It starts off with a gaffe. When I leave the
apartment and reach for my keys to double-lock the door,
I find they're missing. Right away I realize I've left
them inside on the dining table (I always unhook them
from my belt loop to take with me when I go down to pick
up the paper at three or four a.m. these days -- because
by then I've changed out of my street clothes and I
might have to retrieve the paper from the bushes, far
from the door, and need the keys to get back in -- and
this time I neglected to rehook them to the belt loop
afterwards). Without these keys I'm helpless: can't get
into the hideaway or the scope office or, again, back
into the house and apartment. It's five p.m. but I know
Z's going out with "the grrrls" tonight after work. So
within about twenty seconds it dawns on me I have no
choice: I must break down the door.

And I do just that. Which isn't quite the
Herculean feat it might sound like or even appear to be
if anyone were watching (and fortunately no one was).
The molding is so flimsy I've twice broken in by
accident and repaired it with a couple of tiny finishing
nails, the only size it'll take. In fact this time I
put too much shoulder into the lunge and split the
molding clear through. An hour passes before I can mend
things to the point where the door will lock again.

-- And then the walk down. Heavy drizzle. But I'm
in luck: at the old east-depot saloon I find a free
table at the busiest hour of the day. It's in a little
alcove with a TV perched on a shelf directly overhead, a
football game showing soundlessly (as the jukebox blasts

a staticky "Lord, won't you give me a [well-known
German-made luxury vehicle, yeah]"). This alcove is
wood-paneled and even has its own window looking
westward toward the bus terminal, the east depot itself,
and, its top spire lit up although the clock faces
aren't visible, the campanile of the west depot.

This is a working-folks' saloon, a homeless and
single-room-occupancy and just-out-of-jail saloon. Of
sixty or so customers at the moment all but two or three
are men, many wearing ball caps and heavy coats,
unshaven, scruffy, mostly Eurusan but some Afr-, some
Lat-, some Nat-. No Asi- as far as I can see, but
that's probably because this is the Asian quarter where
we're located now and it has scores of saloons and bars
and cafes and restaurants catering pretty much
exclusively to Asi-. (I'm always on the lookout for one
of those places where a Eur- might feel comfortable
doing his jyze thing for an hour or two. Haven't found
one yet. Indoors I'm talking. Outdoors, no problem.)

There's also some good news. For this stretch run
to the millennial rollover I've been made whole again.
My new bank card arrived in today's mail. I'm
financially viable. -- Well, I don't know that for sure
just yet. I need to try the card in a bank machine
first, and I'll do that tonight. But at least in my own
bank's eyes it would appear I'm all right. And how
bizarre it all is.

Water dripping from the eaves outside. Umbrellas
plowing by, many canted forward at roughly thirty
degrees as the drizzle and wind intensify. Windshield
wipers whipping back and forth on vehicles stopped
outside for the light up at the main intersection almost
a full block to the north. Smoke in the air in here:
I'm no longer used to it and it seems to be giving me a
bit of a headache. (For some reason the name of this
joint's been painted over on the awning in front, though
you can still make it out if you peer at it from a
certain angle. New owners, maybe, stalling while they
try to come up with a new name or the money to pay for a
new sign or both.)

[The Battle of Jyze City]

        -- On the way down I was thinking today's jyze
should make a serious attempt to say where things stand.
Now I'm wondering exactly what things I had in mind.
Only two jump into contention. First, Z's not yet in
the clear on the suspiciously thick uterine tissue.
It'll be at least a couple of weeks before we find out
anything more about that (I almost wrote "get to the
bottom of that"). And second, any day now we should be
hearing whether our building's been sold and, if it has,
whether it will be condoized or the rent will be raised
so high we'll be forced out.
        And that's it. All the rest of the things in mind
are a matter of daily doings. Some of those, of course,
are of uncommon interest -- or perhaps I should say of
high common interest -- such as the run-up to the big
meeting of the WTO at the end of this month and then the
countdown to the millennial rollover at the end of next
month with its madly proliferating celebrations not to
mention its massively overhyped Y2Kalypse drama (not to
mention anything beyond the fact of it, that's what I'm
trying to say).
        This upcoming week's daily doings include Aida's
birthday party at which once again I may or may not meet
Z's former lover who is Aida's current lover, the
elusive Kirk M. And on Sunday we'll finally be getting
together with Jess -- the person most responsible for my
meeting Z -- for the first time since her breakup with
Gwen, her partner of seven-plus years. (In fact Z's out
with Jess tonight along with several other lesbian
friends from work. She parcels her girls' nights out
among three groups she sees separately: two straight
ones and one lesbian. -- And by the way, an article in
one of the dailies last week said USAn lesbians now rate
J. City best in the nation as a place for themselves to
live.) (Also, before I forget this, our other friends
whose relationship has gone through a crisis in the past
few months, Leola and Gerry, will be heading off on
Friday for "a romantic weekend at the ocean," so it
would appear they're doing a whole lot better now.)
        One soda is what I paid for here. I've been

nursing it all this time. A buck fifty -- which is a
lot to pay for a soda, I think, in a low-life joint like
this. Meanwhile dozens of folks are standing around
with beer glasses or bottles or cans in hand. Nobody's
bothering me, though, and I'm hardly the only one who's
been occupying a chair for an hour or more without going
for a second or even, in some cases, a first round. I
am, however, the only jyzer at work in here -- in fact
the only scribbler of any kind. And I do feel almost as
if I'm on stage because lots of people are gazing at the
TV right above my head and their eyes drift down
(between plays up there, I suppose, or maybe just during
commercials or some mix of the two), and their faces
crease with puzzlement in some cases, even occasionally
with hostility, or maybe it's just suspicion. It's not
at all unusual for this to happen when I'm jyzing in a
public place, but rarely do I feel so aware of it.
"Psst, that dude a nark writing up a bust?" No doubt
I'm fortunate no drunks have been giving me trouble.

     I expect I'll be coming back here a time or two
over the next five months before this TJM project's
scheduled end (by which point we'll all have moved on,
into a whole new time warp -- or catchment area, call
it, as with septic tanks, if that's not too drastic, and
I say it's not). -- Because in winter J. City offers
few other options for low-cost jyze venues.

[+2]

     So then why ensconced in the armchair at the
hideaway? What happened to being more adventurous?
-- But I do have an excuse. After exiting the movie
house with Jess and Z and stopping by the scope office
to punch in a slew of corrections and print up finals,
it was too late to search for a better spot. And this
afternoon I barely had time to do a half breakfast and
scan the paper (while Z and Jess were at the discount
mart) before it was time to meet them on east hill, as
previously agreed, for dinner. This is the main

drawback with my current two p.m. rising time: it's tough to get out into the world during the afternoon hours, and especially so on weekends.

But I do want to note what a fine foggy night it is. Driving around on the back streets of east hill reminded me of my years in notoriously foggy city 2/7, the headlights beaming off at strange angles because of the steep slopes and twisty turns, the streetlights' glow diffused in soft auras suspended in rows like strange geometrically arrayed nebulae. And later as I walked down the old middle road the great white tower became a spectral presence, slowly materializing as I approached within a block and a half of it. It was lit up, as is the norm, all the way to the top, faint and ghostly yet also somehow even grander and more beautiful than usual in the fog, looking almost as if it were thickly coated with snow. (A few blocks earlier the huge crane perched across the street from the WOC had a similar appearance. And a new sign was hanging above the covered pedestrian walkway there, showing an architect's conception of the building in its finished state along with the words "Defining a New Era." But the words appear to be pure hype because the building, at least as depicted on the sign, looks utterly ordinary. (The new structure housing the operations of local-software-behemoth plutocrat #2 behind the east depot is more deserving of that "New Era" tag.))

-- Two interesting social engagements this past weekend, and both worth looking into for multiple reasons. But before doing that I want to follow up on the new check card and say it really does work and so, yes, I've become financially viable again. (The new ATM screen display trumpets "Ready for 2000!", referring to the bank's preparations to deal with possible Y2K glitches, but I felt it might as well also be referring to me, again able to do business with "America's bank," as this one likes to call itself. -- Probably, however, they're not referring to Central or South or even North America as a whole. But then again they just might be the dominant bank throughout the hemisphere.)

Also I'll note I did tell Z about having to break
the apartment door down. We've been joking about it
ever since. Which is to say: she didn't become paranoid
as I was afraid she might (because if I could do it,
some other brute could too). And yesterday morning she
took the initiative on having a couple of duplicate keys
made so we can stash one in the car and, in case we're
locked out of the car as well, one somewhere else. But
exactly where for that second one? Like maybe under a
stone in the dirt embankment along the side walkway to
the lobby door? But what if all the stones there
already have other people's keys hidden under them? I'd
bet my left (non-jyzing) arm that at least a couple of
them do. (And it turns out that when I banged the door
with my shoulder, I knocked off the white plastic zero
from the middle of our apartment number. I'd noticed it
lying on the floor at the time but assumed it was some
sort of cushion or washer-like pad for the locking
mechanism (the hole in the middle also made it look
something like an extra-large bunion plaster). So now
it appears we're living in apartment No. 23. And I like
this, because 23 was my favorite number for a long spell
until I switched to 42 and then the current 28 on which
the Glennarian calendar is based.)

One more note. Yesterday at Aida's party June told
us about a new condo fourplex which will soon be coming
on the market. It's only a couple of blocks from her
law-school dorm and thus within easy walking distance of
downtown. It would be a good location for us, she
thought, as well as for herself. Today she called and
pretty much sold Z on the idea of our moving there,
saying the units are about a thousand square feet (180
more than our current place), two bedrooms, and though
the price is fairly steep at 184K, she thinks we could
finance it in such a way as to pay $800 a month, or only
$55 more than we're now paying. She wanted us to come
take a look at it immediately, as she'd just done, even
though she warned us the owner is "a jerk." -- But I
wonder how good June really is with numbers. My back-
of-the-hand estimate was that we'd have to pay at least

$1500 a month, and perhaps as much as $1800, and when I
called her to talk about this she quickly agreed with
me. What she'd actually been suggesting, she said, was
that we check out for ourselves what the "middle end,"
as she strangely put it, of the market looks like. Ah,
well, okay then. But in truth I don't see much point in
doing that; the building we're living in right now is
plenty "middle end" enough for us (Thuy had mentioned
that after condoization the units in our building would
go for 150K, I think it was, and up). -- So I'll have
something else besides Aida's party to jaw about with
June when she drops by tonight for help in revising the
remaining ten pages of her appeals brief.

        (Z, by the way, dissolved into tears when I
explained why 184K was likely beyond our means. She
fears I'll feel I should've stayed with Lady U since she
and her family could easily afford such a sum. Z's gone
to pieces several times before over similar issues and
after each time I've thought I've convinced her I don't
see things that way. But then it doesn't hold.
Probably it's more a matter of generalized guilt about
her overall debt; she fears I think that's holding us
back. But again, it just ain't so. And the same with
her fears about the drain of supporting her mother. If
we have to live extremely frugally, so be it. And she
really shouldn't feel guilty on the money score because,
though her debts are big, her income is big too, at
least compared with mine. She also contributes more
financially toward our general upkeep. And I try to
remind her quite often that I'm well aware of all this
and more grateful for it than I can ever fully express.
-- She's a worrier, that's all. On certain kinds of
matters she needs way more reassurance than the average
person. But then on certain other kinds of matters I'm
sure I need way more reassurance than that same average
person, or for that matter any other average person as
long as that person is truly average. And by golly I
believe we both try our best to supply the other with
that reassurance and I think we succeed more often than
anyone ever has any right to expect. And that's just

how it is as I see it, period.)

     And now with time starting to run low I'll say jyze probably shouldn't try to tackle an account of the weekend social engagements tonight. Better to save them for tomorrow -- or no, not so, because Dad's birthday is tomorrow and I'll probably want to focus on that then. So maybe some or all of the weekend stuff will have to wait for another day or perhaps just fall into the abyss like so much else -- or rather like everything else that doesn't make it onto the page. (Taking it up at home tonight is out because June will be there.)

     But okay, a brief mention for Aida's party. The key point is that I did finally meet Kirk. And in truth it was about as anticlimactic as any such meeting of a spouse's ex-lover can be (especially since this is the first time I've met -- to my knowledge anyway -- any ex of Z's -- because, well, Y not?) (say again please?)

     The party itself was fine but considerably smaller than Aida had prepared for. Only ten adults showed up, including Aida, and the senior D's weren't among them (Aida said they were tuckered out after an unexpectedly hard day). Z and I arrived a few minutes early, as planned, and found Dak and Sera already present along with their kids, Tala and Dalisay (half the "L-O-V-E" quartet from our wedding reception; the other half, Marisel and Melisande, couldn't come because their father, Ray the fireman, was on duty and their mother, Vivienne the accountant, has the flu). I actually did move some furniture, with Dak's assistance -- the TV went up to Aida's bedroom, where the kids hung out for most of the evening, with Charles not too wild for a change even though Sera had neglected to give him his ADD medication during an afternoon shopping expedition (and Aida was furious about that oversight). The usual kind of buffet spread was offered on the dining-room table pushed up against one wall, with baked salmon (catered, and probably enough for thirty people) and Filipino side dishes featured along with a potluck mixture of other Asian cuisines (we brought sweet and sour pork from the usual hilltop Chinese restaurant;

Adele U. and Sylva S. both provided Japanese dishes).
     -- So that's it, time's up. Can't say any more.
And obviously the exciting stuff still lies ahead
(including a glance at the letter I received today here
at the hideaway -- from the mayor himself! -- offering
tips about how to prepare for upcoming WTO events).

[+2]

     Here's the new chain coffee shop across from the
public market. Not bad. It actually stays open as late
as nine p.m. on an ordinary weeknight. What, is our
town turning cosmopolitan or something? Another drizzly
mild November evening: the double front doors are
standing wide open twenty or thirty feet from where I
sit and I can barely detect the draft (as an employee
wielding a broom sweeps by and I lift my legs for her:
apparently the countdown to closing is already underway
and yet the big red public-market clock across the
street reads just 7:30: so are signals perhaps crossed
somewhere in the corporate command structure?).
     Sorry to say, a full slate of scoping work awaits
me tonight. It's a good thing I dropped by the office
to check before I came over here, because Naomi took a
rare Tuesday job and I must tend to that as well as the
expected several hundred pages of grand-jury
corrections. So this week it'll be a split C slot for
sure in the eighter jyze entries. The second part of
the split will probably come late tomorrow night, and
that'll be a good time for it because the heavens might
be exploding with a rare showing of Leonid meteorite
pyrotechnics (though the chances of their being visible
within the city limits here under current weather
conditions are slim indeed -- which won't necessarily
detract from the celebration).
     Jazz greats doing "Let's Call The Whole Thing Off"
on the sound system. I say no no no, we don't want to
do that. My seat's in a cluster of four wooden contour
lawn chairs by the west windows. The floor in this area

is sunken a few feet below sidewalk level and so I'm
glimpsing people's legs striding by outside across my
upper visual periphery. Beyond those, rainy neon blurs,
and imposed against it all are windowpane reflections of
the shop interior here with its many yellow hanging
lamps and red and green holiday counter displays. A
large metal planter stands directly to my right, with
swedish-ivy leaves lightly caressing my right, which is
to say jyzin', forearm as it swings across the page
(sort of like a fleshy sleeved windshield wiper).

   Can this franchise coffeehouse hold out for long
against the incursions of cold, wet, hungry drifters and
druggies and homeless folks who infamously congregate in
this area? I wouldn't bet on it. (Several are standing
just inside the front entrance right now, all youngish
males at about my level of scruffiness or slightly
below. Looks to me as though they're casing the joint:
what can they get away with in here? One appears a bit
alarmingly hardcore. Not at all the unflappable
peacekeeper kind of dude we'd like to see more of on the
night streets. The employees on duty at the moment are
two small women and an only slightly taller but also
skinnier late-teens shaved-head dude with lots of
piercings, and he looks rather nervous, I'd say, and
well he should. And well I should also, right.)

   For the remainder of this TJM project I'll be
trying to visit more places like this. (The three guys
just left.) I don't like to have to spend the money and
I don't much like this sterile kind of franchise coffee
shop but I don't really have much choice in the downtown
area in the evening hours unless I want to confine
myself to the two offices, scope and hideaway, for jyze
entries. And I don't want to do that. And this place
here isn't that bad, as I say. No one's hounding me.
The employees might even be glad to have a jyzer around
as a potential ally in case of trouble along the lines
of what they were just now potentially facing. Empty
seats are plentiful. The public-market scene outside is
pleasing to the eye. The sound system is good and so's
the choice of music, at least so far. And the coffee's

all right, although too expensive at two bucks for a
large "venti" cup. (This is after you toss your change,
a couple of dimes, into the tip jar.) In my view it's
only fair to pay a little more to be allowed to sit
indoors for a while. True, I can't really afford to be
doing this as a regular thing. Basically I'm using
savings to do it. Mom's money. I've been investing it
in this jyze project all along -- or rather since Annal
3 -- and I'm sure she'd be happy to know that.

The news out there in the world? It's good. The
U.S. and China have signed a big trade agreement. The
U.S. labor movement will howl about it, but I think
they're failing to see the big picture. It's crucially
important that the world's most populous country be
"brought into" the world economic system, and that will
almost certainly now be happening since the U.S., as
part of the deal, will be supporting China's entry into
the WTO. Only now can it really be said that, like it
or not, the reigning economic system (and we all know
which one that is) is truly a world system.

This doesn't mean the upcoming WTO ministerial will
be lacking matters to protest about. And I have little
doubt those protests will be happening and in a big way.
How effective they'll be, well, that's another matter.
But we're still hoping.

-- And now suddenly this coffee shop is falling
victim to the street scene (that is, to the economic
order as it's working out in practice here at the low
end of one of its most prosperous nodes). The same
three guys are back. They're lurking near the front
entrance and the doors are still wide open. -- But the
shop's closing early; the word just came down. Or maybe
8:17 is now the normal closing time, although the posted
hours, as noted before, say nine. Anyway, I'm outta
here. Gotta exit via the side door, the pierced dude
tells me, his eyes trained on the three guys still
hanging around outside the front entrance, which he just
boldly closed and locked. "In your faces!" (Not that
he actually said that. Or maybe he silently mouthed it
at them in a way that neither they nor I could see.)

[+1]

Well, if they're flashing out there I can't see
them. Not even with the conference-room lights turned
off. Not even looking through the red telescope. Big
white clouds are hanging over the city, low, obscuring
the tops of the tallest buildings -- more like a high
fog really -- and at the moment I can't make out a
single star, to say nothing of what's been billed as one
of the great meteorite showers of the century. But
earlier, walking in, I spotted a few stars of the
(seemingly) stationary variety from the high bridge and
also caught glimpses of the moon as it slid in and out
of gaps in the clouds.

Then again there might not be any meteorite shower
to speak of. The last half-dozen highly touted heavenly
spectaculars I've hoped to observe (including comets)
were all flops, and in several cases complete no-shows.
And if we can't trust a fairly straightforward science
such as astronomy, what about the really far-out stuff
like quantum cybernetics? That's one more reason I'm
glad this jyze has now moved into the era of the far-in.
Where science, that is, including the political kind,
makes way for the personal.

Hear ye, hear ye!

But first...a moment ago I was leafing through a
packet of WTO info put out by the property managers for
this building (the U owns the property itself). This is
not the same letter from the mayor (with attachments) we
received at the hideaway building nor is it the city's
internal packet which Z brought home, but the contents
of all three are similar and in many parts identical.
Here we're only a few blocks from the epicenter for the
gathering at the convention center (three blocks due
east) and just kitty-corner from the many-starred hotel
where a number of the highest of the high honchos will
be staying. Most of the hotel, including the grand
entrance -- its horseshoe drive right now packed with
limousines, some black and some white and one maroon --

is visible from the windows here.

From the looks of the various contingency plans, the security people are leaving nothing to chance. This packet they've distributed at the scope building even provides a questionnaire "script" to tape next to your phone to help deal with anyone calling in a bomb threat. (I suspect if I were to walk into this office unannounced during the daytime hours of WTO week quite a commotion would ensue: swoons, screams, alarms going off. -- In fact it'll be interesting to see how they deal with me down on the street when I come trudging officeward at nine or ten at night. Those squinty-eyed Secret Service guys will just love me, I know it. Chances are high they'll want to run me off as a derelict -- or run me in -- or run me over.)

This is the week before Thanksgiving. And it does have that feeling. Next week the holidays start. And this year they'll all be part of the buildup toward the big quatrorollover. -- And in this TJM project, anyway, they'll keep on rolling right through Chinese New Year in February and then the thousand-year anniversary of the first Christian millennium in March and then domesday (the implosion) probably in April -- and that's it, end of the biggest jyze year of them all. Then the jyzer will take some time off before deciding whether this right here is or is not too hard an act to follow.

So much for politics and political fallout.

Tonight June's coming over again. Her crucial paper's due tomorrow. It's taking more time than I'd like but I'm getting a big kick out of working on it with her. I expect she'll be my friend for life now. (Each night she brings me a cookie. She crashes on the couch for an hour or two as I go over her work with a blue pen -- at times she snores rather loudly -- and then we discuss my suggested changes. Once in a while she starts shivering and I put an arm around her shoulder until she lets me know with a sort of pout that it's been there a little too long but she doesn't want to make me feel too bad by asking me point-blank to take it away. Then at five a.m. or so I walk her to her car.

We both crack wise about how absurd the whole thing is.)
     -- And so a quick trip back to where I left off
several days ago. Aida's living room, Saturday evening.
Nine of us sitting around talking and the doorbell rings
and it's a short stocky guy in a suit and tie and a
formal-looking black cloth winter coat: Kirk for sure.
He has a round face and a trim salt-and-pepper beard and
a deep resonant voice. Introductions. "You know
Zoelie," Aida says with no apparent irony or amusement.
"Hi," says Z with studied casualness, though maybe I'm
the only one who's noticing the studiedness of it.
Probably no one else present except June (and of course
Aida) knows anything about Z's history with Kirk. After
all: they were an item more than twenty years ago. And
now she's married and he and her best friend are an item
and so what's the big deal here? -- And I try to put a
wry raised eyebrow into my own studiedly casual "Hello"
and handshake when I'm introduced, but I doubt either
the wryness or the studiedness communicates to anyone, Z
perhaps excepted. (I had prepared what I thought was a
pretty good opening line -- "Hello, Kirk. So, I hear
you and I have something in common." But I dropped it.
And I also failed to follow Betty's advice: "Just growl
and he'll crawl into the woodwork.")
     And really that's about it. Kirk takes a seat at
the far end of the couch on which Z and I are sitting
with Aida, forcing Aida to come into full-flank contact
with me for the first time ever to my recollection, and
the talk goes on. For a while things break up somewhat,
and I listen in from five or six feet away with my back
turned to Kirk and Adele as they talk city politics
while gnawing on chicken drumsticks near the buffet
table. Kirk's wearing a suit because, I've heard him
say, he's just come from a wedding, but to me he sounds
like a man who always wears a suit: stiff and pompous,
overly sure of himself, a cross between a lawyer and a
professor with perhaps some priest mixed in. But then,
yeah, I'm a bit biased. And I'm trying hard not to
repeat Betty's devastatingly accurate line about the
turkey and the stiff rod -- but there, I've finally gone

and done it. (June said she sees him similarly, but
then June's at least somewhat biased too, and she
certainly doesn't want to get on my wrong side with the
due date looming on her paper.)

     Since that day Aida's again asked Z what she thinks
of the idea of our double-dating. Z says she told Aida
she's not too hot on it because she suspects the four of
us would have little to talk about. But I tried to
encourage it. "Let's give it a shot and see what
happens. Why not?" In truth I'm just thinking it might
be good for spicing up the jyze in the post-rollover
longeurs (which obviously assumes Y2K will fizzle).

     -- As shutdown time looms here in the conference
room I peer out the windows again and still see no
meteorites and no stars either. So much light is the
fog absorbing from the city that it blots out the skies
behind it, and this includes even the parts it's not
hiding directly. Maybe I'll be able to see more from
our hilltop bus stop. (But then up there we're often
hidden in these low clouds ourselves -- which to my mind
is one of the best features of the area.) -- And
there's the evening with Jess still to grapple with, and
the promised deeper meanings of things in general, all
of which are bound to seem anticlimactic now. But, I
ask, is that necessarily bad? (Surely not! And for
certain it's better than nothing, or absence of even a
hint of climax no matter where it falls in the story
line.) (But I think I'll have to leave Dad's birthday
for another year. -- And since jyze has gone into it at
some length in previous annals I guess that'll suffice.)
                    *   *
     -- So all right then (following up), poor Jess.
I'd say she appears okay and generally seems about the
same as before, but her friends all think she's looking
beat-up and haggard and she's obsessing on the question
of why things went wrong with Gwen and she's just about
impossible to get along with. Her best friends at work,
Tobey and Paz, are avoiding her now because her "dark
side" is surfacing too much, to the point where they
feel she's trying to break them up too -- frequently

saying to each of them in various ways, "How do you know
your honey isn't cheating on you? Hm? Hm?" -- and then
pursuing the question until everybody's freaking out.

     So she showed up outside our place at four-thirty
in her pickup and she and Z went off to the discount
mart (the one where, as a gift from Z -- one I never
asked for but couldn't turn down -- I'm now a member as
part of a family-bargain deal). Meanwhile I finished my
half breakfast and read the papers. She didn't come up
to 203: Z had called to warn her it was the usual
cluttery mess, just the opposite of the way Jess keeps
her own house. (But as Jess herself pointed out later,
"It's not as if I haven't seen Zoelie's apartment
hundreds of times" -- and Z's apartment when she was
living alone was usually in even worse shape than our
place is now -- which is to say, as Jess did in fact
say, "You're obviously a good influence on her, Glen,
just like I always knew you would be, except for the
first month or two when I was sure you were a stalker.")

     Jess wanted to go to the discount mart to buy a
stereo system to help nurse her through the lonely hours
at night (to replace the one she and Gwen had borrowed
and she, Jess, recently had to return to its owner).
And while there she did some impulse-buying of other
items in bulk because she thought this would help her
survive financially until she sells the house in May.
(But you have to wonder. That case of semi-expensive
wine supposedly intended to keep her prepared for those
occasions when she's a guest somewhere and is expected
to bring a bottle and doesn't have time beforehand to
run out and buy one, might the presence of that case in
the house tempt her too much on those same lonely nights
which the new stereo is meant to arm her against? And
she with a well-known weakness for good wine? -- This
was a topic we probed in depth during dinner.)

     I met them at the theater at six and after picking
up our tickets we headed a few blocks east to a new
restaurant Jess had spotted earlier. On the way we
passed several lesbian restaurants and hangouts, but
Jess showed no interest in them (and why should she,

especially in her forlorn state?). -- So, yes, I guess I'm saying there was something bedraggled about her. For one thing she looked different: not unhealthy but thinner -- she said she'd lost ten pounds, bringing her down to 102 -- and grimmer. And she was obsessing for sure, numerous times reverting, with no transition at all, to the topic of the breakup -- sometimes in the middle of sentences about totally unrelated matters. (Grimmer yet, a hairpin-like piece of black metal fell out of her burger just as she was chomping into it. Eventually the server determined it was a wire from a grill-cleaning brush; and the restaurant picked up her entire check. Z felt they should've picked up ours too but she didn't push it and I was glad she didn't -- especially given that it's in her DNA to do so.)

     Mostly Jess focused on the question of trust. Why was it Gwen had betrayed her? How can you be dishonest with someone you love? And that's even more true with someone (Gwen) who has such a cute, kind, innocent look about her. Gwen herself had accused Jess of not being trusting enough back when she, Jess, was asking numerous questions about this therapy patient Gwen was taking such a strong interest in. So Jess let the matter drop then, more or less -- this is her version, of course -- and agreed to trust Gwen with the guy, only to have her, Gwen, take advantage of the trust and then lie to her about what was going on and even, finally, justify the lying on the grounds that Jess had been untrusting. - Not such an unusual situation really, but of course no less painful for that. Maybe more painful for that.

     I threw in my two cents' worth a few times and Jess seemed interested enough in it that I suggested we talk things over at length sometime if she'd like. But she hasn't taken me up on it so far and at this point I'm guessing she probably won't. As I said to her, "Maybe I could bring a fresh perspective to it or at the very least a fresh pair of ears to beat on for a while." (I'm not even sure why she's holding back. Maybe she thinks it would cause trouble with Z.) (Jess is the woman Z seems to envy most as far as female

attractiveness goes, and she's a decade or so younger as
well, and famously fit from biking, skiing, backpacking,
working out: she's the one Z did a crying jag over after
seeing her naked in the locker room. "I'm an older
woman now and I can never again have a young woman's
FC." Not that there's any shortage of women out there
who'd love to have Z's FC and not that she doesn't know
that. And this is not even to consider her extremely
rare, I do believe, sexual talents, which have only
flourished with age.) -- Or maybe Jess just thinks I
couldn't offer anything enlightening, because I'm older
too, or because I'm a straight male, or maybe because
she assumes I've always been as out of the loop as I am
now (and by her standards I quite possibly always have
been) -- but I suspect otherwise. I think I probably
could help her out a bit. But so it goes. (And it's
not as if I'm lacking in friends of Z's who're calling
on me for help in one way or another. In this respect I
have to say I'm being a pretty damn good husband and in
fact she says as much herself. -- My relations with
Aida, of course, being a rather notable exception.
-- Not that I haven't tried my utmost with Aida.)

[+1]

     They've been flashing all right but not here. Over
certain Middle Eastern deserts, among other remote
places. That's what the news says.
     Last night after stepping off the bus I gazed up at
the eastern sky for a good fifteen minutes (including a
second session on the balcony here at home) and saw nary
a shooting star. Did see something odd, though: a very
bright double star, as it seemed at first, which over
the course of maybe thirty seconds as I stared at it
revealed itself to be an airliner flying straight at me.
What a citified rube I've become! In the burbs of my
youth was I ever this clueless? Surely not.
     But that was last night. Last of the major
assistance nights for June. I decided I must be living

vicariously the life not chosen; why else would I be
putting so much time into this? Imagine if after
college I'd gone on to law school, as for a short period
I was seriously thinking of doing (though it was never
my first choice). I might've made a fair lawyer but I
can't think I'd ever have been anything but miserable
living a lawyer's life.

   -- Yank my trusty J-stick from its scabbard and
jyze is on again. This right here is the life I want.

   A look around. What's new and different? A stack
of articles I've clipped from newspapers and magazines
over the past few days, most bearing on WTO and Y2K
matters and the rollover in general. Special
supplements in the local weekend papers are already
featuring stories about New Year's Eve entertainment,
and also lots of ads for it, starting with the big
fireworks event and its various preambles at the
fairgrounds (150,000 revelers are expected) and covering
all the swank joints with their ticket prices in the
thousands of dollars and also a millennial ball I hadn't
heard about before at the new exhibition hall featuring
some big names in the national and regional rock and R&B
biz, tickets in the $200 range.   -- And by the way, Sid
and Laila sent us an invitation to a "Scandalous
Millennium Blowout" at our honeymoon resort which sounds
great -- four days, lots of live music and artsy stuff
-- but for us the invite comes too late because we're
firmly committed to house-sitting for Jess. And in
truth I'd rather be in the city for the big night.

   Oddly it's been quite warm lately, and also damp,
foggy, dark, though with occasional sun breaks. All the
flowers in our balcony boxes are still in bloom.

   And here's a review from tonight's paper. It's
discussing what sounds like an abysmally bad made-for-TV
movie about the Y2Kalypse. It's set right here in J.
City, it so happens, and many of the main characters
work for J. City public utilities (a nuclear plant is
melting down), so the reviewer consulted a real live
utilities worker for comment. That worker is none other
than Fletcher D., coordinator of the municipal response

to the millennial bug. Fletcher of Bari and Fletcher,
this is, the couple we were supposed to be kicking back
with tomorrow night ("double-dating"), though I haven't
mentioned this before now. Fletcher the lover of
Chinese poetry, Bari the Korusan math whiz (he's
Eurusan). But it so happens Bari was sent out of town
on very short notice (she's now the school district's
chief financial officer) and they had to cancel -- and
therefore I'll have some free time on my hands tomorrow
night and will be able to continue this then.

     (Ooh ooh, that turns out to be almost an elegant
sign-off!)

                          27

     Well, I did have the free time on my hands Friday
night owing to the Fletcher/Bari cancellation, but I
wound up using most of it just to laze around the
hideaway. There's always reading to be caught up on if
I need some sort of excuse for not doing something else
which for some unknown reason I don't want to be doing
at the moment, and that's what I used as my excuse this
time too. Stretched out on the armchair I was, feet up
on the hassock, shoes off, door open a crack, the usual
Friday-night rap'n'rock cacophony throbbing up from
below.

     (And here's Z now. I recognize her footsteps on
the stairs. Early, as she so often is. ABE-woman!)
                          *
     -- And I'm back after packing the frozen food
rather tightly (nice job!) into the freezer. The lady
made a provisioning run this afternoon, including a stop
to see Rob at the bookstore, but I haven't asked her yet

what he had to say. To talk too much would've been to
suggest the jyze session could be postponed. I'm not
meaning to imply she'd want me to postpone it; I'm
saying I might've yielded to the temptation all on my
own. (Part of her greeting was to fall on her knees,
pull down my shorts, and engage in attempted mouth-to-
genital "Pooshkin resuscitation" -- all just for laughs,
of course -- but surely for real as well -- or so I'd
like to believe. And do believe, yes. And also suspect
she'd confirm if only out of the sheer pleasure she
takes in being unpredictable not to say provocative.)

Now I'm back in the bedroom, the scuzzy old green
armchair covered with its fairly respectable patchwork
quilt, and the jyze sign is hanging in the doorway.
"How long?" she playfully pouted. More provocation.
And I don't doubt I'll yield to it pretty soon here.
Not necessarily any sooner, though, than I should.

-- So I've come bopping out for the start of a new
J-week. About three feet is the net distance I've
traveled so far. Laid out before me in all its shambly
splendor is the unmade marital bed, with Z's untied blue
"hula hoop" stretched out across a mound of white sheets
and hanging limply off the edge, looking like a phallus
that indeed needs resuscitation (that's why it's blue,
see). But no, the phallus it could be said to be
standing for symbolically, precisely by not standing --
ho ho -- is working fine, I'm sure it is. It has no
reason to be blue, either in a breathless sense or in
any other. It's just not having a chance to prove
itself these days (because she's back on the H-rag).

So it's right here the big celebration of the
quatrorollover starts: of the year, of the decade, of
the century, of the millennium. It's the first of the
holiday weeks. It's also run-up week for the big WTO
"ministerial" and thousands of visitors are already
streaming into town, or so it's said (I've encountered
few material signs of any as yet), and the Saturday
morning paper's front-page headline reveals that
facilities are being readied for the legendary Cuban El
Supremo's speech (though the story itself says his

visit's not confirmed yet) (but if he does show up, Kirk
M.'s brother Ed should reap lots of credit for assuring
the man last summer, and drawing mondo pundit flak for
doing so, that he'd be welcome here in J. City no matter
what pushback might occur elsewhere in our rabidly anti-
Commie USA) (and if he does show up and his speech goes
on for five or six -- or ten -- hours, as they've been
known to do quite often, Ed should reap some of the
blame, true).

Thanksgiving week. For the past four years it's
been a mournful time for me because of Mother's death on
the day after Thanksgiving in 1995, and it will be
mournful again this year for another reason as well.
It's now been confirmed Mr. D has cancer, and on
Thanksgiving we'll be joining the D-clan for dinner (and
doing dessert later with Wei and Alison). Just
yesterday Aida told Z about the diagnosis. Monday he's
beginning a chemo regime. But apparently the cancer's a
slow-growing type and he should be able to live with it
for a considerable period if the chemo's effective, and
he's being told it usually is. He's about seventy and Z
says he appears otherwise to be in good health.
Nonetheless the news has of course been hard to take for
the immediate family and that's especially true for
Aida, who dotes on her father to a degree I've seldom
encountered in anyone (though Z at times comes close).

Right now Aida's mainly suffering from "tremendous
exhaustion." Z felt much the same way when she learned
of her own father's terminal diagnosis. And she's being
reminded frequently of that sad period in her life and
it's affecting her quite a bit. Last night upon
arriving home I found, as an instance, she'd covered the
faces of all our clocks. As she explained later, they
reminded her too much of the passage of time and death.
(We had talked about death earlier at the WOC. June had
just learned her friend Peggy's illness had taken an
abrupt turn for the worse. "Death's all around us,"
grumped Z. "Everyone's dying, including you and me."
And then without missing a beat she did one of those
startling instant reversals for which she's known far

and wide: "So let's have fun while we still can!")
    She's been apologizing quite a bit for the
"crankiness" which she now admits lay behind the cold
shoulder she gave me in bed night before last (which in
truth didn't bother me all that much, given my own
exhaustion at the time and awareness of what she was
going through over Aida and Mr. D, among other troubling
matters). Last night she left me a card saying she was
sorry yet again and explaining she thought the real
"concrete slab" underlying her crankiness was distress
over her inability to buy us a house and to pay for
taking care of her mother in the way she'd like to do
during Mama E's declining years. She'd been reminded of
how her father on his deathbed teased her, Z, "You never
did buy me that little house by the sea." (Not that
she'd ever said she would, fortunately, or otherwise
she'd've been hurt even more.) I gave her about twelve
different reasons why she shouldn't be looking at things
so self-disparagingly, but none of them had much effect.
Most of her peers, after all, as she pointed out, own
their own homes or condos, and several have a parent or
even two parents living with them. Nonetheless it's
clearly my own decisions made over a lifetime, much more
than anything she's ever done or failed to do, that
prevent us from having the bucks to buy a house now.
And it's also a social thing: in this shamefully wealthy
society such extreme disparities of means exist between
individuals that more than a third of the adult
population can't afford to own a home and roughly a
seventh are living below the poverty line. So we should
be proud, I tell her, of the choices we've made. (And
I'd say now it helps that she and virtually everyone she
knew while growing up lived in an apartment. I'm the
one who was raised in a big suburban house and therefore
I'm the one who should be feeling bad. Except that
being "declasse'" is exactly what I'm after and
furthermore I believe it's what many or even most of us
(USAns especially if we're above, say, twice the poverty
line) should be seeking in light of the great inequality
between nations and the ever deepening ecocrisis caused

essentially by overconsumption in the wealthy nations.
At times my views on this get me in even more trouble
with Z -- though at other times she esteems me a bit
more because of them, no question. And if this esteem
weren't for real, our own dynamics might be too black
and white for us to survive them.)

    -- And I think this is enough of an introduction in
the face of extreme temptation. June's taking us out to
dinner tonight to celebrate finishing her paper. I need
to jump in the shower. And before that, to see if I can
persuade the Z-wiff to let me crawl back into her good
graces (meaning her pants, yes, among others such, but
not inside the "unners" owing to her current H-state).

[+1]

    -- On the theory that something, even a very small
thing, is better than nothing (a theory with which these
pages are well acquainted) I break out J-book and J-
stick for a forty-minute J-fest. And this when the year
has exactly forty days to run. But it's again the
hideaway, the venue is, and the fan's humming, and the
J-slinger's once again back to slinging.

    I've permanently attached a pillow to the back of
the chair here so I can doze off more comfortably when I
need to (as I did an hour ago). It's held in place by
the chairback itself where it pins it against the wall.
This is one of the thin brown pillows Lady U's mother
made to serve as seat cushions on our hard dining-room
chairs (none of those U's had much in the way of rear-
end padding) (for some reason I've never understood,
Lady U let me take two of the four pillows when we split
up even though her case for taking all four was strong).

    Earlier I used a yellow gel pen to ink in the
windows of the memorial lighthouse model from the
honeymoon, and then I drew in antic little alternating
Z's and G's in black on the yellow. This model stands
in a place of honor atop the long, low notebook cabinet
that runs along the back of the desktop against the

546

wall. The cabinet -- with its nifty sliding frosted
glass doors -- hails from the carriage house up in the
Yuke; Lady U and I were allowed to strip out anything we
wanted before that house was torn down about fourteen
years ago now. Also I brought my altered "King of Jyze"
card down here today. It's protected by a clear plastic
one-piece self-standing frame which I bought earlier
this afternoon during a trip with Z to the south-end
chain arts & crafts superstore. We're gearing up for
Christmas. (The self-standing frames were on sale, half
off, and we bought a dozen. Now I'm thinking I'll go
back and stock up on maybe two dozen more before the
sale ends Wednesday. They come in several sizes, all of
which work for one or another kind of altered postcard.)

Last night's celebratory dinner with June hit a
snag when we found a packed waiting area just inside the
front door at her chosen restaurant (it was raining
heavily at the time), so we wound up trying out a newly
opened place Z had heard about on east hill -- again
southern food and Afrusan-owned, but with a male chef
this time and a more adventurous menu but no strawberry
shortcake. We ordered roast chicken (Z), trout (June),
and pork-but-hold-the-spices (jyzer), and for dessert we
shared a big hunk of freshly baked orange cake with
handmade vanilla ice cream; and the whole thing,
including a double round of drinks (we had to wait at
this second restaurant too) cost June a major bundle.

Afterwards June showed us her dorm room. It's a
small studio but quite nice, with a kitchenette and a
large walk-in closet and a window with a fine southerly
view. Other than that it's austerely furnished and even
though June hadn't known we'd be visiting, it revealed
little about her other than the fact that she's much
more orderly than Z and I are. A couple of Chinese-
language newspapers were lying about on the floor by her
bed and that was about it for clutter. In the hallway
we passed several students and they all looked standard
college age. The woman June usually sits next to in
legal-writing class is twenty-two. "She is very, very
young! I am very, very old!" (But June's a year

younger than me and two and a half years younger than Z,
so for that remark we threatened to have her campused.)
     Some lovely moments with Z this weekend, and also a
couple of minor bumpy ones. She was rubbing against me
and making flattering comments about this or that body
part ("You know your FC turns me on") and telling me how
horny she was and how she'd been fantasizing about
putting some of the blowjob tips from "The Male Body"
into practice. And she did just that, twice, this
afternoon and yesterday afternoon, but both times her
preposterously superior arousability proved too
distracting, and she was still on the H-rag so we had to
go about relieving her "tensions" in "plan B" fashion,
nipply ways mostly and also one of the bun-caress kind,
and there are times when I think she likes these better
anyway (meaning the "plan B" type in general), although
she emphatically denies this. And then today I was
permitted to do some towsing ("unners" pushed to one
side), and as a consequence I had to wash my hand
afterwards and I took my wedding ring off to do that and
forgot to put it back on and that's why I'm not wearing
it now -- for the first time outside the house (except
for visits to the WOC) since our wedding day.
     And that must be it for now.

                        [+1]

     -- Starting up late again tonight. It's seven
o'clock and I'm on the way back in, with a heavy WOC
workout and a long soak (long as I can make it) still
ahead, or so I hope. Stopping meanwhile at the downtown
library, main floor, far northwest corner, a four-table
study area right next to the philosophy section.
     I lingered at home long enough to encounter Z upon
her return from another work-related training session.
Because she'd been sitting all day she walked with me as
far as the south end of the high bridge, even though it
was already dark out, just to get some exercise. She
would've gone a bit farther, at least to the north end

of the bridge, but half a dozen cop cars and fire
engines, all with emergency lights flashing, were
arrayed across the central span. At first we thought it
could be an anti-WTO "action" -- maybe some protesters
dangling with signs above the jam-packed portion of the
east-west freeway that passes underneath -- but it
turned out to be an accident involving a red pickup and
a fancy white SUV much like Leola's. While walking by I
saw a crew lifting someone from the SUV -- a young
skinhead Cawk male, as it happened -- onto a wheeled
gurney as his face pulsated alternately red and blue.

The possibility of an anti-WTO action occurred to
us because radio reports of the first such actions --
taking place downtown -- had been running all afternoon.
In one of these, several protesters scaled the walls of
a chain clothing store in the "retail core" and unfurled
signs decrying the low-wage overseas labor involved in
making most of the chain's clothes. As a reporter
interviewed a group leader, a chant could be heard in
the background: "Don't buy here! Don't buy here!" And
the official opening of the WTO ministerial is still a
week off. The protests against it might turn out to be
even livelier than we've been expecting.

I've been doing a lot of reading lately about the
WTO, both pro and con. Much of the con view to me seems
hopelessly naive and ethnocentric (Western), but the pro
side is far worse on both scores and also the scores of
power, greed, and cynicism, not to mention ecological
obliviousness and/or obstructiveness. (But enough of
that for now. Another time for trying to sort it all
out -- maybe.)

Three Spanish-speaking migrant-worker-type fellows,
sounding tough but probably harmless, or maybe somewhat
harmful but surely only minorly so while bivouacked
inside a library, are yakking it up at one of the other
tables here. Scores of homeless men, and the occasional
homeless woman, occupy seats throughout the building.
These folks basically have nowhere else to go. And
because of this general situation -- the central city's
south end serving as a corral into which the homeless

can be herded -- critics are raising new questions about
the plan to build a big new downtown library. How can
it be designed so that folks like these won't scare away
the middle class? These dudes here are using the
facilities; some are even reading. But they're also
noisy at times and a few are a bit stinky, yeah. So
what's to be done? (Today's headline says crime rates
are continuing to plummet. But the wealth gap is
greater than ever and will almost certainly continue to
widen. Incomes for the bottom sixty percent in this
country have stayed roughly the same for decades while
those for the top ten percent, and especially the top
one percent, have shot up, with CEOs now making upwards
of four hundred times the salary of an average employee
(twenty years ago it was under forty times as much, so
conservatively a mere one thousand percent jump in the
gap).

The problem is, of course, systemic. The rich can
easily evade the negative social consequences of extreme
inequality, including those on display right here in
this room; if necessary, they'll build their own
libraries in their own gated communities. The rest of
us must pay the price for maintaining a system that
because of legal forms of corruption (campaign spending
especially) is more and more tilted in favor of the
wealthy and is at the same time ravaging the planet.
You can see this reflected everywhere. -- And at bottom
I'd say that's what these WTO protests are really about.
Or should be about. Or at least that's a big part of
it. Because it's complex, as I say. This complexity
might even be why I've wound up sitting near the
philosophy section today. Osmosis, do your thing!

-- Unfortunately these dudes here are making quite
a racket. As I've said already, yes, but it's hard not
to be repetitious when the noise is so loud and
persistent you can't think of anything else. Two of
them, I'm realizing now, are seriously drunk. No
library workers are anywhere in sight. As for the
security officers when you really need them -- ha! Nor
am I going to be the one who tells the offenders to shut

up. For one thing, they've got me outnumbered by quite
a lot. But still: this is ridiculous. This makes the
east-depot saloon look as quiet as a mortuary.
     -- So I'd better move on.

                        [+1]

     -- Further notes from a familiar place: brown
chair, hideaway. My own little gated community, could
say, although it's the low-rent type. Relatively. In
much of the world several families could live on what I
fork over for this tiny office. Of course some such
remark might apply to a whole lot of things USAn. In a
sense, everything. -- And does this excuse any of them?
Any of us? Our outrageous behavior? No.
     Turns out grand jury is meeting tomorrow. This'll
tighten up my weekend almost to the shattering point.
That's why I'm back into the jyze today. Tomorrow
afternoon I'll be able to crank out a few pages at some
downtown venue, I hope, but after that I'll probably
have to be snatching paragraphs haphazardly, most of
them late at night. At least that's how it looks from
here.
     The WTO run-up also winds tighter and tighter.
After all this hoopla it'll be sad indeed if the demos
aren't massive and the "actions" aren't riveting. It's
the biggest clash yet between two of the most prominent
Western ways of seeing the world as we head into the
21st century and it's happening right here in J. City.
Even with the millennium rollover coming up people can
talk about little else right now. On the bus going home
last night I could overhear three separate conversations
at once and all three were WTO related. Is the great
Cuban leader coming? How many people will be marching?
Will it be possible to get anywhere downtown by any
means other than hoofing it? (For this occasion my
normal means will be better than most, but still nowhere
near good enough. It's gonna be a war zone out there.
Today two more newspapers came out with WTO special

editions: our venerable alt-weekly and the relatively
new rad fortnightly. Both are excellent from the anti-
WTO vantage. But it's getting to the point I don't even
have a fighting chance to keep up with all the reporting
and commentary on this topic.)

   This afternoon, not yet knowing about grand jury, I
made another run to the corporate arts & crafts
superstore and also did the weekly provisioning. This
trip served as a strong reminder the holidays are coming
up, with the superstore in raucous Christmas mode and
the corporate supermarket athrob with folks piling carts
comically high with turkeys and stuffing mix and all the
other standard fixings (and some of them not so standard
by trad USAn lights, with so many Asiusans and Latusans
and Afrusans of various national ancestries shopping
there). And the same was true of the higher-end co-op
grocery where I looked in vain for the bag of deluxe
taro chips Z asked me to pick up for her.

   The front-page lead story in today's J. City
afternoon paper, which I was also delegated to pick up
since Z had no chance to do so during her current
training session in the next city to the south, reports
on a new study which ranks the freeway interchange that
I walk first over and then under every day (and ride the
bus first under and then over every night) as the third
most congested in the nation. I knew it was bad but I
didn't know it was quite that bad. (More than 280,000
vehicles pass through it daily. An amazing number for
sure considering our city's population is only a bit
more than twice that, and supposing, perhaps foolishly,
at least a few of those vehicles are carrying more than
one passenger -- the hundreds or maybe thousands of
buses as one fair possibility.)

   At home Naomi's message about the grand jury was
awaiting me. She also said the scope firm's been
attempting to reschedule all depositions set for next
week away from the downtown area ("because of this WTO
nonsense") but it's still too early to know whether
she'll be able to come up with any work for the week.
Probably she won't, though, and this will just about

clinch it: I'll have to cancel my Mentoka trip next
spring. When I mentioned this to Z last night she
seemed almost relieved, especially after she'd assured
herself I wasn't all that disappointed about it. Her
own thinking these days is that she should save her
travel funds for two kinds of occasion: when her
mother's either preparing to move out here (if indeed
she decides to do so) or encounters a health emergency
(and obviously this could happen at any time, with the
risks especially high during the next four to six weeks
owing to her cataract surgery). And I've neglected to
mention another major factor involved in the trip
reckoning: our 1999 income taxes due on April 15. At
this point neither of us has more than a vague idea how
our new marital status will affect them. That won't
shake out until February at the earliest.

Nor will we be seeing a "plan A" sex revival
anytime before the weekend at the earliest. This
morning before Z dressed for work I did an outbreak
check, at her request, using my trusty rechargeable
flashlight, and I found recovery is not yet nigh. But
an altered-card revival is already underway, with some
intense work late last night using the new pens from the
arts & crafts superstore resulting in one of my proudest
efforts yet: "Autumn 1999. 'Twas a Very Very Good
Season." The ukiyo-e courtesan pictured is demurely
admiring a profusion of fall colors, and her thought
bubble is saying, "For one thing, I got laid a lot more
than in most seasons up until, oh, about twenty months
ago." (But it's true, from the overall view what a fine
season it's been! And by the Gregorian calendar, at
least, it still has almost a month to run.)

And here's looking at me: a display box for the
special "Limited Series" Millennial M&Ms. I picked it
up at the drugstore tonight (Brad the security guard
wasn't there nor was any other security guard but I paid
for it anyway). And I should note the surprise gift for
me which Z brought home from the discount mart the other
day: a bulk-size package of the special millennial
cereal called "Millennios," with three O-shaped pieces

for every 2-shaped piece. Ooh, the fun, the fun! (And
breaking the jyze rules on brand names twice in one
paragraph, that's fun too! -- But it'll be a long time
before I'll let it happen again and that's a promise.)

[+1]

     Downtown glitter. A window table at yet another
franchise chain coffee shop in the retail core right
across the street from the floodlit white facade of one
of the major chain department stores and just half a
block from the chain young-folks' clothing store that
was the main target of one of Monday's "actions" (of
which not a single trace remains detectable now -- a few
minutes ago I checked). It's a little before six-thirty
and this place closes at eight, though I doubt I'll hang
on here that long. I got work, work, work to do.
     A fine perch. Lots of people are passing by
outside, many carrying shopping bags. This is the heart
of the "glitz strip." And a few of the passersby look
a bit glitzy themselves, at least by local standards.
Most, however, don't. A small number might be called,
like me, conspicuously non-glitzy or anti-glitzy (but
then again I'm wearing one of my newish black cotton
shirts that came from the very corporate chain targeted
by Monday's action, although it was another store in
that chain, and my not-so-new jeans came from a store in
a different chain owned by the same corporation, and my
ancient socks came from a chain store previously owned
by the first-named corporation but they, I believe, sold
it to the corporation that actually made the jeans or
rather had them made by an overseas contractor paying
its workers about a dime an hour -- which of course is
well above the going rate in that country, so what the
heck is all the commotion about?).
     Well okay then, if that's not enough, the shop in
which I sit is a franchise of our locally headquartered
coffee colossus. It's a prime force behind what's
sometimes called "J-town neoliberal neocolonialism,"

which is to say, an avowed proponent of so-called
"socially responsible" globalization, which of course
is a preposterous contradiction in terms if not in
actual meaning, especially if you remember to include
the modifier "corporate" before "globalization" -- and
in this it's just like all those other corporations
mentioned above and also our local software behemoth and
our local aerospace/"defense" giant and the dot-com
gorilla that's taken over our hilltop hood and a whole
slew of other such corporations, here and elsewhere and
of course even in a few places beyond the USA, although
no one has any doubt who's in charge of the overarching
multinational corporate system leading us all straight
to a true apocalypse.

   -- As the fire crackles across the room. And
coffee drinkers lounge in a nest of cushy armchairs.
Not bad, not bad -- though definitely not too homey and
certainly not too funky. Not really, I'd concede, a
jyzer's kind of place. And yet, though perhaps only
because of the lateness of the hour, they're still
letting this jyzer right here do his thing regardless.

   The little round table I've commandeered stands in
a bay formed by the picture windows. I didn't realize
this when I first sat here, but it's almost as if I'm a
live show-window display: the glass is nearly floor to
ceiling and wall to wall. A display for literacy maybe
as I scribble away? Is literacy of the nondigital kind
still considered "socially responsible"? -- And the
table appears to be made of the same kind of wood my
father's last and proudest desk was: cherry.

   (Refills of drip coffee here cost fifty cents. A
sign by the cash register says you must drink all of the
first cup inside the shop in under an hour. Otherwise I
suppose the bench-sitters from the downtown plaza a
block to the west, and any other vagrants or drifters or
jyzers who happen to be in the area, would be buying
one-fourth-price coffee in here all day long using the
same cup.)

   It's an interesting time. Today's one of the big
travel days of the year and the freeways looked even

more jammed than usual as I walked in. (Z was planning
to do dinner in the vicinity of the training session to
avoid the rush-hour crush.) Down here not much is going
on as far as I can see. Lots of Christmas decorations
are in place but not all are turned on yet. The
Christmas carousel is set up in the plaza next to the
fountain but the carved wooden horses are still enclosed
in their crates, and the big asterisk-like star hanging
up to ten stories above the park on the side of the
other main chain department store is dark. But the
white lights strung in the trees lining the avenues are
all shining and the whole area looks glisteningly clean
and even somewhat festive as it awaits the bulk of the
WTO attendees and the Christmas shoppers (but it also
looks faintly ominous: is this just my imagination or
are FBI and Secret Service types already lurking about?
-- Whoever they are, they're plenty steely-eyed).
     I walked up the "very high road" coming in, then
cut through the central plaza, thinking if anything was
going on with the protests it would be happening there.
But I saw nothing unusual. Earlier as I hiked across
the high bridge the city looked spectacular with a low
cloudbank hanging directly above it, engulfing the top
stories of the tallest buildings and aglow with the
colors of the downtown lights, green and pink and yellow
diffused through the mists so the clouds themselves
turned luminous in a multihued way -- and the long two-
toned tongue of the north-south freeway, red on one side
and white on the other, sticking straight out at me --
sassing me! -- while also bending down to lick the AQ
valley. (Underneath the biggest of the overpasses, half
a dozen men were lying in sleeping bags or blankets atop
cardboard. They'll almost certainly be rooted out of
there very soon. One of the largest protest marches
will be going right by that spot. I noticed a couple of
local churches are setting up big tents for the homeless
during WTO, but of course those tents'll be coming down
shortly after the delegates leave town. We wouldn't
want to establish any precedents or instill any bad
habits here. We know when we face a true moral hazard.)

This is the 24th of the month so it's the fourth
anniversary of Mother's death, the first of two this
week (day of the week and date). This afternoon Olwen
called, trying to leave a voicemail for Z, and I picked
up -- and it turns out today is Olwen's mother's
birthday. We had a good talk about mothers and
families. Olwen's mother lived on east hill during her
later years and Z knew her quite well, I learned, and
used to visit her (the mother) on her own, just the two
of them doing tea together. I also told Olwen the story
of my conception day -- triggered by Olwen's mentioning
that she'd be going in for mouth surgery on December
7th. And we revisited the matter of the ominous bee
buzzing around Olwen's hand when she married us. I
admitted I hadn't even noticed it at the time. "well,
you were in another dimension then -- the ecstatic one."
"And I still am!" We set up a meeting for the 16th of
December, after she's had a while to recover from her
surgery. (And I'm still agog that my liaison with Z has
me making such appointments so long in advance, just as
I was flabbergasted to learn about this practice of hers
when we first met. She had luncheon and dinner
engagements blocked in as much as three months in
advance! And now with me to accommodate as well
it's more like four or five months!)
     -- With a coil or two of one ear I'm listening to a
worker from another coffee shop belonging to this same
chain a few blocks up the street near the convention
center talk about what shops and buildings in the area
will or won't be closed next week during the prime demo
hours. According to her, many of them will be boarding
up their show windows.
     Also I should at least mention the morning of
silence Z and I decreed today. The training session is
driving her up the wall, she said in a note, and worst
of all is her coworker Bradley's nonstop jabber during
their hourlong (or longer) commutes back and forth.
"Can this be one of those times," Z asked me, "when we
go for silence?" And so we did, even working it for a
few not-so-silent laughs. The previous night she'd been

557

about to blow her stack because the neighbors were
working on their cars for two hours straight right
outside our dining-area window, engines idling at high
RPMs when not revving hellaciously, black smoke roiling
about, heavy-metal music echoing raucous and loud. If
she'd had a BB gun, she said, she'd've shot out the
Christmas lights they'd just put up on the side of their
house facing us. -- And she grumped playfully about how
I "sleep like a baby" while she's tormented by her
insomnia, waking to find her mind racing on questions
almost always work-related (and in recent days focusing
mainly on the exasperating antics of Gloria G.). "I'm
so envious! You lead such a stress-free life!" -- Ha!
Don't I wish! -- But low-stress, yes, usually, that is,
unless the pressure I put on myself counts. And of
course it does count. And that's why I work very hard
to make the other parts of my life as genuinely myg-
free, I'll dub them in Z's honor, as possible.

[+1]

      And a snatch is what it is, but not that limited a
snatch. Fifty-five minutes until bus time. Down at the
scope office, the conference room. A drizzly night and
all's as quiet as it ever gets in here except wind gusts
are causing frequent taps and creaks in the windows,
sometimes even little pings as if single hailstones or
BBs were hitting them. (I can't help it, I'm thinking
of snipers. This room right here would make a pretty
good perch for one, with the brightly lit horseshoe
drive of the many-starred hotel laid out down below just
half a block away, a Christmas tree ablaze with strings
of white lights standing in the patch of grass at its
center perfectly illuminating the drive and the people
going in and out of the main entrance, almost like decoy
targets on a loop at a shooting gallery. And the
abundance of potential sniper sites in this area
furnishes just one of the many reasons I could run into
trouble myself during my work hours next week.)

But it's Thanksgiving Day (late in the evening of).
Understandably Z moped and pouted about dropping me off
down here after we left Wei and Alison's, but since
we've had plans for weeks or maybe months to see her
friends Fred and Eleanor tomorrow evening I really had
no choice but to tear off a big chunk of grand jury
tonight. And in fact I've already done that, finishing
the morning session, mostly a series of indictments of a
counterfeit-check-cashing ring consisting of an odd mix
of USAns of Vietnamese and Honduran extraction, many of
them down-on-their-luck gamblers. Two to three hours'
work still remains for tomorrow night, but since Z
rarely likes to stay out after ten p.m., I should be
able to grind it out in time to catch my usual last bus
home. And if I haven't finished it by then, I can still
take that same bus home and drive right back down. Even
on a Friday night some street parking should be opening
up at two a.m. (though making the extra round trip is
always a time-wasting pain).

The new tree's up in the main-floor lobby here. A
thirty-footer or so: the angel at the top (yes!) almost
seems to be holding up the ceiling and thus the whole
building with its wingtips. Like the trees of previous
years, this one's a too-deep green; it both looks and
smells artificial. But the smell isn't quite as toxic
as last year's, when tough-guy ex-army lifer Ross the
security guard -- who's still on the job down there --
was sickened by it and had to go home early.

The D-clan's Thanksgiving dinner turned out to be
clannish indeed, with at least thirty relatives showing
up (including us as honoraries) and another carload or
two still expected after we left. It was blessedly
informal and didn't actually become child-dominated
though it often threatened to, with Dak's sister's
daughter and three foster kids under the age of seven --
one a five-month-old girl -- joining Aida's Charles and
the four little girls of "L-O-V-E" serenade fame (for
much of the time all except the infant were billeted
upstairs playing electronic games). Dinner was served
buffet-style at the jam-packed round dining-room table,

with all those present first joining hands in a circle
as Mr. D, who's a lay church official of some sort as
well as the clan patriarch, said an almost professional-
sounding grace. The roast turkey was excellent and the
array of Filipino foods probably was too, though I
wouldn't really know since I only sampled a few for fear
of strong spices, and in any case the whole spread was a
pleasure to look at. No cranberries were on offer,
alas, and Z missed them, as she has at previous D-clan
Thanksgivings. (I missed them too, and also some good
artsy or political talk, but there was really no
opportunity for that.)

     Mr. D seemed in excellent spirits, showing no sign
of disease (other than a large sterile dressing on his
right jaw) or of concern about the chemo ordeal he's
facing. For my benefit Dak broke out the only hard
liquor he had in the house, and that was a fifth of
scotch a friend had given him fifteen or twenty years
ago. When a new batch of cousins arrived, from a branch
of the family even Z hadn't met before, we were
introduced as "our family friend Zoelie and her husband
Glen" -- not quite a first for us but almost. (The one
discordant note, Aida was present but Kirk wasn't, and
that was because Mrs. D had put her foot down and said
she preferred him not to be. Evidently she disapproves
of their relationship because it's sexual and they're
not married. And Aida's a divorcee with an eleven-year-
old kid! As Z said: why did Aida ask her mother for
permission? Why didn't she just bring him? In reply I
told her I wasn't sure but I thought the answer was laid
out somewhere in that book we both read two years ago:
"Culture Shock: The Philippines." At this she rolled
her eyes and said, "Well duh, Glen. I'm talking about
the contradictions in Aida's character, not her mother's
motivation. I shouldn't have to tell you that,
sweetheart, should I?" -- And though I may have blushed
and perhaps even scowled a bit, eventually I had to
admit she had a pretty good point there.)

     We arrived at three and left at quarter to six.
Then we drove about five miles from the D-clan's

festivities in the north end (a few blocks from where
Lady U and I used to buy pet supplies until the owner
was busted for a huge basement marijuana grow) to Wei
and Alison's abode on the western slope of north hill.
We arrived with our special cake, freshly baked earlier
today by a friend of Z's (Z was the high bidder on it at
an office raffle), just as the ten folks gathered around
the candlelit table were finishing up dessert, all of
them groaning in almost choral unison when Z announced
"Dessert's here!" A couple of hours of wide-ranging
small talk followed, much of it with just Wei and Alison
as we helped them clean up after the others left. And
Saturday we'll be seeing W&A again for museum-hopping
and a Christmas-card-making "bee." (I enjoyed gabbing
with Alison's swimming buddy Marj, a retired librarian
and a serious reader. We already knew we liked each
other from W&A's wedding and reception at which she was
the photographer.)
      -- And it's getting stormier out there. More
creaks and pings and some whooshes too. If this turns
into a weeklong spell of bad weather as some forecasters
are predicting, well, the chances that the big anti-WTO
demos will alter the course of the 21st century, already
slight in my view, will diminish still further. (But
many commentators at the national level are still
insisting the impact could be massive. I heard a news
interview in which a veteran political scientist said
this might turn out to be "a crucial moment in American
history.")
      Yipes. "Pedal to metal" time.
                    *   *
(A kwikjyze quote at home. "This is the week that
all good Eurusans give thanks that we've so far escaped
the retribution we so richly deserve for our ethnic
cleansing and in many cases outright genocide
perpetrated against the indigenous occupants of this
land over a period of four centuries and which in many
ways still continue today." -- Those words came to me
and I jotted them down as I waited at the bus stop, and
therefore still on Thanksgiving Day by NUT time.)

[+1]

        The black armchair, unit 203. I've just been
looking through some photocopies of Z's medical records
covering the past few months, including the lab reports
on her pelvic ultrasound and "endometrial ex." They're
a little scarier than she thought, with the presence of
"multiple cysts" noted in the endometrial cavity and
the possibility of cancer not ruled out. After talking
with the specialist today Z's decided to have a D&C
done after all so they can determine for sure what's
going on in there. She'd prefer to wait until after the
Christmas holidays and the quatrorollover to do it, but
I'm urging her to go ahead as soon as possible.

        I don't want to sound glib or resigned but there's
just not much more we can say about this right now.
Oddly, maybe, our spirits are even a little uplifted
because the lab reports found no evidence of malignancy.
Yes, we realize this may be owing to an inadequate
tissue sample; apparently that's always a possibility.
But still and regardless we're thinking it's best to
remain hopeful as long as we can. And I'm even thinking
I'll try to keep going in these pages no matter what
happens. (Yes, this is a reversal. Insofar as possible
I want to include everything in the annal, the bad as
well as the good, and I think I can be tough-minded
about it. I'd rather go out that way myself. And Z's
already told me she'd be really disappointed if I didn't
say to hell with any taunting by the grim reaper and
hold fast to the jyze plan.)

        -- And we learn all this on the day after
Thanksgiving. "Black Friday." Four years ago at this
hour I was snatching a little sleep on the floor at
Mother's apartment after flying down -- or no, that was
the next day. Or maybe the day or even two days after
that? It's all such a blur! I could check Jyze Annal
2 to nail down the details but there's not much point
in doing so. I'll just say it this way: that was the
week when the family I grew up in shattered. It was the

last time Barb, Jeff, Rob, and I were together in one place, probably ever.

But regardless. Jyze goes on about the life I've got now, yes. (And "Hydes of Jyze," the sign, is up too, just in case. And I'll try to come back again tomorrow night for another round since it's already four-thirty a.m., or almost.)

Of interest today, we caught a four o'clock showing of "The Insider" with Fred and Eleanor, then did dinner with them at a north-end Mongolian restaurant, and then I put in the expected three hours of scoping and fortunately that proved to be enough. On the way home Z again let me off downtown, like Thursday night, and I walked to the scope office by way of the central plaza where the Christmas decorations were now all lit up, the carousel spinning merrily as tinny Christmas music echoed off the surrounding buildings, the big holiday tree dazzling everyone with its red and gold lights, the asterisk-shaped department-store star hanging over the whole scene displaying this year a new matching gold and red inner core. Lots of cops were strolling about in various kinds of unfamiliar uniforms (meaning reinforcements are already being called in from the burbs) and several eyed me suspiciously, as did a passenger in one of the horse-drawn Victorian carriages always to be observed clopping around down there at this time of year. "Eek, could that icky man dressed in black be one of those WTO anarchists all the talk shows are warning about?" (Not an actual quote.)

"The Insider" is told from the perspective of a former radical journalist around my age who in his near-dotage has become an investigator for a prestigious hourlong TV news show. The crisis of conscience he goes through in the film is somewhat similar to my own when I left alternative journalism at a much earlier age than he did. It's quite possible I might've followed a career course similar to his if I'd stayed with the game a year or two longer. (And boy, seeing this movie sure did relieve me of any lingering regrets I might've had on that score.)

     -- And then the ongoing livelinesses of life with
Zoelie B. They never do come to an end or even take
more than a brief breather. (As feet sound overhead.
This is the last weekend Doug and Thuy and the kids will
be living here. -- And incidentally we still haven't
heard anything about the status of the rumored sale of
the building. But Z is now saying she's interested in
buying a condo at a new building of artist lofts going
up in the valley just northeast of the hill, only about
eight blocks from here. Except for the newness I
wouldn't mind at all living in a place like that. But
it would probably be too expensive for us, and
construction is only just now starting up and will take
an estimated two years or perhaps longer.)
     -- Last night she tried to pull a little prank on
me. When she heard me coming up the stairs (she was
reading in bed, unable to sleep) she turned off the
bedside light and hid behind the dining table in the
"great room," leaving our bedroom door wide open. But
she failed to figure on one thing: since in the dark I
couldn't see whether she was in bed, I assumed she was
and quietly closed the door and launched into my usual
homecoming routine. After a few minutes she popped up
from behind the dining table, pouting because I hadn't
even noticed her absence or searched for her. A sign,
yeah: she must be feeling neglected, right? And yet
earlier in the day we'd been together for more than
eight hours straight at the two Thanksgiving feasts.
But she says she just can't be, though she tries,
"Norwegian" at all times, by which she means she can't
hold her high-drama impulses in check. Then when she
sees someone who seems to be doing just that, like the
wife of the former radical journalist in the movie
tonight, she asks, "Am I the bad wife or the good wife?"
     Another issue that came up again: she wants to hire
a housecleaner. She says that's the only way she can
hope to (1) stay on top of her job and (2) maintain good
relations with her circle of friends (that is, by
reciprocating invitations as of course proper friends
must do) and at the same time (3) tend to the needs of,

as she says half-jokingly, an "incessantly demanding"
husband. And I grump that this housecleaner thing is a
bad idea because I believe we ought to at least be able
to keep up our small apartment without calling in
outside help, especially when we live in a city where
the services providing such help are mostly staffed by
exploited third-world immigrants, many "illegal").

     And then tonight in the car on the way back home
she suddenly burst out, apropos of nothing, with "I want
more sex!" (And of course I replied, "With whom?" And
she replied, I'm pleased to say: "With you!") -- She's
afraid we'll have even less opportunity now, I think,
because of the cysts. Well, I'll do my very best, I
say. But it wouldn't hurt, I go on, if she'd be just a
little bit more romantic and TLC-ish about it when the
gloves are off and the chips are down and if she'd avoid
just a bit more often putting "the clamp" on me because
she first wants to engage in extended pillow talk
(sometimes also known as venting) even when I'm in a
glaringly ithyfied state which might not last forever.

     All familiar issues, just with slightly new twists.

     And my hour's up, or almost, and I still have a few
chores to do, including locating all the Christmas-
related art supplies which we'll be hauling over to Wei
and Alison's house for the card-making "bee" (which
can't be here, though it should be, since it's our turn;
but the place is just too cluttered).

     Ach, it's frustrating but it's also fun, trying to
do so much and keep the Z-wiff happy and also keep this
TJM project going. (As the neighbors Z loves to hate
pull into their steep driveway with bumpers scraping
concrete and boom box blasting loud enough to wake up
the whole hood -- and this at five-thirty a.m.!)

                         [+1]

     A last snatch of no more than thirty minutes.
Here's the couch. Here's the grossly overgrown
poinsettia from last Christmas, now the de facto holiday

centerpiece for the coffee table and really the whole
"great room." Tomorrow's fat far-coast Sunday paper
(actually today's in Gregorian terms) rests on the seat
of the black armchair to my right. Our WTO story makes
the front page: "Setting the stage for a new century."
Well, no, those words don't actually appear in the story
and they don't even represent its tone, which mainly
deals with the many difficulties facing the WTO. Yet I
think this is how much of the political world is
thinking about it. (Meaning what? Just that it feels
really big, I guess. Certainly more so than it did just
a few days ago, at least for me.)

     The equivalent of an upscale anti-WTO rally took
place last night at the new downtown symphony hall, the
same one outside of which I catch my bus home on scoping
nights. We missed the event because of our prior
commitment to Wei and Alison. But the keynote speaker
was good old Gerry M. from my newshound days in city No.
2/7. Reading the report of what he had to say I
realized the arguments I had with him back then upon my
return from Korea and Japan were much the same as the
arguments USAn labor and ecology groups have with the
WTO today, and especially with the "less developed"
member states of the WTO. Many of those states are
claiming the West is trying to use the WTO to keep their
countries impoverished while at the same time imposing
its values on the world. It's the failure of people
like Gerry M. and the USAn environmental and labor
movements to come to grips with this issue that's
leading to the current impasse. -- But I'm certainly
not saying I know of some formula that would resolve the
dilemma. I just wish less self-righteous certainty were
on display among the people I support -- meaning Gerry
M. and those same movements -- and more willingness to
acknowledge the complexity and depth of the issues and
to include voices from those "less developed" countries
in the discussion (and not just the voices of the elites
who are in cahoots with our own ruling class).

     -- But it's a cauldron. It's nasty. Vast
historical forces are working themselves out and these

people who are trying to avert looming ecological
catastrophe, Gerry M. included, are in my view among the
heroes of our time (yes, even if their vision is too
narrow and purist, according to me, and thus would seem
to be self-canceling).

Sometimes I feel like such a fool to be scribbling
away at my little jyze projects, and never more so than
when I try to come up with a few comments on the burning
issues of the day. It's a moral thing, I guess: at some
level I feel I ought to be out there mixing it up with
the heavyweights or at least trying to. In some way I
just can't give up thinking that's my preferred role --
that's the most admirable, most honorable, most heroic
way to be in our time, and I should try to be that way.
Like the former radical journalist in the movie.

Certainly I have countervoices to that one and on
the whole they're stronger and I believe wiser. But
sometimes I stop hearing them for a while and just have
to go on a kind of blind faith that I've chosen the
right path for myself.

-- Profundities of the crackerbarrel variety from
one whose J-book is his crackerbarrel. -- And so to
bed.

28

-- Comes steppin' on down to the central plaza.
And just this one last time before spring of next year,
most likely, why not try it outdoors, from a park bench,
as the lights shine and a few shoppers straggle by, on
an evening probably less mild than it seems to me right
now. But I'm bundled up. And for maybe an hour I can
stand it, mild or not so mild.

[The Jyze Millennium, Part II]

    The big event is about to begin. Moments ago I was
a chuckling witness to a scene something like a skit
from a bad TV variety show, with a couple of raggedy
half-ripped local Afrusan dudes greeting four sharply
dressed WTO delegates from Pakistan over at my usual
downtown chain burger/cone joint, cleaning off tables
for them and speculating about the real reason
Pakistanis and Indians of the subcontinent type don't
always get along so well. The Pakistanis,
sophisticated-looking men carrying shopping bags from
the plaza chain bookstore right across the street here,
seemed to be enjoying the taste of authentic Jyze City
culture as expressed in such a setting, at least for the
couple of minutes I was sitting nearby.
    Through a gap in a small grove of designer trees
I'm looking at the big gold-and-red silver fir
dominating the plaza (except for the hundred-foot-high
Christmas asterisk hanging over it, affixed to a corner
of the largest of the "glitz strip" chain department
stores). A few feet to my left stands the carousel, now
shut down for the night, behind a circular white picket
fence, and just inside the fence sits a cheerful Cawk
rent-a-cop who's been yukking it up with everybody
passing by, focusing on likely WTO delegates.
    Right now the cops in the square probably outnumber
the non-cops. Ross, the swing-shift guard at the scope
building, told me his security outfit hired a dozen
temps for this week, two for each of their buildings, an
extra day guard and an extra night guard, with twelve-
hour shifts for everyone all week long. And tonight
when I went in, one of those temps was posted at the
counter behind the big lobby Christmas tree and for the
first time in years I had to sign in and out.
Possession of separate swipe cards for the building door
and the elevator and a key for our office door was not
enough. But the guy had a humorous spiel ready. "It's
just for this one week, just to be sure there are no
problems, yadda yadda yadda. All you gotta do is sign
on the dotted line and the whole building is yours."
    Ross said I'd be well advised to take Monday and

Tuesday off. When I told him I almost always have to come in on Tuesday nights and this week would likely be no exception, he warned me to "be very careful out there." To my surprise, though, he didn't ask any questions about whether I'd be rioting and vandalizing buildings with the rest of the protesters. Ross is a hardcore right-winger, a gun nut, a military lifer and a stalwart militia supporter, but I guess the fact that he and I have been joshing and jiving each other for several years now is enough to get me by with him.

So I've been wandering around to see what there is to see. And I'll say there's not a whole lot. A few more fancy limos and cabs than usual are pulling up to the big hotels or lurking nearby. (The cheerful rent-a-cop by the merry-go-round calls out to three obvious probable delegate passersby, "Where are you gentlemen from, India?" "Nepal." "Nepal! Well well, what do you think of Jyze City?" And lights are flashing now as they take photos with the big Christmas tree -- sixty-some feet high -- as a backdrop.) The people you do run into here and there all seem to be looking at each other and wondering, Are you a delegate? An undercover cop? A protester? A genuine native? Or are you a mere street person, a hobo or vagrant or wino or some such reprobate? At various times, depending on the light and what I happen to be doing, I might be taken to fall into any but the first and possibly the second of those categories.

Now and again sirens wail and squad cars speed by, lights flashing. Things are happening in this town tonight, though I don't recall just what. "Actions." This afternoon at the farewell open house for Z's friend Bitha, who's about to move to the far coast with her adopted Chinese infant daughter Josie, one of the attendees was planning to let himself be arrested in a locked-arms-inside-hard-plastic-tubes stop-traffic street sitdown outside the convention center on Tuesday morning. Several others were committed to march. Others, though, weren't; and for a crowd like this, mostly urban liberals in or around their thirties, that

was surprising and disappointing. But this is how it
is: the so-called "new world order," already in place
close to a full decade now since the crumbling of the
Soviet Union, is still causing politics to shake out in
puzzling ways in this country and many others.
      And Mickey and Minnie and Donald are still flashing
their inane grins at us from the second floor of the big
arcade building. But no skateboarders are to be seen or
heard. Apparently they've all been routed from their
usual haunts. For this reason all by itself I could
applaud the city's decision to host this convention.
(Two couples wheel by on bicycles built for two. An odd
sight at this hour. It reminds me, though: a lot of the
people I've witnessed in this area and elsewhere tonight
have been marathoners out on the town celebrating
today's big race, many hobbling about or walking very
gingerly.)
      Meanwhile my hands are about to lock up. For
wandering or strolling about it's a fine night; for
jyzing alfresco it's turning out to be just a few
degrees too chilly. By now all the big department
stores are closed. I can see four of them from here,
making for a box-canyon effect, their walls floodlit and
festooned with seasonal decorations. -- And raindrops
appear suddenly, so I gotta go anyway.
                    *   *
      -- Was it rain or was it someone spraying something
somewhere out of my line of sight? Because those were
the only drops I felt. But then this is the rainy
season and another storm's always about to roll in.
-- And it's Advent Sunday too, at least for many of
those here in evergreen country inclined to observe the
ritual calendars of Mideastern desert religions. (What
is Advent again? I've forgotten. So I should check it
out. But can't do that right now.)
      An uneventful walk from the central plaza down to
the hideaway, not too different from the way it might've
gone any other Sunday at ten-thirty p.m., except for the
two sets of double sentinels, uniformed and armed,
stationed outside the main federal building and the

reserve bank. And Mr. Y at the mom-and-pop store asked
how it was up by the convention center -- "Many people
on street?" -- and told me about the cops and FBI men
who'd come into his store, including one who'd swept
back a trenchcoat when reaching for his wallet and
revealed lots of fancy electronic gear along with a
"big, big" gun in a holster. A Secret Service agent
most likely, we agreed.

"Did he ask if you were going to try to shut down
the WTO?" I queried.

"Shut down? I told him you do it. My friend Mr.
G, arrest him."

The historic quarter is just about dead tonight. I
saw a limo and a few cabs slowly cruising through, all
filled with men looking to be WTO delegates, but they
didn't even bother to stop and check out the only two
clubs open on the triangle proper. And up here in Jyzer
Ink world headquarters it's even quieter, presumably
because many of the officeholders in this building have
left`town for the long Thanksgiving weekend that will
soon be ending. And to my surprise no bands are
blasting away down below.

A note on Bitha's party. She's moving back home,
to the far coast, northern inland section, or if not
home exactly, at least a place where her brother will be
living nearby, and the move is being paid for (as her
adopted daughter was) by proceeds from the stock she
amassed during her years working for our local software
behemoth, where she was a very early hire. She's quite
friendly, New Englandy, small, Eurusan; but other than Z
all her friends who showed up for the party were
likewise Eurusan and, though Z admires her, she can't
help feeling awkward with her at times because of her
extreme lack of awareness on class and racial matters.
Z fears for Josie, the adopted daughter, in much the
same way she's always feared for Kat with Betty,
especially in the lily-pink area where they'll be living
and even though she, Z, thinks Bitha, again like Betty,
has a big heart which usually seems to be in the right
place ("but they're both just so unbelievably naive!").

For most of the evening I wound up sitting at the kitchen table talking with three men, all of whom turned out to be connected in one way or another with my past. One attended my alma mater a decade after I did (he'd just returned from a visit to Taiwan on behalf of his employer, the software behemoth); one lived in my city 2/7 during almost exactly the same period I did and for a few years attended the university where I taught as a guest instructor and he might even have taken one of my classes, though neither of us had any memory of the other; and the third, Kip S., the one who was preparing to be arrested, was and is a playwright/actor/director with experience both here and in city 2/7 and thus might well have been acquainted with one or more of my three previous wives (counting Lady U as a real rather than a zen wife) since all three were seriously involved in theater -- but I didn't get a chance to ask.

I'd like to say a few words about the exhibit of modern Chinese art at the university gallery which we visited with Wei and Alison and also the dinner and card-making "bee" at their house. But the time's all gone and tonight June's dropping by to practice her oral arguments -- which should be a trip and a half for me -- and then tomorrow looks to be too busy to squeeze in any backward looks. -- But maybe not. Can hope. Will.

[+1]

Do numbers matter? Of course they do. So why shouldn't someone take notice we're now in the 333rd day of the year? (I heard someone mention it'll be a thousand years before another year rolls around with three 9's in it -- but that assumes the consensual international basis of number-assigning doesn't change over those years. If we start a whole new calendrical system, it could be up to 1,999 years before three 9's reappear, and that's assuming we start only one such new system. It could be much longer if we start several of them over the turbulent centuries ahead. Or if we

switch to another already existing system -- the Chinese
calendar, say, or the Hindu or the Iranian or the Jewish
or the Ibo or the Navaho or the Mayan or any of hundreds
of others -- those three 9's could reappear much sooner,
though I'd have to do extensive research to figure out
exactly how soon. And that I'm not planning to do.)

Meanwhile we've got the WTO. And so far nothing
terribly exciting has happened. In fact some of the
sizzle has gone out of the event because the stogie-
chawin' Cuban leader has said he won't be coming. And
even more of the sizzle has gone out because today the
rains returned in a big way, complete with strong shifty
gusts, holding down attendance for the first of the
major marches, which I briefly witnessed at three
different times and places tonight. And the forecast
for tomorrow, day of the really big march, is for more
heavy rain -- just what the mayor ordered (and of course
the odds that it would arrive, this being the city it is
and the season it is, were always high).

First I'll note I blew off my tentatively scheduled
meeting with Lynn, guardian of the deep reserves, this
afternoon. She waited until so late to firm up the
details -- calling after I'd left for work last night --
I couldn't return the call; and her message didn't
mention either time or place for the meeting. Nor did I
relish the prospect of wrenching myself out of bed hours
ahead of the normal time so I could try to see her at
2:30 p.m., as tentatively agreed, at a certain twenty-
four-hour cafe over by the fairgrounds, where I knew she
and Rob would be getting together a couple of hours
earlier. Also I recalled her failure to show up for our
scheduled Thanksgiving-week rendezvous two years ago.
And I really just had too many other things on my mind
to be hassling about what I knew would turn out to be
little more than a social confab in which I'd regale her
with my two boffo wedding tales: "Goddess" and
"Glitter." (The punchy new titles. And now I have both
tales down cold, although the laugh-meter always spikes
much higher if Z and I can act out the script together.)

Tomorrow, alas, I'll have to be rising even earlier

in order to join Z near the assembly point at the fairgrounds for the big labor march (ironically we're planning to meet at a different franchise of the same (nonunion) corporate burger chain where I buy my vanilla cones -- and just today protesters reportedly broke some windows in another downtown store belonging to the same chain; a celebrated French farmer, who's leading the charge against the USAn-style fast-fooding of French cuisine, is here for the demos and this "action" was presumably an outgrowth of that cause). Supposedly Betty (Kat's mom) will be dropping by our place and she and I will be busing crosstown together to meet Z, but I wasn't able to reach Betty to confirm this and she runs notoriously late and I won't be waiting around for her if that's the case again tomorrow.

Rather than work out at the WOC and risk being stranded in the area should tonight's demo get out of hand, as many were predicting, Z decided to walk home right after work (bus service was sporadic at best owing to the crowds and blocked-off streets). I decided to delay leaving home so that I could go directly to check out that same demo on my way in. As it happened, our paths crossed in the Asian quarter, roughly two blocks east of the east depot. I was carrying an umbrella, she was wearing her new brown winter raincoat (which leaks, we now know). A lovely moment, a lengthy kiss under the awning of a low-income hotel as several lobby-sitters glumly peered out at us from about two feet away through the big vapor-blurry lobby windows.

Then I walked up to the "very very high road" and the gathering place for the march, which happened to be the same grand old stone church which hosted Z's graduation ceremony two years ago and just a block from city hall. The street was blocked off and the front deck of the church was lined with folks holding umbrellas aloft, drums were pounding, a crowd was packed in tight while sheltering under the overhang of the building across the street, picket signs were bobbing about in the rain. The march, sponsored by the major state association of churches, was calling for cancellation of the debts of the world's poorest countries in the spirit of the Catholic "Jubilee Year" tradition. It was without a doubt the most wholesome-looking and most well-behaved crowd I've ever seen at a protest. And it was relatively small compared to some predictions I'd come across; no more than a thousand people were present at that point, with the march due to start in twenty minutes. I didn't hang around long.

After dropping by the hideaway for forty-five minutes or so I headed off through the HQ and saw the march coming down the hill. I went on ahead to the new stadium exhibition center, which was brightly lit up and Christmas-decorated for the WTO's opening banquet. This center stands midway between the old dome and the new baseball field, but I could get no closer to it than a block and a half, nor could any other observer, as the police had erected a fence at the point where the rounded edge of the dome protrudes into the road and narrows it, and dozens of police were stationed behind the fence (in black ponchos and helmets with transparent visors folded back over their skulls); and a small group of "China out of Tibet" protesters were milling just outside that fence, and a hundred yards to the north a couple of huge union rigs were set up with music blasting, the side of one of the rigs painted with Local No. 174's slogan: "Fighting for Social and Economic Justice." (Yeah, right. Like tell it to the hundreds of millions of Asians and Africans that this same union wants to keep out of any trade agreement. It's regularly endorsed warhawk right-wing presidential candidates for the past three decades.)

Then I doubled back a couple of blocks and watched the march go by. It was only about two blocks long at most, filling up the portion of the street between sidewalks. Lo and behold who should pass about five feet in front of me but Wei and Alison.

"Where's Zoelie?" asked Alison.

"Probably in bed asleep by now," joshed Wei.

"Getting perky for the big one tomorrow," I confirmed.

    And that was about it. They kept going, I went
back to the hideaway. It was hard to imagine the
marchers' numbers would suffice to meet the goal of
creating a linked-hands human chain around the
exhibition center, especially with the expanded police
perimeter surrounding it. And then an hour later I
heard unusual sounds as I was hitting the head and went
down to the lobby to watch the remnant of the march, a
few hundred people -- W&A no longer among them so far as
I could see -- with a couple of squad cars at both ends,
sadly straggle through the triangle headed north, drums
pounding, as the rain continued to pour down.

                        [+1]

    Tonight it's a whole different story. Tonight the
city's in a state of -- "civil emergency"! Tonight our
anti-WTO protests are the lead story on all the national
newscasts in this country and no doubt many around the
world.
    The entire downtown is under a strict curfew
lasting until seven a.m. The hideaway building, where
I'm holed up right now, is at the extreme southwestern
corner of the curfew zone, just inside it. I won't even
try to make it up to the scope office tonight. I know
work's awaiting me there, but the police have announced
anyone who enters the area will be asked to produce ID
and to justify their presence, and I seriously doubt I
could do that in a way they'd accept. Other than my
swipe cards and keys for the scope building I have
nothing to document my need to be there. I suppose I
could rip my Jyzer Ink business license from its spot on
the wall and carry it along, but -- get real! By all
reports the police are in a very surly mood and my
physical appearance all by itself would put me under
intense suspicion.
    It's like Lady S's home city under martial law when
we were living there. It's like Centropolis during the
infamous Days of Rage. -- Oh yes, and the National

Guard's been called out and will be deployed en masse at various strategic spots downtown in the morning.

In short, today's demo was a tremendous success. Before now very few people had even heard of the WTO; by tomorrow it'll be "a household name" throughout the world, and better yet, people will know it's highly controversial and maybe even a few details about why that's so and what could be done about it.

And tomorrow things here in J. City could be still more tense. The president himself just flew in -- this is our U.S. president and therefore of course the self-appointed, more or less, or better to say corporations/plutocrats/oligopolists-appointed, boss of the world -- and he'll be staying at one of the big downtown hotels the next two nights -- nobody's sure just which one -- and from what I hear he'll be delivering a major speech to the WTO ministers and delegates tomorrow afternoon at none other than the many-starred hotel visible from the scope-office windows. No mass actions are scheduled for tomorrow to rival today's big march, but it's my guess that what the media are already calling "the Battle of Jyze City" will continue and perhaps even escalate. The media images radiating out from here -- careening around the planet, yes, I'm sure -- are likely to attract even more protesters from J. City's surrounding metro area and beyond.

The big march itself isn't what did it. That provided a kind of cover, a way to infiltrate tens of thousands of people into the downtown. Then after most of the union people who organized the march and provided perhaps two-thirds of its bodies went home, the remainder of the marchers, including several independent radical groups that had paraded into town from five different directions, were left milling around the core of the commercial area, where they were essentially allowed to take over the streets. It was one of the eeriest sights I've ever witnessed, "almost surreal," as I heard several people observe (one being Zoelie B.), because it was taking place in the retail core where all those Christmas decorations were hanging, within sight

of the big tree, the thousands of lights, the carousel,
the giant star, a huge papier-mache Santa and much more.
And then a few small "violent" incidents occurred
(almost inevitably), clouds of tear gas appeared, masses
of people started swarming this way and that, SWAT teams
materialized, and the battle was on. Five hours later
it was still going strong, with extensive "vandalism"
reported -- lots of graffiti, some broken windows, a few
shops emblematic of major multinational corporations
partially trashed (including my usual downtown chain
burgers hangout and the "glitz strip" chain coffee shop
I was jyzing in last week). By the start of the hastily
announced curfew at seven p.m. the police had cleared
the central downtown, but they had done this by pushing
many of the hardcore protesters up onto east hill. The
last I heard, skirmishes involving hundreds of
protesters and almost as many police were still in
progress there.

Fingers of blame are pointing already. Of course.
The mayor's been too soft. Community policing is the
villain. It's the last straw for the police chief. The
calls heard on reactionary talk radio are hilariously
apoplectic. Liberal talk radio is almost as bad (I've
actually been listening to some of these shows on my
hideaway radio; and earlier at a blues club near the
ORB, with Z, I watched live local TV coverage
alternating with national cable news for a couple of
hours -- the first time literally in decades I've paid
any attention to either kind of media, talk radio or TV
news, not to mention hanging on every word and image).

Bad bad, tsk tsk! And certainly it's true:
lawbreaking is very bad and "violent" lawbreaking is
even worse. But without this lawbreaking the WTO would
still be little-known next week, and what would be known
instead would be bland elements of a mostly false PR
image of it. And if the protesters hadn't done such
very bad things (if they'd all acted respectably and
responsibly, like the union marchers) the media would've
paid little or no attention to them and the march
would've left little or no impression, maybe even here,

not to mention elsewhere, which is to say, again: around
the world.

Z and I, being Glennarian Third Stagers and savvy
vets of many earlier protest campaigns, acted only
slightly less responsibly than those union marchers.
They, after walking downtown, past the convention
center, turned around and walked right back to the
fairgrounds. Along with thousands of other mostly
nonunion people we stayed in the downtown core, hanging
about on the fringes of the big crowds, and when the
tear gas started billowing (lots of pepper spray was
used too, and rubber pellets) we didn't stick around
long to see what would happen next. We made as
dignified an escape as we could, our eyes stinging (and
my throat still feels sore and raw and stiff, some nine
or ten hours later).

It was our first demo as husband and wife. How
about that! And to echo a sentiment we heard expressed
over and over by other grizzled protest vets: it sure
did bring back the good old days. At last: another real
blow against the empire! Far freakin' out! -- Or wait.
Make that far freakin' in! Because of course we're now
into the jyze of the far in.

-- So it's nearly half past twelve. Tonight, with
all the downtown bus stops closed, I can't follow my
usual homegoing routine or anything close to it. I'll
have to hike over to the east-depot bus stop, and who
knows what the streets might be like in the triangle
here and the HQ as a whole tonight. Roving gangs of
rightist goons out to wreak revenge? Petty criminals
freed to do their thing? Rogue cops? National Guard
reconnaissance patrols? Ominous stillness? A suitcase
nuke or two?

After walking Z up to that same east-depot bus stop
at seven and seeing her off within a few minutes on an
actual bus -- it was a miracle! -- I came back here and,
with the portable radio turned on low just inches from
my ear, crashed on the carpet for a couple of hours.
Otherwise I'd've been too wrecked to lay down a single
jyze riff. (And I still haven't managed to gain more

than a few front-page news-rack glimpses of any of
today's newspapers.)

    -- Z was making her first visit to this office, by
the way, as my wife. "Let's fuck on the floor!" she
cried. In our condition it unfortunately had to be a
joke. (Her eyes were nastily red-rimmed from the tear
gas.) But I did show her the "personalized" honeymoon
lighthouse on my desk and she seemed touched by that,
possibly even more so because I worked it up on my own
and put it on display here in a prominent spot without
even telling her about it before today.

    And to top it all off -- also to dive into the
bathos of it -- Min, the landlord, stopped by yesterday
to say the sale of our building would close today. We
should withhold our rent check, he said, until he lets
us know how it's to be made out. From the way he talked
it doesn't seem too likely we'll soon be forced out onto
the street, but then neither of us trusts him, nor do
any of the other tenants, so who knows what might happen.
And he said the new landlord is a certain "Fonzie" (the
goofy character on "Happy Days"?) who owns several
buildings on east hill (where the rents are much higher
than on south hill) and Min doesn't think this Fonzie
dude intends to condoize. So there's a chance we'll be
able to hang on in 203 for a while. My guess, though,
is we'll be hit with a big rent increase later this
month -- a kind of Christmas present in reverse. The
key question: how big an increase?

    Min also thanked us for being "good tenants."
That's a laugh. Z has hounded him mercilessly since the
day we moved in about shortcomings in the building
(involving vents, toilets, heaters, garage door, lobby
safety, and much more), and seeing our cluttered rooms
during his inspections with the bankers must've shocked
him at least a little. About the only way we've been
"good" is our peculiar habit, highly unusual for our
building from what we hear, of paying the rent on time.

    -- So now I'll try to make my getaway. Will the
police perimeter still be established right outside the
building entrance or will it (as seems probable) have

shrunk a bit in the direction of the downtown core
where, along with atop east hill, all the action is
taking place at this time (according to the radio)?

*   *

Home now. As I suspected she would, Naomi had left
a message advising me not to go in tonight because, at
the time of her call, seven p.m., "it seems things are a
little chaotic down there" (since her husband's the
chief federal prosecutor in the war on drugs in the
western half of the state she knows a thing or two about
chaos and law enforcement). So now I've left her a
message saying I'll try again tomorrow night to punch in
those grand-jury corrections.

On the doorstep I found tomorrow's (meaning
Gregorian today's, December 1st's -- last month of the
year, decade, century, millennium) -- tomorrow's far-
coast paper, yes, double-wrapped in blue cellophane
against the rain (which has just started up again after
a day's glorious and crucial respite). And the lead
story in this edition, with a rare four-column hed
above a color photo of cops and protesters mixing it up
amid swirling clouds of tear gas, is "NATIONAL GUARD IS
CALLED TO QUELL TRADE-TALK PROTESTS."

I wound up walking all the way home. Many of the
usual night people were out and about south of the
curfew zone, but no police or troops were in sight and
no roving gangs wreaking revenge (or exacting tribute)
and very little vehicular traffic. In places some of
those same night people were stumbling about in the
mostly empty main streets seemingly for the sheer fun of
it. The buses were running but very sporadically, and
since they were making no stops downtown they too were
nearly empty. Only one person was waiting at the
normally crowded and raucous east-depot stop and he was
sitting on a cement planter wall all bundled up as if
intending to hang on there all night (but a gravelly
voice sounded from between layers of cloth swaddling his
face: "You got a smoke, man?"). Only twice did anyone
try to peddle me anything: one a "You lookin'?" and the
other a "Need anything?" I saw only one person on foot

581

and one vehicle in motion while walking seven blocks up
the incline through the heart of the AQ (in the end I
decided I'd make it home faster by walking). Not a
single hooker was in sight anywhere.

The eeriest moment of all came as I hiked across
the high bridge. During those several minutes of gazing
down at the nation's third-most-congested freeway
intersection I saw only half a dozen vehicles and none
at all on any of the four levels of the east-west
portion. Nothing but bare concrete down there.

And then, also bizarrely, at the moment I'd least
expect it, I finally ran into some cops: of all things
they were making a traffic bust on the hill next to the
DC castle. Hey, what's this I was hearing on right-wing
talk radio about the nefarious protesters drawing all
the police attention, thus allowing criminals free rein
out in the ritsy hoods? -- And it was the very first
traffic bust I've ever seen anywhere on the hill.

But that was it, J. City in a "state of civil
emergency." Except for the absence of freeway traffic,
though, it looked normal from the bridge and in fact
quite lovely on a glittery clear night. The near-total
lack of vehicles probably had something to do with the
clean air. And then just as I reached my home block my
usual bus rolled by without a single passenger aboard.

No doubt some people are viewing all this extreme
oddness as but a faint foretaste of what will happen one
month from now when the calendar rolls over and
Y2Kalypse erupts. But I'd say this is it. It'll be a
long time before J. City sees its like again. Mark my
words, jyze fans!

To recap. (Should I try to do this now? Yes.
It's all but certain lots of new stuff will be going
down tomorrow and this extraordinary day would largely
be lost to TJM account.)

For me it started with the alarm going off at half
past ten, several hours earlier than usual. I made
myself some toast, dressed quickly, and was about to
head out -- Z had left a message saying Betty had
decided to meet us at the fairgrounds later -- when the

first dramatic news of big doings downtown started
coming in on the radio, reporters barely able to speak
because of tear gas affecting their voices (the same way
it later did mine and Z's). There was excited talk of
human chains forming around WTO meeting sites, delegates
trapped in hotel lobbies, proceedings delayed, windows
broken, SWAT teams unleashed.

   My plan was to walk down, across the high bridge
and then west on the main drag, until a bus came along,
and take that bus crosstown and then pick up some coffee
just before joining Z at the chain burger joint close
by the stadium at the fairgrounds. That would be the
site of the labor rally preceding the big march. Z
herself had gone ahead at eight a.m. to meet with
members of her former union (a relatively liberal one),
Local 17 thereof, at a labor-friendly restaurant right
across the street from Rob's bookstore. I got within a
block of the east-depot stop before a bus finally
appeared, and the driver turned out to be a hardcore
right-winger sounding much like Ross the security guard,
raving to his passengers about "outside agitators taking
over the city" (yes!), and he never did tone it down.

   On the way crosstown we saw a phalanx of marchers,
many dressed as sea turtles, gathered in front of the
east depot and a long ominous double column of armed and
masked and shield-bearing riot police emerging from the
financial-district station of the bus tunnel. But
traffic was light on the old "high road" -- at that time
most of the action was several blocks east outside the
convention center -- and we made it uptown quickly; I
actually reached our rendezvous site early. And Z did
too. There, amid a rapidly swelling crowd, we waited in
place for an hour, listening to huge roars throbbing
from the fairgrounds stadium while the monorail glided
by overhead from time to time (and staring at the big
colorful conjoined slabs of software plutocrat #2's
rock-music museum in the shadow of the flying saucer
atop the giant golf tee). For most of that time we
leaned against a fence with Willis E., the county
councilmember, who happened to be in the area; and for a

while he was joined by a key mayoral aide, Dan D., and a
supposedly radical lawyer named Weldon. The start of
the march was delayed half an hour and the route was
changed and I figured it was a matter of the labor
chieftains turning cautious after hearing reports of the
turmoil downtown, but these two stalwarts said no, no,
it was just that the speeches were running over.

    Our friend Jess P. also met us at the same
rendezvous site and she was dragging along her gay pal
Jake, the same guy who escorted her to Ramona's wedding
last spring when Gwen was otherwise occupied. This time
Gwen was truly otherwise occupied, sad to say, and Jess
was already in a bad mood because they'd just run into
Gwen's new boyfriend waving an anti-WTO sign from his
wheelchair (but Gwen wasn't with him). As soon as the
march started, Jess joined her former construction-union
mates and that's the last we saw of her. But then Betty
finally showed up and she stayed with us all the way
down. And we saw Wei and Alison along the route, but
they just waved and bantered from the sidelines in the
same fashion I'd done with them the night before;
exactly what they were up to for the day I don't know.

    It was as colorful a march as I've ever seen, with
forests of picket signs, banners, floats, slogan-bearing
trucks, drummers, stilt-walkers, twelve-foot-tall
puppets, numerous folks in sea-turtle outfits and others
rigged up as walking trees, and plenty of eccentrically
and amusingly dressed individuals, including even a
squadron of bare-breasted "vegan women" in body paint (Z
declining to join them though she said she was tempted).
For -- as I should've mentioned earlier -- the weather,
defying all forecasts, was terrific, temperatures balmy
(in the fifties!), the sun out much of the time.

    We marched with Z's small union group. They
quickly broke up in the swirling mass, but Z and I
traded off carrying the union banner the whole way and
then afterwards hauled it down to the hideaway where it
now stands in a corner. In a blank space just below the
middle of the banner Z wrote, with her largest purple
marker, "No globalization without representation!!!",

and that drew a surprising amount of attention. I loved
the spirited way she would cry out, "If we vote to
protect sea turtles, it should fucking mean something!"
(See, the corporate-corrupted WTO, with full USAn
support, has arrogated itself the right to override the
laws of individual nations regarding trade agreements.)
     So it was a straight run of roughly a mile to the
downtown core, then a left at the central plaza, surging
past the big Christmas tree and eastward up through the
"glitz strip" -- where many of the stores were closed
and boarded up just as promised -- to within a block of
the convention center. And then, surprise, another left
turn and we suddenly found ourselves heading back toward
the fairgrounds. Most of the union people just kept on
marching as directed, but spokespersons for other groups
were pleading with the marchers to stay downtown and
support their actions. One of those was a large faction
sitting in the street outside the theater where the
opening ceremony for the WTO gathering had been
scheduled to be held, across from the convention center
(we could see this sitdown group a block farther up the
"glitz" canyon). Betty felt the call to join them. Z
and I didn't, not wanting to get arrested or to be tear-
gassed, and besides we'd been hearing that the main
action had moved elsewhere. "Kat's all yours if I don't
make it back!" Betty called cheerfully in a touching
moment as she headed off.
     After that Z and I just wandered around, amazed by
the sight of the huge crowds swarming in all the
downtown streets, the surreality and also the
ominousness of it. At every intersection you could look
in four directions and see massed crowds milling about
and police lines standing in formation across street
corridors in the distance, usually two or three or more
blocks away. Most in the crowds were younger people --
scarcely a union jacket in sight -- and some were
dressed for battle, a few even carrying gas masks and
improvised first-aid kits. But the only actual act of
vandalism we witnessed was a fellow who shimmied up a
pole to cut down a beach-towel-size city banner

welcoming the WTO to town. (At the start of the day six
or more of these banners were displayed on every block;
by the end few remained.)

     Along the way Z ran into several friends she hadn't
seen in years and also a few fellow city workers, though
none from her division. I saw no one I knew personally
whom I hadn't met through Z.

     -- All this jyze going down now on the couch at
home, jazz playing low. And it just occurred to me it's
an unusally peaceful night in this building for another
reason: Doug and Thuy and the kids have finally moved
out, as of yesterday. And Z hasn't come wandering out,
which is surprising given all the excitement, but then
she's been sleeping better lately and she did rack up
plenty of exercise today, or rather what from her
perspective is yesterday. Oh: and she told me she's
made an appointment to have the D&C done on December
17th. So if something's seriously wrong with her we'll
be finding out about it the week before Christmas (but
also if all's okay, we'll be finding out about that
instead and can celebrate it right along with the
holidays and the millennium).

                         [+1]

     -- And it continues. A day later and Z and I are
sitting on a couch at a cafe out in the Yuke. We've
just been examining a map of the downtown curfew zone
wondering if there's any way I'll be able to get to the
scope office tonight and we agree the answer is no. As
recently as an hour ago our USAn president was
addressing the WTO at, yes, the many-starred hotel.
Since then more clouds of tear gas have been rolling
through the downtown as phalanxes of police augmented by
National Guard troops pursue "marauding" groups of
protesters. The last I heard, large clashes were
occurring simultaneously at the symphony hall, the
downtown plaza, and the public market. Over both days a
total of more than three hundred arrests have been made.

(Z tells me she's impressed with the coverage of
yesterday's march in the indie weekly, which hit the
stands outside just as I arrived here. How did they
produce it so quickly? Well, they were girding up for
months, that's how. And Earl K. and the staff at the
rad fortnightly were almost uncannily accurate, it's
clear now, in their predictions about how the protests
would play out. This makes the police, who are claiming
their advance analysis said there would be no violence
against property and the number of protesters would be
far lower, look rather bad.)

    Z says no buses were running downtown today except
in the tunnel, which was also just about the only place
free of tear gas. Many of the members of her department
at the utility were out in the streets of the retail
core on official city orders -- sweeping up broken glass
and painting over anti-WTO graffiti, among other tasks.
The word now is that the curfew, which is the first
declared in this city since early in World War II (when
Japusans were restricted to their homes at night, before
the internment), will continue in force downtown from
seven p.m. until midnight through Friday night.

    We're on our way to hear two excellent writers, an
Indian (South Asia type) and a USAn, speak on the issue
of intellectual-property rights and indigenous peoples.
In past years Z has reviewed books by both of these
worthies for the AQ paper. We've had tickets to this
for weeks -- it's part of the university series on "the
meaning of progress" which Z's book group has taken up
-- but it acquires whole new magnitudes of relevance in
light of this week's events.

    (And today, by the way, happens to be World AIDS
Day. "A day without art." The horrifying plague of our
time, millions dying yearly, the numbers mounting
catastrophically, and the medicines which can keep the
disease in check are beyond the reach of all but the
wealthy, and the corporate world is essentially doing
nothing to make them more widely available.)

    -- I'll say this: I've heard snatches of our USAn
president's speech on the radio and read about it in the

papers and it wasn't half bad. It urged the WTO
delegates to listen to the voices outside the hotel and
to include the general populace in the WTO's decision-
making process. In essence, although I'm sure the spin
doctors will try to say otherwise, it supported the
action of the protesters outside, all except the
"violent" ones; and even for those a good case can be
made (though the prexy didn't make it) that they
provided the "peaceful" protesters with the amplifier
that's made their voices audible worldwide. But the
chances that the large corporations which control the
WTO behind the scenes will permit significant reform
remain, in my view, extremely slim.

*   *

     -- Now as I pull my trusty J-stick out again at a
little after midnight the radio is carrying a live
report of another showdown between cops and protesters,
including many local residents, on east hill. Even
conservative talk radio is calling this a police riot.
Four hours ago Z and I ran into the opening skirmishes
when we tried to drive across the hill on our way home
from the campus. We made a quick U-turn and circled
around as much as a mile farther to the east; then we
drove uneventfully west down the main drag through the
AQ and past the depots and then four blocks north to the
southern border of the downtown curfew zone and she
dropped me off and I came upstairs to No. 225 -- here.
     It's a standoff on east hill at the moment,
hundreds of riot police and National Guard troops
arrayed against a group of roughly four or five hundred
civilians. Just who these people are no one can say for
sure. But clouds of tear gas have been rolling down the
main commercial strip up there and lots of residents and
shoppers have been gassed and shot with rubber bullets.
And news reports are saying things could get even worse.
     A full house of about eight hundred heard the two
speakers tonight. Both took a strong stance in favor of
the protesters and backed it up with some sharp analysis
of the WTO and the forces behind it and offered a
surprisingly optimistic prognosis based in part on

588

events happening here in J-town right now. (The USAn
speaker was a last-minute substitute, one who talks my
kind of counterculturese, but an updated version, and is
about my age and I know from reading him over the years
-- having met him and spoken briefly with him long ago
-- that he and I see the world in much the same way, as
is manifest in his latest book. For the past few weeks
a library copy of it has been sitting on the side table
in front of the black armchair and couch at home but
neither Z nor I has had a chance to get to it in depth.)
     The live reports continue. "War zone" is a term
I've been hearing a lot but the standoff is holding so
far, possibly because a couple of popular local
politicians have shown up at the scene and are trying to
defuse the situation. The crowd is shouting at the
police lines: "We'll go home if you'll go home." -- And
it's about time for me to go home too. But I'll mention
first that I didn't even attempt to reach the scope
office tonight. And it looks as though June will
finally be making it over to our place in about an hour
to discuss her oral argument for school, so I probably
won't be returning to these pages until tomorrow. (And
I've been doing a lot of clipping from newspapers over
the past two days. Our living-room floor is littered
with the leavings. -- And hanging on the hat tree here
is one of the two yellow anti-WTO ponchos we bought
yesterday as mementos of the great march.)

                      [+1]

     -- Back at the hideaway about eighteen hours later.
It's dinner hour, and some four blocks to the east the
confrontation continues. I was just up there, wandering
through the crowd of maybe a thousand or twelve hundred
sitting and standing outside the main entrance to the
city jail, with the streets barricaded off for a couple
of blocks in all directions and police massed at the
barricades and in nearby parking lots but holding back
as negotiations proceeded at the mayor's office just a

block away. The crowd was demanding the release of four
hundred demonstrators being held in the jail. The city
has said there will be no release; several hundred
protesters have said they'll stay right where they are
until a release occurs, and if that means facing tear
gas and more arrests, so be it. The main entrance to
the jail was effectively blocked off by the protesters.
The impasse had already persisted for several hours.
And now I'm again listening to radio reports even as
this jyze goes down. If these sentences sound
distracted and disjointed, those reports might have
something to do with it.

The crowd outside the jail didn't seem too surly.
Drums were pounding, people were dancing, media reps
were interviewing authentic protesters. And all this
was taking place right across the street from the county
offices where Z and I obtained our marriage license a
few months ago. Temperatures are plunging into the mid
to low thirties tonight or I'd be jyzing right now on
the same bench where I went at it on that gusty day just
outside those county offices and directly beneath the
skybridge leading to the jail. It would've been a
special kick to be there today because a small group of
protesters dressed as sea turtles was chowing down in
that same area when I checked it out.

Earlier when I left the house two large helicopters
were hovering overhead about a block away and only a
couple of hundred feet up: another ominous sight. A guy
I ran into on the sidewalk said they'd been noisily
flappety-flapping up there for about an hour. It
appeared they were trying to hide behind the massive
facade of the DC castle so as not to be visible from the
area around the jail on the next hill over.

Again Naomi and I have exchanged messages and again
I've decided not to waste time and risk injury or arrest
trying to crack the curfew zone tonight. It's been
reduced in size by a third or so but the scope office is
still well inside it. Given my appearance it's highly
unlikely the security folks at the building would let me
inside even if I did manage to get down there

unhindered, which itself would be highly unlikely.

Despite the showdown just up the hill here, the city is much quieter today. The WTO meeting continues (it officially ends tomorrow afternoon) but our USAn president left town this afternoon. City crews have again been out cleaning up the downtown core (Z herself will be joining one of them tomorrow) and some of the mainline liberal protesters, shamed and embarrassed by the very "violence" that enabled their messages to gain wide play, are down helping with the cleanup, and thus positioning themselves as the responsible, nonviolent alternative. They might not agree, but in my view this is the best possible outcome from the standpoint of anti-corporate-globalization forces.

And the recriminations are mounting. Downtown property owners and business people and conservatives in general are blaming the mayor and the police chief for poor planning and insufficient toughness; these officials in turn are saying (and I admire them for sticking by their guns, or rather their alleged shortage of guns, though I suspect they'll pay a big penalty eventually) -- the officials are saying they did the best they could under the circumstances and they're apologizing for letting things fly out of control, especially during last night's events on east hill (which, mostly thanks to the calming efforts of popular lefty politicians, did wind down without further serious incidents not long after I headed home). The mayor's even saying he's proud the protesters were able to get their message across to the delegates, the president, the world. At times he's seemed to be in way over his head, but in the long run he might look pretty good to everyone to the left of the chamber of commerce, which is to say: to ninety percent of the J. City population. (Z's friend D'Arcy Y. is working in the city's underground command center, "the bunker," and she told Z today it's been, as one might expect, "rather chaotic" down there. She's a PR specialist and she observed, "This administration does not like to put out press releases.")

Downtown business owners are saying property damage
is a couple of million dollars and lost business is
roughly seven million, which I'm sure is a huge
exaggeration (both numbers). But they're also saying
they're still hoping to recoup this lost business and
they'll be holding a big downtown "reopening" party on
Sunday and everyone in the whole region is invited to
attend. It's true, many individuals not directly
associated with major corporations have been
inconvenienced and in some cases hurt a bit financially
(as, for instance, I have: I've lost a week's work and
thus a week's income and at best only a small portion of
it can be made up later). All such losses are
regrettable, but I'd still say they're justified many
times over by the long-term social benefits (already
close to indisputable) arising from this action.

[+1]

-- And now Friday night. The official state of
civil emergency continues and yet life in J. City goes
on. Protesters are still protesting, including the
group up at the jail and another contingent currently
chained to the doors of the main hotel for delegates;
and a report comes on the radio that the WTO's attempts
to produce an agenda for the next round of talks have
collapsed and the ministerial is about to end in failure
(this I hear over the throb of the normal Friday-night
disco dissonance from downstairs). The papers are full
of tales of police and protester misbehavior and citizen
outrage and establishment fingers are pointing in a
hundred directions and heads are going to roll and the
city has supposedly taken a body blow to its reputation
(oh dang!) and I still say this may well turn out to be
one of the most glorious moments in recent USAn history.
-- And then I have a boggling new story from the home
front too.
    I guess I might as well go straight to that home-
front story. (But first I'll mention this big

millennial blowout -- just how big of course is not yet
known -- will occur exactly four weeks from tonight.
Oooeee life is exciting around here these days!)

So right after getting up today I call to check our
messages and hear these words: "Zoelie, this is Martin
W." -- and he said his whole last name. "Do you
recognize the voice?" I skipped to the next message at
that point, but something in the words was teasingly
intimate (and the voice was deep and what I'd call a bit
overly seductive, sort of like a man in a romantic
comedy playfully overdoing a come-on). Later when Z
phoned me from work, just as she was about to hang up
(after excitedly passing on numerous tales of her
interactions with downtown merchants while helping with
the city cleanup), I remembered the unusual voicemail
message and repeated the part I'd heard, minus the man's
last name which I'd forgotten anyway. "Oh my god," she
said, "was the last name W.?" (the same one I'd heard on
the phone). "Yes, that's it." "Oh my god, I don't
believe it! That's Marty!" "You mean THE Marty? YOUR
Marty?" "Yes, THE Marty." And she dissolved into
eardrum-shattering hysterical laughter.

Of course I knew who Marty was: the law student who
was her "cherry man," her very first lover, back when
she was a college sophomore at the U of Centropolis and
he was a first-year law student there (the same law
school my father wanted me to attend). The same Marty
who had her making all those loud love noises for which
she became infamous in his dorm and beyond. The same
Marty who coolly critiqued her body and her performance
after that first sexual act, reducing her to tears. The
same Marty she was soon desperately in love with and
tried to kill herself over.

So she checked out the message and called me back
still agog. Yup, "Martin" was THE Marty all right. He
was in town, the message said, "for all of the WTO stuff
this week." And it said (she laughed wildly as she
tried to mimic his attempt at casualness), "If you're
free sometime maybe we can get together and hang out."
When I asked how long it had been since she'd seen him,

she fumbled a bit and then startled me. "Hmm, hmm, not
since we broke up my sophomore year, so I guess it's --
what? You figure it out." I thought I remembered her
telling me she'd seen him at their U of Centropolis
reunions, maybe even as recently as the one six years
ago, but nope, that was her second big love, Gabe. She
forgave my confusion, however, because Gabe was the
socialist and labor-union organizer who she too thought
would've been much more likely to turn up here for the
protests. And she had mentioned this possibility
several times in the previous few weeks, mainly just to
get a rise out of me, or so it seemed at the time.

     She did talk with Marty on the phone once, though,
and she thinks it was probably seven or eight years ago.
She'd seen his name on the credits for a public-TV
documentary she'd liked -- "It was about feminism, I
think -- or no, maybe it was Cuba. It was, it was Cuba"
-- and she'd called the station where it originated and
somehow managed to wangle his phone number from them and
amazingly enough it was indeed the Martin W. she'd
known. Off the top of her head she didn't recall much
of what they'd talked about or what he'd told her then
about his life, but one cluster of facts did resurface:
he'd adopted the amusing working name "Joe Mondo" and
started a moving company in the main far-coast
megalopolis and made a lot of money. Mondo Movers was
the company name -- sort of like Mighty Movers right
here in J-town. ("Oh great," I said, "my wife's 'cherry
man' comes to town and she's going to hang out with him
and he's one of the biggest movers on the far coast."
"Huh?" she said. "Oh, I get it. Very funny.") (Jyze-
rules exceptions on all three of those names there.)

     Of course I told her I thought she should see him.
(What, I'm going to light up my rebel wife's defiance
circuits by telling her she shouldn't?) So she hung up
to try to call him. Two minutes later she called me
back and said she'd left him a voicemail at the hotel
and the voice on the greeting was a woman who gave the
name Simone. "Well, Z-goose," I said before hanging up,
"when I see you next I guess you've going to have a lot

of interesting things to tell me about and this time
they won't necessarily all be WTO-related.")

   As it happened she arrived home from work right
before I left the house and even though she hadn't yet
talked with Marty in person she still had something
interesting to tell me. Leola had come into Z's office
just as Z and I were finishing up on the phone and --
surely not by mere coincidence -- she and Z had gotten
to talking about first lovers. And to Z's amazement
Leola revealed that her first lover back in college had
been a half-Filipino guy -- a "mestizo" just like Z
herself (except his other half was African). For almost
a decade she and Leola have been bosom buddies and Leola
had never before revealed this important personal fact!
(And by the way, things between Gerry and Leola seem to
be entirely back to normal. Leola hasn't even mentioned
the big Rio crisis in weeks. Whether she and Gerry are
still meeting for lunch once a week and engaging in
those highly earnest Sunday relationship-review
sessions, Z didn't ask and Leola hasn't mentioned.)

   In the meantime I'd altered a card for her and left
it on her pillow. In all lowercase letters the original
said, "art can't get more modern than this," advertising
a website selling artwork (it was from a free-postcard
rack at the art bar); and using a pen whose purple
almost matched that of the word "art," I added an "M" to
the beginning of that word and a "y" to the end of it
and at the bottom of the card in small print something
to the effect that "On the day the Bride of Glennar's
former No. 1 dude and undisputed cherry man invaded her
Husband's homeland." And we sparred, more with delight
than with unease, and then I left.
   -- But it's late, time to go.

[+1]

   On three sides the picture windows of the drive-in.
The premier local chain burger joint, "north pole"
outlet. At the moment, just half a block to the north

and around the corner, Z is meeting with Marty. Atop
the hill, waves are obscenely pulsing up the chains of
Christmas lights adorning the easternmost of the three
huge radio towers. And down here an echoing pulsation
ricochets again and again to the top of the big blue
towerlike neon sign at the national-chain video store,
and a line's forming outside the national-chain movie
theater across the street, probably for the Afrusan-
produced and -directed "The Best Man" since a number of
black and brown folks are in the line and that's unusual
in this hood. And at the next booth here three local
seniors are yakking away, all Cawk men -- no food or
drinks at the table -- and I notice a couple of rolled
sleeping bags and bulging backpacks stashed in the
corner behind their booth. Flophouse talk, memories of
merchant-marine days is what I'm hearing.

Well, it's confirmed now: today's headlines
proclaim the WTO talks a flop. "SUMMIT ENDS IN
FAILURE." Even many WTO insiders are admitting the
protests had a lot to do with this. And so: a great
triumph for the good guys. And the question now is: how
to build on it. And what counterattacks and new
strategies are in store from the bad guys?

This afternoon I finally made it in to the scope
office for the first time all week and cranked out the
corrections for last week's grand jury. Z drove me down
to minimize the chance of my being stopped on the street
but no cops were in sight, including even in the lobby
of the scope building (with its big stinky Christmas
tree still looking and smelling pretty much the same).
Yes, everything was back to normal as far as I could
tell, and in fact I didn't see a single person the whole
time I was in the building. In an effort to lure
shoppers back downtown the city had made street parking
and bus service free all day, and the strategy seemed to
be working. When Z's city cleanup crew passed through
the area, she told me, the holiday carousel was spinning
merrily as ever in normal times and a big crowd
including many excited kids had it surrounded.

Elsewhere in the country the news has mostly moved

on to other matters. What's happened to the polar
lander which was supposed to ease down onto the Martian
surface yesterday; why hasn't it been sending radio
signals? Here in J. City the focus is on "the
aftermath," with special sections in both daily
newspapers addressing the cleanup efforts and protest
ramifications and the crucial question of who's to blame
for the things that went "wrong." From the
establishment perspective this WTO week is being viewed
as a catastrophic failure and a black eye for the city.
Downtown business and the corporate nabobs are the main
champions of this view, of course, the same forces that
lobbied so fiercely to bring the WTO meeting here in the
first place. At the neighborhood level just as at the
international level the matter's likely to be seen much
differently -- if not yet in all or most cases, soon.

     And up next: Marty. In thirty minutes or so I'll
be meeting him. Before I awoke this afternoon Z
arranged to rendezvous with him outside brother Rob's
bookstore (of all places) at seven and then hit the
labor-friendly restaurant across the street for dinner.
Later we discussed the question of whether I should
accompany her. At first she said she wanted me to, but
she quickly agreed with my suggestion that she meet him
alone first so they'd have a chance to talk in an
unconstrained way. I figured I'd feel like a third
wheel or worse to be there, especially at the start.

     For most of the afternoon poor Z had a bad case of
the jitters. At one point she burst into tears and
moments later sobbed out this wrenching phrase: "I don't
think he ever loved me at all!" Last night I arrived
home at 1:30 to find her asleep on the living-room couch
and we wound up talking for a couple of hours about her
relationship with Marty. It turns out I'd misunderstood
quite a few details (but still gotten the general drift
right). Today, when I asked what she remembered most
fondly about him, she thought a moment and said he was
the first man who'd made her feel okay about her feet
and the way the sixth-toe operations had affected her
gait, which he found incredibly sexy (me too!). And she

said she planned to tell him she never dreamed she would
meet her "zolemate" after they broke up but she did --
it just took a bit longer to happen than it should've.
     -- Must stop for now. Out the door and up to the
corner and around it I go -- and Marty won't get any
realer than he'll be then. (Well, I hope he won't.)

[+1]

     Wotta week. I guess I'll probably be closing it
out right here -- or maybe I should try to add a little
something later at home as a good jyzer spoze to do at
eighter's end. But this is the hideaway and the
dissonance is throbbing down below (possibly it'll be
doing so regularly on Sunday nights now through the
holidays and the grand rollover) and I'm still shaking
my head in amazement. I mean, a columnist in today's
far-coast paper suggests a new "progressive-populist"
movement may have been born here in J. City this week,
much like the one that emerged in the 1890s opposing
rapacious corporate control of the country. I'm in a
kind of ecstatic daze. Could it really be? Is all this
happening right before my eyes? Am I dreaming?
     And then Marty the cherry man -- to go once again
from the sublime to the merely personal. Preposterous,
yes, our tripartite interaction and his own with Z, but
also touching, revealing, even marvelous in its peculiar
-- very! -- way. Marty, it turns out, is a kind of
preserved-in-a-time-warp counterculture freak. Or I
guess I could say eccentric. Or oddball, sort of like
me, except, I don't know, is it that he's just better at
it? He runs his own moving company as noted before,
yes, but Mondo Movers (yes!) is a tiny, unlicensed
operation of the type that places small ads in the
classified sections of alternative papers and puts up
handbills on college bulletin boards. He's about my
height, slender, dresses pretty much like me, wears a
big bushy salt-and-pepper beard resembling the Cuban El
Supremo's, and in fact is a passionate fan of that

598

legendary leader and came out here in hopes of hearing him speak at the WTO meeting. He has sparkling eyes ("pretty," Z says, going briefly gooey-eyed herself as she says it) and is highly articulate and charming in a gentle-mad-scientist way and he's utterly monomaniacal about a quasi-astrological system he's dreamed up based on birth dates and the adaptation of human nervous systems to the amount of sun shining on different parts of the planet at different times of year.

I was expecting a fast-talking far-coast-megalopolis lefty legal type but it turns out Marty -- or maybe I should be calling him Joe, or Joe M., since Joe Mondo is his legal name now -- Joe M. is a lot more West Coast hippie than I am. (And remembering now that by upbringing we're also both actually a couple of Greater Centropolis boojie guys.)

Z seemed much less amazed by the changes in him than I was. Nor did she appear to find him particularly interesting. The beard took her aback (she spotted him from well up the block standing outside the bookstore and wondered if that could possibly be him) but his spiel about the birth-date system soon had her rolling-eyes gaga and at the same time almost desperately bored. Nor did she like it that, though she asked many questions about his life during the decades since their last in-person meeting, he asked her virtually none. (He did mention, however, a few things she'd forgotten, including books she'd turned him on to, among them Blake's works (jyze exception for that surname). And two or three times in my hearing he called her "Louise" or "Lou," even though they'd already been together an hour and a half before I joined them and he well knew she'd stopped being Louise or Lou well before he'd stopped being Marty.)

They arrived at the old cine cafe several minutes ahead of schedule. Z immediately went off to the restroom and Marty/Joe's first remark to me was, "I'm afraid I've never learned how to make a success of my life." And my reply: "Yeah, well, I'd say I'm right there with you on that one." Then he launched into a

long-winded spiel on his system, with my encouragement
-- after all, as I eventually managed to tell him, I'd
also come up with a system of sorts of my own based on
solar cycles: the Glennarian calendar. (I didn't even
attempt to go into jyze with its manifesto and its many
strange rules. Maybe another time for that.) Once in a
while I interposed a question about noncalendrical
matters and I learned he'd lived in my city 2/7 for
three years, arriving there the year after I did. It's
quite likely we saw each other at political and other
kinds of events from time to time and knew some of the
same people, though we never did get around to exploring
those matters in any detail.

    After maybe forty minutes of such talk (ranging
from awkward to very awkward, I'd say, with Z clearly
fretting the whole time) Marty/Joe led us down the
street to the independent media center (his other
obsessive interest is video) which had set up shop in a
former Christian bookstore for WTO week and has had a
lot to do with the protest's spectacular success. He
showed us around quickly and then we walked over to an
auditorium at the fairgrounds where a meeting was in
progress that was supposed to be featuring a Cuban
delegation sent in El Supremo's stead. But that
delegation had been indefinitely delayed at U.S. Customs
-- surprise! -- and so a number of local speakers and
musical groups were filling in for them. Marty/Joe had
left one of his video cameras running on a tripod with a
friend watching it, and now he returned to it and was
probably expecting to talk with us some more after the
meeting ended. He'd even, without telling us, paid our
admission fees for the event. But Z wasn't having any
of it; she said she was fading fast and we'd have to be
going. Seeing how stung he obviously was (she was more
than a little abrupt and even cold about it), I tried to
cover for her and floated some dubious excuses. And
that, after an exchange of addresses, was the end of it:
he gave Z one of those hands-on-both-cheeks goodbyes
(it's a Jewish thing of his, she informed me later) and
we left (it was drizzling a little and I shielded his

address book with my hands as he wrote down the address
and phone number of the woman who once tried to kill
herself over insufficiently requited love for him -- or
tried to do it twice actually, as I learned the other
night). And he dug deep in his backpack and came up
with a photocopy of a three-page precis of his geo/neuro
system and also a floppy disk containing a much longer
description of same, complete with dozens of elaborate
diagrams and maps, and these he gave to me along with a
business card for Mondo Movers and asked me to send him
any critique or comments I might have on the system.

     (By the way, the Simone whose voice was on Marty/
Joe's answering machine was the owner of the house where
he was putting up for the week, not his wife or lover.
He does, however, have a lover back in the far-coast
megalopolis. And he did get married once back in his
mid-twenties, I think it was, but it was a fiasco that
far outdid even my own disastrous first marriage at
about the same age: his lasted just three days before he
realized it would never work, and when he revealed this
conclusion to his brand-new wife she beat herself over
the head with a telephone receiver until they were both
splattered with blood. Said Z when I told her this
story: "Sounds like Marty all right." He'd told it to
me at the cine cafe when she was in the restroom --
where she stayed, I might note, for quite a long time.)

     Z and I were in a peculiar state afterwards as we
drove home: strained, joking, awkward. I guess neither
of us wanted to say anything cruel about Marty/Joe and I
certainly didn't want to have her thinking I was
laughing at him (or by extension at her, for instance,
for having loved him so much). She quickly observed,
though, it was obvious I found him a lot more
interesting than she did. Some might think him a bit
loopy, I said, and she agreed, but in my view he was a
fine fellow, admirably well-spoken, certainly still
quite handsome: it wasn't hard at all to see how she
could've fallen so hard for him. (I also noticed he has
very expressive, even beautiful hands.) And I also
said, and I meant it, that more than ever I was feeling

how fortunate we'd been in finding each other; and she
replied almost grimly, and I quote, "Amen to that."

But I'm still puzzled by how calmly -- overall --
she seemed to take all this. As far as I could tell she
wasn't shaken at all, nor was she excited and eager to
talk about the evening. At home she just wanted to rack
out. The only bad moment we had all night, and today as
well for that matter, came in the morning when I wasn't
sexually arousable (this at nine a.m. after I'd been
abed for only three and a half hours after sleeping
maybe five hours the previous night). Earlier we'd
determined by flashlight inspection that she was finally
over her Big H outbreak and now she thought I should be
raring to go after an enforced layoff of close to three
weeks. But for me on this particular morning, no.
Sometimes it's as if I get rusty with disuse during her
quarantine periods and it takes me a while to return to
form again, to build up a head of steam (or head of
whatever), and I tend not to take the initiative because
I fear I won't be able to perform at a time when I know
she's expecting it. "Are you sure you don't think
there's anything wrong?" she asked, meaning between us,
and I assured her I absolutely did not. And after that
we were all right. It seems, again, marriage is helping
here: in the old Deep days, and even more in the
courting days before those, she might've made a big
issue out of all this, hysterics and the whole bit (she
says so herself and even uses that hazardous word).

Tonight we joined Paz and Tobey at a Chinese
seafood place for a birthday dinner party thrown in
June's honor. June's holding up remarkably well
considering the hellish series of events she's going
through, including law-school finals and a battle over
job ratings with her supervisor and, worst of all, a
deathbed ordeal involving her friend Peggy, who just
returned from a trip to Mexico during which she
collapsed while seeking a miracle cure for her stomach
cancer. She's now expected to survive just a few more
days or possibly only hours, leaving behind a frantic
husband and two kids aged nine and eleven. June's been

602

spending hours at the hospital with her every day -- and
this is the fourth friend she'll have lost to cancer in
the past two years. (And she told a story about running
into Guy A., our widely reviled law-and-order city
attorney, who told her with malicious glee ("laughing
like an evil demon!") that the city would "throw the
books" at the six hundred arrested WTO protesters -- but
in fact today the last of them were released from jail
under their own recognizance, and the newspapers all say
only a few of the cases are winnable from the city's
point of view, and the individuals involved in those
will likely seek jury trials, and with so many people
appalled by the brutal police tactics it's doubtful any
local jury would convict.)
     This reminds me, though, Z mentioned the other
night that if it does turn out she has a malignant form
of cancer, she doesn't want to go through all sorts of
convulsions seeking a miracle cure as Peggy has. "Maybe
I'll try one course of chemo or radiation to see what
happens. Other than that it's the Hemlock Society for
me." The proximate cause of this talk was an obit she'd
read of an actress who recently died of ovarian cancer
at exactly Z's age now. But Z feels people are dropping
off like flies all around her, and many are women with
breast or uterine/ovarian cancer, and for the moment she
seems pretty stoic about it all, and I'm trying to be
the same way myself in the face of her upcoming exam.
It'll be two to three weeks before we know the results
and until then we'll both try to think about the matter
as little as possible.
     And finally. Returning to those astounding WTO
events, last night we drove through the downtown and saw
that a few windows were still boarded up on storefronts
of big corporate retail chains targeted by those nasty
anarchists from out of town but otherwise all looked
normal. The damage bemoaned by the establishment
business types was relatively minor and insurance will
cover it all. The newspapers are full of exhortations
to "do your patriotic duty," as one of them says
(unironically!), and get downtown and shop. And the

airwaves are seething with ruling-class and reactionary
talk: fury, blame, recrimination. But most of it's
about strictly local matters (and I'll try to say more
about those next eighter). The bigger picture isn't
being seen much hereabouts except, for the most part, by
the triumphant protesters and their sympathizers. And
that's fine. Because they (we) won and the world just
might turn out to be a lot better off for it. Period.

29

     A wondrous sight as I walked in this evening. A
huge white tumbleweedlike cloud -- one of a formation of
a dozen of more of varying sizes rolling along at low
altitude just above the city and the harbor -- impaled
itself on the upper reaches of downtown's two tallest
and glitteriest skybusters and was somehow held in place
by them -- and illuminated from within -- as the other
clouds kept tumbling by. Cotton candy in the night sky
-- or say the glowing doubly spiked puffball was like a
huge mass of angel's hair with innumerable strings of
Christmas lights sparkling inside it.
     Here at the east-depot saloon it's not so pretty.
Here when one man embraces another who's just been
released from jail it's not too likely either one was a
WTO protester, and I don't care what the commentators
are saying about the new union alignments on the left.
This is a sub-union working-folks' watering hole. Here
you've got the lumpiest of the lumpen. Laughter and
tensions, lots of cigarette smoke, foul language, loud
voices, sudden hot-tempered outbursts. Also lots of
racial diversity as well as abundant diversity-related
sparks (just like me and Z, could say). Country rock on

the box, Monday-night football on four -- or five, I see
now, high-shelved screens, dice cups rattling bones
nonstop at the bar and splashing them on wood clatter
after clatter. And I've grabbed the same seat I had
last time, same table right under one of the screens.

I don't exactly like this place -- its edge is just
a little too jagged for me, or just say too real -- but
I do like being here right now. (Looking out the window
straight at the floodlit great white tower, and by
leaning forward a little I can see that the wondrous
tumblecloud spiked on the two tallest buildings has
already freed itself and moved on.)

It's December. Last night as I walked home on the
hilltop I saw snow for the first time this year. The
flakes were flying near the apexes of the cones of light
beneath the street lamps but by the time they reached my
eye level most had melted and I didn't see a single one
hit the ground, and for some odd reason I was looking
hard. -- Well, I suppose not so odd. So I could tell
Z, "I actually [or "never"] saw one hit the ground."

Back to normality. But it's seasonal normality.
More and more yule decorations popping up, outdoors and
indoors and at the transitional points in between. The
big commercial sell at its peak. It was a giant weekend
for those downtown merchants supposedly "hard hit" by
the protests. The carousel twirled, the Santas chortled,
the carriages clip-clopped. The beer signs, including
the ones right here, have taken on holiday tints of
mixed red and green -- just as the big march itself did
in a different sense (meaning political: red (or at
least pink) unionists and green (but also mostly pink)
enviros). And that was one week ago tomorrow.

Meanwhile "The Battle of Jyze City," sorry to say,
fades from the world's newscasts and front pages. Now
comes the first wave of newspaper wrap-ups and pundit
analyses and spins. Most are noting a new kind of
coalition between big labor and environmentalists --
pinkos, say, and greenies -- and wondering how long it
can last. Some see the birth of a potent new
progressive movement (and of course I hope they're

right). Others see the last gasp of an antiquated labor
movement seeking to ally with even more outmoded or just
plain crazy Luddites and anarchists. In my own view the
battle lines aren't really all that much different from
what they were before the showdown but many of the
familiar arguments have re-emerged newly energized.

My hope is that those who are being left behind by
the cyber-revolution in this country -- and I'd say it's
a majority of the population, possibly as high as sixty
to seventy percent -- will overcome the resistance of
the many social conservatives and reactionaries among
them and unite behind an invigorated democratic left.
My fear is that the movement will turn nationalistic and
split along racial lines, with whites moving toward
formation of a demagogic populist third party.

Here in J. City we're continuing to hear lots of
calls for the mayor and police chief to resign. For the
most part these are the voices of the law-and-order
crowd. Why no demands from them, I wonder, to prosecute
the people responsible for bringing the WTO here in the
first place -- chief among whom would be the CEOs of the
so-called Big Four, the most teratogenically overgrown
corporations around: the software behemoth, the
aerospace giant, the forest products leviathan, and the
coffee colossus. Some groups on the left are also going
after the mayor and the police for the brutal tactics
used after the big march passed through downtown and
then again at frequent times over the succeeding several
days and nights, especially in residential neighborhoods
on or near east hill. The ACLU is suing the city,
asserting that certain aspects of the "civil emergency"
declaration were illegal, especially the creation of
huge "no-protest" zones. I hope these latter efforts
triumph and any attempt by law-and-order forces to bring
down city officials, including councilmembers who
supported the protesters, fail. I don't want to see any
backlash caused by the protests succeed in moving this
relatively liberal and left-leaning city to the right
politically. And I doubt that will happen. But
abundant conflict could arise over this issue in the

weeks and months ahead.

    Meanwhile we're moving into the period of intensive countdown on Y2K and the millennial rollover. One National Guard member who called in to a radio talk show (I'm still listening to some of these, to the point where I'm so sick of them I doubt I ever will again) -- this one caller mentioned in passing, while talking about the deployment of his unit in the downtown battle zone during WTO, that over the previous months they'd been undergoing considerable training for possible Y2K upheavals but had received none at all for WTO. I personally continue to doubt any serious Y2K disruptions will occur in this area or anywhere else in the U.S. But surely there will be plenty of tension and a good deal of suspense and probably some craziness. And so now the focus shifts to all that, at least for the next few weeks. And because of what went down with the WTO demos last week, a lot of nerves are on edge.

    -- And it's my workout night. Z is skipping this one -- I already saw her before leaving home -- or otherwise I couldn't've stopped here. Now I'd better -- like that impaled tumblecloud -- be rolling along.

[+1]

    -- Won't have much time for this. Z's due home in about half an hour, give or take fifteen minutes. And I'll stop abruptly when she arrives (usually I can hear her opening the garage door) because I don't want her to feel jyze is against her. She already does to a degree, of course, and for good reason, because I've asked her to bear with me on this long-running TJM project which has barely reached the three-fifths mark and she knows it's often been responsible for my being too pooped to pop or too busy to do various things with her -- though I've tried to keep such "failures of consortium" (to use a legal phrase I often encounter while scoping) to a minimum and she's by and large been cooperative and understanding and even encouraging. But still, if by moving quickly I can prevent the project from racking up a few more demerits in her eyes, I will, and that's why this J-book will shut down pronto when she gets here.

So why try to do any jyzing at all under these conditions? Because today's the "day that will live in infamy," December 7th, Pearl Harbor Day and also, not at all by coincidence, my conception day, and I want to be sure to lay down at least a few J-riffs on this day. Since Naomi didn't call I'm assuming a job awaits me at the office, and if it's more than a certain length, say fifty or sixty pages, I won't have time for jyzing down there, and then when I return home tonight the story might be the same because Z seems to be moving back into an insomniac phase owing to stress at the utility along with worries about the D&C, holiday obligations, losing the apartment, her mother's operation, relations with Aida, on and on and on. And since I've been performing so poorly in the sack lately -- dang it anyway! -- I feel increased pressure myself to stick around the house for a couple of hours after she gets home and see if I can ravish her up a bit before I head off to work.

Oh the complexities, the pushes and pulls and feints and compromises of married life -- and for damn sure I wouldn't want to do away with a single one of them if that meant I had to give up married life itself. Which of course it would. As I sit here in my old green terrycloth bathrobe with one of its two front belt loops missing and a three-inch rip in the left armpit and listen to the dryer spin squeakily in the hall. And I'm sitting at an odd angle because the undercarriage (or whatever it's called) of the seat of the black armchair partially gave way the other day when I sat down in it a bit heedlessly, I'll say, snapping a couple of the wires I repaired it with a year ago.

And there's this: today Cal C., the Jyze City chief of police and an occasional fellow iron-pumper at the WOC (though I've spoken with him only once and that very briefly), resigned. He did it, he said, not because of the cries for his head from certain quarters, both left and right, and not because the mayor asked for his badge

(the mayor confirmed he hadn't), but to "depoliticize"
the process of investigating complaints about police
performance during WTO week "so that the real truth can
come out." Z whispered the news to me this morning when
she came in to kiss me goodbye. Now those seeking
blood will probably shift their focus to the mayor
himself. Oh it's gonna be a circus over the coming
months, with hearings, task forces, investigations
galore by all sorts of agencies and groups, both
governmental and private, and of course droves of
lawsuits. But the horse of in ---
                          *   *
     Will try for a while anyway. Past four in the
morning now. June showed up unexpectedly tonight,
presenting me with a one-page critique for inspection.
She was already a day late in turning it in because her
friend Peggy died Sunday night just an hour or two after
June's birthday party. But tonight June was in
surprisingly good spirits, and I could hardly turn her
away. She also brought a hand-me-down sweater for me, a
black cardigan, a baggy fit for one of her sons but
still, as it turns out, too small for me, because on the
standard human scale, as she amusingly observed, I'm
"too extra." Then she presented me with four free one-
ride bus passes which she happened to have in her purse.
(And earlier this week Z, with my okay, gave her the
message phone I bought almost four years ago for use in
good old B-2. (We have no need for two of them and Z's
is far superior.) -- But a pang when I let that phone
go. I first heard Z's fabulous voice on it -- and the
marvelous hearty laugh which, just like the voice, still
regularly blows me away some thirty-three months later
-- as of day after tomorrow.)
     And tonight's scoping job was tough; I was lucky to
finish it up (and with just minutes to spare). But then
I'd gotten a late start on it because I was checking out
last week's papers on the out-of-town racks at
newsstands and bookstores. It was both fascinating and
appalling -- even thrilling in a few cases -- to see the
wide array of opinion and the varying types of news

coverage of the WTO events. And it was gratifying
indeed to learn just how massive the coverage has been.
"The Battle of Jyze City" is also on the cover of one of
the weekly U.S. national news magazines (but the other
major newsweekly makes it a minor story and condemns the
protesters -- the same kind of blatantly biased right-
wing coverage it regularly gave major antiwar demos
during the Vietnam War era). And then there's our
heroic local radical fortnightly that triumphantly
declares victory. And I have yet to catch up on the
local dailies, the stories about today's resignation of
Chief C. and the rest of the ongoing WTO fallout.
      I'd like to make room for the personal stuff too.
Z's "jump my bones" dream one night (I was the dreamy
jumper!), "gamboling baby elephants" the next. Her
principled stand against a mainstream-based ad campaign
prepared for the utility and the grief that stand is
causing her. Her promise to be patient with me.
("Don't you just love having such a demanding wife?")
      And a complicated story about Aida. Her father's
not reacting well to the chemo and her mother's in the
hospital after "forgetting" to take her blood-pressure
medication (Z says the real reason she "forgot" was that
Mrs. D can't stand not being the one who's in the
spotlight and being extravagantly cared for). And now
Aida's hesitating to accept "the ideal job" (admin type)
despite strong efforts to recruit her for it; she's
afraid caring for her parents will interfere too much
with the job duties. Z's advising her not to take on
more than her share with her parents, but her four
siblings have convenient ways of sidestepping their
responsibilities (especially the two in the U.S. armed
forces who're living with their families overseas). But
when Z's father died Aida was there for her, "for years
and years," and Z wants to be there for Aida now. And
Aida's saying Z's "still in a cocoon" with me (because
Z's often unavailable at the times Aida proposes to see
her -- usually on Saturdays or Sunday afternoons, which
just happen to be, as Aida well knows, the only times Z
and I can realistically schedule to do things together

for more than an hour or two during which neither of us
is asleep). Also, Kirk's now telling Aida he loves her,
and she's backing away from him for those same family-
related reasons, or at least that's what she tells Z.
And Aida's ex, Tom, has started taking Charles to a non-
Catholic church on the alternate weekends when he has
him. So for Aida, yes, things are definitely tensing
up.

And Jess, I can report, received a long letter from
Gwen in which, Z says, Gwen describes her dream of how
beautiful things would be with them now if only Jess
would forgive her. Yet the letter has no return address,
indicating Gwen's probably staying with or living with
her wheelchair-bound boyfriend. And Jess is going
around telling people this letter shows just how sick
Gwen really is. Says Z: "I don't think she's aware of
what that suggests about her as a person who fell in
love with Gwen." (And so I turn right around and say
it's not so uncommon for people to fall in love "on the
rebound" and for reasons that aren't completely
"healthy," and that might even apply to us too, ZAG &
GAZ, just maybe -- but only in the past, of course, and
before we met, back in the days when we didn't have it
together to the extent we do now. Ho ho.)

And and and. And now I arrive at the Pearl Harbor
story. Day of Infamy. Z's comment: "I can't believe
your mother told you all this. Even the hour they were
schtupping?" Well, not the exact hour. The night it
must've happened, yes. That night was the only
possibility because they were using contraceptives
before the attack and Dad was confined to base the next
afternoon and had to stay there until several days later
when his troop train rolled out for distant parts (and
soon he shipped out for the South Pacific).

-- But the anniversary's passed us by already.
It's the morning of the 8th now, though still dark here
-- end of the long night on which I popped into
existence exactly as many years ago as my father was
alive on this earth, in total, excluding his own period
"in the oven."

[+1]

-- On the way in tonight I'm stopping at the ORB
cafe for a jyze session. I've got something close to
the usual: a bottle of root beer and a table next to the
plumbing apparatus in one of the back corners. Oil
paintings perhaps a bit overly reminiscent of those of a
certain famous Mexican muralist hang on the brick walls,
unusually big canvases for this smallish space. Lumens
flood down -- one of the ceiling spotlights used for
wall art is inadvertently, I assume, aimed directly at
my table. My fold-up umbrella is lying on the floor by
my chair like a beached fish still shedding water as it
twitches -- or true, I'm likely just imagining the
twitches even if the umbrella undeniably resembles a
silky all-black northern pike. The paycheck I picked up
last night and then earlier this afternoon placed in an
ATM envelope for deposit later tonight somehow acquired
a damp spot while it rode inside my wallet inside the
red protective bag inside my backpack during my walk
down. It's very, very wet out there.
     But I enjoyed the trek anyway. Not just the
freeways but the streets up by our house and the one on
the high bridge were all jammed with traffic usually
creeping along at a pace slower than my normal walking
speed. Glittery streets, lots and lots of white and red
lights in view, headlights and taillights, and here and
there some more variegated Christmas lights as well. A
couple of nights ago the floodlights at the DC castle
flipped on again (for some reason they were out of
commission for several weeks; people were beginning to
suspect a plot on the dot-com's part to ignore the
landmark board's ruling that those lights must stay on),
and at the very top of the building a huge white
Christmas star materialized. Oh holy digital night!
     Even earlier, just as I was about to leave the
apartment, I stepped on an envelope near the front door.
It turned out to be a letter announcing the purchase of
the building by a Raphael and Dana D. (not someone named

"Fonzie," as we'd been told, or at least that's what I
thought I'd heard), and it contained, by omission, some
surprisingly good news. It said nothing about a rent
increase. Our deposit will be upped by $345 to a full
month's rent of $745, but that's the only increase, and
since the letter said the $345 could be paid in
installments, it seemed to be implying that no rent
increase is contemplated at this time. Which is a far
cry -- a far cry of joy! -- from what we expected.

Tonight, as it happens, Z's attending the inital
session of a three-part "class for first-time
homebuyers" put on by one of the city employees' unions.
Our present hope, which we talked about even before the
arrival of this letter from the new landlords, is that
we'll be able to hang on at 1511 for another eighteen
months to two years and then move into the "artist
lofts" condos some five or six blocks east of the high
bridge (they won't be ready for occupation until then).
Now our chances of being able to do that look much
better, although they're probably still quite low. At
this point we don't even know what the market-value loft
units will be going for. And though Z and I taken
together are roughly forty K in the red at this point,
we don't come anywhere near qualifying for one of the
partially subsidized units (in essence because Z makes
too much in her new job).

And today, I noticed while checking out the
calendar for the week, is called Immaculate Conception
Day by -- someone. Probably the Catholic Church, I
suppose. Why it's called that I haven't the faintest
idea, unless the church would have us believe their main
man's gestation period was just seventeen days (but then
we are talking miracles here) or maybe he was born three
and a half months beyond his due date (in which case
much howling must've come from his mother in that
stable). Or maybe it's the mother's conception itself
that's being referred to? In any case it's amusing that
my own conception day is either adjacent to or actually
coincides with (if the two progenitors of me were
humping away after midnight) an official one, and an

immaculate one no less, for Christianity.
       And here on the table, more WTO-aftermath analysis.
This time it's filling up a big chunk of the neopunk
indie weekly's first special Christmas shopping issue.
The headline on this morning's J. City daily, a copy of
which, threaded through a library stick, lies atop a
nearby table, says "FOCUS NOW MOVES TO MAYOR." The
first WTO hearings at the city council opened today.
       And then as part of my own aftermath musings
covering the same period I want to note for the record
just a few things Z told me about her affair with Marty
back in the day. First, they were together only about
thirteen months or so, starting the fall of her
sophomore year at the U of Centropolis when he was a
first-year student in the law school there. His father
was a prosperous merchant who owned several downtown
menswear shops and also quite a bit of real estate,
including, not far from the UC campus, a medical
building which she and Marty used to visit at night to
"play doctor," she told me, "as it was meant to be,"
meaning atop the examination tables. Marty had two
younger brothers and a very attractive mother with whom
he was unusually close. In her first meeting with Z
Marty's mother took Z's face in her hands, looked at her
hard, and said, "She's not THAT beautiful, Martin." For
understandable reasons Z never got along very well with
this woman but Marty's two brothers doted on Z (one now
lives in Norway and manufactures candy molds; the other
is some sort of industrial scientist somewhere back in
the USA heartland). Almost from the start Marty told Z
he was helplessly drawn to blue-eyed blond women, and in
the end this is what broke them up, because he said he
wanted to date others, meaning blue-eyed blonds (his
mother was a blue-eyed redhead). -- And yes, Z said his
family was a lot like the one in "Portnoy's Complaint"
and Marty himself in that period physically resembled
the book's author, just as he psychosexually resembled
the book's protagonist (and maybe the author too,
absolutely). After seeing him last week she now wonders
even more than before if he ever loved her at all.

[The Battle of Jyze City]

    The first time she really lost it with him she cut
herself in the thigh and went to the campus infirmary.
The second time, outside her house, he was taking her
home for what he said would be the last time. She was
prepared: she'd stashed a razor blade in her purse. She
slashed her right wrist (as a lefty, she said, she found
that "more natural"). He drove her to the emergency
room at a nearby hospital and told the admissions nurse,
"She's a pseudo-masochist." The nurse looked at her
sympathetically and said to her, "So you don't speak
English, honey?" (I misheard her before; I thought the
nurse said that sarcastically to him, not
sympathetically to her, and I don't recall the "honey"
part at all.) Then, to be admitted, since she was
underage, her parents had to be called. This turned out
to be a blessing, Z says now, because as a result her
father for the first time was willing to let her seek
psychiatric help. That was how she met Dr. T., the
shrink she was to continue seeing for the next eight
years (he was the one Mama E called before Z left on her
world trip at the end of those eight years, saying --
this is Mama E -- "I'll kill myself if she goes"). Dr.
T. himself tried, unsuccessfully, to seduce Z. And
years later she somehow ran into him again and he'd
become the head of a women's psychiatric unit at a
university hospital in another state.)
    Z likes to remind me that lots of men were chasing
her at the time she decided to shuck her virginity. She
picked Marty as her designated deflowerer at least in
part because he was very handsome and charming (she told
me this before I met him; in person I could easily see
why he was so attractive to her). He also left her with
a legacy of self-consciousness about her physical
attributes, which he rated out loud to her face one by
one, and not just about her face (he told her he did
this with all his women). Her nose was too big, her
cheeks too wide, her breasts too small, blah blah blah
-- all of which is nonsense. It was simply part of his
way of controlling women, as her shrink pointed out to
her (he called him "a controlling Hitler").

[+2]

     -- A big change. Z's fractured a bone in her arm
and let's just say neither of us is dealing with the
injury very well. Because of this I didn't make it in
to work until half past ten on a very heavy night, and
at last-bus time I had to go home and then come back
down in the Z-mobile, and now it's quarter to four in
the a.m. and I've finally finished up the week's work
and I'm taking this opportunity to jyze a bit here in
the conference room because it's not too likely I'll be
able to do so at home tonight and god only knows what
tomorrow may bring.

     (If I stand up and go over to the window, some
fifteen to seventeen stories down I can see a city-
block-size planter containing numerous deciduous trees
spangled with white Christmas lights, all shimmery and
glittery in the wind, and also the gigantic upside-down
carpenter's pencil of the highrise across the street --
I don't even know the building's name now -- rising up
out of that same planter, which is actually the dark
gravelly roof of the three-story base of the highrise;
and only a single car is visible anywhere on the
streets, and that car is our own Dalmation-spotted Z-
wagon parked almost directly below.)

     Yesterday Z went out as a volunteer on a city-
sponsored salmon-counting expedition. The accident
happened in a stretch of a north-end creek that the team
leader, who just happened to be our friend Jess, had
warned everyone was tricky, but Z made it through okay
the first time and so was a little careless the second.
Her foot slipped on a log and she lost her balance and
tried to break her fall with her left arm. Instead the
arm broke. She fell into the water too but managed to
stay pretty much upright and she was wearing hip waders
and so didn't get too wet. Oddly, it was because Jess
herself had taken a similar spill on the very same log
(but without breaking anything) that she had described
it to the whole group beforehand as a tricky spot.

    My first awareness of this accident came from a
terse note I found in my armchair when I got up
yesterday -- or today actually by NUT measure -- at the
current normal hour, one p.m. In an unfamiliar, very
shaky hand it read: "Hurt wrist in a fall into creek.
Gone to Doc." I'd thought I'd heard someone come in
earlier, but whoever it was hadn't tried to awaken me
and soon left (I suspected it was June, who has a key).
From Z's note I assumed the "hurt" was fairly minor, and
at the time of writing the note so did she, although it
was already swelling up quite a bit. A sprain maybe,
she thought. But then she called me at three and said
the wrist was broken, it was in a cast, she couldn't
drive because of pain drugs, she needed me to come and
take her home. She seemed in surprisingly good spirits,
I thought -- trying to be "Norwegian" probably.
    That didn't last long. I hiked all the way over to
the hospital on east hill, a couple of miles (we agreed
this would be faster than waiting for a taxi), and when
I walked in I cracked an ill-advised joke about being
stoic on pain -- very harmless, I thought, and even
affectionate -- and she fell apart, began bawling openly
and loudly, making for an awkward scene in the seriously
crowded lobby. It didn't help at all that I hadn't
shaved in a couple of days and was dressed in my usual
street rags. Was I a batterer who'd broken this poor
woman's arm and was now verbally abusing her, perhaps an
evil anti-WTO protester as well, maybe a bum off the
street asking for handouts and harassing not only her
but everyone in the lobby, potentially if not overtly
just yet? It was very uncomfortable there for a while.
    -- And it's pretty much continued that way ever
since. I've been doing my best to deal with what to me
is a whole lot of craziness on her part -- some of it
truly outrageous -- and my patience is just about gone.
Hospitals freak her out. They always have, ever since
she spent several traumatic months in one as an infant
because of the botched sixth-toe removals. In her
twenties she forked over thousands of dollars to shrinks
trying to help her cope with her hospital phobia (among

other psych maladies). And her "way" of being sick, and
she's made no secret of this with me, is to do lots of
whining and make lots of demands, and if her caretaker
-- I, for instance, caretaker G-hub right here at her
service -- if he bridles at any of this or pleads that
he has other things he must tend to, she breaks into
loud sobs or shifts into outraged vindictive martyr mode
and acts as if he's treating her horribly. In fact I,
the caretaker, have faced all this with her before and
this time I thought I was prepared to "serve" anyway --
as she isn't failing to remind me I must, according to
our wedding vows -- but she's being extremely nasty and
-- well. Best to go get myself a glass of water right
now and see if maybe I can chill out a bit, yeah.

*

     Roughly a decade ago Z broke up with Jerry II
because he supposedly didn't want to take care of her
when she came home from the hospital after her
fibroidectomy. Several times in the past she's painted
him to me as a monster for acting as he did back then.
Now I think I have a better idea what actually happened
between them. I mean, she demands, and not in anything
close to a friendly way. She orders. She freaks out,
melts down, goes ballistic over nothing at all. Yike!
     So now we've fought about it. When I stopped in
briefly several hours ago while picking up the car (the
fight was earlier in the evening) she woke up and came
out to observe, "That was the worst fight we've had
since before we were married." And I said: "Right now
I'm about as bummed as I can possibly be." She let it
go. (In her pathetically shaky hand -- unfortunately
it's her writing arm, the left, that's broken -- she'd
written a brief note about Jerry II and about hospitals
freaking her out.) She didn't start anything this time.
I told her I had my own horror stories, the worst having
to do with being terrorized by cascades of demands from
Lady V, though only a few of those had anything to do
with hospitals. (And in my rush to get back down here
to finish up the scoping job I was wearing my shoes in
the kitchen while rustling up a bite to eat when Z first

618

came out. More horrors. Was I a total barbarian
intentionally trying to drive her insane?)

    This afternoon she almost succeeded in pushing me
to the point where I would have to get nasty with her.
Somehow I managed to keep a lid on it. At one point my
eyes were welling over at the sadness and frustration of
it all. And though I tried to conceal this she spotted
it and asked why and I said, "Because I don't like to
let you down." Only then did she seem to realize how
serious this whole matter was to me and to compose
herself somewhat and put an end to the hysterics (dread
word) -- flying into rages because she thinks I want her
to be "stoic" when I just want her to stop attacking me.
(But then I'm not moving fast enough in doing whatever
she's demanding, so she's taking it as an insult to
her.)

    She'll be wearing the cast for six weeks. It's
dark blue, not too unsightly (in a sling of the same
color), and extends above the elbow and makes many of
her normal movements awkward and sometimes difficult or
impossible, but except for an occasional slight dull
ache she's no longer in pain. She's saying the accident
itself is a message from the cosmos that she's been
trying to do too much and she should take it easy for
the holidays. The mygs have obviously been swarming
because of her mother's cataract operation (which
apparently was a success; it took place yesterday and,
though Mama E was groggy at first, she's fine now --
Tito's with her -- and she can "even see dust!"). And
still more stressful is Z's own D&C scheduled for just a
week from today to determine the nature of the growths
in her uterus. And on top of all this it's been a bad
week for her at work, with an infuriated walkout -- her
own, that is -- from a meeting with a clueless team of
Eurusan ad consultants followed by a tiff with her
friend Kendra. And then there's the usual seasonal
stress and all the excitement around the WTO protests
and their aftermath and Marty's appearance in the middle
of it all. And while we're at it why not throw in her
husband's recent mediocre performance as a lover.

-- So it's understandable, I guess, that she would lose it. But such extreme nastiness can never be understandable when you're actually facing it. She goes so far over the top it can be terrifying even to, yes, a monster like me. And it sure doesn't help that she won't take any responsibility at all for its effects. -- Or maybe later on she'll say she will, well after the damage is done and while still sounding resentful about it all.

What a terrible temper she has! What rage is in her!

I don't know what to do. Just hang in and slog on. There's no talking reason with her about any of this (she heaps scorn on the very idea of being "reasonable" at such a time). I tell her what effect her ongoing outbursts have on me and on this TJM project I'm committed to completing -- with great reluctance do I even bring this up with her -- and of course she leaps on my candid disclosure as proof that I think she's a bad wife, uncaring, insensitive, demanding, and flies off into yet another rage over that.

So what am I supposed to do, beg her to lay off? That'd be no good anyway; I know because I've already tried it. Pleaded. Explained everything in detail. And she promised to bear with me -- this was last summer -- or at least I thought she did. At most times she seems to be making the effort but then earlier this week that vow started cracking at the edges and now it's shattered.

I dread -- I'll repeat -- playing the jyze card here. "You're not letting me do my jyze thing." If I bring this up too much she'll just start hating jyze and resenting me for putting it "above" her. The ancient conflict -- and I never want to believe it's inevitable, and I refuse to believe it is now. But my confidence about this is facing a severe test. (I was lulled into such confidence, one might say, by the years with Lady U. With her my writing -- this was during the protojyze era, or most of it was -- my writing never did pose a conflict, not a single time. Why, I don't know. A

miracle, I guess. And even with that miracle as a major
strength in the relationship the thing still fell
apart.)

     Hang in and slog on. Right. It's gonna be grim.
Maybe not at all times, but more often than I'd like.
And then some. Probably. Almost certainly.

     She's still wearing the same red sweater and T-
shirt she had on when she fell. Somehow they didn't get
wet except in one small spot. Eventually I'll have to
cut them off her. But at this point she's not ready for
that. There's something consoling to her about keeping
that red sweater on, and the T-shirt seems to have
become a de facto part of the sweater.

     Memo to self: try to muster maximum sympathy for
the Z-woman no matter what her attitude. I too once had
a cast on my left hand and forearm. On another occasion
I suffered through several lousy months with a huge cast
on my left leg owing to a ruptured Achilles tendon.
And: be prepared. For six weeks she's gonna be a
nonstop pain in the ass. She's told me so herself --
promised me so. From the appearance of things she'd
feel totally out of sorts if she weren't being a pain in
the ass. She'd think it was a kind of self-betrayal.
It's like a matter of honor with her: when you're sick
you must be whiny and demanding and hard to get along
with, and when you're seriously injured (or anyway think
you are) you must push all these to the max, and when
what you're doing has a strongly negative effect on your
spouse, the love of your goddamn life, you must melt
down and fly into the mother of all rages.

     I don't understand it. It's shocking. It's
colossally foolish. It's monstrously selfish and it's
about as unloving as you can get. Sez I. But then --
we're different. Yes. She sees things her way and I
see things mine. It's her "acorn" we're talking about
here. It's how she was raised. Very sorry, she's not
from some "nice" privileged suburban family. Very
sorry, she's not gracious when the chips are down and
never will be (though she quite often is when she wants
to be). Very sorry, she's gonna be who she is and fuck

you, G-hub, if it causes you a whole lotta grief.
     -- Wind blowing hard. Just like me. It'd be nice
if a massive storm swept over the city right about now.
Wotta fine hunka pathetic fallacy that would be! But
it's ten to six. In the morning, yes. Ten minutes from
now, I think -- could be wrong -- the car must be off
the street down there. Could be towed and draw a big
impoundment fee as well as a fine. And I gotta go home
sometime, so it might as well be now. (This on the
night exactly three weeks from the millennial rollover.)

[+2]

     -- Well, we're lucky. Or (which is to say the same
thing) (or almost) (okay, it's not the same thing at all
but the effect's the same): we're well matched. Or it's
both of those things and maybe some others too, though I
can't think of any in particular right now -- don't even
want to try. But we're out of the woods. Crisis over.
Already. The newlyweds rock!
     It happened that same morning when I arrived home
(now roughly forty hours ago) and went straight to bed.
She got up when I first came in, I made it plain I was
still plenty unhappy with her, then she returned to bed
and I once again, at her request, laid out the reasons
why. I said I was willing to make up and move on, but I
wanted to be clear that as far as I was concerned she'd
totally lost it for more than a day and it wouldn't be
acceptable to me if she kept up the same kind of
treatment of me, meaning the impossible demands followed
by raging attacks when I couldn't meet those demands.
And I pointed out she'd already admitted she'd "freaked
out" over being in the hospital, so in effect I was only
telling her what she'd said herself. And I said she
just had to pull herself together because we'd be facing
some tough times in the six weeks ahead (of her being in
the cast) -- and when she started to dissolve into tears
again over these statements of mine I said she had to
stop that, the high drama had to end, this was too

serious for such self-indulgence. Harsh words, yes.

     And then to my surprise and great relief she did
pull herself out of it. And much more quickly than I
ever would've thought possible. True, she did say she
thought the term "raging attacks" was a little strong
and she'd like me to take it back, but she said it
fairly calmly. And though I didn't think the term was
too strong, I said I'd do that -- take it back -- as
long as she'd agree to cease and desist on whatever kind
of acts those were that the term was referring to. And
that was all okay by her.

     So we made up. And so now I take it back, all of
it, as promised. And in writing!

     "You're good, you know," she said a bit later.
"You're really good. I don't think anyone else I've
known could've talked me out of that."

     My difficult wife. Somehow I eventually hit the
right note this time. Maybe I'm becoming a bit wiser,
or maybe she was more afraid of the consequences of
letting herself go all the way berserko and so was more
ready to back down. Or let's just say maybe we're both
becoming a bit wiser and also we've now built up a
bigger reserve of trust to fall back on when the going
gets dangerously rough. And this said, I suppose I
should also concede that if she's my difficult wife, as
after all I openly declared a few sentences back, then
it must be equally true I'm her difficult husband. It
even seems to make a kind of logical and symmetrical
sense. So how could I have even the slightest objection
to it? And I don't. None. I'm totally good with it.

     Since that morning she's been careful to be "nice"
(though she grits her teeth over it sometimes) and I've
been helping her in every way I can. I've taken her to
the library so she could stock up on whodunits along
with a serious read or two, to a mall so she could buy
some tops that will work with her ungainly cast, to the
co-op so she could lay in some types of food she'll be
able to prepare one-handed when I'm away. I've cut off
her consolatory red sweater and T-shirt. I've clipped
her fingernails and -- be careful! -- toenails. I've

helped her bathe, first tying a drawstring trash bag
around her cast to keep it dry. I've cleaned up after
her, washed her dishes, paid her bills, wrapped several
of her Christmas presents for friends and relatives (and
written in the captions for the dozen of our blown-up
wedding photos she'd picked out to appear in a custom-
made year 2000 calendar she's sending her mother -- a
wonderful gift which I must say shows Z at her finest).
And of course I'm constantly fetching things for her,
answering the phone, assisting her in dressing and even
in moving, including if the move's just a few inches to
change positions in bed or elsewhere, because sometimes
the cast seems to clamp down on her every bit as tightly
as she likes to clamp down on my hands in bed if I'm
getting inappropriately frisky when she's not up for it.

    All this is taking a whole lot of time, yes. But I
don't mind -- I even like the closeness it fosters --
just so long as I can hang on to enough space for myself
to grind out my Jyzer Ink work and keep this TJM project
going as it approaches millennium crunch time. Or call
it clamp time. On that Jyzer Ink/TJM score, so far, so
good. And I think it'll stay that way, because I think
Z is now ready to listen and to adapt if I ask her to.

    The next three weeks will be tough, though, and
each one for a different reason. This coming week
she'll be going to work every day while still wearing
the big cast. I'll have to stay up quite a bit later
than usual to help get her out the door in the morning.
And at the end of the week, Friday, the cast will be
replaced with a smaller, lighter, more maneuverable one,
but that same day she'll also be going in for her D&C
and she's plenty worried about that, as am I.

    The week after that we'll be waiting to hear the
results on the D&C and she'll be home on vacation the
entire time -- she'll be bored, restless, needy, scared,
clingy, touchy, moody, myggy. Christmas Day is at the
end of that week. (We've agreed it would be way too
much to try to follow through on our plan to have Rob
and Gail over for Christmas dinner. We still might try
to take them out somewhere. But...probably not.)

     The third week she goes back to work but that's the
week we're still scheduled to do the house-sitting for
Jess (last year when we did the same thing for Jess --
and for Gwen then -- Z found it increasingly frustrating
to be away from home, and then she badly sprained her
toe). That's also most likely the week we'll be finding
out the results of the D&C, though they could come in
earlier. And it's the week of the final countdown to
the millennial rollover, which falls on that Friday
night. And -- who knows -- maybe that same night the
madness of Y2Kalypse will break out as well and the
planet will blow to smithereens. Or that could happen
the next day, meaning the first day of the new year,
decade, century, etc. Or it could happen two days after
that, the first working day of the new -- yeah. The
quatro. That's the day when most of the world's
computers will be cranking up for the first time post-
rollover, with the post-holiday restart of business.
     Oho, the curse of interesting times. Has its
foulness ever been fouler? -- But we love it, yes we
do. I do anyway, in my way. And I think she does too,
in hers; I don't think she's just saying it.
     So that settles that.
     Meanwhile the WTO fallout continues. On the
national scene it's dropped out of the spotlight but in
J-town it's still stage center. Hundreds of people
showed up at the city council hearings to testify about
firsthand experience with police brutality (the
hearings were held in the library auditorium just up the
hill and the scene was much like the one with the crowd
ringing the jail last week; long lines were waiting
outside the chamber to testify and the cops were present
in force). Property owners and law-and-order
conservatives had their own love-in for the police
yesterday at the central plaza. The city seems to be
divided down the middle about how to view the protests
and the police actions. All sorts of investigations
into causation are planned, but my own sense of the
matter is that the divisions will remain pretty much as
they are no matter what conclusions the panels and

commissions and editorial pages reach. The mayor seems
to be hanging tough.

The WTO itself is in regroup mode. It's not likely
to make any serious effort to start up a new round of
negotiations until after the U.S. elections next fall.
Opponents of the WTO's brand of "free trade" have bought
themselves at least an additional year to organize and
make their case. For that reason alone -- but there are
others -- this protest must be judged a huge success.

The other reasons, I guess I'll mention a few right
now. First, the protest has shown that corporate power
can be successfully challenged at the international
level (a way exists to fight it, in part owing to the
same digitization that's doing so much to foster
international movement of capital). Second, it's made
the WTO a household name in this country and around the
world; and this can only be good because people are
asking what it is and how it functions; and when (and
if) they get some accurate answers, it's likely many
will oppose it. Third, it's demonstrated that a
coalition of labor and environmental groups can work
together (it's created a new coalition, however shaky).
Fourth, it's begun the process of radicalizing and/or
activating a new generation of young people who, in this
country at least, have in recent times been largely
apolitical. And fifth, it's actually changing minds,
even among the media elite and the opinion-setters.
(Dennis Q., former editor of the alt-weekly and now a
columnist for J. City's afternoon paper, comes right out
and says this about his own views on the WTO -- he now
opposes it -- but you can see changes of a less overt
nature in many other places.)

-- And it's that season again. Plummeting
temperatures. Talk of snow. Fear of ice on the hills
(I'm afraid Z will lose her balance on the steep and
slippery leaf-strewn south-hill sidewalks -- maybe fall
down and break her other arm or a leg). But the
Christmas lights are still fine to behold, especially
when they appear in unexpected places. I encountered
several instances of this on the way down tonight: a

Chinese restaurant in the AQ with Santa's sleigh and the usual eight scraggly reindeer brightly lit up while navigating the tiles of a traditional Chinese flying-eaves rooftop at a very steep angle; the waterfront streetcar jouncing along, its electric whistle blowing and strings of colored lights twinkling, including part of one string that had come loose and was dragging like a tiny sparking tail on the rail bed; and then on the waterfront itself a huge fish-processing ship whose bow and superstructure were ablaze with multicolored lights which in turn revealed a massive white Christmas bell hanging from the rigging high above.

Just nineteen days to go until the day when (I'm paraphrasing a newspaper lede here) we'll no longer have to be hearing about how many days remain before the millennium. (But I'll bet we do then too, on that very day. At least once. Someone will point out it's only 365,242 revolutions of the earth until the next millennium -- unless, that is, an unexpectedly large planetary wobble occurs. And also if I've done the math correctly. Which is not that hard, really: 365.242 days per year (a figure from the almanac) times 1,000.)

[+1]

A tack-on note at home. The black armchair. A small air cleaner whirring in Z's half-bathroom around the corner to combat the tobacco fumes that have recently resumed migrating there by way of the vent for the overhead fan. Clocks ticking, refrigerator and wheeled portable radiator heater creaking. A jet flying low overhead, coming in from who knows where but it's likely a "red eye" flight since the time is 5:05 a.m. And I in my green sweatshirt and long-legged black sweatpants (not the cutoffs) have just settled in for this no doubt very brief winter's jyze.

Poor Z. All these other things and now this: a piece of hate mail. It's signed only "Your co-workers," but the body of the brief note makes clear it was sent

by one or more of the attendees at the meeting Z walked
out of a week ago today. That was the one featuring the
all-Cawk ad agency team working up the big campaign on
recycling for next year, a task force of utility people
attending to be briefed on the campaign, and Z objected
strenuously because neither of the two proposed plans
were directed toward or showed any concern at all about
the "underserved" or people of color, and those two
categories combined make up about forty percent of the
utility's customers.

And now this letter, which not only accuses her of
being "unprofessional" for walking out and states "most
of us" are "sick of" her "grandstanding" and
"manipulating with tears" (she was weeping at one point)
but goes on to attack her personally, saying she should
quit "playing the race card" and dressing "like a
sixties radical" and other outrageous things.

She told me about it on the phone this afternoon --
"Talk about high drama!" -- but didn't reveal the
contents until she arrived home. She was surprisingly
poised about it -- calm -- maybe because she was in a
state of shock or close to it. But also her friends at
work are standing firmly behind her and, maybe even more
important, and much more surprising for sure, her boss,
Dale, is furious about the letter and is determined to
get to the bottom of its origin by holding another
meeting with the same group but minus the clueless
outside-ad-agency bunch. And I was fuming over it
myself all evening, and when I came in at 1:30 a.m. and
found June unexpectedly here, we fumed over it together.

Only later tonight did Z shed a few tears over the
letter itself, and those were quiet, in bed, as I
massaged her aching cast-weight-bearing left shoulder.
She was remembering how her mother didn't really do
anything to fight back when Z was the victim of racial
baiting as a kid -- just repeated the "sticks and
stones" mantra. "It means so much now to have my
husband and my friends and even my boss standing behind
me...." I'm also suggesting various defenses and lines
she can use in obtaining justice and maybe a measure of

comeuppance, I'll call it. I wish I could play a
frontline role in the counterattack. But on the other
hand it's probably a good thing I can't because I'd be
liable to go off like a bomb -- throttle the perp or
perps if I found out who he/she/they were. The cowards
-- cloaking themselves in anonymity like Ku Kluxers.

     I also have to say I'm aware of a certain irony
here, and so's she. It wasn't all that long ago I was
warning her she'd be sabotaging herself at work if she
unleashed her hot temper on people there as she was
doing on me at home. And she said then she absolutely
agreed -- that was one of the things she'd learned at
the leadership institute. In fact we've been hashing
out this issue since the very day we met -- when she
observed brightly near the drawbridge where we were to
part, "I think we're having our first fight!"

     -- And so the end of another wild jyze eighter.
And the millennium's still more than a fortnight away!

30

     Probably won't last long down here. There's no
heat and I can tell I'll have to take a leak pretty
soon. But this is the AQ station of the underground and
I'm sitting on a bench halfway between bay A and bay B,
directly beneath one of the large red-and-white metal
origami sculptures that line the upper part of the high
wall on this side. Buses roll by from time to time,
very quietly except for the sizzle of their tires
(they're dual gas/electric and here they're running as
trolleys). Small crowds gather and then are swallowed
up by buses at each of the bays and also at the matching
ones on the southbound side across the tunnel.

I've never been down here before. And it's the
start of the last of the eighters before this jyze
project shifts into high millennial gear (at which point
the length of J-weeks will shrink from eight days to
five, with the number of pages to be filled remaining --
in theory -- the same). And it's the day on which the
United States officially returns the Panama Canal to the
country of Panama, which the U.S. itself created by
expropriating land from Colombia almost a century ago,
back in the primitive early days of our country's period
of blatant overseas colonialism (as opposed to the
period of blatant overseas neocolonialism we're in now).
And it's also the birthday of that high-profile French
prognosticator of the 16th century, "Nasty-doom-us," of
whom it seems certain woo-woo types can less than ever
get enough as the big quatrorollover looms dead ahead.

Crossing the high bridge at six-thirty I couldn't
see the sunset (it had taken place two hours earlier)
but it's now occurring almost as far south as it ever
does, with the solstice falling on the last day of this
eighter (and Friday night we'll be attending a solstice
party at Craig A.'s house if Z's feeling up to it after
her D&C). What I did see from the bridge, though, was a
city crew working to install the floodlights which will
be part of the municipal Year 2000 celebration,
illuminating the great green arched ironwork structure
from below for the benefit of everyone for miles around,
and especially for the thousands passing beneath the
span every hour in vehicles on the freeways. The lights
were being adjusted atop poles bordering the street
roughly a hundred feet down, with helmeted workers
riding dozers and bucket cranes. At one point they
turned the lights on experimentally while I was directly
above them and I waved down to confirm that they -- the
lights -- were working and several crew members waved
back. Excitement to die for! Of course I can't wait to
tell Z all about it. She may even know some of those
guys as work colleagues.

The lead story in this afternoon's paper, city
edition, reports that last week's warning about

terrorist activities expected on New Year's Eve or
January 1 was prompted by the arrest in an unnamed
Middle Eastern country of twelve people planning just
such activities. Ross, the scope-building security
guard, says his outfit's received alerts about local
"citizen militias" -- not the ones he's told me about
which his friends belong to, I presume -- expected to
stage protest events downtown on those same days.
Personally I doubt any of the threats (and there have
been many others, here and elsewhere) will amount to
much. But I guess I'm not above exploiting the
possibility for a little drama in these pages, at least
to the extent of mentioning it. Or a little suspense,
say. And that's because almost daily the media are
issuing soothing stories about the Y2K-bug disruptions,
saying in this country and probably most others they'll
be only minor and local. All major computer-dependent
systems in the U.S. have been checked out and the
vulnerable ones recalibrated or replaced (at a cost of
billions, true, but hey, we can't be chintzy about
maintaining our national digital infrastructure,
especially with whopping corporate revenues at stake).

     Z walked with me as far as the DC castle. Tonight
the realtors holding the lease for that property are
throwing a Christmas party for neighborhood groups, a
little PR massage action intended to keep the serfs
living nearby in line, ourselves so magnanimously
included. Z wasn't feeling up to attending, but she had
a petition she wanted to turn in (it calls for creation
of residential-parking zones to prevent dot-com workers
from grabbing all the spaces as they're doing now; such
zones have existed for decades in many north-end hoods).
I hesitated to let her walk back to the house alone for
fear she'd slip on the steep leaf-plastered sidewalks
(and also because we'd seen several nasty-looking dudes
unloading a beater pickup along the way) but she said
she really needed the exercise and insisted, and I mean
quite forcefully insisted, she'd be okay.

     She still seems to be doing fine with the hate
letter. Today she attended a training session with

leaders of regional environmental-justice groups and was
even able to use the letter to gain a little street cred
with the obstreperous Rowena of JCEJ. Before now Rowena
had always seemed to treat Z as just another honky city
bureaucrat, even though Z was a cofounder of JCEJ and is
only half honky (roughly the same proportion Rowena is,
I'd guess, judging solely by skin color).

     -- And my fingers are about to fall off and my
bladder's about to burst. Therefore, sayonara, origami
sculpture and excellent AQ tunnel station. (But I'll
note very quickly the only sign of holiday cheer in this
place is a single bedraggled poinsettia on view inside
the transit offices in the basement of the east depot
visible across the way, behind the southbound bays.)

[+2]

     All's well, at least as far as I know. And how far
is that? No way to tell, really, especially concerning
the time dimension. The bubble of perceived well-being:
how large can it ever be? Or you could call it the
bubble of self-delusion. Yet don't most people live in
such a bubble (dual-purpose!) most of the time? And
these are moving bubbles; they go where we go, and
that's especially true for those of us drifting hither
and yon right here in the good ol' USA -- in the
historic quarter of Jyze City, say. And here or
anywhere else such bubbles can interlock and overlap and
combine, just like soap bubbles. They can even pop.
     Same goes, of course, for bubbles of the economic
or financial kind, here or elsewhere. But especially
here.
     Or then again all this is probably nonsense. (Not
that you couldn't build a tolerable socioeconomic theory
out of it, expand it to book length, include elaborate
charts and graphs. It might even have been done already,
though if so, I haven't read the book or heard about it
as far as I can recall. But, again, how far is that?
-- So maybe I should ask Z to check the web for the

existence of such a study. -- But it's not too likely
I'll do that, no. Because my plate is already just
about as full as it can ever get.)

   -- Jyzing in the brown armchair. Therefore this
must be the hideaway. (Another sign being that the
armchair, unlike the one at home, has no large gap in
its undercarriage.) The blinking red digital clock on
the radio says it's 11:46 p.m. I would've taken up this
J-book twenty minutes earlier but I had to read the
full-page story in this afternoon's paper about the
fateful behind-the-scenes decision-making on Tuesday of
WTO week, the main "Battle of J. City" day. The account
is riveting even though the mayor and his staff, citing
attorney warnings about possible lawsuits against the
city, are still refusing to comment on all that world-
shaking -- and world-remaking! -- chaos.

   This afternoon and evening, the early part anyway,
I was out at Olwen's place and most of the time after
Trent's arrival home from work we were trading WTO
horror stories. No doubt a good many other J-towners
have been doing the same over the past couple of weeks.
Trent was an officially designated "peacekeeper" for the
forgive-the-debt march on Monday night and participated
in several other events. Because the upper-echelon law
firm where he works as a paralegal threw the
"schmoozefest," as he called it, for WTO delegates and
local politicos and business types outside which our
sole Afrusan city councilmember, on his way in to do
some schmoozing, was brutalized by the cops, Trent was
able to give me the inside story on that outrageous
incident (a female Afrusan attorney from Trent's firm
was escorting the councilmember when the cops descended).
Also, a friend of Trent's, a Eurusan, was tackled by
three cops without warning late Tuesday afternoon about
a block and a half south of my scope office, thrown to
the ground, and one pointed a gun (a real one; not a
rubber-pellet type or a water pistol) at his head while
another held him down and a third searched his backpack,
spilling all its contents on the sidewalk; and then
without saying another word the trio of berserko lawmen

ran off and did the same to someone else. I've heard
numerous stories like this and read many more. And I
would've walked right by that spot myself that same
night if I hadn't abandoned my attempt to go to work.

     Olwen and I had a couple of hours to ourselves and
those also were enjoyable for me -- and for her as well,
I hope. Each time we get together we're a little more
comfortable. We sat at the dining-room table; a half-
finished jigsaw puzzle of formidable complexity lay on a
nearby card table and I think Olwen had figured we would
work on it -- something Trent said suggested as much --
but we never did. Mostly we talked jyze, poetry,
genealogy, and the unending turmoil in the life of one
Zoelie B.: the fall in the creek, the Marty meet-up, the
hate letter, the frantic husband, the upcoming D&C. I
also learned Olwen's return to college helped
precipitate the breakup of her marriage of seventeen
years. That breakup came right at the time almost a
quarter century ago when she first met Z. Some fellow
students in a writing class she was taking recommended a
certain woman-led radical-therapy group in which Z
turned out to be a member; and then they, Z and Olwen,
discovered they both were contributors to the same local
poetry mag. Even in those days, Olwen says, Z was
carrying around a big bag stuffed full of pills that
rattled audibly from around corners and outside windows
(at first she was commuting from fifty miles south for
the meetings -- not that I'm saying the rattles could he
heard from that distance) (thirty miles maybe). And
they've been friends ever since.

     -- But I can't go much longer now. To arrive at
Olwen's by three o'clock I had to peel myself out of bed
ninety minutes early after crashing almost an hour late
and then, half an hour after that, being called upon to
help Z don her backpack (she gets a charge from the way
I rise up naked on my knees to do this from the edge of
the bed and so I like to ham it up even more and soon
I'm wide awake and panting for more of her hand action
just as she's bridling to head out the door).

     Her spirits remain high. Even at work people are

telling her she's holding up remarkably well under all
the strains. But her biggest test yet will come
tomorrow when she faces the cast replacement in the
morning, with associated rigmarole that will take hours,
and then the D&C in the afternoon. On her own she's
decided to catch a bus to east hill in the morning so I
can abide by something fairly close to my normal sleep
pattern and then drive over to join her before the D&C.
She's also heroically planning to attend Craig A.'s
solstice party tomorrow evening and the city employee
union's Christmas dinner and dance Saturday evening.
And of course I'll be accompanying her to those too, if
the plans don't fall through, which I hereby predict at
least one of them, and quite possibly both, will do.

     Meanwhile I've been putting in lots of late-night
hours helping June, whose final-exam paper was due at
nine this morning. For the past several days she's been
dealing with her friend Peggy's family, assisting with
planning the funeral and then attending it yesterday
(and also writing a one-page eulogy which came to me via
Z for editing). Last night she confessed she's afraid
her debt to me is "getting much too big" -- but also let
it slip that even assuming a successful conclusion of
this semester she'll have completed only forty of the
ninety credits she needs for a degree, clearly implying
she's hoping our collaboration will continue. And I'm
hoping for that also. But maybe with a few more
constraints in place. Which I'm quite sure is Z's view
as well.

     And then the time that goes to helping Z -- doing
her dishes, cleaning up, assisting her with washing up
and getting dressed, things like that. And now the
deadline for Christmas cards is looming and, though Z's
done all of hers (and I've added a few words and signed
most of the cards) I haven't even begun my own, except
for the one sorry attempt I eked out at Wei and Alison's
"carding bee" Thanksgiving weekend. And after the
cards, Christmas presents, or at least one, for Z. And
I've got a rep to live up to! And in her condition
she'll be needing and expecting -- and without question

deserving -- some special treatment this year.

At work, I should note, she's been showing the hate letter to anyone and everyone. She's focusing her efforts on converting this painful experience into an AFLO (another fucking learning opportunity) for the utility as a whole, and especially for its non-Cawk employees, by developing a protocol to be distributed citywide about what to do if you receive such a letter. She's afraid Dale is backing away somewhat from his intention to pursue the matter strongly but she's trying to withhold judgment about that because he's extremely busy these days. She did show Kendra the letter and from her shocked reaction to it Z's sure she's not the perp. Z's suspicions at this point are focused on Cassie B., the incorrigible never-rock-the-boat blond Eurusan from my own city 2/7 with whom she's had several run-ins over the years. But today is Z's last day at work until after Christmas Day, and many of her coworkers, including Cassie, will be taking off the week between Christmas and New Year's, and by the time normal operations resume in January (next decade! next century! next millennium!) all this may look like just what it will be, at least in a sense: ugly stuff that took place in a radically previous era which everyone would prefer to forget about. But I hope not. And certainly she's not the type to let it slide if she can help it.

Regarding our circle of friends I can think of only one other piece of news. Z says she made it a specific point to ask Leola on my behalf how the reconciliation with Gerry is coming along. And Leola said it's proceeding pretty well except she's the one who has to provide all the initiative concerning the "healing steps" they vowed to take together. Gerry, even though he's the purported villain in this drama, is just sort of agreeably going along with whatever she asks. (Z's remark: "Poor Gerry. More and more I'm seeing his side of this. While Leola was talking on the phone with me and watching TV at the same time -- which I hate! -- he was out in the driveway in a heavy drizzle flocking the

Christmas tree she'd volunteered to take to her
workplace without even asking him first.") -- But what
we both see as the bottom line is that Gerry and Leola
in their many years of marriage have learned how to
weather the storms. There's a whole spectrum of opinion
among the circle of friends about how this should be
regarded -- from wholly admirable to sadly spineless --
but to my way of thinking the truth about it is not
something that's available to outsiders. All we can do
is acknowledge L&G are somehow able to do something not
too common these days, which is to guide their
couplehood through to the next day and then the one
after that and then on and on down through the months
and years. Among the circle the next-oldest living-
together relationship is four or five years (Paz and
Tobey, who are Deeps) and the next-oldest marriage is
seven and a half months (Ramona and Pepe).

    And I guess I should stop now. I don't really know
what's happening with Mr. D. Z is well aware Aida will
be needing her support in the coming weeks and months
(years maybe), but for the moment Aida is absorbed in
other things -- perhaps as a way to deal with the pain,
which even three months after her father's original
diagnosis is still fresh to her -- and not telling Z
much, having called off several planned get-togethers
with her. -- And there are many WOC tales I might go
into, especially regarding WTO week and the aftermath,
but I think I'll just blow them off. I'm tired. Need
some shut-eye real bad.

[+1]

    Here's the waiting room at Z's clinic. A moment
ago she was called in for her "procedure." "It's just
like an abortion, you know," she reminded me as we were
leaving the house (and passing within a few feet of the
mail carrier, who was startled enough at what he
undoubtedly overheard to raise an eyebrow and shoot us a
quizzical glance despite the heavy pre-Christmas sorting

job he was engaged in at 1511's tilt-down box cluster --
and a "pineapple express" has warmed things up enough
around here that he was wearing shorts).

So it turns out I've been through something like
this a few times before. But the other times the doc
was taking out a growth we knew was in there; this time,
of course, the hope is nothing's in there that needs
taking out.

Considering her extensive history of bad
experiences in hospitals -- not least the one just eight
days ago in which I supposedly contributed to the
badness (not that I'm actively disputing the matter) --
Z's been remarkably composed and cheerful in the face of
today's ordeal. But earlier, at home, she was quick to
take up my suggestion that we rattle our marital good-
luck "twanger" a few times before leaving. And there
was, understandably enough, a little edge to her banter
as she waited for me to finish my breakfast. (No doubt
a good portion of this edge was induced by the four or
five hours she'd already spent tussling with the medical
system today.) -- And I now know her resolve to be
early for everything includes even her own partial
internal dismemberment, so to speak.

Her new cast, besides being shorter and lighter, is
also a new color: purple. Her favorite! But it pinches
a little in the upper forearm when she bends her arm and
her wrist "pings" once in a while, especially if she
squeezes her pen too firmly. And that goes also for
squeezing the G-hub's copulatory organ (she did
experiment with this "just to see how 'abled' I am now"
as I was wolfing down my cereal at the dining table).

How long the D&C will take I don't know. Nor did
she when I last saw her. (She's never had an abortion,
by the way, although she's accompanied several friends
who have.) -- But not too long, I'm thinking. Unless,
of course, complications arise. That happened once
during one of Lady U's "procedures" when her abnormally
slow heartbeat slowed even more, to the point the nurses
thought she was "about to flatline," as the lady herself
always liked to put it in telling the story.

Fortunately -- in a sense -- something similar had
happened to her twice before during other kinds of
operations and she knew what to inform the nurses to do.
-- But my guess now with Z is an hour or so.

   The Christmas decorations hanging on the wall here,
including one suspended directly above my head, are
handsome and surprisingly opulent, I'd say, even for a
doctor's office: a collection of old-timey life-size
brass horns, presumably authentic -- a trumpet, a
cornet, a couple of more exotic medieval-looking musical
instruments whose names I don't know -- they could also
be gynecological instruments, almost -- and each is
adorned with plaid ribbon and bow and sprig of holly and
"swag" of evergreen ---

                    *   *

   -- At that point (way earlier than expected) Z
emerged from the inner office quietly weeping and
looking devastated. "I made a big mistake," she said,
but she wouldn't tell me what it was until we reached
the car in the underground parking garage. And so for
the whole way, trudging through labyrinthine corridors,
waiting for the elevator, riding down with a packed
carload of people pretending not to notice Z's sorry
condition but sneaking glances anyway, then stumbling
through the dark moldy cavelike slanting-floor depths of
the garage, I was left to wonder what terrible thing she
could've done to reduce herself to this state. Maybe
something involving failure to let the doc know in
advance about her previous fibroidectomy? But that
didn't seem very likely. What else could it be, though?

   Inside the car she revealed what it was with a
fresh burst of sobs. Somehow she'd misremembered a
medical term and told the gynecologist on the phone a
week ago that she'd be coming in for an apelleloma
(sic?) something or other, not a D&C. And this other
operation is much simpler than a D&C, which requires a
day or two of preparations including a preliminary visit
for an EKG (a heart test, I guess). Therefore Dr. W
couldn't operate today and the next open date isn't
until January 5th, and to Z that seems about as far away

as it sounds when you say "next decade," "next century,"
etc. She'd had her heart set on getting this thing over
with as soon as possible (in part because I've favored
that approach). Now she admitted it had been very hard
to psych herself up for going in today -- and to keep up
her "stoic pose" while doing so -- and the thought of
repeating the whole ordeal in January was more than she
could bear at the moment. "You have no idea how much I
hate hospitals. I just can't stand this!"

So, time for some consoling. And I think I must've
done all right at it, because after a few minutes' good
weep she started pulling herself out of the pit and
before long she decided we might as well stop at the
east-hill co-op on the way home so she could buy a
certain kind of makeup to disguise or maybe do away with
the swelling and redness around her eyes caused by
crying. -- And the fact that she'd garbled the info Doc
Karen gave her to pass on to the gynecologist was also
highly upsetting to her. "I'm just falling apart these
days! How could I have become so confused?" (I told
her it must've been the same thing that caused her to
plunge into the creek last week: yet another powerful
burst of vertiginous postnup euphoria. But an
unconscious one, apparently, since she admitted to
having no memory of anything like that.)

-- So now I'm briefly stopping by the hideaway
before heading back home once again. In between was the
solstice party for her gay coworkers (all males), a
soggy walk downtown on a very windy and stormy night, a
browse at the central-plaza chain bookstore, a brief
stop at the scope office to do finals on two short jobs,
and the hike back down here (which afforded fine views,
during a welcome break in the rain, of low white clouds
in the southern sky streaming at fantastic speeds in
front of a moon slightly more than half full -- and also
of the DC castle lit up with its crowning Christmas star
at one end of the "middle road" corridor and at the
other end the golf-tee city icon decked out in its
Christmas peaked dunce hat perched atop the saucer).
Down here in the HQ the triangle's quite lively tonight

with holiday revelry and I'm riding the complex
vibrations produced by the dueling sound systems turned
up high in the clubs below.

     The "swag" I mentioned right before breaking off in
the doctor's office, by the way, represents a usage of
the term which, much to Z's surprise, I'd never heard
before. A "swag" of evergreen -- a single branch or
group of branches used as decoration.

     This morning as Z and I talked in bed -- much
longer than usual, probably because of her mostly
hidden, at that point, anxiety about the "procedure" --
she updated me on several "circle of friends" stories.
But I'll have to save those and also an account of the
gay solstice party for another time. The klaxon in my
head is now sounding its de facto pre-curfew warning of
one a.m. (personal curfew I'm talking here, not city).

                         [+2]

     -- I'm doing the best I can but it's turning out
to be not so good. Duties of all sorts intervened and
now I'm back in these pages a day later than I expected
to be. And for a setting I'm again falling back on the
hideaway. And in only a little over an hour it'll be
time to go home and wrestle with another batch of those
same duties. The main one tonight will be to come up
with a Christmas card which I can take to a copy shop
tomorrow afternoon and then sign the copies individually
and try to get them out to the core list by having Z
drop them off at the utility's postal station the
following morning.

     In the meantime some big news. In the first entry
of this eighter on Tuesday this jyzer right here noted
the government warning about millennium-related
terrorism and pretty much pooh-poohed it. That, it
turns out, was a mistake. Because at virtually the same
time he was doing so, an alleged terrorist with
suspected ties to the nasty Al Qaeda group in
Afghanistan was detained at a border port of entry just

fifty miles north of here. He arrived on an auto ferry,
and agents found more than a hundred pounds of bomb-
making materials along with four ignition devices hidden
in the trunk tire compartment of his rental car.

     The story didn't hit the papers until Friday
afternoon and the jyzer didn't see it until he arrived
home that night, after finishing the previous entry.
But he's now learned, from that story and several
follow-ups, that the detainee's believed to be an
Algerian "sleeper" who was living in Canada for the past
year and his immediate destination was a motel near the
J-town fairgrounds. The authorities suspect the bomb
was intended to disrupt the millennial celebration there
on New Year's Eve -- perhaps by blowing up the golf-tee/
saucer icon itself (the bomb was powerful enough "to
take out a large building"). This of course is the same
celebration which the jyzer and the Z-woman were
planning to attend (along with a hundred and fifty
thousand other revelers) and as far as we know still
are, though that could change at any moment, yes.

     Also: the detainee was scheduled to stay just one
night at the motel and carried airline tickets for a
flight the next morning bound for the far coast and
onward to England. Authorities are assuming he was just
a courier, also called a "mope," for the explosives.
And they're currently searching for a second man, still
on the loose, believed to have been traveling with the
"mope" or set to meet him at the motel (or "mopel"?),
where the reservations were for two people.

     Beyond this apparently not much is known. The
detainee is refusing to talk and little useful evidence
was found on his person or in the car, other than the
bomb itself. But Wednesday, five days from now and just
three days before Christmas, he'll be appearing in court
right here in J. City. And it's also quite possible the
grand jury will be taking up the matter, as it's done
with several similar, but lesser, incidents that
occurred in the past at that same port of entry. The
jyzer knows a thing or two about those because his
nightscoper avatar has worked on transcripts of

testimony concerning them (but most of those involved drug smuggling or illegal immigration).

Today, meanwhile, was the day for Kat. Best for jyze to tackle that immediately before the cascade of events washes it away. (But first this, speaking of washing things away: a trip to the head.)

*

And back to first-person jyze.

So this afternoon the four of us -- Betty and Kat, Z and I -- caught a remake of "The King and I" (retitled "Anna and the King") at a downtown theater. Overall I thought it mediocre or worse, just as have the reviews I've come across, but for some reason I don't really understand Z was keenly interested in seeing it. And she loved it. "I don't care," she said afterwards, "how politically incorrect I am for feeling this way -- I thought it was gorgeous." Was it because it's a tale of cross-cultural love with an Asian man in the lead -- not the usual imbecilic Western stereotype of a "weak" Asian man but a virile king (though a stereotype in many other ways) -- and a blond European beauty (in my view every bit as stereotypical) slowly won over by his manly and kingly charms? Could this be how Z views her own parents, or anyway would like to at times, if only unconsciously, say for three hours at a stretch? And does this way of seeing them perhaps represent part of the impetus for her choice some seventeen years ago to change her given name so that it would be an amalgam of the names her parents went by with each other and most of their friends, Zo and El -- i.e., Zoelie?

I don't really know. She just laughed when I asked her these questions. And a moment later said, referring to the amalgam question only, I think, "Maybe!"

Then, after the movie, a stop for burgers and onward to unit 203 for an early exchange of Christmas gifts, or rather completion of the exchange since the movie itself along with the dinner afterwards had been Kat and Betty's gift to us. For them we had the big picture book on Mayan culture (ordered months ago) and a bag of small gifts for each, and for both the goofball animated clock which I worked on for many hours over the past few nights to decorate and personalize. A bar above the clock face tilts every second like a teeter-totter and causes two marionettelike figurines dangling from its ends to jump around and shimmy hilariously -- one a male musician newly labeled "G" sitting at a piano with his hands attached to the keyboard (and an affixed cartoon speech bubble saying "The Kat & Betty Song, Z-goose -- hit it!"), the other a female singer labeled "Z" who's belting out a number with her hands wrapped around a standing mic (the words to the tune, in her speech bubble, being "Lub lub lub, we lub 'em to the nub!"). Alas, the speech bubbles, with their armatures fashioned by me from de-cottoned cotton ear swabs and rubber cement, proved too heavy for the battery-run tilt mechanism and as a result the two figurines could just barely shudder in place. So once I'd shown everyone how I'd hoped the thing would work -- moving the tilt bar myself with finger power -- I removed the speech bubbles and after that it functioned pretty well (though not quite as well as before I started messing with it -- probably owing to the weight of the rubber cement that remained, looking like huge wads of gum, in the marionettes' mouths). And Betty said she would place the clock on the mantel at home to keep it out of reach of the cats and she'd prop the detached speech bubbles against the bricks behind it for easy reference.

This exchange of gifts was happening early because B&K are going away for the holidays, mainly to see Wanda and Nick in their southwestern home state but with several other stops en route (including one in my own city 2/7). And the movie and dinner was a last-minute substitution; they'd hoped to take us to see the Christmas show put on by the J-town gay men's chorus, but Betty dawdled on ordering the tickets (and few can out-dawdle Betty when she's on her game) and the show surprised everyone by selling out much earlier than usual this year.

Kat, sad to say, continues to seem less interested in us than she used to be. At one point she even came

right out and said to Z, but referring to us both, "You
aren't even real relatives!" (Of course in a sense
she's not a "real" member of her own family either,
being adopted -- not that anyone would ever dream of
pointing this out to her under such circumstances.) At
the movie I was personally disappointed -- like a
rejected suitor! -- because she wanted to sit between Z
and Betty instead of between Z and me. My only hope to
coax her away from her particular preoccupation of the
moment (usually it's a book or some electronic game) is
to challenge her to a wrestling match or a wall-ball
game, but unless we have an extended free period at our
apartment or her house there's rarely enough time for
either of those. And meanwhile she's growing fast, soon
to turn age ten and move into a preadolescent stage in
which she'll probably be even less sociable with her
"subunk" -- or for that matter with all of us.

     It's a shame. But I suppose she's just being
normal. I shouldn't expect her to be otherwise and I
certainly shouldn't make demands on her out of some
unconscious hope she'll be a surrogate for my own kid.
I chose this course in life! And I'm grateful for the
many wonderful moments I've had with her! And I'll be
pleased if I'm simply able to follow her own course from
nearby over the years ahead as she becomes a young
woman! (And I'll confess -- talk about little aches
here -- at certain moments when we're face-to-face up
close she almost becomes, with her wide full lips and
oval countenance, high cheekbones, Mayan nose, dark
eyes, brown skin and vivid coloring -- Lady V. And I've
told Z about this and she admits it makes her "a little"
jealous but also says she's glad of the fact that
there's an "added attractor" for me just as there is for
her, because she wants me to be as strongly attached to
Kat as she is; and in her case that "added attractor" is
her own best-buddy closeness to Manny, Kat's adoptive
father. Also she'd like me to play the same role with
Kat as her artist brother-in-law Ben did with her -- and
there was plenty of "added attractor" in that, as she's
never been shy to let me know.)

     -- And time's up.

                    [+1]

     Same hour, same chair, next day. And oh what
fascinating days these are. Today the city's in an
uproar over the terrorist incident. "The King of
Terror," he's being dubbed in certain circles, in honor
of the centuries-old "Nasty-doom-us" prediction. (Yes,
this is all for real.) -- And yet things still stand
just about where they did two days ago, which is to say
that basically nobody knows much of anything about
what's going on.
     One thing that is known, however, is that city
authorities are tightening security measures for the
millennial fireworks on New Year's Eve, with a gated
fence to go up around the fairgrounds and some twelve
hundred police to be deployed in the area. And there's
also this: the droves of media folks who not long ago
left town with the wind-down of the WTO protests are
back. Maybe not quite as many, but still -- plenty. Z
herself saw a gaggle of them lurking around the federal
courthouse today, along with a number of "mean-looking
dudes," some uniformed and some not, carrying what she
thought were machine guns "or maybe bazookas" (seems
doubtful to me).
     Also today the abominable national weekly newsmag
with the red-bordered cover announced its person of the
year and it turns out to be a neighbor of ours. A guy
who usually hangs out a little over a block down the
street from our apartment. None other than -- that's
right! -- the widely despised high muckety-muck of the
dot-com that's taken over the DC castle. As far as the
book world's concerned, this man is the true "King of
Terror" of our time. -- And I say it's incredible how
1999 is turning out to be such a J-town-oriented year.
Astounding. Jyze serendipity, I can't deny, far beyond
the imaginable and also far beyond the allowable if this
were a standard work of fiction as opposed to the jyze

kind. No sooner did the J-man break out the J-stick
back in April for this TJM project than our drowsy
little burg suddenly became an untoppable world-class
hot spot.

And then also today almost half a millennium of
old-school Western colonialism in Asia comes to an end
as control of Macau reverts from Portugal to China. In
tandem with our own USAn return of the Panama Canal to,
yes, Panama last week this sets the stage admirably for
a new half millennium of -- what? New-school
colonialism, correct! Or just call it expanded world
domination. Well, or that's our plan anyway. No one
denies this except maybe nominally or tongue in cheek.
It's even set forth in chapter and verse in a certain
high-level foundation's "Plan for the New USAn Century."

And finally, tomorrow is the solstice. And it's
not just any solstice but one for which forecasters are
saying the moon will be larger in the sky than it's been
for a century, and it won't be this large again for
another century. I saw it up there tonight, swathed in
fast-moving clouds but fully visible for periods of up
to maybe thirty seconds (which is about the longest any
kind of lunar visibility can be expected in this city at
this time of year), and yes, it's already huge even if
not quite completely huge.

And one particularly interesting footnote about the
solstice is that with it the season of the wedding of
ZAG and GAZ -- when planets Z and G went into tight,
tight orbit as those jagged lightning bolts flashed
between them -- will officially come to an end. Yes,
autumn 1999 I'm talking about. And at this point I'll
venture way out on a limb and say I think this marriage
is already firmly established. It's a keeper. -- Even
though earlier today Z was on a "You're my hubbin'!?!?"
kick, saying it at least half a dozen times as we swung
through an afternoon series of errands, and each time
with a semi-mock wide-eyed puzzled look both a little
goofier and a little more serious than the previous one.
(Another phrase she's been taking great pleasure in
bandying about lately is "There's a strange man in my

bed" -- or "in the kitchen," "in the shower," "driving
my car," "sitting in the living room," "pooshing his
Pooshkin into me" -- and sometimes with the word "naked"
subbing for or augmenting "strange.")

    Z's on vacation now, so she needs lots of whodunits
to pass the time, especially since I'm preternaturally
busy with this jyze and various Christmas projects and
also still doing for her lots of the things she can't do
for herself owing to the condition of that same upper
left limb, which means she has even more free time on
her hands (one of which is of course close to fully
immobilized) during which she'd like to be entertained,
and since I can't be doing it all that often during this
frenzied period, the only other recourse for her is
thrillers/mysteries/whodunits (or as a distant second
choice, TV, but she usually avoids that, particularly if
I'm around). So while I was making copies of my
Christmas card at a nearby shop, she picked up a batch
of books at the downtown library (which is across the
street from the courthouse where she observed the wild
militarized "King of Terror" scene). And we stood in
line for twenty or thirty minutes to mail a package at
the main south-end post office, and we did a
provisioning run which was brightened at the natural-
food chain store by the appearance for the very first
time, at least to our knowledge, of cut-rate frozen
organic blueberries, of which we bought no fewer than
eight bags which then forced us to perform triage in the
freezer of our fridge at home to fit them all in (two
packages of brown rice got tossed; the chunk of our
wedding cake in its zip-lock bag stayed).

    The good wiff has also taken to moaning
histrionically about how she's afraid that by the time
this jyze project whirls to an end almost exactly four
months from now I'll have forgotten how to be with her
and maybe won't even be able to recognize her. For the
moment this seems to be little more than a teasing kind
of hyperbole but I'm still taking it as a warning sign.
"I'm expecting a big reward," she cries, "when April
22nd finally gets here!" (A newspaper article yesterday

about the new edition of the diagnostic manual for
shrinks, DSM-IV, nails her in its description of
"histrionic personality disorder," which as the article
points out seems to describe a perfectly normal kind of
person found in especially large clusters in Hollywood.
As expected she loved the article and is planning to
make copies for all her friends, with, written at the
top, "Comments? Suggestions? Links?")
   And: I'm sorry to say it appears she's about to be
waylaid by another outbreak of the dreaded H social
disease. (She told me last night it's the thing she
least likes to talk about. This had the feeling of a
preface, and it turned out to be just that. She does
talk about it despite the pain, she pointed out, and she
likes to think we, as authentic, accredited "zolemates,"
should be able to talk about anything, so why won't I
talk with her about my teeth? -- "Individually or en
masse?" I asked. And pointed out we've talked about
them plenty of times -- their tiny but admittedly still
regrettable imperfections, I'm saying, which to most
people aren't even visible, though I'll admit she's
definitely not most people. But that doesn't mean I
have to want to talk about them or think we should be
stripped of our "zolemate" tag if I ask her not to bring
them up so often. Like say couldn't she at least hold
back on this matter until after the TJM project has run
its course and the J-slinger can no longer claim to
deserve special handling?)
   Craig A.'s party, will jyze ever get down with it?
Yes -- tomorrow. It was billed, after all, as a
solstice party and tomorrow's the solstice. And in fact
I think I'd be much better off stopping right here and
using the time to put together the last batch of
Christmas cards. Solstice day will be no good for that
because the cards must be in the mail before five p.m.
to have any hope at all of arriving at their
destinations before Christmas (and precious little hope
even if they do go out before five -- but just a little
hope is enough for me as things stand now).
   Cards coming in for me so far? One from Lynn at

the deep reserves which I've neglected to open. One
from Naomi at the scope firm saying she'd be lost
without me and commending my "unfailing good humor"
during certain bumpy stretches this past year and
including a hundred-dollar bonus check. And the usual
printed-up holiday newsletter from cousin Kar detailing
his triumphs of the past year in appallingly shameless
self-congratulatory purple prose, with a hand-jotted
squib saying he and Kerani might be in our town
"briefly" during the holidays. Just what we need!
Let's clear our calendar for the next two weeks on the
off chance Kar and Kerani will show up sometime! (And
we've moved the dinner with Rob and Gail a day later,
from Christmas to Boxing Day/Kwanzaa, but we're still
planning to go ahead with it; and the delay means Z and
I can now spend, and are planning to, a relaxed
Christmas Day all by ourselves at home -- even if the
phone rings on that day and it's Kar and they're on the
way over. Which to be sure is just the way he likes to
operate.)

[+1]

     Exactly nine minutes before the newest magical
moment. (Though confusion abounds about this. One of
the J-town dailies states flat-out the solstice is
tomorrow. And that's correct -- but not for us. It
takes place after midnight in the other three
continental USA time zones but at 11:44 p.m. here -- if
my sources are right. And lord knows they've let me
down any number of times in the past. I could even say
I'm letting myself down by continuing to use them as
sources. -- But no, because the truth is I have no
other choice. Not if I want to remain a jyzer. And I
do want that. Anyone would!)
     A few fog puffs have rolled in tonight but the
moon's still visible, and dramatically so, just as
billed, even through the puffs, many of which are close
to diaphanous. The lunar orb's just a few degrees or

maybe even only a few minutes or seconds short of true
roundness and at first glance appears to be all the way
there and unbelievably huge.

    -- Blink, it's 11:44. Solstice. Right there. The
thousand-year period moves into its final season, and a
partial one at that. Or say highly partial: it's just
ten days. The up-close millennial countdown (and solar
bounceback, in which the sun starts ratcheting back up
the plain and eventually into the peaks of the coastal
range) begins right now. Or rather a moment ago now.
An almost complete jyze paragraph ago. Ten, nine,
eight...or no, eleven (at the moment), ten (starting in
about ten minutes, at midnight), nine....

    Through it all the familiar sound of the hoover
firing up and roaring energetically and shutting down,
the janitorial cart rolling from room to room.

    For me the real magical moment of the day came at
sunset on the south-hill high bridge -- or two or three
minutes after sunset, actually, since I arrived a little
late despite frantic efforts not to let that happen
(these are far from the easiest of times for the still-
green-around-the-gills newlyweds at home, especially for
the Z-woman with her immobilized flipper). To the west
a spectacular sunset, nearby roundish black clouds
drifting in front of low horizontal streaks shading from
glowing white to, right at the horizon, incandescent
pink, and all this as far to the south as the sun ever
goes, just about on a direct line above the twin green
mermaids riding the spires atop the industrial-district
tower belonging to the coffee colossus here in J. City.
And to the east an even more spectacular moonrise
through a grayish-rose haze clinging to the mountains
and floating just above them. The huge lunar orb
surprised me -- stopped me in my tracks -- by first
popping into view, well before I was expecting to see
it, through the winter-stripped trees of the greenbelt
directly across from the DC castle (yes, the very one
haunted at all hours by the newsmag's omnivorous mogul
king of the year). What's more, the sky was otherwise
perfectly clear and blue -- an anomaly indeed for the

shortest day of the year and also the darkest month in terms of both hours of daylight and, I'm pretty sure, hours of cloud cover (though I could be wrong about the latter if November's even cloudier, and it may be) (so further research is called for, yes, but it will have to involve those same regrettably fallible sources mentioned before).

Tonight, the longest night of the year in the northern hemisphere, will last just thirteen minutes short of sixteen hours in Jyze City. Or so they say.

But is the apparent size of the moon tonight really such a rarity? Once again the experts are dueling. One set would have us believe a couple of naive reporters were taken in by an internet hoax. They say a night of equal or even greater lunar largeness occurred just six years ago (the other set say it's been 133 years). Of course in this case jyze, like most of us, is once again at the mercy of the experts; it lacks the equipment not to mention the skill to undertake its own independent measurements. Faith in the experts: more than ever our necessary fate as the apocalypse (the real one) looms.

And I was the only pedestrian on the bridge taking in the awesome sight. To most inhabitants of the Digital Age, let's face it, none of this astronomical stuff means a whole lot. But just think of all those lunations (the technical term, I learned just this week, for one complete orbit of the moon around the earth, taking about 29.3 days) -- all those lunations since the Gregorian/Julian calendar last showed three zeroes. (Roughly 12,400 lunations if my head math is correct.)

And it suddenly occurs to me the reason for the moon's unusual size is of course that its orbit has brought it so close to the earth, and in just two weeks the same will be true of the earth itself with respect to the sun -- the "far in" moment of perihelion -- and thus it could be said this is the fortnight of close encounters of the planetary kind, where our planet right here is the one doing the encountering, and with the millennium going down more or less in the middle of this same fortnight. And is this not a savory fascinoma?

[The Battle of Jyze City]

Out (far) with the old, in (far) with the new!
                    *   *
     -- Home now roughly an hour later and I'm tired as
hell, even though dazed with weird happiness because
jyze has managed to make it to this milestone in its
project. From the start two solstices were slated to
take place in this J-sling annal and now they're both in
here, along with one of the two equinoxes. On the
wheels of just two such major calendrical events this
four-wheeled J-sling vehicle, I'll call it, couldn't
stand straight or go anywhere. Now it can do both. But
for true stability and mobility, yes, the fourth wheel
-- the second equinox -- will be necessary.
     Why so tired? One little thing went wrong last
night (Monday night) in my personal Christmas-card-
making "bee": nowhere in the exceptionally proliferant
clutter of our apartment here could I find the book of
blank postcards I was planning to use. I sized the
photocopies for gluing on those cards, and without them
I had to improvise with my stock of free advertising
postcards picked up in bars and taverns over the years,
and all but one of those had to be trimmed with scissors
and several with a razor knife as well. Altogether I
lost more than three hours and didn't finish up until
eight a.m. In the meantime Z was giving me a hard time,
once again rightfully declaring I wasn't showing her
enough of the attention she fully deserves, especially
in her sorry broken-limbed state, and also in her fear
of the D&C operation once again looming not very far
ahead. Several times she shouted incoherently in her
sleep and once she stumbled in to tell me about a scary
dream. Twice she accosted me directly in the living
room and then when I finally did hit the bed, dead
tired, she was on my case because I had nothing left for
schtupping (and making matters worse, I knew in advance
all her systems were go, or at least the crucial one
was, or better to say one of the crucial ones, because
earlier we'd done an exam with the flashlight and I
could detect no sign of the outbreak she'd suspected).
     The long-suffering Z! And the long-suffering G!

But then this afternoon when I wrenched myself out of
bed -- after five hours' sleep -- she burst into tears
of apology for hounding me so mercilessly at Christmas
crunch time; and I apologized too for all my
distractedness and obsessiveness; and I truly believe I
can honestly say we both felt much better.

     In the dream she was in the hospital where she had
her fibroidectomy and the building was disintegrating
around her because of a flood (this imagery inspired,
she said, by her viewing of gruesome TV news reports on
the current deluges in Venezuela which have already
killed some twenty thousand people, mostly in mudslides).
As her operating theater was about to go live, Aida
somehow came barreling right into the ward in her car
and rescued her. That was basically what happened back
when the actual fibroidectomy went down, she told me,
Aida standing by her while Jerry II epically messed up,
acting as if he resented having to be there for both her
admission and her release (his failure to show for the
latter being the infamous final straw for their
relationship). It caused me a little twinge when Z
mentioned that she'd checked with Jerry II before
scheduling that operation so she'd be sure it would
happen on a day when he was available. -- And was
there a message somewhere in this dream for me? None,
I'm happy to say, or at least none she insisted on. But
I suppose maybe she's feeling I resent having to take
care of her so much, or why would she tell me about the
dream at all? (She's also saying she wants copious
compensation from the city for failing to provide her
with adequate boots for the salmon-counting expedition.
It's realizing just how much trouble this dysfunctional
arm will be causing her that's prodding her to think
this way. -- And I'm hoping to dissuade her from making
a big issue about it with the city.)

     Also she wasn't too pleased I'd made separate cards
of my own for several of the same friends -- originally
just hers -- for whom she'd already made cards in much
more timely fashion and then had me sign before sending
them out. The message in my own separate cards I made

last night joked about how preposterously demanding
she's become in her casted-up state. She didn't like
that much either, though she realized it was my way of
trying to balance out the story she's been telling
everyone about her "stoicism meltdown" supposedly
provoked by me at the hospital last week.

But I'm probably making things sound a lot worse
than they are -- or than I hope they are, anyway.
Actually my suspicion is they're very good right now and
especially relative to how they might've been. But...
we'll see.

On the way in earlier tonight I stopped by the
wooden-toy shop in the HQ in hopes of finding another
"cabaret" clock like the one I gave Betty and Kat. No
such luck. The best I could do is order one, and the
owner said it might not arrive for months. So with
Christmas just four days off I have only one present for
Z: a similar clock featuring a different scene, "The
Little Train that Could." I'm intending to decorate it
one of these nights. (I was thinking two clocks, one
for her office and one for home, might wow her, not
least because she'd said of the one I did for Betty and
Kat, "I want one of those!")

-- And I'm just about ready to kiss this volume
goodbye. I'm out of gas. I'd like to crash right here
and right now. But first a few last details and then
some dinner and then the crash. And maybe squeeze in a
glance or two at the far-coast paper if it arrives
between now and then.

I churned out a total of thirty-three cards this
year, and that might be a personal record. All by
itself it might also suggest I'm a happily married man.
And: today we were startled to learn Betty has canceled
her and Kat's holiday road trip, feeling she, Betty,
needs to rest up instead. This is especially good news
because it means the burial of the millennial time
capsule, previously scheduled for next week in B&K's
backyard, then canceled owing to the suddenly hatched
plan for their excursion, is now back on. And yesterday
June finished her last exam -- and tomorrow Z's making a

special trip of her own into the office so she can stand
at June's side during a meeting with a notoriously
uptight Cawk supervisor who's been giving June a hard
time because of "communication and attitudinal issues"
(meaning Chinese accent and stubborn Kung-family pride).
    Any other jyzebits? No. In an ideal world I'd
like to add more, or rather at least something, about
Craig's party and the dance of the city employees -- and
in fact this is an ideal world, come to think of it, if
only of its type (but as far as we know the only one of
its type and therefore perfection itself, or so goes the
old saw, which itself, it follows Q.E.D., is perfect
since it's part of this perfect world) -- but still,
regardless, no more at this time. I'm just too damn
woozy. And so "The Battle of Jyze City" stands pat. On
to -- what? "Millennial J" maybe. If, that is, the
terrorist bomb has truly been defused as they say it
has, and nobody has another one ready to go.
                            *

    -- Well, but I shouldn't fail to mention this: the
terrorist himself is currently locked up for
interrogation in a special cell at the immigration jail
on the southern fringe of the AQ -- the utility
grapevine has passed this piece of news along to me via
Z -- and the streets down there look "just like they did
during WTO but with more pigs and bigger guns." I
actually overheard the latter statement on the bus
tonight.

BOOK G

[Millennial]

31

    J. City lies unrepentant under a blanket of mist.
Above the mist the brightest moon of the century --
well, by some accounts anyway -- tries to shed its
silvery grace on us but has big trouble with the last
few hundred feet. And regardless we denizens of the
east-depot saloon disdain all this celestial hokum. We
got "work to do" (the catchy tune is once again
blasting) and not only that, we got schooners to drain
(of beer of the root kind in my case, non-alcoholic, as
in the sarsaparilla of the white hat in old westerns).
    And this the first day of winter. And the first
day of Book G by Jyzer G which is also the book of the
official millennium and its J. And the first day of the
first standard five-day J-week ever, also to be known as
a fiver. -- And spray-painted in white on the window
next to my table are the words "OH OH" -- orgasmic
cries, could say. From outside, however, they read in
mirror-image order as either, first, the jolly Santa
comment on the purported goodness of earthly petitioners
for gifts, or second, a hint you can buy some love in
here cheap. And you almost certainly can do just that.
But what else you might get with it could be far from
jolly. And that's a fact. The STD stats for this city
were an issue in a dep I scoped a few months back.
    The TV's roaring overhead, and other TVs are doing
likewise elsewhere in the room, all showing the usual
dullsville football even though it's not Monday night.
It's Wednesday night, or late afternoon really, but
we're into the holidays: the programming has turned
special. (And "work to do" has yielded to a local

659

anthem performed by a homegrown talent not so
coincidentally describing the very phenomenon visible
everywhere outside the window: purple haze.)

   ("What you got to do is, you reel 'em in real
slow." A woman's slurred voice is saying that. She's
offering advice to a man just released from city jail
this afternoon who's told her he's hot for a friend of
hers who's currently hunkered down in the ladies' room
-- or anyway doing something in there, if only, perhaps,
to avoid him. These two here are leaning against the
outside of the slatted wooden wall of the niche,
apparently unaware I'm sitting on the inside about a
foot away from them and can hear every word they say.)

   For me, big doings, relatively speaking, coming
up soon. They're related to the banner hed topping
tonight's paper: "U.S. ON 'HIGHEST LEVEL OF ALERT'."
Today a grand jury right here in J. City indicted the
Algerian-national "King of Terror" caught with the bomb
at the border port. Was he planning to blow up our
iconic golf-tee saucer and symbol of never-ending
technological progress? Or as a mere "Mope of Terror"
was he possibly planning to pass the bomb along to
someone else who would do the job, perhaps killing off a
few hundred (or thousand) "children of Satan," and thus
usurping the title "King of Terror"? No one knows for
sure just yet, but speculation is -- rife, yes. About
as rife, I'd say, as it ever gets.

   Government spokespersons continue to describe this
incident as part of a terrorist plot fomented by
"radical Muslims" associated with Al Qaeda (once an
extremely well-paid subcontractor for our CIA in
Afghanistan, now gone renegade). The bomb's makings are
similar to those used by that same outfit to blow up two
U.S. embassies in Africa last year and to attempt to
topple the titanic "twin towers" in the U.S. far-coast
megalopolis a few years back (the two towers together
triumphantly proclaimed to be, it's relevant to recall,
the center of world trade, with three of those last four
words capped and "center" shifted to the end and "of"
dropped). Meanwhile, because two ferry ticket stubs

660

were found in the detainee's pocket, a "massive manhunt"
is underway across the U.S. and Canada for a second
suspect who may have walked off the ferry undetected.
     We've also had another bomb threat right here in J.
City. It tied up ferry service for some six hours
yesterday, afternoon rush hour included, stranding
thousands before the all-clear was sounded (no bomb was
found and the last I heard a few hours ago the source of
the threat was still unknown).
     And: the grand jury mentioned above is presumably
the one Naomi served as reporter for today -- the
transcript of the proceedings of which I'll be scoping
tonight. It'll be part of the paperwork on which the
indictment of the alleged terrorist ("King of Terror")
will be based when it's issued in its entirety.
     Never a dull moment in J-town.
     (Now I'm overhearing a squabble about the moon.
Yes! I can scarcely believe my ears. Closest,
brightest -- massive tides expected -- will it trigger
killer quakes? "Aw, you're full of it, asshole. You're
saying it's gonna do all this and it's not even up
there. Go out and see for your own fucking self, man!"
-- So it seems seleno stuff does still matter after all,
at least in some precincts of the more raucous type.)
     Earlier today Z briefly joined Madge I. and several
other work friends in a march to city hall on behalf of
the homeless (roughly a thousand of whom have been
sleeping on downtown streets during recent nights, along
with another two thousand in city shelters). A short
time later her presence at the meeting between June and
June's supervisor made quite a difference, according to
a message June left me (and then Z, when she arrived at
home just as I was leaving, said she thought it had too).
Suddenly the bad marks on June's yearly evaluation all
moved up into the "satisfactory" range. And now, with
June's two sons flying in tomorrow for the holidays, the
celebrations begin: the first being dinner for the whole
group Friday night at what June declares to be the best
restaurant in the AQ (I often walk by it just up the
street here but I've never been inside -- or maybe once

long ago in my former life).

A story buried in the local section of this
morning's J. City daily (Z pointed it out to me) says
the downtown business district has now caught up with
the rest of the region in its Christmas sales. This
refers to overall seasonal sales since well before the
anti-WTO protests. So much for all the editorial
anguishing over the terrible damage those "violent
protesters" supposedly did to downtown sales.

At nine this morning Z had to roust me out of bed
to turn off the water in the tub. The plastic knob on
the faucet is cracked and her one-hand grip isn't strong
enough to turn it back to "off" if she twists it too
far in turning it on. She said, "You always look so
cute when you do that" -- meaning I'm naked and
genitally loosey-goosey or maybe even still partially
tumefied owing to some hot dream, probably starring her,
which she's just so rudely awakened me from.

-- Kicking a small inflated brown paper bag ahead
of me as I walked through the upper AQ on the way here.
Seeing the familiar homeless man sitting with his dog
and his high-bundled grocery cart on the front stoop of
the food bank (first in line for tomorrow morning?).
Warily eyeing a couple of single Natusan males slouching
along -- just as they were warily eyeing me (as was also
a briskly striding Afrusan woman in tony business garb).
Glancing in the windows of the Asian curio shops and
restaurants, most of which I'll probably never enter.
Thinking about recent stories I've read about how
community policing has eased crime problems in the AQ
(and I believe those stories) as I uneasily glance back
to make sure a couple of ornery-looking Cawk drifter
types I've passed under the freeway aren't doubling back
on me. Not that I think the chances are all that high
they'll have done so. But: always watch your back when
you're on the move after dark in the AQ or HQ or many
other places downtown or near downtown, yeah.

I'm disappointed with myself for failing to come up
with a blockbuster Christmas present for Z this year. I
overdid it the past couple of years -- for her birthdays

too -- and now I must pay the price for stoking high
expectations on those occasions. Ever since
Thanksgiving I've been apologizing in advance for not
being able to do much this year. But I've done the same
sort of thing in the past as a misdirection ploy and I
can tell she thinks I'm up to the same old tricks again.
And I don't see how I can break out of this bind. We've
limited ourselves to spending twenty-five bucks or less
on each other this year and I've already coughed up
thirty-five for the one krazy klock and it's not even
the one she likes.

Stymied. Three days to go, really just two, and
I'll have little free time.

Oh well. Such is the cost of taking on a major
jyze project. And most of the time, even while caught
up in the project -- this one, TJM, I'm talking about,
yes indeed -- I don't have to sacrifice much, if
anything. That's the truth. But now's the exception.
Mostly it's my own doing -- other than the broken-arm-
related duties -- and therefore I must take my medicine.
So just do it then. A glass of water, please. Gulp.
So taken! -- And now can I please stop obsessing about
this matter? I'd like to see jyze tackle a few other
things. And I'm not even saying they all have to be
millennium and/or terrorist and/or WTO related.

Twinkling Christmas lights above the bar. I hadn't
noticed them before. (As the intoxicated tablefuls
whoop and groan and shout encouragement or complaint or
instruction to the TV gridders.) Up on the hill I was
thinking about the seasonal lights on the houses,
especially the run-down ones, and the plaintive glow
they shed on the overall scene. And then here's the
huge castle of the newsmag's Scrooge-like person of the
year who's worth billions because he's managed to take
so much business away from so many other businesses
which now are collectively worth billions less, and the
vast majority of them are small businesses -- mostly
independent bookstores! -- but overall somehow we're all
better off, supposedly. Or so the economists say.
Progress. Limits. Extinctions. Land of the rich.

"Our business is business." Power. Domination.
Hegemony. "A Second USAn Century." Nukes. Terror.
Blowback. (And also calls on the internet, Z tells me,
for a boycott of the person of the year's dot-com, which
is in fact now the world's largest bookseller -- though
I've never bought a book from it and never will. (She
has, though. Along with just about everyone else I
know. Brother Rob being the one certain exception.))
     -- And then the high bridge, the grand view, the
fog and the mist and the glittery lights, rivers of
traffic flowing sluggishly below, a helicopter thumping
above, no moon anywhere in sight (as previously noted)
but the mist truly does seem a little brighter shade of
purple than usual, as if moonlight is mixed in there
somehow. -- A solitary figure, the jyzer, ambling
across that bridge, perplexed smile and all, undeniably
feeling personally blessed even if knowing it shouldn't
count for much in an account like this and it shouldn't
color his views of life at the millennium too much
(because blessing in this country nine times out of ten
is just another word for unearned and/or coerced
privilege -- we all know this! -- and it's nowhere more
true than right here and right now in J. City).

[+1]

     Here's the conference room at the scope office. In
eleven minutes we'll officially be into Gregorian
Christmas Eve, sort of (since this will also still be
the night before the night before Christmas, the eve of
the Eve). A couple hundred feet across the street the
crossword-puzzle-like patterns of lighted offices in the
tower are barely visible through swirling fog. And over
here I've just finished doing the finals for our most
mediagenic grand-jury case yet.
     This morning's local paper plays the story with a
big bold four-column hed, "BOMB SUSPECT IS INDICTED,"
and next to it on the far right is a courtroom sketch of
none other than assistant U.S. attorney Larry H. -- this

is Naomi's husband, yes -- arguing the case before a
judge, with the defendant and his translator and public
defender Will E. (whom I met at Larry's and Naomi's
house on their wedding day) sitting behind him. It's
the first time I can recall any part of our little cog
in the wheels of justice being deemed worthy of a front-
page newspaper visual (and indeed this case, just like
the WTO protest, is drawing headlines worldwide).

So now I'm a contributor of sorts to the "war on
terror." Of course I've long been a contributor to most
of the dubious or even outright bad things our
government does, so this latest venture doesn't feel all
that new. And really now, we USAns are all contributors
to this same monstrous cause in one way or another and
often in many ways. We pay taxes, don't we? We vote?
We apply for licenses? We obey laws? In short: We're
all complicit! -- Or anyhow seeing things this way
helps me to justify and live with my own share of the
complicity. And I suspect I'm far from the only one who
thinks this way.

This newest alleged terrorist threat is now
specifically being tied in with the Y2K rollover.
Supposedly the "radical Muslim extremist factions" want
to expose the vulnerability of the Christian West by
setting off bombs in a number of the West's major cities
on the day the two-thousandth anniversary of
Christianity's founding will be celebrated. In the land
of the crusader hegemon, our very own USA, the targeted
cities are supposedly the two largest -- that is, the
major megalopoli, one on each coast -- and then for some
unknown reason our city right here: good old J-town.

(One theory about why us: it turns out the
architect for the building across the street (it's like
a carpenter's pencil forty stories high whose point
thrusts into the earth, but a pencil with many, many
windows) -- the architect for this structure was the
same Japusan man, born right here, who designed the
previously mentioned twin trade towers on the other side
of the country. And he also designed, as it happens,
some buildings out at the fairgrounds, right next to the

golf tee/saucer "symbol of technological progress.")
     Did I not say speculation was rife?
     So then I might as well kick in another two cents'
worth. Could the vengeful alleged plot perhaps have
something to do with our civic boosters' hubris (not to
say greed) in inviting the WTO to town? Could they, the
boosters, in some sense be indicted as co-conspirators?
     And then why is this incident drawing so much media
attention? It's a dramatic story, no doubt about that.
But the government could be playing it down just as it's
doing, and has been all along, with the possibility of
cataclysms linked to the Y2K bug. Instead it's fanning
the flames. And I'd say the reason is obvious: to
portray our civilization as endangered by these
outsiders is to pump up support for the military, the
security state, and chauvinistic law-and-order
conservative values in general. That is: it's the same
reason the anti-WTO protests were portrayed by the
mainstream media as they were.
     -- So of course. The dynamics of great historical
forces. "The clash of civilizations." Or is it the
clash of the elites of civilizations who fear losing
their power and their fortunes? In any case: the
casualties caused by these clashes keep mounting, to the
point now where all life on earth is threatened as never
before. "Civilizations clash while the planet burns."
     And what's happening meanwhile? At the quotidian
level? (Because life goes on, yeah, so far anyway, and
jyze has its commitments.)
     This afternoon when Z and I were heading out on a
quick errand we found someone had tried to break into
the Z-mobile. The lock on the front passenger-side door
had been jimmied and part of its mechanism was lying on
the concrete garage floor. Where the lock face with the
keyhole had been there was now nothing but a gaping hole
in the metal door panel about the size of a nickel.
Some other items were also scattered on the floor nearby,
including AAA-size batteries and what looked like a kid-
leather golfing glove (white), indicating the thief had
probably succeeded in breaking into the car parked next

to ours (the space was now empty). How a prowler had
gained entrance to the locked garage we don't know. The
remote for the garage vehicle door wasn't working at the
time, but the door itself showed no sign of forced entry,
nor did the human-size one next to it or the lobby doors
half a flight of stairs up. The building has seen lots
of turnover in the past few months and it has a history
of garage break-ins (especially involving Ciro's car).
Does the thief have a key? If so, that's scary. The
door between the garage and the interior stairs isn't
lockable.

We had no time to do anything about it at that
point, but Z's supposed to be writing a note to the new
landlords tonight. And she had met one of them earlier,
a tall fortyish man who, although he was apparently
taking a break from painting the apartment above ours,
had a "pampered-class look about him." (She would've
talked with him if he hadn't surprised her as she was
padding down to fetch the paper wearing just her
slippers and bathrobe.)

I'm not quite sure how to view this latest break-in
from the standpoint of ongoing neighborhood
gentrification. Is it a sign there's still some life in
the old hilltop street culture and the gentrifiers might
find the going a little harder up there than they
thought? Or does it indicate that a new set of crooks
of a different type -- "higher class" -- has been drawn
to the hood by the wealth of the gentrifiers? I lean
toward the first view, but only in the sense that this
is probably a kind of rearguard action or a last gasp.
Most likely before too much longer buildings like ours
will have video alarm systems or door guards -- maybe
even, who knows, moats with crocodiles (or mini nuke-
bearing digital submarines?).

And then a bit of unalloyed good news. I got my
mojo workin' again. The fleshy tubular crotchety
accoutrement of a certain vintage, I mean. In fact it
worked twice in one night all the way to invag ejac for
the first time in quite a while -- possibly close to a
month. When I came home I found a note from Z saying

all right, she was backing down, she would make it a
"solstice resolution" to put "more TLC" into her loving.
It sounded a little grumpy or grudging in the written
version, but it didn't feel that way at all in her
verbal and bodily expressions of it (via lips, hands,
eyes, tongue) when I hit the bed, or again this
afternoon when she crept in to wake me up.

I've found this generally to be true: When I'm not
just sparring with Z in standard marital-friction
fashion but rather seriously concerned about something,
she pays close attention, thinks things over, and often
makes changes designed to address the concern. She
battles hard and it may take a while for her to see the
light -- or it may take no time at all -- but she's not
one of those rigid types who refuse to compromise or to
try "walking in the other's moccasins" (a favorite
slogan of hers, in fact, a few years back). And could
anything be more important to the well-being and
longevity of a hitch-up? (Of course these words should
apply equally to the staff half -- assuming "staff" is
the binary opposite of "distaff" -- and in this case I
believe they do.)

And right now, sooner than I'd like -- but of
course there's not a damn thing I can do about it --
bus time.

*   *

I didn't mention this earlier (home now, black
chair), but tonight Aida and Charles picked us up at
half past five and we once again did dinner, the four of
us, at our current favorite southern Afrusan restaurant.
It's still extremely popular: twenty minutes before the
doors opened we found a long line standing out in the
misty cold (the joint takes no reservations) and we
barely landed a table. Partially de-spiced cooking,
very fine, again reminding me of Charles and Ernelle C.
in Mentoka Falls and also of some of my own mother's
specialties -- as did the fried chicken I went with
tonight (Z-wiff chose the porkchops and a bite from one
of those had the same nostalgic effect on me).

As almost always things seemed awkward between me

668

and Aida. I've given up trying to figure out why this
is or what to do about it. Lately, though, she's been
going through some tough times, especially owing to her
father's lymphoma diagnosis. Also, Charles has been
acting up again -- in the latest instance bashing his
bedroom walls, apparently with the very same baseball
bat he used on the door last time (why doesn't she take
that damn bat away from him?) -- and he's still not
cottoning to Kirk. And Aida and her ex, Tom, are
skirmishing -- to repeat, Tom's now started hauling
Charles off to a different church (non-Catholic) in the
alternate weeks he has him -- and one day not long ago
Tom called to say he was about to commit Charles to the
mental ward at some (again, non-Catholic) hospital.
Aida cooled him down and now all three are starting to
see a "counselor" -- whether Catholic or otherwise I
don't know -- and that seems to be helping.
     Charles is small for his age, slight, and very
active. I've noticed he likes jockish challenges. But
Aida keeps him on too tight a leash for me to show more
interest in him, and to my mind the form this leashing
takes is both way too moralistic and way too
tempestuous, in effect teaching him that temper tantrums
are acceptable and even necessary to get your way. (I
learned today Aida suffered seizures as a child -- not
epileptic, though they were thought to be that for a
while -- and I can't help wondering, as Z does too, if
Charles's problems might somehow be related to this.
But Aida has told Z the doctors say they're not.)
     Tonight Charles ate only a few bites and then
announced he was suffering from a tummyache and refused
to touch anything more. It took major efforts to keep
him in line, with Z providing many of them by playing
"hangman's noose" and other games with him. Aida and I
were able to talk seriously for only a few moments, and
even then we had trouble hearing each other over the
music and chatter. But one thing she said came through
loud and clear: "Zo tells me you're working on the 'King
of Terror' case! It must be very exciting!" (Z's not
supposed to be talking about the grand-jury stuff. I

had to remind her of this -- gently! -- afterward. If
there were ever a case where a breach of secrecy could
get me in trouble, this terrorist case is it.)
     -- So, it's Christmas. Huge crowds downtown.
Numerous interesting sights. While I waited in the
parked car outside the symphony hall (Z was inside
buying a gift certificate for Gail and Rob as their
Christmas present from us) a Samoan-looking woman in a
heavy winter coat came walking up the hill with a large
potted poinsettia balanced atop her head -- that was the
best sight of them all. And I liked watching a very
skinny and lithe and bearded Santa-suited woman helping
people into horse-drawn carriages, of which there was a
long line of about a dozen across from the carousel
at the downtown plaza, with scores of people including,
again, lots of excited kids waiting to take rides.
     -- And I gotta say something about yesterday's
Christmas party at the scope office, or rather its
aftermath. Since the party went down at noon, I
couldn't attend (and probably wouldn't've anyway, even
if it had overlapped with my normal working hours), but
when I arrived for work I found the carpets almost
literally covered (or carpeted, could say) with, among
other things, glitter. It was indistinguishable from
the type that played such a large role with Z and me on
our honeymoon and continues to do so to this day,
considering how it led directly to her being scheduled
for a D&C last week and now again for week after next.
If she had come in to the office with me last night she
might've had a heart attack -- or maybe some kind of
vaginal seizure. (And the janitors didn't like that
glitter too much either. The industrial-strength vacuum
couldn't suck it all up, and when the supervisor came
around and noticed this, he soon had the janitor, and
then himself as well, crawling around trying to pry out
deeply set pieces with kitchen knives.)
     -- And this is all the jyzer can squeeze out for
now. What's happening with the various millennial
doings, that will have to wait for next time. He hopes.
Meanwhile: work work work to do.

[+1]

A little on Christmas Eve. Probably very little.
It's twenty to six in the morning -- of Christmas Day,
actually, by Gregorian count -- and Zoelie in her blue
hula hoop (and nothing else) has already been tucked in
bed for more than her standard eight hours (quite
possibly with X-rated visions of former bed partners
dancing in her head: and I say this because she relishes
telling me about her erotic dreams and does so quite
often, at least once every few weeks or so, probably
depending on the degree to which she thinks I'm in need
of a provocative jolt). -- But it's a wondrously foggy
night and I just finished decorating and wrapping her
one present from me and I jes gotta weigh in here.
     Kneeling on the floor to wrap this altered krazy
klock with extreme awkwardness, coming away from the
task with rug-burns on my knees and possibly elbows too.
But that's nothing compared with the J-slinger's pride
in the ill-wrapped package itself, now resting all smug
and sparkly on the couch (as I find myself flashing back
to pressing my index finger on the ribbon for young Mom
as she tied bows on gifts atop her and Dad's big double
bed a whole lotta Christmas Eves in the rearview).
     Oh the holiday nostalgia. It's traditional! It's
a prereq for human flourishing no matter what your
tradition! And on the radio a report of a hijacked
plane and the pope opening some rarely used Vatican door
at midnight Friday (the same night that's just about to
come to an end here) to inaugurate the so-called
"Jubilee Year" of the millennium, which just out of some
popish whimsy or perhaps schadenfreude they're declaring
to fall out of sync by seven days with the rollover into
year 2000 of their very own Gregorian calendar. But
then again this does make the opening day coincide with
the official birthday of the eponymous Christmas holy
man. -- And so wrap a couple of millennial jyze ribbons
around all that and press your finger on the bow!
     On the last possible day a card arrived from Angie

and brother Jeff, written solely by Angie but signed by
both, with Angie supplying the ampersand between their
first names (Z does the same when she leaves a card for
me to sign). Brother Rob's card came in one day before:
a very fine specimen which he'd found in a bargain bin,
featuring a dynamite snowman with a top hat and green
scarf and big red oven mitts, it would appear: twenty
cards for $2.50 "including, of course, envelopes" (he
wrote up the tale in his usual gently humorous fashion,
by hand, in the card itself) (and he signed for Gail as
well, ampersand included, which is the norm for them).

    Also we picked up a parcel from Mama E, an official
"gift pack," as it turned out, of candies and coffee
from the famous Centropolis department store where she
worked for years so that her only child might one day be
able to go off to college. And the sight of that gift
pack also took me back, since my own family often
visited a branch of the same store at the mall near
Gatewood, and the store is still using the same classy
green wrapping paper and gold ribbon and those same gold
seals embossed with the store's initials (MF as it
happens, as in MFer, for example, or one who lives in
Mentoka Falls, among other interpretations).

    Then we drove over to the alehouse in the Scandi
quarter in hopes of picking up tickets for next Friday's
millennium blues bash featuring Isaac S., celebrated
local bandleader/vocalist/axman supreme and favorite of
Zoelie B. (and me), but found it closed for the day. So
we'll try again Sunday. It was Z who spotted the ad and
said she'd love to see him again, and of course I was
delighted with the idea so long as we could still make
it to the fairgrounds by ten to position ourselves for
the big millennium fireworks blowout at midnight (the
city's "fire ceremony" previously scheduled for eight
p.m. has now been canceled) and she was agreeable to
this (with only a few arm-twists necessary owing to the
size of the expected crowd, the high security levels,
and the lateness of the hour by her standards).

    Then a stop in her old hood for co-op groceries,
coffee, a browse at the funky retro/head/counterculture

variety shop there (soon to close down for good after a
twenty-year run), and another nostalgic moment at the
entrance to the magazine shop where she and I first (as
far as we know) set eyes on each other some thirty-three
months ago. -- And exactly three months ago today,
since it's Gregorianly the 25th now, we got hitched.
Nuptially conjoined. Best day of the rest of my life, I
hereby predict, as well as best of the part preceding
that same period, and therefore best of all of it, yes.
     Mush mush ye reindeer!
     The main event of this day was the dinner with June
and her two boys, Adam and Michael, both handsome and
sturdy lads, both very polite and pleasant even in their
somewhat jet-lagged state (both planes were delayed by
the fog). It was quite a feast with all sorts of exotic
dishes, not a single one of which I could name by sight
and several of which I could barely manage to sample for
fear of strong spices. Adam explained at length just
exactly what he does as a compliance engineer for a
fiberoptics company (and this bored Z so much she
started kicking me under the table because I was asking
too many questions and encouraging Adam to rattle on).
But what nonsense it is that this young guy in his early
twenties is now making ungodly sums through stock
options for doing what amounts to standard engineering
work. The economy these days is like a roulette wheel
gone wild. (I don't believe I've mentioned it before:
we now have sixty thousand millionaires living in J.
City and environs. Sixty K -- and CQ that, which in
newsroomese means it's not a misprint. Or another way
to think of it, as I pointed out to June: it's one
thousand millionaires for every single year of the
sixty-year Chinese astrological cycle. How about that!
-- And isn't it a trip that a descendant of Confucius is
named Adam? June says this was her husband's idea and
she had no choice but to go along with him. "Why do you
think we are divorced now? Never any choice for me to
decide! Divorce is only one!" -- And the boys didn't
even blink when she said this.)
     -- I could go more into June's family dynamics and

I probably will one of these days -- possibly Monday when we'll be having dinner together again, this time with a number of her and Z's friends from work. For now, though, I'll move on to the other main event of the day: another roll in the hay. Consecrated ejaculatorily yet again! What's going on here? All Z has to do is wax a little bit tender with her G-hub and he's immediately super-aroused! Again and again and again! (And is yet again right now, albeit to a lesser but still palpable extent, just thinking about it.) A coupla "freakin' fookin' fogeys" is what we're suddenly becoming. I even wrote that three-word F-phrase right there on the krazy klock Christmas gift. It's a choo-choo, by the way, whose moving parts are a puff of smoke, a couple of birds in flight, and a mustachioed engineer nodding at the cab window. "The Li'l Hitch-up That Could," as I labeled it on the base. (The triple-F term adorns the engine.) Very nicely kitschy and mushy and gushy, yes. I'm just hoping she doesn't cry because this year's offering falls so far short of those of previous years. I've been joking about it all day in one last effort to prepare her for disappointment.

The news, meanwhile, is full of terrorist stories, and J. City continues to feature in many of them even at the national and international levels. It's all so absurd and preposterous and at the same time so pathetic and exasperating that I scarcely know what to say about it. Larry H., Naomi's husband, is suddenly a star, given a lengthy sidebar profile in the J. City afternoon paper as the prosecutor in our case here. (I've known Larry for more than a decade but much of what's revealed in the profile is new to me. I knew he liked baseball and umpiring, but I learn now he's president of the umpire association for the whole western half of the state. His favorite line about why he likes umping so much, which I've definitely heard before, shows up again in the story: "Because there can be no appeals.")

Also: part of the city's millennial celebration at the fairgrounds has been canceled owing to the alleged terrorist plot to blow up the golf-tee-cum-flying-saucer

icon which is ordinarily at the center of it. This same
plot has caused the estimated size of the crowd expected
to attend the midnight fireworks display launched from
atop the saucer to fall by two-thirds, from a high of
150,000 to 50,000. To my way of thinking it's absurd
that the government is being so alarmist about these
purported plots. I can't help but suspect the alarmism
is itself part of a plot of a very familiar kind to drum
up support for the security state and further expansion
of the ludicrously overblown USAn military budget.
(When I mentioned this at the Chinese restaurant I could
see Adam and Michael thought I was nuts. Yet they had
no trouble believing those same hawkish factions in and
out of the U.S. government are trying to puff up China
as the next big enemy -- or that there's a government
plot against the Chiusan physician recently indicted for
alleged spying on behalf of China.)
     As a child on Christmas morning Z almost always
snuck out of bed very early -- just as I suspect she's
about to do right now (as I can hear her stirring --
"not even a mouse" no longer -- so I in my kerchief will
drop this jyze and head on in there. With a bound!).

[+1]

     Even more than last night a token appearance. The
whole night gone -- and most of it to a single project,
reminding me of Christmases of deep family yore. Dad
putting in long hours assembling a layout for the
electric train which had been his as a boy and now
became mine. Or another time struggling with a tin
filling station whose sharp-edged tabs refused to fit
into their slots and caused him to cut his finger. (I
can still see the blood: index finger right hand,
yellowish-brown nicotine-stained skin sliced into just
below the fingernail.) Or my own goofball schemes of my
late-teen years, best among them the "authentic"
education trust fund (real penny stocks!) for Dad.
     Tonight I've been refurbing the daytimer cover I

made for Z a year ago. Around three a.m. I sprayed
fixative on it in the garage as the fog hung like cotton
candy just outside the meshed garage door, little wisps
sifting in here and there (in some places not so wispy
or little: more like a huge marshmallow being grated).
Then I applied what I hope is enough bookbinding tape to
keep the cover from falling apart at the seams for
another year. This woman subjects her daytimers, and
for that matter the days themselves, to one helluva
workout. -- But jyze has mentioned this a few times
before, indeed it has: because it's important!

A lovely peaceful home-dwelling day, the only
outdoor venture a walk down to the corner to pick up the
afternoon paper -- unsuccessful; the box was empty --
followed by a drive to the gas station down at the
junction (the one across the street from the site of our
wedding reception, with the usual dubious dudes on duty
and even surlier than usual, I suppose because of having
to be in the job harness on Christmas Day) -- where I
got the very last copy.

Now I'm working on my second glass of bourbon.
It's still the same 1.75-liter bottle we received as a
wedding gift, and probably enough remains in it to carry
me well into the new year/decade/century/millennium (Z
never touches the stuff).

She gave me five small and lovely gifts, each one
personalized with scribbles applied by her still-very-
shaky left hand. My favorite is a nine-by-twelve-inch
painted tin box from the coffee colossus with the lid
showing the colossus's original shop (they say now, and
falsely) at the public market, and Z has altered it to
make it look trashed by the anti-WTO protest, with the
circle-A anarchist symbol drawn on plywood-covered
windows. Also there's a bottle of a Scandi drink
originally called "Glogg" (with double dots over the
"o") which she's altered to "Glen" (also with the same
double dots over the "e" as well as a double-wide "n" --
which in editing lingo might be called an em "n"), a
magnetized figurine with bendable limbs, a "Kissing
Machine" cardboard contraption which I still haven't

quite figured out, and a glittery mica heart with "Lub!"
written on it to add to our "hearts of stone"
collection. The krazy klock I decorated for her seems
to have been a hit; at this very moment it's doing its
antic thing under the branches of the potted Norwegian
pine Rob and Gail gave us for Christmas a year ago --
and which this year is serving as our official Yuletide
evergreen, decorated with ornaments of various sorts and
provenances (Z's and mine) and two strings of
multicolored mini-lights (new).

     While I slept, Z made a dozen or more phone calls
to friends and family here and across the country. It's
something she's always liked to do on Christmas Day.
Later I talked with Rob, Mama E, and Kat and Betty (who
surprised us by calling from Betty's friend Maggie's
place, a five-hour drive south of here) (Kat was hard at
work on a small spiral notebook of diary entries and
drawings to bury in our millennial time capsule this
coming week) (we're all doing such notebooks) (Z's
idea). I read the papers, I clipped, I cleaned up, I
worked on the daytimer project. And I wrapped Rob and
Gail's present, the symphony gift certificate, which for
a few panicky moments we thought we'd accidentally
thrown out (until I discovered it in my bag, though I
had no memory of putting it there -- and Z only half-
jokingly attributed this gaffe to the effect of the
toxic chemicals in the oil-based ultra-markers I often
use for my cards). And Z earlier whirled into near
meltdown over the neighbor's revving his engine for
thirty minutes straight -- on Christmas Day! -- but
fortunately that was before I got up and she had mostly
recovered from it by then and the air cleaners had
successfully scrubbed away most of the fumes.

     The papers are full of the usual Christmas and end-
of-year stuff, but this year the available space must be
divided among four end-ofs instead of just the usual
single one and so a kind of confusion reigns, with none
of the four receiving the kind of attention one might
expect. The focus is on the millennium, of course, and
to a lesser extent the century, with the year and

especially the decade getting short shrift. The
possibility of terrorist attacks is still commanding the
spotlight -- no surprise there -- forcing the Y2Kalypse
fears into a subsidiary position (though the two
obviously overlap in some ways).

For dinner fish stew and peach pie with vanilla soy
ice cream (and on Z's, hot fudge sauce). And all day
the apartment's been unusually chilly because the units
above and below ours are both vacant at the moment,
meaning their heat is off, and the temperature outside
has hovered just barely above freezing. Only in the
past few days did we start wondering if Aboula and his
family had left without saying goodbye, and today, while
peering from the sidewalk ledge through the partially
open blinds into their apartment, we confirmed that they
had. It's entirely empty down there. We'll miss them
-- for their unfailing friendliness, for the African
"flash of the spirit" they brought to the building, and
certainly not least for the way they kept their
apartment extremely well heated and thus it also warmed
ours considerably. From the few times I knocked on
their door for one reason or another I'd guess they
never let their thermometer fall below eighty degrees.

Today is probably the first time since last year's
Christmas holidays that I've stayed in my houseclothes
all day (the winter version): black sweatpants and a
heavy long-sleeve henley (the blue one, which is falling
apart at the wrists and around the placket but I still
can't bear to give it up).

Also today I learned that the little groaning and/
or muttering sounds Z sometimes makes as she putters
around the apartment started out as an intentional
imitation of what her father used to do. Now they've
become a habit -- a sporadic one -- which she's usually
not even aware of having fallen into. -- And she
informed me that when her father read the papers for an
hour or two every night after arriving home from work
(which she'd told me about before) he whacked at pages
that crinkled across the fold using the edge of his hand
karate-style exactly the way I do it.

[Millennial J]

    And that's about it. The jyzer's one helluva lucky
guy, yes he is. The music's been wonderful all day,
with tonight's special four-hour Christmas blues show on
our local public radio station a rare treat. Many of
the cuts I'd never heard before. The thick fog makes
for a different, maybe even more beautiful, white
Christmas, visible right outside the window even at the
darkest time of night. And now -- yippee! -- to bed.

                          [+1]

    Final hours of the long holiday weekend. And a
splendid five days it's been, including the eve of the
Eve and the day before that, but for jyze itself
undeniably far from the best of times. Because that
very thing, but in the singular -- time -- has been so
short. Here I've left myself another thirty minutes or
so and that's it, end of fiver.
    By the krazy klock, as it happens, it's five to
five in the morning. And so far the little battery-
driven engine of this klock appears to be staying right
on track, which is to say, yes, on time. Because of the
extra weight I've added to the moving parts, I'd been
wondering if it would be able to do that (because look
what happened to the other one, the "cabaret" klock).
    More fog and it's even denser tonight. I can peer
out at an extremely faint but still perfectly
symmetrical volcano with steep pale-yellow slopes that's
standing beneath the down-facing hemiglobe of the
street lamp maybe forty feet away. Distant foghorns
sounding, nearby trees dripping with condensation. I
walked into town through all this gorgeous eerieness at
nine-thirty fully intending to squeeze in a jyze session
but promptly had to catch some zees on the conference-
room carpet once I'd done the corrections (corrections
of corrections, actually, but these are important
transcripts since they involve the alleged "King of
Terror"; by the time I climb out of bed this afternoon
they'll probably have been illegally leaked to the

                          679

media. It was a rare night: the first of our hilltop
era when I've been out on foot and found all the mom-
and-pop stores between here and downtown closed,
including even the east-depot minimart. (And this was
several minutes before ten!)

     Prior to that a fine evening with Rob and Gail at a
restaurant near the beach on their side (west) of town.
Z and I left the hill around ten after five, forty
minutes later than planned, but we still managed to pick
up the Isaac S. tickets in the Scandi quarter (no longer
trusting the internet way of purchasing them, which has
failed us too many times before) and then Rob and Gail
at their house, and to arrive at the restaurant only a
minute or two past six-thirty, the time of our
reservations. We guzzled our way through two bottles of
wine and got quite jolly and Z and I found ourselves
running through our whole repertoire of postnup stories
for the first time in quite a while, because Gail had
previously heard only brief summaries of them from Rob
(and hadn't seen the wedding pictures at all, so Z
brought along the "My Wedding" binder to show her). An
exchange of gifts; Rob was startled that for the first
time in many years I laid not a single book on him (but
he gave me several, along with snickerdoodles and wine).
And it was clear his disappointment went deep, as I
expected it to, when I told him Z and I have decided we
have no choice but to cancel the Mentoka trip for this
spring. But otherwise all was excellent, and Rob tossed
off some amusing lines, especially about my "vigor for
your age" (it's becoming a jyze leitmotif!) and "your
artwork is improving a lot," and he and I vowed to make
a Mentoka trip of our own another year -- as soon as we
can both rack up sufficient ka-chings on our giant slot
machine of an economy.

     And I'd better let it go right there. With regret!
The problem is a massive sinkload -- counterload too --
of Z's dishes still to run through the dishwasher, and a
host of other chores to tend to. And I'm the likely one
-- the usual suspect, I'll say -- to be doing all that.
Because this is one husband-dude who takes his "serve

you...in sickness and health" vow seriously. Damn
right! -- This being, by the way, Boxing Day and the
first day of Kwanzaa as well as the last Sunday of the
DYCM (that's Z's handy office acronym for decade/year/
century/millennium, pronounced "diss 'em," although she
prefers "dick 'em" outside the office setting) (I wish
she'd told me about it earlier; it could've saved me a
lot of writing time and space). And of course the
Sunday papers are groaningly heavy with DYCM-end wrap-
ups and I've scarcely had a chance to look at any of
them. And tomorrow, besides attending the second of the
June dinners, we need to ready ourselves for the move up
to Jess's the following afternoon. So it'll be another
hectic day. But with Z returning to work I should have
a little more free time than has been the case for the
past ten days. A good thing too, because this is the
week the J-slinger's been building toward for months --
or actually for years, right from the start-up of jyze
(which occurred in part so he'd be able to chronicle
this grand occasion -- because how could any self-
respecting journalizer pass up not just a once-in-a-
millennium event but the millennial event itself, and in
a sense -- not to be too apocalyptic here -- the
apocalypse itself, or at the very least the opening day
of the era thereof as looks highly probable now.)

32

  -- Came staggering out of the bedroom at half past
two to start the big quatrorollover fiver (today's
Monday the 27th) and so far haven't made it out of the
apartment. But I'll have to do that, make it out, in
about thirty-five minutes in order to hike down to the

AQ by six for June's party. And before leaving I'll
want to dry my hair and get dressed, yes. As here I sit
towel-headed. Tick, tick, tick -- three different
clocks/klocks are nattering away about jyze time limits
and the approaching millennium. A jet roars overhead.
Cars pass below. But outdoor sounds are muffled, much
like the outside light, by the continuing thick fog.
(And I'm delighted it's continuing. It's far better
than the usual wind-driven cold rain or the occasional
snow encountered at this time of year. But as a former
cross-sound commuter for almost seven years I know fog
is no favorite of ferry riders. Just from the
frequency of the foghorns I've been hearing all
afternoon I'm sure their boats are again being delayed
today, their trips prolonged, their total travel time
doubled or tripled or worse.)
     The small triumphs and the small slipups. One such
triumph is my makeshift repair of the cracked bathtub
spigot knob with rubber bands. It works -- and for Z
too; it helps her get a better grip on the knob. One
such slipup, on the other hand, is my failure to do some
of the corrections awaiting me at the office last night.
Only at four this afternoon did I realize this (with a
conk upside the head) and call Naomi immediately,
fearful this blunder, though seemingly small, could turn
out to be big, even huge, maybe even massively huge,
possibly affecting international relations, who knows
what, since it involves the fast-track indictment of the
alleged terrorist bomber. But it turned out to be small
after all: they told her they don't need the transcripts
until tomorrow (I say "they" because that's the term she
used; but it was undoubtedly her husband Larry who did
the telling since he's the chief prosecutor in the case)
(is this a small city or what?) and so she didn't go
down to the office today and won't until tomorrow
morning. (I blamed my screwup on the distractions and
confusions of being a newlywed with a fractured-flipper
spouse on a big holiday weekend, one fraught with
obligations to friends and relatives among others, and
she laughed and said she forgave me.)

But I'm not kidding about the possible, although now discounted, ramifications. Late last night and all of today the lead story on the national news dealt with the arrest yesterday of seven suspected terrorists at the main border crossing point some ninety miles north of here. It turns out now the incident had nothing to do with terrorism but rather involved a wife wanting to see her husband -- they had the misfortune of being Jordanians and thus matching the profile of Muslim terrorists -- but this shows the kind of panic mode the government and media are in these days. The smallest matter might be taken to be part of a conspiratorial plot. "Nightscoper with known leftist tendencies delays terrorist prosecution" -- headline around the world.

Hyperbole to the near max, of course. But it fits the moment. Sort of. At a certain level.

Meanwhile regular life grinds on. Millennial sightings are so common now it's hard to believe a major Y2K disruption could occur. The polls say this too. By "sightings" I mean things like luncheon appointments being made for dates in January 2000, bills arriving with due dates in 2000 -- like that. In other words, the computers seem to be handling the date rollover quite well.

And now, dash to the bathroom, blow-dry hair, brush, apply ponytail loop, dress, and -- because the bed's already made and all other chores are done -- zip on outta here and down the hill and across the bridge and down again from there into the central AQ.

*   *

Now, six and a quarter hours later, kicking back for a brief spell in the hideaway office I'm still so delighted to have as my very own, even if only on month-to-month lease. "Jyzer Ink World Headquarters." Truly that descriptor, though maybe it's not all that grand, is still a lot grander than the physical appearance of the office. But this matters not one iota. Such a fine little hideaway it is. At an earlier stage of my life I might've preferred to be hanging out in bars or clubs at an hour like this. Now, with this haven to fall back

683

on, that prospect wholly lacks sizzle for me.

Plenty of bars and clubs around here where I could be hanging out. Could be jyzing there too. But to be sure I wouldn't be hassled I'd need to cultivate a relationship with the place first -- with any of the places -- and that's entirely out of the question. No time for that. Right here is where it's at for me. (Except when I'm exploring or going somewhere for a reason, a jyze tie-in or some such thing.)

Such an entrancing walk down the old edge road, figures materializing in the clam-chowder-thick fog as foghorns boomed nearby (one almost loud enough to blow me against a wall like a burst of wind). Two of the materializing figures were Mr. Y and his wife, locking the iron grate in front of their market (right next to the three-story-high storefront where the portrait of J-town's most celebrated rock guitarist, painted there maybe two decades back or more, has now been painted over). Their huge shiny silver SUV was quivering at the curb like a horse raring to go. "Big," I said to Mr. Y; "big, big, big. Yours?" "Yes." "Big. Damn!" Then several blocks up the street four guys reverse-faded into view as they fished for an inner door handle with a coat hanger in a car they'd locked themselves out of, and the one directing the operation (whose voice I recognized long before I could see him or the others or the car itself) was Darren the street cartoonist.

The fog also had me thinking about gas -- swirling clouds of tear gas at the WTO protest -- and gas masks. From an article in the paper a day or two back I learned of a hue and cry for gas masks in Seoul. The U.S. Army has suddenly issued some thirteen thousand of them to its personnel stationed there and the residents of Seoul are figuring the U.S. must know something the South Koreans don't know about North Korean intentions. It's the latest twist in the Cold War standoff that's been going on there for more than half a century and that continues now ten years after the Cold War's end. (And just why are our troops still there? Well, it seems we'd be a less credible boss of the world if they

weren't. And the same goes for the hundreds of other
overseas U.S. bases in countries around the globe.)
     I finally did punch in those corrections I messed
up on last night. I also sent out three final holiday
cards and a pair of delayed Boxing Day gifts (checks for
ten bucks) to our paper-delivery people (who happened to
be sitting in the musical chair at the right moment,
because their low-paying job with such lousy hours sees
tremendous turnover in these days of low unemployment).
And I withdrew a hundred bucks in cash from the usual
ATM to carry me through millennium weekend (noting the
media are saying the massive cash withdrawals which were
anticipated for this week aren't happening -- but gun
sales are "soaring"). And the headline on the night
final, I noticed, called yesterday's terrorist brouhaha
at the border a "false alarm" (so does that mean the
Jordanians were wrong to be alarmed?).
     In the end only seven of the dozen expected
attendees showed up for June's dinner at the Chinese
fish house. Jess decided she needed the time for
packing, Aida chose to see Emiko about something or
other, June's son Michael came down with what his
brother Adam described as "a minor case of food
poisoning" and was last seen curled up fetally on a
couch at the family home in the northern burbs (and
groaning pitiably by all reports), and Adele apparently
just spaced it out (we considered giving her a "group
wake-up call" at home but decided against it). The
attendees, in addition to our four from Friday night,
included June's former coworker Karen K., who now has a
job elsewhere with the city. (In shaking my hand Karen
said, "I get to meet you at last -- could I ever burn
your ears with the things I've heard about you!" Nor
would she give me any specifics on these ear-burners,
even when I pleaded. "I want people to keep trusting
me," she said, "with their nasty little secrets.")
     The dinner itself was magnificent but June has now
decided the only Chinese food my pusillanimous "Viking
stomach" can stand in any volume is fried rice and so
she ordered a specially bland plate of same just for me.

And the sad fact is that, except for some sample nibbling, that's the only dish I ate. Of course I had my usual night-worker excuse that my breakfast was still digesting, and I didn't fail to use it.

Among the main topics of conversation -- prompting much banter and teasing -- were Z's broken arm and the infamous piece of hate mail she received. A new theory is gaining ground: that a certain former coworker of Paz and Tobey's, widely thought to be unbalanced and super-bitchy, a notorious racist and homophobe and also a friend of Kendra's right-leaning daughter, was the culprit. She left the city's employ two or three weeks ago after offending everyone in sight. The thought is she probably dispatched the letter on her own for the sheer mean-spirited pleasure of it and certainly without Kendra's knowledge, although Kendra's daughter might know about it. But in the end it's really just speculation. (So then why repeat it here? Well, why not? It stirred up lots of talk at the dinner. And I'm not naming the alleged perpetrator at this point. But that could change, because Z tells me I did meet her at one of the weddings this past summer.)

Earlier in the afternoon Z called to report on the latest developments regarding the recycling campaign and the fallout from the hate mail. She read aloud a letter she'd written criticizing the campaign, focusing on a draft of an official explanatory letter that's ready to go out to all recipients of recycling service in the city. This official letter sounded as though it were written for holders of postgraduate degrees. Incredible. And she asked for my advice about certain phrases in her own letter and about whether she should send a "blind CC" to Dale, her boss (I said yes). She'd also had a meeting about the hate letter with the city's EEO rep who told her this is exactly the kind of thing the city wants to crack down on. And Dale and his boss will be meeting with the task force for the campaign to discuss the whole sorry business and find ways to ensure it won't happen again.

So I'd say Z's approach on the matter is working

quite well. As hoped, she's jujitsu'd it into something
positive.
     -- And what? The windows in the triangle down
below have been decorated for the holidays. Half say
"Merry Christmas," the other half "Happy Millenum [sic]"
-- and that's the first time I've seen the latter
phrase written out anywhere, (sic) version or not (and
the error is repeated at least four times in other
'rangle windows).
     Four days left. Much prep work still to do on my
computers at the scope office, mostly involving
downloading copies of files. I'm sticking with my
gamble that the oldest of the machines will muddle
through. But if it doesn't, the laptop should serve
adequately as a stopgap until I can come up with a full-
size replacement (though it'll be a pain in the ass --
both using the laptop and finding a replacement). And I
alerted Naomi to the situation in our phone talk.
     -- Okay, time to go home.

[+1]

     Oh the boggling twists. Today J. City is once
again leading the national news, this time because the
city is canceling most of its New Year's Eve bash at the
fairgrounds. The "biggest party in a generation" --
struck. Erased. All that'll be left will be the
fireworks launched from the top of the flying saucer --
and those'll be seen on TV across the nation and around
the world, and probably even more so now, because the
media will be able to show a striking contrast: the
empty fairgrounds some six hundred feet beneath the
saucer. The only people allowed in will be a coterie of
rich folks who've rented the saucer's rotating
restaurant for the night (and their elite presence, and
that of several hundred cops around the periphery of the
grounds, possibly even wearing our city's now world-
infamous black Darth Vader police gear, will spice up
the visuals still more).

It was the mayor's call. This time, though, he has
what appears to be across-the-board support among city
officials and councilmembers. They're all extremely
wary of the combination of explicit terrorist threats,
Y2K/millennnial/apocalytic craziness, and leftover
jitters and resentment from the WTO protest. Renewed
rumblings are also sounding about far-right militia
actions along the lines of the bombing of the plains-
state federal building several years ago. A propane
truck was stolen two weeks ago in a Jyze City exurb and
has been missing ever since. "Better safe than sorry."

From a distance, though, the mayor's decision
appears to be a cave-in to terrorist intimidation. Some
national figures -- such as the execrable mayor of the
major far-coast megalopolis -- are coming right out and
saying this. None of the other cities reportedly
targeted by millennial terrorist threats are canceling
their celebrations, and the crowds expected for those
are much larger than that predicted for the one here
(because the cities themselves are all much larger,
including Centropolis and the national capital). An
accomplice of the so-called "King of Terror" arrested
here is thought to have flown on to Las Vegas, but that
city is going ahead with its celebration. At this point
we appear to be the odd city out. But then again a lot
could happen in the next couple of days.

It's a good thing Z and I bought our tickets for
the Isaac S. show when we did. Now a hundred fifty
thousand people (up from a hundred thousand a week ago)
will be looking for something to do on that momentous
night. (Will some of them decide the best remaining
option is to taunt the cops downtown and engage in a
little hit-and-run "anarchism"? It could happen, sure.)

So at this point about all that's left of the
city's millennium festival is some tame daytime stuff at
the fairgrounds and the ceremonial lighting of our very
own south-hill high bridge Thursday afternoon (which
just happens to be, I noticed in checking the calendar,
Jose Rizal Day in the Philippines, the anniversary of
his martyrdom in the anticolonial uprising against Spain

a few years before the beginning of the century now
ending -- the very man whose looks remind Z of her
father and whom our high bridge and hilltop strip park
are named after). It'll call for some fancy footwork on
Thursday but I'm hoping to be present for the ceremony.
-- And earlier this evening I saw the bridge lit up
again in what was probably a rehearsal for Thursday.

     It's odd, too, how I'm jyzing here. I'm stretched
out on Z's chair in the living room, fully dressed, even
wearing my shoes, and it's ten after three in the
morning. Before sitting here (to be near the portable
radiator) I loaded up the car with gear we'll be needing
for our stay at "the wedding house" -- Jess's -- over
the next six days. Z went there directly after work,
leaving me a number of voicemails about what to bring
and the location of the key at Jess's (under a blue cup
to the left of the door on the side-entry porch).
Yesterday she showed me an e-mail from Jess's block-
watch group describing an attempted break-in robbery the
previous night at the house next door to Jess's -- and
the house was occupied at the time -- so Z's surely not
sleeping easily out there alone tonight. Not even the
company of Jess's two dogs can keep her mygs in check on
this. True, the dogs are small. (But they scare me, or
at least the one I haven't met does. This is Erfa,
Kiba's replacement. I may get a very raucous reception
when I arrive there in the middle of the night.)

     Z's Y2Kalypse fears have subsided a lot, though,
along with most other people's (though definitely not
those of the lunatic/paranoid fringe and those who can
profit, financially or politically, from stirring them
up). The only remaining signs of Z's fears in the items
I loaded earlier were the big two-gallon container of
bottled water and the crank-powered radio she ordered
from a catalog last month. And we have a couple hundred
bucks of extra cash we ordinarily wouldn't be carrying.
Beyond those things, though, we're going into the End of
the World unprotected. In fact we'll be leaving all our
hoarded food -- mostly mine, and I originally set it
aside with no thought at all about Y2K -- right here.

If the sky does fall we'll be stuck at Jess's and most
of the supplies will be about eight miles distant.
(Question: do crank-powered radios pick up only crank
call-in shows? Guess we'll soon be finding out.)
     The supermarket tabloids are out with their
apocalypse issues. The indie weekly hit the stands
tonight with a parody of same. At this point everyone
seems to be sick of the subject but also a little edgy
about what might actually happen. You know just on
principle a few newsworthy disruptions must take place,
if only because the intelligence services (our USAn ones
especially) will want to exploit the opportunity to make
other countries look bad (as indeed they're already
doing in inflating the alleged terrorist threats into
what sound like near certainties of attacks with mass
casualties).
     As for me, I woke up with a headache from sleeping
in an odd position -- somehow the pillow jammed up under
my neck -- and I haven't been able to shake it
completely even with the help of a WOC waterfall massage
followed by an hourlong soak in the whirlpool. Actual
moneymaking work at the scope office will be light but
much else remains to be done, especially on my
precautionary backups of files, and I'll also be taking
the Z-mobile in for servicing tomorrow and picking it up
Thursday and I'll be in charge of walking Jess's dogs
and lord only knows what else will be coming up. But
I'll still be popping back into these pages for kwikjyze
bursts as often as I can.
     -- A pause to admire once again the wiggy krazy
klock. Nodding engineer, flapping birds, tumbling smoke
puffs. Oh yez, a splendid addition to the postnup scene
here. -- And now water the plants and make sure all's
shipshape -; the heaters turned off, the fridge doors
fully closed, the toilet flush balls pulled all the way
up, etc. -- and I should be hitting the freeway
northbound through the foggy heart of the city at about
3:40 a.m., arriving just about exactly at the promised
4:00 (living up to my "JIT guy" rep, "just in time") (as
opposed to Z's "ABE gal" rep, "always be early," right)

-- and I say this just in case ("JIC") I didn't say it before ("SIB") -- because acronyms matter! ("BAM!").

[+1]

I've stopped by the Z-geist cafe to see if it can help spark a few new thoughts about the big picture. So far not much luck. But the place feels good. I'm up in the balcony, a low-ceilinged loftlike space overlooking the high-ceilinged first-floor seating area. Those sloshy dishwashing sounds are coming from the service zone directly below the loft.

Old brick walls, original artwork, exposed piping, plants, a vintage dictionary laid out on a podium, a reading lamp standing on each table, folksy music playing on a good sound system. Most excellent. If only the place stayed open later than seven so I could come here more often.

It's ten to six now. Tonight's the night for my last major effort of just-in-case millennial downloading at the scope office -- partly of my own stuff but mostly of Naomi's. I've held off on reading today's newspapers so I'll have something relatively undemanding to do while the computer's grinding away at its tiresome tasks (mainly formatting scores of disks, with each one taking a couple of minutes). I did scan the headline story in the morning paper about the "lockdown" at the fairgrounds. It confirmed that anger and scorn are widespread regarding this "Nervous Nellie" shutdown and some J-towners see it as an intentional slight of "the people" by local power brokers as payback for the WTO protests; a few are even threatening the kind of New Year's Eve guerrilla warfare I was speculating about myself yesterday. The one bit of real news is that the elite private group that rented the saucer restaurant for the night has also canceled its own party, which involved seven hundred invitees and has been in the works for several years. So the fairgrounds will be a "no-protest zone" and "no-noninvitees zone" and a "no-

one-allowed zone." -- Well, no one allowed except for
the cops and a few fireworks technicians, I suppose.

I bused down after dropping off the car at the shop
in the Scandi quarter (a new lock's on order for our
jimmied passenger-door lock hole, I learned, but it
won't arrive in time for installation tomorrow and so
I'll have to go through the whole drill again in a week
or two). I exited the bus early to take a look at the
ballyhooed millennium shop at one of the flagship
downtown department stores, but I found most of it had
already been dismantled to make way for the next big
thing, whatever that might be. (Valentine's Day?
Certainly not M.L. King's birthday; that's more like
Devil's Day to the downtown stores.) All that remained
in the shop space were half a dozen teetering stacks of
boxes of the store's signature candy, which is probably
deemed appropriate to celebrate any and all big events
and occasions. But the store itself, like most of the
others I passed by in the retail zone, was thronged;
there was no sign at all of any harm done from the
protests which the downtown powers-that-be were bleating
about as being of federal-disaster proportions a few
weeks ago. The business news services confirm it:
overall holiday sales for the downtown area, including
the period of the protests, were up about eight percent
this year, right at the national average. But of course
the newspapers bury this story near the obituaries.

With one exception the first night at Jess's place
went smoothly. At seven Z awoke me because a fuse blew
as she was making her breakfast (she's "the boss" at the
office this week with Dale on vacation) and she couldn't
figure out how to reset the circuit breakers. This
stirred memories of our last house-sitting stay for Jess
when the furnace itself blew, taking one of the
electrical circuits with it. So I did a grumbly naked
clamber downstairs, to much nervous laughter and ribbing
from Z, and luckily was able to get things up and
running again. Otherwise the only snag was in bed: both
Cy and Erfa, it turns out, are accustomed to sleeping
there with Jess (now that Gwen's gone) and they take up

a lot of room and the bed isn't that large (twin size as compared with the full size we're used to, and of course we're not sharing our bed at home with a pair of mutts). Jess had moved the furniture around a bit, what little there is of it in her austere scheme, and installed a new round oak dining table, but otherwise things looked much the same. Nonetheless the feeling was quite different, as if Jess no longer cared at all about the place with Gwen out of the picture. (All traces of Gwen that could be removed have been: photos, artwork, plants, miscellaneous small gifts and purchases.) The house, and the garden especially, was their joint creation, even though Jess was the original owner, and the whole place now seems dead. It's almost appropriate that Jess, without Gwen to cover half the payments, is forced to put it up for sale. Her plan is to stay on only long enough to pour the slab for a new house on her land on southwest island in early spring and then to move over there and live in a tent while she builds the new place. She'll be putting her current house on the market shortly after returning from her travels in January.

Erfa, a black longhair hound with lots of cocker spaniel in her, turns out to be meek, mild, friendly, and quite amusing with her unique bark that sounds just like her name but with a questioning uptone as part of the second syllable. For much of the day she slept with her snout resting on my bare right upper arm. She lacks Kiba's high-energy sparkiness but that's not necessarily bad. Cy defers to her anyway, perhaps just out of habit as inculcated by the overbearing Kiba.

Stopping in at the ORB on the way here I read a couple of articles in periodicals, one about the twentieth century and one about the nineties, the current decade now coming to an end. Big-picture stuff. The new issue of the alt-weekly is out (its cover shows a Pinocchio figure and the caption "The Year of the Liar," cleverly using this as a theme to link the presidential impeachment, the Jyze City ballparks, Kosovo and Iraq, WTO and a good deal else) -- and the

estimable Earl K. also does a nineties piece in the rad
fortnightly along with his usual entertaining end-of-
year feature on overhyped and underhyped stories. Once
again (in a return to form after his overwrought WTO
pieces coming down hard on the dastardly out-of-town
anarchists) Earl seems dead-on to me. And as soon as I
find other people saying something I lose interest in
trying to say it again myself but differently. Often I
regret this later. This time too probably.

Z called me at Jess's at two p.m. today, waking me
up. (She knew I wouldn't be in the house long. First
the dog-walking, then the drive to the repair shop.)
She regretted to inform her "night-worker hubbin" that
her clinic does D&C surgery only in the morning, on
Wednesdays and Fridays. She'd had to schedule hers for
nine days from now at seven-thirty a.m. She sounded
anxious because she knows how exasperated I get with
day-worker scheduling which forces me to turn my own
life upside down. But of course I said I would
accompany her. It's a big deal for both of us. For
sure! (But her jokey line about it took me aback a bit:
"It's almost like they'll be aborting our baby.")
-- And the surgery might not be part of the
millennial-rollover big picture to anyone else but it
sure is to us. (I say this as a long-skirted young
woman wearing a black-knit "anarchist's cap" -- complete
with eyeholes, I see -- appears with a mop and pail and
starts cleaning the loft area here at Z-geist. Think
maybe she's hinting it's time for me to move on.)

[+1]

So the big rollover moment, or rather the first of
some two dozen of them, is now just hours away. Exactly
how many hours away still isn't quite clear to me -- but
more on that later. For starters I'm holed up at the
hideaway with my Jeep cap on and my "Time Capsule for
the 21st Century" propped like a leaning tower, rampant
and orangishly florid, between my left thigh and the arm

of the brown armchair. (With Kat and Betty out of town
again it appears -- alas! -- we won't be burying it in
their yard until next week.)

     I'll stroke out a few paragraphs here and then ride
the bus to the hilltop and continue with the entry in
unit 203 and then drive over to Jess's place and finish
it there as (if I've got the time zones right) the first
authentic crack giving onto the 21st Century and the
Third Millennium C.E. opens.

     I thought the alley bar at the public market would
be the perfect place to launch this entry. That's
because it uses the word "alibi" in its official name,
presumably playing off its location (by the alley). I'm
guessing the first question future generations might
want to ask about us -- inhabitants of the late
twentieth and early twenty-first centuries, back when
the dangers of global roasting and species extinction
and genetic tinkering and mass nuclear irradiation or
holocaust should've been evident to all -- is: And
what's your alibi? Do you think you have one? And
they'll go on: If you do, that's a delusion. Any alibi
you cook up is a phony. You were there at the scene of
the crime and you did nothing to stop it and in fact you
abetted it; you are guilty as a co-conspirator. You are
sentenced to burn in eternal shame. The only question
still open is this: Are there any mitigating factors
that should be considered in your case to reduce the
degree of shame from first to second or third? And I
say: As of now it's likely the answer in every case --
especially those involving USAns -- will be no.

     -- But to my shock I found the alley bar has gone
glitzy. It's still holding forth in the same funky
brick portion of the alley at the lower level of the
market near the south end but I stuck my head in the
door and saw scores of poshly dressed people, heard
awful disco-y music ("house tech," I guess maybe), and
witnessed a maitre'd registering alarm at the sight of
one of my shabby longhair drifterlike ilk lurking inside
the doorway. I vamoosed before he could get over to
usher me out (and he was moving my way fast).

Of course I enjoyed the rude welcome. I wear it as
a badge of pride. And yet I also hereby blow off the
alley bar for the entire coming millennium. It's become
a place of unmitigable first-degree shame, yes.

Here's the puzzler about the hours. Both of our
local dailies published hour-by-hour chronologies of the
arrival of the year 2000 as the crucial moment sweeps
around the world, but one of these says it will all
begin at two a.m. our time and the other at four a.m.
our time. With utter mindlessness I've been going by
the two a.m. all day, but now I realize that can't be
right; it must be four a.m. For eighteen years I was
constantly assuring my zen wife Lady U that the time on
her home island was three hours behind us, and the
International Dateline is one hour the far side of that
island. And at this time of year there's no Daylight
Savings Time to confuse the matter still further.

Yes, I'm settling for four a.m. But when I arrive
home -- meaning unit 203 -- I'll turn on something
electronic -- even Z's little black-and-white TV, may
the gods help me, if the radio proves to be of no use --
just to be sure.

Meanwhile I'm boggled to be able to say that at the
very last moment I've solved my own Y2K problem. Or at
least I think I have. By sheer happenstance I came
across a magazine article with instructions on how to
change what's called the "inception date" on old
computers. I was able to move the date on the more
antique of my machines back to 1980, meaning it should
have no problems for another twenty years, and I'm
figuring my need to use this computer will end long
before then. I'd hoped to be able to change the date
even further back, to 1972, because that would fit with
the "Glennarian calendar" and all the dates and days of
the week would match for another hundred years, but for
some reason the computer is programmed so that it can go
back no further than 1980.

Sheer serendipity. -- But I doubt I would've had a
problem anyway. Still I don't want to deny I'm
breathing more easily now.

Earlier this afternoon I witnessed the ceremonial
lighting of our high bridge named after the Philippine
hero. It was both hokey and intriguing, even inspiring.
In my own mind what I was seeing was Jyze City's
celebration of the end of 442 years of Western
imperialism and colonialism in Asia, although none of
the speakers mentioned this. For about ten minutes I
was standing very close to our embattled mayor, Jon H.,
and I suppose I could've humbly suggested to him that he
refer to this matter in his speech, but I never had the
gumption to break in on his conversations with others.
And I doubt even a major surge of gumption could've
spurred me to do it. Because then I wouldn't't've known
whether he would mention the matter on his own without a
prompt from one of his constituents, namely me. And
I'll just end the suspense on that right now: he didn't
do it. But he did give a pretty good speech anyway. I
stood right in front of his podium about eight feet away
with no one between us and he seemed to be speaking
directly to me and looking me in the eye the whole time.
It was all just seeming, though; he was speaking to and
looking at the TV camera right next to me.
     -- But it's bus time. Gotta leave the capsule
behind now. It didn't climax but I can tell it's ready.
                    *   *
     -- Forty-five minutes later. I guess I was wrong.
I don't understand why. But the TV's turned on here at
203 (not at Jess's yet) and tuned to an unintentionally
comical live broadcast from the South Pacific,
alternating between Tonga and Kiribati. We're about to
observe the first witnessing in a thousand years of a
millennial rollover of Christian or Gregorian or so-
called Common Era time. (What does this system have in
"common" with the Muslim or Chinese or Indian way of
measuring time, to name just a few? Not a whole lot.)
The comedy comes from the nonstop technical screwups and
the utter confusion and vapidity of the TV commentators
as they try to conceal them extemporaneously. But never
mind. Grass-skirted dancers, a local king, ukuleles,
words being sung in their language, whatever it may be

-- no one is telling us or translating -- and my clock
here by the bed says it's two a.m. but the announcer now

    -- And that extra-long dash right there, that's it,
the first crack. The bridge leading to the new
millennium. It snuck up on me. And suddenly a huge
Tongan choir is singing the "Hallelujah Chorus"! How
bizarre this is! And yet...watching the introduction to
this special twenty-five-hour show as it switched
quickly, for preview purposes, from site to site around
the world, some two dozen of them, I'll say I felt what
seemed to be one of those earth-seen-from-space moments
(and now here's the rousing finale, the choir of ten
thousand belting it out as fireworks explode just like
at "tater time" above the old ball yard): felt a surge
of hope, I say, for the world to come. Hula waggles, a
torch handed by an elder to a young boy to light the
whole world -- a torch of peace -- the boy climbing into
a canoe and paddling out to sea to meet the sunrise.
Sappy hope, yes. As I lie jyzing. (And recalling jyze
never lies in that other sense.) Stretched out atop my
and Zoelie's bed atop south hill, directly above the
probable earthquake fault line, facing the pillows,
glancing at the black-and-white screen to my right as
the King of Tonga (I've since learned) prays aloud in
highly elegant English.
    -- But enough for now. The program's moving ahead
to the next time zone, New Zealand's, and we're being
teased with a foretaste of the next midnight ceremony.
And I'm hongry. Back in a while.
            *   *
    -- What a night it's turning out to be. The
celebration on the tube continues, I don't know where.
New Guinea maybe. Thousands of spear carriers gathered
on a beach, that much I can see. But I've turned the
sound down so low I can't make out what's being said.
Meanwhile a WHAP echoes outside as the far-coast paper
arrives, I retrieve it, "last issue of the millennium"
but also "first issue of the new millennium" (though
that's not how it's dated), and the lead story tells of

the arrest in the far-coast megalopolis itself of
another accomplice of the "King of Terror" here who, the
feds say, met with him in this very city -- J. City,
yes -- a few weeks ago, well before he tried to smuggle
in the bomb. More and more evidence suggests a radical
Algerian Islamic group is now targeting the U.S. And a
TV news flash: the booze-crazy pro-democracy Russian
president has just now resigned! "Chasing the
millennium right off the front pages in Moscow."

     Nothing yet about any Y2K-bug computer foul-ups or
ensuing mass panic.

     -- The first half hour of this telecast, though,
was extraordinary. Part of this was because it seemed
utterly unrehearsed, as if it had just been learned the
millennium was about to arrive and it would be happening
on a remote South Pacific island and a hasty uplink had
been patched together to bring the story to the world.
With all the boggles and fumbles and urgent tones it was
more like the live broadcast of the immediate aftermath
of a president's assassination while all was still
confusion.

     Too bad Z's not here to see this. But she was bone
tired and ready to crash at eight p.m. Tomorrow's
continuing telecast would be enough for her, she said.
The official "world" time of the new day and the
quatrorollover or DYCM-changing event is four p.m. by
our local time -- midnight Greenwich time (sure does
confirm that a few centuries of classic imperialism can
provide delayed payoffs) (and by coincidence on TV right
now they're showing Greenwich, a castlelike building, a
folksinger performing inside, I think -- or maybe the
singer is elsewhere even if the official clock isn't).

     Z arrived a few minutes late for the high-bridge
Millennium Light ceremony, having loyally trusted the
time given out by the mayor's office over the one
published in the newspapers. This was unfortunate,
because she missed speeches delivered by several
Filusans she's worked with off and on for years,
although she's not really close to any of them (she
feels they look down their noses at her because she's

biracial and "too assimilated" and originally from
Centropolis and therefore "too east coast" and "not
demure enough"). The gathering took place under a
couple of small open-sided tents, white and red, perched
on the bluffside overlooking the bridge from its raised
southeast end. A Filusan women's choir sang too, all
dressed traditionally. But the illumination of the
bridge as seen from the tents was not too impressive,
especially considering the symbolic meaning it had to
carry as one of the few remnants of the city's official
Millennial Project (though the mayor did note the
planting of twenty thousand trees and cleanup of several
urban creeks -- including the one Z fell into when she
broke her wrist (not that he mentioned that fall
specifically, of course)). Z said she'd expected
something a bit fancier, like Christmas lights maybe;
not just an underlighting of the green girders of the
support arch above the freeway and the city streets far
below. "It's more like turning on the night lights in a
shipyard," she said, "or a steel mill or something."
     But TV was there, three trucks with uplinks
quivering high overhead like "War of the World" eye pods.
Lots of red "on air" lights burning and blinking.
     Earlier I had walked from Z's old hood to the
Scandi quarter, some three miles, to pick up the wagon.
The repairs came to $275, about a third of which went
for replacing the jimmied lock. They were able to dig
one up locally after all. Another unexpected third paid
for realignment of tires knocked awry by potholes. Our
insurance will eventually pay for the lock replacement.
     And after the high-bridge ceremony Z and I walked
down to the HQ, on an impulse, hoping to do dinner at
the Last Supper Club (just because of the name) (which I
mention here as a special millennial jyze exception).
Finding that restaurant closed, we hit the well-regarded
Italian place nearby for the first time as a couple.
She'd always hesitated to suggest our going there,
fearing the spicy Italian sauces would disagree with me,
and that's exactly what they did. I managed to get down
only a couple of bites and suddenly seemed to be running

a high fever and felt my bowels were about to explode.
But glugging down a glass of whole milk saved me, and
after a suitable recovery period I was able to walk Z up
to the bus stop where she caught a coach out to Jess's
place (as I learned almost too late last night, the
route I used to take out to Z's apartment when she lived
a block away from Jess is no longer running). At the
bus stop Z noticed a woman eyeballing me (she said) and
observed, "You know, it's real easy to tell you're not
wearing any underwear. And it looks like maybe those
red peppers are having an unexpected effect." (Could
that be true? Will I have to start gobbling peppers and
damn the stomach-trouble costs?)

The mayor's speech, I was starting to say a while
back, was unexpectedly good even if poorly delivered.
It talked about the "many ways" the bridge could be seen
as a symbol, linking the most diverse parts of the city,
the central area and the south end, with perhaps a
hundred different languages being spoken in homes and
apartments within less than a mile of the structure
itself, and also linking the downtown with the new e-
commerce growth zone symbolized by the dot-com
headquarters in the DC castle atop the hill right behind
us (and lit up with its own new lighting scheme; and
seen through the grove of mostly leaf-barren deciduous
trees in the greenbelt it looked magnificent).

A moment to treasure. To my utter surprise it was,
yes, exactly that. And I should note that only
afterwards did it occur to me I could've introduced
myself as a possible former teacher of the mayor's. I
know he attended Mezzu and I know he has an engineering
degree, so it's at least theoretically possible he was
in one of those technical-writing classes for which I
was a TA in the engineering college. He's a few years
older than I am, but maybe he received his degree late
-- I don't know. It's an odd connection, though. Maybe
a subconscious awareness of the possible link also had
something to do with the sympathy I felt for him as he
fumbled his way through the WTO crisis, pretty much the
same way he did with this speech.

[The Jyze Millennium, Part II]

      -- The show goes on ---
                              *
      (The phone rang then and it was Z. "I woke up and
it was 4:15 and you weren't here! Why aren't you here?"
-- But she knew why. And I told her I'd gotten hooked a
little bit on the extraordinary live telecast. -- And
right now even as this jyze goes down the tube's showing
an Indonesian dance in silhouette, a single female
dancer, on a beach before the rising sun -- it's hard to
tear myself away. -- But Z says Jess called and she'll
be coming back early, on New Year's Day, because the
mountains are short on snow for snowboarding and she
hasn't met anyone even slightly interesting and she's
bored to tears. And today D'Arcy, in giving Z a copper
heart -- "just for being alive" -- mentioned she thinks
that Jess, who's currently her officemate, will
reconcile with Gwen despite everything "because she's
still crazy in love with her.")

                           [+1]

      -- Now it's about twenty-three-and-a-half hours
later, and though for most of the globe the new year/
decade/century/millennium -- DYCM! -- have all begun, a
tiny slice far out in the Pacific is still clinging to
1999, the '90s, the 1900s, the second millennium. And
so in a sense the globe as a whole is doing the same.
For about twenty-six more minutes.
      Here's the important news first. As far as anyone
knows -- or anyway is reporting in the media -- no Y2K-
bug glitches of significance have occurred and the
same's true for homegrown militia terror incidents and
new Islamic terror incidents. The end of the world this
is not. At least not yet. But of course the likelihood
that we're heading for climate and ecology devastation
in the decades ahead -- to say nothing of centuries or
millennia -- seems as great as ever, or greater.
      Here in Jyze City, TV did the best it could to make
the occasion look festive. The fireworks shot off from

atop the saucer burst into a spectacular display,
writing out in flame the numbers "2000" so they were
visible for many miles in all directions. Crowds
gathered outside the police-lined fences at the
fairgrounds, atop north hill and east hill and even
south hill (at the strip park), on scores of boats on
the largest of the inner-city lakes and on the bay, and
no doubt in many, many other places. Z and I watched
from Jess's small outdoor garret balcony, our view
neatly blocked (symbolically too, as Z pointed out) by a
big evergreen standing next door. But the pyrotechnics
were still partially visible through the branches, and
we could see flashes reflecting off downtown buildings.
Numerous skyrockets also went off locally and in more
distant parts of the city and the burbs, including a
private display ignited by the world's richest person
from a barge on the big lake to the east, near the posh
waterfront burb where he lives, and the upper portions
of those eruptions were visible to us. At the first
sighting of the saucer display -- this was exactly at
midnight, right on schedule -- a cheer went up in Jess's
hood and lots of horns sounded, firecrackers went off,
ship steam whistles blasted. Z and I kissed and clung
and rubbed and vowed we'd make our first full decade/
century/millennium together, to the extent we survive
it/them (given our standard mammalian three-billion-
heartbeat limits), every bit as good as our mutual
partial D/C/M set now converted to ancient history.

     And that was pretty much it. A minute or two more
and most of the sounds and sights had died away and it
was too cold to stay out there (a jagged little wind was
slicing away) and we went inside to watch it all on tape
delay on Jess's TV in the basement. And after ten
minutes of that Z was fading fast and I took her up to
bed and lay there for a while pondering the momentous
occasion with her asleep in my arms.

     -- And in less than a minute it'll be two o'clock
-- midnight in the westernmost USAn state way out there
in the central Pacific -- and all these time periods at
issue, meaning the full DCYM bunch, will themselves

convert to ancient history everywhere.

Here's where it happens, when the dot goes down inside the brackets:

[.]

(Might there be some isolated spots in a time belt between that westernmost USAn state and the International Dateline which still have an hour to go until midnight? I don't think so but I'm not sure. The map in the paper makes it appear there could be -- and maybe the same's true for slices of Siberia and Antarctica -- but I don't trust these maps. I'll just say it's possible the old-DYCM group is still clinging to life and will continue doing so for about fifty-eight more minutes. I sort of like the ambiguity. I'll try to finish up this account before three o'clock so that only with tomorrow's new jyze entry -- start of a new fiver -- will it be certain, from the highly local jyze point of view, that the new era is fully underway.)

I'm stretched out on Jess's green leather couch. The two dogs are lying on the bed upstairs with Z, replacing me for her just as they replaced Gwen for Jess (though it's not an exact analogy, I sure do hope). All's quiet except for the humming furnace and some occasional creaking in the vents and an even more occasional car rolling by on the street outside.

Through an odd series of circumstances we wound up doing dinner this past evening -- millennium eve! -- at the cafe, funky yet also highly plastic and noisy, in the Scandi quarter's prime bowling alley. Z nearly melted down over our inability to find an open eatery that would accept us (private parties had taken over many of them), but as soon as she had a little bowling-alley "Combo Burger" in her she was all right and even congratulated me on handling her tantrum so well (I thought I did a good job too -- although I nearly snapped at one point and was about to suggest we go back to the house). At a high-toned deli where a few couples in formal evening wear were sitting primly at the usual standard deli tables (looking very odd) I asked if it was too late to order a sandwich and the woman behind

the counter said icily, "It's all one setup for a
hundred dollars per person." A nearby Scandi restaurant
was less snooty but gave essentially the same reply, the
cost there being just eighty per.

    But the blues show was fine. The alehouse isn't
large, just a single brick-walled room with a bar on one
side and maybe a dozen tables on the other and a small
dancefloor in between, with the band set up on a riser
in back. We arrived just in time to grab the last two
adjacent empty seats (at a table already occupied by a
young couple playing gin rummy). By sheer coincidence a
woman sitting at the table behind Z turned out to be her
physical therapist from the medical building downtown, a
twenty-something blond who'd once promised Z to "get you
ready for your honeymoon." She asked Z in a whisper (as
Z reported to me a moment later), "So is this the guy
all the excitement was about?" She scoped me out rather
boldly, I thought -- including a blatant up-and-down FC
check when I came back from the restroom -- and never
did stop staring at me from time to time. "Have you
noticed," Z asked, "my therapist seems quite taken with
you?" I had. This was the second time in two nights
something like this has happened (the woman at the east-
depot bus stop being the first). "Being crazy in love
with you," I said, "must give me some special glow a
certain kind of woman finds fascinating" -- and I think
there may be some truth to that (though probably not
much). And saying it seemed to give Z a special glow
too. And got me off the hook, it did, at least so far.

    Our other adventure of the day was a walk down the
hill to hood central in pursuit of coffee and newspapers
and a few groceries from the co-op. We took "the
dogies" (pronounced as in "get along little...") with us
and that turned out to be a mistake because Cy is easily
frightened by traffic and I wound up having to carry him
much of the way in both directions.

    -- Back to the alehouse. A color TV with the
sound turned off was flickering above the bar and we
followed the New Year's Eve events on it from time to
time as the hour struck in different time zones. First

the main far-coast megalopolis with a massive crowd and
what appeared to be exploding buildings as the ball fell
(only fireworks), then Centropolis, then my old city No.
11 in the mountains, then my old city No. 2/7 on our
coast here but that one only in previews: all the major
urban zones of my own pre-Jyze City life odyssey, with
the main far-coast megalopolis standing in for my
college town roughly a hundred thirty miles north of it.
Scenes from J. City itself also appeared from time to
time and like everyone around us we were hyper-alert to
the possibility of trouble -- probably no one would've
been shocked if a gaggle of cops had burst in and
proclaimed another state of civil emergency like the
one of WTO days and ordered us all to go home or perhaps
line up to be herded into black mariahs -- but nothing
like that happened.

Back at Jess's place we watched replays of the
festivities in other countries. They all looked slick
and professionally spectacular, and I decided I'd seen
the best part of the broadcast live from Tonga the
previous night. But there was the Eiffel Tower shooting
off fireworks, the top of the Great Pyramid in Egypt lit
up, the pope muttering blessings from the Vatican, the
queen in England, so on and so forth. The linked world.
Just how linked and to what effect, that remains to be
seen. But still, a rare show. How long will it be
before its like comes along -- if ever?

I have no special millennial resolutions. Just
want to do all I can to keep things in my own life and
in particular my life with (A) Z and (B) jyze going
pretty much as they've been going -- and that's been a
kind of daily renewable resolution of mine for almost
three years now with Z, six years with jyze.

Tomorrow, New Year's Day, we'll be packing up and
leaving here shortly after I awaken and later we're
planning to attend Adele's annual party and maybe Leola
and Gerry's too, though probably not. In any event I
won't have a chance to jyze here again tomorrow, and
this is probably the last time we'll be house-sitting
for Jess before she sells the place. This means it's

almost certainly the last time Z and I will be able to
return to the spot where we were married and probably
also the last time we'll be able to hang out like this
in the hood where Z was living when we met. Her former
apartment, we've noticed, is now occupied by someone
with a set of large, fancy-looking bookcases -- we could
see their upper reaches as we gazed up from the street
toward the fourth-floor balcony that used to be hers --
and the cars in the parking lot look somewhat posher.
The hood as a whole still seems less than upscale to me
-- just ordinary middle class, if anything a bit more
nondescript than most in the north end -- but also a cut
or two above our part of south hill. People of color
are few and far between. Then again techies are taking
over both hoods -- a different huge dot-com dominates
each one -- and so Z and I bristle in the same way over
developments in both. (On TV tonight all three local
stations ran stories from the nearby "Center of the
Universe Ball," which was described as the biggest and
daffiest gathering in the city. Some seventeen hundred
partiers were present -- we'd been thinking we might be
among them until Z noticed the ad for Isaac S.'s
appearance at the alehouse -- and a lot of them, I'm
sorry to say, had that familiar nerdy and overly
prosperous dot-com look. The party was thrown as one
final blowout by the owners of the locally famous
counterculture-ish variety store right next door to the
magazine shop where Z and I first met. The variety
store's closing down for good after a twenty-year run,
signaling for many the end of an era in Z's old hood and
no doubt well beyond.)

    In the mail I brought over for Z last night were
two items of interest. One confirmed our names have
been added to the list of those interested in purchasing
a condo at the lofts place. This may never work out,
but for the next couple of years we'll probably be
thinking of that as our, to cite the going term, "dream
home." We still haven't heard anything about rent
increases or condoizing of our present building by the
new owners, but we have little doubt we'll eventually --

and more likely sooner than later -- be driven out of
there. That's already our apartment of the past, not of
the future. We'll probably wind up thinking of it as
our Deep apartment: the only one where we lived as
domestic partners.

     Second, Z received notice from the Social Security
Administration, as everyone with an account there will
soon be doing if they haven't already (I haven't), of
the exact value of the benefits she can expect to
receive. If she were to retire at sixty-five she'd be
looking at monthly payments of around $1400, and those
would be on top of her city pension payments of $2500 or
more. Adding in my own paltry Social Security of about
$700 a month (I'm just estimating, but I'm sure I'll be
at or near the minimum) this means the two of us
together will likely have close to $60,000 a year to
live on, and unless inflation goes crazy that should be
enough to allow us to afford a small condo in the city.
And so for our first full millennium together --
whatever small portion of it we live to see -- it would
appear we'll be secure as far as the basics go. And
what more could we ask or want?

     One other small item. Z pointed out something
neither she nor I had realized before: if she
"predeceases" her spouse, her full Social Security
benefits go to the spouse for the rest of his life.
Even given the upcoming medical tests Z's facing I think
the odds still favor my croaking first. Nonetheless: it
comes as a relief to know this money would be there if I
lost her to death. And it means I can go ahead and use
the deep (uncapped, yes) reserves as a down payment on a
condo or a house for us, since I now know I won't be
needing the interest from that account to supplement my
own meager Social Security payments.

     Dry stuff -- but important. The coast now looks as
clear as it could possibly be for me to concentrate on
my jyze projects for the rest of my life. I've got me a
splendid wife and, as far as I know, passably good
health and now it appears a basic financial security as
well. So I'm ready for the new (and for me final) age.

33

So if things were going the way the TV commentators
predicted, it would be as if a layer of skin had been
ripped off everyone's eyes or like a curtain had opened
on a glistening new era. And for a moment last night it
seemed as if it might be just that way for me -- both
ways at once -- and that moment is still producing faint
after-tremors: for example, when I say to myself
everything in my life up to midnight last night was a
1900s kind of thing.
     But piffle, never mind. Already I'm trying to
focus on March 25, date of what I insist is the true
millennium, and saying until we hit that anniversary
none of the real meaning of the big rollover can even
begin to come into view. And before that the Year of
the Dragon roars in, and that's year 4698, I believe, of
the Chinese lunar calendar and so it's obviously way
beyond any mere millennium or two in significance of the
longevity or cumulative kind.
     But here it is, January 1, 2000, according to the
Gregorian solar calendar which I've lived by most of my
life. Not just any Saturday or just any first day of
the month or even of the year, the decade, the century.
So it's big. And a huge stack of newspapers is resting
on the couch here to prove how big it is. For banner
front-page headlines two of them run a massive block
"2000" and one chooses "01-01-00." It'll take a week
to wade through all this stuff. (Included in the stack
will be the two Sunday papers -- one's already here --
and the three Friday papers. "Millennium Weekend." Our
Jyze City evening paper is offering a three-day

commemorative edition enclosed in a special millennial
shrink-wrap with the date printed on it in, again, very
big numerals -- but available only through the newspaper
itself, from what I hear, or at local franchises of a
certain schlocky national corporate convenience-store
chain.

It's four a.m. and Z and I are back at home and
she's asleep. Our cluttery apartment -- I do see it, at
least, with fresh eyes after living in Jess's austere
and immaculately clean home for most of the past week.
But to say this doesn't mean I'm disapproving! (Z at
first thought it might.) We didn't make a major effort
to decorate No. 203 for the holidays but we did put out
a few seasonal items here and there. My favorite of
these is the extra-large "Noel" stocking Z hung on the
seat-back of the couch. It features big block red
letters (except for a green wreath standing in for the
"O") on a white background with bright blue trim --
truly a handsome old sock. -- Noel, by the way, is also
the name of the tall Asian guy we've been seeing in the
garage for the past week. It turns out he and his wife
or roommate or whatever she is -- we just met them
tonight, and we didn't even get her name -- have moved
into Ciro's old place. This is startling; it means Ciro
moved out a day or two after we last talked with him and
at that time he gave us no hint he was going. He was an
unhappy camper, though, we know, because Min, our now-
former landlord, had assured him the building wasn't
about to be sold, and a few days later it was sold, and
then the new owners immediately advised Ciro his
services as manager were no longer needed.

So now Z will be, as far as we know, the only
person of at least partial Philippine ancestry in the
building. And a hand-lettered sign will no longer hang
on the tree in front offering seamstress services (by,
it turns out, both Ciro's mother and his wife, neither
of whom we've ever really met). And from the looks of
things so far, upkeep will be even worse than it was
while Ciro was in charge. -- But Z and I will try to
maintain a low profile until the new owners have tipped

their hand on condoizing and rent increases.

Earlier in the evening we drove up to Adele U.'s place in a fancy-pants first-tier burb for her annual New Year's party. This is a small at-home affair for family and friends with a Japanese-accented buffet dinner and it's the third time I've attended it so I'm almost feeling I'm part of the family. All the various children and grandchildren are, without question, growing. After some rusty mental gear-shifting I'm back into the family tales, picking up from a year ago. Colin, Adele's date two years ago who acted scandalously by soliciting Aida's phone number at the party (at that point Aida didn't know he was there with Adele) and then showing up at a party of Aida's the next week, where he repeated his dastardliness by hitting on Emiko -- all this stirring up a big flap among the circle of politically astute Asiusan women of whom those three and Z are charter members from many years back -- that same smooth-talking Colin showed up this time too and with Emiko in tow! I thought this must've been hard on Adele but Z assured me it wasn't; Adele and Emiko made up long ago and they've even traveled together twice since then, to Costa Rica, I think it was, and Bali. And Emiko and Colin, though they've had their ups and downs, have been together for most of the past two years, according to Z, with each maintaining a separate residence.

Otherwise this party, it must be said, was a dud. In part it was because neither Aida nor her sister Sera could be present. Mr. D developed a case of pneumonia a few days ago and with Mrs. D also in bad health the two older daughters living nearby have been taking turns watching over him at the hospital, and the task became even more complicated when one of Sera's daughters fell victim to a virus last night. Z hasn't been able to talk with Aida about any of this as yet (and she's not on very good terms with Sera at the moment and won't even try to call her) and so she doesn't know how serious the situation is, but it's her guess Aida will be needing her support and lots of it, and of course Z has her own D&C coming up this week. And lately she's

begun talking again about how she just doesn't schmooze
with Aida as much these days -- because she now tells me
things first and then finds it boring to go over the
same stuff again with Aida -- and they aren't as close
as they were. "You're the most important person in my
life now" -- she's told me this twice in the past week
alone and both times with such unexpected gravity I'm
sure she's freshly realizing it and perhaps seeing new
ramifications which I'm not yet aware of myself. -- Not
that she seems unhappy about it. But as she says, it
can be sobering to realize you have only so much in the
way of emotional resources and you can't spread them too
thin without causing worrisome consequences.

Jess arrived home, chauffeured from the airport by
Madge I., not long after I rolled out of bed and
staggered downstairs. She snuck up from behind and gave
me a big hug as I was washing dishes -- the first time
she's ever done anything like that with me. Was I
pleased! The only story she had to tell about her trip
was that Gwen had sent Jess's mother a Christmas card --
and Jess's mother hadn't even come up to the mountains
for the holiday, as she was supposed to do; Jess learned
about the card by phone. So it appears D'Arcy was
right: the obsession continues. Z and I are scheduled
to do dinner with Jess next weekend, so maybe we'll find
out more then. (Z has urged me several times to take
the initiative in talking with Jess but for some reason
I shy away from doing so. But Z's been saying for weeks
that Jess felt she got a lot from my comments when the
three of us met up last month (and Jess almost chomped
into the grill-brush wire in her burger). My own guess
is that it was Z herself who was interested to hear me
talking "philosophically" about love and romance; to me,
at least, it all seemed to bounce off Jess leaving no
mark at all. She's said nothing about any of it to me
since then.)

Lots of packing. Lots of driving. Lots of helping
Z on and off with her coat, buckling her in, cutting her
food, tying her shoes, etc. etc. -- and it's a drag
sometimes, there's no denying, but it's also good to

feel so useful for a change. (Haw -- that's a joke,
though not without a certain underlying seriousness.) A
stop at bro Rob's bookstore -- he was their designated
New Year's Day "point man" -- to wish him a happy new
DYCM, but we missed him by a few minutes after he'd
called it a day (and it had been a glitch-free one, his
co-employee at the register said, all company and
supplier computers performing well -- in fact far better
than usual, he said, owing to the exceptional amount of
IT care lavished upon them). We bought a birthday cake
to take over to Betty's for our birthday/time-capsule
celebration tomorrow. For the fourth day in a row my
morning coffee was a paper cup of house drip from a
franchise shop -- ugh. (But better that than the only
real alternative, a paper cup from a convenience store.
Hauling the makings for coffee over to Jess's place just
hadn't seemed worth the effort given the afternoon time
constraints.) -- And dog hair all over everything. Z's
now convinced I'm aching to have a dog of my own. I do
enjoy the highly expressive Erfa -- her personality,
once she overcomes her shyness, turns out to be a lot
like that of brother Jeff's Monty from Gatewood days if
Monty had had that truly bizarre Erfa bark -- but at
this stage in my life I wouldn't want to take on the
care and feeding of a critter, whether cat or dog or
even bird or turtle. Z-goose herself (as I joked) is
the one exception, just as I hope I am for her. But
things might change when an even more advanced stage of
dotage sets in on one side or the other, Z or me -- and
eventually, of course, on both. Unless, that is,
something else takes down one or the other of us first.

     Last night on the way up to bed I gazed out for a
while, through the glass door leading onto the garret
balcony, at the downtown skyline where we'd been
watching the fireworks earlier. Some puffy white clouds
were trailing out to the east of the flying-saucer/golf-
tee icon, looking almost as if they could've been
lingering smoke from the pyrotechnical explosions,
except the wind had been strong and gusty all night.
And the "sky beam" which has been a matter of

controversy for the past couple of months (though I
don't think I've ever mentioned it before) was shooting
straight up from the top of the saucer, rapidly
diffusing after a few hundred feet in the swirling
clouds. It was the first time I'd actually seen it and
it did indeed look tacky, like something that belonged
at Disneyland or our own countrified state fair. A
story in the paper said permission for the "sky beam"
was granted for just a short period; then the city will
launch a full examination of the issue. (A north-hill
neighborhood group strongly opposes the beam. Naomi,
although she's not a member of the group, does also.)
     This jyze is drifting perilously close to the
sheer-drivel zone. In a way it seems entirely apt on
such a massively hyped day. And this is no less true
just because I'm as guilty as anyone of the hyping. And
what's more it's a hype I believe in! We need things to
find meaning in even if we know it's all our own
creation and thus, on the cosmic scale, close to
meaningless (yet still also as close to meaningful as we
can get or know of). -- Well yes, of course! Wotta
lotta hooey here! (And with so many talented
wordslingers taking on the millennium as a topic these
days I can't help but be hugely humbled. Even if they
weren't talented you can only read so much before
feeling that everything that could be said about all
this fascinating bunkum has indeed been said again and
again -- and yet here you are with the blank J-book
lying open before you and a fierce jyze itch needing to
be scratched, including in the sense of, first, being
scratched out on paper, and then, in many if not most or
even all cases, scratched as in deleted; except jyze,
unless the rules change significantly at this late stage
of the game, has no delete button. But of course
civilization has plenty of those, and nature even more.

                        [+1]

     -- Only a few minutes for this. But I can't fail

to deliver a few strokes on First Stroke Day. It's
Kakizome! All the calligraphers in the land (and in the
actual land of First Stroke Day that's just about
everyone) -- all the calligraphers break out their
inkstones and brushes and position themselves just so in
a state of serene alertness and wait for inspiration to
strike. Then -- slash slash slash, and each a slash of
at least attempted grace -- and the shape of the year to
come is set for eternity in wondrous ragged black ink.
Or colored ink, I suppose, in at least a few cases. And
the raggedness is so important in this computer age that
always wants to disregard the outliers and the boggling
complexities and shifting perviousness (not to say
perviness) of its ever more elusive boundaries.

These J-stick strokes right here going down
(wondrous or not but proudly ragged for sure) at the
hideaway. I stopped in briefly -- because that was the
only possibility left to me after the festivities at
Betty and Kat's place, the drive in, the walk downtown,
the corrections and printing at the scope office, the
trot down to the triangle -- and then paid the rent
(newly raised at the COLA rate by $4, to $175), watered
the plants, put up the new five-by-seven-inch year 2000
calendars from the newsstand at the public market -- and
they continue to give them away free! With each and
every employee quirkily depicted thereon!

But a fine walk down. For some reason the sight of
the dome just waiting for implosion (first coming into
view as I crossed the now routinely all-lit-up south-
hill high bridge) inspired me to think of implosion as
closure. Implosion is due to happen in late March, the
papers say, in the same general time as my celebration
of the self-proclaimed, which is to say (also) jyze-
proclaimed, true millennium. Why not combine the two
and invite everyone in the city to attend? So much
frustration's in the air because of the lingering WTO
tensions and the cancellation of the fairgrounds
fireworks gala; people are aching to participate in a
big celebratory communal ritual. And it just so happens
that March 25th is the "real" millennium date -- meaning

it's technically correct from a historical standpoint --
since it falls exactly a thousand years after the date
of the previous and only other millennium celebration of
the Christian variety, which in the year 1000 (as with
every such New Year's celebration after that up into the
17th century) was observed on March 25th. (And what's
more, for the religiously minded who also happen to be
at least somewhat open-minded, and especially the
Christian subset of that group, and most especially the
fundamentalist and Catholic subsubsets, vanishingly tiny
though they may be, March 25th from the start was the
designated date of Christ's conception; and don't all
the Right-to-Lifers of our day insist that the fetus
becomes a fully human being at the moment of conception
-- and therefore the Christ fetus must become an even
more than fully human being on that date -- a flesh-and-
blood deity no less -- and therefore isn't March 25th
the date Christians should celebrate the appearance of
their lord and savior on this earth?)
     But I wonder if I really want to do it. Write a
letter to the editor or maybe publish a small "Common
Sense"-style pamphlet? Could any approach along those
lines possibly work? (Would it matter even slightly if
it did?) -- Is that (any such approach) my style? Is
that the kind of thing jyze, with the high value it puts
on nondisruption or minimal disruption (since "non" is
impossible) of the surrounding life which it's
chronicling, wants to be doing?
     Best to let it percolate for a while.
                        *

     -- An amusing moment at the time-capsule ceremony.
Kat slipped on the mud and fell halfway into the hole
I'd just dug on the edge of Betty's garden, a few feet
beyond Manny's shed. This in a light but quite cold
rain at four p.m. as Z and Betty held our large "just-
in-case" wedding umbrella over all four of us. Kat, in
other words, aped her aunt's plunge into the creek that
broke her wrist -- she "did a Zoelie." Except the only
thing she broke was -- into laughter! And then she had
to go in and change into some dry pants.

What else was, and is, in that capsule? Each of us provided five items, including a small notebook with quotes, drawings, poems, recipes, messages for the future, etc. -- we had a hoot reading these aloud at the kitchen table. Other items: a group photo, a G&Z love rock, a gummy bear, a spaceman from our wedding cake.

It was a touching moment for all of us, reminding everyone of the rainy evening two years ago when we memorialized Manny's death. At the end each of us tossed one of Betty's yellow birthday mums onto the orange capsule before I filled the hole in. The capsule will rise again, I should note, in a thousand years, self-propelled by a small faux "time-sensitive battery-powered surfacing mechanism" that was also among the contents. The highly evolved beetle or jellyfish people controlling the earth in the year 3000 will surely be intrigued by all this.

-- A relaxed birthday dinner followed. Manny's brother Reuben and Betty's friend Yvonne arrived at six, an hour late. I had a devil of a time prying the cork out of a bottle of fancy sparkling apple juice. Reuben told of his WTO experiences as a guard at the swankiest shopping center in town, at the heart of the downtown glitz strip, most of the time near an outlet of a certain upscale chain clothing store which was high on every serious protester's target list (but not a single one got to it, Reuben said with extremely annoying pride). Kat showed off her "new room" -- she's moved upstairs to Manny's remodeled pine-paneled garret workroom. For dinner, meatloaf and scalloped corn and buttermilk biscuits; for dessert a fudge cake with a gimmicky candle that hilariously screeched out a sloweddown version of "Happy Birthday." No wrestling, but while Kat was out of the room Betty let it be known the first budding of the "Kat bosoms" is occurring right now. Betty helped Z apply moleskin to a rough edge on her cast (and also prescribed liberal usage of vaseline all along the edges and warned that no matter what precautions Z takes the stink will soon become close to unbearable).

And time's up. Mainstream millennium weekend's
coming to an end. Tomorrow morning a second chance for
Y2Kalypse to erupt will present itself when most
businesses reopen after the New Year holiday and turn on
their computers or try to use them for the first time
since the rollover -- and this will be, it's said, about
ninety percent of the world's computers. Still a chance
for a little major chaos and pandemonium to break out so
that the more wild-eyed of the prognosticators won't
look as bad as they do right now. (Wei my friend, is
the shame upon you yet?)

[+1]

And here we are at Perihelion Day -- the day when
Earth swings in closest to the sun. If there's any one
day when the planet's wings would most likely fall off
Icarus-like, this is it. But it hasn't happened.
Apparently all's hanging together to just about the same
degree it was hanging together before. To my knowledge
the media have failed to discover a single instance of
significant damage caused by the Y2K bug. In fact I've
seen no reports of any damage at all, not so much as a
briefly frozen screen or hooting error message. And as
a result, according to a headline I did see, the stock
markets are going crazy, soaring off once again into
record territory. It's as if the so-called digital
revolution has passed its final test and is now free to
pull out every last goddamn stop, greasing the chute for
the true global-roasting ecocidal apocalypse.
May the gods stop fighting each other and help us!
I had thought today would be a day off for jyze,
but I can't let such an exceptional occasion slip by
without a burst or two. (I'd been thinking tomorrow was
Perihelion Day. But that's by Greenwich time, starting
at midnight in England. Here in J. City the exact
moment of shortest distance to the sun came at nine p.m.
tonight as I was soaking up some chlorine in the WOC
whirlpool while watching the waterfall calve off its

usual unending parade of poolside-clinging foambergs.)

Somehow I misplaced my "Jyze" pendant somewhere at home and so I'm now wearing its "Celebrate" twin, borrowed back from Z. It's a good day to have it on display, too, because today life returns to at least the appearance of normality for most people, myself included to be sure. The party's over, if not forever, certainly for a while. Now the resolutions kick in, and so it came as no surprise that I found the WOC more crowded than I've ever seen it before. Probably more tons of iron were pumped and more treadmill loops run today than on any other day of the year. -- Me, I took it fairly easy. I have no resolutions to live up to or to regret falling short on. I'm just trying to work slowly back into my routine after basically taking a couple of weeks off for the holidays. And I must've succeeded in not overdoing it because so far I'm not sore at all. Which of course is all the more reason for celebrating.

Z returned to work today too, but for her the restart didn't last long. She's come down with a sore throat and will take tomorrow off. Aida's sick too, with the flu, and this afternoon Z asked me to do her a big favor: to pick up some prescriptions and drop them off at Aida's. As I'd just spent a couple of hours subbing for Z on her weekly cleaning chores (the ones she can't do owing to her broken arm), I told her this was a bit much. She got the point quickly and said she would pick up the prescriptions herself; in turn I volunteered to stay on at the house an hour later than planned and drive the medicine over to Aida's when Z arrived home. And then when she did arrive home, she felt well enough to go with me for the drop-off. (I stayed in the car while Z took the meds in; we agreed this would improve the odds we wouldn't have to stick around too long. But I must confess I was a bit peeved Aida didn't even wave from her front stoop or tell Z to thank me for being the courier for her medicine. It was typical Aida, though.)

So it's sick time again. I'll probably be next. But I've had a fairly long run of good health vis-a-vis

communicable diseases, as has Z, after both of us
suffered through a bad couple of years for colds, sore
throats, flus, viruses. Probably we've begun to build
up immunity to the new sets of germs each of us has
introduced into the other's life (and especially Z into
mine; for me she was like the explorer from the teeming
industrial country -- that is, the utility offices --
arriving at my little pristine B-2 and 225 backwaters).
-- And will she have to postpone the D&C again because
of her current illness? That's what we're both fearing
now. And that's why she's staying home from work
tomorrow, in hopes of beating the bug before it gains a
firm grip on her. As always she hates the thought of
going into the hospital and doesn't want to have to
think about it any more than necessary. (And likewise
me. And if something is seriously wrong with her, the
sooner the diagnosis the better.)

    -- But actually it still is celebration time, I've
been thinking while noting these other matters. For one
thing we're only at the ninth day of Christmas, with
three more days to go before Epiphany ("Twelfth Night")
with its dozen crazy-ass drummers drumming. And Ramadan
has a few days to run as well, and we're still more than
a month away from Chinese New Year and some eleven weeks
from the true millennium, and almost a month more than
that until the end of the city's official Millennium
Project along with jyze's unofficial yet far more
personally significant TJM curtain-drop. It's a kind of
interregnum here, a time when ordinary life truly does
remain suspended in some ways.

    But will I try to sell my "true millennium" notion
to the city? The idea of municipal closure as the dome
blows? I ran it by Z and she scarcely batted an eye; in
fact I thought if I went on any longer about it she
might bop me over the head with her cast. So I've
decided -- tentatively, for now -- to let the matter
rest. Will something come along to light a fire under
it? I think probably not. I think everyone's had their
fill and then some of millennium ballyhoo. But maybe in
a few weeks that will change. (But I doubt it.)

[+1]

Just inside the door when I arrived home last
night, next to the laundry closet whose light we leave
on when all the others are off, I saw a piece of
notepaper lying on the floor. "Temp 101.6" appeared
on it in Z's shakiest "see, I'm sick and at the same
time my wrist's broken" hand. Then as I sat down to
take off my shoes a croak issued from the darkened
bedroom. "Glllennnnn?"

The woman is sicker than any dog I've ever known
(or no, with the exception of the rabies-maddened one in
Seoul). Cough, sore throat, chills and sweats, nausea.
And the way she talks in that dramatic croak and moans
aloud for minutes at a time in bed make it seem even
worse. But she's actually being quite good -- trying to
show she too can be "stoic," especially given that this
new malady comes on top of the broken wrist -- and she
admits the production of dramatic croaks and groans is
just Z being Z, and also standard for the home she grew
up in. She apologizes a lot for this and says the
apologizing itself is a Catholic thing she also learned
at home. In other words, it's all pure FOO.

She insisted I sleep on the couch in the living
room. "I don't want you to get this too! You need your
sleep!" After a strictly perfunctory show of reluctance
I complied, but regardless didn't rack up a whole lot of
sleep. The construction noise upstairs started about an
hour after I turned off the lights and it went on all
day. Z called for me only once during that time (she's
shaking our good-luck Buddhist "twanger" from the
country fair when she needs me -- thus getting a twofer).

When I rose at two p.m. her temperature was up to
102.9. She uses an automated thermometer that gives an
electronic beep when it's ready for reading. "If I
didn't have you," she groaned, "I don't know what I
would do!" I called Doc Karen's office for her but the
doc herself was out and the nurse in charge never did
call back, despite my twice updating the message. But

by four p.m. Z's temperature had dropped to 101.6, and
shortly after that we heard a report on the news about
the "savage" flu that's going around and this made her
feel better -- good enough to eat a dish of Neapolitan
soy ice cream, her first "solid" food in thirty-six
hours except for a couple of pieces of toast which I
rustled up for her at three a.m. and she, after a
dramatic show of thorough chewing, promptly regurgitated,
thereby inspiring me to change the sheets.

When I arrive home tonight (about an hour from now)
I'll be making -- the deal's already cut -- a grocery
run to the 24/7 east-hill co-op. Juice and soup and
more soy ice cream. The incubation period on this flu
is said to be four or five days, so my phase of biggest
personal danger probably won't come for another couple
of days. It's a big grand-jury week too: more on the
millennium-terror case. I'm just hoping I can hang on
until the weekend.

Of course Z's had to cancel the D&C again. So
that'll be hanging over our heads for at least another
two to three weeks.

Meanwhile the world spins insouciantly on, now
starting to move farther away from the sun again on the
way to next year's Far Out Day (or rather it must be
later this year, since the last one was just slightly
more than six months ago). Today's headlines tell us
the city's dropping charges against 280 more anti-WTO
protesters, meaning only about 35 out of the original
600-plus arrestees still face charges. Two police
organizations, state and county, have called for the
mayor's resignation because of "poor planning" regarding
WTO. A dozen Chinese stowaways have been arrested in
regional ports after being found locked inside standard
shipping containers on a freighter arriving from Hong
Kong (this has been happening at ports up and down the
coast the past week or so). And the volatile stock
market has plummeted 350 points or about three percent
(apparently the squashing of the Y2K bug wasn't such a
big deal after all). -- And I neglected to mention
yesterday was a holiday in many countries and so the

Y2Kalypse doomsayers had still another chance to shout
that the sky would fall, but again today I can say it
just hasn't happened. (So now they're focusing on
February 29 as the next day the computers might rebel in
their human-caused confusion. Ordinarily this wouldn't
be a leap year, coming at the end of a century -- even
though it's four years since the last leap year -- but
the Gregorian calendar declares every fourth year ending
in two zeroes to be an exception and this is the
exceptional year, as I may have mentioned before. It's
the exception to an exception really: in Gregorian
calendrical terms the most unusual year of them all.
The last one of these, apparently, was the year 1600,
although that was just eighteen years after the
inception of the new calendar, so it seems odd a double
exception would occur so soon.)
     Work for me is light this week, and this also is
owing to Y2Kalypse fears: lawyers didn't want to
schedule depositions until next week. A small but
reliable percentage of deponents, they figured, would
fail to show because they were hiding under their beds
or in their bomb shelters until the all-clear sounded.
But the work I do have this week is also a result of
that same kind of fear along with the WTO riots, because
it would appear it was the combination of those two
events that brought the "King of Terror" (alleged) and
his accomplices to our city in the first place.
     And now: home.

[+1]

     Hangin' in there on Twelfth Night. I did spot one
beat-up, tinsel-bestrewn evergreen "swag" lying in the
gutter on the street outside but otherwise who'd know
what day it is. Poor Z just schlepped herself back to
the bedroom. She'd stumbled out half an hour earlier
groaning about being restless and unable to sleep. Was
I sure those two pills I'd given her were sleeping
pills? I was; I even showed her the bottle they came

from, which was still standing open on the kitchen counter, as "proof." A short while later she asked me to make her a peanut-butter-and-jelly sandwich using my bread (it's turned out she dislikes the new kind of spelt bread she bought to try out). I complied, happy to have something to do, because she wasn't talking much. She tried reading tonight's paper, stopping for a while to mutter "I think I'm losing it." But actually it would appear she's a lot better than she was. Last night her temperature spiked to 103.5. Tonight it's back down to a steady 101. "I think maybe I'm hypoglycemic from not being able to eat anything," she announced. She courageously chomped into the sandwich I'd thrown together for her but managed only a few bites. Her right shoulder's hurting too, even worse than the broken (left) wrist is. And she helpfully passed along the information, imparted by a TV "News at Eleven" segment on the flu, that the symptoms are much like those of last year's bug "except it lasts longer."

It's a good thing the grand-jury session I had to scope tonight wasn't too tough or I might've lost it myself by now. Sometimes this "in sickness or in health" business can be brutal. But I'm doing my best not to let the effects show. For one thing, I'm afraid she really would lose it if they did show.

-- Meanwhile, perhaps nudged along by this health crisis at home, I seem to be doing better at reconciling myself to the likelihood that the final two fivers of this Book G will be lacking in the grand themes and high drama of the other fivers already gone by. I can even say this is probably how it oughta be. Once in a while a jyze volume might take on dramatic shape more or less by accident, but in general they should be like life -- petering out just when you'd expect the sturm and drang. Going nowhere in particular, but just keepin' on keepin' on although also from time to time grinding to sporadic inexplicable halts or near-halts.

Today's grand-jury session, by the way, turned out to have nothing to do with the millennium terrorists. It was run-of-the-mill drug and immigration cases --

although it was mentioned that the Chinese stowaways
currently being rousted out of container ships might
come up during the next session. And a front-page story
tells about behind-the-scenes jockeying between U.S.
Attorney's offices here and on the far coast to win the
assignment to prosecute the "King of Terror" case.
(Also on that front page, a report that the cost to the
city of hosting the WTO meeting has risen to nine
million dollars, half again what was planned for; and
the private host organization, which had originally
promised to kick in up to three million of the cost, is
now saying it'll be lucky to come up with a hundred
grand. Presumably that's the big corporate group co-
chaired by J-town plutocrat #1, the world's richest man,
and the chairman of the world's biggest airplane
manufacturer. But of course everyone already knew that
those slick dudes are wholly unreliable.)
     My tax forms for 1999 came in the mail today. The
packet is incomplete, though; it contains only the forms
I filed in previous years as a single man. Now Z and I
both face onerous perplexities as we try to figure out
how to file jointly. (So there's a hot topic for the
rest of Book G. My first quarterly self-employment-
tax prepayment, after all, falls due on the ides of this
month, the very last day of Millennial J. -- Or no,
that's wrong. That's a Saturday, so the due date's the
following Monday -- or probably Tuesday, since Monday's
a holiday, M.L. King Day -- or in other words I'll have
that prepayment as a gangbusters opener for the first
fiver of the presumably even more drama-starved Book H.
But after that, yes, jyze will be back to eighters in
Book I -- that "I" right there is not a Roman numeral --
and all the way through to the grand finale of the
entire TJM project, whatever that might turn out to be.)
     And whither the weather? It's chilly but nowhere
near as cold or wet -- not to mention snowy -- as usual.
Most of our balcony geraniums are in bloom again, just
like the marigolds at Jess's place. So far this is not
at all the severe La Nina winter that was predicted.
     Next a good solid eight hours of sweaty thrashing

on the couch. The noise from the remodel upstairs
continues unabated during daytime hours, in fact with a
bonus: one of the workers has taken to playing a boom
box and occasionally singing along with it. And the
power saw was going for a while this morning.

    This chapter started with a potential apocalypse, a
Big Bang for our time, and ends like this, with whines
and whimpers. -- But actually things are not bad at all
on the personal level as long as Z recovers from the flu
and nothing too terrible is found when she finally goes
under the knife. It's not a matter of "one damn thing
after another," it's more like "one damn fine thing
after another" -- but with an occasional temporary
setback just to keep us on our toes. Knock on wood.
Quaff some blackberry wine too. (It's the most
soporific drink I know of, much like cough syrup.)

34

    The bare minimum and no more, or not much more.
The wrong place, the wrong time. The scope-office
conference room, Thursday night, already it's past two
a.m. and here I am with many pages still to scope in a
dep that's referring to stacks of documents for quotes
that must be checked or filled in, jumping around
without specifying exactly where things are going --
"Here on page 1 you say da da da but over here, three
lines up from the bottom, starting with 'Grantor
agrees,' you say blah blah blah" -- on and on like this.
    And on Twelfth Night. Feast of the Epiphany!
    I'm way behind schedule because I had to run
some errands for Z, and the medicine -- herbal stuff
from Lorraine stashed in a desk drawer on her front

porch in a spooky part of eastern east hill with the
wind whooing in the trees -- the medicine wasn't ready
until seven p.m. The Z-mobile is parked on the street
down around the corner so I can stay here as late as
necessary, and that might turn out to be pretty damn
late, except I'm worn to a frazzle from losing too much
sleep owing to those damn hammers and power saws and
boom boxes and singing carpenters upstairs. -- If ever
there was a prime candidate for the flu, I'm it.

Z's doing better, though. Her fever's dropped
below a hundred and she's back to provocative teasing
and mock flattery and occasional goosing and groping,
meaning her hormones are pumping again. Then too I
wouldn't be surprised to see some of those herbal
potions from Lorraine knock her flat on her back again.
But the hope is she'll at least be strong enough to
start some reciprocal catering to me when the same bug
takes me down, most likely in the next day or two.

Computer humming away a few feet to my left.
Janitor passed through on his final quick-check round --
it's the short Latino guy with the high voice, very
friendly, a voracious reader, always has newspapers and
a paperback or two tucked into his cart -- and now,
already, I have the office, the floor, probably the
whole damn building all to myself. It's like the old
days when I was working graveyard every night. And in
those days this would've been the time for my magic-
carpet nap, hidden from view on the rug behind the
conference table (just in case security entered the
office during its three-thirty a.m. round). I could go
for one of those refreshers right now. But better not.
Z-wiff might be worrying about me. And she might be
counting on me to make her some soup or something.

I've been impressed, though, with how undemanding
she's become. She's wrestling with her FOOs, not
wanting to impose on me too much. At times she loses it
briefly but then she pulls herself back together. She's
still too weak to shower or take a bath and she barely
touches the food I make for her or bring to her --
chicken soup, cereal, chili, toast, soy Neapolitan ice

cream, frozen waffle with maple syrup, peanut-butter-
and-jelly sandwich, Chinese takeout. She has no fresh
whodunits to read and lacks the mental energy to tackle
anything too serious. TV's okay for a while but then
suddenly it's giving her the screaming meemies with its
nonstop hard-sell inanity and banality. Mostly she just
lies in bed with glazed eyes. Usually in her red
bathrobe. And almost always wearing the blue hula hoop
because her shoulder/back/hip are hurting too, at least
in part from all the enforced inactivity. And the cast
is bothering her, becoming itchier and stinkier by the
day. And she's starved for company and I arrive home
and I have all these things I should be doing and she's
worried she's sabotaging my jyze project and maybe I'm a
little less attentive than I oughta be and suddenly
she's weeping -- but it turns out it's because she's
just heard a poem read on public radio by a woman who's
lost her husband. "I want to be the first to die!" Z
wails. "Please, please, don't die before me!"
     And that's it, the limit for tonight. I've reached
it. And the whole time chawing on a mouthful of dried
apricots. (The latest scoop is that fruit does nothing
to prevent cancer, and especially not prostate cancer;
veggies are the magic bullet, and particularly
cruciferous veggies, the very ones I like least and eat
least: cauliflower and brussels sprouts and cabbage. So
it is I'm again suddenly feeling a lot less healthy than
I was, especially for the few months back there when it
appeared blueberries were the magic bullet; and I was
also on a high in earlier periods during the tomato,
fish, and beta carotene crazes. -- But any or all of
these could reverse again at any time. And probably
what really counts is a good overall diet without too
much fat, and on that score I do fairly well. But I'm
still way short on vegetables. I drink lots of veggie
juice and get some lettuce and tomatoes, green peas,
broccoli sprouts in capsules and daily green supplements
-- though many researchers believe these capsules and
pills do little or no good other than making for "very
expensive urine." -- Ach, never mind, all of a sudden

[Millennial J]

I'm obsessed with health? More like it's a matter of
procrastination I'd say. Back to work!)

                        [+3]

     After giving the matter some intense thought I
decided I'd better take it easy for a while -- on the
jyze front, I mean. That's why the three days off.
     I feared if I kept driving myself so hard when I
had so much else to do I'd fall sick for sure and then I
wouldn't be able to do any jyzing anyway. Better to
give it a rest for a while in the hopes I'd be able to
take better care of myself as a result and thus avoid
true illishness. In other words, better to take a break
from jyze and be well during it than to take a break
from jyze and be sick during it.
     So far so good. Z-wiff thinks I might be out of
the woods; I'm not so sure. Nowhere have I seen it
stated with any real confidence what the incubation
period on this abominable flu is. But as of now, Sunday
night, no symptoms for me. And Z herself is feeling
much better. Today her temp's back to normal and we
even made a run to the natural-food chain store (though
we used only one cart instead of the usual two -- she
wasn't feeling strong enough to push her own). She's
also still struggling with a nasty cough, and because of
that she's insisting I continue sleeping on the couch
for a couple more days, and I'm planning to do just that.
If all goes well she'll try returning to work on Tuesday,
but only for half a day at the start.
     Meanwhile I'm thinking I'll jyze only once or twice
more this week (Gregorian week, that is). Even if the
flu weren't going around and Z didn't require lots of
help because of her broken wrist I'd probably still be
needing a break. Starting back in July or early August
it's been nonstop crisis for six straight months, one
big story after another. And even before July there was
plenty of turbulence that now, however, although only in
retrospect and relatively, seems minor. In any case I

need a little R&R before launching into the final
quarter of this TJM project. Hopefully events will
permit me to cut back to a less frenzied pace.
-- Though I'm not forgetting for a moment that the dome
implosion and the true millennium are still to come, and
these will be preceded by the high-stress February-March
period of birthdays and anniversaries. And of course
for morbid thrills there's the cast removal and Z's D&C.
     Meanwhile I've already been missing some
interesting occasions. Friday was Christmas Day for the
main branches of Orthodox Christianity and Saturday
marked the end of Ramadan. All week playoff fever was
building and today our gridders made their final stand
in the dome. Because they lost, it'll be the last game
ever played there and the implosion will reportedly go
ahead as planned at the end of March or possibly early
in April. Those who believe the city's reputation took
a terrible hit during the WTO protests and then over the
cancellation of the millennium bash were hoping our lads
would restore some civic pride by beating the bejeezus
out of the hated far-coast bullies they played today.
Guess they'll just have to keep suffering, the poor
deprived machoites and ball-game-Babbitts (not that I
fail to show symptoms of both of these maladies myself
under certain kinds of enticement).
     Yesterday we cut the strings holding our wreath in
place on the outside of the 203 entrance door. Today we
noticed the star had disappeared from the top of the DC
castle. Here and there in the hood a few decorations
are still hanging on, looking with each passing day,
just as one would expect, more bedraggled and forlorn --
but none more so than the clusters of red lights still
dangling from the pergola in the HQ triangle.
     This morning Z-wiff noticed the sun was shining in
on me as I slept on the couch. She tried to protect me
by planting an umbrella over my head, and then was so
struck by how innocent my sleeping face appeared -- and
it's true, I slept through the whole thing -- that she
wrote a poem about it. To read it in her pathetic shaky
cast-impaired hand was enough to make me vow never ever

again to be impatient with her. -- But soon she was
back in more normal form, venting some feistinesses
she'd suppressed during the flu period (to name just two
of many, she thinks I've been poking too much fun about
her herbs and her whodunits) and suddenly I no longer
felt I should remain so abjectly subservient.

A few more quick notes and then jyze won't return
until maybe Tuesday, Wednesday, even Thursday. Wei and
Alison are off to Mexico (their travels never cease and
I never cease to react to this fact by thinking I'm sure
glad Z doesn't want to live that way). Betty is
reporting that Manny's brother Reuben wants to take Kat
back east for a week next summer (and Z and I both have
serious doubts about this, and in addition I'm in
mourning because I've pretty much lost Kat to this man;
no longer can there be any doubt I've fallen from the
top spot on her surrogate-uncle list). And I've opened
the very last of my boxes of honeymoon cornflakes. Life
just keeps rolling right along, occasionally tossing up
crispy little flakes of nostalgia which, however, soon
go soggy in the two-percent milk of contemplation.
-- But no, I don't really mean that, because there are
always new supplies of cornflakes out there (so far).

As for the millennium -- the "official" one -- and
the Y2Kalypse and all that, it's pretty much ancient
history already. The media, just like this jyze, are
casting frantically about for new material. The cost to
the city and other local agencies of the WTO fiasco (as
the corporate boosters see it) is now supposedly up to
fifteen million dollars, but the mayor nonetheless
appears to be weathering the storm. The stock of our
south-hill dot-com is down a bit, that of the local
software behemoth up a bit, those of the local
aerospace/"defense" megacorp and the local coffee
colossus up quite a bit. We've still heard nothing more
about a rent increase or condoization at 1511. The
remotely operated opener for the garage door is still
broken. Jess is still resisting Gwen's pleas for
reconciliation. Mama E is still sending me tabloid
clips and she's also thanking me for taking such good

care of her daughter (and still not saying anything
about moving out here). We've heard of no change in Mr.
D.'s condition. The flu is everywhere. -- And I'm now
playing hookey from jyze, as of this moment.

                         35

     A brief break from the break to say that the break
(the nonjyzing one, or rather the one from jyze rather
than the one back into it) -- the break is going well.
Z returned to work today, Tuesday, beginning as planned
with a half day. I'm still, as far as I know, bug-free,
as are most of the Y2K computers, including mine.
Snow's in the forecast, though so far only for outlying
and higher-altitude regions. The new landlady has
called, leaving a message saying she's too busy to send
out the new rental agreements this month and we can pay
up the increased deposit at the rate of $200 a month.
As of last night I'm back to sleeping in our bed. Today
a dot-com outfit bought up one of the major old-line
media companies in the biggest corporate merger in
history, proving that the internet economy is truly for
real and that it won't halt -- in fact, will intensify
-- the giganticizing of corporate control of the media
(or really, let's face it, corporate control of just
about everything). And I still haven't found my missing
"Jyze" pendant -- but it must be around somewhere.

                        [+4]

     Here's how the break breaks off for good at the far
border of the fiver. It begins happening under a new

lamp at an unfamiliar end of the couch at ten minutes
before six a.m. I just assembled the lamp while
sprawled on the rug, reminding myself of the time about
five years ago now (give or take a few weeks) when I
assembled the very similar lamp that's hanging above the
black armchair right in front of me, about three feet
away -- and that one's a twin of the one that hangs over
my brown armchair at the hideaway, and those two came
into full operational form within days of each other.
And all three are brass floor lamps with fold-out arms
at the top. -- This new one, we bought it so Z can sit
at this end of the couch, by the door to the balcony,
and we can be closer together while reading, our feet
stretched out on the low wooden table, toes interlaced
as is only appropriate for the red-hot Freakin' Fookin'
Fogeys we're almost ready to return to being.

    It's been a crazy week. Z worked only half days,
returning home each day at noon. Friday, which is to
say yesterday by NUT time, her back went out again while
she was sitting on a stool at the coffee shop where she
often takes morning breaks. When I woke up that
afternoon I found her stretched out on our living-room
carpet. "I'm falling to pieces," she groaned. "They
should just take me out and shoot me." Earlier today
her back was much better but some of her flu symptoms
had returned and we had to cancel tonight's plans to
attend Dak and Sera's party for Mark and Ben, who are in
town for the weekend. (These are the husband and nine-
year-old son of the deceased Julie K., another charter
member of the Asiusan women's group.) But then around
five-thirty Z felt better and we drove down to the HQ
for dinner -- big burgers at the best of the blues clubs
-- and to pick up some books and magazines at the ORB.
-- What wore her out earlier today, I should mention,
and no doubt helped to bring back the symptoms, was an
energetic blowjob she performed in waking me up.

    I'm taking a lot of grief for continuing to be
healthy through all this. It's a mystery why I've
failed to come down with anything. My newest theory is
that my long stays in the whirlpool at the WOC are

having the same effect as a very high fever, killing off
the bugs.

   The other morning the hills across the lake were
strikingly snow-covered, visible out the window behind
me now. But I never saw any flakes here and today
another warming trend is setting in. The weather
honchos are declaring themselves mystified: what's
happened to the vaunted La Nina effect? Are the new
patterns caused by global roasting already strong enough
to offset La Nina? Is El Nino coming back so soon?
(Another long news story has appeared confirming that
climate breakdown is a fact. Even a few of the die-hard
skeptics are admitting it now. Which is not to say
they're ready to try to do something about it.)

   And one night I flicked the toilet handle in the
big bathroom a bit too emphatically and broke it off.
The whole flush arm inside the tank would have to be
replaced, at a cost of $4.99. (If we'd bought the same
brand that broke, it would've been $1.99; if we'd gone
for top of the line, it would've been $29.99.) My fix-
up task for tomorrow is installing the new mechanism.
(We could've asked the landlord to do it but we don't
want him or his wife coming in here if we can help it --
and Z's in full agreement on this now, unlike earlier in
our 203 stay when she wanted to call in the landlord to
fix every little broken thing. She's readjusting to the
working-class level of existence she grew up in and said
she was hoping to find embodied in a man before she met
me. And guess what: I'm doing better than she ever
dreamed possible at meeting her ideal. (Yes, she told
me this herself.)) -- Meanwhile we've kept the lid off
the toilet tank so we can easily pull the chain or the
flushball itself by hand. And we're continuing to turn
the knob on the shower with a Phillips screwdriver, as
we've been doing for more than a week now, after my
original rubber-band fix proved to be too flimsy.

   -- And here she is. "You're late, LOML," says she.
"You're way late. You're being very bad." -- But it's
okay. I was about done anyway. And I can show off the
new lamp, assembled by my own proudly ink-stained hands.

BOOK H

[Jyze Reboot]

36

Stormy night. Out I come pinwheeling but not in the usual way. By Z-mobile! On a mission! But first a stop at the scope office for finals work and now at our primo local burger chain's north-pole outlet for the good greasy stuff; and then after this, on the way home, another stop at the east-hill co-op to pick up some items Z's wanting and in one case avowedly craving (and I believe her).

I was pretty sure but not certain this joint would still be open at half past ten. That shows how far I've drifted away from my pre-Z life. When I pulled up outside, the interior looked dark and the visible part of the seating section was entirely empty. "I don't believe it!" I cried out loud, startling myself. -- But they were just in a slow period. Now the movie theater across the street's let out and the place is packed. Or half full actually as far as the seating goes, but the lines are long, with four registers open (of five). And glary headlights keep distracting me. These come from two directions, the parking lot and the street, leaving me nowhere to turn to get away from them.

All day gusts were rattling unit 203 -- roiling the trees and thwacking the power line against the side of the house. The bridge across the lake to the east was closed and power was reported to be down in several outlying areas. But it's a warm storm, an overwrought pineapple express.

Z awakened me at around nine a.m. "I found a pimple on my heinie. I know it probably won't do any good this long after but I'd like you to wash Poosh

anyway." "Sure, okay. I'll do it." She had a
washcloth all prepared. I threw off the covers and
rolled over onto my back and scrubbed/fondled as she
gazed in rapt wonder at my naked assets. "I'm sorry,"
she said. "I'm sorry too." "No, I mean really."
"Please don't be saying that -- you know it's not your
fault. It makes me feel like you think I really do
think it's your fault." -- We go through a version of
this dialogue just about every damn time she fears an H-
outbreak is imminent.

     Poor Z. The ills just keep piling on. Earlier
we'd horsed around a bit -- and she'd gotten off more
than a bit via hand (mine) after Poosh (we've pretty
much dropped the "kin" now, yes) had done a classic slow
deflate -- but this had the delayed effect of tiring her
out so much she had to cancel our moviegoing plans for a
second straight day. Mark offered to drop by our place
with son Ben but she nixed that too. Then around six
her energy level started rising again.

      This was supposed to be our weekend for "reviewing"
her financial situation. Probably it won't happen now.
But I did assemble the lamp and fix the toilet. "My
baby is a real man! He does real-man things!"
(Excepting, alas, today's humping. And I'll admit the
foozle brought back a traumatic memory or two from our
courtship era. But she was very understanding about it.
"We haven't done it for so long because I was sick.
Poosh figures he might as well go south and hit the
beach." -- But I've been loving her up "plan B" style
at least once a day, with or without penile consummation.
And now she's vowing to jack me off more so I don't go
rusty during the down times. But being as she's still
one-handed -- and that hand being her off hand, her
right -- it might not be so easy. It's the two-handers
I really go for, and of course even more so with lips
and tongue as accompaniments.)
      Meanwhile this is looking to be a fine week for
climbing back into the jyze saddle. At the front end
we've got the M.L. King holiday -- it's tomorrow,
although the man's actual birthday was yesterday -- and

at the end what's being billed as a spectacular total
eclipse of the moon. Just two nights ago I caught a
glimpse of the moon for the first time in the new year/
decade/century/millennium -- DYCM, right (I could've
saved myself ten seconds there if I'd remembered the
acronym in time). Now this first moon of the DYCM will
blot itself out -- a wink to celebrate its specialness.

Ahead is the TJM stretch run. As of today just one
more J-book to go after this one until the true
millennium and then the end. "The end is near."

Meanwhile the ongoing stories keep playing
themselves out or at least onward. The news is full of
horrific tales of the suffering of "undocumented"
Chinese immigrants trying to sneak into the country
while hidden inside containers on cargo ships. The
world's richest man has turned over the reins of our
local software behemoth to an underling so he, the primo
plutocrat of them all, can concentrate on software
design, or so he says. The investigation into the
alleged millennium terrorist's alleged bombing attempt
on the flying-saucer icon continues. The letters pages
are still full of rants about WTO and the mayor and,
especially, the police. Market analysts are predicting
a big shakeout in dot-com stocks. The U.S. economy is
only weeks away from achieving the longest "peacetime"
expansion ever. Chinese New Year is three weeks from
yesterday.

I don't have much to report about the circle of
friends. Well, a few things. Kat's "uncle" Nick has
decided to move to the northern quadrant of the far
coast, in a sense ending his nearly three-year-long
period of mourning over his wife's -- Manny's daughter's
-- death. Jess is visiting an old friend in my city
No. 11 thirteen hundred miles to the southeast, where
Lady U and I first met and lived together for almost two
years before moving here. Olwen is reading her poetry
tomorrow night at a mall bookstore out in the Yuke and
I'll be attending, although the less than fully
convalesced Z probably won't. Leola is visiting the
next big city to the north (in Canada) where the storm

[The Jyze Millennium, Part II]

is having even wilder effects (and when she decided to
go up there on her own with a friend, Gerry asked if
she'd mind if he went skiing on his own -- better put
that in quotes, "on his own" -- and she okayed it!).
Leola invited us to join her and Gerry at a jazz club
next month but the tickets are sixty-five bucks apiece
(and yet we might do it anyway because Z feels she still
owes Leola for her many exertions around our wedding).
      This week Z will try to return to work full time.
The big issues of the recycling campaign and the hate
mail still remain to be dealt with, but the brouhahas
stirred up by both have died down quite a bit.
Bombshell Gloria has broken up with her out-of-state
fiance Bud (citing as the reason her inability to deal
any longer with his hormone-saturated thirteen-year-old
son) but Z sees no sign of sadness or mourning and
predicts Gloria will find someone new within a week or
two. ("She's always up to her neck in men chasing after
her -- almost reminds me of myself back in the day" --
and I ask: is she maybe thinking of like the day before
yesterday?) If Z feels well enough she'll go ahead and
reschedule the D&C, probably for sometime early in
February. In theory, at least, my period of maximum
caretaking should start easing back at the end of this
week when her cast comes off. No doubt other such
periods lie ahead for both of us. This has been a kind
of dry run for the fogey era of our future decades.
(Does having her as a lover and companion make all the
trouble worthwhile? Absolutely! -- But I wouldn't want
to imply that means I enjoy every second of it, any more
than she does when I'm the invalid. We've long ago
gotten real about this kind of thing. And even so,
three or four ailments piled on top of each other can,
as in the past few months, exact a heavy toll.)
      Midnight coming on. Time to wad up my greasy bags
and napkins and drain the last drops of soda from the
cup and move on. (The scurvy old Cawk street dude who
was sitting in the corner booth this whole time just
staggered off lugging a beat-up white suitcase that
looks just like one I used to have. And by the way:

740

this guy's been hanging out here preying on fast-fooders
for years. Not a bad scam, I guess. Personally,
though, I'll admit I long ago lost all patience with
him. For some reason he's nonstop prickly about pretty
much everything.)

[+1]

    So now to struggle against that feeling of jyzerly
futility. (It may vanish with the first stroke of the
J-stick. Or the hundredth. Or it may deepen. Or it
may become troublingly elusive in its meaning and its
effects. I'd even say it already has -- both of those.)
    A few feet from the spot where I sit, Olwen read
her poems. That was an hour ago, more or less. I was
moved: by the beauty of her words, by their thoughtful
and sensuous content, by her fine speaking voice. I
cradled my chin in my palms and made ear trumpets of my
hands and closed my eyes much of the time so I could
concentrate on the flow of the words. It wasn't always
easy to hear her, in part because she wasn't familiar
with that particular kind of hand-held mike. It worked
best when she tipped it up at a forty-five-degree angle
just millimeters in front of her lips, but she found
that position, as she said -- sparking a good laugh
which she then joined, in what I thought a very winning
way -- "awkwardly intimate."
    I liked listening to her and felt I knew her better
as I did so -- feel that now. But I still maintain my
longstanding gripe against readings. You miss too much.
You can't linger over a meaning or go back to pick up
something crucial that slid past you. It's more like a
game you're playing in solitary fashion, say for example
pinball. Concentrate on superficial word movements, try
to keep the meaning in play and regardless you're
eventually going to lose it. Flip it toward targets
with high scores (symbolism, memory) and avoid all traps
and side-exits (irrelevant thoughts, the cough in the
next row).

741

    Olwen's older brother, Carey, also attended, a tall
graying man, outdoorsy looking, wearing a blue quilted
down jacket which he never did take off, and I met him.
But I couldn't remember what she'd told me about him,
other than the general impression -- perhaps wrong --
that he was some sort of engineer and very conservative,
though in recent years he'd made an effort to be more
accepting of her radic-lib and woo-woo views. (After
the reading, when Olwen was telling someone that her
Sufi group isn't really Muslim -- which makes it a
highly unusual Sufi group, I'd say -- Carey joked, "You
mean we don't have to look for bombs in their cars?"
"Frees us up to go after our homegrown militias," I
should've said, but what if he was packing heat?)
-- Even so I felt for him as he stood nearby listening
to his only sister read poems about the childhood and
teen years they shared, about fishing and swimming in
the mountains in the eastern part of the state, and also
a very personal one (not involving him) about lovemaking.
How much of it was getting through to him? What was he
thinking? (I didn't consciously come up with this at
the time, but I suppose I might've been projecting
myself into his shoes, with Olwen standing in for my own
sister who also writes poetry. In her mixture of
earthiness and refinement Olwen has always reminded me a
little of Barb.)
    She had to leave shortly afterwards because the
chemical-laden institutional air was bothering her.
Olwen in a green turtleneck and a floppy gray beret
gliding down the escalator and waving back to us. I
followed moments later but after buying a book for Z (at
her request) I've now returned to the scene of the
reading. It's a cozy corner, relatively speaking, with
a big fireplace and a wooden floor maybe fifteen by
thirty feet, and clustered around it are a dozen
armchairs (fully occupied all the way through the
reading by students apparently doing classwork, no doubt
mostly from the U) and a couple of square black wooden
tables, at one of which I sat then and am again sitting
now. This area is separated from the rest of the huge

second floor only by low partitional bookcases.

Years ago I bought a couple of pairs of pants in this building when it housed an outlet of a now-defunct department store. Since then the mall as a whole has remade itself, mostly in the past two or three years, upscaling significantly. Now it's even more burbanly ritzy and I feel even more uncomfortable here than I used to. -- But then again this bookstore is a little easier to take now than it was when it first opened a few years ago. It's weathered a bit. It doesn't seem at all uptight about the scores of students using the place as a library or a hangout cafe -- or even about the older near-derelict types like myself who can be spotted here and there (though I'm sure if our numbers increased a bit as a regular matter the store's laissez-faire policy would change quickly). A good half of the poetry audience, incidentally, looked as out of place and uncomfortable with the idea of finding themselves at a reading in this mall-like setting as I was. And am. (Not mall-"like." It is a mall. But nowadays malls are being talked about as yesteryear's fad. They're not virtual, see; they're "brick and mortar." And because they're tainted with obsolescence, perhaps they're gaining -- in an effort to survive -- a little soul. They're suffering. You can feel for them. Or almost.)

And today's a holiday, though perhaps the least holidaylike of major USAn holidays: M.L. King Day. In the eyes of many Eurusans it's either not a legitimate holiday or it's just not something they're used to yet. It's the day when a large number of Eurusans defer, often quite grudgingly, to the need of a smaller number of Eurusans to pretend they really care about race relations, while a still smaller number actually do celebrate racial diversity on this day. And yes, I'm one of the ones celebrating; I'm even wearing my "Celebrate" pendant and a rainbow-star button. But then again I'm also skeptical about this country's reception of the holiday. And I'll just mention that of the hundreds of faces I've seen in here today only one was Afrusan, and not too surprisingly that person was

743

working a cash register. (Though now I see another, a cornrowed student walking along with a heavy bookbag.)

     Zoelie B., for instance, takes this holiday very seriously. She's focusing on books by Afrusan authors (I just bought "Paradise" for her). That sort of thing is a bit much for me. It's almost like shouting out, "I don't really care about this matter the other fifty-one weeks of the year." (Yet that's not the case with Z. She cares consistently and acts on it -- as much as or more than anyone I've ever known. It's one of the many ways she both touches and impresses me.)

     But enough of this out-of-control praise. What a dweeb I'm sounding like. Mr. Earnest here! And I've got places to go (work) and things to do (work). And for the second night in a row I'm driving the Z-mobile and I'll be parking it downtown. This makes me uncomfortable too, relying on private wheels, even if they're my own wife's and I help pay for them. I must be afraid I'll go soft or something. Gotta keep walking, gotta hold to the love-my-way-of-life way of living. (Well, as much as I can.) (Can't stop myself with this over-the-top stuff! So shut it down already!)

[+2]

     -- A crew of some two dozen was working on the tracks down below street level near the entrance to the downtown tunnel -- lots of noise and glary lights, workers bundled up against the cold, then clapping their hands and jumping in place off to the side to keep warm as a very long container train rolled through -- so now I've stopped by at the west depot to check it all out. But I can't tell much. The doors to the loading area are locked and only one person's around, a janitor with a rather hostile look.

     The board says six of today's seven arrivals are "OT," meaning not overtime, as in sports, or over time, but on time. Only the continental that passes through Mentoka was late, by three hours, coming in at noon.

744

[Jyze Reboot]

     Meanwhile the moon's doing a warm-up for tomorrow
evening's eclipse, rising bright and full and fetchingly
blurry through a fine mist. I walked alongside a
Natusan man while crossing the bridge, admiring the
moon, but he was too caught up in yammering about a
friend he'd been riding with to reveal anything about
himself, such as his tribe, his story, its story. In a
front-page headline tonight's paper laments "Clouds May
Spoil Moon's Big Show" ("NSDT," Z would say, "in this
city in winter?"). (Once again that's Dick Tracy she's
addressing there.)
     I did a good card for her this afternoon. I'm
still chortling over it. It's too complicated to
describe in detail, but it has to do with a "Sleepless
on South Hill" scene she threw at four a.m. last night.
Tani, her masseuse -- city insurance pays for her
services (but only six sessions per year) -- suggested
to Z that the string of misfortunes she's been suffering
through since our wedding might be related to her
feeling "ungrounded." (First Tani had asked if she was
unhappy with the marriage and Z said, according to what
she told me, "Oh no, it's not that, I'm very happy with
it" -- and when I said, "You're making that up just so
I'll doubt the whole story," she assured me in somewhat
mocking tones that oh no, she really did say it.)
Anyway: being highly suggestible, Z had merely taken
Tani's theory and run with it. The mygs are flying
again! And when she found herself unable to sleep (it's
almost always related to planning for work, she thinks)
the thought struck her that things would keep going
badly until we could come up with a secure housing plan.
We need to know right now what the new owners will be
doing with the building. We need a backup plan in case
we're unable to stay on in unit 203.
     I admit I didn't take very well to all this
fretting. We'd already agreed on a plan -- hang on and
hope, make no waves -- and I was trying to get some
important backed-up reading done. It was as if she had
to come up with something to fill her worry quotient.
She, meanwhile, thought I was being "cranky." The kind

745

of secure plan she wanted was unavailable to us, I said,
so why worry about it. We're victims, sure, but let's
not make things worse by panicking. We're a lot more
fortunate than most people, etc. etc. And we're
certainly not short on other things to worry about.
Insofar as possible I want to devote my energies to
jyzing and loving and not to worrying. How much time
are we allotted on this earth? Let's try to minimize
the portion of it we burn up in worrying.

        She was a little placated and went back to bed.
Ten minutes later she reappeared and said she'd come up
with a plan. She would ask Betty to let her have a
"tiny plot" in her garden, just a square foot or so,
where she could grow something. That way she would feel
more grounded.

        Great! Go for it! (Except she'll soon be worrying
she's not watering the thing properly. What, our
schedule's not tight enough already without trying to
work in regular trips over to Betty's for gardening
purposes? -- But the idea of growing something of her
own in authentic grounded soil did seem to make her feel
better. It all comes back to Mother Earth! -- But what
she'd really, really like, she's already made clear, is
a much more concrete backup plan: if we had to move out
we could move in with June, something like that.)

        So quiet here. Did the crew leave? It's the same
old nondescript depot, though, a sad shadow of its
former High Railroad Era self. (And earlier I heard my
old ferry-riding friend Tom T.'s name mentioned at the
desk, except they called him Henry, his real name --
same as Taj. I guess Tom's still dispatching from the
new headquarters in the southwestland.)

        It's warm here. Why my lingering presence is
tolerated on this particular day I don't know. The fact
that I'm jyzing sometimes makes them pause a second --
maybe he isn't a bum, maybe he's a traveler arriving
early, one of those weird Eurotrash types with a
national pass, something like that. In fact in all my
years of visits here I've never been seriously hassled
by security, other than the several times they've told

me to move on because the place was closing early.

One other news tidbit. Z and I have pretty much decided to forgo a true-millennium blowout, meaning one to which we'd invite a big crowd. Better, we agree, to make it an intimate affair. Especially since the date coincides with our six-month wedding anniversary. (The one-year anniversary of our "wedding before the gods" is coming up next week and I think she's totally forgotten about it. She mentioned she has plans for that night: Aida asked her to come see Charles perform in his school orchestra. So I'll keep quiet about it in advance and just give her a card on the day itself and then blow her away with lots of loving recompense.)

-- Time's short. This is my heavy week and I need to pick up a pound of coffee on the way in. (Another train's rolling through. Screeches, thumps. Feels kind of important, this place, in a regular everyday way: keeps things moving right along. No better place for jyzin' than a railroad depot during the slow hours.)

[+1]

Yup, the clouds have it. I'm hunkered down on the couch fifteen minutes before eclipse time and I'm gazing out into the misty darkness to the east and seeing not even a faint sign of the main player. (I must've sounded downright fanatical about taking in this show. Z suggested I could drive to the other side of the mountains where clear skies are forecast. But I had resolved to see it only if it was here, casting its blush-red moonshine over J. City.)

I can be holed up in unit 203 doing this now because it's girls' night out for Z. Tonight the gang's gathering at the pub across the street from my old B-2 digs, the same joint where Z and I grabbed dinner before our very first "horseplay" scene in the loft. But I've got to get going soon: grand jury is indeed heavy this week, mainly because it's finally taking up the case of the Chinese stowaways. Stride on in fast through a cold

drizzle (I can see the myriad droplets angling down in
the aura around the half-moon-shaped streetlight --
particles swarming as on the inside of a closed eyelid).

   -- And tomorrow Z goes in to have her cast removed.
In some ways I'll miss the old purple clunker. Also the
struggles to help her on with her coat or her "shower
protector" and especially toweling her off after the
shower. And the scrape and bulk on my flank where she
rests it, or did, while spooning from behind in bed.

   One last glance. Nope, nothin' but those same
swarmings. But I'll keep my eyes out for any cloud-
break cameos the orb might make over the next few hours.

                    *   *

   -- Now five a.m. And I can report I caught two
quick glimpses of the moon in eclipse, but the veiling
effect of the mist was so great I could barely tell
anything was different. And even then I thought I might
just be imagining the slight orangish hue I thought I
was seeing, perhaps. I did finally get a considerably
less obscured view -- straight overhead -- when I hopped
off the bus atop the hill at a few minutes past one-
thirty a.m., but by then the phenomenon was over.

   The other developments, such as they are -- and
actually there are a couple of some interest -- I'll
save until tomorrow. Right now I'm brain-fried-
exhausted and I still have a bunch of cleanup work to do
around here. So let this J-week be over.

                     37

   The grumpiness is upon me. Came grinding out of
the house at four p.m. without benefit of coffee-stoking
or cereal-fueling (just toast!) and trudged across the

high bridge, through the AQ, past the north sides of the
two depots, into the HQ and onward to the ORB cafe for
a quick cup of java and a grouchy jyze strokedown.

Along the way I observed layered clouds dominating
the sweeping high-bridge vista, with a slot opening up
showing rugged western peaks seemingly transported much
closer than usual by the clear cold air. I saw a
Chinese-looking man emerge from the Chinese Christian
church in the upper AQ to chew out the Cawk homeless man
with the hugely overloaded grocery-cart who's again been
pitching camp on the front stoop of the foodbank next
door (though I suspect this cart man is not actually
homeless -- I've seen him pushing his massive load into
the subsidized-housing area behind the Natusan center in
the late evening). From street level near the west
depot I watched a southbound continental train pull out
down below, standing (me) near a ragged Cawk man with a
huge backpack and several black trash sacks arrayed
around him like sandbags protecting an artillery
emplacement. I saw lots of urban sights. I thought
about the mystery of how they all hang together in their
boggling complexity and ultimate human imponderability.

I left the house before Z returned with her
liberated arm. It would've been a kick to be present
late this morning at the doc's office for the cracking
of the cast, the hatching of the reborn or at least
reknit limb. A kick if not an elbow poke, that is. But
-- I'm too uptight right now to deal with a big upheaval
in my sleep schedule. I'm facing hundreds of pages of
scoping today, including a rush job that must go out in
final form first thing Monday morning (it's Friday now).
And most of those pages involve the two high-profile
cases the grand jury is currently grappling with: the
Chinese stowaways and the millennium terrorists.
Another indictment regarding these latter, based on the
testimony I'll be scoping tonight, has already been
handed down and drawn a screaming five-column front-page
hed in this morning's J. City paper: "INDICTMENT DETAILS
BOMB CONSPIRACY." I'm carrying a copy of that article
in my bag right now in hopes it will help with spellings

and any garbled transcription.

     And one of the interesting little stories I
mentioned last night has to do with the Chinese
stowaways. Halfway through the night's scoping the
printer broke down, causing me to lose big chunks of
time and also fomenting all sorts of chaos as I moved
various items around to get at the machines in hopes I
could make a repair on my own (it turned out I couldn't
-- but Naomi left me a message this morning saying the
day crew called in a repairman and the printer's working
again). Later before leaving I gathered some sheets of
what I thought was scrap paper and took them with me to
dispose of in the street trash can (I do this quite
often so as not to make the janitors look bad by filling
up the trash cans they've just emptied). In the process
of ripping up these pages I noticed with shock that
several had photographs on them. They were grand-jury
exhibits -- photos of the bloated face of one of the
three stowaways who had died en route, who was the
cousin of a voyage survivor who had testified before
the grand jury through an interpreter. I had already
torn these photos into halves and one set of the halves
into quarters before I realized what I was doing.

     These were just standard photocopies but they were
also official numbered grand-jury exhibits, four of them
actually, including one with lots of scribbling on
it in Chinese, accompanied by English translations in
brackets. I'm carrying all the pieces in my bag right
now and I'm planning to tape them together when I reach
the office and leave a note throwing myself on Naomi's
mercy and just hope the feds won't be pounding on my
door tomorrow morning with arrest warrants in hand and
pistols drawn.

     -- And speaking of irony, the other little story is
that Naomi left me a note yesterday, before I mutilated
the exhibits, saying she was unilaterally raising the
page rate for grand jury by fifteen cents, from eighty-
five cents to a dollar even. "Lord knows you deserve
it!" the note says, and goes on to explain she's doing
this even though it appears the feds won't be boosting

their page rate to her on our new grand-jury contract
(though they might sweeten her hourly appearance fee a
bit). What moved her to do it at this particular time
I don't know, other than maybe she was feeling sorry for
me after our phone talk last week about the agonies of
being chronically broke as a newlywed, the effects of
inflation on bottom-feeders like me in this millionaire-
infested city -- and so on. Also, she left me some
promotional literature about a new transcription system
she's thinking of switching to at a cost of some ten
grand and she knows this would force me to move up to a
more powerful computer myself at an expense of maybe
three grand, not counting the many hours or days lost
while learning the new system (all of which would be on
my own dime). And in my note responding to this I said
I'd be willing to do it -- to upgrade -- and hoped this
way we'd be able to keep our collaboration going for a
few more years at the very least (she's often muttering
about switching to another kind of work because of her
slowly worsening case of CTS -- carpal tunnel syndrome).
     This raise -- if she doesn't rescind it after
finding out about the mutilated exhibits -- will amount
to about a hundred bucks a month. It's been five years
since we last boosted my pay rate on GJ and this
increase won't even cover the effect of inflation over
that period, but it'll still help plenty -- give me a
chance to scrape by without resorting to more
withdrawals from the deep reserves. -- And on that
score, I've just about demolished the eight K which Z
borrowed on my behalf last year so I wouldn't have to
deplete those reserves any further. I've set aside
twelve hundred bucks for this year's taxes but that's it
for the cushion. If I do have to go to the well again,
I'm thinking maybe it'd be wiser to take everything out
of the reserves and put it into savings to be sure I'd
have the bulk of it for a condo down payment a year or
two from now, if needed.
     Worries, worries. I'm trying not to let them drag
me down. Z's already firmly established her status as
not only the chief family bacon-bringer but also the

chief family tsuri. (Last night she said people at the
office were surprised when she showed them the "3 Faces
of Z" card about her worry quota: they hadn't even
realized she was a worrier. To most of her office-mates
she seems very confident and aggressive -- or at least
when she's not on one of those infamous strategic crying
jags, I suppose.) -- She was unable to sleep again --
because of the worry mygs buzzing about, of course --
and joined me in the living room and we wound up going
through a thick "plan book" she'd brought home
concerning the city-subsidized lofts development. She'd
obtained it from Leola, whose office for some reason
sets up one of the many hurdles the project must clear.
The estimated market-level price for a loft (about a
thousand square feet) would be $148,000, or $2,000 less
than what we've set as our upper limit. But those
prices may be outdated already and of course not in the
direction we'd like. Nonetheless we're allowing
ourselves to fantasize a little. -- And the townhouses
in the same development look good too and might cost a
little less since their floor space is about the same
and their ceilings much lower.

    -- So it's a new jyze fiver. Off to a rushed and
shaky start but things are rolling now. And since
nothing major looms this week in the way of engagements
or important occasions like birthdays or anniversaries
I'm thinking this is the week -- finally -- to review
the ever-mounting pile of WTO commentary, among other
things. (And I'm still wavering about whether to buy
the WTO tapes. And I'm again feeling the urge to hatch
some sort of jyze scheme around the true millennium and
the dome implosion. And Z and I have a bit of catching
up to do in bed as she comes off the outbreak-disabled
list. And maybe I'll find myself with a little more
free time now as she starts to slip back into harness on
her domestic chores and the broken-wrist emergency
slowly fades into the past -- though this also means
we'll soon be facing the D&C ordeal again. After
putting it off, if I'm remembering correctly, for two
months now, cumulatively.

[+1]

A few notes from deep in a Saturday night. Way
deep. The black armchair now, but for most of the night
I sat in the green armchair in the bedroom overlooking Z
as she snoozed with her white sleep mask on. A single
lamp glowing. A cup of wine at hand on the shaky
chairside table, a stack of newspapers and magazines to
go through. Paradise almost. If only the jazz station
could've been playing. But Z needs to get back into her
sleep routine. And that's why I was sitting in the
chair -- at her request -- rather than lying next to her
with the reading lamp on. (And the good-night kiss
turned into nipple nookie with her newly uncasted left
hand limply and sort of kinkily holding my aroused male
appendage -- for it's still too soon in the outbreak
cycle for us to indulge in any hardcore action. And
then dozing in each other's arms for a while. All in
all quite a lovely quiet night, and it's left me with
all my juice for future copulative endeavors.)

And all day her arm's been the center of attention
and rightly so. It's like both the mother and her
newborn babe freshly out of the hospital, the big
bloated "pregnant" casted arm having given birth to its
pitifully weak and pink mended offspring, little flakes
of dried skin still clinging to it like afterbirth. Her
arm muscles are atrophied and slack, her wrist wooden,
her fingers incapable of gripping or lifting anything
much heavier than a marshmallow (although she can
scribble by propping the pen in the gap between ring and
index fingers so that it's almost weightless and then
sort of dragging it along).

It'll be a while before she's ready to wash her own
dishes again. Six months maybe? That's her joke
anyway. I told her I'll happily continue doing them
just as long as she'll also let me keep washing her off
in the shower and toweling her dry afterwards. "You've
got yourself a deal, Buster Brown!" she cried.

And meanwhile her cough's much better. This means

she can soon go in to make another D&C appointment (they
bar you from doing so if you have any sort of
respiratory illness). Her stamina's still low, however,
from her bout with the flu and the four-day return to
full-time work, so today we again canceled the movie
outing we'd overoptimistically planned, and we instead
limited ourselves to a relatively short provisioning
run. This included stops for office goods, art supplies,
pharmaceuticals, and groceries. It was my first visit
to this particular art-supply store in about a dozen
years, and though I don't think it's changed much, my
perception of it has: it just can't crack up to the new
arts & crafts superstores. For serious artists this
might not be the case but for rank amateurs such as
myself it's sadly lacking in low-end supplies.
     -- Not that this day was without rough patches.
It's pretty much par for the course that we encounter at
least one of these while spending so many hours in a row
together, and part of what keeps us going is that we
both enjoy extricating ourselves from them. She turns
pushy, I turn grumpy. One or another of our hundred
different ongoing minor disputes or political fracases
kicks up. The sore spots, the disappointed expectations
("You're not going to have a glass of wine with me when
I've been looking forward to it all day?"). At one
point in the bedroom earlier tonight she asked whether
I'd mind if she flipped on the TV to watch the news, if
it would disturb my reading, and I said it was okay with
me, but after a few minutes I found it too distracting
(as I was doing the kind of reading that doesn't lend
itself to involuntary multitask mode) and said I'd go in
the living room until the news was over, and she said
no, she'd turn it off, and did, but she was pouting and
displeased and I said no, really, she should just watch
it and call me back in when it was over, it was no big
deal, but she insisted it was -- and so the solution
this time was that she didn't watch the news and I
didn't read and, strangely enough, we smooched instead
and everything was good again.
     And we both talked with June on the phone for a

while, serially, and this was my first direct contact
with her since the holidays and she reported she was
unhappy with her grades on the papers we'd worked on
together (only one 'A' and that was a minus) but she'd
passed the courses all right, and I filled her in --
sketchily, in deference to my vow of secrecy (which,
through the feds' oversight, I've never actually vowed)
-- on the latest developments in several different
cases which touch her life in one way or another,
including the Chinese stowaways and a businessman of
Taiwanese descent, well known to her personally, who's
being pursued on major tax-evasion charges and has now
absconded to mainland China, and also a pair of third-
year students (Cawk) at her very own law school involved
in a bank-fraud ring.

    -- And I haven't mentioned this before, but in the
past week D'Arcy has offered us the use of her condo
down in a megastate desert resort town as a wedding gift
and I've said to Z I really couldn't afford to do it
this year and reminded her of our pledge to "save money
in aughty-aught," but last night I suggested if she
really wanted to go down there maybe she should do as
she'd forewarned me she'd want to do from time to time
after we got hitched and use this offer as a chance to
steal away on her own or to travel with Aida (as they've
done quite often, averaging once or twice a year, Z
thinks, over the past fifteen years). And to my
surprise -- because I'd brought this up with some
trepidation suspecting she'd seize on it as proof I
don't care as much as I used to or I should -- she said
she liked the idea, though she doubted Aida would be
able to do it. (And so will I grasp at this as proof
that Z doesn't care as much as she used to or she
should? Hell no! -- But I do admit to feeling a tiny
sting.)

    This as the three old-fashioned clocks in here tick
ever onward in an interesting triple near-synchrony,
reminding me of the flags on 32nd notes of the musical
kind, and all now closing in on six o'clock a.m. And we
again have plans for the early afternoon -- early, that

is, from the perspective of my current daily wake-up
call: three p.m. -- and I don't want to be missing too
much sleep in these flu-risky days.

[+2]

   -- A quickie from the hideaway. Not much is new
around here, and for today, tentatively, I'll say that's
good.
   At home Z has requested a "transition week" on the
cleaning and various other chores. I've said sure. And
in general things are much better. For most personal
tasks she no longer needs my help, and her disposition,
now that she can get out and about a bit, is much
sunnier. Yesterday she even told me she realized she'd
feel imposed upon if I emerged from the bedroom and
wanted to talk or be entertained during her "meditation
time" (by which she's referring in this case to all the
many hours she's up on weekend days before I roll out),
and so she'll make more of an effort not to impose on me
during my equivalent hours after I get home at 1:35 a.m.
   Meanwhile I'm in the first day of another schedule
reset. I'm trying to go back to a four-thirty a.m.
bedtime. Tonight I made a point of soaking an hour in
the whirlpool at the WOC in hopes it would, first,
compensate for last night's reduced sleep and keep my
immune system in fighting trim (the flu's still raging
all over town and for that matter the whole country, or
so the news says), but also would let me remain tired
enough to go to bed tonight, again, like last night,
ninety minutes earlier than I'm currently accustomed to.
   Yesterday we dropped by Olwen's for a long-
scheduled visit. Trent was down with a migraine so we
couldn't do board games. Instead the three of us set
off on a walk around "Manny Lake." Z soon started to
weaken, however, and we turned back at about the one-
fifth mark. Olwen herself had gone through a tough week
because of reaction to the nasty chemical stuff in the
air at the chain bookstore during her reading. But she

was still glad she'd done the reading. Now she's
angling to place an essay in the Sunday magazine of the
main-far-coast-megalopolis newspaper. In response to my
questions she told some detailed stories about her
brother, Carey. It turns out this was only the second
time he's heard her read her own work in public or
anywhere else. And she said about Chance M. -- who's a
member of her poetry group -- that she was shocked to
hear him sounding so bitter and macho when he read right
before she did. Later she learned his boss at the
oceanic agency was present for the event and she chalked
up the change in Chance to an attempt to please this man
and stay in character with some sort of male-bonded
shipboard tough-guy image he has or thinks he has.

    -- And that's it. Has to be. Bus stop here I come
-- better hustle too.

[+1]

    Starting out at the hideaway again. Maybe I'll end
here as well, but the ideal would be to tack on a page
or two at home. I'm trying to get back in the groove,
finishing up the J-week at night and at home (after
starting it out in the morning -- the night worker's
version thereof -- and on the way into town). But the
change in sleep schedules, even though it involves only
a ninety-minute shift, makes this hard. I'm tired all
the time. And I have to squeeze a lot into those three
hours before bedtime after arriving home, especially
since I'm still trying to do most of Z's chores as well
as my own.
    Two days in a row I've run into her on the hillside
as she returned from work while I was heading in. It's
not entirely a coincidence; I usually try to time my
departure so that a meeting would at least be possible.
But I can never be sure she won't linger at the office a
few extra minutes or do something downtown before
setting off for home. These days she's taking the bus
to the bridge road, then walking the rest of the way,

mostly uphill, trying to build herself back into shape. Next week she's hoping to restart her WOC workouts.

"Express Yourself." (The golden oldie playing on the radio right now.) -- And we usually do a lot of such expressing when we meet on the bridge or the hillside above it. At the very least a bit of sidewalk smooching. "Necking late-midlifers, ugh ugh." That was her laughing comment today, projected onto the busload of gawkers groaning by on the steep uphill climb by the DC castle. Or more like half a busload, I suppose, since the ones in the seats on the far side of the bus probably couldn't see much out the windows on our side.

I'm starting to take up the card thing again. Why now in particular I don't know, but in the back of my mind I hear the whisper of the "Thousand Cards for Z" wedding-present promise. And it's still just as it always was: I enjoy doing them. And that oughta be enough all by itself, yes. In any case that's why I got such a late start in leaving 203 today.

Meanwhile the results of the first caucuses in the U.S. presidential race are in and the two front-runners for the past two years, both of whose names are four-letter words -- which actually do read as ordinary English-language words when uncapped, and not even profane ones -- are the winners. No surprises. If these two also win in the first primary next week the race will be all but over. I expect them to be the nominees. Both are trying to come off as centrists. The former president's son is actually pretty far to the right, but both are corporatists and it's hard to rev up any excitement about the other guy. The crucial issues will be the same either way and neither candidate will address them at all. That's how it looks as we near the end of the first month of the new millennium.

*   *

-- A little earlier than usual for a late-night J-week closer. Quarter to four. But I lost some steam on this one because Z, despite what she said the other day about not disturbing me during these hours, showed up in the living room at three to read the paper. I told her

758

I'd planned to do some jyzing and after a few minutes
she stood up and said she'd read in the bedroom -- after
first asking me if I wanted her to leave. I said no, it
was fine if she stayed, but best if we didn't talk.

I don't like being put in this position. But
neither do I want jyze to be disrupting our lives. So
is it so terrible that I find myself wishing Z would do
what she says she'll do? But in her eyes such an
expectation makes me "rigid." When she complained about
this to Aida last week they branded me as a stodgy, set-
in-his-ways "perceiver" type -- something like that --
as defined by some business-oriented psych study that's
making the rounds, while Z and Aida were both fluid,
spontaneous "sensators." I don't like it! And I must
ask: how else can one ever get things done?

(It's not as if this isn't a familiar issue in my
life. I imagine it is for most writers and of course
virtually all jyzers. I'm sure it's scuttled many a
relationship, possibly including a few of my own. In a
sense I could even say jyze came into being as a way of
trying to cope with this very predicament. But a
fundamental truth on such matters is that flexibility
can't be limitless. Even a jellyfish has an exoskeleton
of sorts -- or I suppose it might be better called a
thin skin.)

-- I don't think any serious damage has been done
here. Not tonight. On the surface at least she didn't
seem miffed at all.

The other things I was hoping to touch on I think
I'll save for tomorrow. Yesterday the mayor gave his
annual "state of the city" address to the council; I was
planning to comment on that and relate it to my own idea
for a celebration of the true millennium. I'll still
try to do that. And say something about the weather:
I've sort of let it go largely or maybe even completely
unobserved in these pages for a week or two or more.
And I'd thought I would say something about my late-
night bus rides home -- how long's it been since I've
mentioned those? -- but they'll have to wait a while
longer, it appears.

38

"Ya gotta be kiddin' me!" It's the first time I've
been carded in, oh, say a couple of decades. A guy
dressed just about like me, ponytail and all, but
wearing a ball cap and windbreaker (both beer-company-
branded, but competing brands) -- that guy was the
checker. Taken aback, I suspected he was crazy or up to
no good and asked him for ID proving he was the checker.
He produced something from his pocket and remained
easygoing so I decided he must be for real and showed
mine, which he didn't even look at. "What it is, the
State Liquor Board's come through and it's a five-
hundred-dollar fine for every underage they find in here
and you know they'd just love to shut us down."
     East-depot saloon in the AQ. The usual table under
the TV. For some reason no one's ever sitting here, not
even when every other seat in the place is taken. Folks
must think it has a hex on it. (And now with everyone
who comes in -- and this is through the side door just a
few feet away -- the same scene repeats itself as the
guy in the beer-branded gear asks for ID. "I'm forty-
five fuckin' years old! You playin' me?") -- And every
other seat is indeed taken at the moment. Country music
throbbing, lots of laughter and smoke. You can almost
see wrinkles deepening and life expectancies shrinking
with every breath taken in.
     The next big deal here is the Super Bowl on Sunday.
Beer handbills (the same multinational corporation
that's on the checker's cap) hype it. A hand-lettered
sign says spaghetti will be just three bucks from one to
three p.m. on "Supe Day." (Afrusan dude screaming now,

760

"I just wanna see if you check anyone else!" A bunch
of us pipe up, "He did me!" "He got me, man." Afrusan
dude is somewhat mollified but still grumpy -- and
rightfully so! -- as he stomps over to the bar.
Somebody buy that man a beer!)

     -- Came lightly tripping out at dusk. (Removed
half a dozen books from my bag before leaving.) Scoped
out the headlines at the bus-stop news rack at the north
end of the bridge and saw a big feature on the upcoming
dome implosion. Wouldn't one of the weekly papers love
to call for a celebration of the true millennium in
which the reprobate Jyze City past as symbolized by the
dome itself would be blown away? Also lots of play is
going to the three-hundredth anniversary today of the
great quake and tidal wave that devastated much of our
coastal region a hundred years before European
"explorers" first set eyes on it (and hooks in it).
Such seismic events happen once every three- to five-
hundred years, geologists say, so the next one could
occur at any time. When it does, the damage will be
all but unimaginable. As just one indication, the tidal
wave would breach the entire twenty-mile-long peninsula
where Z and I did our honeymoon. It would basically be
swept clear. Nothing but sand and rock left, and maybe
not all that much sand. It's happened numerous times
before. And exponentially more people live there now.
(The native people probably were smart enough and had
cultural memory reaching back far enough to stay away.)

     Also coming up: tomorrow is the first anniversary
of our "real marriage before the assembled personal
deities." It was something I just spontaneously asked Z
to agree to a year ago as we talked about setting a date
for the official wedding "before the tribe." I made a
fairly big deal of it at the time -- put together some
cards and such -- but I think Z's entirely forgotten
about it. The plans are still on for her to see
Charles's concert with Aida tomorrow night. I haven't
said anything so far, but I'm planning to buy some cut
flowers and balloons at a twenty-four-hour corporate
supermarket late tonight and make a card similar to the

best one from a year ago and leave all these on her
pillow so she'll find them there when she comes home
from the concert tomorrow night. (Maybe I'll put them
under the covers in hopes she won't stumble upon them
when she arrives home after work. -- This'll be her
first time behind the wheel since breaking her wrist so
she might not be noticing too much at home.)

     What to say about the "state of the city" speech?
The mayor's still hanging in there, refusing to let
himself be run out of office over the WTO "fiasco," as
others are calling it (but not him and certainly not
me). He didn't propose much of anything, but he has a
good excuse for this: he can say he's heeding his
critics' advice and discussing his ideas privately with
councilmembers before taking those ideas public. All he
really needs to do is sit tight and ride out the storm,
and that's what he's been doing. Truth is, the storm's
already blown itself almost entirely out. (This is why
he'd be unlikely to support a celebration of the true
millennium: it would risk stirring up another brouhaha
over some of the same sore issues.)

     As I walked under the freeway tonight some Chinese-
looking kids were setting off firecrackers. It's the
first truly convincing sign I've seen of the Chinese New
Year's approach. The luckiest of years is coming in:
the Dragon. (Z checked out a website dispensing Chinese
horoscopes. It seems we Horse and Snake people are
"strongly attracted" and make a fiery match with lots
of sparky/snarky disputes.) -- June called this
afternoon, by the way, wanting to talk about the arrest
of the law students from her classes. It's now proven
I'm an insider guy, well worth knowing, as she joked.
Probably Z and I will get together with her a week from
Saturday to welcome in the Dragon. (And as I jyze I'm
half-listening to a gent ranting about how the world
will be ending a month from this Saturday on Leap Year
Day when Y2Kalypse will finally show up.)

     Onward. I'm hoping for a light worknight so I can
fit in a workout. -- But I also have a bit of a
headache. Start of the flu? I'm still worrying.

[Jyze Reboot]

[+1]

     -- Now it's the downtown glitz strip, back at that
same franchise coffee shop jyze visited during WTO days.
Less than an hour before closing time and I'm the only
customer in the place. They obviously don't like me
much here and it's entirely because of my looks --
sweatshirt, jeans, ponytail, a day's growth, big beat-up
backpack. Counter dudes -- they're young, peroxided,
pierced, tattooed, and shiny pink -- condescendingly
"sirring" me with a sneer. Oh well.

     No big protest march going by, no nasty tensions in
the air. The status quo is back. And did this district
lose anything at all financially from the protests?
Probably not. The media seem to have themselves lost
interest in pursuing the question, presumably because
the answer would embarrass the big downtown property
owners and merchants who were doing all the whining a
month ago. Many of them are of course major advertisers
in those same media.

     Earlier I walked along the local "sidewalk of fame"
outside one of the department stores and was hit by
roughly 1.5 panhandlers for every set of famous
footprints engraved in metal on the concrete. The top
two local plutocrats, the rock-guitar legend, and maybe
the glass-blowing super-artist are the only names that
would be widely recognizable outside the region, I
suspect, although technically speaking, since I don't
happen to know the panhandlers' names and didn't ask for
them, I can't be sure about this. But I do know a damn
good photo op is available over there, the show windows
full of luxury goods standing right behind the
panhandlers with their ragged clothes and bundles and
their mix of sickly and tragic and defiant faces.

     This as our U.S. president delivers his final
"state of the union" address. "Last quacks of the lame
duck." I imagine he's proclaiming the union's state to
be pretty damn good, with a few strategically placed
hedges and qualifiers so he can't be accused of

outright lies. The state of the world, of course, is
another matter, as I don't think he'd have any trouble
conceding, and so's the state of the future. And what
are the odds a president of the United States will ever
give another millennium-year "state of the union"
address?

I didn't make it down to today's grand reopening
ceremony for the great white tower. I'd hoped to, but
then I got caught up in altering some cards for Z (three
of them!) about today's first "before the gathered
personal deities" wedding anniversary. She came in just
as I was leaving and showed no sign of realizing what
kind of grand occasion had been going down all day and
still was. (I'd just hidden the cards under her pillow
so she wouldn't see them until bedtime. And to make
sure she wouldn't miss them at that point I placed a
piece of paper bearing a big red arrow and the words
"Isn't there something MOMENTOUS you should've
remembered about today?" between the sheets and pointing
up under the pillow. -- All in the spirit of good fun,
of course. Of course! Of course of course! -- But
under the covers there was -- nothing else. No flowers,
no balloons, no healthful fancy snack. Because -- no
time to go out and buy them. And regardless they
would've been too conspicuous under there and flowers
might've dampened her slumber.)

On the way down here I stopped at the scope office
to check on tonight's workload. As it happened I ran
into Naomi in the elevator as she returned from today's
job, which ran late. "It's just a good thing Larry was
available to pick up the kids today or I'd've been in
big trouble." (Yes, this is the same Larry who probably
was the major source for today's front-page lead story
in all the papers, far coast included, saying a firm
link has been established between the alleged millennial
terrorists from Algeria and the notorious top-dog
terrorist of our time, the leader of Al Qaeda.) In the
past week Naomi and I have been exchanging notes about a
number of topics, so it was good to have a chance to
talk with her about those matters. Her hair looked

different: she's dyed it an auburn brown, I'd call it.
(And I wonder how she thought I looked. She momentarily
stiffened when I stepped onto the elevator, I noticed,
until she recognized me.)
     (I thought it was kind of her not to mention the
grand-jury exhibits I accidentally tore up. And I'm
sure it's only by coincidence that she wants to learn
how to operate the computer enough to tran a job so she
can send it to Doris on the far coast via internet "just
in case there's another WTO type of thing and you can't
get down to the office." And happily she's in no hurry
to switch over to the latest transcription system if
it's of no benefit to me, and I assured her it isn't.
And she said she's pleased to know I won't after all be
going on vacation in March, since that means she won't
need to start sending Doris stuff anytime soon. -- And
little would I have dreamed ten or fifteen years ago
that Doris would still be trying to steal Naomi's work
away from me after all this time. And from a distance
of three thousand miles! -- But I guess they've kept in
touch, though I never could understand the basis of
their friendship. -- And I learned the person who'd
been using my computer at the office was, as I suspected,
reporter Fran, but she was just checking out something
at Naomi's behest; and that's a relief to know.)
     -- And best that be it for now. Naomi's job
running late means I have lots of work to do, though I
can space it out over two nights. "Way more than two
hundred pages," she said. Next stop: midtown chain
burgers for two double-stacks to go, hold the cheese.
     -- But first: I also want to mention the news about
our hilltop building. Upon arrival home last night I
found a note on my armchair. "Lotsa bad news," I
thought it said at first. Then I saw that what I'd
taken to be the "a" in "bad" was actually a stunted "l"
and the seeming tail on the "d" was a "g" and the word
was an abbreviation for "building" -- "bldg" -- mauled
by Z's still-very-shaky left hand. "Lotsa bldg news."
And the news wasn't bad at all; it was good.
     She explained it when I joined her in bed. Ciro,

765

who we thought had moved out, was back; he'd merely been
subletting while visiting the Philippines on vacation.
And he said he'd met the new owners of the property and
they were fine people and they weren't planning to
condoize the place and he also thought they wouldn't be
raising the rents. They will, however, be remodeling
the apartments one by one as they fall vacant, and
they're already starting in on that work for 103 and
303, the ones below and above ours. Ciro took Z on a
tour of 103 -- formerly Aboula's place -- and Z said
it's in the process of becoming much fancier now, and
Ciro told her 303 will be even fancier, with parquet
floors and tiled bathrooms and new all-wood cabinets and
even "standalone kitchen sinks," whatever that means
(and why that would be viewed as an upgrade I don't know
either, but Z assured me it is). For the redone 303
they'll be asking nine hundred something, Ciro said, a
bump of roughly two hundred or twenty-five percent. Not
all that bad, really, under current conditions.

     -- So yes, we can at least hope to be able to hang
on in 203 for another year, maybe even two years,
without paying too much more. Yayhoo! (And Ciro said
the automatic garage-door opener is working again as of
today, after being on the fritz for more than a month.)

[+2]

     A pot of water is heating on the stove. In a
moment I'll pour it in the bathroom sink to flush away
the drain cleaner I put in there an hour ago (the
powerful but highly toxic kind this time). And an
extremely bright crescent moon has just come creeping
above the eastern horizon at an almost sideways tilt
(looks like an albino turtle tipped on its back with its
head and legs pulled in) and I'm peering at it with one
eye as I jyze. -- And the boiling pour please, maestro.
                         *
     -- And back. The drain's better now but still very
slow. I'll try another round in a day or two. Or maybe

by then tonight's round will have had more effect and I
won't need to.

Again tonight I'm just trying to keep a hand in on
the jyze. But I can't pass up the chance to say it's
been a fine couple of days, though for me short on
sleep. And Z and I are back at it again! Three full-
service copulations in thirty-six hours! (Also it
appears I've again entered a phase where I need to crow
a bit about such things, yeah.)

Also we saw a superb movie, "Flowers of Shanghai."
Z didn't much care for it, though; the pace was too slow
for her and the subject matter -- fin de nineteenth
siecle brothel life -- "too dependent on the erotic
exotic." June at one point was supposed to be seeing it
with us (her family on both sides lived in Shanghai
during that era) but she backed out because of a heavy
law-school workload.

As we sat in the lobby at the theater Z remarked,
"You're a little grayer than when we met. Has your new
wife been giving you a hard time?" I suspect she was
just retaliating for my failure to wax joyous about the
new haircut she came home with this afternoon. She'd
been muttering about having something radically
different done -- like shaving half or a third of her
scalp bald -- but at crunch time she chose something
only a little different, a bit more randomly spiky on
top, as if she'd forgotten to brush it after getting up
in the morning. Which probably makes it sound as if I
don't like it, but that's not the case. In fact I think
it's quite striking. But I was distracted when she
first showed it to me and I failed to rave enough and
that's been a hard hole to dig myself out of.

Then there's the news. Another arrest in the
terrorist case. Also, protesters are being jailed at
the annual meeting of financial and political bigwigs at
Davos, Switzerland, where the head of the WTO is now
admitting that the protests in our city have
considerably set back his organization's cause, perhaps
permanently. And as an indication of this, the Canadian
conference on biofoods has agreed, to the extreme

displeasure of corporados everywhere, to accept the very
precautionary principle demanded by protesters here. If
there's ever been a quick showing of how small but
determined groups of people can make a large political
difference for the better, this is it.

Some bad news too. The knee pain Betty's been
suffering from for some time has worsened and spread.
It's affecting both legs now to the extent she's often
unable to sleep. She's had all sorts of tests done but
the docs haven't been able to determine the cause. Z
made Betty promise to see a naturopath for a second (or
maybe it's a third) opinion before embarking on any
drastic course of treatment such as having a knee (or
both knees) replaced.

Here in the living room two new plants have taken
up positions on the window ledge above the couch, one a
swedish ivy shaped like a small tree and the other a mix
of colorfully blooming flowers in a wooden box. They
displaced the blue ceramic hippos and the wood-framed
watercolors which all now perch elsewhere in the room.
Five plants in a row make for a cheery scene (the half
moon of the street lamp hanging just above the middle of
the row, the albino-turtle real moon having somehow
righted itself and scuttled mostly horizontally into the
left side of the next window where the half-canted
blinds fracture it unless I move my head quickly up and
down to recompose it visually, finding it on its back
again, legs and head retracted again -- that being the
dying first moon of the new millennium -- nontrue or
just call it false new millennium, due to come to an end
on March 25 -- and when a fresh moon is born a week from
last night it'll bring with it the Year of the Dragon.)

[+1]

I hiked over to the fast-food joint at the state
ferry dock with the idea of doing some jyzing there but
inspiration refused to strike. Or rather I should say
it went on strike over the utter sterility of in-house

jyzing conditions. (The one business the protesters at Davos managed to trash, at least a little bit, was a franchise licensed by this same fast-food chain, just as one of the first ones targeted here was.) So I concluded I'd really just used the possibility of jyzing there as a rationale for depositing myself within buying distance of one of their vanilla cones. If this seems politically incorrect, so be it -- because it is. Society so arranges things that only a saint could maneuver through an entire day without being politically -- and maybe even morally -- incorrect numerous times. The rest of us have to pick and choose the occasions where we're going to take a stand and also learn to live with the ones where we must cave.

Now I'm back at the hideaway. Not much time left -- the usual situation.

Today is Super Bowl Sunday -- "Supe Day." No doubt that's why traffic was so light on the freeway when I walked down. The event is just as hyped as ever but I'm now much better able to dodge or ignore all that nonsense. Because I didn't hit the WOC during the hours of high jock concentration this week I didn't have to talk about it at all, with a single exception when the janitor at the scope office asked if I'd be watching it -- and he's Mexican (the voracious reader) and was asking, I think, mainly to show he's no slouch at gringo culture.

Z and I spent most of the pregame and first-half hours at the dining table going over her finances. This is something we've scheduled and then put off doing on numerous occasions over at least a six-month period, and both the scheduling and the putting off was always, at least as I recall, at her request. Finances and herpes are the two hardest things for her to talk about: she says so herself. In both cases she feels she's revealing moral weaknesses and their consequences, or shameful "addictive behavior" (sex and shopping are two of the three addictions she long ago diagnosed in herself and for a period tried to counter through participation in twelve-step groups; and I just remembered the third, workaholism).

I thought it went well. Several times she asked some version of "You sure you still love me after you've seen all this?" But I don't really view these issues as moral ones, or at least not with regard to the way they've played out in her life. Probably I'm just as "addicted" in all three areas as she is. Far from disapproving, I'm proud she's always been sexually brave and adventurous, she's always been generous with the money she earns, she's always been fiercely dedicated to her work (and that includes the voluntary and political and artistic kind as well as the vocational).

As for the actual numbers, she's quite a bit less in debt than I'd been thinking -- only 68K, not 88. But we worked out a rough budget and it turns out she's spending $300 a month more than she's bringing home, so we identified areas where she could cut back, and I've been appointed the official finger-wagger. She'll run big-ticket purchases by me first and if she can't buy the item without busting her budget, I'm supposed to veto it. Also she'll be cutting back on deli food purchases and on lunching out in general. (Yes, it's a little risky for me to be the designated naysayer. But I think it'll be all right. It might even help foster a new kind of closeness.)

The other major problem is that she owes her debt to seven or eight different finance and credit-card outfits. She's going crazy trying to keep up with all the paperwork and the tricky rules which apply to the low-interest accounts (which suddenly become high-interest if she breaks the rules or doesn't get a payment in the mail within a certain period, in most cases five days). So I've agreed to join her in attending the meeting of a city-accredited finances group which will show us how to consolidate all the loans into one and eliminate all but one of her credit cards. The hope is she'll be able to cut back her expenses enough to pay down the loans and thus make it easier for us to afford a condo loft or a small house a year or two down the road. (But obviously a lot of this

will simply be a matter of luck -- and especially where
her mother's health is concerned.)

     Her current take-home is just under three K a
month. After retirement her pension will pay almost
exactly that amount per month before taxes, and in
addition she'll be pulling down a bit more than half
that much in Social Security. So we'll be doing quite
well if we can find a relatively inexpensive place to
live. -- And obviously again I'm very fortunate to be
with her, since my own post-retirement take-home,
including income from the deep reserves, will be about a
fifth of hers. (By then I'll probably be using the
reserves in a different way -- as a condo or house down
payment -- but that's beside the point here since they
would still essentially be going for rent.)

39

     -- Came trotting out at ten to five. That was
about seven hours ago. Now I'm cooped up again at the
hideaway because I can't think of any other place I'd
rather be. (Or no, I can think of plenty such, but none
reachable within the time and money constraints.)

     Today Z and I made our first return together to the
WOC since a few days before she broke her wrist. Most
of the old gang was in attendance pumping away at their
usual machines and freeweights. At times high hilarity
prevailed. Jay and Melanie, Clio, Marcus, Estella,
Willis, Mitch -- they all wanted to know just what I'd
had to do for Z with her dominant left arm out of action
-- like brush her teeth maybe? The New-Year's-
resolution crowd was still much in evidence and so Z and
I had to wait fifteen or twenty minutes before we could

nab adjacent treadmills.

Poor Z. She could do only twenty minutes on the treadmill. Her list of ailments is so long she almost needs a checklist to determine her overall status. As of the last time I saw her before she left, nothing was bothering her particularly: neither left foot nor right knee nor lower back nor right shoulder nor neck nor -- though it still looked pathetically atrophied, as everyone agreed -- left wrist. And hand and forearm.

As in the old days she caught me up on developments at work while we treadmilled in tandem (and also while we waited to do that). Dale is backing her one hundred percent in her efforts to whip the new recycling publicity campaign into shape. Marvin, Dale's boss, is revising his divisionwide letter about Z's hate mail based on her critique of an earlier draft (she felt it focused too much on her specifically and not enough on the general issue). D'Arcy, returning well-tanned from a week at her condo a thousand miles to the south, is saying she just can't stand her job (in PR) anymore. Kendra is ready for early retirement in April or maybe even March if the recycling campaign turns out to be too arduous. Gloria is behaving admirably at the moment but still dressing far too provocatively (though this may be why Marvin's asked her to come work in his office).

And then there's Jess. First, it would appear she's settled her differences with Paz and Tobey because those two will be house-sitting for her next week and all three will be attending a one-person show put on by a gay Filusan actor this Sunday, as will we as part of the group. Second, because of the strong likelihood that ferry service will be sharply curtailed owing to Initiative FTG (Fuck the Government) cutbacks, Jess is having second thoughts about selling her house and moving to southwest island. Now she's cursing herself for having bought the land as a kind of revenge measure against Gwen: "I'll show you; even though we split up I'll buy the land anyway and go and live there by myself in the sticks on that remote island and you'll be sorry." And third, Gwen and Jess met by chance outside

an indie bookstore on east hill over the weekend and,
when Gwen pursued Jess down the street demanding to know
why she'd said certain things in her response to Gwen's
most recent letter (something to do with Gwen's moving
to a house on south hill not far from us and also not
far from her new, or actually not so new now, boyfriend)
-- after all that, yes, they flew off into a nasty
screaming match (but it didn't get physical).

About other important circle-of-friends matters --
Betty's leg pain, Mr. D.'s cancer -- Z had nothing new
to pass along. She did learn over the weekend, though,
that Kat's "uncle" Nick is now having second thoughts
about his projected move to the northern far coast. All
it took was one big snowstorm to do it. (But Z suspects
his new flame -- who lives out there and, I should've
mentioned before, is definitely a woman -- will turn him
around again.) Betty, meanwhile, is still hoping to
drive down with Kat to see Nick and also Wanda (whose
new romance is still going strong) over spring break,
and if she's able to do that (it's a 2400-mile round
trip), Z and I will be house-sitting for them, tending
to Arnie and the cats and the thirteen hamsters, or by
then maybe it'll be a hundred and thirteen hamsters.
And it would be the perfect time for Z to plant the
one-square-yard (not foot) "grounding" patch of garden
Betty has kindly allotted to her, which is just a step
or two from where the millennial capsule is buried.

-- And so another week. This should be an amusing
one with Groundhog Day coming up day after tomorrow.
And then the Year of the Metal Dragon clanks in.

Last night I altered a corny fifties S&M card
showing a voluptuous cartoon babe tied to a post: made
the babe into Z as best I could and inscribed the legend
"Z-goose savors the EXQUISITE TORTURE...of her KINKY NEW
BUDGET CONSTRAINTS." Today on the phone she proudly
reported she'd bought a loaf of bread for the office
refrigerator and then made herself a peanut-butter
sandwich (using the jar of organic stuff I mixed for her
last night, since there was just no way she could do the
deed one-handed, and she did try, she swears, before

writing me a note begging me to take over for her when I
arrived home). I also suggested a new "gold-star
challenge plan" in which she would set aside whatever's
left over from her monthly checks into a savings account;
but she didn't seem too excited about the idea.

Eeps, gotta quit right here. (And not even a
mention yet of this being the day of the first national
primary. Or the plane bound for our city going down in
the ocean this afternoon with all aboard -- eighty or
so, I believe -- lost, meaning dead.)

[+1]

One delay after another pushed this entry back to
half past three in the morning. Peanut butter still
clinging to my lips (as I swirl my tongue around the
bristly outer lip edges: mmm, good! -- though not
organic). "Grooveyard" on the radio. Vites & supps
already washed down with veggie juice (this ritual now
preceding the meal in an attempt to cut down on hunger).

Interesting day. The media are focusing on the
plane crash (our friend Madge I. knew two of the dead
crew members) and now the results coming in from the
presidential primary (it's a horse race, folks!) and
also the fact that today the nation moves into its 107th
consecutive month of economic expansion, topping the old
record of 106 set in the sixties. (At what cost it's
happening, and to whose benefit and at whose expense,
both immediate and long term, are hardly being discussed
at all.)

And some personal news: this afternoon I spoke for
a few minutes with one of the new building owners, Dana
D., when she called to thank us for sending the letter
with our rent. She does indeed, as Matt D. a/k/a Zonker
assured us she would, seem friendly and even "refined"
(his term). And I learned something important: she and
her husband, Raphael, are definitely planning to go
condo with the building, which is one of several they
own, early next year. They haven't decided on prices

yet, but she said if we're interested we could choose either to keep our unit as it is, and presumably pay less, or have it "upgraded" as they're doing now with the units directly below and above us, 103 and 303. She also mentioned that the other tenants on our floor, in 201 and 202 (with both of which units we share an entranceway), will be moving out at the end of the month and that Raphael and his crew, when they finish up with 103 and 303, will then start rehabbing those two other units. (I had already told her, before the topic of condoizing came up, that ours is in "pretty bad" shape.) She even kindly apologized for the inconvenience of having construction work going on all day every day both above and below us (though she kept silent on this until I'd mentioned twice, and perhaps a bit grumpily the second time, that I'm a night worker and so I'm around here most of the day trying to sleep).

I called Z right away to tell her about all this. She agreed with me: if we can afford to buy a condo here we should probably do it. If we don't, we'll have to move out sometime later this year, most likely, and then we'd have to find a temporary place somewhere and wait at least a year to learn whether we would qualify for one of the subsidized lofts, or we could try to hunt down some other spot that would be more permanent. To make two moves in such a short period would be expensive and a lot of trouble. This place right here would almost surely be better than anything else we could find, especially in terms of location. And didn't we agree when we moved in that we'd try to stay here, or if not in this building at least in this hilltop hood, permanently? (Yes we did.)

By the time she got home she was saying she's decided not to worry about the housing predicament anymore; whatever happens happens; we'll find something. And she's set up a meeting with the financial advisor for later in the month. My thought now is that this year we should concentrate on whittling down her debt as much as possible. That should be our big project.

-- And speaking of projects: I did some research at

the library and found three reputable sources confirming
that in England in the year 1000, New Year's was
celebrated on March 25th. So all the elements except
one are in place for what I'd like to call -- maybe -- a
"True Millennium Blowout" campaign, and that one element
probably won't be knowable until too late and probably
should itself become part of the campaign. And that one
element is: on what date will the dome implosion take
place? For the past month newspaper stories have been
saying nothing more specific than that it will be a
weekend morning in late March or early April. March
25th is a Saturday.

    It's surprising no one else has come forth with
this idea. Except possibly for the fact that the 25th
is the actual millennium date it seems almost blindingly
obvious, and you'd expect that anyone who started
thinking about optimum dates would've become curious
about historical echoes and wondered about what was
happening on that date in the year 1000. (It occurred
to me a hook exists here even for the wonky literalists
who insist -- wrongly in my view -- that January 1,
2001, is the true millennium date; for if the two-
thousandth anniversary of the birth of Christ is to be
celebrated on that date, it only figures that the two-
thousandth anniversary of his "conception" would be
celebrated nine months earlier, on what Christians call
"Annunciation Day," I've now learned, and what back
then the English called, and maybe still do, "Lady Day,"
because that was the day the Angel Gabriel announced to
"the Lady," meaning Mary the Jesus mama, that she would
give birth to a divinity -- and thus that was the day on
which, as one of the books I looked at puts it, "the
Divine Presence was first da da da on earth.") (Can't
come up with the "da da da" word right now. Maybe will
fill in later if it seems important. Or in journalese:
TK, meaning: to come. Though it might not come.)

    Fascinating stuff. And now I have a few more days
to think about what I want to do with it, if anything.
Grand jury meets the next two days and so I'll be busy
with that until the weekend -- that and jyze, of course.

So I'll set late this weekend as the deadline for deciding.

[+2]

    -- Had no chance to scribble a word on Groundhog Day. Whether Punxatawny Phil ("Punx Phil") saw his shadow I don't know yet. If he'd poked his head up in this area he wouldn't've, not yesterday, but on an unusually large number of recent days he would've, including, the forecast says, the four coming up. Climate-chaos weather. Still not a single sticking snowflake in J. City this winter, or at least not that I know of. Today I again watered the flowers on the balcony and all four of the large boxes and several of the small ones still had at least a bloom or two on view: geraniums, marigolds, pansies, even some bright blue lobelia (along with, to be sure, plenty of scraggly dead stuff).

    And fittingly we're just a day away from the end of what I think of as the winter doldrums, the period between Western and Eastern New Year, solar and lunar. (For the Chinese, Saturday is the first day of not just the Year of the Dragon but also, and ipso facto, of spring. So the doldrums are what East and West, or at least big parts of both which also happen to be in the northern hemisphere, agree are winter.)

    -- This being as well First Thursday I've taken a little detour on my way in to work, stopping at Z-geist for a root beer. It's half past six and the place is bustling with artwalkers, including some I can hear stomping on the floor above me. And it's confirmed now, this will be the last time the five floors of studios and lofts up above will be open for artwalks. All the building's residents are being booted out at the end of April, I think it is, and most if not all are artists. Rumors of a conversion to upscale condos and offices have been swirling for at least a year. It's part of the redevelopment that's changing the nature of life

around here (though of course it's the crazy so-called
new economy that's really driving it). The number of
artists who can afford to live or work in the area is
rapidly shrinking. Epitaphs are everywhere. Artwalks
might continue as long as a critical mass of galleries
remains -- and that's iffy too -- but they won't be the
same with so many of the working-artist spaces gone.
     Now if the roulette wheel had spun a little
differently four years ago -- almost to the day -- and
I'd wound up sharing a loft upstairs, as once seemed
quite likely, I'd probably be up against it today,
scrambling to find some affordable place to live. And
almost certainly Zoelie B. would not be in my life.
     I hiked down at dusk, admiring the remnants of
sunset rosifying bands of dark clouds at the horizon
above the darkened bulk of the dome. Most dome
attachments, including the lights and the flagpole at
its highest point, have already been removed in
preparation for the demolition. The structure is so big
there's something ominous about seeing it in this state
of desuetude (a favorite word of mine right there!).
-- And in the upper AQ I noticed that the big pit-bull
watchdog usually prowling the alley behind one of the
produce exchanges now gives only a couple of meek yips
and sniffs the air almost happily when he sees me.
We've become friends! (But I'm still glad we're
separated by a heavy ten-foot-high chain-link fence.)
     The inner streets of the AQ were crackling with
excitement as exceptionally large numbers of shoppers
ran last-minute New Year's errands. Literally crackling
in places: firecracker crackling. Under the freeway
overpass a couple of hookers were working the south side
of the street -- the first I've seen there in months --
and I was reminded of a story in the paper about the
conviction in the far southeastern corner of the country
of a former resident of our city now known as "America's
Pimp." The story mentioned that he used to run a ring
on the streets in the AQ here -- probably in the very
spot where I was walking. The pair I saw might even be
former members of his "stable." "America's Hookers."

Appropriately enough, I suppose, one looked Eurusan and the other like an Afr/Asiusan mix including Korean.

The AQ's main English-language paper (for which Z did occasional book reviews until recently, and may yet do more) carries a story this week about the possibility a new kind of restaurant might soon be coming to the AQ, to a prime corner a few doors down from the east-depot saloon. A national-corporate-chain burger joint! It would be the first fast-food franchise of any type in the AQ. Many people in the community oppose it, but others, including our former upstairs neighbor Doug T. (quoted in the article), have mixed feelings about it, thinking the large numbers of low-income folks living in the area would be pleased to have a place where they could buy a burger for a buck. Whether this chain should be allowed in -- if indeed it can be stopped -- will probably be one of the big AQ issues of the year (but largely too late, I'd imagine, for this TJM project to keep tabs on it). That corner's pretty nasty already; a corporate burger joint there would be a magnet for more trouble, much like the one at the downtown plaza where I buy my cones (which is part of the same chain, I should note, as is the one at the ferry dock and the one across from the fairgrounds where Z and I met before the big WTO march -- along with, of course, many other franchises in other parts of the city and also the ones Mama E favors in Centropolis).

Z arrived home early this afternoon, popping in as I worked on yet another card for her. "Can't come in here, Z-goose, big secret stuff going on!" She takes injunctions like this more in stride now. Heads for the "big" bathroom, which is near the front door, and waits until I've finished up and put my art stuff away.
-- Today her favorite magazine arrived so it was hard getting any sustained talk going with her but easy for me to do lots of sustained teasing, including a little striptease and then an "N'dow wag" right in front of her nose to see if I could arouse her attention. She did chortle a bit. (Loving was out of the question, I should note, because she's been hit by another outbreak.

It's come puzzlingly soon after the last one, she thinks
probably owing to stress over the finances talk.)
    -- Now a big commotion outside. I stop for a
moment to lean out the balcony window and see a crowd
blocking the street, a small band with drummers pounding
away, a line of dragon dancers snaking back and forth in
front of the entrance to the lobby serving the studios
upstairs. Some bystanders are waving black flags.
Anarchist artists protesting the closure? Maybe so. Or
possibly just mourners. But it seems more celebratory
than anything. -- And in here a story is being typed
out paragraph by paragraph by a group of writers, I
guess, all women in vintage fifties dresses, with the
results being projected onto a big screen that reaches
almost to the ceiling. It's official entertainment, it
appears, which you don't often see at Z-geist. Applause
and laughter, carriage-return bells dinging and hand-
squeezed oogah horns sounding. An artsy crowd has taken
over all the tables up here too, as I shrink back into
my brick-lined corner. All sorts of sparky goings-on.
In fact, too much so for jyze to keep on keeping up, I'd
say. And -- gotta go anyway. "And so to work."

[+1]

    Late for bed. But I must at least note the magical
day has arrived. The Year of the Dragon is, yup,
lumbering in right on time. (Clanking in I think I said
last time, picturing metallic claws and scales.) -- But
on a quiet night in the "great room." Unable to decide
between the north or south end of the couch, each with
its own lamp now, I've plopped myself down in the middle
(but mainly because a big pillow is occupying each end
and I didn't have a hand free to toss either of them
aside). At my back the long, narrow, homemade wooden
flowerbox riding the ledgelike inside windowsill offers
a full panoply of blooms, purple and red and yellow,
with all but the primroses and the mini-irises nameless
for me. -- And I'll have to be getting up early.

[Jyze Reboot]

    Meanwhile I'm recalling that today, Friday (it's
also Saturday morning), is the first day of spring by
the lunar calendar but the exact midpoint of winter by
the solar, with forty-five days gone by since winter
began and forty-five more to go until the first day of
spring of the solar, meaning Gregorian, kind. It seems
I prefer to think of myself as inhabiting spring now,
though by the same token I suppose I must therefore also
think of winter having started early -- unless, of
course, the seasons can be unbalanced, or irregular,
some longer than others. And why can't they? Must
everything be regular and efficient and globalized?
    I've altered an "Enter the Dragon" movie postcard
for Z, calling this the beginning of our superlucky
first full lunar year together as a fully hitched couple
and not just a pair of hokey "Deeps." The Year of the
Rabbit we were married all the way through by my lights
(as well as those of the "Norski deities") but not by
hers and certainly not by those of the Gregorian
solarians in general. On this card the Asiusan star of
"Enter the Dragon" can be seen to be saying via cartoon
speech bubble, "They're unbelievably hot, folks,"
meaning we two, Z and me, the newlyweds.
    (I'm surrounded right now by big plants, most at
eye level, and love being so -- peace lily, poinsettia,
fern, Rob and Gail's potted live Christmas tree with
the original miniature ornaments obscured deep within
its fast-growing branches.)
    -- And to Z it was a springlike day, the way the
air was. At the club, Jay the juggler and I bantered
and Gene the pilot appeared for the first time looking
tan but emphatically unpumped and unripped -- in fact
paunchy and dissolute -- but still quite happy -- after
his six-week "layover" in Mexico.
    -- But I must stop, the Saturday-morning news is
about to start (but I'll mention that the kitchen wall
clock, after my recalibration of it earlier tonight at
Z's request, is no longer three minutes fast, and so now
she'll more easily be able to time her morning bus).
-- And, and, Z came up with a new dragon stamp, of the

781

rubber type, and inked it up six different ways and
wound the sentences of tonight's note to me among the
images -- hard to read because her hand remains shaky,
but still: wotta splendid notion!

40

     -- Comes creeping to the same spot he nabbed last,
but one cushion over, to the north, toward the balcony
door. And skoal! Here's to the Dragon! With a cup of
wine I've been nursing for hours.
     (I hear a heavy splat. Would that be the Sunday
far-coast paper? I just checked moments ago and it
wasn't there. Now glancing down at the street I see not
the usual red van but a Cawk dude on a motorcycle -- and
then another Cawk dude appears from our south walkway
and hops on a skateboard and they roll on together.
Bizarre. But I'll go check for the paper again. At
this hour what else could be landing down there?)
                              *
     The paper is what it was. I glanced through it:
nothing much new. Is our gunslinger nation picking
another fight, this one in Colombia? What's behind the
hotheaded militaristic ex-war-prisoner's success in the
first primary? (And I was reminded that our state's
primary is coming up a month from Tuesday. In walking
to the WOC last night I noticed a certain wishywashy
liberal Cawk and former pro-hoops star has opened a
presidential campaign office two hundred feet east of
the hideaway building's side entrance along what's often
described as one of the most crime-ridden stretches in
the city.)
     A little loving before Z drifted off to sleep

tonight. Actually I slid in next to her as she read --
nap time, I announced -- but then I couldn't help
myself, I got playful, really just goofing around or so
I thought. Suddenly I was stiffening up. And she was
amenable. Mutual jerk-offs followed, with more or less
simultaneous comes, although for her it was the fifth
or sixth or who knows how many there were, as is almost
always the case with her and that's just how it is and
sometimes I almost take it for granted now -- though
truth to tell not all that often. (She's still
vaginally off limits tonight, I should mention, owing to
the Big H.)

Then the nap, for an hour or so, and reading in the
bedroom chair as she slept on. At one point sudden
movement of her foot startled me: I thought it was a
cat! And we don't have a cat! (Her foot had crept
outside the covers on the side of the bed, as it often
does. She once said she thinks this happens because I
don't compliment her toenail polish enough.)

This afternoon, following the pre-agreed scenario,
we went down to the AQ at three, stopping by the east
depot to check out the Year of the Dragon festival, then
hitting the nearby Japanese department store (A-mart) to
spend a thirty-dollar gift certificate that was our last
uncashed wedding present. I bought a copy of "A Brief
History of Imbecility" and Z found a very fine paper-
lantern-style lamp for her bedroom (and she razzed me
about some haughty fashion-plate Japanese college girls
in short skirts who seemed to be eyeballing me in the
bookstore, probably in shock or horror, although they
kindly kept poker faces -- "Does that bring back your
Kyoto days, dear?").

In walking through Chinatown we saw crowds gathered
outside several restaurants to watch lion dances as the
gongs and drums pounded antically away. The sidewalks
were littered with firecracker wrappings and the shops
were unusually crowded. Best moment: on the way back to
the car we came upon two lion-dance crews taking a break
together under the freeway bridge, wearing colorful
orange-and-black leggings below ragged sweatshirts that

would be hidden beneath the lion's cloth body when they
were back in full costume. The huge lion heads were
carefully propped on the curb and staring up at us
trancelike as we walked by. A small crowd had gathered
to watch the crew members smoke and to listen in as they
swapped ribald jokes in mixed English and Chinese. Only
the lion heads were not laughing.

Then onward by Z-mobile to our usual provisioning
destinations, with a stop along the way at Z's office to
drop off a box of dishes. It was my first visit up
there in many months -- since before the wedding. She
couldn't resist letting me know she's expecting flowers
on Valentine's Day. "Oh good, I'm so glad you mentioned
that because now I couldn't live with myself if I came
up with some, as I'd been planning to do until now,
because then you'd think I'm just meekly following your
orders and you'd despise me." (Each year it gets a
little harder to think of something to surprise her with
on V. Day -- which itself is of course no surprise.)

A doubly unusual dinner tonight. Not only did we
eat together at home but we cooked. Mostly she did the
honors. She'd come across some free-range "natural"
hamburger meat at the co-op -- no hormones in the feed
and so forth (of course the meat's much more expensive
without the additives) -- and also, in preparing the
freezer for the new influx, uncovered a bag of frozen
so-called American fries that must've been in there
since we moved in -- it probably came from my fridge at
B-2. (I toasted the buns and tossed the salad and
warmed up the chocolate sauce for the ice cream. And I
set the table and cleaned up afterwards too.)

Earlier we had decided to change our plans for the
two pieces of frozen wedding cake in a ziplock bag which
is taking up a big chunk of freezer space.
Traditionally, according to Z, you keep them for a year
and eat them on your first anniversary for good luck.
But she was feeling so bad about having forgotten our
Norski-deities anniversary, she suggested we could thaw
them -- that is, the pieces of cake (look out if you try
to thaw a Norski deity!) -- for tonight's dessert in

delayed honor of that anniversary. I suggested a compromise: we bring them out as part of our six-month Sufi and standard-municipal wedding anniversary on March 25th. (I'd be grateful for anything that would lend some ceremonial weight to the occasion.) She went for it and we bought the ice cream and chocolate sauce for tonight instead: her idea.

All day we've been sparring over chores. It's been low-level, mostly good-natured skirmishing but with a little edge to it every now and then. While cleaning the bathrooms this morning (the first time the task's fallen to her in months -- probably since well before the wedding) she got it into her head that her chores demand more "intense exertion" than mine. True enough, I said; but that's because of the way she does hers, putting them off for weeks or months until a massive effort is required, whereas I usually try to do a little bit every day. Nonetheless she made out a list of all her chores and intends to note not just the amount of time each takes but also the degree of exertion.

I have to admit I was -- am -- a little miffed that she'd come on like this so soon after I've gone through an extended period of doing all those same chores, both hers and mine, and also lots of other things she couldn't do -- for seven weeks straight! And the truth is I do a bunch more than she does anyway, and that's been the case ever since we moved in, and lots of it is stuff she's supposed to do. Furthermore I'd rather do those things and not even mention them in an effort to keep our life together going smoothly, and in fact I intend to continue doing just that. Nor do I really mind her getting in my face about her chores -- I like her spiritedness! But I want to be appreciated too. Usually if I take out the recycling, mop the kitchen floor, clean the tub and toilets and sinks, wash her dishes, she doesn't even notice. It's the flip side of a quality in her I like a lot: an ability to overlook messes and not worry too much about things being spic and span.

-- Ach, so enough about all that. Enough period.

what is jyze coming to? Nor can I stay up too late,
because again we have Sunday-afternoon plans. That's
why we did the weekly shopping on a Saturday. (And this
wine's getting to me. We started in on it shortly after
arriving home around seven, so ten hours straight --
minus the nap -- sipping at wine. It's a miracle I
don't have a headache. And no surprise I've been
feeling so sleepy the past hour or two.)

[+2]

     Carved out an hour for this. Yesterday I missed
entirely and so now jyze has returned on what was
supposed to be a day of rest. And a Monday too!
-- Third day of the Chinese New Year celebration. The
shops in the AQ will remain closed for one more day.
(And then ten more days of celebration will follow but
they'll be of a less-focused kind, with the Festival of
Lanterns as a concluding ceremony on the 19th. I like
the way Chinese do New Year.)
     Today Z read aloud a couple of passages from her
journal to "prove" she loves me a lot. She didn't have
to do that. But it's true, she "mushed me up" by going
ahead with it despite my protests. (She was also
teasing me for behaving "weirdly" this morning in
refusing to let her escape from the bed until we'd
indulged in, at the very least, a little nipple nookie.
I didn't think of it at the time, but I should've
reminded her of the way she'd strong-armed me into
getting her off the night before (I was stone asleep and
all but unarousable, in either sense; but eventually she
got me in both).)
     We're now talking about looking for a condo in the
AQ. Z surprised me by saying she'd be willing to live
there as long as we had a secure building with a safe
parking space and an in-unit washer/dryer. After the
east-depot celebration the other day we saw an
affordable condo for sale in a nearby six-story building
-- it was right at what we're still thinking of as our

upper limit, 150K -- but it was a studio and quite a bit smaller than 203. It was closer, in fact, to the size of my old B-2 studio, which was 385 square feet. (It's odd I remember that number. Why is it numbers stick in my head but I have a hard time memorizing poetry? Could this have something to do with why I became a jyzer? -- That is, as a matter of rebellion against my own inner nature, except for my natural rebelliousness?)

We're thinking the chances are not great -- though not nonexistent either -- that our current apartment will be priced within our range. The new owners bought the building for 900K and it has nine units, and ours would be in the middle range or average. For 203 to be priced at 150K the owners would have to be satisfied with a mere fifty percent return on their investment in a single year (assuming they would, as Dana the landlady said they would on the phone, let us have our unit without remodeling it). In today's outrageous market it's far from a sure thing that that size of markup would be enough for them.

-- But then again, I'm now wondering if our chances might be better than I thought. I hadn't really looked closely at the numbers before. -- And I'd say the odds are good that the real-estate market will have cooled off a bit by this summer. Most likely we'll have to be making a decision one way or the other by fall, because if we don't want the unit, they'll be needing to remodel it before the building goes condo across the board early next year.

(I figure the real reason for Dana's call the other day was to inform us we'd have to be moving out by a certain date. It probably hadn't occurred to her that we might be interested in buying the unit. Apparently none of the other tenants are going for theirs. Our guess is she'd already talked with at least some of them, including the occupants of the two other units on our floor, and their response was to say they'd be leaving. What Z and I can't figure out is what will happen to 103 and 303, the units below and above ours, when their remodeling is complete by the end of the

month. Will they sit empty until next January? Who
would want to rent those units knowing they'd have to
move out in a few months? Or will they go on the market
immediately as condos? -- In which case it might be
possible for us to buy our unit now, or soon, before the
price goes up even more. Or on the other hand we might
learn now, or soon, we can't afford it, in which case
we'd want to start looking elsewhere right away, and if
we found something we'd want to move quickly on it.)
     -- All of which I'm mentioning here to explain why
it's possible, though not likely, we'll be moving from
1511 even before this jyze project ends. And of course
making such a move would seriously crimp the amount of
time left for jyzing. It's one of the last things I'd
want but it might happen.
     -- And one final observation, though maybe it's so
obvious it needn't be said: it appears less and less
likely we'll ever realize our hope of securing a place
in the subsidized-loft development. The units there
won't become available until too far down the road. I
don't think we'll want to go through the ordeal of
buying a condo twice within a couple of years. -- But
who knows. Two years ago I was hoping we'd never have
to move again (and in fact I still am). And of course
two years before that I was thinking B-2 would be my
home for the rest of my days.
     We found ourselves talking about all this again
yesterday while walking around the AQ before and after
the one-man show. "I Remember Mapa" wasn't bad at all,
and the mostly gay/lesbian and Asian audience (including
many Asian gays and lesbians) seemed to get a large
charge out of it. Z did too, mainly because of the
frequent references to various difficulties a second-
generation Filusan kid faces while growing up in the
USA, many of which she had experienced herself. For me
I have to admit it all seemed a little stale. Also, a
lot of the humor was theater-world insider stuff of the
type I encountered all too often during earlier eras of
my life, and another large portion was the kind of
politically incorrect ethnic-bashing-for-laffs that's

standard on Lady U's home turf and that, indeed, she and
I used to go to the mat on from time to time during our
years together. But I still enjoyed it.

     -- And now my time's up, and much remains to be
said. Can I return later tonight for an encore? -- Can
hope so.

[+1]

     It didn't happen. With my bedtime back to half
past four the late-night window for jyze is not big and
I must fit in lots of other stuff as well, including
chores, dinner, reading the local papers, and working up
a card or note for Z, not to mention making at least a
perfunctory effort to keep up on more serious reading.

     So now ground zero, the art bar. One of the last
remaining really good places. And then only if you
arrive here early enough to do your thing and ease out
before nine, at which point the live or DJ'd music
starts and you must pay the cover charge to stay on.

     A little side table with an audibly and sniffably
as well as visibly guttering candle. Paintings hanging
perilously askew nearby on both sides. Bizarre music.
Pool balls clicking and rolling and dropping into
pockets with big klunks. A stronger Afrusan presence
here now than in its early days (its fourth anniversary
is coming up) with different forms and mixes of hip-hop,
funk, and jazz featured most nights. Everything painted
black or, along one lower side wall, red.

     A windy evening, squally at times -- meaning
windblown wet -- but I happened to hit on a dry period
for my walk down. Z had raved about the clouds and I
saw why. (She had also stripped down to show off her
new black thong underwear and I raved about those and
also about how she looked in them. "Oooh, sexy vintage
woman," she murmured, eyeing herself in the mirror.
Getting away was not easy.)

     A grisly head-on collision on the high bridge had
left two cars crumpled and smoking in an interlocked

state, with two big fire trucks, an ambulance, and
several police cars still present, all lined up in the
middle two lanes so rush-hour traffic could squeeze by
in the outer two, blue and red flashing lights
reflecting on chrome and glass everywhere. I see lots
of speeders on that bridge and lately the odds have been
catching up with them. This is the third major accident
I've witnessed there -- or rather witnessed the
aftermath of there -- in the past year.

I've already stopped by the scope office and
learned that tonight's docket is corrections only. So
after finishing those I'll start drafting a letter to
the editor of the alt-weekly. Yes, I've decided to do
it. Probably nothing will come of it. Certainly I
won't be putting a lot of effort into it. Just a
suggestion: that they publish an open letter to the
mayor calling for him to proclaim a citywide celebration
geared around the implosion of the dome on March 25th,
"domesday," which also happens to be, in case they
didn't know, the "true millennium." Let's put our city
back together again! -- And so on. J. City's morale is
even lower now because of this most recent plane crash.
Let's put it all behind us with a big bang! (I'm so
cheesy I can't believe it. Just shaking my head and
rolling my eyes over this nonsense. But of course it's
fun anyway. And even if nonsense it's still nonsense
that makes a kind of sense.)

-- An amusing moment when I walked up to the front
desk at the WOC to check in last night. Van, handing me
my towel, said, "I have to tell you this. I had a dream
about you last night. My girlfriend was giving you a
blowjob." No more details than that. "Ooh, the levels
of meaning!" observed Z when I told her about it. I
figure it's a simple matter of rivalry, whether
unconscious or not: Van and I, after all, are the only
two people either of us knows or has heard about who are
keeping some sort of millennium journal or J-book. As
for his girlfriend, I've never met her or even seen her
as far as I know. But she looks real good in the photo
he showed me and somehow sort of familiar. I imagine

the jyzer in the dream must've been enjoying himself
even if also perhaps feeling a bit guilty, although then
again why be guilty -- the dream was Van's! The jyzer
was trapped in it! Captive! Even the Z-woman
understands this point and agrees with it.)

   In quasi-family news, the results of Betty's MRI
tests came back yesterday and they can be interpreted in
two ways: either it's a virus of the spinal cord she's
suffering from or it's a recurrence of the polio she
contracted as an infant. More tests lie ahead. This
was the first that Z and I had heard about Betty's
polio. Apparently she was exposed to it after the
vaccine's creation but before its use was widespread.
(Earlier Z and Betty had gone heart to heart on their
financial problems. Betty doesn't know where her money
goes either. She makes 44K a year as an elementary-
school nurse and is never able to save a penny. Over
the past three months she's had to pay the astounding
sum of $500 on bounced checks at $25 a pop.)

   (Half a dozen Afrusan dudes are working on their
raps at the table behind me, two making drum sounds with
pursed-lip explosions. One came up and watched me
jyzing away for maybe fifteen seconds, then handed me a
sheet of paper and asked me to write down the name of
his company using the J-stick. "Your penmanship's worth
money, man!" Hey, I'm flattered! -- But he didn't give
me any money. Then again I didn't ask for any. -- And
it occurs to me that in a sense this is the first
autograph I've ever signed. So this is how they feel,
those washed-up sports heroes who appear at the
collectible shows. Hey over there, who's next in line?
-- Oh, and no more free samples, dudes!)

   In other news, Z informed me Aida and Kirk are
parting ways. It may or may not be temporary. Kirk
told Aida he thinks they should stop being lovers -- he
has "issues" he wants to work on. Aida said these have
to do with being abused as a kid. When she asked him if
this meant they had to stop being friends too, Kirk said
he'd just assumed she would realize that. To Z's
puzzlement, Aida didn't seem upset by any of this. "She

and I relate to men so differently. I've seen it before
with Kavi and others but it never stops amazing me.
With a man I'm either in or I'm out. This on-and-off,
half-ass stuff dragging out forever, I could never stand
it."

     And June called yesterday with an offer to help on
our taxes. She convinced me it would be all right and
then I convinced Z. "Just so she doesn't know about my
credit-card debt," she, Z, cautioned. "Because she'll
rake me over the coals on that." June's volunteering
six Saturday mornings between now and April 15 to help
low-income folks with their taxes; apparently we're to
be a kind of extension of that. Perhaps this way she
can feel less obligated to us for the help we're giving
her on law-school papers. "And now I can come over at
two in the morning," she joked, "and you can make me
coffee and orange-bread toast with honey and butter
while I do your taxes."

     One other matter to mention. Maybe I've already
said something about it, but just to be sure. When Z
and I talked about the serious conflicts we both have
with our sisters I mentioned the cruel note Barb had
sent Gail about never wanting to hear about her ferrets
again. So the other day Z came home with a book of
ferret postcards and suggested we send one to Gail and
Rob from time to time with personalized touches. And
today I'm carrying the first of these, a Valentine's Day
special, two ferrets sniffing each other's noses in
front of a heart-shaped box of chocolates, one ferret
saying, "Hope Rob and Gail have a notably vigorous
February." (Rob likes to chaff us that for a couple of
ancients we're still "notably vigorous.") -- It's
hopelessly corny and smarmy, this card, no question, but
I'm quite touched Z would think of doing it and then
follow through as she did.

     And going back to "I Remember Mapa," I should
mention Paz and Tobey attended it with us, as did Jess
and Jess's friend Courtney from construction-worker days
and also Courtney's new partner Hannah. Jess was still
wearing her outdoor work clothes, denim coveralls and

heavy work boots, because the ferry was running late and she couldn't make it home to change. She was embarrassed to be dressed that way, but she looked as good as I've seen her in recent months and was in high spirits. Again I wished she'd seek me out to talk about her travails, but I guess it just won't be happening. I'm a male! What do I know about loving women! -- So then I hope she'll pair up with someone again soon so Z and I will be able to see more of her with her new partner. (Z feels the same way. Everybody has a thing for Jess even when she's impossible to get along with. Hannah was reduced to a gibbering idiot in front of her. Just like me, I suppose. Certainly like Z.)

[+1]

     -- Late late late. I blew it. Almost an hour past my bedtime and Z's alarm might go off at any moment. I just have time to say I worked up a draft of the "True Millennium" proposal and it's looking pretty good and I'm planning to go over it one more time tomorrow and deliver it to the alt-weekly Friday. I even left myself two hours for jyzing at the hideaway tonight, but when I returned there I found a large amount of lumber and plywood stacked in the "free" zone in the building's entrance hallway and an old dream flamed up again: I'd build a loft in my office! And with a fourteen-foot-high ceiling it's an actual possibility. So I spent most of the next two hours hauling the wood upstairs and making room to store it.
     More on all that another time. It's the fifth day of Chinese New Year, the shops are open again, life's returning to normal. Except that today the engineers union at our local aerospace/"defense" leviathan went out on strike, and probably within a few days the whole company will shut down for a spell. Around here that's big news. We're thinking of sending Fred and Eleanor W. a CARE package (because he's an engineer for the leviathan). -- And also big news, an "attack" against

the internet by unknown "antisocial" hackers -- or maybe
just one -- is now into its third day and is wreaking
lots of havoc, I'm pleased to say, among the techies and
their financial backers. Average response times at the
big e-commerce companies have doubled, from four to
eight seconds (that's the time consumers must wait
online before placing an order). Oh lovely lovely.
Maybe the whole internet will collapse in a big cloud of
dust and we can return to our former moderately
consumerist way of living (ha!). -- And I just made
Valentine's anklets for Betty, Kat, and Jess, to go in
cards Z bought for them. Just on a lark, but now I
think I'll do the same for Z herself and that'll be it,
my Valentine's duty done! (But this declaration is
subject to almost certain major revision over the next
few days.)

BOOK I

[Infinite Jyze]

41

Came sizzling out a little early this time and with a wad of hot copy in hand. Unusual for this era -- but old memories were crowding back in. While crossing the high bridge I saw the dome looking sadly used and beaten, splotchy portions of its fluted roof turned an odd powdery blue. The copy -- in my bag actually -- was a memo offering a "story idea" based on the upcoming demolition for which the dome is now being prepped.

Straight down to the alt-weekly's office on the old "low road," just four blocks or so from the hideaway, and there I handed the manila envelope to the receptionist, saying, "Could you please see that he gets this?" -- "he" being the name I pointed at on the outside of the envelope, "Emil H." (followed by "(Personal)") -- and she said, "Surely"; and it was my impression she was about to take it straight in to him. But I didn't stick around to find out. Pivoted, made myself scarce. But my phone number and address are in the memo.

I did the best I could on it. Gave over most of yesterday afternoon to writing it and then fiddled with it for two hours on the computer at the scope office last night before printing it -- that's why I'm a day late in starting this entry. It was journalism deja vu, the referent here being my own era with various weeklies, some alt and some not, in other cities. Just as back then it was both exciting and disturbing to feel so intensely invested. In such circumstances it's tough to focus on anything else or even work up an interest in anything else. But the interest in other kinds of

writing is always there, underneath, gnawing away, and
in my case back then often leaving me feeling quite
frustrated. So it's still good to be reminded every
once in a while why I got out of deadline journalism.

Now the ORB cafe, my favorite table in the rear
corner. (Some jerk talking loud on his cellphone -- I
finally had to ask him to dial it back a bit, and to my
surprise he did -- even apologized!) An ice-cold root
beer. This preceded by more than an hour of browsing
upstairs, half an hour each with two hardcovers way too
expensive to buy and a few minutes flipping through the
current issue of the main-far-coast-megalopolis review
of books which Z and I subscribe to (but I've let the
subscription lapse; it's under Z's name, and we'll hold
off on starting another one in my own name until a
bargain-rate offer comes in, because that way is much
cheaper than renewing). And after this jyze session
here, a workout and a soak at the WOC.

Will the alt-weekly bite on the idea? Maybe. I'd
say it's about fifty/fifty. I wouldn't be surprised to
find a message from Emil H. on our answering machine
sometime next week, maybe even this weekend or tonight.
But I shouldn't set myself up for disappointment. I've
done what I wanted to do. From here on in it's out of
my hands. (Hard to think, it's so noisy down here.
This is not the way a bookshop cafe should be. -- But
then again I guess it is, because a couple of large and
enthusiastic book groups at the long tables in the
adjoining section are the main high-decibel offenders.
And I'd be pushing my luck for sure if I asked them to
tone it down.)

In the meantime an interesting couple of days. On
arrival at home last night I found a six-page letter
from Z lamenting her discovery at a home-buying class
that she's blown it on credit and we'll probably never
be able to buy a condo or a house. She was weeping as
she wrote it, and then she began weeping again later
when I joined her in bed and she was telling me the
story. High drama -- as she said herself. I said we'd
be fine; we'll just keep on keeping on as before until

we can't do that anymore, at which point we'll adjust.
Simple! Yes, true, it's a drag that we'll have to move
soon -- probably by summer, I'd guess -- but so it goes.
On balance and looking at all aspects of our lives can
we say we're unlucky? When we've got each other, Z-
woman? Eh? Eh? -- And this afternoon I found a note
on my armchair thanking me for putting up with "my
freakwent freakouts" and saying how grateful she is for
having "such a rock of a hubbin" (and "zoelmate, lover,
friend"). Hey, and likewise I'm sure!

The rest of the news can wait. It's already time
to move on. But I'm feeling good, yes I am. As we head
into Valentine's weekend. I'm even a little prepared on
Valentine's gifts for Z and others. And how could I not
be happy when a new collection of essays by "the most
interesting philosopher in the world today" is out and
I'm reading one essay a day, "like fine wine" as that
hopeless reprobate not to say blockhead reactionary
Marcus G. at the WOC might say if he went for this
particular liberal and truly progressive, in a sense not
just radical but beyond radical, neoprag thinker, which
he definitely would never do.

        *   *

-- Carrying on now -- briefly -- at the hideaway
some five hours later. Nightclub activity below is
shaking the joint in the usual paroxysmal Friday-night
way. What's not so usual is the tropical climate up
here tonight. Presumably it's a result of
overcompensation with regard to the predicted cold spell
which is turning out to be not so cold after all -- but
building staff left the furnaces blasting for the
weekend anyway, just in case, before they went home -
and this has me stripped down to a pair of black gym
shorts and the sleeveless brown "NJA" muscle henley with
the sleeves chopped off because Z likes them that way.

Also unusual, three sheets of plywood are leaning
against the bookcase to my left and pressing against the
cushion of this chair, reducing its de facto sitting
width by a third so that it's more like an airline seat
in tourist class. And in the two corners of the room

I'm facing, northeast and northwest, two-by-four studs
poke straight up to almost two-thirds of ceiling height
(eight-fourteenths, to be exact), ten of them in all.
These are the makings for my hideaway loft of the
future. And now with the likelihood increasing markedly
that Z and I will be renting forever -- will never have
a home of our own to stash books in -- the loft project
here takes on new urgency of a sort. But then this
assumes I'll be able to keep this place longer than any
apartment we may rent, and with all the changes around
the HQ that's probably a false assumption. Old Allen
W., the owner of this building, by and large treats his
tenants well -- never raises the rent by more than the
yearly increase in the cost of living -- but he's in his
eighties. When he goes, my occupancy here will almost
surely soon come to an end also.
     Okay, time's up. And despite the summer gear I'm
sweating heavily: need to sponge myself down real fast
in the men's room before hitting the streets.

                         [+2]

     And to the opening entry for Book I of this
seemingly never-ending TJM project -- once again that's
the ninth letter of the alphabet there, and this is also
book the penultimate, of ten -- I can now add a brief
postscript and that's it. Saturday night, four a.m. No
response yet to the memo I left for Emil H. at the alt-
weekly. Z asleep, probably still in a state of shock --
now dreamified shock -- over the size of the bill for
tonight's jazz-club outing. Over three hundred bucks!
That was for four of us and included a virtually taste-
free light snack which the menu called dinner and a
watered-down drink or two apiece and one set of a Cuban
trumpet/piano maestro and his jazzed-up seven-piece
mariachi band (as I saw it in my Latin-music
benightedness) -- though the man is extremely talented
and I enjoyed the spectacle, including the chance to
observe a roomful of massively overaffluent digerati so

nerdily at play. And Gerry and Leola's company is always a pleasure. -- On which more next time, I hope.

This was Z's "treat" for my having nursed her through her fractured flipper and flu. Maybe it's a good way to kick off the frugality era, sort of like polishing off an entire butterscotch cream pie the night before going on a drastic diet. And today she resumed vacuuming after a hiatus of months. And we discussed the possibility that she had panicked about her credit score on the self-administered test at the home-buying class; and tonight Gerry, who frequently deals with credit matters at his job with FHA, gave her some encouragement on this: he thinks she'll be just fine. So perhaps it's not really settled after all that we'll be moving from here and never owning a home -- or at least not settled with a hundred percent certainty. But the likelihood's still very high, I'd say.

-- And we sparred a bit, with Z confessing after some time that her crankiness might have something to do not just with her return to vacuuming but also with my blowing off her blunt "sex-on-demand" move in bed this morning (I was exhausted and scarcely remember it). We recovered from the sparring, but I won't be surprised if she rebuffs me right back on my own next move, which might or might not come a few minutes from now. She's off the injured list, I'll note, and also off the H-rag. (And some great-looking half-Norski guy at the utility supposedly has a big crush on her and of course she hasn't shied away from letting me know about that.)

Tomorrow Kat and Betty. On the way home tonight we bought a rotisserie chicken -- free range to be sure (if indeed one can be sure) -- and Z will warm it up for dinner tomorrow. And I'm feeling those Valentine's Day anxieties again: will my little schemes beget enough to keep the Z-wiff happy? She's let me know she's working hard on something for me in her room -- off-limits to me until after the 14th -- and when I caught a glimpse of her actually doing this, or something like it, as I passed her wide-open door, I suddenly sensed the gross inadequacy of my own efforts. But at this late moment I

may be stymied. It might even be Christmas all over
again. -- And, in a first, we could see all the way
through the dome as we drove across the high bridge
tonight. Saw the sunset through it! -- As the ramps
and walls come off the sides to make the imminent
demolition go more easily (but also less thunderously).

[+1]

     A surprise at dinner tonight. Betty served up a
couple of presents and a raspberry pie as a birthday
gift -- for me! The presents were a gorgeous picture
book about fountain pens that once belonged to Manny and
a Norski calendar for the millennial year. On the cover
of the calendar a photo of my face is affixed to a
drawing of a knight from medieval days; his (my) arms
are cradling a religious statue labeled, by Betty, "the
Kitchen Goddess," with a headful of Zoelie-like spiked
black hair added. (Also included in the package were a
batch of photos Z and I hadn't seen before, taken -- by
Betty's friend Wanda -- during our first group trip to
what a year later turned out to be our honeymoon resort
-- and six years earlier was Betty and Manny's
honeymoon resort.) (Z's amused comment afterwards:
"Well, do you believe me now that Betty has an
incorrigible lateness problem?" My birthday was five
and a half months ago! -- Yeah, and Z herself, as I
reminded her, forgot all about it at the time and wound
up spending it in Centropolis two thousand miles away!)
     Kat and I squeezed in a good rasslin' session this
time. Her tenth birthday's coming up in a week and a
half, but she and Betty will be flying off to see Nick
and Wanda that week because it's also winter break.
She, Kat, hadn't even begun (except for five lame
attempts at an opening sentence) the paper Z and I were
supposed to help her "rewrite" tonight. She's heard so
much talk from adults about her high test scores that
her eyes glaze over when the topic comes up. When Betty
openly wished she could find better ways to motivate

her, Kat quipped, "Green money will always do it!"

As we arrived we caught a lovely unguarded view of Kat through the dining-room window, her eyes wide as she carefully lit a candle in the mostly darkened room already aflicker with scattered flames. Z and I were both stunned by the beauty of that scene -- just stood there staring, first at Kat and then at each other.

The entire evening Kat seemed to be "testing" her mother, doing the opposite of whatever Betty asked her to do or dawdling on it to eternity. "Do you think I'm overreacting?" Betty finally asked us when Kat left the room for a moment. Well, maybe, I said, but only with respect to the fact that she might want to save some of it for the truly tough tests coming up over the next eight or ten years -- best not to shoot her wad at this early stage. Z said, as she has once or twice before, that what Kat really needs at such times, and also when she dawdles too much on her homework, is "a good Filipino pinch."

For the first time I noticed a slightly humped area on Betty's upper back that might've resulted from her childhood polio (I didn't ask). And I tried to help her disassemble a table which Manny built in the garret room and in its finished form is much too large to navigate the narrow staircase, but the socket-wrench set I brought along turned out to offer nothing large enough for the task and the standard wrench couldn't reach the recessed nuts (Manny was clearly quite the woodworker). And both Betty and Kat kept quiet, as I had asked them to, about the anklets I sent them to wear on Valentine's Day. That's because tonight I'll be working up, starting in about thirty minutes, a number of similar items for Z fashioned from the same two-inch-wide cloth tape -- it's very thick, stiffened somewhat with plastic wires, and bears a colorful hearts-and-flowers pattern -- including a choker, earrings, bracelets, and a "truly intimate" liner for her "unners." I'll be inscribing messages on all of them with textile markers. -- But will this be enough? I'm still worried. Should I rise at the crack of dawn and dress myself as a bicycle

messenger and deliver some flowers to her office? (I'd
like to but it would mangle the rest of the day and that
I can't afford to let happen.)
     This from the hideaway, a typical quiet Sunday
night. I've had less time than hoped for, though,
because I decided to crash on the floor for half an hour
and it turned into an hour and a half. A sweet morning
lovemaking session -- "plan A" all the way -- Z to my
surprise initiating things almost before I was fully in
bed with the kind of long slow lip-and-tongue-dragging
back kisses I love (on my back and shoulders, I'm
saying, and ass and back of thighs too, as her hands
wandered in front) -- that fine session left me long on
languorous after-tremors, yes, but also short on sleep.

                        [+1]

     So now it's late in the evening of Valentine's Day.
And I guess I can say it turned out all right. I came
up with two new twists on the charm idea -- both
bubbling up as I worked with a sense of mounting anxiety
on the "packet of charms" at four a.m., having earlier
found Z's set of Valentine gifts awaiting me when I
arrived home. These included a string of little
cardboard hearts with a message hand-drawn on each one
("Ooh, jyze me, baby"), a couple of altered commercial
cards, a box of chocolate hearts, and some message
handbills scattered throughout the apartment (one by the
entrance to the kitchen said "Food and Drink"; one next
to the bedroom door had an arrow pointing in and said
"Entertainment").
     So it occurred to me to add another item to my
packet for her: a hearts-and-flowers "kiri" ribbon like
the one in the "twisting in the wind" box I sent her
after she broke our very first date, this one saying
"For us every day is Valentine's Day." Stone lame,
yeah, but I went with it anyway. And then I wrapped the
packet and boxed it and made a "Merc's Valentine
Special" label for it, playing off the name of the

messenger service which delivered that first box, whose
arrival as her officemates looked on has become a
favorite story of hers to tell. And she liked this.
Spurning my note saying she should open it at the
office, she ripped off all the wrappings on the spot and
then came rushing back to the bedroom to thank me. And
she did wear the charms all day, she told me later in a
phone call, including the "intimate" one pinned inside
her tap pants. (In that same call she did grump a
little about how I'd been "so stubborn" in not giving
her flowers which she could show off at the office, but
she didn't seem seriously upset. Her friends had raved
about the new kiri ribbon, she assured me, and also the
various charms -- the ones she could show them. When we
met at the WOC at five she handed me a package saying
"My Stubborn Valentine" on the outside, but inside was
a giant cinnamon cookie frosted with "I love you.")
     Bullet safely dodged? I think so. But another may
be coming my way a month from tomorrow: her birthday.
And two weeks after that, our We Meet! anniversary.
     In the meantime, though, maybe I can take a few
deep breaths.
     And I'm feeling lucky because during the
housecleaning finale on Sunday my missing jyze pendant
turned up. Unfortunately it was the vacuum cleaner that
found it (under the bed -- Z was wielding the vacuum)
and by the time it coughed it up the pendant was fairly
well mangled. But I was able to hammer it back into
something vaguely resembling its former shape and to put
a new cord on it and I'm wearing it right now. If it
was "primitive copper" before, now it's ur-primitive.
But I like it better, I think. An intriguing storm-
tossed look it has to it. This pendant has been around
the mulberry bush a few times -- and now around the
vacuum spin-sweeper, or whatever it's called, as well.
     Still no response to my T/M (true millennium) memo.
But if it's flopped, it's flopped. No big deal.
Nonetheless I'll still keep an eye out for references to
it, direct or indirect, in the alt-weekly itself. Or
who knows, maybe Emil H. has magnanimously passed it

along to the indie weekly and I should keep an eye out
there as well, or even the J. City dailies. The far-
coaster, I'll admit that's a stretch.

     The last few days, by the way, have seen major new
developments in the Kirk and Aida story. On Friday Z
learned it was all over: Kirk had told Aida he'd given
the matter "a great deal of serious thought" and decided
to make their breakup complete and permanent. On Sunday
morning Aida called Z and wanted to schmooze with her
about it in person that afternoon, but Z had to turn her
down owing to our prior engagement with Betty and Kat.
By the time we returned from that, Aida had caved and
called Kirk and asked him to reconsider, and in the end
they agreed to keep seeing each other as "friends." Z's
comment: "I can't believe she went crawling back to him
like that! She's a total masochist. Now he'll be
exploiting her for months or years just like Kavi did.
She'll be neither fish nor fowl."

     -- June too was aghast about the latest twist in
the Aida/Kirk soap opera in her Valentine's call to me
this afternoon (she was thanking me for a card Z gave
her from both of us, though I never even saw it and
didn't know what it said and therefore had to fake
things a bit on the phone). "It might be different,"
June said, "if she really loved him or he cared a lot
about her. But neither one is true! Glen! She has no
pride!" (And then she told me about the big new scandal
in her own family: her older brother's daughter, at
twenty-one a recent graduate from the elite far-coast
tech school where he teaches, has joined an our-coast
(megastate) internet start-up firm, and she's in love
with a classmate who's followed her out there -- an
Ethiopian! Suddenly June's brother's wife is afraid of
disturbing the spirits of all those Kung family
ancestors she was always so sarcastic about before.
June is cackling like crazy over this. What matters to
her, she says, isn't race, it's culture, and she figures
this young man must come from a high-ranking family if
they could afford to send him to that elite school; and
also she views Ethiopian culture as ancient and proud --

enough so to fight off many of the insidious effects
of westernization -- though her only real evidence for
this, she admits, comes from certain observations she's
made while eating at an Ethiopian restaurant she
occasionally visits a block from her dorm on east hill.)

I also want to note Mad Mitch showed up at the WOC
tonight for the first time in weeks. He's now an
ultimate fighter in the over-forty division. He's also
serving as a doorman at a gay nightclub ("Sodom and
Gomorrha," he calls it, though that's not its actual
name), and he's added a couple of new tattoos, a Mohawk
'do, and about thirty pounds to his already
horrifically fearsome appearance (especially when he
pops out his artificial left eyeball). And he's again
spouting nonsense about a physics paper he wrote which
supposedly was published in some important scientific
journal. But I always enjoy talking with him anyway,
and never more so than when he's waxing enthusiastic
about my T/M plan. He's the only one at the WOC who's
shown genuine interest in it -- especially concerning
the astrological aspects of the upcoming planetary
"grand alignment," although that, alas, will be arriving
too late for this annal except in preliminary form. For
sure we both like the name.

-- This again from the hideaway. I worked out too
hard and then soaked too long: I'm a molten lump of
soreness and exhaustion. And hunger as well, having
skipped dinner except for a banana and a power bar.
It'll be cold up there at the bus stop: temperatures
below freezing, snow in outlying areas (and Gene the
pilot's now living on the peninsula and must drive about
ninety miles to get home; we walked out of the WOC
together tonight and he was pining for Mexico as so many
people around here do at this time of year; and he just
returned from there!).

[+1]

-- Here's another new twist on housing. (Oh the

buffetings! Back and forth we go!)
     Shortly after Z popped in the door this evening we
heard a loud dripping sound coming from the kitchen
area. Visual inspection revealed water leaking from one
of the recessed ceiling light fixtures and dropping onto
the counter next to the sink (one of Z's designated
personal zones -- where she keeps her pills and water-
purifying bottles, among other things, including big
stacks of dirty dishes). At first the drip was very
slow but it gradually speeded up even as we were peering
at it, increasing to a total of about five or six drops
per second, most originating from three or four spots
around the circular rim of the fixture.
     We called the number Dana D. had left with us and
were immediately able to reach Raphael, Dana's husband
who's been remodeling the unit above ours, and he said
he was at home (on east hill) but he'd be right over.
For us this was a dreaded moment of truth: we were about
to let the new landlord enter our unit and he'd see for
the first time what kind of state we keep it in. Well,
no, maybe not the first time: he and Dana had probably
toured it with Min during the inspection before they
bought the building. But that was likely when we were
away on our honeymoon and, to our minds anyway, had a
good excuse for the place looking as it did. This time
we'd have none. So we set about tidying up a bit. But
neither of us panicked. After all, how much of a dent
could we hope to make in the mess in such a short time?
And besides, why should we care? We'd soon be moving
out anyway and they'd be remodeling our place too. And
luckily Z had done a full vacuuming this past weekend.
So we just tended to the most obvious stuff in and near
the kitchen and pushed things out of sight in other
areas.
     Within fifteen minutes Raphael appeared. From what
Z had told me I was expecting an arrogant prep-school
type, but he turned out to be an unassuming, soft-spoken
fellow with a twinkle in his eye, tall, trim, somewhat
Italian looking, with a shock of dark hair falling
over his forehead (indeed fitting Zonker's description

of him and Dana as "handsome people" and reminding me a bit of brother Jeff -- and maybe even a tiny bit of the Fonz, or the Fonzie, as our previous landlord Min called him). He said he'd already found the source of the leak, a valve or faucet beneath the sink which one of his workers must've nudged open accidentally just before leaving. He was hoping any damage would be minor.

While waiting for the dripping to slow down -- after he turned off the valve/faucet and mopped up in 303 above us -- we talked about the building and their plans for it. To our surprise we learned the condoizing scheme is much less firm than we'd been thinking. It's their intent to rent out the currently empty units above and below ours on one-year leases, so the official condoizing couldn't begin before March of 2001 at the earliest. And from the way he was talking Z and I both got the impression it might happen much later than that. It would appear they're thinking the hood won't be ready for condos -- that is, won't be respectable enough to support the marketing of upscale condos at ungodly prices -- for several more years. It depends on the city's housing market in general, of course. But until some of the rattletrap houses and apartment buildings across the street and on the next block to the north are replaced, for example, Raphael and Dana probably won't be able to maximize their profits and would be better off keeping the building as a source of rental income.

That was the big news. Raphael also passed along some information we hadn't heard before. The two other sets of tenants on our floor just happened to give notice at the same time, he said; he and Dana hadn't even spoken to them about the condo possibility or for that matter anything else. And the remodeling of those units will proceed at a slower pace than planned because the crew foreman just this past weekend broke his leg. Also: Aboula and family, in the unit below ours, moved out shortly before R&D bought the building, leaving their unit, he said, "totally trashed." As for the backup of cigar and cigarette smoke through the vent system which has upset Z at times, he said the baffles

should prevent that and he doesn't know why they're
failing to do so, but in the future we shouldn't have
any problem because all the new leases will include no-
smoking provisions.

Currently he's painting the hallways and stairwell;
later his crew will be replacing the defective outdoor
siding at no cost to tenants (hurrah!). In his view the
construction quality of this building is "typical" for
the period when it went up roughly a decade ago. Their
other buildings are all from sixty to almost a hundred
years old and in some ways this one is far superior.
And he knew there had been a problem with our wall
heaters but seemed unaware of the big recall of that
brand and asked us to provide more information if we had
it (and we do, somewhere, though not much).

All in all I liked the guy. Dana handles the sales
end of things; Raphael seems more like a natural-born
carpenter/builder -- again something like brother Jeff.
Z admitted her earlier impression of him as a
"privileged-class wheeler-dealer in a fancy suit" had
been way off.

After he left she and I talked awhile and she
seemed quite relieved. Her "panic mygs" had been
stirred up a bit by the credit-scoring revelation, to
the point that she'd written letters to a number of
friends asking them to be on the lookout for rental
prospects for us; those letters had been awaiting my
signature for a couple of days. But I'd told her I
thought it might be better to hold off on sending them
until her credit reports came in (the ones Gerry advised
her to ask for, which she immediately did), and now we
were both glad the letters hadn't gone out yet. "Hey,"
she conceded, "maybe my husband-person has a better
sense for this kind of financial stuff than he likes to
let on most of the time." (Busted!) (Ha.)

We agreed to put off any housing decisions for the
rest of this year. If her credit score does turn out to
be good enough to swing a mortgage -- we know mine won't
since I don't have one -- then this apartment we're in
right now will be our first choice for a permanent

residence when it becomes available, as long as the
price is within reach. (And Raphael did confirm what
his wife had told us: we could have it as-is at a lower
price if that's our preference.) If a mortgage is
beyond our reach, then we'll stay on here as long as we
can and not even think about looking elsewhere until
next year. (Raphael also assured us we'd receive
"plenty" of advance notice about any condoizing
decision. -- And after our talk today I think I trust
him enough on that to say the hell with worrying. At
the very least we're guaranteed ninety days' notice
under a city ordinance and that should suffice by itself
-- especially since he's the one who mentioned it.)
     Incidentally, it happened that tonight the hilltop
neighborhood association was meeting. It was obvious
Raphael hadn't heard about it before and knew little
about the hood itself beyond what's on our block. He
didn't even know the former marine hospital is being
subleased to the dot-com by a realty company, nor was he
aware several new buildings will be going up there or
that the hood has a new street parking plan (which Z
helped draw up). It appeared he might even think we'd
be useful tenants to have around, if only to keep him
apprised of such things. (And I saw him give only one
lingering glance at Z's kitchen counter piled high with
dirty dishes and bottles of herbs, etc.; otherwise he
did a good job of pretending he wasn't seeing the rest
of the apartment at all.)

[+1]

     The amusing news is that Z's already made other
plans for herself for the day of the true millennium,
which is still more than five weeks in the future. She
spaced out another of my most significant days! And
more boggling yet, Aida plays a part in the drama!
     Lately Z's again been moaning about how much harder
it is now for her to talk with Aida. "I always feel
like she's going to disapprove -- be judgmental." But

811

Z's also worrying because of the problems Aida's having
with Charles and her father's poor health and now the
fiasco with Kirk, who just last night told her he
doesn't think they can cut it as friends either and
again broke off all contact with her. Weeks ago I had
suggested that Z take a trip with Aida as a way to
bolster their own friendship, and though that notion
didn't go anywhere at the time, last night she came up
with the idea of spending a weekend alone with Aida at
Jess's house when Jess would be on the island working on
the new place (as she is most weekends now). Today Z
called Aida and she liked the idea and they settled on
the first mutually workable dates: March 25th and 26th,
which is to say: weekend of the true millennium.

    Despite all my talk about March 25th, Z had never
bothered to mark it off on her calendar! But what am I
gonna do? Certainly I don't want to stand between these
two tempestuous longtime buddies. (Aida's comment to Z,
which to me sounded vaguely hostile: "So you're finally
ready to come out of your cocoon?" -- But she did tell
Z something apparently favorable too: "I think Glen's a
lot more in touch with his emotions than Kirk is.") Z
also says Aida is upset with her parents because they're
suddenly back to making it much harder for her to have a
social life, disapproving of her "boyfriends" and
refusing to let her invite them to family gatherings (as
with the infamous incident involving Kirk's banishment
at Thanksgiving). But this would also suggest to me
she's become more accepting of her father's declining
health -- maybe because he seems to be responding well
to the ministrations of the Chinese herbalist (whom Z
located for him through Lorraine, her naturopath).

    But I also tell Z I think she may be setting
herself up for a big disappointment. I remind her it's
possible she and Aida are just naturally growing apart.
On political matters Aida seems to be moving steadily
rightward, becoming more and more involved with the
church, even "looking at" the so-called maverick ex-
prisoner of war (in most matters I'd say he's actually a
belligerent reactionary) as a presidential candidate she

might campaign for. But she and Tom are regularly
seeing a counselor together about Charles and this seems
to be helping, and maybe Aida will accordingly be
feeling less pressure to seek support from the church
and its conservative worldview -- its reassuring
certainties.

With Z and me, meanwhile, our sex life has taken a
sudden somewhat negative turn, and the past few days
she's been putting "the clamp" on me in various ways --
discouraging me from touching her sexually -- and she's
announced she's feeling feisty and rebellious. The
mushy period leading up to Valentine's Day is over.
She's even back to openly denouncing me for failing to
give her flowers on that day. Maybe this is how she
reacts when she feels she's been overdoing the mush
(I've noticed the pattern a couple of times before).
-- But I should also say she's doing it with elan, in a
generally spirited, nonhostile way, even a playfully
mischievous and seductive one now and then, respecting
limits, and so it's not that bad and maybe -- probably
-- it's good. Her mercurial changes keep life
interesting around here, just as they always have.

Another amusing note: at the hood meeting last
night it was announced that a group of eight hilltop
homeowners are suing the realty company that's leasing
the marine hospital ("the DC castle") from the city for
failing to follow proper municipal procedures in
subleasing it to the dot-com. I don't know the details
yet, but the story should soon be hitting the papers.
The realty company is shamelessly trying to buy off the
homeowners, asserting the lawsuit can't win but offering
to give the legal fees it would cost them to fight it --
$30,000, they say -- to the nearest of the hilltop
elementary schools for upgrading of the dusty playground
there if the homeowners will drop the suit, which
threatens to tie up the construction program at the
castle for years. Matt B., "Zonker," chaired the
meeting. Suddenly it's all too clear how the realty
company is manipulating and exploiting this little
citizens' group (of which Z's apparently the only member

who's a renter, or so she believes).
   A couple other unusual items:
   ** Last Friday evening as I walked through the
warehouse district in the upper AQ a woman popped out
from between two parked cars and took a totally
unprovoked roundhouse swing at me. Luckily I saw her
coming -- and also heard a man calling "Look out! Look
out!" as he chased her -- and I was able to duck away
from the swing, do a little dance to get around her and
keep going on my way as the man now called back to me,
"It's all right, it's cool." They were both Natusan,
I'm pretty sure, heading up to the Natusan center or the
"rez" beyond it, and I suspect alcohol was involved and
the man was trying to get her to sell her body for him
(I've seen her doing that around there before but he's
new to me). As I walked on I ran into two other men
she'd gone after with her fists. Laughter and
amazement. "That crazy bitch tried to punch me, man!"
   ** The other was a road-rage incident Sunday
afternoon as Z and I drove over the west-side bridge on
the way to Betty's. A red pickup had been weaving from
lane to lane at high speed with sudden dangerous veers
and bursts of acceleration, passing us on the right at
about a hundred miles an hour (no exaggeration), but
then getting blocked behind a clot of slow-moving
vehicles so that we caught up with it in the double
left-turn lane at the light near the top of the hill on
the far side of the bridge. We were right behind him
when another car he'd passed, towing a boat, pulled up
next to him and the driver cussed him out -- "Fuckin'
asshole!" -- before continuing on when the light turned
green as our lane waited for the turn arrow. Suddenly
the red pickup squealed out in pursuit of the boat-
tower, nearly causing a pile-up as it roared into heavy
traffic, and we saw it pull even with the boat-tower and
the two drivers (both Cawk males to be sure) jawing away
red-faced as traffic tried to avoid them. And then they
went around a bend and we lost sight of them.
   It was the first such incident Z had ever witnessed.
"Suddenly I think I have a better idea why you think I

shouldn't be yelling 'Eat shit and die, motherfucker' at
our neighbors," she observed. Yes, she actually said
that. But then: "You know what? We're just a couple of
sedate old goo-goos." -- "Hey," says I, "let's not be
glamorizing that kind of idiocy, all right?" She: "Wait
a minute, wait a minute, you can't be more politically
correct than me!"

    ** And then something definitely less amusing.
Day after tomorrow Z goes in for her long-delayed D&C.
This fact is also a likely contributor to her recent
bursts of high feistiness. As her note here by the
black armchair says, "Meltdowns over hospital waxing and
waning." I'll be taking her in at seven in the morning
and holing up in that god-awful waiting room for as long
as it takes -- probably several hours. I'm doing the
best I can to keep my worries down and so's she. She's
even managed to sleep pretty well for the past couple of
weeks, including tonight and last night (though she did
call me in when the portable screen we use to shield us
from the air cleaner somehow toppled over onto the bed
in the dark, momentarily trapping her beneath it)
(fortunately it's all but weightless, or she might've
been injured; and this would not have been an optimal
time for anything like that to happen).

    And by the way: the new alt-weekly is out and it
shows not a single trace of my T/M memo. This doesn't
mean my hope for it is dead, but it is fading a bit.
Maybe I should've sent the damn thing to the indie
(neopunk) weekly. I'm guessing now the idea for the
open letter is kookier than I realized -- especially
with the tie-in to the "grand alignment" -- and the
indie weekly does do kookie better (and kinky better
yet). It could be the alt-weekly itself has become, in
Z's excellent term, a "sedate old goo-goo," too
concerned with being taken as a serious political player
to want to risk going with something so (apparently)
outre. -- But regardless a T/M ceremony will take place
on the 25th. Z won't be there with me, so -- fittingly
enough, I suppose -- I might be the only attendee who's
truly in the know.

42

Came dragging out this time at quarter to seven in
the morning. But it's what I usually think of (by sheer
force of habit) as a new day, simply because it's past
dawn. A rosy-fingered sunrise -- more like a cherry
layer cake, really, with bands of white-sugar filling --
and a shimmery downtown inside a diaphanous silvery fog.
Quite beautiful and startling, not to say riveting, and
I'm sure not just because I so rarely see a morning
downtown view at all in this current life.
     -- And up the south flank of east hill to the main
road and north to the clinic, where I now sit in the
surgery section's waiting area (a lucky thirteen
upholstered chairs, mine included, stand here, each with
hard glossy-tan metal arms; also present are a coffee
machine, three lamps, a single large framed oil painting
of a riverine woodland scene in what might be called
USAn nineteenth-century primitive realistic style, and a
large TV hovering on a wall-mounted shelf at about the
seven-foot level (just as at the east-depot saloon) and
that TV right now is thankfully turned off).
     The nurse in her sea-green outfit just came out to
fetch Z's glasses. There's been a delay: Dr. W. isn't
here yet. For the first twenty minutes or so of this
delay -- which was not yet official at that point -- I
sat with Z in a small cubicle back by the operating
area. She had already changed into a blue seersucker
hospital-issue robe which she found "hilariously
unflattering." I, the husband, was trying to play the
role in the way it oughta be done. What little talking
I did, however, had to be in a misdirected whisper, as

if I were speaking to the ominous medical machine five
or six feet to her left, because, as it happens, I'm
currently being assaulted by a cold bug. Great timing.
And probably no coincidence, to be sure. This bug's
been trying to gain a choke hold on me for weeks. This
past week, with the D&C coming up, I've been sleeping
less and stressing out more (though doing my damndest
not to let it show, because Z truly does do better in
times of high stress if I can be a rock for her).

Once the doc straggles in -- and I probably won't
know when that happens -- I'll have only thirty more
minutes to wait, forty at most, and then I can go back
to Z's cubicle and be with her as she comes off the
anesthetic. Or at least this is what the
anesthesiologist told me earlier.

Z upbraided me for admitting -- when she asked
about it -- I've accompanied other women to hospitals
for D&C's in my day. "Ooh," she cried, "so nonchalant!"
I wish she hadn't brought up that topic, but she did.
Fortunately she'd just been talking about an item in her
U of Centropolis alum mag describing the recent exploits
of the first man she was engaged to, back in her
welfare-worker days. Gabe. Her second big love, after
she'd gotten over Marty (a/k/a Joe Mondo of Mondo
Movers, yes). Her having mentioned Gabe kept the
situation from becoming too emotionally unbalanced. He
was the number-two guy at the social workers' union she
was a highly active member of; that's how she met him.
Unions became his lifework. But his real love (as with
my father) was tennis, of all things, and recently,
despite the handicap of a quadruple heart bypass, he's
returned to it, becoming the top-rated player in his age
group in the far southeastern state where he now lives
with his second wife. For the first time I revealed to
Z that my parents actually met on a tennis court, though
each was accompanied by someone else at the time. Z
confessed that despite serious efforts, which included
taking private lessons, she'd never been able to offer
Gabe any serious competition on the court. And I
admitted that, despite being a proud jock, I never did

much better with my father.)
     Tonight I'll have to go down to the scope office
just as on so many others. Because the printout
material describing the D&C recommends that an observer
be present with the recovering patient for the first
twenty-four hours after the procedure, Z asked June to
come over and sub for me, which she'll be doing. Now my
task is to remember to tell June to avoid anything too
spicy when she picks up dinner in the AQ on the way
over. Also I'm supposed to remind Z to take an herb
prescribed by Lorraine to help heal the internal wounds.
Arnica I think it's called ("sounds like a Cubist
painting about a war scene but with the 'G' -- that's
me! -- left out": this is my mnemonic device).
     Meanwhile -- what? Today's another primary-
election day, and the results on this one could go far
in determining the candidate of the more right-wing of
the two major parties, both of which in my view are
seriously right-wing to start with. The hot-tempered
"maverick" Vietnam vet who was a prisoner of war for
five years is coming on strong. Bad news. But the
literacy-challenged faux-cowboy son of the former
president is equally bad or worse. Both are what I
would call very close to hard right. If the economy
keeps rolling along I'd guess neither has much of a
chance to win.
     Geez, I hate to see myself acting as a cheerleader
for continuing U.S. economic expansion in the era of
global roasting and ecocide, but that's what I've just
been doing: pulling for the economy to boom in order to
keep the raging right "party of business" out of power.
-- Not a new dilemma really even if paradoxical.
     An article about the lawsuit against the realty
company that's subleasing the marine hospital to the
dot-com did appear. In fact it was in the same issue of
the alt-weekly I was glancing through in search of a
reference to 3/25. For some odd reason the dailies
haven't picked up on it yet. The story says "the Hill,"
which of course includes Z and me, has "warmed up" to
the dot-com's massive presence thanks to ---

[Infinite Jyze]

*

(The doc just appeared and introduced herself.
Z's on the way out! They're finished! -- And
everything went fine, the doc sez. "But she's just a
little bit groggy right now. Someone'll be out in a few
minutes to let you know you can go back." Bright-faced
thirty-something, not someone you'd guess was a surgeon
and not just because she's a young-looking woman. I
could see her as a city worker though. Radiates
confidence and competence too. Reminds me a little of
Z's friend Madge I. (who's redoing her houseboat decking
these days). -- So now I'll pack up and be ready to
move on.) ("...thanks to some smooth PR work," back
there just before the doc popped in.)

[+1]

-- A quick note at four a.m. to say Z's still doing
well. Other than some light bleeding -- "I'm having a
period again!" (a sensation seemingly more welcome than
worrisome, at least for a while) -- other than this, I
say, she's had no adverse reactions at all: no pain, no
nausea, no heavy, clotty bleeding -- all of which she
was warned to be prepared for.
June did stay with us last night, but mostly she
just caught up on sleep. Today Z not only was ready to
drive Betty and Kat to the airport, but she suggested we
take in a movie, "American Beauty," which she's been
wanting to see for some time, and especially since its
recent nomination for an Academy Award, and so we caught
it at a theater near the airport (and chowed down
beforehand at the attached bowling alley). Turned out
we both hated the movie. It was like a roll call of
cheap shots and black humor chiches with "Pulp Fiction"
twists, an "Ordinary People" for the late nineties
(thank god they're over now!) with not a single
believable character (although the villainous right-wing
colonel did remind me somewhat of the "maverick"
reactionary presidential candidate).

-- But I had a few very good moments goofing with
Kat in her backyard before leaving for the airport.
Best of all was one in which I chased her up the cherry
tree and then she surprised me when I was looking away
by jumping down on my shoulders like a fun-loving chimp.
But it was awful seeing Betty in so much pain in the
backseat and trying (Z and I both) to talk brightly to
keep her distracted. "Crampers," Betty calls what
happens in her legs, but they're far worse than mere
cramps -- more like severe spastic spasms -- and the new
set of tests has slightly lengthened the list of
possible causes, to MS, lupus, or postpolio syndrome.
Z's talking about our possibly moving out to that part
of town (where housing is still relatively inexpensive)
so we could provide Betty with more support.

     Meanwhile Z's displeased and hurt that Aida hasn't
even called to check on how she's doing after the D&C.
All her other good friends have done so but her best
friend of all, who wanted to marry her if she'd been
born (or sex-changed to?) a man, hasn't. After my
arrival at home last night June and I talked at length
about what's happening with Aida (though I couldn't do
much of the talking with my throat so gravelly sore and
still can't croak out more than a few words at a time).
Everyone agrees the recent series of setbacks with
Charles, Mr. D., and Kirk, along with some serious
political infighting at work, have been more than Aida
can handle and she'll just have to be indulged for a
while. Z says Aida "blew up" at her the other day after
suggesting they hang out together next weekend, to which
Z responded that she had a couple other things on the
calendar, including an important meeting of JCEJ, her
environmental-justice group. And Z told me Aida used to
lose it entirely in fights with Tom during the declining
years of their marriage -- shrieking, throwing things,
even physically attacking him -- and she thinks this has
a lot to do with the tantrums Charles, who witnessed
much of that, throws now. My own fear is that in her
current neediness Aida will react to Z's inability to be
there for her to the degree she was in former times by

820

escalating her attempts to turn her against me. Even
under the best of circumstances Aida still seems to view
me as a rival and maybe as a political/religious/
philosophical enemy. -- Ironically, one of the reasons
Z wanted to see "American Beauty" was Aida's rave about
it. But then Betty also liked it a lot.

On the way home tonight a stop at the east-hill co-
op so Z could pick up a quart of Neapolitan soy ice
cream and half a dozen of her favorite chocolate toffee
bars. She said it was almost as if the D&C had set off
a series of "shadow pregnancy cravings."

(And Thursday afternoon, by the way, I witnessed a
nasty fight in the driveway of the "bad neighbors"'
house directly to our south. One guy was working on a
car, another was pacing around shouting epithets at him
-- then physically attacked him. They were rolling
around on the ground wrestling and slugging each other
until the original attacker gained the upper hand and
the other guy, pinned on his back, was calling out
piteously, "I don't want to die, I don't want to die."
I might've tried to do something -- to intervene somehow
maybe, if only by shouting out the window -- but two
other men, also residents of that house or possibly
visiting friends there, were standing right next to them
with arms crossed, observing and doing nothing. Even
then I might've called the cops if it had gone on much
longer. But the attacker triumphantly let the other guy
get up, and then for the next several minutes the loser
wailed and wept. It was pitiful and it was ugly.
-- And I should mention we've seen no sign of Mikey,
their big black dog, in weeks. But the auto engines
continue to roar at odd hours. Drug deliveries? It's
hard to imagine they'd be this blatant about it.)

[+1]

A brief one, probably, down at the scope office.
Late. Well past bus time. But I arrived late too,
driving in at eleven. The Z-mobile's parked right in

front of the building entrance, in a spot likely to
be free only after two a.m. except on nights when the
janitors are off. And this is such a night because
today is Presidents Day. That is, we're already three
hours into it by Gregorian measure. This is how it
works: the maintenance crew gets the night before the
holiday off, not the night of the holiday itself.

     Two long, tough grand-jury sessions this week, well
over four hundred pages combined. I still have much to
do on the last quarter of the job, Thursday afternoon's
testimony, a couple of financial-fraud cases bristling
with names and numbers, many of which I'll have to look
up in exhibits because they came too fast for Naomi and
she could get only partials (a/k/a "markers") on the
steno. So I'll have to finish it up tomorrow night. I
forewarned Naomi about this, reminding her of the
holiday and referring to "family plans" with little glow
quotes set around the words (she likes to tease me about
being a newlywed, no longer able to live my wild "rogue
male" life of yore -- but that life also freed me up to
take more odd-hours scoping jobs for her).

     Z and I hit the discount mart as well as the usual
stops on our provisioning run this week. Left at four,
returned home before seven. Then read in the living
room. Right now she's in an enforced state of what the
hospital form calls "pelvic rest," meaning no douches,
no tampons, and no intercourse. We interpret that to
mean no towsing (clit/vulva diddling) either. But
nipples, they're a different story, and by tonight she
was horny enough to offer herself up for tweaking
("limited plan B") despite my pesky cold. A series of
explosive nipple comes and, for me, an extended blowjob/
wank-off followed, with the Sunday-night blues show as
soundtrack (Z thinks I'd love to shack up with the
hostess of that show because she's so knowledgeable
about blues -- and she, Z, says so!). (She also says I
have by far the hairiest dick of any man she's ever
known, but I think she must be blanking out or
generalizing past wangers of her life -- and that's
good, right? She makes it sound as if I'm furry from

base to tip. In fact it's the bottom inch or so, that's
all. And besides, she likes it. It adds a little
something extra during "full penetration," i.e., all the
way to the hairy hilt, like a cock ring or certain kinds
of dildos or condoms with bells and ticklers attached --
not that I've ever tried any of those. But she has --
all the permutes and combos. And more. Many times. On
her own even. "Whatever gets you through the night.")
     Lots of other matters I could address here.
However, it's, as noted earlier, late, and now of course
even later. So I'll limit myself to mentioning the
arrival of the first of Z's credit reports. It looks
okay to me -- but then what do I know about credit
reports? I, to repeat (again!), have no credit
whatsoever and never have had any so far as I know. She
on the other hand apparently has not a single black mark
on her record. She's always paid her bills on time.
Lifetime we're talking about. And she's starting to
regain some confidence about such things, perhaps just
because she now has my record as a contrast. (Later
this week I'll be going in with her to meet some sort of
credit counselor. Her main goal is to consolidate all
her payments into one. Unfortunately it turns out doing
this looks bad on your credit record, suggesting you
can't properly manage your money without help. But I
think she's probably better off getting out from under
the stress. This is an unorthodox view, though. I know
she's worrying about whether it's the wise thing to do.
Usually for things like this she seeks advice from June,
the business-school grad and savvy investor, and I
expect she'll do it this time too.)
     And so the final paragraph begins of yet another
conference-table entry. My seemingly dull work life.
Been doing this for so long! Like a laborer from
another era! -- Or like a milkman, say, if the cliche
itself weren't too cheesy, delivering on the same route
for decades. But it's hardly a traditional kind of job
or life. And it's so close to ideal for me I can't stop
believing I'd be a fool to give it up.
     This table (can't help myself, one more paragraph

here), I remember when it first came on the scene
thirteen or fourteen years ago. The chairs arrived then
too, but they've been reupholstered twice during the
interim. And the watercolors, all featuring tugboats,
hanging on the walls, I also remember when those first
appeared. The red telescope. The little black-and-
white TV mostly hidden on a lower shelf. Oh the tales I
could tell! And have! And no one's wanted to listen!
(And will any of this knowledge and experience ever
matter even slightly to anyone who works here in future
years -- be something for someone to learn from? Nope.)

[+1]

    -- Patching this in again at the scope office, the
front desk this time. The pendulum swings on the fake
old-fashioned wall clock. 12:33 it says up there, but
it always runs seven minutes fast -- not six, not eight.
The red message light flashes on the master phone with
its dozens of buttons and the screen there gives the
date and a time that, oddly enough, is nine minutes fast
(the clock in the copy room is the only accurate one in
the whole suite, including the one on my computer, which
is now off not just by a full hour plus, as always, but,
with the new Y2K adjustment, an additional nineteen
years). The screen on the phone also says "headset
enabled." It fails to mention today's a holiday.
    I worked out earlier tonight but at less than full
strength (and full strength itself is a lot less than
I'd like it to be). Just took a spin through the
office, in fact, to fetch a cough drop and to double-
check whether that statement about the copy-room clock
being accurate is itself, again, still accurate. It is.
Two radios and three fans, an air cleaner, a fax
machine, a desktop computer, an ancient electric
typewriter, and two photocopiers have been running in
there the whole three-day weekend. One radio's playing
classic music, the other indie rock, and they're about
three feet apart on the shelf above the main worktable.

[Infinite Jyze]

Looks as though another feud's broken out in there, but
maybe not as bad as some in the past: the volume on both
radios is set fairly low.
      Z walked in with me this evening as far as the AQ,
and she was carrying wrist weights in lieu of visiting
the WOC. She also had an umbrella tucked under her coat
and was wearing a blue beret. She can look quite
menacing if she wants to -- and up at the apartment I'm
not so sure she wanted to, but she apparently appeared
that way regardless to the Christian missionary who
presumably entered the building through the broken lobby
entrance and was going door to door upstairs asking for
donations. I had been impatiently listening to his
spiel, but when Z spotted him and demanded to know how
he'd gotten in the building he skedaddled right off.
This startled her. "Am I so scary then?"
      But what I started out to say is it was a lovely
little walk. Our walks have always had a mushy/gushy/
sappy effect on me. Then after we parted I rounded the
corner and found three cop cars parked in the middle of
the street with flashing lights, two men spread-eagled
on hoods (Afrusan men of course, and all Eurusan cops,
of course, though one was a woman). From the looks of
things it was an attempted robbery of someone who'd just
used the cash machine at the nearby branch bank, across
the alley from the east-depot minimart.
      And now with the scene all set, I gotta go. Bus
time. Too bad, because there's some disturbing news.
Maybe I'll be able to squeeze in a few words about that
when I return home (as I so often say I'll do or at
least think I'll do but so rarely manage to do, I know).

[+1]

      -- And didn't manage to do it this time either. So
now we've gone from Presidents Day, the official
holiday, to what used to be the official holiday
observing the birth date of the first of those
presidents, the one who was a slaveholder/Indian killer.

825

Interestingly, though, that president wasn't actually
born on this date but rather on February 11, one day
before, instead of ten days after, the birth date of the
other president (the reluctant freer of slaves) whose
birth date was celebrated yesterday. The true date of
the first of these presidents' birth matters at least a
little, or rather the ambiguity with respect to it does,
because that ambiguity was caused by an adjustment in
the Gregorian calendar made in the year 1752, a couple
of decades after that birth. Eleven days were added to
the calendar, so what had been February 11 now became
the 22nd. And at the same time the date of the New Year
celebration was changed from March 25th to January 1st.
Otherwise there would be no question whether this year's
millennium celebration a few days short of eight weeks
ago was false or true or jyze or jive.

I just picked up this little tidbit today from a
column in the far-coast paper. And it resonates in two
other ways. First, it suggests March 25 was the start
of the new year in England for almost exactly three-
quarters of that same millennium. And second, it
reveals something I hadn't really thought about before,
in that it wasn't only Europe where New Year's was
celebrated on 3/25; it was the same in this country, or
say this part of the world, in certain North American
colonies of England (as was their status at the time,
since this was before 1776). Depending on what date one
accepts for the establishment of the first English
colony here, it could be said 3/25 was the New Year's
date for a third to a half of this country's "recorded
history."

By a happy coincidence this afternoon's paper gives
the first solid dates for the dome demolition here in
Jyze City, saying it will be either the 19th or the 26th
of March. These two dates are called tentative, but the
reasons cited for rejecting the weekend following that
of the 25th/26th (baseball season starting up at the
nearby new stadium) and the one preceding that of the
18th/19th (not enough time to finish the preparations
for demolition) suggest it'll have to be one or the

other. And for purposes of the T/M celebration and the
story idea I gave the alt-weekly, these dates are just
about perfect. "Hey Mr. Mayor, how about moving the
demolition one day!" -- My hope is that this news will
light a fire under the alt-weekly editors, or blast the
scales off their eyes about the magnitude of the
journalistic possibilities. (The same article says the
first test blast at the dome will take place tomorrow
morning -- and it'll be within easy hearing distance of
the hilltop and also the alt-weekly offices.)

In any event, all this has jolted me to the brink
of taking new action. I've now decided if there's no
sign of the "Open Letter" in this week's issue of the
alt-weekly (due out later tomorrow or Thursday) I'll go
ahead and pass the idea on to the indie weekly, which,
as I realized after dropping off the packet for Emil H.,
might find it more congenial, and especially at this
late date, just as a snarky, in-your-face kind of jape,
since that's their basic approach to the world. (I'm
still mulling whether I should contact the alt-weekly
first before doing this. But if they're planning to go
with the story in a future issue, they haven't shown me
the courtesy of informing me of this, so why should I
owe them that kind of courtesy myself?)

Meanwhile it's a grand-jury corrections night. Z
dropped me off at the scope office and I'm estimating I
have about three hours' work up there. So now I've
stopped by at the art bar and I'm holding down the same
table where jyze did its thing last week. The two large
tables across the aisle are occupied by Eurusan twenty-
somethings, a dozen of them in all, and seven of the
nine males are wearing baseball caps with V'd brims
facing backward (same way I wore my cap during Little
League days when I played catcher, but not for any of my
other waking hours, indoors or out, during most of which
I wore that same cap, but always with the brim facing
forward) (for one thing, it kept the bright summer sun
out of your eyes). Some raw paintings on the walls,
knockoffs of works by the eighties main-far-coast-
megalopolis Afrusan dude who's become so popular lately

(including with me). Same Afrusan hip-hop crowd ruling
in the pool-table area, and one of these was the sharp
fellow who last time wanted to hire me as a calligrapher
(this time he doesn't know me).

     What's new, a thirtyish Cawk woman in black was
over here checking out what I'm doing. Coming on to the
jyzer, no question about it, maybe thinking he must be
someone important to be scribbling away like this in
such a setting. And she was smoking too; I can still
smell it. I tried not to be rude but I didn't ask her
to sit down (my bag and coat and sweatshirt are piled on
the free chair). Now she's sitting with another Cawk
woman, a purple-haired one, up at the bar. I don't
think I exist for her anymore. And that's good -- but I
do owe her for the flattering show of interest. And
it's something I can mention to Z if she starts boasting
about some guy who's been trying to hit on her at the
coffee shop or on a utility elevator or at the bus stop
or on the bus itself, as she often likes to do.

     So this news. First, Z. After our "plan B" action
Sunday evening she started spotting, and the next
morning she called the doctor's office. The nurse there
asked a series of questions and one was about sex: had
she been having any? Z answered negatively at first but
then said, "Well no, wait. I haven't had intercourse
but...." The nurse asked if she'd "orgasmed clitorally
then?" Z fumbled a moment and then admitted to a
"nipple orgasm." The nurse was taken aback -- "Well, I
think this might be a first for me." -- And then
sternly admonished her: "No more sex of any kind!" It
seems the physiological workings of the orgasm, because
they involve convulsions or spasms of the cervix, can
cause bleeding after an operation like hers.

     Of course Z delighted in telling me this story.
She likes showing off her uncommon sexual talents -- and
why shouldn't she? "I think she was especially
surprised that a vintage woman could be doing it like
that. And I didn't even tell her there were at least
four or five of them, not just one." Since then we've
been teasing each other about avoiding all sexual and

even just sexy behavior -- touches, glances, whatever.
"Too risky." Because anything at all might set the old
Z-cervix raucously aflutter.

    -- And then the disturbing news. Again it features
Aida. There's been another worrisome incident involving
Charles, or maybe more than one, but one exceptionally
bad tantrum in which he locked himself in his room,
threw things, battered the walls -- with a hockey stick
this time -- and hurled obscenities at Aida for an hour
and a half straight and she could do nothing with him.
Finally she had to call Tom over to restrain him. And
afterwards she decided, and Tom agreed, Charles should
now live full-time with Tom. Of course this is painful
for Aida, and it will be doubly so because of the way
her tightly knit and highly religious family, and
especially her parents, are sure to react to it. Add
this to her heartbreak over Kirk and her father's cancer
diagnosis and her ongoing troubles at work and she's
obviously going through some extremely hard times.

    Unfortunately I can be of little help with any of
this. Aida doesn't want support from me and probably
would tell me to get lost if I did try to offer some.
But Z can try to help her, and I can do my part by
supporting her in doing this. "We were so close
before," Aida told her yesterday, "because we were
always there for each other. But since you met Glen you
haven't needed me to be there for you." That's not
exactly true, I'd say, but still, she's basically right:
it's an unsymmetrical situation now. And it might even
be an unsustainable one. I say this because, to put
things in the best light possible, Aida doesn't seem
very sensitive about the ramifications on me of her
behavior with Z. Or in the worst light, she seems to
resent me and to misunderstand me and probably (though
maybe only as a consequence of the first two) dislike me
if not, let's face it, hate me. But it would be more
than Z could bear for her to fail Aida now. So it's
clear what I must do: be supportive of Z in whatever she
feels she must do to be supportive of Aida. So -- okay.
Just do it.

-- They're clearing the floor now. Disco dance time. Again. Either skedaddle soon or pay the cover.

[+2]

A jyze stop at the downtown library on the way in to work, this time seeking refuge out in the open in the magazine/newspaper section upstairs. Not too many rowdies hang out in this area, I suppose mainly because the presence of three library workers at the nearby "research station" makes them uncomfortable. -- But just now a security guard moseyed through, so maybe the calm is only momentary. (He didn't even give me a second look, though. So who knows. -- But just like the dome, this whole building will soon be blown up and a bigger, badder, far uglier new version will replace it. The postmodern or maybe better to say hypermodern design by a trendy Dutch architect is stirring up some opposition -- "looks like Darth Vader's helmet" -- but probably nowhere near enough to cause any significant alterations.)

So what's new? Lots of stuff, though I suppose it doesn't really amount to much. It appears Z and I may be able to swing a condo purchase after all. The political spotlight is moving toward our state for the upcoming primary and it'll be more intense than previously expected. I've decided to make one more effort to gain my T/M idea a public airing. And today is Kat's birthday -- though neither Z this morning nor I this evening was able to reach her at uncle Nick's place in the U.S. southwest borderlands and all we could do was leave goofy phone messages including a harmonizing "Happy Birthday" duet.

To tackle the political stuff first, it just happens that this state's primary next Tuesday -- the only one in the nation between now and "Super Tuesday" the week after that -- has become crucially important for both major parties. This was the subject of front-page stories in all of yesterday's papers, including the

far-coaster -- and a banner head in the J-town morning
paper. Suddenly all the major candidates are here
stumping or soon will be. The two pre-primary favorites
are now being pressed by challengers supposedly a bit
more moderate, with the reactionary "maverick" hothead
seeming to have seized "the Big Mo" from the hapless
right-wing president's son; and with the shambling
middle-of-the-road hoopster suddenly proclaiming himself
to be an old-fashioned liberal, desperately trying to
keep his campaign alive against the cautious and pompous
and sanctimonious reigning middle-of-the-road veep. In
truth there's not much to choose from between the two
MOR types, and of course both would be far preferable to
either of the hard-rightists -- especially the hothead,
who might turn out to be dangerously bellicose once in
office -- but it's a virtual certainty I'll be opposed
to nearly all of the policies of whoever of the four
wins since they're all safely in corporate pockets. And
it should be noted: all four are pro-WTO.
     -- But it's a hoot to have the national political
spotlight swing back this way and to see the state
energized over larger issues because the election
results will matter nationally. It rarely happens here.
Owing to our far-western location, by the time the state
finishes voting in national elections they've usually
been decided, and the electorate is too small to matter
in the primaries -- usually. But this year our
primary's taking place earlier in the process and, by
happenstance, yes, it matters. Or maybe our new
position in the process -- right before so-called Super
Tuesday -- means this will often be the case in the
future, so long as it does precede Super Tuesday (that
is, Super Tuesday itself doesn't move earlier).
     -- So then the personal. I shaved and showered and
dressed up as much as possible -- which is not all that
much -- for the visit to the "consumer counseling
service." It turned out Nelson C., who, when he called
on Tuesday to confirm the appointment, sounded like a
cut-and-trimmed yuppie gladhander, was a heavyset and
casually dressed longhair with whom Z and I both felt

quite comfortable. By his own account he was a
sociology major in college who, unlikely as it might
seem, took up his current line of work for idealistic
reasons. He needed only a glance at Z's salary stubs
and credit report and the summary of her debts to assure
us she'd be able to swing a "medium-size" mortgage.
Payments on her debts amount to just slightly more than
half the forty percent of gross salary which credit
officers for banks regard as the cutoff for mortgages.
He even instilled enough confidence in Z about her
credit-card debt -- on a large portion of which she has
among the lowest interest rates he's seen recently --
that she probably won't seek to consolidate them after
all, since he confirmed doing so would put a black mark
on her unblemished lifetime credit record. He also
tipped her to the fact that if she were to telephone the
companies with the highest interest rates -- two of her
loans are due to jump to higher rates in coming months
-- they'd probably offer her a deal rather than risk
losing her business.

     Afterwards she and I stopped at a nearby cafe to
talk things over. Although she'd been pleased enough
with the results of the meeting to make a donation to
the counseling outfit as we exited, now she suddenly
seemed less happy. Already, it turned out, she was
focusing on her next big worry, the meeting with Dr. W.
on March 7th to learn the results of the lab tests on
her uterine tissue. (And she was disturbed because she
thought she felt a new herpes outbreak coming on --
confirmed later -- and this so soon after the previous
one.) Later she apologized for being "such a nonstop
worrywart." But in this instance who can really blame
her? (Which isn't to say her self-description is
inaccurate. She worries things like no one I've ever
known. She thinks this comes from her mother. "For her
the sky was always falling." But then: "I realize now I
should honor her more for having survived such a
hardscrabble life. I mean, she had a lot of very good
reasons to worry, starting with being sexually abused by
her father at a very young age.")

So we set some tentative plans for the rest of the year. We won't worry at all about housing until after May (when this TJM project has finally concluded and she's past her current major project at work of directing the rollout of the newly revamped citywide recycling program). Then we'll try to find out what Dana and Raphael would charge us for our unit when the place condoizes. And for the minimum of eight months or so after that until the unit actually becomes available -- and it could be longer or even much longer -- we'll look around to see what else is available and we'll go through the preapproval process for the city's "first-time home-buyer" program so we can move quickly if we find something we like. But we both think the chances are slim we'll stumble across anything better than what we already have, if that indeed remains affordable for us. And if it doesn't, at least we'll have those eight months (or more) to find something else. And we might even be able to hang on long enough to have a legitimate shot -- admittedly a long one -- at one of the subsidized lofts we've already looked into.

Under the circumstances this seems a pretty good outcome for us. The fear, though, is that by waiting too long -- as we already may have done -- we'll be priced out of the market. But again, if this turns out to be the case, we're more ready for it now. Z won't be feeling it's her fault because she screwed up on her credit. -- Whereas the truth is it's only her relative financial strength that's giving us a shot at buying a house or a condo. If it depended on me we'd barely qualify for a tiny low-end condo out in the sticks somewhere (this would be if I cashed in the deep reserves and paid that cash on the barrelhead, since, to repeat yet again, I'm entirely without credit -- by design! -- and intend to keep it that way).

-- Now they're making the closing-time announcement. Outta here! So I'm thinking rather than scrawl out the rest of today's news real quickly I'll move on and return to these pages later, at home, for a proper eighter close-out.

[+1]

     -- Well, it's later, yes, but a full day later, and
I'm not at home either. Just as I was about to start in
on the jyze last night (AHH-CHOOO! -- I just sneezed, a
monster one!) Z ambled into the living room, unable to
sleep for worrying about various thorny situations at
work (mainly recycling mess-ups) along with D&C results,
Aida, etc. She left after twenty minutes but then
reappeared before I'd rebuilt enough steam for another
attempt at a jyze follow-on. "I need skin!" she pouted.
She curled up at my feet as I sat in the black armchair,
and just then I was hit by a bad coughing spell and had
to split for the bathroom and the cough medicine. That
was it for the jyze plans as well as the skin hopes.
(But she did kindly fashion a wedge of pillows for me in
bed. It tilted my head up enough to aid "drainage"
without causing a neck crick, and so I slept better than
I have in several days.)
     And now it's the hideaway before heading home. And
the new deal is this: I'll put off the decision about
contacting the indie weekly until next Wednesday after
the new edition of the alt-weekly hits the streets. If
the alt again fails to go with the T/M idea, I'll work
up a packet for the indie immediately. And at the same
time I'll contact the publicity director for the HQ
community council to see if they'd bite on a "Dome
Blowout Weekend" publicity stunt also pegged on the true
millennium. (As it happens, the HQ starts its weeklong
"Mardi Gras 2000" celebration next Wednesday and
they're pushing it as a substitute for the canceled
1/1/2000 millennium party. So why not, I ask, push the
notion a step or two further? The Mardi Gras posters
are up all over town (and they feature a graphic of the
front-entrance arch of the hideaway building itself).
     This should be one heckuva week coming up. Another
calendrical rarity, an anniversary, a shadow birthday,
an eleven-year peak in a natural cycle which could do
more damage than the Y2K bug did (as could also the

calendrical rarity). And we have a family birthday as
well, we have First Thursday (another housing protest by
artists at the "shoe" lofts above Z-geist?) -- on and
on. Jyze material galore! And it starts tomorrow with
a highly unusual Saturday when I'll be on my own
(because Z will be seeing Aida).

Meanwhile front-page stories about the dome
implosion are appearing daily. Today it was announced
the freeways will be shut down for the occasion and a
safety zone declared, meaning the crowds on south hill
and the high bridge will be even bigger than previously
anticipated. (It's almost as if they're about to blow
up a whole city here.) All four major presidential
candidates are in town at the moment, incidentally,
their motorcades officiously bustling about. And the
stock market is suddenly falling precipitously -- to
below ten thousand for the first time in a year.

And that has to be it. (As the cacophonous meat-
market music whooms on below.)

43

-- Came rolling out in the Z-mobile at two-forty
p.m., zipped across the high bridge, up and over to the
freeway and through downtown to Z's former hood, making
it to her old dry cleaner's just moments before the
three p.m. closing time to pick up my "dress" pants and
shirt (cleaned at the preposterous cost of nine bucks!).

On a day both very, very good and also, though on a
different kind of scale, pretty damn bad. And sometimes
it's hard not to mix up the scales themselves with the
things they're measuring. -- But before inquiring into
any of that I'll mention I'm holding forth at a window

table in an old favorite hang, the Yuke cine cafe,
gazing out at the rain-slick wooden fence and staircase
leading to the red wooden theater door, which is flanked
by twin lanterns shedding a warm dim light on a pair of
noirish door-size movie posters in glass boxes. "Ikiru"
is playing in there at the moment (and maybe I'll see
the next show at seven-thirty). And a real fire is
crackling in the redbrick fireplace in here and this
small low-ceilinged room is very warm and the four
potted poinsettia lined up on the windowsill are looking
as wilted as I suddenly feel -- as now a guy at a nearby
table strips off his sweater and I realize I could do
the same with my outer shirt -- and will.

*

   -- Done. And while at it I fetched myself a glass
of ice water. The hot chocolate, gone now, I ordered
before I realized how warm the room was.
   Ah, but it's good to be back here. Maybe it's my
favorite commercial kind of room in the whole city. For
a while it seemed this cafe would go belly up, but both
the theater and the cafe were saved by new owners. The
only significant difference I see between the remodeled
cafe and the earlier version is the absence of a long
couch in front of the fireplace. In its place is a row
of two-seater wooden tables. I used to do some serious
cogitating on that couch while gazing into the fire.
Not too often, no, but maybe once every couple of months,
and sometimes weekly or even daily for short bursts,
over a period of a decade. And sometimes I'd do a bit
of protojyzing there too. So yes, to me the word
"significant" is justified for the absence of the couch.
-- But again, that's a different scale too.
   Here's how the day's very, very good. When I got
home last night Z called out from the darkened bedroom,
"Guess what! Doc W. called. I'm okay! No problems at
all!" What a relief! I jumped into bed with her and we
rolled around exuberantly. -- And so there goes the
cloud I expected this week to be under as well as the
one hanging over the past three months. -- And after
a while we stopped rolling around. She was tired -- had

836

been asleep for four hours, as is usually the case when
I arrive home -- and I was hungry; and besides, we
couldn't get it on because of my cough and her possible
H-outbreak (she thought she might be okay after all on
this score as well, but we'd need to check first, and
she wasn't ready for that at the moment).

So I bade her good night and moved on as if it were
just a normal evening: chores, dinner, papers, jazz
radio, listening for the delivery of the night paper,
making her a card (about how lucky we are -- a frequent
theme! -- and this afternoon upon arising I found she'd
framed it). Only two differences: I poured myself a
drink, bourbon and water, with ice cubes no less, to
celebrate. And footsteps sounded overhead, sheerly by
coincidence of course, because earlier that afternoon
the new tenants, owners of a spiffy silver SUV but
otherwise completely unknown to us, had begun moving in.

So now I'll show just how disparate the scales are.
For the bad news is that when I left the house this
afternoon we were upset and angry with each other. She
didn't say goodbye and neither did I -- the first such
parting in many months. Also the first serious fight in
just that many months. -- Or I guess it's a fight. It
happened so fast and I had to leave so soon afterwards
it's hard to be sure what's going on. But what a time
for it! And then again, there's never been a swifter or
apter demonstration of Z's fully acknowledged inability
to stand prosperity. Two pieces of extremely good news
in two days -- too too much! Let's rumble!

She arrived home at two in a fury, curses ringing
out, her backpack and coat and other items flying
against walls. "The fuckers! Someone parked in our
place in the garage! The yuppie bastards, they should
eat shit and die!" And that was it! -- Or no, there
was something else. This morning Betty had called
asking Z to pick up her and Kat at the airport --
apparently Reuben had been unable to do it after all --
and then when Z did so, Kat was in a foul mood, "acting
like a stuck-up little bitch the way she does so well."
And earlier there had been another incident involving

the bad neighbors to the south, the same two, with loud
voices, things breaking, the one guy wailing and moaning
horrendously (this time the repeated phrase was "I wish
you hadn't done that!") and Z had very nearly called the
cops but then the wailing stopped and all seemed okay --
and moments later three cop cars rolled up and the nasty
tall guy, ball-cap wearer, owner of the missing dog
Mikey, was arrested, cuffed, and taken away. (Not the
end of the saga, I suspect; but nothing more happened
today as far as I know -- and I slept through all but
the initial incident this morning, Z having turned the
air cleaners up high to mask the sound.)
     -- So as I went about preparing to leave, she
stormed around the apartment vociferating and
philippicking (it's a Filipino thing). I said little,
thinking this was one of her inexplicable overreactions
to perceived social slights that happen once in a while,
hoping she'd quickly cool off, hesitating to say
anything for fear of enraging her further. (Maybe I
should've joined in on the philippicking, tried to get
her laughing by showing how ludicrously overblown it
sounded. That's sometimes worked in the past. But her
explosion caught me so much by surprise at such an early
hour I wasn't able to think fast enough.) Then she
grabbed a handful of paper and announced she was going
to write a nasty note. "Follow the rules, motherfuckers!
No parking anarchy around here!" -- And worse.
     "You don't want to do that," I said.
     "Well then you write it if you're so fucking smart!"
-- and she threw down the paper and marker and stormed
out of the room and into our bedroom, slamming the door
violently, then throwing things around inside -- I could
hear them crashing against the walls.
     I didn't react further to any of this, but now I
also was furious. When, after a few minutes, she calmed
down and came out of the room, going for a while into
her own room and then into the living room where she sat
in her armchair, I said nothing and neither did she.
When I was almost ready to go I picked up my bag from
behind her chair (where I usually set it down), stopping

for a moment to look her in the eye, and said very
seriously, "I think you owe me an apology." She didn't
respond until I was about to close the door on my way
out and then she shrieked in an acid tone, "I'm sorry!"
-- a mockery. So I left.

Out in the hall I noticed the door to unit 201 was
open -- formerly the motorcycle woman's place -- and
that a post-move-out cleanup was underway. A short
Latino-looking guy in carpenter overalls was patching a
wall nearby and I asked him if his car might be parked
in our slot downstairs. He could just barely understand
English, but after a few variations I made myself
understood. "Ah, yes! Car! I am sorry! I did not
know!" He followed me down. As it turned out, his car
was parked in someone else's slot and that person's car
was parked in ours. That person is another new resident
-- I recognized the car but I don't know who the owner
is -- and so I left a short note on his/her windshield.
Not an angry note -- why start a feud over a first
offense by someone who may not know the protocol and who
had nowhere else to park? And then I drove off
wondering if I'd even be able to reach the dry cleaner's
on time. We'd been putting off this pickup for weeks
and feared they might've confiscated the clothes.

-- And so now the Yuke. At the moment here in the
cafe it's all probable students except for me, just as
it usually was back in the old days (not counting the
Christian evangelizers who hung out at the church next
door and sometimes made a nuisance of themselves here
with attempted recruitment talk). But today they're
mostly liberal-arts students, I'd guess, many of them
older, foreign students, literary types -- the kind who
come to see the esoteric foreign films shown here.
Quiet, intelligent, sometimes a bit pompous talkers just
as you'd expect (maybe they'd say the same of me -- but
I hope not -- and I don't talk much here, if at all).
Folk music and classical mixing it up on the PA.

This is the day Z is spending with Aida. It's been
planned for a couple of weeks. My own trip over here to
the Yuke has been in the works for several days. I told

Z I might take advantage of the opportunity to see a
couple of movies I knew she wasn't much interested in,
one Chinese and one ("Ikiru") Japanese. She's already
seen a Japanese film in the festival at the Asian art
museum -- and that's, as she said, her quota for the
month. But she still pretended to be miffed, or maybe
she was genuinely miffed but chose not to make an issue
of it, when I told her about my plans. "Of course I'd
much rather you stayed home," she pouted, "and pined
away for me." (At the time she seemed genuinely good-
humored about it; only now, after the outburst this
afternoon, am I wondering if something else was going on
even then.)

What next? For the first couple of hours after
leaving the house I was thinking I shouldn't let this
donnybrook with Z drop immediately. (I did say one
other thing to her before the line about her owing me an
apology: "I just want you to know, in case it's not
obvious, I don't appreciate your treating me this way.")
Being hot-tempered, as she notoriously is, is one thing;
throwing things against walls is another. So is cursing
out your husband (that's me!) when he has absolutely
nothing to do with the inciting incident. In this case
the disproportion of the reaction was so extreme it
seems to me I can't let her conclude I'll just meekly
put up with it. But I guess it all depends on how she's
acting when I get home.

So here I am "out on my own." In a place like this
I'm seen as a somewhat intriguing character, I think;
maybe that's one reason I like coming here. Mainly it's
just because I'm comfortable here. "Temptations" abound
in the form of attractive and even sometimes flirtatious
women but they're no more truly tempting now than they
were back in Lady U days, which is to say: they're not
at all, other than to merit a glance here and there.
The lack of any such real interest must itself be, for
me, part of the pleasure of being here: knowing, being
reminded, of just how happily attached to the monogamous
life I once again am. That's how it was with Lady U and
now it's just as much or more that way with Z, although

today may not be the best of days to make such a claim.
     Speaking of the best of days: by an amusing
coincidence today is the third anniversary of my first
communication from Z -- the first one directed
personally to me, that is: the postcard from the
mountain resort. She'd forgotten all about it when I
mentioned it on Thursday and then she disputed my
recollection of the timing of events back then. I
showed her my calendar from that year. Those thirteen
days between the card and the phone call which the card
promised look even longer when laid out one by one in
their own little squares on the calendar -- and the
nineteen days between the call and the first face-to-
face meeting look like an eternity. We got to talking
about this; she said if she hadn't met me then she
wouldn't be with anyone now. I asked why she thought
that. She said she just knew. What about that other
guy she was seeing then, the one who spoke fluent
Spanish and knew so much about Guatemala and thus
would've been perfect, as she's told me before, to help
out on her relationship with Kat? My remembering about
him seemed to take her aback for a moment, but then she
said, "No, that never would've lasted." Again I asked
why she thought that. She said: "He didn't know what to
do with me." "Hey, I didn't know what to do with you
either." "Yeah, but even when you didn't, you still did
something. You had the confidence. He was intimidated
by me."
     Hah! -- So then maybe I'm writing down this story
as a way of beefing up my resolve to be firm with her
tonight.
     -- I think I've blown it with "Ikiru." Jyze must
come first! And even without seeing a single movie this
has been a fruitful outing. In addition to picking up
the cleaning I've come across several good used books
(again at my same old haunts which I rarely get to visit
anymore: the half-price place and two smaller used-book
shops here on the Ave). Also I've found some magazines
and journals I rarely see for sale anywhere else in the
city and I've bought a new backpack umbrella -- for just

seven bucks! -- to replace my old one (which, during yesterday's rainy walk in to the scope office, revealed itself to have developed two holes in annoying spots). And I've found some three dozen new art postcards with high alteration potential.

   -- But it's a bad time to be caught up in a fight with Z. What if it drags on for a while? Her birthday's a little over two weeks away. I'd like to be able to concentrate on that -- hoping to spark some powerful inspiration -- and also on the campaign for the T/M celebration. Don't want to be losing a lot of time to morbid brooding and imaginary dialogues while trying to work things out with the Z-woman.

   And now for dinner I'll stop in at another familiar spot: the chain burger joint standing across the street to the west. It's a different chain from the two I patronize downtown but at one time it was every bit as familiar to me as those two are now. I confess it: I'm curious to see if their double-stacks are better than the ones I buy now, as they certainly have been all these years in my taste-memory bank. And I don't want to forget to pick up a quart of whole milk before going home, and I'll do that at the corporate chain supermarket right behind the burger joint; and that's where I used to do most of our grocery shopping back in Lady U days. This is the same chain I occasionally visit down in the valley below south hill. Yes! Am I true to my school or what? (The milk is for measuring out into my wake-up coffee by the babyfood jarful which I first nuke for twenty-two seconds (or call it morning coffee by NUT time).) (Am I compulsive or something? I hope not. But I do like to go with what works well -- for example, the babyfood jar, twenty-two seconds -- and you don't have to be a wild-eyed neoprag to believe habits can often be useful and maybe even invaluable.)

[+1]

   -- Just a note, next night at the scope office

(break time, conference room) to report we seem to have
steered our way through the crisis all right. After
arriving home I managed to hold my ground firmly for six
hours or so, but mainly because she was asleep for most
of that time. She wanted to make up from the start, but
I insisted we had to come to an understanding first
about these rage explosions. I had decided to go to the
mat with her on this, and I did. And three different
times she did a stomp-out, declaring the situation
hopeless. How quickly things could change! We weren't
"zoelmates" after all, we were "fundamentally
incompatible." So we hauled out our old "Moskstraumen
Rules," the first time we've done that since, what, last
summer? We talked at length, me in my armchair and she
in hers, black denim v. rattan.

     Basically my position was that those outbursts were
unacceptable to me, they were beyond my limits. Her
position was that, first, I was exaggerating what had
happened, but, second, in any case she should be free to
be herself. We were different types, had I forgotten?
At times she'd threaten to go to the opposite extreme:
clamp down completely on her anger, the implication
being she'd close herself behind thick walls and go dead
on me -- and how would I like that? Finally we settled
on a concrete plan, concocted by her: she'd close
herself in her room when her hot buttons get pushed to
the point where she must break things and/or throw
things. If necessary I should leave the apartment. Any
lesser outburst I could accept, I said (and indeed have
done so many times though not always with delight).

     We didn't rack up a whole lot of sleep. Today she
kept the phone turned off and covered the faces of all
the clocks. At five a.m. we tumbled into bed (in her
case, back into bed) and hanky-panked and canoodled and
made nice and basically made up for two and a half
hours, including catnaps (but it turned out she was
still suffering an H-outbreak so we were limited to
"plan B," which was maybe for the better, because this
meant I could be sure I wouldn't do a foozle on her at a
time when she might freak over it).

One thing I regretted during the argument: a phrase slipped out, something about her "playing the deprived-childhood card" too much. That hurt her. I didn't mean it the way it sounded, and she does refer to her "FOO issues" as an excuse for or cause of her behavior quite often, especially in the context of emphasizing our "class differences," which I think she makes way too much of. (Other lenses on our differences can be useful too, as I like to remind her. We don't have to be one-dimensional!) -- This afternoon she gave me a touching poem she'd written about all this while I slept.

[+1]

-- If my mother had been born a few hours later she'd've turned twenty tomorrow, if she were also still alive. But how many hours later? If she ever told me her exact time of birth, I can't recall it now. Maybe I wrote it down somewhere, though I have no idea where. In hopes of digging it up I pulled out her babybook (I keep it here at the hideaway) and browsed in it for what turned out to be more than an hour. Earlier in the day my direct appeal to memory hadn't worked very well to summon ol' Mom, but this unplanned journey through the first dozen years of her life (when I suppose I could say I was traveling with her at all times although only in incomplete and highly undeveloped form as an unfertilized and not even faintly conscious ovum: my mama half) -- somehow this reading of her babybook did bring her alive for me. Seance on a rainy J-town Sunday night. I learned lots of new or new-seeming things (for I've looked through this babybook a number of times before, including once with her). I didn't, however, learn the hour of her birth.
(The most interesting discovery was the first letter her father -- Popeye to me -- wrote her mother -- Nana -- asking her out for a date. He wrote it three years before ol' Mom's birth, which is to say the same year ol' Dad was born. This reminded me of my first

letter to Z, also written three years ago as of
Valentine's Day just past. Both were single-page
letters -- short and to the point. Popeye at that time
was considerably less than half my age now but his
letter is surely the more gracefully written, and I do
mean by quite a lot. But in the end, yes, both letters,
his and mine, did the trick.) (On the other hand, my
first letter to Elgie's mother, Lady S, was written
almost nine years before Elgie's birth.)

        Yes, I often miss my mother. I converse with her
in my head just as much as ever, I think, if not a bit
more since I've been with Z. This of course is because
Z often reminds me of her in ways both small and large.
Their family (FOO!) backgrounds could scarcely be more
different but they have the same high energy level,
social interest and involvement, big-heartedness, love
of being at the center of things, easy laughter, high
drama, need to be pampered at times, fierce focus,
easily triggered sense of outrage. If Dad knew Z he'd
probably call her Snorty II.

        Mom. Snorty I. In this room she's always a
presence. Her ashes -- a dusting of them -- are here.
Several pictures of her stand on my desk and more atop
her old antique glass-doored bookcase, some with me
included, some with Dad, some with the whole family, one
with Jim Q. The framed poster showing the celebrated
hilltop where most of her ashes are scattered hangs
above that bookcase (it used to ride the wall by her
desk in the apartment on the slope of that same hill (in
my old city No. 2/7)) and I frequently gaze up at it as
I sit in the brown armchair where I'm battened down now.
On the wall to the left of that one, between framed
paintings done by Ladies S and V, is the large mola of a
parrot and flowers I gave her, Mom, as a birthday gift
some sixteen or seventeen years ago (it came from the
folk-arts shop out in the Yuke, and that shop is still
there; I walked by it yesterday and would've gone in to
look for something for Z's birthday had it been open,
but it was already closed for the day).

        -- Otherwise today's main interests have been

politics and millennial brainstorming. All four major
presidential candidates are still in town doing last-
minute storming of another kind -- barn kind, I'm
thinking -- with the primary taking place tomorrow, and
the candidates of the more right-wing of the two de
facto (in my view) right-wing parties are savaging each
other and their own fundamentalist Christian far-right
wing and I love it. About time! Unusually spirited WOC
talk with Marcus about this. He, being a churchgoing
Afrusan conservative, is agog at it all. But then so
are lots of other folks.

The brainstorming took place with Z on the
treadmill (yup, the reconciliation is holding just fine
so far). I've been trying to rough out a proposal to
present to the HQ boosters group for what I'm now
thinking of calling the "Domesday Jubilee." Z came up
with a good bit today: have a booth that peddles little
pieces of concrete from the dome implosion with the
proceeds going to charity; call the booth "Rubble with a
Cause." But right now everything depends on one more
little piece of serendipity -- the date scheduled for
the implosion must be the 26th, not the 19th. According
to the newspapers it's all up to the big kahunas at the
demolition company, and for them the major factor is
probably the weather. Usually it's a cinch that'll be
bad in this city in March, but lately it's been fairly
good -- for the whole winter, really -- so maybe the
odds favoring the 26th aren't all that great. A few
more days and we'll know. (So here's another dollop of
suspense to go along with the question of whether the
alt-weekly will run with the T/M idea -- last chance!
And who'll win our crucial -- ha! -- state primary is
another.)

[+1]

It's the exception to an exception, the rarest of
all days on the Gregorian calendar. Once-every-four-
centuries leap day finds me hunkered down near the

arrivals/departures board in the waiting room of the
west train depot. Nobody else in here but me and a
counter clerk and he's stepped into the back room for a
moment (or more than a moment, right). My feet are wet
from the rain. And this on the day our city became a
real city! -- By one reckoning at least.

   Back in 44 B.C.E. a caesar named Julius proclaimed
an extra day would be tacked on at the end of February
every fourth year to keep the calendar in sync with the
seasons. Some sixteen centuries later a pope named
Gregory noticed seasonal creep was occurring anyway
despite the caesar's good intentions and ordered a
calendar correction of ten days and also a new
calendrical rule, a modification of the Julian version:
on leap years ending in double zeroes, which is to say
the last year of each century, the extra day at the end
of February would be dropped. But then to tighten the
synchrony still further, an exception to that rule would
be made at the end of every fourth century, when a leap
day would be added or, in effect, restored. Thus
today's rareness. The last day like it, and the only
other one ever before now under the Gregorian calendar,
occurred four hundred years ago today.

   Nobody's made much of it, though. The print media
didn't mention it until today, and the three stories
I've seen all focus on how nobody ever gives leap day
its due even though it's supposedly highly significant:
"It's what keeps our calendar in sync with the
universe," one deep-thinking pundit is quoted as saying.
What little notice was taken of it beforehand had to do
with the possibility of computer screwups, but after the
earlier failures of Y2Kalypse to arrive the doom-criers
were too embarrassed to start wailing again about this
highly exceptional leap day. And indeed this
afternoon's paper reports computer disruptions have been
even more minor than they were on January 1 or 3.

   -- And I'm happy to say it's a rainy miserable day.
The odds that domesday will fall on the weekend of the
25th/26th increase a bit.

   As I was crossing the high bridge beneath my spiffy

new black umbrella I could see a news helicopter
hovering in the drizzly gray mist above the west depot
down here. I thought I'd misremembered the time for the
departure ceremony of the city's very first commuter
train of the modern era. But the helicopter must've
arrived on the scene a bit early, because I did make it
here just in time to touch the back fin of the last car
about two minutes before the train pulled out. When the
whistle sounded, in fact, and the train started to roll,
I was standing at a publicity table picking up free
cardboard engineer caps and other giveaway items and the
train's sudden absence -- for it had indeed left the
station -- allowed a rainy gust of wind to roar into the
previously sheltered area and it toppled the large "Ride
of the Century" sign above the table. As it happened I
became a momentary hero of sorts: I caught the aluminum
tubing at the top of the sign on the way down or it
would've taken out the table and perhaps injured a
couple of PR workers standing behind it who had their
backs turned and didn't see the sign falling. One
even cried rapturously: "You're our hero!" Alas, the TV
cameras were already being packed up.

The waiting room's still empty. The next train,
according to the board here, isn't due in until 8:35 --
the continental from the south. But I have my line
ready in case anyone asks why I'm sitting here. "Well,
I just missed the five-thirty commuter train so I'm
waiting for the next one." The next one, however, won't
be leaving until -- ho ho -- October, more than six
months from now. Today's run was just an introductory
publicity stunt.

In the prefeminist era leap day was observed also
as a kind of Sadie Hawkins Day, the one twenty-four-hour
period in a four-year stretch when a woman could propose
to a man. In my high-school days, so-called turnabout
dances were held every year in late February for which
the girls invited the boys. Z also grew up in that era,
of course, and for her the tradition may have been
doubly strong because the due date for her birth was St.
Patrick's Day, and St. Patrick was said to be one of the

originators of the leap day tradition (Z's actual birth
came two days early, on St. Louise's Day: hence her
birth name of Louise). So, in a repeat of sorts of our
Sadie Hawkins dispute of last fall, she was disappointed
during her call this afternoon when I said I'd already
made plans for later. She'd hoped we could meet at
home where she'd slip into her black teddy "and read off
a whole list of things I'd like you to do to me." (Her
notion of how the tradition should play out differs from
mine. To me it's the gal who ought to be performing a
list of desiderata provided by the guy. We're talking
turnabout!) -- I invited her to meet me here at the
station for the "Ride of the Century" but she quipped
that the only place I was going to get a "Ride of the
Century" was in bed at home. I told her I'd already
signed an ironclad jyze contract calling for me to make
a personal appearance down here, and she said in that
case she'd go shopping for the clothes hamper she's been
hankering for but up until now had been hampered in
shopping for by her busy schedule. (Z in zesty pun
mode: I always like it and try to fire right back.)

     And then today's also election day. The national
news broadcasts are all focusing here. If the liberal
hoopster doesn't win in our state -- and the final polls
say he won't even come close -- it's pretty much all
over for him. The party of the farther right will keep
duking it out among themselves no matter what happens,
but a victory here by the "maverick" ex-POW could add
still more fire to his attack on the bigoted Christian
extreme far right and possibly lead to a major split in
the party. So these primaries are turning out to be
quite a bit more interesting than most people, myself
included, expected. Some important issues are actually
being debated. Then again, many aren't -- most aren't
-- and the way the country will be governed for the
next four years won't be much affected, if at all, by
any of this. But the national mood could be and
probably will be. -- So I soon ought to be making
another visit to the Z-geist cafe, which is the place
where I like best to ponder the national mood. Day

after tomorrow maybe for that -- which just happens to be First Thursday again, and therefore Z-geist stays open an hour or two later than the usual seven p.m.

This station sits right next to the dome. On domesday it'll be well within what they're calling the safety zone, so train traffic will be halted for a period of an hour or more. If the wind is from the southwest, as it's likely to be this time of year (or almost any time of year), the area will be covered with concrete dust, making the coating of volcanic ash left by the major volcano eruption two decades ago just down the road a piece look like a light frost compared to a blizzard. Or so they say. (Who's this "they" I keep mentioning? Folks on the street, at the bus stops, in the minimarts, on the airwaves, on the internet, in the newspapers -- everyone's talking domesday now almost nonstop. But no one's calling it that yet. Ooh ooh ooh these next few weeks gonna be fun.)

(And by the way I haven't heard a single word about the sunspot cycle which was supposed to reach its eleven-year peak today. Did it knock any planes out of the sky or disable any major electronic systems as certain experts were saying it very well might? Is the peak perhaps still to come, between now and midnight? -- Oh, and I ran into Caleb, our across-the-hall neighbor in 202, on the stairs as he returned from taking a load down to his big rental truck. For him and his partner -- whom I've never seen again since the fire alarm last fall and I don't believe I've ever known her name -- it's move-out day. I asked why they're leaving and he said it's because the place is being condoized and they expect rents will be going up still more and they were able to find a cheaper rental farther south on the hill, outside the zone of highest impact of the DC castle and the "new economy." "Might as well start saving the money now -- we'll be getting the same amount of space for almost two hundred a month less, and that's before the rents go up here." Heh heh. -- But goofy Aaron from 101 with his stubbly cheeks and backward ball cap, the other night I ran into him coming in the front

door at three a.m. as I went down to fetch the paper and
he had a little packet of weed in his hand -- turned
beet red, he did, when he saw me see it. Thinking the
longhair jyzer might assume he's one of our antiquated
old-school pothead ilk, I wonder?)

[+1]

A window seat at the HQ-triangle sandwich shop. I
just stood on the steps outside watching a brass band
march by playing "When the Saints Go Marching In." A
couple hundred partiers straggled along behind,
including mimes in whiteface and pirates and clowns with
humongous red clodhoppers and a pair of puppets about
twelve feet tall representing I don't know what (but a
man and a woman -- whom I thought I recognized from the
big WTO parade). And so: the Jubilee Mardi Gras is now
underway. -- With the parade having vanished around the
corner but an impromptu five-piece bongo band still
banging away beneath the pergola. And all five faces on
the totem pole some twenty feet north of them seem to be
grinning in excellent "Can you believe this?" synchrony.
     In here four of the tables besides mine are
occupied and the language spoken is English at one,
Spanish at two, and Korean at the last, that of the
owners (and one of those, the father, is now barking at
a super-grungy Cawk woman panhandler who's been a
fixture around here in recent months to get out).
     The new edition of the alt-weekly hit the racks a
few hours ago. Not a word in it about domesday or the
T/M (true millennium, that's right). Nor in the new
edition of the indie weekly for that matter. But for me
to take the next step I need to know the day of
demolition and that's not yet been announced. (But hey,
another hook just suggested itself: a demolition derby.
And how about a play on the ambiguity of the term "demo"
-- the big domesday demo demo? Nah, forget it.) -- But
I'm losing the sense that I know what to propose to the
indie weekly. Again the moment may have passed. It's

all a matter of reading the civic mood. Even so,
though, I still want to pitch my domesday jubilee idea
to our local HQ community council. (And by the way, the
HQ business improvement district just sent me four
letters dunning for past-due BID assessments, a total of
probably a hundred bucks or so. I don't know the exact
amount; I've opened only one of the envelopes and that
covered '97 and '98 and was for $49. I'm protesting
because of the extreme regressiveness of the tax, as I
explained to them in a letter back in '97, I believe.
They never even bothered to reply. But now their
cumulative assessment plus penalties and interest is a
lot less than I thought it would be. -- And that's an
issue to look into another day.)

     The election results are not exciting but they're
relatively good. The hapless fake-cowboy son of the ex-
president (himself a former CIA operative and director)
beat the rabid "maverick" ex-POW here and in the other
two states holding primaries yesterday, but in doing so
he's had to wed himself openly to the extreme Christian
right. He should be easy pickings for the current veep
in November. This particular veep thrashed the hoopster
by a three-to-one margin here; everyone expects the
hoopster will now be bowing out of the national race.
(The hoopster's campaign headquarters just up the street
were a sorry sight at one a.m. last night. Then at the
bus stop I had to ask the desk clerk at the nearby
shelter to call 911 because a Natusan man -- or possibly
a First Nations man from Canada -- appeared to be
suffering a seizure of some sort right outside the door,
but no one inside was paying any attention.)

     -- Other than the parade and the bongo corps I'm
afraid Mardi Gras isn't amounting to much so far. Looks
like the sandwich shop will soon be closing for the
night. Darren's out there with his cartoons on display
under the far end of the pergola. Many of the usual
suspects and "persons of interest" are drifting about.
Windows are painted with party scenes here and there.
Bands will be striking up at a dozen different clubs
later in the evening -- but I'd better be moving on to

the scope office right about now. (And with a heavy
backpack -- containing weekly papers, drinks, a banana,
new mags and several remaindered books from the ORB.)

[+1]

     -- Must jyze quickly here. Upstairs at Z-geist,
the end table by the fence rail overlooking the lower
entrance, the cushioned window seat at my back. Some
very fine old blues playing on the sound system. Eight
minutes after five. Z'll be here in a few minutes.
She's stopping at a couple of card shops on the way, but
she may well have left work early too. She has this
applecart-upsetting penchant for arriving everywhere
early. "ABE" -- always be early, yes. (Between us we
use so many acronyms the U.S. military might be envious.
And neither I nor Z can be blamed for that groaner right
there; her friend D'Arcy the flack dropped it on us.)
     Speaking of early: today is Z's shadow birthday --
meaning if the Julian calendar had still been in effect
when she was born (and if my calculations are correct)
her date of birth would've been today: March 2nd.
     By the entrance to "the shoe" a poster hangs
proclaiming "The End is Near," referring not to the
domesday demo but "the shoe" evictions. I hadn't seen
this poster before today so I'm guessing it hasn't
received wide play and the turnout for the demo it seems
to be announcing, though without giving any particulars,
will be small. But I hope I'm wrong.
     (And here she is! "Where's the bathroom in this
place? I've completely forgotten!" -- She's carrying a
paper bag containing several cards destined for various
recipients on particular special occasions coming up but
she doesn't have one for her own shadow birthday! Nor,
alas, do I. I should've been more prepared. But this
is heavy week for me and last night was another
"sleepless on south hill" night for her and so I had
about an hour less time to myself than hoped for and
expected. And she's been griping because we've been

seeing too little of each other. -- As I say hello to
her straight down through the rail, and she flashes that
high-megawatt smile of hers straight up at me. This is
a whole new experience -- looking down at the top of her
head now as she waits in line -- and I tell her that. I
don't know if she heard me. She's ordering chai, her
usual coffeehouse preference these days.)

     She left the local afternoon paper folded in two on
the table here. No news visible about domesday. (And
it's a sunny day out there, contrary to forecasts. As
seen from the west-depot parking lot the dome looked
especially hulky and also bedraggled in the bright
light, almost as if it could crumble at any moment. The
north parking lot is packed with the trucks and RVs of
the demolition crew and a huge blue flag, maybe the
state's, stirs restlessly on the flagpole there, way too
big for the pole. Possibly it came from the much larger
pole that used to poke up atop the roof.) -- And this
is the next-to-last edition of the afternoon paper.
"Penultimate." (Scribo ultimo.) After a century as an
evening paper it goes to mornings next week, done in by
J-town's burgeoning cityhood and almost as much a sign
of that as Tuesday's "Ride of the Century." Traffic
congestion lies behind both developments. But so do
media changes. This is said to be, by the paper itself
but I suspect it's true anyway, the last successful,
which is to say profitable, afternoon paper in a major
city in the entire country.

     -- But she's here now and I should stop.
"Attention, attention, I want attention!" (Verbatim Z-
geist Z-quote.)

                    [+1]

     The news is out and it's good. Serendipity. D-day
will be March 26th. Z called and left a message this
morning and then the headline in the last-ever edition
of the afternoon J-town paper -- it's D-day for it too
-- in just those words. "And the Walls Will Come

Tumbling Down." Not only that, but the implosion will
be broadcast live on TV and the internet (maybe they're
one and the same by now?), and the main sponsor of this
really big show -- or simply call it the spectacle --
will be, aptly enough, our local software behemoth. One
of its cofounders, local plutocrat #2 (world #4), is the
major force behind the phase-out of the dome, which will
be replaced by an open-air stadium for our J-town pro-
football team which he also owns.

Later Z passed along a story she heard from D'Arcy.
At one point the baseball club, owned by competing
plutocrats of somewhat lesser standing, was planning to
invite people to its new stadium, one long block south
of the dome, and charge them to view the implosion. In
response plutocrat #2 saw to it that the safety zone was
expanded by a block to include the baseball stadium.

Z also said she wants to view the spectacle with me
from the hill. She'll still be spending the weekend
with Aida -- and also attending an all-day "Jubilee
2000" conference with her as well as Wei and Alison next
weekend (most of it's too early in the day for me) --
but Aida goes to mass on Sunday mornings (may the jyze
gods forgive her) and Z will sneak back to be with me
for the big event. She's still feeling guilty for
having spaced out the date of the all-important true
millennium when she set up the weekend with Aida.
-- But she doesn't want to stand on the south-hill high
bridge for the occasion, even though that may offer the
best view. She's afraid the contractors skimped in
building it and the vibrations from the big blast --
which will actually be a series of smaller blasts
altogether lasting about fifteen seconds -- will take
down the bridge too.

So what do I do now? Maybe not as much as I'd been
thinking. Mostly I just want to be sure the word gets
out to the main print media and to the HQ people. I
suspect the energy's just not there (in the city, that
is) to take advantage of the opportunity for a great
celebration, whether from the subversive or the civic-
booster or the save-the-planet perspective. This coming

Sunday we'll be seeing Olwen, who's been associated with
neighborhood organizing in the HQ for years, and we'll
do some more brainstorming with her and Trent. Then
Monday I'll start making the rounds -- HQ community
council and indie weekly being the key stops. Early in
the week ending on the 26th I might send letters to
the daily papers if the word's still not out.
        Meanwhile -- what? I'm brain-fried. It's four-
thirty a.m. and the "Hydes of Jyze" poster is propped on
a chair in the hall. But Z doesn't work tomorrow, it
being Saturday, and so she may well sleep through the
night. Tomorrow we'll have Kat for most of the day and
we both need to be well rested for that. Last night Z
was up for two hours in the middle of the night, from
two to four. Then when I went to bed I was the randy
one, as she observed numerous times later in the day --
it became a theme in calls and cards -- and shot off
with unusual force as a result of her splendid hand job
(which started out as a "perfunk" but then I ithyfied a
bit more than usual, or more quickly, I should say, or
maybe both, and she brought on her best "plan B" game).
        The tour of "the shoe" last night was both
inspirational and infuriating. Z had never been up
there before. Five floors of artist lofts and studios,
each floor a colorful maze offering wonder after wonder
of the aesthetic kind (and some of the intentional art
was pretty good too). I revisited the space I almost
lived in and mused about fate. I'd've loved living
there, I don't doubt it, but not for that or for
anything would I give up the past three years of high-
test partnered-up life with Z. And we're just starting!
We're woman and husband! (Also we saw some grand views
of the avenue below, the downtown skyline with the great
white tower prominent in the foreground, the docks, and
especially the hulking dome, all lit up and looming
stunningly close-by across the parking lot to the south
as the night shift prepping for the implosion labored
away inside, huge shadows cast by spotlights and welding
torches playing eerily on the interior walls.)
        For news there's this. Charles has moved in with

his dad and it's going well so far (and by the way, it
might not be permanent after all if his behavior
improves). Z's and Aida's friend Emiko has a tumor
behind her right ear and it may be malignant but Z
doesn't know much yet. And the outrageous Gloria G. at
the utility has done it again, revealing she's had an
affair going for the past two months with an "older guy"
down in the megastate's major megalopolis -- she met him
on the internet -- and now she's planning to move down
there in August -- and moments after the revelation she
asked Z to approve a training request for herself that
would cost the city big bucks. And with what return?
-- Not that anyone would bet a bundle Gloria will
actually leave the job and move to be with the older
guy. Plenty of time between March and August for more
of the lady's boggling swerves and flip-flops.

Can't push the J-stick any farther tonight. And
tomorrow I'll definitely be taking off from J no matter
what. So the D-day countdown is about to move to twenty
by the time of the next entry. -- And for Z's birthday,
what? Ten! And if I don't come up with something good
for her birthday the D-day doings the following J-week
might seem a minor distraction owing to the consequences
of her disappointment. So I gotta do her right and do
her good. (And want to anyway but of course.)

44

Back at the sandwich shop as the HQ triangle's big
night gets underway. It's Fat Tuesday, the orgiastic
climax of Mardi Gras, also known in some realms as
Carnival or (maybe) the Feast of Fools. A radio
station's broadcast trailer is set up outside the window

here, about thirty feet away, its white strobes flashing
annoyingly, and just moments ago the live DJ patter
started blasting on the PA. The triangle is decked out
in numerous colorful Mardi Gras pennants and banners
provided by beer companies and a few people are starting
to show up. It's just dusk. The big doings won't take
place until eleven or so, and I'm hoping to be here for
those. (But will they really be big? Compared with HQ
Fat Tuesdays a decade or two ago, probably not.
Compared with Fat Tuesdays in renowned Mardi Gras/
Carnival cities in more southern climes, forget it.
-- And besides, though no one knows this yet, and many
or most or maybe even every last one will never know it,
it's all just part of the buildup for the grandest
celebration of them all on the 25th/26th of this month.)
     It's also Super Tuesday. Exit polls are already
saying the primary campaign season will to all extents
and purposes end today. No surprises will be left to
spring -- and we're still twelve days short of the first
day of spring. It'll be the pompous silver-spoon veep
versus the arrogant silver-spoon faux cowboy in the
fall. This is just how it is. (But Ralph N. -- yes,
I've met him in the journalistic long-ago and thus by
the jyze rules can use his name this way -- Ralph N. has
jumped into the race on the Green ticket. He says he
intends to make a serious run this year. Of course he
has no chance to win, but those with a certain kind of
social hope can be buoyed a bit by the thought that
he'll be getting the message out at least a shade more
than otherwise would've been the case.)
     So this is a combined entry. It's Sunday's as well
as today's. Two causes for this delay: first, the
effort to spread the message about the true millennium,
and second, another disheartening squabble with Z. The
T/M info is out there now, at least to the extent it's
going to be. I'm making no more efforts. I'm shifting
my focus to Z's birthday. The aftereffects of this new
squabble are lingering and I expect they'll keep doing
so for a while. But the marriage doesn't seem to be
imperiled or anything like that. As I said to her this

morning (and her hearty laughter seemed to indicate she
agreed): "Looks like this hitch has hit a slippery
patch."

Last night I polished up a three-hundred-word
letter to the editor of the original morning paper and
sent it off. Even with the polishing I'm afraid it
didn't read very well. Needed more punch. Which I was
plumb out of. Today I gave copies of this lame letter
to two other people, one of them being the Z-wiff. If
she had the time today, she said, she'd try to work up a
version to send under her name to the former afternoon
paper (which is indeed appearing in the mornings now,
making everything throughout the day seem slightly
cockeyed or dissonant, with the two major "Fifth Estate"
voices coming in simultaneously rather than serially).
The other person I gave a copy to is Paige I., the
director of our business district and a force on the HQ
community council, and though I tried three times, I
wasn't able to see her personally and had to leave the
copy in a manila envelope on her desk.

Either the original morning paper or Paige I. could
be calling in the next day or two. Or there's still a
slim possibility the alt-weekly will do something, and
that paper's due to hit the streets tomorrow. If none
of these three pan out, that'll be it. Celebration of
the true millennium will go ahead regardless, of course,
but on a purely private basis. And that's okay, because
isn't this the age of privatization? (In fact, the
first of two "shadow" true millenniums falls this week.
And the second one, which occurs in April if this matter
stays, again, strictly private, that will actually be a
little truer than the true millennium on the 25th/26th,
for complicated calendrical reasons I won't even try to
explain now -- or maybe ever.)

More partiers going by, usually in small groups.
Some are wearing costumes or at least masks. One couple
appears to be Dracula and Vampira and for some reason --
or maybe no reason at all -- they're on roller skates.
At the moment a long-legged human-size playing card
wearing bright red tights is standing right outside the

door while her, or maybe his, male companion in silver
robot gear orders something at the counter. The card,
I'll have jyze readers know, is a 4 of Hearts.

All the tables in here are occupied -- that's eight
of them, I see, and each with four chairs -- and two are
offering the very loud in-person half of cellphone
conversations (very loud because "Black Magic Woman" is
playing at high volume on the box -- and it's not the
tune the payer, a Latusan dude, wanted, and he squawked,
"This isn't my song, this thing's fuckin' with me, man!"
and went over to the register to demand his money back,
but I don't think he'll get it).

I'm on my way to the scope office to punch in GJ
corrections. I'm hoping to finish those off in about
two hours and won't have any new scoping to do. On
Tuesdays the odds are strongly against new work. But if
they don't hold up this time, what's going down right
here must serve, if appropriate at all, as my one and
only Feast of Fools entry (my "feast" -- I had to buy
something, of course, to be allowed to sit here -- is a
can of guava juice, to which I now say: bottoms up!).

Too bad Z can't be here, but she had her follow-up
appointment with the D&C doc late this afternoon. She
could've come anyway, I think, but she showed no
interest when I suggested it. A little payback there,
I'm guessing -- aftereffect of the new squabble -- but I
didn't make an issue of it and neither did she. Then
again she didn't call today or leave a message and
that's highly unusual. (Now an exceptionally obnoxious
Cawk dude at the next table is griping loudly because
the live radio broadcast outside is interfering with his
cellphone reception. Wotta shame! Owner, owner, help
this dominant-culture man patch in again!)

[+1]

The odds didn't come through for jyze last night,
nor did they earlier tonight. To my surprise a big
scoping job awaited me last night and then another one,

even bigger but less of a surprise, tonight. And when I
arrived home last night Z descended on the living room
before I could even finish my dinner and that was it for
the night (though we eventually had some good pillow
talk and it was by no means a lost night). -- But her
sleep pattern is messed up for sure and she'll probably
be roaming around again tonight; and if she's not, jyze
doesn't want to be too disruptive. So I'm squeezing in
forty minutes at the scope-office reception desk before
catching that last bus home.

But earlier today one of my promotion efforts
finally scored. When I rolled out of bed at quarter to
one I found an eleven a.m. voicemail from the original
morning paper saying they wanted to use my letter, "or
most of it anyway," in tomorrow's edition. But they
needed me to call to confirm I was the author and also
to give them either a first name or a middle initial,
since I had signed the letter "G. Sandefjord" and their
policy forbids single initials.

Good enough. But then when I called back, the
letters coordinator, a certain Sharon L., said they were
now "a little late in the cycle" for letters for
tomorrow's edition and she "couldn't guarantee" they'd
get it in. The implication was it might run on Friday,
but she didn't come right out and say that. She did
volunteer she thought the letter was "real cute," and I
don't think she meant that pejoratively. She just
chuckled when I asked her to change the name of the
county executive I used to that of the current one; the
one I mentioned, after all, left office years ago. "We
caught it, yeah."

After I hung up it occurred to me that a one-day
delay might be fatal for my letter. That's because Z
had written one also -- shorter and punchier but
offering the same basic shtick -- and e-mailed it to the
former afternoon paper. She showed it to me last night.
And if that were to appear in tomorrow's edition, Sharon
L. and her staff would be sure to see it during this
first week of head-to-head a.m. competition between the
two papers and would probably yank the version I sent

them. -- Oh well, so it goes. Did I have some sort of
egotistical thing about the letter? The truth was, and
is, Z's version of it would likely be more effective
than mine. (Manny used to tell her, she mentioned last
night, she has "a real talent for polemic." Not for
nothing her long stint of editing the feisty utility
newsletter, whose circulation after all is greater than
that of both J. City dailies combined.)

But then when I saw her at the WOC -- where she was
meeting with a trainer to work up a new exercise program
in hopes of coping better with her ever-growing list of
physical ailments -- she said she hadn't thought to
check her e-mail to see if her letter had made the cut
and the newspaper needed a confirmation as it had with
mine. Presumably this means the earliest hers could run
would be Friday, and so it shouldn't have any effect on
mine at the other paper.

The new alt-weekly has hit the streets and it makes
no use of the packet I left with them. Now that's
disappointing. The HQ is their own hood, or if their
office isn't technically inside the borders, it's very
close, and they still can't see the potential here. I'm
strongly reminded of my own alt-weekly days (several
different alt-weeklies in different cities in a
different state) and the unending efforts to pitch
promotional and editorial ideas to the editor/publisher/
staff. It must be the vision thing! -- And our HQ
community council is even worse. The March issue of
their newsletter finally arrived today. It focuses on
Mardi Gras, which lurched to an end yesterday, but all
the stories about it are in the future tense. It runs a
story about the dome implosion but says nothing about
special doings in the HQ for that weekend. The
promotional opportunity of a lifetime is kicking them in
the head and they still don't get it.

So I'm girding up to make one more attempt to talk
with them. And if I can go in there with the letter
published in one of the dailies so I can wave it in
their faces, maybe they'll actually listen to me. Maybe
a published letter by itself would wake them up and I

wouldn't need to do anything in person. Maybe they'd
connect the name on the letter to the name on the packet
I left them and they'd be calling me.

So this is the Ash Wednesday report. The long
penance beginneth (run-up to the Easter weekend when, by
sheer coincidence, the jyze finale will also be taking
place). Super Tuesday results are just as expected and
the races are essentially over. -- Oh, and the pope has
announced he's asking for forgiveness for the sins of
Catholics over the past two thousand years. Just like
that, poof, they're forgiven and all's good again!
Covers quite a few sins, I'd say, both individual and
collective. Hopefully the major Catholic deity -- I
presume that's whom he's asking to accord the
forgiveness -- has super-powerful computers to deal with
such big numbers. (It's sort of a trip pondering
whether the major Catholic deity should be "who" or
"whom" in that last sentence.)

[+1]

Things can change fast. -- I think yet again as
the up-escalator at the glitz-strip chain bookstore
keeps right on rumbling by just inches from my right ear.
I've wound up here on a Thursday evening, still fairly
early, in the never-ending pursuit of art postcards with
a potential for quick and easy alteration of the
humorous and yet maybe also pointed kind. Tomorrow,
after all, is First Call Day.

The news is this. My letter didn't run in today's
original morning paper; in its place was someone else's
screed about the dome implosion. And I liked it: it
lays out the underlying economic issues quite well,
though it sounds a bit cranky ("Get with the times,
boy," Dad would urge, back when the times were leaving
him behind for good, I'm sorry to say -- though I'll
also admit I wasn't so sorry to say it then). To learn
all this I had to go down to the corner to buy a paper
after I woke up this afternoon; Z had taken our home-

delivery copy with her, as is her standard practice (and agreed to by me), to read on the bus going in. And then in leaving me a "gush" phone message during lunch hour she'd neglected to mention whether the letter had appeared or not. I guess maybe she figured I didn't care that much one way or the other -- and for good reason, since that's what I've been telling her -- and myself -- for the past several days. But at the same time I was fantasizing about the big splash the letter might make. Had I inadvertently provided fodder for Annunciation Day sermons all over town? Would the TV stations be calling for interviews in the wake of the mayor's snap decision to adopt the domesday idea? Could I prevent myself from being corrupted by my sudden fifteen minutes of fame? Would Z perhaps now see me as a more romantic figure, not just a meat-and-potatoes hubbin with whom the thrill is, if not entirely gone, slowly embering, at least in her view, which itself has become, I must say, a bit jaundiced at times?

     While I was out I also picked up today's edition of the former afternoon paper. Z's letter wasn't in there either (and I hadn't really expected it to be, since she'd told me before leaving the house this morning that she'd received no e-mail asking for confirmation of authorship). But in glancing through the printed letters I saw one, tagged as being received "by e-mail," referring to a Mardi Gras riot in and around the HQ triangle. This puzzled me until I came across a couple of stories about such an event in the local section. It happened Tuesday night not long after the parade ended -- when I would've been present if I hadn't had the unexpected work to do -- but too late to make Wednesday morning's papers (and of course there is no Wednesday afternoon paper now). It involved roughly a thousand people getting rowdy, the SWAT team swooping in, a dozen arrests and a couple of serious injuries. A columnist said it was all caused by drunken men jumping atop benchbacks and vehicle hoods or roofs to scope out women going topless. Ordinarily idiocy like this might've merited a paragraph or two in the police-beat section,

but the city's still extremely jittery as a result of
the WTO uprising (and the stories say lots of WTO-
related insults were hurled at the cops during this
Mardi Gras incident). In addition the head-to-head
newspaper war is inspiring more intensive coverage of
local news and also more sensational treatment of it,
especially in headlines. (Today's edition of the
original morning paper pulled out all the stops: the
lead hed was "FIERY CRASH ON BRIDGE STRANGLES COMMUTE."
Wow! -- As if the commute isn't "strangled" virtually
every day!)

But even if the "riot" wasn't much -- more like
spring-break hormonal hijinx -- the way it was covered
is bound to stir up even more city apprehension about
large gatherings. And that's doubly true for the
pusillanimous HQ community council.

So my letter now has two strikes against it. Would
any newspaper want to lead its letters section with a
dome-implosion-related epistle two days in a row?
Doubtful. And now the editors might have second
thoughts about encouraging a gathering down near the
dome, just blocks from the epicenter of the Fat Tuesday
"riot." And the letter itself, even if it were
published, would be tainted by datedness, because it
calls for a "Mardi Gras-like" midnight parade with no
reference to the rowdiness at the actual Mardi Gras
parade Tuesday night.

-- So that's it. This time I really mean it: my
campaign to make the true millennium into a cathartic
public event, one weighty with true millennial portent,
is over. I'm not going to bang my head against the wall
with the HQCC. Whatever happens happens.

In a few minutes I'll have to be moving on. I'll
just say, though, it feels very odd to be jyzing here.
It's not all that bad a place; it's just too slick, too
commercial, too franchisey for my liking. But then
again it is a bookstore and a "brick-and-mortar" one,
though really more steel-and-glass-and-plastic, but
still: how can I squawk? (And by the way, a story in
the original morning paper mentions that downtown

businesses -- the same ones that were moaning about WTO losses back in December and January, including this one I'm sitting in, just half a block from the epicenter of those protests -- increased their profits by fifteen percent overall last year, with the glitz strip right here leading the way. -- And in another story a professor at the U predicted the WTO upheaval would be strongly reverbing in city politics for at least a decade -- and of course the reluctance to make the dome implosion festive in a meaningful way is part of that reverbing.)

   "On December 31st ours was the only city in the country to cancel its millennium celebration; on March 25th/26th, to compensate for this loss, we were the only city in the country to celebrate what scholars agree should be recognized as the true millennium." But no, they won't be saying that.

[+1]

   My hunch was correct. No letter today either -- it got scratched. Nor did Z's appear. Couple of irrelevant old dinosaurs -- might as well just confine ourselves to mating in that grinding, slow-churning dinosaur fashion that takes days to complete. Or I guess it's giant tortoises I'm thinking of.
   But no, I don't mean it. We're fine. I all by myself am fine. At the moment I'm holed up in the spa at the WOC. Roaring waterfall, slowly circling white "foambergs," wiggling shadows of palm leaves. Fake palm leaves actually, of course, and that thought a few moments ago dislodged the makings of a title which then slowly surfaced: "Fake Idols Cast Real Shadows." Sounds almost Socratic, it does, at least to me. Now I just need to find something it doesn't apply to.
   A few moments ago a shapely young woman in a black bikini was cavorting in the water here. Now she's gone but two guys have taken her place, including one I know, Jojo, who's about ten shades darker than he was the last

time I saw him. He's an out gay man but for some reason
he seems to think I don't know that, so I act as if I
don't and he appears pleased.

When Z was here, upstairs, we were sniping at each
other a bit on the same sexuality issue that's been on
our docket for a while now. Maybe halfway through her
workout she came up and said she wanted to apologize for
the things she said last weekend, mostly, along with a
few brief reiterations since then. And so I returned
the favor. But the issue probably won't be going away
anytime soon and in fact we said we ought to try to talk
it out a little this weekend. Some questions associated
with the issue: Did my bad experience with Lady V
really and truly oversensitize me or traumatize me about
S/M sex? What's Z really and truly asking for when she
says she wants more "more 'Story of O'-type drama"? Is
there a cause other than aging for my more frequent
slowness to get aroused in recent months? (Or to put it
differently, is there something about the way she makes
love that fails to excite me or turns me off?) Are
control or power issues involved on either side? Should
she keep her criticism of me as a lover to herself to a
greater degree? And so on. It's been a week of jokes
and teasing about my being a "meat and potatoes" kind of
guy, about "the thrill is gone," about "formula" and
formulaic lovemaking. Some edge to it too, though I
think not all that much. I still tend to believe she's
not really serious in what she's saying: it's more like
a plea for attention or an effort to stir up a little
drama, which after all is one of her self-acknowledged
favorite things to do.

And meanwhile it's First Call Day. She didn't seem
much impressed with the special card I labored over for
her last night. "Three years ago today we were babes in
the woods. Now we're out of the woods but of course
we're still babes." These words laid out around a
bizarre-banal photo of a diapered infant holding an old-
fashioned telephone receiver to his/her (gender is not
clear) ear and mouth as if a conversation were going on,
with a conceptual forest of blue and green trees (the

"woods") inked in on the photo by the jyzer himself.
-- Then she forgot to leave the promised voicemail for
me saying whether either of the letters had appeared in
the dailies and so I again had to hike down to the
corner boxes and waste more coins, this time in a nasty
blowy rain. And tonight she was supposed to tell me
what she was expecting me to look like after talking
with me during that first call three years ago -- she'd
teased me with it this morning; it's something she's
never mentioned before -- but we both forgot about it.

     This morning I did break down and give her a little
loving. Yeah. But only "plan B." "Plan A" I didn't
even attempt, though she was not on the H-rag and I was
not slow to tumefy a/k/a ithyfy (ithify?). She,
however, was in a hurry because she had to get to the
office early to prepare for an 8:30 meeting.

     Last night she left me a poem she'd written about
an elderly mixed-race couple she'd seen on the bus.
They were like her parents, the man Filusan, the woman
Eurusan "and sort of Slavic-looking, with a babushka,"
and what moved her most -- caused her to tear up on the
bus and wish she could follow them home and check out
their domestic life -- was that they were holding hands
and openly showing affection for each other in public,
something her parents never dared to do when she was
growing up in viciously racist Centropolis. (And
yesterday Brooke, a trainer at the WOC, advised her not
to walk with her feet "sticking out so much." I
would've expected this directive to bother her because
of its associations with her childhood foot trauma, all
those hours over a period of an entire decade spent
learning to walk "correctly" under the guidance of
snippy Cawk nurses at the charity hospital after the
operations on her feet, but she didn't seem at all
perturbed. She said her father walked in a somewhat
similar splay-footed fashion and she didn't think the
operations had much to do with hers. And besides, she
knows I think her gait is terrifically sexy (as do
plenty of others) and it was one of the first things
to catch my eye when we actually met in the flesh

(although lips and eyes and cheekbones and hair and body
shape preceded gait: perhaps because she was standing
still at first). -- During the First Call, however, it
was her voice and laugh that did it. And the First
Call, like the First Cut, is the deepest. It's still
her voice that's her sexiest quality of all for me --
except, of course, for her extraordinary sexuality.)
        -- This reminds me, she ran into a former friend
she hadn't seen in years. This friend has been married
even longer than the period I was living with Lady U --
that's eighteen years and five months, folks! -- and was
telling her "the issues" in marriage never change and
never go away; they just keep reappearing in slightly
different forms and contexts and sometimes with a
different spin or valency to them, including once in a
while a mirror-image reversal. A lot of truth in all
that, I think. -- This sexuality issue, it's because
we've been around the mulberry bush on it numerous times
before -- with each other, I mean -- that I'm not so
worried about it now. I'm confident we can find our way
back to the same balanced (though also in some ways
tacit) compromise which has usually worked quite well
for us in the past, the one in which she offers more TLC
and "mutuality" in bed than she's accustomed to giving
(and her extreme sexuality in a sense often prevents her
from giving) and I accept less of both than I'd like to
get.
        -- If no one pushes the button on the wall, the
jets in the pool turn off automatically after fifteen
minutes. The roar ceases; the only remaining sound is
the steady tumbling splash of the waterfall. As now.
-- And the foambergs keep drifting around the edges but
they don't move as fast. ("Foambergs," I still go for
that term. Reminds me of a certain very short Japanese
book from the twelfth or thirteenth century, the exile
living in his tiny hut by a creek, the froth and foam he
watches going by and likens to our lives.)
        Birthday presents for Z. I've hit on a few new
ideas but not a really good one.
        As for the true millennium, domesday, all that, I'm

trying just to go with the flow -- froth and foam
included. "Let the cosmos decide." I nurse a few last
slim hopes one of the letters to the editor will run or
one of the weeklies will do something exciting at the
last moment or the HQ community council will come up
with a new angle on it or something totally unexpected
will happen -- who knows, perhaps someone else will
arrive spontaneously, or already has, at the same
domesday idea. Otherwise I'll have to be satisfied with
trying to come up with something appropriate I can do on
my own. This, after all, is the big penultimate
climactic moment for this whole TJM project. By
default. Simply as a matter of structure. It must fit
in right about here. But I'll wait until after Z's
birthday to focus on the details.

[+1]

     Closing it out on the offbeat. And with some good
news, although it probably comes too late to make much,
if any, difference. And also another boggling
coincidence in the realm of former romances. And also
an amusing discovery that explains a longstanding
mystery jyze recently took note of in these pages, maybe
a week or two back. (This now coming from the hideaway
after putting in two hours doing corrections at the
scope office and then hiking down here late.)
     The good news is the T/M letter finally ran in
yesterday's original morning paper. (Should I call it
the OMP, and the former afternoon paper the FAP? I
think I'll do that, yes.) It was the very last of the
letters in order, way down in the right-hand bottom
corner of the page, and it had a dull hed, and it
contained a couple of typos and some awkward editorial
revisions, but it still did the job: got the concept of
the true millennium out there and tied it in with the
big implosion. Hizonner the mayor has not yet called,
however, to congratulate me and say he'd be adopting the
concept posthaste, and neither have I been able to

detect any sign of a grass-roots T/M groundswell. In
fact I have yet to run into anyone or be contacted by
anyone who's even noticed the letter. And the people
I've shown it to didn't seem to be blown away by it or
by the proposal it put forward. But nonetheless its
appearance in print still might lead to a little
something more in the way of T/M celebration than would
otherwise have occurred.

The coincidence revealed itself as Z and I sat with
Fred and Eleanor W. in the upstairs theater at the
multiplex nearest the U waiting for "Being John
Malkovich" to begin. Suddenly Z said to me, "You know,
that voice behind us sounds just like" -- and turning,
said, "Yes! It is you, Gordon! I thought I recognized
that voice!" It was Gordon F., the instructor in her
master's program who was a proximate cause, so to speak,
of her meeting me. It was because she felt strongly
attracted to him and feared the fallout of acting on it
-- mainly that she might fall in love with him -- that
she decided she'd better meet some new guys. And she
revealed all this to Jess, and Jess took it from there
and wrote up the ad (with Gwen's help) and ran it (after
Z made a few edits and okayed it). He's tall, blond,
bearded, well built, good-looking, in his mid forties,
I'd guess, and has a pronounced Australian accent, and
he was seated directly behind me (so I easily could've
reached under my seat and given him a hotfoot). He was
there with his wife, also an instructor in the same
program and somewhat of a sourpuss, I thought, though Z
later told me she's highly respected by the students
(they were married back then too, albeit secretly, and
of course she might've had suspicions about Z and Gordon
at the time, though Z says she's always gotten along
quite well with her).

Not a whole lot happened. The three of them
exchanged pleasantries and then I became part of the
proceedings when Gordon asked what she'd been up to
since graduation and Z said, "Well, for one thing, I got
married." "And this would be the lucky man, I presume,"
Gordon inquired with a smarmy chuckle, perhaps pointing

or nodding at the back of my head (or just my ponytail).
I turned and said, "I'm the one all right," and shook
his hand and worked in a question to him: "So then are
you still teaching in the same program?" It drew a
surprising answer: "Well, no, I'm not; it's a little
embarrassing but I've gone over to" -- and here he named
our local software behemoth. At which point the whole
theater seemed to fall silent, as in that famous TV ad
for an investment company -- though I guess it was
mainly just the four of us. He did seem genuinely
embarrassed, though, and his wife displeased, somehow,
with his embarrassment, as if she'd perhaps been
instrumental in convincing him to make the move,
possibly because the behemoth's salary was a whole lot
better than what he was pulling down at the leadership
institute (not to mention the behemoth's stock options).

He and Z talked a little more and Eleanor W. leaned
across to me and asked in a whisper, "So who is this
guy?" I whispered back something like, "This is the
leadership instructor Zoelie had a crush on and because
of that she met me -- we'll tell you the whole sordid
story later." Z meanwhile had turned back toward the
screen as the movie was about to begin and she heard
most of what I said and she scolded me in a hushed voice
because she thought Gordon and his wife might have heard
it too. No way, I insisted -- but I'll admit now I
wouldn't've been too bothered if they had. Maybe I was
just jealous, but I thought there was something slick
and condescending about the man and took an instant
dislike to him. (Aida had reacted to him in much the
same way, I learned later. Of course she might've been
jealous too -- maybe even more so, since she attended
the institute before Z did and strongly recommended it
to her. For all I know Aida might've tried to put the
moves on him herself. She and Z might even have done it
tag-team fashion. And if so, he wouldn't've been their
first such mutual target.)

Then an oddity. About a third of the way through
the movie I heard the man -- Gordon -- get up and I
assumed he was hitting the men's room. But he didn't

return, and a few moments later his wife left too.
Neither of them said goodbye. My theory, mainly based
on how sour the wife looked, was that they'd been
fighting earlier and the incident with us just
intensified it; otherwise if they'd merely disliked the
movie I suspect they'd've said goodbye.

It gave Z and me something to razz each other about
the rest of the night. And I'll admit I was quite
pleased with myself for eliciting Gordon's "I'm
embarrassed" statement about his move from the academic
to the business world. It was unintentional or
unconscious but it also might've looked like a quick
rapier thrust to deflate his condescending tone. My
standing with the Z-woman might even have risen a bit.

So that's the coincidence. Next is the discovery.
That took place here in the hideaway and it was a simple
one. I noticed the corner of a piece of mail sticking
out from under the filing cabinet (which is wheeled,
thus creating a narrow gap between the bottom of the
frame and the carpet) and in retrieving it I realized
some other mail might've scooted a few inches across the
rug after being shoved under the door at just the right
angle and wound up out of sight and lost under there.
That indeed turned out to be the case; I fished out half
a dozen envelopes, all inconsequential except one: the
official reply to my letter refusing to pay the
regressive BID tax two and a half years ago. So that's
why I thought no action was taken! -- But this
discovery makes no practical difference; the letter just
says, in essence, it's the law, period, and it's legal,
you can't beat it, if you try to beat it you'll just be
paying a high interest rate and stiff lateness penalties
and if you also refuse to do that you'll eventually go
to debtor's prison or be burned at the stake or
something along those lines.

So be it.

And now it's time to go home. Again I'm hoping
I'll be able to add a bit more jyze here before the last
vibes of this off-the-beat entry trail off.

*   *

Maybe a thirty-minute wrap tops. Black armchair.
A newly altered card drying ("Bone Trouble," from a
Mickey Mouse cartoon). A few sentences written inside a
dinosaur shape in a Girls Day card for Kat. A card for
me from Z propped on the side table at eye level (on
which card she's drawn in a Woman of the West, with
spiky black hair like Z's own, asking, "Is it really so
hard to believe I know you're the one?" -- referring to
a few "just making sure" questions I asked her after the
Gordon incident). (On my card the bulldog guarding the
big bone says, "Dis dawg don't do kink.")

It was a day on which I attended to some of those
"manly-man chores" around the house. Finally glued the
zero back in its proper place between the 2 and the 3 on
the hallway door, for one (or for zero). It seemed to
be making a symbolic statement that we're at least
temporarily reclaiming this place for the future. Also
fixed the loose bracket for the blinds in the bedroom
(luckily found the necessary longer screw in my toolbox)
(yes, this is a true story). -- And then I timed Z as
she rehearsed the speech she'll give tomorrow at her old
neighborhood association, the one serving the hood where
she was living when we met. She'll be sharing the
platform with three other political activists she's
known for years. The handbill for the program (which
I've seen posted all over town) styles her as
"Environmental Justice Crusader Zoelie B." She liked
that so much she's planning to wear a cape during the
speech. (She said she'd prefer me not to come to watch
her in action this time and I agreed. I sort of like it
that my presence can still make her nervous under
certain conditions.)

Here at home it appears she's embarking on a
different kind of crusade (or maybe she'd say it's not
so different) against the two guys who've moved in
directly above us in Doug and Thuy's former place. They
play loud music and so she blasts our big console right
back at them. (This is in the evenings when I'm not
around.) She's had several run-ins with them but so far
without serious incident. One of the guys drives the

fancy SUV which happens to bear Mentoka plates. So now
she's considering trying a friendly "We're from Mentoka
too" approach. The trouble is, we're at a distinct
disadvantage being right under them. The new parquet
floors up there act like a tight drumskin for hard-soled
shoes and boots, and that seems to be what these guys
wear at all times. Or possibly they're pounding on the
floor with their feet or hands or any heavy items handy
just for -- especially regarding the feet -- kicks.)
     Meanwhile I've finally decided what my main
birthday presents for Z will be and the key components
are a couple of metal boxes I've had on hand all along.
But a lot of work will be involved and I have only two
days to do it in. And I haven't even started yet.

45

     Came squishing out about as late as I ever do. A
gentle pre-spring rain was just heavy enough to induce
use of the still-all-but-virginal fold-up umbrella (and
a moment ago when I reached into the middle zip
compartment of my backpack for this J-stick I found it,
the J-stick, beaded with condensation, almost as if it
were nervous, "sweating" this jyze appearance).
     In the greenery at the south end of the high
bridge, across the street from the "prow" of the dot-com
campus, a Cawk drifter dude was standing a little off to
the side relieving himself, the yellow stream and most
of his personal drainage spout fully visible to me and
to anyone driving by. "Excuse me, brother," he said as
I tried to slip unobtrusively past him, "but I gotta pee
real bad." Less and less is this an unusual sight
around town, but rarely is the act quite this brazen and

even more rarely is the perp in any way apologetic.

As I crossed the bridge it occurred to me I do it -- cross it -- differently than I used to at night. The millennial lights shining up from below are blinding if you walk too close to the rail, say within three feet or so. Suddenly it's as if you're on stage and can't see out beyond the footlights. The hulking dome, the shimmering bay, the brooding mountains, the thrusting skyline, the streaming freeway traffic -- they all disappear. (And the other day a new high-bridge experience: the entire structure started to shake under my feet and I thought this was it, the recently discovered south-hill fault had ruptured, the big quake was underway and I was going to crash down with the bridge just as Z's been fearing might happen to us both along with hundreds or thousands of others on domesday -- but it was merely a huge truck pulling an extra-wide load of earthmoving equipment, coasting downhill behind me, the engine not even audible until it was passing a few feet to my right).

And down through the AQ to the east-depot saloon, much of the way peering up at the gigantic crane that's still hanging over software plutocrat #2's headquarters building -- as it was already doing when I started this TJM project almost eleven months ago, and as it probably will still be doing when I shut it down, knock on wood, in six weeks (J-weeks I'm saying, so forty-eight days) -- and at this very moment I can see its brawny lower reaches out the window from my usual table in the niche under the TV shelf.

Right about now my caped-crusader spouse is delivering her rousing speech (and I know just how rousing it is because she practiced it with me). Aware she wouldn't be coming home after work, I stuck around the house longer than usual, intending to start painting the twin art boxes I'll be giving her for her birthday. They're like fifties school lunchboxes made of brushed aluminum; I picked them up on sale at a great price at a franchise coffee shop a couple of months ago, thinking then I would make them into art boxes for Kat and Z

(they were being sold as letter-writing kits with
stationery inside, original cost nineteen bucks apiece,
but I guess they didn't sell too well because they'd
been marked down to five). I never did get around to
doing one for Kat and I need something special for Z, so
-- this'll have to be it. Two personalized art boxes!
One for home and one for work! How fabulous! -- But I
advanced no further in the painting than opening a
squeeze container of red acrylic paint. I gave it a
tentative squeeze and a glop of paint shot out and split
in two in midair, with one glob (defined for this
incident report as half a glop) landing on one of the
old leather moccasins I was wearing and the other on the
light gray living-room carpet right next to Z's chair.
Cleanup efforts on the carpet took the next thirty or
forty minutes and weren't very successful, each round
making the stain a little fainter but also a little
bigger. Finally I decided to hell with it, the stain
would be like a boxer's scar from winning a big fight, a
badge of honor -- and the same would go for the one on
the moccasin. (No way will I be able to cover up the
carpet stain where it is and I don't think Z will be
oblivious to it.)
     Should her birthday this year be a "modest" one?
She's used to my making a very big deal of this
occasion: banners, balloons, surprises, lots of
presents. I hate to disappoint her. I still have the
banners from the past two years and the pushpins for
mounting them are still up on the walls. I even have
the shrunken remains of last year's balloons hidden in
a box in my bedroom closet. Until maybe twenty minutes
ago I was thinking I'd skip all that this year. But no,
now the itch is upon me to hit the party store tomorrow
afternoon. Probably they can reinflate the balloons.
I'll see what else I can come up with. And I suppose I
might as well drop by the public market and pick out a
big bunch of flowers for her. (Yesterday she hinted
again about flowers. We certainly don't want a repeat
of the Valentine's Day fiasco.)
     -- The dreaded birthday week! But no, not really.

Not dreaded. Far from it. In fact it's already become
one of my favorite weeks, a high point of the year.
This year, however, is a little different with the true
millennium coming up at the end of the following week.
But still the birthday week makes for an excellent lead-
in. And this year it includes not only St. Patrick's
Day and the Muslim Feast of Sacrifice but also the
vernal equinox. It's the last week of winter and also
the last week of "Infinite Jyze," as I'm calling this
volume just because I can and because I like the name.
I'm sure the good-humored author of "Infinite Jest" --
an alum of the same college I attended, although I've
never met him and he wouldn't know me from Adam -- or
from Adams, the college -- I'm sure would urge me on
with it.

     -- So I'm feeling festive. Let the good times
roll! -- But here at the saloon nothing like that's
happening tonight, except for right here under the TV.
For some reason the joint's almost empty. Has the
Liquor Board cracked down on it again? Ever since I
came in tonight a couple of grizzled Cawk dudes have
been trading off at the mechanical ticket lottery games
behind me, about a foot from my left ear, the sound of
the coin plunger much like an old-time adding machine or
cash register. The only exciting moment occurred when
another Cawk dude, this one ungrizzled and smallish and
wearing a yellow poncho, stepped inside the door and
started shaking himself off like a dog, with water
flying in all directions and making me jump up from the
chair with this J-book in hand. For a second he
apparently thought I was coming after him and he cringed
away -- "Sorry, man, sorry!" -- And that's two
apologies I've incurred in one night! (Am I turning
into a really scary Cawk dude myself, even without being
all that seriously grizzled, or what? Of course I'd be
very proud of myself if I have. And I'd probably add a
few years to my life expectancy if potential aggressors
of all sizes were to be frightened away just by the
sight of me as this shaking-dog dude was.

     Now onward. Tonight I'll hit the WOC for a soak

but I won't work out; instead I'll use the time to go
through today's papers at the hideaway to free up an
extra hour for painting when I return home.

      (And is the domesday letter published in Saturday's
original morning paper -- OMP! -- nibbling away at the
city's unconscious? Still not a single sign that it is.
On the phone Z told me she posted three copies, one on
each of her office bulletin boards and the other on the
"community board" at the coffee shop downstairs.
Otherwise no one's mentioned it. But D'Arcy and Leola
both howled over the Gordon F. story (our coincidental
meeting at the theater). And Calamity Gloria missed her
plane back from the megastate last night and this put Z
in a bind at work and she didn't have much time to talk
with me on the phone this afternoon.)

[+2]

      Just to get in a few words on the right day. The
on-beat. The Ides. Sprinkles of rain at four a.m. and
the big cluster of birthday balloons is twirling slowly
overhead, anchored by ribbons attached to the coffee
table. Banners, streamers, and bouquets of cut flowers
everywhere. Tulips and daffodils. A big new toucan
balloon lording it over the reinflated ones from
previous years. I've been nibbling on peach pie. The
two newly painted and decorated art boxes rest on the
table. The gold medal from the party store, inscribed
with "Da bestest wiff dere ever could be" (ooh, lame!),
hangs by its yellow ribbon from the chairback. Z's card
thanking me for the "exquisite birthday" and teasing me
about my happily revived sexuality graces the usual spot
for her cards on the table by the black armchair. I'm
holding down the corner of the couch by the big peace
lily and I've just turned the krazy klock around so it's
facing out again, the fookin' fogeys whooing down the
track on their antic steam engine as it poofs up puff
after puff of white plastic smoke. Time was once again
banished for the day (and still is on the other side of

the room, with each of the two clock faces there covered
by a sheet of blue construction paper held in place by
masking tape).

     A fine day, yes. And baffling too. How is it all
of a sudden I'm a stud again? Four times in thirty-six
hours, and that's counting only those complete with
ejac. A miracle! And it's not pill-induced either. Of
course I don't expect it to continue at such a clip or
for that matter ever to happen again, though I suppose
it might under just the right conditions. But could it
portend a new, "more vigorous" era? Or is it just a
freak occurrence?

     But wotta day. Wotta wife. How lucky I am.
-- And will continue with this boasting, gloating,
marveling tomorrow.

                          [+2]

     -- For our St. Patrick's Day party Z and I met on
the high bridge. This was an hour ago and it was half
coincidental, half intentional. She said she'd be
walking home; I left the house when I figured I'd run
into her somewhere on my way in. Before I reached the
bridge I spotted her hurrying along about halfway across
(she was walking fast for the exercise value) and waited
to surprise her at the south end by the prow of the dot-
com campus, all but literally in the shadow of the
castle itself.

     "Fancy meeting you here!"

     "Hey -- this is where I always crawl out of the
bushes."

     (At the army-surplus store in my old edgy hood -- I
ducked in for a look-see the other day while picking up
her birthday flowers at the public market -- I
discovered they're carrying hooded jackets which are
almost identical knockoffs of my green one which is
getting a little frayed now. Well, okay, a lot frayed.
Z says it always makes me look as if I've just emerged
from one or another of those same "jungle" or "rez"

paths -- especially when I'm wearing an extra-large gray
sweatshirt beneath it, as I was today. But for me
that's just the point of the jacket: blending into the
world of the Jyze City night streets. So as soon as I
have the money I'll buy one of the knockoffs and start
intentionally "stressing" it a bit so I can nail down my
street cred for another five years or so.)

     At the corner we schmoozed about weekend plans.
The main question right now is whether Z will be
attending the art-fire show at the fairgrounds with me
on Sunday evening. This is one of the main events
originally scheduled to take place on December 31st as
part of the millennium celebration but then canceled
because of the terrorist threat. Now it will coincide
nicely with the equinox that same Sunday night. And
it's also right on the way for our usual alternate-
Sundays north-hill provisioning run. But Z's moving
into the budget-crunch period at work and doesn't know
if she'll have enough free time on this particular
Sunday. (Tomorrow I'll be watching Kat while Z and
Betty enjoy their long-delayed Christmas pedicure. Noon
was the latest hour they could arrange it for, so I'll
have to be rising before the crack of my personal NUT-
time dawn. Z noticed I was looking tired at the bridge
and the reason was I'd gotten up early today to prepare
myself for getting up even earlier tomorrow. -- And
after they do the pedicure we'll all, Kat included, be
attending an adult puppet show up in the north end.
-- And then at home I'll be tackling the taxes.)

     Also on the bridge we talked about just where we'll
stand for T/M domesday. Somewhere up by the strip park
on the west side of the hill would be best -- it'll
still be early enough in spring that greenery won't be
blocking the view -- but the crowds there might be
formidable. It's hard to say for sure. But the media
buildup for this thing has been fierce, the OMP leading
the pack with its front-page "Countdown to Implosion"
series (we're at nine days now), and many of those
stories declare the best view will be from the northwest
end of our hill. And the safety zone around the dome

itself has been expanded by several blocks in all
directions, meaning the number of direct viewpoints at
ground level has shrunk considerably.

       Z also mentioned she'd heard the police were
girding up for another rough night in the triangle
tonight owing to St. Patrick's revelry. Rowdy packs of
drunken frat-boy types in glossy green cardboard hats
were already raucously in evidence when I walked through
the area an hour ago. And the police are said to be in
an unusually nasty mood caused by the release of an
outside expert's report severely criticizing their
performance during WTO week. (But this expert is from
the southernmost of the two megalopoli in the megastate
to the south with its history of riots and notoriously
out-of-control cops and is himself a known brook-no-
nonsense authoritarian.) -- But in any case I won't be
down here when the St. Pat's action gets hot and heavy,
if it does, because a full docket of scoping awaits me.

       Today Z had lunch with Dale, her boss, and he
showered her with praise for the job she's been doing.
So she's on a roll right now. And the cards are still
pouring in for her birthday. And her husband's got his
mojo workin' again.   -- But never mind that, even if
it's pretty damn important. Time to move on.

       -- Oh, but wait. I should at least mention the
news. First a judge threw out most of Initiative FTG
(Fuck the Government), scuttling the tax-vote portion
but leaving the license-tabs reduction intact for now.
Then just this morning the aerospace/"defense" leviathan
settled with the engineers and the strike is over.
-- And yesterday the stock market shot up 499 points,
the biggest single-day gain in history. Volatility.
Exciting times. We twist up a few more loops on the
great ecopocalyptic death spiral.

                         [+2]

       -- At last the millennium is again almost upon
us! It's twenty past eleven in the evening and in just

fifteen minutes the vernal equinox occurs. (That's
generalized for this time zone. Won't try to calibrate
it any more finely than that.) Since the vernal
equinoctial turn signaled the start of the new year a
thousand years ago in England, this will arguably be the
millennial anniversary of that occasion -- the truly
true millennium. Truly true too, though, back then
March 25th was thought to be equinox day and therefore
another celebration should occur on that date, six days
from now, and will, at least here in these pages if
nowhere else. And then still another one a week after
that, representing a further refinement of calendrical
adjustments over the thousand years, and that one will
be even more private. "My own private true shadow
millennium."
     Still eight minutes to go. Since I'm at the scope
office I have to figure in the seven-minute discrepancy
between their clocks and the correct time. But the
actual celebration -- and it was an official one, though
also in a sense coincidental -- took place about four
hours ago. And at the exact moment when the bonfire
consumed the giant egg at the fairgrounds to reveal the
great phoenix seemingly poised to take flight from
inside (this beneath a spectacular full moon and the
iconic saucer slowly spinning atop its tee about six
hundred feet almost directly overhead), someone -- not
me! -- in the crowd of five thousand or so yelled out,
"Belated happy new year!", sparking scattered laughter.
-- And then the phoenix fell back into the ashes and
within moments Z and I along with just about everyone
else were scrambling for the exits.
     -- As now occurs the true moment at least of this
iteration. When the dot goes down inside the brackets:

[.]

     Millennial felicitations! -- And winter's over
too. Of whose discontent? Well not mine! Because for
me right now all's at least seemingly just about as good
as it could possibly get. Truly true millennium season

and all's for the best!

     Even the taxes look good. Over the past hour I put
together my rough estimates on the various forms for the
first time and it appears we'll be owing somewhere
between one and two thousand dollars less than we've
already forked over through withholding and quarterly
payments. It's the so-called "marriage penalty" factor
at work; but because of the extreme difference in our
incomes it actually works in our favor. In effect on
about half of her income Z now is taxed at a
considerably lower rate than she's withheld on. Or to
put it differently, her being hitched to such a hapless
financially challenged nightscoping ne'er-do-well as
myself is saving her up to a coupla grand a year.

     I still have to run all this by June, our self-
appointed (and happily acceded to) tax expert. I won't
be at all surprised if she catches me out in some goofs
and they might be fairly large by my standards, worth
maybe hundreds of bucks -- because I'm venturing into a
whole new territory here in filing a joint return in
which the co-filer actually has significant income.
Unlike, say, Lady U. No longer am I working on the
first page of the tax tables. -- But I'm sure I've got
the basic drift right. I was prepared to be delighted
if the amount I still owed was under a thousand dollars.
Now it appears that not only will I owe nothing but I'll
even be getting a few hundred bucks back. Hallelujah!
Happy truly true millennium!

     Z and I left the house around half past five and
were lucky enough to find a free parking spot within a
few blocks of the fairgrounds. The ceremony itself was
free too, as was entrance to the grounds. The carnival
was in operation as per normal on a Sunday and a fairly
large crowd was on hand. We glanced in the old armory
(food arcade way back when) and I offered to show her
the place where my booth used to stand during the
world's fair, but since I'd already done that twice
before I felt I shouldn't insist when she shrugged and
went "Enh." Lots of history for me in that area within
a few hundred yards of the armory, though, with at least

one personal event of high significance going down there
in each of the previous four decades. But: that stuff
is all basically beyond the pale for jyze. And in any
case: it was a good place to witness a ceremonial
burning.

The outdoor central fountain was turned off for the
occasion and its great sunken concrete bowl became a
natural amphitheater, with maybe a quarter of the open
space around it roped off for the "sculptures": some
dozen or more wood-and-paper-mache figures up to fifteen
feet tall, including a number on horseback separated
from the central gathering around the egg. The two
figures there supposedly represented pestilence and
death, but I must confess the symbolism of the display
as a whole was never quite clear to me. The artist, a
local fellow, based his creation on an annual ceremony
held somewhere in Spain in which hundreds of similar
statues on a much larger scale (some seventy feet high)
are torched. This was to have been the centerpiece of
the city's official millennium celebration prior to the
explosion of fireworks from atop the saucer on December
31st. The artist had an ironclad contract, according to
what Z's told me, and was able to force the city to
allow him to present the work on a date of his choosing.
He chose well. (But I wish he'd picked next weekend
instead -- the truliest true "true millennium." Or
maybe I don't. I do like it that two of the three
rolling true millennium dates have a kind of public
celebration attached, leaving me the third for my own
private one.

We had about an hour's wait for darkness to fall.
During that time Z and I stood on the lip of the bowl
just a few feet from the fenced-off fire area. Live
music played from a tent on the far side of that same
area, flute and electric piano, and the bowl gradually
filled up, with the crowd growing to the aforementioned
five thousand or so by the time of the burning. The
moon rose from directly behind one of the horseback
figures as seen from our angle (it had been a fine sunny
day, chilly but with the sky mostly clear except for

cloud banks looming above the eastern mountains which went pink -- the clouds did -- in tiers at sunset and also coughed up the moon). Next to us on the lip a mother tried to keep a hyperactive five-year-old under control. He knocked over a big box of buttered popcorn, making the steep sides of the bowl perilously slippery for people trying to pass by in that area. I was bundled up in my old black winter coat, but it didn't do me much good because the zipper was broken. It had been so long since the last time I wore the coat -- a couple of years -- I'd forgotten about the disabled zipper. By the time I discovered it didn't work we were already approaching the fairgrounds on foot.

The burning itself lasted only about forty minutes. The main surprise was that all the figures contained sparkling fireworks ignited by the heat. And the egg, I should've mentioned, offered an impressive lightshow of its own from within, a succession of primitive art faces each of whose expressions burned through a series of horrific changes as the flames consumed the countenances one by one before the phoenix appeared.

Yesterday, too, I want to say, was fine, with the puppet show enjoyable, my three hours alone with Kat the usual merry ordeal (but a little more of an ordeal than expected, actually, because I was going on so little sleep, having to rise three and a half hours earlier than usual), and an amusing coincidence on the way home, after a north-hill grub stop, when we spotted brother Rob ambling down the old middle road on his way to the downtown bus stop and pulled over to chat with him a bit. (He said I was "looking pretty slick" in my glossy black army-surplus raincoat -- not the black winter coat -- as though suddenly I'd moved up in the world.)

And so I must yield to the penultimatum: yes, here it comes, Book the Standalone. Be done with this wintry stuff. Ratchet the countdown down down down down down to five -- in days to T/M dome doom and in J-weeks to J-end.

BOOK J

[Jyze of the True Millennium]

46

Came padding out on a warm sunny afternoon. Got
only as far as our balcony outside the apartment where I
sit now. But then this is as far as I or anyone could
go on this path; one more step in any direction and --
oops! Splat! But handily the mess would be right by
the dumpster.

In my slippers. This doddering start to the last
of the books of the TJM project (and to what I've been
looking at from the start, although through a good many
different mood prisms, as its climactic week) -- this
start only befits the elder I'm all too obviously
becoming. Or at least so Z says. Personally I'd prefer
to think she's just up to her old pot-stirring tricks.
She utters such heresies as "You're sure a lot grayer
than you were three years ago!" and "I keep finding
these long gray hairs all over the place and I know
whose they are. You're not just graying, you're
shedding! ...I don't want to split hairs here, so I'll
just say you're literally losing it!"

So if she doesn't like to see my hair turn gray,
shouldn't she be happy that I'm losing it?

Even Kat joined the assault this past weekend,
suggesting I could do as her science teacher has
recently done and shave my head. "Of course he's
really, really old, Glen. He's forty-three!" (That's
more Kat humor. She knows just how old I am -- just
like she knows my every last anatomical detail.)

But I don't believe a word of any of this. I'm
vigorous! I'm flashy! And I'm on a roll -- a J-roll!

Perhaps it would be best to make it explicit right

889

at, or anyway near, the top: it's absolutely appropriate
that the last J-book of this annal should be Book J.
     Then again I'll admit it's not so warm out here.
In a heavy long-sleeve henley and a thermal hooded
sweatshirt I'm shivering. Nor does sunshine ever reach
this spot at this time of day. It's raying in just
around the corner, though, and I'm admiring the complex
way the facades of the buildings across the street are
lighting up in response to it, and the same for sunlight
and shadows on the slopes of the in-city ridge across
the valley and the wooded island in the lake (itself
barely visible) and the hills across the lake. The
mountains, though, many still snow-shrouded, are cloaked
in what looks like hazy brown sunscreen.
     But I'll be out here just a few more minutes. As
soon as Z arrives home we're taking off for the south-
end A&C superstore where a big sale on art supplies is
starting up. This is the only day we can go.
     It's the 21st of March. First day of spring for
many. In Japan today is the vernal-equinox holiday. In
Iran, among numerous other countries, it's the first day
of a new year. (An Iranian festival was underway at
the fairgrounds when we were there Sunday. I've been
seeing an unusual number of Muslims of likely Middle
Eastern ancestry wearing trad gear on the buses.)
-- And on this balcony every single one of the dozen or
so geraniums is already in bloom. Or I could say
they're still in bloom, because, as we've been
speculating about disbelievingly for months, they've
never stopped producing new flowers all winter long.
     (Now I see the Z-mobile roll up and I call down to
the lady herself as she turns into the driveway. She
stops and waves. And then varooms ahead so as to beat
the closing of the remote-controlled garage door.)
     -- Better wrap it up here. Didn't have a chance to
talk about this afternoon's trolley-bus depoling -- the
usual comic scene -- but I do want to note they're still
happening. And of course this is it, I absolutely must
mention: the week the dome blows. Big-time excitement
ahead.

*   *

Pushing on some four hours later in a booth at midtown chain burgers across the "very high road" from the scope office. This is the booth closest to the service counter but also the one most hidden from it (by a six-foot-wide stretch of wall immediately behind me). At eight they stop giving out trays at the counter, hoping to discourage table-sitters like me. A few more minutes and they'll close the front dining area, leaving just these three booths here for anyone who wants to eat in-house sitting down. Half an hour after that the big surge of swing-shift janitors on lunch break starts -- their orders are all to go -- and half an hour after that the place closes for the night.

I guess I'm noting all this to explain why it is I rarely jyze here. And the reasons are similar for the only other restaurant I can afford that's open at night in the central downtown area, the chain burger joint with the excellent softie cones. And there a cop's on duty to roust anyone who sits at a table beyond the allotted thirty minutes. Here the joint simply doesn't provide places to sit, except for these three booths, all of which are usually occupied at this hour.

Life in the big city. J-town USA. Fast-food franchises. They drive everyone else at the low end out of business. I don't want to patronize them but I'm pretty much forced to. (Reminds me of those mainstream critics who ripped WTO protesters for wearing shoes or clothes made by the chains they were protesting against. Hypocrisy, they said. But it wasn't. Essentially people have no choice but to patronize the giant corporations, and that's just what the protesters were upset about -- among other things. But of course you can't expect mainstream critics to look at things too far beneath the surface when that surface is the very one holding them aloft in the world.)

A slow Tuesday. I have only corrections to do, no scoping.

Z was in an irritable mood today. The minute she arrived upstairs she pouted about my failure to come in

from the balcony to open the door for her. What, I'm
not even supposed to finish up the paragraph I'm jyzing?
I expect her to be a little more understanding and
supportive. And then when I told her this she jumped on
me for being "cranky"! It's a familiar tactic of hers
for disarming criticism, accusing me of what she's
already guilty of herself.

And she kept it up the whole time we were together,
and I griped back, but it all stayed on a low level.
The real villain, as she admitted herself, is the
biennial budget-time pressure she's under at work. The
reason she had the car this afternoon was that she'd
needed it to see Lorraine, her naturopath, who'd given
her a "homeopathic" which is supposed to help keep her
calm for the next two months as the budget process plays
itself out (and later Z asked me not to tease her too
much about her alternative medicine, and I agreed not to
do that, although just last night she'd been explaining
that she likes to tease me about all sorts of things
because she grew up in a home where her parents teased
each other constantly and so she's used to that kind of
banter -- this matter coming up when I objected to a
series of what I considered complaints, and fairly
hostile ones, not just mere teasing).

But no, I don't think we're facing any serious
problems here. Just another friction patch. By and
large we seem to handle them pretty well. In fact we
run into many fewer of them than I would've expected,
given our numerous differences. It's just too bad one
such patch has to come up during the opening day of what
may be jyze's biggest eighter of the entire project.

So what's she on my case about now? Wanting her to
be "too nice." Asking her to be "stoic." Being
"avuncular" myself in offering my opinions about things
she asks me about. Being too hard on her in objecting
(too mildly if you ask me!) to her carelessly bending,
crinkling, wrinkling, mutilating the cards I make for
her. ("They're mine!" she cries. "You gave them to me!
I can do whatever I want to them!")

Ecch, so what am I doing here, trying to polish up

my kvetching style? Enough.

    -- She was also irascible today, by the way, owing
to new incidents involving the incorrigible Gloria G.
Last night she, Gloria, drank a bit too much wine and
called Dale, the department chief, at home and moaned
about her troubles. Her elderly mother in Manila now
wants to return to the States and live with her, and
this is threatening to queer Gloria's relationship with
her new "older guy" boyfriend in the megastate to the
south (they'll be talking about it with his therapist
when she flies down there later this week). Gloria's
what Filipinos call an "ate," an oldest daughter, and
thus is morally obligated to provide care for her
parents (like Serafina in the D. family or sort of like
Zoelie herself in the half-Filipino B. family).

    Dale called Z this morning and they tried to find a
way out. Z suggested having Gloria seek help from a
Filipino therapist, but it turns out Gloria prefers the
Western kind; a Filipino would be "too embarrassing."
And there are other issues; she's going behind Z's back
to get training which the city will have to pay for even
though Gloria's leaving soon -- and so forth and so on.
It's all driving poor Z half-mad. (Does she make any
connection between Gloria's histrionics and her own
penchant for same? I know she does to an extent. But
sometimes I wish the extent were a little greater.)

    -- They're sweeping up here. The guy's doing it
too energetically, trying to be funny about it, now
sweeping backward between his legs, and a little chunk
of something -- was it a French fry? -- landed all the
way up here on my booth tabletop and then skittered off.
But it means time's short.

    Our trip to the A&C superstore flopped. We found
it closed down -- permanently. The next-closest outlet
of the same chain with the big sale going on is twenty
miles away, down by the airport. So instead we motored
over to our local paper store just to feed our
heightened art-supply jonesing; then Z dropped me off in
the HQ triangle.

    On the way in we passed right by the dome. With

its outer walls stripped away it looks pathetic from
every angle and distance but from nowhere more so than
up close. -- And in the HQ triangle not a sign of
festivity or celebration, no posters announcing any kind
of special activity for this exceptional weekend.
Nuttin'.
     -- No more stays. Must split.
                    *   *

     Tacking on a few paragraphs up in the conference
room. Work done, bus not due for forty minutes, why
not jyze? It's T/M week! (A nap might be better right
now but the janitor's still around. He's not here at
the moment but his red vacuum cleaner is. He's a new
guy, by the way -- the short Mexusan book lover is gone,
replaced by a slightly taller balding Eurusan I can't
figure out at all; he's sort of like a throwback punk
with some serious attitude but in a suit he could pass
for a banker. The janitors change but the vacuum
cleaner stays the same. The Mexusan guy, I even showed
him how to reattach the loose grate on the bottom of the
machine -- a trick I learned a few years ago because a
previous janitor in fear of losing his job if he had to
call in the supervisor asked for my help in figuring out
how to do it and together we somehow succeeded.) (We
night workers gotta stick together, see.)
     So I'll move on into the meat of things and mention
that the millennium terrorist ("King of Terror") will be
rippling out a delayed effect on my life this summer.
Once again local politics will be costing me dough.
Naomi left a note in the safe saying she'll be joining
Larry in the megastate for at least a week this summer
when he's down there to try the man. The trial has been
transferred there because of the massive amounts of
prejudicial publicity the incident received up here (in
essence the same publicity that caused the fairgrounds
pyrotechnics to be canceled and the fire ceremony to be
postponed until this past weekend). It's possible
she'll be gone for two weeks or even more, and in that
case I'd lose a bundle. -- So I get bashed from both
sides of the political spectrum, in a way, first by the

WTO and then by one of the groups -- the most extreme of
them all -- fighting it: the "radical Islamic"
terrorists. Or I could look at it differently and say
I'm an unintended (except in a broader sense) victim of
neoimperialist USAn law enforcement both times.

My total loss will probably just about balance what
I'm unexpectedly gaining from the "marriage penalty" on
this year's taxes. And meanwhile the stock market's
zooming back up again, so I suppose I could say I'm
sitting pretty, financially speaking, as a participating
capitalist. But volatility is the word. Potential
flip-flops lurk everywhere. This is always the case, of
course, and it's so for everybody if you include
emotional attachments and health among the variables,
but right now for me it's a bit more than usual, and I'm
always up at the high end of the potential volatility
spectrum -- except, I like to think, regarding emotional
attachments. And in the past five years that exception
has failed to apply several times -- with Mother, with
Barb, with Lady U.

So what else is there? Aida is now saying she
wants to join us Sunday at the strip park to view the
implosion. Excitement is building about the anti-IMF/
World Bank protests slated for the U.S. capital the
middle of next month (some folks are expecting them to
be even more effective than the anti-WTO ones here were,
and I hope they're right; but this time neither the feds
nor the cops will be taken by surprise). And it now
appears we have not one but two Eurusan men living in
the apartment above ours, each owning a large SUV, each
unfriendly, and each possibly -- Z thinks -- gay (I've
had only brief glimpses of them from a distance).

At the WOC I haven't seen Marcus in a couple of
weeks. Is he lying low because of the hothead ex-POW's
flameout in the presidential primaries? Clio is keeping
me informed on the Taiwan situation (the Nationalists
have lost the presidency, tensions with China are up,
and Clio's grandmother wants to move to the U.S. before
war breaks out). (June hasn't called to talk about
developments over there, presumably because she's right

at the center of the city's budget crunch.) Estella
told me she's getting serious again about publishing her
poetry and wants to meet for coffee to talk about it,
even though there's really nothing I can do for her and
I've told her this. Z and I have set a movie date with
Melanie and Jay for sometime in mid April, a meshing of
Melanie's and Z's packed calendars having finally been
achieved after months of failed attempts.
     And so it is: the items I could fit in during a
forty-minute jyze.

[+2]

     What the heck: I'll try my luck at downtown chain
burgers. The place closes in a little under an hour.
I'm partially hidden in a corner of the back section
looking out on the old "high road." Around the corner I
hear the rent-a-cop talking with one of the regulars
(both of them right-wingers who backed the hothead ex-
POW in the presidential primaries before he denounced
certain fundamentalist preachers as "evil," which from
my point of view of course they are; then both of these
jokers flipped to the knucklehead faux cowboy who sucked
up to the fundamentalists).
     It's Thursday of T/M week. I'm taking a break from
a blessedly short and easy scoping job which is already
almost a wrap. It's chilly out there but not raining.
And still all the tables in here are occupied and mostly
by people trying to get some respite from the streets.
Many of the faces are at least slightly familiar to me.
The old Afrusan dude in the beat-up baseball cap who
just sat down at the corner table by the back door
(where it's a lot chillier owing to the door's frequent
openings), he usually grabs the seat I have here when he
can. He's not upset though. If I bring a newspaper
with me he often winds up with most of it (though
reading it must be annoying because I almost always clip
an article or two) (though rarely from the sports pages,
true, and those he always goes for first).

What news? The pope visiting the Holy Land, he's
supposedly trying to mend Jewish/Catholic relations.
The U.S. president visiting India, he's supposedly
aiming at reversing USAn "neglect" of the subcontinent
(not that anyone's noticed India complaining about it).
    Onward. Hereabouts the city's whipping itself into
a frenzy over domesday. Too bad nothing politically
progressive (in my sense of the term, which has little
to do with the conventional usage which makes it a mere
synonym for liberalism) -- is going on around it. We're
all but buried alive in long articles from the daily
papers about the technical details regarding the
demolition, the elite viewing parties (and places the
hoi polloi can congregate, with the high bridge and the
Filipino strip park across from the DC castle always
near the top of the list), about dome history,
objections to public expenditures, pro and con opinions
on dome architecture, safety precautions regarding the
blast, on and on and on -- but little or nothing about
the political and economic forces behind the decision to
replace the dome and the impact of their massive clout
on future life here.
    The new editions of the weeklies are a big
disappointment. Both limit their domesday coverage to a
brief satirical piece taking up less than half a page.
    Meanwhile Z and I are seeing each other mostly in
passing this week. She's caught up in the intensifying
budget matters at work and also delayed birthday
luncheons and dinners with various friends, and this
weekend she'll be staying with Aida for a day. This
morning when I crawled into bed a bit early she was
unexpectedly frisky but the timing was bad: I was barely
able to keep my eyes open. Tonight I ran into her in
the garage on my way out just as she returned from a
hair appointment in the north end. A heartening moment
then: she told me Nika at work had come over to her and
said, "You know, it just occurred to me you have
everything you want. You're in love, you love your job,
you have so many friends." And Z to me: "You know what?
I realized she's right! -- But I'm too superstitious

to let myself see it. I'm afraid the gods will punish
me!"

     Then again I think she's going through a period of
adjusting to the settledness of having been in a love
relationship for three years (as of next Wednesday).
There's now no question about it: this is her longest-
lasting ever. And it's with a male and she'd given up
males forever!

     -- And my jyzing here is done. Cleanup is
starting, the doors are open, a cold wind is whistling
through, the intentionally abominable country music
that's been playing all this time on the PA has now been
turned up deafeningly loud.

                         [+1]

     Kicking off Big Date Broke Day with a whole new
experience: a late dinner in the back room at the
firehouse saloon. This is just a block from the HQ
triangle and it's the beginning of domesday weekend and
the joint is jumpin'. As is the whole quarter. Makes
you wanna weep when you think about what could've been.
     I rarely come in here because the place always
draws an ultra-straight crowd -- lots of law-
enforcement types, the majority being firemen from
citywide department headquarters just a block to the
south -- and not too surprisingly it always feels
hostile to me. One tipoff: a sign on the door says no
one with a backpack will be admitted. That's meant to
keep the drifters and the homeless out, but I always
wonder if they'll apply it to me too. When my pack's
full it's almost as big as some of the vagabond packs
often seen in this area, although mine lacks the typical
rolled-up sleeping bag affixed to the top or bottom.
     So tonight when I set out from the hideaway I
didn't bring my pack. Carried the J-book in my hand
(probably looking something like -- but not too much
like, I hope -- a friar with his good book) and my
pocket watch in my pocket (for the first time in

months). Did a quick tour of nearby nightspots and sure
enough this was the only one I could enter without
paying the joint cover charge or, prospectively, a huge
dinner bill. And even so I'll be laying out over ten
bucks for one of the cheapest firehouse meals, chicken
strips with fries. Right now it's cooling on the other
side of the booth tabletop. It was either order dinner
or sit at the bar, where jyzing would've been just about
impossible. And I was hungry anyway, and am. So will
dig in.

     -- But do the digging left-handed and meanwhile
keep the jyze going. A glance around: ancient woodwork,
brick walls with underlit classic soft-drink posters of
bathing beauties (all Cawk), antiquated firefighter
outfits and gear hanging here and there from the walls
or ceiling, twirling overhead fans (the ceiling must be
at least fifteen feet high), a pair of spiffy old-style
pinball machines, three wall-mounted big-screen TVs
tuned to sports, sound off. About thirty people in
here, all in groups of at least six, including a
tableful of thirtyish women, a couple of whom check out
the mysterious blackshirted ponytailed J-slinger from
time to time, presumably for want of anything better to
do (everyone else in here is coupled). Golden oldies on
the box right now. "Oh Darlin', Please Believe Me."
I'm almost certainly the only one present who's been
around long enough to remember hearing that one when it
first came out.

     Earlier Z and I revisited the site of Big Date
Broke at the ORB cafe. We sat at the very table where I
huddled alone morosely trying to commune with her spirit
and contemplating my likely strike-out with her. It's
become part of our March ritual to do this. Tonight she
asked me again: "Did you really think I'd show up down
here after I'd told you I couldn't?" "Very slim chance,
sure. But I'd say it was more like the near-utter
hopelessness of the gesture that did it for me." (And
of course I enjoyed jyzing about it as well. And
sending her a card about it I wrote on the spot.)

     Last night I made her another card celebrating that

same occasion and today at her birthday luncheon with
her office pals at a downtown grill she showed it around
and told the story. "Everyone thought it was really
cute." Tobey raved about the card and said I ought to
go into business making funny T-shirts. Z tut-tutted
her, saying her "high-culture hubbin" probably wouldn't
think that was a compliment. But she's wrong! On both
counts! (That is, I ain't high culture either. My
culture thing is a whole lot more complicated than that.
And she, Z, knows it too. And I'm quite sure of this
because sometimes she comes right out and says it
baffles her. And it always pleases me when she does so
and inspires me to think of new ways to complexify it.)
     And we were sparring a bit over a misfire in bed
this morning. When I tried to get something going she
applied "the clamp," barring me from access to any of
her more crucial erogenous zones. Perhaps this was
payback for my unresponsiveness the previous night (when
I was just too tired). So I gave up, but then she
griped that I'd done so too quickly. But I wouldn't be
re-enticed. I don't like that clamp one bit. I take it
seriously. She'd like me to try to fight through it.
     But it's no big deal. Culture clash, another
example of the many differences which keep things
interesting for both of us. But she dislikes it that I
see our dispute about the clamp as a probable Catholic/
Protestant thing and admit I've run into something much
like it a few times before with others (and I know she
hates hearing this and that may be why I mention it,
because I want to rile her after she's riled me with,
this time, talk about how other men reacted to "the
clamp" as she applied it to them).
     And in my view it's good her temper isn't triggered
by this sort of thing as it might've been (and often
was) a couple of years ago. She doesn't stifle it
completely but now she's much more likely to pull back
from overly heated displays. "You think you've tamed
me," she likes to say with a snort. Maybe a little,
yeah, sez I. Any problem with that? In the name of
cross-couple peacekeeping? And I think it's good for

900

her too, all on her own, and I think she does too, at least most of the time. She knows what the cost would be of going too far and she chooses not to. It's wisdom. It's equals. (It's love, sure. Not only that, we're married.)

   -- Lotsa noise in here right now. The nighttime entertainment world is rowdier these days, here and everywhere else in the quarter. More and more it's a bread-and-circuses kind of operation (I'm sorry to say). Last night when I came hiking down from the scope office at about eleven-thirty a big group had gathered outside the best of the blues joints as some sort of topless contest -- wet T-shirts would be my educated guess -- went down on the stage just inside the window. Whoops and hollers as a big blond from the peninsula (as she announced) flashed her enormous mammaries to the gapers outside. The chant went up inside: "Show your tits! Show your tits!" All this may be in part a response to the cops' overreaction to a similar incident in the triangle two weeks ago during Mardi Gras, setting off the "riot." It's also a cause of that kind of police overreaction. The whole scene is degenerating. I guess that's why (putting the best possible face on things) the powers-that-be wouldn't risk any special domesday celebration despite the obvious promotional and immediate moneymaking potential. -- But I still say this doesn't excuse the city's lack of imagination.

   "Implosion Party Planner" reads the OMP's front-page overline. It's the elite who will be partying in their private clubs and office suites with a view. All the highrises at the south end of the downtown cluster and most of the smaller buildings in the civic center and nearby have events on tap. For everyone else it's just like this past New Year's Eve: watch from a distance behind heavily patrolled fences while braving the weather, or watch on TV at home. (Up on south hill they must be expecting a huge crowd. Temporary no-parking signs have been set out all week for Sunday from five a.m. until noon along all the streets within six blocks of the strip park and the high bridge, and this

includes the street in front of our house.)
    Just thirty-two hours until the big boom. -- And
smaller booms will be taking place tonight between three
and four a.m. Seismic experts are jumping at the chance
to map the area's fault lines when the quakelike
domesday implosion occurs, and tonight they'll be
setting off small explosions in various parts of the
city to calibrate their instruments. They also admit,
because true scientists must admit surprises are always
possible, that the implosion could set off a real
earthquake, even a severe one. But of course the
chances are vanishingly slim, in rough proportion to the
puniness of humanity's power compared with nature's.
(But if it did happen, our 1511 apartment building would
likely be affected and might even disappear into the
abyss opened along the same fault line that passes
underneath our block and also within a block of the dome
itself. Except, true, we've been told this isn't the
abyss-opening kind of fault line but rather the tectonic-
grinding type, which presumably means we'd just get a
real good shake and not an actual grind.)
    "Mustang Sally" now. Goodness the nostalgia. "All
you wanna do is ride around, Sally." Huh! That true,
Sally? Not even for a moment wanna stop all that riding
whoop-de-do and watch the true millennium go down? If
only symbolically? -- But I'll be heading myself out
now. Need to stop by the hideaway on the way to the bus
stop, pick up my pack (the one banned in here).

[+1]

    And here's the true millennium as seen from another
HQ nightclub. What do I know about the entertainment
zone anyway? I'd always assumed this dive was part of
the "joint [or dive] cover charge" circuit -- at least
for the couple of years it's been located where it is
now, after moving here from a block to the east -- and
maybe for a while it was. But now on a Saturday evening
the back section with its dancefloor and bandstand is

902

closed. I'm seated by the jukebox in the games and
computers section, separated from the bar by a low
partition. Skateboarders over here, a row of folks in
faux S&M gear at the bar (tattooed woman in see-through
full-body fishnets over black lingerie, also wearing
spike heels and sporting a ton of chains and piercings).

If anything the quarter seems a bit slow for a
nonrainy Saturday night during what for many students is
spring break. Too bad. But no more carping from me.

It's a little eerie over near the dome too, just
five or six blocks from here, with streets blocked off,
whole buildings up to six stories tall cloaked in black
cloth or transparent plastic, lots of cops and private
guards around. Yet you can walk right up to the fence
in the middle of the dome's north parking lot, as I did
myself maybe thirty minutes ago, only a few hundred feet
from the hulking stripped-down structure with all its
innards exposed. A dozen other sightseers were standing
there with me, including a group of five who'd flown
more than three thousand miles from the northern far
coast just to witness the implosion up close and in
person. Seven daffodils were stuck in the fence. Just
behind us a white TV truck with broadcast tower fully
erect was setting up a live feed for the news at eleven.
Rental lifts for use by official observer crews were
standing ready and under guard. The west train depot
was open and as I stood there I could see one of the
continentals slowly backing in. A dozen taxis were
parked in a row outside, a group of mostly turbaned
drivers gabbing on the sidewalks, many squatting. And
here and there people were camped out for the night, a
number with cameras set up on tripods. Several of these
stood on the raised deck of the new transit headquarters
building. Earlier I'd walked across that deck and found
bags of some sort of saltlike chemical deposited on
rubber mats laid out every fifty feet or so, presumably
for use in clearing off cement dust after the blast.

Up on south hill it was a wild scene truly worthy
of domesday eve and the true millennial blowout to come
(very soon!). The main roads on both sides of the DC

castle were lined with RVs parked for the night, many
with the vehicles leveled up on the hillside, which is
quite steep in some places, with jacks and wooden blocks
and wedges under the wheels and/or chassis frame at the
lower end. Cooking units were arrayed along the
sidewalks and hundreds of people were milling around
almost as if for football tailgate parties. Over at the
strip park and on the edges of the dot-com's campus
various media outfits had staked out territories and set
up observation stands, with the biggest of the cable
sports networks boasting the largest, a thirty-foot-
square platform rising ten to twelve feet above street
level, a fancy white tent pitched atop it at the back
behind a fenced viewing area and lots of chairs and
electronic gear set up inside the tent. Humming media
trucks with satellite dishes and broadcast towers and
flashing lights were scattered here and there nearby. A
large police van stood alongside the park's permanent
shelter and cops were going around enforcing the two-
hour parking limit in the lot itself. A hundred or so
people with blankets and sleeping bags were camped out
on the grass along the edge of the view ridge; it wasn't
clear whether the usual park curfew of eleven would be
enforced. The night wasn't too chilly and the sky was
clear and so was the air; the view to the west and north
was looking its spectacular best.

   I walked across the high bridge with a friendly
Afrusan dude who said he'd graduated from high school
the year the dome opened, almost a quarter century ago.
He'd lived in this city ever since but had been inside
the dome only five or six times, he said, twice for
baseball games and three or four times for basketball --
just about the same as me. "Poof, it'll be gone at
eight-thirty."

   How big will the crowd be in the morning? Could
reach fifty thousand or more just at the strip park and
on the bridge. That's what they're saying. I know
this: Z and I, and also maybe June and Aida, will be
part of it. We'll be observing "the symbolic end of the
twentieth century," in the words of a commentary I heard

on the radio last night. Yeah, that and a few other
symbolic endings, I'd say myself.

     (Upstairs they're playing pool here at the dive.
Every so often one of the bartenders on our level flips
off the volume on the jukebox and uses the PA to remind
the players up there not to tap their pool cues on the
floor in time with the music. -- Actually if they did
it in time with the music it might not be so annoying;
but most of the time it sounds strictly random. In any
event I have no trouble at all seeing how it must drive
the bartenders nuts after a while.)

     (Lots of jerks and assholes around here. Those are
the two pervading types, I'd say (and I should know,
right). Here's one now yelling "I gotta be a boy!" to a
woman asking him to pipe down. -- Not that the current
jerk-and-asshole quotient in this sort of setting is any
greater, proportionately, than it was one, two, three,
many decades back. But nonetheless it's a fact that in
a certain kind of crowd this is the way to be nowadays.
In-your-face ugliness is admired. Yuck. But even here
the offenders are probably a minority. And even those
skateboarders desist from bugging me when I answer their
surprisingly polite questions about what the heck I'm
doing over here in the corner by saying it's just what
it looks like and I can't do it if I'm talking: the same
line I've been using since long before any of them were
born and always try to offer as pleasantly as possible
at least on the first go-round. Tonight I've had to say
some version of those words six or seven times, but
never to any one questioner twice. Two wanted their
names put in these pages: Devin and Selena (sp?). One
asked with suspicion verging on hostility, "You writing
about us?" "Naw, domesday," I said, and that brought a
puzzled frown and then a shrug as he wandered away.)

     -- And now I'll pack it in a little early, giving
myself an hour or so to poke around the quarter before I
go home.

*   *

     Four or five hours later and here's the empty bed.
But no "Empty Bed Blues" for me. This bed is full.

905

(This life's full too. Yup. And I'm not embarrassed to be repeating the assertion. Proud. Don't care how much sheer luck is involved. Know it's not all just luck. Plenty of loving work is involved -- loving work at loving, so loving work squared or at least doubled. On both sides, yes. -- And now it's almost time for the truly true millennium and I can start celebrating.)

Didn't hear the calibrating kabooms for the earthquake faults. I turned the radio off and kept my ears alert for the whole hour between three and four a.m. Nothing. -- Or plenty, but not a single kaboom. Several car alarms, several sirens going by on the street below, two of the next-door vehicles bouncing up the steep driveway (each with a boom box blasting and bumpers scraping on concrete just as always), frequent yakking bypassers on the sidewalk, occasional loud footsteps on the ceiling, an unusually high amount of vehicular traffic -- but no kabooms.

From the bus windows on the way up I surveyed the hillside RV encampments. The west side of the road by the DC castle had been completely cleared but on the hilltop both sides were packed all the way up past the forked turnoff leading onto our street. Even in our block here there were several, including one visible from our living-room window, across the street and three buildings south. But all seemed peaceful, and that was equally true down in the HQ and AQ.

It's clear not a whole lot of people out there are thinking of this as the true millennium. I wonder: are any at all? How many are even aware of the arguability of the proposition? Not just on the hill here; how many in the city? In the country? In all of Christendom? On the planet?

I was thinking myself: if you stretch things far enough, a credible justification exists for saying 8:30 a.m. on the 26th here in J-town, the hour of the implosion, is also the exact hour of the true millennium. The logic goes like this. The Angel Gabriel when he came down to visit Mary the Jesus-mama-to-be on the 25th probably waited until after dark when

the odds improved that he'd find her alone in her room.
Probably he waited until her family was asleep, keeping
him away until about 10:30 p.m., say. And might there
not be about ten hours' difference between here and that
hallowed spot in the Middle East? Jyze City would spin
in right there at 8:30 a.m. on the 26th?

Of course I'm not truly serious about any of this.
I just like playing with it. Seeking the raw makings
for possible meanings. It's from such small connections
that large myths can be inflated and often are, here and
everywhere. The Annunciation Day myth itself must be
something like that, a backwards projection to fill out
the "Son of God" story in a humanly credible way (for
the ones who want to, or are raised to, believe).

My next task here is to grab a few winks. It
shouldn't be too hard: I poured myself a stiff drink as
part of the celebration and I'm still feeling a little
woozy. Once again this pour came from the big bottle of
bourbon that was one of our wedding gifts, the same one
I hit again at New Year's/New Decade's/New Century's/New
Millennium's -- a/k/a New DYCM's, yes. Tonight I
finally polished it off for New Truly True Millennium's.
Call it the ceremonial bottle of the TJM year.

And now the last of the major ceremonies for this
year is almost over, with just the big T/M kaboom
remaining. And then the ceremonies of denouement begin.

[+1]

And blow it did. Poof! -- End of an era! On a
day when the north end of south hill was the center of
the universe. And won't see its like again for many a
moon, or more probably ever. A fitting climax for this
jyze project, no question. But just how it's fitting
I'm still pondering and no doubt will continue to do so
for a good long time.

When I awoke at seven a.m., people were already
streaming by on the sidewalks in front of our building
beneath a white sunrise almost blindingly glaring. Z

didn't arrive home until 7:25, the short trip from
Aida's taking forty minutes instead of the usual fifteen
or less -- meaning domesday observers were swarming in
from all directions and the crowd would be immense.

     And it was. We waited until quarter to eight as
June had asked us to do half an hour earlier by phone,
but when she didn't appear (and I should mention that
Aida had decided not to join us) we walked the two short
blocks and one long one over to the lookout area of the
strip park. Soon it became obvious the question was,
for us, as for tens of thousands of others who hadn't
shown up hours early, whether we'd even be able to find
a viewing spot from which the dome would be visible.
The first glimpse of the high bridge was stunning: it
was jammed with people all the way across, not just on
the wide sidewalks but in two of the four traffic lanes,
and a single beleaguered cop car at each end was trying
to keep the other two lanes open (and eventually they
both gave up).

     What a scene! At one point no fewer than seven
helicopters were buzzing around overhead. The largest
of the TV platforms was on live (we recognized several
of the celebrities sitting on folding chairs up there,
including former national and local sports stars who
actually played in the dome; they were positioned so the
dome itself would be visible behind and above them from
the angle of a camera set up on a higher platform-on-
the-platform). Elsewhere folks were climbing fences and
trees and plunging into the thick hillside shrubbery of
"the jungle" and overrunning all the hobo camps farther
down the hillside; they were gathered on the roofs of
the DC castle, up at the Natusan center at the far end
of the bridge, and in every other conceivable spot with
a view as far as my eye, even when aided by my small
monocular, could see, including the roofs of warehouses
in the upper AQ and of the tallest downtown buildings
and the Chinese room with its viewing balcony atop the
great white tower in the HQ (where Z and I once stood
peering at the very spot where we now stood, wondering
how we'd look from there). A huge flotilla of small

boats was visible just offshore to either side of the
dome itself -- which was facing its final moments with
utter stoicism, no signs of movement or life of any
kind visible -- no last meal, no last drag on a
cigarette, nothing -- just squatting there in its
pathetic stripped-down state, many of the peglike
explosive charges visible on its roof like clamps
attached to the head of a condemned convict strapped
into an electric chair (and that really was the first
thought to come to mind and then hard to get rid of as
you stared at that gigantic wired concrete skull).

Z and I did eventually find a spot where the view
was only partially obscured by the limbs of shrubbery
just starting to bud and a guy sprawled, like many
others just below the edge of the overlook, in the
branches of a small tree. This spot we wound up in was
on the grassy hillside strip just above the bridge,
across the street from the prow of the dot-com campus
(hundreds of people, presumably employees of the giant
monopolistic dot-com bookseller and all-around robotic
merchandiser, lined the iron-grillwork fences up there,
just four or five feet in front of the fencepost where I
once sat jyzing last summer). The ground was damp and
cold, but bearably so. Z had brought a blanket and we
both sat on it from time to time as we waited and
observed the scene with astonishment. We had an
excellent view of the high bridge and the full downtown
skyline, the HQ and the AQ and the freeways, all of
which were utterly traffic-free -- shut down tight --
another aspect of the uniqueness of the scene.

A well-behaved crowd it was. Lots of kids, Sunday
bicyclists in full gear, obvious sports fanatics (as
opposed to mere fans) -- but mostly just ordinary folks,
on the whole recognizably local because of the
preponderance of casual outdoor gear and rainwear,
mostly Eurusan but with a good mix of Asi- and Lat- and
a few Afr- and Nat-, with the sexily or punkily or
fancily or hip-hoppishly dressed sticking out (though
for the grungies to stick out even slightly, as always
in this city, the grunge had to be extreme). It wasn't

much different from the kind of crowd you might've
expected to see inside the dome -- or well, no. Take it
back. Proportionally more women, more older people,
more kids were on the hill, I think. (How can I say for
sure when I haven't been inside the dome in so long?)
-- Well, it's been two and a half years actually, the
baseball game with Jim Q. and brother Rob, back when Z
and I had known each other just a few months.

No one nearby had a radio so we just went by
watches (next to me stood a big towheaded Cawk man with
his blond wife and young son; an older son of this
couple and the son's friend had plunged down into the
bushes in search of a better view). As eight-thirty
approached, the crowd became tensely expectant, all eyes
trained on the dome, and several times cries went up
over false alarms caused by sunlight flashing off boats.
It was five more minutes before ignition (it turned out
this delay of five minutes had been planned, although
eight-thirty sharp was the announced demolition time).
And then it went suddenly and without warning: sounded
like a string of huge firecrackers going off, lasting
about fifteen seconds at most, and the first collapsing
movements of the implosion were visible among grayish-
white puffs before suddenly the dustcloud mushroomed in
something like atomic-bomb fashion. Very quickly that
cloud obscured the entire dome area and the dome itself
within it, rapidly puffing outward and upward, with a
light wind pushing it across the historic quarter and
downtown just as the demolition company had hoped.
Within a minute or less the forty-two-story great white
tower was fading from sight, the cloud by then as high
as the tallest downtown skyscraper well up the hill, and
within a few more minutes the entire skyline all the way
down to street level had disappeared. A minute or two
after that, Z and I both thought we detected a whiff of
the concrete dust, but this may just have been our
imaginations feeding off each other.

It seemed to be about ten minutes or so before the
air above the site itself had cleared enough that the
pile of rubble started to become visible, like a movie

dissolve in reverse. From our vantage we could make out
only a small part of it -- but could now see the black-
shrouded buildings which prior to the implosion had been
hidden behind the dome itself -- and we had to wait
until we'd walked up the hill to the very top of the
strip park to get a good view of the jumbled rubble,
which even from that distance reminded me of the
fountain near the ferry building in my city No. 2/7 with
its tangle of fallen and oddly tilted concrete beams --
a gargantuan version of that.

     Then the short walk home through gridlocked traffic
like nothing we've ever seen before on the hill. I ate
a piece of the birthday cake Aida had baked for Z; then
I went back to bed and slept until three. Z said it
took about two hours for the streets outside to return
to normal.

     A spectacle but one with no real theme or focus and
no clear public meaning. That was the shame of it.
What a missed opportunity! Aside from one guy hawking
"I was there" T-shirts and a plane pulling a "Stamp out
tobacco" message, there was nothing. An empty ceremony
-- not even a ceremonious one. And with "the whole
world" watching. -- I suppose we should just be
grateful it was so relatively uncommercialized. But of
course whatever part of the rest of the world that was
actually watching live saw it differently -- with
commercials.

     For purposes of providing a climactic moment to
this tale of a year in jyze, though, I was tickled pink.
A cast of thousands! Maximum exposure! Symbolic drama!
And that it should all be happening a thousand years "to
the day" (if not "to the hour" except maybe by NUT time)
after the previous (and only other) millennial
celebration in all Christendom -- though I wonder if
even a single person in that entire crowd was aware of
this ("other than you and me, dear," scolded Z) -- this
was a J-slinger's dream supreme. "We leave you our
ceremonies. Give them their meaning."

     Tonight in coming to work -- getting a late start,
too, at eight, after a shopping expedition -- I retraced

my steps of last night. From the high bridge I couldn't
see the rubble at all in the dark -- and wouldn't have
been able to see much even in daylight -- but still
things looked quite different. Where before the massive
darkened hulk of the dome had stood, lights were now
shining from a whole "new" set of buildings and parts of
waterfront shipyards and even homes clustered on the
hills across the bay, all of which the dome had blocked
before from that perspective. It was a vaguely Buddhist
thought that came to mind: I was seeing the absence of
an emptiness. In a few months, though, a different kind
of emptiness will return as the new stadium starts to go
up in its place. Construction lights might even be
trained on it, in which case it will be a well-lit
emptiness. And once in use it would still be empty on
most nights and for that matter for the larger part of
all nights and most days, just as is true of the new
baseball stadium a couple of blocks to its south.

     I was curious about the effect of the dust, but I
didn't find much until I'd trekked all the way down to
the HQ and entered the former restricted zone, and even
then the amounts were nowhere near what I expected.
Much of it had already been cleaned up. (As I walked by
the AQ bus station it was being hosed down.) In
isolated spots yet to be reached by the cleanup crews I
found a thin coating, usually a quarter to half an inch
thick, of something like dirty powdery snow, and even
more like the coatings of volcanic ash from the big
volcano eruption of two decades ago, which took place
ninety-some miles to the south. Even areas that had
been cleaned still bore traces of dome dust in tire
tracks and footprints like those seen near construction
sites. The south and west sides of the dark brick
campanile of the west depot were noticeably whitened,
lending it a spectral aura. The dark wrappings on the
buildings, most of which were still in place, were
grayer now in spots and also spectral in a different
way, billowing eerily in the frisky evening breeze off
the bay. Otherwise I saw few traces of any impact and
no sign of any unexpected damage, although some nearby

streets were still blocked off and I couldn't get a
close-up look there.
    But I could get a piece of rubble. In the north
parking lot near the fence stood several small piles of
it and some two dozen people were pawing through them as
a TV cameraman filmed the scene. I heard him tell
someone that same footage would be going out on the air
in a few minutes, and he pointed to the big white van
which was at that moment telescoping up its broadcast
tower. Then he turned off the camera and I decided what
the heck, why not me too. And picked up half a dozen
small rubbly chunks and jammed them in my jacket pocket.
    And now those chunks are lined up on the desk here
at the hideaway. In size and texture they're a lot like
the pieces of sandstone debris I picked up at the base
of the arboretum fence in Lahontan some seven years ago
(the only other rocklike objects I can recall --
speaking lifetime now -- keeping on hand as memorabilia).
I'll add one of these new chunks to the shelf atop
Mother's antique bookcase and also take a couple home
for Z and Kat. "A Fragment from the Implosive Climax of
the True Millennium. Rubble with a Cause." (And I
thank you, Z-wiff, for the phrase.)

[+1]

    The naked man. Perches now on the couch with his
back to the night. Except he's still got his socks on.
Buffoon! And the jyze pendant he wears every day, that
he's got on too. The news (which he just flipped off on
the radio): USAn pressure on the oil cartel builds
inexorably: produce more so prices will fall! Our way
of life depends on it! (Well of course it does, as does
its coming self-inflicted extinction -- an odds-on wager
now, I'd say -- which everyone else will have no choice
but to share in.)
    Deep in the night of the last on-beat day of the
domesday eighter. Already the ash from the blowout has
all been swept up (except, of course, for the tons of it

that will drift about in the atmosphere for days or
weeks or longer). The posters for the special
commemorative domesday newspaper issues have been
removed from the street racks to make way for this
morning's new news, whatever it may be -- probably the
oil thing. Or maybe it'll be something about our local
software behemoth (the one located mostly out in the
burbs) which today lost its claim to being the world's
highest-valued company (another digital corporation
headquartered about eight hundred miles to the south
took its place) and may also learn of the judgment in
its antitrust case as efforts to settle it have
reportedly failed.

The papers confirm what I observed myself: damage
from the domesday blast was negligible, just a few
broken windows. In the century-old underground passages
beneath the HQ "not even the spider webs were
disturbed."

Here at home Z was in a touchy mood when she
returned from her first day of budget training class at
the U. Sometimes her quick shifts of mood can stun me;
I have to scramble to get back on her good side. It's
not so easy to know what will be comforting to her, if
anything will, when she's feeling so insecure. This
time it was a question she asked in the training class
that "went plop" and reminded her of college days. Her
classmates this week are almost all Cawk and the teacher
is a pompous far-coast specimen of same -- an elite
waspy male not yet dead but sounding close to it, yet
even so still in a declining-days lash-out state. I
foolishly said something about how numbers aren't her
thing anyway so why be bothered? Bad. Tears. Anger.
Her father used to say something like that. Yeek!

Keeps me off-balance, she does. Loving ain't
always easy. -- Not the first time jyze has so
pontificated and the chances are excellent for many more
instances of same to come.

Now I've made her a card about being a "rookie wiff
at spring training," altering an old ukiyo-e print of a
kimonoed woman in an orchard of blooming cherry trees (Z

had told me the Japanese cherry trees at the U, visible
from her training classroom windows, were gorgeously
abloom). Is it funny, this card? Maybe not. But I'm
planning to toss it out there anyway. Out onto the seat
of my armchair where she'll find it when she gets up.

     A couple of the birthday balloons were sagging
badly so I moved the whole cluster to the side of the
cabinet at the far end of the dining table. At this
moment the big proud yellow-beak toucan is eyeing me
from there, looking none too happy because the ceiling
is making his/her whole body tilt to one side. (High-
flying birds don't like low ceilings!) The rest of the
birthday decorations are still in place, except for
those short-lived tulips. Now I'm pondering whether I
want to make another run to the party store tomorrow to
pick up a couple of items for the upcoming anniversary
-- on Wednesday -- of our first meeting in the flesh.
We Meet! Day. I've already laid in a few small gifts.

     The fete-ful month of March. It's well into the
lamb end now. And I like all the commotion, the
celebrating. If at all possible I like to be the
instigator where the Z-wiff's concerned. But she likes
to be that too, and often is, and usually in wholly
unpredictable fashion. (And she may be getting up now,
if I'm hearing right, or in any case she'll be doing it
soon, so I'll just stop right here.)

47

     Trying to get a grip. A late start, late coffee,
and now I'm perched on a rocking chair back where it all
began, by which I mean the Z portion of it. It's
another of the long string of special March

anniversaries: We Meet! Day. And in just forty minutes
we'll be meeting again some eight or ten blocks up the
hill and then returning here to reenact We Meet! Day.

"Our Love Is Here To Stay" has aptly commandeered
the sound system. Every table is taken, including the
one where we, Z and I, sat back then. Bright sun's
making for a warm room even though the front door's open
-- but the overhead fan's not spinning. Early spring it
is. On the car radio coming over I heard that the
highest of the major mountain passes that close for the
winter will be opening tomorrow, much earlier than usual
-- which is standard in this era of accelerating global
roasting -- but also much earlier than last year, which
could mean we've found a new accelerant to throw on the
global fire (or not) (or not yet but likely soon).

In the freezer bag in the Z-mobile parked just
outside, our two slices of thawing wedding cake await
us. We'll be bringing them in here. Z's arriving by
bus from her budget training session at the U and I'll
pick her up at the bus stop near a market we both know
well half a mile straight up the hill.

Just caught a glimpse of a stretch bus rolling
across the high bridge -- another high bridge -- visible
through a window across the room directly above where we
were sitting on the first day. And it occurred to me:
that's within yards of the spot where a similar bus
plunged off the bridge a year ago when the driver was
shot by a passenger. To see such a thing happening from
this vantage, how hallucinatory it must've been. Would
you believe your own lying eyes? Surely not. And the
likelihood of my ever meeting a Zoelie B. in this
lifetime? Considerably less, no question.

*

-- "Our" table suddenly opened up, so I've moved
over to it. I'm perched on the bench with my back to
the wall beneath the window of the flying bus. This is
where Z seated herself on that fateful late Saturday
afternoon. Several incidents from the hour or so we
spent here then have become part of our "origins legend":
the way her arm recoiled when I lightly touched it while

916

making a point, the way she casually shrugged off the
"Comet Zoelie" card I'd made for her ("I'll look at it
again later"), the fierce mutual gaze we found ourselves
locked into but just for an instant. I especially
remember the painful sensation of being struck dumb --
fumblingly tongue-tied -- numerous times by either her
dazzling smile, her bizarrely guarded or unexpected
questions and responses (or, just as much if not more,
absences of questions and responses), or simply my own
self-consciousness after almost two years of near-total
reclusion. I was trying hard not to show it but it was
one of the most intensely awkward yet also intensely
exciting -- shockingly so -- hours of my life.
     Three years later she retains the ability to knock
me off-balance at will and for the most part I still try
not to let her know she's done it.   "Hey, I'm cool."
And in general this works out just fine.
     For my primary We Meet! Day gift I tied together a
couple of small furry toy-store-bought green dinosaurs
with heart tape left over from Valentine's Day and wrote
this on the tag: "Just a coupla hinckety geezer dinos
lashed together by a merciful fate."
     Time's up. Maybe she'll be agreeable to a bit of
tandem jyzing when we return here. If not, this is
heavy week for me and it's highly doubtful I'll make it
back to these pages tonight.

                         [+1]

     Carrying on now at the same spot, one seat over but
one day later. By coincidence an errand brings me back
to the same part of town, or a bit north of it actually,
and rather than fight some nasty crosstown traffic at
five p.m. to motor back to the south end I'm stopping
off here again. "Jyze City's No. 1 Neighborhood
Hangout," says the fancy framed award certificate from
the alt-weekly hanging by the door -- which is open
again today as the intimations of real spring continue.
     The errand? Having a couple of dings removed from

the Z-mobile's windshield. It's one of my voluntary
chores, taking the car in for the various kinds of
upkeep work, all of which Z pays for. Seems the least I
can do (although I'm also kicking in fifty bucks a
month, still, for my occasional use of the car). And
it's a way I can use my flip-flopped night worker's
schedule to our advantage, since she's usually not free
to take care of things like this on weekdays. Also it
gives me a chance to vary my routine and to run the kind
of personal errands that would be a major pain if I
attempted them on foot or by bus. So along the way
today I've stopped at the Yuke bookstore and a couple of
my special north-end postcard and magazine sources. And
now I'm back here again, also a special pleasure.

     Yesterday we wound up sitting across the room,
several tables removed from our original seats on that
glorious first day. A young woman had claimed "our"
table and she stayed there the whole time reading a
calendrically near-appropriate paperback copy of what Z
calls her "birthday book": "Middlemarch." Once the
woman raised our hopes by standing and putting on her
coat, but then she sat right back down and read on.
Apparently she'd just picked up a little chill.

     That wooden rocking chair I was holding forth from
at the start yesterday, by the way, was stabilized with
the back of its legs and the seatback braced against the
inside corner of the entrance-foyer wall, as it still is
now as a fellow in a cloth cap reads today's FAP in it
(I almost wrote "afternoon paper," but of course that's
an obsolete term now -- and not just here but in most
USAn cities and probably worldwide).

     Z-wiff spoiled me here yesterday. At the very spot
on the sidewalk outside where, exactly three years
earlier, I gave her the fake doctor's certificate
affirming my toes were fungus-free, along with a package
containing the removed fungus (actually green-dyed bread
crumbs), she now presented me with a card proclaiming a
doctor-verified "Love Attack" along with a package of
"comet's-tail glitter." Then inside the cafe she handed
me a bag containing two more gifts: an upward extender

for our shower nozzle (so I can stand beneath it without
bending over) and a cigar box altered for pen storage,
with a host of Z-isms inscribed on it and in it.

This morning in bed, alas, did not work out well.
"I don't want things to go smoothly!" she cried. Just
because what usually turns me on most is her being
tenderly loving doesn't mean she'll always try to be
that way when she wants some loving herself. Au
contraire! Once again I find myself in the embarrassing
position of trying to defend my sadly conventional
lovemaking taste -- "vanilla," "meat and potatoes,"
"formulaic." I swear it's not really any of those
horrible things; if you open yourself to slow-it-down
TLC, it intensifies sensation, both physical and
emotional, and merges them to a degree far beyond any
other means I know of. Or at least it works that way
for me. And most of the women in my life have come to
see it the same way, even though in some instances they
at first had notions more like Z's. (Then there were a
few who were Z-like at the start and stayed that way, or
were "vanilla" but gradually became Z-like as they came
to know their own sexuality -- especially Lady V.)

It becomes a kind of power struggle, playful but
also serious. She doesn't want me to think I can change
her. Why not? Isn't it more courageous to let yourself
be changed -- if not a lot, at least somewhat -- by
love? But I hold back too at times, because I don't
want her to think she can control me. It's a dance --
as she says. Nor do I disagree. But I say we could
move beyond it to a more mutually satisfying kind of
dance. And I think we will. And I think we are.
Slowly. I don't doubt we can still go much further.

Three years. It's uncharted territory. For her
it's already been that for six months or more. And is
it really any different for me? Off the charts from day
one! But she worries, worries, worries. Moving away
from the sexual realm here, her big "new" anxiety
(actually one I'm all too familiar with by now) has to
do with buying a house or condo. Her budget class has
introduced her to a concept entirely new to her: the

difference between an operating budget and a capital
budget. "It's such an eye-opener! How could it be no
one's ever explained this to me? You don't go into debt
for operating expenses -- it's so simple! But I didn't
know it and certainly it never occurred to me that it
might apply to my own private life and so now I might
not be able to afford capital investment!" -- But if
so, it's not really her fault. The market's doing it to
us. Its propaganda is everywhere. It's providing every
last material good thing in our lives without exception
and never mind the life-obliterating ecoclysm it's also
bringing on. -- But...enough soapbox for today.

    -- In fact it's late. They're putting candles out
on the tables. And I got work to do! And got to get
the Z-mobile home first and then hike in! Must move on
now!

[+1]

    It's the new Z-geist cafe. The timing could
scarcely be better. It just opened today, half a block
east of the old site, still on the AQ/HQ main drag but
at an intersection now, the southwest corner, with good
city views in several directions.

    It's a big funky space, maybe two and a half or
three times the size of the old one, with twenty-foot-
high ceilings and brick walls and exposed beams and
ductwork. Worthy, certainly, though it lacks a balcony
and I do like balconies. And in a nod to all the
techies in the hood (with many more coming, including
those who'll be replacing the artists chased out of "the
shoe" next door) its news racks now feature, along with
the normal fare, the house organ of a certain
conurbation zone in the megastate to the south -- the
zone Z likes to call Silly-Con Valley.

    "Will the last artist leaving this city please turn
out the lights." The cover of the current alt-weekly
emblazons those words on a photo of "the shoe" with the
old Z-geist visible down at the bottom, its signature

stainless-steel tables set up on the sidewalk, just as
they are now right outside the window where I sit.

Likewise today's weather is very fine. I could
comfortably be sitting in shirtsleeves at one of those
tables out there, at least until the sun drops down a
bit lower. It's, what -- a readable clock is mounted
above the counter! -- five-twenty. A quick jyze, a
quick workout, a good solid five hours' scoping (but it
can't be a single minute more than that).

Z arrived home early this afternoon, before three,
and immediately started razzing me about not seizing the
occasion to tear off some nookie. But I'm sparring with
her right now. Low key. And she with me. In a current
weekly news magazine feature on boomer aging she read a
piece about the prevalence of "permanent impotence" in
males; now she's trying to provoke me into action by
muttering "Permanent?" at moments of physical closeness.
It fits right in with her "iffy ithy" crack of a couple
days ago -- for which she was now profusely apologizing.
Go figure! But she's also saying she wants us to start
wearing "short kimonos" around the house so our "assets"
are showing and easily accessible. And she's back to
insisting she'll never be romantic. "Sexy, sensual,
affectionate, loving, yes, but romantic, huh-uh. For me
romantic is heroines dying tragically." And then she
spoofs me with, "You thought I'd be the noble wife,
didn't you. 'I'll stay home and pine away, darling,
while you pursue your visions. Go forth and jyze!'"
And though I didn't dig the content of this a whole lot
I did go for the sassy way she delivered it.

Today is the second day of the second three years.
We're due for some adjustments, some fine-tuning. But
not all that much, really, I'd say. I don't even want
to paint over the rust spots or smooth out the dings.
As she said, inspired by memories of those grand old
cherry trees she's been admiring this week at the U, she
wants us both to be "super-gnarly." And so do I. But
tenderly super-gnarly. Even lovingly super-gnarly. No
better way to get twisted than that.

Walking down from the hill an hour ago I was struck

by the sight of the clouds of cherry blossoms floating
above the hillside community garden a block up east hill
from the main drag. All that aberrant blossoming I was
seeing all winter long, impressive as it was at the time,
was nothing as compared to this. Obviously the big
bloomers had been holding out for real spring. -- And
then I approached the freeway underpass and saw the sun
framed under it, straight ahead right down the center of
the road, very close to due west. By that measure we're
still in equinox and thus T/M territory.

These window seats at the new Z-geist are great for
people-watching. Our changing HQ. Some domesday ash
still whitens the brick, I see, of the ancient three-
story hotel building across the street, site of an
underground dance club and a Korean antique shop (one of
my favorite places to window-gaze) and another popular
nightclub just around the corner.

The shift of the Z-geist. In physical distance
it's not much and maybe spiritually it's not either --
not yet anyway -- but symbolically it's very good, at
least for me. Think of it as the zeitgeist of the new
century. The grappling-with-the-ecocrisis spirit. But
no, it doesn't know this quite yet. It thinks it's more
the redoubled information-revolution spirit. (I didn't
mention: bouquets are on display everywhere in here.
Quite a sight. "Welcome to your new spot in the old
hood." Should've noted the flowers in the first
paragraph and meant to. Got distracted. Old story.)

Onward.

[+1]

Here's another climax -- not necessarily the final
one but the final main one. "My own private jyze true
millennium." Sitting sideways on the couch, back
propped up by a couple of pillows, totally naked, sick
as not a dog but whatever creature gets about half that
sick. On the window to my right the gaudy interior 203
reflection overlays an inky dark night; to my left the

203 "great room" interior itself -- surprise! -- is laid out in much more expansive but far less shimmery liquid detail (shimmery especially on the window when a car goes by down below). Jazz playing, my thighs aching (something to do with being sick). And a lot to say here in not very much time as a buildup to the big moment -- which as a matter of fact won't even exist.

The "grand alignment" is still gathering for its double appearance which will soon put a couple of exclamation points on these proceedings. But right now is an alignment of sorts too and one that I, lately accused of being, and in return acknowledging myself to be, obsessive on the subject, find fascinating.

For one thing, it's April Fool's Day, or at least the Saturday which is still ongoing although it's past midnight is, so the NUT version thereof. All Fools, all of us, and never more in human history, I'd say, than right now, with us USAns far far far FAR in the lead.

Related to that, the 1st of April is also the last day of the traditional weeklong New Year's celebration which began on March 25th and in medieval times was known as the Feast of Fools. (When the Gregorian shift occurred, country people who hadn't heard about, or who had simply resisted, the change of New Year's from March 25 to January 1 were called April fools. That's the origin of the term. And that's why at one point I was using the term "January fools" for those who resisted the timing of the true millennium. Not that it really mattered to anyone, of course, and in a sense one could say that includes me. But then in another sense....)

Third, it's now actually, by Gregorian as opposed to NUT time, April 2nd. And by one of those wondrous serendipitous coincidences which have marked this entire TJM year (and still may ruin it, even though this is jyze fiction and thus coincidences are welcome instead of frowned upon as in standard fiction -- and without a doubt there are more ahead) -- today, I say, happens to be the Julian/Gregorian-adjusted true millennium, the truest of the truly true, one could say, since it's actually today that exactly one thousand revolutions of

the earth around the sun (to the inch!) have passed
since the celebration of the last millennium in the year
1000 in northern and western Europe, land of my
ancestors (and half of Z's). Of course a margin of
error's still involved, but it's only seconds or minutes
or at the extreme possibly hours, not days or weeks.

And fourth, it just so happens -- because I decided
to wait until one-fifteen a.m. to pick up the J-stick to
start this account -- that Daylight Savings Time starts
in just seventeen minutes and the clock "springs ahead"
to three o'clock. Actually it doesn't "spring ahead,"
implying a time of transit will exist as the entire
country or rather the part of it in our time zone sails
from one spot of time to another like a steroid-bloated
long jumper. Nope -- it happens instantaneously.
Intercalary entanglement! Which is to say the entire
hour between two and three, minus some infinitesimally
small fraction of a second (always smaller than however
small it can be said or computed to be), will not exist.
It'll be two/three a.m., and the slash will have no
width. And in that entirely imaginary hour -- aptly!
sez I, who in any case am the supreme authority on the
matter at least as I'm seeing it at this moment -- will
exist the utterly truly truest of true jyze millenniums.

And fifth, tonight is the start of the last month
of this TJM project, the full yearlong project, yet this
is also its thirteenth month because it began with eight
days (a J-week) still left in April, way back in the
previous decade/year/century/millennium -- or DYCM, yes.
(I always remember the acronym too late!)

So here comes the instant. At two during the break
on the public radio station a ping will sound and
that'll be the moment sharing two different designations
on the clock. As before on similar occasions I'll make
a little box with brackets. The ping will be the dot
inside the box. And that dot, sort of like a black hole
but quite a bit smaller -- dimensionless! -- will
contain infinite jyze worlds, so to speak. And then on
the far side of the right bracket begins the new era
(according to this jyzer right here):

[Jyze of the True Millennium]

[.]

   -- And so it is.
   And with this I declare my work for the day
complete -- almost. I still have to change all the
clocks. (And I'll mention that somewhere two or three
paragraphs back footsteps sounded outside and the Sunday
far-coast paper arrived with a thud somewhat louder than
usual, perhaps because the editors realized this is such
a weighty day. The less cosmic news events of this day
-- one of them very worrisome and possibly bearing large
consequences for Z and me and our life together -- jyze
should have time to tackle tomorrow night.) -- And I
should pour myself a celebratory drink of some kind.
Wine is what it'll have to be. Since this is a strictly
private great occasion it's okay that Z should snooze
right on through it in the bedroom. I'll toast her,
though, and mention I sure am glad to be going into this
ecoclysmic era with her at my side. Even if by now
she's got her ears plugged to all this jyze-millennium
jive -- because why should what is or isn't stuffed into
her ears matter in the slightest? (But of course it
does anyway. But I can live with it and so can jyze.)

[+1]

   It seemed appropriate for the first entry of the
new era to go down at the hideaway. So here I am,
having just rushed HQ-ward from the scope office after
punching in some corrections (less than an hour's worth)
so I'd be here while it's still April the 2nd, the,
again, utterly truly truest of the true-millennium days
by adjusted Julian/Gregorian reckoning, and I made it
with fifteen minutes to spare. Or a little more,
actually, because since arriving I've unpacked my bag,
watered the plant (which is now doing splendidly after a
worrisome yellow-leaf episode last month), changed the
clocks, ripped a page off the calendars, and made up a

list of things I need to do here later this week.
     Meanwhile boxes and trashbags and miscellaneous
other items are landing on the carpet just outside the
door with the usual loud crashes, although I think more
of those explosions are sounding than I've ever heard
before in a single barrage. Since packing chips are
scattered all over the place, it's a good bet another
internet start-up or two moved in over the weekend.
(The janitors toss things down as a matter of efficiency,
sometimes from four floors up. Because the atrium
starts here on the second floor, this is where the trash
stops when it's thrown down. One of these days a flying
box will brain a second-floor visitor or officeholder
and that person will have a terrific negligence lawsuit
and the building will quickly pass into other hands and
rents will triple overnight and I'll be out of here.
Better that than to be out of a brain, though, so I'm
not tempted to venture out there to see if I can cherry-
pick a lawsuit.)
     Jyzing is tough right now. The muscles in my upper
legs and hips are still aching. I can't stay in any one
position for long. Last night in bed I had to elevate
my legs on a big cushion before I could get any sleep at
all, and even then I was waking up off and on throughout
the night (day).
     This date (now ending) has another significance.
For me and Z it's the fourth day of our fourth year
together. And we've treated it that way too, as a
special day, endowing it with no fewer than two meltdown
scenes. Both can be chalked up to the same old sex
conundrums, but that doesn't mean I'm about to
acknowledge they're a real threat to us. They're just
part of our dialectic of love, that's all. Sure, I wish
they didn't have to be, but who wouldn't? Of course Z
does too. But she can't stop herself from wondering
every now and then if it's her "fault" and becoming
upset about it. Best to try not to take too much issue
with her when this happens. But I can't always stop
myself either. So then we thrash it out and things can
get a little ugly. Yes they can. And then we have to

926

wait for the incident to pass, almost as if it were more like a loud fight in a next-door apartment. And it always does pass. Today, as I say, the first passed so quickly it left time for a second.

Maybe I'll try to describe one or both of these incidents later. But first I want to mention the truly worrisome news that came in yesterday. Betty's finally received a "definitive" diagnosis for her problems with her legs and it doesn't look good. After yet another battery of tests the doctors are telling her she's suffering from "subcortical dementia" as evidenced by white spots showing in that area of her brain and that the disease is ordinarily progressive. "Are you experiencing incontinence yet?" one doctor asked, implying it was inevitable. The "dementia" part sounds so generic, I'm guessing it's really just a way of indicating they don't know what the cause is. But they told her the white spots are showing on only one side of her brain, just as the symptoms are affecting only one side of her body -- the opposite one -- and therefore MS and postpolio syndrome can be ruled out. (Olwen, who herself suffers from postpolio syndrome, isn't so sure about this, and her doctor is a leading specialist in the field. Up until now Betty's put off talking with Olwen, but she's promised to do so soon.)

Just ahead for Betty, still more batteries of tests. Also, Z-wiff has volunteered her services to accompany her next time she sees the doctors, because for some reason Betty feels too intimidated to ask the hard questions. Usually this isn't the case -- she's a nurse! -- but she thinks it's happening now because she's gone into "farmgirl stoic" mode. She's also been trying to shield Kat from her anxiety and consequently, as she says herself, finds it too easy to slip over the line into a kind of denial in which she hypnotizes herself into believing what she wants Kat to believe.

And what if the disease is confirmed to be serious and rapidly worsening? Z and I were talking about this. Essentially Kat would have two options: to go back to live with Betty's brother's family on the farm in the upper midwest (they have a couple of kids around Kat's age) or to live with us. without even having to think about it Z and I agreed we would certainly take in Kat if Betty wanted us to, and of course Kat's wishes would probably be the prime determinant for Betty. (Z worries a lot more than Betty does, clearly, about the troubles Kat might face in that highly conservative and lily-white area of the country Betty hails from, but the inferior educational opportunities available there might give her even more pause.) One interim solution, possibly leading to a long-term one, would be for us to move in with Betty and Kat, so if Betty's illness should prove fatal, at least Kat would be able to stay on in the same house. As an adopted child who within four years of adoption lost her adoptive father, in a sense she may be more prepared for another loss than anyone's thinking right now. But Z says she, Z, would go nuts trying to live in such close quarters if we didn't at least have a bathroom of our own and preferably a whole separate area, so her idea would be to add a second-floor "granny apartment" above the current single-story and flat-roofed rec room, which used to be a porch.

It'll be a while before we have to make any decisions about all this. But then things could change quickly, so we need to be ready just in case. It's stressful, to be sure, and Z even said it was probably the real reason for her meltdowns today. It may well turn out to have a major impact on our personal life in the period right after this TJM project closes down and possibly right on through the years ahead.

-- So never mind about the latest twist in the sex squabbles, the detailed description. I'll hold that in abeyance in case nothing else arises to keep jyze occupied during the next couple of days.

And...why not a few jyzebits. Let's see. The fine weather's holding (it's mild enough that I could be going at this outside tonight if I weren't afraid of worsening my cold). The attempt to mediate the case involving the software behemoth has failed, but the threatened strike by the garbage workers has been called

off (the companies caved, just as Z said she thought
they would, probably because their contract with the
city calls for them to pay big penalties if they don't
perform for any reason, and that includes a strike).
Z's worrying again about the messy state of our
apartment and we're talking about bestowing a higher
priority on our cleanup and maintenance efforts (but the
work itself must be something we undertake together and
therefore it can't happen right now).

     And...why not a few more. Yesterday we bought some
fuchsia starters on sale at a discount mart, six for
three bucks, but failed to find the kind of "short
kimonos" she'd like us to wear around the house to make
sexual access, both visual and tactile, easy and quick
and sure to happen inadvertently from time to time
(genital flashes!). And Z surprised me with an April
Fool's gag which had the landlords requiring us to take
all the plants and even the door off our 203 balcony to
bring it into conformance with building regulations.
(She's big on April Fool's gags. Left scary messages
with lots of friends, the main one being that a certain
officious blond coworker had filed a sexual-harassment
charge against the highly earnest Afrusan Roy.) And I
got her back, leaving an envelope outside the 203 front
door with her name written on it (misspelled) in decoy
handwriting. She hesitated to open it, feeling sure it
would be another hate letter or the rantings of an irate
neighbor. But instead it was an autographed photo of a
certain female Italian movie star, the message saying
she was a bit tired of being told how much she looks
like the fabulous Zoelie B. in Jyze City USA ("but I
surely am envious of you for having a dashingly handsome
husband with such an admirable head of hair").

                          [+2]

     Yesterday, as it happens, was the first ordinary
day of the new thousand-year period whose completion may
or may not be celebrated when it occurs on March 25,

3000. And so jyze decided to skip it as far as jyzing
goes. But a few interesting things happened anyway.
For one, the city's new recycling program, with Zoelie
B. a major player in its fashioning and rollout, got
underway. For another, the sanitation workers, after a
last-minute wobble, voted to accept a new contract,
ensuring that the new recycling era can begin.

And then the truly big news. The antitrust
decision involving our local software behemoth finally
came down. And it was sternly anti-behemoth. The
company's stock was battered, and therefore technology
stocks in general took a beating. Markets gyrated
crazily, with old-line stocks gaining hugely as new ones
lost even more hugely. The behemoth's market valuation
fell by something like fifteen percent, and because this
one company constitutes almost sixty percent of the
total corporate value for our region -- that's five
states -- this was no small hit around here.

Will it hold? The behemoth is making a confident
show that it will prevail on appeal. Legal experts say
this is possible but not too likely; and even if it does
prevail, it's all but certain a major portion of
corporate energies will have to go to battling
litigation. The behemoth is probably on a downward
course now. And with it, perhaps, a measure of realism
will return to the technofantasyland in which so many,
and among them a high proportion of the residents of
Jyze City, have been living.

For the larger picture, though, this decision has
little meaning. If anything it could worsen matters,
allowing the digital revolution to pick up speed again,
thus accelerating the countdown to ecoclysm.

-- Today, meanwhile, is a less ordinary day as far
as scheduled events go, because today's opening day of
baseball season. I even see it reflected here at
midtown chain burgers at nine p.m., with a number of
obvious game attendees standing in the unusually long
line right now. As I hiked across our south-hill high
bridge earlier I could see the lights of the new
ballpark turned on for the first time (as far as I know

anyway) since last fall.

Otherwise today's pretty ordinary too. Z arrived home an hour early because she had a work-related meeting to attend tonight. Although I think I've succeeded in beating back the cold and achy-muscle syndrome, I was feeling a little tired and crashed briefly on the couch. She came over to wake me after thirty minutes and oddly I found myself becoming quickly aroused (under circumstances in which ordinarily nothing much has been happening lately). She found this highly amusing. For that matter so did I. Here I was panting away, ready to jump her bones -- just what she'd been calling for over the weekend -- and now she was the one who wasn't particularly interested. She was already half-dressed for her meeting.

Aiiieee! But so it goes. This morning she had suddenly asked me to "pleasure" her -- or rather griped because I wasn't doing it -- and I pointed out she hadn't responded at all during the several earlier times I'd nuzzled in to see if she might be interested. It was that old "put some heart into it" thing. But as noted a number of times before, she doesn't go for romancey TLC stuff (except when she does -- which is when she decides to do so, for reasons which I've never been able to understand, and isn't very often). She'd been reading an encomium to testosterone in the far-coast paper's Sunday mag the night before and now she remarked that the men of her life had always been asking her why she didn't act more like a girl. No doubt about it: she shows many of the symptoms this article cites for the highly testoed. Even her arousal patterns are more like those of typical males, though I don't know if that has anything to do with testosterone (and the article is so full of confusions and contradictions and conservative bias, there's no telling from it). ---
*
-- That's when the franchise manager showed up to say he was about to lock the front door. I could've stayed on a while, but then letting me out would've been a nuisance for him (he works in back but must walk all

931

the way up front to unlock the door for each person
leaving, meaning it's that much longer before his work's
done and he can go home).

Down in the street a work crew was, and still is,
sending up a huge racket while breaking the surface to
lay more fiberoptic cable. This has been going on for
the entire year of this TJM project and they're still
nowhere near finished. Now I'm listening to it from the
scope-office conference room. The street is blocked off
for a whole, yes, block. Looking down I'm reminded of
WTO days, the pitched street battles that went on up at
the corner in front of the many-starred hotel. One of
the daytime staffers here wrote an account of those days
for a court-reporting magazine (edited by reporter Fran,
of all people) describing, among other things, the weird
sight of wisps of tear gas climbing up the side of the
building and clinging to these windows right here (and
they suffered from that gas on this side of the windows
too, throughout the office, though not terribly).

Back to the funny testo talk. Or no, designate
that "Back to" sentence instead to be the lead-in to
last weekend's two meltdowns. Yes, I've decided I'd
better mention those after all just in case they
repercuss further down the line. But only in brief.

The first came as Z was reading a mystery in which
a male character in his early Glennarian Third Stage --
like me -- is wildly attracted to women and "loses all
self-control" in sex with them. Z wanted to know when
the last time was I'd lost all self-control like that.
To her this is the way a man in love oughta be. I told
her the truth: I was never like that. Nor is it my idea
of what good sex is about. She's often heard me say
this before, but it melted her down anyway. She's "not
interested" in trying it my way or meeting halfway --
and regardless I may not be up to winning her over.
(But I still foresee no real problems. Once she's
turned on -- and flicking her switch usually isn't hard
at all -- she doesn't care about any of this theoretical
stuff. It's more a kind of leftover neurotic thing --
fear of being seen as inferior to some other woman.

Lord knows she must see me as inferior testo-wise to a whole lot of other men in her life. And that's a shame. But I take some solace in the belief she'd surely see me much less that way if I could be the lover I was at the age of those men she's comparing me with back when she knew them. -- And I don't think she makes a huge number of those invidious comparisons either. Just every now and then when one sneaks up on her, as when she was reading this whodunit.)

The other meltdown, Sunday, happened because I didn't react as she thought I should to the "let's make up" apology she'd written regarding the first meltdown. It contained a line which I read at first as a kind of threat, and all I said about it was that I didn't quite get that one line; but that was enough to send her stomping out of the room -- wailing that we'd never make it, it was hopeless, she'd never write me a note again: in short, all her usual sorts of flamingly over-the-top responses (though her meltdowns have become a lot less frequent than they used to be). It was just another example of the standard type of overreaction or call it the standard extremely intense reaction for which she's celebrated and held in awe and at times dreaded by all who know her, with absolutely no exceptions I'm aware of. Even after three years of intimate living with her these extreme reactions of hers can still stun me and knock me completely off balance -- it's hard to imagine how they could be any stronger if I were to commit mass murder before her eyes -- but nowadays I can usually get myself back together much more quickly, and so can she. And that's what happened this time.

(But there's no question: she's got the power, baby. Put it that way. The woman herself doesn't fully realize the extent of it.)

*

Other news, let's see. The main thing is she's decided to give up hope on doing any serious housecleaning until after the budget brouhaha at work passes. She's been worrying more about this lately. "You know," she observed the other day, "we really are a

couple of slobs." Much of the blame for this falls on
me because I won't have any "outside help" coming in.
After reading yet another article I'd given her about
exploitation of maids (this one written by a woman she
much admires) Z's more or less agreed to go along with
me, at least for now, but even so some old "class
anxieties," as she calls them, keep nibbling at her.
"Before, my apartments could always pass as being sort
of middle class" -- because in the past she's always had
outside help, usually from one of her Cawk radical-
therapy-group friends who badly needed to make some
extra money. Last night when I came home I found she'd
posted a new "White Glove Advisory" just inside the
front door, along the same lines as the "Abandon Martha
Stewart all ye who enter here" it replaced but much more
detailed and defensive sounding. -- So, as mentioned
before, I'm intending to take on more of the cleaning
tasks just as a kind of unspoken gift to her. As noted
many times before, I already do much more than she does
-- she simply doesn't have time to work up the head of
steam she needs to undertake any serious cleaning, and
knocking off a little bit each day isn't her way and
seems beyond her reach -- but I can still justify my
doing more on an egalitarian basis since she spends a
lot more money on us than I do or most likely ever could
do. (And slap a "Jyze Rules Exception" sticker on
that branded Cawk woman's name up there.)
     Oh yes, and a diagnosis at Z's office: the docs are
telling Gloria G. she's suffering from bipolar syndrome
(and so are her kids). No one's ever come up with
anything like this before. And it's happening because Z
talked her into getting help from a counselor.
     Today I saw Ciro down in the garage polishing his
car. He'd been away for weeks -- vacationing in
Singapore, it turns out. He observed that only he and Z
and I and the couple in 101 remain from the "old gang"
of two years ago. Then his eyes went wide when I
mentioned Raphael ("Fonzie") and Dana's tentative
condoizing plan -- it was the first he'd heard of it.
But he was relieved to know he'd be able to stay on in

102 at least another year even if he doesn't want to buy
the unit. His biggest fear while overseas was that he'd
be facing a big rent increase when he returned. I told
him I didn't think that was too likely -- yet. But the
new owners might be coming after him to vacate so they
could refurb his unit, maybe sometime this summer, if he
doesn't want to, or can't, buy it. (Z and I are
planning to talk to them in June or July about this --
what price they'd ask for 203.)
     -- And it's bus time. No more jyze tonight or
tomorrow, unless something big happens. Then: the
launch, in terms of chapters, of the penultimate to the
penultimate. (Yay for pens! In jyze they're the true
ultimates!) (Scratch that pen paren but -- cain't.)

48

     Deep in hostile territory at the east-depot saloon.
My usual table under the TV is taken. At the one where
I've landed instead my back's not covered. The milling
nasties. And they smoke a lot too. I'm halfway between
the entrances to the men's and women's rooms, left arm
pressed against a wall of worn and greasy cedar paneling.
A tin cigar sign maybe eighteen inches by two feet is
tacked to this wall just above a standing person's head
level (if the sign fell it could slice off my left arm,
and it looks shaky up there).
     So in chapters this is the three count, as in
three-two-one BLAST-OFF, of the TJM countdown. The Lent
countdown is also at three, I believe, in days, and
regarding Earth Day and the final curtain for the city's
official Millennium Project (and for this jyze project
here as well), we're at something like, in days, maybe

fifteen or sixteen. And today's a day of celebration
for lots of folks -- Mormons, for whom it's Founders Day
(the church is 170 years old); Thais, for whom it's
Dynasty Day (the current one's been in power for 218
years) -- and above all for Muslims, for whom this is
New Year's Day, the 1st of Muharrana, the year 1421.
And in the HQ right here in J. City it's another First
Thursday, the last for this annal, and since I have only
about two hours' scoping work to do tonight I'm thinking
about stopping by at Z-geist. This, I'll note again, is
the one night in the month it's open past seven.

     Z surprised me this afternoon, first calling to say
she'd be leaving for home at four, then calling again
(deploying the new double-three system, two warning
calls of three rings each, which is easy for her using
her office phone's redial feature) to say since I
wouldn't be around (as I'd let her know during the first
call) she'd work late down there, and then surprising me
again by showing up at home early after all, about ten
past four, catching me at work on a batch of cards for
her. "Wait! Don't come in here! Mad cardiac at work!"
     "Limerence must be back in effect," she called in
from the foyer (she sat on the bench and leafed through
catalogs from the mail while waiting). "Or why would I
always be looking for you on the bridge and the hill
when I come home? I always love to catch you!" And she
had an idea: she'd buy a whistle for signaling to me
over the din of bridge traffic. When I suggested this
might seem a little odd -- woman blows whistle to summon
husband -- she said I'm starting to sound just like that
gynophobic macho man at the gym, Marcus G. (whose
birthday, I remind myself now, is Saturday).
     Her spirits are good today. This morning we got
into some extended "plan B" canoodling. "It seems like
every time we do that for so long, people are telling me
all day how happy I look." It does put a little extra
color in her face, I think, and maybe mellows her out a
bit. But she's back on the H-rag so for a while we
can't indulge in the ultimate mellowing experience -- by
which I refer to "plan A" -- and this afternoon that

936

fact probably kept us from tumbling back into bed.

A trio of Eurusans are still camped out at my usual table under the TV shelf, I see, puffing up a storm and raucously ripped (ever since I came in one's been sporadically cussing out the bartender for refusing to crank up the jukebox volume). Buses are rolling by with horns blaring; half a dozen Latusans are horsing around just outside the door against the backdrop of pink and purple and green Victorian ironwork at the AQ bus station. Today's the final game of the baseball series against a certain hated far-coast team and one guy at the bar is wearing that team's pinstriped cap and spouting the usual kind of in-your-face nonsense, though not succeeding in rousing much hometown chauvinism. After all the Kid is gone, traded away to a team in the other league, long live the Kid.

A letter from Jim Q. came in yesterday -- the first we've heard from him since the wedding. It's good to know (A) he's okay and (B) he's not miffed at me about something. It's a struggle for him to write (I still vividly recall watching his tangles with it during our overnight stop while driving up here in the rental truck containing Rob's and my shares of Mother's household goods a month after her death) -- and so when he does write it means something. But this time he doesn't mention getting together again, and this past Christmas for the first time he didn't send me or Rob a gift, so it appears the relationship is fading now that he's living with Nancy. Could be she doesn't take well to his staying close to the kids of his previous big love.

Other news? The police are out with a report on their own performance at WTO, and they're admitting to errors -- but nothing too serious, mind you, and certainly nothing in the brutality category. They're saying they should've been better prepared and that's it. No surprise here, although many of the protest groups are expressing outrage. This is as it should be, the morality play continuing as the world burns.

(But I'm going to cut out now. A super-scruffy street dude is bugging me. Intentionally blowing smoke

in my face. Not just mine, but still. His call card
isn't working. Now he's demanding I write its number on
a napkin for him because the digits are too small for
him to read without his glasses, or so he says. He's
becoming even more irate because the card -- which I'd
wager he ripped off somewhere -- isn't working in the
phone ---)

*   *

   -- Whew, yeah, that was getting heavy back there.
And it was followed by a comical scene as three of us
waited to use the tiny men's room with its low-doored
crapper (in urgent splat-sploosh use) and single urinal
where a good-humored Cawk geezer was more or less
permanently camped out. "When you guys're as old as me
it'll take you forever too."

   So now Z-geist, the same corner window table as
last week. Golden-oldie sixties British Invasion rock
playing. For a First Thursday the crowd is surprisingly
small; only half the tables are in use. This means I
have my very own old-fashioned metal gooseneck desk lamp
to light up this page and devilishly underlight my face
as revealed by the window reflection. For jyze settings
it just don't get any better than this. I'm even part
of the arts tour for some of these folks. But politely
so. By and large the crowd is a fairly straight mix of
boomerish suburban couples and Gen-X-ish downtown
workers, all Eurusan, with a sprinkling of racially
diverse younger arty types (but also including a
dreadlocked Cawk trio slouching at the metal table just
outside the window, high-schoolers I'd guess, and all
three puffing away on cigarettes with a truly comical
and yet touching show of attempted sophistication).

   By leaning close to the glass I can see a few
people going into "the shoe." Tonight is its last
hurrah, but it's a muted one because most of the artists
have already decamped for good. "The shoe's" countdown
is running eight days behind Earth Day's and just one
day behind this jyze project's.

   "Who'll be the next in line?" That's what the
sound system's now asking. It's the original recording,

938

and after all these years it still sounds good and seems
on point.

     For a couple of days I was goofing with Z about her
latest diagnosis of an imperfection in our relationship.
This time, in only a slight twist on some earlier
findings, it's marital boredom. "He's always here!" We
don't go at it with quite the same degree of wild
exultation or desperation or something. She's such a
sensitive mineshaft canary -- she alerts to the mere
thought of something going wrong. Not that I'm saying
this is necessarily bad. This talent of hers often
helps us dispose of such conflicts while they're still
manageable. But it can be wearing at times. It can
bring on a kind of cry-wolf numbing. I kidded her about
this, saying I'd checked it out in the J-books and this
was the twelfth straight week in which she's spotted
something objectionable in her hubbin's behavior and
wailed about it. Wasn't this becoming a bit one-sided?
She answered in typical Z fashion by producing a chart
for the next six weeks, today through the 18th of May,
with a space for stars to be drawn in if she manages to
keep from announcing something new to worry about.

     The darkening bricks out there. Candles in here.
A bit of excitement. A band's arriving, an artist is
about to be feted, an art film shown. A claque of
dressed-up folks carrying official artwalk folders has
me penned in. Fancy cars and SUVs are double-parking
outside as the glitterati arrive (oh no, not more
glitter!). The intersection of the picture windows and
the glassed-in entrance foyer is making for some
fascinating multiple reflections, offering the illusion
of layer after layer of deep surfaces (candlelit
tablefuls of art-conversers swimming like distant
galaxies on the far side of the foyer, massive vehicles
hurtling by outside and, at times, with the door angled
open just right, seemingly into the room itself before
they vanish without a sound into thin air). With an old
Polaroid camera and some matte frames I could be making
a mint off this infinitely regressive imagery, slapping
the prints on the wall right now for sale at the

shockingly high prices required by today's art world.

[+1]

    This might not work for long. That familiar twin-
tined peak across the water is about to fork the sun. A
wino's coming up. But dozens of kids are still playing
on the slides and swings and jungle gym and merry-go-
round, tennis players are dancing and lunging, hoopsters
are banging away (hitting the rims so hard they sound
like a steel-drum band warming up), swarms of soccer
players are surging up and down the infamously dusty
field in clouds of their own making -- all of this at
the hilltop playground. (And here's a comely Asiusan
mama at the fence a few feet behind me calling her child
over from the slides and now she's gently reproving him
in a language I don't recognize. Is it maybe Burmese?)
    Through gaps between houses mountains rise to the
left, right, and dead ahead, or south, where it's the
iconic volcano. A train whistle toots somewhere down in
the former tideflats to the west. A squad of pigeons
patrols the desolate expanses of the wading pool, which
is shaped like a kidney bean or an artist's palette but
it's still unfilled, dry as desert adobe. A squirrel
scrabbles overhead in the biggest tree in the park,
maybe a cottonwood, the trunk about eight feet around at
eye level (my eye level, I'm saying, as I'm seated), a
profusion of early buds fuzzing the branches above.
    Such a fine day it is to be celebrating Buddha's
birthday. Reckoning time from his birth we're already
close to halfway into the third millennium thereof, as
would be the case also for Platonic time or Confucian
time; and today, by a quirk of the Western calendar,
happens also to be the Confucian spring ancestor-
honoring holiday (Qing Ming in China). It's a good bet
well over half the folks in this park now are observing
one or the other, if not both, of these holidays in some
way, or at least thinking they oughta be. -- Or on
second thought, maybe not. But surely some are.

[Jyze of the True Millennium]

    Me, I'm paying my respects to Buddha today, yes,
but saving Confucius and Qing Ming for tomorrow.
    These days the great relativity scientist's words
about Buddhism being the most appropriate religion of
the future seem more apt than ever. (In part, perhaps,
because he's been declared "person of the century" by
the same weekly USAn news mag that proclaimed our evil
hilltop dot-com's CEO "person of the year" for 1999.)
And I'm thinking this scientist would probably look well
upon Taoism too. But then whole library wings are
packed with books written about the compatibility of
science and Taoism, so this is no scoop for jyze.
    WHOOM! Somebody just set off a cherry bomb behind
the restrooms. For about ten seconds all activity in
the park froze; then it resumed just as before.
    Today Z's off on a long-planned outing, tiptoeing,
with friends Leola and D'Arcy, through abundant tulip
fields right now grandly abloom two counties to the
north. They departed far too early for me to go along
-- in fact at seven a.m., shortly after my bedtime. Z-
wiff left the wagon behind, and earlier this afternoon I
took advantage of its unconditional availability to do
my weekly provisioning and then some art-goods shopping.
But I didn't figure on a full-house baseball game
letting out while I was down at the paper shop, just a
block or two from the stadium. (I was thinking today's
game would be under the lights.) As a result I was
caught up in traffic for nearly an hour and that's why I
arrived here so late.
    The sun's fully set, I see, though the volcano's
still lit up, a good deal more rosily now than a few
minutes ago. A quiet rosy-golden sunset, skimpy clouds
incandescing in places above the western mountains and a
pale sickle of moon hanging high overhead. Z's due back
at nine, about an hour from now, and she mentioned the
possibility of our walking over to the high bridge to
view the three planets currently in close conjunction,
an early harbinger of the grand alignment scheduled for
four weeks from yesterday. A couple of articles about
these astronomic/astrological phenomena appeared in

yesterday's papers, and both quoted the same scientist
as declaring the grand alignment has "no significance."
He was referring to forecasts for a grand-alignment-
linked shift in Earth's magnetic pole which would
supposedly cause widespread chaos, and I suspect he's
right about that. But he didn't qualify his remarks in
any way. No significance at all? None? Zero? Not
even any jyze significance? Science is just so blind
sometimes. Which of course is why it can have such
impressive predictive powers at other times.

     Or if not jyze significance, what about
significance with respect to the current Age of Pisces
and the approaching Age of Aquarius? Tens or hundreds
of millions of people grew up hearing about these. At
least a few of those people are convinced the rollover
between the two will be happening next month. And how
many USAns, not to mention people of other lands, take
astrology seriously? Well, jyze has an answer to that
one: a great many. And it's not just the scientists who
are blind to this kind of significance. Media people
are even worse. An upcoming astrological event has to
smack them between the eyes before they have any idea at
all what it might be about.

     -- Almost as if everyone could somehow read the
nonsense I'm spouting in here, the park is suddenly
emptying out fast. Two kids on the swings, a die-hard
hoopster, a few folks scattered here and there -- the
last holdouts. I smell something burning, possibly a
fire started in a washroom trash barrel by the cherry
bomb (though no smoke's visible over there). And a
chill's upon me. -- As a plane with its headlights on
comes roaring straight at us from the south, but now I
see, as I crane my head around, it's turning sharply
eastward in the very way that's drawing a lot of flak
(not literally -- but maybe soon) from the high-status
folks living in that direction. Yet the truly high-
decibel zone for flight paths is to the south where the
planes are much closer to the ground, and the south end
of J-town lacks the financial and political clout to
throw up flak about it, literally or otherwise, no

942

matter how much worse they have it. (A map showing
these decibel zones is laid out on the coffee table at
home. Z's getting interested in the problem. Look
out, airlines!) -- And here's another plane.

*   *

   -- Seven hours later and I still haven't managed to
lift my jaw back to its normal location. Today has
turned out to be Qing Ming day for me, all right, and
with a vengeance -- or no, I don't want to say that.
Vengeance is the last word I want to use. But Qing Ming
with my own twist on it and I hope all for the better.
   It's quarter past eleven now and I'm down at the
hideaway. A moment ago I dusted off the "ancestral
tablet" area atop my ancient glass-doored bookcase,
including the photos showing the spots (located two
thousand miles apart) where my parents' ashes were
scattered. This is about as close as I can get to
cleaning their gravesites in traditional Confucian
fashion. For me this room right here is the place where
their spirits reside. And since I visit it most every
day throughout the year, I feel, yes, about as closely
in touch with them as I could, I think, or would want to
under the circumstances (meaning with them in their
ashen state).
   But seven hours ago the phone rang as I was sitting
in my armchair at home reading the Sunday paper, almost
as usual for that hour except I was working on an early
deadline, because at half past four Z and I were
planning to go out and do our bit in the city-sponsored
annual spring Adopt-a-Block cleanup. Z answered it, as
she usually does owing to the fact that almost all calls
are for her anyway, and after a moment she said, "He's
right here," and handed the phone to me with a wide-
eyed, raised-eyebrows quizzical look (later she told me
she'd thought the accent she heard might be Scandinavian
and wondered if this could be one of my long-lost
Norwegian cousins calling from the old country).
   Hearing just a couple of words was enough for me to
recognize the voice. "Is it really you, Glen?" A voice
I hadn't heard in four or five years. Mother of a kid

943

bearing my name of whom I'm very likely the father --
for sure neither of us would ever dispute it -- but for
whom the fates, I guess I'll say, have never allowed me
to be an active on-scene father, except for a brief
period of roughly a year a quarter century ago.
Without any doubt one of the most influential people in
my life-before-Zoelie -- probably the most so. A woman
I loved a lot. And deep down no doubt still do, in the
way of powerful relationships that have ended as far as
physical presence goes. Former wife. Woman over whom
I've suffered a lot, as has she over me.

　　　So we talked for ten or fifteen minutes. Z said
she's never seen me looking "so nervous" before,
sweating profusely, face flushed one moment and pale the
next. I think she was exaggerating more than a little
-- but that's not to say I was completely agitation-
free. And Z stayed in the room the whole time, keeping
me skewered with her eyes (I mouthed the words "It's
Jang!" after a moment and Z's jaw dropped too); in fact,
after a while she moved closer, sitting at my feet. "I
was gonna guard my turf!" she explained later.

　　　It was a cautious talk on both sides. In the past
during similar calls Jang's often started out sounding
polite and friendly but things always fell apart when
they got personal. This time they never did get
personal, or at least not very. She was calling from
Koreatown in the megastate to the south's major
megalopolis and she said she's currently living there
with Elgie when he's around, but he travels a lot,
including to Korea, and she goes there herself from time
to time. I got the impression they've been living down
there a while, but she was vague on this, as on many
things, in a way that's totally familiar to me. I
didn't press for answers. Instead we talked mostly
about people we've both known, starting with each
other's families. She was stunned and also embarrassed
to learn my mother had died (I didn't talk about our
failed efforts to reach her, Jang, or even locate her
after she decamped again for Korea, and supposedly
"permanently" this time). "I can't believe it. No....

My mother is so much older and she's still alive so I never even thought...." (I tense up while jyzing that line -- start shaking my head in dismay, even tearing up when I think of what Jang and my mother went through together -- so I'd better not go there right now.)
*

Jang. Lady S. She lost her middle brother, Nim, to pancreatic cancer, but the other three siblings are doing well. Hyu, three years her senior, is still teaching at the same elite university in Seoul although he's technically retired. She said she asked him to look me up once when he was in our area to attend some sort of literary festival; "Of course I don't think he did." I could confirm that: yes, he did not. Interestingly, my first big run-in with Hyu in Korea came over Jang's opposition to his plans to take me up to their father's gravesite in the mountains for spring cleanup on this same weekend we're in now, Cold Food Day, the Korean version of Qing Ming. (I wonder: did the filial-ethics vibes set off by this weekend in the megastate's megalopolitan Koreatown -- largest outside of Korea itself -- have anything to do with her calling today? Probably did. It can't be merely a matter of coincidence. She'd be thinking about her son's ancestors on both sides of the family. But why this year as opposed to some other I have no idea at all. Could it be simply because of its millennial specialness? I rather doubt it.)

We also talked about mutual acquaintances from the world of writing, but this was more to note publishing successes of others and our own lack of same in recent years, not to mention more of the very same lack (with a few minor exceptions, mostly on her side) in earlier years as well.

And then the most important matter. She said, when I asked about Elgie, that I "should talk with him." But when I asked if that was what he wanted, she again went vague on me. "Well, we don't really speak about it...." I gather he's expressed no interest. I said I'd be delighted to talk with him, of course, but also that I

945

didn't think I ought to be initiating anything if it's
not something he would want. But we left this hanging,
and I guess she'll -- maybe -- sound him out on it.

(I should also mention: she told a touching story
of briefly listening at the door of a nearby university
auditorium as an unfamiliar poet read to a large crowd,
"a white-haired old man," and deciding not to go in, and
only later learning the poet had been Kurt T., one
of her first instructors in the poetry workshop at
Mezzu; she lived as a renter in his house during her
first semester in town, before my arrival there.)

After, to repeat, ten or fifteen minutes I'd had
more than enough and said I had to be going. Since Z
had answered the phone, Jang obviously knew I was with
someone and she may have assumed it was still the same
person as before -- a decade earlier or even two decades
earlier, which is to say Lady U. Neither of us asked
any questions about romantic involvements, nor did I say
anything about the divorce proceedings, the attempts to
reach her, the wedding last fall. It would've been too
difficult to broach those subjects, especially with Z
sitting right there gripping my knees. Next time will
be soon enough for that, or maybe I'll try to do it in a
letter. Early in the call I gave her my address and she
said she would write, so I let it go at that and didn't
ask for her address. If she does write, and if the good
vibes persist, I'll write back and tell her about my new
life, and I'll also send along a couple of copies of the
genealogy compiled by our son's great-grandfather and
readied for publication by our son's father, meaning,
yes, me; and I'll also append some notes about what
we've learned about the Sandefjord family in the fifteen
years since our last sustained contact.

Not that I'm not leery here. Can't help but be.
Has she got some agenda? Too many times in the past
she's had one, and invariably I haven't liked it, and
I've believed she was overstepping boundaries we'd
agreed to. Lots of old pains and sorrows could be
kicked up. But on the other hand, there's reason to be
hopeful. So I'll try to let the hope prevail as long as

I can see no concrete reason not to.

    -- So after that brief delay for the phone call, Z and I went out in the street with our gloves, our blue plastic bags, and our pickers, and we cleaned up both sides of the block all the way to the cross streets in both directions. Both of us still agog over the new development. Z groused that I was now acting like the cock of the walk, lording it over her because my old lover was "after me again." But this was just games. Little jealousies and envies. Thank god for Marty's call last fall and their subsequent meeting; I now have that to use as a counterweight. Z would be delighted to meet Elgie -- she's always said so -- and I don't think she'd even oppose my meeting with Jang, since she could use that as a bargaining chip in trying to persuade me to okay her meeting with her former lover Bradley. She's been half-seriously lobbying for such a rendezvous all along. Today I even jokingly proposed that the four of us could get together in my old city No. 2/7, which is where Bradley's lived for many years. He's like Jang in that Z met him in college and they've been meeting on and off ever since, often as lovers, up until seven or eight years ago. But the difference is they were never "serious" lovers.

    Another quid pro quo, she suggested, would be Jerry II, her last "serious" lover before me. And then of course there's also Kirk, but after last fall that would be a stretch for sure. And it probably wouldn't go over at all well with Aida. But then again Z could reassert her rights because she did have first dibs on Kirk, just as Aida reasserted (with Adele) her first dibs on Colin.

    In any event these sorts of things won't be developing for some time, if ever. And probably they never will. Right now I'm just astonished that Jang -- Lady S! -- would reappear in my life. And also I'm almost chagrined by the timing as far as this TJM project is concerned. Z thought I'd be cackling over it -- one more in a long string of happy coincidences and serendipities of the plot-churning type -- and in a way I was. But it's also almost too good to be true. "But

it is true!" Z objected. "All this stuff is really
happening! It's not fiction. That's what the big
difference is with jyze, right? One of them? It's not
really fiction? That's why you call it jyze fiction?"
Well, yeah, but...talk about the appearance of
contrivance. You can say it's too good to be true about
real life too. The creaky deus ex machina. "What did
he do, secretly look up the most important figure from
his early adult years and ask her to get in touch with
him in April of 2000 as a way to enliven what was
looking to be a dull ending in a writing project? And
maybe tie up a few loose strings?"
     Yikes. It is boggling.
     -- So then I walked into town, still rattled. And
all the way, as I know from past experience will be
happening for the next several weeks, though I hope with
dwindling frequency, my trigger finger for the Adopt-a-
Block trash-picker was involuntarily twitching at every
sight of a cigarette butt or scrap of paper or even an
errant leaf on the sidewalk. To the scope office,
where I did a few corrections and then finally finished
up our income-tax forms for last year, and they came out
within fifty bucks of my estimate of a month ago (and
would've been on the money if Z hadn't neglected to give
me one form). Quite possibly this is the earliest I've
ever finished the taxes. I don't even think it's smart
to send them in early -- more likely to trigger an audit
since we're owed a hefty refund, most of which will go
to Z -- but I'd rather risk that than startle a squadron
of Zoelie B. anxiety mygs into flight over my "last-
minuteness," also known as JITness, "just-in-timeness."
(This morning I found a note on my chair: "Is there some
way I can help you finish the taxes?" She worries!)

                        [+2]

     If the aurora borealis were to make an appearance
in our area tonight, this is one of the more likely
spots where it would be visible. It's the lookout park

adjoining the public market, high above the waterfront
-- maybe a hundred feet or more -- and it has a good
open vista to the north, with the city lights not much
of a factor. And now's the time too, just about
midnight. And that bright sickle moon is hanging up
there again, to the northwest, at about a forty-five-
degree angle above the mouth of the harbor.
     But it's also hazy tonight, just enough so to block
out the stars but not the moon, which seems to be
surrounded by a raggedy gray halo, as the rest of the
sky seemingly keeps trying to close in around the hole.
The eleven-year sunspot cycle is at its peak, but the
peak may not be high enough this time to power a
northern-lights phenomenon that could overcome this
haze. It's not turning out to be the gangbusters
sunspot year many were predicting. The news stories of
its disruptive effects on earthbound electronic systems
are few and far between. But still -- it's worth a
shot. Do something, sunspots! (But not too much,
right, or we'll all be fried on, and by, the spot.)
     For this time of year the night's unusually mild,
but it's still not all that mild. I'm wearing four
layers on top and feel I could use one more. A slight
breeze is blowing in off the bay, and it's also pushing
an acrid urine smell this way from the base of the
viewing-deck fence. A guy's lying on a bench under the
pergola about thirty feet to the south -- he just
started playing a harmonica -- and he's bundled up in
blankets inside a large transparent plastic wrap, sort
of like a spectator at a late-season football game for
which rain is predicted and seems imminent.
     Some other shady characters are lurking about, as
is often the case down here at this hour, and they're
making me a little nervous. I'm sitting so my back's
protected.
     It's a big sky. I see two sets of airplane lights
off to the north. But except for the moon and the haze,
nothing else above the cityscape in any direction.
     (A freight train is screeching through a curve car
by car at the tunnel entrance down below. I can hear it

through the vents and feel it a little bit, much as I
sometimes can when a heavily laden truck goes by on the
viaduct which is also down below -- feel it with my toes
mostly, a slight vibration.)

    An interesting bit of world news: the leaders of
North and South Korea will soon be meeting for the first
time since the fifties, or maybe ever (depending on how
"leader" is defined), aiming to move toward
reconciliation. It's another fine coincidence that this
would first be announced on the very day Lady S called
me. One of the ironies of our relationship is that it
never would've existed had it not been for (1) the USA's
defeat of Japan in World War II and (2) the Cold War and
particularly its Korean component -- which is two
ironies in one, right. (Yesterday was also, as it
happens, the anniversary of the end of the USAn Civil
War, without which my parents never would've met.)

    This guy stretched out on the bench can't blow
harp. That's not stopping him from trying, though.
From here, unless I stand up, I can see only his
plastic-wrapped feet. -- And now a suspicious-looking
dude is snooping about along the fence, probably
searching for cigarette butts. These are homeless men
and they're also probable hostiles. No cops around. A
big empty park. -- Well, but here come four tourists
and that's a bit of a relief and also quite a surprise
at this hour. They're checking out the totem pole and
glancing about nervously, just like me. I'm glad the
light here is good and I'm sure they are too.

    Wooden table, lots of carvings, the usual sort of
thing, linked initials prevailing. This is exactly
where I was sitting while gazing at the moon last
September shortly before the wedding. (That is: when
the mermaid-like salmon goddess rose up so auspiciously
from the waters and her face was Zoelie B.'s.)

    She's been spreading the word about Lady S's call.
She told June she's sure glad now we took the precaution
of fail-safeing the divorce. June, who's seen some
pictures of Lady S and who knows she herself -- June --
reminds me of Lady S in certain ways, is eager, Z says,

to talk with me about the call and especially about
Elgie. Now with a real possibility of our seeing him,
the fact that June's son Michael is within a few months
of his age takes on greater relevance.

Quiet harbor, lights shimmering along the shoreline
all the way around to the south, none of the big cranes
at work tonight. Downtown skyscrapers lit up in
swatches for the janitors and other night workers such
as myself, tier upon tier. The sickle of moon, cutting
edge facing down like a certain kind of chopping knife
(designed to work in bowls, one of which the harbor
could be said to be a fairly shallow example), is slowly
sinking, possibly in the early stages of a gigantic
chop. Three guys who descended on another of these
tables a moment ago are adjusting their backpacks -- big
ones, probably holding all their worldly possessions --
and one has a stack of fuzzy white blankets. They're
leaving now. The tourists have drifted to the park's
north end; they're hunkered down in what I'd call a very
tentative way, as if ready to take flight at any second,
at a table right by my old lucky spot. (Splatter of
liquid -- a new guy's taking a leak against the fence.
Looks Natusan. I'm seeing all types tonight.)

I surreptitiously pull out my pocket watch -- not
that it's actually worth a whole lot, but it might seem
to be to other eyes -- and observe it's a little past
twelve-thirty. The northern lights are taking their
time if they're still fixing to show. -- As an
inwardbound ferry glides silently in mid-bay, its four
decks fully lit up and blurrily reflected on the water
in a double or sometimes triple stack, almost as if it's
some fancy kind of catamaran. The night's too dark to
be able to make out the ferry's wake unless you don't
look at it directly but instead focus on something
nearby; then it emerges sort of like invisible writing
(or a dimly glowing, slightly sinuous white line painted
on velvet under a blacklight).

Week of the Passion, Christianly speaking. I don't
see or hear much about it except through the religion
pages of the papers (which I almost always skim very

quickly). And it's hinted at by the annual resurrection
of the Easter candy bowls at the scope office. Z sent
off a Passover card to Kat -- Z feels a responsibility
to Manny's spirit to keep Kat in touch with his Jewish
roots. For Betty she sent a Nurses Day card. Meanwhile
the two of them, Betty and Kat, have driven two hundred
miles south to visit Betty's nurse friend Maggie for the
weekend. There's nothing new to report on Betty's
diagnosis, at least so far as we know. We're both
afraid Betty will try to keep any further bad news to
herself to spare Kat.

Now as the moon keeps sinking it's starting to fade
into the haze. The aura has vanished and the sickle's
sharp edges have dulled. It's no longer a chopper, just
a blob or maybe a pale makeup sponge facing heavy odds
if it hopes to wipe off all those clouds up there.

The same three guys are back at the other table and
getting a bit beyond merely raucous. So I think I'll
toss in the towel on the northern lights right here.

[+2]

No new incidents back at the lookout and no
celestial displays either. Now, some fifty hours down
the road and worn to a frazzle from a tough night at
work -- and tired regardless because I'm running on too
little sleep, though for good carnal reasons -- I'm
curled up in the black armchair and I know I won't be
able to do a whole lot in the way of a wrap-up on this
eighter. But -- must do something.

Resting on the couch arm is the potted tulip Z
brought back from her tiptoeing field trip Saturday.
Attached to it is a note in her hand: "I'm fading -- plz
put me outside." Our east-facing inside windowsill
didn't work for the tulip; the lips of its four petals
are curling back and shriveling. So I'll try it on the
balcony as Z's note suggests. Yesterday I cleaned up a
bit out there and started planting the new -- what
else? -- starters. The unseasonably fine and dry days

continue. I was shirtless for that session yesterday,
wearing just a wholly unobjectionable pair of shorts.

The utility's budget crunch is grinding ever harder
on the Z-woman. She says it's the only thing she dreams
about now. But she hasn't been getting up at night and
we've been able to squeeze in a little "plan B" loving
here and there, including this morning (she induced
quite the gusher from me by hand -- she's still a day or
two from going off the H-rag). Her job right now is
basically to ride herd on the section heads who each
provide a piece of the ten-million-dollar budget. It's
unlike anything she's ever done before, though, so she's
worrying even more than usual.

Most of the J-town buzz, meanwhile, is clustering
around two oddly related nodes: the big sell-off in
high-tech "new economy" stocks and the big week of
protests against the IMF and the World Bank ratcheting
up toward their peak this weekend in the U.S. capital.
Today the mail brought two publications with articles
that should intensify the talk even more. The glossy
far-coast weekly lit mag features a long "After Jyze
City" piece analyzing the protests here and describing
the birth of what they call a new kind of anarchism.
The glossy far-coast political fortnightly's cover story
is an "insider" critique of the IMF written by none
other than my old college classmate Ben Z., who was the
USAn president's chief economic advisor before taking a
job as the number-two guy at the World Bank a couple of
years ago, and last fall he was forced out of that job
because of his perceived incipient anti-corporate-
globalization leanings. What he has to say may seem
mild and timid from the standpoint of anyone who's been
opposing these institutions for decades -- it sure does
to me -- but I suppose it'll have some influence for the
better at the power points.

In my own little world of the TJM project I've been
doing some frenzied research on the matter of the "grand
alignment" and also the "Ice" prediction of a cataclysm
to befall the world on May 5th (first of two days of
planetary alignment, on both of which I'm now intending

to return to these pages for a TJM coda) as well as the proposition advanced in some quarters, and I'm pretty sure noted in here before, that these alignments represent the point at which the Age of Pisces ends and that of Aquarius begins.

And here's what I've come up with. Basically it's all a crock. Of course I thought that anyway from the start in the sense I'm no believer in the astrological system on which it's all based, but it turns out that even to most believers in that system it's nonsense. Such alignments as these apparently aren't particularly rare -- it seems they happen several times every year - and the most authoritative account I could find on the end of the Piscean age has it occurring in about 225 years, although other accounts are all over the map on it. And the "Ice" hypothesis is based on the slenderest reed imaginable, although it does have some resonance just because it resembles certain forecasts regarding the catastrophic effects of global roasting. It exploits the entirely justified fears about that and flogs them into a lather in essence by concentrating all the effects in one dramatic moment that's to occur, as it happens, exactly three weeks from today. This was predicted, and the book was written, some two decades ago when the media and certain isolated segments of the population at large were just starting to take seriously the global-roasting hypothesis.

So it's all hooey except for those entirely justified fears that are being exploited. But it's still interesting, and it's what's happening now. And for the me of now, this G right here, it's part of the TJM plot. I'm going to stay on it all the way to the end. The end of what? The TJM project, of course. Beyond that, anything goes. (You read it here first!)

*

I'd also like to do an update on Z's gang.

Last week Leola left a message saying things had blown up again with Gerry and she and her sister Renny were hunting for an apartment to share. It took Z a day to find out what happened on that, and by then the

954

blowup had blown over. Gerry's been remodeling the
upstairs of their house and Leola got on his case for
being too slow about it, keeping the place a mess when
she's scheduled some important entertaining for the near
future. Gerry said he had a headache and this wasn't
the time to talk about it. Leola persisted. Gerry hit
the roof. But Leola admitted to Z that her lawyer had
advised her not to move out and, besides, she knew very
well she'd never be able to live with Renny. A day
later Z learned Gerry and Leola were still planning to
vacation next week in the palm desert of the our-coast
megastate (presumably staying at D'Arcy's place) and she
said Leola was lying low out of "chagrin." And earlier
Leola had been upset with Z because she, Z, hadn't
automatically sided with her, Leola, and said the right
kind of comforting things. And this has happened over
and over! Z's side-of-head-bonking comment: "When am I
going to learn?"
     Then Jess. She's been under extensive pressure
lately because the millennial creekfest program she's
been working on for two years is climaxing this weekend.
Coming on top of the lingering emotional upset over the
breakup with Gwen it's been too much for her. Several
times she's seriously lost her temper at work, throwing
screaming tantrums. The third time Z and Madge became
so concerned they decided an intervention was called
for, and when they went up to confront Jess she at first
blew up at them too. But after a while she broke down
and the three of them started hugging and weeping. Jess
admitted she hadn't been taking the powerful tranks
she'd been prescribed. A day later she called to say
she was taking them now -- seeing auras around people
and so forth. Saturday we'll be attending the creekfest
-- one of two festivals symbolizing the end of the
city's Millennial Project. The other is a week from
Saturday, Earth Day, the official end. (I'm not even
sure what the event itself is or where it is. But I'll
be taking part in it if at all possible.)
     I suppose I should stop right here. Four-forty.
No new altered card for Z tonight, but then again she

wasn't able to leave one for me. Visually it's not yet
even hinting at dawn out there, but a few birds are
cheeping in a slow, half-awake, undeniably groggy
fashion. And I should note I did mail off the taxes.
Home free for another year, knock on wood. But yeah, my
confidence level on this is fairly high.

49

    Jyzeweek the penultimate. When ultimate is -- the
J-stick! Again! As always!
    Yes. But the week's not getting off to the kind of
start I hoped for. Late this afternoon, as I was about
to leave the house, a call came in to notify me of a
rush job and messed up all my plans. Lacking the
slightest clue as to how long the rush job would take I
had to head straight downtown, and I already had four
hours' scoping work awaiting me anyway.
    Now at midtown chain burgers, the back corner
booth, break time, I can say tonight jyze will go for
about forty minutes and it's starting right here and six
minutes of it have already ticked by (according to my
not-so-trusty pocket watch which is spread open on the
tabletop to J-book's left).
    Yesterday the weather broke and it's still bad out
there, windy and wet. Everyone's worried about
tomorrow's creekfest concert. Jess has been working on
it, as noted earlier, for two years. It was risky
scheduling it for outdoors at this time of year and yet
there's no indoor fallback venue. But Z and I will be
attending no matter what. It's all about loyalty to
Jess. Z says it's crucially important to Jess that all
her friends show up. She's been feeling unappreciated

-- part of the reason for her recent blowups (or a
symptom of the same underlying problems, better to say).
Today she was out racing around trying to come up with
various items a local rock star is demanding for her
dressing room. These include ten towels which Jess
wound up "borrowing," with Z's help, from the WOC.

     Today Z arrived home from work earlier than
expected and brought with her a printout of a news
story. Otherwise I probably wouldn't have known at this
time about today's big market sell-off. What a couple
of weeks it's been! Crunch time is here for those
who've been investing heavily in the dot-coms and
various other technology stocks of the "new economy."
Those values are down more than a quarter in just a
week. The investors are by and large the same people
who are generally viewed as lording it over the rest of
us, so not too many of the rest of us are crying for
them now. Of course it's entirely possible the stocks
could regain their pre-sell-off value and exceed it as
quickly as they lost it. As of now I'm personally not
expecting anything more than a temporary slowdown in the
new economy's triumphant march. Of course in the long
run I still believe that march will almost certainly
lead to political and ecological disaster.

     This should be a fascinating week for other reasons
as well. Passion Week segues into Holy Week for
Christians. Will Lady S write? Today, by the way, is a
date which always resonates for me: birthday of that
other great love of my early Glennarian Stage II years,
Lady V. Z, meanwhile, squabbled with Aida today when
she tried to tell her about the Lady S call and Aida
accused her of not wanting to listen to her own tales of
woe about Charles and Tom; Z was still alternately
fuming and weeping about this when she arrived home.

     The storm was bad last night -- I got soaked three
times in less than eight hours -- but not as bad as it
seemed. As I sat in the black armchair I heard tapping
sounds on the big east window and I assumed the wind was
blowing leaves and branches against it. It turned out
our upstairs neighbors had hung an antenna wire with

some sort of plasticized weight at its tip and that
weight was thrashing wildly about. For the most part
these neighbors have been pretty good, though not
particularly friendly -- they seemed to get the message
we sent by playing our sound system loud when they had
the volume way up on theirs; since then we've heard
little from upstairs except for occasional foot-tapping,
perhaps in time to music on earphones -- so we'll wait
until we see them to mention their disruptive antenna.

     -- I've stayed here five minutes too long. And
I've been too distracted by three loud Cawk women in the
next booth chattering on a cellphone, passing it from
hand to hand (it just rang again -- more of the same --
lemme outta here!).

                        [+1]

     Yah, I made it. Now lying on a blanket on asphalt,
sun shining down (maybe only for a little while), city
council member Margaret P. speaking a few yards away,
introducing the mayor, our good buddy Jon H. -- polite
applause. Right off he's taking full credit for the
sunshine: "Mayor gets the blame, mayor gets the credit,
right?" In a few minutes Z's fave and, to repeat, one
of mine too, bluesman Isaac S. and his band.
     Now hizonner's telling us what the city's
Millennium Project has been all about -- not fireworks
and parties but...well, this right here, the park,
restoration of the creek...and lighting of the high
bridge, planting trees, art, suchlike. I for one still
sort of admire the guy.
     -- But the speech is over already, it's Isaac S.
Rolling out in his wheelchair. As on New Year's Eve.
Celebratory junctures! A couple of hundred people
scattered around the parking lot here, mostly midlifers,
I'd say, jeans, Saturday casual, folding chairs and
blankets spread on the asphalt. The moment most of us
have been waiting for. The other entertainment, enh.
     Z's working the recycling booth on the other side

of the creek, up the hill, with Tobey and David. A
couple of dozen informational and food booths up there,
a "Kidz Stage." And when you cross the creek itself an
authentic "wild" beaver pops its head out down below; I
myself saw this critter do just that. "Nature's double-
edged sword -- or should I say double-edged teeth," as
the MC quipped a while back. (I see Jess prowling
behind the stage with her clipboard. Looking good.
Looking intense and relaxed at the same time -- fully in
charge.) -- Already this beaver's felled several trees
in the area and you can inspect its gnaw marks on a
couple more, now protected with chicken-wire fencing.
The beaver looked right back at me and does the same
with everyone else. No one could doubt he feels he
belongs right where he is. And this of course is how it
should be, with beavers and with the rest of us too.
Getting there of course is something different. But at
least this beaver has pulled it off. For now.
     (This creek, by the way, is not the one into which
Z took a tumble back in December. That's about ten
miles northeast of here. But I'll affirm this one can
still cause her more than a little phantom wrist pain.)
     "Going to Centropolis, sorry but I can't take you."
Blues are ordinarily nighttime music but they can still
sound pretty damn good in the sun at high noon. We're
over in the western part of town, a creek named after a
poet (another Mezzu guy, in fact), an industrial zone on
one side, residential on the other, hills and trees, a
big old warehouse not far behind the stage and a glassy
modern corporate headquarters type of place, maybe five
stories, over behind where the Z-mobile's parked. "When
you see me comin', raise your window high." Isaac in
shades. Two of the band members look and dress a
lot like me -- wotta coupla bad dudes! Said the mayor
to Isaac, "They tell me you're really good at this and I
should stay and listen" -- and this mayor's been living
in greater Jyze City longer than I have! And he hasn't
heard Isaac S. play before! And he's now confessed this
in public! -- So, yes, there are limits to how much
this mayor can be admired. He is, after all, a high-

powered, high-wealth multimillionaire real-estate
developer. This is the USA.

     Of course the crowd is close to a hundred percent
Cawk, except for Isaac on stage and roughly half the
city workers, and those workers are easy to spot because
they're all in orange vests. And behind me to my left a
lissome Asian lady is straddling a bicycle -- didn't
notice her before. A couple of cherry trees are
shedding their blossoms late on the other side of the
chain-link fence which has let dozens of pinkish blooms
drift over this way, two of which are now clinging to my
shirt like moths. Black long-sleeve shirt, many-penned
pocket, and the sun is hot. My right shoulder and left
thigh are burning, seems like. I hardly ever see the
sun at full midday power but here it is.

     Applause! Yes, this is a fine way to ease the jyze
along toward its last TJM spasms. "A little more
keyboard in the mix, please." That's Isaac. (And
here's Z. Let's give it up for Z! -- Half the blanket,
that is. "I was standing in back -- got here just in
time. Isn't he fabulous? I was riveted in place. He's
in great voice today!" -- And you also, Z-duck!)

[+1]

     Chawing on three dried apricots. Again a night
hasn't gone according to plan -- this night right here.
I thought I'd need to spend only an hour at the scope
office but it's turned out to be closer to three. Now
with only an hour or so until bus time there's no point
in trying to make it down to the hideaway. Once again
the conference room will have to do.

     The good news is that the rope burns on my fingers
aren't cramping my keyboard style. I sustained these
burns this afternoon when Z and I were up at Jess's
place walking her dogs -- she's left for a conference in
the our-coast megastate southland that's really a
vacation in disguise, and a well-deserved one too -- and
the sudden appearance of a huge dog a few feet away

(behind a fence) caused Jess's two mutts to panic and
then attack. The rope-like wire of Erfa's leash was
looped across my index and middle fingers, left hand,
and I instinctively clamped down on the wire with my
thumb as it spun out. The pain was intense, and though
it eased off fairly quickly, especially when I got some
ice on the burns back at Jess's place, the incident left
a couple of half-inch-long white welts rimmed with angry
red and even now they're still smarting a bit.

        (Easing the pain still more, a half-drunk woman hit
on me a little bit when I stopped at midtown chain
burgers on my way up here. She was with a group of
three other women and a man and they'd all just attended
a symphony performance at the concert hall a block to
the west and were dressed to the nines, or for this city
say the tens. I was reading a lit journal to one side
as she and I both awaited our orders. I'd noticed her
checking me out before -- very bold eyes -- and now even
more boldly she put her hand on my journal-holding hand
and asked what I was reading -- and kept her hand there
as we talked, and she moved in so close she was pressing
against me with most of the length of her body. Boozy
breath, big eyes, lots of makeup -- fortyish, a sparkly
black dress with frills under a silver coat. "Carol!"
one of her friends called from the condiment table
across the room, "What are you doing!" The woman's
three friends stood there gaping -- the man had gone off
to the restroom -- and laughing hysterically as I
shrugged to them and Carol ignored them. But then our
orders arrived and I took the chance to get away. "May
God be with you," Carol said to me, as her friends'
laughter continued. "Carol, what in the world....")
        -- Why me? Why them? Maybe because I was flushed
from the burns. Or because I too was wearing black,
"Looking just like what's-his-name in the movie," as Z
had commented earlier, although I don't think she meant
it in a flattering way -- this was "Holy Smoke" which we
saw with Jay and Melanie last night and Z had found
"what's-his-name" (I knew just who she was referring
to) repulsive in the deprogrammer role: the old guy

having the tables turned on him and being seduced by the
young woman he was trying to wrest away from some
nefarious swami's hold. But Z always says she thinks I
look sexy in black. Well! Yeah! (I can't help but
notice I must be engaged in some utterly futile vanity
project here -- as if I'm still in the game or could be
if I wanted. And I don't want! -- But sure, I'd like Z
to think I still can do it, as it's clear to me she'd
like me to think she can too -- and often lets me know
one way or another, and usually not at all subtly, when
guys try to hit on her -- and I'm glad she does want
this, so I should realize maybe she'd be glad if I
wanted her to know when a gal tried to hit on me, so
maybe tonight or tomorrow I should tell her about this
little incident after all -- because earlier I'd been
thinking I'd better keep it quiet.)

    Halt right there. Those tricky quicksand marshes
of vanity, ego, fear of aging, etc. etc. -- And on Palm
Sunday! On one of the climactic days of the big
protests in our U.S. capital city and thus the world
capital city. Z and I had been planning to watch the
news when we arrived at Jess's, but to our surprise we
discovered she no longer has a TV. "Maybe she's trying
to emulate you," Z said flatteringly. I suspect it's
part of Jess's effort to get over the pain of losing
Gwen by cutting her home-life activities to the bare
necessities. In the entire house there were only half a
dozen pieces of furniture; everything looked and felt
even more austere than usual, almost to the point of
desolation. I noticed the nails and hangers which used
to support pictures of Gwen or of the two of them
together or of Gwen's family are still in place but no
new pictures have been put on them, while all the other
pictures and photos are as they were before. The garden
looked good, but then it must if Jess is to fetch top
dollar when the property goes on the market next month.
But working on that garden must be painful for her,
seeing the flowers blooming which Gwen planted or they
worked on together. The tulips are spectacular this
year. (And I gazed a while, Z and I both did, at the

driveway and Jess's truck parked there -- parked right
above the patch where we were married. Atop the grease
stain which Jess on our wedding day had earlier covered
with newspapers and an old blanket which we then topped
with cushions and Z's Nepalese dragon rug. -- And
the weatherworn deck chair where Jess sat alone looking
so forlorn at the end of the wedding, way at the back of
the garden, is still right where it was then, although
appearing another J. City winter more weathered and
probably nearing collapse.)
     Earlier Z had been following IMF/World Bank protest
developments on the internet. Up to that point the
capital police, cracking down hard with hugely superior
force, seemed to have things pretty much under control.
Yesterday's six hundred arrests along with preemptive
raids on the protest headquarters (under the
transparently phony pretext of mitigating a fire hazard)
seem to have left the protesters in disarray. But maybe
not. Several ministers of foreign countries were unable
to get to the World Bank meeting. Tomorrow's actually
supposed to be the biggest day, and it's possible the
decentralizing of the protest leadership structure will
allow the action to continue.
     So tomorrow, Monday, will be a big news day for a
couple of reasons. First, the protests. Second, and
probably more important to many people -- the movers and
shakers especially -- what will happen to the financial
markets after their closure for the weekend. Will the
free fall of tech stocks continue? Is the boom really
over? Is a bust starting, a real one? Is this 1929 all
over again? Scary moments for lots of folks. And who
can gloat? That's the irony; if the U.S. economy
collapses, the poor will of course suffer most, at least
in this country. Elsewhere, maybe less so. And in the
long run the overall effects might be good. Give
everyone a chance to think a little bit more about the
likely consequences of all this commoditizing and
privatizing and deregulating and the headlong rush into
across-the-board digitization. A chance to break the
spell of deranged climate-collapse denial.

[+1]

     -- Back at the same spot. It's a few minutes
before midnight. On the west side of the street
seventeen stories straight down I can see (not now, but
when I stand at the window) a long line of idling cars,
and it continues around the corner and all the way up to
the post office. Although today's the 17th of the
month, it's nonetheless tax day because the 15th fell on
Saturday. At least a dozen postal employees are working
the curbsides, including one right in front of our
building to whom I gave the envelope containing my
quarterly payment a short while ago. In return a shill
for a radio station gave me a tube of lip gloss. Sure,
okay, I'll toss it in my bag, why the heck not: the z-
woman might go for it as a quirky kind of backup lube.
     It's not quite as lively as in past years down
there. I took a quick spin through the area and saw two
radio stations broadcasting live, each with its own
tent, and two TV crews interviewing last-minute
"procrastinators" in klieg-lit doorways. Inside the
post office people were filling out tax forms or gravely
peering at them at every one of the stand-up tables and
along the window ledges and there was no sign of levity
anywhere. But that's not so unusual. What was strange
was the absence of tax protesters or for that matter any
kind of protesters. In every other year I can recall
scores of them have swarmed the area to keep things
lively.
     Is this another reflection of the well-known fact
that the "booming new economy" has taken a lot of the
steam out of tax protest? After all it was only last
Friday that this part of the new economy may've stopped
booming, or begun the process thereof, and the effects
haven't quite had time to trickle down to the average
taxpayer. -- And besides, today the markets are up
again, and for new-economy stocks they're up
significantly. No one doubts the long-dreaded shakeout
of dot-coms is getting underway, but for tech stocks as

a whole the general course might still be upward.

Nor does it appear the new coalition of forces protesting corporate control of globalization is growing at the rate necessary to score more successes in the near future. The protests in the U.S. capital have drawn lots of media attention but they haven't succeeded in shutting down the meetings of the World Bank and the IMF. Today's final big day led to another six hundred arrests but the police appeared in full control and by late in the day the protests were no longer even a major story on cable news. More worrisome to me, the number of protesters drawn to the capital for this protest week was much smaller than the 1960s kind of mass turnouts many were hoping for. Ten to fifteen thousand was the estimate I heard today -- which at most would be less than a third the size of the largest crowd for J-town's anti-WTO protests last November. The far coast hasn't produced. Of course this isn't to say the movement won't keep growing there or anywhere else. But I'd guess it will remain confined for now mostly to local hot spots in the U.S. and Europe, and many of those will probably be right here on our coast, and our northern portion of it may well remain in the lead -- and if this is indeed how it shakes out, we might easily become isolated and marginalized.

Just guesses. It's really far too early to get a good feel for what's going on here. And regardless one must maintain hope. The world economy will have to change in major ways and the changes must be in the direction of greater income equality within and between nations and vastly reduced consumption and coal/oil energy use in the wealthy nations. The alternative is too horrible to contemplate. The calamities already produced by treading the path we've been on, and are still on, are bad enough all by themselves.

Of course! But here we are and life is as it is and none of the needed changes can happen quickly. You gotta be in this thing for the long haul and your tolerance for ambivalence, irony, and massive missteps not to mention backward slides must be high.

-- And so what am I doing down here tonight? I
executed a one-eighty on my tax plan. I was looking to
stop making quarterly prepayments on my puny Jyzer Ink
scoping business -- because the deductions from Z's
salary amount to an overpayment far larger than what I
owe -- but at the last moment I decided that course was
too risky in the sense it would likely increase the odds
of an audit. The IRS might decide Jyzer Ink can't call
itself an independent contractor since it's basically
working for only one person now -- Naomi -- and that
would mean it couldn't deduct the expense of renting an
office, e.g., the hideaway. And other ramifications
might emerge, including heightened scrutiny of returns
from previous years. All this could happen anyway, but
I want to keep the odds that it will do so as low as
possible. This means I might need to make more
withdrawals from the deep reserves at a very bad time
for them (though of course the times might well worsen
still more in that same respect). But -- like it or
not, this is the way I'd better go.

And then I remembered I didn't have any checks in
my checkbook. I made the final decision last night to
continue the quarterly prepays but only when I arrived
downtown today did I remember about the checkbook. So I
had to take the unusual step of riding the bus back home
at nine-thirty p.m. and then scaring the heck out of Z
as I used a flashlight to retrieve the checks from the
bedroom where she was already asleep. (The bus driver
even did a double take: "What're you doing going home so
early? You sick or something?" -- This is Ken, the one
who's always asking me what I'm reading. He seems to be
some sort of Christian do-gooder; he often has young
reform-school-type kids riding the bus with him, sitting
on the front bench seats and asking him lots of tedious
questions. Which is to say: regardless of the Christian
part, he seems to be a highly admirable person.)

So from now on I'll be living from check to check,
hoping I can eke out enough to pay my bills. In the
back of my mind, but more foregrounded now, is that
$1500 to $2000 sister Barb set aside after Mother's

death for each of the four of us to cover possible
future tax problems regarding the estate. Supposedly
that was to be kept in a special account for two or
three years, but it's been over four now. Rob checked
into it last year but nothing came of that. I might
suggest he look into it again. I certainly wouldn't ask
Barb about it myself. I'd rather write it off entirely,
and my hunch is I'll probably wind up doing just that.
     -- For once I don't need to worry about catching
the bus. It's a little after one now, the time I'd
usually start packing up, but tonight I've got the Z-
mobile. It's parked a few blocks down the street in
front of the library (and that reminds me: the architect
for the new library, the plans for which I dislike so
much, won some big prize this weekend, meaning it'll be
that much harder to argue against the appropriateness of
this kind of triumphalist in-your-face hyper-modernistic
design for J. City). -- But then again I'm tired and I
don't want to arrive home too late. My injured fingers
are still bothering me -- they're both bloating up a bit
from the rope burns -- and the sunburn I picked up at
creekfest Saturday is still causing little chills now
and then. It's nothing serious and it might even all be
in my mind, an effect of the shift to spring weather --
I don't know what. I do have the leisure to say the
Boston Marathon was run today and I have no idea how it
came out. Our baseball team is stunning the sports
world -- locally anyway -- by winning big in the early
going without the Kid. Big Bad Mad Mitch from the WOC
-- he's reappeared -- has recently gone to work at the
ballpark and is offering to sneak his WOC buddies in for
free, myself included. While Z and I were treadmilling
today she revealed that she had a "big gush" about me
earlier, realizing she'd always wished she could be in
love with a genuinely "nice" person and now it's finally
happened. (Lately she's been on this kick of describing
me as being "nice." It makes me nervous, I admit that.
It would do so even if she didn't like to proclaim "I am
not a nice person!" regarding herself and even if she
hadn't confessed to me about her S/M leanings. Just the

other day a shudder ran through me when she said, "You
have no idea some of the things I used to do." I don't
like it when I start feeling urges to be tough with her
-- "the brute!" -- just so she won't be thinking I'm
some kind of Boy Scout whose virtue she can take
advantage of at will; and I don't doubt at all she
sometimes, or even often, thinks exactly that way.)

[+1]

     Third night in a row the same place. Or almost.
One seat farther on from the head of the table, moving
clockwise, so I'm now roughly halfway between one and
two o'clock on this long dark-wood oval, looking across
at our two windows and then the night and nothing but
banks of windows on two other big buildings. Every
break I take a slightly different crossword puzzle of
lit windows appears out there, one formed by the tower
directly across the street that I'm still thinking of as
a potential terrorist target and the other by that big
bank building a couple of blocks to the east, fifty-
eight stories I think it is, with a huge spotlit Old
Glory often flapping up there late into the evening.
     Purely a holding action tonight. Time's almost
gone already.
     Where'd it go? I didn't get down here until about
half past eight. Dinner at midtown chain burgers and a
vanilla softie at downtown chain burgers, both while
reading a new quarterly with its fine array of "After
Jyze City" articles concerning the WTO and the
"washington consensus" (ha!) and market mania in
general (and a monthly mag's new issue is just as good
on the same topics), with some browsing at the central-
plaza chain bookstore in between -- my usual itinerary
for a Tuesday or Thursday if the scoping load is not too
heavy. Then back here to churn out several hundred
pages of grand-jury finals and lock them in the safe for
Naomi to pick up in the morning. And atop these I place
my bill for the first half of the month, $631, about

half again larger than average (but only because this
one happens to include four grand-jury sessions rather
than the usual two).

*

     -- And I've just discovered my old Russian
pocket watch isn't working. It was doing fine until a
few moments ago when I reset it. Did I overwind it?
The second hand isn't moving. There's no tick. Damn!
And such a fine watch it is, with its incandescent
purple face embossed with flowers and its protective
hinged stainless-steel cover embossed with a corny red
star. But cheap, true -- that being one of its main
attractions. Not worth repairing if it's even possible.
So one of these days I'll probably head back to the
army-surplus store and buy another just like it, funds
permitting. I know the store still carries them, or it
did as of a month or two ago.
     Damn!

[+2]

     Marvelous afternoon. The wedding-reception gazebo.
Sun and birds and tulips and a light earthy breeze.
"You might not believe this, but I got hitched here last
year": my prepared line in case someone should ask what
the heck I'm up to. "I can't help myself, I'm
irresistibly drawn back to the scene of the crime -- I
mean, of the sublime!"
     It's the right day for it in another way too. The
culture says this is a week of miracles and even a day
of miracles. "Holy Thursday." -- Or Maundy Thursday,
as it's also called. It's the first day of Passover, or
I guess in some interpretations it actually is Passover
-- maybe until sundown? Last night was Seder night,
Jews celebrating their escape from Egypt, and I suppose
this was the mass exeunt where the Red Sea parted (and I
teased Kat that some very early Vikings rowed down to
help rescue Manny's ancestors but by the time they got
there the emergency had long been over and the Red Seal

969

stopped parting its hair). And isn't this the day the
Christian top dog of all time arrived in Jerusalem for
what turned out to be (as he should've known anyway, and
I think supposedly did) the Last Supper, time of
betrayal, the snitch, crucifixion and resurrection soon
to follow, miracles, birth of a big-time long-lasting
religion and way of life, major reorg of space and time,
eventual cause for millennial celebration and occasion
for the one and only (barring the super-slim long-term
possibility of epigoni) jyze true millennium.

Dozens of yellow and red tulips nodding gaily and a
blossom-choked bluish-white hydrangea bush shuddering
brightly. Burn, baby, burn! Here in the gazebo I'm far
advanced in a meltdown of the blissful kind. Lawn so
USAn and neatly clipped around the edges. This spot I'm
anointing as the ritual center, so to speak, of my
life's third act: Glennarian Stage III. (As I've been
scribbling and musing, the bottom edge of the gazebo
roof's shadow has been climbing up my chest and neck and
face and just now made it to my eyes -- a bedazzlement
ensuing. Even with my shades on.)

Early rush-hour traffic backs up on the two-lane
street in front. A couple of times I've noticed drivers
with nothing better to do while waiting for the light to
change than to glance this way, and the second time I
gave a little wave with the fingers of my non-J-sticking
hand (while continuing to hold the J-book's upright
left-side fold of pages and cover in the crook between
thumb and upper palm). All this to no particular effect
except that in doing so I happened to notice the "Z & G"
(or "ZAG") inscribed on the copper wedding ring and was
pleased at how spontaneously that noticing occurred.

Swivel my head: nothing but residences in sight,
all sides, except the garden club itself to the left.
The alleyway behind me is a delight to the eye: the
jumble of fences, trees, flowers, garages, weeds,
children's playthings (a pink plastic tricycle tipped on
its side!). Domestic sounds too: kid voices, kitchen
clinkings, a small dog barking excitedly, a radio
station playing hip-hop, a low-rider car rolling by a

moment ago with its boom box sounding so splintery it seemed the car must disintegrate on the spot (which of course must be precisely the effect a certain kind of boom-box-car owner aims for, or so I'd presume).

As for the world and news thereof, at times it appears the financial markets are recovering. Roughly half the two trillion dollars of wealth "destroyed" last week has been "recreated" this week. (Gee, why is it I don't hear J. City's downtown business people raging at the so-called free market for the way it, much like WTO protesters except on an infinitely larger scale, "destroys property"?) A plane loaded with homebound Easter week revelers goes down in the Philippines -- where Aida assures me, via Z, that Easter is taken a whole lot more seriously than it is here -- and once again this fallen aircraft is one of our local creations, quite possibly built during the period when the workers were unusually restless, as Z points out. Commentary on the IMF/World Bank protests in the U.S. capital piles up; everyone is agreed on two things: the side they favor was victorious and "it was no Jyze City!" Next the focus moves to the WTO meeting in Eastern Europe and also to the major-party political conventions in this country, but those are all months away. Maybe it's just the influence of narrative-shaping, but as this TJM project nears its end it seems the major convulsions it's been trying to follow -- because they've been there -- involving the "new economy" and "globalization" -- have also peaked and moved into a period of relative quiet. By coincidence, it would seem, this is turning out to be a pretty good -- "natural" -- time to bring this project to a close. (It's certainly not entirely a coincidence. A year and a half ago when I was thinking about the structure for TJM it appeared late April would be the best "natural" ending time. And of course it's also far from entirely "natural." It was constructed at many levels -- "fabricated," "contrived" -- including by this jyze right here. The timing for the wedding, for one crucial example.)

Shadows lengthening. My favorites are those laid
out across the gazebo's wooden benches -- a four-
slatted, cream-colored octagon, with the side that's
directly facing the afternoon sun open -- shadows cast
by the beveled railing supports, a grid of squiggly
lines that almost seems to shimmer in its stillness as
the leaves and blossoms on all sides shake and wave in
the wind. Bugs walking. Buds trembling -- rosebuds I'm
talking about, plenty of beauty and mystery enfolded in
them to fascinate this Citizen Jyze right here. They're
even leaning in over the railing by my shoulders, on
both sides, as if to check out what's being jyzed about
(and one nuzzles against my back, just below the left
shoulder blade, making me wonder from time to time if
that's a thorn I'm feeling).

Oyez oyez. -- And Z and Aida have once again made
peace. Emiko's merely gone through brain surgery -- but
hallelujah, the tumor behind her ear turned out to be
benign. Gloria, newly energized by her diagnosis as a
"borderline personality," is presently off in the
Philippines conferring with her mother about the ill-
advisedness of her moving to the U.S. to live with her
daughter at this perilous time in the daughter's work
and love life (though Gloria's told Z the affair with
the guy down in the megastate "has been slowed down" and
she won't, after all, be moving down there or quitting
her job here this summer).

Quieter now. Dinner hour. And for me it's time to
move on. The scope job awaiting me, I'd been thinking I
could stretch it out over two nights, but this afternoon
I learned Z's managed to hook up with the almost
mythical Bari and Fletcher for some sort of get-together
tomorrow evening. This means, in case the job turns out
to be unexpectedly long and/or difficult, I need to go
in early tonight. (As a jet roars overhead, reminding
me that the dispute continues to grow over whether we'll
be hearing even more of these planes as they fly over
the hill on the proposed new flight path, a public
hearing having been held a couple of nights ago --
hundreds of angry people, many threatening lawsuits, and

this matter is still in the early stages.)
    -- Life on the hill. Ya gotta love it. Such a
fine setting for a jyzer's Stage III years. I'll say it
yet again, once more (if not more than that): this J-
dude right here has lucked out for sure. (Knock hard on
gazebo wood and hope the structure won't collapse.)

[+1]

    Up goes the jyze sign. Half past three in the a.m.
I tried it last night as well, or rather was about to,
though I hadn't put up the sign yet. But Z's again not
sleeping well these days, after a period of several
weeks when she was doing much better. The past two
nights she's ambled into the living room and stayed for
an hour or two and that raises the odds it'll happen
again tonight.
    I still find it strange that this is the part of my
plan for the TJM jyzarama that's worked out least well.
In the end it's toughest to bring it on home.
    -- So tonight's the last time for finishing up a
TJM eighter with the knowledge that at least one more is
still to come. And it's Good Friday. The most solemn
day for Christians, it's said, but I don't know why that
should be so. Why such great meaning in the crucifixion
of an immortal? If the Christian god decided to walk
the earth for a while in human form, why should
Christians worry the matter any more than any other of
that deity's decisions? As religious myths go I suppose
it's no more far-fetched than many others; but still
it's puzzling to me how it could've caught on as it has,
to be believed by billions of earth-dwelling humanoids
over the course of two millennia.
    Here in the living room it's more peaceful than
usual for a Friday night. Neither upstairs nor next
door has been acting up -- though plenty of time still
remains for that (but upstairs by and large over the
past month has kept it within what I consider reasonable
bounds). -- As right then the first bird of the new day

started up, quickly joined by a second. Quarter to
four. Radio jazz on low. Stack of discarded newspapers
mounting ever higher. Otherwise our clutter level,
although near its all-time peak, seems to be holding
steady. Spring cleaning is for later (after all, as of
today the season still has two months to run). Plants
thriving, but not all are in their usual places.
Adjustments. Variety. But the only really noticeable
newness in the room is the large fan-shaped wire
cardholder Z brought back from an antique shop in a town
near the tulip fields. It's standing on the coffee
table now with eight of the cards she's made for me
displayed on it. (The other day I looked through the
cards I've done for her and guessed their number at
about four hundred. Her stack for me isn't quite as big
but then she's just been keeping me company, as it were;
and lately we've been churning them out at about the
same rate. It's impressive that she can do this given
her time constraints. Such responsiveness! It's a big
part of what makes her the terrific companion she is, in
the sexual realm for sure but in so many other ways as
well -- and never mind the few ways she's not.)
     We finally have some new info about Betty's ills.
Her diagnosis now is "undifferentiated autoimmume
disease." It's something like lupus, but they don't
know what the cause is. It's even possible it's
iatrogenic, if that's the right term, a side effect of
medicine she's been taking for high blood pressure and
allergies. She'll try dropping those meds immediately
and see what happens. To my way of thinking the news is
good in that it's nowhere near as bad as it might've
been (and Z and I were both bracing ourselves for the
worst). But it would be premature to think she's out of
danger. She's been granted a breathing spell and more
reason than before to hope -- and that's a lot.
     For me there's news regarding my job and its
future. Naomi left a note saying the grand-jury
contract will expire in a couple of weeks and the feds
will be putting it up for open bid. She'll be bidding
and, in expectation of tough competition, will keep our

bid rates the same as last time. Her long experience
will count strongly in her favor as will the quality of
her work -- it's always been high, and she works fast
too -- but price will be the feds' first consideration.
It seems this city has an oversupply of court reporters
these days, as do most cities across the country --
mostly owing to digitization in various forms, including
experimental "electronic courtrooms" which dispense with
reporters entirely -- and so she may well be underbid.
The X factor is what effect her being married to the
assistant U.S. attorney (AUSA) who runs one of the three
grand juries will have. And she's close with several
other AUSAs as well. I suspect this will help her quite
a bit (it certainly hasn't hurt in the past), but it
could be they'll suddenly decide to bend over backwards
to avoid the appearance of conflict of interest. -- If
she does win the contract, though, it should boost our
workload significantly, since both existing grand juries
along with a third that's to convene soon are being put
up for bid as a group, meaning if you win the contract,
you get all of Jyze City's GJ-related reporting
assignments. Currently they're being split with another
firm. More work I can handle; I'd be grateful for it.
It might even enable me to scrape by without further
depleting the deep reserves. But if she doesn't win the
contract, the pickings will be slim and I'll probably be
forced to look for additional revenue elsewhere.
Scoping work's much harder to come by in this digital
era, so I might also need to seek a different kind of
job, and that might easily conflict with scoping for
Naomi, especially if it involves daytime hours.

        So, big changes could lie ahead. Or not. It's one
of those time-will-tell things and there's no good
reason to start worrying about it now. Hence I'll try
to push it onto the back burner or better yet some of
that hard shiny white space behind the back burner.

        Tonight's dinner with Fletcher and Bari (another
Eurusan-Asiusan mixed marriage, though Bari's ancestry
is fully Korean) was enjoyable, yes. A couple of hours
at a delightfully funky vegan restaurant on east hill

(it's run by a lesbian couple who describe themselves as
refugees from the far coast). It took almost two years
for Z and Bari to make their schedules intersect again
after our last get-together. Fletcher's an interesting
fellow -- runs the city's computer program but studied
Chinese in grad school -- and he and I hit it off well.
Bari and Zoelie's friendship goes back more than twenty
years and they have plenty to talk about that neither of
us husband-persons can contribute much to, so the talk
tends to go off on two separate tracks with occasional
brief crossings. At one point I brought out this very
J-book for Fletcher to inspect. The questions he asked
about it showed genuine interest: those are always
a pleasure to try to answer. And I learned another
possible reason for our seeming ease with each other:
his father, like my grandfather, was a sociologist.

    Fatigue setting in. Tomorrow I want to be alert --
it's Earth Day and thus the official ending day of the
city's millennium project (and in a way for this TJM
Project as well, though I long ago decided purely for
reasons of form to stretch the "day" out to a full J-
week). As of tomorrow -- in fact as of now by Gregorian
count, since it's well past midnight -- I've completed a
full year. "A Year in the Life." Earth Day was the day
this thing began.

50

    Came rolling out at half past two so we could make
it to the Earth Day and Jyze City Millennium Project
grand finale at the fairgrounds at four. And we made
it, and it was good, and I just wish it could've been
better. Then we wandered around the old "north pole"

976

hood for a couple of hours, and then we came rolling
back home, and that was about nine hours ago. But this
is really my first chance all day to break out the J-
book with the hope of laying down a few uninterrupted
riffs. And the hope's not all that great, really. And
that's all right, just so long as something gets jyzed
here. -- And now in fact something is getting jyzed
here, so the rest is gravy.

This time I'm hanging out at the dining table, the
back end where I usually work on my cards for Z. Had to
sweep aside a mess of pens, papers, mugs, rolls of tape,
stickies, bananas -- or bulldoze aside, more accurately,
as with construction debris, deploying as a dozer the
rectangular wooden-legged tray that ordinarily serves as
our plant-bearing centerpiece. Such splendid clutter
here. Our way of life, I'm crazy about it. It couldn't
possibly be topped except by even more of the same,
which is to say: that's how it'll be a year from now
(unless, of course, we're not so lucky).

Standing on the table here, a surprise Easter
present from the Z-goose: a six-inch-tall G-duck --
cartoon figurine kind -- in a black leather jacket and a
duck's-ass haircut. Half a dozen messages inscribed on
it. Funny stuff! And I've been caught almost totally
unprepared. I have a set of colored plastic eggs in
which I'd planned to leave her messages to be hidden
around unit 203 but they're just not on the same level
at all. I've been one-upped. What to do here?

Meanwhile:

-- So it billed itself as the biggest celebration
of all time, with five hundred million participants
around the world. I don't know the truth value of
that claim. But there was the mayor again and he was
lauded by a contingent of environmentalists before
delivering his speech. Earlier in the morning he had
indeed planted the symbolic twenty-thousandth tree in
the old-growth grove near the south end of the big east
lake, literally in the shade of a three-hundred-foot-
tall Douglas fir. He looked proud and "vigorously"
healthy in his rumpled grandfatherly way -- certainly a

different look from the shell-shocked hizonner of some
four or five months ago. Z and I were sitting on the
grass about ten feet directly in front of the speaker's
podium and when the mayor referred to "diversity in
government" he looked straight at her and it was clear
he remembered presenting her with the city's diversity
award and for a moment I thought he was about to say
something about that. But no -- he kept things short.
(And again, except among the city workers who set up the
event, not a whole lot of diversity was present.)
     Bari's boss, the superintendent of schools, also
gave a short talk. I can't deny it, I was sort of
grudgingly impressed. Things are being done. Compared
with most places this is ecotopia. From an ecology
standpoint Jyze City and especially its public utilities
are probably tops in the country if not the world. But
right now it's easy, and doubly so because of the
economic flush times. The task ahead is immense and
it's gonna be ugly and it may well fail.
     -- And we forge on with our day-to-day life. After
the ceremony Z and I stopped in at Rob's bookstore just
two blocks from the fairgrounds and were lucky to catch
him still there; he said some big changes are about to
go down at the store and he and I agreed to meet Tuesday
afternoon to talk about them along with the many other
things we're behind on. And then for Z and me a lazy
dinner at north-pole local-chain burgers around the
corner, and then home. (But first we shopped briefly at
my old corporate chain supermarket, near which an
apparently demented Afrusan man was shot and killed by
the cops last week after he allegedly shoplifted a
carton of milk from the market and then fired a couple
of shots in the air when a security guard pursued him.)
     All day it's been "Opening Day of the Last J-Week."
This G-duck Z gave me is celebrating that as well as
Earth Day and Easter; it says so right on the back of
his leather jacket. A bunch of flowers in a vase by the
window, yellow daisies included. Two boxes of fresh
strawberries. And some early-evening loving with the
blues show on -- my male member didn't distinguish

itself but my hands and tongue did all right -- followed
by a two-hour Third-Stager nap. At eleven Z watched the
hot news on TV, having first heard about it when calling
her mother with Easter greetings: this morning the feds
finally went in and grabbed the Cuban kid from his
childnapping relatives down in the far southeastern
corner of the nation, or rather the heavily populated
sun-worshipping peninsula extending therefrom, and ever
since then that area has been rocked by riots. With any
luck at all this will kill off the myth of the political
importance of the right-wing Cuban refugee community.
     Never mind that. And for that matter, this. Time
to close up shop for the night. -- But I'll just say
first I've been feeling really good all day about having
made it through the year, jyzing away from beginning to
end pretty much according to plan. And what a year it's
been! I thought of that especially last night while
trying to fill in Fletcher and Bari on what had happened
during the course of the long TJM rollout. So many
surprises! So many good stories!

[+1]

     Easter Sunday isn't making much of a stir here at
the east-depot saloon. Or is it? The crowd's small,
but is it smaller than usual for a Sunday dinner hour?
I go by the thickness of the carpet of pulltags by the
bar. That seems about normal. Passing through it is
something like kicking through leaves on a sidewalk on a
dry afternoon at the height of autumn.
     A nondescript baseball game is playing on all five
screens. Earlier this afternoon our Jyze City nine was
going at it a few blocks from here. Maybe the postgame
influx, now dispersed, is the reason the pulltag carpet
looks normal.
     Shortly before sundown. I'm looking out the
window. The campanile tower of the west depot stands
proud (except for that ugly microwave dish clinging to
the top) against a gray cloudbank with billowing white

and gold underlighting. In the gap between the back of
the east depot and the front of plutocrat #2's giant
green-glass diesel-locomotive-shaped building a patch of
blue sky is visible at the horizon where the dome used
to bulge up. A row of gulls perches on the terminal
roofline with numerous others banking and wheeling above
in an endless airshow that puts those blasted summerfest
U.S. Navy jets to shame and what's more is virtually
silent, at least from here (and it's lovely the way the
wings at certain angles flash golden with the sunset).
    -- A face speckled with dried blood just leaned
around the wooden partition, two fingers to lips and
brows raised in the universal smoke-cadger's query. A
Latusan I'd guess, as maybe a third of the bar crowd is
at the moment, and he's deploying a cane, I see, as he
hobbles around the room and hits up others. -- And now
snagging a burst of late sunshine is the red Chinatown
banner attached to the light pole across the street, the
dragon emblazoned on it undulating slightly and yet also
ominously in the breeze.
    A quiet afternoon reading the Sunday papers.
Sliced fresh strawberries on my cereal. Z did some
bathroom cleaning, first moving everything out of them
-- both -- in her usual fashion. (The Victorian-globe
outdoor lights at the AQ bus station across the street
just blinked on as I glanced at a cluster of them,
sparking the odd thought that they're activated by a
movement-sensitive device so finely tuned it detected
the movement of my eyeballs.) Later she sat crosslegged
on her opened-out convertible couch, Z did, ensconced
amid stacks of books and papers and all kinds of boxes,
working on bills. She also wrote a note asking the guys
upstairs to move the dangling wire antenna which I
mentioned in these pages last week: it distracts her too
much when she's meditating. Then I rewrote the note,
with her permission, so it didn't sound quite so blunt.
Her comment: "Well, you've very nicely nice-ified it.
No, I really do agree it's better. I'm just mean
sometimes, that's all. But you already knew that and
you love me anyway."

Just so.
-- June called shortly after I stumbled out of the
bedroom this afternoon and Z covered for me, saying I
was still asleep (and it wasn't that far from being
true). This led to some talk later about Lady S -- June
had asked Z some questions about her which Z couldn't
answer -- and in the course of that talk Z told me she'd
prefer to have Elgie come up here to my going down
there, should the opportunity arise, but in any case she
thinks I ought to cut my hair before seeing him. At her
request I described the last two times I saw him twelve
and fifteen years ago, the twice-raised and then twice-
dashed hopes of reestablishing a regular relationship.
It's always tough to explain the issues behind the clash
between Lady S and me: this time it was at least a
little easier because of our discussion about it with
Bari Friday night and her confirmation then of what I'd
been telling Z about certain aspects of traditional
Korean morality and childraising practices.
    Well anyway: it went okay. Talking with Z about
former loves and lovers is always a little delicate --
no surprise there -- but it's no longer the perilous
matter it once was. Or so it seems to me. And that
ought to count for something, especially right here in
my own J-book.
    Easter Sunday. Resurrection. Of the earth, or at
least the mid and higher latitudes of the northern
hemisphere. Cycles. Baseball. Bonnets. Parades.
-- As an aid car with flashing lights but silent siren
zips by outside. And inside here's a young Cawk woman
in a strategically ripped black miniskirt, slurred talk,
staggering, flashing red "unners." -- And I've been at
it long enough: time to be moving on. (And now that
same guy with dried blood on his face is pressing up
against the window from outside, arms spread, shape of
his face distorted by the glass like a bank robber in a
nylon mask -- a truly sorry and grotesque sight. But
it's cold out there -- I forgot to mention the change of
weather -- and he's doing this at least partly to get
warm, I think, and also to spite the east-depot saloon

here because between the time this entry began and now
he's been, as I overheard someone remark, 86'd.)

[+1]

    I suppose this'll be the last time for the
hideaway. All times are probable last times now --
talking about with respect to this TJM project, of
course. But after a nine-month sabbatical -- and any
TJM codas to one side -- jyze does intend to return.
Back to its regular old ways, until death do us part.
(Intentions, intentions, right. But these are about as
strong as intentions get -- mine anyway.)
    Meanwhile things are winding down fast. At times I
want to squeeze in as much as I can before the final
curtain but at other times the story itself seems to
forbid that. Because...isn't this pretty much how the
last stages of denouement ought to be?
    Regardless, however, life keeps barreling along on
all cylinders just as one might expect it would. Or on
all organo-energy-exchangers, say. Roars along even if
you happen upon one of the isolated still spots or
backwaters -- such as this one right here (brown
armchair, floor lamp on, fan spinning).
    I've got me four Easter eggs hand-decorated by Kat.
Betty brought them along to the doctor appointment this
morning, offering them in apology for a certain rude
moment of Kat's on the phone with Z yesterday (more and
more, Betty tells Z, Kat's engaging in "adolescent
boundary-testing"). Three of the eggs have a 'Z' on
them, I might note, and only one a 'G.' I'm relatively
neglected again, and by a large margin! But I'm sure
I'll be able to reconnect with Kat when the chance
presents itself, and that should be happening a number
of times in the weeks ahead. In the long run there
might be many more -- regular and steady -- because Z
and I are quite serious about providing as much support
to Betty as she wants and needs and will allow.
    The news from Betty's appointment today isn't good.

Z proclaimed herself to be in a state of shock over it
when I talked with her on the phone this afternoon;
earlier she'd broken down and bawled while telling
bossman Dale about it. The diagnosis of subcortical
dementia has been dropped -- this is the second-opinion
doc now, and Betty likes her and is angling to move her
up to number one -- but it's still a disease of the
autoimmune system and MS has not been ruled out. A
spinal tap is coming up next week.

Obviously no one can make any long-term decisions
until a firm diagnosis is in hand, and also a firm
prognosis. But Z seems quite determined about moving to
the west side to be near Betty and Kat if that's what
they want. (And truth to tell she doesn't use that
qualifying "if" phrase at the end. Not yet. But Betty
may have other ideas, such as moving back to the farm.
And in my view Z needs to be more realistic about how
much of a caretaker role she can take on, especially in
light of the fact that her mother will be turning
eighty-five in two months and will likely be needing her
only child's caretaking help before much longer. Then
again I don't really expect that kind of realism to
deter Z. And assuming it won't, I'm ready to go along
with her all the way and to pitch in as much as
possible.) (Jess, by the way, keeps trying to talk us
into moving to the area where "creekfest" was held a
couple of weeks ago. "It's the coming hood." And it's
not far from Betty's place. It's not quite within
walking distance of downtown, but I could still go for
it if Z did. Good bus connections out there, Betty
tells us, though she rarely uses them herself.)

Other news? Right-wingers are screaming about the
"child-snatching" by the feds in Miami. Fine, let 'em
scream. Around here the big buzz is about a new plan,
apparently likely to be ordered by the court, to break
up the software behemoth as the penalty for its
antitrust violations. (I'm thinking about writing a
letter to the editor about the complicity of the entire
metro area -- the way it's benefited, at the community
level as well as the individual, from the company's ill-

gotten wealth. It's tainted and we're tainted! And
this is far from our only taint!) (T'aint so? Sez who?
It's true of the whole country and of many corporations!)
     The guys upstairs reeled in their dangling wire
antenna. Better yet, they left a note outside our door
(written on the back of our note to them): "Mi scusi."
So, a rising hope of neighborliness here. And down in
the lobby a six-foot-high potted plant has appeared,
"the kind you'd expect to find in a funeral home," as Z
observed. But still: this is the first step we've seen
the new landlords take toward upgrading the premises.
We both regard it as promising.
     Here at the hideaway little is changed. The sheets
of plywood and the two-by-fours still dominate the room,
awaiting the start of the loft-construction project.
I've penciled that in for sometime this summer. I'll be
seeing less of the place for a while as I type up the
ten J-books of TJM on the scope-office computers. Once
that's finished I expect to be here a lot. (And now --
outta here! Bus stop! Be bused or bust! -- Or be
busted, yeah, because...you never know.)

                         [+1]

     Funny thing: a familiar name jumped out at me last
night as I was glancing through the local section of the
FAP (former afternoon paper). The jyzer's name! This
jyzer's! His surname, that is.
     It was an item in the gossip column. I probably
would've glanced through the column eventually but at
that point I hadn't; it was one of those instinctive
things, like a mother instantly spotting her kid's face
in a crowd of thousands. In this case it was brother
Rob's name. The item was about the words on his
bookstore's spinning sign, which say (though the item
garbled them, I learned later), "Eat garlic / drink red
wine / go for a walk / write a poem." And Rob was cited
as their author, and also quoted to the effect that
although National Poetry Month occasioned the verse, the

first three lines had drawn more comments.

    "My ten seconds of fame," he dryly observed this afternoon when we met. -- And then we talked for a couple of hours at the pub directly across the street from that spinning sign, and then walked into town together, parting along the way so I could angle over to the old digi-cafe to do some jyzing -- which turns out to be these very words going down at this moment. As electronic music plays and a couple of guys puzzle over a chessboard (they're still doing that in here!). I just closed two of the same old industrial swing-out windows, pulling them in by a small attached chain: it's suddenly getting cold out there with the sun sinking below the building line (the gallery for homeless artists across the street and also, a block farther west, the upper two-thirds of the new eight-story structure going up, and nearly complete now, next door to my old apartment building -- and again I'm thanking my stars I didn't have to be living there during the construction phase, which was just starting when I moved out to take up living with Z on south hill).

    For Rob and me it was our first extended meeting in many months. Last night I jotted down a dozen items on a Z-style list of things I wanted to ask him about and then today added a few more as I bused crosstown (cheating on my resolution to walk all the way but only because I was running so late). The most amusing, it turned out, was the one that elicited Rob's description of the night he and Gail attended the symphony using the tickets Z and I gave them for Christmas. "Best seats in the house," he assured me (and afterwards they made an all-around big night of it by hitting a nearby grill for steaks, and then they bused home). The "Roy Harris No. 3," his favorite work by a USAn: he was rhapsodic about it. "It's stunning how much our symphony has improved. It's world class now." All night long he heard only one bad note, a trombone trailing on too long in the "Pathetique." It's a kick to think I have a brother who knows so much about such things -- and he's a longhair, scruffily-dressed sixties leftover just like me, only

ten years younger, and working a skanky job too, also
just like me. And he's still smoking that pipe. Which
worries me. The waitress at the pub, recognizing him as
a bookstore employee -- they hold staff meetings there
-- let him get away with smoking in a nonsmoking area
since no one else was around. -- And we were both
carrying bags from the drugstore that stands kittycorner
on the upper level of the mall, each of us having
independently gone there today on the first day of the
new coupon sale and having bought the same item: vitamin
D. In this sun-starved city you gotta stay stocked up
on your vitamin D.

     The big news is that the bookstore's mother company
is downsizing and reorging to meet internet competition.
Many longtime employees are being let go and the ones
spared from this will be stripped of their more
interesting duties -- bookbuying, for example, will be
centralized -- and they'll be expected to spend all
their time on the floor. If Rob chooses to stay on --
he's one of the spared ones -- he'll have to close the
store at eleven p.m. at least twice a week and arrive
early in the morning the other days. He's afraid he
won't be able to hack that extreme kind of split
schedule again -- it took him years to be able to escape
those closing tasks. So just yesterday he sent out a
batch of resumes to other bookstores in the area,
including the two big corporate chains. If he gets a
solid offer -- especially one that involves a classic-
music department -- he'll leave his present employer.

     On other matters, he was relieved to read the
letter from Jim Q. because he and Gail had both been
worrying about him and were afraid, just as I was
regarding myself, that they'd somehow offended him last
fall (and the letter doesn't really relieve him on that
score). We agreed Jim had probably realized during the
wedding week that he wasn't as attached to our family as
he'd thought; he had clung to us as a form of mourning,
in a sense, after Mother's death and now that he'd found
another woman he no longer needed us as much in that
way. Or, as I'd theorized earlier, his new wife, Nancy,

frowned on his keeping up the old contacts. Or both.
     And regarding sister Barb and the tax money, he's
as baffled as I am. He's heard nothing from her. "I
live in the same city as you, see you frequently --
could just be I'm tainted by association." (Another
taint, yes.) He'll see if he can find some excuse to
write her a note about it. But we're not holding our
breaths. Nor are we expecting to hear from brother
Jeff. Rob regards Jeff's failure to get in touch with
me about the wedding (other than the one call beforehand
when he said he couldn't attend) the same way I do: he
must still be going through tough times over money.
     Finally, Rob was, as I feared, familiar with the
book I bought for him about our claimed ancestor --
claimed by Popeye, of course -- Eleanor of Aquitaine.
He'd just finished reading another book about roughly
the same era by the same author, but he hadn't bought
the Eleanor book yet. And he said he was so backed up
on reading, he could wait until his birthday for me to
give it to him.
     -- And I'd better be moving on soon. A few
swallows of root beer left. Small crowd (same two chess
players just now starting another new game). Bizarro
nineties neopunk jazz, I'll call it, on the PA. As I
understand it, the dot-com that owns this place is
thriving as an internet service provider -- even with
all the market "shakeout" volatility -- and thus the
existence of the cafe itself is no longer threatened. I
think of the many hours I spent here back during my pre-
Z B-2 era -- usually sitting in one of the armchairs
over in the corner. (Upholstered benches are set up
there now but the feeling of the area's about the same
-- and right next to me here on the raised section by
the windows is an armchair with a hassock, but without a
reading light.) At some level I was usually hoping to
meet a woman during those times I was sitting in here,
but I was always well aware the chances of that
happening were poor. I was pretty much resigned, but
not completely so, to continuing on indefinitely in a
life of jyze-devoted solitude (boohoo...but true!). By

and large I wasn't unhappy, although I was sometimes
despondent -- especially sitting here on Friday or
Saturday evenings -- and could never feel fully pleased
with my life for long. That things could turn out as
they have would've been beyond my imagination back then
-- or say too fantasylike to merit anything but scorn.

So I return in triumph. Yes I do! Yee-ha! -- And
now bottoms up on the root beer and make ready to move
on -- the old hike down the middle road, cutting
diagonally through parking lots across to the high road
and then, where the street grids shift, the very high
road, and then on to work, at the same reporting firm's
office on the same floor but now, unlike then, at the
south end of the hall instead of the north end. Then
the bus ride home, also southbound, to the hill on the
far side of downtown. (For me it's the new world order
as it oughta be.)

[+1]

A quickie. Clock above the entrance to the west
terminal says quarter to five. At half past I'm due to
meet Z at the WOC (still our usual time). -- And now a
twin diesel blast. Rumble of a passenger train rolling
by down below, pulling into the tunnel just far enough
for a flip of the switch and then the train can back up
into the station. (Will the excitement never end? But
in just four days, alas, yes, it will, regarding the
tiny fraction of it that makes it into these pages.)
Didn't want to pass up this opportunity. A fine
sunny afternoon, a chance to sit on the flowerbox bench
at one of my favorite corners, just four or five feet in
front of the endstop on the tracks for the waterfront
streetcar. Diagonally across the intersection the
corner street-level area of the three-story brick
building now stands empty, probably awaiting its
makeover into a spiffy burger-chain franchise. To the
left the east-depot minimart, to the right the east-
depot saloon with its tacky blank sign. Straight ahead

behind the AQ bus terminal the row of new office
buildings, soon to open for business and provide throngs
of fast-food chompers for the burger-chain franchise;
and those buildings are owned by the newly straitened
plutocrat #2, now worth only a bit more than half what
he was three weeks ago, so maybe he's fallen off the
list of the top ten richest in the world. U.S. and
state and transit flags rippling on their poles in front
of the east station. Buses thundering by. (The old
dome's gone, yes, but it never was visible from here.)
-- And new AQ dragon banners rippling handsomely -- even
if also, again, ominously, as is only proper for dragons
at least in the Western world -- on light poles on both
sides of the street in all four directions.

    Ah, it's a lively scene. A group of drifters and
dealers hangs out along the parking-lot fence just to
the south. A woman, forty-something 1970s vet in jeans,
long blond hair, says hello to me and suddenly calls
back to one of the drifter guys for no apparent reason,
or maybe to no one in particular, or maybe even to me
though I doubt it, "I'm not married, no." (Or probably
the drifter dude asked in a low voice and I couldn't
hear it.) -- Struts across at the light. A block
uphill the sign atop the big low-income hotel says -- at
the seventh-floor level -- "MODERN FIREPROOF LOW RATES";
I'm pretty sure she lives there. Or at least I've seen
her going in or out a few times.

    -- And I've got a little hunk of news. Can't wait
to tell Z. As I was putting on my shoes just inside the
apartment door I heard voices in the hallway outside, a
woman and a small girl who were themselves just leaving
the unit next to ours, 202, saying goodbye to the
workmen who've been putting the finishing touches on the
remodels there and in 201. When I went out and asked
the longhair workman who they were, he said, "Oh, that's
Raphael's wife and kid. They're going to be moving in
here on Friday." "Raphael's going to be moving in
here?" "Yup. Sold their house, movin' in."

    So! The landlord will be living next door! Two
next doors, in fact, and also two landlords -- the ones

Matt B. called "handsome people." And a third, a
handsome little landlord in training! Presumably Dana
is the woman Z saw yesterday and of whom she said, "She
looks like a young woman who grew up very privileged."
So now I'm guessing I'll probably have to be persuading
Z to give them half a chance. -- We'll also need to be
cleaning up some, I'd say, and especially out on our
balcony, which, as noted before, is just a couple of
feet away from the 202 balcony and fully visible -- and
jumpable -- from there.

The other quick news is that Betty's spinal tap is
scheduled for Friday and Z will be accompanying her,
taking most of the early part of the day off. And
Saturday we'll be seeing "My Sex Life" with Wei and
Alison, but the early show, not the late show as
formerly agreed. And Kat can't go to southwest island
with us next Saturday to celebrate the completion of the
recycling campaign -- Lou G. from Z's office is throwing
a big bash at his farmette there -- because it turns out
that's her children's-theater day.

Oh yeah. Fine corner. Nothing abloom in the box
here at the moment, though, and the ground cover looks
more like weeds. But at least they appear to be
authentic weeds. (Tall Afrusan dude lays a wad of bills
on the far end of this six-foot-long bench, says rather
forcefully to another Afrusan -- though at first I think
he's talking to me -- "There it is, the shit's right
there, just pick it up." And the other dude does just
that and off they go, four dudes in all and all Afrusan.
Drug deal? Who knows. But lots of 'em go down around
here. Bold doings -- and right in the man's face. "The
man": that's me of course. I mean, how could they be
sure I wasn't? It's curious. Cawk nark scribbling just
as fast as he can -- would've been my first thought for
sure if I were them.) -- But onward.

[+1]

-- And now the last attempt to get up close to the

spirit of the age. Z-geist cafe. But they might not
have the right spirit-contacting modem installed here, I
recognize that. In fact I don't see a single computer
in the place at the moment. And at six p.m. I'm one of
only three customers. Good for the concentration. (But
the music's bad for that same faculty, some sort of
wiggy neobubblegum stuff, likely meant to be parodic,
if only in a setting like this.)

A block south of here in the parking lot for the
former dome the piles of domesday rubble are looking
impressive. This is the processed rubble, broken down
into baseball-size chunks and smaller. From where I
stood I could see none of the original large jumbly
boulders. Four huge cranes hovered above the area where
at least some of those boulders used to be. And on the
back side of the lot the walls of the new stadium are
already visible. Things move fast when, as here, a key
part of the spectacle that keeps so many of us going has
been blown to bits in order to be replaced and upgraded.

Mainstream critics continue to pile on with their
pans of the U.S. capital protests, the left, "Jyze City
man," all the usual hooey. As a cartoon in this week's
edition of our local radical rag observes: so what are
we supposed to do, just sit back and enjoy the pillage
of the earth and ruination of the future for generations
to come (if indeed any more complete generations are to
come)?

Today, by the way, is an interesting anniversary.
It's a repeat for this TJM project but so it goes.
1521, the Spaniard who first circumnavigated the globe
(or rather his fleet did) is killed (and maybe eaten) in
a Southeast Asian archipelago that, thanks in
considerable part to that very Spaniard's efforts, would
soon be called the Philippines. It's a holiday there,
as well it should be, though the reasons they give for
public consumption, so to speak, are of course not the
true ones. A celebration of the beginning of four
centuries of Spanish colonialism! Yayhoo! When we were
talking about this, Z was moved to tears by memories of
the proud way her father used to assure her their family

in the Philippines had not one drop of Spanish blood.
But maybe, since they lived in the right area -- the
Visayans -- it did have a residual taste of Spanish
flesh. This week the media have been carrying accounts
of indigenous people's protests mounted against the
celebration in Brazil of the five-hundredth anniversary
of the first Cawk invader's landing there; I'd imagine
some of that same spirit must be found in Z's father's
ancestral land. Certainly it's found in Z herself. And
in me too, by what I consider, as Z does also and even
more so, a kind of miracle.
     Oh what a millennium it's been.
     Meanwhile it's now confirmed: Dana and Raphael and
their daughter will be occupying both 201 and 202 on our
floor. Z happened to arrive home when furniture was
being brought up to both apartments. Fancy stuff, she
says. We had an amusing talk about her "making nice"
with them. If she likes drama, well, "making nice" is a
kind of acting too. And I think she'll be okay with the
new setup, at least for a while. But she's highly
sensitive to any suggestions of status differences. It
bugs her that the door mat which materialized yesterday
outside the entrance to 202 -- a kind of partially
rubberized Turkish carpet, it appears -- is a lot
fancier than ours. But she's happy about the upgrades
to the house, including the new deluxe automatic garage
door installed yesterday. And yet another large new
plant appeared, the third in less than a week, this one
on the landing outside the second-floor entranceway that
we'll be sharing with all three new landlords.
     What else? Scattered talk about Vietnam days as
the twenty-fifth anniversary of the frantic U.S.
evacuation of Saigon approaches this weekend. The
effort to shape the history of the war from the USAn
vantage continues unabated. It's appalling to see the
same old debunked lies cropping up again and again.
That goddamn domino theory, it still lives!
     Today, as in previous years, Kat was supposed to
accompany Z on Take Our Daughters to Work Day. But it
didn't happen; the child's involved in three consecutive

days of state testing (the hateful WASL tests -- but I'm
not going to let myself get started on those).
     -- Now I see Z-geist is gearing up to bring in the
chairs and tables. I'm the last one out here. If I try
to jyze much more I'll wind up stacked and pressed into
a tight Z-shape in the entranceway -- or at least the
look on the face of this young woman who's doing the
hauling and stacking is very resolute. (And I notice
she's dressed exactly as I am: black-and-white chucks,
jeans, three-button placket-neck black short-sleeve
henley. -- People, we're on the comeback trail! (We
dedicated followers of....) -- But in facial piercings
and tattoos she's way out ahead and I'm nowheresville.
-- As the old near-Mentokan troubadour cracks up at the
beginning of "I was riding on the Mayflower," now
playing top volume on the Z-geist PA. Yes, a good note
to end on, that cackle, the start of yet another epic
Cawk invasion.)

                      [+1]

     -- Didn't think I'd be able to jyze today (and
today would've been the last chance for an on-beat
entry, and is). This morning it was raining and the
forecast called for more of the same, possibly with what
they dubbed "frozen rain" tonight. (Is that the same as
sleet? Snow? Hail? Probably any or all of those.)
But now at a little past five p.m. a massive sun break
is taking up over half the heavens (that's with the blue
part included as well as the yellow). And I'm standing
here as ready as I know how to be for chill winds, the
green jacket worn over the gray hooded sweatshirt over
the heavy black denim shirt over the heavy black long-
sleeve henley, and shades on too, and feeling pretty
damn good right now.
     This is the cement pedestal/podium at the upper end
of the south-hill high bridge, hard by one of the prime
entrances to the "jungle/rez." It's where I started
this TJM thing and now where I'll be finishing it --

almost. But not quite, because tomorrow night, on the
last offbeat night of these fifty J-weeks, I'm fixing to
tack on a few final words at home. And then that'll be
it: jyze is outta here. Except maybe for a coda or two.
     And today's a special day as well, including in a
way I hadn't expected. But later for that. Meanwhile
it's Arbor Day, and it's spinal-tap day for Betty, and
it's move-in day for Dana and Raphael and their
daughter, whose name is Bethany, I just found out an
hour ago, and she's seven. And handsome in the family
way, yes. And it's also Good Friday again, this time
for the orthodox Christians. Seems like you just can't
get away from this event-filled Christian calendar. And
of course that's true, you can't avoid it, just as you
can't disentangle yourself from the story that's
associated with it, certainly not around here but
basically not anywhere. All you can do is live with it
as best you can, like it or not, and try to build on it
in a way that will minimize the massive damage it
symbolizes and continues to create worldwide.
     Bridges! Rush-hour traffic whizzing, creeping,
lumbering, rattling, roaring, moving in all directions
(when it's moving at all) on all sides and at a dozen
different levels. Business. "Got work to do." This on
the day it's confirmed the plaintiffs -- us, the U.S.,
as well as some nineteen industrial states of the union
-- are proposing breakup into two companies of our local
mega money machine. (And I glance to my left and
there's the orange-brick DC castle currently occupied by
another such machine but one in an earlier stage of
attempted total domination of the planet.) The trees
are well turned out for their special day. The
greenbelt area around the freeways is at, or anyway
close to, its most multifarious springtime green. So
far no one's emerged from or entered the pathway
starting just a few feet from this jyze soapbox made of
concrete and leading down into, to repeat, "the jungle/
rez." Several walkers whom I've taken as likely
candidates for that steeply descending and perilous
journey have passed by on the sidewalk but they've just

kept on going southwestward, perhaps to access other
entrances farther up the hill.

Cottony clouds are clinging to the peaks of the
western mountains so it's hard to guess just where the
sun will bed down for the night over there. And it's a
bit early in the afternoon to be projecting its path,
though the orb itself is already lighting up a silvery
corridor across the bay and out into the sound. And it
occurs to me that a lot more of that corridor is visible
from here now with the dome gone -- though it won't be
visible for long. The walls of the new stadium, as
noted earlier, are rising. A few months, a year tops
for the corridor. Right now is as good as it gets.

The downtown skyline. Yuh, I like it. You jyze
about it as much as I do, you become even more attached.
-- A big old heavily laden freighter is slowly making
its way out into the bay from the river docks. Sun
winking. A gargantuan crane swinging over plutocrat
#2's buildings. The economic forecast tilts this way
and that but the boom still seems to be happening.
Maybe it's just a matter of lag time. (And it's a scary
day too. Scientists announce what they're calling the
first big breakthrough in gene therapy. Will they use
it to refashion us all into scientists? Or maybe just
into scientists' apprentices?)

Earlier I had a chat with landlord Raphael down in
the garage. He tells me they haven't decided yet about
condoizing -- haven't really thought about it. He and
the rest of his family might even be moving back to the
far coast at the end of the year. But they'll be our
neighbors at least through December, and they'll let us
know as soon as possible whether they're condoizing and
what the prices on the units will be. He promises. (He
has zero credibility, of course, since with landlords
and credibility it's the opposite of ordinary people and
innocence.) (Should that remark stand? I don't think I
really understand it but yes, let it stand anyway.
-- As the end nears I'm sorry to say but it's obvious
regardless: the jyze standards are seriously slipping.)

And there's a bit of bad news which I do believe

without equivocation: our building is one of the ones
that has defective siding (we've been reading about this
issue for the past year or two). It'll cost forty K to
replace. How it'll be paid for I didn't ask, but I
don't doubt we tenants will bear a good portion of it.
The company which made the siding is kicking in only a
thousand bucks, Raphael said, and I gather it's now gone
bankrupt. -- Raphael the gentleman contractor. I
confess I sort of like the guy. In his easygoing
casualness he reminds me more and more of brother Jeff
(who for years did a similar kind of work -- building
houses, renting them out or selling them -- and he may
be doing it again now, though almost certainly without
Raphael's kind of financial assets or returns).

     -- And leave it to Z to come up with a way of
tweaking this jyze project -- providing a climax for it,
no less, and not just so to speak. A bit of well-timed
drama with a sexy twist. What she does is this morning
she succeeds for the first time ever in getting me off
completely fellatiously, meaning all the way to, and
including -- fully mouthed -- ejac. A perfunk that
turned out not to be perfunk! She had the time because
she'd taken the day off from work but she wasn't due to
pick up Betty until eleven. But why she decided to hang
in there on this occasion as opposed to some other --
instead of going for "the visual," as she's always said
she prefers ("I'm just a visual kind of person") --
well, if she didn't do it for its jyze impact, she's not
saying what it was for. She did, however, remind me I'd
told her this was the "penultimate day" for this TJM
project and she couldn't resist the pun (as far as I
know she never even tries to resist a pun) about pen,
penis, "The Pen is Ultimate Day." And afterwards I left
her a "First Swallow" (at Capistrano) card I'd been
holding in reserve for months, now suitably doctored to
memorialize April 28th.

     So some raunchiness for the endpiece. What could
be finer? -- As now I shift again to put most of my
weight on my left leg, leaning my right flank against
the podium, facing up the hill so I can see some big

gray clouds rolling in at breakneck speed above the
castle. Lots of 'em. A sneak attack from the rear! So
I think it's best to evacuate this position right now.
Mosey on across the bridge -- but better go with a fast
mosey -- and straight downtown, try to make it to the
scope office without getting soaked. At this point I'd
have to say the odds look poor.

[+1]

     Guess the black armchair is as good a place as any
for the last entry of the annal's main body. Being
naked except for the jyze pendant is good also. Jazz
playing, likewise good. A crescent of last-quarter moon
due to rise out there at just about daybreak, good as
well. (I won't stick around long enough to see that
crescent, but it was also present last night about this
time and a marvelous sight as the sky slowly blued
around it, revealing long sinuous horizontal black
brushstrokes just below its level, like mountains of
dark ash propelling it up phoenixlike -- like a
flameless version, say, of the millennial fire ceremony
we saw last month at the fairgrounds.)
     At four a.m. on this particular night Z-wiff is
abed and most likely asleep. The same is true for
everyone else in the building, it would appear,
including the newly ensconced Raphael and family.
Earlier tonight -- but past ten p.m. -- he was outside
replacing the bulbs in several of the globe lamps
overhanging the side walkway leading to the lobby
entrance, each globe shining amid the leafy branches
like a full moon viewed through bamboo (as I often think
coming home at night when those lights are working).
     The last of 374 days -- a leap year plus a J-week.
As it happens, this is also the 25th anniversary of the
end of the Vietnam War. Or I could say, since by
Gregorian measure we're actually four hours into the
375th day, it's orthodox Easter. A good day for
phoenixes and also for putting things to an end. And

also, yes, just for being alive on this earth (that's right!).

On this day, just as planned, Z and I saw "My Sex Life" at the Little Theater with Wei and Alison. It wasn't the movie I'd been hoping for -- my expectations had spiraled way too high since I missed it the first time around a few months after Z and I met -- and it was two minutes short of three hours long. The four of us made up about a third of the audience. Even in that small theater (with its hundred or so seats) the crowd seemed tiny. When we got out, the line for the restaurant two doors down easily tripled our numbers. Life and love playing out among a bookish French group of twenty-somethings: that was the movie. Seemed to me they were only just at the beginning of the path of learning what life and love and sex are all about, and that was also true of the movie itself with respect to its being a work of art, and so also for the writers, the director, et al. But at least it tried to put before us something thoughtful and admirable.

Afterwards another vegetarian restaurant a few blocks up the street from the theater. Dishes from a number of Asian cuisines, and where the traditional dish has some form of meat, fish, or fowl, this restaurant substitutes soy but still uses the traditional name of the dish -- teriyaki, bulgogi, you name it (or rather tradition does). Sounds a little tacky maybe but it was tastefully done and gastronomically tasty as well. Even Wei, who's an excellent cook himself and usually quite critical of anyone else's cooking, had nothing but good things to say about it.

Alison, as Z had forewarned me after seeing her at book group on Tuesday, looked tired and gaunt. She's been sleeping poorly lately, at least in part from stress over the lump in her breast which is slated to be MRI'd next week. Wei was being touchingly affectionate with her to an extent we hadn't seen before, calling her "darling" and embracing her several times in the booth seat. They never brought up the lump and so we didn't either. I had the feeling I often do with them: we must

see more of each other to be able to bump the friendship
up to a more intimate level. I'd like for that to
happen, and I think the others would too, but somehow it
never quite does. Why, I'm not sure. Maybe it still
can.

And last night another kind of touching scene.
Earlier in the day Betty had given Z "a piercing look"
when Z mentioned she was planning to send her mother
money rather than use it to visit her on her eighty-
fifth birthday in June. At three a.m. she, Z, got up,
again unable to sleep (though Betty's spinal tap had
gone about as well as it possibly could've; apparently
that kind of procedure is no longer the horrifically
painful ordeal it used to be and which Betty had been
prepping herself for, as had Z as her support person) --
Z got up, as I say, and we talked it over and she
decided to travel to Centropolis for the birthday after
all. She realized she would feel terrible later about
missing it, especially if her mother's health doesn't
hold up. She wept as she recalled her ex-post-facto
regrets about being unable to return home to see her
father in his last months twenty years ago, and also
about missing her mother's eightieth birthday because of
grad-school commitments. So she cranked up her computer
and within twenty minutes had all the information she
needed on flights and hotels, and this morning she
called Mama E and she was delighted Z could come (and
it's out of character for her mother to express this so
directly and go along with such a proposed visit so
easily -- usually she'd object "You shouldn't spend the
money" and would need much persuading). By the time I'd
gotten up, all the arrangements were set, including a
family birthday party at the same Italian restaurant
where we all gathered during our Centropolis visit in
'98. Her nephew Jacob would be throwing the party this
time in lieu of the promised wedding banquet for us.

I won't be able to go with her, but I don't think
that's a problem. It'll just be four or five days. I
couldn't afford it anyway, but as it happens that
workweek is a heavy one for me. And besides: it'll

probably be good for Z-wiff to have this chance to be
alone with her mother. (Or maybe not so alone. Said Z
to Mama E: "Be sure to invite Tito to the dinner."
Replied Mama E: "Oh, he'll be there." This is the
twenty-years-younger (not just ten as we'd thought
before) Greek man who's been staying with her and
recently, having broken up with his former girlfriend in
Canada, sold his wheels and appears to be shacking up
with Mama E for good. So it could be Mama E will never
be moving out to Jyze City.)

Ought to have a paragraph or two here about other
last-entry kinds of things. Can think of some
possibilities but -- to heck with it. Birds are
awakening and tomorrow we again have plans: a big
afternoon with Olwen and Trent, dinner included, to make
up for the get-together canceled last weekend. Such a
very social life I lead now in the high Zoelie era
(though rarely more than two or three days of the week,
and even on those days I usually have some time to
myself, as right now, because of the extreme differences
in the hours she and I keep; and despite occasional
qualms we both agree in general it's a very good thing
that our schedules work as they do while still leaving
plenty of -- or "just enough" -- overlap).

Birds of the love-train krazy klock swooping and
smokestack steampuffs rising in the usual antic way.
Some cut flowers here. Books and papers and magazines.
Stacks of altered cards. Plants. Colorful Nepalese
dragon rug. The not-so-faint red paint stain from last
month on the regular carpet. Familiar clutter. Old
albums, knickknacked bookcases, the Jeep cap. The new
G-duck. Mash notes. This is it, scene of the good life
-- thank the old lucky stars and the crescent moon just
gathering strength to resurrect itself once again from
the mountains out there -- oh what a terrific year it's
been! -- and if our luck holds, who knows, maybe more of
such blessings lie ahead -- but this TJM project must
end. Now. While it's still the page I was aiming all
along to end it on. Don't wanna overshoot! (And one
way or another I'll make sure I don't.)

1000

[THREE JYZE CODAS]

                     Coda 1

    He's baaaad and he's baaaack! It's a jyze
millennium that never ends!
    And it had to be here (as a car alarm goes off,
bells and whistles and whoops sound for about a minute
from the lot a hundred feet to the north) simply because
it had to be here, though I didn't realize this until
earlier today. South-hill strip park. Early Friday
evening, sun rays shafting silverishly through
impressive swirly clouds, and fitfully too, as angry
gray rain puffballs tumble overhead. I'm both indoors
and outdoors, sitting at a picnic table at the corner of
the wall-less park shelter. Orange-brick DC castle
behind, jagged city skyline and water/mountain vista
ahead, bust of the Filipino national hero and the
colorful triptych celebrating local Filusans up the
hill to the left, fields of flowers and cars to the
right, trees shakin' their assets here and there and
most everywhere -- and right behind me is a dazzling
bloom-laden camellia bush whose embrace I can almost
lean back and fold myself into.
    It's Grand Alignment day! (Everyone else is
capping it so jyze will too.)
    Yes, I feel well aligned on this day. Things going
just as they oughta. I'm again ready to move on to
concocting another project (after a few days of dazed
wandering). -- As a posse of pigeons races by on foot.
    Meanwhile all the electronic world's in an uproar
over a new computer virus known as the "I love you" bug.
It's tearing up files and whole systems everywhere, with
damage estimated to be in the billions of USAn dollars

(and maybe tens of billions if copycats proliferate, as
many are predicting they will). Supposedly the
perpetrator is a twenty-three-year-old twenty-first-
century brainiac prodigy residing in, as fortune would
have it, the Philippines, although this last-named
purported fact may turn out to be a ruse. But whoever
it is, I'd say the person is a kind of hero for
demonstrating not only the vulnerability of the system
but also the folly of having the entire world depend so
heavily on an unimaginably complex single digital
operation. -- Or say this is part of the ongoing
"conversation" about priorities for the new century.
Power is being addressed. So far it's scarcely begun to
listen. Is it likely it will at some point? Well, no,
it's not. It's got what it considers more important
things to do, such as maintaining itself in power. And
making a few zillion bucks while doing so, of course.
That way the kids of power will inherit the power of
their parents and the oligopoly will be self-sustaining.
Or so it hopes. Of course other oligopolies could arise
and turn out to be unkind to the existing ones. They
might even be doing so as I scratch these words onto
paper the old-school way, via J-stick.

It's also Cinco de Mayo. Tonight's another one of
those "grrrls' nights out" for Zoelie B. and well in
advance she's predicting the infamous margaritas at such
and such downtown watering hole will just about do her
in. (But only now do I recall Cinco de Mayo is strictly
a Mexican holiday and not one observed by all the former
Spanish colonies, for example the Philippines, except
maybe sort of vicariously.) For me it's to be a hard-
working night at the scope office, unexpectedly, with a
sudden cascade of back orders hitting yesterday.

In Korea and Japan it's Children's Day, as I've
been reminded all week by posters thickly plastered
throughout the Asian quarter, and that's relevant
here too. On Children's Day the parks and other public
places in those distant (but happily more than a little
familiar to me) lands are packed with excited and
colorfully dressed kids being taken out to mingle with

society, as tradition decrees, by their parents. And
for me the chances I'll soon be doing something like
that with my own son (in age-appropriate fashion to be
sure) got a bit of a boost just yesterday when the
promised letter from Lady S finally arrived.

     Well, not really a letter. A short note, scrawled
with obvious haste on one side of a white five-by-seven
notecard, with her address and phone number on the other.
She apologizes for the delay, saying that learning my
mother, which is to say Elgie's grandmother, was no
longer alive left her too shocked to be able to write
about "worldly things." And she says I'm welcome to
contact Elgie "if you would like to." But there's a
worrisome undertone as well -- if I'm not imagining it
-- which seems to be hinting (in Lady S's inimitable
way) that such a move might not be welcomed by Elgie.
Since our talk it's been "a sad time" for them, she
says, but she doesn't explain why. Is it because of the
news about Mother or are they fighting or what? She
says in the interim she (and he?) returned to Korea and
now this note comes from a south-central U.S. state, and
I have no idea why she might be there or what her
connection, if any, to the place is.

     So I'm mulling. Z and I talked it over in bed this
morning. I'm not about to rush in. Where Lady S is
concerned it's always wise to be cautious (and lord
knows I've often been unwise about relations with her in
the past). Nor do I want to be barging into Elgie's
life if I'm not really wanted. Move slowly, feel out
the situation, show willingness to forgive, forget,
repair, reconcile, but don't commit to anything until
things are much clearer than they are now: that's the
ticket. Z thinks so too.

     -- And the sun reappears, very bright, just above
the mountain-swaddling clouds. Within a few degrees in
one direction or another the moon and all those planets
are hanging together, from the earthly perspective,
"lined up like ducks in a row," though only the sun
itself is visible. An astronomical/astrological rarity
to be sure, this "Grand Alignment," though exactly how

rare it's tough to determine because no one with any
credibility in astronomy cares to weigh in on the matter.
I prefer to go with the view that this configuration
won't be happening again for 650 years and we're moving
into another "age" right now, today, the so-called
Aquarian. From an astrological standpoint it doesn't
make a whole lot of sense, apparently, but from a
broader "perspective of the planet" and "life on Earth"
I believe it does, or at least it could. And it had
better, or whatever life remains on Earth for human
beings, if any, won't be much worth living.

    Brrr, sun sinking, wind picking up. Traffic is
moving surprisingly well in all directions on the
freeways so topographically displayed down below. On
the grass here crows are walking. "These crows, yes,
they're made for walking. So let them walk!" -- The
economy, as of now, is still booming along. Our hilltop
dot-com headquartered in the picturesque old sixteen-
story hospital a few hundred feet directly behind me is
holding steady even as other dot-coms crash all around
it -- and that can be said for the stock market as a
whole. But for how long? To me massive economic
troubles look inevitable. How long can this grace
period at the beginning of the new era last? (The big
topic locally is still the antitrust case against the
software behemoth. Is a breakup of the company good or
bad? If it really happens, what will the effects be
locally?)

    -- May 5 is also our FF Day. Z's and mine, right.
Today we didn't celebrate it in proper fashion, or at
least not yet. And tonight probably won't be good for
that either. But all's fine on the F front, I insist,
deliciously carnal and sparky and exciting, and on the
overall nuptial front as well, and I expect all that to
continue -- our very own two-planet Grand Alignment.
(As atop the wedding cake the lightning bolts flash!)

Coda 2

The folk dancers are circling, hands linked, on the
stage in front of the friendship mural, a Norwegian flag
rippling just above their heads. Fiddles sawing away,
buses roaring by. Trees shuddering with delight. But
it's a gray day and the parade, due to start in about an
hour, could get rained on.

Yes, a fine way to end the voyage. It's the second
of this year's amazing twin Grand Alignment days -- the
next such astonishment won't arise for more than six
centuries, even the soberest observers are now saying --
and it's also the last of the millennial days of
allegedly apocalyptic portent. As of today planetary
survival appears highly probable, at least for a few
more decades. Which is not to suggest the odds for the
time after that, say four or five decades out from here,
are improving. On the contrary: they're worsening at
the fastest rate ever, and many credible experts project
this worsening will continue and even accelerate until
civilization itself collapses, or comes very close to
it.

A dark blue cross outlined with white on a red
field: here, there, everywhere. A crowd of several
hundred, mostly seated on folding chairs set up in an
arc facing the covered stage, or standing behind the
sitters. And then there's the jyzer, this jyzer right
here -- still the same Jyzer G, yup, however irrevocably
changed he may be by the events of the millennial year
-- Jyzer G hunkered down at a picnic table next to the
sound truck, back pressed against the chain-link fence
protecting the friendship mural from this madding Scandi

throng. The building just behind the mural, the old
brick hotel, burned almost to the ground a couple of
weeks ago. When the wind blows from the south you can
still smell the charred timbers.

Prior to the folk dancers, a men's chorus from the
old country. I found myself fascinated. At least a
third of the members looked like potential or likely
relatives. So do lots of folks in the audience right
now, and most of all the ones wearing budan, I think
they're called: national costumes of the trad sort. Or
is it all just psychological that so many faces seem so
familiar? (No, not all -- just a large percentage of
it. But there are good genealogical reasons to think
substantial relatedness is on display here and that the
G-genes are included. As for the meaning of this in
terms of the big picture -- enh, not so much.)

The Z-mobile's parked in a metered space a couple
of blocks down the road to the southeast. Its window of
vulnerability for a ticket is down to twenty minutes.
Earlier I stopped by Z's car-repair garage to have a
brake light replaced (the bulb was half full of water!).
Then I took a walk around the business district here,
buying a couple of cards and a hyper-kitschy fridge
magnet for the Z-wiff ("Happiness is being married to a
Norwegian") (and perhaps I should mention here I'm
wearing my "Skanky Scandi" button bought on the day of
last year's parade) and I've partaken of free milk and
cookies at no fewer than three separate shops. Is there
an ethnicity anywhere even half so corny and schmaltzy
as my own? -- Referring to the leading line of my
mongrel mix. Or the power quarter, could say, because
it's actually just a bit more than twenty-five percent
and therefore can win every internal vote, unless two or
all three of the other quarters form a bloc.

This, by the way, will be a two-part entry. Right
here is an excellent spot to bid farewell to the dragon
boat I've been sailing in for the past year (plus four
weeks or so), but an even better spot for this ceremony
lies a mile or two down the road to the west, and that's
where I'll be heading for the second part. Hint: it has

to do with this spring being the thousandth anniversary
of the first known European encounter with what much,
much later became known as the North American continent.

The small triangular park right here is named after
J-town's sister city in Norway. Those Vikings of a
millennium ago often set out on their maraudings from
the central fjord area near that city. My own
Sandefjord ancestors of the time were tending their
cows, most likely, within a few days' walking distance
of the city, and probably some were on those marauding
boats too. 1070, it says on the mural, was the founding
date for the sister city. The first Norwegian arrived
here in J-town, it also says, 150 years ago.

(Problems with the sound system. Too loud. A
Norwegian folksinger, deep voice, Knute somebody
wouldn't you know, he's telling us he just got off a
fishing boat this morning. He's backed by a truly
dynamic accordionist.) -- A lot's being made here of
the local anniversary, the 150th, but not of the
1,000th. But the latter's been hot nationally. Vikings
everywhere: on the covers of the national weekly
newsmagazines, in all the newspapers -- even the
ultimate, a documentary on public TV (which I missed).

To my left I see big crowds gathering along the
sidewalks of the main drag. It's just about parade
time. The folksinger's slowly losing his audience even
though the accordionist is wheezing it out in ever more
virtuoso fashion. Before much longer the two of them
may be serenading me alone.

-- Also earlier today -- much earlier, as in an
hour past midnight -- I mailed off my reply to Lady S's
note. It's just a couple of pages and it's trying hard
to be friendly and encouraging. But I do ask her to
pass the word along to Elgie that he should drop me a
line if he's interested. I gave the matter a lot of
thought. I'm sure his mother means well (and always
did), but I'm also afraid she's the one who's pushing
this reconciliation and she's refusing to acknowledge
the degree to which she's, to use my mother's favored
term for the lady's influence on him, "poisoned his

mind" against me (and the lady did this, of course, for what she believed were excellent moral reasons) and he's not really interested. And if he's not, I don't believe it would be good for either of us to try to force the issue. And if he does want to go ahead, then I think we should go slowly, starting with snail mail -- give ourselves plenty of time to absorb any shocks.

    -- Concert now ending. All chairs suddenly empty. A few people standing around chatting, and above the chatter, the sound of a distant brass band. The parade's coming! As a news helicopter thwack-thwacks by directly overhead, flying low. Dozens of small flags, U.S. and Norwegian, flutter energetically, still attached to the empty chairs. Police motorcycles rumble. The sound-system guy warns me he needs to pull in the orange heavy-duty wire running along the base of the fence right beneath me and now he's doing that.

*   *

    -- Finishing up at the marina. Couldn't be a better spot -- but the weather might be improved upon. No rain, though, yet. Late sun illuminating some thin seams here and there in the clouds but haze clinging to the water. The jagged mountains on the other side, so spectacular when they can be seen from here, are hidden today.

    Calm water in the enclosed marina. Hundreds of masts but not one is moving even slightly. I'm looking up an aisle between two rows of good-size sailboats, roughly two dozen on each side, a breakwater at the end, a big oceanbound freighter chugging by on the far side of that and also a little chartreuse-sailed sailboat limping along -- reminds me of my father and his sorry fate.

    As does this spot itself. It's a memorial to the Norwegian national hero of a thousand years ago. Two pine trees, or junipers maybe, flank a reflecting pool right at my back -- no water in it, but lots of pinecones -- and just behind it, maybe ten yards distant, a statue of the great man stands atop a pedestal. It's well-greened bronze, the statue is,

1010

roughly double life-size, and the pedestal's another
twelve feet tall. The hero in a tunic, sword at his
waist, hand resting on a long-handled ax. He's wearing
a historically correct hornless Viking helmet, gazing
out across the water. (As now, halfway up the bluff on
the far side of the parking lot and road, a freight
train appears with a screeching rumble and a long line
of double-stack container cars goes rolling by through
the trees, heading north along the edge of the sound and
then through the mountains and into the interior.) (And
a big white dog comes sniffing up, friendly, his nose
twitching for a moment right above this page -- could be
an exceptionally well-trained narc dog, I'm thinking --
followed, though, by a smiling young Cawk woman in a
maroon track suit. But no one else is around, except, I
now see, a Glennarian second-stager Cawk couple in a
rowboat down below, and now that I know they're there I
can even hear their oarlocks creaking with each stroke.)

     This statue, I learn from the inscription, was
dedicated on June 17 of 1962, the summer of the world's
fair and probably within a week of the day I arrived in
this city for the first time. But until last week, when
I came across a mention of the statue in the paper, I
didn't even know it existed. Or if I did, I took so
little notice of it I'd entirely forgotten about it.

     On this side of the statue the great Norseman's
name is spelled in a bizarre way with three more letters
than one usually sees. On the other side it's the plain
old USAnized version -- and the statue was presented to
the citizens of Jyze City by a local Scandi-quarter club
named after the hero, and they too go with the standard
USAn spelling. (As another freight train appears, this
one rumbling along in the opposite direction.) -- And
if this bronze statue were flesh-and-blood and had eagle
eyes, as it indeed appears to, it could be reading this
jyze tribute to itself/himself over my left shoulder.

     The statue is modeled after one in the Norwegian
sister city. A close-up photo of the head of that one
appears on the cover of this month's Scandi newsletter,
a copy of which I picked up last week when I was out

here in the SQ. When Z saw the photo she said she
thought it looked a lot like me.   "It's the bones. And
that resolute look. Got to, got to, just got to put
that TJM project to bed." (I showed her the newly typed
version of Book A and she likes the title.) But I can't
make too much of the resemblance -- can't, for example,
start calling myself by the hero's first name -- because
she once had a boyfriend by that same first name, Leif.
Leif L. I'd totally forgotten about him. This kind of
thing can happen, though, because she's got the right
kind of ex-boyfriend numbers for it. A fact which I
like because in some deep sense it keeps me honest and
also alert, I'll say.

The Norskis who left Norway to settle Iceland in
the ninth and tenth centuries C.E. also established a
settlement in Greenland about the same time as they
explored the eastern coast of North America and settled
in for a short period at L'Auxe Meadows in Nova Scotia.
Greenland was probably the base for the North American
expedition. But eventually, right around the start in
the 1400s of what's known as the Little Ice Age, the
Norse settlement on Greenland disappeared. And now,
just weeks ago, scientists have discovered it's likely
the ice in Greenland is melting because of global
warming. They're saying that if it all melts, as many
expect will happen, sea levels will rise as much as
twenty feet. And if the Greenland ice goes, the
Antarctic ice will all but certainly follow, causing a
further sea-level rise of roughly two hundred feet and
unimaginable catastrophe worldwide.

So this seemed to be the ideal spot to bring TJM to
a close. -- And the moon should itself be rising just
about now (it will go full tomorrow and was gorgeous at
midnight last night, a glowing white ball at the center
of a "galloping galleon" riding atop a sea of storm-
tossed clouds in which were submerged the hidden
nautical hazards of downtown J. City's skyscrapers) --
but tonight the clouds are hiding the moon. And I, on a
Wednesday night, must be getting down to the scope
office.

1012

Coda 3

One more time, just one.

End of the Gregorian year. This way, should some future tribunal decide the "real" millennium year wasn't the year 2000 after all but rather 2001, TJM still gets to put at least a toe down in the newly declared year one of the third millennium and twenty-first century of the so-called Common Era. And also just so the J-slinger can tighten up a few loose slings, so to speak. And just so the J-slinger can sling, period. Got to, got to, got to. After this the rationales for any further codas become too strained to pass muster.

We're about four hours into the last day of December of the year 2000 by Julian/Gregorian count. Later today I'm planning to do a bit of jyzing downtown -- I've set aside the time for this well in advance -- and then Z and I will be heading up to east hill in search of a spot where we can tandem-jyze out the year (jyze bougaloos down main street at the midnight hour!). And then, after a night's sleep, a few last thoughts on the first day of the new year and that'll be it. (I was thinking of stretching this coda out a day or two further yet, with one final postscript on the Feast of the Epiphany, 6th of January, last day of Christmas, anniversary day for the sages' arrival from the East to bestow empathetic blessing on the aborning religion of the West. And maybe I will do that. When I write it out the idea starts to sound pretty good again. But if I don't do it, this ever-expanding parenthesis right here partakes at least a little, I hope, of the

epiphanic glow.)
     So I'm jyzing again. Self-indulgently too. But
discipline is hard after such a long period away from
the game. And I'm working on a celebratory house
bourbon on the rocks. As the fifth hour of jazz plays.
Usually the news starts at four a.m. but on Friday and
Saturday nights the music runs for an extra hour. It's
canned and sometimes it's completely jockless.
Talkless. Spotless, in the sense of being without
public-service announcements or any other kind. And
that's tonight. Best hour of radio all week as far as
I'm concerned.
     Secrets of the night people.
     -- This from the black armchair. I suppose all's
pretty much the same as it was the last time jyze went
down at this spot (though I don't recall exactly when
that was). The clutter in this room's probably a little
ranker than it was back then, but for a good reason, and
I'll be getting to that in a bit. But through the
windows, I want to say, I see the same row of white
icicle holiday lights as were on display last year
hanging from the second-story eaves of the motel-like
building across the street, with "Seasons [sic]
Greetings" and the vague outline of a Santa face blazing
from the sign at the center, also just as last year.
But something's different there too: an energy crisis is
upon us and city officials are requesting that residents
light holiday displays only "as necessary." And a whole
lot of folks seem to be interpreting this to mean they
should keep them on constantly. And so, as the wag
says: more power to them, of the electrical variety.
But therefore that much less, alas, to everyone else.
     A whole year to catch up on. Or actually no, just
seven months and a couple of weeks. But that still
requires an extremely high level of generality and
abstractness (almost like that Santa face, could say --
or no, maybe not).
     For world news it's been the year of the burst dot-
com bubble (and of deepening crises involving AIDS and
refugees and global roasting and species extinction --

but these have become so much a part of the landscape
they've scarcely even been noticed -- or because they're
so inconvenient to the aims of the power brokers they're
flat-out denied or swept under the rug: and of course
nothing new here either).

Nationally it's been the year of the dead-heat
presidential election eventually stolen with Supreme
Court connivance by the more rightward of the two major
parties, putting that wing of the establishment back in
power (starting just twenty-two days from now): and oh
is it gonna be an ugly four years (and just pray it
won't be twelve or more, like the last go-round starting
twenty years ago with pretty much this same hard-right
bunch in charge).

Locally it's been the year of WTO aftershocks and,
again, dot-com shakeouts, with last year's Man of the
Year, who's still installed in the DC castle a little
over a block from our apartment here, now more likely to
be chosen "Schmuck of the Year." His company's stock
has lost eighty-five percent of its value! But this
also means, when that shocking loss is combined with
similar ones for other former high-flying high-tech
companies in our area, that the real-estate boom in Jyze
City is over. And this directly impinges on our lives,
Z's and mine, in important ways (for us).

Another big local story is the strike that began in
mid-November against the two daily newspapers. Just in
the past day or two it's been half-settled. The paper
that hasn't settled, the former afternoon one (FAP), I'm
giving up on entirely because of the shoddy union-
busting tactics it's used. I'm seizing the day: less
time reading news means more time for jyzing or jyze
typing. (Z sees it the same way: she too is done with
the FAP. And we'll both miss the strike tabloid put out
three times weekly by the best writers from the staffs
of both dailies operating independently.)

On a personal level, I've tallied them up and I can
think of three big surprises. Two of these involve
detailed explanations so I'll save them until later, but
one is general and simple: it's the fact that by and

large on all fronts the personal news is good. And I
guess it follows syllogistically that the other two big
surprises must therefore be good too. -- And I'm
furiously knocking on wood here, literally, on the
chairside table, using my left hand, as the J-stick
scrawls onward.

Tonight we saw a movie with our co-explorers of
Glennarian Third Stage racially mixed marriage, Wei and
Alison. It was the Chinese swordfight flick "Crouching
Tiger, Flying Dragon." Talk about overhype -- yeeesh!

After the movie a late dinner at W&A's place, the
Christmas tree (a five-buck special and even so quite
handsome) blazing away right next to the dinner table
but still more impressively, even hypnotically so for me
-- better than anything in the movie -- in double
reflection on the wavy glass of the French doors leading
out to the porch and also, but differently, on the porch
windows, with the standing lights farther down the
hillside and in the valley seeming to shift in place as
I moved my head and the doubly reflected lights from the
living room holding steady behind them. Some dazzling
parallaxes there. And some warm and sappy moments
during the lengthy dinner. I was especially touched
when Wei brought forth for our inspection the year 2001
journal he'd made for Alison, the cover a blend of
digital photos of the two of them he'd put together on
his computer.

-- Perched across the room on the art table (back
here in 203 now) is my own Christmas present for Z.
It's a thirty-by-forty canvas, acrylic, bearing a much
enlarged likeness of the first postcard she sent me
(from the mountain resort) and various other emblems of
those very early weeks in our time together. It also
contains twenty-six reduced-size pages of jyze written
after the reception of that postcard but before we'd
actually met. The title is written in large letters on
the painting itself, sort of like on a dust-jacket front
cover for a book except the long dimension of the
rectangle here is horizontal rather than vertical: "Jyze
Meditations on the Disembodied Zoelie B. (Part 2)."

[Three Jyze Codas]

(Part 1, not yet in existence, will cover the period
from first sighting of her ad to arrival of the card she
sent me from the mountain resort where her classes were
meeting that week.)
     I'm still working on the painting. But I also gave
her a printed booklet version of the "Jyze Meditations"
and that was a big hit. At five a.m. Christmas morning
she read it all the way through right after I presented
it. She was sitting in the green armchair in the
bedroom, I was stretched out on the bed. Every time she
chuckled or laughed out loud or reacted in any other
detectable way I asked her to tell me what she was
reacting to. It was a magical hour. "This reads like a
novel." She bawled a couple of times. "This is my best
Christmas present ever. It's like a dream."
     Jyze's first venture into the real world. Z is its
first reader other than me. (Well, and Lady U and old
Mom. What am I thinking? So, a correction: it's jyze's
third such venture, but the first in five years.)
     Her gifts were marvelous too. There were two: a
wall hanging featuring the conservative Hollywood icon
her mother amusingly thinks I look like -- this shows
him in his Rooster Cogburn role in "True Grit" -- and a
beer tray (to replace my rusted-out "From the Land of
Sky-blue Waters" tray) and both personalized with
numerous painterly additions of her own.
     But I won't try to deny it: I'm still wholly caught
up in "Jyze Meditations." This is a crucial time for
me. I love the way this stuff is turning out.
     And I love the way this marriage is turning out.
It's only got fifteen months on its nuptometer, of
course, but as of tomorrow we'll be entering our fourth
year of living together. I'm more deeply attached than
ever to this Zoelie B. And still crazy in love. Just
wanna say so right now. Repeat. Repeat. Gush gush
gush. (Love is farcical this way, oh is it ever.)
     -- But more for the lovey-dovey stuff later. The
love interest herself will be putting in a personal
appearance right here in these pages -- taking a well-
deserved bow! Meanwhile I'll just mention a few more

things "of topical interest" (he said hopefully) and
I'll be outta here for now since it's almost six (and
now here's the tap-tap on 203's windows of rain starting
up, almost as if the game's been suspended and the
ground crew's preparing to roll out the tarp across the
jyze infield).

First, a huge plant with leaves like hands (but
closer to baseball mitts in size) stands majestically
atop our dining table at the far end of the room. It
belongs to Dana and Raphael, our landlords, who are away
in Italy for three months. But they'll be returning,
and when they do they'll be staying on in this city,
moving out of their current double apartment across the
hall from us (both 201 and 202) and probably into a
house on east hill, though maybe temporarily into
another apartment upstairs here. After spending several
weeks with their families on the far coast this past
summer they decided to drop the idea of moving back
there permanently: too much in-law friction on both
sides. And because of the drastic change in the real-
estate market here (especially in this hood) they've
decided to drop for at least the next couple of years
their plans to condoize this building. And because
their apartment across the hall on the west side of the
building (number 201) will be opening up and because it
offers several advantages over this one, Z and I are
pretty well agreed we'll move there. (But I'll come
back to this later if I can: the twisted course of the
housing saga.)

Another extremely topical matter, about as topical
as they get, is the hair-dissolving drain cleaner I
applied tonight in yet another effort to unclog the sink
in the big bathroom. I checked right before starting
back in on the jyze and it appears not to have worked.
More drastic measures will be called for, namely the
truly heavy-duty industrial stuff they sell at the home-
goods superstore.

Don't want to stop. But must. (And by the way,
the krazy klock is still chugging away atop the record-
album boxes directly across the room. A huge geranium

graces the center of the coffee table, with blooms
aplenty still in view though winter scraggliness is
gaining. A dozen newly framed altered-art cards from
my ongoing wedding-present project are on display here
and there around the room. (The card count is up to
about seven hundred now but the project's on hold until
I put the last of the finishing touches on the Christmas
canvas, which will probably take weeks.) And here's a
stack of Z's dust-jacketed mysteries from the library --
here on the rug near my feet, I mean, and these are
mysteries of the whodunit kind in which all the
detectives are female. And at the far end of the coffee
table a batch of Christmas cards standing half open,
including even, already, a couple of thank-you notes.
     Okay, stop.

                        [+1]

     East-depot saloon. Still pretty much the same old
dive. Just not so crowded as I would've expected at
five p.m. on the last day of -- to yield to the hype du
jour -- the week, the month, the quarter, the year, the
decade, the century, and the millennium. And yeah,
that's the old DYCM and then some. By one kind of
calendar anyway, and one way of reading it.
     My favorite secluded booth beneath one of the high-
mounted TVs is occupied at the moment. Instead I'm
looking straight at it from across the room. I've
grabbed the small table set alongside the cedar-paneled
wall (reminds me of my shed of peninsula days) midway
between the doors for the men's and women's restrooms
and across a narrow aisle from the rear counter with its
row of high backless barstools, none occupied at the
moment; and behind that counter (which is used only for
grill customers) are three shelves of Christmas
knickknacks, including, on top, an idealized English
village with each building lit up from inside and
angel's hair serving as huge snowdrifts. Odd to see
such a display set up here among all the grungy street

folks, hardcore urbanites, pensioners, recently released
jailbirds, and (probably the majority right now) Latusan
day workers, and also a few probable Natusans.
(Football on the tube, and on the box country'n'western
fighting it out with classic hard-driving rock.)
     The walk down. A nostalgic feel to it. Right at
sunset I gazed out from the high bridge at the deeply
familiar yet ever-changing panoramic scene. Latest
noticeable big change: framework for the new football
stadium's bleachers has risen where the domed stadium
used to be. At this stage it looks sort of like the
hull of a huge wooden ship being constructed upside
down. And above me to my left stood the orange-brick DC
castle with its big white holiday star ablaze on top and
the full-building floodlights already turned on for the
evening. One infuriating change there is that the new
parking garage is now up and running (where a splendid
grove of evergreens used to stand just west of the main
building), but a bigger change is not visible and won't
be and is therefore positive: the two large towers which
were to rise in the parking lot, completely blocking the
view of the main landmark edifice not just from the
bridge but from much of the valley, downtown, east hill
and many other points north -- that construction plan
has now been shelved indefinitely owing to the
precarious financial condition of the dot-com occupying
the DC castle. (Today's far-coast paper's year-end
wrap-up in the business pages shows the dot-com's CEO
pictured in a red-bordered parody of the "Man of the
Year" magazine cover and it's labeled "Tank." No doubt
that photo will be serving as a dartboard in a lot of
venues around this town tonight.)
     And down below the high bridge, in the greenbelt
"jungle/rez" between freeway sections and to either side
of them, at least a dozen small, scattered drifter
encampments were visible. In the bushes just a few feet
from where that first TJM entry went down on the bridge
some twenty months ago, two men were talking; their
somewhat menacing look and sound persuaded me to move
farther out on the bridge. -- And two blocks past that,

nearing the foodbank, I had to cross the street twice,
winding up on the same side where I started, to avoid
clusters of rowdy homeless men. It's gotten a bit
chancier down there in recent months and now I usually
stick to the main roads on my way in.

    But I still love the walk. And it's livelier than
before, with more businesses opening up, mostly in the
Vietnamese section as it expands in all directions from
its epicenter two blocks north of the bridge. (Right
now I'm feeling it for all the people being turned away
here at the saloon for want of ID or being asked to
leave because they're not buying anything -- and the
woman whose job it is to do the eighty-sixing. Many of
these men are carrying big packs and blanket rolls and
appear to be living on the streets. According to the
strike newspaper the homeless population sleeping
outdoors downtown is about the same as it was last year
-- somewhere slightly over a thousand. Over two
thousand more are sleeping in city shelters.)

    -- It's filling up rapidly here and there's
pressure from the milling crowd, some folks in a
belligerent state, so I'm thinking I'll move on.
(Sudden shift of plans.) "Good place to write down your
memories, man," opines one cheery dude. No doubt he's
got more than a few highly jyzable tales of his own.

                    *   *

    -- And now, a few minutes later, it's the lobby of
the west depot one block west of the east-depot saloon.
The room's almost empty -- I can still hear the clanging
of a train's bell as it pulls out. An Afrusan janitor
maybe about my age, a woman, pushes a broom and
eventually she'll get to my area but I don't think
she'll question my presence. I bought a vending-machine
soda and I have lots of railroad travel handouts stacked
on the seat next to me. By looks alone I'm a borderline
case at best, even now while wearing my best black
"dress" jeans. But I'm sitting right by the arrivals/
departures board adjacent to Door 1 and I'm ready to
gaze at that board with a puzzled look and fiddle with
a brochure or two if doing so seems advisable.

Those big new buildings put up by plutocrat #2,
who's back again now to being one of the world's five
richest people even though his holdings have shrunk in
value by an eleven-figure sum in just the past year --
the buildings standing in the block between here and the
east-depot saloon, I'm talking about -- they've all
opened for business, and so has the new home of the A-
mart right across from several of those same buildings.
So far, however, the Asian quarter feels little
different, and in fact the attempt to open a corporate
fast-food burger franchise has been beaten back. But
the pressures for development in the area are still
immense and growing despite the economic slowdown.
        One other item. The wooden bench I used to like to
sit on by the streetcar terminus is gone. A streetcar
lost its brakes and plowed through it, injuring dozens
of bystanders. Now the bench and flowerbox have been
replaced by a large concrete block intended to stop any
future runaways. (And here's the same janitor, pulling
a rickety old metal-wheeled baggage cart loaded with
upright black-plastic inner linings she's lifting from
the trash cans, slowly moving around the waiting room --
pulling the cart herself like a horse or a rickshaw
woman.) (And poking out from the top of one bag,
several red leaves of a still intact poinsettia.)
        Six p.m. New Year's Eve. The next train's not due
in until 8:25 and that's the continental I used to ride
for my visits to see old Mom and the board says it's
"OT," meaning on time. (The board probably lies. It
says everything up there is "OT" and that's unheard of.
Whoever's responsible for updating it probably figures
the night's too slow to bother. Or just a skeleton
crew's working tonight and has too much else to do.)
        When I left the apartment today I found a card from
Z leaning against the wall outside our unit 203 door.
(She'd taken off an hour earlier to do some shopping
after a plan to see "Chocolat" with Aida and Adele fell
through at the last moment.) "Happy 2001!" A fine
surprise. Typical Z though: she just loves to surprise
me (and I her). -- And inside the card a note

concerning our long-ongoing conversation, I'll call it,
about romance and TLC. I'd like her to be a little more
romantic in loving (that is, lovemaking; that is, sex);
she has her doubts about romance because of its
patriarchal roots. But then I have similar doubts, and
have explored them ad nauseam for a quarter of a century
or so. I'm pleased as punch to be with a woman who's
interested in advancing this conversation and wants to
think about such things critically. Just so long as it
won't interfere too much with the loving. And she says
much the same thing.

   -- So I wound up going back inside and writing her
a note. I also left a paperback book about Romanticism
on my chair next to the note and also a big fat
dictionary open to its definition of romance, with the
note saying definitions B and C were the ones I was
referring to -- having to do with "ardent emotional
attachment" and "aura of enchantment" (but I should note
I'm going by memory here).

   Her note points out that her doubts about romance
evolved in much the same way as did mine about S&M.
This is where the balancing point lies right now: if I'd
like her to be a little mushier and smoochier, she'd
like me to be a little more machoistically dominating at
certain times. So issues of political correctness
arise. In fact it's a conversation we've been having
since very early on, breaking out sporadically, until we
hit the sore-point limits and realize once again the
matter's better left as a tacit compromise in which
neither of us is too critical or demanding of the other.

   I expect we'll hit that point again later tonight,
possibly while we're up bougalooing down main street.

   Empty room. Hum of the vending machines but no
other sounds. Well, no, a lower hum of the heating
system. Still the same shamefully ugly room, a false
ceiling hung low so that the old cathedral vastness is
hidden, with only the intricately patterned floor tiles
suggesting the former glory. -- And no freight trains
going by tonight. New Year's Eve, and it's also Sunday.
And I'm thinking I'll move on again: make this into a

night of many jyze venues.

*   *

     -- Now the hideaway. The stop here must be brief.
In seventy minutes I'll be meeting Z up at the scope
office -- or no, I'll be calling her then and it would
just about have to be from there (most downtown pay
phones are shut off at night and of course I don't carry
a cellphone). Then she'll be picking me up there,
outside, an hour later.
     I blew thirty minutes here reading some old jyze.
Then just when I was about to hit the head, the janitors
showed up and temporarily shut down both of them, men's
and women's (it's the same Hmong family as before). My
bathroom keys work on only those two bathrooms and none
of the other dozen in the building. Pretty soon I
discovered I couldn't wait for the crew to finish the
cleaning: and so I used the jumbo peanut-butter jar
(empty, yes) I keep on hand for just such emergencies.
(And right now the boxes and bags of trash tossed down
from the balconies of the upper floors are exploding
outside my door and windows. No problem, though; I'm
totally used to it. As one of the negative trade-offs
for being a night worker it's easily acceptable.)
     This office is basically the same as it was eight
months ago but it's been through a lot, as has the rest
of the building. For years a leak in the northwest
corner of the roof went undetected and finally this past
fall a toxic mold originating there got into the
ventilation system. From what I hear, a dozen people
were hospitalized and many more sickened -- most of them
from the upper floors in that corner of the building.
But the whole structure and everything inside it had to
be decontaminated, and that was a complicated process
that took three months (the last blowers were removed
ten days ago) and caused massive disruption for resident
businesses. Making matters far worse, the entire
process was poorly managed -- outrageously so -- and now
I'm told a number of the tenants are suing. (To manage
matters so badly in a building roughly one-quarter
tenanted by law firms hurting for business is foolish

1024

indeed.)
     This office right here was invaded -- with no
forewarning at all -- five separate times, and the fifth
time it was pretty much turned upside down, with
everything shifted about and all freestanding items on
desks and shelves unceremoniously tossed into eight
large cardboard boxes which were then stacked atop the
desk and the armchair in which I now sit. The window
above my left shoulder was forced open and left that
way, meaning anyone could've climbed in. What a shock
it was when I opened the door upon arrival that day!
(The boxed items included all my research clippings and
notes, many of which had been mixed up willy-nilly.)
For the next month the office was unusable as a huge
blower roared right outside the open window. Trying to
put things back in order was pointless because there was
no assurance they wouldn't be rudely disordered again.
     I could've done like the lawyers and some others:
gone postal. Z thought I should. But I love this place
and I appreciate the relatively low rent. Nothing like
this would be available elsewhere downtown at twice or
maybe even three times the price. So I held back and
simply enclosed notes with my monthly payment, which for
the past two months I've unilaterally reduced by eighty
percent (and will do so again this month, probably for
the last time). I also provided written explanations,
"objectively" couched. They've accepted them so far,
and I think they'll continue to do so.
     As a result I'll have saved, assuming the owner
accepts this month's reduced check like the others, a
little over four hundred bucks. Since I was able to do
all my work elsewhere the only real loss to me was the
dozen or so hours it took to shape the place up again
(including gluing back together the large filing cabinet
which the invaders damaged). So, ironically I feel like
I'm coming out ahead. But it might easily have been
otherwise, because my office is in the northeast corner
and I'm told someone in the office two doors from mine
fell sick and was hospitalized for several days. So I
lucked out in a big way. (From what I hear, all the

damage is covered by insurance. There's even reason to believe the annual rent hike won't exceed the expected cost-of-living increase.)

     -- As now, at six minutes to eight, I can hear the band starting to warm up for the New Year's Eve bash at the rock venue down below. And there'll be one at the hip-hop club as well.

     Another change in here is that the three large sheets of plywood and the dozen or so two-by-four studs are gone. I've given up on the idea of constructing a hideaway loft. As I'm seeing things now, my hold on the place is too tenuous to justify the labor. And the contamination uproar enabled me to unload all that wood with no problem at all: I simply left it out in the hall. A good half of the contents of the offices on this floor was already out there. And within a few days two of the plywood sheets were cut up to cover broken windows and doors -- there was a fire too, confined to a single office directly across the hall from mine, the one where the jungle animals used to dwell, seemingly, their cries emanating from an audio tape intended to comfort a pet parrot while the tenant was away at night -- and the studs had completely vanished. (As has Robert the Afrusan acupuncturist, by the way, from his office whose entrance shares the vestibule with mine -- gone as of today. He moved in early this past summer.)

     And then for a week before Christmas I worked here on painting the Christmas "Jyze Meditations" canvas for Z. That's why a few specks of acrylic paint can be spotted on the carpet where none ever appeared before. And several hours of cleanup work remain for me before the place will be truly back to normal. As yet few of the tchotchkes have returned to the shelves. The little family memorial corner is a shambles. And many of the clippings for this TJM project will have to be redistributed. -- But as I say, I'm okay with all of this. "Shit happens." On balance it's been a helluva lucky year.

     -- Those two big surprises I mentioned earlier, they both have to do with family, and one with my own

preexisting family, so I thought I'd lay them out here.
Now I see the time's too short. But I can at least
mention a couple of other surprises. And one's a piece
of bad news: just yesterday Rob called to let us know
the company he works for will be shutting down all its
bookselling operations, including his store, sometime in
January, and for good. Although his store is still
profitable, the company's overall book division isn't,
or is just marginally so. It can't compete with the big
chains and especially not with internet operations, and
mainly those of the dot-com headquartered on our hilltop
(yes, the one whose CEO Wall Street has labeled, perhaps
prematurely, "Tank"). Rob himself has been offered his
old position as manager of the classical-music section
at the company's store out in the Yuke and he's also
eligible for what he described as a "real good severance
package"; he's undecided on which way he'll go. But he
was depressed over the news, and all of the lower north-
hill area will be too, I'm sure, when they hear about
it. His shop is the heart of the commercial zone there.
     At home, though, he has something to lift his
spirits: a skylight which a carpenter installed in his
garret study. He proudly showed it off when Z and I
dropped by the other day -- Christmas Eve -- with our
gifts, including an electronic singing Christmas card.
     That'll have to be it for now. I've left myself
just barely enough time to make it up to the scope
office for the call.

*   *

     -- This is interesting. A whole tableful -- a
spread, farther than my arms can reach! -- of Christmas
goodies. Cookies, candy, cake, canes. And another
tableful of much the same, but smaller portions across
the board, up by the receptionist's desk.
     I'm throwing all caution aside. This is pig-out
night. (But first I dutifully downed my minipack of
canned tuna salad and crackers.) Gobble gobble.
Crunch. Suck.)
     I hadn't figured on doing the jyze thing up here
tonight. But what the heck. Both of my usual chain

1027

burger joints are closed for New Year's Eve and so are
the two backup grills and the ground-zero teriyaki place
(I walked by 'em all on the way here). And the digital
clock on the phone says it's 9:05. Forty minutes to
blow. If I jyze hard and fast maybe I'll pig out less
and no extra WOC workouts will be required this week.

On the phone I changed the meeting time to quarter
to ten. How come, Z wanted to know. "I need every
minute!" I cried. "Whoa!" she exclaimed. "You sound
just a little hyper!" And I was. As revelers swarmed
on all sides -- including a guy whose silver cardboard
top hat bopped me as he rolled by: "Happy New Year to
you too!" Dressed-up folks. Babes and foxes and hunks
and studs. Street drunks getting into it. -- This from
the pay phone down in the HQ triangle, right in front of
where the sandwich shop used to be. That shop closed
about four months ago; the windows are covered on the
inside now with butcher paper. I'd say the triangle at
this point is probably at the nadir of its boom/bust
cycle. But it still rocks out every now and then, and
tonight will be one of those times.

Straight up the old edge road I hoofed it, past the
long lines of twenty-somethings standing outside the
main performance venue near the public market. (A funk
group is the headliner there tonight and I'm glad to see
that kind of music seems to be coming back.) And then
over to the middle road, trudging directly toward the
hovering Christmas-cone-bedecked saucer of the Jyze City
icon-of-icons (it appears to be wearing a dunce hat).
Will someone nefarious try to take it out tonight?
(Last year's alleged terrorist bombers are still
languishing in jail, the trial having been postponed
several times. Naomi's Larry remains on the case, doing
lots of traveling, she tells me, but so far the
government's come up with no breakthrough evidence.)
-- Big crowds are expected at the fairgrounds for the
fireworks show at midnight. For me it was a matter of
choosing between that and someplace where I could hope
to sit down across a table from Z and we could do some
tandem jyzing. If no place better with empty seats

presents itself on the east-hill strip we're thinking we
might wind up in the cafe section of one of the twenty-
four-hour supermarkets. Surely they're not charging a
bundle at the door there.

     As I mostly unconsciously munch my way through a
bag of chocolate-covered cherries. Whoa, gotta leave at
least a few in there!

     New doings right here -- the table itself. Brand-
new. The old oval conference table which had served the
firm ever since my first days as a nightscoper -- two
decades ago -- and which I'd worked at and napped under
hundreds of times if not thousands, just in the past
week it was unceremoniously sawed into pieces and hauled
off to make room for this new monster. Glass-covered.
Rectangular with forty-five-degree truncated corners.
And matching new wheeled lean-back armchairs to go with
it. And two new rolling cupboards like huge consoles,
also matching. My poor little computer's been shoved
into a corner -- and it's not even mine anymore!

     It's like this. The scope firm (which is to say,
reporter Naomi) won the new grand-jury contract, and one
clause of it stipulates that the firm must own the
computers used for working on the transcripts. So I
sold those ancient machines back to the firm for a grand
total of fifty bucks, with the spoken (but not written)
understanding they'll sell them back to me at the same
price when the contract ends or if I leave. And this
contract is for five years! Which means, unless Naomi
falls sick or is newly injured or her old carpal tunnel
worsens or she must move to another city, I've pretty
much got a job guaranteed right up to my earliest
possible Social Security retirement age. So most likely
I'll be winding up my "day job" career right here, doing
the same old same old. And that's just fine with me.

     -- But I'd better pack it in now. 9:37. Z the
ABE's probably parked down there already. I'll be back
here tomorrow night to do GJ finals and if time allows
I'll carry on with this then. (And part of what I'm
packing in is a big baggy of the office cinnamon
Christmas cookies.)

[The Jyze Millennium]

                    *   *

   -- The waiter led me over to the bar so I could set
my watch by the TV. (Make that server, not waiter.
Waiters ceased to exist decades ago. What am I
thinking?) "They're doing the countdown in there," he
said. But they weren't. "Nah, too early," the
bartender said. But then a customer at the bar brought
out a truly fancy pocket watch and assured me he had set
it by "the atomic clock" earlier today. So I calibrated
my watch with his. And now, back at the table, the same
server just returned, wanting to calibrate the main
microwave clock in the kitchen with my watch because the
customer had left! The cafe's celebration is dependent
on my totally untrustworthy watch!
   Chain cafe on the east-hill main drag, up at the
north end, just around the corner from the movie
theater. A fine low-rent joint, it turns out, much
better than either of us expected, with pop-culture
decor and reasonable prices. Even a couple of students
with books and laptops laid out on booth tables. And
two-thirds of the tables are unoccupied, meaning there's
no pressure to make room for someone else. We're here
for the long haul into 01/01/01. And it won't be that
long actually: just nineteen minutes now. And I was
warned that the "Dutch Baby" I ordered takes at least
twenty minutes to rise in the oven. (A Dutch Baby is a
custard-filled pancake. I never knew.)
   Two glasses of wine. Tandem jyze. "Sunglasses" on
the box at the moment, the double Z's and they're tops.
   Nothing could be finer!
   The Z-mobile is parked down at the other end of the
main drag, across from the community-college campus. As
we pulled up, a big crowd of several hundred was milling
around on the campus lawn, drums pounding, we knew not
why and no one we asked could tell us. We left them and
walked north, stopping at the hoppin' cheapo local
drive-in chain for burgers and fries which we ate
standing up outdoors at the one table, beneath the sign.
Then we hiked all the way to the north end of the strip,
spotting three or four potential jyze sites, including

this one, en route, then trekked all the way back to see
if the supermarket cafe (a block past the campus) was
open, since it seemed more promising at that point, but
it was closed -- a janitor inside was lifting chairs
atop tables. So then we hoofed it back up here.
     (The server just told us everyone will be gathering
in the bar at five to twelve for the countdown. We're
welcome to join them (meaning, it would seem, we've not
previously been considered part of the aforementioned
"everyone"). Z thinks this guy, who's surely gay (and
Cawk), is flirting with me. I think we're his best
prospect for a decent tip.)
     -- And our orders arrive. Wow: Z's plate of
blueberry pancakes is huge. And the Dutch Baby ain't
bad. Sort of like a hot apple fritter. It's sitting
picture perfect, almost -- just one bite missing -- only
inches to the right of my jyzing hand and giving off
some real fine fragrance. But it's four minutes before
the hour.
     "Say goodbye," I say.
     "To what?"
     "To DYCM."
     "Omigod, I'd forgotten all about DYCM! -- But does
that still work for this year too?"
     "It's the same old DYCM, just slightly revised."
     "Because jyze says so?"
     "Yeah."
     A cry goes up from the chef: "Two minutes!"
     We're staying at our corner window table,
nonsmoking section near the door.
     (Mmmm, good, bite number two of Dutch Baby.)
     Once again the dot inside the brackets means we're
there and the celebration of a thousand years of history
is now itself finally history:

[.]

     (And then we raise our wine glasses, clink! And I
step around the table to present Z-wiff with an ardent
celebratory kiss -- surprises her, this does. Good!

-- As earlier she surprised me, twice, but in different
ways, after the "Happy 2001" card of this afternoon.
Tonight when we met she was wearing -- and still is -- a
homemade heart-shaped pin-on button proclaiming
"ardently emotional attachment," as specified by
dictionary definition number two of "romance." And then
as we started walking up the strip she brought forth an
"uncertified" envelope containing "tween-toe fungus," in
echoance of my gag from way back on the day we first
met. -- Ooh, she's so fine! -- But felt self-conscious
about the scarf she was wearing, the fancy "suburban"
model Aida gave her for Christmas.)

     Now on the box, "Let the Good Times Roll."
Meanwhile little's changed in here. A dozen-person
cheer went up as the hour struck and that was about it.
No one going around bestowing kisses and we're not doing
it either, except for the doozer with each other.

     During the second leg of our lengthy walk, heading
back south, we encountered a parade coming our way. It
was that same drumming bunch from the campus, maybe six,
seven hundred strong now, with several cop cars rolling
in front and behind with blue and red lights flashing
and two large "Celebrate Weirdness!" banners at the head
of the parade itself, followed by a raucous local
radical band we've seen several times before, including
at the WTO march. A gaudily dressed and spirited bunch
these paraders were, many carrying signs proclaiming
"Save the Monolith." We still haven't figured out what
that was all about. In other cities "Hail to the Thief"
parades were slated for tonight in honor of the bonehead
president-elect's tainted victory in November. Was this
parade related to those? Or was this another instance
of student nose-thumbing at the cops who overreacted so
badly in this same area during WTO week? Or a largely
gay and lesbian good-times outing? High spirits
prevailed. "Come join us!" Painted faces, zany
outfits. We sidewalk-hugging Third Stagers waved and
shouted our encouragement but stayed right where we
were. Then passing by the campus corner Z spotted a
pikelike strip of wood with half-a-dozen brightly

colored ribbons and streamers of various sizes attached
to one end. Apparently someone in the parade had left
it behind and it was destined to become trash. So we
picked it up and now it's stashed in the back of the Z-
mobile. A decade or two down the road, we're thinking,
we'll bring it out to commemorate this night and all the
other millennial hooha, and of course with a special
emphasis on the jyze and the true versions of same.
     -- And am I achingly full. "The mythical year is
finally here!" declares the server -- lets us know his
all-time favorite movie is "2001: A Space Odyssey." (He
looks a whole lot like a coworker of brother Rob's named
Greg but says regretfully he doesn't have a brother
himself -- and we didn't ask! -- nor does he know anyone
who works at that bookstore but he likes it.)
     "I got you three times in one day!" cackles Z.
     She did. Three very fine surprises. Of course
she's got me for good anyway but -- as the button says,
the stone heart I lay on her pillow every day now,
usually with a new altered card for her: "Marry me anew
every day." Yup, she's got me anew every day, no
question. Don't care how corny it sounds: it stands.
     Ink's out, so why not stop here for now.

                        [+1]

     Again I must yield to melodrama. It's 01/01/01
I'm waking up into. Or did so wake some six hours ago.
(And to the tune of a wiff-administered wank which
caused her to say, "Ooh, baby!" -- She being once again
on the H-rag. A straight-up vertical two-handed white-
fountain wank! Jizz spurts like bleached candy canes
with hooks on the end!) -- But 01/01/01, it sounds way
too digital and binary to be anything I could personally
get excited about.
     A relaxed first afternoon of the expanded new DYCM
-- "the rest of your life." (Call it DYCM-E, sort of
like the revised psych diagnostic manual.) Z hauled out
her windup radio and we listened to the Rose Bowl

because our local university team was involved and Z's
very likable but mentally challenged buddy at work,
Roland (he's permanently frozen at emotional age eight,
I think it is), gave her a ball cap with that team's
logo on it for Christmas and she promised to wear it all
day January 1st. (And she did, starting with wake-up --
and even kept it on while so lovingly servicing her
horny old hubbin -- and said she'd keep doing so,
meaning keep wearing the cap, until bedtime.)
   I left around five and now it's past seven and I'm
holed up at the hideaway again. Just like yesterday I
got involved in rereading some old jyze "just for fun."
Procrastination really (though fun it was!). Some part
of me is looking at tying up the loose ends and laying
out the two big surprises as a chore, I guess. There's
too much catchup involved here. Much better the all-out
jyze improv.
   But okay. Quiet building, good time for doing the
chores. Not all. But some.
   So start out with the loose-end list. The friends
list. What's been happening with them? They're all
basically Z's friends; I'm just a bonus or a tack-on,
and in some cases one to be suffered, I don't doubt.
Aida's case especially.
   Aida I've reached the end of my rope with. From
now on I just smile nicely when I see her and I avoid
being with her if I can do so diplomatically. The
condescending way she talked to me at the credit union's
Christmas banquet is what did it. But she and Z are
still close (though Z wonders why Aida's seemingly
becoming ever more religious and boojie). Lately she's
started dating a guy she met through an alt-weekly ad
(his), a Jewish lawyer. At least I can say I had a
little positive influence here. If Z hadn't procured a
husband out of the alt-weekly ads Aida wouldn't't've been
willing to try them.
   The others in a nutshell:
   ** June went through a crisis over the difficulty
of law school but she's still hanging in there and I'm
still her late-night tutor. Both of her sons are now

living in the megastate to the south, or soon will be.
Adam has met a good wife candidate and she's Chinese and
highly educated, so June can scarcely restrain her
excitement.
     **   Gerry and Leola are still together, with
Gerry's remodel of the house putting paid to the Rio
disaster (and now they both have something else to focus
on in their daughter Jaz's upcoming marriage).
     **   Jess has sold the house where Z and I were
married (sold it for a fabulous sum right at the peak of
the boom) and is well along in constructing her dream
house in a woodsy area of her "island redoubt." She's
also back to seeing Gwen, but in a "low-profile way."
This has been going on for months with Z being one of
the last to learn about it because she'd so strongly
advised Jess never to see Gwen again. Supposedly we'll
be joining the two of them together at one of the
lesbian-group dinners later this month.
     **   Paz and Tobey sold their house on east hill and
bought a new one five miles due south, within a block or
so of a co-op branch where Z occasionally shops. But
we haven't seen their new digs yet. As a whole we've
been interacting less with the lesbian group -- Madge I.
too -- because of the Gwen/Jess imbroglio in which
everyone's taken sides and some in surprisingly
impassioned ways.
     **   Wei and Alison seem to be doing well and are
planning new trips, at this point to the southwest USA
and somewhere else -- is it West Africa? We see them
together every month or two and Z runs into Wei often at
work and book group and JCEJ. My hope that Wei and I
might become good friends on our own now seems
increasingly misplaced. In Z's view it's because we're
both too much "alpha males" -- "not necessarily 24/7 but
when you're together."
     **   Similarly with Olwen and Trent. They married
us, Z goes way back with both of them, we see them every
couple of months or so for a Sunday afternoon of
conversation over a board game or maybe during a walk
around "Manny Lake," but possible friendships between me

and either of them are not developing beyond this. I
think Olwen feels she'd face too much conflict in her
friendship with Z (probably true) and I'm guessing the
age gap between me and Trent is just too large. But the
occasional Sunday-afternoon get-togethers remain good
fun.

     ** And Z's seeing less and less of the D-clan as a
whole (including Aida's boy Charles). Chemo seems to
have stabilized Mr. D's cancer; the four granddaughters
living in town are cute as ever but I rarely get to
spend any time with them. Z is disappointed that "the
D's" don't make a bigger deal of socializing with us,
but so it is. Because we don't have kids we don't
really fit in their world anyway. I don't think she's
all that upset about it. She depends on them much less
for emotional support now -- needs them less. I think
both sides are well enough satisfied with the new, less
intense relationship.

     ** As for others: "average artichoke" Lee M.'s
still stuck out in the boonies arbitrating nuclear
disputes; we don't hear much from him anymore. Evan W.
and Doug T. seem to want to keep their distance. D'Arcy
Y. shows little interest in us as a couple, possibly
because she's not coupled herself, but she and Z still
do lunch regularly.

     -- And I'll stop there for now. No doubt I've
forgotten some people (Irene, Madge I., Ramona come
immediately to mind) and I haven't gotten to the most
important, Betty and Kat. So, later. Right now it's
time to hoof it up to the scope office to do some actual
paid work. (I'd hoped to stop by the art bar for a jyze
session. I guess it won't be happening. The all-night
cafe on New Year's Eve was this coda's venture out into
the world beyond my normal beaten paths. -- I didn't
mention it before, but that was only the second time
I've been inside a franchise of that particular all-
night chain, in J-town or anywhere.)

*   *

     The mighty third and final coda charges on. At the
new scope-office conference table now, again, with the

night's scoping work done. It's one a.m. just about,
and that means it's technically no longer day one of
week one of month one, etc. -- no longer DYCM-E Day --
except it still is in the simple animal sense that the
day's not over until you go to sleep at night (animals
with calendars, I'm saying).

     Is this also the last day for jyze, or at least for
G's jyze, the real thing, not an imitation? Maybe it
is. I hope not. I've cooked up a few ideas for
bringing it back, but not until 2002. This year will be
for whipping some of the old jyze and protojyze/urjyze
into shape, to the extent possible. Working up the
"Jyze Meditations" excerpt for Z boosted my confidence
that there's some readerly value in this stuff. I want
to see if I can tease out some more of it. If I do make
it as far as 2002 with most of my faculties intact (my
J-slinging arm and various organs and nerves attached
thereto, directly and indirectly) I'll decide then
whether I've got another yearlong jyze season in me.
Still the same hunger for the game? That will most
likely be the determining factor.

     But back to the current effort. Earlier on the way
up here I took a stroll through the downtown plaza just
to listen to the echoes of WTO days. They're still
present, no question. An "N30" demo might even become
an annual event in this town, and if that happens, Z and
I will probably be attending them as long as we're able
to toddle along with the rest of the marchers (and
scurry out of harm's way when the riot cops swoop down).
We did that this past year, a little over a month ago.
And just to make sure, we scurried away well before the
swoop, which did eventually come, although this second
time around it was more a choreographed kind of thing,
almost a ritual if not quite a farce.

     Is the world paying attention? More than it was
before 11/30/99, that's for sure. But the road ahead is
winding, it's mined, it doubles back on itself in
numerous places, it runs through long twisty canyons of
mirrors and booby traps and so forth. And yet:
eventually the issues raised by N30 will have to be

addressed. And the longer the delay, the greater the
price to be paid. The reactionary period immediately
ahead, as signaled by the U.S. presidential election,
will make this more obvious than ever.

     Am I absolutely sure about all this? As much so as
it's possible to be sure about anything. (Maybe a ramp
will drop down from the sky and all the creatures still
remaining on Earth will be able to escape to Mars before
our own planet becomes a giant toxic dump? And even in
a case like that we also must hope superior beings from
a distant star will be grooming Mars for us so it's just
the way we want it, which is to say: the way Earth used
to be before we ruined it.)

     -- So enough of that. Back to my own slice of
life. It's time for big surprise number one.

     Which would be a letter from sister Barbara. Out
of the blue. Just a few sentences, but saying she's
sorry. I chewed at it for a while and decided not to
inquire further on what exactly she's sorry about (she
doesn't specify) or what assurances she's offering that
she won't engage in the same sort of outrageous behavior
in the future. Instead I proposed that we start up a
correspondence and see how things go. And we've done
that, a couple of short letters apiece. It's, yes, a
start. She says she now can wake up feeling much better
about things in general. I don't know if that's true
for me. I still see no sign we'll ever arrive at the
point where we'll talk on the phone, much less meet in
person. But the door's open a crack now. I'm pleased
this is so. And yet for a true reconciliation to take
place we'll have to come to grips with the real basis of
our longstanding conflict and I continue to doubt she'll
ever be ready to do that. She's certainly shown no sign
of it so far.

     Still, it's a happy surprise. That was one of the
two biggest negatives in my life and now it's showing
some movement in a positive direction.

     Same with big surprise number two. I got to talk
with Elgie on the phone for a few minutes. It was our
first direct contact in about a dozen years. Lady S

finally called again and owned up to her real purpose in
contacting me earlier, although this (as is so often the
case with things regarding Lady S) remains somewhat
mysterious. Elgie is applying to grad school -- for an
MBA, I'm not so thrilled to say -- and she wants me to
help with the application. Help how? Well, that's not
so clear. She says they need some information, but is
she really asking for money? She doesn't come right out
and say that, but just in case I did let her know, and
as tactfully as I could, that, as we agreed long ago, I
won't be supplying any. And then as I learn more about
the situation it appears maybe the kid won't be needing
money. Maybe he's making enough on his own.

He was present at the apartment in the main
megalopolis of the this-coast megastate (it could be
they're both currently living in that apartment; this
wasn't clear either) and she thrust the phone at him.
"Hi, Dad," he said. A very quiet, restrained voice.
And then I had to do almost all the talking. He had no
questions, or rather just one: when I said I don't do
e-mail and have little interest in the internet, he came
up with a puzzled-sounding "Why?" He has his own
website, I learned from his mother, and he makes his
living producing CDs. He also does DJ stints for
parties, I gather, and for a while he appeared in films
and commercials in Korea. And he must've done well in
college because the grad schools he's applying to are
good ones. Very quickly it was obvious, though, he
didn't want to be talking on the phone. Before he got
off I said, "Now that we've finally made contact I hope
you'll want to continue with it. We could write, we
could talk, whatever. I'm completely open and available
to you on this. But I'm also well aware you may not be
too interested in doing any of these things so I have to
say: it's really up to you. I'd like it if we could
establish a relationship with some regular contact
between us." He said, "Sure. Okay." And then a few
final amenities and he was gone.

That was in October. I haven't heard anything more
from him, nor from Lady S. (I also said I'd be happy to

help out with the grad-school applications, offer tips
on universities and living conditions in various towns
and cities and anything else he might be interested in.)
And I did let Lady S know that if we hadn't been
officially divorced before, we are now. She seemed a
little surprised, as I expected, but not at all upset.
(And when I asked she said no, she hadn't gotten a
divorce from me as she'd said she would. She'd been far
too busy with other things. And she's "too busy" now
even to be interested in my sending down the genealogy
or the Turtle Rapids book or the Norwegian material
relating to her son's heritage, and he expressed no
interest in them either.)

     -- But still, a surprise, a big one, and again
movement in what I consider a positive direction. He
heard my voice for the first time since he was fourteen
or fifteen. Maybe it'll be possible for him to conceive
the idea that I might not be the kind of person he's
probably thinking I am. Maybe curiosity will get the
better of him one of these days. I hope so. And for me
it was a great pleasure hearing his voice and knowing he
seems to be quite pleased with his life and wants to
push on academically.

     -- And now, two a.m., I'm going to push on again
myself. One last entry at home before I crash. (The Z-
mobile's parked down on the street, meaning that for a
change I won't be taking a bus home tonight. -- That
last bus, by the way, is as "colorful" as ever. I like
it. And the WOC's fine too, though the turnover in
staff has been close to a hundred percent. Floyd,
Myles, Van -- all gone. But most of the members who
were my workout friends are still there and are still my
workout friends, including Estella and Jay and Melanie
and Clio and Marcus. Pilot Gene's moved on to Arizona.
Mad Mitch has disappeared.

     (And a couple of other quick notes now occurring to
me. Sister Barb did, at my urging, distribute that
final chunk of Mother's estate she'd been advised to
hold back in case of a tax audit. My share of $1500 --
same as for the other three -- came in at an opportune

time and enabled me to get all the way through the year
2000 without withdrawing a single dollar from the
principal in my deep-reserves account. But because of
the bad year with the markets that principal has shrunk
anyway, by about ten percent. It's just about to the
point where I'll need to cut back on my quarterly income
checks, which in turn means those checks will no longer
pay the full rent on the storage unit and the hideaway.
No question about it: financially the next five to eight
years will be tight for me. Then Social Security will
kick in. -- And this: Initiative FTG has basically been
stopped in its tracks by the courts. Part of it was
passed into law anyway -- by the abysmal rural-dominated
state legislature -- but our county and city are fairly
well insulated against its negative effects owing to the
tax benefits of the high-tech boom, even though that
boom is now slowing across the board. At this point,
I'm happy to say, the buses are still running, the
libraries are still open.)

*   *

     -- Couch. Over here by the big peace lily, the
record albums, the krazy klock, the Rob & Gail
evergreen, the immortalized wedding shoes (Z's) on their
wooden stand, the cedar boxes, the window corner (that's
southeast), the miniature Norwegian flag stuck in the
soil of the new asparagus fern, the big "Jyze
Meditations" canvas visible through the pine needles
where it's propped up on the art table.
     It's the last and final TJM close-out time.
     A celebratory drink. A blue hippo. A shaky-legged
zebra. A "Chinatown" (the movie) postcard morphed to
"South Hill." And a new card from Z, tonight's creation.
     Just gotta, just gotta, just gotta be stopping this
thing.
     But first the last of the big surprises. It turns
out all those frightening diagnoses of Betty's malady
were wrong. It's not anything fatal. It's something
she can live with. (Just what it is, though, is not so
clear. -- But it's obvious her condition has stabilized
and even improved.) -- Back before this news came in,

1041

Betty told us she'd decided she'd rather have us
bringing up Kat if she couldn't do it. She struck the
names of the high plains relatives off the papers and
put ours in their place (after asking for our okay --
and saying "I just really like the kind of relationship
you two have"). And we're still next in line should
anything happen to Betty. But she's been lucky too in
having one of Kat's friends, Celine, and her mother,
Faye, who's a picture framer and a very interesting and
likable woman (smart and ribald and soulful and a heavy
toker), move into the upstairs rooms at their place, and
after some awkward times at first it looks to be working
out for them as a foursome (and Celine is biracial,
father Afrusan and mother Eurusan). Over the holidays Z
and I attended a party at their place and also went out
with Betty and Kat on Christmas Day, seeing the new
infant elephant at the zoo and then a movie ("Miss
Congeniality") before coming here for present-opening
and ball-playing (me and Kat down in the garage). Kat
turns eleven next month and she's just entering
pubescence; she's bright, beautiful, funny, a handful.
I'm the father figure in her life, Z thinks, and I hope
it's true and will become more true and stay that way.
     -- And a fine Christmas it's been. Did I already
mention Z roasted her first turkey ever? That was
Christmas Eve. She failed to extricate an aluminum-foil
package of giblets from the innards before roasting but
by and large the experiment was a success -- enough so
that she's saying she'd like to do it again in a few
years (but only if the leftovers from the current bird
are gone by then, and that appears doubtful). And the
day after Christmas she finally met my cousin Kar and
his wife Kerani as we joined them and Rob and Gail for
dinner at a Thai restaurant in the same block where Z
and I, in a manner of speaking, met: the block in which
are located the offices of the alt-weekly in which her
ad ran (and my proposal regarding the true millennium
didn't run). Making the arrangements for this get-
together was a boggling task spread over a period of
more than six months. Z found Kar both less arrogant

and more boojie than she expected from my descriptions.
     Z's work life, I should also note, is about to
undergo a shake-up. Dale, the department head she's
been working closely with for the past year and a half
-- in what I consider a terrific adaptive triumph for
both of them -- is now being transferred to head up a
different division. He wants her to come along and
she'd like to do it, but the utility probably won't
let her. Yet she has a poor relationship with the man
who will be the new boss of her department. She's
pondering her options. Transfer to the sustainability
unit? Leave city employment and seek work elsewhere,
maybe with the county? Stay on and fight it out with
the benighted new boss? The next few months promise to
be tumultuous. (Meanwhile her biggest personal work
headache, Gloria, is still around after a transfer
engineered by Dale was vetoed by the utility head,
Roberta C. -- who's gone and gotten married! So if Z
stays with her current job it appears likely she'll also
continue to have a feisty Filipina prima donna to deal
with. And of course I tell her I fully sympathize with
her and offer to give her tips based on a similar kind
of situation I happen to be involved in myself.)
     She and I have our issues too, yes we do. Of
course we do. But they're emphatically not, sez I, of
the relationship-threatening kind. There's the sexual
impasse, "romance" v. "S&M." There's the cleanup issue:
I've agreed to consider her proposal to bring in a
cleaning person once a month or however often she thinks
is best (personally I still hate the idea): but
January's our month for talking this out. We're also
supposed to be drawing up wills this month. And by the
end of April we want to finish up the preapproval papers
needed to apply for a city-sponsored low-interest
mortgage. Z seems to be more seriously attached than
I'd realized to the notion of our owning a house or
condo (it's the security issue again). I'm of a
different mind on all these matters but I'm ready to
bend and I expect I'll be pretzeled to a fare-thee-well
before it's all over. But as long as she remains as

understanding as she's been all along -- by and large --
about my needs as a nightscoper and jyzeslinger, I think
I can take all that bending and whatever else may be
required.

     For tonight's card she got me again. It's an
altered "Spirit of Jyzetown" oversize postcard featuring
a photo of the big anti-WTO parade, a large puppet at
the center, and she's made that puppet look recognizably
like me, ponytail and all. "Up with ardent two-
handers!" she has me saying, referring to last night's
romance squabble and this morning's successful wank job
(in which for a change she accepted my advice to take
her time and use both hands). One of the banners shown
on the card is altered to read "Celebrate Weirdness" as
in last night's parade (she's admitted, by the way, she
was "almost shocked" by the rawness and roughness of the
late-night street scene up there on east hill). And
then on the back side of the card there's a heart made
of X's and O's with an "01/01/01" worked in and the
words "lub from da feisty evolving Z-wiff."
     How I love this Zoelie B.!
     And so now I can wander off in the direction of the
sunset (which by happy coincidence is also the direction
in which our bedroom lies). She'll be waking up -- her
alarm going off -- in fifty-five minutes and gearing up
for the first workday of the new DYCM-E era. But first
pillow talk and who knows what else, maybe right up to
our current agreed deadline of quarter to six. And
before all that I need to reply to a couple of her
notes. Would also like to alter a card in response to
hers but, to summon yet again a well-worn phrase, "it's
not in the cards" on this busy night. (Wotta card!)
And gotta go down and pick up tomorrow's -- today's
actually, or in Gregorian terms by USAn styling
01/02/01's -- paper. Just heard it arrive with the
usual loud THWACK (and then a squeal of tires -- sounds
like we've got us a fast-moving new delivery person).

END

1044